THE BEST OF
ERNEST
HEMINGWAY

Ernest Hemingway was born in Oak Park, Illinois, in 1899, and began his writing career for *The Kansas City Star* in 1917. During the First World War he volunteered as an ambulance driver on the Italian front but was invalided home, having been seriously wounded while serving with the infantry.

In 1921 Hemingway settled in Paris, where he became part of the expatriate circle of Gertrude Stein, F. Scott Fitzgerald, Ezra Pound, and Ford Madox Ford. His first book, *Three Stories and Ten Poems*, was published in Paris in 1923 and was followed by the short story selection *In Our Time*, which marked his American debut in 1925.

With the appearance of *The Sun Also Rises* in 1926, Hemingway became not only the voice of the 'lost generation' but the preeminent writer of his time. This was followed by Men Without Women in 1927, when Hemingway returned to the United States, and his novel of the Italian front, *A Farewell to Arms* (1929).

In the 1930s, Hemingway settled in Key West, and later in Cuba, but he traveled widely—to Spain, Italy, and Africa—and wrote about his experiences in *Death in the Afternoon* (1932), his classic treatise on bullfighting, and *Green Hills of Africa* (1935), an account of big-game hunting in Africa. Later he reported on the Spanish Civil War, which became the background for his brilliant war novel, *For Whom the Bell Tolls* (1939), hunted U-boats in the Caribbean, and covered the European front during the Second World War.

Hemingway's most popular work, *The Old Man and the Sea*, was awarded the Pulitzer Prize in 1953, and in 1954 Hemingway won the Nobel Prize in Literature 'for his powerful, style-forming mastery of the art of narration.'

One of the most important influences on the development of the short story and novel in American fiction, Hemingway has seized the imagination of the American public like no other twentieth-century author. He died, by suicide, in Ketchum, Idaho, in 1961.

His other works include *The Torrents of Spring* (1926), *Winner Take Nothing* (1933), *To Have and Have Not* (1937), *The Fifth Column and the First Forty-nine Stories* (1938), *Across the River and Into the Trees* (1950), and posthumously, *A Moveable Feast* (1964), *Islands in the Stream* (1970), *The Dangerous Summer* (1985), and *The Garden of Eden* (1986).

THE BEST OF
ERNEST
HEMINGWAY

First published by
Rupa Publications India Pvt. Ltd 2025
161-B/4, Gulmohar House,
Yusuf Sarai Community Centre,
New Delhi 110049

Sales centres:
Bengaluru Chennai
Hyderabad Kolkata Mumbai

Edition copyright © Rupa Publications India Pvt. Ltd. 2025

This is a work of fiction. Names, characters, places and incidents are either the product of the author's imagination or are used fictitiously and any resemblance to any actual person, living or dead, events or locales is entirely coincidental.

All rights reserved.
No part of this publication may be reproduced, transmitted, or stored in a retrieval system, in any form or by any means, electronic, mechanical, photocopying, recording or otherwise, without the prior permission of the publisher.

P-ISBN: 978-93-6156-076-7
E-ISBN: 978-93-6156-675-2

Second impression 2026

10 9 8 7 6 5 4 3 2

Printed in India

This book is sold subject to the condition that it shall not, by way of trade or otherwise, be lent, resold, hired out, or otherwise circulated, without the publisher's prior consent, in any form of binding or cover other than that in which it is published.

CONTENTS

A Farewell to Arms	1
The Sun Also Rises	187
Men without Women	333
The Old Man and the Sea	418
For whom the Bell Tolls	463

A FAREWELL TO ARMS

BOOK ONE

1

In the late summer of that year we lived in a house in a village that looked across the river and the plain to the mountains. In the bed of the river there were pebbles and boulders, dry and white in the sun, and the water was clear and swiftly moving and blue in the channels. Troops went by the house and down the road and the dust they raised powdered the leaves of the trees. The trunks of the trees too were dusty and the leaves fell early that year and we saw the troops marching along the road and the dust rising and leaves, stirred by the breeze, falling and the soldiers marching and afterward the road bare and white except for the leaves.

The plain was rich with crops; there were many orchards of fruit trees and beyond the plain the mountains were brown and bare. There was fighting in the mountains and at night we could see the flashes from the artillery. In the dark it was like summer lightning, but the nights were cool and there was not the feeling of a storm coming.

Sometimes in the dark we heard the troops marching under the window and guns going past pulled by motor-tractors. There was much traffic at night and many mules on the roads with boxes of ammunition on each side of their pack-saddles and gray motor trucks that carried men, and other trucks with loads covered with canvas that moved slower in the traffic. There were big guns too that passed in the day drawn by tractors, the long barrels of the guns covered with green branches and green leafy branches and vines laid over the tractors. To the north we could look across a valley and see a forest of chestnut trees and behind it another mountain on this side of the river. There was fighting for that mountain too, but it was not successful, and in the fall when the rains came the leaves all fell from the chestnut trees and the branches were bare and the trunks black with rain. The vineyards were thin and bare-branched too and all the country wet and brown and dead with the autumn. There were mists over the river and clouds on the mountain and the trucks splashed mud on the road and the troops were muddy and wet in their capes; their rifles were wet and under their capes the two leather cartridge-boxes on the front of the belts, gray leather boxes heavy with the packs of clips of thin, long 6.5 mm. cartridges, bulged forward under the capes so that the men, passing on the road, marched as though they were six months gone with child.

There were small gray motor cars that passed going very fast; usually there was an officer on the seat with the driver and more officers in the back seat. They splashed more mud than the camions even and if one of the officers in the back was very small and sitting between two generals, he himself so small that you could not see his face but only the top of his cap and his narrow back, and if the car went especially fast it was probably the King. He lived in Udine and came out in this way nearly every day to see how things were going, and things went very badly.

At the start of the winter came the permanent rain and with the rain came the cholera. But it was checked and in the end only seven thousand died of it in the army.

2

The next year there were many victories. The mountain that was beyond the valley and the hillside where the chestnut forest grew was captured and there were victories beyond the plain on the plateau to the south and we crossed the river in August and lived in a house in Gorizia that had a fountain and many thick shady trees in a walled garden and a wistaria vine purple on the side of the house. Now the fighting was in the next mountains beyond and was not a mile away. The town was very nice and our house was very fine. The river ran behind us and the town had been captured very handsomely but the mountains beyond it could not be taken and I was very glad the Austrians seemed to want to come back to the town some time, if the war should end, because they did not bombard it to destroy it but only a little in a military way. People lived on in it and there were hospitals and cafés and artillery up side streets and two bawdy houses, one for troops and one for officers, and with the end of the summer, the cool nights, the fighting in the mountains beyond the town, the shell-marked iron of the railway bridge, the smashed tunnel by the river where the fighting had been, the trees around the square and the long avenue of trees that led to the square; these with there being girls in the town, the King passing in his motor car, sometimes now seeing his face and little long necked body and gray beard like a goat's chin tuft; all these with the sudden interiors of houses that had lost a wall through shelling, with plaster and rubble in their gardens and sometimes in the street, and the whole thing going well on the Carso made the fall very different from the last fall when we had been in the country. The war was changed too.

The forest of oak trees on the mountain beyond the town was gone. The forest had been green in the summer when we had come into the town but now there were the stumps and the broken trunks and the ground torn up, and one day at the end of the fall when I was out where the oak forest had been I saw a cloud coming over the mountain. It came very fast and the sun went a dull yellow and then everything was gray and the sky was covered and the cloud came on down the mountain and suddenly we were in it and it was snow. The snow slanted across the wind, the bare ground was covered, the stumps of trees projected, there was snow on the guns and there were paths in the snow going back to the latrines behind trenches.

Later, below in the town, I watched the snow falling, looking out of the window of the bawdy house, the house for officers, where I sat with a friend and two glasses drinking a bottle of Asti, and, looking out at the snow falling slowly and heavily, we knew it was all over for that year. Up the river the mountains had not been taken; none of the mountains beyond the river had been taken. That was all left for next year. My friend saw the priest from our mess going by in the street, walking carefully in the slush, and pounded on the window to attract his attention. The priest looked up. He saw us and smiled. My friend motioned for him to come in. The priest shook his head and went on. That night in the mess after the spaghetti course, which every one ate very quickly and seriously, lifting the spaghetti on the fork until the loose strands hung clear then lowering it into the mouth, or else using a continuous lift and sucking into the mouth, helping ourselves to wine from the grass-covered gallon flask; it swung in a metal cradle and you pulled the neck of the flask down with the forefinger and the wine, clear red, tannic and lovely, poured out into the glass held with the same hand; after this course, the captain commenced picking on the priest.

The priest was young and blushed easily and wore a uniform like the rest of us but with a cross in dark red velvet above the left breast pocket of his gray tunic. The captain spoke pidgin Italian for my doubtful benefit, in order that I might understand perfectly, that nothing should be lost.

'Priest to-day with girls,' the captain said looking at the priest and at me. The priest smiled and blushed and shook his head. This captain baited him often.

'Not true?' asked the captain. 'To-day I see priest with girls.'

'No,' said the priest. The other officers were amused at the baiting.

'Priest not with girls,' went on the captain. 'Priest never with girls,' he explained to me. He took my glass and filled it, looking at my eyes all the time, but not losing sight of the priest.

'Priest every night five against one.' Every one at the table laughed. 'You understand? Priest every night five against one.' He made a gesture and laughed loudly. The priest accepted it as a joke.

'The Pope wants the Austrians to win the war,' the major said. 'He loves Franz Joseph. That's where the money comes from. I am an atheist.'

'Did you ever read the "Black Pig"?' asked the lieutenant. 'I will get you a copy. It was that which shook my faith.'

'It is a filthy and vile book,' said the priest. 'You do not really like it.'

'It is very valuable,' said the lieutenant. 'It tells you about those priests. You will like it,' he said to me. I smiled at the priest and he smiled back across the candle-light. 'Don't you read it,' he said.

'I will get it for you,' said the lieutenant.

'All thinking men are atheists,' the major said. 'I do not believe in the Free Masons however.'

'I believe in the Free Masons,' the lieutenant said. 'It is a noble organization.' Some one came in and as the door opened I could see the snow falling.

'There will be no more offensive now that the snow has come,' I said.

'Certainly not,' said the major. 'You should go on leave. You should go to Rome, Naples, Sicily—'

'He should visit Amalfi,' said the lieutenant. 'I will write you cards to my family in Amalfi. They will love you like a son.'

'He should go to Palermo.'

'He ought to go to Capri.'

'I would like you to see Abruzzi and visit my family at Capracotta,' said the priest. 'Listen to him talk about the Abruzzi. There's more snow there than here. He doesn't want to see peasants. Let him go to centres of culture and civilization.'

'He should have fine girls. I will give you the addresses of places in Naples. Beautiful young girls—accompanied by their mothers. Ha! Ha! Ha!' The captain spread his hand open, the thumb up and fingers outspread as when you make shadow pictures.

There was a shadow from his hand on the wall. He spoke again in pidgin Italian. 'You go away like this,' he pointed to the thumb, 'and come back like this,' he touched the little finger. Every one laughed.

'Look,' said the captain. He spread the hand again. Again the candle-light made its shadows on the wall. He started with the upright thumb and named in their order the thumb and four fingers, 'soto-tenente (the thumb), tenente (first finger), capitano (next finger), maggiore (next to the little finger), and tenentecolonello (the little finger). You go away soto-tenente! You come back soto-colonello!' They all laughed. The captain was having a great success with finger games. He looked at the priest and shouted, 'Every night priest five against one!' They all laughed again.

'You must go on leave at once,' the major said.

'I would like to go with you and show you things,' the lieutenant said.

'When you come back bring a phonograph.'

'Bring good opera disks.'

'Bring Caruso.'

'Don't bring Caruso. He bellows.'

'Don't you wish you could bellow like him?'

'He bellows. I say he bellows!'

'I would like you to go to Abruzzi,' the priest said. The others were shouting. 'There is good hunting. You would like the people and though it is cold it is clear and dry. You could stay with my family. My father is a famous hunter.'

'Come on,' said the captain. 'We go whorehouse before it shuts.'

'Good-night,' I said to the priest.

'Good-night,' he said.

3

When I came back to the front we still lived in that town. There were many more guns in the country around and the spring had come. The fields were green and there were small green shoots on the vines, the trees along the road had small leaves and a breeze came from the sea. I saw the town with the hill and the old castle above it in a cup in the hills with the mountains beyond, brown mountains with a little green on their slopes. In the town there were more guns, there were some new hospitals, you met British men and sometimes women, on the street, and a few more houses had been hit by shell fire. It was warm and like the spring and I walked down the alleyway of trees, warmed from the sun on the wall, and found we still lived in the same house and that it all looked the same as when I had left it. The door was open, there was a soldier sitting on a bench outside in the sun, an ambulance was waiting by the side door and inside the door, as I went in, there was the smell of marble floors and hospital. It was all as I had left it except that now it was spring. I looked in the door of the big room and saw the major sitting at his desk, the window open and the sunlight coming into the room. He did not see me and I did not know whether to go in and report or go upstairs first and clean up. I decided to go on upstairs.

The room I shared with the lieutenant Rinaldi looked out on the courtyard. The window was open, my bed was made up with blankets and my things hung on the wall, the gas mask in an oblong tin can, the steel helmet on the same peg. At the foot of the bed was my flat trunk, and my winter boots, the leather shiny with oil, were on the trunk. My Austrian sniper's rifle with its blued octagon barrel and the lovely dark walnut, cheek- fitted, schutzen stock, hung over the two beds. The telescope that fitted it was, I remembered, locked in the trunk. The lieutenant, Rinaldi, lay asleep on the other bed. He woke when he heard me in the room and sat up.

'Ciaou!' he said. 'What kind of time did you have?'

'Magnificent.'

We shook hands and he put his arm around my neck and kissed me.

'Oughf,' I said.

'You're dirty,' he said. 'You ought to wash. Where did you go and what did you do?

Tell me everything at once.'

'I went everywhere. Milan, Florence, Rome, Naples, Villa San Giovanni, Messina, Taormina—'

'You talk like a time-table. Did you have any beautiful adventures?'

'Yes.'

'Where?'

'Milano, Firenze, Roma, Napoli—'

'That's enough. Tell me really what was the best.'

'In Milano.'

'That was because it was first. Where did you meet her? In the Cova? Where did you go? How did you feel? Tell me everything at once. Did you stay all night?'

'Yes.'

'That's nothing. Here now we have beautiful girls. New girls never been to the front before.'

'Wonderful.'

'You don't believe me? We will go now this afternoon and see. And in the town we have beautiful English girls. I am now in love with Miss Barkley. I will take you to call. I will probably marry Miss Barkley.'

'I have to get washed and report. Doesn't anybody work now?'

'Since you are gone we have nothing but frostbites, chilblains, jaundice, gonorrhea, self-inflicted wounds, pneumonia and hard and soft chancres. Every week some one gets wounded by rock fragments. There are a few real wounded. Next week the war starts again. Perhaps it start again. They say so. Do you think I would do right to marry Miss Barkley—after the war of course?'

'Absolutely,' I said and poured the basin full of water.

'To-night you will tell me everything,' said Rinaldi. 'Now I must go back to sleep to be fresh and beautiful for Miss Barkley.'

I took off my tunic and shirt and washed in the cold water in the basin. While I rubbed myself with a towel I looked around the room and out the window and at Rinaldi lying with his eyes closed on the bed. He was good-looking, was my age, and he came from Amalfi. He loved being a surgeon and we were great friends. While I was looking at him he opened his eyes.

'Have you any money?'

'Yes.'

'Loan me fifty lire.'

I dried my hands and took out my pocket-book from the inside of my tunic hanging on the wall. Rinaldi took the note, folded it without rising from the bed and slid it in his breeches pocket. He smiled, 'I must make on Miss Barkley the impression of a man of sufficient wealth. You are my great and good friend and financial protector.'

'Go to hell,' I said.

That night at the mess I sat next to the priest and he was disappointed and suddenly hurt that I had not gone to the Abruzzi. He had written to his father that I was coming and they had made preparations. I myself felt as badly as he did and could not understand why I had not gone. It was what I had wanted to do and I tried to explain how one thing had led to another and finally he saw it and understood that I had really wanted to go and it was almost all right. I had drunk much wine and afterward coffee and Strega and I explained, winefully, how we did not do the things we wanted to do; we never did such things.

We two were talking while the others argued. I had wanted to go to Abruzzi. I had gone to no place where the roads were frozen and hard as iron, where it was clear cold and dry and the snow was dry and powdery and hare-tracks in the snow and the peasants took off their hats and called you Lord and there was good hunting. I had gone to no such place but to the smoke of cafés and nights when the room whirled and you needed to look at the wall to make it stop, nights in bed, drunk, when you knew that that was all there was, and the strange excitement of waking and not knowing who it was with you, and the world all unreal in the dark and so exciting that you must resume again unknowing and not caring in the night, sure that this was all and all and all and not caring. Suddenly to care very much and to sleep to wake with it sometimes morning and all that had been there gone and everything sharp and hard and clear and sometimes a dispute about the cost.

Sometimes still pleasant and fond and warm and breakfast and lunch. Sometimes all niceness gone and glad to get out on the street but always another day starting and then another night. I tried to tell about the night and the difference between the night and the day and how the night was better unless the day was very clean and cold and I could not tell it; as I cannot tell it now. But if you have had it you know. He had not had it but he understood that I had really wanted to go to the Abruzzi but had not gone and we were still friends, with many tastes alike, but with the difference between us. He had always known what I did not know and what, when I learned it, I was always able to forget. But I did not know that then, although I learned it later. In the meantime we were all at the mess, the meal was finished, and the argument went on. We two stopped talking and the captain shouted, 'Priest not happy. Priest not happy without girls.'

'I am happy,' said the priest.

'Priest not happy. Priest wants Austrians to win the war,' the captain said. The others listened. The priest shook his head.

'No,' he said.

'Priest wants us never to attack. Don't you want us never to attack?'

'No. If there is a war I suppose we must attack.'

'Must attack. Shall attack!'

The priest nodded.

'Leave him alone,' the major said. 'He's all right.'

'He can't do anything about it anyway,' the captain said. We all got up and left the table.

4

The battery in the next garden woke me in the morning and I saw the sun coming through the window and got out of the bed. I went to the window and looked out. The gravel paths were moist and the grass was wet with dew. The battery fired twice and the air came each time like a blow and shook the window and made the front of my pajamas flap. I could not see the guns but they were evidently firing directly over us. It was a nuisance to have them there but it was a comfort that they were no bigger. As I looked out at the garden I heard a motor truck starting on the road. I dressed, went downstairs, had some coffee in the kitchen and went out to the garage.

Ten cars were lined up side by side under the long shed. They were top-heavy, blunt-nosed ambulances, painted gray and built like moving-vans. The mechanics were working on one out in the yard. Three others were up in the mountains at dressing stations.

'Do they ever shell that battery?' I asked one of the mechanics.

'No, Signor Tenente. It is protected by the little hill.'

'How's everything?'

'Not so bad. This machine is no good but the others march.' He stopped working and smiled. 'Were you on permission?'

'Yes.'

He wiped his hands on his jumper and grinned. 'You have a good time?' The others all grinned too.

'Fine,' I said. 'What's the matter with this machine?'

'It's no good. One thing after another.'

'What's the matter now?'

'New rings.'

I left them working, the car looking disgraced and empty with the engine open and parts spread on the work bench, and went in under the shed and looked at each of the cars. They were moderately clean, a few freshly washed, the others dusty. I looked at the tires carefully, looking for cuts or stone bruises. Everything seemed in good condition. It evidently made no difference whether I was there to look after things or not. I had imagined that the condition of the cars, whether or not things were obtainable, the smooth functioning of the business of removing wounded and sick from the dressing stations, hauling them back from the mountains to the clearing station and then distributing them to the hospitals named on their papers, depended to a considerable extent on myself.

Evidently it did not matter whether I was there or not.

'Has there been any trouble getting parts?' I asked the sergeant mechanic.

'No, Signor Tenente.'

'Where is the gasoline park now?'

'At the same place.'

'Good,' I said and went back to the house and drank another bowl of coffee at the mess table. The coffee was a pale gray and sweet with condensed milk. Outside the window it was a lovely spring morning. There was that beginning of a feeling of dryness in the nose that meant the day would be hot later on. That day I visited the posts in the mountains and was back in town late in the afternoon.

The whole thing seemed to run better while I was away. The offensive was going to start again I heard. The division for which we worked were to attack at a place up the river and the major told me that I would see about the posts for during the attack. The attack would cross the river up above the narrow gorge and spread up the hillside. The posts for the cars would have to be as near the river as they could get and keep covered. They would, of course, be selected by the infantry but we were supposed to work it out. It was one of those things that gave you a false feeling of soldiering.

I was very dusty and dirty and went up to my room to wash. Rinaldi was sitting on the bed with a copy of Hugo's English grammar. He was dressed, wore his black boots, and his hair shone.

'Splendid,' he said when he saw me. 'You will come with me to see Miss Barkley.'

'No.'

'Yes. You will please come and make me a good impression on her.'

'All right. Wait till I get cleaned up.'

'Wash up and come as you are.'

I washed, brushed my hair and we started.

'Wait a minute,' Rinaldi said. 'Perhaps we should have a drink.' He opened his trunk and took out a bottle.

'Not Strega,' I said.

'No. Grappa.'

'All right.'

He poured two glasses and we touched them, first fingers extended. The grappa was very strong.

'Another?'

'All right,' I said. We drank the second grappa, Rinaldi put away the bottle and we went down the stairs. It was hot walking through the town but the sun was starting to go down and it was very pleasant. The British hospital was a big villa built by Germans before the war. Miss Barkley was in the garden. Another nurse was with her. We saw their white uniforms through the trees and walked toward them. Rinaldi saluted. I saluted too but more moderately.

'How do you do?' Miss Barkley said. 'You're not an Italian, are you?'

'Oh, no.'

Rinaldi was talking with the other nurse. They were laughing. 'What an odd thing—to be in the Italian army.'

'It's not really the army. It's only the ambulance.'

'It's very odd though. Why did you do it?'

'I don't know,' I said. 'There isn't always an explanation for everything.'

'Oh, isn't there? I was brought up to think there was.'

'That's awfully nice.'

'Do we have to go on and talk this way?'

'No,' I said.

'That's a relief. Isn't it?'

'What is the stick?' I asked. Miss Barkley was quite tall. She wore what seemed to me to be a nurse's uniform, was blonde and had a tawny skin and gray eyes. I thought she was very beautiful. She was carrying a thin rattan stick like a toy riding-crop, bound in leather.

'It belonged to a boy who was killed last year.'

'I'm awfully sorry.'

'He was a very nice boy. He was going to marry me and he was killed in the Somme.'

'It was a ghastly show.'

'Were you there?'

'No.'

'I've heard about it,' she said. 'There's not really any war of that sort down here. They sent me the little stick. His mother sent it to me. They returned it with his things.'

'Had you been engaged long?'

'Eight years. We grew up together.'

'And why didn't you marry?'

'I don't know,' she said. 'I was a fool not to. I could have given him that anyway. But I thought it would be bad for him.'

'I see.'

'Have you ever loved any one?'

'No,' I said.

We sat down on a bench and I looked at her.

'You have beautiful hair,' I said.

'Do you like it?'

'Very much.'

'I was going to cut it all off when he died.'

'No.'

'I wanted to do something for him. You see I didn't care about the other thing and he could have had it all. He could have had anything he wanted if I would have known. I would have married him or anything. I know all about it now. But then he wanted to go to war and I didn't know.'

I did not say anything.

'I didn't know about anything then. I thought it would be worse for him. I thought perhaps he couldn't stand it and then of course he was killed and that was the end of it.'

'I don't know.'

'Oh, yes,' she said. 'That's the end of it.'

We looked at Rinaldi talking with the other nurse.

'What is her name?'

'Ferguson. Helen Ferguson. Your friend is a doctor, isn't he?'

'Yes. He's very good.'

'That's splendid. You rarely find any one any good this close to the front. This is close to the front, isn't it?'

'Quite.'

'It's a silly front,' she said. 'But it's very beautiful. Are they going to have an offensive?'

'Yes.'

'Then we'll have to work. There's no work now.'

'Have you done nursing long?'

'Since the end of 'fifteen. I started when he did. I remember having a silly idea he might come to the hospital where I was. With a sabre cut, I suppose, and a bandage around his head. Or shot through the shoulder. Something picturesque.'

'This is the picturesque front,' I said.

'Yes,' she said. 'People can't realize what France is like. If they did, it couldn't all go on. He didn't have a sabre cut. They blew him all to bits.'

I didn't say anything.

'Do you suppose it will always go on?'

'No.'

'What's to stop it?'

'It will crack somewhere.'

'We'll crack. We'll crack in France. They can't go on doing things like the Somme and not crack.'

'They won't crack here,' I said.

'You think not?'

'No. They did very well last summer.'

'They may crack,' she said. 'Anybody may crack.'

'The Germans too.'

'No,' she said. 'I think not.'

We went over toward Rinaldi and Miss Ferguson.

'You love Italy?' Rinaldi asked Miss Ferguson in English.

'Quite well.'

'No understand,' Rinaldi shook his head.

'Abbastanza bene,' I translated.

He shook his head.

'That is not good. You love England?'

'Not too well. I'm Scotch, you see.'

Rinaldi looked at me blankly.

'She's Scotch, so she loves Scotland better than England,' I said in Italian.

'But Scotland is England.'

I translated this for Miss Ferguson.

'Pas encore,' said Miss Ferguson.

'Not really?'

'Never. We do not like the English.'

'Not like the English? Not like Miss Barkley?'

'Oh, that's different. You mustn't take everything so literally.'

After a while we said good-night and left. Walking home Rinaldi said, 'Miss Barkley prefers you to me. That is very clear. But the little Scotch one is very nice.'

'Very,' I said. I had not noticed her. 'You like her?'

'No,' said Rinaldi.

5

The next afternoon I went to call on Miss Barkley again. She was not in the garden and I went to the side door of the villa where the ambulances drove up. Inside I saw the head nurse, who said Miss Barkley was on duty—'there's a war on, you know.'

I said I knew.

'You're the American in the Italian army?' she asked.

'Yes, ma'am.'

'How did you happen to do that? Why didn't you join up with us?'

'I don't know,' I said. 'Could I join now?'

'I'm afraid not now. Tell me. Why did you join up with the Italians?'

'I was in Italy,' I said, 'and I spoke Italian.'

'Oh,' she said. 'I'm learning it. It's beautiful language.'

'Somebody said you should be able to learn it in two weeks.'

'Oh, I'll not learn it in two weeks. I've studied it for months now. You may come and see her after seven o'clock if you wish. She'll be off then. But don't bring a lot of Italians.'

'Not even for the beautiful language?'

'No. Nor for the beautiful uniforms.'

'Good evening,' I said.

'A rivederci, Tenente.'

'A rivederla.' I saluted and went out. It was impossible to salute foreigners as an Italian, without embarrassment. The Italian salute never seemed made for export.

The day had been hot. I had been up the river to the bridgehead at Plava. It was there that the offensive was to begin. It had been impossible to advance on the far side the year before because there was only one road leading down from the pass to the pontoon bridge and it was under machine-gun and shell fire for nearly a mile. It was not wide enough either to carry all the transport for an offensive and the Austrians could make a shambles out of it. But the Italians had crossed and spread out a little way on the far side to hold about a mile and a half on the Austrian side of the river. It was a nasty place and the Austrians should not have let them hold it. I suppose it was mutual tolerance because the Austrians still kept a bridgehead further down the river. The Austrian trenches were above on the hillside only a few yards from the Italian lines. There had been a little town but it was all rubble. There was what was left of a railway station and a smashed permanent bridge that could not be repaired and used because it was in plain sight.

I went along the narrow road down toward the river, left the car at the dressing station under the hill, crossed the pontoon bridge, which was protected by a shoulder of the mountain, and went through the trenches in the smashed-down town and along the edge of the slope. Everybody was in the dugouts. There were racks of rockets standing to be touched off to call for help from the artillery or to signal with if the telephone wires were cut. It was quiet, hot and dirty. I looked across the wire at the Austrian lines. Nobody was in sight. I had a drink with a captain that I knew in one of the dugouts and went back across the bridge.

A new wide road was being finished that would go over the mountain and zig-zag down to the bridge. When this road was finished the offensive would start. It came down through the forest in sharp turns. The system was to bring everything down the new road and take the empty trucks, carts and loaded ambulances and all returning traffic up the old narrow road. The dressing station was on the Austrian side of the river under the edge of the hill and stretcher-bearers would bring the wounded back across the pontoon bridge. It would be the same when the offensive started. As far as I could make out the last mile or so of the new road where it started to level out would be able to be shelled steadily by the Austrians. It looked as though it might be a mess. But I found a place where the cars would be sheltered after they passed that last badlooking bit and could wait for the wounded to be brought across the pontoon bridge. I would have liked to drive over the new road but it was not yet finished. It looked wide and well made with a good grade and the turns looked very impressive where you could see them through openings in the forest on the mountain side. The cars would be all right with their good metal-to-metal brakes and anyway, coming down, they would not be loaded. I drove back up the narrow road.

Two carabinieri held the car up. A shell had fallen and while we waited three others fell up the road. They were seventy-sevens and came with a whishing rush of air, a hard bright burst and flash and then gray smoke that blew across the road. The carabinieri waved us to go on. Passing where the shells had landed I avoided the small broken places and smelled the high explosive and the smell of blasted clay and stone and freshly shattered flint. I drove back to Gorizia and our villa and, as I said, went to call on Miss Barkley, who was on duty.

At dinner I ate very quickly and left for the villa where the British had their hospital.

It was really very large and beautiful and there were fine trees in the grounds. Miss Barkley was sitting on a bench in the garden. Miss Ferguson was with her. They seemed glad to see me and in a little while Miss Ferguson excused herself and went away.

'I'll leave you two,' she said. 'You get along very well without me.'

'Don't go, Helen,' Miss Barkley said.

'I'd really rather. I must write some letters.'

'Good-night,' I said.

'Good-night, Mr. Henry.'

'Don't write anything that will bother the censor.'

'Don't worry. I only write about what a beautiful place we live in and how brave the Italians are.'

'That way you'll be decorated.'

'That will be nice. Good-night, Catherine.'

'I'll see you in a little while,' Miss Barkley said. Miss Ferguson walked away in the dark.

'She's nice,' I said.

'Oh, yes, she's very nice. She's a nurse.'

'Aren't you a nurse?'

'Oh, no. I'm something called a V.A.D. We work very hard but no one trusts us.' 'Why not?'

A Farewell to Arms • 13

'They don't trust us when there's nothing going on. When there is really work they trust us.'

'What is the difference?'

'A nurse is like a doctor. It takes a long time to be. A V. A. D. is a short cut.'

'I see.'

'The Italians didn't want women so near the front. So we're all on very special behavior. We don't go out.'

'I can come here though.'

'Oh, yes. We're not cloistered.'

'Let's drop the war.'

'It's very hard. There's no place to drop it.'

'Let's drop it anyway.'

'All right.'

We looked at each other in the dark. I thought she was very beautiful and I took her hand. She let me take it and I held it and put my arm around under her arm.

'No,' she said. I kept my arm where it was.

'Why not?'

'No.'

'Yes,' I said. 'Please.' I leaned forward in the dark to kiss her and there was a sharp stinging flash. She had slapped my face hard. Her hand had hit my nose and eyes, and tears came in my eyes from the reflex.

'I'm so sorry,' she said. I felt I had a certain advantage.

'You were quite right.'

'I'm dreadfully sorry,' she said. 'I just couldn't stand the nurse's-evening off aspect of it. I didn't mean to hurt you. I did hurt you, didn't I?'

She was looking at me in the dark. I was angry and yet certain, seeing it all ahead like the moves in a chess game.

'You did exactly right,' I said. 'I don't mind at all.'

'Poor man.'

'You see I've been leading a sort of a funny life. And I never even talk English. And then you are so very beautiful.' I looked at her.

'You don't need to say a lot of nonsense. I said I was sorry. We do get along.'

'Yes,' I said. 'And we have gotten away from the war.'

She laughed. It was the first time I had ever heard her laugh. I watched her face.

'You are sweet,' she said.

'No, I'm not.'

'Yes. You are a dear. I'd be glad to kiss you if you don't mind.'

I looked in her eyes and put my arm around her as I had before and kissed her. I kissed her hard and held her tight and tried to open her lips; they were closed tight. I was still angry and as I held her suddenly she shivered. I held her close against me and could feel her heart beating and her lips opened and her head went back against my hand and then she was crying on my shoulder.

'Oh, darling,' she said. 'You will be good to me, won't you?'

What the hell, I thought. I stroked her hair and patted her shoulder. She was crying.

'You will, won't you?' She looked up at me. 'Because we're going to have a strange life.'

After a while I walked with her to the door of the villa and she went in and I walked home. Back at the villa I went upstairs to the room. Rinaldi was lying on his bed. He looked at me.

'So you make progress with Miss Barkley?'

'We are friends.'

'You have that pleasant air of a dog in heat.'

I did not understand the word.

'Of a what?' He explained.

'You,' I said, 'have that pleasant air of a dog who—'

'Stop it,' he said. 'In a little while we would say insulting things.' He laughed.

'Good-night,' I said.

'Good-night, little puppy.'

I knocked over his candle with the pillow and got into bed in the dark.

Rinaldi picked up the candle, lit it and went on reading.

6

I was away for two days at the posts. When I got home it was too late and I did not see Miss Barkley until the next evening. She was not in the garden and I had to wait in the office of the hospital until she came down. There were many marble busts on painted wooden pillars along the walls of the room they used for an office. The hall too, that the office opened on, was lined with them. They had the complete marble quality of all looking alike. Sculpture had always seemed a dull business—still, bronzes looked like something. But marble busts all looked like a cemetery. There was one fine cemetery though—the one at Pisa. Genoa was the place to see the bad marbles. This had been the villa of a very wealthy German and the busts must have cost him plenty. I wondered who had done them and how much he got. I tried to make out whether they were members of the family or what; but they were all uniformly classical. You could not tell anything about them.

I sat on a chair and held my cap. We were supposed to wear steel helmets even in Gorizia but they were uncomfortable and too bloody theatrical in a town where the civilian inhabitants had not been evacuated. I wore one when we went up to the posts and carried an English gas mask. We were just beginning to get some of them. They were a real mask. Also we were required to wear an automatic pistol; even doctors and sanitary officers. I felt it against the back of the chair. You were liable to arrest if you did not have one worn in plain sight. Rinaldi carried a holster stuffed with toilet paper. I wore a real one and felt like a gunman until I practised firing it. It was an Astra 7.65 caliber with a short barrel and it jumped so sharply when you let it off that there was no question of hitting anything. I practised with it, holding below the target and trying to master the jerk of the ridiculous short barrel until I could hit within a yard of where I aimed at twenty paces and then the ridiculousness of carrying a pistol at all came over me and I soon forgot it and carried it flopping against the small of my back with no feeling at all except a vague sort of shame when I met English-speaking people. I sat now in the chair and an orderly of some sort looked at me disapprovingly from behind a desk while I looked at the marble floor, the pillars with the marble busts, and the frescoes on the wall and waited for Miss Barkley.

The frescoes were not bad. Any frescoes were good when they started to peel and flake off.

I saw Catherine Barkley coming down the hall, and stood up. She did not seem tall walking toward me but she looked very lovely.

'Good-evening, Mr. Henry,' she said.

'How do you do?' I said. The orderly was listening behind the desk.

'Shall we sit here or go out in the garden?'

'Let's go out. It's much cooler.'

I walked behind her out into the garden, the orderly looking after us. When we were out on the gravel drive she said, 'Where have you been?'

'I've been out on post.'

'You couldn't have sent me a note?'

'No,' I said. 'Not very well. I thought I was coming back.'

'You ought to have let me know, darling.'

We were off the driveway, walking under the trees. I took her hands, then stopped and kissed her.

'Isn't there anywhere we can go?'

'No,' she said. 'We have to just walk here. You've been away a long time.'

'This is the third day. But I'm back now.'

She looked at me, 'And you do love me?'

'Yes.'

'You did say you loved me, didn't you?'

'Yes,' I lied. 'I love you.' I had not said it before.

'And you call me Catherine?'

'Catherine.'

We walked on a way and were stopped under a tree.

'Say, "I've come back to Catherine in the night."'

'I've come back to Catherine in the night.'

'Oh, darling, you have come back, haven't you?'

'Yes.'

'I love you so and it's been awful. You won't go away?'

'No. I'll always come back.'

'Oh, I love you so. Please put your hand there again.'

'It's not been away.' I turned her so I could see her face when I kissed her and I saw that her eyes were shut. I kissed both her shut eyes. I thought she was probably a little crazy. It was all right if she was. I did not care what I was getting into. This was better than going every evening to the house for officers where the girls climbed all over you and put your cap on backward as a sign of affection between their trips upstairs with brother officers. I knew I did not love Catherine Barkley nor had any idea of loving her. This was a game, like bridge, in which you said things instead of playing cards. Like bridge you had to pretend you were playing for money or playing for some stakes. Nobody had mentioned what the stakes were. It was all right with me.

'I wish there was some place we could go,' I said. I was experiencing the masculine difficulty of making love very long standing up.

'There isn't any place,' she said. She came back from wherever she had been.

'We might sit there just for a little while.'

We sat on the flat stone bench and I held Catherine Barkley's hand. She would not let me put my arm around her.

'Are you very tired?' she asked.

'No.'

She looked down at the grass.

'This is a rotten game we play, isn't it?'

'What game?'

'Don't be dull.'

'I'm not, on purpose.'

'You're a nice boy,' she said. 'And you play it as well as you know how. But it's a rotten game.'

'Do you always know what people think?'

'Not always. But I do with you. You don't have to pretend you love me. That's over for the evening. Is there anything you'd like to talk about?'

'But I do love you.'

'Please let's not lie when we don't have to. I had a very fine little show and I'm all right now. You see I'm not mad and I'm not gone off. It's only a little sometimes.'

I pressed her hand, 'Dear Catherine.'

'It sounds very funny now—Catherine. You don't pronounce it very much alike. But you're very nice. You're a very good boy.'

'That's what the priest said.'

'Yes, you're very good. And you will come and see me?'

'Of course.'

'And you don't have to say you love me. That's all over for a while.' She stood up and put out her hand. 'Good-night.'

I wanted to kiss her.

'No,' she said. 'I'm awfully tired.'

'Kiss me, though,' I said.

'I'm awfully tired, darling.'

'Kiss me.'

'Do you want to very much?'

'Yes.'

We kissed and she broke away suddenly. 'No. Good-night, please, darling.' We walked to the door and I saw her go in and down the hall. I liked to watch her move. She went on down the hall. I went on home. It was a hot night and there was a good deal going on up in the mountains. I watched the flashes on San Gabriele.

I stopped in front of the Villa Rossa. The shutters were up but it was still going on inside. Somebody was singing. I went on home. Rinaldi came in while I was undressing.

'Ah, ha!' he said. 'It does not go so well. Baby is puzzled.' 'Where have you been?'

'At the Villa Rossa. It was very edifying, baby. We all sang. Where have you been?'

'Calling on the British.'

'Thank God I did not become involved with the British.'

7

I came back the next afternoon from our first mountain post and stopped the car at the smistimento where the wounded and sick were sorted by their papers and the papers marked for the different hospitals. I had been driving and I sat in the car and the driver took the papers in. It was a hot day and the sky was very bright and blue and the road was white and dusty. I sat in the high seat of the Fiat and thought about nothing. A regiment went by in the road and I watched them pass. The men were hot and sweating. Some wore their steel helmets but most of them carried them slung from their packs. Most of the helmets were too big and came down almost over the ears of the men who wore them.

The officers all wore helmets; better-fitting helmets. It was half of the brigata Basilicata. I identified them by their red and white striped collar mark. There were stragglers going by long after the regiment had passed—men who could not keep up with their platoons. They were sweaty, dusty and tired. Some looked pretty bad. A soldier came along after the last of the stragglers. He was walking with a limp. He stopped and sat down beside the road. I got down and went over.

'What's the matter?'

He looked at me, then stood up.

'I'm going on.'

'What's the trouble?'

'—the war.'

'What's wrong with your leg?'

'It's not my leg. I got a rupture.'

'Why don't you ride with the transport?' I asked. 'Why don't you go to the hospital?'

'They won't let me. The lieutenant said I slipped the truss on purpose.'
'Let me feel it.' 'It's way out.'
'Which side is it on?'
'Here.'
I felt it.
'Cough,' I said.
'I'm afraid it will make it bigger. It's twice as big as it was this morning.'
'Sit down,' I said. 'As soon as I get the papers on these wounded I'll take you along the road and drop you with your medical officers.'
'He'll say I did it on purpose.'
'They can't do anything,' I said. 'It's not a wound. You've had it before, haven't you?'
'But I lost the truss.'
'They'll send you to a hospital.'
'Can't I stay here, Tenente?'
'No, I haven't any papers for you.'
The driver came out of the door with the papers for the wounded in the car.
'Four for 105. Two for 132,' he said. They were hospitals beyond the river.
'You drive,' I said. I helped the soldier with the rupture up on the seat with us.
'You speak English?' he asked.
'Sure.'
'How you like this goddam war?'
'Rotten.'
'I say it's rotten. Jesus Christ, I say it's rotten.'
'Were you in the States?'
'Sure. In Pittsburgh. I knew you was an American.'
'Don't I talk Italian good enough?'
'I knew you was an American all right.'
'Another American,' said the driver in Italian looking at the hernia man.
'Listen, lootenant. Do you have to take me to that regiment?'
'Yes.'
'Because the captain doctor knew I had this rupture. I threw away the goddam truss so it would get bad and I wouldn't have to go to the line again.'
'I see.'
'Couldn't you take me no place else?'
'If it was closer to the front I could take you to a first medical post. But back here you've got to have papers.'
'If I go back they'll make me get operated on and then they'll put me in the line all the time.'
I thought it over.
'You wouldn't want to go in the line all the time, would you?' he asked.
'No.'
'Jesus Christ, ain't this a goddam war?'

'Listen,' I said. 'You get out and fall down by the road and get a bump on your head and I'll pick you up on our way back and take you to a hospital. We'll stop by the road here, Aldo.' We stopped at the side of the road. I helped him down.

'I'll be right here, lieutenant,' he said.

'So long,' I said. We went on and passed the regiment about a mile ahead, then crossed the river, cloudy with snow-water and running fast through the spiles of the bridge, to ride along the road across the plain and deliver the wounded at the two hospitals. I drove coming back and went fast with the empty car to find the man from Pittsburgh. First we passed the regiment, hotter and slower than ever: then the stragglers. Then we saw a horse ambulance stopped by the road. Two men were lifting the hernia man to put him in. They had come back for him. He shook his head at me. His helmet was off and his forehead was bleeding below the hair line. His nose was skinned and there was dust on the bloody patch and dust in his hair.

'Look at the bump, lieutenant!' he shouted. 'Nothing to do. They come back for me.'

When I got back to the villa it was five o'clock and I went out where we washed the cars, to take a shower. Then I made out my report in my room, sitting in my trousers and an undershirt in front of the open window. In two days the offensive was to start and I would go with the cars to Plava. It was a long time since I had written to the States and I knew I should write but I had let it go so long that it was almost impossible to write now. There was nothing to write about. I sent a couple of army Zona di Guerra post-cards, crossing out everything except, I am well. That should handle them. Those post-cards would be very fine in America; strange and mysterious. This was a strange and mysterious war zone but I supposed it was quite well run and grim compared to other wars with the Austrians. The Austrian army was created to give Napoleon victories; any Napoleon. I wished we had a Napoleon, but instead we had Ii Generale Cadorna, fat and prosperous and Vittorio Emmanuele, the tiny man with the long thin neck and the goat beard. Over on the right they had the Duke of Aosta. Maybe he was too good-looking to be a. great general but he looked like a man. Lots of them would have liked him to be king. He looked like a king. He was the King's uncle and commanded the third army. We were in the second army. There were some British batteries up with the third army. I had met two gunners from that lot, in Milan. They were very nice and we had a big evening.

They were big and shy and embarrassed and very appreciative together of anything that happened. I wish that I was with the British. It would have been much simpler. Still I would probably have been killed. Not in this ambulance business. Yes, even in the ambulance business. British ambulance drivers were killed sometimes. Well, I knew I would not be killed. Not in this war. It did not have anything to do with me. It seemed no more dangerous to me myself than war in the movies. I wished to God it was over though.

Maybe it would finish this summer. Maybe the Austrians would crack. They had always cracked in other wars. What was the matter with this war? Everybody said the French were through. Rinaldi said that the French had mutinied and troops marched on Paris. I asked him what happened and he said, 'Oh, they stopped them.' I wanted to go to Austria without war. I wanted to go to the Black Forest. I wanted to go to the Hartz Mountains.

Where were the Hartz Mountains anyway? They were fighting in the Carpathians. I did not want to go there anyway. It might be good though. I could go to Spain if there was no war. The sun was going down and the day was cooling off. After supper I would go and see Catherine Barkley. I wish she were here now. I wished I were in Milan with her. I would like to eat at the Cova and then walk down the Via Manzoni in the hot evening and cross over and turn off along the canal and go to the hotel with Catherine Barkley. Maybe she would. Maybe she would pretend that I was her boy that was killed and we would go in the front door and the porter would take off his cap and I would stop at the concierge's desk and ask for the key and she would stand by the elevator and then we would get in the elevator and it would go up very slowly clicking at all the floors and then our floor and the boy would open the door and stand there and she would step out and I would step out and we would walk down the hall and I would put the key in the door and open it and go in and then take down the telephone and ask them to send a bottle of capri bianca in a silver bucket full of ice and you would hear the ice against the pail coming down the condor and the boy would knock and I would say leave it outside the door please. Because we would not wear any clothes because it was so hot and the window open and the swallows flying over the roofs of the houses and when it was dark afterward and you went to the window very small bats hunting over the houses and close down over the trees and we would drink the capri and the door locked and it hot and only a sheet and the whole night and we would both love each other all night in the hot night in Milan. That was how it ought to be. I would eat quickly and go and see Catherine Barkley.

They talked too much at the mess and I drank wine because tonight we were not all brothers unless I drank a little and talked with the priest about Archbishop Ireland who was, it seemed, a noble man and with whose injustice, the injustices he had received and in which I participated as an American, and of which I had never heard, I feigned acquaintance. It would have been impolite not to have known something of them when I had listened to such a splendid explanation of their causes which were, after all, it seemed, misunderstandings. I thought he had a fine name and he came from Minnesota which made a lovely name: Ireland of Minnesota, Ireland of Wisconsin, Ireland of Michigan. What made it pretty was that it sounded like Island. No that wasn't it. There was more to it than that. Yes, father. That is true, father. Perhaps, father. No, father. Well, maybe yes, father. You know more about it than I do, father. The priest was good but dull. The officers were not good but dull. The King was good but dull. The wine was bad but not dull. It took the enamel off your teeth and left it on the roof of your mouth.

'And the priest was locked up,' Rocca said, 'because they found the three per cent bonds on his person. It was in France of course. Here they would never have arrested him. He denied all knowledge of the five per cent bonds. This took place at Béziers. I was there and reading of it in the paper, went to the jail and asked to see the priest. It was quite evident he had stolen the bonds.'

'I don't believe a word of this,' Rinaldi said.

'Just as you like,' Rocca said. 'But I am telling it for our priest here. It is very informative. He is a priest; he will appreciate it.'

The priest smiled. 'Go on,' he said. 'I am listening.'

'Of course some of the bonds were not accounted for but the priest had all of the three per cent bonds and several local obligations, I forget exactly what they were. So I went to the jail, now this is the point of the story, and I stood outside his cell and I said as though I were going to confession, "Bless me, father, for you have sinned."'

There was great laughter from everybody.

'And what did he say?' asked the priest. Rocca ignored this and went on to explain the joke to me. 'You see the point, don't you?' It seemed it was a very funny joke if you understood it properly. They poured me more wine and I told the story about the English private soldier who was placed under the shower bath. Then the major told the story of the eleven Czecho-slovaks and the Hungarian corporal. After some more wine I told the story of the jockey who found the penny. The major said there was an Italian story something like that about the duchess who could not sleep at night. At this point the priest left and I told the story about the travelling salesman who arrived at five o'clock in the morning at Marseilles when the mistral was blowing. The major said he had heard a report that I could drink. I denied this. He said it was true and by the corpse of Bacchus we would test whether it was true or not. Not Bacchus, I said. Not Baëchus. Yes, Bacchus, he said. I should drink cup for cup and glass for glass with Bassi, Fillipo Vincenza. Bassi said no that was no test because he had already drunk twice as much as I. I said that was a foul lie and, Bacchus or no Bacchus, Fillipo Vincenza Bassi or Bassi Fillippo Vicenza had never touched a drop all evening and what was his name anyway? He said was my name Frederico Enrico or Enrico Federico? I said let the best man win, Bacchus barred, and the major started us with red wine in mugs. Half-way through the wine I did not want any more. I remembered where I was going.

'Bassi wins,' I said. 'He's a better man than I am. I have to go.'

'He does really,' said Rinaldi. 'He has a rendezvous. I know all about it.'

'I have to go.'

'Another night,' said Bassi. 'Another night when you feel stronger.' He slapped me on the shoulder. There were lighted candles on the table. All the officers were very happy. 'Good-night, gentlemen,' I said.

Rinaldi went out with me. We stood outside the door on the patch and he said, 'You better not go up there drunk.'

'I'm not drunk, Rinin. Really.'

'You'd better chew some coffee.'

'Nonsense.'

'I'll get some, baby. You walk up and down.' He came back with a handful of roasted coffee beans. 'Chew those, baby, and God be with you.'

'Bacchus,' I said.

'I'll walk down with you.'

'I'm perfectly all right.'

We walked along together through the town and I chewed the coffee. At the gate of the driveway that led up to the British villa, Rinaldi said good-night.

'Good-night,' I said. 'Why don't you come in?'

He shook his head. 'No,' he said. 'I like the simpler pleasures.'

'Thank you for the coffee beans.'

'Nothing, baby. Nothing.'

J started down the driveway. The outlines of the cypresses that lined it were sharp and clear. I looked back and saw Rinaldi standing watching me and waved to him.

I sat in the reception hail of the villa, waiting for Catherine Barkley to come down.

Some one was coming down the hallway. I stood up, but it was not Catherine. It was Miss Ferguson.

'Hello,' she said. 'Catherine asked me to tell you she was sorry she couldn't see you this evening.'

'I'm so sorry. I hope she's not ill.'

'She's not awfully well.'

'Will you tell her how sorry I am?'

'Yes, I will.'

'Do you think it would be any good to try and see her tomorrow?'

'Yes, I do.'

'Thank you very much,' I said. 'Good-night.'

I went out the door and suddenly I felt lonely and empty. I had treated seeing Catherine very lightly, I had gotten somewhat drunk and had nearly forgotten to come but when I could not see her there I was feeling lonely and hollow.

8

The next afternoon we heard there was to be an attack up the river that night and that we were to take four cars there. Nobody knew anything about it although they all spoke with great positiveness and strategical knowledge. I was riding in the first car and as we passed the entry to the British hospital I told the driver to stop. The other cars pulled up. I got out and told the driver to go on and that if we had not caught up to them at the junction of the road to Cormons to wait there. I hurried up the driveway and inside the reception hall I asked for Miss Barkley.

'She's on duty.'

'Could I see her just for a moment?'

They sent an orderly to see and she came back with him.

'I stopped to ask if you were better. They told me you were on duty, so I asked to see you.'

'I'm quite well,' she said, 'I think the heat knocked me over yesterday.'

'I have to go.'

'I'll just step out the door a minute.'

'And you're all right?' I asked outside.

'Yes, darling. Are you coming to-night?'

'No. I'm leaving now for a show up above Plava.'

'A show?'

'I don't think it's anything.'

'And you'll be back?'

'To-morrow.'

She was unclasping something from her neck. She put it in my hand. 'It's a Saint Anthony,' she said. 'And come to-morrow night.'

'You're not a Catholic, are you?'

'No. But they say a Saint Anthony's very useful.'

'I'll take care of him for you. Good-by.'

'No,' she said, 'not good-by.' 'All right.'

'Be a good boy and be careful. No, you can't kiss me here. You can't.'

'All right.'

I looked back and saw her standing on the steps. She waved and I kissed my hand and held it out. She waved again and then I was out of the driveway and climbing up into the seat of the ambulance and we started. The Saint Anthony was in a little white metal capsule. I opened the capsule and spilled him out into my hand.

'Saint Anthony?' asked the driver.

'Yes.'

'I have one.' His right hand left the wheel and opened a button on his tunic and pulled it out from under his shirt.

'See?'

I put my Saint Anthony back in the capsule, spilled the thin gold chain together and put it all in my breast pocket.

'You don't wear him?'

'No.'

'It's better to wear him. That's what it's for.'

'All right,' I said. I undid the clasp of the gold chain and put it around my neck and clasped it. The saint hung down on the Outside of my uniform and I undid the throat of my tunic, unbuttoned the shirt collar and dropped him in under the shirt. I felt him in his metal box against my chest while we drove. Then I forgot about him. After I was wounded I never found him. Some one probably got it at one of the dressing stations.

We drove fast when we were over the bridge and soon we saw the dust of the other cars ahead down the road. The road curved and we saw the three cars looking quite small, the dust rising from the wheels and going off through the trees. We caught them and passed them and turned off on a road that climbed up into the hills. Driving in convoy is not unpleasant if you are the first car and I settled back in the seat and watched the country. We were in the foothills on the near side of the river and as the road mounted there were the high mountains off to the north with snow still on the tops. I looked back and saw the three cars all climbing, spaced by the interval of their dust. We passed a long column of loaded mules, the drivers walking along beside the mules wearing red fezzes. They were bersaglieri.

Beyond the mule train the road was empty and we climbed through the hills and then went down over the shoulder of a long hill into a river-valley. There were trees along both sides of the road and through the right line of trees I saw the river, the water clear, fast and shallow. The river was low and there were stretches of sand and pebbles with a narrow channel of water and sometimes the water spread like a sheen over the pebbly bed. Close to the bank I saw deep pools, the water blue like the sky. I saw arched stone bridges over the river where tracks turned off from the road and we passed stone farmhouses with pear trees candelabraed against their south walls and low stone walls in the fields. The road went up the valley a long way and then we turned off and commenced to climb into the hills again. The road climbed steeply going up and back and forth through chestnut woods to level finally along a ridge. I could look down through the woods and see, far below, with the sun on it, the line of the river that separated the two armies. We went along the rough new military road that followed the crest of the ridge and I looked to the north at the two ranges of mountains, green and dark to the snow-line and then white and lovely in the sun. Then, as the road mounted along the ridge, I saw a third range of mountains, higher snow mountains, that looked chalky white and furrowed, with strange planes, and then there were mountains far off beyond all these that you could hardly tell if you really saw. Those were all the Austrians' mountains and we had nothing like them.

Ahead there was a rounded turn-off in the road to the right and looking down I could see the road dropping through the trees. There were troops on this road and motor trucks and mules with mountain guns and as we went down, keeping to the side, I could see the river far down below, the line of ties and rails running along it, the old bridge where the railway crossed to the other side and across, under a hill beyond the river, the broken houses of the little town that was to be taken.

It was nearly dark when we came down and turned onto the main road that ran beside the river.

9

The road was crowded and there were screens of corn-stalk and straw matting on both sides and matting over the top so that it was like the entrance at a circus or a native village. We drove slowly in this matting-covered tunnel and came out onto a bare cleared space where the railway station had been. The road here was below the level of the river bank and all along the side of the sunken road there were holes dug in the bank with infantry in them. The sun was going down and looking up along the bank as we drove I saw the Austrian observation balloons above the hills on the other side dark against the sunset. We parked the cars beyond a brickyard. The ovens and some deep holes had been equipped as dressing stations. There were three doctors that I knew. I talked with the major and learned that when it should start and our cars should be loaded we would drive them back along the screened road and up to the main road along the ridge where there would be a post and other cars to clear them. He hoped the road would not jam. It was a one-road show. The road was screened because it was in sight of the Austrians across the river. Here at the brickyard we were sheltered from rifle or machine-gun fire by the river bank. There was one smashed bridge across the river. They were going to put over another bridge when the bombardment started and some troops were to cross at the shallows up above at the bend of the river. The major was a little man with upturned mustaches. He had been in the war in Libya and wore two woundstripes. He said that if the thing went well he would see that I was decorated. I said I hoped it would go well but that he was too kind. I asked him if there was a big dugout where the drivers could stay and he sent a soldier to show me. I went with him and found the dugout, which was very good. The drivers were pleased with it and I left them there. The major asked me to have a drink with him and two other officers. We drank rum and it was very friendly. Outside it was getting dark. I asked what time the attack was to he and they said as soon as it was dark. I went back to the drivers. They were sitting in the dugout talking and when I came in they stopped. I gave them each a package of cigarettes, Macedonias, loosely packed cigarettes that spilled tobacco and needed to have the ends twisted before you smoked them. Manera lit his lighter and passed it around. The lighter was shaped like a Fiat radiator. I told them what I had heard.

'Why didn't we see the post when we came down?' Passini asked.

'It was just beyond where we turned off.'

'That road will be a dirty mess,' Manera said.

'They'll shell the—out of us.'

'Probably.'

'What about eating, lieutenant? We won't get a chance to eat after this thing starts.'

'I'll go and see now,' I said.

'You want us to stay here or can we look around?'

'Better stay here.'

I went back to the major's dugout and he said the field kitchen would be along and the drivers could come and get their stew. He would loan them mess tins if they did not have them. I said I thought they had them. I went back and told the drivers I would get them as soon as the food came. Manera said he hoped it would come before the bombardment started. They were silent until I went out. They were all mechanics and hated the war.

I went out to look at the cars and see what was going on and then came back and sat down in the dugout with the four drivers. We sat on the ground with our backs against the wall and smoked. Outside it was nearly dark. The earth of the dugout was warm and dry and I let my shoulders back against the wall, sitting on the small of my back, and relaxed.

'Who goes to the attack?' asked Gavuzzi.

'Bersaglieri.'

'All bersaglieri?'

'I think so.'

'There aren't enough troops here for a real attack.'

'It is probably to draw attention from where the real attack will be.'

'Do the men know that who attack?'

'I don't think so.'

'Of course they don't,' Manera said. 'They wouldn't attack if they did.'

'Yes, they would,' Passini said. 'Bersaglieri are fools.'

'They are brave and have good discipline,' I said.

'They are big through the chest by measurement, and healthy. But they are still fools.' man?' them.'

'The granatieri are tall,' Manera said. This was a joke. They all laughed.

'Were you there, Tenente, when they wouldn't attack and they shot every tenth

'No.'

'It is true. They lined them up afterward and took every tenth man. Carabinieri shot

'Carabinieri,' said Passini and spat on the floor. 'But those grenadiers; all over six feet. They wouldn't attack.'

'If everybody would not attack the war would be over,' Manera said.

'It wasn't that way with the granatieri. They were afraid. The officers all came from such good families.'

'Some of the officers went alone.'

'A sergeant shot two officers who would not get out.'

'Some troops went out.'

'Those that went out were not lined up when they took the tenth men.'

'One of those shot by the carabinieri is from my town,' Passini said. 'He was a big smart tall boy to be in the granatieri. Always in Rome. Always with the girls. Always with the carabinieri.' He laughed. 'Now they have a guard outside his house with a bayonet and nobody can come to see his mother and father and sisters and his father loses his civil rights and cannot even vote. They are all without law to protect them. Anybody can take their property.'

'If it wasn't that that happens to their families nobody would go to the attack.'

'Yes. Alpini would. These V. E. soldiers would. Some bersaglieri.'

'Bersaglieri have run too. Now they try to forget it.'

'You should not let us talk this way, Tenente. Evviva l'esercito,' Passini said sarcastically.

'I know how you talk,' I said. 'But as long as you drive the cars and behave—'

'—and don't talk so other officers can hear,' Manera finished. 'I believe we should get the war over,' I said. 'It would not finish it if one side stopped fighting. It would only be worse if we stopped fighting.'

'It could not be worse,' Passini said respectfully. 'There is nothing worse than war.' 'Defeat is worse.'

'I do not believe it,' Passini said still respectfully. 'What is defeat? You go home.'

'They come after you. They take your home. They take your sisters.'

'I don't believe it,' Passini said. 'They can't do that to everybody. Let everybody defend his home. Let them keep their sisters in the house.'

'They hang you. They come and make you be a soldier again. Not in the auto-ambulance, in the infantry.'

'They can't hang every one.'

'An outside nation can't make you be a soldier,' Manera said. 'At the first battle you all run.'

'Like the Tchecos.'

'I think you do not know anything about being conquered and so you think it is not bad.'

'Tenente,' Passini said. 'We understand you let us talk. Listen. There is nothing as bad as war. We in the auto-ambulance cannot even realize at all how bad it is. When people realize how bad it is they cannot do anything to stop it because they go crazy. There are some people who never realize. There are people who are afraid of their officers. It is with them the war is made.'

'I know it is bad but we must finish it.'

'It doesn't finish. There is no finish to a war.'

'Yes there is.'

Passini shook his head.

'War is not won by victory. What if we take San Gabriele? What if we take the Carso and Monfalcone and Trieste? Where are we then? Did you see all the far mountains to-day? Do you think we could take all them too? Only if the Austrians stop fighting. One side must stop fighting. Why don't we stop fighting? If they come down into Italy they will get tired and go away. They have their own country. But no, instead there is a war.'

'You're an orator.'

'We think. We read. We are not peasants. We are mechanics. But even the peasants know better than to believe in a war. Everybody hates this war.'

'There is a class that controls a country that is stupid and does not realize anything and never can. That is why we have this war.'

'Also they make money out of it.'

'Most of them don't,' said Passini. 'They are too stupid. They do it for nothing. For stupidity.'

'We must shut up,' said Manera. 'We talk too much even for the Tenente.'

'He likes it,' said Passini. 'We will convert him.'

'But now we will shut up,' Manera said.

'Do we eat yet, Tenente?' Gavuzzi asked.

'I will go and see,' I said. Gordini stood up and went outside with me.

'Is there anything I can do, Tenente? Can I help in any way?' He was the quietest one of the four. 'Come with me if you want,' I said, 'and we'll see.'

It was dark outside and the long light from the search-lights was moving over the mountains. There were big search-lights on that front mounted on camions that you passed sometimes on the roads at night, close behind the lines, the camion stopped a little off the road, an officer directing the light and the crew scared. We crossed the brickyard, and stopped at the main dressing station. There was a little shelter of green branches outside over the entrance and in the dark the night wind rustled the leaves dried by the sun. Inside there was a light. The major was at the telephone sitting on a box. One of the medical captains said the attack had been put forward an hour. He offered me a glass of cognac. I looked at the board tables, the instruments shining in the light, the basins and the stoppered bottles. Gordini stood behind me. The major got up from the telephone.

'It starts now,' he said. 'It has been put back again.'

I looked outside, it was dark and the Austrian search-lights were moving on the mountains behind us. It was quiet for a moment still, then from all the guns behind us the bombardment started.

'Savoia,' said the major.

'About the soup, major,' I said. He did not hear me. I repeated it.

'It hasn't come up.'

A big shell came in and burst outside in the brickyard. Another burst and in the noise you could hear the smaller noise of the brick and dirt raining down.

'What is there to eat?'

'We have a little pasta asciutta,' the major said.

'I'll take what you can give me.'

The major spoke to an orderly who went out of sight in the back and came back with a metal basin of cold cooked macaroni. I handed it to Gordini.

'Have you any cheese?'

The major spoke grudgingly to the orderly who ducked back into the hole again and came out with a quarter of a white cheese.

'Thank you very much,' I said.

'You'd better not go out.'

Outside something was set down beside the entrance. One of the two men who had carried it looked in.

'Bring him in,' said the major. 'What's the matter with you? Do you want us to come outside and get him?'

The two stretcher-bearers picked up the man under the arms and by the legs and brought him in.

'Slit the tunic,' the major said.

He held a forceps with some gauze in the end. The two captains took off their coats. 'Get out of here,' the major said to the two stretcher-bearers.

'Come on,' I said to Gordini.

'You better wait until the shelling is over,' the major said over his shoulder.

'They want to eat,' I said.

'As you wish.'

Outside we ran across the brickyard. A shell burst short near the river bank. Then there was one that we did not hear coming until the sudden rush. We both went flat and with the flash and bump of the burst and the smell heard the singing off of the fragments and the rattle of falling brick. Gordini got up and ran for the dugout. I was after him, holding the cheese, its smooth surface covered with brick dust. Inside the dugout were the three drivers sitting against the wall, smoking.

'Here, you patriots,' I said.

'How are the cars?' Manera asked.

'All right.'

'Did they scare you, Tenente?'

'You're damned right,' I said.

I took out my knife, opened it, wiped off the blade and pared off the dirty outside surface of the cheese. Gavuzzi handed me the basin of macaroni.

'Start in to eat, Tenente.'

'No,' I said. 'Put it on the floor. We'll all eat.'

'There are no forks.'

'What the hell,' I said in English.

I cut the cheese into pieces and laid them on the macaroni.

'Sit down to it,' I said. They sat down and waited. I put thumb and fingers into the macaroni and lifted. A mass loosened.

'Lift it high, Tenente.'

I lifted it to arm's length and the strands cleared. I lowered it into the mouth, sucked and snapped in the ends, and chewed, then took a bite of cheese, chewed, and then a drink of the wine. It tasted of rusty metal. I handed the canteen back to Passini.

'It's rotten,' he said. 'It's been in there too long. I had it in the car.'

They were all eating, holding their chins close over the basin, tipping their heads back, sucking in the ends. I took another mouthful and some cheese and a rinse of wine. Something landed outside that shook the earth.

'Four hundred twenty or minnenwerfer,' Gavuzzi said.

'There aren't any four hundred twenties in the mountains,' I said.

'They have big Skoda guns. I've seen the holes.'

'Three hundred fives.'

We went on eating. There was a cough, a noise like a railway engine starting and then an explosion that shook the earth again.

'This isn't a deep dugout,' Passini said.

'That was a big trench mortar.'

'Yes, sir.'

I ate the end of my piece of cheese and took a swallow of wine. Through the other noise I heard a cough, then came the chuh-chuhchuh-chuh—then there was a flash, as when a blast-furnace door is swung open, and a roar that started white and went red and on and on in a rushing wind. I tried to breathe but my breath would not come and I felt myself rush bodily out of myself and out and out and out and all the time bodily in the wind. I went out swiftly, all of myself, and I knew I was dead and that it had all been a mistake to think you just died. Then I floated, and instead of going on I felt myself slide back. I breathed and I was back. The ground was torn up and in front of my head there was a splintered beam of wood. In the jolt of my head I heard somebody crying. I thought somebody was screaming. I tried to move but I could not move. I heard the machine-guns and rifles firing across the river and all along the river. There was a great splashing and I saw the star-shells go up and burst and float whitely and rockets going up and heard the bombs, all this in a moment, and then I heard close to me some one saying Mama Mia!

Oh, mama Mia!' I pulled and twisted and got my legs loose finally and turned around and touched him. It was Passini and when I touched him he screamed. His legs were toward me and I saw in the dark and the light that they were both smashed above the knee. One leg was gone and the other was held by tendons and part of the trouser and the stump twitched and jerked as though it were not connected. He bit his arm and moaned, 'Oh mama mia, mama Mia,' then, 'Dio te salve, Maria. Dio te salve, Maria. Oh Jesus shoot me Christ shoot me mama mia mama Mia oh purest lovely Mary shoot me. Stop it. Stop it.

Stop it. Oh Jesus lovely Mary stop it. Oh oh oh oh,' then choking, 'Mama mama mia.' Then he was quiet, biting his arm, the stump of his leg twitching.

'Porta feriti!' I shouted holding my hands cupped. 'Porta feriti!' I tried to get closer to Passini to try to put a tourniquet on the legs but I could not move. I tried again and my legs moved a little. I could pull backward along with my arms and elbows. Passini was quiet now. I sat beside him, undid my tunic and tried to rip the tail of my shirt. It would not rip and I bit the edge of the cloth to start it. Then I thought of his puttees. I had on wool stockings but Passini wore puttees. All the drivers wore puttees but Passini had only one leg. I unwound the puttee and while I was doing it I saw there was no need to try and make a tourniquet because he was dead already. I made sure he was dead. There were three others to locate. I sat up straight and as I did so something inside my head moved like the weights on a doll's eyes and it hit me inside in back of my eyeballs. My legs felt warm and wet and my shoes were wet and warm inside. I knew that I was hit and leaned over and put my hand on my knee. My knee wasn't there. My hand went in and my knee was down on my shin. I wiped my hand on my shirt and another floating light came very slowly down and I looked at my leg and was very afraid. Oh, God, I said, get me out of here. I knew, however, that there had been three others. There were four drivers. Passini was dead. That left three. Some one took hold of me under the arms and somebody else lifted my legs.

'There are three others,' I said. 'One is dead.'

'It's Manera. We went for a stretcher but there wasn't any. How are you, Tenente?'

'Where is Gordini and Gavuzzi?'

'Gordini's at the post getting bandaged. Gavuzzi has your legs. Hold on to my neck, Tenente. Are you badly hit?'

'In the leg. How is Gordini?'

'He's all right. It was a big trench mortar shell.'

'Passini's dead.'

'Yes. He's dead.'

A shell fell close and they both dropped to the ground and dropped me. 'I'm sorry, Tenente,' said Manera. 'Hang onto my neck.'

'If you drop me again.'

'It was because we were scared.'

'Are you unwounded?'

'We are both wounded a little.'

'Can Gordini drive?'

'I don't think so.'

They dropped me once more before we reached the post.

'You sons of bitches,' I said.

'I am sorry, Tenente,' Manera said. 'We won't drop you again.'

Outside the post a great many of us lay on the ground in the dark. They carried wounded in and brought them out. I could see the light come out from the dressing station when the curtain opened and they brought some one in or out. The dead were off to one side. The doctors were working with their sleeves up to their shoulders and were red as butchers. There were not enough stretchers. Some of the wounded were noisy but most were quiet. The wind blew the leaves in the bower over the door of the dressing station and the night was getting cold. Stretcher-bearers came in all the time, put their stretchers down, unloaded them and went away. As soon as I got to the dressing station Manera brought a medical sergeant out and he put bandages on both my legs. He said there was so much dirt blown into the wound that there had not been much hemorrhage. They would take me as soon as possible. He went back inside. Gordini could not drive, Manera said. His shoulder was smashed and his head was hurt. He had not felt bad but now the shoulder had stiffened. He was sitting up beside one of the brick walls. Manera and Gavuzzi each went off with a load of wounded. They could drive all right. The British had come with three ambulances and they had two men on each ambulance. One of their drivers came over to me, brought by Gordini who looked very white and sick. The Britisher leaned over.

'Are you hit badly?' he asked. He was a tall man and wore steel-rimmed spectacles.

'In the legs.'

'It's not serious I hope. Will you have a cigarette?'

'Thanks.'

'They tell me you've lost two drivers.'

'Yes. One killed and the fellow that brought you.'

'What rotten luck. Would you like us to take the cars?'

'That's what I wanted to ask you.'

'We'd take quite good care of them and return them to the villa. 206 aren't you?'

'Yes.'

'It's a charming place. I've seen you about. They tell me you're an American.'

'Yes.'

'I'm English.'

'No!'

'Yes, English. Did you think I was Italian? There were some Italians with one of our units.'

'It would be fine if you would take the cars,' I said.

'We'll be most careful of them,' he straightened up. 'This chap of yours was very anxious for me to see you.' He patted Gordini on the shoulder. Gordini winced and smiled. The Englishman broke into voluble and perfect Italian. 'Now everything is arranged. I've seen your Tenente. We will take over the two cars. You won't worry now.' He broke off, 'I must do something about getting you out of here. I'll see the medical wallahs. We'll take you back with us.'

He walked across to the dressing station, stepping carefully among the wounded. I saw the blanket open, the light came out and he went in.

'He will look after you, Tenente,' Gordini said.

'How are you, Franco?'

'I am all right.' He sat down beside me. In a moment the blanket in front of the dressing station opened and two stretcherbearers came out followed by the tall Englishman. He brought them over to me.

'Here is the American Tenente,' he said in Italian.

'I'd rather wait,' I said. 'There are much worse wounded than me. I'm all right.'

'Come, come,' he said. 'Don't be a bloody hero.' Then in Italian: 'Lift him very carefully about the legs. His legs are very painful. He is the legitimate son of President Wilson.' They picked me up and took me into the dressing room. Inside they were operating on all the tables. The little major looked at us furious. He recognized me and waved a forceps.

'Ca va bien?'

'Ca va.'

'I have brought him in,' the tall Englishman said in Italian. 'The only son of the American Ambassador. He can be here until you are ready to take him. Then I will take him with my first load.' He bent over me. 'I'll look up their adjutant to do your papers and it will all go much faster.' He stooped to go under the doorway and went out. The major was unhooking the forceps now, dropping them in a basin. I followed his hands with my eyes. Now he was bandaging. Then the stretcher-bearers took the man off the table.

'I'll take the American Tenente,' one of the captains said. They lifted me onto the table. It was hard and slippery. There were many strong smells, chemical smells and the sweet smell of blood. They took off my trousers and the medical captain commenced dictating to the sergeant-adjutant while he worked, 'Multiple superficial wounds of the left and right thigh and left and right knee and right foot. Profound wounds of right knee and foot. Lacerations of the scalp (he probed—Does that hurt?—Christ, yes!) with possible fracture of the skull. Incurred in the line of duty. That's what keeps you from being court- martialled for self-inflicted wounds,' he said. 'Would you like a drink of brandy? How did you run into this thing anyway? What were you trying to do? Commit suicide? Antitetanus please, and mark a cross on both legs. Thank you. I'll clean this up a little, wash it out, and put on a dressing. Your blood coagulates beautifully.'

The adjutant, looking up from the paper, 'What inflicted the wounds?'

The medical captain, 'What hit you?'

Me, with the eyes shut, 'A trench mortar shell.'

The captain, doing things that hurt sharply and severing tissue—"Are you sure?'

Me—trying to lie still and feeling my stomach flutter when the flesh was cut, 'I think so.'

Captain doctor—(interested in something he was finding), 'Fragments of enemy trench-mortar shell. Now I'll probe for some of this if you like but it's not necessary. I'll paint all this and—Does that sting? Good, that's nothing to how it will feel later. The pain hasn't started yet. Bring him a glass of brandy. The shock dulls the pain; but this is all right, you have nothing to worry about if it doesn't infect and it rarely does now. How is your head?'

'Good Christ" I said.

'Better not drink too much brandy then. If you've got a fracture you don't want inflammation. How does that feel?'

Sweat ran all over me.

'Good Christ!' I said.

'I guess you've got a fracture all right. I'll wrap you up and don't bounce your head around.' He bandaged, his hands moving very fast and the bandage coming taut and sure. 'All right, good luck and Vive la France.'

'He's an American,' one of the other captains said.

'I thought you said he was a Frenchman. He talks French,' the captain said. 'I've known him before. I always thought he was French.' He drank a half tumbler of cognac. 'Bring on something serious. Get some more of that Antitetanus.' The captain waved to me. They lifted me and the blanket-flap went across my face as we went out. Outside the sergeant-adjutant knelt down beside me where I lay, 'Name?' he asked softly. 'Middle name? First name? Rank? Where born? What class? What corps?' and so on. 'I'm sorry for your head, Tenente. I hope you feel better. I'm sending you now with the English ambulance.'

'I'm all right,' I said. 'Thank you very much.' The pain that the major had spoken about had started and all that was happening was without interest or relation. After a while the English ambulance came up and they put me onto a stretcher and lifted the stretcher up to the ambulance level and shoved it in. There was another stretcher by the side with a man on it whose nose I could see, waxy-looking, out of the bandages. He breathed very heavily. There were stretchers lifted and slid into the slings above. The tall English driver came around and looked in, 'I'll take it very easily,' he said. 'I hope you'll be comfy.' I felt the engine start, felt him climb up into the front seat, felt the brake come off and the clutch go in, then we started. I lay still and let the pain ride.

As the ambulance climbed along the road, it was slow in the traffic, sometimes it stopped, sometimes it backed on a turn, then finally it climbed quite fast. I felt something dripping. At first it dropped slowly and regularly, then it pattered into a stream. I shouted to the driver. He stopped the car and looked in through the hole behind his seat.

'What is it?'

'The man on the stretcher over me has a hemorrhage.'

'We're not far from the top. I wouldn't be able to get the stretcher out alone.' He started the car. The stream kept on. In the dark I could not see where it came from the canvas overhead. I tried to move sideways so that it did not fall on me. Where it had run down under my shirt it was warm and sticky. I was cold and my leg hurt so that it made me sick. After a while the stream from the stretcher above lessened and started to drip again and I heard and felt the canvas above move as the man on the stretcher settled more comfortably.

'How is he?' the Englishman called back.

'We're almost up.'

'He's dead I think,' I said.

The drops fell very slowly, as they fall from an icicle after the sun has gone. It was cold in the car in the night as the road climbed. At the post on the top they took the stretcher out and put another in and we went on.

10

In the ward at the field hospital they told me a visitor was coming to see me in the afternoon. It was a hot day and there were many flies in the room. My orderly had cut paper into strips and tied the strips to a stick to make a brush that swished the flies away. I watched them settle on the ceiling. When he stopped swishing and fell asleep they came down and I blew them away and finally covered my face with my hands and slept too. It was very hot and when I woke my legs itched. I waked the orderly and he poured mineral water on the dressings. That made the bed damp and cool. Those of us that were awake talked across the ward. The afternoon was a quiet time. In the morning they came to each bed in turn, three men nurses and a doctor and picked you up out of bed and carried you into the dressing room so that the beds could be made while we were having our wounds dressed. It was not a pleasant trip to the dressing room and I did not know until later that beds could be made with men in them. My orderly had finished pouring water and the bed felt cool and lovely and I was telling him where to scratch on the soles of my feet against the itching when one of the doctors brought in Rinaldi. He came in very fast and bent down over the bed and kissed me. I saw he wore gloves.

'How are you, baby? How do you feel? I bring you this—' It was a bottle of cognac.

The orderly brought a chair and he sat down, 'and good news. You will be decorated.

'They want to get you the medaglia d'argento but perhaps they can get only the bronze.'

'What for?'

'Because you are gravely wounded. They say if you can prove you did any heroic act you can get the silver. Otherwise it will be the bronze. Tell me exactly what happened. Did you do any heroic act?'

'No,' I said. 'I was blown up while we were eating cheese.'

'Be serious. You must have done something heroic either before or after. Remember carefully.'

'I did not.'

'Didn't you carry anybody on your back? Gordini says you carried several people on your back but the medical major at the first post declares it is impossible. He had to sign the proposition for the citation.'

'I didn't carry anybody. I couldn't move.'

'That doesn't matter,' said Rinaldi.

He took off his gloves.

'I think we can get you the silver. Didn't you refuse to be medically aided before the others?'

'Not very firmly.'

'That doesn't matter. Look how you are wounded. Look at your valorous conduct in asking to go always to the first line. Besides, the operation was successful.'

'Did they cross the river all right?'

'Enormously. They take nearly a thousand prisoners. It's in the bulletin. Didn't you see it?'

'No.'

'I'll bring it to you. It is a successful coup de main.'

'How is everything?'

'Splendid. We are all splendid. Everybody is proud of you. Tell me just exactly how it happened. I am positive you will get the silver. Go on tell me. Tell me all about it.' He paused and thought. 'Maybe you will get an English medal too. There was an English there. I'll go and see him and ask if he will recommend you. He ought to be able to do something. Do you suffer much? Have a drink. Orderly, go get a corkscrew. Oh you should see what I did in the removal of three metres of small intestine and better now than ever. It is one for The Lancet. You do me a translation and I will send it to The Lancet.

Every day I am better. Poor dear baby, how do you feel? Where is that damn corkscrew? You are so brave and quiet I forget you are suffering.' He slapped his gloves on the edge of the bed.

'Here is the corkscrew, Signor Tenente,' the orderly said.

'Open the bottle. Bring a glass. Drink that, baby. How is your poor head? I looked at your papers. You haven't any fracture. That major at the first post was a hog-butcher. I would take you and never hurt you. I never hurt anybody. I learn how to do it. Every day I learn to do things smoother and better. You must forgive me for talking so much, baby. I am very moved to see you badly wounded. There, drink that. It's good. It cost fifteen lire. It ought to be good. Five stars. After I leave here I'll go see that English and he'll get you an English medal.'

'They don't give them like that.'

'You are so modest. I will send the liaison officer. He can handle the English.'

'Have you seen Miss Barkley?'

'I will bring her here. I will go now and bring her here.'

'Don't go,' I said. 'Tell me about Gorizia. How are the girls?'

'There are no girls. For two weeks now they haven't changed them. I don't go there any more. It is disgraceful. They aren't girls; they are old war comrades.'

'You don't go at all?'

'I just go to see if there is anything new. I stop by. They all ask for you. It is a disgrace that they should stay so long that they become friends.'

'Maybe girls don't want to go to the front any more.'

'Of course they do. They have plenty of girls. It is just bad administration. They are keeping them for the pleasure of dugout hiders in the rear.'

'Poor Rinaldi,' I said. 'All alone at the war with no new girls.'

Rinaldi poured himself another glass of the cognac.

'I don't think it will hurt you, baby. You take it.'

I drank the cognac and felt it warm all the way down. Rinaldi poured another glass. He was quieter now. He held up the glass. 'To your valorous wounds. To the silver medal. Tell me, baby, when you lie here all the time in the hot weather don't you get excited?'

'Sometimes.'

'I can't imagine lying like that. I would go crazy.'

'You are crazy.'

'I wish you were back. No one to come in at night from adventures. No one to make fun of. No one to lend me money. No blood brother and roommate. Why do you get yourself wounded?'

'You can make fun of the priest.'

'That priest. It isn't me that makes fun of him. It is the captain. I like him. If you must have a priest have that priest. He's coming to see you. He makes big preparations.'

'I like him.'

'Oh, I knew it. Sometimes I think you and he are a little that way. You know.'

'No, you don't.'

'Yes, I do sometimes. A little that way like the number of the first regiment of the Brigata Ancona.'

'Oh, go to hell.'

He stood up and put on his gloves.

'Oh I love to tease you, baby. With your priest and your English girl, and really you are just like me underneath.'

'No, I'm not.'

'Yes, we are. You are really an Italian. All fire and smoke and nothing inside. You only pretend to be American. We are brothers and we love each other.'

'Be good while I'm gone,' I said.

'I will send Miss Barkley. You are better with her without me. You are purer and sweeter.'

'Oh, go to hell.'

'I will send her. Your lovely cool goddess. English goddess. My God what would a man do with a woman like that except worship her? What else is an Englishwoman good for?'

'You are an ignorant foul-mouthed dago.'

'A what?'

'An ignorant wop.'

'Wop. You are a frozen-faced . . . wop.'

'You are ignorant. Stupid.' I saw that word pricked him and kept on. 'Uninformed.

Inexperienced, stupid from inexperience.'

'Truly? I tell you something about your good women. Your goddesses. There is only one difference between taking a girl who has always been good and a woman. With a girl it is painful. That's all I know.' He slapped the bed with his glove. 'And you never know if the girl will really like it.'

'Don't get angry.'

'I'm not angry. I just tell you, baby, for your own good. To save you trouble.'

'That's the only difference?'

'Yes. But millions of fools like you don't know it.'

'You were sweet to tell me.'

'We won't quarrel, baby. I love you too much. But don't be a fool.'

'No. I'll be wise like you.'

'Don't be angry, baby. Laugh. Take a drink. I must go, really.'

'You're a good old boy.'

'Now you see. Underneath we are the same. We are war brothers. Kiss me good-by.'

'You're sloppy.'

'No. I am just more affectionate.'

I felt his breath come toward me. 'Good-by. I come to see you again soon.' His breath went away. 'I won't kiss you if you don't want. I'll send your English girl. Good-by, baby. The cognac is under the bed. Get well soon.'

He was gone.

11

It was dusk when the priest came. They had brought the soup and afterward taken away the bowls and I was lying looking at the rows of beds and out the window at the tree-top that moved a little in the evening breeze. The breeze came in through the window and it was cooler with the evening. The flies were on the ceiling now and on the electric light bulbs that hung on wires. The lights were only turned on when some one was brought in at night or when something was being done. It made me feel very young to have the dark come after the dusk and then remain. It was like being put to bed after early supper. The orderly came down between the beds and stopped. Some one was with him. It was the priest. He stood there small, brown-faced, and embarrassed.

'How do you do?' he asked. He put some packages down by the bed, on the floor.

'All right, father.'

He sat down in the chair that had been brought for Rinaldi and looked out of the window embarrassedly. I noticed his face looked Very tired.

'I can only stay a minute,' he said. 'It is late.'

'It's not late. How is the mess?'

He smiled. 'I am still a great joke,' he sounded tired too. 'Thank God they are all well.

'I am so glad you are all right,' he said. 'I hope you don't suffer.' He seemed very tired and I was not used to seeing him tired. 'Not any more.'

'I miss you at the mess.'

'I wish I were there. I always enjoyed our talking.'

'I brought you a few little things,' he said. He picked up the packages. 'This is mosquito netting. This is a bottle of vermouth. You like vermouth? These are English papers.'

'Please open them.'

He was pleased and undid them. I held the mosquito netting in my hands. The vermouth he held up for me to see and then put it on the floor beside the bed. I held up one of the sheaf of English papers. I could read the headlines by turning it so the half-light from the window was on it. It was The News of the World

'The others are illustrated,' he said.

'It will be a great happiness to read them. Where did you get them?'

'I sent for them to Mestre. I will have more.'

'You were very good to come, father. Will you drink a glass of vermouth?'

'Thank you. You keep it. It's for you.'

'No, drink a glass.'

'All right. I will bring you more then.'

The orderly brought the glasses and opened the bottle. He broke off the cork and the end had to be shoved down into the bottle. I could see the priest was disappointed but he said, 'That's all right. It's no matter.'

'Here's to your health, father.'

'To your better health.'

Afterward he held the glass in his hand and we looked at one another. Sometimes we talked and were good friends but to-night it was difficult.

'What's the matter, father? You seem very tired.'

'I am tired but I have no right to be.'

'It's the heat.'

'No. This is only the spring. I feel very low.'

'You have the war disgust.'

'No. But I hate the war.'

'I don't enjoy it,' I said. He shook his head and looked out of the window.

'You do not mind it. You do not see it. You must forgive me. I know you are wounded.'

'That is an accident.'

'Still even wounded you do not see it. I can tell. I do not see it myself but I feel it a little.'

'When I was wounded we were talking about it. Passini was talking.'

The priest put down the glass. He was thinking about something else.

'I know them because I am like they are,' he said.

'You are different though.' 'But really I am like they are.'

'The officers don't see anything.'

'Some of them do. Some are very delicate and feel worse than any of us.' 'They are mostly different.'

'It is not education or money. It is something else. Even if they had education or money men like Passini would not wish to be officers. I would not be an officer.'

'You rank as an officer. I am an officer.'

'I am not really. You are not even an Italian. You are a foreigner. But you are nearer the officers than you are to the men.'

'What is the difference?'

'I cannot say it easily. There are people who would make war. In this country there are many like that. There are other people who would not make war.'

'But the first ones make them do it.'

'Yes.'

'And I help them.'

'You are a foreigner. You are a patriot.'

'And the ones who would not make war? Can they stop it?' I do not know.

He looked out of the window again. I watched his face.

'Have they ever been able to stop it?'

'They are not organized to stop things and when they get organized their leaders sell them out.'

'Then it's hopeless?'

'It is never hopeless. But sometimes I cannot hope. I try always to hope but sometimes I cannot.'

'Maybe the war will be over.'

'I hope so.'

'What will you do then?'

'If it is possible I will return to the Abruzzi.'

His brown face was suddenly very happy.

'You love the Abruzzi?'

'Yes, I love it very much.'

'You ought to go there then.'

'I would be too happy. If I could live there and love God and serve Him.'

'And be respected,' I said.

'Yes and be respected. Why not?'

'No reason not. You should be respected.'

'It does not matter. But there in my country it is understood that a man may love God. It is not a dirty joke.'

'I understand.'

He looked at me and smiled.

'You understand but you do not love God.'

'No.'

'You do not love Him at all?' he asked.

'I am afraid of Him in the night sometimes.'

'You should love Him.'

'I don't love much.'

'Yes,' he said. 'You do. What you tell me about in the nights. That is not love. That is only passion and lust. When you love you wish to do things for. You wish to sacrifice for. You wish to serve.'

'I don't love.'

'You will. I know you will. Then you will be happy.'

'I'm happy. I've always been happy.'

'It is another thing. You cannot know about it unless you have it.'

'Well,' I said. 'If I ever get it I will tell you.'

'I stay too long and talk too much.' He was worried that he really did.

'No. Don't go. How about loving women? If I really loved some woman would it be like that?'

'I don't know about that. I never loved any woman.'

'What about your mother?'

'Yes, I must have loved my mother.'

'Did you always love God?'

'Ever since I was a little boy.'

A Farewell to Arms • 41

'Well,' I said. I did not know what to say. 'You are a fine boy,' I said.

'I am a boy,' he said. 'But you call me father.'

'That's politeness.'

He smiled.

'I must go, really,' he said. 'You do not want me for anything?' he asked hopefully.

'No. Just to talk.'

'I will take your greetings to the mess.'

'Thank you for the many fine presents.'

'Nothing.'

'Come and see me again.'

'Yes. Good-by,' he patted my hand.

'So long,' I said in dialect.

'Ciaou,' he repeated.

It was dark in the room and the orderly, who had sat by the foot of the bed, got up and went out with him. I liked him very much and I hoped he would get back to the Abruzzi some time. He had a rotten life in the mess and he was fine about it but I thought how he would be in his own country. At Capracotta, he had told me, there were trout in the stream below the town. It was forbidden to play the flute at night. When the young men serenaded only the flute was forbidden. Why, I had asked. Because it was bad for the girls to hear the flute at night. The peasants all called you 'Don' and when you met them they took off their hats. His father hunted every day and stopped to eat at the houses of peasants. They were always honored. For a foreigner to hunt he must present a certificate that he had never been arrested. There were bears on the Gran Sasso D'Italia but it was a long way.

Aquila was a fine town. It was cool in the summer at night and the spring in Abruzzi was the most beautiful in Italy. But what was lovely was the fall to go hunting through the chestnut woods. The birds were all good because they fed on grapes and you never took a lunch because the peasants were always honored if you would eat with them at their houses. After a while I went to sleep.

12

The room was long with windows on the right-hand side and a door at the far end that went into the dressing room. The row of beds that mine was in faced the windows and another row, under the windows, faced the wall. If you lay on your left side you could see the dressing-room door. There was another door at the far end that people sometimes came in by. If any one were going to die they put a screen around the bed so you could not see them die, but only the shoes and puttees of doctors and men nurses showed under the bottom of the screen and sometimes at the end there would be whispering.

Then the priest would come out from behind the screen and afterward the men nurses would go back behind the screen to come out again carrying the one who was dead with a blanket over him down the corridor between the beds and some one folded the screen and took it away.

That morning the major in charge of the ward asked me if I felt that I could travel the next day. I said I could. He said then they would ship me out early in the morning. He said I would be better off making the trip now before it got too hot.

When they lifted you up out of bed to carry you into the dressing room you could look out of the window and see the new graves in the garden. A soldier sat outside the door that opened onto the garden making crosses and painting on them the names, rank, and regiment of the men who were buried in the garden. He also ran errands for the ward and in his spare time made me a cigarette lighter out of an empty Austrian rifle cartridge. The doctors were very nice and seemed very capable. They were anxious to ship me to Milan where there were better X-ray facilities and where, after the operation, I could take mechano-therapy. I wanted to go to Milan too. They wanted to get us all out and back as far as possible because all the beds were needed for the offensive, when it should start.

The night before I left the field hospital Rinaldi came in to see me with the major from our mess. They said that I would go to an American hospital in Milan that had just been installed. Some American ambulance units were to be sent down and this hospital would look after them and any other Americans on service in Italy. There were many in the Red Cross. The States had declared war on Germany but not on Austria.

The Italians were sure America would declare war on Austria too and they were very excited about any Americans coming down, even the Red Cross. They asked me if I thought President Wilson would declare war on Austria and I said it was only a matter of days. I did not know what we had against Austria but it seemed logical that they should declare war on her if they did on Germany. They asked me if we would declare war on Turkey. I said that was doubtful. Turkey, I said, was our national bird but the joke translated so badly and they were so puzzled and suspicious that I said yes, we would probably declare war on Turkey. And on Bulgaria? We had drunk several glasses of brandy and I said yes by God on Bulgaria too and on Japan. But, they said, Japan is an ally of England. You can't trust the bloody English. The Japanese want Hawaii, I said.

Where is Hawaii? It is in the Pacific Ocean. Why do the Japanese want it? They don't really want it, I said. That is all talk. The Japanese are a wonderful little people fond of dancing and light wines. Like the French, said the major. We will get Nice and Savoia from the French. We will get Corsica and all the Adriatic coast-line, Rinaldi said. Italy will return to the splendors of Rome, said the major. I don't like Rome, I said. It is hot and full of fleas. You don't like Rome? Yes, I love Rome. Rome is the mother of nations. I will never forget Romulus suckling the Tiber. What? Nothing. Let's all go to Rome.

Let's go to Rome to-night and never come back. Rome is a beautiful city, said the major. The mother and father of nations, I said. Roma is feminine, said Rinaldi. It cannot be the father. Who is the father, then, the Holy Ghost? Don't blaspheme.

I wasn't blaspheming, I was asking for information. You are drunk, baby. Who made me drunk? I made you drunk, said the major. I made you drunk because I love you and because America is in the war. Up to the hilt, I said. You go away in the morning, baby, Rinaldi said. To Rome, I said. No, to Milan. To Milan, said the major, to the Crystal Palace, to the Cova, to Campari's, to Biffi's, to the galleria. You lucky boy. To the Gran Italia, I said, where I will borrow money from George. To the Scala, said Rinaldi. You will go to the Scala. Every night, I said. You won't be able to afford it every night, said the major.

The tickets are very expensive. I will draw a sight draft on my grandfather, I said. A what? A sight draft. He has to pay or I go to jail. Mr. Cunningham at the bank does it. I live by sight drafts. Can a grandfather jail a patriotic grandson who is dying that Italy may live? Live the American Garibaldi, said Rinaldi. Viva the sight drafts, I said. We must be quiet, said the major. Already we have been asked many times to be quiet. Do you go to-morrow really, Federico? He goes to the American hospital I tell you, Rinaldi said. To the beautiful nurses. Not the nurses with beards of the field hospital. Yes, yes, said the major, I know he goes to the American hospital. I don't mind their beards, I said. If any man wants to raise a beard let him. Why don't you raise a beard, Signor Maggiore? It could not go in a gas mask. Yes it could. Anything can go in a gas mask. I've vomited into a gas mask.

Don't be so loud, baby, Rinaldi said. We all know you have been at the front Oh, you fine baby, what will I do while you are gone? We must go, said the major. This becomes sentimental. Listen, I have a surprise for you. Your English. You know? The English you go to see every night at their hospital? She is going to Milan too. She goes with another to be at the American hospital. They had not got nurses yet from America. I talked to-day with the head of their riparto. They have too many Women here at the front. They send some back. How do you like that, baby? All right. Yes? You go to live in a big city and have your English there to cuddle you. Why don't I get wounded? Maybe you will, I said.

We must go, said the major. We drink and make noise and disturb Federico. Don't go. Yes, we must go. Good-by. Good luck. Many things. Ciaou. Ciaou. Ciaou. Come back quickly, baby. Rinaldi kissed me. You smell of lysol. Good-by, baby. Good-by. Many things. The major patted my shoulder. They tiptoed out. I found I was quite drunk but went to sleep.

The next day in the morning we left for Milan and arrived forty-eight hours later. It was a bad trip. We were sidetracked for a long time this side of Mestre and children came and peeked in. I got a little boy to go for a bottle of cognac but he came back and said he could only get grappa. I told him to get it and when it came I gave him the change and the man beside me and I got drunk and slept until past Vicenza where I woke up and was very sick on the floor. It did not matter because the man on that side had been very sick on the floor several times before. Afterward I thought I could not stand the thirst and in the yards outside of Verona I called to a soldier who was walking up and down beside the train and he got me a drink of water. I woke Georgetti, the other boy who was drunk, and offered him some water. He said to pour it on his shoulder and went back to sleep. The soldier would not take the penny I offered him and brought me a pulpy orange. I sucked on that and spit out the pith and watched the soldier pass up and down past a freight-car outside and after a while the train gave a jerk and started.

BOOK TWO

13

We got into Milan early in the morning and they unloaded us in the freight yard. An ambulance took me to the American hospital. Riding in the ambulance on a stretcher I could not tell what part of town we were passing through but when they unloaded the stretcher I saw a market-place and an open wine shop with a girl sweeping out. They were watering the street and it smelled of the early morning. They put the stretcher down and went in. The porter came out with them. He had gray mustaches, wore a doorman's cap and was in his shirt sleeves. The stretcher would not go into the elevator and they discussed whether it was better to lift me off the stretcher and go up in the elevator or carry the stretcher up the stairs. I listened to them discussing it. They decided on the elevator. They lifted me from the stretcher. 'Go easy,' I said. 'Take it softly.'

In the elevator we were crowded and as my legs bent the pain was very bad. 'Straighten out the legs,' I said.

'We can't, Signor Tenente. There isn't room.' The man who said this had his arm around me and my arm was around his neck. His breath came in my face metallic with garlic and red wine.

'Be gentle,' the other man said.

'Son of a bitch who isn't gentle!'

'Be gentle I say,' the man with my feet repeated.

I saw the doors of the elevator closed, and the grill shut and the fourth-floor button pushed by the porter. The porter looked worried. The elevator rose slowly.

'Heavy?' I asked the man with the garlic.

'Nothing,' he said. His face was sweating and he grunted. The elevator rose steadily and stopped. The man holding the feet opened the door and stepped out. We were on a balcony. There were several doors with brass knobs. The man carrying the feet pushed a button that rang a bell. We heard it inside the doors. No one came. Then the porter came up the stairs.

'Where are they?' the stretcher-bearers asked.

'I don't know,' said the porter. 'They sleep down stairs.'

'Get somebody.'

The porter rang the bell, then knocked on the door, then he opened the door and went in. When he came back there was an elderly woman wearing glasses with him. Her hair was loose and half-falling and she wore a nurse's dress.

'I can't understand,' she said. 'I can't understand Italian.'

'I can speak English,' I said. 'They want to put me somewhere.'

'None of the rooms are ready. There isn't any patient expected.' She tucked at her hair and looked at me near-sightedly.

'Show them any room where they can put me.'

'I don't know,' she said. 'There's no patient expected. I couldn't put you in just any room.'

'Any room will do,' I said. Then to the porter in Italian, 'Find an empty room.'

'They are all empty,' said the porter. 'You are the first patient.' He held his cap in his hand and looked at the elderly nurse.

'For Christ's sweet sake take me to some room.' The pain had gone on and on with the legs bent and I could feel it going in and out of the bone. The porter went in the door, followed by the grayhaired woman, then came hurrying back. 'Follow me,' he said. They carried me down a long hallway and into a room with drawn blinds. It smelled of new furniture. There was a bed and a big wardrobe with a mirror. They laid me down on the bed.

'I can't put on sheets,' the woman said. 'The sheets are locked up.'

I did not speak to her. 'There is money in my pocket,' I said to the porter. 'In the buttoned-down pocket.' The porter took out the money. The two stretcher-bearers stood beside the bed holding their caps. 'Give them five lire apiece and five lire for yourself. My papers are in the other pocket. You may give them to the nurse.'

The stretcher-bearers saluted and said thank you. 'Good-by,' I said. 'And many thanks.' They saluted again and went out.

'Those papers,' I said to the nurse, 'describe my case and the treatment already given.'

The woman picked them up and looked at them through her glasses. There were three papers and they were folded. 'I don't know what to do,' she said. 'I can't read Italian. I can't do anything without the doctor's orders.' She commenced to cry and put the papers in her apron pocket. 'Are you an American?' she asked crying.

'Yes. Please put the papers on the table by the bed.'

It was dim and cool in the room. As I lay on the bed I could see the big mirror on the other side of the room but could not see what it reflected. The porter stood by the bed. He had a nice face and was very kind.

'You can go,' I said to him. 'You can go too,' I said to the nurse. 'What is your name?'

'Mrs. Walker.'

'You can go, Mrs. Walker. I think I will go to sleep.'

I was alone in the room. It was cool and did not smell like a hospital. The mattress was firm and comfortable and I lay without moving, hardly breathing, happy in feeling the pain lessen. After a while I wanted a drink of water and found the bell on a cord by the bed and rang it but nobody came. I went to sleep.

When I woke I looked around. There was sunlight coming in through the shutters. I saw the big armoire, the bare walls, and two chairs. My legs in the dirty bandages, stuck straight out in the bed. I was careful not to move them. I was thirsty and I reached for the bell and pushed the button. I heard the door open and looked and it was a nurse. She looked young and pretty.

'Good-morning,' I said.

'Good-morning,' she said and came over to the bed. 'We haven't been able to get the doctor. He's gone to Lake Como. No one knew there was a patient coming. What's wrong with you anyway?'

'I'm wounded. In the legs and feet and my head is hurt.'

'What's your name?'

'Henry. Frederic Henry.'

'I'll wash you up. But we can't do anything to the dressings until the doctor comes.'

'Is Miss Barkley here?'

'No. There's no one by that name here.'

'Who was the woman who cried when I came in?'

The nurse laughed. 'That's Mrs. Walker. She was on night duty and she'd been asleep. She wasn't expecting any one.'

While we were talking she was undressing me, and when I was undressed, except for the bandages, she washed me, very gently and smoothly. The washing felt very good. There was a bandage on my head but she washed all around the edge.

'Where were you wounded?'

'On the Isonze north of Plava.'

'Where is that?'

'North of Gorizia.'

I could see that none of the places meant anything to her.

'Do you have a lot of pain?'

'No. Not much now.'

She put a thermometer in my mouth.

'The Italians put it under the arm,' I said.

'Don't talk.'

When she took the thermometer out she read it and then shook it.

'What's the temperature?'

'You're not supposed to know that.'

'Tell me what it is.'

'It's almost normal.'

'I never have any fever. My legs are full of old iron too.'

'What do you mean?'

'They're full of trench-mortar fragments, old screws and bedsprings and things.'

She shook her head and smiled.

'If you had any foreign bodies in your legs they would set up an inflammation and you'd have fever.'

A Farewell to Arms • 47

'All right,' I said. 'We'll see what comes out.'

She went out of the room and came back with the old nurse of the early morning.

Together they made the bed with me in it. That was new to me and an admirable proceeding.

'Who is in charge here?'

'Miss Van Campen.'

'How many nurses are there?'

'Just us two.'

'Won't there be more?'

'Some more are coming.'

'When will they get here?'

'I don't know. You ask a great many questions for a sick boy.'

'I'm not sick,' I said. 'I'm wounded.'

They had finished making the bed and I lay with a clean smooth sheet under me and another sheet over me. Mrs. Walker went out and came back with a pajama jacket. They put that on me and I felt very clean and dressed.

'You're awfully nice to me,' I said. The nurse called Miss Gage giggled. 'Could I have a drink of water?' I asked.

'Certainly. Then you can have breakfast.'

'I don't want breakfast. Can I have the shutters opened please?'

The light had been dim in the room and when the shutters were opened it was bright sunlight and I looked out on a balcony and beyond were the tile roofs of houses and chimneys. I looked out over the tiled roofs and saw white clouds and the sky very blue.

'Don't you know when the other nurses are coming?' 'Why? Don't we take good care of you?'

'You're very nice.'

'Would you like to use the bedpan?'

'I might try.'

They helped me and held me up but it was not any use. Afterward I lay and looked out the open doors onto the balcony.

'When does the doctor come?'

'When he gets back. We've tried to telephone to Lake Como for him.'

'Aren't there any other doctors?'

'He's the doctor for the hospital.'

Miss Gage brought a pitcher of water and a glass. I drank three glasses and then they left me and I looked out the window a while and went back to sleep. I ate some lunch and in the afternoon Miss Van Campen, the superintendent, came up to see me. She did not like me and I did not like her. She was small and neatly suspicious and too good for her position. She asked many questions and seemed to think it was somewhat disgraceful that I was with the Italians.

'Can I have wine with the meals?' I asked her.

'Only if the doctor prescribes it.'

'I can't have it until he comes?'

'Absolutely not.'

'You plan on having him come eventually?'

'We've telephoned him at Lake Como.'

She went out and Miss Gage came back.

'Why were you rude to Miss Van Campen?' she asked after she had done something for me very skilfully.

'I didn't mean to be. But she was snooty.'

'She said you were domineering and rude.'

'I wasn't. But what's the idea of a hospital without a doctor?'

'He's coming. They've telephoned for him to Lake Como.'

'What does he do there? Swim?'

'No. He has a clinic there.'

'Why don't they get another doctor?'

'Hush. Hush. Be a good boy and he'll come.'

I sent for the porter and when he came I told him in Italian to get me a bottle of Cinzano at the wine shop, a fiasco of chianti and the evening papers. He went away and brought them wrapped in newspaper, unwrapped them and, when I asked him to, drew the corks and put the wine and vermouth under the bed. They left me alone and I lay in bed and read the papers awhile, the news from the front, and the list of dead officers with their decorations and then reached down and brought up the bottle of Cinzano and held it straight up on my stomach, the cool glass against my stomach, and took little drinks making rings on my stomach from holding the bottle there between drinks, and watched it get dark outside over the roofs of the town. The swallows circled around and I watched them and the night-hawks flying above the roofs and drank the Cinzano. Miss Gage brought up a glass with some eggnog in it. I lowered the vermouth bottle to the other side of the bed when she came in.

'Miss Van Campen had some sherry put in this,' she said. 'You shouldn't be rude to her. She's not young and this hospital is a big responsibility for her. Mrs. Walker's too old and she's no use to her.'

'She's a splendid woman,' I said. 'Thank her very much.'

'I'm going to bring your supper right away.'

'That's all right,' I said. 'I'm not hungry.'

When she brought the tray and put it on the bed table I thanked her and ate a little of the supper. Afterward it was dark outside and I could see the beams of the search-lights moving in the sky. I watched for a while and then went to sleep. I slept heavily except once I woke sweating and scared and then went back to sleep trying to stay outside of my dream. I woke for good long before it was light and heard roosters crowing and stayed on awake until it began to be light. I was tired and once it was really light I went back to sleep again.

14

It was bright sunlight in the room when I woke. I thought I was back at the front and stretched out in bed. My legs hurt me and I looked down at them still in the dirty bandages, and seeing them knew where I was. I reached up for the bell-cord and pushed the button. I heard it buzz down the hall and then some one coming on rubber soles along the hall. It was Miss Gage and she looked a little older in the bright sunlight and not so pretty.

'Good-morning,' she said. 'Did you have a good night?'

'Yes. Thanks very much,' I said. 'Can I have a barber?'

'I came in to see you and you were asleep with this in the bed with you.'

She opened the armoire door and held up the vermouth bottle. It was nearly empty. 'I put the other bottle from under the bed in there too,' she said. 'Why didn't you ask me for a glass?'

'I thought maybe you wouldn't let me have it.'

'I'd have had some with you.'

'You're a fine girl.'

'It isn't good for you to drink alone,' she said. 'You mustn't do it.'

'All right.'

'Your friend Miss Barkley's come,' she said.

'Really?'

'Yes. I don't like her.'

'You will like her. She's awfully nice.'

She shook her head. 'I'm sure she's fine. Can you move just a little to this side? That's fine. I'll clean you up for breakfast.' She washed me with a cloth and soap and warm water. 'Hold your shoulder up,' she said. 'That's fine.'

'Can I have the barber before breakfast?'

'I'll send the porter for him.' She went out and came back. 'He's gone for him,' she said and dipped the cloth she held in the basin of water.

The barber came with the porter. He was a man of about fifty with an upturned mustache. Miss Gage was finished with me and went out and the barber lathered my face and shaved. He was very solemn and refrained from talking.

'What's the matter? Don't you know any news?' I asked.

'What news?'

'Any news. What's happened in the town?'

'It is time of war,' he said. 'The enemy's ears are everywhere.'

I looked up at him. 'Please hold your face still,' he said and went on shaving. 'I will tell nothing.'

'What's the matter with you?' I asked.

'I am an Italian. I will not communicate with the enemy.'

I let it go at that. If he was crazy, the sooner I could get out from under the razor the better. Once I tried to get a good look at him. 'Beware,' he said. 'The razor is sharp.'

I paid him when it was over and tipped him half a lira. He returned the coins.

'I will not. I am not at the front. But I am an Italian.'

'Get the hell out of here.'

'With your permission,' he said and wrapped his razors in newspaper. He went out leaving the five copper coins on the table beside the bed. I rang the bell. Miss Gage came in. 'Would you ask the porter to come please?'

'All right.'

The porter came in. He was trying to keep from laughing.

'Is that barber crazy?'

'No, signorino. He made a mistake. He doesn't understand very well and he thought I said you were an Austrian officer.'

'Oh,' I said.

'Ho ho ho,' the porter laughed. 'He was funny. One move from you he said and he would have—' he drew his forefinger across his throat.

'Ho ho ho,' he tried to keep from laughing. 'When I tell him you were not an Austrian. Ho ho ho.'

'Hoho ho,' I said bitterly. 'How funny if he would cut my throat. Ho ho ho.'

'No, signorino. No, no. He was so frightened of an Austrian. Ho ho ho.'

'Ho ho ho,' I said. 'Get out of here.'

He went out and I heard him laughing in the hall. I heard some one coming down the hallway. I looked toward the door. It was Catherine Barkley.

She came in the room and over to the bed.

'Hello, darling,' she said. She looked fresh and young and very beautiful. I thought I had never seen any one so beautiful.

'Hello,' I said. When I saw her I was in love with her. Everything turned over inside of me. She looked toward the door, saw there was no one, then she sat on the side of the bed and leaned over and kissed me. I pulled her down and kissed her and felt her heart beating.

'You sweet,' I said. 'Weren't you wonderful to come here?'

'It wasn't very hard. It may be hard to stay.'

'You've got to stay,' I said. 'Oh, you're wonderful.' I was crazy about her. I could not believe she was really there and held her tight to me.

'You mustn't,' she said. 'You're not well enough.'

'Yes, I am. Come on.'

'No. You're not strong enough.'

'Yes. I am. Yes. Please.'

'You do love me?'

'I really love you. I'm crazy about you. Come on please.'

'Feel our hearts beating.'

'I don't care about our hearts. I want you. I'm just mad about you.'

'You really love me?'

'Don't keep on saying that. Come on. Please. Please, Catherine.'

'All right but only for a minute.'

'All right,' I said. 'Shut the door.'

'You can't. You shouldn't.'

'Come on. Don't talk. Please come on.'

Catherine sat in a chair by the bed. The door was open into the hall. The wildness was gone and I felt finer than I had ever felt.

She asked, 'Now do you believe I love you?'

'Oh, you're lovely,' I said. 'You've got to stay. They can't send you away. I'm crazy in love with you.'

'We'll have to be awfully careful. That was just madness. We can't do that.'

'We can at night.'

'We'll have to be awfully careful. You'll have to be careful in front of other people.'

'I will.'

'You'll have to be. You're sweet. You do love me, don't you?'

'Don't say that again. You don't know what that does to me.'

'I'll be careful then. I don't want to do anything more to you. I have to go now, darling, really.'

'Come back right away.'

'I'll come when I can.'

'Good-by.'

'Good-by, sweet.'

She went out. God knows I had not wanted to fall in love with her. I had not wanted to fall in love with any one. But God knows I had and I lay on the bed in the room of the hospital in Milan and all sorts of things went through my head but I felt wonderful and finally Miss Gage came in.

'The doctor's coming,' she said. 'He telephoned from Lake Como.'

'When does he get here?'

'He'll be here this afternoon.'

15

Nothing happened until afternoon. The doctor was a thin quiet little man who seemed disturbed by the war. He took out a number of small steel splinters from my thighs with delicate and refined distaste. He used a local anaesthetic called something or other 'snow,' which froze the tissue and avoided pain until the probe, the scalpel or the forceps got below the frozen portion. The anxsthetized area was clearly defined by the patient and after a time the doctor's fragile delicacy was exhausted and he said it would be better to have an X-ray. Probing was unsatisfactory, he said.

The X-ray was taken at the Ospedale Maggiore and the doctor who did it was excitable, efficient and cheerful. It was arranged by holding up the shoulders, that the patient should see personally some of the larger foreign bodies through the machine. The plates were to be sent over. The doctor requested me to write in his pocket notebook, my name, and regiment and some sentiment. He declared that the foreign bodies were ugly, nasty, brutal. The Austrians were sons of bitches. How many had I killed? I had not killed any but I was anxious to please—and I said I had killed plenty. Miss Gage was with me and the doctor put his arm around her and said she was more beautiful than Cleopatra.

Did she understand that? Cleopatra the former queen of Egypt. Yes, by God she was. We returned to the little hospital in the ambulance and after a while and much lifting I was upstairs and in bed again. The plates came that afternoon, the doctor had said by God he would have them that afternoon and he did. Catherine Barkley showed them to me. They were in red envelopes and she took them out of the envelopes and held them up to the light and we both looked.

'That's your right leg,' she said, then put the plate back in the envelope. 'This is your left.'

'Put them away,' I said, 'and come over to the bed.'

'I can't,' she said. 'I just brought them in for a second to show you.'

She went out and I lay there. It was a hot afternoon and I was sick of lying in bed. I sent the porter for the papers, all the papers he could get.

Before he came back three doctors came into the room. I have noticed that doctors who fail in the practice of medicine have a tendency to seek one another's company and aid in consultation. A doctor who cannot take out your appendix properly will recommend to you a doctor who will be unable to remove your tonsils with success. These were three such doctors.

'This is the young man,' said the house doctor with the delicate hands.

'How do you do?' said the tall gaunt doctor with the beard. The third doctor, who carried the X-ray plates in their red envelopes, said nothing.

'Remove the dressings?' questioned the bearded doctor.

'Certainly. Remove the dressings, please, nurse,' the house doctor said to Miss Gage. Miss Gage removed the dressings. I looked down at the legs. At the field hospital they had the look of not too freshly ground hamburger steak. Now they were crusted and the knee was swollen and discolored and the calf sunken but there was no pus.

'Very clean,' said the house doctor. 'Very clean and nice.'

'Urn,' said the doctor with the beard. The third doctor looked over the house doctor's shoulder.

'Please move the knee,' said the bearded doctor.

'I can't.'

'Test the articulation?' the bearded doctor questioned. He had a stripe beside the three stars on his sleeve. That meant he was a first captain.

'Certainly,' the house doctor said. Two of them took hold of my right leg very gingerly and bent it.

'That hurts,' I said.

'Yes. Yes. A little further, doctor.'

'That's enough. That's as far as it goes,' I said.

'Partial articulation,' said the first captain. He straightened up. 'May I see the plates again, please, doctor?' The third doctor handed him one of the plates. 'No. The left leg, please.'

'That is the left leg, doctor.'

'You are right. I was looking from a different angle.' He returned the plate. The other plate he examined for some time. 'You see, doctor?' he pointed to one of the foreign bodies which showed spherical and clear against the light. They examined the plate for some time.

'Only one thing I can say,' the first captain with the beard said. 'It is a question of time. Three months, six months probably.'

'Certainly the synovial fluid must re-form.'

'Certainly. It is a question of time. I could not conscientiously open a knee like that before the projectile was encysted.'

'I agree with you, doctor.'

'Six months for what?' I asked.

'Six months for the projectile to encyst before the knee can be opened safely.'

'I don't believe it,' I said.

'Do you want to keep your knee, young man?'

'No,' I said.

'What?'

'I want it cut off,' I said, 'so I can wear a hook on it.'

'What do you mean? A hook?'

'He is joking,' said the house doctor. He patted my shoulder very delicately. 'He wants to keep his knee. This is a very brave young man. He has been proposed for the silver medal of valor.'

'All my felicitations,' said the first captain. He shook my hand. 'I can only say that to be on the safe side you should wait at least six months before opening such a knee. You are welcome of course to another opinion.'

'Thank you very much,' I said. 'I value your opinion.'

The first captain looked at his watch.

'We must go,' he said. 'All my best wishes.'

'All my best wishes and many thanks,' I said. I shook hands with the third doctor. 'Capitano Varini—Tenente Enry,' and they all three went out of the room.

'Miss Gage,' I called. She came in. 'Please ask the house doctor to come back a minute.'

He came in holding his cap and stood by the bed. 'Did you wish to see me?'

'Yes. I can't wait six months to be operated on. My God, doctor, did you ever stay in bed six months?'

'You won't be in bed all the time. You must first have the wounds exposed to the sun. Then afterward you can be on crutches.'

'For six months and then have an operation?'

'That is the safe way. The foreign bodies must be allowed to encyst and the synovial fluid will re-form. Then it will be safe to open up the knee.'

'Do you really think yourself I will have to wait that long?'

'That is the safe way.'
'Who is that first captain?'
'He is a very excellent surgeon of Milan.'
'He's a first captain, isn't he?'
'Yes, but he is an excellent surgeon.'
'I don't want my leg fooled with by a first captain. If he was any good he would be made a major. I know what a first captain is, doctor.'
'He is an excellent surgeon and I would rather have his judgment than any surgeon I know.'
'Could another surgeon see it?'
'Certainly if you wish. But I would take Dr. Varella's opinion myself.'
'Could you ask another surgeon to come and see it?'
'I will ask Valentini to come.'
'Who is he?'
'He is a surgeon of the Ospedale Maggiore.'
'Good. I appreciate it very much. You understand, doctor, I couldn't stay in bed six months.'
'You would not be in bed. You would first take a sun cure. Then you could have light exercise. Then when it was encysted we would operate.'
'But I can't wait six months.'
The doctor spread his delicate fingers on the cap he held and smiled. 'You are in such a hurry to get back to the front?'
'Why not?'
'It is very beautiful,' he said. 'You are a noble young man.' He stooped over and kissed me very delicately on the forehead. 'I will send for Valentini. Do not worry and excite yourself. Be a good boy.'
'Will you have a drink?' I asked.
'No thank you. I never drink alcohol.'
'Just have one.' I rang for the porter to bring glasses.
'No. No thank you. They are waiting for me.'
'Good-by,' I said.
'Good-by.'
Two hours later Dr. Valentini came into the room. He was in a great hurry and the points of his mustache stood straight up. He was a major, his face was tanned and he laughed all the time.
'How did you do it, this rotten thing?' he asked. 'Let me see the plates. Yes. Yes. That's it. You look healthy as a goat. Who's the pretty girl? Is she your girl? I thought so. Isn't this a bloody war? How does that feel? You are a fine boy. I'll make you better than new. Does that hurt? You bet it hurts. How they love to hurt you, these doctors. What have they done for you so far? Can't that girl talk Italian? She should learn. What a lovely girl. I could teach her. I will be a patient here myself. No, but I will do all your maternity work free. Does she understand that? She will make you a fine boy. A fine blonde like she is.

A Farewell to Arms • 55

That's fine. That's all right. What a lovely girl. Ask her if she eats supper with me. No I won't take her away from you. Thank you. Thank you very much, Miss. That's all.'

'That's all I want to know.' He patted me on the shoulder. 'Leave the dressings off.' 'Will you have a drink, Dr. Valentini?'

'A drink? Certainly. I will have ten drinks. Where are they?'

'In the armoire. Miss Barkley will get the bottle.'

'Cheery oh. Cheery oh to you, Miss. What a lovely girl. I will bring you better cognac than that.' He wiped his mustache.

'When do you think it can be operated on?'

'To-morrow morning. Not before. Your stomach must be emptied. You must be washed out. I will see the old lady downstairs and leave instructions. Good-by. I see you to-morrow. I'll bring you better cognac than that. You are very comfortable here. Good-by. Until to-morrow. Get a good sleep. I'll see you early.' He waved from the doorway, his mustaches went straight up, his brown face was smiling. There was a star in a box on his sleeve because he was a major.

16

That night a bat flew into the room through the open door that led onto the balcony and through which we watched the night over the roofs of the town. It was dark in our room except for the small light of the night over the town and the bat was not frightened but hunted in the room as though he had been outside. We lay and watched him and I do not think he saw us because we lay so still. After he went out we saw a searchlight come on and watched the beam move across the sky and then go off and it was dark again. A breeze came in the night and we heard the men of the anti-aircraft gun on the next roof talking. It was cool and they were putting on their capes. I worried in the night about some one coming up but Catherine said they were all asleep. Once in the night we went to sleep and when I woke she was not there but I heard her coming along the hall and the door opened and she came back to the bed and said it was all right she had been downstairs and they were all asleep. She had been outside Miss Van Campen's door and heard her breathing in her sleep. She brought crackers and we ate them and drank some vermouth. We were very hungry but she said that would all have to be gotten out of me in the morning. I went to sleep again in the morning when it was light and when I was awake I found she was gone again. She came in looking fresh and lovely and sat on the bed and the sun rose while I had the thermometer in my mouth and we smelled the dew on the roofs and then the coffee of the men at the gun on the next roof.

'I wish we could go for a walk,' Catherine said. 'I'd wheel you if we had a chair.'

'How would I get into the chair?'

'We'd do it.'

'We could go out to the park and have breakfast outdoors.' I looked out the open doorway.

'What we'll really do,' she said, 'is get you ready for your friend Dr. Valentini.'
'I thought he was grand.'
'I didn't like him as much as you did. But I imagine he's very good.'
'Come back to bed, Catherine. Please,' I said.
'I can't. Didn't we have a lovely night?'
'And can you be on night duty to-night?'
'I probably will. But you won't want me.'
'Yes, I will.'
'No, you won't. You've never been operated on. You don't know how you'll be.'
'I'll be all right.'
'You'll be sick and I won't be anything to you.'
'Come back then now.'
'No,' she said. 'I have to do the chart, darling, and fix you up.'
'You don't really love me or you'd come back again.'
'You're such a silly boy.' She kissed me. 'That's all right for the chart. Your temperature's always normal. You've such a lovely temperature.'
'You've got a lovely everything.'
'Oh no. You have the lovely temperature. I'm awfully proud of your temperature.'
'Maybe all our children will have fine temperatures.'
'Our children will probably have beastly temperatures.'
'What do you have to do to get me ready for Valentini?'
'Not much. But quite unpleasant.'
'I wish you didn't have to do it.'
'I don't. I don't want any one else to touch you. I'm silly. I get furious if they couch you.'
'Even Ferguson?'
'Especially Ferguson and Gage and the other, what's her name?'
'Walker?'
'That's it. They've too many nurses here now. There must be some more patients or they'll send us away. They have four nurses now.'
'Perhaps there'll be some. They need that many nurses. It's quite a big hospital.'
'I hope some will come. What would I do if they sent me away? They will unless there are more patients.'
'I'd go too.'
'Don't be silly. You can't go yet. But get well quickly, darling, and we will go somewhere.'
'And then what?'
'Maybe the war will be over. It can't always go on.'
'I'll get well,' I said. 'Valentini will fix me.'
'He should with those mustaches. And, darling, when you're going under the ether just think about something else—not us. Because people get very blabby under an anaesthetic.'

A Farewell to Arms • 57

'What should I think about?'

'Anything. Anything but us. Think about your people. Or even any other girl.'

'No.'

'Say your prayers then. That ought to create a splendid impression.'

'Maybe I won't talk.'

'That's true. Often people don't talk.'

'I won't talk.'

'Don't brag, darling. Please don't brag. You're so sweet and you don't have to brag.'

'I won't talk a word.'

'Now you're bragging, darling. You know you don't need to brag. Just start your prayers or poetry or something when they tell you to breathe deeply. You'll be lovely that way and I'll be so proud of you. I'm very proud of you anyway. You have such a lovely temperature and you sleep like a little boy with your arm around the pillow and think it's me. Or is it some other girl? Some fine Italian girl?'

'It's you.'

'Of course it's me. Oh I do love you and Valentini will make you a fine leg. I'm glad I don't have to watch it.'

'And you'll be on night duty to-night.'

'Yes. But you won't care.'

'You wait and see.'

'There, darling. Now you're all clean inside and out. Tell me. How many people have you ever loved?'

'Nobody.'

'Not me even?'

'Yes, you.'

'How many others really?'

'None.'

'How many have you—how do you say it?—stayed with?'

'None.'

'You're lying to me.'

'Yes.'

'It's all right. Keep right on lying to me. That's what I want you to do. Were they pretty?'

'I never stayed with any one.'

'That's right. Were they very attractive?'

'I don't know anything about it.'

'You're just mine. That's true and you've never belonged to any one else. But I don't care if you have. I'm not afraid of them. But don't tell me about them. When a man stays with a girl when does she say how much it costs?'

'I don't know.'

'Of course not. Does she say she loves him? Tell me that. I want to know that.'

'Yes. If he wants her to.'

'Does he say he loves her? Tell me please. It's important.'
'He does if he wants to.'
'But you never did? Really?'
'No.'
'Not really. Tell me the truth.'
'No,' I lied.
'You wouldn't,' she said. 'I knew you wouldn't. Oh, I love you, darling.'

Outside the sun was up over the roofs and I could see the points of the cathedral with the sunlight on them. I was clean inside and outside and waiting for the doctor.

'And that's it?' Catherine said. 'She says just what he wants her to?' 'Not always.'
'But I will. I'll say just what you wish and I'll do what you wish and then you will never want any other girls, will you?' She looked at me very happily. 'I'll do what you want and say what you want and then I'll be a great success, won't I?'
'Yes.'
'What would you like me to do now that you're all ready?'
'Come to the bed again.'
'All right. I'll come.'
'Oh, darling, darling, darling,' I said.
'You see,' she said. 'I do anything you want.'
'You're so lovely.'
'I'm afraid I'm not very good at it yet.'
'You're lovely.'
'I want what you want. There isn't any me any more. Just what you want.'
'You sweet.'
'I'm good. Aren't I good? You don't want any other girls, do you?'
'No.'
'You see? I'm good. I do what you want.'

17

When I was awake after the operation I had not been away. You do not go away. They only choke you. It is not like dying it is just a chemical choking so you do not feel, and afterward you might as well have been drunk except that when you throw up nothing comes but bile and you do not feel better afterward. I saw sandbags at the end of the bed. They were on pipes that came out of the cast. After a while I saw Miss Gage and she said, 'How is it now?'
'Better,' I said.
'He did a wonderful job on your knee.'
'How long did it take?'
'Two hours and a half.'
'Did I say anything silly?'
'Not a thing. Don't talk. Just be quiet.'

I was sick and Catherine was right. It did not make any difference who was on night duty.

There were three other patients in the hospital now, a thin boy in the Red Cross from Georgia with malaria, a nice boy, also thin, from New York, with malaria and jaundice, and a fine boy who had tried to unscrew the fuse-cap from a combination shrapnel and high explosive shell for a souvenir. This was a shrapnel shell used by the Austrians in the mountains with a nose-cap which went on after the burst and exploded on contact.

Catherine Barkley was greatly liked by the nurses because she would do night duty indefinitely. She had quite a little work with the malaria people, the boy who had unscrewed the nose-cap was a friend of ours and never rang at night, unless it was necessary but between the times of working we were together. I loved her very much and she loved me. I slept in the daytime and we wrote notes during the day when we were awake and sent them by Ferguson. Ferguson was a fine girl. I never learned anything about her except that she had a brother in the Fifty-Second Division and a brother in Mesopotamia and she was very good to Catherine Barkley.

'Will you come to our wedding, Fergy?' I said to her once.

'You'll never get married.'

'We will.'

'No you won't.'

'Why not?'

'You'll fight before you'll marry.'

'We never fight.'

'You've time yet.'

'We don't fight.'

'You'll die then. Fight or die. That's what people do. They don't marry.'

I reached for her hand. 'Don't take hold of me,' she said. 'I'm not crying. Maybe you'll be all right you two. But watch out you don't get her in trouble. You get her in trouble and I'll kill you.'

'I won't get her in trouble.'

'Well watch out then. I hope you'll be all right. You have a good time.'

'We have a fine time.'

'Don't fight then and don't get her into trouble.'

'I won't.'

'Mind you watch out. I don't want her with any of these war babies.'

'You're a fine girl, Fergy.'

'I'm not. Don't try to flatter me. How does your leg feel?'

'Fine.'

'How is your head?' She touched the top of it with her fingers.

It was sensitive like a foot that had gone to sleep.

'It's never bothered me.'

'A bump like that could make you crazy. It never bothers you?'

'No.'

'You're a lucky young man. Have you the letter done? I'm going down.'

'It's here,' I said.

'You ought to ask her not to do night duty for a while. She's getting very tired.'

'All right. I will.'

'I want to do it but she won't let me. The others are glad to let her have it. You might give her just a little rest.'

'All right.'

'Miss Van Campen spoke about you sleeping all the forenoons.'

'She would.'

'It would be better if you let her stay off nights a little while.'

'I want her to.'

'You do not. But if you would make her I'd respect you for it.'

'I'll make her.'

'I don't believe it.' She took the note and went out. I rang the bell and in a little while Miss Gage came in.

'What's the matter?'

'I just wanted to talk to you. Don't you think Miss Barkley ought to go off night duty for a while? She looks awfully tired. Why does she stay on so long?'

Miss Gage looked at me.

'I'm a friend of yours,' she said. 'You don't have to talk to me like that.'

'What do you mean?'

'Don't be silly. Was that all you wanted?'

'Do you want a vermouth?'

'All right. Then I have to go.' She got out the bottle from the armoire and brought a glass.

'You take the glass,' I said. 'I'll drink out of the bottle.' 'Here's to you,' said Miss Gage.

'What did Van Campen say about me sleeping late in the mornings?'

'She just jawed about it. She calls you our privileged patient.'

'To hell with her.'

'She isn't mean,' Miss Gage said. 'She's just old and cranky. She never liked you.'

'No.'

'Well, I do. And I'm your friend. Don't forget that.'

'You're awfully damned nice.'

'No. I know who you think is nice. But I'm your friend. How does your leg feel?'

'Fine.'

'I'll bring some cold mineral water to pour over it. It must itch under the cast. It's hot outside.'

'You're awful nice.'

'Does it itch much?'

'No. It's fine.'

'I'll fix those sandbags better.' She leaned over. 'I'm your friend.'

'I know you are.'

'No you don't. But you will some day.'

Catherine Barkley took three nights off night duty and then she came back on again. It was as though we met again after each of us had been away on a long journey.

18

We had a lovely time that summer. When I could go out we rode in a carriage in the park. I remember the carriage, the horse going slowly, and up ahead the back of the driver with his varnished high hat, and Catherine Barkley sitting beside me. If we let our hands touch, just the side of my hand touching hers, we were excited. Afterward when I could get around on crutches we went to dinner at Biffi's or the Gran Italia and sat at the tables outside on the floor of the galleria. The waiters came in and out and there were people going by and candles with shades on the tablecloths and after we decided that we liked the Gran Italia best, George, the headwaiter, saved us a table. He was a fine waiter and we let him order the meal while we looked at the people, and the great galleria in the dusk, and each other. We drank dry white capri iced in a bucket; although we tried many of the other wines, fresa, barbera and the sweet white wines. They had no wine waiter because of the war and George would smile ashamedly when I asked about wines like fresa.

'If you imagine a country that makes a wine because it tastes like strawberries,' he said.

'Why shouldn't it?' Catherine asked. 'It sounds splendid.'

'You try it, lady,' said George, 'if you want to. But let me bring a little bottle of margaux for the Tenente.' 'I'll try it too, George.'

'Sir, I can't recommend you to. It doesn't even taste like strawberries.'

'It might,' said Catherine. 'It would be wonderful if it did.'

'I'll bring it,' said George, 'and when the lady is satisfied I'll take it away.'

It was not much of a wine. As he said, it did not even taste like strawberries. We went back to capri. One evening I was short of money and George loaned me a hundred lire. 'That's all right, Tenente,' he said. 'I know how it is. I know how a man gets short. If you or the lady need money I've always got money.'

After dinner we walked through the galleria, past the other restaurants and the shops with their steel shutters down, and stopped at the little place where they sold sandwiches; ham and lettuce sandwiches and anchovy sandwiches made of very tiny brown glazed rolls and only about as long as your finger. They were to eat in the night when we were hungry. Then we got into an open carriage outside the galleria in front of the cathedral and rode to the hospital. At the door of the hospital the porter came out to help with the crutches. I paid the driver, and then we rode upstairs in the elevator.

Catherine got off at the lower floor where the nurses lived and I went on up and went down the hall on crutches to my room; sometimes I undressed and got into bed and sometimes I sat out on the balcony with my leg up on another chair and watched the swallows over the roofs and waited for Catherine. When she came upstairs it was as though she had been away on a long trip and I went along the hall with her on the crutches and carried the basins and waited outside the doors, or went in with her; it depending on whether they were friends of ours or not, and when she had done all there was to be done we sat out on the balcony outside my room. Afterward I went to bed and when they were all asleep and she was sure they would not call she came in. I loved to take her hair down and she sat on the bed and kept very still, except suddenly she would dip down to kiss me while I was doing it, and I would take out the pins and lay them on the sheet and it would be loose and I would watch her while she kept very still and then take out the last two pins and it would all come down and she would drop her head and we would both be inside of it, and it was the feeling of inside a tent or behind a falls.

She had wonderfully beautiful hair and I would lie sometimes and watch her twisting it up in the light that came in the open door and it shone even in the night as water shines sometimes just before it is really daylight. She had a lovely face and body and lovely smooth skin too. We would be lying together and I would touch her cheeks and her forehead and under her eyes and her chin and throat with the tips of my fingers and say, 'Smooth as piano keys,' and she would stroke my chin with her finger and say, 'Smooth as emery paper and very hard on piano keys.'

'Is it rough?'

'No, darling. I was just making fun of you.'

It was lovely in the nights and if we could only touch each other we were happy. Besides all the big times we had many small ways of making love and we tried putting thoughts in the other one's head while we were in different rooms. It seemed to work sometimes but that was probably because we were thinking the same thing anyway.

We said to each other that we were married the first day she had come to the hospital and we counted months from our wedding day. I wanted to be really married but Catherine said that if we were they would send her away and if we merely started on the formalities they would watch her and would break us up. We would have to be married under Italian law and the formalities were terrific. I wanted us to be married really because I worried about having a child if I thought about it, but we pretended to ourselves we were married and did not worry much and I suppose I enjoyed not being married, really. I know one night we talked about it and Catherine said, 'But, darling, they'd send me away.'

'Maybe they wouldn't.'

'They would. They'd send me home and then we would be apart until after the war.'

'I'd come on leave.'

'You couldn't get to Scotland and back on a leave. Besides, I won't leave you. What good would it do to marry now? We're really married. I couldn't be any more married.' 'I only wanted to for you.'

'There isn't any me. I'm you. Don't make up a separate me.'

'I thought girls always wanted to be married.'

'They do. But, darling, I am married. I'm married to you. Don't I make you a good wife?'

'You're a lovely wife.'

'You see, darling, I had one experience of waiting to be married.'

'I don't want to hear about it.'

'You know I don't love any one but you. You shouldn't mind because some one else loved me.'

'I do.'

'You shouldn't be jealous of some one who's dead when you have everything.'

'No, but I don't want to hear about it.'

'Poor darling. And I know you've been with all kinds of girls and it doesn't matter to me.'

'Couldn't we be married privately some way? Then if anything happened to me or if you had a child.'

'There's no way to be married except by church or state. We are married privately.

You see, darling, it would mean everything to me if I had any religion. But I haven't any religion.'

'You gave me the Saint Anthony.'

'That was for luck. Some one gave it to me.'

'Then nothing worries you?'

'Only being sent away from you. You're my religion. You're all I've got.'

'All right. But I'll marry you the day you say.'

'Don't talk as though you had to make an honest woman of me, darling. I'm a very honest woman. You can't be ashamed of something if you're only happy and proud of it.

Aren't you happy?'

'But you won't ever leave me for some one else.'

'No, darling. I won't ever leave you for some one else. I suppose all sorts of dreadful things will happen to us. But you don't have to worry about that.'

'I don't. But I love you so much and you did love some one else before.' 'And what happened to him?'

'He died.'

'Yes and if he hadn't I wouldn't have met you. I'm not unfaithful, darling. I've plenty of faults but I'm very faithful. You'll be sick of me I'll be so faithful.'

'I'll have to go back to the front pretty soon.'

'We won't think about that until you go. You see I'm happy, darling, and we have a lovely time. I haven't been happy for a long time and when I met you perhaps I was nearly crazy. Perhaps I was crazy. But now we're happy and we love each other. Do let's please just be happy. You are happy, aren't you? Is there anything I do you don't like? Can I do anything to please you? Would you like me to take down my hair? Do you want to play?'

'Yes and come to bed.'

'All right. I'll go and see the patients first.'

19

The summer went that way. I do not remember much about the days, except that they were hot and that there were many victories in the papers. I was very healthy and my legs healed quickly so that it was not very long after I was first on crutches before I was through with them and walking with a cane. Then I started treatments at the Ospedale Maggiore for bending the knees, mechanical treatments, baking in a box of mirrors with violet rays, massage, and baths. I went over there afternoons and afterward stopped at the café and had a drink and read the papers. I did not roam around the town; but wanted to get home to the hospital from the café. All I wanted was to see Catherine. The rest of the time I was glad to kill. Mostly I slept in the mornings, and in the afternoons, sometimes, I went to the races, and late to the mechanotherapy treatments. Sometimes I stopped in at the AngloAmerican Club and sat in a deep leather-cushioned chair in front of the window and read the magazines. They would not let us go out together when I was off crutches because it was unseemly for a nurse to be seen unchaperoned with a patient who did not look as though he needed attendance, so we were not together much in the afternoons. Although sometimes we could go out to dinner if Ferguson went along. Miss Van Campen had accepted the status that we were great friends because she got a great amount of work out of Catherine. She thought Catherine came from very good people and that prejudiced her in her favor finally. Miss Van Campen admired family very much and came from an excellent family herself. The hospital was quite busy, too, and that kept her occupied. It was a hot summer and I knew many people in Milan but always was anxious to get back home to the hospital as soon as the afternoon was over. At the front they were advancing on the Carso, they had taken Kuk across from Plava and were taking the Bainsizza plateau. The West front did not sound so good. It looked as though the war were going on for a long time. We were in the war now but I thought it would take a year to get any great amount of troops over and train them for combat. Next year would be a bad year, or a good year maybe. The Italians were using up an awful amount of men. I did not see how it could go on. Even if they took all the Bainsizza and Monte San Gabriele there were plenty of mountains beyond for the Austrians. I had seen them. All the highest mountains were beyond. On the Carso they were going forward but there were marshes and swamps down by the sea. Napoleon would have whipped the Austrians on the plains. He never would have fought them in the mountains. He would have let them come down and whipped them around Verona. Still nobody was whipping any one on the Western front. Perhaps wars weren't won any more. Maybe they went on forever. Maybe it was another Hundred Years' War. I put the paper back on the rack and left the club. I went down the steps carefully and walked up the Via Manzoni. Outside the Gran Hotel I met old Meyers and his wife getting out of a carriage. They were coming back from the races. She was a big-busted woman in black satin. He was short and old, with a white mustache and walked flat-footed with a cane.

'How do you do? How do you do?' She shook hands. 'Hello,' said Meyers.

'How were the races?'

'Fine. They were just lovely. I had three winners.'

'How did you do?' I asked Meyers.

'All right. I had a winner.'

'I never know how he does,' Mrs. Meyers said. 'He never tells me.'

'I do all right,' Meyers said. He was being cordial. 'You ought to come out.' While he talked you had the impression that he was not looking at you or that he mistook you for some one else.

'I will,' I said.

'I'm coming up to the hospital to see you,' Mrs. Meyers said. 'I have some things for my boys. You're all my boys. You certainly are my dear boys.'

'They'll be glad to see you.'

'Those dear boys. You too. You're one of my boys.'

'I have to get back,' I said.

'You give my love to all those dear boys. I've got lots of things to bring. I've some fine marsala and cakes.'

'Good-by,' I said. 'They'll be awfully glad to see you.'

'Good-by,' said Meyers. 'You come around to the galleria. You know where my table is. We're all there every afternoon.' I went on up the street. I wanted to buy something at the Cova to take to Catherine. Inside, at the Cova, I bought a box of chocolate and while the girl wrapped it up I walked over to the bar. There were a couple of British and some aviators. I had a martini alone, paid for it, picked up the box of chocolate at the outside counter and walked on home toward the hospital. Outside the little bar up the street from the Scala there were some people I knew, a vice-consul, two fellows who studied singing, and Ettore Moretti, an Italian from San Francisco who was in the Italian army. I had a drink with them. One of the singers was named Ralph Simmons, and he was singing under the name of Enrico DelCredo. I never knew how well he could sing but he was always on the point of something very big happening. He was fat and looked shopworn around the nose and mouth as though he had hayfever. He had come back from singing in Piacenza. He had sung Tosca and it had been wonderful.

'Of course you've never heard me sing,' he said.

'When will you sing here?'

'I'll be at the Scala in the fall.'

'I'll bet they throw the benches at you,' Ettore said. 'Did you hear how they threw the benches at him in Modena?'

'It's a damned lie.'

'They threw the benches at him,' Ettore said. 'I was there. I threw six benches myself.'

'You're just a wop from Frisco.'

'He can't pronounce Italian,' Ettore said. 'Everywhere he goes they throw the benches at him.'

'Piacenza's the toughest house to sing in the north of Italy,' the other tenor said. 'Believe me that's a tough little house to sing.' This tenor's name was Edgar Saunders, and he sang under the name of Edouardo Giovanni.

'I'd like to be there to see them throw the benches at you.' Ettore said. 'You can't sing Italian.'

'He's a nut,' said Edgar Saunders. 'All he knows how to say is throw benches.'

'That's all they know how to do when you two sing,' Ettore said. 'Then when you go to America you'll tell about your triumphs at the Scala. They wouldn't let you get by the first note at the Scala.'

'I'll sing at the Scala,' Simmons said. 'I'm going to sing Tosca in October.'

'We'll go, won't we, Mac?' Ettore said to the vice-consul. 'They'll need somebody to protect them.'

'Maybe the American army will be there to protect them,' the vice-consul said. 'Do you want another drink, Simmons? You want a drink, Saunders?'

'All right,' said Saunders.

'I hear you're going to get the silver medal,' Ettore said to me. 'What kind of citation you going to get?'

'I don't know. I don't know I'm going to get it.'

'You're going to get it. Oh boy, the girls at the Cova will think you're fine then. They'll all think you killed two hundred Austrians or captured a whole trench by yourself. Believe me, I got to work for my decorations.'

'How many have you got, Ettore?' asked the vice-consul.

'He's got everything,' Simmons said. 'He's the boy they're running the war for.'

'I've got the bronze twice and three silver medals,' said Ettore. 'But the papers on only one have come through.'

'What's the matter with the others?' asked Simmons.

'The action wasn't successful,' said Ettore. 'When the action isn't successful they hold up all the medals.'

'How many times have you been wounded, Ettore?'

'Three times bad. I got three wound stripes. See?' He pulled his sleeve around. The stripes were parallel silver lines on a black background sewed to the cloth of the sleeve about eight inches below the shoulder.

'You got one too,' Ettore said to me. 'Believe me they're fine to have. I'd rather have them than medals. Believe me, boy, when you get three you've got something. You only get one for a wound that puts you three months in the hospital.'

'Where were you wounded, Ettore?' asked the vice-consul.

Ettore pulled up his sleeve.

'Here,' he showed the deep smooth red scar. 'Here on my leg. I can't show you that because I got puttees on; and in the foot. There's dead bone in my foot that stinks right now. Every morning I take new little pieces out and it stinks all the time.'

'What hit you?' asked Simmons.

'A hand-grenade. One of those potato mashers. It just blew the whole side of my foot off. You know those potato mashers?' He turned to me.

'Sure.'

'I saw the son of a bitch throw it,' Ettore said. 'It knocked me down and I thought I was dead all right but those damn potato mashers haven't got anything in them. I shot the son of a bitch with my rifle. I always carry a rifle so they can't tell I'm an officer.'

'How did he look?' asked Simmons.

'That was the only one he had,' Ettore said. 'I don't know why he threw it. I guess he always wanted to throw one. He never saw any real fighting probably. I shot the son of a bitch all right.'

'How did he look when you shot him?' Simmons asked.

'Hell, how should I know?' said Ettore. 'I shot him in the belly. I was afraid I'd miss him if I shot him in the head.'

'How long have you been an officer, Ettore?' I asked.

'Two years. I'm going to be a captain. How long have you been a lieutenant?'

'Going on three years.'

'You can't be a captain because you don't know the Italian language well enough,' Ettore said. 'You can talk but you can't read and write well enough. You got to have an education to be a captain. Why don't you go in the American army?'

'Maybe I will.'

'I wish to God I could. Oh, boy, how much does a captain get, Mac?'

'I don't know exactly. Around two hundred and fifty dollars, I think.'

'Jesus Christ what I could do with two hundred and fifty dollars. You better get in the American army quick, Fred. See if you can't get me in.'

'All right.'

'I can command a company in Italian. I could learn it in English easy.'

'You'd be a general,' said Simmons.

'No, I don't know enough to be a general. A general's got to know a hell of a lot. You guys think there ain't anything to war. You ain't got brains enough to be a second- class corporal.'

'Thank God I don't have to be,' Simmons said.

'Maybe you will if they round up all you slackers. Oh, boy, I'd like to have you two in my platoon. Mac too. I'd make you my orderly, Mac.'

'You're a great boy, Ettore,' Mac said. 'But I'm afraid you're a militarist.'

'I'll be a colonel before the war's over,' Ettore said.

'If they don't kill you.'

'They won't kill me.' He touched the stars at his collar with his thumb and forefinger. 'See me do that? We always touch our stars if anybody mentions getting killed.'

'Let's go, Sim,' said Saunders standing up.

'All right.'

'So long,' I said. 'I have to go too.' It was a quarter to six by the clock inside the bar. 'Ciaou, Ettore.'

'Ciaou, Fred,' said Ettore. 'That's pretty fine you're going to get the silver medal.'

'I don't know I'll get it.'

'You'll get it all right, Fred. I heard you were going to get it all right.'

'Well, so long,' I said. 'Keep out of trouble, Ettore.'

'Don't worry about me. I don't drink and I don't run around. I'm no boozer and whorehound. I know what's good for me.'

'So long,' I said. 'I'm glad you're going to be promoted captain.'

'I don't have to wait to be promoted. I'm going to be a captain for merit of war. You know. Three stars with the crossed swords and crown above. That's me.'

'Good luck.'

'Good luck. When you going back to the front?'

'Pretty soon.'

'Well, I'll see you around.'

'So long.'

'So long. Don't take any bad nickels.'

I walked on down a back street that led to a cross-cut to the hospital. Ettore was twenty-three. He had been brought up by an uncle in San Francisco and was visiting his father and mother in Torino when war was declared. He had a sister, who had been sent to America with him at the same time to live with the uncle, who would graduate from normal school this year. He was a legitimate hero who bored every one he met. Catherine could not stand him.

'We have heroes too,' she said. 'But usually, darling, they're much quieter.'

'I don't mind him.'

'I wouldn't mind him if he wasn't so conceited and didn't bore me, and bore me, and bore me.'

'He bores me.'

'You're sweet to say so, darling. But you don't need to. You can picture him at the front and you know he's useful but he's so much the type of boy I don't care for.'

'I know.'

'You're awfully sweet to know, and I try and like him but he's a dreadful, dreadful boy really.'

'He said this afternoon he was going to be a captain.'

'I'm glad,' said Catherine. 'That should please him.'

'Wouldn't you like me to have some more exalted rank?'

'No, darling. I only want you to have enough rank so that we're admitted to the better restaurants.'

'That's just the rank I have.'

'You have a splendid rank. I don't want you to have any more rank. It might go to your head. Oh, darling, I'm awfully glad you're not conceited. I'd have married you even if you were conceited but it's very restful to have a husband who's not conceited.'

We were talking softly out on the balcony. The moon was supposed to rise but there was a mist over the town and it did not come up and in a little while it started to drizzle and we came in. Outside the mist turned to rain and in a little while it was raining hard and we heard it drumming on the roof. I got up and stood at the door to see if it was raining in but it wasn't, so I left the door open.

'Who else did you see?' Catherine asked.

'Mr. and Mrs. Meyers.'

'They're a strange lot.'

'He's supposed to have been in the penitentiary at home. They let him out to die.'

'And he lived happily in Milan forever after.'

'I don't know how happily.'

'Happily enough after jail I should think.'

'She's bringing some things here.'

'She brings splendid things. Were you her dear boy?'

'One of them.'

'You are all her dear boys,' Catherine said. 'She prefers the dear boys. Listen to it rain.'

'It's raining hard.'

'And you'll always love me, won't you?' 'Yes.'

'And the rain won't make any difference?'

'No.'

'That's good. Because I'm afraid of the rain.'

'Why?' I was sleepy. Outside the rain was falling steadily.

'I don't know, darling. I've always been afraid of the rain.'

'I like it.'

'I like to walk in it. But it's very hard on loving.'

'I'll love you always.'

'I'll love you in the rain and in the snow and in the hail and—what else is there?'

'I don't know. I guess I'm sleepy.'

'Go to sleep, darling, and I'll love you no matter how it is.'

'You're not really afraid of the rain are you?'

'Not when I'm with you.' 'Why are you afraid of it?'

'I don't know.'

'Tell me.'

'Don't make me.'

'Tell me.'

'No.'

'Tell me.'

'All right. I'm afraid of the rain because sometimes I see me dead in it.'

'No.'

'And sometimes I see you dead in it.'

'That's more likely.'

'No, it's not, darling. Because I can keep you safe. I know I can. But nobody can help themselves.'

'Please stop it. I don't want you to get Scotch and crazy tonight. We won't be together much longer.'

'No, but I am Scotch and crazy. But I'll stop it. It's all nonsense.' 'Yes it's all nonsense.'

'It's all nonsense. It's only nonsense. I'm not afraid of the rain. I'm not afraid of the rain. Oh, oh, God, I wish I wasn't.' She was crying. I comforted her and she stopped crying. But outside it kept on raining.

20

One day in the afternoon we went to the races. Ferguson went too and Crowell Rodgers, the boy who had been wounded in the eyes by the explosion of the shell nose- cap. The girls dressed to go after lunch while Crowell and I sat on the bed in his room and read the past performances of the horses and the predictions in the racing paper.

Crowell's head was bandaged and he did not care much about these races but read the racing paper constantly and kept track of all the horses for something to do. He said the horses were a terrible lot but they were all the horses we had. Old Meyers liked him and gave him tips. Meyers won on nearly every race but disliked to give tips because it brought down the prices. The racing was very crooked. Men who had been ruled off the turf everywhere else were racing in Italy. Meyers' information was good but I hated to ask him because sometimes he did not answer, and always you could see it hurt him to tell you, but he felt obligated to tell us for some reason and he hated less to tell Crowell.

Crowell's eyes had been hurt, one was hurt badly, and Meyers had trouble with his eyes and so he liked Crowell. Meyers never told his wife what horses he was playing and she won or lost, mostly lost, and talked all the time.

We four drove out to San Siro in an open carriage. It was a lovely day and we drove out through the park and out along the tramway and out of town where the road was dusty. There were villas with iron fences and big overgrown gardens and ditches with water flowing and green vegetable gardens with dust on the leaves. We could look across the plain and see farmhouses and the rich green farms with their irrigation ditches and the mountains to the north. There were many carriages going into the race track and the men at the gate let us in without cards because we were in uniform. We left the carriage, bought programmes, and walked across the infield and then across the smooth thick turf of the course to the paddock. The grand-stands were old and made of wood and the betting booths were under the stands and in a row out near the stables. There was a crowd of soldiers along the fence in the infield. The paddock was fairly well filled with people and they were walking the horses around in a ring under the trees behind the grandstand. We saw people we knew and got chairs for Ferguson and Catherine and watched the horses.

They went around, one after the other, their heads down, the grooms leading them.

One horse, a purplish black, Crowell swore was dyed that color. We watched him and it seemed possible. He had only come out just before the bell rang to saddle. We looked him up in the programme from the number on the groom's arm and it was listed a black gelding named Japalac. The race was for horses that had never won a race worth one thousand lire or more. Catherine was sure his color had been changed. Ferguson said she could not tell. I thought he looked suspicious. We all agreed we ought to back him and pooled one hundred lire. The odds sheets showed he would pay thirty-five to one. Crowell went over and bought the tickets while we watched the jockeys ride around once more and then go out under the trees to the track and gallop slowly up to the turn where the start was to be.

We went up in the grand-stand to watch the race. They had no elastic barrier at San Siro then and the starter lined up all the horses, they looked very small way up the track, and then sent them off with a crack of his long whip. They came past us with the black horse well in front and on the turn he was running away from the others. I watched them on the far side with the glasses and saw the jockey fighting to hold him in but he could not hold him and when they came around the turn and into the stretch the black horse was fifteen lengths ahead of the others. He went way on up and around the turn after the finish.

'Isn't it wonderful,' Catherine said. 'We'll have over three thousand lire. He must be a splendid horse.'

'I hope his color doesn't run,' Crowell said, 'before they pay off.'

'He was really a lovely horse,' Catherine said. 'I wonder if Mr. Meyers backed him.'

'Did you have the winner?' I called to Meyers. He nodded.

'I didn't,' Mrs. Meyers said. 'Who did you children bet on?'

'Japalac.'

'Really? He's thirty-five to one!'

'We liked his color.'

'I didn't. I thought he looked seedy. They told me not to back him.'

'He won't pay much,' Meyers said.

'He's marked thirty-five to one in the quotes,' I said.

'He won't pay much. At the last minute,' Meyers said, 'they put a lot of money on him.'

'No.'

'Kempton and the boys. You'll see. He won't pay two to one.'

'Then we won't get three thousand lire,' Catherine said. 'I don't like this crooked racing!'

'We'll get two hundred lire.'

'That's nothing. That doesn't do us any good. I thought we were going to get three thousand.'

'It's crooked and disgusting,' Ferguson said.

'Of course,' said Catherine, 'if it hadn't been crooked we'd never have backed him at all. But I would have liked the three thousand lire.'

'Let's go down and get a drink and see what they pay,' Crowell said. We went out to where they posted the numbers and the bell rang to pay off and they put up 18.50 after Japalac to win. That meant he paid less than even money on a ten-lira bet.

We went to the bar under the grand-stand and had a whiskey and soda apiece. We ran into a couple of Italians we knew and McAdams, the vice-consul, and they came up with us when we joined the girls. The Italians were full of manners and McAdams talked to Catherine while we went down to bet again. Mr. Meyers was standing near the pari- mutuel.

'Ask him what he played,' I said to Crowell.

'What are you on, Mr. Meyers?' Crowell asked. Meyers took out his programme and pointed to the number five with his pencil.

'Do you mind if we play him too?' Crowell asked.

'Go ahead. Go ahead. But don't tell my wife I gave it to you.'

'Will you have a drink?' I asked.

'No thanks. I never drink.'

We put a hundred lire on number five to win and a hundred to place and then had another whiskey and soda apiece. I was feeling very good and we picked up a couple more Italians, who each had a drink with us, and went back to the girls. These Italians were also very mannered and matched manners with the two we had collected before. In a little while no one could sit down. I gave the tickets to Catherine.

'What horse is it?'

'I don't know. Mr. Meyers' choice.'

'Don't you even know the name?'

'No. You can find it on the programme. Number five I think.'

'You have touching faith,' she said. The number five won but did not pay anything.

Mr. Meyers was angry.

'You have to put up two hundred lire to make twenty,' he said. 'Twelve lire for ten.'

'It's not worth it. My wife lost twenty lire.'

'I'll go down with you,' Catherine said to me. The Italians all stood up. We went downstairs and out to the paddock.

'Do you like this?' Catherine asked.

'Yes. I guess I do.'

'It's all right, I suppose,' she said. 'But, darling, I can't stand to see so many people.'

'We don't see many.'

'No. But those Meyers and the man from the bank with his wife and daughters—'

'He cashes my sight drafts,' I said.

'Yes but some one else would if he didn't. Those last four boys were awful.'

'We can stay out here and watch the race from the fence.'

'That will be lovely. And, darling, let's back a horse we've never heard of and that Mr. Meyers won't be backing.'

'All right.'

We backed a horse named Light For Me that finished fourth in a field of five. We leaned on the fence and watched the horses go by, their hoofs thudding as they went past, and saw the mountains off in the distance and Milan beyond the trees and the fields.

'I feel so much cleaner,' Catherine said. The horses were coming back, through the gate, wet and sweating, the jockeys quieting them and riding up to dismount under the trees.

'Wouldn't you like a drink? We could have one out here and see the horses.'

'I'll get them,' I said.

'The boy will bring them,' Catherine said. She put her hand up and the boy came out from the Pagoda bar beside the stables. We sat down at a round iron table.

'Don't you like it better when we're alone?' 'Yes,' I said.

'I felt very lonely when they were all there.'

'It's grand here,' I said.

'Yes. It's really a pretty course.'

'It's nice.'

'Don't let me spoil your fun, darling. I'll go back whenever you want.'

'No,' I said. 'We'll stay here and have our drink. Then we'll go down and stand at the water jump for the steeplechase.'

'You're awfully good to me,' she said.

After we had been alone awhile we were glad to see the others again. We had a good time.

21

In September the first cool nights came, then the days were cool and the leaves on the trees in the park began to turn color and we knew the summer was gone. The fighting at the front went very badly and they could not take San Gabriele. The fighting on the Bainsizza plateau was over and by the middle of the month the fighting for San Gabriele was about over too. They could not take it. Ettore was gone back to the front. The horses were gone to Rome and there was no more racing. Crowell had gone to Rome too, to be sent back to America. There were riots twice in the town against the war and bad rioting in Turin. A British major at the club told me the Italians had lost one hundred and fifty thousand men on the Bainsizza plateau and on San Gabriele. He said they had lost forty thousand on the Carso besides. We had a drink and he talked. He said the fighting was over for the year down here and that the Italians had bitten off more than they could chew. He said the offensive in Flanders was going to the bad. If they killed men as they did this fall the Allies would be cooked in another year. He said we were all cooked but we were all right as long as we did not know it. We were all cooked. The thing was not to recognize it. The last country to realize they were cooked would win the war. We had another drink. Was I on somebody's staff? No. He was. It was all balls. We were alone in the club sitting back in one of the big leather sofas. His boots were smoothly polished dull leather. They were beautiful boots. He said it was all balls. They thought only in divisions and man-power. They all squabbled about divisions and only killed them when they got them. They were all cooked. The Germans won the victories. By God they were soldiers. The old Hun was a soldier. But they were cooked too. We were all cooked. I asked about Russia. He said they were cooked already. I'd soon see they were cooked. Then the Austrians were cooked too. If they got some Hun divisions they could do it. Did he think they would attack this fall? Of course they would. The Italians were cooked. Everybody knew they were cooked. The old Hun would come down through the Trentino and cut the railway at Vicenza and then where would the Italians be? They tried that in 'sixteen, I said. Not with Germans. Yes, I said. But they probably wouldn't do that, he said. It was too simple.

They'd try something complicated and get royally cooked. I had to go, I said. I had to get back to the hospital. 'Good-by,' he said. Then cheerily, 'Every sort of luck!' There was a great contrast between his world pessimism and personal cheeriness.

I stopped at a barber shop and was shaved and went home to the hospital. My leg was as well as it would get for a long time. I had been up for examination three days before. There were still some treatments to take before my course at the Ospedale.

Maggiore was finished and I walked along the side street practising not limping. An old man was cutting silhouettes under an arcade. I stopped to watch him. Two girls were posing and he cut their silhouettes together, snipping very fast and looking at them, his head on one side. The girls were giggling. He showed me the silhouettes before he pasted them on white paper and handed them to the girls.

'They're beautiful,' he said. 'How about you, Tenente?'

The girls went away looking at their silhouettes and laughing. They were nice-looking girls. One of them worked in the wine shop across from the hospital.

'All right,' I said.

'Take your cap off.'

'No. With it on.'

'It will not be so beautiful,' the old man said. 'But,' he brightened, 'it will be more military.'

He snipped away at the black paper, then separated the two thicknesses and pasted the profiles on a card and handed them to me.

'How much?'

'That's all right.' He waved his hand. 'I just made them for you.'

'Please.' I brought out some coppers. 'For pleasure.'

'No. I did them for a pleasure. Give them to your girl.' 'Many thanks until we meet.'

'Until I see thee.'

I went on to the hospital. There were some letters, an official one, and some others.

I was to have three weeks' convalescent leave and then return to the front. I read it over carefully. Well, that was that. The convalescent leave started October fourth when my course was finished. Three weeks was twenty-one days. That made October twenty-fifth. I told them I would not be in and went to the restaurant a little way up the street from the hospital for supper and read my letters and the Corriere Della Sera at the table. There was a letter from my grandfather, containing family news, patriotic encouragement, a draft for two hundred dollars, and a few clippings; a dull letter from the priest at our mess, a letter from a man I knew who was flying with the French and had gotten in with a wild gang and was telling about it, and a note from Rinaldi asking me how long I was going to skulk in Milano and what was all the news? He wanted me to bring him phonograph records and enclosed a list. I drank a small bottle of chianti with the meal, had a coffee afterward with a glass of cognac, finished the paper, put my letters in my pocket, left the paper on the table with the tip and went out. In my room at the hospital I undressed, put on pajamas and a dressing-gown, pulled down the curtains on the door that opened onto the balcony and sitting up in bed read Boston papers from a pile Mrs. Meyers had left for her boys at the hospital. The Chicago White Sox were winning the American League pennant and the New York Giants were leading the National League. Babe Ruth was a pitcher then playing for Boston. The papers were dull, the news was local and stale, and the war news was all old. The American news was all training camps. I was glad I wasn't in a training camp. The baseball news was all I could read and I did not have the slightest interest in it. A number of papers together made it impossible to read with interest. It was not very timely but I read at it for a while. I wondered if America really got into the war, if they would close down the major leagues. They probably wouldn't. There was still racing in Milan and the war could not be much worse. They had stopped racing in France. That was where our horse Japalac came from. Catherine was not due on duty until nine o'clock. I heard her passing along the floor when she first came on duty and once saw her pass in the hall.

She went to several other rooms and finally came into mine.

'I'm late, darling,' she said. 'There was a lot to do. How are you?'

I told her about my papers and the leave.

'That's lovely,' she said. 'Where do you want to go?'

'Nowhere. I want to stay here.'
'That's silly. You pick a place to go and I'll come too.'
'How will you work it?'
'I don't know. But I will.'
'You're pretty wonderful.'
'No I'm not. But life isn't hard to manage when you've nothing to lose.'
'How do you mean?'
'Nothing. I was only thinking how small obstacles seemed that once were so big.'
'I should think it might be hard to manage.'
'No it won't, darling. If necessary I'll simply leave. But it won't come to that.'
'Where should we go?'
'I don't care. Anywhere you want. Anywhere we don't know people.'
'Don't you care where we go?'
'No. I'll like any place.'
She seemed upset and taut.
'What's the matter, Catherine?'
'Nothing. Nothing's the matter.'
'Yes there is.'
'No nothing. Really nothing.'
'I know there is. Tell me, darling. You can tell me.'
'It's nothing.'
'Tell me.'
'I don't want to. I'm afraid I'll make you unhappy or worry you.'
'No it won't.'
'You're sure? It doesn't worry me but I'm afraid to worry you.'
'It won't if it doesn't worry you.'
'I don't want to tell.'
'Tell it.'
'Do I have to?'
'Yes.'
'I'm going to have a baby, darling. It's almost three months along. You're not worried, are you? Please please don't. You mustn't worry.'
'All right.'
'Is it all right?'
'Of course.'
'I did everything. I took everything but it didn't make any difference.'
'I'm not worried.'
'I couldn't help it, darling, and I haven't worried about it. You mustn't worry or feel badly.'
'I only worry about you.'
'That's it. That's what you mustn't do. People have babies all the time. Everybody has babies. It's a natural thing.'

A Farewell to Arms • 77

'You're pretty wonderful.'

'No I'm not. But you mustn't mind, darling. I'll try and not make trouble for you. I know I've made trouble now. But haven't I been a good girl until now? You never knew it, did you?'

'No.'

'It will all be like that. You simply mustn't worry. I can see you're worrying. Stop it.

Stop it right away. Wouldn't you like a drink, darling? I know a drink always makes you feel cheerful.'

'No. I feel cheerful. And you're pretty wonderful.'

'No I'm not. But I'll fix everything to be together if you pick out a place for us to go. It ought to be lovely in October. We'll have a lovely time, darling, and I'll write you every day while you're at the front.'

'Where will you be?'

'I don't know yet. But somewhere splendid. I'll look after all that.'

We were quiet awhile and did not talk. Catherine was sitting on the bed and I was looking at her but we did not touch each other. We were apart as when some one comes into a room and people are self-conscious. She put out her hand and took mine.

'You aren't angry are you, darling?'

'No.'

'And you don't feel trapped?'

'Maybe a little. But not by you.'

'I didn't mean by me. You mustn't be stupid. I meant trapped at all.'

'You always feel trapped biologically.'

She went away a long way without stirring or removing her hand.

"Always" isn't a pretty word.'

'I'm sorry.'

'It's all right. But you see I've never had a baby and I've never even loved any one.

And I've tried to be the way you wanted and then you talk about "always".'

'I could cut off my tongue,' I offered.

'Oh, darling!' she came back from wherever she had been. 'You mustn't mind me.' We were both together again and the self-consciousness was gone. 'We really are the same one and we mustn't misunderstand on purpose.'

'We won't.'

'But people do. They love each other and they misunderstand on purpose and they fight and then suddenly they aren't the same one.'

'We won't fight.'

'We mustn't. Because there's only us two and in the world there's all the rest of them. If anything comes between us we're gone and then they have us.'

'They won't get us,' I said. 'Because you're too brave. Nothing ever happens to the brave.'

'They die of course.'

'But only once.'

'I don't know. Who said that?'

'The coward dies a thousand deaths, the brave but one?'

'Of course. Who said it?'

'I don't know.'

'He was probably a coward,' she said. 'He knew a great deal about cowards but nothing about the brave. The brave dies perhaps two thousand deaths if he's intelligent. He simply doesn't mention them.'

'I don't know. It's hard to see inside the head of the brave.'

'Yes. That's how they keep that way.'

'You're an authority.'

'You're right, darling. That was deserved.'

'You're brave.'

'No,' she said. 'But I would like to be.'

'I'm not,' I said. 'I know where I stand. I've been out long enough to know. I'm like a ball-player that bats two hundred and thirty and knows he's no better.'

'What is a ball-player that bats two hundred and thirty? It's awfully impressive.'

'It's not. It means a mediocre hitter in baseball.'

'But still a hitter,' she prodded me.

'I guess we're both conceited,' I said. 'But you are brave.' 'No. But I hope to be.'

'We're both brave,' I said. 'And I'm very brave when I've had a drink.'

'We're splendid people,' Catherine said. She went over to the armoire and brought me the cognac and a glass. 'Have a drink, darling,' she said. 'You've been awfully good.'

'I don't really want one.'

'Take one.'

'All right.' I poured the water glass a third full of cognac and drank it off. 'That was very big,' she said. 'I know brandy is for heroes. But you shouldn't exaggerate.'

'Where will we live after the war?'

'In an old people's home probably,' she said. 'For three years I looked forward very childishly to the war ending at Christmas. But now I look forward till when our son will be a lieutenant commander.'

'Maybe he'll be a general.'

'If it's an hundred years' war he'll have time to try both of the services.'

'Don't you want a drink?'

'No. It always makes you happy, darling, and it only makes me dizzy.'

'Didn't you ever drink brandy?'

'No, darling. I'm a very old-fashioned wife.'

I reached down to the floor for the bottle and poured another drink.

'I'd better go to have a look at your compatriots,' Catherine said. 'Perhaps you'll read the papers until I come back.'

'Do you have to go?'

'Now or later?'
'All right. Now.'
'I'll come back later.'
'I'll have finished the papers,' I said.

22

It turned cold that night and the next day it was raining. Coming home from the Ospedale Maggiore it rained very hard and I was wet when I came in. Up in my room the rain was coming down heavily outside on the balcony, and the wind blew it against the glass doors. I changed my clothing and drank some brandy but the brandy did not taste good. I felt sick in the night and in the morning after breakfast I was nauseated.

'There is no doubt about it,' the house surgeon said. 'Look at the whites of his eyes, Miss.'

Miss Gage looked. They had me look in a glass. The whites of the eyes were yellow and it was the jaundice. I was sick for two weeks with it. For that reason we did not spend a convalescent leave together. We had planned to go to Pallanza on Lago Maggiore. It is nice there in the fall when the leaves turn. There are walks you can take and you can troll for trout in the lake. It would have been better than Stresa because there are fewer people at Pallanza. Stresa is so easy to get to from Milan that there are always people you know. There is a nice village at Pallanza and you can row out to the islands where the fishermen live and there is a restaurant on the biggest island. But we did not go.

One day while I was in bed with jaundice Miss Van Campen came in the room, opened the door into the armoire and saw the empty bottles there. I had sent a load of them down by the porter and I believe she must have seen them going out and come up to find some more. They were mostly vermouth bottles, marsala bottles, capri bottles, empty chianti flasks and a few cognac bottles. The porter had carried out the large bottles, those that had held vermouth, and the straw-covered chianti flasks, and left the brandy bottles for the last. It was the brandy bottles and a bottle shaped like a bear, which had held kümmel, that Miss Van Campen found. The bear shaped bottle enraged her particularly. She held it up, the bear was sitting up on his haunches with his paws up, there was a cork in his glass head and a few sticky crystals at the bottom. I laughed.

'It is kümmel,' I said. 'The best kümmel comes in those bearshaped bottles. It comes from Russia.'

'Those are all brandy bottles, aren't they?' Miss Van Campen asked.

'I can't see them all,' I said. 'But they probably are.'

'How long has this been going on?'

'I bought them and brought them in myself,' I said. 'I have had Italian officers visit me frequently and I have kept brandy to offer them.'

'You haven't been drinking it yourself?' she said.

'I have also drunk it myself.'

'Brandy,' she said. 'Eleven empty bottles of brandy and that bear liquid.'

'Kümmel.'

'I will send for some one to take them away. Those are all the empty bottles you have?'

'For the moment.'

'And I was pitying you having jaundice. Pity is something that is wasted on you.'

'Thank you.'

'I suppose you can't be blamed for not wanting to go back to the front. But I should think you would try something more intelligent than producing jaundice with alcoholism.'

'With what?'

'With alcoholism. You heard me say it.' I did not say anything. 'Unless you find something else I'm afraid you will have to go back to the front when you are through with your jaundice. I don't believe self-inflicted jaundice entitles you to a convalescent leave.'

'You don't?'

'I do not.'

'Have you ever had jaundice, Miss Van Campen?'

'No, but I have seen a great deal of it.'

'You noticed how the patients enjoyed it?'

'I suppose it is better than the front.'

'Miss Van Campen,' I said, 'did you ever know a man who tried to disable himself by kicking himself in the scrotum?'

Miss Van Campen ignored the actual question. She had to ignore it or leave the room. She was not ready to leave because she had disliked me for a long time and she was now cashing in.

'I have known many men to escape the front through self-inflicted wounds.'

'That wasn't the question. I have seen self-inflicted wounds also. I asked you if you had ever known a man who had tried to disable himself by kicking himself in the scrotum. Because that is the nearest sensation to jaundice and it is a sensation that I believe few women have ever experienced. That was why I asked you if you had ever had the jaundice, Miss Van Campen, because—' Miss Van Campen left the room. Later Miss Gage came in.

'What did you say to Van Campen? She was furious.'

'We were comparing sensations. I was going to suggest that she had never experienced childbirth—'

'You're a fool,' Gage said. 'She's after your scalp.'

'She has my scalp,' I said. 'She's lost me my leave and she might try and get me court-martialled. She's mean enough.'

'She never liked you,' Gage said. 'What's it about?'

'She says I've drunk myself into jaundice so as not to go back to the front.'

'Pooh,' said Gage. 'I'll swear you've never taken a drink. Everybody will swear you've never taken a drink.'

'She found the bottles.'

'I've told you a hundred times to clear out those bottles. Where are they now?'

'In the armoire.'

'Have you a suitcase?'

'No. Put them in that rucksack.'

Miss Gage packed the bottles in the rucksack. 'I'll give them to the porter,' she said. She started for the door.

'Just a minute,' Miss Van Campen said. 'I'll take those bottles.' She had the porter with her. 'Carry them, please,' she said. 'I want to show them to the doctor when I make my report.'

She went down the hall. The porter carried the sack. He knew what was in it.

Nothing happened except that I lost my leave.

23

The night I was to return to the front I sent the porter down to hold a seat for me on the train when it came from Turin. The train was to leave at midnight. It was made up at Turin and reached Milan about half-past ten at night and lay in the station until time to leave. You had to be there when it came in, to get a seat. The porter took a friend with him, a machine-gunner on leave who worked in a tailor shop, and was sure that between them they could hold a place. I gave them money for platform tickets and had them take my baggage. There was a big rucksack and two musettes.

I said good-by at the hospital at about five o'clock and went out. The porter had my baggage in his lodge and I told him I would be at the station a little before midnight. His wife called me 'Signorino' and cried. She wiped her eyes and shook hands and then cried again. I patted her on the back and she cried once more. She had done my mending and was a very short dumpy, happy-faced woman with white hair. When she cried her whole face went to pieces. I went down to the corner where there was a wine shop and waited inside looking out the window. It was dark outside and cold and misty. I paid for my coffee and grappa and I watched the people going by in the light from the window. I saw Catherine and knocked on the window. She looked, saw me and smiled, and I went out to meet her. She was wearing a dark blue cape and a soft felt hat. We walked along together, along the sidewalk past the wine shops, then across the market square and up the street and through the archway to the cathedral square. There were streetcar tracks and beyond them was the cathedral. It was white and wet in the mist. We crossed the tram tracks. On our left were the shops, their windows lighted, and the entrance to the galleria. There was a fog in the square and when we came close to the front of the cathedral it was very big and the stone was wet.

'Would you like to go in?'

'No,' Catherine said. We walked along. There was a soldier standing with his girl in the shadow of one of the stone buttresses ahead of us and we passed them. They were standing tight up against the stone and he had put his cape around her.

'They're like us,' I said.

'Nobody is like us,' Catherine said. She did not mean it happily.

'I wish they had some place to go.'

'It mightn't do them any good.'

'I don't know. Everybody ought to have some place to go.'

'They have the cathedral,' Catherine said. We were past it now. We crossed the far end of the square and looked back at the cathedral. It was fine in the mist. We were standing in front of the leather goods shop. There were riding boots, a rucksack and ski boots in the window. Each article was set apart as an exhibit; the rucksack in the centre, the riding boots on one side and the ski boots on the other. The leather was dark and oiled smooth as a used saddle. The electric light made high lights on the dull oiled leather.

'We'll ski some time.'

'In two months there will be ski-ing at Mflrren,' Catherine said.

'Let's go there.'

'All right,' she said. We went on past other windows and turned down a side street.

'I've never been this way.'

'This is the way I go to the hospital,' I said. It was a narrow street and we kept on the right-hand side. There were many people passing in the fog. There were shops and all the windows were lighted. We looked in a window at a pile of cheeses. I stopped in front of an armorer's shop.

'Come in a minute. I have to buy a gun.'

'What sort of gun?'

'A pistol.' We went in and I unbuttoned my belt and laid it with the empty holster on the counter. Two women were behind the counter. The women brought out several pistols.

'It must fit this,' I said, opening the holster. It was a gray leather holster and I had bought it second-hand to wear in the town.

'Have they good pistols?' Catherine asked.

'They're all about the same. Can I try this one?' I asked the woman.

'I have no place now to shoot,' she said. 'But it is very good. You will not make a mistake with it.'

I snapped it and pulled back the action. The spring was rather strong but it worked smoothly. I sighted it and snapped it again.

'It is used,' the woman said. 'It belonged to an officer who was an excellent shot.' 'Did you sell it to him?'

'Yes.'

'How did you get it back?'

A Farewell to Arms • 83

'From his orderly.'

'Maybe you have mine,' I said. 'How much is this?'

'Fifty lire. It is very cheap.'

'All right. I want two extra clips and a box of cartridges.'

She brought them from under the counter.

'Have you any need for a sword?' she asked. 'I have some used swords very cheap.'

'I'm going to the front,' I said.

'Oh yes, then you won't need a sword,' she said.

I paid for the cartridges and the pistol, filled the magazine and put it in place, put the pistol in my empty holster, filled the extra clips with cartridges and put them in the leather slots on the holster and then buckled on my belt. The pistol felt heavy on the belt. Still, I thought, it was better to have a regulation pistol. You could always get shells.

'Now we're fully armed,' I said. 'That was the one thing I had to remember to do. Some one got my other one going to the hospital.'

'I hope it's a good pistol,' Catherine said.

'Was there anything else?' the woman asked.

'I don't believe so.'

'The pistol has a lanyard,' she said.

'So I noticed.'

The woman wanted to sell something else.

'You don't need a whistle?'

'I don't believe so.'

The woman said good-by and we went out onto the sidewalk. Catherine looked in the window. The woman looked out and bowed to us.

'What are those little mirrors set in wood for?'

'They're for attracting birds. They twirl them out in the field and larks see them and come out and the Italians shoot them.'

'They are an ingenious people,' Catherine said. 'You don't shoot larks do you, darling, in America?'

'Not especially.'

We crossed the street and started to walk up the other side.

'I feel better now,' Catherine said. 'I felt terrible when we started.'

'We always feel good when we're together.'

'We always will be together.'

'Yes, except that I'm going away at midnight.'

'Don't think about it, darling.'

We walked on up the street. The fog made the lights yellow.

'Aren't you tired?' Catherine asked.

'How about you?'

'I'm all right. It's fun to walk.'

'But let's not do it too long.'

'No.'

We turned down a side street where there were no lights and walked in the street. I stopped and kissed Catherine. While I kissed her I felt her hand on my shoulder. She had pulled my cape around her so it covered both of us. We were standing in the street against a high wall.

'Let's go some place,' I said.

'Good,' said Catherine. We walked on along the street until it came out onto a wider street that was beside a canal. On the other side was a brick wall and buildings. Ahead, down the street, I saw a streetcar cross a bridge.

'We can get a cab up at the bridge,' I said. We stood on the bridge in the fog waiting for a carriage. Several streetcars passed, full of people going home. Then a carriage came along but there was some one in it. The fog was turning to rain.

'We could walk or take a tram,' Catherine said.

'One will be along,' I said. 'They go by here.'

'Here one comes,' she said.

The driver stopped his horse and lowered the metal sign on his meter. The top of the carriage was up and there were drops of water on the driver's coat. His varnished hat was shining in the wet. We sat back in the seat together and the top of the carriage made it dark.

'Where did you tell him to go?'

'To the station. There's a hotel across from the station where we can go.'

'We can go the way we are? Without luggage?'

'Yes,' I said.

It was a long ride to the station up side streets in the rain.

'Won't we have dinner?' Catherine asked. 'I'm afraid I'll be hungry.'

'We'll have it in our room.'

'I haven't anything to wear. I haven't even a night-gown.'

'We'll get one,' I said and called to the driver.

'Go to the Via Manzoni and up that.' He nodded and turned off to the left at the next corner. On the big street Catherine watched for a shop.

'Here's a place,' she said. I stopped the driver and Catherine got out, walked across the sidewalk and went inside. I sat back in the carriage and waited for her. It was raining and I could smell the wet street and the horse steaming in the rain. She came back with a package and got in and we drove on.

'I was very extravagant, darling,' she said, 'but it's a fine night-gown.'

At the hotel I asked Catherine to wait in the carriage while I went in and spoke to the manager. There were plenty of rooms. Then I went out to the carriage, paid the driver, and Catherine and I walked in together. The small boy in buttons carried the package.

The manager bowed us toward the elevator. There was much red plush and brass.

The manager went up in the elevator with us.

'Monsieur and Madame wish dinner in their rooms?'

'Yes. Will you have the menu brought up?' I said.

'You wish something special for dinner. Some game or a soufflé?'

The elevator passed three floors with a click each time, then clicked and stopped.

'What have you as game?'

'I could get a pheasant, or a woodcock.'

'A woodcock,' I said. We walked down the corridor. The carpet was worn. There were many doors. The manager stopped and unlocked a door and opened it.

'Here you are. A lovely room.'

The small boy in buttons put the package on the table in the centre of the room. The manager opened the curtains.

'It is foggy outside,' he said. The room was furnished in red plush. There were many mirrors, two chairs and a large bed with a satin coverlet. A door led to the bathroom.

'I will send up the menu,' the manager said. He bowed and went out.

I went to the window and looked out, then pulled a cord that shut the thick plush curtains. Catherine was sitting on the bed, looking at the cut glass chandelier. She had taken her hat off and her hair shone under the light. She saw herself in one of the mirrors and put her hands to her hair. I saw her in three other mirrors. She did not look happy. She let her cape fall on the bed.

'What's the matter, darling?'

'I never felt like a whore before,' she said. I went over to the window and pulled the curtain aside and looked out. I had not thought it would be like this.

'You're not a whore.'

'I know it, darling. But it isn't nice to feel like one.' Her voice was dry and flat. 'This was the best hotel we could get in,' I said. I looked out the window. Across the square were the lights of the station. There were carriages going by on the street and I saw the trees in the park. The lights from the hotel shone on the wet pavement. Oh, hell, I thought, do we have to argue now?

'Come over here please,' Catherine said. The flatness was all gone out of her voice. 'Come over, please. I'm a good girl again.' I looked over at the bed. She was smiling.

I went over and sat on the bed beside her and kissed her.

'You're my good girl.'

'I'm certainly yours,' she said.

After we had eaten we felt fine, and then after, we felt very happy and in a little time the room felt like our own home. My room at the hospital had been our own home and this room was our home too in the same way.

Catherine wore my tunic over her shoulders while we ate. We were very hungry and the meal was good and we drank a bottle of Capri and a bottle of St. Estephe. I drank most of it but Catherine drank some and it made her feel splendid. For dinner we had a woodcock with soufflé potatoes and purée de marron, a salad, and zabaione for dessert.

'It's a fine room,' Catherine said. 'It's a lovely room. We should have stayed here all the time we've been in Milan.'

'It's a funny room. But it's nice.'

'Vice is a wonderful thing,' Catherine said. 'The people who go in for it seem to have good taste about it. The red plush is really fine. It's just the thing. And the mirrors are very attractive.'

'You're a lovely girl.'

'I don't know how a room like this would be for waking up in the morning. But it's really a splendid room.' I poured another glass of St. Estephe.

'I wish we could do something really sinful,' Catherine said. 'Everything we do seems so innocent and simple. I can't believe we do anything wrong.'

'You're a grand girl.'

'I only feel hungry. I get terribly hungry.'

'You're a fine simple girl,' I said.

'I am a simple girl. No one ever understood it except you.'

'Once when I first met you I spent an afternoon thinking how we would go to the Hotel Cavour together and how it would be.'

'That was awfully cheeky of you. This isn't the Cavour is it?'

'No. They wouldn't have taken us in there.'

'They'll take us in some time. But that's how we differ, darling. I never thought about anything.'

'Didn't you ever at all?' 'A little,' she said.

'Oh you're a lovely girl.'

I poured another glass of wine.

'I'm a very simple girl,' Catherine said.

'I didn't think so at first. I thought you were a crazy girl.'

'I was a little crazy. But I wasn't crazy in any complicated manner. I didn't confuse you did I, darling?'

'Wine is a grand thing,' I said. 'It makes you forget all the bad.'

'It's lovely,' said Catherine. 'But it's given my father gout very badly.'

'Have you a father?'

'Yes,' said Catherine. 'He has gout. You won't ever have to meet him. Haven't you a father?'

'No,' I said. 'A step-father.'

'Will I like him?'

'You won't have to meet him.'

'We have such a fine time,' Catherine said. 'I don't take any interest in anything else any more. I'm so very happy married to you.'

The waiter came and took away the things. After a while we were very still and we could hear the rain. Down below on the street a motor car honked.

'But at my back I always hear Time's winged chariot hurrying near,' I said. 'I know that poem,' Catherine said. 'It's by Marvell. But it's about a girl who wouldn't live with a man.'

My head felt very clear and cold and I wanted to talk facts.
'Where will you have the baby?'
'I don't know. The best place I can find.'
'How will you arrange it?'
'The best way I can. Don't worry, darling. We may have several babies before the war is over.'
'It's nearly time to go.'
'I know. You can make it time if you want.'
'No.'
'Then don't worry, darling. You were fine until now and now you're worrying.'
'I won't. How often will you write?'
'Every day. Do they read your letters?'
'They can't read English enough to hurt any.'
'I'll make them very confusing,' Catherine said.
'But not too confusing.'
'I'll just make them a little confusing.'
'I'm afraid we have to start to go.' 'All right, darling.'
'I hate to leave our fine house.'
'So do I.'
'But we have to go.'
'All right. But we're never settled in our home very long.'
'We will be.'
'I'll have a fine home for you when you come back.'
'Maybe I'll be back right away.'
'Perhaps you'll be hurt just a little in the foot.'
'Or the lobe of the ear.'
'No I want your ears the way they are.'
'And not my feet?'
'Your feet have been hit already.'
'We have to go, darling. Really.'
'All right. You go first.'

24

We walked down the stairs instead of taking the elevator. The carpet on the stairs was worn. I had paid for the dinner when it came up and the waiter, who had brought it, was sitting on a chair near the door. He jumped up and bowed and I went with him into the side room and paid the bill for the room. The manager had remembered me as a friend and refused payment in advance but when he retired he had remembered to have the waiter stationed at the door so that I should not get out without paying. I suppose that had happened; even with his friends. One had so many friends in a war.

I asked the waiter to get us a carriage and he took Catherine's package that I was carrying and went out with an umbrella. Outside through the window we saw him crossing the street in the rain. We stood in the side room and looked out the window.

'How do you feel, Cat?'

'Sleepy.'

'I feel hollow and hungry.'

'Have you anything to eat?'

'Yes, in my musette.'

I saw the carriage coming. It stopped, the horse's head hanging in the rain, and the waiter stepped out, opened his umbrella, and came toward the hotel. We met him at the door and walked out under the umbrella down the wet walk to the carriage at the curb.

Water was running in the gutter.

'There is your package on the seat,' the waiter said. He stood with the umbrella until we were in and I had tipped him.

'Many thanks. Pleasant journey,' he said. The coachman lifted the reins and the horse started. The waiter turned away under the umbrella and went toward the hotel. We drove down the street and turned to the left, then came around to the right in front of the station. There were two carabinieri standing under the light just out of the rain. The light shone on their hats. The rain was clear and transparent against the light from the station. A porter came out from under the shelter of the station, his shoulders up against the rain.

'No,' I said. 'Thanks. I don't need thee.'

He went back under the shelter of the archway. I turned to Catherine. Her face was in the shadow from the hood of the carriage.

'We might as well say good-by.' 'I can't go in?'

'No.'

'Good-by, Cat.'

'Will you tell him the hospital?' 'Yes.'

I told the driver the address to drive to. He nodded.

'Good-by,' I said. 'Take good care of yourself and young Catherine.'

'Good-by, darling.'

'Good-by,' I said. I stepped out into the rain and the carriage started. Catherine leaned out and I saw her face in the light. She smiled and waved. The carriage went up the street, Catherine pointed in toward the archway. I looked, there were only the two carabinieri and the archway. I realized she meant for me to get in out of the rain. I went in and stood and watched the carriage turn the corner. Then I started through the station and down the runway to the train.

The porter was on the platform looking for me. I followed him into the train, crowding past people and along the aisle and in through a door to where the machine-gunner sat in the corner of a full compartment. My rucksack and musettes were above his head on the luggage rack. There were many men standing in the corridor and the men in the compartment all looked at us when we came in.

There were not enough places in the train and every one was hostile. The machine-gunner stood up for me to sit down. Some one tapped me on the shoulder. I looked around. It was a very tall gaunt captain of artillery with a red scar along his jaw. He had looked through the glass on the corridor and then come in.

'What do you say?' I asked. I had turned and faced him. He was taller than I and his face was very thin under the shadow of his cap-visor and the scar was new and shiny. Every one in the compartment was looking at me.

'You can't do that,' he said. 'You can't have a soldier save you a place.'

'I have done it.'

He swallowed and I saw his Adam's apple go up and then down. The machine-gunner stood in front of the place. Other men looked in through the glass. No one in the compartment said anything.

'You have no right to do that. I was here two hours before you came.'

'What do you want?'

'The seat.'

'So do I.'

I watched his face and could feel the whole compartment against me. I did not blame them. He was in the right. But I wanted the seat. Still no one said anything.

Oh, hell, I thought.

'Sit down, Signor Capitano,' I said. The machine-gunner moved out of the way and the tall captain sat down. He looked at me. His face seemed hurt. But he had the seat. 'Get my things,' I said to the machine-gunner. We went out in the corridor. The train was full and I knew there was no chance of a place. I gave the porter and the machine-gunner ten lire apiece. They went down the corridor and outside on the platform looking in the windows but there were no places.

'Maybe some will get off at Brescia,' the porter said.

'More will get on at Brescia,' said the machine-gunner. I said good-by to them and we shook hands and they left. They both felt badly. Inside the train we were all standing in the corridor when the train started. I watched the lights of the station and the yards as we went out. It was still raining and soon the windows were wet and you could not see out.

Later I slept on the floor of the corridor; first putting my pocket-book with my money and papers in it inside my shirt and trousers so that it was inside the leg of my breeches. I slept all night, waking at Brescia and Verona when more men got on the train, but going back to sleep at once. I had my head on one of the musettes and my arms around the other and I could feel the pack and they could all walk over me if they wouldn't step on me. Men were sleeping on the floor all down the corridor. Others stood holding on to the window rods or leaning against the doors. That train was always crowded.

BOOK THREE

25

Now in the fall the trees were all bare and the roads were muddy. I rode to Gorizia from Udine on a camion. We passed other camions on the road and I looked at the country. The mulberry trees were bare and the fields were brown. There were wet dead leaves on the road from the rows of bare trees and men were working on the road, tamping stone in the ruts from piles of crushed stone along the side of the road between the trees. We saw the town with a mist over it that cut off the mountains. We crossed the river and I saw that it was running high. It had been raining in the mountains. We came into the town past the factories and then the houses and villas and I saw that many more houses had been hit. On a narrow street we passed a British Red Cross ambulance. The driver wore a cap and his face was thin and very tanned. I did not know him. I got down from the camion in the big square in front of the Town Major's house, the driver handed down my rucksack and I put it on and swung on the two musettes and walked to our villa. It did not feel like a homecoming.

I walked down the damp gravel driveway looking at the villa through the trees. The windows were all shut but the door was open. I went in and found the major sitting at a table in the bare room with maps and typed sheets of paper on the wall.

'Hello,' he said. 'How are you?' He looked older and drier.

'I'm good,' I said. 'How is everything?'

'It's all over,' he said. 'Take off your kit and sit down.' I put my pack and the two musettes on the floor and my cap on the pack. I brought the other chair over from the wall and sat down by the desk.

'It's been a bad summer,' the major said. 'Are you strong now?'

'Yes.'

'Did you ever get the decorations?'

'Yes. I got them fine. Thank you very much.'

'Let's see them.'

I opened my cape so he could see the two ribbons.

'Did you get the boxes with the medals?'

'No. Just the papers.'

'The boxes will come later. That takes more time.'

'What do you want me to do?'

'The cars are all away. There are six up north at Caporetto. You know Caporetto?'

'Yes,' I said. I remembered it as a little white town with a campanile in a valley. It was a clean little town and there was a fine fountain in the square.

'They are working from there. There are many sick now. The fighting is over.'

'Where are the others?'

'There are two up in the mountains and four still on the Bainsizza. The other two ambulance sections are in the Carso with the third army.'

'What do you wish me to do?'

'You can go and take over the four cars on the Bainsizza if you like. Gino has been up there a long time. You haven't seen it up there, have you?'

'No.'

'It was very bad. We lost three cars.'

'I heard about it.'

'Yes, Rinaldi wrote you.'

'Where is Rinaldi?'

'He is here at the hospital. He has had a summer and fall of it.'

'I believe it.'

'It has been bad,' the major said. 'You couldn't believe how bad it's been. I've often thought you were lucky to be hit when you were.'

'I know I was.'

'Next year will be worse,' the major said. 'Perhaps they will attack now. They say they are to attack but I can't believe it. It is too late. You saw the river?'

'Yes. It's high already.'

'I don't believe they will attack now that the rains have started. We will have the snow soon. What about your countrymen? Will there be other Americans besides yourself?'

'They are training an army of ten million.'

'I hope we get some of them. But the French will hog them all. We'll never get any down here. All right. You stay here to-night and go out to-morrow with the little car and send Gino back. I'll send somebody with you that knows the road. Gino will tell you everything. They are shelling quite a little still but it is all over. You will want to see the Bainsizza.'

'I'm glad to see it. I am glad to be back with you again, Signor Maggiore.'

He smiled. 'You are very good to say so. I am very tired of this war. If I was away I do not believe I would come back.'

'Is it so bad?'

'Yes. It is so bad and worse. Go get cleaned up and find your friend Rinaldi.'

I went out and carried my bags up the stairs. Rinaldi was not in the room but his things were there and I sat down on the bed and unwrapped my puttees and took the shoe off my right foot. Then I lay back on the bed. I was tired and my right foot hurt. It seemed silly to lie on the bed with one shoe off, so I sat up and unlaced the other shoe and dropped it on the floor, then lay back on the blanket again. The room was stuffy with the window closed but I was too tired to get up and open it. I saw my things were all in one corner of the room. Outside it was getting dark. I lay on the bed and thought about Catherine and waited for Rinaldi. I was going to try not to think about Catherine except at night before I went to sleep. But now I was tired and there was nothing to do, so I lay and thought about her. I was thinking about her when Rinaldi came in. He looked just the same. Perhaps he was a little thinner.

'Well, baby,' he said. I sat up on the bed. He came over, sat down and put his arm around me. 'Good old baby.' He whacked me on the back and I held both his arms.

'Old baby,' he said. 'Let me see your knee.'

'I'll have to take off my pants.'

'Take off your pants, baby. We're all friends here. I want to see what kind of a job they did.' I stood up, took off the breeches and pulled off the knee-brace. Rinaldi sat on the floor and bent the knee gently back and forth. He ran his finger along the scar; put his thumbs together over the kneecap and rocked the knee gently with his fingers.

'Is that all the articulation you have?'

'Yes.'

'It's a crime to send you back. They ought to get complete articulation.'

'It's a lot better than it was. It was stiff as a board.'

Rinaldi bent it more. I watched his hands. He had fine surgeon's hands. I looked at the top of his head, his hair shiny and parted smoothly. He bent the knee too far.

'Ouch!' I said.

'You ought to have more treatment on it with the machines,' Rinaldi said.

'It's better than it was.'

'I see that, baby. This is something I know more about than you.' He stood up and sat down on the bed. 'The knee itself is a good job.' He was through with the knee. 'Tell me all about everything.'

'There's nothing to tell,' I said. 'I've led a quiet life.'

'You act like a married man,' he said. 'What's the matter with you?'

'Nothing,' I said. 'What's the matter with you?'

'This war is killing me,' Rinaldi said, 'I am very depressed by it.' He folded his hands over his knee.

'Oh,' I said.

'What's the matter? Can't I even have human impulses?'

'No. I can see you've been having a fine time. Tell me.'

'All summer and all fall I've operated. I work all the time. I do everybody's work. All the hard ones they leave to me. By God, baby, I am becoming a lovely surgeon.'

'That sounds better.'

'I never think. No, by God, I don't think; I operate.'

'That's right.'

'But now, baby, it's all over. I don't operate now and I feel like hell. This is a terrible war, baby. You believe me when I say it. Now you cheer me up. Did you bring the phonograph records?'

'Yes.'

They were wrapped in paper in a cardboard box in my rucksack. I was too tired to get them out.

'Don't you feel good yourself, baby?'

'I feel like hell.'

'This war is terrible,' Rinaldi said. 'Come on. We'll both get drunk and be cheerful. Then we'll go get the ashes dragged. Then we'll feel fine.'

'I've had the jaundice,' I said, 'and I can't get drunk.'

'Oh, baby, how you've come back to me. You come back serious and with a liver. I tell you this war is a bad thing. Why did we make it anyway.'

'We'll have a drink. I don't want to get drunk but we'll have a drink.'

Rinaldi went across the room to the washstand and brought back two glasses and a bottle of cognac.

'It's Austrian cognac,' he said. 'Seven stars. It's all they captured on San Gabriele.'

'Were you up there?'

'No. I haven't been anywhere. I've been here all the time operating. Look, baby, this is your old tooth-brushing glass. I kept it all the time to remind me of you.'

'To remind you to brush your teeth.'

'No. I have my own too. I kept this to remind me of you trying to brush away the Villa Rossa from your teeth in the morning, swearing and eating aspirin and cursing harlots. Every time I see that glass I think of you trying to clean your conscience with a toothbrush.' He came over to the bed. 'Kiss me once and tell me you're not serious.'

'I never kiss you. You're an ape.'

'I know, you are the fine good Anglo-Saxon boy. I know. You are the remorse boy, I know. I will wait till I see the Anglo-Saxon brushing away harlotry with a toothbrush.'

'Put some cognac in the glass.'

We touched glasses and drank. Rinaldi laughed at me.

'I will get you drunk and take out your liver and put you in a good Italian liver and make you a man again.'

I held the glass for some more cognac. It was dark outside now. Holding the glass of cognac, I went over and opened the window. The rain had stopped falling. It was colder outside and there was a mist in the trees.

'Don't throw the cognac out the window,' Rinaldi said. 'If you can't drink it give it to me.'

'Go something yourself,' I said. I was glad to see Rinaldi again. He had spent two years teasing me and I had always liked it. We understood each other very well.

'Are you married?' he asked from the bed. I was standing against the wall by the window.

'Not yet.'

'Are you in love?'

'Yes.'

'With that English girl?'

'Yes.'

'Poor baby. Is she good to you?'

'Of course.'

'I mean is she good to you practically speaking?'

'Shut up.'

'I will. You will see I am a man of extreme delicacy. Does she—?' 'Rinin,' I said. 'Please shut up. If you want to be my friend, shut up.' 'I don't want to be your friend, baby. I am your friend.'

'Then shut up.'

'All right.'

I went over to the bed and sat down beside Rinaldi. He was holding his glass and looking at the floor.

'You see how it is, Rinin?'

'Oh, yes. All my life I encounter sacred subjects. But very few with you. I suppose you must have them too.' He looked at the floor.

'You haven't any?'

'Not any?'

'No.'

'I can say this about your mother and that about your sister?'

'And that about your sister,' Rinaldi said swiftly. We both laughed.

'The old superman,' I said.

'I am jealous maybe,' Rinaldi said.

'No, you're not.'

'I don't mean like that. I mean something else. Have you any married friends?'

'Yes,' I said.

'I haven't,' Rinaldi said. 'Not if they love each other.'

'Why not?'

'They don't like me.'

'Why not?'

'I am the snake. I am the snake of reason.'

'You're getting it mixed. The apple was reason.'

'No, it was the snake.'

He was more cheerful.

'You are better when you don't think so deeply,' I said.

'I love you, baby,' he said. 'You puncture me when I become a great Italian thinker. But I know many things I can't say. I know more than you.'

'Yes. You do.'

'But you will have a better time. Even with remorse you will have a better time.'

'I don't think so.'

'Oh, yes. That is true. Already I am only happy when I am working.' He looked at the floor again.

'You'll get over that.'

'No. I only like two other things; one is bad for my work and the other is over in half an hour or fifteen minutes. Sometimes less.'

'Sometimes a good deal less.'

'Perhaps I have improved, baby. You do not know. But there are only the two things and my work.'

'You'll get other things.'

'No. We never get anything. We are born with all we have and we never learn. We never get anything new. We all start complete. You should be glad not to be a Latin.'

'There's no such thing as a Latin. That is "Latin" thinking. You are so proud of your defects.' Rinaldi looked up and laughed.

'We'll stop, baby. I am tired from thinking so much.' He had looked tired when he came in. 'It's nearly time to eat. I'm glad you're back. You are my best friend and my war brother.'

'When do the war brothers eat?' I asked.

'Right away. We'll drink once more for your liver's sake.'

'Like Saint Paul.'

'You are inaccurate. That was wine and the stomach. Take a little wine for your stomach's sake.'

'Whatever you have in the bottle,' I said. 'For any sake you mention.'

'To your girl,' Rinaldi said. He held out his glass.

'All right.'

'I'll never say a dirty thing about her.'

'Don't strain yourself.'

He drank off the cognac. 'I am pure,' he said. 'I am like you, baby. I will get an English girl too. As a matter of fact I knew your girl first but she was a little tall for me. A tall girl for a sister,' he quoted.

'You have a lovely pure mind,' I said.

'Haven't I? That's why they call me Rinaldo Purissimo.'

'Rinaldo Sporchissimo.'

'Come on, baby, we'll go down to eat while my mind is still pure.'

I washed, combed my hair and we went down the stairs. Rinaldi was a little drunk. In the room where we ate, the meal was not quite ready.

'I'll go get the bottle,' Rinaldi said. He went off up the stairs. I sat at the table and he came back with the bottle and poured us each a half tumbler of cognac.

'Too much,' I said and held up the glass and sighted at the lamp on the table.

'Not for an empty stomach. It is a wonderful thing. It burns out the stomach completely. Nothing is worse for you.' 'All right.'

'Self-destruction day by day,' Rinaldi said. 'It ruins the stomach and makes the hand shake. Just the thing for a surgeon.'

'You recommend it?'

'Heartily. I use no other. Drink it down, baby, and look forward to being sick.'

I drank half the glass. In the hall I could hear the orderly calling. 'Soup! Soup is ready!'

The major came in, nodded to us and sat down. He seemed very small at table.

'Is this all we are?' he asked. The orderly put the soup bowl down and he ladled out a plate full.

'We are all,' Rinaldi said. 'Unless the priest comes. If he knew Federico was here he would be here.'

'Where is he?' I asked.

'He's at 307,' the major said. He was busy with his soup. He wiped his mouth, wiping his upturned gray mustache carefully. 'He will come I think. I called them and left word to tell him you were here.'

'I miss the noise of the mess,' I said.

'Yes, it's quiet,' the major said.

'I will be noisy,' said Rinaldi.

'Drink some wine, Enrico,' said the major. He filled my glass. The spaghetti came in and we were all busy. We were finishing the spaghetti when the priest came in. He was the same as ever, small and brown and compact looking. I stood up and we shook hands. He put his hand on my shoulder.

'I came as soon as I heard,' he said.

'Sit down,' the major said. 'You're late.'

'Good-evening, priest,' Rinaldi said, using the English word. They had taken that up from the priest-baiting captain, who spoke a little English. 'Good-evening, Rinaldo,' the priest said. The orderly brought him soup but he said he would start with the spaghetti.

'How are you?' he asked me.

'Fine,' I said. 'How have things been?'

'Drink some wine, priest,' Rinaldi said. 'Take a little wine for your stomach's sake. That's Saint Paul, you know.'

'Yes I know,' said the priest politely. Rinaldi filled his glass.

'That Saint Paul,' said Rinaldi. 'He's the one who makes all the trouble.' The priest looked at me and smiled. I could see that the baiting did not touch him now.

'That Saint Paul,' Rinaldi said. 'He was a rounder and a chaser and then when he was no longer hot he said it was no good. When he was finished he made the rules for us who are still hot. Isn't it true, Federico?'

The major smiled. We were eating meat stew now.

'I never discuss a Saint after dark,' I said. The priest looked up from the stew and smiled at me.

'There he is, gone over with the priest,' Rinaldi said. 'Where are all the good old priest-baiters? Where is Cavalcanti? Where is Brundi? Where is Cesare? Do I have to bait this priest alone without support?'

'He is a good priest,' said the major.

'He is a good priest,' said Rinaldi. 'But still a priest. I try to make the mess like the old days. I want to make Federico happy. To hell with you, priest!'

I saw the major look at him and notice that he was drunk. His thin face was white. The line of his hair was very black against the white of his forehead.

'It's all right, Rinaldo,' said the priest. 'It's all right.'

'To hell with you,' said Rinaldi. 'To hell with the whole damn business.' He sat back in his chair.

'He's been under a strain and he's tired,' the major said to me. He finished his meat and wiped up the gravy with a piece of bread.

'I don't give a damn,' Rinaldi said to the table. 'To hell with the whole business.' He looked defiantly around the table, his eyes flat, his face pale.

'All right,' I said. 'To hell with the whole damn business.'

'No, no,' said Rinaldi. 'You can't do it. You can't do it. I say you can't do it. You're dry and you're empty and there's nothing else. There's nothing else I tell you. Not a damned thing. I know, when I stop working.'

The priest shook his head. The orderly took away the stew dish.

'What are you eating meat for?' Rinaldi turned to the priest. 'Don't you know it's Friday?'

'It's Thursday,' the priest said.

'It's a lie. It's Friday. You're eating the body of our Lord. It's God-meat. I know. It's dead Austrian. That's what you're eating.'

'The white meat is from officers,' I said, completing the old joke.

Rinaldi laughed. He filled his glass.

'Don't mind me,' he said. 'I'm just a little crazy.'

'You ought to have a leave,' the priest said.

The major shook his head at him. Rinaldi looked at the priest.

'You think I ought to have a leave?'

The major shook his head at the priest. Rinaldi was looking at the priest.

'Just as you like,' the priest said. 'Not if you don't want.'

'To hell with you,' Rinaldi said. 'They try to get rid of me. Every night they try to get rid of me. I fight them off. What if I have it. Everybody has it. The whole world's got it.

First,' he went on, assuming the manner of a lecturer, 'it's a little pimple. Then we notice a rash between the shoulders. Then we notice nothing at all. We put our faith in mercury.'

'Or salvarsan,' the major interrupted quietly.

'A mercurial product,' Rinaldi said. He acted very elated now. 'I know something worth two of that. Good old priest,' he said. 'You'll never get it. Baby will get it. It's an industrial accident. It's a simple industrial accident.'

The orderly brought in the sweet and coffee. The dessert was a sort of black bread pudding with hard sauce. The lamp was smoking; the black smoke going close up inside the chimney.

'Bring two candles and take away the lamp,' the major said. The orderly brought two lighted candles each in a saucer, and took out the lamp blowing it out. Rinaldi was quiet now. He seemed all right. We talked and after the coffee we all went out into the hall.

'You want to talk to the priest. I have to go in the town,' Rinaldi said. 'Good-night, priest.'

'Good-night, Rinaldo,' the priest said.

'I'll see you, Fredi,' Rinaldi said.

'Yes,' I said. 'Come in early.' He made a face and went out the door. The major was standing with us. 'He's very tired and overworked,' he said. 'He thinks too he has syphilis. I don't believe it but he may have. He is treating himself for it. Good-night. You will leave before daylight, Enrico?'

'Yes.'

'Good-by then,' he said. 'Good luck. Peduzzi will wake you and go with you.'

'Good-by, Signor Maggiore.'

'Good-by. They talk about an Austrian offensive but I don't believe it. I hope not. But anyway it won't be here. Gino will tell you everything. The telephone works well now.'

'I'll call regularly.'

'Please do. Good-night. Don't let Rinaldi drink so much brandy.'

'I'll try not to.'

'Good-night, priest.'

'Good-night, Signor Maggiore.'

He went off into his office.

26

I went to the door and looked out. It had stopped raining but there was a mist.

'Should we go upstairs?' I asked the priest.

'I can only stay a little while.'

'Come on up.'

We climbed the stairs and went into my room. I lay down on Rinaldi's bed. The priest sat on my cot that the orderly had set up. It was dark in the room.

'Well,' he said, 'how are you really?'

'I'm all right. I'm tired to-night.'

'I'm tired too, but from no cause.'

'What about the war?'

'I think it will be over soon. I don't know why, but I feel it.'

'How do you feel it?'

'You know how your major is? Gentle? Many people are like that now.'

'I feel that way myself,' I said.

'It has been a terrible summer,' said the priest. He was surer of himself now than when I had gone away. 'You cannot believe how it has been. Except that you have been there and you know how it can be. Many people have realized the war this summer.

Officers whom I thought could never realize it realize it now.'

'What will happen?' I stroked the blanket with my hand.

'I do not know but I do not think it can go on much longer.'
'What will happen?'
'They will stop fighting.'
'Who?'
'Both sides.'
'I hope so,' I said.
'You don't believe it?'
'I don't believe both sides will stop fighting at once.'
'I suppose not. It is too much to expect. But when I see the changes in men I do not think it can go on.'
'Who won the fighting this summer?'
'No one.'
'The Austrians won,' I said. 'They kept them from taking San Gabriele. They've won. They won't stop fighting.'
'If they feel as we feel they may stop. They have gone through the same thing.'
'No one ever stopped when they were winning.'
'You discourage me.'
'I can only say what I think.'
'Then you think it will go on and on? Nothing will ever happen?'
'I don't know. I only think the Austrians will not stop when they have won a victory.
It is in defeat that we become Christian.'
'The Austrians are Christians—except for the Bosnians.'
'I don't mean technically Christian. I mean like Our Lord.'
He said nothing.
'We are all gentler now because we are beaten. How would Our Lord have been if Peter had rescued him in the Garden?'
'He would have been just the same.'
'I don't think so,' I said.
'You discourage me,' he said. 'I believe and I pray that something will happen. I have felt it very close.'
'Something may happen,' I said. 'But it will happen only to us. If they felt the way we do, it would be all right. But they have beaten us. They feel another way.'
'Many of the soldiers have always felt this way. It is not because they were beaten.'
'They were beaten to start with. They were beaten when they took them from their farms and put them in the army. That is why the peasant has wisdom, because he is defeated from the start. Put him in power and see how wise he is.'
He did not say anything. He was thinking.
'Now I am depressed myself,' I said. 'That's why I never think about these things. I never think and yet when I begin to talk I say the things I have found out in my mind without thinking.'
'I had hoped for something.'

'Defeat?'
'No. Something more.'
'There isn't anything more. Except victory. It may be worse.'
'I hoped for a long time for victory.'
'Me too.'
'Now I don't know.'
'It has to be one or the other.'
'I don't believe in victory any more.'
'I don't. But I don't believe in defeat. Though it may be better.'
'What do you believe in?'
'In sleep,' I said. He stood up.
'I am very sorry to have stayed so long. But I like so to talk with you.'
'It is very nice to talk again. I said that about sleeping, meaning nothing.'
We stood up and shook hands in the dark.
'I sleep at 307 now,' he said.
'I go out on post early to-morrow.'
'I'll see you when you come back.'
'We'll have a walk and talk together.' I walked with him to the door.
'Don't go down,' he said. 'It is very nice that you are back. Though not so nice for you.' He put his hand on my shoulder.
'It's all right for me,' I said. 'Good-night.'
'Good-night. Ciaou!'
'Ciaou!' I said. I was deadly sleepy.

27

I woke when Rinaldi came in but he did not talk and I went back to sleep again. In the morning I was dressed and gone before it was light. Rinaldi did not wake when I left.

I had not seen the Bainsizza before and it was strange to go up the slope where the Austrians had been, beyond the place on the river where I had been wounded. There was a steep new road and many trucks. Beyond, the road flattened out and I saw woods and steep hills in the mist. There were woods that had been taken quickly and not smashed.

Then beyond where the road was not protected by the hills it was screened by matting on the sides and over the top. The road ended in a wrecked village. The lines were up beyond. There was much artillery around. The houses were badly smashed but things were very well organized and there were signboards everywhere. We found Gino and he got us some coffee and later I went with him and met various people and saw the posts. Gino said the British cars were working further down the Bainsizza at Ravne. He had great admiration for the British. There was still a certain amount of shelling, he said, but not many wounded. There would be many sick now the rains had started. The Austrians were supposed to attack but he did not believe it. We were supposed to attack too, but they had not brought up any new troops so he thought that was off too. Food was scarce and he would be glad to get a full meal in Gorizia. What kind of supper had I had? I told him and he said that would be wonderful. He was especially impressed by the dolce. I did not describe it in detail, only said it was a dolce, and I think he believed it was something more elaborate than bread pudding.

Did I know where he was going to go? I said I didn't but that some of the other cars were at Caporetto. He hoped he would go up that way. It was a nice little place and he liked the high mountain hauling up beyond. He was a nice boy and every one seemed to like him. He said where it really had been hell was at San Gabriele and the attack beyond Lom that had gone bad. He said the Austrians had a great amount of artillery in the woods along Ternova ridge beyond and above us, and shelled the roads badly at night. There was a battery of naval guns that had gotten on his nerves. I would recognize them because of their flat trajectory. You heard the report and then the shriek commenced almost instantly. They usually fired two guns at once, one right after the other, and the fragments from the burst were enormous. He showed me one, a smoothly jagged piece of metal over a foot long. It looked like babbitting metal.

'I don't suppose they are so effective,' Gino said. 'But they scare me. They all sound as though they came directly for you. There is the boom, then instantly the shriek and burst. What's the use of not being wounded if they scare you to death?'

He said there were Croats in the lines opposite us now and some Magyars. Our troops were still in the attacking positions. There was no wire to speak of and no place to fall back to if there should be an Austrian attack. There were fine positions for defense along the low mountains that came up out of the plateau but nothing had been done about organizing them for defense. What did I think about the Bainsizza anyway?

I had expected it to be flatter, more like a plateau. I had not realized it was so broken up.

'Alto piano,' Gino said, 'but no piano.'

We went back to the cellar of the house where he lived. I said I thought a ridge that flattened out on top and had a little depth would be easier and more practical to hold than a succession of small mountains. It was no harder to attack up a mountain than on the level, I argued. 'That depends on the mountains,' he said. 'Look at San Gabriele.'

'Yes,' I said, 'but where they had trouble was at the top where it was flat. They got up to the top easy enough.'

'Not so easy,' he said.

'Yes,' I said, 'but that was a special case because it was a fortress rather than a mountain, anyway. The Austrians had been fortifying it for years.' I meant tactically speaking in a war where there was some movement a succession of mountains were nothing to hold as a line because it was too easy to turn them. You should have possible mobility and a mountain is not very mobile. Also, people always over-shoot downhill. If the flank were turned, the best men would be left on the highest mountains. I did not believe in a war in mountains. I had thought about it a lot, I said. You pinched off one mountain and they pinched off another but when something really started every one had to get down off the mountains.

What were you going to do if you had a mountain frontier? he asked.

I had not worked that out yet, I said, and we both laughed. 'But,' I said, 'in the old days the Austrians were always whipped in the quadrilateral around Verona. They let them come down onto the plain and whipped them there.'

'Yes,' said Gino. 'But those were Frenchmen and you can work out military problems clearly when you are fighting in somebody else's country.'

'Yes,' I agreed, 'when it is your own country you cannot use it so scientifically.'

'The Russians did, to trap Napoleon.'

'Yes, but they had plenty of country. If you tried to retreat to trap Napoleon in Italy you would find yourself in Brindisi.'

'A terrible place,' said Gino. 'Have you ever been there?'

'Not to stay.'

'I am a patriot,' Gino said. 'But I cannot love Brindisi or Taranto.'

'Do you love the Bainsizza?' I asked.

'The soil is sacred,' he said. 'But I wish it grew more potatoes. You know when we came here we found fields of potatoes the Austrians had planted.'

'Has the food really been short?'

'I myself have never had enough to eat but I am a big eater and I have not starved. The mess is average. The regiments in the line get pretty good food but those in support don't get so much. Something is wrong somewhere. There should be plenty of food.'

'The dogfish are selling it somewhere else.'

'Yes, they give the battalions in the front line as much as they can but the ones in back are very short. They have eaten all the Austrians' potatoes and chestnuts from the woods. They ought to feed them better. We are big eaters. I am sure there is plenty of food. It is very bad for the soldiers to be short of food. Have you ever noticed the difference it makes in the way you think?'

'Yes,' I said. 'It can't win a war but it can lose one.'

'We won't talk about losing. There is enough talk about losing. What has been done this summer cannot have been done in vain.'

I did not say anything. I was always embarrassed by the words sacred, glorious, and sacrifice and the expression in vain. We had heard them, sometimes standing in the rain almost out of earshot, so that only the shouted words came through, and had read them, on proclamations that were slapped up by billposters over other proclamations, now for a long time, and I had seen nothing sacred, and the things that were glorious had no glory and the sacrifices were like the stockyards at Chicago if nothing was done with the meat except to bury it. There were many words that you could not stand to hear and finally only the names of places had dignity. Certain numbers were the same way and certain dates and these with the names of the places were all you could say and have them mean anything. Abstract words such as glory, honor, courage, or hallow were obscene beside the concrete names of villages, the numbers of roads, the names of rivers, the numbers of regiments and the dates. Gino was a patriot, so he said things that separated us sometimes, but he was also a fine boy and I understood his being a patriot. He was born one. He left with Peduzzi in the car to go back to Gorizia.

It stormed all that day. The wind drove down the rain and everywhere there was standing water and mud. The plaster of the broken houses was gray and wet. Late in the afternoon the rain stopped and from out number two post I saw the bare wet autumn country with clouds over the tops of the hills and the straw screening over the roads wet and dripping. The sun came out once before it went down and shone on the bare woods beyond the ridge. There were many Austrian guns in the woods on that ridge but only a few fired. I watched the sudden round puffs of shrapnel smoke in the sky above a broken farmhouse near where the line was; soft puffs with a yellow white flash in the centre. You saw the flash, then heard the crack, then saw the smoke ball distort and thin in the wind. There were many iron shrapnel balls in the rubble of the houses and on the road beside the broken house where the post was, but they did not shell near the post that afternoon. We loaded two cars and drove down the road that was screened with wet mats and the last of the sun came through in the breaks between the strips of mattings. Before we were out on the clear road behind the hill the sun was down. We went on down the clear road and as it turned a corner into the open and went into the square arched tunnel of matting the rain started again.

The wind rose in the night and at three o'clock in the morning with the rain coming in sheets there was a bombardment and the Croatians came over across the mountain meadows and through patches of woods and into the front line. They fought in the dark in the rain and a counter-attack of scared men from the second line drove them back. There was much shelling and many rockets in the rain and machine-gun and rifle fire all along the line. They did not come again and it was quieter and between the gusts of wind and rain we could hear the sound of a great bombardment far to the north.

The wounded were coming into the post, some were carried on stretchers, some walking and some were brought on the backs of men that came across the field. They were wet to the skin and all were scared. We filled two cars with stretcher cases as they came up from the cellar of the post and as I shut the door of the second car and fastened it I felt the rain on my face turn to snow. The flakes were coming heavy and fast in the rain.

When daylight came the storm was still blowing but the snow had stopped. It had melted as it fell on the wet ground and now it was raining again. There was another attack just after daylight but it was unsuccessful. We expected an attack all day but it did not come until the sun was going down. The bombardment started to the south below the long wooded ridge where the Austrian guns were concentrated. We expected a bombardment but it did not come. It was getting dark. Guns were firing from the field behind the village and the shells, going away, had a comfortable sound.

We heard that the attack to the south had been unsuccessful. They did not attack that night but we heard that they had broken through to the north. In the night word came that we were to prepare to retreat. The captain at the post told me this. He had it from the Brigade. A little while later he came from the telephone and said it was a lie. The Brigade had received orders that the line of the Bainsizza should be held no matter what happened. I asked about the break through and he said that he had heard at the Brigade that the Austrians had broken through the twenty-seventh army corps up toward Caporetto. There had been a great battle in the north all day.

'If those bastards let them through we are cooked,' he said.

'It's Germans that are attacking,' one of the medical officers said. The word Germans was something to be frightened of. We did not want to have anything to do with the Germans.

'There are fifteen divisions of Germans,' the medical officer said. 'They have broken through and we will be cut off.'

'At the Brigade, they say this line is to be held. They say they have not broken through badly and that we will hold a line across the mountains from Monte Maggiore.'

'Where do they hear this?'

'From the Division.'

'The word that we were to retreat came from the Division.'

'We work under the Army Corps,' I said. 'But here I work under you. Naturally when you tell me to go I will go. But get the orders straight.'

'The orders are that we stay here. You clear the wounded from here to the clearing station.'

'Sometimes we clear from the clearing station to the field hospitals too,' I said. 'Tell me, I have never seen a retreat—if there is a retreat how are all the wounded evacuated?'

'They are not. They take as many as they can and leave the rest.'

'What will I take in the cars?'

'Hospital equipment.'

'All right,' I said.

The next night the retreat started. We heard that Germans and Austrians had broken through in the north and were coming down the mountain valleys toward Cividale and Udine. The retreat was orderly, wet and sullen. In the night, going slowly along the crowded roads we passed troops marching under the rain, guns, horses pulling wagons, mules, motor trucks, all moving away from the front. There was no more disorder than in an advance.

That night we helped empty the field hospitals that had been set up in the least ruined villages of the plateau, taking the wounded down to Plava on the river-bed: and the next day hauled all day in the rain to evacuate the hospitals and clearing station at Plava. It rained steadily and the army of the Bainsizza moved down off the plateau in the October rain and across the river where the great victories had commenced in the spring of that year. We came into Gorizia in the middle of the next day. The rain had stopped and the town was nearly empty. As we came up the street they were loading the girls from the soldiers' whorehouse into a truck. There were seven girls and they had on their hats and coats and carried small suitcases. Two of them were crying. Of the others one smiled at us and put out her tongue and fluttered it up and down. She had thick full lips and black eyes.

I stopped the car and went over and spoke to the matron. The girls from the officers' house had left early that morning, she said. Where were they going? To Conegliano, she said. The truck started. The girl with thick lips put out her tongue again at us. The matron waved. The two girls kept on crying. The others looked interestedly out at the town. I got back in the car.

'We ought to go with them,' Bonello said. 'That would be a good trip.'

'We'll have a good trip,' I said.

'We'll have a hell of a trip.'

'That's what I mean,' I said. We came up the drive to the villa.

'I'd like to be there when some of those tough babies climb in and try and hop them.'

'You think they will?'

'Sure. Everybody in the Second Army knows that matron.'

We were outside the villa.

'They call her the Mother Superior,' Bonello said. 'The girls are new but everybody knows her. They must have brought them up just before the retreat.'

'They'll have a time.'

'I'll say they'll have a time. I'd like to have a crack at them for nothing. They charge too much at that house anyway. The government gyps us.'

'Take the car out and have the mechanics go over it,' I said. 'Change the oil and check the differential. Fill it up and then get some sleep.'

'Yes, Signor Tenente.'

The villa was empty. Rinaldi was gone with the hospital. The major was gone taking hospital personnel in the staff car. There was a note on the window for me to fill the cars with the material piled in the hall and to proceed to Pordenone. The mechanics were gone already. I went out back to the garage. The other two cars came in while I was there and their drivers got down. It was starting to rain again.

'I'm so—sleepy I went to sleep three times coming here from Plava,' Piani said. 'What are we going to do, Tenente?'

'We'll change the oil, grease them, fill them up, then take them around in front and load up the junk they've left.'

'Then do we start?'

'No, we'll sleep for three hours.'

'Christ I'm glad to sleep,' Bonello said. 'I couldn't keep awake driving.'

'How's your car, Aymo?' I asked.

'It's all right.'

'Get me a monkey suit and I'll help you with the oil.'

'Don't you do that, Tenente,' Aymo said. 'It's nothing to do. You go and pack your things.'

'My things are all packed,' I said. 'I'll go and carry out the stuff that they left for us. Bring the cars around as soon as they're ready.'

They brought the cars around to the front of the villa and we loaded them with the hospital equipment which was piled in the hallway. When it was all in, the three cars stood in line down the driveway under the trees in the rain. We went inside.

'Make a fire in the kitchen and dry your things,' I said.

'I don't care about dry clothes,' Piani said. 'I want to sleep.'

'I'm going to sleep on the major's bed,' Bonello said. 'I'm going to sleep where the old man corks off.'

'I don't care where I sleep,' Piani said.

'There are two beds in here.' I opened the door.

'I never knew what was in that room,' Bonello said.

'That was old fish-face's room,' Piani said.

'You two sleep in there,' I said. 'I'll wake you.'

'The Austrians will wake us if you sleep too long, Tenente,' Bonello said.

'I won't oversleep,' I said. 'Where's Aymo?'

'He went out in the kitchen.'

'Get to sleep,' I said.

'I'll sleep,' Piani said. 'I've been asleep sitting up all day. The whole top of my head kept coming down over my eyes.'

'Take your boots off,' Bonello said. 'That's old fish-face's bed.'

'Fish-face is nothing to me.' Piani lay on the bed, his muddy boots straight out, his head on his arm. I went out to the kitchen. Aymo had a fire in the stove and a kettle of water on.

'I thought I'd start some pasta asciutta,' he said. 'We'll be hungry when we wake up.'

'Aren't you sleepy, Bartolomeo?'

'Not so sleepy. When the water boils I'll leave it. The fire will go down.'

'You'd better get some sleep,' I said. 'We can eat cheese and monkey meat.'

'This is better,' he said. 'Something hot will be good for those two anarchists. You go to sleep, Tenente.'

'There's a bed in the major's room.'

'You sleep there.'

'No, I'm going up to my old room. Do you want a drink, Bartolomeo?'

'When we go, Tenente. Now it wouldn't do me any good.'

'If you wake in three hours and I haven't called you, wake me, will you?'

'I haven't any watch, Tenente.'

'There's a clock on the wall in the major's room.'

'All right.'

I went out then through the dining-room and the hall and up the marble stairs to the room where I had lived with Rinaldi. It was raining outside. I went to the window and looked out. It was getting dark and I saw the three cars standing in line under the trees.

The trees were dripping in the rain. It was cold and the drops hung to the branches. I went back to Rinaldi's bed and lay down and let sleep take me.

We ate in the kitchen before we started. Aymo had a basin of spaghetti with onions and tinned meat chopped up in it. We sat around the table and drank two bottles of the wine that had been left in the cellar of the villa. It was dark outside and still raining. Piani sat at the table very sleepy.

'I like a retreat better than an advance,' Bonello said. 'On a retreat we drink barbera.'

'We drink it now. To-morrow maybe we drink rainwater,' Aymo said.

'To-morrow we'll be in Udine. We'll drink champagne. That's where the slackers live. Wake up, Piani! We'll drink champagne tomorrow in Udine!'

'I'm awake,' Piani said. He filled his plate with the spaghetti and meat. 'Couldn't you find tomato sauce, Barto?'

'There wasn't any,' Aymo said.

'We'll drink champagne in Udine,' Bonello said. He filled his glass with the clear red barbera.

'We may drink—before Udine,' Piani said.

'Have you eaten enough, Tenente?' Aymo asked.

'I've got plenty. Give me the bottle, Bartolomeo.'

'I have a bottle apiece to take in the cars,' Aymo said.

'Did you sleep at all?'

'I don't need much sleep. I slept a little.'

'To-morrow we'll sleep in the king's bed,' Bonello said. He was feeling very good.

'To-morrow maybe we'll sleep in—,' Piani said.

'I'll sleep with the queen,' Bonello said. He looked to see how I took the joke.

'You'll sleep with—,' Piani said sleepily.

'That's treason, Tenente,' Bonello said. 'Isn't that treason?'

'Shut up,' I said. 'You get too funny with a little wine.' Outside it was raining hard. I looked at my watch. It was half-past nine.

'It's time to roll,' I said and stood up.

'Who are you going to ride with, Tenehte?' Bonello asked.

'With Aymo. Then you come. Then Piani. We'll start out on the road for Cormons.'

'I'm afraid I'll go to sleep,' Piani said.

'All right. I'll ride with you. Then Bonello. Then Aymo.'

'That's the best way,' Piani said. 'Because I'm so sleepy.'

'I'll drive and you sleep awhile.'

'No. I can drive just so long as I know somebody will wake me up if I go to sleep.'

'I'll wake you up. Put out the lights, Barto.'

'You might as well leave them,' Bonello said. 'We've got no more use for this place.'

'I have a small locker trunk in my room,' I said. 'Will you help take it down, Piani?'

'We'll take it,' Piani said. 'Come on, Aldo.' He went off into the hall with Bonello. I heard them going upstairs.

'This was a fine place,' Bartolomeo Aymo said. He put two bottles of wine and half a cheese into his haversack. 'There won't be a place like this again. Where will they retreat to, Tenente?'

'Beyond the Tagliamento, they say. The hospital and the sector are to be at Pordenone.'

'This is a better town than Pordenone.'

'I don't know Pordenone,' I said. 'I've just been through there.'

'It's not much of a place,' Aymo said.

28

As we moved out through the town it was empty in the rain and the dark except for columns of troops and guns that were going through the main street. There were many trucks too and some carts going through on other streets and converging on the main road. When we were out past the tanneries onto the main road the troops, the motor trucks, the horse-drawn carts and the guns were in one wide slow-moving column. We moved slowly but steadily in the rain, the radiator cap of our car almost against the tailboard of a truck that was loaded high, the load covered with wet canvas. Then the truck stopped. The whole column was stopped. It started again and we went a little farther, then stopped. I got out and walked ahead, going between the trucks and carts and under the wet necks of the horses. The block was farther ahead. I left the road, crossed the ditch on a footboard and walked along the field beyond the ditch. I could see the stalled column between the trees in the rain as I went forward across from it in the field. I went about a mile. The column did not move, although, on the other side beyond the stalled vehicles I could see the troops moving. I went back to the cars. This block might extend as far as Udine. Piani was asleep over the wheel. I climbed up beside him and went to sleep too.

Several hours later I heard the truck ahead of us grinding into gear. I woke Piani and we started, moving a few yards, then stopping, then going on again. It was still raining.

The column stalled again in the night and did not start. I got down and went back to see Aymo and Bonello. Bonello had two sergeants of engineers on the seat of his car with him. They stiffened when I came up.

'They were left to do something to a bridge,' Bonello said. 'They can't find their unit so I gave them a ride.'

'With the Sir Lieutenant's permission.'

'With permission,' I said.

'The lieutenant is an American,' Bonello said. 'He'll give anybody a ride.'

One of the sergeants smiled. The other asked Bonello if I was an Italian from North or South America.

'He's not an Italian. He's North American English.'

The sergeants were polite but did not believe it. I left them and went back to Aymo.

He had two girls on the seat with him and was sitting back in the corner and smoking. 'Barto, Barto,' I said. He laughed.

'Talk to them, Tenente,' he said. 'I can't understand them. Hey!' He put his hand on the girl's thigh and squeezed it in a friendly way. The girl drew her shawl tight around her and pushed his hand away. 'Hey!' he said. 'Tell the Tenente your name and what you're doing here.'

The girl looked at me fiercely. The other girl kept her eyes down. The girl who looked at me said something in a dialect I could not understand a word of. She was plump and dark and looked about sixteen.

'Sorella?' I asked and pointed at the other girl.

She nodded her head and smiled.

'All right,' I said and patted her knee. I felt her stiffen away when I touched her. The sister never looked up. She looked perhaps a year younger. Aymo put his hand on the elder girl's thigh and she pushed it away. He laughed at her.

'Good man,' he pointed at himself. 'Good man,' he pointed at me. 'Don't you worry.' The girl looked at him fiercely. The pair of them were like two wild birds.

'What does she ride with me for if she doesn't like me?' Aymo asked. 'They got right up in the car the minute I motioned to them.' He turned to the girl. 'Don't worry,' he said. 'No danger of—,' using the vulgar word. 'No place for—.' I could see she understood the word and that was all. Her eyes looked at him very scared. She pulled the shawl tight. 'Car all full,' Aymo said. 'No danger of—. No place for—.' Every time he said the word the girl stiffened a little. Then sitting stiffly and looking at him she began to cry. I saw her lips working and then tears came down her plump cheeks. Her sister, not looking up, took her hand and they sat there together. The older one, who had been so fierce, began to sob.

'I guess I scared her,' Aymo said. 'I didn't mean to scare her.'

Bartolomeo brought out his knapsack and cut off two pieces of cheese. 'Here,' he said. 'Stop crying.'

The older girl shook her head and still cried, but the younger girl took the cheese and commenced to eat. After a while the younger girl gave her sister the second piece of cheese and they both ate. The older sister still sobbed a little.

'She'll be all right after a while,' Aymo said.

An idea came to him. 'Virgin?' he asked the girl next to him. She nodded her head vigorously. 'Virgin too?' he pointed to the sister. Both the girls nodded their heads and the elder said something in dialect.

'That's all right,' Bartolomeo said. 'That's all right.'

Both the girls seemed cheered.

I left them sitting together with Aymo sitting back in the corner and went back to Piani's car. The column of vehicles did not move but the troops kept passing alongside. It was still raining hard and I thought some of the stops in the movement of the column might be from cars with wet wiring. More likely they were from horses or men going to sleep. Still, traffic could tie up in cities when every one was awake. It was the combination of horse and motor vehicles. They did not help each other any. The peasants' carts did not help much either. Those were a couple of fine girls with Barto. A retreat was no place for two virgins. Real virgins. Probably very religious. If there were no war we would probably all be in bed. In bed I lay me down my head. Bed and board. Stiff as a board in bed.

Catherine was in bed now between two sheets, over her and under her. Which side did she sleep on? Maybe she wasn't asleep. Maybe she was lying thinking about me. Blow, blow, ye western wind. Well, it blew and it wasn't the small rain but the big rain down that rained. It rained all night. You knew it rained down that rained. Look at it. Christ, that my love were in my arms and I in my bed again. That my love Catherine. That my sweet love Catherine down might rain. Blow her again to me. Well, we were in it. Every one was caught in it and the small rain would not quiet it. 'Good-night, Catherine,' I said out loud. 'I hope you sleep well. If it's too uncomfortable, darling, lie on the other side,' I said. 'I'll get you some cold water. In a little while it will be morning and then it won't be so bad. I'm sorry he makes you so uncomfortable. Try and go to sleep, sweet.'

I was asleep all the time, she said. You've been talking in your sleep. Are you all right? us.

Are you really there?

Of course I'm here. I wouldn't go away. This doesn't make any difference between

You're so lovely and sweet. You wouldn't go away in the night, would you?

Of course I wouldn't go away. I'm always here. I come whenever you want me.

'—,' Piani said. 'They've started again.'

'I was dopey,' I said. I looked at my watch. It was three o'clock in the morning. I reached back behind the seat for a bottle of the barbera.

'You talked out loud,' Piani said.

'I was having a dream in English,' I said.

The rain was slacking and we were moving along. Before daylight we were stalled again and when it was light we were at a little rise in the ground and I saw the road of the retreat stretched out far ahead, everything stationary except for the infantry filtering through. We started to move again but seeing the rate of progress in the daylight, I knew we were going to have to get off that main road some way and go across country if we ever hoped to reach Udine.

In the night many peasants had joined the column from the roads of the country and in the column there were carts loaded with household goods; there were mirrors projecting up between mattresses, and chickens and ducks tied to carts. There was a sewing machine on the cart ahead of us in the rain. They had saved the most valuable things. On some carts the women sat huddled from the rain and others walked beside the carts keeping as close to them as they could. There were dogs now in the column, keeping under the wagons as they moved along. The road was muddy, the ditches at the side were high with water and beyond the trees that lined the road the fields looked too wet and too soggy to try to cross. I got down from the car and worked up the road a way, looking for a place where I could see ahead to find a side-road we could take across country. I knew there were many side-roads but did not want one that would lead to nothing. I could not remember them because we had always passed them bowling along in the car on the main road and they all looked much alike. Now I knew we must find one if we hoped to get through. No one knew where the Austrians were nor how things were going but I was certain that if the rain should stop and planes come over and get to work on that column that it would be all over. All that was needed was for a few men to leave their trucks or a few horses be killed to tie up completely the movement on the road.

The rain was not falling so heavily now and I thought it might clear. I went ahead along the edge of the road and when there was a small road that led off to the north between two fields with a hedge of trees on both sides, I thought that we had better take it and hurried back to the cars. I told Piani to turn off and went back to tell Bonello and Aymo.

'If it leads nowhere we can turn around and cut back in,' I said.

'What about these?' Bonello asked. His two sergeants were beside him on the seat. They were unshaven but still military looking in the early morning.

'They'll be good to push,' I said. I went back to Aymo and told him we were going to try it across country.

'What about my virgin family?' Aymo asked. The two girls were asleep.

'They won't be very useful,' I said. 'You ought to have some one that could push.' 'They could go back in the car,' Aymo said. 'There's room in the car.'

'All right if you want them,' I said. 'Pick up somebody with a wide back to push.' 'Bersaglieri,' Aymo smiled. 'They have the widest backs. They measure them. How do you feel, Tenente?' 'Fine. How are you?'

'Fine. But very hungry.'

'There ought to be something up that road and we will stop and eat.'

'How's your leg, Tenente?'

'Fine,' I said. Standing on the step and looking up ahead I could see Piani's car pulling out onto the little side-road and starting up it, his car showing through the hedge of bare branches. Bonello turned off and followed him and then Piani worked his way out and we followed the two ambulances ahead along the narrow road between hedges. It led to a farmhouse. We found Piani and Bonello stopped in the farmyard. The house was low and long with a trellis with a grape-vine over the door. There was a well in the yard and Piani was getting up water to fill his radiator. So much going in low gear had boiled it out. The farmhouse was deserted. I looked back down the road, the farmhouse was on a slight elevation above the plain, and we could see over the country, and saw the road, the hedges, the fields and the line of trees along the main road where the retreat was passing. The two sergeants were looking through the house. The girls were awake and looking at the courtyard, the well and the two big ambulances in front of the farmhouse, with three drivers at the well. One of the sergeants came out with a clock in his hand.

'Put it back,' I said. He looked at me, went in the house and came back without the clock.

'Where's your partner?' I asked.

'He's gone to the latrine.' He got up on the seat of the ambulance. He was afraid we would leave him.

'What about breakfast, Tenente?' Bonello asked. 'We could eat something. It wouldn't take very long.'

'Do you think this road going down on the other side will lead to anything?'

'Sure.'

'All right. Let's eat.' Piani and Bonello went in the house.

'Come on,' Aymo said to the girls. He held his hand to help them down. The older sister shook her head. They were not going into any deserted house. They looked after us.

'They are difficult,' Aymo said. We went into the farmhouse together. It was large and dark, an abandoned feeling. Bonello and Piani were in the kitchen.

'There's not much to eat,' Piani said. 'They've cleaned it out.' Bonello sliced a big cheese on the heavy kitchen table.

'Where was the cheese?'

'In the cellar. Piani found wine too and apples.'

'That's a good breakfast.'

Piani was taking the wooden cork out of a big wicker-covered wine jug. He tipped it and poured a copper pan full.

'It smells all right,' he said. 'Find some beakers, Barto.'

The two sergeants came in.

'Have some cheese, sergeants,' Bonello said.

'We should go,' one of the sergeants said, eating his cheese and drinking a cup of wine.

'We'll go. Don't worry,' Bonello said. 'An army travels on its stomach,' I said.

'What?' asked the sergeant.

'It's better to eat.'

'Yes. But time is precious.'

'I believe the bastards have eaten already,' Piani said. The sergeants looked at him. They hated the lot of us.

'You know the road?' one of them asked me.

'No,' I said. They looked at each other.

'We would do best to start,' the first one said.

'We are starting,' I said. I drank another cup of the red wine. It tasted very good after the cheese and apple.

'Bring the cheese,' I said and went out. Bonello came out carrying the great jug of wine.

'That's too big,' I said. He looked at it regretfully.

'I guess it is,' he said. 'Give me the canteens to fill.' He filled the canteens and some of the wine ran out on the stone paving of the courtyard. Then he picked up the wine jug and put it just inside the door.

'The Austrians can find it without breaking the door down,' he said.

'We'll roll.' I said. 'Piani and I will go ahead.' The two engineers were already on the seat beside Bonello. The girls were eating cheese and apples. Aymo was smoking. We started off down the narrow road. I looked back at the two cars coming and the farmhouse. It was a fine, low, solid stone house and the ironwork of the well was very good. Ahead of us the road was narrow and muddy and there was a high hedge on either side. Behind, the cars were following closely.

29

At noon we were stuck in a muddy road about, as nearly as we could figure, ten kilometres from Udine. The rain had stopped during the forenoon and three times we had heard planes coming, seen them pass overhead, watched them go far to the left and heard them bombing on the main highroad. We had worked through a network of secondary roads and had taken many roads that were blind, but had always, by backing up and finding another road, gotten closer to Udine. Now, Aymo's car, in backing so that we might get out of a blind road, had gotten into the soft earth at the side and the wheels, spinning, had dug deeper and deeper until the car rested on its differential. The thing to do now was to dig out in front of the wheels, put in brush so that the chains could grip, and then push until the car was on the road. We were all down on the road around the car.

The two sergeants looked at the car and examined the wheels. Then they started off down the road without a word. I went after them.

'Come on,' I said. 'Cut some brush.'

'We have to go,' one said.

'Get busy,' I said, 'and cut brush.'

'We have to go,' one said. The other said nothing. They were in a hurry to start. They would not look at me.

'I order you to come back to the car and cut brush,' I said. The one sergeant turned. 'We have to go on. In a little while you will be cut off. You can't order us. You're not our officer.'

'I order you to cut brush,' I said. They turned and started down the road.

'Halt,' I said. They kept on down the muddy road, the hedge on either side. 'I order you to halt,' I called. They went a little faster. I opened up my holster, took the pistol, aimed at the one who had talked the most, and fired. I missed and they both started to run. I shot three times and dropped one. The other went through the hedge and was out of sight. I fired at him through the hedge as he ran across the field. The pistol clicked empty and I put in another clip. I saw it was too far to shoot at the second sergeant. He was far across the field, running, his head held low. I commenced to reload the empty clip. Bonello came up.

'Let me go finish him,' he said. I handed him the pistol and he walked down to where the sergeant of engineers lay face down across the road. Bonello leaned over, put the pistol against the man's head and pulled the trigger. The pistol did not fire.

'You have to cock it,' I said. He cocked it and fired twice. He took hold of the sergeant's legs and pulled him to the side of the road so he lay beside the hedge. He came back and handed me the pistol.

'The son of a bitch,' he said. He looked toward the sergeant. 'You see me shoot him, Tenente?'

'We've got to get the brush quickly,' I said. 'Did I hit the other one at all?' 'I don't think so,' Aymo said. 'He was too far away to hit with a pistol.'

'The dirty scum,' Piani said. We were all cutting twigs and branches. Everything had been taken out of the car. Bonello was digging out in front of the wheels. When we were ready Aymo started the car and put it into gear. The wheels spun round throwing brush and mud. Bonello and I pushed until we could feel our joints crack. The car would not move.

'Rock her back and forth, Barto,' I said.

He drove the engine in reverse, then forward. The wheels only dug in deeper. Then the car was resting on the differential again, and the wheels spun freely in the holes they had dug. I straightened up.

'We'll try her with a rope,' I said.

'I don't think it's any use, Tenente. You can't get a straight pull.'

'We have to try it,' I said. 'She won't come out any other way.'

Piani's and Bonello's cars could only move straight ahead down the narrow road. We roped both cars together and pulled. The wheels only pulled sideways against the ruts.

'It's no good,' I shouted. 'Stop it.'

Piani and Bonello got down from their cars and came back. Aymo got down. The girls were up the road about forty yards sitting on a stone wall.

'What do you say, Tenente?' Bonello asked.

'We'll dig out and try once more with the brush,' I said. I looked down the road. It was my fault. I had led them up here. The sun was almost out from behind the clouds and the body of the sergeant lay beside the hedge.

'We'll put his coat and cape under,' I said. Bonello went to get them. I cut brush and Aymo and Piani dug out in front and between the wheels. I cut the cape, then ripped it in two, and laid it under the wheel in the mud, then piled brush for the wheels to catch. We were ready to start and Aymo got up on the seat and started the car. The wheels spun and we pushed and pushed. But it wasn't any use.

'It's—ed,' I said. 'Is there anything you want in the car, Barto?'

Aymo climbed up with Bonello, carrying the cheese and two bottles of wine and his cape. Bonello, sitting behind the wheel, was looking through the pockets of the sergeant's coat.

'Better throw the coat away,' I said. 'What about Barto's virgins?'

'They can get in the back,' Piani said. 'I don't think we are going far.'

I opened the back door of the ambulance.

'Come on,' I said. 'Get in.' The two girls climbed in and sat in the corner. They seemed to have taken no notice of the shooting. I looked back up the road. The sergeant lay in his dirty long-sleeved underwear. I got up with Piani and we started. We were going to try to cross the field. When the road entered the field I got down and walked ahead. If we could get across, there was a road on the other side. We could not get across. It was too soft and muddy for the cars. When they were finally and completely stalled, the wheels dug in to the hubs, we left them in the field and started on foot for Udine.

When we came to the road which led back toward the main highway I pointed down it to the two girls.

'Go down there,' I said. 'You'll meet people.' They looked at me. I took out my pocket-book and gave them each a ten-lira note. 'Go down there,' I said, pointing.

'Friends! Family!'

They did not understand but they held the money tightly and started down the road.

They looked back as though they were afraid I might take the money back. I watched them go down the road, their shawls close around them, looking back apprehensively at us. The three drivers were laughing.

'How much will you give me to go in that direction, Tenente?' Bonello asked.

'They're better off in a bunch of people than alone if they catch them,' I said.

'Give me two hundred lire and I'll walk straight back toward Austria,' Bonello said. 'They'd take it away from you,' Piani said.

'Maybe the war will be over,' Aymo said. We were going up the road as fast as we could. The sun was trying to come through. Beside the road were mulberry trees. Through the trees I could see our two big moving-vans of cars stuck in the field. Piani looked back too.

'They'll have to build a road to get them out,' he said.

'I wish to Christ we had bicycles,' Bonello said.

'Do they ride bicycles in America?' Aymo asked.

'They used to.'

'Here it is a great thing,' Aymo said. 'A bicycle is a splendid thing.'

'I wish to Christ we had bicycles,' Bonello said. 'I'm no walker.'

'Is that firing?' I asked. I thought I could hear firing a long way away.

'I don't know,' Aymo said. He listened.

'I think so,' I said.

'The first thing we will see will be the cavalry,' Piani said.

'I don't think they've got any cavalry.'

'I hope to Christ not,' Bonello said. 'I don't want to be stuck on a lance by any—cavalry.'

'You certainly shot that sergeant, Tenente,' Piani said. We were walking fast.

'I killed him,' Bonello said. 'I never killed anybody in this war, and all my life I've wanted to kill a sergeant.'

'You killed him on the sit all right,' Piani said. 'He wasn't flying very fast when you killed him.'

'Never mind. That's one thing I can always remember. I killed that—of a sergeant.'

'What will you say in confession?' Aymo asked.

'I'll say, "Bless me, father, I killed a sergeant." ' They all laughed.

'He's an anarchist,' Piani said. 'He doesn't go to church.'

'Piani's an anarchist too,' Bonello said.

'Are you really anarchists?' I asked.

'No, Tenente. We're socialists. We come from Imola.'

'Haven't you ever been there?'

'No.'

'By Christ it's a fine place, Tenente. You come there after the war and we'll show you something.'

'Are you all socialists?'

'Everybody.'

'Is it a fine town?'

'Wonderful. You never saw a town like that.'

'How did you get to be socialists?'

'We're all socialists. Everybody is a socialist. We've always been socialists.'

'You come, Tenente. We'll make you a socialist too.'

Ahead the road turned off to the left and there was a little hill and, beyond a stone wall, an apple orchard. As the road went uphill they ceased talking. We walked along together all going fast against time.

30

Later we were on a road that led to a river. There was a long line of abandoned trucks and carts on the road leading up to the bridge. No one was in sight. The river was high and the bridge had been blown up in the centre; the stone arch was fallen into the river and the brown water was going over it. We went on up the bank looking for a place to cross. Up ahead I knew there was a railway bridge and I thought we might be able to get across there. The path was wet and muddy. We did not see any troops; only abandoned trucks and stores. Along the river bank there was nothing and no one but the wet brush and muddy ground. We went up to the bank and finally we saw the railway bridge.

'What a beautiful bridge,' Aymo said. It was a long plain iron bridge across what was usually a dry river-bed.

'We'd better hurry and get across before they blow it up,' I said.

'There's nobody to blow it up,' Piani said. 'They're all gone.'

'It's probably mined,' Bonello said. 'You cross first, Tenente.'

'Listen to the anarchist,' Aymo said. 'Make him go first.'

'I'll go,' I said. 'It won't be mined to blow up with one man.'

'You see,' Piani said. 'That is brains. Why haven't you brains, anarchist?'

'If I had brains I wouldn't be here,' Bonello said.

'That's pretty good, Tenente,' Aymo said.

'That's pretty good,' I said. We were close to the bridge now. The sky had clouded over again and it was raining a little. The bridge looked long and solid. We climbed up the embankment.

'Come one at a time,' I said and started across the bridge. I watched the ties and the rails for any trip-wires or signs of explosive but I saw nothing. Down below the gaps in the ties the river ran muddy and fast. Ahead across the wet countryside I could see Udine in the rain. Across the bridge I looked back. Just up the river was another bridge. As I watched, a yellow mud-colored motor car crossed it. The sides of the bridge were high and the body of the car, once on, was out of sight. But I saw the heads of the driver, the man on the seat with him, and the two men on the rear seat. They all wore German helmets. Then the car was over the bridge and out of sight behind the trees and the abandoned vehicles on the road. I waved to Aymo who was crossing and to the others to come on. I climbed down and crouched beside the railway embankment. Aymo came down with me.

'Did you see the car?' I asked.

'No. We were watching you.'

'A German staff car crossed on the upper bridge.'

'A staff car?'

'Yes.'

'Holy Mary.'

The others came and we all crouched in the mud behind the embankment, looking across the rails at the bridge, the line of trees, the ditch and the road.

'Do you think we're cut off then, Tenente?'

'I don't know. All I know is a German staff car went along that road.'

'You don't feel funny, Tenente? You haven't got strange feelings in the head?'

'Don't be funny, Bonello.'

'What about a drink?' Piani asked. 'If we're cut off we might as well have a drink.' He unhooked his canteen and uncorked it.

'Look! Look!' Aymo said and pointed toward the road. Along the top of the stone bridge we could see German helmets moving. They were bent forward and moved smoothly, almost supernaturally, along. As they came off the bridge we saw them. They were bicycle troops. I saw the faces of the first two. They were ruddy and healthy-looking.

Their helmets came iow down over their foreheads and the side of their faces. Their carbines were clipped to the frame of the bicycles. Stick bombs hung handle down from their belts. Their helmets and their gray uniforms were wet and they rode easily, looking ahead and to both sides. There were two—then four in line, then two, then almost a dozen; then another dozen—then one alone. They did not talk but we could not have heard them because of the noise from the river. They were gone out of sight up the road.

'Holy Mary,' Aymo said.

'They were Germans,' Piani said. 'Those weren't Austrians.'

'Why isn't there somebody here to stop them?' I said. 'Why haven't they blown the bridge up? Why aren't there machine-guns along this embankment?'

'You tell us, Tenente,' Bonello said.

I was very angry.

'The whole bloody thing is crazy. Down below they blow up a little bridge. Here they leave a bridge on the main road. Where is everybody? Don't they try and stop them at all?'

'You tell us, Tenente,' Bonello said. I shut up. It was none of my business; all I had to do was to get to Pordenone with three ambulances. I had failed at that. All I had to do now was get to Pordenone. I probably could not even get to Udine. The hell I couldn't. The thing to do was to be calm and not get shot or captured.

'Didn't you have a canteen open?' I asked Piani. He handed it to me. I took a long drink. 'We might as well start,' I said. 'There's no hurry though. Do you want to eat something?'

'This is no place to stay,' Bonello said.

'All right. We'll start.'

'Should we keep on this side—out of sight?'

'We'd be better off on top. They may come along this bridge too. We don't want them on top of us before we see them.'

We walked along the railroad track. On both sides of us stretched the wet plain. Ahead across the plain was the hill of Udine. The roofs fell away from the castle on the hill. We could see the campanile and the clock-tower. There were many mulberry trees in the fields. Ahead I saw a place where the rails were torn up. The ties had been dug out too and thrown down the embankment.

'Down! down!' Aymo said. We dropped down beside the embankment. There was another group of bicyclists passing along the road. I looked over the edge and saw them go on.

'They saw us but they went on,' Aymo said.

'We'll get killed up there, Tenente,' Bonello said.

'They don't want us,' I said. 'They're after something else. We're in more danger if they should come on us suddenly.'

'I'd rather walk here out of sight,' Bonello said.

'All right. We'll walk along the tracks.'

'Do you think we can get through?' Aymo asked.

'Sure. There aren't very many of them yet. We'll go through in the dark.'

'What was that staff car doing?'

'Christ knows,' I said. We kept on up the tracks. Bonello tired of walking in the mud of the embankment and came up with the rest of us. The railway moved south away from the highway now and we could not see what passed along the road. A short bridge over a canal was blown up but we climbed across on what was left of the span. We heard firing ahead of us.

We came up on the railway beyond the canal. It went on straight toward the town across the low fields. We could see the line of the other railway ahead of us. To the north was the main road where we had seen the cyclists; to the south there was a small branch- road across the fields with thick trees on each side. I thought we had better cut to the south and work around the town that way and across country toward Campoformio and the main road to the Tagliamento. We could avoid the main line of the retreat by keeping to the secondary roads beyond Udine. I knew there were plenty of side-roads across the plain. I started down the embankment.

'Come on,' I said. We would make for the side-road and work to the south of the town. We all started down the embankment. A shot was fired at us from the side-road. The bullet went into the mud of the embankment.

'Go on back,' I shouted. I started up the embankment, slipping in the mud. The drivers were ahead of me. I went up the embankment as fast as I could go. Two more shots came from the thick brush and Aymo, as he was crossing the tracks, lurched, tripped and fell face down. We pulled him down on the other side and turned him over. 'His head ought to be uphill,' I said. Piani moved him around. He lay in the mud on the side of the embankment, his feet pointing downhill, breathing blood irregularly. The three of us squatted over him in the rain. He was hit low in the back of the neck and the bullet had ranged upward and come out under the right eye. He died while I was stopping up the two holes. Piani laid his head down, wiped at his face, with a piece of the emergency dressing, then let it alone.

'The—,' he said.

'They weren't Germans,' I said. 'There can't be any Germans over there.' 'Italians,' Piani said, using the word as an epithet, 'Italiani!' Bonello said nothing.

He was sitting beside Aymo, not looking at him. Piani picked up Aymo's cap where it had rolled down the embankment and put it over his face. He took out his canteen.

'Do you want a drink?' Piani handed Bonello the canteen.

'No,' Bonello said. He turned to me. 'That might have happened to us any time on the railway tracks.'

'No,' I said. 'It was because we started across the field.'

Bonello shook his head. 'Aymo's dead,' he said. 'Who's dead next, Tenente? Where do we go now?'

'Those were Italians that shot,' I said. 'They weren't Germans.'

'I suppose if they were Germans they'd have killed all of us,' Bonello said.

'We are in more danger from Italians than Germans,' I said. 'The rear guard are afraid of everything. The Germans know what they're after.'

'You reason it out, Tenente,' Bonello said. 'Where do we go now?' Piani asked.

'We better lie up some place till it's dark. If we could get south we'd be all right.'

'They'd have to shoot us all to prove they were right the first time,' Bonello said.

'I'm not going to try them.'

'We'll find a place to lie up as near to Udine as we can get and then go through when it's dark.'

'Let's go then,' Bonello said. We went down the north side of the embankment. I looked back. Aymo lay in the mud with the angle of the embankment. He was quite small and his arms were by his side, his puttee-wrapped legs and muddy boots together, his cap over his face. He looked very dead. It was raining. I had liked him as well as any one I ever knew. I had his papers in my pocket and would write to his family. Ahead across the fields was a farmhouse. There were trees around it and the farm buildings were built against the house. There was a balcony along the second floor held up by columns.

'We better keep a little way apart,' I said. 'I'll go ahead.' I started toward the farmhouse. There was a path across the field.

Crossing the field, I did not know but that some one would fire on us from the trees near the farmhouse or from the farmhouse itself. I walked toward it, seeing it very clearly. The balcony of the second floor merged into the barn and there was hay coming Out between the columns. The courtyard was of stone blocks and all the trees were dripping with the rain. There was a big empty two-wheeled cart, the shafts tipped high up in the rain. I came to the courtyard, crossed it, and stood under the shelter of the balcony. The door of the house was open and I went in. Bonello and Piani came in after me. It was dark inside. I went back to the kitchen. There were ashes of a fire on the big open hearth. The pots hung over the ashes, but they were empty. I looked around but I could not find anything to eat.

'We ought to lie up in the barn,' I said. 'Do you think you could find anything to eat, Piani, and bring it up there?'

'I'll look,' Piani said.

'I'll look too,' Bonello said.

'All right,' I said. 'I'll go up and look at the barn.' I found a stone stairway that went up from the stable underneath. The stable smelt dry and pleasant in the rain. The cattle were all gone, probably driven off when they left. The barn was half full of hay. There were two windows in the roof, one was blocked with boards, the other was a narrow dormer window on the north side. There was a chute so that hay might be pitched down to the cattle. Beams crossed the opening down into the main floor where the hay-carts drove in when the hay was hauled in to be pitched up. I heard the rain on the roof and smelled the hay and, when I went down, the clean smell of dried dung in the stable. We could pry a board loose and see out of the south window down into the courtyard. The other window looked out on the field toward the north. We could get out of either window onto the roof and down, or go down the hay chute if the stairs were impractical. It was a big barn and we could hide in the hay if we heard any one. It seemed like a good place. I was sure we could have gotten through to the south if they had not fired on us. It was impossible that there were Germans there. They were coming from the north and down the road from Cividale. They could not have come through from the south. The Italians were even more dangerous. They were frightened and firing on anything they saw. Last night on the retreat we had heard that there had been many Germans in Italian uniforms mixing with the retreat in the north. I did not believe it. That was one of those things you always heard in the war. It was one of the things the enemy always did to you. You did not know any one who went over in German uniform to confuse them. Maybe they did but it sounded difficult. I did not believe the Germans did it.

I did not believe they had to. There was no need to confuse our retreat. The size of the army and the fewness of the roads did that. Nobody gave any orders, let alone Germans. Still, they would shoot us for Germans. They shot Aymo. The hay smelled good and lying in a barn in the hay took away all the years in between. We had lain in hay and talked and shot sparrows with an air-rifle when they perched in the triangle cut high up in the wall of the barn. The barn was gone now and one year they had cut the hemlock woods and there were only stumps, dried tree-tops, branches and fireweed where the woods had been. You could not go back. If you did not go forward what happened? You never got back to Milan. And if you got back to Milan what happened? I listened to the firing to the north toward Udine. I could hear machine-gun firing. There was no shelling.

That was something. They must have gotten some troops along the road. I looked down in the half-light of the hay-barn and saw Piani standing on the hauling floor. He had a long sausage, a jar of something and two bottles of wine under his arm.

'Come up,' I said. 'There is the ladder.' Then I realized that I should help him with the things and went down. I was vague in the head from lying in the hay. I had been nearly asleep.

'Where's Bonello?' I asked.

'I'll tell you,' Piani said. We went up the ladder. Up on the hay we set the things down. Piani took out his knife with the corkscrew and drew the cork on a wine bottle.

'They have sealing-wax on it,' he said. 'It must be good.' He smiled.

'Where's Bonello?' I asked.

Piani looked at me.

'He went away, Tenente,' he said. 'He wanted to be a prisoner.'

I did not say anything.

'He was afraid we would get killed.'

I held the bottle of wine and did not say anything.

'You see we don't believe in the war anyway, Tenente.'

'Why didn't you go?' I asked.

'I did not want to leave you.'

'Where did he go?'

'I don't know, Tenente. He went away.'

'All right,' I said. 'Will you cut the sausage?'

Piani looked at me in the half-light.

'I cut it while we were talking,' he said. We sat in the hay and ate the sausage and drank the wine. It must have been wine they had saved for a wedding. It was so old that it was losing its color.

'You look out of this window, Luigi,' I said. 'I'll go look out the other window.'

We had each been drinking out of one of the bottles and I took my bottle with me and went over and lay flat on the hay and looked out the narrow window at the wet country. I do not know what I expected to see but I did not see anything except the fields and the bare mulberry trees and the rain falling. I drank the wine and it did not make me feel good. They had kept it too long and it had gone to pieces and lost its quality and color. I watched it get dark outside; the darkness came very quickly. It would be a black night with the rain. When it was dark there was no use watching any more, so I went over to Piani. He was lying asleep and I did not wake him but sat down beside him for a while. He was a big man and he slept heavily. After a while I woke him and we started.

That was a very strange night. I do not know what I had expected, death perhaps and shooting in the dark and running, but nothing happened. We waited, lying flat beyond the ditch along the main road while a German battalion passed, then when they were gone we crossed the road and went on to the north. We were very close to Germans twice in the rain but they did not see us. We got past the town to the north without seeing any Italians, then after a while came on the main channels of the retreat and walked all night toward the Tagliamento. I had not realized how gigantic the retreat was. The whole country was moving, as well as the army. We walked all night, making better time than the vehicles. My leg ached and I was tired but we made good time. It seemed so silly for Bonello to have decided to be taken prisoner. There was no danger. We had walked through two armies without incident. If Aymo had not been killed there would never have seemed to be any danger. No one had bothered us when we were in plain sight along the railway. The killing came suddenly and unreasonably. I wondered where Bonello was.

'How do you feel, Tenente?' Piani asked. We were going along the side of a road crowded with vehicles and troops.

'Fine.'

'I'm tired of this walking.'

'Well, all we have to do is walk now. We don't have to worry.'

'Bonello was a fool.'

'He was a fool all right.'

'What will you do about him, Tenente?'

'I don't know.'

'Can't you just put him down as taken prisoner?'

'I don't know.'

'You see if the war went on they would make bad trouble for his family.' 'The war won't go on,' a soldier said. 'We're going home. The war is over.'

'Everybody's going home.'

'We're all going home.'

'Come on, Tenente,' Piani said. He wanted to get past them.

'Tenente? Who's a Tenente? A basso gli ufficiali! Down with the officers!'

Piani took me by the arm. 'I better call you by your name,' he said. 'They might try and make trouble. They've shot some officers.' We worked up past them.

'I won't make a report that will make trouble for his family.' I went on with our conversation.

'If the war is over it makes no difference,' Piani said. 'But I don't believe it's over.'

'It's too good that it should be over.'

'We'll know pretty soon,' I said.

'I don't believe it's over. They all think it's over but I don't believe it.'

'Viva la Pace!' a soldier shouted out. 'We're going home!'

'It would be fine if we all went home,' Piani said. 'Wouldn't you like to go home?'

'Yes.'

'We'll never go. I don't think it's over.'

'Andiamo a casa!' a soldier shouted.

'They throw away their rifles,' Piani said. 'They take them off and drop them down while they're marching. Then they shout.'

'They ought to keep their rifles.'

'They think if they throw away their rifles they can't make them fight.'

In the dark and the rain, making our way along the side of the road I could see that many of the troops still had their rifles. They stuck up above the capes.

'What brigade are you?' an officer called out.

'Brigata di Pace,' some one shouted. 'Peace Brigade!' The officer said nothing. 'What does he say? What does the officer say?'

'Down with the officer. Viva la Pace!'

'Come on,' Piani said. We passed two British ambulances, abandoned in the block of vehicles.

'They're from Gorizia,' Piani said. 'I know the cars.'

'They got further than we did.'

'They started earlier.'

'I wonder where the drivers are?'

'Up ahead probably.'

'The Germans have stopped outside Udine,' I said. 'These people will all get across the river.'

'Yes,' Piani said. 'That's why I think the war will go on.'

'The Germans could come on,' I said. 'I wonder why they don't come on.'

'I don't know. I don't know anything about this kind of war.'

'They have to wait for their transport I suppose.'

'I don't know,' Piani said. Alone he was much gentler. When he was with the others he Was a very rough talker.

'Are you married, Luigi?'

'You know I am married.'

'Is that why you did not want to be a prisoner?'

'That is one reason. Are you married, Tenente?'

'No.'

'Neither is Bonello.'

'You can't tell anything by a man's being married. But I should think a married man would want to get back to his wife,' I said. I would be glad to talk about wives.

'Yes.'

'How are your feet?' 'They're sore enough.'

Before daylight we reached the bank of the Tagliamento and followed down along the flooded river to the bridge where all the traffic was crossing.

'They ought to be able to hold at this river,' Piani said. In the dark the flood looked high. The water swirled and it was wide. The wooden bridge was nearly three-quarters of a mile across, and the river, that usually ran in narrow channels in the wide stony bed far below the bridge, was close under the wooden planking. We went along the bank and then worked our way into the crowd that were crossing the bridge. Crossing slowly in the rain a few feet above the flood, pressed tight in the crowd, the box of an artillery caisson just ahead, I looked over the side and watched the river. Now that we could not go our own pace I felt very tired. There was no exhilaration in crossing the bridge. I wondered what it would be like if a plane bombed it in the daytime.

'Piani,' I said.

'Here I am, Tenente.' He was a little ahead in the jam. No one was talking. They were all trying to get across as soon as they could: thinking only of that. We were almost across. At the far end of the bridge there were officers and carabinieri standing on both sides flashing lights. I saw them silhouetted against the sky-line. As we came close to them I saw one of the officers point to a man in the column. A carabiniere went in after him and came out holding the man by the arm. He took him away from the road. We came almost opposite them. The officers were scrutinizing every one in the column, sometimes speaking to each other, going forward to flash a light in some one's face. They took some one else out just before we came opposite. I saw the man. He was a lieutenantcolonel. I saw the stars in the box on his sleeve as they flashed a light on him. His hair was gray and he was short and fat. The carabiniere pulled him in behind the line of officers. As we came opposite I saw one or two of them look at me. Then one pointed at me and spoke to a carabiniere. I saw the carabiniere start for me, come through the edge of the column toward me, then felt him take me by the collar.

'What's the matter with you?' I said and hit him in the face. I saw his face under the hat, upturned mustaches and blood coming down his cheek. Another one dove in toward us.

'What's the matter with you?' I said. He did not answer. He was watching a chance to grab me. I put my arm behind me to loosen my pistol.

'Don't you know you can't touch an officer?'

The other one grabbed me from behind and pulled my arm up so that it twisted in the socket. I turned with him and the other one grabbed me around the neck. I kicked his shins and got my left knee into his groin.

'Shoot him if he resists,' I heard some one say.

'What's the meaning of this?' I tried to shout but my voice was not very loud. They had me at the side of the road now.

'Shoot him if he resists,' an officer said. 'Take him over back.'

'Who are you?'

'You'll find out.'

'Who are you?'

'Battle police,' another officer said.

'Why don't you ask me to step over instead of having one of these airplanes grab me?'

They did not answer. They did not have to answer. They were battle police.

'Take him back there with the others,' the first officer said. 'You see. He speaks Italian with an accent.'

'So do you, you,' I said.

'Take him back with the others,' the first officer said. They took me down behind the line of officers below the road toward a group of people in a field by the river bank. As we walked toward them shots were fired. I saw flashes of the rifles and heard the reports. We came up to the group. There were four officers standing together, with a man in front of them with a carabiniere on each side of him. A group of men were standing guarded by carabinieri. Four other carabinieri stood near the questioning officers, leaning on their carbines. They were wide-hatted carabinieri. The two who had me shoved me in with the group waiting to be questioned. I looked at the man the officers were questioning. He was the fat gray-haired little lieutenant-colonel they had taken out of the column. The questioners had all the efficiency, coldness and command of themselves of Italians who are firing and are not being fired on.

'Your brigade?'

He told them.

'Regiment?'

He told them.

'Why are you not with your regiment?'

He told them.

'Do you not know that an officer should be with his troops?' He did.

That was all. Another officer spoke.

'It is you and such as you that have let the barbarians onto the sacred soil of the fatherland.'

'I beg your pardon,' said the lieutenant-colonel.

'It is because of treachery such as yours that we have lost the fruits of victory.'

'Have you ever been in a retreat?' the lieutenant-colonel asked.

'Italy should never retreat.'

We stood there in the rain and listened to this. We were facing the officers and the prisoner stood in front and a little to one side of us.

'If you are going to shoot me,' the lieutenant-colonel said, 'please shoot me at once without further questioning. The questioning is stupid.' He made the sign of the cross. The officers spoke together. One wrote something on a pad of paper.

'Abandoned his troops, ordered to be shot,' he said.

Two carabinieri took the lieutenant-colonel to the river bank. He walked in the rain, an old man with his hat off, a carabinieri on either side. I did not watch them shoot him but I heard the shots. They were questioning some one else. This officer too was separated from his troops. He was not allowed to make an explanation. He cried when they read the sentence from the pad of paper, and they were questioning another when they shot him. They made a point of being intent on questioning the next man while the man who had been questioned before was being shot. In this way there was obviously nothing they could do about it. I did not know whether I should wait to be questioned or make a break now. I was obviously a German in Italian uniform. I saw how their minds worked; if they had minds and if they worked. They were all young men and they were saving their country. The second army was being re-formed beyond the Tagliamento. They were executing officers of the rank of major and above who were separated from their troops.

They were also dealing summarily with German agitators in Italian uniform. They wore steel helmets. Only two of us had steel helmets. Some of the carabinieri had them. The other carabinieri wore the wide hat. Airplanes we called them. We stood in the rain and were taken out one at a time to be questioned and shot. So far they had shot every one they had questioned. The questioners had that beautiful detachment and devotion to stern justice of men dealing in death without being in any danger of it. They were questioning a full colonel of a line regiment. Three more officers had just been put in with us.

'Where was his regiment?'

I looked at the carabinieri. They were looking at the newcomers. The others were looking at the colonel. I ducked down, pushed between two men, and ran for the river, my head down. I tripped at the edge and went in with a splash. The water was very cold and I stayed under as long as I could. I could feel the current swirl me and I stayed under until I thought I could never come up. The minute I came up I took a breath and went down again. It was easy to stay under with so much clothing and my boots. When I came up the second time I saw a piece of timber ahead of me and reached it and held on with one hand. I kept my head behind it and did not even look over it. I did not want to see the bank. There were shots when I ran and shots when I came up the first time. I heard them when I was almost above water. There were no shots now. The piece of timber swung in the current and I held it with one hand. I looked at the bank. It seemed to be going by very fast. There was much wood in the stream. The water was very cold. We passed the brush of an island above the water. I held onto the timber with both hands and let it take me along. The shore was out of sight now.

31

You do not know how long you are in a river when the current moves swiftly. It seems a long time and it may be very short. The water was cold and in flood and many things passed that had been floated off the banks when the river rose. I was lucky to have a heavy timber to hold on to, and I lay in the icy water with my chin on the wood, holding as easily as I could with both hands. I was afraid of cramps and I hoped we would move toward the shore. We went down the river in a long curve. It was beginning to be light enough so I could see the bushes along the shore-line. There was a brush island ahead and the current moved toward the shore. I wondered if I should take off my boots and clothes and try to swim ashore, but decided not to. I had never thought of anything but that I would reach the shore some way, and I would be in a bad position if I landed barefoot. I had to get to Mestre some way.

I watched the shore come close, then swing away, then come closer again. We were floating more slowly. The shore was very close now. I could see twigs on the willow bush. The timber swung slowly so that the bank was behind me and I knew we were in an eddy. We went slowly around. As I saw the bank again, very close now, I tried holding with one arm and kicking and swimming the timber toward the bank with the other, but I did not bring it any closer. I was afraid we would move out of the eddy and, holding with one hand, I drew up my feet so they were against the side of the timber and shoved hard toward the bank. I could see the brush, but even with my momentum and swimming as hard as I could, the current was taking me away. I thought then I would drown because of my boots, but I thrashed and fought through the water, and when I looked up the bank was coming toward me, and I kept thrashing and swimming in a heavy-footed panic until I reached it. I hung to the willow branch and did not have strength to pull myself up but I knew I would not drown now. It had never occurred to me on the timber that I might drown. I felt hollow and sick in my stomach and chest from the effort, and I held to the branches and waited. When the sick feeling was gone I pulled into the willow bushes and rested again, my arms around some brush, holding tight with my hands to the branches. Then I crawled out, pushed on through the willows and onto the bank. It was halfdaylight and I saw no one. I lay flat on the bank and heard the river and the rain.

After a while I got up and started along the bank. I knew there was no bridge across the river until Latisana. I thought I might be opposite San Vito. I began to think out what I should do. Ahead there was a ditch running into the river. I went toward it. So far I had seen no one and I sat down by some bushes along the bank of the ditch and took off my shoes and emptied them of water. I took off my coat, took my wallet with my papers and my money all wet in it out of the inside pocket and then wrung the coat out. I took off my trousers and wrung them too, then my shirt and under clothing. I slapped and rubbed myself and then dressed again. I had lost my cap.

Before I put on my coat I cut the cloth stars off my sleeves and put them in the inside pocket with my money. My money was wet but was all right. I counted it. There were three thousand and some lire. My clothes felt wet and clammy and I slapped my arms to keep the circulation going. I had woven underwear and I did not think I would catch cold if I kept moving. They had taken my pistol at the road and I put the holster under my coat. I had no cape and it was cold in the rain. I started up the bank of the canal. It was daylight and the country was wet, low and dismal looking. The fields were bare and wet; a long way away I could see a campanile rising out of the plain. I came up onto a road. Ahead I saw some troops coming down the road. I limped along the side of the road and they passed me and paid no attention to me. They were a machine-gun detachment going up toward the river. I went on down the road.

That day I crossed the Venetian plain. It is a low level country and under the rain it is even flatter. Toward the sea there are salt marshes and very few roads. The roads all go along the river mouths to the sea and to cross the country you must go along the paths beside the canals. I was working across the country from the north to the south and had crossed two railway lines and many roads and finally I came out at the end of a path onto a railway line where it ran beside a marsh. It was the main line from Venice to Trieste, with a high solid embankment, a solid roadbed and double track. Down the tracks a way was a flag-station and I could see soldiers on guard. Up the line there was a bridge over a stream that flowed into the marsh. I could see a guard too at the bridge. Crossing the fields to the north I had seen a train pass on this railroad, visible a long way across the flat plain, and I thought a train might come from Portogruaro. I watched the guards and lay down on the embankment so that I could see both ways along the track. The guard at the bridge walked a way up the line toward where I lay, then turned and went back toward the bridge. I lay, and was hungry, and waited for the train. The one I had seen was so long that the engine moved it very slowly and I was sure I could get aboard it. After I had almost given up hoping for one I saw a train coming. The engine, coming straight on, grew larger slowly. I looked at the guard at the bridge. He was walking on the near side of the bridge but on the other side of the tracks. That would put him out of sight when the train passed. I watched the engine come nearer. It was working hard. I could see there were many cars. I knew there would be guards on the train, and I tried to see where they were, but, keeping out of sight, I could not.

The engine was almost to where I was lying. When it came opposite, working and puffing even on the level, and I saw the engineer pass, I stood up and stepped up close to the passing cars. If the guards were watching I was a less suspicious object standing beside the track. Several closed freight-cars passed. Then I saw a low open car of the sort they call gondolas coming, covered with canvas. I stood until it had almost passed, then jumped and caught the rear hand-rods and pulled up. I crawled down between the gondola and the shelter of the high freight-car behind. I did not think any one had seen me. I was holding to the hand-rods and crouching low, my feet on the coupling. We were almost opposite the bridge. I remembered the guard. As we passed him he looked at me. He was a boy and his helmet was too big for him. I stared at him contemptuously and he looked away. He thought I had something to do with the train.

We were past. I saw him still looking uncomfortable, watching the other cars pass and I stooped to see how the canvas was fastened. It had grummets and was laced down at the edge with cord. I took out my knife, cut the cord and put my arm under. There were hard bulges under the canvas that tightened in the rain. I looked up and ahead. There was a guard on the freight-car ahead but he was looking forward. I let go of the hand-rails and ducked under the canvas. My forehead hit something that gave me a violent bump and I felt blood on my face but I crawled on in and lay flat. Then I turned around and fastened down the canvas.

I was in under the canvas with guns. They smelled cleanly of oil and grease. I lay and listened to the rain on the canvas and the clicking of the car over the rails. There was a little light came through and I lay and looked at the guns. They had their canvas jackets on. I thought they must have been sent ahead from the third army. The bump on my forehead was swollen and I stopped the bleeding by lying still and letting it coagulate, then picked away the dried blood except over the cut. It was nothing. I had no handkerchief, but feeling with my fingers I washed away where the dried blood had been, with rainwater that dripped from the canvas, and wiped it clean with the sleeve of my coat. I did not want to look conspicuous. I knew I would have to get out before they got to Mestre because they would be taking care of these guns. They had no guns to lose or forget about. I was terrifically hungry.

32

Lying on the floor of the flat-car with the guns beside me under the canvas I was wet, cold and very hungry. Finally I rolled over and lay flat on my stomach with my head on my arms. My knee was stiff, but it had been very satisfactory. Valentini had done a fine job. I had done half the retreat on foot and swum part of the Tagliamento with his knee. It was his knee all right. The other knee was mine. Doctors did things to you and then it was not your body any more. The head was mine, and the inside of the belly. It was very hungry in there. I could feel it turn over on itself. The head was mine, but not to use, not to think with, only to remember and not too much remember.

I could remember Catherine but I knew I would get crazy if I thought about her when I was not sure yet I would see her, so I would not think about her, only about her a little, only about her with the car going slowly and clickingly, and some light through the canvas and my lying with Catherine on the floor of the car. Hard as the floor of the car to lie not thinking only feeling, having been away too long, the clothes wet and the floor moving only a little each time and lonesome inside and alone with wet clothing and hard floor for a wife.

You did not love the floor of a flat-car nor guns with canvas jackets and the smell of vaselined metal or a canvas that rain leaked through, although it is very fine under a canvas and pleasant with guns; but you loved some one else whom now you knew was not even to be pretended there; you seeing now very clearly and coldly—not so coldly as clearly and emptily. You saw emptily, lying on your stomach, having been present when one army moved back and another came forward. You had lost your cars and your men as a floorwalker loses the stock of his department in a fire. There was, however, no insurance. You were out of it now. You had no more obligation. If they shot floorwalkers after a fire in the department store because they spoke with an accent they had always had, then certainly the floorwalkers would not be expected to return when the store opened again for business. They might seek other employment; if there was any other employment and the police did not get them.

Anger was washed away in the river along with any obligation. Although that ceased when the carabiniere put his hands on my collar. I would like to have had the uniform off although I did not care much about the outward forms. I had taken off the stars, but that was for convenience. It was no point of honor. I was not against them. I was through. I wished them all the luck. There were the good ones, and the brave ones, and the calm ones and the sensible ones, and they deserved it. But it was not my show any more and I wished this bloody train would get to Mestre and I would eat and stop thinking. I would have to stop.

Piani would tell them they had shot me. They went through the pockets and took the papers of the people they shot. They would not have my papers. They might call me drowned. I wondered what they would hear in the States. Dead from wounds and other causes. Good Christ I was hungry. I wondered what had become of the priest at the mess. And Rinaldi. He was probably at Pordenone. If they had not gone further back. Well, I would never see him now. I would never see any of them now. That life was over. I did not think he had syphilis. It was not a serious disease anyway if you took it in time, they said. But he would worry. I would worry too if I had it. Any one would worry.

I was not made to think. I was made to eat. My God, yes. Eat and drink and sleep with Catherine. To-night maybe. No that was impossible. But to-morrow night, and a good meal and sheets and never going away again except together. Probably have to go damned quickly. She would go. I knew she would go. When would we go? That was something to think about. It was getting dark. I lay and thought where we would go. There were many places.

BOOK FOUR

33

I dropped off the train in Milan as it slowed to come into the station early in the morning before it was light. I crossed the track and came out between some buildings and down onto the street. A wine shop was open and I went in for some coffee. It smelled of early morning, of swept dust, spoons in coffee-glasses and the wet circles left by wine-glasses. The proprietor was behind the bar. Two soldiers sat at a table. I stood at the bar and drank a glass of coffee and ate a piece of bread. The coffee was gray with milk, and I skimmed the milk scum off the top with a piece of bread. The proprietor looked at me.

'You want a glass of grappa?'

'No thanks.'

'On me,' he said and poured a small glass and pushed it toward me. 'What's happening at the front?'

'I would not know.'

'They are drunk,' he said, moving his hand toward the two soldiers. I could believe him. They looked drunk.

'Tell me,' he said, 'what is happening at the front?'

'I would not know about the front.'

'I saw you come down the wall. You came off the train.'

'There is a big retreat.'

'I read the papers. What happens? Is it over?'

'I don't think so.'

He filled the glass with grappa from a short bottle. 'If you are in trouble,' he said, 'I can keep you.'

'I am not in trouble.'

'If you are in trouble stay here with me.'

'Where does one stay?'

'In the building. Many stay here. Any who are in trouble stay here.'

'Are many in trouble?'

'It depends on the trouble. You are a South American?'

'No.'

'Speak Spanish?'

'A little.'

He wiped off the bar.

'It is hard now to leave the country but in no way impossible.'

'I have no wish to leave.'

'You can stay here as long as you want. You will see what sort of man I am.'

'I have to go this morning but I will remember the address to return.'

He shook his head. 'You won't come back if you talk like that. I thought you were in real trouble.'

'I am in no trouble. But I value the address of a friend.'

I put a ten-lira note on the bar to pay for the coffee.

'Have a grappa with me,' I said.

'It is not necessary.'

'Have one.'

He poured the two glasses.

'Remember,' he said. 'Come here. Do not let other people take you in. Here you are all right.'

'I am sure.'

'You are sure?'

'Yes.'

He was serious. 'Then let me tell you one thing. Do not go about with that coat.'

'Why?'

'On the sleeves it shows very plainly where the stars have been cut away. The cloth is a different color.'

I did not say anything.

'If you have no papers I can give you papers.'

'What papers?'

'Leave-papers.'

'I have no need for papers. I have papers.'

'All right,' he said. 'But if you need papers I can get what you wish.'

'How much are such papers?'

'It depends on what they are. The price is reasonable.'

'I don't need any now.'

He shrugged his shoulders.

'I'm all right,' I said.

When I went out he said, 'Don't forget that I am your friend.'

'No.'

'I will see you again,' he said.

'Good,' I said.

Outside I kept away from the station, where there were military police, and picked up a cab at the edge of the little park. I gave the driver the address of the hospital. At the hospital I went to the porter's lodge. His wife embraced me. He shook my hand.

'You are back. You are safe.'

'Yes.'

'Have you had breakfast?'

'Yes.'

'How are you, Tenente? How are you?' the wife asked.

'Fine.'

'Won't you have breakfast with us?'

'No, thank you. Tell me is Miss Barkley here at the hospital now?'

'Miss Barkley?'

'The English lady nurse.'

'His girl,' the wife said. She patted my arm and smiled.

'No,' the porter said. 'She is away.'

My heart went down. 'You are sure? I mean the tall blonde English young lady.'

'I am sure. She is gone to Stresa.'

'When did she go?'

'She went two days ago with the other lady English.'

'Good,' I said. 'I wish you to do something for me. Do not tell any one you have seen me. It is very important.'

'I won't tell any one,' the porter said. I gave him a ten-lira note. He pushed it away.

'I promise you I will tell no one,' he said. 'I don't want any money.'

'What can we do for you, Signor Tenente?' his wife asked.

'Only that,' I said.

'We are dumb,' the porter said. 'You will let me know anything I can do?'

'Yes,' I said. 'Good-by. I will see you again.'

They stood in the door, looking after me.

I got into the cab and gave the driver the address of Simmons, one of the men I knew who was studying singing.

Simmons lived a long way out in the town toward the Porta Magenta. He was still in bed and sleepy when I went to see him.

'You get up awfully early, Henry,' he said.

'I came in on the early train.'

'What's all this retreat? Were you at the front? Will you have a cigarette? They're in that box on the table.' It was a big room with a bed beside the wall, a piano over on the far side and a dresser and table. I sat on a chair by the bed. Simmons sat propped up by the pillows and smoked.

'I'm in a jam, Sim,' I said.

'So am I,' he said. 'I'm always in a jam. Won't you smoke?'

'No,' I said. 'What's the procedure in going to Switzerland?'

'For you? The Italians wouldn't let you out of the country.'

'Yes. I know that. But the Swiss. What will they do?'

'They intern you.'

'I know. But what's the mechanics of it?'

'Nothing. It's very simple. You can go anywhere. I think you just have to report or something. Why? Are you fleeing the police?'

'Nothing definite yet.'

'Don't tell me if you don't want. But it would be interesting to hear. Nothing happens here. I was a great flop at Piacenza.'

'I'm awfully sorry.'

'Oh yes—I went very badly. I sung well too. I'm going to try it again at the Lyrico here.'

'I'd like to be there.'

'You're awfully polite. You aren't in a bad mess, are you?'

'I don't know.'

'Don't tell me if you don't want. How do you happen to be away from the bloody front?'

'I think I'm through with it.'

'Good boy. I always knew you had sense. Can I help you any way?'

'You're awfully busy.'

'Not a bit of it, my dear Henry. Not a bit of it. I'd be happy to do anything.'

'You're about my size. Would you go out and buy me an outfit of civilian clothes? I've clothes but they're all at Rome.'

'You did live there, didn't you? It's a filthy place. How did you ever live there?'

'I wanted to be an architect.'

'That's no place for that. Don't buy clothes. I'll give you all the clothes you want. I'll fit you out so you'll be a great success. Go in that dressing room. There's a closet. Take anything you want. My dear fellow, you don't want to buy clothes.'

'I'd rather buy them, Sim.'

'My dear fellow, it's easier for me to let you have them than go out and buy them. Have you got a passport? You won't get far without a passport.' 'Yes. I've still got my passport.'

'Then get dressed, my dear fellow, and off to old Helvetia.'

'It's not that simple. I have to go up to Stresa first.'

'Ideal, my dear fellow. You just row a boat across. If I wasn't trying to sing, I'd go with you. I'll go yet.'

'You could take up yodelling.'

'My dear fellow, I'll take up yodelling yet. I really can sing though. That's the strange part.'

'I'll bet you can sing.'

He lay back in bed smoking a cigarette.

'Don't bet too much. But I can sing though. It's damned funny, but I can. I like to sing. Listen.' He roared into 'Africana,' his neck swelling, the veins standing out. 'I can sing,' he said. 'Whether they like it or not.' I looked out of the window. 'I'll go down and let my cab go.'

'Come back up, my dear fellow, and we'll have breakfast.' He stepped out of bed, stood straight, took a deep breath and commenced doing bending exercises. I went downstairs and paid off the cab.

34

In civilian clothes I felt a masquerader. I had been in uniform a long time and I missed the feeling of being held by your clothes. The trousers felt very floppy. I had bought a ticket at Milan for Stresa. I had also bought a new hat. I could not wear Sim's hat but his clothes were fine. They smelled of tobacco and as I sat in the compartment and looked out the window the new hat felt very new and the clothes very old. I myself felt as sad as the wet Lombard country that was outside through the window. There were some aviators in the compartment who did not think much of me. They avoided looking at me and were very scornful of a civilian my age. I did not feel insulted. In the old days I would have insulted them and picked a fight. They got off at Gallarate and I was glad to be alone. I had the paper but I did not read it because I did not want to read about the war. I was going to forget the war. I had made a separate peace. I felt damned lonely and was glad when the train got to Stresa.

At the station I had expected to see the porters from the hotels but there was no one. The season had been over a long time and no one met the train. I got down from the train with my bag, it was Sim's bag, and very light to carry, being empty except for two shirts, and stood under the roof of the station in the rain while the train went on. I found a man in the station and asked him if he knew what hotels were open. The Grand-Hotel & des Isles Borromées was open and several small hotels that stayed open all the year. I started in the rain for the Isles Borromées carrying my bag. I saw a carriage coming down the street and signalled to the driver. It was better to arrive in a carriage. We drove up to the carriage entrance of the big hotel and the concierge came out with an umbrella and was very polite.

I took a good room. It was very big and light and looked out on the lake. The clouds were down over the lake but it would be beautiful with the sunlight. I was expecting my wife, I said. There was a big double bed, a _letto matrimoniale_ with a satin coverlet. The hotel was very luxurious. I went down the long halls, down the wide stairs, through the rooms to the bar. I knew the barman and sat on a high stool and ate salted almonds and potato chips. The martini felt cool and clean.

'What are you doing here in borghese?' the barman asked after he had mixed a second martini.

'I am on leave. Convalescing-leave.'

'There is no one here. I don't know why they keep the hotel open.'

'Have you been fishing?'

'I've caught some beautiful pieces. Trolling this time of year you catch some beautiful pieces.'

'Did you ever get the tobacco I sent?'

'Yes. Didn't you get my card?'

I laughed. I had not been able to get the tobacco. It was American pipe-tobacco that he wanted, but my relatives had stopped sending it or it was being held up. Anyway it never came.

'I'll get some somewhere,' I said. 'Tell me have you seen two English girls in the town? They came here day before yesterday.'

'They are not at the hotel.'

'They are nurses.'

'I have seen two nurses. Wait a minute, I will find out where they are.'

'One of them is my wife,' I said. 'I have come here to meet her.'

'The other is my wife.'

'I am not joking.'

'Pardon my stupid joke,' he said. 'I did not understand.' He went away and was gone quite a little while. I ate olives, salted almonds and potato chips and looked at myself in civilian clothes in the mirror behind the bar. The bartender came back. 'They are at the little hotel near the station,' he said.

'How about some sandwiches?'

'I'll ring for some. You understand there is nothing here, now there are no people.'

'Isn't there really any one at all?'

'Yes. There are a few people.'

The sandwiches came and I ate three and drank a couple more martinis. I had never tasted anything so cool and clean. They made me feel civilized. I had had too much red wine, bread, cheese, bad coffee and grappa. I sat on the high stool before the pleasant mahogany, the brass and the mirrors and did not think at all. The barman asked me some question.

'Don't talk about the war,' I said. The war was a long way away. Maybe there wasn't any war. There was no war here. Then I realized it was over for me. But I did not have the feeling that it was really over. I had the feeling of a boy who thinks of what is happening at a certain hour at the schoolhouse from which he has played truant.

Catherine and Helen Ferguson were at supper when I came to their hotel. Standing in the hallway I saw them at table. Catherine's face was away from me and I saw the line of her hair and her cheek and her lovely neck and shoulders. Ferguson was talking. She stopped when I came in.

'My God,' she said.

'Hello,' I said.

'Why it's you!' Catherine said. Her face lighted up. She looked too happy to believe it. I kissed her. Catherine blushed and I sat down at the table.

'You're a fine mess,' Ferguson said. 'What are you doing here? Have you eaten?'

'No.' The girl who was serving the meal came in and I told her to bring a plate for me. Catherine looked at me all the time, her eyes happy.

'What are you doing in mufti?' Ferguson asked. 'I'm in the Cabinet.'

'You're in some mess.'

'Cheer up, Fergy. Cheer up just a little.'

'I'm not cheered by seeing you. I know the mess you've gotten this girl into. You're no cheerful sight to me.'

Catherine smiled at me and touched me with her foot under the table.

'No one got me in a mess, Fergy. I get in my own messes.'

'I can't stand him,' Ferguson said. 'He's done nothing but ruin you with his sneaking Italian tricks. Americans are worse than Italians.'

'The Scotch are such a moral people,' Catherine said.

'I don't mean that. I mean his Italian sneakiness.'

'Am I sneaky, Fergy?'

'You are. You're worse than sneaky. You're like a snake. A snake with an Italian uniform: with a cape around your neck.'

'I haven't got an Italian uniform now.'

'That's just another example of your sneakiness. You had a love affair all summer and got this girl with child and now I suppose you'll sneak off.'

I smiled at Catherine and she smiled at me.

'We'll both sneak off,' she said.

'You're two of the same thing,' Ferguson said. 'I'm ashamed of you, Catherine Barkley. You have no shame and no honor and you're as sneaky as he is.'

'Don't, Fergy,' Catherine said and patted her hand. 'Don't denounce me. You know we like each other.'

'Take your hand away,' Ferguson said. Her face was red. 'If you had any shame it would be different. But you're God knows how many months gone with child and you think it's a joke and are all smiles because your seducer's come back. You've no shame and no feelings.' She began to cry. Catherine went over and put her arm around her. As she stood comforting Ferguson, I could see no change in her figure.

'I don't care,' Ferguson sobbed. 'I think it's dreadful.'

'There, there, Fergy,' Catherine comforted her. 'I'll be ashamed. Don't cry, Fergy.

Don't cry, old Fergy.'

'I'm not crying,' Ferguson sobbed. 'I'm not crying. Except for the awful thing you've gotten into.' She looked at me. 'I hate you,' she said. 'She can't make me not hate you.

You dirty sneaking American Italian.' Her eyes and nose were red with crying.

Catherine smiled at me.

'Don't you smile at him with your arm around me.'

'You're unreasonable, Fergy.'

'I know it,' Ferguson sobbed. 'You mustn't mind me, either of you. I'm so upset. I'm not reasonable. I know it. I want you both to be happy.'

'We're happy,' Catherine said. 'You're a sweet Fergy.'

Ferguson cried again. 'I don't want you happy the way you are. Why don't you get married? You haven't got another wife have you?'

'No,' I said. Catherine laughed.

'It's nothing to laugh about,' Ferguson said. 'Plenty of them have other wives.'

'We'll be married, Fergy,' Catherine said, 'if it will please you.'

'Not to please me. You should want to be married.'

'We've been very busy.'

'Yes. I know. Busy making babies.' I thought she was going to cry again but she went into bitterness instead. 'I suppose you'll go off with him now to-night?'

'Yes,' said Catherine. 'If he wants me.'

'What about me?'

'Are you afraid to stay here alone?'

'Yes, I am.'
'Then I'll stay with you.'
'No, go on with him. Go with him right away. I'm sick of seeing both of you.'
'We'd better finish dinner.'
'No. Go right away.' 'Fergy, be reasonable.'
'I say get out right away. Go away both of you.'
'Let's go then,' I said. I was sick of Fergy.
'You do want to go. You see you want to leave me even to eat dinner alone. I've always wanted to go to the Italian lakes and this is how it is. Oh, Oh,' she sobbed, then looked at Catherine and choked.

'We'll stay till after dinner,' Catherine said. 'And I'll not leave you alone if you want me to stay. I won't leave you alone, Fergy.'

'No. No. I want you to go. I want you to go.' She wiped her eyes. 'I'm so unreasonable. Please don't mind me.'

The girl who served the meal had been upset by all the crying. Now as she brought in the next course she seemed relieved that things were better.

That night at the hotel, in our room with the long empty hall outside and our shoes outside the door, a thick carpet on the floor of the room, outside the windows the rain falling and in the room light and pleasant and cheerful, then the light out and it exciting with smooth sheets and the bed comfortable, feeling that we had come home, feeling no longer alone, waking in the night to find the other one there, and not gone away; all other things were unreal. We slept when we were tired and if we woke the other one woke too so one was not alone. Often a man wishes to be alone and a girl wishes to be alone too and if they love each other they are jealous of that in each other, but I can truly say we never felt that. We could feel alone when we were together, alone against the others. It has only happened to me like that once. I have been alone while I was with many girls and that is the way that you can be most lonely. But we were never lonely and never afraid when we were together. I know that the night is not the same as the day: that all things are different, that the things of the night cannot be explained in the day, because they do not then exist, and the night can be a dreadful time for lonely people once their loneliness has started. But with Catherine there was almost no difference in the night except that it was an even better time. If people bring so much courage to this world the world has to kill them to break them, so of course it kills them. The world breaks every one and afterward many are strong at the broken places. But those that will not break it kills. It kills the very good and the very gentle and the very brave impartially. If you are none of these you can be sure it will kill you too but there will be no special hurry.

I remember waking in the morning. Catherine was asleep and the sunlight was coming in through the window. The rain had stopped and I stepped out of bed and across the floor to the window. Down below were the gardens, bare now but beautifully regular, the gravel paths, the trees, the stone wall by the lake and the lake in the sunlight with the mountains beyond. I stood at the window looking out and when I turned away I saw Catherine was awake and watching me.

'How are you, darling?' she said. 'Isn't it a lovely day?'

'How do you feel?'

'I feel very well. We had a lovely night.'

'Do you want breakfast?'

She wanted breakfast. So did I and we had it in bed, the November sunlight coming in the window, and the breakfast tray across my lap.

'Don't you want the paper? You always wanted the paper in the hospital?'

'No,' I said. 'I don't want the paper now.'

'Was it so bad you don't want even to read about it?'

'I don't want to read about it.'

'I wish I had been with you so I would know about it too.'

'I'll tell you about it if I ever get it straight in my head.'

'But won't they arrest you if they catch you out of uniform?'

'They'll probably shoot me.'

'Then we'll not stay here. We'll get out of the country.'

'I'd thought something of that.'

'We'll get out. Darling, you shouldn't take silly chances. Tell me how did you come from Mestre to Milan?'

'I came on the train. I was in uniform then.'

'Weren't you in danger then?'

'Not much. I had an old order of movement. I fixed the dates on it in Mestre.'

'Darling, you're liable to be arrested here any time. I won't have it. It's silly to do something like that. Where would we be if they took you off?'

'Let's not think about it. I'm tired of thinking about it.'

'What would you do if they came to arrest you?' 'Shoot them.'

'You see how silly you are, I won't let you go out of the hotel until we leave here.'

'Where are we going to go?'

'Please don't be that way, darling. We'll go wherever you say. But please find some place to go right away.'

'Switzerland is down the lake, we can go there.'

'That will be lovely.'

It was clouding over outside and the lake was darkening.

'I wish we did not always have to live like criminals,' I said.

'Darling, don't be that way. You haven't lived like a criminal very long. And we never live like criminals. We're going to have a fine time.'

'I feel like a criminal. I've deserted from the army.'

'Darling, please be sensible. It's not deserting from the army. It's only the Italian army.'

I laughed. 'You're a fine girl. Let's get back into bed. I feel fine in bed.'

A little while later Catherine said, 'You don't feel like a criminal do you?' 'No,' I said. 'Not when I'm with you.'

'You're such a silly boy,' she said. 'But I'll look after you. Isn't it splendid, darling, that I don't have any morning-sickness?'

'It's grand.'

'You don't appreciate what a fine wife you have. But I don't care. I'll get you some place where they can't arrest you and then we'll have a lovely time.'

'Let's go there right away.'

'We will, darling. I'll go any place any time you wish.'

'Let's not think about anything.'

'All right.'

35

Catherine went along the lake to the little hotel to see Ferguson and I sat in the bar and read the papers. There were comfortable leather chairs in the bar and I sat in one of them and read until the barman came in. The army had not stood at the Tagliamento.

They were falling back to the Piave. I remembered the Piave. The railroad crossed it near San Dona going up to the front. It was deep and slow there and quite narrow. Down below there were mosquito marshes and canals. There were some lovely villas. Once, before the war, going up to Cortina D'Ampezzo I had gone along it for several hours in the hills. Up there it looked like a trout stream, flowing swiftly with shallow stretches and pools under the shadow of the rocks. The road turned off from it at Cadore. I wondered how the army that was up there would come down. The barman came in.

'Count Greffi was asking for you,' he said.

'Who?'

'Count Greffi. You remember the old man who was here when you were here before.'

'Is he here?'

'Yes, he's here with his niece. I told him you were here. He wants you to play billiards.'

'Where is he?'

'He's taking a walk.'

'How is he?'

'He's younger than ever. He drank three champagne cocktails last night before dinner.'

'How's his billiard game?'

'Good. He beat me. When I told him you were here he was very pleased. There's nobody here for him to play with.'

Count Greffi was ninety-four years old. He had been a contemporary of Metternich and was an old man with white hair and mustache and beautiful manners. He had been in the diplomatic service of both Austria and Italy and his birthday parties were the great social event of Milan. He was living to be one hundred years old and played a smoothly fluent game of billiards that contrasted with his own ninety-four-year-old brittleness. I had met him when I had been at Stresa once before out of season and while we played billiards we drank champagne. I thought it was a splendid custom and he gave me fifteen points in a hundred and beat me.

'Why didn't you tell me he was here?'

'I forgot it.'

'Who else is here?'

'No one you know. There are only six people altogether.'

'What are you doing now?'

'Nothing.'

'Come on out fishing.'

'I could come for an hour.'

'Come on. Bring the trolling line.'

The barman put on a coat and we went out. We went down and got a boat and I rowed while the barman sat in the stern and let out the line with a spinner and a heavy sinker on the end to troll for lake trout. We rowed along the shore, the barman holding the line in his hand and giving it occasional jerks forward. Stresa looked very deserted from the lake. There were the long rows of bare trees, the big hotels and the closed villas. I rowed across to Isola Bella and went close to the walls, where the water deepened sharply, and you saw the rock wall slanting down in the clear water, and then up and along to the fisherman's island. The sun was under a cloud and the water was dark and smooth and very cold. We did not have a strike though we saw some circles on the water from rising fish.

I rowed up opposite the fisherman's island where there were boats drawn up and men were mending nets.

'Should we get a drink?'

'All right.'

I brought the boat up to the stone pier and the barman pulled in the line, coiling it on the bottom of the boat and hooking the spinner on the edge of the gunwale. I stepped out and tied the boat. We went into a little café, sat at a bare wooden table and ordered vermouth.

'Are you tired from rowing?'

'I'll row back,' he said.

'I like to row.'

'Maybe if you hold the line it will change the luck.'

'All right.'

'Tell me how goes the war.'

'Rotten.'

'I don't have to go. I'm too old, like Count Greffi.'

'Maybe you'll have to go yet.'

'Next year they'll call my class. But I won't go.'

'What will you do?'

'Get out of the country. I wouldn't go to war. I was at the war once in Abyssinia. Nix.

Why do you go?'

'I don't know. I was a fool.'

'Have another vermouth?'

'All right.'

The barman rowed back. We trolled up the lake beyond Stresa and then down not far from shore. I held the taut line and felt the faint pulsing of the spinner revolving while I looked at the dark November water of the lake and the deserted shore. The barman rowed with long strokes and on the forward thrust of the boat the line throbbed. Once I had a strike: the line hardened suddenly and jerked back. I pulled and felt the live weight of the trout and then the line throbbed again. I had missed him.

'Did he feel big?'

'Pretty big.'

'Once when I was out trolling alone I had the line in my teeth and one struck and nearly took my mouth out.'

'The best way is to have it over your leg,' I said. 'Then you feel it and don't lose your teeth.'

I put my hand in the water. It was very cold. We were almost opposite the hotel now.

'I have to go in,' the barman said, 'to be there for eleven o'clock. L'heure du cocktail.'

'All right.'

I pulled in the line and wrapped it on a stick notched at each end. The barman put the boat in a little slip in the stone wall and locked it with a chain and padlock.

'Any time you want it,' he said, 'I'll give you the key.'

'Thanks.'

We went up to the hotel and into the bar. I did not want another drink so early in the morning so I went up to our room. The maid had just finished doing the room and Catherine was not back yet. I lay down on the bed and tried to keep from thinking.

When Catherine came back it was all right again. Ferguson was downstairs, she said. She was coming to lunch.

'I knew you wouldn't mind,' Catherine said.

'No,' I said.

'What's the matter, darling?'

'I don't know.'

'I know. You haven't anything to do. All you have is me and I go away.'

'That's true.'

'I'm sorry, darling. I know it must be a dreadful feeling to have nothing at all suddenly.'

'My life used to be full of everything,' I said. 'Now if you aren't with me I haven't a thing in the world.'

'But I'll be with you. I was only gone for two hours. Isn't there anything you can do?' 'I went fishing with the barman.'

'Wasn't it fun?'

'Yes.'

'Don't think about me when I'm not here.'

'That's the way I worked it at the front. But there was something to do then.'

'Othello with his occupation gone,' she teased.

'Othello was a nigger,' I said. 'Besides, I'm not jealous. I'm just so in love with you that there isn't anything else.'

'Will you be a good boy and be nice to Ferguson?'

'I'm always nice to Ferguson unless she curses me.'

'Be nice to her. Think how much we have and she hasn't anything.'

'I don't think she wants what we have.'

'You don't know much, darling, for such a wise boy.'

'I'll be nice to her.'

'I know you will. You're so sweet.'

'She won't stay afterward, will she?'

'No. I'll get rid of her.'

'And then we'll come up here.'

'Of course. What do you think I want to do?'

We went downstairs to have lunch with Ferguson. She was very impressed by the hotel and the splendor of the dining-room. We had a good lunch with a couple of bottles of white capri. Count Greffi came into the dining-room and bowed to us. His niece, who looked a little like my grandmother, was with him. I told Catherine and Ferguson about him and Ferguson was very impressed. The hotel was very big and grand and empty but the food was good, the wine was very pleasant and finally the wine made us all feel very well. Catherine had no need to feel any better. She was very happy. Ferguson became quite cheerful. I felt very well myself. After lunch Ferguson went back to her hotel. She was going to lie down for a while after lunch she said.

Along late in the afternoon some one knocked on our door.

'Who is it?'

'The Count Greffi wishes to know if you will play billiards with him.'

I looked at my watch; I had taken it off and it was under the pillow.

'Do you have to go, darling?' Catherine whispered.

'I think I'd better.' The watch was a quarter-past four o'clock. Out loud I said, 'Tell the Count Greffi I will be in the billiard-room at five o'clock.'

At a quarter to five I kissed Catherine good-by and went into the bathroom to dress. Knotting my tie and looking in the glass I looked strange to myself in the civilian clothes. I must remember to buy some more shirts and socks.

'Will you be away a long time?' Catherine asked. She looked lovely in the bed. 'Would you hand me the brush?'

I watched her brushing her hair, holding her head so the weight of her hair all came on one side. It was dark outside and the light over the head of the bed shone on her hair and on her neck and shoulders. I went over and kissed her and held her hand with the brush and her head sunk back on the pillow. I kissed her neck and shoulders. I felt faint with loving her so much.

'I don't want to go away.'

'I don't want you to go away.'

'I won't go then.'

'Yes. Go. It's only for a little while and then you'll come back.' 'We'll have dinner up here.'

'Hurry and come back.'

I found the Count Greffi in the billiard-room. He was practising strokes, looking very fragile under the light that came down above the billiard table. On a card table a little way beyond the light was a silver icing-bucket with the necks and corks of two champagne bottles showing above the ice. The Count Greffi straightened up when I came toward the table and walked toward me. He put out his hand, 'It is such a great pleasure that you are here. You were very kind to come to play with me.'

'It was very nice of you to ask me.'

'Are you quite well? They told me you were wounded on the Isonzo. I hope you are well again.'

'I'm very well. Have you been well?'

'Oh, I am always well. But I am getting old. I detect signs of age now.'

'I can't believe it.'

'Yes. Do you want to know one? It is easier for me to talk Italian. I discipline myself but I find when I am tired that it is so much easier to talk Italian. So I know I must be getting old.'

'We could talk Italian. I am a little tired, too.'

'Oh, but when you are tired it will be easier for you to talk English.'

'American.'

'Yes. American. You will please talk American. It is a delightful language.'

'I hardly ever see Americans.'

'You must miss them. One misses one's countrymen and especially one's countrywomen. I know that experience. Should we play or are you too tired?'

'I'm not really tired. I said that for a joke. What handicap will you give me?'

'Have you been playing very much?'

'None at all.'

'You play very well. Ten points in a hundred?'

'You flatter me.'

'Fifteen?'

'That would be fine but you will beat me.'

'Should we play for a stake? You always wished to play for a stake.'

'I think we'd better.'

'All right. I will give you eighteen points and we will play for a franc a point.'

He played a lovely game of billiards and with the handicap I was only four ahead at fifty. Count Greffi pushed a button on the wall to ring for the barman.

'Open one bottle please,' he said. Then to me, 'We will take a little stimulant.' The wine was icy cold and very dry and good.

'Should we talk Italian? Would you mind very much? It is my weakness now.'

We went on playing, sipping the wine between shots, speaking in Italian, but talking little, concentrated on the game. Count Greffi made his one hundredth point and with the handicap I was only at ninety-four. He smiled and patted me on the shoulder.

'Now we will drink the other bottle and you will tell me about the war.' He waited for me to sit down.

'About anything else,' I said.

'You don't want to talk about it? Good. What have you been reading?'

'Nothing,' I said. 'I'm afraid I am very dull.'

'No. But you should read.'

'What is there written in war-time?'

'There is "Le Feu" by a Frenchman, Barbusse. There is "Mr. Britling Sees Through It."'

'No, he doesn't.'

'What?'

'He doesn't see through it. Those books were at the hospital.'

'Then you have been reading?'

'Yes, but nothing any good.'

'I thought "Mr. Britling" a very good study of the English middle-class soul.'

'I don't know about the soul.'

'Poor boy. We none of us know about the soul. Are you Croyant?'

'At night.'

Count Greffi smiled and turned the glass with his fingers. 'I had expected to become more devout as I grow older but somehow I haven't,' he said. 'It is a great pity.' 'Would you like to live after death?' I asked and instantly felt a fool to mention death. But he did not mind the word.

'It would depend on the life. This life is very pleasant. I would like to live forever,' he smiled. 'I very nearly have.'

We were sitting in the deep leather chairs, the champagne in the ice-bucket and our glasses on the table between us.

'If you ever live to be as old as I am you will find many things strange.'

'You never seem old.'

'It is the body that is old. Sometimes I am afraid I will break off a finger as one breaks a stick of chalk. And the spirit is no older and not much wiser.'

'You are wise.'

'No, that is the great fallacy; the wisdom of old men. They do not grow wise. They grow careful.'

'Perhaps that is wisdom.'
'It is a very unattractive wisdom. What do you value most?'
'Some one I love.'
'With me it is the same. That is not wisdom. Do you value life?'
'Yes.'
'So do I. Because it is all I have. And to give birthday parties,' he laughed. 'You are probably wiser than I am. You do not give birthday parties.'

We both drank the wine.

'What do you think of the war really?' I asked.
'I think it is stupid.'
'Who will win it?'
'Italy.'
'Why?'
'They are a younger nation.'
'Do younger nations always win wars?'
'They are apt to for a time.'
'Then what happens?'
'They become older nations.'
'You said you were not wise.'
'Dear boy, that is not wisdom. That is cynicism.'
'It sounds very wise to me.'
'It's not particularly. I could quote you the examples on the other side. But it is not bad. Have we finished the champagne?'
'Almost.'
'Should we drink some more? Then I must dress.'
'Perhaps we'd better not now.'
'You are sure you don't want more?'
'Yes.' He stood up.
'I hope you will be very fortunate and very happy and very, very healthy.'
'Thank you. And I hope you will live forever.'
'Thank you. I have. And if you ever become devout pray for me if I am dead. I am asking several of my friends to do that. I had expected to become devout myself but it has not come.' I thought he smiled sadly but I could not tell. He was so old and his face was very wrinkled, so that a smile used so many lines that all gradations were lost.
'I might become very devout,' I said. 'Anyway, I will pray for you.'
'I had always expected to become devout. All my family died very devout. But somehow it does not come.'
'It's too early.'
'Maybe it is too late. Perhaps I have outlived my religious feeling.'
'My own comes only at night.'
'Then too you are in love. Do not forget that is a religious feeling.'
'You believe so?'

'Of course.' He took a step toward the table. 'You were very kind to play.'
'It was a great pleasure.'
'We will walk up stairs together.'

36

That night there was a storm and I woke to hear the rain lashing the window-panes. It was coming in the open window. Some one had knocked on the door. I went to the door very softly, not to disturb Catherine, and opened it. The barman stood there. He wore his overcoat and carried his wet hat.

'Can I speak to you, Tenente?'
'What's the matter?'
'It's a very serious matter.'

I looked around. The room was dark. I saw the water on the floor from the window. 'Come in,' I said. I took him by the arm into the bathroom; locked the door and put on the light. I sat down on the edge of the bathtub.

'What's the matter, Emilio? Are you in trouble?'
'No. You are, Tenente.'
'Yes?'
'They are going to arrest you in the morning.'
'Yes?'
'I came to tell you. I was out in the town and I heard them talking in a café.'
'I see.'

He stood there, his coat wet, holding his wet hat and said nothing.

'Why are they going to arrest me?'
'For something about the war.'
'Do you know what?'
'No. But I know that they know you were here before as an officer and now you are here out of uniform. After this retreat they arrest everybody.'

I thought a minute.

'What time do they come to arrest me?'
'In the morning. I don't know the time.'
'What do you say to do?'

He put his hat in the washbowl. It was very wet and had been dripping on the floor. 'If you have nothing to fear an arrest is nothing. But it is always bad to be arrested—especially now.'

'I don't want to be arrested.'
'Then go to Switzerland.'
'How?'
'In my boat.'
'There is a storm,' I said.
'The storm is over. It is rough but you will be all right.'
'When should we go?'

'Right away. They might come to arrest you early in the morning.'
'What about our bags?'
'Get them packed. Get your lady dressed. I will take care of them.'
'Where will you be?'
'I will wait here. I don't want any one to see me outside in the hall.'

I opened the door, closed it, and went into the bedroom. Catherine was awake.

'What is it, darling?'

'It's all right, Cat,' I said. 'Would you like to get dressed right away and go in a boat to Switzerland?'

'Would you?'

'No,' I said. 'I'd like to go back to bed.'

'What is it about?'

'The barman says they are going to arrest me in the morning.'

'Is the barman crazy?'

'No.'

'Then please hurry, darling, and get dressed so we can start.' She sat up on the side of the bed. She was still sleepy. 'Is that the barman in the bathroom?'

'Yes.'

'Then I won't wash. Please look the other way, darling, and I'll be dressed in just a minute.'

I saw her white back as she took off her night-gown and then I looked away because she wanted me to. She was beginning to be a little big with the child and she did not want me to see her. I dressed hearing the rain on the windows. I did not have much to put in my bag.

'There's plenty of room in my bag, Cat, if you need any.'

'I'm almost packed,' she said. 'Darling, I'm awfully stupid, but why is the barman in the bathroom?'

'Sh—he's waiting to take our bags down.'

'He's awfully nice.'

'He's an old friend,' I said. 'I nearly sent him some pipetobacco once.'

I looked out the open window at the dark night. I could not see the lake, only the dark and the rain but the wind was quieter.

'I'm ready, darling,' Catherine said.

'All right.' I went to the bathroom door. 'Here are the bags, Emilio,' I said. The barman took the two bags.

'You're very good to help us,' Catherine said.

'That's nothing, lady,' the barman said. 'I'm glad to help you just so I don't get in trouble myself. Listen,' he said to me. 'I'll take these out the servants' stairs and to the boat. You just go out as though you were going for a walk.'

'It's a lovely night for a walk,' Catherine said.

'It's a bad night all right.'

'I'm glad I've an umbrella,' Catherine said.

We walked down the hall and down the wide thickly carpeted stairs. At the foot of the stairs by the door the porter sat behind his desk.

He looked surprised at seeing us.

'You're not going out, sir?' he said.

'Yes,' I said. 'We're going to see the storm along the lake.'

'Haven't you got an umbrella, sir?'

'No,' I said. 'This coat sheds water.'

He looked at it doubtfully. 'I'll get you an umbrella, sir,' he said. He went away and came back with a big umbrella. 'It is a little big, sir,' he said. I gave him a ten-lira note. 'Oh you are too good, sir. Thank you very much,' he said. He held the door open and we went out into the rain. He smiled at Catherine and she smiled at him. 'Don't stay out in the storm,' he said. 'You will get wet, sir and lady.' He was only the second porter, and his English was still literally translated.

'We'll be back,' I said. We walked down the path under the giant umbrella and out through the dark wet gardens to the road and across the road to the trellised pathway along the lake. The wind was blowing offshore now. It was a cold, wet November wind and I knew it was snowing in the mountains. We came along past the chained boats in the slips along the quay to where the barman's boat should be. The water was dark against the stone. The barman stepped out from beside the row of trees.

'The bags are in the boat,' he said.

'I want to pay you for the boat,' I said.

'How much money have you?'

'Not so much.'

'You send me the money later. That will be all right.'

'How much?'

'What you want.'

'Tell me how much.'

'If you get through send me five hundred francs. You won't mind that if you get through.'

'All right.'

'Here are sandwiches.' He handed me a package. 'Everything there was in the bar. It's all here. This is a bottle of brandy and a bottle of wine.' I put them in my bag. 'Let me pay you for those.'

'All right, give me fifty lire.'

I gave itto him. 'The brandy is good,' he said. 'You don't need to be afraid to give itto your lady. She better get in the boat.' He held the boat, it rising and falling against the stone wall and I helped Catherine in. She sat in the stern and pulled her cape around her.

'You know where to go?'

'Up the lake.'

'You know how far?'

'Past Luino.'

'Past Luino, Cannero, Cannobio, Tranzano. You aren't in Switzerland until you come to Brissago. You have to pass Monte Tamara.'

'What time is it?' Catherine asked.

'It's only eleven o'clock,' I said.

'If you row all the time you ought to be there by seven o'clock in the morning.'

'Is it that far?'

'It's thirty-five kilometres.'

'How should we go? In this rain we need a compass.'

'No. Row to Isola Bella. Then on the other side of Isola Madre go with the wind.

The wind will take you to Pallanza. You will see the lights. Then go up the shore.'

'Maybe the wind will change.'

'No,' he said. 'This wind will blow like this for three days. It comes straight down from the Mattarone. There is a can to bail with.'

'Let me pay you something for the boat now.'

'No, I'd rather take a chance. If you get through you pay me all you can.'

'All right.'

'I don't think you'll get drowned.'

'That's good.'

'Go with the wind up the lake.'

'All right.'

I stepped in the boat.

'Did you leave the money for the hotel?'

'Yes. In an envelope in the room.'

'All right. Good luck, Tenente.'

'Good luck. We thank you many times.'

'You won't thank me if you get drowned.'

'What does he say?' Catherine asked.

'He says good luck.'

'Good luck,' Catherine said.

'Thank you very much.'

'Are you ready?'

'Yes.'

He bent down and shoved us off. I dug at the water with the oars, then waved one hand. The barman waved back deprecatingly. I saw the lights of the hotel and rowed out, rowing straight out until they were out of sight. There was quite a sea running but we were going with the wind.

37

I rowed in the dark keeping the wind in my face. The rain had stopped and only came occasionally in gusts. It was very dark, and the wind was cold. I could see Catherine in the stern but I could not see the water where the blades of the oars dipped. The oars were long and there were no leathers to keep them from slipping out. I pulled, raised, leaned forward, found the water, dipped and pulled, rowing as easily as I could. I did not feather the oars because the wind was with us. I knew my hands would blister and I wanted to delay it as long as I could. The boat was light and rowed easily. I pulled it along in the dark water. I could not see, and hoped we would soon come opposite Pallanza.

We never saw Pallanza. The wind was blowing up the lake and we passed the point that hides Pallanza in the dark and never saw the lights. When we finally saw some lights much further up the lake and close to the shore it was Intra. But for a long time we did not see any lights, nor did we see the shore but rowed steadily in the dark riding with the waves. Sometimes I missed the water with the oars in the dark as a wave lifted the boat. It was quite rough; but I kept on rowing, until suddenly we were close ashore against a point of rock that rose beside us; the waves striking against it, rushing high up, then falling back. I pulled hard on the right oar and backed water with the other and we went out into the lake again; the point was out of sight and we were going on up the lake.

'We're across the lake,' I said to Catherine.

'Weren't we going to see Pallanza?'

'We've missed it.'

'How are you, darling?'

'I'm fine.'

'I could take the oars awhile.'

'No, I'm fine.'

'Poor Ferguson,' Catherine said. 'In the morning she'll come to the hotel and find we're gone.'

'I'm not worrying so much about that,' I said, 'as about getting into the Swiss part of the lake before it's daylight and the custom guards see us.'

'Is it a long way?'

'It's some thirty kilometres from here.'

I rowed all night. Finally my hands were so sore I could hardly close them over the oars. We were nearly smashed up on the shore several times. I kept fairly close to the shore because I was afraid of getting lost on the lake and losing time. Sometimes we were so close we could see a row of trees and the road along the shore with the mountains behind. The rain stopped and the wind drove the clouds so that the moon shone through and looking back I could see the long dark point of Castagnola and the lake with white- caps and beyond, the moon on the high snow mountains. Then the clouds came over the moon again and the mountains and the lake were gone, but it was much lighter than it had been before and we could see the shore. I could see it too clearly and pulled out where they would not see the boat if there were custom guards along the Pallanza road. When the moon came out again we could see white villas on the shore on the slopes of the mountain and the white road where it showed through the trees. All the time I was rowing.

The lake widened and across it on the shore at the foot of the mountains on the other side we saw a few lights that should be Luino. I saw a wedgelike gap between the mountains on the other shore and I thought that must be Luino. If it was we were making good time. I pulled in the oars and lay back on the seat. I was very, very tired of rowing. My arms and shoulders and back ached and my hands were sore.

'I could hold the umbrella,' Catherine said. 'We could sail with that with the wind.'

'Can you steer?'

'I think so.'

'You take this oar and hold it under your arm close to the side of the boat and steer and I'll hold the umbrella.' I went back to the stern and showed her how to hold the oar. I took the big umbrella the porter had given me and sat facing the bow and opened it. It opened with a clap. I held it on both sides, sitting astride the handle hooked over the seat. The wind was full in it and I felt the boat suck forward while I held as hard as I could to the two edges. It pulled hard. The boat was moving fast.

'We're going beautifully,' Catherine said. All I could see was umbrella ribs. The umbrella strained and pulled and I felt us driving along with it. I braced my feet and held back on it, then suddenly, it buckled; I felt a rib snap on my forehead, I tried to grab the top that was bending with the wind and the whole thing buckled and went inside out and I was astride the handle of an inside-out, ripped umbrella, where I had been holding a wind-filled pulling sail. I unhooked the handle from the seat, laid the umbrella in the bow and went back to Catherine for the oar. She was laughing. She took my hand and kept on laughing.

'What's the matter?' I took the oar.

'You looked so funny holding that thing.'

'I suppose so.'

'Don't be cross, darling. It was awfully funny. You looked about twenty feet broad and very affectionate holding the umbrella by the edges—" she choked.

'I'll row.'

'Take a rest and a drink. It's a grand night and we've come a long way.'

'I have to keep the boat out of the trough of the waves.'

'I'll get you a drink. Then rest a little while, darling.'

I held the oars up and we sailed with them. Catherine was opening the bag. She handed me the brandy bottle. I pulled the cork with my pocket-knife and took a long drink. It was smooth and hot and the heat went all through me and I felt warmed and cheerful. 'It's lovely brandy,' I said. The moon was under again but I could see the shore. There seemed to be another point going out a long way ahead into the lake.

'Are you warm enough, Cat?'

'I'm splendid. I'm a little stiff.'

'Bail out that water and you can put your feet down.'

Then I rowed and listened to the oarlocks and the dip and scrape of the bailing tin under the stern seat.

'Would you give me the bailer?' I said. 'I want a drink.'

'It's awful dirty.'

'That's all right. I'll rinse it.'

I heard Catherine rinsing it over the side. Then she handed it to me dipped full of water. I was thirsty after the brandy and the water was icy cold, so cold it made my teeth ache. I looked toward the shore. We were closer to the long point. There were lights in the bay ahead.

'Thanks,' I said and handed back the tin pail.

'You're ever so welcome,' Catherine said. 'There's much more if you want it.'

'Don't you want to eat something?'

'No. I'll be hungry in a little while. We'll save it till then.'

'All right.'

What looked like a point ahead was a long high headland. I went further out in the lake to pass it. The lake was much narrower now. The moon was out again and the guardia di finanza could have seen our boat black on the water if they had been watching.

'How are you, Cat?' I asked. 'I'm all right. Where are we?'

'I don't think we have more than about eight miles more.'

'That's a long way to row, you poor sweet. Aren't you dead?'

'No. I'm all right. My hands are sore is all.'

We went on up the lake. There was a break in the mountains on the right bank, a flattening-out with a low shore line that I thought must be Cannobio. I stayed a long way out because it was from now on that we ran the most danger of meeting guardia. There was a high dome-capped mountain on the other shore a way ahead. I was tired. It was no great distance to row but when you were out of condition it had been a long way. I knew I had to pass that mountain and go up the lake at least five miles further before we would be in Swiss water. The moon was almost down now but before it went down the sky clouded over again and it was very dark. I stayed well out in the lake, rowing awhile, then resting and holding the oars so that the wind struck the blades.

'Let me row awhile,' Catherine said.

'I don't think you ought to.'

'Nonsense. It would be good for me. It would keep me from being too stiff.'

'I don't think you should, Cat.'

'Nonsense. Rowing in moderation is very good for the pregnant lady.'

'All right, you row a little moderately. I'll go back, then you come up. Hold on to both gunwales when you come up.'

I sat in the stern with my coat on and the collar turned up and watched Catherine row. She rowed very well but the oars were too long and bothered her. I opened the bag and ate a couple of sandwiches and took a drink of the brandy. It made everything much better and I took another drink.

'Tell me when you're tired,' I said. Then a little later, 'Watch out the oar doesn't pop you in the tummy.'

'If it did'—Catherine said between strokes—'life might be much simpler.'

I took another drink of the brandy.

'How are you going?'

'All right.'

'Tell me when you want to stop.'

'All right.'

I took another drink of the brandy, then took hold of the two gunwales of the boat and moved forward.

'No. I'm going beautifully.'

'Go on back to the stern. I've had a grand rest.'

For a while, with the brandy, I rowed easily and steadily. Then I began to catch crabs and soon I was just chopping along again with a thin brown taste of bile from having rowed too hard after the brandy.

'Give me a drink of water, will you?' I said.

'That's easy,' Catherine said.

Before daylight it started to drizzle. The wind was down or we were protected by mountains that bounded the curve the lake had made. When I knew daylight was coming I settled down and rowed hard. I did not know where we were and I wanted to get into the Swiss part of the lake. When it was beginning to be daylight we were quite close to the shore. I could see the rocky shore and the trees.

'What's that?' Catherine said. I rested on the oars and listened. It was a motor boat chugging out on the lake. I pulled close up to the shore and lay quiet. The chugging came closer; then we saw the motor boat in the rain a little astern of us. There were four guardia di finanza in the stern, their alpini hats pulled down, their cape collars turned up and their carbines slung across their backs. They all looked sleepy so early in the morning. I could see the yellow on their hats and the yellow marks on their cape collars. The motor boat chugged on and out of sight in the rain.

I pulled out into the lake. If we were that close to the border I did not want to be hailed by a sentry along the road. I stayed out where I could just see the shore and rowed on for three quarters of an hour in the rain. We heard a motor boat once more but I kept quiet until the noise of the engine went away across the lake.

'I think we're in Switzerland, Cat,' I said.

'Really?'

'There's no way to know until we see Swiss troops.'

'Or the Swiss navy.'

'The Swiss navy's no joke for us. That last motor boat we heard was probably the Swiss navy.'

'If we're in Switzerland let's have a big breakfast. They have wonderful rolls and butter and jam in Switzerland.'

It was clear daylight now and a fine rain was falling. The wind was still blowing outside up the lake and we could see the tops of the white-caps going away from us and up the lake. I was sure we were in Switzerland now. There were many houses back in the trees from the shore and up the shore a way was a village with stone houses, some villas on the hills and a church. I had been looking at the road that skirted the shore for guards but did not see any. The road came quite close to the lake now and I saw a soldier coming out of a café on the road. He wore a gray-green uniform and a helmet like the Germans.

He had a healthy-looking face and a little toothbrush mustache. He looked at us. 'Wave to him,' I said to Catherine. She waved and the soldier smiled embarrassedly and gave a wave of his hand. I eased up rowing. We were passing the waterfront of the village.

'We must be well inside the border,' I said.

'We want to be sure, darling. We don't want them to turn us back at the frontier.' 'The frontier is a long way back. I think this is the customs town. I'm pretty sure it's Brissago.'

'Won't there be Italians there? There are always both sides at a customs town.'

'Not in war-time. I don't think they let the Italians cross the frontier.'

It was a nice-looking little town. There were many fishing boats along the quay and nets were spread on racks. There was a fine November rain falling but it looked cheerful and clean even with the rain.

'Should we land then and have breakfast?'

'All right.'

I pulled hard on the left oar and came in close, then straightened out when we were close to the quay and brought the boat alongside. I pulled in the oars, took hold of an iron ring, stepped up on the wet stone and was in Switzerland. I tied the boat and held my hand down to Catherine.

'Come on up, Cat. It's a grand feeling.'

'What about the bags?'

'Leave them in the boat.'

Catherine stepped up and we were in Switzerland together.

'What a lovely country,' she said.

'Isn't it grand?'

'Let's go and have breakfast!'

'Isn't it a grand country? I love the way it feels under my shoes.'

'I'm so stiff I can't feel it very well. But it feels like a splendid country. Darling, do you realize we're here and out of that bloody place?'

'I do. I really do. I've never realized anything before.'

'Look at the houses. Isn't this a fine square? There's a place we can get breakfast.'

'Isn't the rain fine? They never had rain like this in Italy. It's cheerful rain.'

'And we're here, darling! Do you realize we're here?'

We went inside the café and sat down at a clean wooden table. We were cockeyed excited. A splendid clean-looking woman with an apron came and asked us what we wanted.

'Rolls and jam and coffee,' Catherine said.
'I'm sorry, we haven't any rolls in war-time.'
'Bread then.'
'I can make you some toast.'
'All right.'
'I want some eggs fried too.'
'How many eggs for the gentleman?'
'Three.'
'Take four, darling.'
'Four eggs.'

The woman went away. I kissed Catherine and held her hand very tight. We looked at each other and at the café.

'Darling, darling, isn't it lovely?'
'It's grand,' I said.
'I don't mind there not being rolls,' Catherine said. 'I thought about them all night.

But I don't mind it. I don't mind it at all.'
'I suppose pretty soon they will arrest us.'
'Never mind, darling. We'll have breakfast first. You won't mind being arrested after breakfast. And then there's nothing they can do to us. We're British and American citizens in good standing.'
'You have a passport, haven't you?'
'Of course. Oh let's not talk about it. Let's be happy.'
'I couldn't be any happier,' I said. A fat gray cat with a tail that lifted like a plume crossed the floor to our table and curved against my leg to purr each time she rubbed. I reached down and stroked her. Catherine smiled at me very happily. 'Here comes the coffee,' she said.

They arrested us after breakfast. We took a little walk through the village then went down to the quay to get our bags. A soldier was standing guard over the boat.

'Is this your boat?'
'Yes.'
'Where do you come from?'
'Up the lake.'
'Then I have to ask you to come with me.'
'How about the bags?'
'You can carry the bags.'

I carried the bags and Catherine walked beside me and the soldier walked along behind us to the old custom house. In the custom house a lieutenant, very thin and military, questioned us.

'What nationality are you?'
'American and British.'
'Let me see your passports.'
I gave him mine and Catherine got hers out of her handbag.

He examined them for a long time.

'Why do you enter Switzerland this way in a boat?'

'I am a sportsman,' I said. 'Rowing is my great sport. I always row when I get a chance.'

'Why do you come here?'

'For the winter sport. We are tourists and we want to do the winter sport.'

'This is no place for winter sport.'

'We know it. We want to go where they have the winter sport.'

'What have you been doing in Italy?'

'I have been studying architecture. My cousin has been studying art.'

'Why do you leave there?'

'We want to do the winter sport. With the war going on you cannot study architecture.'

'You will please stay where you are,' the lieutenant said. He went back into the building with our passports.

'You're splendid, darling,' Catherine said. 'Keep on the same track. You want to do the winter sport.'

'Do you know anything about art?'

'Rubens,' said Catherine.

'Large and fat,' I said.

'Titian,' Catherine said.

'Titian-haired,' I said. 'How about Mantegna?'

'Don't ask hard ones,' Catherine said. 'I know him though—very bitter.'

'Very bitter,' I said. 'Lots of nail holes.'

'You see I'll make you a fine wife,' Catherine said. 'I'll be able to talk art with your customers.'

'Here he comes,' I said. The thin lieutenant came down the length of the custom house, holding our passports.

'I will have to send you into Locarno,' he said. 'You can get a carriage and a soldier will go in with you.'

'All right,' I said. 'What about the boat?'

'The boat is confiscated. What have you in those bags?'

He went all through the two bags and held up the quarterbottle of brandy. 'Would you join me in a drink?' I asked.

'No thank you.' He straightened up. 'How much money have you?'

'Twenty-five hundred lire.'

He was favorably impressed. 'How much has your cousin?'

Catherine had a little over twelve hundred lire. The lieutenant was pleased. His attitude toward us became less haughty.

'If you are going for winter sports,' he said, 'Wengen is the place. My father has a very fine hotel at Wengen. It is open all the time.'

'That's splendid,' I said. 'Could you give me the name?'

'I will write it on a card.' He handed me the card very politely.

'The soldier will take you into Locarno. He will keep your passports. I regret this but it is necessary. I have good hopes they will give you a visa or a police permit at Locarno.'

He handed the two passports to the soldier and carrying the bags we started into the village to order a carriage. 'Hi,' the lieutenant called to the soldier. He said something in a German dialect to him. The soldier slung his rifle on his back and picked up the bags.

'It's a great country,' I said to Catherine.

'It's so practical.'

'Thank you very much,' I said to the lieutenant. He waved his hand.

'Service!' he said. We followed our guard into the village.

We drove to Locarno in a carriage with the soldier sitting on the front seat with the driver. At Locarno we did not have a bad time. They questioned us but they were polite because we had passports and money. I do not think they believed a word of the story and I thought it was silly but it was like a law-court. You did not want something reasonable, you wanted something technical and then stuck to it without explanations. But we had passports and we would spend the money. So they gave us provisional visas.

At any time this visa might be withdrawn. We were to report to the police wherever we went.

Could we go wherever we wanted? Yes. Where did we want to go?

'Where do you want to go, Cat?'

'Montreux.'

'It is a very nice place,' the official said. 'I think you will like that place.'

'Here at Locarno is a very nice place,' another official said. 'I am sure you would like it here very much at Locarno. Locarno is a very attractive place.'

'We would like some place where there is winter sport.'

'There is no winter sport at Montreux.'

'I beg your pardon,' the other official said. 'I come from Montreux. There is very certainly winter sport on the Montreux Oberland Bernois railway. It would be false for you to deny that.'

'I do not deny it. I simply said there is no winter sport at Montreux.'

'I question that,' the other official said. 'I question that statement.'

'I hold to that statement.'

'I question that statement. I myself have luge-ed into the streets of Montreux. I have done it not once but several times. Luge-ing is certainly winter sport.'

The other official turned to me.

'Is luge-ing your idea of winter sport, sir? I tell you you would be very comfortable here in Locarno. You would find the climate healthy, you would find the environs attractive. You would like it very much.'

'The gentleman has expressed a wish to go to Montreux.'

'What is luge-ing?' I asked.

'You see he has never even heard of luge-ing!'

That meant a great deal to the second official. He was pleased by that.

'Luge-ing,' said the first official, 'is tobogganing.'

'I beg to differ,' the other official shook his head. 'I must differ again. The toboggan is very different from the luge. The toboggan is constructed in Canada of flat laths. The luge is a common sled with runners. Accuracy means something.'

'Couldn't we toboggan?' I asked.

'Of course you could toboggan,' the first official said. 'You could toboggan very well. Excellent Canadian toboggans are sold in Montreux. Ochs Brothers sell toboggans. They import their own toboggans.'

The second official turned away. 'Tobogganing,' he said, 'requires a special piste.

You could not toboggan into the streets of Montreux. Where are you stopping here?' 'We don't know,' I said. 'We just drove in from Brissago. The carriage is outside.'

'You make no mistake in going to Montreux,' the first official said. 'You will find the climate delightful and beautiful. You will have no distance to go for winter sport.'

'If you really want winter sport,' the second official said, 'you will go to the Engadine or to Mürren. I must protest against your being advised to go to Montreux for the winter sport.'

'At Les Avants above Montreux there is excellent winter sport of every sort.' The champion of Montreux glared at his colleague.

'Gentlemen,' I said, 'I am afraid we must go. My cousin is very tired. We will go tentatively to Montreux.'

'I congratulate you,' the first official shook my hand.

'I believe that you will regret leaving Locarno,' the second official said. 'At any rate you will report to the police at Montreux.'

'There will be no unpleasantness with the police,' the first official assured me. 'You will find all the inhabitants extremely courteous and friendly.'

'Thank you both very much,' I said. 'We appreciate your advice very much.'

'Good-by,' Catherine said. 'Thank you both very much.'

They bowed us to the dooi the champion of Locarno a little coldly. We went down the steps and into the carriage.

'My God, darling,' Catherine said. 'Couldn't we have gotten away any sooner?' I gave the name of a hotel one of the officials had recommended to the driver. He picked up the reins.

'You've forgotten the army,' Catherine said. The soldier was standing by the carriage. I gave him a ten-lira note. 'I have no Swiss money yet,' I said. He thanked me, saluted and went off. The carriage started and we drove to the hotel.

'How did you happen to pick out Montreux?' I asked Catherine. 'Do you really want to go there?'

'It was the first place I could think of,' she said. 'It's not a bad place. We can find some place up in the mountains.'

'Are you sleepy?'

'I'm asleep right now.'

'We'll get a good sleep. Poor Cat, you had a long bad night.'

'I had a lovely time,' Catherine said. 'Especially when you sailed with the umbrella.'

'Can you realize we're in Switzerland?'

'No, I'm afraid I'll wake up and it won't be true.'

'I am too.'

'It is true, isn't it, darling? I'm not just driving down to the stazione in Milan to see you off.'

'I hope not.'

'Don't say that. It frightens me. Maybe that's where we're going.'

'I'm so groggy I don't know,' I said.

'Let me see your hands.'

I put them out. They were both blistered raw.

'There's no hole in my side,' I said.

'Don't be sacrilegious.'

I felt very tired and vague in the head. The exhilaration was all gone. The carriage was going along the Street.

'Poor hands,' Catherine said.

'Don't touch them,' I said. 'By God I don't know where we are. Where are we going, driver?' The driver stopped his horse.

'To the Hotel Metropole. Don't you want to go there?'

'Yes,' I said. 'It's all right, Cat.'

'It's all right, darling. Don't be upset. We'll get a good sleep and you won't feel groggy to-morrow.'

'I get pretty groggy,' I said. 'It's like a comic opera to-day. Maybe I'm hungry.'

'You're just tired, darling. You'll be fine.' The carriage pulled up before the hotel.

Some one came out to take our bags.

'I feel all right,' I said. We were down on the pavement going into the hotel.

'I know you'll be all right. You're just tired. You've been up a long time.'

'Anyhow we're here.'

'Yes, we're really here.'

We followed the boy with the bags into the hotel.

BOOK FIVE

38

That fall the snow came very late. We lived in a brown wooden house in the pine trees on the side of the mountain and at night there was frost so that there was thin ice over the water in the two pitchers on the dresser in the morning. Mrs.

Guttingen came into the room early in the morning to shut the windows and started a fire in the tall porcelain stove. The pine wood crackled and sparked and then the fire roared in the stove and the second time Mrs. Guttingen came into the room she brought big chunks of wood for the fire and a pitcher of hot water. When the room was warm she brought in breakfast. Sitting up in bed eating breakfast we could see the lake and the mountains across the lake on the French side. There was snow on the tops of the mountains and the lake was a gray steel- blue.

Outside, in front of the chalet a road went up the mountain. The wheel ruts and ridges were iron hard with the frost, and the road climbed steadily through the forest and up and around the mountain to where there were meadows, and barns and cabins in the meadows at the edge of the woods looking across the valley. The valley was deep and there was a stream at the bottom that flowed down into the lake and when the wind blew across the valley you could hear the stream in the rocks.

Sometimes we went off the road and on a path through the pine forest. The floor of the forest was soft to walk on; the frost did not harden it as it did the road. But we did not mind the hardness of the road because we had nails in the soles and heels of our boots and the heel nails bit on the frozen ruts and with nailed boots it was good walking on the road and invigorating. But it was lovely walking in the woods.

In front of the house where we lived the mountain went down steeply to the little plain along the lake and we sat on the porch of the house in the sun and saw the winding of the road down the mountain-side and the terraced vineyards on the side of the lower mountain, the vines all dead now for the winter and the fields divided by stone walls, and below the vineyards the houses of the town on the narrow plain along the lake shore.

There was an island with two trees on the lake and the trees looked like the double sails of a fishing-boat. The mountains were sharp and steep on the other side of the lake and down at the end of the lake was the plain of the Rhone Valley flat between the two ranges of mountains; and up the valley where the mountains cut it off was the Dent du Midi. It was a high snowy mountain and it dominated the valley but it was so far away that it did not make a shadow.

When the sun was bright we ate lunch on the porch but the rest of the time we ate upstairs in a small room with plain wooden walls and a big stove in the corner. We bought books and magazines in the town and a copy of 'Hoyle' and learned many two-handed card games. The small room with the stove was our living-room. There were two comfortable chairs and a table for books and magazines and we played cards on the dining-table when it was cleared away. Mr. and Mrs. Guttingen lived downstairs and we would hear them talking sometimes in the evening and they were very happy together too. He had been a headwaiter and she had worked as maid in the same hotel and they had saved their money to buy this place. They had a son who was studying to be a headwaiter. He was at a hotel in Zurich. Downstairs there was a parlor where they sold wine and beer, and sometimes in the evening we would hear carts stop outside on the road and men come up the steps to go in the parlor to drink wine.

There was a box of wood in the hall outside the living-room and I kept up the fire from it. But we did not stay up very late. We went to bed in the dark in the big bedroom and when I was undressed I opened the windows and saw the night and the cold stars and the pine trees below the window and then got into bed as fast as I could. It was lovely in bed with the air so cold and clear and the night outside the window. We slept well and if I woke in the night I knew it was from only one cause and I would shift the feather bed over, very softly so that Catherine would not be wakened and then go back to sleep again, warm and with the new lightness of thin covers. The war seemed as far away as the football games of some one else's college. But I knew from the papers that they were still fighting in the mountains because the snow would not come.

Sometimes we walked down the mountain into Montreux. There was a path went down the mountain but it was steep and so usually we took the road and walked down on the wide hard road between fields and then below between the stone walls of the vineyards and on down between the houses of the villages along the way. There were three villages; Chernex, Fontanivent, and the other I forget. Then along the road we passed an old square-built stone château on a ledge on the side of the mountain-side with the terraced fields of vines, each vine tied to a stick to hold it up, the vines dry and brown and the earth ready for the snow and the lake down below flat and gray as steel. The road went down a long grade below the château and then turned to the right and went down very steeply and paved with cobbles, into Montreux.

We did not know any one in Montreux. We walked along beside the lake and saw the swans and the many gulls and terns that flew up when you came close and screamed while they looked down at the water. Out on the lake there were flocks of grebes, small and dark, and leaving trails in the water when they swam.

In the town we walked along the main street and looked in the windows of the shops. There were many big hotels that were closed but most of the shops were open and the people were very glad to see us. There was a fine coiffeur's place where Catherine went to have her hair done. The woman who ran it was very cheerful and the only person we knew in Montreux. While Catherine was there I went up to a beer place and drank dark Munich beer and read the papers. I read the Corriere della Sera and the English and American papers from Paris. All the advertisements were blacked out, supposedly to prevent communication in that way with the enemy. The papers were bad reading.

Everything was going very badly everywhere. I sat back in the corner with a heavy mug of dark beer and an opened glazed-paper package of pretzels and ate the pretzels for the salty flavor and the good way they made the beer taste and read about disaster. I thought Catherine would come by but she did not come, so I hung the papers back on the rack, paid for my beer and went up the street to look for her. The day was cold and dark and wintry and the stone of the houses looked cold. Catherine was still in the hairdresser's shop. The woman was waving her hair. I sat in the little booth and watched. It was exciting to watch and Catherine smiled and talked to me and my voice was a little thick from being excited. The tongs made a pleasant clicking sound and I could see Catherine in three mirrors and it was pleasant and warm in the booth. Then the woman put up Catherine's hair, and Catherine looked in the mirror and changed it a little, taking out and putting in pins; then stood up. 'I'm sorry to have taken such a long time.'

'Monsieur was very interested. Were you not, monsieur?' the woman smiled.

'Yes,' I said.

We went out and up the street. It was cold and wintry and the wind was blowing. 'Oh, darling, I love you so,' I said.

'Don't we have a fine time?' Catherine said. 'Look. Let's go some place and have beer instead of tea. It's very good for young Catherine. It keeps her small.'

'Young Catherine,' I said. 'That loafer.'

'She's been very good,' Catherine said. 'She makes very little trouble. The doctor says beer will be good for me and keep her small.'

'If you keep her small enough and she's a boy, maybe he will be a jockey.'

'I suppose if we really have this child we ought to get married,' Catherine said. We were in the beer place at the corner table. It was getting dark outside. It was still early but the day was dark and the dusk was coming early.

'Let's get married now,' I said.

'No,' Catherine said. 'It's too embarrassing now. I show too plainly. I won't go before any one and be married in this state.'

'I wish we'd gotten married.'

'I suppose it would have been better. But when could we, darling?'

'I don't know.'

'I know one thing. I'm not going to be married in this splendid matronly state.'

'You're not matronly.'

'Oh yes, I am, darling. The hairdresser asked me if this was our first. I lied and said no, we had two boys and two girls.'

'When will we be married?'

'Any time after I'm thin again. We want to have a splendid wedding with every one thinking what a handsome young couple.'

'And you're not worried?'

'Darling, why should I be worried? The only time I ever felt badly was when I felt like a whore in Milan and that only lasted seven minutes and besides it was the room furnishings. Don't I make you a good wife?'

'You're a lovely wife.'

'Then don't be too technical, darling. I'll marry you as soon as I'm thin again.'

'All right.'

'Do you think I ought to drink another beer? The doctor said I was rather narrow in the hips and it's all for the best if we keep young Catherine small.'

'What else did he say?' I was worried.

'Nothing. I have a wonderful blood-pressure, darling. He admired my blood-pressure greatly.'

'What did he say about you being too narrow in the hips?'

'Nothing. Nothing at all. He said I shouldn't ski.'

'Quite right.'

'He said it was too late to start if I'd never done it before. He said I could ski if I wouldn't fall down.'

'He's just a big-hearted joker.'

'Really he was very nice. We'll have him when the baby comes.'

'Did you ask him if you ought to get married?'

'No. I told him we'd been married four years. You see, darling, if I marry you I'll be an American and any time we're married under American law the child is legitimate.'

'Where did you find that out?'

'In the New York World Almanac in the library.'

'You're a grand girl.'

'I'll be very glad to be an American and we'll go to America won't we, darling? I want to see Niagara Falls.'

'You're a fine girl.'

'There's something else I want to see but I can't remember it.'

'The stockyards?'

'No. I can't remember it.'

'The Woolworth building?'

'No.'

'The Grand Canyon?'

'No. But I'd like to see that.'

'What was it?'

'The Golden Gate! That's what I want to see. Where is the Golden Gate?'

'San Francisco.'

'Then let's go there. I want to see San Francisco anyway.'

'All right. We'll go there.'

'Now let's go up the mountain. Should we? Can we get the M.O.B.?'

'There's a train a little after five.'

'Let's get that.'

'All right. I'll drink one more beer first.'

When we went out to go up the street and climb the stairs to the station it was very cold. A cold wind was coming down the Rhone Valley. There were lights in the shop windows and we climbed the steep stone stairway to the upper street, then up another stairs to the station. The electric train was there waiting, all the lights on. There was a dial that showed when it left. The clock hands pointed to ten minutes after five. I looked at the station clock. It was five minutes after. As we got on board I saw the motorman and conductor coming out of the station wine-shop. We sat down and opened the window. The train was electrically heated and stuffy but fresh cold air came in through the window.

'Are you tired, Cat?' I asked.

'No. I feel splendid.'

'It isn't a long ride.'

'I like the ride,' she said. 'Don't worry about me, darling. I feel fine.'

Snow did not come until three days before Christmas. We woke one morning and it was snowing. We stayed in bed with the fire roaring in the stove and watched the snow fall. Mrs. Guttingen took away the breakfast trays and put more wood in the stove. It was a big snow storm. She said it had started about midnight. I went to the window and looked out but could not see across the road. It was blowing and snowing wildly. I went back to bed and we lay and talked.

'I wish I could ski,' Catherine said. 'It's rotten not to be able to ski.'

'We'll get a bobsled and come down the road. That's no worse for you than riding in a car.'

'Won't it be rough?'

'We can see.'

'I hope it won't be too rough.'

'After a while we'll take a walk in the snow.'

'Before lunch,' Catherine said, 'so we'll have a good appetite.'

'I'm always hungry.'

'So am I.'

We went out in the snow but it was drifted so that we could not walk far. I went ahead and made a trail down to the station but when we reached there we had gone far enough. The snow was blowing so we could hardly see and we went into the little inn by the station and swept each other off with a broom and sat on a bench and had vermouths.

'It is a big storm,' the barmaid said.

'Yes.'

'The snow is very late this year.'

'Yes.'

'Could I eat a chocolate bar?' Catherine asked. 'Or is it too close to lunch? I'm always hungry.'

'Go on and eat one,' I said.

'I'll take one with filberts,' Catherine said.

'They are very good,' the girl said, 'I like them the best.'

'I'll have another vermouth,' I said.

When we came out to start back up the road our track was filled in by the snow.

There were only faint indentations where the holes had been. The snow blew in our faces so we could hardly see. We brushed off and went in to have lunch. Mr. Guttingen served the lunch.

'To-morrow there will be ski-ing,' he said. 'Do you ski, Mr. Henry?'

'No. But I want to learn.'

'You will learn very easily. My boy will be here for Christmas and he will teach you.'

'That's fine. When does he come?'

'To-morrow night.'

When we were sitting by the stove in the little room after lunch looking out the window at the snow coming down Catherine said, 'Wouldn't you like to go on a trip somewhere by yourself, darling, and be with men and ski?'

'No. Why should I?'

'I should think sometimes you would want to see other people besides me.'

'Do you want to see other people?'

'No.'

'Neither do I.'

'I know. But you're different. I'm having a child and that makes me contented not to do anything. I know I'm awfully stupid now and I talk too much and I think you ought to get away so you won't be tired of me.'

'Do you want me to go away?'

'No. I want you to stay.' 'That's what I'm going to do.'

'Come over here,' she said. 'I want to feel the bump on your head. It's a big bump.' She ran her finger over it. 'Darling, would you like to grow a beard?'

'Would you like me to?'

'It might be fun. I'd like to see you with a beard.'

'All right. I'll grow one. I'll start now this minute. It's a good idea. It will give me something to do.'

'Are you worried because you haven't anything to do?'

'No. I like it. I have a fine life. Don't you?'

'I have a lovely life. But I was afraid because I'm big now that maybe I was a bore to you.'

'Oh, Cat. You don't know how crazy I am about you.'

'This way?'

'Just the way you are. I have a fine time. Don't we have a good life?'

'I do, but I thought maybe you were restless.'

'No. Sometimes I wonder about the front and about people I know but I don't worry.

I don't think about anything much.'

'Who do you wonder about?'

'About Rinaldi and the priest and lots of people I know. But I don't think about them much. I don't want to think about the war. I'm through with it.'

'What are you thinking about now?'

'Nothing.'

'Yes you were. Tell me.'

'I was wondering whether Rinaldi had the syphilis.'

'Was that all?'

'Yes.'

'Has he the syphilis?'
'I don't know.'
'I'm glad you haven't. Did you ever have anything like that?'
'I had gonorrhea.'
'I don't want to hear about it. Was it very painful, darling?'
'Very.'
'I wish I'd had it.'
'No you don't.'
'I do. I wish I'd had it to be like you. I wish I'd stayed with all your girls so I could make fun of them to you.'
'That's a pretty picture.'
'It's not a pretty picture you having gonorrhea.'
'I know it. Look at it snow now.'
'I'd rather look at you. Darling, why don't you let your hair grow?'
'How grow?'
'Just grow a little longer.'
'It's long enough now.'
'No, let it grow a little longer and I could cut mine and we'd be just alike only one of us blonde and one of us dark.'
'I wouldn't let you cut yours.'
'It would be fun. I'm tired of it. It's an awful nuisance in the bed at night.'
'I like it.'
'Wouldn't you like it short?'
'I might. I like it the way it is.'
'It might be nice short. Then we'd both be alike. Oh, darling, I want you so much I want to be you too.'
'You are. We're the same one.'
'I know it. At night we are.'
'The nights are grand.'
'I want us to be all mixed up. I don't want you to go away. I just said that. You go if you want to. But hurry right back. Why, darling, I don't live at all when I'm not with you.'
'I won't ever go away,' I said. 'I'm no good when you're not there. I haven't any life at all any more.'
'I want you to have a life. I want you to have a fine life. But we'll have it together, won't we?'
'And now do you want me to stop growing my beard or let it go on?'
'Go on. Grow it. It will be exciting. Maybe it will be done for New Year's.'
'Now do you want to play chess?'
'I'd rather play with you.'
'No. Let's play chess.'
'And afterward we'll play?'
'Yes.'

'All right.'

I got out the chess-board and arranged the pieces. It was still snowing hard outside.

One time in the night I woke up and knew that Catherine was awake too. The moon was shining in the window and made shadows on the bed from the bars on the window- panes.

'Are you awake, sweetheart?'

'Yes. Can't you sleep?'

'I just woke up thinking about how I was nearly crazy when I first met you. Do you remember?'

'You were just a little crazy.'

'I'm never that way any more. I'm grand now. You say grand so sweetly. Say grand.'

'Grand.'

'Oh, you're sweet. And I'm not crazy now. I'm just very, very, very happy.'

'Go on to sleep,' I said.

'All right. Let's go to sleep at exactly the same moment.'

'All right.'

But we did not. I was awake for quite a long time thinking about things and watching Catherine sleeping, the moonlight on her face. Then I went to sleep, too.

39

By the middle of January I had a beard and the winter had settled into bright cold days and hard cold nights. We could walk on the roads again. The snow was packed hard and smooth by the hay-sleds and wood-sledges and the logs that were hauled down the mountain. The snow lay over all the country, down almost to Montreux. The mountains on the other side of the lake were all white and the plain of the Rhone Valley was covered.

We took long walks on the other side of the mountain to the Bains de l'Alliaz. Catherine wore hobnailed boots and a cape and carried a stick with a sharp steel point. She did not look big with the cape and we would not walk too fast but stopped and sat on logs by the roadside to rest when she was tired.

There was an inn in the trees at the Bains de l'Alliaz where the woodcutters stopped to drink, and we sat inside warmed by the stove and drank hot red wine with spices and lemon in it. They called it gluhwein and it was a good thing to warm you and to celebrate with. The inn was dark and smoky inside and afterward when you went out the cold air came sharply into your lungs and numbed the edge of your nose as you inhaled. We looked back at the inn with light coming from the windows and the woodcutters' horses stamping and jerking their heads outside to keep warm. There was frost on the hairs of their muzzles and their breathing made plumes of frost in the air. Going up the road toward home the road was smooth and slippery for a while and the ice orange from the horses until the wood-hauling track turned off. Then the road was clean-packed snow and led through the woods, and twice coming home in the evening, we saw foxes.

It was a fine country and every time that we went out it was fun.

'You have a splendid beard now,' Catherine said. 'It looks just like the woodcutters'. Did you see the man with the tiny gold earrings?'

'He's a chamois hunter,' I said. 'They wear them because they say it makes them hear better.'

'Really? I don't believe it. I think they wear them to show they are chamois hunters.

Are there chamois near here?'

'Yes, beyond the Dent de Jaman.'

'It was fun seeing the fox.'

'When he sleeps he wraps that tail around him to keep warm.'

'It must be a lovely feeling.'

'I always wanted to have a tail like that. Wouldn't it be fun if we had brushes like a fox?'

'It might be very difficult dressing.'

'We'd have clothes made, or live in a country where it wouldn't make any difference.'

'We live in a country where nothing makes any difference. Isn't it grand how we never see any one? You don't want to see people do you, darling?'

'No.'

'Should we sit here just a minute? I'm a little bit tired.'

We sat close together on the logs. Ahead the road went down through the forest. 'She won't come between us, will she? The little brat.'

'No. We won't let her.' 'How are we for money?'

'We have plenty. They honored the last sight draft.'

'Won't your family try and get hold of you now they know you're in Switzerland?'

'Probably. I'll write them something.'

'Haven't you written them?'

'No. Only the sight draft.'

'Thank God I'm not your family.'

'I'll send them a cable.'

'Don't you care anything about them?'

'I did, but we quarrelled so much it wore itself out.'

'I think I'd like them. I'd probably like them very much.'

'Let's not talk about them or I'll start to worry about them.' After a while I said, 'Let's go on if you're rested.'

'I'm rested.'

We went on down the road. It was dark now and the snow squeaked under our boots. The night was dry and cold and very clear.

'I love your beard,' Catherine said. 'It's a great success. It looks so stiff and fierce and it's very soft and a great pleasure.'

'Do you like it better than without?'

'I think so. You know, darling, I'm not going to cut my hair now until after young Catherine's born. I look too big and matronly now. But after she's born and I'm thin again I'm going to cut it and then I'll be a fine new and different girl for you. We'll go together and get it cut, or I'll go alone and come and surprise you.'

I did not say anything.

'You won't say I can't, will you?'

'No. I think it would be exciting.'

'Oh, you're so sweet. And maybe I'd look lovely, darling, and be so thin and exciting to you and you'll fall in love with me all over again.'

'Hell,' I said, 'I love you enough now. What do you want to do? Ruin me?'

'Yes. I want to ruin you.'

'Good,' I said, 'that's what I want too.'

40

We had a fine life. We lived through the months of January and February and the winter was very fine and we were very happy. There had been short thaws when the wind blew warm and the snow softened and the air felt like spring, but always the clear hard cold had come again and the winter had returned. In March came the first break in the winter. In the night it started raining. It rained on all morning and turned the snow to slush and made the mountain-side dismal. There were clouds over the lake and over the valley. It was raining high up the mountain. Catherine wore heavy overshoes and I wore Mr. Guttingen's rubber-boots and we walked to the station under an umbrella, through the slush and the running water that was washing the ice of the roads bare, to stop at the pub before lunch for a vermouth. Outside we could hear the rain.

'Do you think we ought to move into town?'

'What do you think?' Catherine asked.

'If the winter is over and the rain keeps up it won't be fun up here. How long is it before young Catherine?'

'About a month. Perhaps a little more.'

'We might go down and stay in Montreux.'

'Why don't we go to Lausanne? That's where the hospital is.'

'All right. But I thought maybe that was too big a town.'

'We can be as much alone in a bigger town and Lausanne might be nice.'

'When should we go?'

'I don't care. Whenever you want, darling. I don't want to leave here if you don't want.'

'Let's see how the weather turns out.'

It rained for three days. The snow was all gone now on the mountain-side below the station. The road was a torrent of muddy snow-water. It was too wet and slushy to go out. On the morning of the third day of rain we decided to go down into town.

'That is all right, Mr. Henry,' Guttingen said. 'You do not have to give me any notice. I did not think you would want to stay now the bad weather is come.'

'We have to be near the hospital anyway on account of Madame,' I said.

'I understand,' he said. 'Will you come back some time and stay, with the little one?'

'Yes, if you would have room.'

'In the spring when it is nice you could come and enjoy it. We could put the little one and the nurse in the big room that is closed now and you and Madame could have your same room looking out over the lake.'

'I'll write about coming,' I said. We packed and left on the train that went down after lunch. Mr. and Mrs. Guttingen came down to the station with us and he hauled our baggage down on a sled through the slush. They stood beside the station in the rain waving good-by.

'They were very sweet,' Catherine said.

'They were fine to us.'

We took the train to Lausanne from Montreux. Looking out the window toward where we had lived you could not see the mountains for the clouds. The train stopped in Vevey, then went on, passing the lake on one side and on the other the wet brown fields and the bare woods and the wet houses. We came into Lausanne and went into a medium-sized hotel to stay. It was still raining as we drove through the streets and into the carriage entrance of the hotel. The concierge with brass keys on his lapels, the elevator, the carpets on the floors, and the white washbowls with shining fixtures, the brass bed and the big comfortable bedroom all seemed very great luxury after the Guttingens. The windows of the room looked out on a wet garden with a wall topped by an iron fence.

Across the street, which sloped steeply, was another hotel with a similar wall and garden. I looked out at the rain falling in the fountain of the garden.

Catherine turned on all the lights and commenced unpacking. I ordered a whiskey and soda and lay on the bed and read the papers I had bought at the station. It was March, 1918, and the German offensive had started in France. I drank the whiskey and soda and read while Catherine unpacked and moved around the room.

'You know what I have to get, darling,' she said.

'What?'

'Baby clothes. There aren't many people reach my time without baby things.'

'You can buy them.'

'I know. That's what I'll do to-morrow. I'll find out what is necessary.'

'You ought to know. You were a nurse.'

'But so few of the soldiers had babies in the hospitals.'

'I did.'

She hit me with the pillow and spilled the whiskey and soda.

'I'll order you another,' she said. 'I'm sorry I spilled it.'
'There wasn't much left. Come on over to the bed.'
'No. I have to try and make this room look like something.'
'Like what?'
'Like our home.'
'Hang out the Allied flags.'
'Oh shut up.'
'Say it again.'
'Shut up.'
'You say it so cautiously,' I said. 'As though you didn't want to offend any one.'
'I don't.'
'Then come over to the bed.'
'All right.' She came and sat on the bed. 'I know I'm no fun for you, darling. I'm like a big flour-barrel.'
'No you're not. You're beautiful and you're sweet.'
'I'm just something very ungainly that you've married.'
'No you're not. You're more beautiful all the time.'
'But I will be thin again, darling.'
'You're thin now.'
'You've been drinking.'
'Just whiskey and soda.'
'There's another one coming,' she said. 'And then should we order dinner up here?'
'That will be good.'
'Then we won't go out, will we? We'll just stay in to-night.'
'And play,' I said.
'I'll drink some wine,' Catherine said. 'It won't hurt me. Maybe we can get some of our old white capri.'
'I know we can,' I said. 'They'll have Italian wines at a hotel this size.'
The waiter knocked at the door. He brought the whiskey in a glass with ice and beside the glass on a tray a small bottle of soda.
'Thank you,' I said. 'Put it down there. Will you please have dinner for two brought up here and two bottles of dry white capri in ice.'
'Do you wish to commence your dinner with soup?'
'Do you want soup, Cat?'
'Please.'
'Bring soup for one.'
'Thank you, sir.' He went out and shut the door. I went back to the papers and the war in the papers and poured the soda slowly over the ice into the whiskey. I would have to tell them not to put ice in the whiskey. Let them bring the ice separately. That way you could tell how much whiskey there was and it would not suddenly be too thin from the soda. I would get a bottle of whiskey and have them bring ice and soda. That was the sensible way. Good whiskey was

very pleasant. It was one of the pleasant parts of life.

'What are you thinking, darling?'

'About whiskey.'

'What about whiskey?'

'About how nice it is.'

Catherine made a face. 'All right,' she said.

We stayed at that hotel three weeks. It was not bad; the diningroom was usually empty and very often we ate in our room at night. We walked in the town and took the cogwheel railway down to Ouchy and walked beside the lake. The weather became quite warm and it was like spring. We wished we were back in the mountains but the spring weather lasted only a few days and then the cold rawness of the breaking-up of winter came again.

Catherine bought the things she needed for the baby, up in the town. I went to a gymnasium in the arcade to box for exercise. I usually went up there in the morning while Catherine stayed late in bed. On the days of false spring it was very nice, after boxing and taking a shower, to walk along the streets smelling the spring in the air and stop at a café to sit and watch the people and read the paper and drink a vermouth; then go down to the hotel and have lunch with Catherine. The professor at the boxing gymnasium wore mustaches and was very precise and jerky and went all to pieces if you started after him. But it was pleasant in the gym. There was good air and light and I worked quite hard, skipping rope, shadowboxing, doing abdominal exercises lying on the floor in a patch of sunlight that came through the open window, and occasionally scaring the professor when we boxed. I could not shadow-box in front of the narrow long mirror at first because it looked so strange to see a man with a beard boxing. But finally I just thought it was funny. I wanted to take off the beard as soon as I started boxing but Catherine did not want me to.

Sometimes Catherine and I went for rides out in the country in a carriage. It was nice to ride when the days were pleasant and we found two good places where we could ride out to eat. Catherine could not walk very far now and I loved to ride out along the country roads with her. When there was a good day we had a splendid time and we never had a bad time. We knew the baby was very close now and it gave us both a feeling as though something were hurrying us and we could not lose any time together.

41

One morning I awoke about three o'clock hearing Catherine stirring in the bed.

'Are you all right, Cat?'

'I've been having some pains, darling.'

'Regularly?'

'No, not very.'

'If you have them at all regularly we'll go to the hospital.'

I was very sleepy and went back to sleep. A little while later I woke again.

'Maybe you'd better call up the doctor,' Catherine said. 'I think maybe this is it.'

I went to the phone and called the doctor. 'How often are the pains coming?' he asked.

'How often are they coming, Cat?'

'I should think every quarter of an hour.'

'You should go to the hospital, then,' the doctor said. 'I will dress and go there right away myself.'

I hung up and called the garage near the station to send up a taxi. No one answered the phone for a long time. Then I finally got a man who promised to send up a taxi at once. Catherine was dressing. Her bag was all packed with the things she would need at the hospital and the baby things. Outside in the hall I rang for the elevator. There was no answer. I went downstairs. There was no one downstairs except the night-watchman. I brought the elevator up myself, put Catherine's bag in it, she stepped in and we went down. The night-watchman opened the door for us and we sat outside on the stone slabs beside the stairs down to the driveway and waited for the taxi. The night was clear and the stars were out. Catherine was very excited.

'I'm so glad it's started,' she said. 'Now in a little while it will be all over.'

'You're a good brave girl.'

'I'm not afraid. I wish the taxi would come, though.'

We heard it coming up the street and saw its headlights. It turned into the driveway and I helped Catherine in and the driver put the bag up in front.

'Drive to the hospital,' I said.

We went out of the driveway and started up the hill.

At the hospital we went in and I carried the bag. There was a woman at the desk who wrote down Catherine's name, age, address, relatives and religion, in a book. She said she had no religion and the woman drew a line in the space after that word. She gave her name as Catherine Henry.

'I will take you up to your room,' she said. We went up in an elevator. The woman stopped it and we stepped out and followed her down a hall. Catherine held tight to my arm.

'This is the room,' the woman said. 'Will you please undress and get into bed? Here is a night-gown for you to wear.'

'I have a night-gown,' Catherine said.

'It is better for you to wear this night-gown,' the woman said.

I went outside and sat on a chair in the hallway.

'You can come in now,' the woman said from the doorway. Catherine was lying in the narrow bed wearing a plain, square-cut night-gown that looked as though it were made of rough sheeting. She smiled at me.

'I'm having fine pains now,' she said. The woman was holding her wrist and timing the pains with a watch.

'That was a big one,' Catherine said. I saw it on her face.

'Where's the doctor?' I asked the woman.

'He's lying down sleeping. He will be here when he is needed.'

'I must do something for Madame, now,' the nurse said. 'Would you please step out again?'

I went out into the hall. It was a bare hall with two windows and closed doors all down the corridor. It smelled of hospital. I sat on the chair and looked at the floor and prayed for Catherine.

'You can come in,' the nurse said. I went in.

'Hello, darling,' Catherine said.

'How is it?'

'They are coming quite often now.' Her face drew up. Then she smiled.

'That was a real one. Do you want to put your hand on my back again, nurse?'

'If it helps you,' the nurse said.

'You go away, darling,' Catherine said. 'Go out and get something to eat. I may do this for a long time the nurse says.'

'The first labor is usually protracted,' the nurse said.

'Please go out and get something to eat,' Catherine said. 'I'm fine, really.'

'I'll stay awhile,' I said.

The pains came quite regularly, then slackened off. Catherine was very excited. When the pains were bad she called them good ones. When they started to fall off she was disappointed and ashamed.

'You go out, darling,' she said. 'I think you are just making me self-conscious.' Her face tied up. 'There. That was better. I so want to be a good wife and have this child without any foolishness. Please go and get some breakfast, darling, and then come back. I won't miss you. Nurse is splendid to me.'

'You have plenty of time for breakfast,' the nurse said.

'I'll go then. Good-by, sweet.'

'Good-by,' Catherine said, 'and have a fine breakfast for me too.'

'Where can I get breakfast?' I asked the nurse.

'There's a café down the street at the square,' she said. 'It should be open now.'

Outside it was getting light. I walked down the empty street to the café. There was a light in the window. I went in and stood at the zinc bar and an old man served me a glass of white wine and a brioche. The brioche was yesterday's. I dipped it in the wine and then drank a glass of coffee.

'What do you do at this hour?' the old man asked.

'My wife is in labor at the hospital.'

'So. I wish you good luck.' 'Give me another glass of wine.'

He poured it from the bottle slopping it over a little so some ran down on the zinc. I drank this glass, paid and went out. Outside along the street were the refuse cans from the houses waiting for the collector. A dog was nosing at one of the cans.

'What do you want?' I asked and looked in the can to see if there was anything I could pull out for him; there was nothing on top but coffee-grounds, dust and some dead flowers.

'There isn't anything, dog,' I said. The dog crossed the street. I went up the stairs in the hospital to the floor Catherine was on and down the hall to her room. I knocked on the door. There was no answer. I opened the door; the room was empty, except for Catherine's bag on a chair and her dressing-gown hanging on a hook on the wall. I went out and down the hall, looking for somebody. I found a nurse.

'Where is Madame Henry?'

'A lady has just gone to the delivery room.'

'Where is it?'

'I will show you.'

She took me down to the end of the hall. The door of the room was partly open. I could see Catherine lying on a table, covered by a sheet. The nurse was on one side and the doctor stood on the other side of the table beside some cylinders. The doctor held a rubber mask attached to a tube in one hand.

'I will give you a gown and you can go in,' the nurse said. 'Come in here, please.' She put a white gown on me and pinned it at the neck in back with a safety pin. 'Now you can go in,' she said. I went into the room.

'Hello, darling,' Catherine said in a strained voice. 'I'm not doing much.'

'You are Mr. Henry?' the doctor asked.

'Yes. How is everything going, doctor?'

'Things are going very well,' the doctor said. 'We came in here where it is easy to give gas for the pains.'

'I want it now,' Catherine said. The doctor placed the rubber mask over her face and turned a dial and I watched Catherine breathing deeply and rapidly. Then she pushed the mask away. The doctor shut off the petcock.

'That wasn't a very big one. I had a very big one a while ago. The doctor made me go clear out, didn't you, doctor?' Her voice was strange. It rose on the word doctor.

The doctor smiled.

'I want it again,' Catherine said. She held the rubber tight to her face and breathed fast. I heard her moaning a little. Then she pulled the mask away and smiled.

'That was a big one,' she said. 'That was a very big one. Don't you worry, darling.

You go away. Go have another breakfast.'

'I'll stay,' I said.

We had gone to the hospital about three o'clock in the morning. At noon Catherine was still in the delivery room. The pains had slackened again. She looked very tired and worn now but she was still cheerful.

'I'm not any good, darling,' she said. 'I'm so sorry. I thought I would do it very easily. Now—there's one—' she reached out her hand for the mask and held it over her face. The doctor moved the dial and watched her. In a little while it was over.

'It wasn't much,' Catherine said. She smiled. 'I'm a fool about the gas. It's wonderful.'

'We'll get some for the home,' I said.

'There one comes,' Catherine said quickly. The doctor turned the dial and looked at his watch.

'What is the interval now?' I asked.

'About a minute.'

'Don't you want lunch?'

'I will have something pretty soon,' he said.

'You must have something to eat, doctor,' Catherine said. 'I'm so sorry I go on so long. Couldn't my husband give me the gas?'

'If you wish,' the doctor said. 'You turn it to the numeral two.'

'I see,' I said. There was a marker on a dial that turned with a handle.

'I want it now,' Catherine said. She held the mask tight to her face. I turned the dial to number two and when Catherine put down the mask I turned it off. It was very good of the doctor to let me do something.

'Did you do it, darling?' Catherine asked. She stroked my wrist.

'Sure.'

'You're so lovely.' She was a little drunk from the gas.

'I will eat from a tray in the next room,' the doctor said. 'You can call me any moment.' While the time passed I watched him eat, then, after a while, I saw that he was lying down and smoking a cigarette. Catherine was getting very tired.

'Do you think I'll ever have this baby?' she asked.

'Yes, of course you will.'

'I try as hard as I can. I push down but it goes away. There it comes. Give it to me.'

At two o'clock I went out and had lunch. There were a few men in the café sitting with coffee and glasses of kirsch or marc on the tables. I sat down at a table. 'Can I eat?' I asked the waiter.

'It is past time for lunch.'

'Isn't there anything for all hours?'

'You can have choucroute.'

'Give me choucroute and beer.'

'A demi or a bock?'

'A light demi.'

The waiter brought a dish of sauerkraut with a slice of ham over the top and a sausage buried in the hot wine-soaked cabbage. I ate it and drank the beer. I was very hungry. I watched the people at the tables in the café. At one table they were playing cards. Two men at the table next me were talking and smoking. The café was full of smoke. The zinc bar, where I had breakfasted, had three people behind it now; the old man, a plump woman in a black dress who sat behind a counter and kept track of everything served to the tables, and a boy in an apron. I wondered how many children the woman had and what it had been like.

When I was through with the choucroute I went back to the hospital. The street was all clean now. There were no refuse cans out. The day was cloudy but the sun was trying to come through.

I rode upstairs in the elevator, stepped out and went down the hail to Catherine's room, where I had left my white gown. I put it on and pinned it in back at the neck. I looked in the glass and saw myself looking like a fake doctor with a beard. I went down the hail to the delivery room. The door was closed and I knocked. No one answered so I turned the handle and went in. The doctor sat by Catherine. The nurse was doing something at the other end of the room.

'Here is your husband,' the doctor said.

'Oh, darling, I have the most wonderful doctor,' Catherine said in a very strange voice. 'He's been telling me the most wonderful story and when the pain came too badly he put me all the way out. He's wonderful. You're wonderful, doctor.'

'You're drunk,' I said.

'I know it,' Catherine said. 'But you shouldn't say it.' Then 'Give it to me. Give it to me.' She clutched hold of the mask and breathed short and deep, pantingly, making the respirator click. Then she gave a long sigh and the doctor reached with his left hand and lifted away the mask.

'That was a very big one,' Catherine said. Her voice was very strange. 'I'm not going to die now, darling. I'm past where I was going to die. Aren't you glad?'

'Don't you get in that place again.'

'I won't. I'm not afraid of it though. I won't die, darling.'

'You will not do any such foolishness,' the doctor said. 'You would not die and leave your husband.'

'Oh, no. I won't die. I wouldn't die. It's silly to die. There it comes. Give it to me.'

After a while the doctor said, 'You will go out, Mr. Henry, for a few moments and I will make an examination.'

'He wants to see how I am doing,' Catherine said. 'You can come back afterward, darling, can't he, doctor?'

'Yes,' said the doctor. 'I will send word when he can come back.'

I went out the door and down the hall to the room where Catherine was to be after the baby came. I sat in a chair there and looked at the room. I had the paper in my coat that I had bought when I went out for lunch and I read it. It was beginning to be dark outside and I turned the light on to read. After a while I stopped reading and turned off the light and watched it get dark outside. I wondered why the doctor did not send for me.

Maybe it was better I was away. He probably wanted me away for a while. I looked at my watch. If he did not send for me in ten minutes I would go down anyway.

Poor, poor dear Cat. And this was the price you paid for sleeping together. This was the end of the trap. This was what people got for loving each other. Thank God for gas, anyway. What must it have been like before there were anaesthetics? Once it started, they were in the mill-race. Catherine had a good time in the time of pregnancy. It wasn't bad. She was hardly ever sick. She was not awfully uncomfortable until toward the last. So now they got her in the end. You never got away with anything. Get away hell! It would have been the same if we had been married fifty times. And what if she should die? She won't die. People don't die in childbirth nowadays. That was what all husbands thought. Yes, but what if she should die? She won't die. She's just having a bad time. The initial labor is usually protracted. She's only having a bad time. Afterward we'd say what a bad time and Catherine would say it wasn't really so bad. But what if she should die? She can't die. Yes, but what if she should die? She can't, I tell you. Don't be a fool. It's just a bad time. It's just nature giving her hell. It's only the first labor, which is almost always protracted. Yes, but what if she should die? She can't die. Why would she die? What reason is there for her to die? There's just a child that has to be born, the by-product of good nights in Milan. It makes trouble and is born and then you look after it and get fond of it maybe. But what if she should die? She won't die. But what if she should die? She won't. She's all right. But what if she should die? She can't die. But what if she should die? Hey, what about that? What if she should die?

The doctor came into the room.

'How does it go, doctor?'

'It doesn't go,' he said.

'What do you mean?'

'Just that. I made an examination—' He detailed the result of the examination. 'Since then I've waited to see. But it doesn't go.'

'What do you advise?'

'There are two things. Either a high forceps delivery which can tear and be quite dangerous besides being possibly bad for the child, and a Caesarean.'

'What is the danger of a Caesarean?' What if she should die!

'It should be no greater than the danger of an ordinary delivery.'

'Would you do it yourself?'

'Yes. I would need possibly an hour to get things ready and to get the people I would need. Perhaps a little less.'

'What do you think?'

'I would advise a Caesarean operation. If it were my wife I would do a Caesarean.' 'What are the after effects?'

'There are none. There is only the scar.'

'What about infection?'

'The danger is not so great as in a high forceps delivery.'

'What if you just went on and did nothing?'

'You would have to do something eventually. Mrs. Henry is already losing much of her strength. The sooner we operate now the safer.'

'Operate as soon as you can,' I said.

'I will go and give the instructions.'

I went into the delivery room. The nurse was with Catherine who lay on the table, big under the sheet, looking very pale and tired.

'Did you tell him he could do it?' she asked.

'Yes.'

'Isn't that grand. Now it will be all over in an hour. I'm almost done, darling. I'm going all to pieces. Please give me that. It doesn't work. Oh, it doesn't work!'

'Breathe deeply.'

'I am. Oh, it doesn't work any more. It doesn't work!'

'Get another cylinder,' I said to the nurse.

'That is a new cylinder.'

'I'm just a fool, darling,' Catherine said. 'But it doesn't work any more.' She began to cry. 'Oh, I wanted so to have this baby and not make trouble, and now I'm all done and all gone to pieces and it doesn't work. Oh, darling, it doesn't work at all. I don't care if I die if it will only stop. Oh, please, darling, please make it stop. There it comes. Oh Oh Oh!' She breathed sobbingly in the mask.

'It doesn't work. It doesn't work. It doesn't work. Don't mind me, darling. Please don't cry. Don't mind me. I'm just gone all to pieces. You poor sweet. I love you so and I'll be good again. I'll be good this time. Can't they give me something? If they could only give me something.'

'I'll make it work. I'll turn it all the way.'

'Give it to me now.'

I turned the dial all the way and as she breathed hard and deep her hand relaxed on the mask. I shut off the gas and lifted the mask. She came back from a long way away.

'That was lovely, darling. Oh, you're so good to me.'

'You be brave, because I can't do that all the time. It might kill you.'

'I'm not brave any more, darling. I'm all broken. They've broken me. I know it now.' 'Everybody is that way.'

'But it's awful. They just keep it up till they break you.'

'In an hour it will be over.'

'Isn't that lovely? Darling, I won't die, will I?'

'No. I promise you won't.'

'Because I don't want to die and leave you, but I get so tired of it and I feel I'm going to die.'

'Nonsense. Everybody feels that.'

'Sometimes I know I'm going to die.'

'You won't. You can't.'

'But what if I should?'

'I won't let you.'

'Give it to me quick. Give it to me!'

Then afterward, 'I won't die. I won't let myself die.'

'Of course you won't.'

'You'll stay with me?' 'Not to watch it.' 'No, just to be there.'

'Sure. I'll be there all the time.'

'You're so good to me. There, give it to me. Give me some more. It's not working!'

I turned the dial to three and then four. I wished the doctor would come back. I was afraid of the numbers above two.

Finally a new doctor came in with two nurses and they lifted Catherine onto a wheeled stretcher and we started down the hall. The stretcher went rapidly down the hall and into the elevator where every one had to crowd against the wall to make room; then up, then an open door and out of the elevator and down the hall on rubber wheels to the operating room. I did not recognize the doctor with his cap and mask on. There was another doctor and more nurses.

'They've got to give me something,' Catherine said. 'They've got to give me something. Oh please, doctor, give me enough to do some good!'

One of the doctors put a mask over her face and I looked through the door and saw the bright small amphitheatre of the operating room.

'You can go in the other door and sit up there,' a nurse said to me. There were benches behind a rail that looked down on the white table and the lights. I looked at Catherine. The mask was over her face and she was quiet now. They wheeled the stretcher forward. I turned away and walked down the hall. Two nurses were hurrying toward the entrance to the gallery.

'It's a Caesarean,' one said. 'They're going to do a Caesarean.'

The other one laughed, 'We're just in time. Aren't we lucky?' They went in the door that led to the gallery.

Another nurse came along. She was hurrying too.

'You go right in there. Go right in,' she said.

'I'm staying outside.'

She hurried in. I walked up and down the hall. I was afraid to go in. I looked out the window. It was dark but in the light from the window I could see it was raining. I went into a room at the far end of the hall and looked at the labels on bottles in a glass case. Then I came out and stood in the empty hall and watched the door of the operating room.

A doctor came out followed by a nurse. He held something in his two hands that looked like a freshly skinned rabbit and hurried across the corridor with it and in through another door. I went down to the door he had gone into and found them in the room doing things to a new-born child. The doctor held him up for me to see. He held him by the heels and slapped him.

'Is he all right?'

'He's magnificent. He'll weigh five kilos.'

I had no feeling for him. He did not seem to have anything to do with me. I felt no feeling of fatherhood.

'Aren't you proud of your son?' the nurse asked. They were washing him and wrapping him in something. I saw the little dark face and dark hand, but I did not see him move or hear him cry. The doctor was doing something to him again. He looked upset.

'No,' I said. 'He nearly killed his mother.'

'It isn't the little darling's fault. Didn't you want a boy?'

'No,' I said. The doctor was busy with him. He held him up by the feet and slapped him. I did not wait to see it. I went out in the hall. I could go in now and see. I went in the door and a little way down the gallery. The nurses who were sitting at the rail motioned for me to come down where they were. I shook my head. I could see enough where I was.

I thought Catherine was dead. She looked dead. Her face was gray, the part of it that I could see. Down below, under the light, the doctor was sewing up the great long, forcep-spread, thickedged, wound. Another doctor in a mask gave the anaesthetic. Two nurses in masks handed things. It looked like a drawing of the Inquisition. I knew as I watched I could have watched it all, but I was glad I hadn't. I do not think I could have watched them cut, but I watched the wound closed into a high welted ridge with quick skilful-looking stitches like a cobbler's, and was glad. When the wound was closed I went out into the hall and walked up and down again. After a while the doctor came out.

'How is she?'

'She is all right. Did you watch?'

He looked tired.

'I saw you sew up. The incision looked very long.'

'You thought so?'

'Yes. Will that scar flatten out?'

'Oh, yes.'

After a while they brought out the wheeled stretcher and took it very rapidly down the hallway to the elevator. I went along beside it. Catherine was moaning. Downstairs they put her in the bed in her room. I sat in a chair at the foot of the bed. There was a nurse in the room. I got up and stood by the bed. It was dark in the room. Catherine put out her hand. 'Hello, darling,' she said. Her voice was very weak and tired.

'Hello, you sweet.'

'What sort of baby was it?' 'Sh—don't talk,' the nurse said.

'A boy. He's long and wide and dark.'

'Is he all right?'

'Yes,' I said. 'He's fine.'

I saw the nurse look at me strangely.

'I'm awfully tired,' Catherine said. 'And I hurt like hell. Are you all right, darling?' 'I'm fine. Don't talk.'

'You were lovely to me. Oh, darling, I hurt dreadfully. What does he look like?'

'He looks like a skinned rabbit with a puckered-up old-man's face.'

'You must go out,' the nurse said. 'Madame Henry must not talk.'

'I'll be outside.'

'Go and get something to eat.'

'No. I'll be outside.' I kissed Catherine. She was very gray and weak and tired. 'May I speak to you?' I said to the nurse. She came out in the hall with me. I walked a little way down the hall.

'What's the matter with the baby?' I asked.
'Didn't you know?'
'No.'
'He wasn't alive.'
'He was dead?'
'They couldn't start him breathing. The cord was caught around his neck or something.'
'So he's dead.'
'Yes. It's such a shame. He was such a fine big boy. I thought you knew.' 'No,' I said. 'You better go back in with Madame.'

I sat down on the chair in front of a table where there were nurses' reports hung on clips at the side and looked out of the window. I could see nothing but the dark and the rain falling across the light from the window. So that was it. The baby was dead. That was why the doctor looked so tired. But why had they acted the way they did in the room with him? They supposed he would come around and start breathing probably. I had no religion but I knew he ought to have been baptized. But what if he never breathed at all.

He hadn't. He had never been alive. Except in Catherine. I'd felt him kick there often enough. But I hadn't for a week. Maybe he was choked all the time. Poor little kid. I wished the hell I'd been choked like that. No I didn't. Still there would not be all this dying to go through. Now Catherine would die. That was what you did. You died. You did not know what it was about. You never had time to learn. They threw you in and told you the rules and the first time they caught you off base they killed you. Or they killed you gratuitously like Aymo. Or gave you the syphilis like Rinaldi. But they killed you in the end. You could count on that. Stay around and they would kill you.

Once in camp I put a log on top of the fire and it was full of ants. As it commenced to burn, the ants swarmed out and went first toward the centre where the fire was; then turned back and ran toward the end. When there were enough on the end they fell off into the fire. Some got out, their bodies burnt and flattened, and went off not knowing where they were going. But most of them went toward the fire and then back toward the end and swarmed on the cool end and finally fell off into the fire. I remember thinking at the time that it was the end of the world and a splendid chance to be a messiah and lift the log off the fire and throw it out where the ants could get off onto the ground. But I did not do anything but throw a tin cup of water on the log, so that I would have the cup empty to put whiskey in before I added water to it. I think the cup of water on the burning log only steamed the ants.

So now I sat out in the hall and waited to hear how Catherine was. The nurse did not come out, so after a while I went to the door and opened it very softly and looked in. I could not see at first because there was a bright light in the hall and it was dark in the room. Then I saw the nurse sitting by the bed and Catherine's head on a pillow, and she was all flat under the sheet. The nurse put her finger to her lips, then stood up and came to the door.

'How is she?' I asked.

'She's all right,' the nurse said. 'You should go and have your supper and then come back if you wish.'

I went down the hall and then down the stairs and out the door of the hospital and down the dark street in the rain to the café. It was brightly lighted inside and there were many people at the tables. I did not see a place to sit, and a waiter came up to me and took my wet coat and hat and showed me a place at a table across from an elderly man who was drinking beer and reading the evening paper. I sat down and asked the waiter what the plat du jour was.

'Veal stew—but it is finished.'

'What can I have to eat?'

'Ham and eggs, eggs with cheese, or choucroute.'

'I had choucroute this noon,' I said.

'That's true,' he said. 'That's true. You ate choucroute this noon.' He was a middle-aged man with a bald top to his head and his hair slicked over it. He had a kind face.

'What do you want? Ham and eggs or eggs with cheese?'

'Ham and eggs,' I said, 'and beer.'

'A demi-blonde?'

'Yes,' I said.

'I remembered,' he said. 'You took a demi-blonde this noon.'

I ate the ham and eggs and drank the beer. The ham and eggs were in a round dish—the ham underneath and the eggs on top. It was very hot and at the first mouthful I had to take a drink of beer to cool my mouth. I was hungry and I asked the waiter for another order. I drank several glasses of beer. I was not thinking at all but read the paper of the man opposite me. It was about the break through on the British front. When he realized I was reading the back of his paper he folded it over. I thought of asking the waiter for a paper, but I could not concentrate. It was hot in the café and the air was bad. Many of the people at the tables knew one another. There were several card games going on. The waiters were busy bringing drinks from the bar to the tables. Two men came in and could find no place to sit. They stood opposite the table where I was. I ordered another beer. I was not ready to leave yet. It was too soon to go back to the hospital. I tried not to think and to be perfectly calm. The men stood around but no one was leaving, so they went out. I drank another beer. There was quite a pile of saucers now on the table in front of me. The man opposite me had taken off his spectacles, put them away in a case, folded his paper and put it in his pocket and now sat holding his liqueur glass and looking out at the room. Suddenly I knew I had to get back. I called the waiter, paid the reckoning, got into my coat, put on my hat and started out the door. I walked through the rain up to the hospital.

Upstairs I met the nurse coming down the hall.

'I just called you at the hotel,' she said. Something dropped inside me.

'What is wrong?'

'Mrs. Henry has had a hemorrhage.'

'Can I go in?'

'No, not yet. The doctor is with her.'

'Is it dangerous?'

'It is very dangerous.' The nurse went into the room and shut the door. I sat outside in the hall. Everything was gone inside of me. I did not think. I could not think. I knew she was going to die and I prayed that she would not. Don't let her die. Oh, God, please don't let her die. I'll do anything for you if you won't let her die. Please, please, please, dear God, don't let her die. Dear God, don't let her die. Please, please, please don't let her die. God please make her not die. I'll do anything you say if you don't let her die. You took the baby but don't let her die. That was all right but don't let her die. Please, please, dear God, don't let her die.

The nurse opened the door and motioned with her finger for me to come. I followed her into the room. Catherine did not look up when I came in. I went over to the side of the bed. The doctor was standing by the bed on the opposite side. Catherine looked at me and smiled. I bent down over the bed and started to cry.

'Poor darling,' Catherine said very softly. She looked gray.

'You're all right, Cat,' I said. 'You're going to be all right.'

'I'm going to die,' she said; then waited and said, 'I hate it.'

I took her hand.

'Don't touch me,' she said. I let go of her hand. She smiled. 'Poor darling. You touch me all you want.'

'You'll be all right, Cat. I know you'll be all right.'

'I meant to write you a letter to have if anything happened, but I didn't do it.'

'Do you want me to get a priest or any one to come and see you?'

'Just you,' she said. Then a little later, 'I'm not afraid. I just hate it.'

'You must not talk so much,' the doctor said.

'All right,' Catherine said.

'Do you want me to do anything, Cat? Can I get you anything?'

Catherine smiled, 'No.' Then a little later, 'You won't do our things with another girl, or say the same things, will you?'

'Never.'

'I want you to have girls, though.'

'I don't want them.'

'You are talking too much,' the doctor said. 'Mr. Henry must go out. He can come back again later. You are not going to die. You must not be silly.'

'All right,' Catherine said. 'I'll come and stay with you nights,' she said. It was very hard for her to talk.

'Please go out of the room,' the doctor said. 'You cannot talk.' Catherine winked at me, her face gray. 'I'll be right outside,' I said.

'Don't worry, darling,' Catherine said. 'I'm not a bit afraid. It's just a dirty trick.'

'You dear, brave sweet.'

I waited outside in the hall. I waited a long time. The nurse came to the door and came over to me. 'I'm afraid Mrs. Henry is very ill,' she said. 'I'm afraid for her.'

'Is she dead?'

'No, but she is unconscious.'

It seems she had one hemorrhage after another. They couldn't stop it. I went into the room and stayed with Catherine until she died. She was unconscious all the time, and it did not take her very long to die.

Outside the room, in the hall, I spoke to the doctor, 'Is there anything I can do to- night?'

'No. There is nothing to do. Can I take you to your hotel?'

'No, thank you. I am going to stay here a while.'

'I know there is nothing to say. I cannot tell you—'

'No,' I said. 'There's nothing to say.'

'Good-night,' he said. 'I cannot take you to your hotel?'

'No, thank you.'

'It was the only thing to do,' he said. 'The operation proved—'

'I do not want to talk about it,' I said.

'I would like to take you to your hotel.'

'No, thank you.'

He went down the hall. I went to the door of the room.

'You can't come in now,' one of the nurses said.

'Yes I can,' I said.

'You can't come in yet.'

'You get out,' I said. 'The other one too.'

But after I had got them out and shut the door and turned off the light it wasn't any good. It was like saying good-by to a statue. After a while I went out and left the hospital and walked back to the hotel in the rain.

THE SUN ALSO RISES

BOOK ONE

1

Robert Cohn was once middleweight boxing champion of Princeton. Do not think that I am very much impressed by that as a boxing title, but it meant a lot to Cohn. He cared nothing for boxing, in fact he disliked it, but he learned it painfully and thoroughly to counteract the feeling of inferiority and shyness he had felt on being treated as a Jew at Princeton. There was a certain inner comfort in knowing he could knock down anybody who was snooty to him, although, being very shy and a thoroughly nice boy, he never fought except in the gym. He was Spider Kelly's star pupil. Spider Kelly taught all his young gentlemen to box like featherweights, no matter whether they weighed one hundred and five or two hundred and five pounds. But it seemed to fit Cohn. He was really very fast. He was so good that Spider promptly overmatched him and got his nose permanently flattened. This increased Cohn's distaste for boxing, but it gave him a certain satisfaction of some strange sort, and it certainly improved his nose. In his last year at Princeton he read too much and took to wearing spectacles. I never met any one of his class who remembered him. They did not even remember that he was middleweight boxing champion.

I mistrust all frank and simple people, especially when their stories hold together, and I always had a suspicion that perhaps Robert Cohn had never been middleweight boxing champion, and that perhaps a horse had stepped on his face, or that maybe his mother had been frightened or seen something, or that he had, maybe, bumped into something as a young child, but I finally had somebody verify the story from Spider Kelly. Spider Kelly not only remembered Cohn. He had often wondered what had become of him.

Robert Cohn was a member, through his father, of one of the richest Jewish families in New York, and through his mother of one of the oldest. At the military school where he prepped for Princeton, and played a very good end on the football team, no one had made him race-conscious. No one had ever made him feel he was a Jew, and hence any different from anybody else, until he went to Princeton. He was a nice boy, a friendly boy, and very shy, and it made him bitter. He took it out in boxing, and he came out of Princeton with painful self-consciousness and the flattened nose, and was married by the first girl who was nice to him. He was married five years, had three children, lost most of the fifty thousand dollars his father left him, the balance of the estate having gone to his mother, hardened into a rather unattractive mould under domestic unhappiness with a rich wife; and just when he had made up his mind to leave his wife she left him and went off with a miniature-painter. As he had been thinking for months about leaving his wife and had not done it because it would be too cruel to deprive her of himself, her departure was a very healthful shock.

The divorce was arranged and Robert Cohn went out to the Coast. In California he fell among literary people and, as he still had a little of the fifty thousand left, in a short time he was backing a review of the Arts. The review commenced publication in Carmel, California, and finished in Provincetown, Massachusetts. By that time Cohn, who had been regarded purely as an angel, and whose name had appeared on the editorial page merely as a member of the advisory board, had become the sole editor. It was his money and he discovered he liked the authority of editing. He was sorry when the magazine became too expensive and he had to give it up.

By that time, though, he had other things to worry about. He had been taken in hand by a lady who hoped to rise with the magazine. She was very forceful, and Cohn never had a chance of not being taken in hand. Also he was sure that he loved her. When this lady saw that the magazine was not going to rise, she became a little disgusted with Cohn and decided that she might as well get what there was to get while there was still something available, so she urged that they go to Europe, where Cohn could write. They came to Europe, where the lady had been educated, and stayed three years. During these three years, the first spent in travel, the last two in Paris, Robert Cohn had two friends, Braddocks and myself. Braddocks was his literary friend. I was his tennis friend.

The lady who had him, her name was Frances, found toward the end of the second year that her looks were going, and her attitude toward Robert changed from one of careless possession and exploitation to the absolute determination that he should marry her. During this time Robert's mother had settled an allowance on him, about three hundred dollars a month. During two years and a half I do not believe that Robert Cohn looked at another woman. He was fairly happy, except that, like many people living in Europe, he would rather have been in America, and he had discovered writing. He wrote a novel, and it was not really such a bad novel as the critics later called it, although it was a very poor novel. He read many books, played bridge, played tennis, and boxed at a local gymnasium.

I first became aware of his lady's attitude toward him one night after the three of us had dined together. We had dined at l'Avenue's and afterward went to the Café de Versailles for coffee. We had several *fines* after the coffee, and I said I must be going. Cohn had been talking about the two of us going off somewhere on a weekend trip. He wanted to get out of town and get in a good walk. I suggested we fly to Strasbourg and walk up to Saint Odile, or somewhere or other in Alsace. 'I know a girl in Strasbourg who can show us the town,' I said.

Somebody kicked me under the table. I thought it was accidental and went on: 'She's been there two years and knows everything there is to know about the town. She's a swell girl.'

I was kicked again under the table and, looking, saw Frances, Robert's lady, her chin lifting and her face hardening.

'Hell,' I said, 'why go to Strasbourg? We could go up to Bruges, or to the Ardennes.'

Cohn looked relieved. I was not kicked again. I said good-night and went out. Cohn said he wanted to buy a paper and would walk to the corner with me. 'For God's sake,' he said, 'why did you say that about that girl in Strasbourg for? Didn't you see Frances?'

'No, why should I? If I know an American girl that lives in Strasbourg what the hell is it to Frances?'

'It doesn't make any difference. Any girl. I couldn't go, that would be all.'

'Don't be silly.'

'You don't know Frances. Any girl at all. Didn't you see the way she looked?'

'Oh, well,' I said, 'let's go to Senlis.'

'Don't get sore.'

'I'm not sore. Senlis is a good place and we can stay at the Grand Cerf and take a hike in the woods and come home.'

'Good, that will be fine.'

'Well, I'll see you to-morrow at the courts,' I said.

'Good-night, Jake,' he said, and started back to the café.

'You forgot to get your paper,' I said.

'That's so.' He walked with me up to the kiosque at the corner. 'You are not sore, are you, Jake?' He turned with the paper in his hand.

'No, why should I be?'

'See you at tennis,' he said. I watched him walk back to the café holding his paper. I rather liked him and evidently she led him quite a life.

2

That winter Robert Cohn went over to America with his novel, and it was accepted by a fairly good publisher. His going made an awful row I heard, and I think that was where Frances lost him, because several women were nice to him in New York, and when he came back he was quite changed. He was more enthusiastic about America than ever, and he was not so simple, and he was not so nice. The publishers had praised his novel pretty highly and it rather went to his head. Then several women had put themselves out to be nice to him, and his horizons had all shifted. For four years his horizon had been absolutely limited to his wife. For three years, or almost three years, he had never seen beyond Frances. I am sure he had never been in love in his life.

He had married on the rebound from the rotten time he had in college, and Frances took him on the rebound from his discovery that he had not been everything to his first wife. He was not in love yet but he realized that he was an attractive quantity to women, and that the fact of a woman caring for him and wanting to live with him was not simply a divine miracle. This changed him so that he was not so pleasant to have around. Also, playing for higher stakes than he could afford in some rather steep bridge games with his New York connections, he had held cards and won several hundred dollars. It made him rather vain of his bridge game, and he talked several times of how a man could always make a living at bridge if he were ever forced to.

Then there was another thing. He had been reading W. H. Hudson. That sounds like an innocent occupation, but Cohn had read and reread 'The Purple Land.' 'The Purple Land' is a very sinister book if read too late in life. It recounts splendid imaginary amorous adventures of a perfect English gentleman in an intensely romantic land, the scenery of which is very well described. For a man to take it at thirty-four as a guide-book to what life holds is about as safe as it would be for a man of the same age to enter Wall Street direct from a French convent, equipped with a complete set of the more practical Alger books. Cohn, I believe, took every word of 'The Purple Land' as literally as though it had been an R. G. Dun report. You understand me, he made some reservations, but on the whole the book to him was sound. It was all that was needed to set him off. I did not realize the extent to which it had set him off until one day he came into my office.

'Hello, Robert,' I said. 'Did you come in to cheer me up?'

'Would you like to go to South America, Jake?' he asked.

'No.'

'Why not?'

'I don't know. I never wanted to go. Too expensive. You can see all the South Americans you want in Paris anyway.'

'They're not the real South Americans.'

'They look awfully real to me.'

I had a boat train to catch with a week's mail stories, and only half of them written.

'Do you know any dirt?' I asked.

'No.'

'None of your exalted connections getting divorces?'

'No; listen, Jake. If I handled both our expenses, would you go to South America with me?'

'Why me?'

'You can talk Spanish. And it would be more fun with two of us.'

'No,' I said, 'I like this town and I go to Spain in the summer-time.'

'All my life I've wanted to go on a trip like that,' Cohn said. He sat down. 'I'll be too old before I can ever do it.'

'Don't be a fool,' I said. 'You can go anywhere you want. You've got plenty of money.'

'I know. But I can't get started.'

'Cheer up,' I said. 'All countries look just like the moving pictures.'

But I felt sorry for him. He had it badly.

'I can't stand it to think my life is going so fast and I'm not really living it.'

'Nobody ever lives their life all the way up except bull-fighters.'

'I'm not interested in bull-fighters. That's an abnormal life. I want to go back in the country in South America. We could have a great trip.'

'Did you ever think about going to British East Africa to shoot?'

'No, I wouldn't like that.'

'I'd go there with you.'

'No; that doesn't interest me.'

'That's because you never read a book about it. Go on and read a book all full of love affairs with the beautiful shiny black princesses.'

'I want to go to South America.'

He had a hard, Jewish, stubborn streak.

'Come on down-stairs and have a drink.'

'Aren't you working?'

'No,' I said. We went down the stairs to the café on the ground floor. I had discovered that was the best way to get rid of friends. Once you had a drink all you had to say was: 'Well, I've got to get back and get off some cables,' and it was done. It is very important to discover graceful exits like that in the newspaper business, where it is such an important part of the ethics that you should never seem to be working. Anyway, we went down-stairs to the bar and had a whiskey and soda. Cohn looked at the bottles in bins around the wall. 'This is a good place,' he said.

'There's a lot of liquor,' I agreed.

'Listen, Jake,' he leaned forward on the bar. 'Don't you ever get the feeling that all your life is going by and you're not taking advantage of it? Do you realize you've lived nearly half the time you have to live already?'

'Yes, every once in a while.'

'Do you know that in about thirty-five years more we'll be dead?'

'What the hell, Robert,' I said. 'What the hell.'

'I'm serious.'

'It's one thing I don't worry about,' I said.

'You ought to.'

'I've had plenty to worry about one time or other. I'm through worrying.'

'Well, I want to go to South America.'

'Listen, Robert, going to another country doesn't make any difference. I've tried all that. You can't get away from yourself by moving from one place to another. There's nothing to that.'

'But you've never been to South America.'

'South America hell! If you went there the way you feel now it would be exactly the same. This is a good town. Why don't you start living your life in Paris?'

'I'm sick of Paris, and I'm sick of the Quarter.'

'Stay away from the Quarter. Cruise around by yourself and see what happens to you.'

'Nothing happens to me. I walked alone all one night and nothing happened except a bicycle cop stopped me and asked to see my papers.'

'Wasn't the town nice at night?'

'I don't care for Paris.'

So there you were. I was sorry for him, but it was not a thing you could do anything about, because right away you ran up against the two stubbornnesses: South America could fix it and he did not like Paris. He got the first idea out of a book, and I suppose the second came out of a book too.

'Well,' I said, 'I've got to go up-stairs and get off some cables.'

'Do you really have to go?'

'Yes, I've got to get these cables off.'

'Do you mind if I come up and sit around the office?'

'No, come on up.'

He sat in the outer room and read the papers, and the Editor and Publisher and I worked hard for two hours. Then I sorted out the carbons, stamped on a by-line, put the stuff in a couple of big manila envelopes and rang for a boy to take them to the Gare St. Lazare. I went out into the other room and there was Robert Cohn asleep in the big chair. He was asleep with his head on his arms. I did not like to wake him up, but I wanted to lock the office and shove off. I put my hand on his shoulder. He shook his head. 'I can't do it,' he said, and put his head deeper into his arms. 'I can't do it. Nothing will make me do it.'

'Robert,' I said, and shook him by the shoulder. He looked up. He smiled and blinked.

'Did I talk out loud just then?'

'Something. But it wasn't clear.'

'God, what a rotten dream!'

'Did the typewriter put you to sleep?'

'Guess so. I didn't sleep all last night.'

'What was the matter?'

'Talking,' he said.

I could picture it. I have a rotten habit of picturing the bedroom scenes of my friends. We went out to the Café Napolitain to have an *apéritif* and watch the evening crowd on the Boulevard.

3

It was a warm spring night and I sat at a table on the terrace of the Napolitain after Robert had gone, watching it get dark and the electric signs come on, and the red and green stop-and-go traffic-signal, and the crowd going by, and the horse-cabs clippety-clopping along at the edge of the solid taxi traffic, and the *poules* going by, singly and in pairs, looking for the evening meal. I watched a good-looking girl walk past the table and watched her go up the street and lost sight of her, and watched another, and then saw the first one coming back again. She went by once more and I caught her eye, and she came over and sat down at the table. The waiter came up.

'Well, what will you drink?' I asked.

'Pernod.'

'That's not good for little girls.'

'Little girl yourself. Dites garçon, un pernod.'

'A pernod for me, too.'

'What's the matter?' she asked. 'Going on a party?'

'Sure. Aren't you?'

'I don't know. You never know in this town.'

'Don't you like Paris?'

'No.'

'Why don't you go somewhere else?'

'Isn't anywhere else.'

'You're happy, all right.'

'Happy, hell!'

Pernod is greenish imitation absinthe. When you add water it turns milky. It tastes like licorice and it has a good uplift, but it drops you just as far. We sat and drank it, and the girl looked sullen.

'Well,' I said, 'are you going to buy me a dinner?'

She grinned and I saw why she made a point of not laughing. With her mouth closed she was a rather pretty girl. I paid for the saucers and we walked out to the street. I hailed a horse-cab and the driver pulled up at the curb. Settled back in the slow, smoothly rolling *fiacre* we moved up the Avenue de l'Opéra, passed the locked doors of the shops, their windows lighted, the Avenue broad and shiny and almost deserted. The cab passed the New York *Herald* bureau with the window full of clocks.

'What are all the clocks for?' she asked.

'They show the hour all over America.'

'Don't kid me.'

We turned off the Avenue up the Rue des Pyramides, through the traffic of the Rue de Rivoli, and through a dark gate into the Tuileries. She cuddled against me and I put my arm around her. She looked up to be kissed. She touched me with one hand and I put her hand away.

'Never mind.'

'What's the matter? You sick?'

'Yes.'

'Everybody's sick. I'm sick, too.'

We came out of the Tuileries into the light and crossed the Seine and then turned up the Rue des Saints Pères.

'You oughtn't to drink pernod if you're sick.'

'You neither.'

'It doesn't make any difference with me. It doesn't make any difference with a woman.'

'What are you called?'

'Georgette. How are you called?'

'Jacob.'

'That's a Flemish name.'

'American too.'

'You're not Flamand?'

'No, American.'

'Good, I detest Flamands.'

By this time we were at the restaurant. I called to the *cocher* to stop. We got out and Georgette did not like the looks of the place. 'This is no great thing of a restaurant.'

'No,' I said. 'Maybe you would rather go to Foyot's. Why don't you keep the cab and go on?'

I had picked her up because of a vague sentimental idea that it would be nice to eat with some one. It was a long time since I had dined with a *poule*, and I had forgotten how dull it could be. We went into the restaurant, passed Madame Lavigne at the desk and into a little room. Georgette cheered up a little under the food.

'It isn't bad here,' she said. 'It isn't chic, but the food is all right.'

'Better than you eat in Liège.'

'Brussels, you mean.'

We had another bottle of wine and Georgette made a joke. She smiled and showed all her bad teeth, and we touched glasses. 'You're not a bad type,' she said. 'It's a shame you're sick. We get on well. What's the matter with you, anyway?'

'I got hurt in the war,' I said.

'Oh, that dirty war.'

We would probably have gone on and discussed the war and agreed that it was in reality a calamity for civilization, and perhaps would have been better avoided. I was bored enough. Just then from the other room some one called: 'Barnes! I say, Barnes! Jacob Barnes!'

'It's a friend calling me,' I explained, and went out.

There was Braddocks at a big table with a party: Cohn, Frances Clyne, Mrs. Braddocks, several people I did not know.

'You're coming to the dance, aren't you?' Braddocks asked.

'What dance?'

'Why, the dancings. Don't you know we've revived them?' Mrs. Braddocks put in.

'You must come, Jake. We're all going,' Frances said from the end of the table. She was tall and had a smile.

'Of course, he's coming,' Braddocks said. 'Come in and have coffee with us, Barnes.'

'Right.'

'And bring your friend,' said Mrs. Braddocks laughing. She was a Canadian and had all their easy social graces.

'Thanks, we'll be in,' I said. I went back to the small room.

'Who are your friends?' Georgette asked.

'Writers and artists.'

'There are lots of those on this side of the river.'

'Too many.'

'I think so. Still, some of them make money.'

'Oh, yes.'

We finished the meal and the wine. 'Come on,' I said. 'We're going to have coffee with the others.'

Georgette opened her bag, made a few passes at her face as she looked in the little mirror, re-defined her lips with the lipstick, and straightened her hat.

'Good,' she said.

We went into the room full of people and Braddocks and the men at his table stood up.

'I wish to present my fiancée, Mademoiselle Georgette Leblanc,' I said. Georgette smiled that wonderful smile, and we shook hands all round.

'Are you related to Georgette Leblanc, the singer?' Mrs. Braddocks asked.

'Connais pas,' Georgette answered.

'But you have the same name,' Mrs. Braddocks insisted cordially.

'No,' said Georgette. 'Not at all. My name is Hobin.'

'But Mr. Barnes introduced you as Mademoiselle Georgette Leblanc. Surely he did,' insisted Mrs. Braddocks, who in the excitement of talking French was liable to have no idea what she was saying.

'He's a fool,' Georgette said.

'Oh, it was a joke, then,' Mrs. Braddocks said.

'Yes,' said Georgette. 'To laugh at.'

'Did you hear that, Henry?' Mrs. Braddocks called down the table to Braddocks. 'Mr. Barnes introduced his fiancée as Mademoiselle Leblanc, and her name is actually Hobin.'

'Of course, darling. Mademoiselle Hobin, I've known her for a very long time.'

'Oh, Mademoiselle Hobin,' Frances Clyne called, speaking French very rapidly and not seeming so proud and astonished as Mrs. Braddocks at its coming out really French. 'Have you been in Paris long? Do you like it here? You love Paris, do you not?'

'Who's she?' Georgette turned to me. 'Do I have to talk to her?'

She turned to Frances, sitting smiling, her hands folded, her head poised on her long neck, her lips pursed ready to start talking again.

'No, I don't like Paris. It's expensive and dirty.'

'Really? I find it so extraordinarily clean. One of the cleanest cities in all Europe.'

'I find it dirty.'

'How strange! But perhaps you have not been here very long.'

'I've been here long enough.'

'But it does have nice people in it. One must grant that.'

Georgette turned to me. 'You have nice friends.'

Frances was a little drunk and would have liked to have kept it up but the coffee came, and Lavigne with the liqueurs, and after that we all went out and started for Braddocks's dancing-club.

The dancing-club was a *bal musette* in the Rue de la Montagne Sainte Geneviève. Five nights a week the working people of the Pantheon quarter danced there. One night a week it was the dancing-club. On Monday nights it was closed. When we arrived it was quite empty, except for a policeman sitting near the door, the wife of the proprietor back of the zinc bar, and the proprietor himself. The daughter of the house came downstairs as we went in. There were long benches, and tables ran across the room, and at the far end a dancing-floor.

'I wish people would come earlier,' Braddocks said. The daughter came up and wanted to know what we would drink. The proprietor got up on a high stool beside the dancing-floor and began to play the accordion. He had a string of bells around one of his ankles and beat time with his foot as he played. Every one danced. It was hot and we came off the floor perspiring.

'My God,' Georgette said. 'What a box to sweat in!'

'It's hot.'

'Hot, my God!'

'Take off your hat.'

'That's a good idea.'

Some one asked Georgette to dance, and I went over to the bar. It was really very hot and the accordion music was pleasant in the hot night. I drank a beer, standing in the doorway and getting the cool breath of wind from the street. Two taxis were coming down the steep street. They both stopped in front of the Bal. A crowd of young men, some in jerseys and some in their shirt-sleeves, got out. I could see their hands and newly washed, wavy hair in the light from the door. The policeman standing by the door looked at me and smiled. They came in. As they went in, under the light I saw white hands, wavy hair, white faces, grimacing, gesturing, talking. With them was Brett. She looked very lovely and she was very much with them.

One of them saw Georgette and said: 'I do declare. There is an actual harlot. I'm going to dance with her, Lett. You watch me.'

The tall dark one, called Lett, said: 'Don't you be rash.'

The wavy blond one answered: 'Don't you worry, dear.' And with them was Brett.

I was very angry. Somehow they always made me angry. I know they are supposed to be amusing, and you should be tolerant, but I wanted to swing on one, any one, anything to shatter that superior, simpering composure. Instead, I walked down the street and had a beer at the bar at the next Bal. The beer was not good and I had a worse cognac to take the taste out of my mouth. When I came back to the Bal there was a crowd on the floor and Georgette was dancing with the tall blond youth, who danced big-hippily, carrying his head on one side, his eyes lifted as he danced. As soon as the music stopped another one of them asked her to dance. She had been taken up by them. I knew then that they would all dance with her. They are like that.

I sat down at a table. Cohn was sitting there. Frances was dancing. Mrs. Braddocks brought up somebody and introduced him as Robert Prentiss. He was from New York by way of Chicago, and was a rising new novelist. He had some sort of an English accent. I asked him to have a drink.

'Thanks so much,' he said, 'I've just had one.'

'Have another.'

'Thanks, I will then.'

We got the daughter of the house over and each had a *fine à l'eau*.

'You're from Kansas City, they tell me,' he said.

'Yes.'

'Do you find Paris amusing?'

'Yes.'

'Really?'

I was a little drunk. Not drunk in any positive sense but just enough to be careless.

'For God's sake,' I said, 'yes. Don't you?'

'Oh, how charmingly you get angry,' he said. 'I wish I had that faculty.'

I got up and walked over toward the dancing-floor. Mrs. Braddocks followed me. 'Don't be cross with Robert,' she said. 'He's still only a child, you know.'

'I wasn't cross,' I said. 'I just thought perhaps I was going to throw up.'

'Your fiancée is having a great success,' Mrs. Braddocks looked out on the floor where Georgette was dancing in the arms of the tall, dark one, called Lett.

'Isn't she?' I said.

'Rather,' said Mrs. Braddocks.

Cohn came up. 'Come on, Jake,' he said, 'have a drink.' We walked over to the bar. 'What's the matter with you? You seem all worked up over something?'

'Nothing. This whole show makes me sick is all.'

Brett came up to the bar.

'Hello, you chaps.'

'Hello, Brett,' I said. 'Why aren't you tight?'

'Never going to get tight any more. I say, give a chap a brandy and soda.'

She stood holding the glass and I saw Robert Cohn looking at her. He looked a great deal as his compatriot must have looked when he saw the promised land. Cohn, of course, was much younger. But he had that look of eager, deserving expectation.

Brett was damned good-looking. She wore a slipover jersey sweater and a tweed skirt, and her hair was brushed back like a boy's. She started all that. She was built with curves like the hull of a racing yacht, and you missed none of it with that wool jersey.

'It's a fine crowd you're with, Brett,' I said.

'Aren't they lovely? And you, my dear. Where did you get it?'

'At the Napolitain.'

'And have you had a lovely evening?'

'Oh, priceless,' I said.

Brett laughed. 'It's wrong of you, Jake. It's an insult to all of us. Look at Frances there, and Jo.'

This for Cohn's benefit.

'It's in restraint of trade,' Brett said. She laughed again.

'You're wonderfully sober,' I said.

'Yes. Aren't I? And when one's with the crowd I'm with, one can drink in such safety, too.'

The music started and Robert Cohn said: 'Will you dance this with me, Lady Brett?'

Brett smiled at him. 'I've promised to dance this with Jacob,' she laughed. 'You've a hell of a biblical name, Jake.'

'How about the next?' asked Cohn.

'We're going,' Brett said. 'We've a date up at Montmartre.' Dancing, I looked over Brett's shoulder and saw Cohn, standing at the bar, still watching her.

'You've made a new one there,' I said to her.

'Don't talk about it. Poor chap. I never knew it till just now.'

'Oh, well,' I said. 'I suppose you like to add them up.'

'Don't talk like a fool.'

'You do.'

'Oh, well. What if I do?'

'Nothing,' I said. We were dancing to the accordion and some one was playing the banjo. It was hot and I felt happy. We passed close to Georgette dancing with another one of them.

'What possessed you to bring her?'

'I don't know, I just brought her.'

'You're getting damned romantic.'

'No, bored.'

'Now?'

'No, not now.'

'Let's get out of here. She's well taken care of.'

'Do you want to?'

'Would I ask you if I didn't want to?'

We left the floor and I took my coat off a hanger on the wall and put it on. Brett stood by the bar. Cohn was talking to her. I stopped at the bar and asked them for an envelope. The patronne found one. I took a fifty-franc note from my pocket, put it in the envelope, sealed it, and handed it to the patronne.

'If the girl I came with asks for me, will you give her this?' I said. 'If she goes out with one of those gentlemen, will you save this for me?'

'C'est entendu, Monsieur,' the patronne said. 'You go now? So early?'

'Yes,' I said.

We started out the door. Cohn was still talking to Brett. She said good night and took my arm. 'Good night, Cohn,' I said. Outside in the street we looked for a taxi.

'You're going to lose your fifty francs,' Brett said.

'Oh, yes.'

'No taxis.'

'We could walk up to the Pantheon and get one.'

'Come on and we'll get a drink in the pub next door and send for one.'

'You wouldn't walk across the street.'

'Not if I could help it.'

We went into the next bar and I sent a waiter for a taxi.

'Well,' I said, 'we're out away from them.'

We stood against the tall zinc bar and did not talk and looked at each other. The waiter came and said the taxi was outside. Brett pressed my hand hard. I gave the waiter a franc and we went out. 'Where should I tell him?' I asked.

'Oh, tell him to drive around.'

I told the driver to go to the Parc Montsouris, and got in, and slammed the door. Brett was leaning back in the corner, her eyes closed. I got in and sat beside her. The cab started with a jerk.

'Oh, darling, I've been so miserable,' Brett said.

4

The taxi went up the hill, passed the lighted square, then on into the dark, still climbing, then levelled out onto a dark street behind St. Etienne du Mont, went smoothly down the asphalt, passed the trees and the standing bus at the Place de la Contrescarpe, then turned onto the cobbles of the Rue Mouffetard. There were lighted bars and late open shops on each side of the street. We were sitting apart and we jolted close together going down the old street. Brett's hat was off. Her head was back. I saw her face in the lights from the open shops, then it was dark, then I saw her face clearly as we came out on the Avenue des Gobelins. The street was torn up and men were working on the car-tracks by the light of acetylene flares. Brett's face was white and the long line of her neck showed in the bright light of the flares. The street was dark again and I kissed her. Our lips were tight together and then she turned away and pressed against the corner of the seat, as far away as she could get. Her head was down.

'Don't touch me,' she said. 'Please don't touch me.'

'What's the matter?'

'I can't stand it.'

'Oh, Brett.'

'You mustn't. You must know. I can't stand it, that's all. Oh, darling, please understand!'

'Don't you love me?'

'Love you? I simply turn all to jelly when you touch me.'

'Isn't there anything we can do about it?'

She was sitting up now. My arm was around her and she was leaning back against me, and we were quite calm. She was looking into my eyes with that way she had of looking that made you wonder whether she really saw out of her own eyes. They would look on and on after every one else's eyes in the world would have stopped looking. She looked as though there were nothing on earth she would not look at like that, and really she was afraid of so many things.

'And there's not a damn thing we could do,' I said.

'I don't know,' she said. 'I don't want to go through that hell again.'

'We'd better keep away from each other.'
'But, darling, I have to see you. It isn't all that you know.'
'No, but it always gets to be.'
'That's my fault. Don't we pay for all the things we do, though?'

She had been looking into my eyes all the time. Her eyes had different depths, sometimes they seemed perfectly flat. Now you could see all the way into them.

'When I think of the hell I've put chaps through. I'm paying for it all now.'

'Don't talk like a fool,' I said. 'Besides, what happened to me is supposed to be funny. I never think about it.'

'Oh, no. I'll lay you don't.'

'Well, let's shut up about it.'

'I laughed about it too, myself, once.' She wasn't looking at me. 'A friend of my brother's came home that way from Mons. It seemed like a hell of a joke. Chaps never know anything, do they?'

'No,' I said. 'Nobody ever knows anything.'

I was pretty well through with the subject. At one time or another I had probably considered it from most of its various angles, including the one that certain injuries or imperfections are a subject of merriment while remaining quite serious for the person possessing them.

'It's funny,' I said. 'It's very funny. And it's a lot of fun, too, to be in love.'

'Do you think so?' her eyes looked flat again.

'I don't mean fun that way. In a way it's an enjoyable feeling.'

'No,' she said. 'I think it's hell on earth.'

'It's good to see each other.'

'No. I don't think it is.'

'Don't you want to?'

'I have to.'

We were sitting now like two strangers. On the right was the Parc Montsouris. The restaurant where they have the pool of live trout and where you can sit and look out over the park was closed and dark. The driver leaned his head around.

'Where do you want to go?' I asked. Brett turned her head away.

'Oh, go to the Select.'

'Café Select,' I told the driver. 'Boulevard Montparnasse.' We drove straight down, turning around the Lion de Belfort that guards the passing Montrouge trams. Brett looked straight ahead. On the Boulevard Raspail, with the lights of Montparnasse in sight, Brett said: 'Would you mind very much if I asked you to do something?'

'Don't be silly.'

'Kiss me just once more before we get there.'

When the taxi stopped I got out and paid. Brett came out putting on her hat. She gave me her hand as she stepped down. Her hand was shaky. 'I say, do I look too much of a mess?' She pulled her man's felt hat down and started in for the bar. Inside, against the bar and at tables, were most of the crowd who a been at the dance.

'Hello, you chaps,' Brett said. 'I'm going to have a drink.'

'Oh, Brett! Brett!' the little Greek portrait-painter, who called himself a duke, and whom everybody called Zizi, pushed up to her. 'I got something fine to tell you.'

'Hello, Zizi,' Brett said.

'I want you to meet a friend,' Zizi said. A fat man came up.

'Count Mippipopolous, meet my friend Lady Ashley.'

'How do you do?' said Brett.

'Well, does your Ladyship have a good time here in Paris?' asked Count Mippipopolous, who wore an elk's tooth on his watch-chain.

'Rather,' said Brett.

'Paris is a fine town all right,' said the count. 'But I guess you have pretty big doings yourself over in London.'

'Oh, yes,' said Brett. 'Enormous.'

Braddocks called to me from a table. 'Barnes,' he said, 'have a drink. That girl of yours got in a frightful row.'

'What about?'

'Something the patronne's daughter said. A corking row. She was rather splendid, you know. Showed her yellow card and demanded the patronne's daughter's too. I say it was a row.'

'What finally happened?'

'Oh, some one took her home. Not a bad-looking girl. Wonderful command of the idiom. Do stay and have a drink.'

'No,' I said. 'I must shove off. Seen Cohn?'

'He went home with Frances,' Mrs. Braddock put in.

'Poor chap, he looks awfully down,' Braddocks said.

'I dare say he is,' said Mrs. Braddocks.

'I have to shove off,' I said. 'Good night.'

I said good night to Brett at the bar. The count was buying champagne. 'Will you take a glass of wine with us, sir?' he asked.

'No. Thanks awfully. I have to go.'

'Really going?' Brett asked.

'Yes,' I said. 'I've got a rotten headache.'

'I'll see you to-morrow?'

'Come in at the office.'

'Hardly.'

'Well, where will I see you?'

'Anywhere around five o'clock.'

'Make it the other side of town then.'

'Good. I'll be at the Crillon at five.'

'Try and be there,' I said.

'Don't worry,' Brett said. 'I've never let you down, have I?'

'Heard from Mike?'

'Letter to-day.'

'Good night, sir,' said the count.

I went out onto the sidewalk and walked down toward the Boulevard St. Michel, passed the tables of the Rotonde, still crowded, looked across the street at the Dome, its tables running out to the edge of the pavement. Some one waved at me from a table, I did not see who it was and went on. I wanted to get home. The Boulevard Montparnasse was deserted. Lavigne's was closed tight, and they were stacking the tables outside the Closerie des Lilas. I passed Ney's statue standing among the new-leaved chestnut-trees in the arc-light. There was a faded purple wreath leaning against the base. I stopped and read the inscription: from the Bonapartist Groups, some date; I forget. He looked very fine, Marshal Ney in his top-boots, gesturing with his sword among the green new horse-chestnut leaves. My flat was just across the street, a little way down the Boulevard St. Michel.

There was a light in the concierge's room and I knocked on the door and she gave me my mail. I wished her good night and went up-stairs. There were two letters and some papers. I looked at them under the gas-light in the dining-room. The letters were from the States. One was a bank statement. It showed a balance of $2432.60. I got out my check-book and deducted four checks drawn since the first of the month, and discovered I had a balance of $1832.60. I wrote this on the back of the statement. The other letter was a wedding announcement. Mr. and Mrs. Aloysius Kirby announce the marriage of their daughter Katherine—I knew neither the girl nor the man she was marrying. They must be circularizing the town. It was a funny name. I felt sure I could remember anybody with a name like Aloysius. It was a good Catholic name. There was a crest on the announcement. Like Zizi the Greek duke. And that count. The count was funny. Brett had a title, too. Lady Ashley. To hell with Brett. To hell with you, Lady Ashley.

I lit the lamp beside the bed, turned off the gas, and opened the wide windows. The bed was far back from the windows, and I sat with the windows open and undressed by the bed. Outside a night train, running on the street-car tracks, went by carrying vegetables to the markets. They were noisy at night when you could not sleep. Undressing, I looked at myself in the mirror of the big armoire beside the bed. That was a typically French way to furnish a room. Practical, too, I suppose. Of all the ways to be wounded. I suppose it was funny. I put on my pajamas and got into bed. I had the two bull-fight papers, and I took their wrappers off. One was orange. The other yellow. They would both have the same news, so whichever I read first would spoil the other. *Le Toril* was the better paper, so I started to read it. I read it all the way through, including the Petite Correspondance and the Cornigrams. I blew out the lamp. Perhaps I would be able to sleep.

My head started to work. The old grievance. Well, it was a rotten way to be wounded and flying on a joke front like the Italian. In the Italian hospital we were going to form a society. It had a funny name in Italian. I wonder what became of the others, the Italians. That was in the Ospedale Maggiore in Milano, Padiglione Ponte. The next building was the Padiglione Zonda. There was a statue of Ponte, or maybe it was Zonda. That was where the liaison colonel came to visit me. That was funny. That was about the first funny thing. I was all bandaged up. But they had told him about it. Then he made that wonderful speech: 'You, a foreigner, an Englishman" (any foreigner was an Englishman) 'have given more than your life.' What a speech! I would like to have it illuminated to hang in the office. He never laughed. He was putting himself in my place, I guess. 'Che mala fortuna! Che mala fortuna!'

I never used to realize it, I guess. I try and play it along and just not make trouble for people. Probably I never would have had any trouble if I hadn't run into Brett when they shipped me to England. I suppose she only wanted what she couldn't have. Well, people were that way. To hell with people. The Catholic Church had an awfully good way of handling all that. Good advice, anyway. Not to think about it. Oh, it was swell advice. Try and take it sometime. Try and take it.

I lay awake thinking and my mind jumping around. Then I couldn't keep away from it, and I started to think about Brett and all the rest of it went away. I was thinking about Brett and my mind stopped jumping around and started to go in sort of smooth waves. Then all of a sudden I started to cry. Then after a while it was better and I lay in bed and listened to the heavy trams go by and way down the street, and then I went to sleep.

I woke up. There was a row going on outside. I listened and I thought I recognized a voice. I put on a dressing-gown and went to the door. The concierge was talking down-stairs. She was very angry. I heard my name and called down the stairs.

'Is that you, Monsieur Barnes?' the concierge called.

'Yes. It's me.'

'There's a species of woman here who's waked the whole street up. What kind of a dirty business at this time of night! She says she must see you. I've told her you're asleep.'

Then I heard Brett's voice. Half asleep I had been sure it was Georgette. I don't know why. She could not have known my address.

'Will you send her up, please?'

Brett came up the stairs. I saw she was quite drunk. 'Silly thing to do,' she said. 'Make an awful row. I say, you weren't asleep, were you?'

'What did you think I was doing?'

'Don't know. What time is it?'

I looked at the clock. It was half-past four. 'Had no idea what hour it was,' Brett said. 'I say, can a chap sit down? Don't be cross, darling. Just left the count. He brought me here.'

'What's he like?' I was getting brandy and soda and glasses.

'Just a little,' said Brett. 'Don't try and make me drunk. The count? Oh, rather. He's quite one of us.'

'Is he a count?'

'Here's how. I rather think so, you know. Deserves to be, anyhow. Knows hell's own amount about people. Don't know where he got it all. Owns a chain of sweetshops in the States.'

She sipped at her glass.

'Think he called it a chain. Something like that. Linked them all up. Told me a little about it. Damned interesting. He's one of us, though. Oh, quite. No doubt. One can always tell.'

She took another drink.

'How do I buck on about all this? You don't mind, do you? He's putting up for Zizi, you know.'

'Is Zizi really a duke, too?'

'I shouldn't wonder. Greek, you know. Rotten painter. I rather liked the count.'

'Where did you go with him?'

'Oh, everywhere. He just brought me here now. Offered me ten thousand dollars to go to Biarritz with him. How much is that in pounds?'

'Around two thousand.'

'Lot of money. I told him I couldn't do it. He was awfully nice about it. Told him I knew too many people in Biarritz.'

Brett laughed.

'I say, you are slow on the up-take,' she said. I had only sipped my brandy and soda. I took a long drink.

'That's better. Very funny,' Brett said. 'Then he wanted me to go to Cannes with him. Told him I knew too many people in Cannes. Monte Carlo. Told him I knew too many people in Monte Carlo. Told him I knew too many people everywhere. Quite true, too. So I asked him to bring me here.'

She looked at me, her hand on the table, her glass raised. 'Don't look like that,' she said. 'Told him I was in love with you. True, too. Don't look like that. He was damn nice about it. Wants to drive us out to dinner to-morrow night. Like to go?'

'Why not?'

'I'd better go now.'

'Why?'

'Just wanted to see you. Damned silly idea. Want to get dressed and come down? He's got the car just up the street.'

'The count?'

'Himself. And a chauffeur in livery. Going to drive me around and have breakfast in the Bois. Hampers. Got it all at Zelli's. Dozen bottles of Mumms. Tempt you?'

'I have to work in the morning,' I said. 'I'm too far behind you now to catch up and be any fun.'

'Don't be an ass.'

'Can't do it.'

'Right. Send him a tender message?'

'Anything. Absolutely.'

'Good night, darling.'

'Don't be sentimental.'

'You make me ill.'

We kissed good night and Brett shivered. 'I'd better go,' she said. 'Good night, darling.'

'You don't have to go.'

'Yes.'

We kissed again on the stairs and as I called for the cordon the concierge muttered something behind her door. I went back up-stairs and from the open window watched Brett walking up the street to the big limousine drawn up to the curb under the arc-light. She got in and it started off. I turned around. On the table was an empty glass and a glass half-full of brandy and soda. I took them both out to the kitchen and poured the half-full glass down the sink. I turned off the gas in the dining-room, kicked off my slippers sitting on the bed, and got into bed. This was Brett, that I had felt like crying about. Then I thought of her walking up the street and stepping into the car, as I had last seen her, and of course in a little while I felt like hell again. It is awfully easy to be hard-boiled about everything in the daytime, but at night it is another thing.

5

In the morning I walked down the Boulevard to the rue Soufflot for coffee and brioche. It was a fine morning. The horse-chestnut trees in the Luxembourg gardens were in bloom. There was the pleasant early-morning feeling of a hot day. I read the papers with the coffee and then smoked a cigarette. The flower-women were coming up from the market and arranging their daily stock. Students went by going up to the law school, or down to the Sorbonne. The Boulevard was busy with trams and people going to work. I got on an S bus and rode down to the Madeleine, standing on the back platform. From the Madeleine I walked along the Boulevard des Capucines to the Opéra, and up to my office. I passed the man with the jumping frogs and the man with the boxer toys. I stepped aside to avoid walking into the thread with which his girl assistant manipulated the boxers. She was standing looking away, the thread in her folded hands. The man was urging two tourists to buy. Three more tourists had stopped and were watching. I walked on behind a man who was pushing a roller that printed the name CINZANO on the sidewalk in damp letters. All along people were going to work. It felt pleasant to be going to work. I walked across the avenue and turned in to my office.

Up-stairs in the office I read the French morning papers, smoked, and then sat at the typewriter and got off a good morning's work. At eleven o'clock I went over to the Quai d'Orsay in a taxi and went in and sat with about a dozen correspondents, while the foreign-office mouthpiece, a young Nouvelle Revue Française diplomat in horn-rimmed spectacles, talked and answered questions for half an hour. The President of the Council was in Lyons making a speech, or, rather he was on his way back. Several people asked questions to hear themselves talk and there were a couple of questions asked by news service men who wanted to know the answers. There was no news. I shared a taxi back from the Quai d'Orsay with Woolsey and Krum.

'What do you do nights, Jake?' asked Krum. 'I never see you around.'

'Oh, I'm over in the Quarter.'

'I'm coming over some night. The Dingo. That's the great place, isn't it?'

'Yes. That, or this new dive, The Select.'

'I've meant to get over,' said Krum. 'You know how it is, though, with a wife and kids.'

'Playing any tennis?' Woolsey asked.

'Well, no,' said Krum. 'I can't say I've played any this year. I've tried to get away, but Sundays it's always rained, and the courts are so damned crowded.'

'The Englishmen all have Saturday off,' Woolsey said.

'Lucky beggars,' said Krum. 'Well, I'll tell you. Some day I'm not going to be working for an agency. Then I'll have plenty of time to get out in the country.'

'That's the thing to do. Live out in the country and have a little car.'

'I've been thinking some about getting a car next year.'

I banged on the glass. The chauffeur stopped. 'Here's my street,' I said. 'Come in and have a drink.'

'Thanks, old man,' Krum said. Woolsey shook his head. 'I've got to file that line he got off this morning.'

I put a two-franc piece in Krum's hand.

'You're crazy, Jake,' he said. 'This is on me.'

'It's all on the office, anyway.'

'Nope. I want to get it.'

I waved good-by. Krum put his head out. 'See you at the lunch on Wednesday.'

'You bet.'

I went to the office in the elevator. Robert Cohn was waiting for me. 'Hello, Jake,' he said. 'Going out to lunch?'

'Yes. Let me see if there is anything new.'

'Where will we eat?'

'Anywhere.'

I was looking over my desk. 'Where do you want to eat?'

'How about Wetzel's? They've got good hors d'œuvres.'

In the restaurant we ordered hors d'œuvres and beer. The sommelier brought the beer, tall, beaded on the outside of the steins, and cold. There were a dozen different dishes of hors d'œuvres.

'Have any fun last night?' I asked.

'No. I don't think so.'

'How's the writing going?'

'Rotten. I can't get this second book going.'

'That happens to everybody.'

'Oh, I'm sure of that. It gets me worried, though.'

'Thought any more about going to South America?'
'I mean that.'
'Well, why don't you start off?'
'Frances.'
'Well,' I said, 'take her with you.'
'She wouldn't like it. That isn't the sort of thing she likes. She likes a lot of people around.'
'Tell her to go to hell.'
'I can't. I've got certain obligations to her.'
He shoved the sliced cucumbers away and took a pickled herring.
'What do you know about Lady Brett Ashley, Jake?'
'Her name's Lady Ashley. Brett's her own name. She's a nice girl,' I said. 'She's getting a divorce and she's going to marry Mike Campbell. He's over in Scotland now. Why?'
'She's a remarkably attractive woman.'
'Isn't she?'
'There's a certain quality about her, a certain fineness. She seems to be absolutely fine and straight.'
'She's very nice.'
'I don't know how to describe the quality,' Cohn said. 'I suppose it's breeding.'
'You sound as though you liked her pretty well.'
'I do. I shouldn't wonder if I were in love with her.'
'She's a drunk,' I said. 'She's in love with Mike Campbell, and she's going to marry him. He's going to be rich as hell some day.'
'I don't believe she'll ever marry him.'
'Why not?'
'I don't know. I just don't believe it. Have you known her a long time?'
'Yes,' I said. 'She was a V. A. D. in a hospital I was in during the war.'
'She must have been just a kid then.'
'She's thirty-four now.'
'When did she marry Ashley?'
'During the war. Her own true love had just kicked off with the dysentery.'
'You talk sort of bitter.'
'Sorry. I didn't mean to. I was just trying to give you the facts.'
'I don't believe she would marry anybody she didn't love.'
'Well,' I said. 'She's done it twice.'
'I don't believe it.'
'Well,' I said, 'don't ask me a lot of fool questions if you don't like the answers.'
'I didn't ask you that.'
'You asked me what I knew about Brett Ashley.'
'I didn't ask you to insult her.'
'Oh, go to hell.'
He stood up from the table his face white, and stood there white and angry

behind the little plates of hors d'œuvres.

'Sit down,' I said. 'Don't be a fool.'

'You've got to take that back.'

'Oh, cut out the prep-school stuff.'

'Take it back.'

'Sure. Anything. I never heard of Brett Ashley. How's that?'

'No. Not that. About me going to hell.'

'Oh, don't go to hell,' I said. 'Stick around. We're just starting lunch.'

Cohn smiled again and sat down. He seemed glad to sit down. What the hell would he have done if he hadn't sat down? 'You say such damned insulting things, Jake.'

'I'm sorry. I've got a nasty tongue. I never mean it when I say nasty things.'

'I know it,' Cohn said. 'You're really about the best friend I have, Jake.'

God help you, I thought. 'Forget what I said,' I said out loud. 'I'm sorry.'

'It's all right. It's fine. I was just sore for a minute.'

'Good. Let's get something else to eat.'

After we finished the lunch we walked up to the Café de la Paix and had coffee. I could feel Cohn wanted to bring up Brett again, but I held him off it. We talked about one thing and another, and I left him to come to the office.

6

At five o'clock I was in the Hotel Crillon waiting for Brett. She was not there, so I sat down and wrote some letters. They were not very good letters but I hoped their being on Crillon stationery would help them. Brett did not turn up, so about quarter to six I went down to the bar and had a Jack Rose with George the barman. Brett had not been in the bar either, and so I looked for her up-stairs on my way out, and took a taxi to the Café Select. Crossing the Seine I saw a string of barges being towed empty down the current, riding high, the bargemen at the sweeps as they came toward the bridge. The river looked nice. It was always pleasant crossing bridges in Paris.

The taxi rounded the statue of the inventor of the semaphore engaged in doing same, and turned up the Boulevard Raspail, and I sat back to let that part of the ride pass. The Boulevard Raspail always made dull riding. It was like a certain stretch on the P. L. M. between Fontainebleau and Montereau that always made me feel bored and dead and dull until it was over. I suppose it is some association of ideas that makes those dead places in a journey. There are other streets in Paris as ugly as the Boulevard Raspail. It is a street I do not mind walking down at all. But I cannot stand to ride along it. Perhaps I had read something about it once. That was the way Robert Cohn was about all of Paris. I wondered where Cohn got that incapacity to enjoy Paris. Possibly from Mencken. Mencken hates Paris, I believe. So many young men get their likes and dislikes from Mencken.

The taxi stopped in front of the Rotonde. No matter what café in Montparnasse you ask a taxi-driver to bring you to from the right bank of the river, they always take you to the Rotonde. Ten years from now it will probably be the Dome. It was near enough, anyway. I walked past the sad tables of the Rotonde to the Select. There were a few people inside at the bar, and outside, alone, sat Harvey Stone. He had a pile of saucers in front of him, and he needed a shave.

'Sit down,' said Harvey, 'I've been looking for you.'

'What's the matter?'

'Nothing. Just looking for you.'

'Been out to the races?'

'No. Not since Sunday.'

'What do you hear from the States?'

'Nothing. Absolutely nothing.'

'What's the matter?'

'I don't know. I'm through with them. I'm absolutely through with them.'

He leaned forward and looked me in the eye.

'Do you want to know something, Jake?'

'Yes.'

'I haven't had anything to eat for five days.'

I figured rapidly back in my mind. It was three days ago that Harvey had won two hundred francs from me shaking poker dice in the New York Bar.

'What's the matter?'

'No money. Money hasn't come,' he paused. 'I tell you it's strange, Jake. When I'm like this I just want to be alone. I want to stay in my own room. I'm like a cat.'

I felt in my pocket.

'Would a hundred help you any, Harvey?'

'Yes.'

'Come on. Let's go and eat.'

'There's no hurry. Have a drink.'

'Better eat.'

'No. When I get like this I don't care whether I eat or not.'

We had a drink. Harvey added my saucer to his own pile.

'Do you know Mencken, Harvey?'

'Yes. Why?'

'What's he like?'

'He's all right. He says some pretty funny things. Last time I had dinner with him we talked about Hoffenheimer. "The trouble is," he said, "he's a garter snapper." That's not bad.'

'That's not bad.'

'He's through now,' Harvey went on. 'He's written about all the things he knows, and now he's on all the things he doesn't know.'

'I guess he's all right,' I said. 'I just can't read him.'

'Oh, nobody reads him now,' Harvey said, 'except the people that used to read the Alexander Hamilton Institute.'

'Well,' I said. 'That was a good thing, too.'
'Sure,' said Harvey. So we sat and thought deeply for a while.
'Have another port?'
'All right,' said Harvey.
'There comes Cohn,' I said. Robert Cohn was crossing the street.
'That moron,' said Harvey. Cohn came up to our table.
'Hello, you bums,' he said.
'Hello, Robert,' Harvey said. 'I was just telling Jake here that you're a moron.'
'What do you mean?'
'Tell us right off. Don't think. What would you rather do if you could do anything you wanted?'
Cohn started to consider.
'Don't think. Bring it right out.'
'I don't know,' Cohn said. 'What's it all about, anyway?'
'I mean what would you rather do. What comes into your head first. No matter how silly it is.'
'I don't know,' Cohn said. 'I think I'd rather play football again with what I know about handling myself, now.'
'I misjudged you,' Harvey said. 'You're not a moron. You're only a case of arrested development.'
'You're awfully funny, Harvey,' Cohn said. 'Some day somebody will push your face in.'
Harvey Stone laughed. 'You think so. They won't, though. Because it wouldn't make any difference to me. I'm not a fighter.'
'It would make a difference to you if anybody did it.'
'No, it wouldn't. That's where you make your big mistake. Because you're not intelligent.'
'Cut it out about me.'
'Sure,' said Harvey. 'It doesn't make any difference to me. You don't mean anything to me.'
'Come on, Harvey,' I said. 'Have another porto.'
'No,' he said. 'I'm going up the street and eat. See you later, Jake.'
He walked out and up the street. I watched him crossing the street through the taxis, small, heavy, slowly sure of himself in the traffic.
'He always gets me sore,' Cohn said. 'I can't stand him.'
'I like him,' I said. 'I'm fond of him. You don't want to get sore at him.'
'I know it,' Cohn said. 'He just gets on my nerves.'
'Write this afternoon?'
'No. I couldn't get it going. It's harder to do than my first book. I'm having a hard time handling it.'
The sort of healthy conceit that he had when he returned from America early in the spring was gone. Then he had been sure of his work, only with these personal longings for adventure. Now the sureness was gone. Somehow I feel I

have not shown Robert Cohn clearly. The reason is that until he fell in love with Brett, I never heard him make one remark that would, in any way, detach him from other people. He was nice to watch on the tennis-court, he had a good body, and he kept it in shape; he handled his cards well at bridge, and he had a funny sort of undergraduate quality about him. If he were in a crowd nothing he said stood out. He wore what used to be called polo shirts at school, and may be called that still, but he was not professionally youthful. I do not believe he thought about his clothes much. Externally he had been formed at Princeton. Internally he had been moulded by the two women who had trained him. He had a nice, boyish sort of cheerfulness that had never been trained out of him, and I probably have not brought it out. He loved to win at tennis. He probably loved to win as much as Lenglen, for instance. On the other hand, he was not angry at being beaten. When he fell in love with Brett his tennis game went all to pieces. People beat him who had never had a chance with him. He was very nice about it.

Anyhow, we were sitting on the terrace of the Café Select, and Harvey Stone had just crossed the street.

'Come on up to the Lilas,' I said.

'I have a date.'

'What time?'

'Frances is coming here at seven-fifteen.'

'There she is.'

Frances Clyne was coming toward us from across the street. She was a very tall girl who walked with a great deal of movement. She waved and smiled. We watched her cross the street.

'Hello,' she said, 'I'm so glad you're here, Jake. I've been wanting to talk to you.'

'Hello, Frances,' said Cohn. He smiled.

'Why, hello, Robert. Are you here?' She went on, talking rapidly. 'I've had the darndest time. This one'—shaking her head at Cohn—'didn't come home for lunch.'

'I wasn't supposed to.'

'Oh, I know. But you didn't say anything about it to the cook. Then I had a date myself, and Paula wasn't at her office. I went to the Ritz and waited for her, and she never came, and of course I didn't have enough money to lunch at the Ritz—'

'What did you do?'

'Oh, went out, of course.' She spoke in a sort of imitation joyful manner. 'I always keep my appointments. No one keeps theirs, nowadays. I ought to know better. How are you, Jake, anyway?'

'Fine.'

'That was a fine girl you had at the dance, and then went off with that Brett one.'

'Don't you like her?' Cohn asked.

'I think she's perfectly charming. Don't you?'

Cohn said nothing.

'Look, Jake. I want to talk with you. Would you come over with me to the Dome? You'll stay here, won't you, Robert? Come on, Jake.'

We crossed the Boulevard Montparnasse and sat down at a table. A boy came up with the *Paris Times*, and I bought one and opened it.

'What's the matter, Frances?'

'Oh, nothing,' she said, 'except that he wants to leave me.'

'How do you mean?'

'Oh, he told every one that we were going to be married, and I told my mother and every one, and now he doesn't want to do it.'

'What's the matter?'

'He's decided he hasn't lived enough. I knew it would happen when he went to New York.'

She looked up, very bright-eyed and trying to talk inconsequentially.

'I wouldn't marry him if he doesn't want to. Of course I wouldn't. I wouldn't marry him now for anything. But it does seem to me to be a little late now, after we've waited three years, and I've just gotten my divorce.'

I said nothing.

'We were going to celebrate so, and instead we've just had scenes. It's so childish. We have dreadful scenes, and he cries and begs me to be reasonable, but he says he just can't do it.'

'It's rotten luck.'

'I should say it is rotten luck. I've wasted two years and a half on him now. And I don't know now if any man will ever want to marry me. Two years ago I could have married anybody I wanted, down at Cannes. All the old ones that wanted to marry somebody chic and settle down were crazy about me. Now I don't think I could get anybody.'

'Sure, you could marry anybody.'

'No, I don't believe it. And I'm fond of him, too. And I'd like to have children. I always thought we'd have children.'

She looked at me very brightly. 'I never liked children much, but I don't want to think I'll never have them. I always thought I'd have them and then like them.'

'He's got children.'

'Oh, yes. He's got children, and he's got money, and he's got a rich mother, and he's written a book, and nobody will publish my stuff; nobody at all. It isn't bad, either. And I haven't got any money at all. I could have had alimony, but I got the divorce the quickest way.'

She looked at me again very brightly.

'It isn't right. It's my own fault and it's not, too. I ought to have known better. And when I tell him he just cries and says he can't marry. Why can't he marry? I'd be a good wife. I'm easy to get along with. I leave him alone. It doesn't do any good.'

'It's a rotten shame.'

'Yes, it is a rotten shame. But there's no use talking about it, is there? Come on, let's go back to the café.'

'And of course there isn't anything I can do.'

'No. Just don't let him know I talked to you. I know what he wants.' Now for the first time she dropped her bright, terribly cheerful manner. 'He wants to go back to New York alone, and be there when his book comes out so when a lot of little chickens like it. That's what he wants.'

'Maybe they won't like it. I don't think he's that way. Really.'

'You don't know him like I do, Jake. That's what he wants to do. I know it. I know it. That's why he doesn't want to marry. He wants to have a big triumph this fall all by himself.'

'Want to go back to the café?'

'Yes. Come on.'

We got up from the table—they had never brought us a drink—and started across the street toward the Select, where Cohn sat smiling at us from behind the marble-topped table.

'Well, what are you smiling at?' Frances asked him. 'Feel pretty happy?'

'I was smiling at you and Jake with your secrets.'

'Oh, what I've told Jake isn't any secret. Everybody will know it soon enough. I only wanted to give Jake a decent version.'

'What was it? About your going to England?'

'Yes, about my going to England. Oh, Jake! I forgot to tell you. I'm going to England.'

'Isn't that fine!'

'Yes, that's the way it's done in the very best families. Robert's sending me. He's going to give me two hundred pounds and then I'm going to visit friends. Won't it be lovely? The friends don't know about it, yet.'

She turned to Cohn and smiled at him. He was not smiling now.

'You were only going to give me a hundred pounds, weren't you, Robert? But I made him give me two hundred. He's really very generous. Aren't you, Robert?'

I do not know how people could say such terrible things to Robert Cohn. There are people to whom you could not say insulting things. They give you a feeling that the world would be destroyed, would actually be destroyed before your eyes, if you said certain things. But here was Cohn taking it all. Here it was, all going on right before me, and I did not even feel an impulse to try and stop it. And this was friendly joking to what went on later.

'How can you say such things, Frances?' Cohn interrupted.

'Listen to him. I'm going to England. I'm going to visit friends. Ever visit friends that didn't want you? Oh, they'll have to take me, all right. 'How do you do, my dear? Such a long time since we've seen you. And how is your dear mother?' Yes, how is my dear mother? She put all her money into French war bonds. Yes, she did. Probably the only person in the world that did. 'And what about Robert?' or else very careful talking around Robert. 'You must be most careful not to mention him, my dear. Poor Frances has had a most unfortunate experience.' Won't it be fun, Robert? Don't you think it will be fun, Jake?'

She turned to me with that terribly bright smile. It was very satisfactory to her to have an audience for this.

'And where are you going to be, Robert? It's my own fault, all right. Perfectly my own fault. When I made you get rid of your little secretary on the magazine I ought to have known you'd get rid of me the same way. Jake doesn't know about that. Should I tell him?'

'Shut up, Frances, for God's sake.'

'Yes, I'll tell him. Robert had a little secretary on the magazine. Just the sweetest little thing in the world, and he thought she was wonderful, and then I came along and he thought I was pretty wonderful, too. So I made him get rid of her, and he had brought her to Provincetown from Carmel when he moved the magazine, and he didn't even pay her fare back to the coast. All to please me. He thought I was pretty fine, then. Didn't you, Robert?

'You mustn't misunderstand, Jake, it was absolutely platonic with the secretary. Not even platonic. Nothing at all, really. It was just that she was so nice. And he did that just to please me. Well, I suppose that we that live by the sword shall perish by the sword. Isn't that literary, though? You want to remember that for your next book, Robert.

'You know Robert is going to get material for a new book. Aren't you, Robert? That's why he's leaving me. He's decided I don't film well. You see, he was so busy all the time that we were living together, writing on this book, that he doesn't remember anything about us. So now he's going out and get some new material. Well, I hope he gets something frightfully interesting.

'Listen, Robert, dear. Let me tell you something. You won't mind, will you? Don't have scenes with your young ladies. Try not to. Because you can't have scenes without crying, and then you pity yourself so much you can't remember what the other person's said. You'll never be able to remember any conversations that way. Just try and be calm. I know it's awfully hard. But remember, it's for literature. We all ought to make sacrifices for literature. Look at me. I'm going to England without a protest. All for literature. We must all help young writers. Don't you think so, Jake? But you're not a young writer. Are you, Robert? You're thirty-four. Still, I suppose that is young for a great writer. Look at Hardy. Look at Anatole France. He just died a little while ago. Robert doesn't think he's any good, though. Some of his French friends told him. He doesn't read French very well himself. He wasn't a good writer like you are, was he, Robert? Do you think he ever had to go and look for material? What do you suppose he said to his mistresses when he wouldn't marry them? I wonder if he cried, too? Oh, I've just thought of something.' She put her gloved hand up to her lips. 'I know the real reason why Robert won't marry me, Jake. It's just come to me. They've sent it to me in a vision in the Café Select. Isn't it mystic? Some day they'll put a tablet up. Like at Lourdes. Do you want to hear, Robert? I'll tell you. It's so simple. I wonder why I never thought about it. Why, you see, Robert's always wanted to have a mistress, and if he doesn't marry me, why, then he's had one. She was his mistress for over two years.

See how it is? And if he marries me, like he's always promised he would, that would be the end of all the romance. Don't you think that's bright of me to figure that out? It's true, too. Look at him and see if it's not. Where are you going, Jake?'

'I've got to go in and see Harvey Stone a minute.'

Cohn looked up as I went in. His face was white. Why did he sit there? Why did he keep on taking it like that?

As I stood against the bar looking out I could see them through the window. Frances was talking on to him, smiling brightly, looking into his face each time she asked: 'Isn't it so, Robert?' Or maybe she did not ask that now. Perhaps she said something else. I told the barman I did not want anything to drink and went out through the side door. As I went out the door I looked back through the two thicknesses of glass and saw them sitting there. She was still talking to him. I went down a side street to the Boulevard Raspail. A taxi came along and I got in and gave the driver the address of my flat.

7

As I started up the stairs the concierge knocked on the glass of the door of her lodge, and as I stopped she came out. She had some letters and a telegram.

'Here is the post. And there was a lady here to see you.'

'Did she leave a card?'

'No. She was with a gentleman. It was the one who was here last night. In the end I find she is very nice.'

'Was she with a friend of mine?'

'I don't know. He was never here before. He was very large. Very, very large. She was very nice. Very, very nice. Last night she was, perhaps, a little—' She put her head on one hand and rocked it up and down. 'I'll speak perfectly frankly, Monsieur Barnes. Last night I found her not so gentille. Last night I formed another idea of her. But listen to what I tell you. She is très, très gentille. She is of very good family. It is a thing you can see.'

'They did not leave any word?'

'Yes. They said they would be back in an hour.'

'Send them up when they come.'

'Yes, Monsieur Barnes. And that lady, that lady there is some one. An eccentric, perhaps, but quelqu'une, quelqu'une!'

The concierge, before she became a concierge, had owned a drink-selling concession at the Paris race-courses. Her life-work lay in the pelouse, but she kept an eye on the people of the pesage, and she took great pride in telling me which of my guests were well brought up, which were of good family, who were sportsmen, a French word pronounced with the accent on the men. The only trouble was that people who did not fall into any of those three categories were very liable to be told there was no one home, chez Barnes. One of my friends, an extremely underfed-looking painter, who was obviously to Madame Duzinell neither well brought up, of good family, nor a sportsman, wrote me a letter asking if I could get him a pass to get by the concierge so he could come up and see me occasionally in the evenings.

I went up to the flat wondering what Brett had done to the concierge. The wire was a cable from Bill Gorton, saying he was arriving on the *France*. I put the mail on the table, went back to the bedroom, undressed and had a shower. I was rubbing down when I heard the door-bell pull. I put on a bathrobe and slippers and went to the door. It was Brett. Back of her was the count. He was holding a great bunch of roses.

'Hello, darling,' said Brett. 'Aren't you going to let us in?'

'Come on. I was just bathing.'

'Aren't you the fortunate man. Bathing.'

'Only a shower. Sit down, Count Mippipopolous. What will you drink?'

'I don't know whether you like flowers, sir,' the count said, 'but I took the liberty of just bringing these roses.'

'Here, give them to me.' Brett took them. 'Get me some water in this, Jake.' I filled the big earthenware jug with water in the kitchen, and Brett put the roses in it, and placed them in the centre of the dining-room table.

'I say. We have had a day.'

'You don't remember anything about a date with me at the Crillon?'

'No. Did we have one? I must have been blind.'

'You were quite drunk, my dear,' said the count.

'Wasn't I, though? And the count's been a brick, absolutely.'

'You've got hell's own drag with the concierge now.'

'I ought to have. Gave her two hundred francs.'

'Don't be a damned fool.'

'His,' she said, and nodded at the count.

'I thought we ought to give her a little something for last night. It was very late.'

'He's wonderful,' Brett said. 'He remembers everything that's happened.'

'So do you, my dear.'

'Fancy,' said Brett. 'Who'd want to? I say, Jake, *do* we get a drink?'

'You get it while I go in and dress. You know where it is.'

'Rather.'

While I dressed I heard Brett put down glasses and then a siphon, and then heard them talking. I dressed slowly, sitting on the bed. I felt tired and pretty rotten. Brett came in the room, a glass in her hand, and sat on the bed.

'What's the matter, darling? Do you feel rocky?'

She kissed me coolly on the forehead.

'Oh, Brett, I love you so much.'

'Darling,' she said. Then: 'Do you want me to send him away?'

'No. He's nice.'

'I'll send him away.'

'No, don't.'

'Yes, I'll send him away.'

'You can't just like that.'

'Can't I, though? You stay here. He's mad about me, I tell you.'

She was gone out of the room. I lay face down on the bed. I was having a bad time. I heard them talking but I did not listen. Brett came in and sat on the bed.

'Poor old darling.' She stroked my head.

'What did you say to him?' I was lying with my face away from her. I did not want to see her.

'Sent him for champagne. He loves to go for champagne.'

Then later: 'Do you feel better, darling? Is the head any better?'

'It's better.'

'Lie quiet. He's gone to the other side of town.'

'Couldn't we live together, Brett? Couldn't we just live together?'

'I don't think so. I'd just *tromper* you with everybody. You couldn't stand it.'

'I stand it now.'

'That would be different. It's my fault, Jake. It's the way I'm made.'

'Couldn't we go off in the country for a while?'

'It wouldn't be any good. I'll go if you like. But I couldn't live quietly in the country. Not with my own true love.'

'I know.'

'Isn't it rotten? There isn't any use my telling you I love you.'

'You know I love you.'

'Let's not talk. Talking's all bilge. I'm going away from you, and then Michael's coming back.'

'Why are you going away?'

'Better for you. Better for me.'

'When are you going?'

'Soon as I can.'

'Where?'

'San Sebastian.'

'Can't we go together?'

'No. That would be a hell of an idea after we'd just talked it out.'

'We never agreed.'

'Oh, you know as well as I do. Don't be obstinate, darling.'

'Oh, sure,' I said. 'I know you're right. I'm just low, and when I'm low I talk like a fool.'

I sat up, leaned over, found my shoes beside the bed and put them on. I stood up.

'Don't look like that, darling.'

'How do you want me to look?'

'Oh, don't be a fool. I'm going away to-morrow.'

'To-morrow?'

'Yes. Didn't I say so? I am.'

'Let's have a drink, then. The count will be back.'

'Yes. He should be back. You know he's extraordinary about buying champagne. It means any amount to him.'

We went into the dining-room. I took up the brandy bottle and poured Brett a drink and one for myself. There was a ring at the bell-pull. I went to the door and there was the count. Behind him was the chauffeur carrying a basket of champagne.

'Where should I have him put it, sir?' asked the count.

'In the kitchen,' Brett said.

'Put it in there, Henry,' the count motioned. 'Now go down and get the ice.' He stood looking after the basket inside the kitchen door. 'I think you'll find that's very good wine,' he said. 'I know we don't get much of a chance to judge good wine in the States now, but I got this from a friend of mine that's in the business.'

'Oh, you always have some one in the trade,' Brett said.

'This fellow raises the grapes. He's got thousands of acres of them.'

'What's his name?' asked Brett. 'Veuve Cliquot?'

'No,' said the count. 'Mumms. He's a baron.'

'Isn't it wonderful,' said Brett. 'We all have titles. Why haven't you a title, Jake?'

'I assure you, sir,' the count put his hand on my arm. 'It never does a man any good. Most of the time it costs you money.'

'Oh, I don't know. It's damned useful sometimes,' Brett said.

'I've never known it to do me any good.'

'You haven't used it properly. I've had hell's own amount of credit on mine.'

'Do sit down, count,' I said. 'Let me take that stick.'

The count was looking at Brett across the table under the gas-light. She was smoking a cigarette and flicking the ashes on the rug. She saw me notice it. 'I say, Jake, I don't want to ruin your rugs. Can't you give a chap an ash-tray?'

I found some ash-trays and spread them around. The chauffeur came up with a bucket full of salted ice. 'Put two bottles in it, Henry,' the count called.

'Anything else, sir?'

'No. Wait down in the car.' He turned to Brett and to me. 'We'll want to ride out to the Bois for dinner?'

'If you like,' Brett said. 'I couldn't eat a thing.'

'I always like a good meal,' said the count.

'Should I bring the wine in, sir?' asked the chauffeur.

'Yes. Bring it in, Henry,' said the count. He took out a heavy pigskin cigar-case and offered it to me. 'Like to try a real American cigar?'

'Thanks,' I said. 'I'll finish the cigarette.'

He cut off the end of his cigar with a gold cutter he wore on one end of his watch-chain.

'I like a cigar to really draw,' said the count 'Half the cigars you smoke don't draw.'

He lit the cigar, puffed at it, looking across the table at Brett. 'And when you're divorced, Lady Ashley, then you won't have a title.'

'No. What a pity.'

'No,' said the count. 'You don't need a title. You got class all over you.'

'Thanks. Awfully decent of you.'

'I'm not joking you,' the count blew a cloud of smoke. 'You got the most class of anybody I ever seen. You got it. That's all.'

'Nice of you,' said Brett. 'Mummy would be pleased. Couldn't you write it out, and I'll send it in a letter to her.'

'I'd tell her, too,' said the count. 'I'm not joking you. I never joke people. Joke people and you make enemies. That's what I always say.'

'You're right,' Brett said. 'You're terribly right. I always joke people and I haven't a friend in the world. Except Jake here.'

'You don't joke him.'

'That's it.'

'Do you, now?' asked the count. 'Do you joke him?'

Brett looked at me and wrinkled up the corners of her eyes.

'No,' she said. 'I wouldn't joke him.'

'See,' said the count. 'You don't joke him.'

'This is a hell of a dull talk,' Brett said. 'How about some of that champagne?'

The count reached down and twirled the bottles in the shiny bucket. 'It isn't cold, yet. You're always drinking, my dear. Why don't you just talk?'

'I've talked too ruddy much. I've talked myself all out to Jake.'

'I should like to hear you really talk, my dear. When you talk to me you never finish your sentences at all.'

'Leave 'em for you to finish. Let any one finish them as they like.'

'It is a very interesting system,' the count reached down and gave the bottles a twirl. 'Still I would like to hear you talk some time.'

'Isn't he a fool?' Brett asked.

'Now,' the count brought up a bottle. 'I think this is cool.'

I brought a towel and he wiped the bottle dry and held it up. 'I like to drink champagne from magnums. The wine is better but it would have been too hard to cool.' He held the bottle, looking at it. I put out the glasses.

'I say. You might open it,' Brett suggested.

'Yes, my dear. Now I'll open it.'

It was amazing champagne.

'I say that is wine,' Brett held up her glass. 'We ought to toast something. "Here's to royalty."'

'This wine is too good for toast-drinking, my dear. You don't want to mix emotions up with a wine like that. You lose the taste.'

Brett's glass was empty.

'You ought to write a book on wines, count,' I said.

'Mr. Barnes,' answered the count, 'all I want out of wines is to enjoy them.'

'Let's enjoy a little more of this,' Brett pushed her glass forward. The count poured very carefully. 'There, my dear. Now you enjoy that slowly, and then you can get drunk.'

'Drunk? Drunk?'

'My dear, you are charming when you are drunk.'

'Listen to the man.'

'Mr. Barnes,' the count poured my glass full. 'She is the only lady I have ever known who was as charming when she was drunk as when she was sober.'

'You haven't been around much, have you?'

'Yes, my dear. I have been around very much. I have been around a very great deal.'

'Drink your wine,' said Brett. 'We've all been around. I dare say Jake here has seen as much as you have.'

'My dear, I am sure Mr. Barnes has seen a lot. Don't think I don't think so, sir. I have seen a lot, too.'

'Of course you have, my dear,' Brett said. 'I was only ragging.'

'I have been in seven wars and four revolutions,' the count said.

'Soldiering?' Brett asked.

'Sometimes, my dear. And I have got arrow wounds. Have you ever seen arrow wounds?'

'Let's have a look at them.'

The count stood up, unbuttoned his vest, and opened his shirt. He pulled up the undershirt onto his chest and stood, his chest black, and big stomach muscles bulging under the light.

'You see them?'

Below the line where his ribs stopped were two raised white welts. 'See on the back where they come out.' Above the small of the back were the same two scars, raised as thick as a finger.

'I say. Those are something.'

'Clean through.'

The count was tucking in his shirt.

'Where did you get those?' I asked.

'In Abyssinia. When I was twenty-one years old.'

'What were you doing?' asked Brett. 'Were you in the army?'

'I was on a business trip, my dear.'

'I told you he was one of us. Didn't I?' Brett turned to me. 'I love you, count. You're a darling.'

'You make me very happy, my dear. But it isn't true.'

'Don't be an ass.'

'You see, Mr. Barnes, it is because I have lived very much that now I can enjoy everything so well. Don't you find it like that?'

'Yes. Absolutely.'

'I know,' said the count. 'That is the secret. You must get to know the values.'

'Doesn't anything ever happen to your values?' Brett asked.

'No. Not any more.'

'Never fall in love?'

'Always,' said the count. 'I am always in love.'

'What does that do to your values?'

'That, too, has got a place in my values.'

'You haven't any values. You're dead, that's all.'

'No, my dear. You're not right. I'm not dead at all.'

We drank three bottles of the champagne and the count left the basket in my kitchen. We dined at a restaurant in the Bois. It was a good dinner. Food had an excellent place in the count's values. So did wine. The count was in fine form during the meal. So was Brett. It was a good party.

'Where would you like to go?' asked the count after dinner. We were the only people left in the restaurant. The two waiters were standing over against the door. They wanted to go home.

'We might go up on the hill,' Brett said. 'Haven't we had a splendid party?'

The count was beaming. He was very happy.

'You are very nice people,' he said. He was smoking a cigar again. 'Why don't you get married, you two?'

'We want to lead our own lives,' I said.

'We have our careers,' Brett said. 'Come on. Let's get out of this.'

'Have another brandy,' the count said.

'Get it on the hill.'

'No. Have it here where it is quiet.'

'You and your quiet,' said Brett. 'What is it men feel about quiet?'

'We like it,' said the count. 'Like you like noise, my dear.'

'All right,' said Brett. 'Let's have one.'

'Sommelier!' the count called.

'Yes, sir.'

'What is the oldest brandy you have?'

'Eighteen eleven, sir.'

'Bring us a bottle.'

'I say. Don't be ostentatious. Call him off, Jake.'

'Listen, my dear. I get more value for my money in old brandy than in any other antiquities.'

'Got many antiquities?'

'I got a houseful.'

Finally we went up to Montmartre. Inside Zelli's it was crowded, smoky, and noisy. The music hit you as you went in. Brett and I danced. It was so crowded we could barely move. The nigger drummer waved at Brett. We were caught in the jam, dancing in one place in front of him.

'Hahre you?'

'Great.'

'Thaats good.'

He was all teeth and lips.

'He's a great friend of mine,' Brett said. 'Damn good drummer.'

The music stopped and we started toward the table where the count sat. Then the music started again and we danced. I looked at the count. He was sitting at the table smoking a cigar. The music stopped again.

'Let's go over.'

Brett started toward the table. The music started and again we danced, tight in the crowd.

'You are a rotten dancer, Jake. Michael's the best dancer I know.'

'He's splendid.'

'He's got his points.'

'I like him,' I said. 'I'm damned fond of him.'

'I'm going to marry him,' Brett said. 'Funny. I haven't thought about him for a week.'

'Don't you write him?'

'Not I. Never write letters.'

'I'll bet he writes to you.'

'Rather. Damned good letters, too.'

'When are you going to get married?'

'How do I know? As soon as we can get the divorce. Michael's trying to get his mother to put up for it.'

'Could I help you?'

'Don't be an ass. Michael's people have loads of money.'

The music stopped. We walked over to the table. The count stood up.

'Very nice,' he said. 'You looked very, very nice.'

'Don't you dance, count?' I asked.

'No. I'm too old.'

'Oh, come off it,' Brett said.

'My dear, I would do it if I would enjoy it. I enjoy to watch you dance.'

'Splendid,' Brett said. 'I'll dance again for you some time. I say. What about your little friend, Zizi?'

'Let me tell you. I support that boy, but I don't want to have him around.'

'He is rather hard.'

'You know I think that boy's got a future. But personally I don't want him around.'

'Jake's rather the same way.'

'He gives me the willys.'

'Well,' the count shrugged his shoulders. 'About his future you can't ever tell. Anyhow, his father was a great friend of my father.'

'Come on. Let's dance,' Brett said.

We danced. It was crowded and close.

'Oh, darling,' Brett said, 'I'm so miserable.'

I had that feeling of going through something that has all happened before.

'You were happy a minute ago.'

The drummer shouted: 'You can't two time—'

'It's all gone.'

'What's the matter?'

'I don't know. I just feel terribly.'

'.....' the drummer chanted. Then turned to his sticks.

'Want to go?'

I had the feeling as in a nightmare of it all being something repeated, something I had been through and that now I must go through again.

'.....' the drummer sang softly.

'Let's go,' said Brett. 'You don't mind.'

'.....' the drummer shouted and grinned at Brett.

'All right,' I said. We got out from the crowd. Brett went to the dressing-room.

'Brett wants to go,' I said to the count. He nodded. 'Does she? That's fine. You take the car. I'm going to stay here for a while, Mr. Barnes.'

We shook hands.

'It was a wonderful time,' I said. 'I wish you would let me get this.' I took a note out of my pocket.

'Mr. Barnes, don't be ridiculous,' the count said.

Brett came over with her wrap on. She kissed the count and put her hand on his shoulder to keep him from standing up. As we went out the door I looked back and there were three girls at his table. We got into the big car. Brett gave the chauffeur the address of her hotel.

'No, don't come up,' she said at the hotel. She had rung and the door was unlatched.

'Really?'

'No. Please.'

'Good night, Brett,' I said. 'I'm sorry you feel rotten.'

'Good night, Jake. Good night, darling. I won't see you again.' We kissed standing at the door. She pushed me away. We kissed again. 'Oh, don't!' Brett said.

She turned quickly and went into the hotel. The chauffeur drove me around to my flat. I gave him twenty francs and he touched his cap and said: 'Good night, sir,' and drove off. I rang the bell. The door opened and I went up-stairs and went to bed.

BOOK TWO

8

I did not see Brett again until she came back from San Sebastian. One card came from her from there. It had a picture of the Concha, and said: 'Darling. Very quiet and healthy. Love to all the chaps. Brett.'

Nor did I see Robert Cohn again. I heard Frances had left for England and

I had a note from Cohn saying he was going out in the country for a couple of weeks, he did not know where, but that he wanted to hold me to the fishing-trip in Spain we had talked about last winter. I could reach him always, he wrote, through his bankers.

Brett was gone, I was not bothered by Cohn's troubles, I rather enjoyed not having to play tennis, there was plenty of work to do, I went often to the races, dined with friends, and put in some extra time at the office getting things ahead so I could leave it in charge of my secretary when Bill Gorton and I should shove off to Spain the end of June. Bill Gorton arrived, put up a couple of days at the flat and went off to Vienna. He was very cheerful and said the States were wonderful. New York was wonderful. There had been a grand theatrical season and a whole crop of great young light heavyweights. Any one of them was a good prospect to grow up, put on weight and trim Dempsey. Bill was very happy. He had made a lot of money on his last book, and was going to make a lot more. We had a good time while he was in Paris, and then he went off to Vienna. He was coming back in three weeks and we would leave for Spain to get in some fishing and go to the fiesta at Pamplona. He wrote that Vienna was wonderful. Then a card from Budapest: 'Jake, Budapest is wonderful.' Then I got a wire: 'Back on Monday.'

Monday evening he turned up at the flat. I heard his taxi stop and went to the window and called to him; he waved and started up-stairs carrying his bags. I met him on the stairs, and took one of the bags.

'Well,' I said, 'I hear you had a wonderful trip.'

'Wonderful,' he said. 'Budapest is absolutely wonderful.'

'How about Vienna?'

'Not so good, Jake. Not so good. It seemed better than it was.'

'How do you mean?' I was getting glasses and a siphon.

'Tight, Jake. I was tight.'

'That's strange. Better have a drink.'

Bill rubbed his forehead. 'Remarkable thing,' he said. 'Don't know how it happened. Suddenly it happened.'

'Last long?'

'Four days, Jake. Lasted just four days.'

'Where did you go?'

'Don't remember. Wrote you a post-card. Remember that perfectly.'

'Do anything else?'

'Not so sure. Possible.'

'Go on. Tell me about it.'

'Can't remember. Tell you anything I could remember.'

'Go on. Take that drink and remember.'

'Might remember a little,' Bill said. 'Remember something about a prize-fight. Enormous Vienna prize-fight. Had a nigger in it. Remember the nigger perfectly.'

'Go on.'

'Wonderful nigger. Looked like Tiger Flowers, only four times as big. All of a sudden everybody started to throw things. Not me. Nigger'd just knocked local boy down. Nigger put up his glove. Wanted to make a speech. Awful noble-looking nigger. Started to make a speech. Then local white boy hit him. Then he knocked white boy cold. Then everybody commenced to throw chairs. Nigger went home with us in our car. Couldn't get his clothes. Wore my coat. Remember the whole thing now. Big sporting evening.'

'What happened?'

'Loaned the nigger some clothes and went around with him to try and get his money. Claimed nigger owed them money on account of wrecking hall. Wonder who translated? Was it me?'

'Probably it wasn't you.'

'You're right. Wasn't me at all. Was another fellow. Think we called him the local Harvard man. Remember him now. Studying music.'

'How'd you come out?'

'Not so good, Jake. Injustice everywhere. Promoter claimed nigger promised let local boy stay. Claimed nigger violated contract. Can't knock out Vienna boy in Vienna. 'My God, Mister Gorton,' said nigger, 'I didn't do nothing in there for forty minutes but try and let him stay. That white boy musta ruptured himself swinging at me. I never did hit him.'"

'Did you get any money?'

'No money, Jake. All we could get was nigger's clothes. Somebody took his watch, too. Splendid nigger. Big mistake to have come to Vienna. Not so good, Jake. Not so good.'

'What became of the nigger?'

'Went back to Cologne. Lives there. Married. Got a family. Going to write me a letter and send me the money I loaned him. Wonderful nigger. Hope I gave him the right address.'

'You probably did.'

'Well, anyway, let's eat,' said Bill. 'Unless you want me to tell you some more travel stories.'

'Go on.'

'Let's eat.'

We went down-stairs and out onto the Boulevard St. Michel in the warm June evening.

'Where will we go?'

'Want to eat on the island?'

'Sure.'

We walked down the Boulevard. At the juncture of the Rue Denfert-Rochereau with the Boulevard is a statue of two men in flowing robes.

'I know who they are.' Bill eyed the monument. 'Gentlemen who invented pharmacy. Don't try and fool me on Paris.'

We went on.

'Here's a taxidermist's,' Bill said. 'Want to buy anything? Nice stuffed dog?'

'Come on,' I said. 'You're pie-eyed.'

'Pretty nice stuffed dogs,' Bill said. 'Certainly brighten up your flat.'

'Come on.'

'Just one stuffed dog. I can take 'em or leave 'em alone. But listen, Jake. Just one stuffed dog.'

'Come on.'

'Mean everything in the world to you after you bought it. Simple exchange of values. You give them money. They give you a stuffed dog.'

'We'll get one on the way back.'

'All right. Have it your own way. Road to hell paved with unbought stuffed dogs. Not my fault.'

We went on.

'How'd you feel that way about dogs so sudden?'

'Always felt that way about dogs. Always been a great lover of stuffed animals.'

We stopped and had a drink.

'Certainly like to drink,' Bill said. 'You ought to try it some times, Jake.'

'You're about a hundred and forty-four ahead of me.'

'Ought not to daunt you. Never be daunted. Secret of my success. Never been daunted. Never been daunted in public.'

'Where were you drinking?'

'Stopped at the Crillon. George made me a couple of Jack Roses. George's a great man. Know the secret of his success? Never been daunted.'

'You'll be daunted after about three more pernods.'

'Not in public. If I begin to feel daunted I'll go off by myself. I'm like a cat that way.'

'When did you see Harvey Stone?'

'At the Crillon. Harvey was just a little daunted. Hadn't eaten for three days. Doesn't eat any more. Just goes off like a cat. Pretty sad.'

'He's all right.'

'Splendid. Wish he wouldn't keep going off like a cat, though. Makes me nervous.'

'What'll we do to-night?'

'Doesn't make any difference. Only let's not get daunted. Suppose they got any hard-boiled eggs here? If they had hard-boiled eggs here we wouldn't have to go all the way down to the island to eat.'

'Nix,' I said. 'We're going to have a regular meal.'

'Just a suggestion,' said Bill. 'Want to start now?'

'Come on.'

We started on again down the Boulevard. A horse-cab passed us. Bill looked at it.

'See that horse-cab? Going to have that horse-cab stuffed for you for Christmas. Going to give all my friends stuffed animals. I'm a nature-writer.'

A taxi passed, some one in it waved, then banged for the driver to stop. The taxi backed up to the curb. In it was Brett.

'Beautiful lady,' said Bill. 'Going to kidnap us.'

'Hullo!' Brett said. 'Hullo!'

'This is Bill Gorton. Lady Ashley.'

Brett smiled at Bill. 'I say I'm just back. Haven't bathed even. Michael comes in to-night.'

'Good. Come on and eat with us, and we'll all go to meet him.'

'Must clean myself.'

'Oh, rot! Come on.'

'Must bathe. He doesn't get in till nine.'

'Come and have a drink, then, before you bathe.'

'Might do that. Now you're not talking rot.'

We got in the taxi. The driver looked around.

'Stop at the nearest bistro,' I said.

'We might as well go to the Closerie,' Brett said. 'I can't drink these rotten brandies.'

'Closerie des Lilas.'

Brett turned to Bill.

'Have you been in this pestilential city long?'

'Just got in to-day from Budapest.'

'How was Budapest?'

'Wonderful. Budapest was wonderful.'

'Ask him about Vienna.'

'Vienna,' said Bill, 'is a strange city.'

'Very much like Paris,' Brett smiled at him, wrinkling the corners of her eyes.

'Exactly,' Bill said. 'Very much like Paris at this moment.'

'You *have* a good start.'

Sitting out on the terraces of the Lilas Brett ordered a whiskey and soda, I took one, too, and Bill took another pernod.

'How are you, Jake?'

'Great,' I said. 'I've had a good time.'

Brett looked at me. 'I was a fool to go away,' she said. 'One's an ass to leave Paris.'

'Did you have a good time?'

'Oh, all right. Interesting. Not frightfully amusing.'

'See anybody?'

'No, hardly anybody. I never went out.'

'Didn't you swim?'

'No. Didn't do a thing.'

'Sounds like Vienna,' Bill said.

Brett wrinkled up the corners of her eyes at him.

'So that's the way it was in Vienna.'

'It was like everything in Vienna.'

Brett smiled at him again.

'You've a nice friend, Jake.'

'He's all right,' I said. 'He's a taxidermist.'

'That was in another country,' Bill said. 'And besides all the animals were dead.'

'One more,' Brett said, 'and I must run. Do send the waiter for a taxi.'

'There's a line of them. Right out in front.'

'Good.'

We had the drink and put Brett into her taxi.

'Mind you're at the Select around ten. Make him come. Michael will be there.'

'We'll be there,' Bill said. The taxi started and Brett waved.

'Quite a girl,' Bill said. 'She's damned nice. Who's Michael?'

'The man she's going to marry.'

'Well, well,' Bill said. 'That's always just the stage I meet anybody. What'll I send them? Think they'd like a couple of stuffed race-horses?'

'We better eat.'

'Is she really Lady something or other?' Bill asked in the taxi on our way down to the Ile Saint Louis.

'Oh, yes. In the stud-book and everything.'

'Well, well.'

We ate dinner at Madame Lecomte's restaurant on the far side of the island. It was crowded with Americans and we had to stand up and wait for a place. Some one had put it in the American Women's Club list as a quaint restaurant on the Paris quais as yet untouched by Americans, so we had to wait forty-five minutes for a table. Bill had eaten at the restaurant in 1918, and right after the armistice, and Madame Lecomte made a great fuss over seeing him.

'Doesn't get us a table, though,' Bill said. 'Grand woman, though.'

We had a good meal, a roast chicken, new green beans, mashed potatoes, a salad, and some apple-pie and cheese.

'You've got the world here all right,' Bill said to Madame Lecomte. She raised her hand. 'Oh, my God!'

'You'll be rich.'

'I hope so.'

After the coffee and a *fine* we got the bill, chalked up the same as ever on a slate, that was doubtless one of the 'quaint' features, paid it, shook hands, and went out.

'You never come here any more, Monsieur Barnes,' Madame Lecomte said.

'Too many compatriots.'

'Come at lunch-time. It's not crowded then.'

'Good. I'll be down soon.'

We walked along under the trees that grew out over the river on the Quai d'Orléans side of the island. Across the river were the broken walls of old houses that were being torn down.

'They're going to cut a street through.'

'They would,' Bill said.

We walked on and circled the island. The river was dark and a bateau mouche went by, all bright with lights, going fast and quiet up and out of sight under the bridge. Down the river was Notre Dame squatting against the night sky. We crossed to the left bank of the Seine by the wooden foot-bridge from the Quai de Bethune, and stopped on the bridge and looked down the river at Notre Dame. Standing on the bridge the island looked dark, the houses were high against the sky, and the trees were shadows.

'It's pretty grand,' Bill said. 'God, I love to get back.'

We leaned on the wooden rail of the bridge and looked up the river to the lights of the big bridges. Below the water was smooth and black. It made no sound against the piles of the bridge. A man and a girl passed us. They were walking with their arms around each other.

We crossed the bridge and walked up the Rue du Cardinal Lemoine. It was steep walking, and we went all the way up to the Place Contrescarpe. The arc-light shone through the leaves of the trees in the square, and underneath the trees was an S bus ready to start. Music came out of the door of the Negre Joyeux. Through the window of the Café Aux Amateurs I saw the long zinc bar. Outside on the terrace working people were drinking. In the open kitchen of the Amateurs a girl was cooking potato-chips in oil. There was an iron pot of stew. The girl ladled some onto a plate for an old man who stood holding a bottle of red wine in one hand.

'Want to have a drink?'

'No,' said Bill. 'I don't need it.'

We turned to the right off the Place Contrescarpe, walking along smooth narrow streets with high old houses on both sides. Some of the houses jutted out toward the street. Others were cut back. We came onto the Rue du Pot de Fer and followed it along until it brought us to the rigid north and south of the Rue Saint Jacques and then walked south, past Val de Grâce, set back behind the courtyard and the iron fence, to the Boulevard du Port Royal.

'What do you want to do?' I asked. 'Go up to the café and see Brett and Mike?'

'Why not?'

We walked along Port Royal until it became Montparnasse, and then on past the Lilas, Lavigne's, and all the little cafés, Damoy's, crossed the street to the Rotonde, past its lights and tables to the Select.

Michael came toward us from the tables. He was tanned and healthy-looking.

'Hel-lo, Jake,' he said. 'Hel-lo! Hel-lo! How are you, old lad?'

'You look very fit, Mike.'

'Oh, I am. I'm frightfully fit. I've done nothing but walk. Walk all day long. One drink a day with my mother at tea.'

Bill had gone into the bar. He was standing talking with Brett, who was sitting on a high stool, her legs crossed. She had no stockings on.

'It's good to see you, Jake,' Michael said. 'I'm a little tight you know. Amazing, isn't it? Did you see my nose?'

There was a patch of dried blood on the bridge of his nose.

'An old lady's bags did that,' Mike said. 'I reached up to help her with them and they fell on me.'

Brett gestured at him from the bar with her cigarette-holder and wrinkled the corners of her eyes.

'An old lady,' said Mike. 'Her bags *fell* on me. Let's go in and see Brett. I say, she is a piece. You *are* a lovely lady, Brett. Where did you get that hat?'

'Chap bought it for me. Don't you like it?'

'It's a dreadful hat. Do get a good hat.'

'Oh, we've so much money now,' Brett said. 'I say, haven't you met Bill yet? You *are* a lovely host, Jake.'

She turned to Mike. 'This is Bill Gorton. This drunkard is Mike Campbell. Mr. Campbell is an undischarged bankrupt.'

'Aren't I, though? You know I met my ex-partner yesterday in London. Chap who did me in.'

'What did he say?'

'Bought me a drink. I thought I might as well take it. I say, Brett, you *are* a lovely piece. Don't you think she's beautiful?'

'Beautiful. With this nose?'

'It's a lovely nose. Go on, point it at me. Isn't she a lovely piece?'

'Couldn't we have kept the man in Scotland?'

'I say, Brett, let's turn in early.'

'Don't be indecent, Michael. Remember there are ladies at this bar.'

'Isn't she a lovely piece? Don't you think so, Jake?'

'There's a fight to-night,' Bill said. 'Like to go?'

'Fight,' said Mike. 'Who's fighting?'

'Ledoux and somebody.'

'He's very good, Ledoux,' Mike said. 'I'd like to see it, rather'—he was making an effort to pull himself together—'but I can't go. I had a date with this thing here. I say, Brett, do get a new hat.'

Brett pulled the felt hat down far over one eye and smiled out from under it. 'You two run along to the fight. I'll have to be taking Mr. Campbell home directly.'

'I'm not tight,' Mike said. 'Perhaps just a little. I say, Brett, you are a lovely piece.'

'Go on to the fight,' Brett said. 'Mr. Campbell's getting difficult. What are these outbursts of affection, Michael?'

'I say, you are a lovely piece.'

We said good night. 'I'm sorry I can't go,' Mike said. Brett laughed. I looked back from the door. Mike had one hand on the bar and was leaning toward Brett, talking. Brett was looking at him quite coolly, but the corners of her eyes were smiling.

Outside on the pavement I said: 'Do you want to go to the fight?'

'Sure,' said Bill. 'If we don't have to walk.'

'Mike was pretty excited about his girl friend,' I said in the taxi.
'Well,' said Bill. 'You can't blame him such a hell of a lot.'

9

The Ledoux-Kid Francis fight was the night of the 20th of June. It was a good fight. The morning after the fight I had a letter from Robert Cohn, written from Hendaye. He was having a very quiet time, he said, bathing, playing some golf and much bridge. Hendaye had a splendid beach, but he was anxious to start on the fishing-trip. When would I be down? If I would buy him a double-tapered line he would pay me when I came down.

That same morning I wrote Cohn from the office that Bill and I would leave Paris on the 25th unless I wired him otherwise, and would meet him at Bayonne, where we could get a bus over the mountains to Pamplona. The same evening about seven o'clock I stopped in at the Select to see Michael and Brett. They were not there, and I went over to the Dingo. They were inside sitting at the bar.

'Hello, darling.' Brett put out her hand.

'Hello, Jake,' Mike said. 'I understand I was tight last night.'

'Weren't you, though,' Brett said. 'Disgraceful business.'

'Look,' said Mike, 'when do you go down to Spain? Would you mind if we came down with you?'

'It would be grand.'

'You wouldn't mind, really? I've been at Pamplona, you know. Brett's mad to go. You're sure we wouldn't just be a bloody nuisance?'

'Don't talk like a fool.'

'I'm a little tight, you know. I wouldn't ask you like this if I weren't. You're sure you don't mind?'

'Oh, shut up, Michael,' Brett said. 'How can the man say he'd mind now? I'll ask him later.'

'But you don't mind, do you?'

'Don't ask that again unless you want to make me sore. Bill and I go down on the morning of the 25th.'

'By the way, where is Bill?' Brett asked.

'He's out at Chantilly dining with some people.'

'He's a good chap.'

'Splendid chap,' said Mike. 'He is, you know.'

'You don't remember him,' Brett said.

'I do. Remember him perfectly. Look, Jake, we'll come down the night of the 25th. Brett can't get up in the morning.'

'Indeed not!'

'If our money comes and you're sure you don't mind.'

'It will come, all right. I'll see to that.'

'Tell me what tackle to send for.'

'Get two or three rods with reels, and lines, and some flies.'
'I won't fish,' Brett put in.
'Get two rods, then, and Bill won't have to buy one.'
'Right,' said Mike. 'I'll send a wire to the keeper.'
'Won't it be splendid,' Brett said. 'Spain! We *will* have fun.'
'The 25th. When is that?'
'Saturday.'
'We *will* have to get ready.'
'I say,' said Mike, 'I'm going to the barber's.'
'I must bathe,' said Brett. 'Walk up to the hotel with me, Jake. Be a good chap.'
'We *have* got the loveliest hotel,' Mike said. 'I think it's a brothel!'

'We left our bags here at the Dingo when we got in, and they asked us at this hotel if we wanted a room for the afternoon only. Seemed frightfully pleased we were going to stay all night.'

'*I* believe it's a brothel,' Mike said. 'And *I* should know.'
'Oh, shut it and go and get your hair cut.'

Mike went out. Brett and I sat on at the bar.
'Have another?'
'Might.'
'I needed that,' Brett said.

We walked up the Rue Delambre.
'I haven't seen you since I've been back,' Brett said.
'No.'
'How *are* you, Jake?'
'Fine.'

Brett looked at me. 'I say,' she said, 'is Robert Cohn going on this trip?'
'Yes. Why?'
'Don't you think it will be a bit rough on him?'
'Why should it?'
'Who did you think I went down to San Sebastian with?'
'Congratulations,' I said.

We walked along.
'What did you say that for?'
'I don't know. What would you like me to say?'

We walked along and turned a corner.
'He behaved rather well, too. He gets a little dull.'
'Does he?'
'I rather thought it would be good for him.'
'You might take up social service.'
'Don't be nasty.'
'I won't.'
'Didn't you really know?'
'No,' I said. 'I guess I didn't think about it.'

The Sun Also Rises • 233

'Do you think it will be too rough on him?'

'That's up to him,' I said. 'Tell him you're coming. He can always not come.'

'I'll write him and give him a chance to pull out of it.'

I did not see Brett again until the night of the 24th of June.

'Did you hear from Cohn?'

'Rather. He's keen about it.'

'My God!'

'I thought it was rather odd myself.'

'Says he can't wait to see me.'

'Does he think you're coming alone?'

'No. I told him we were all coming down together. Michael and all.'

'He's wonderful.'

'Isn't he?'

They expected their money the next day. We arranged to meet at Pamplona. They would go directly to San Sebastian and take the train from there. We would all meet at the Montoya in Pamplona. If they did not turn up on Monday at the latest we would go on ahead up to Burguete in the mountains, to start fishing. There was a bus to Burguete. I wrote out an itinerary so they could follow us.

Bill and I took the morning train from the Gare d'Orsay. It was a lovely day, not too hot, and the country was beautiful from the start. We went back into the diner and had breakfast. Leaving the dining-car I asked the conductor for tickets for the first service.

'Nothing until the fifth.'

'What's this?'

There were never more than two servings of lunch on that train, and always plenty of places for both of them.

'They're all reserved,' the dining-car conductor said. 'There will be a fifth service at three-thirty.'

'This is serious,' I said to Bill.

'Give him ten francs.'

'Here,' I said. 'We want to eat in the first service.'

The conductor put the ten francs in his pocket.

'Thank you,' he said. 'I would advise you gentlemen to get some sandwiches. All the places for the first four services were reserved at the office of the company.'

'You'll go a long way, brother,' Bill said to him in English. 'I suppose if I'd given you five francs you would have advised us to jump off the train.'

'Comment?'

'Go to hell!' said Bill. 'Get the sandwiches made and a bottle of wine. You tell him, Jake.'

'And send it up to the next car.' I described where we were.

In our compartment were a man and his wife and their young son.

'I suppose you're Americans, aren't you?' the man asked. 'Having a good trip?'

'Wonderful,' said Bill.

'That's what you want to do. Travel while you're young. Mother and I always wanted to get over, but we had to wait a while.'

'You could have come over ten years ago, if you'd wanted to,' the wife said. 'What you always said was: "See America first!" I will say we've seen a good deal, take it one way and another.'

'Say, there's plenty of Americans on this train,' the husband said. 'They've got seven cars of them from Dayton, Ohio. They've been on a pilgrimage to Rome, and now they're going down to Biarritz and Lourdes.'

'So, that's what they are. Pilgrims. Goddam Puritans,' Bill said.

'What part of the States you boys from?'

'Kansas City,' I said. 'He's from Chicago.'

'You both going to Biarritz?'

'No. We're going fishing in Spain.'

'Well, I never cared for it, myself. There's plenty that do out where I come from, though. We got some of the best fishing in the State of Montana. I've been out with the boys, but I never cared for it any.'

'Mighty little fishing you did on them trips,' his wife said.

He winked at us.

'You know how the ladies are. If there's a jug goes along, or a case of beer, they think it's hell and damnation.'

'That's the way men are,' his wife said to us. She smoothed her comfortable lap. 'I voted against prohibition to please him, and because I like a little beer in the house, and then he talks that way. It's a wonder they ever find any one to marry them.'

'Say,' said Bill, 'do you know that gang of Pilgrim Fathers have cornered the dining-car until half past three this afternoon?'

'How do you mean? They can't do a thing like that.'

'You try and get seats.'

'Well, mother, it looks as though we better go back and get another breakfast.'

She stood up and straightened her dress.

'Will you boys keep an eye on our things? Come on, Hubert.'

They all three went up to the wagon restaurant. A little while after they were gone a steward went through announcing the first service, and pilgrims, with their priests, commenced filing down the corridor. Our friend and his family did not come back. A waiter passed in the corridor with our sandwiches and the bottle of Chablis, and we called him in.

'You're going to work to-day,' I said.

He nodded his head. 'They start now, at ten-thirty.'

'When do we eat?'

'Huh! When do I eat?'

He left two glasses for the bottle, and we paid him for the sandwiches and tipped him.

'I'll get the plates,' he said, 'or bring them with you.'

The Sun Also Rises • 235

We ate the sandwiches and drank the Chablis and watched the country out of the window. The grain was just beginning to ripen and the fields were full of poppies. The pastureland was green, and there were fine trees, and sometimes big rivers and chateaux off in the trees.

At Tours we got off and bought another bottle of wine, and when we got back in the compartment the gentleman from Montana and his wife and his son, Hubert, were sitting comfortably.

'Is there good swimming in Biarritz?' asked Hubert.

'That boy's just crazy till he can get in the water,' his mother said. 'It's pretty hard on youngsters travelling.'

'There's good swimming,' I said. 'But it's dangerous when it's rough.'

'Did you get a meal?' Bill asked.

'We sure did. We set right there when they started to come in, and they must have just thought we were in the party. One of the waiters said something to us in French, and then they just sent three of them back.'

'They thought we were snappers, all right,' the man said. 'It certainly shows you the power of the Catholic Church. It's a pity you boys ain't Catholics. You could get a meal, then, all right.'

'I am,' I said. 'That's what makes me so sore.'

Finally at a quarter past four we had lunch. Bill had been rather difficult at the last. He buttonholed a priest who was coming back with one of the returning streams of pilgrims.

'When do us Protestants get a chance to eat, father?'

'I don't know anything about it. Haven't you got tickets?'

'It's enough to make a man join the Klan,' Bill said. The priest looked back at him.

Inside the dining-car the waiters served the fifth successive table d'hôte meal. The waiter who served us was soaked through. His white jacket was purple under the arms.

'He must drink a lot of wine.'

'Or wear purple undershirts.'

'Let's ask him.'

'No. He's too tired.'

The train stopped for half an hour at Bordeaux and we went out through the station for a little walk. There was not time to get in to the town. Afterward we passed through the Landes and watched the sun set. There were wide fire-gaps cut through the pines, and you could look up them like avenues and see wooded hills way off. About seven-thirty we had dinner and watched the country through the open window in the diner. It was all sandy pine country full of heather. There were little clearings with houses in them, and once in a while we passed a sawmill. It got dark and we could feel the country hot and sandy and dark outside of the window, and about nine o'clock we got into Bayonne. The man and his wife and Hubert all shook hands with us. They were going on to LaNegresse to change for Biarritz.

'Well, I hope you have lots of luck,' he said.

'Be careful about those bull-fights.'

'Maybe we'll see you at Biarritz,' Hubert said.

We got off with our bags and rod-cases and passed through the dark station and out to the lights and the line of cabs and hotel buses. There, standing with the hotel runners, was Robert Cohn. He did not see us at first. Then he started forward.

'Hello, Jake. Have a good trip?'

'Fine,' I said. 'This is Bill Gorton.'

'How are you?'

'Come on,' said Robert. 'I've got a cab.' He was a little near-sighted. I had never noticed it before. He was looking at Bill, trying to make him out. He was shy, too.

'We'll go up to my hotel. It's all right. It's quite nice.'

We got into the cab, and the cabman put the bags up on the seat beside him and climbed up and cracked his whip, and we drove over the dark bridge and into the town.

'I'm awfully glad to meet you,' Robert said to Bill. 'I've heard so much about you from Jake and I've read your books. Did you get my line, Jake?'

The cab stopped in front of the hotel and we all got out and went in. It was a nice hotel, and the people at the desk were very cheerful, and we each had a good small room.

10

In the morning it was bright, and they were sprinkling the streets of the town, and we all had breakfast in a café. Bayonne is a nice town. It is like a very clean Spanish town and it is on a big river. Already, so early in the morning, it was very hot on the bridge across the river. We walked out on the bridge and then took a walk through the town.

I was not at all sure Mike's rods would come from Scotland in time, so we hunted a tackle store and finally bought a rod for Bill up-stairs over a drygoods store. The man who sold the tackle was out, and we had to wait for him to come back. Finally he came in, and we bought a pretty good rod cheap, and two landing-nets.

We went out into the street again and took a look at the cathedral. Cohn made some remark about it being a very good example of something or other, I forget what. It seemed like a nice cathedral, nice and dim, like Spanish churches. Then we went up past the old fort and out to the local Syndicat d'Initiative office, where the bus was supposed to start from. There they told us the bus service did not start until the 1st of July. We found out at the tourist office what we ought to pay for a motor-car to Pamplona and hired one at a big garage just around the corner from the Municipal Theatre for four hundred francs. The car was to pick us up at the hotel in forty minutes, and we stopped at the café on the square where we had eaten breakfast, and had a beer. It was hot, but the town had a cool, fresh, early-morning smell and it was pleasant sitting in the café. A breeze started to blow, and you could feel that the air came from the sea. There were pigeons out in the square, and the houses were a yellow, sun-baked color, and I did not want to leave the café. But we had to go to the hotel to get our bags packed and pay the bill. We paid for the beers, we matched and I think Cohn paid, and went up to the hotel. It was only sixteen francs apiece for Bill and me, with ten per cent added for the service, and we had the bags sent down and waited for Robert Cohn. While we were waiting I saw a cockroach on the parquet floor that must have been at least three inches long. I pointed him out to Bill and then put my shoe on him. We agreed he must have just come in from the garden. It was really an awfully clean hotel.

Cohn came down, finally, and we all went out to the car. It was a big, closed car, with a driver in a white duster with blue collar and cuffs, and we had him put the back of the car down. He piled in the bags and we started off up the street and out of the town. We passed some lovely gardens and had a good look back at the town, and then we were out in the country, green and rolling, and the road climbing all the time. We passed lots of Basques with oxen, or cattle, hauling carts along the road, and nice farmhouses, low roofs, and all white-plastered. In the Basque country the land all looks very rich and green and the houses and villages look well-off and clean. Every village had a pelota court and on some of them kids were playing in the hot sun. There were signs on the walls of the churches saying it was forbidden to play pelota against them, and the houses in the villages had red tiled roofs, and then the road turned off and commenced to climb and we were going way up close along a hillside, with a valley below and hills stretched off back toward the sea. You couldn't see the sea. It was too far away. You could see only hills and more hills, and you knew where the sea was.

We crossed the Spanish frontier. There was a little stream and a bridge, and Spanish carabineers, with patent-leather Bonaparte hats, and short guns on their backs, on one side, and on the other fat Frenchmen in kepis and mustaches. They only opened one bag and took the passports in and looked at them. There was a general store and inn on each side of the line. The chauffeur had to go in and fill out some papers about the car and we got out and went over to the stream to see if there were any trout. Bill tried to talk some Spanish to one of the carabineers, but it did not go very well. Robert Cohn asked, pointing with his finger, if there were any trout in the stream, and the carabineer said yes, but not many.

I asked him if he ever fished, and he said no, that he didn't care for it.

Just then an old man with long, sunburned hair and beard, and clothes that looked as though they were made of gunny-sacking, came striding up to the bridge. He was carrying a long staff, and he had a kid slung on his back, tied by the four legs, the head hanging down.

The carabineer waved him back with his sword. The man turned without saying anything, and started back up the white road into Spain.

'What's the matter with the old one?' I asked.

'He hasn't got any passport.'

I offered the guard a cigarette. He took it and thanked me.

'What will he do?' I asked.

The guard spat in the dust.

'Oh, he'll just wade across the stream.'

'Do you have much smuggling?'

'Oh,' he said, 'they go through.'

The chauffeur came out, folding up the papers and putting them in the inside pocket of his coat. We all got in the car and it started up the white dusty road into Spain. For a while the country was much as it had been; then, climbing all the time, we crossed the top of a Col, the road winding back and forth on itself, and then it was really Spain. There were long brown mountains and a few pines and far-off forests of beech-trees on some of the mountainsides. The road went along the summit of the Col and then dropped down, and the driver had to honk, and slow up, and turn out to avoid running into two donkeys that were sleeping in the road. We came down out of the mountains and through an oak forest, and there were white cattle grazing in the forest. Down below there were grassy plains and clear streams, and then we crossed a stream and went through a gloomy little village, and started to climb again. We climbed up and up and crossed another high Col and turned along it, and the road ran down to the right, and we saw a whole new range of mountains off to the south, all brown and baked-looking and furrowed in strange shapes.

After a while we came out of the mountains, and there were trees along both sides of the road, and a stream and ripe fields of grain, and the road went on, very white and straight ahead, and then lifted to a little rise, and off on the left was a hill with an old castle, with buildings close around it and a field of grain going right up to the walls and shifting in the wind. I was up in front with the driver and I turned around. Robert Cohn was asleep, but Bill looked and nodded his head. Then we crossed a wide plain, and there was a big river off on the right shining in the sun from between the line of trees, and away off you could see the plateau of Pamplona rising out of the plain, and the walls of the city, and the great brown cathedral, and the broken skyline of the other churches. In back of the plateau were the mountains, and every way you looked there were other mountains, and ahead the road stretched out white across the plain going toward Pamplona.

We came into the town on the other side of the plateau, the road slanting up steeply and dustily with shade-trees on both sides, and then levelling out through the new part of town they are building up outside the old walls. We passed the bull-ring, high and white and concrete-looking in the sun, and then came into the big square by a side street and stopped in front of the Hotel Montoya.

The driver helped us down with the bags. There was a crowd of kids watching the car, and the square was hot, and the trees were green, and the flags hung on their staffs, and it was good to get out of the sun and under the shade of the arcade that runs all the way around the square. Montoya was glad to see us, and shook hands and gave us good rooms looking out on the square, and then we washed and cleaned up and went down-stairs in the dining-room for lunch. The driver stayed for lunch, too, and afterward we paid him and he started back to Bayonne.

There are two dining-rooms in the Montoya. One is up-stairs on the second floor and looks out on the square. The other is down one floor below the level of the square and has a door that opens on the back street that the bulls pass along when they run through the streets early in the morning on their way to the ring. It is always cool in the down-stairs dining-room and we had a very good lunch. The first meal in Spain was always a shock with the hors d'œuvres, an egg course, two meat courses, vegetables, salad, and dessert and fruit. You have to drink plenty of wine to get it all down. Robert Cohn tried to say he did not want any of the second meat course, but we would not interpret for him, and so the waitress brought him something else as a replacement, a plate of cold meats, I think. Cohn had been rather nervous ever since we had met at Bayonne. He did not know whether we knew Brett had been with him at San Sebastian, and it made him rather awkward.

'Well,' I said, 'Brett and Mike ought to get in to-night.'

'I'm not sure they'll come,' Cohn said.

'Why not?' Bill said. 'Of course they'll come.'

'They're always late,' I said.

'I rather think they're not coming,' Robert Cohn said.

He said it with an air of superior knowledge that irritated both of us.

'I'll bet you fifty pesetas they're here to-night,' Bill said. He always bets when he is angered, and so he usually bets foolishly.

'I'll take it,' Cohn said. 'Good. You remember it, Jake. Fifty pesetas.'

'I'll remember it myself,' Bill said. I saw he was angry and wanted to smooth him down.

'It's a sure thing they'll come,' I said. 'But maybe not to-night.'

'Want to call it off?' Cohn asked.

'No. Why should I? Make it a hundred if you like.'

'All right. I'll take that.'

'That's enough,' I said. 'Or you'll have to make a book and give me some of it.'

'I'm satisfied,' Cohn said. He smiled. 'You'll probably win it back at bridge, anyway.'

'You haven't got it yet,' Bill said.

We went out to walk around under the arcade to the Café Iruña for coffee. Cohn said he was going over and get a shave.

'Say,' Bill said to me, 'have I got any chance on that bet?'

'You've got a rotten chance. They've never been on time anywhere. If their money doesn't come it's a cinch they won't get in to-night.'

'I was sorry as soon as I opened my mouth. But I had to call him. He's all right, I guess, but where does he get this inside stuff? Mike and Brett fixed it up with us about coming down here.'

I saw Cohn coming over across the square.

'Here he comes.'

'Well, let him not get superior and Jewish.'

'The barber shop's closed,' Cohn said. 'It's not open till four.'

We had coffee at the Iruña, sitting in comfortable wicker chairs looking out from the cool of the arcade at the big square. After a while Bill went to write some letters and Cohn went over to the barber-shop. It was still closed, so he decided to go up to the hotel and get a bath, and I sat out in front of the café and then went for a walk in the town. It was very hot, but I kept on the shady side of the streets and went through the market and had a good time seeing the town again. I went to the Ayuntamiento and found the old gentleman who subscribes for the bull-fight tickets for me every year, and he had gotten the money I sent him from Paris and renewed my subscriptions, so that was all set. He was the archivist, and all the archives of the town were in his office. That has nothing to do with the story. Anyway, his office had a green baize door and a big wooden door, and when I went out I left him sitting among the archives that covered all the walls, and I shut both the doors, and as I went out of the building into the street the porter stopped me to brush off my coat.

'You must have been in a motor-car,' he said.

The back of the collar and the upper part of the shoulders were gray with dust.

'From Bayonne.'

'Well, well,' he said. 'I knew you were in a motor-car from the way the dust was.' So I gave him two copper coins.

At the end of the street I saw the cathedral and walked up toward it. The first time I ever saw it I thought the façade was ugly but I liked it now. I went inside. It was dim and dark and the pillars went high up, and there were people praying, and it smelt of incense, and there were some wonderful big windows. I knelt and started to pray and prayed for everybody I thought of, Brett and Mike and Bill and Robert Cohn and myself, and all the bull-fighters, separately for the ones I liked, and lumping all the rest, then I prayed for myself again, and while I was praying for myself I found I was getting sleepy, so I prayed that the bull-fights would be good, and that it would be a fine fiesta, and that we would get some fishing. I wondered if there was anything else I might pray for, and I thought I would like to have some money, so I prayed that I would make a lot of money, and then I started to think how I would make it, and thinking of making money reminded me of the count, and I started wondering about where he was, and regretting I hadn't seen him since that night in Montmartre, and about something funny Brett told me about him, and as all the time I was kneeling with my forehead on the wood in front of me, and was thinking of myself as praying, I was a little ashamed, and regretted that I was such a rotten Catholic, but realized there was nothing I could do about it, at least for a while, and maybe never, but that anyway it was a grand religion, and I only wished I felt religious and maybe I would the next time; and then I was out in the hot sun on the steps of the cathedral, and the forefingers and the thumb of my right hand were still damp, and I felt them dry in the sun. The sunlight was hot and hard, and I crossed over beside some buildings, and walked back along side-streets to the hotel.

At dinner that night we found that Robert Cohn had taken a bath, had had a shave and a haircut and a shampoo, and something put on his hair afterward to make it stay down. He was nervous, and I did not try to help him any. The train was due in at nine o'clock from San Sebastian, and, if Brett and Mike were coming, they would be on it. At twenty minutes to nine we were not half through dinner. Robert Cohn got up from the table and said he would go to the station. I said I would go with him, just to devil him. Bill said he would be damned if he would leave his dinner. I said we would be right back.

We walked to the station. I was enjoying Cohn's nervousness. I hoped Brett would be on the train. At the station the train was late, and we sat on a baggage-truck and waited outside in the dark. I have never seen a man in civil life as nervous as Robert Cohn—nor as eager. I was enjoying it. It was lousy to enjoy it, but I felt lousy. Cohn had a wonderful quality of bringing out the worst in anybody.

After a while we heard the train-whistle way off below on the other side of the plateau, and then we saw the headlight coming up the hill. We went inside the station and stood with a crowd of people just back of the gates, and the train came in and stopped, and everybody started coming out through the gates.

They were not in the crowd. We waited till everybody had gone through and out of the station and gotten into buses, or taken cabs, or were walking with their friends or relatives through the dark into the town.

'I knew they wouldn't come,' Robert said. We were going back to the hotel.

'I thought they might,' I said.

Bill was eating fruit when we came in and finishing a bottle of wine.

'Didn't come, eh?'

'No.'

'Do you mind if I give you that hundred pesetas in the morning, Cohn?' Bill asked. 'I haven't changed any money here yet.'

'Oh, forget about it,' Robert Cohn said. 'Let's bet on something else. Can you bet on bull-fights?'

'You could,' Bill said, 'but you don't need to.'

'It would be like betting on the war,' I said. 'You don't need any economic interest.'

'I'm very curious to see them,' Robert said.

Montoya came up to our table. He had a telegram in his hand. 'It's for you.' He handed it to me.

It read: 'Stopped night San Sebastian.'

'It's from them,' I said. I put it in my pocket. Ordinarily I should have handed it over.

'They've stopped over in San Sebastian,' I said. 'Send their regards to you.'

Why I felt that impulse to devil him I do not know. Of course I do know. I was blind, unforgivingly jealous of what had happened to him. The fact that I took it as a matter of course did not alter that any. I certainly did hate him. I do not think I ever really hated him until he had that little spell of superiority at lunch—that and when he went through all that barbering. So I put the telegram in my pocket. The telegram came to me, anyway.

'Well,' I said. 'We ought to pull out on the noon bus for Burguete. They can follow us if they get in to-morrow night.'

There were only two trains up from San Sebastian, an early morning train and the one we had just met.

'That sounds like a good idea,' Cohn said.

'The sooner we get on the stream the better.'

'It's all one to me when we start,' Bill said. 'The sooner the better.'

We sat in the Iruña for a while and had coffee and then took a little walk out to the bull-ring and across the field and under the trees at the edge of the cliff and looked down at the river in the dark, and I turned in early. Bill and Cohn stayed out in the café quite late, I believe, because I was asleep when they came in.

In the morning I bought three tickets for the bus to Burguete. It was scheduled to leave at two o'clock. There was nothing earlier. I was sitting over at the Iruña reading the papers when I saw Robert Cohn coming across the square. He came up to the table and sat down in one of the wicker chairs.

'This is a comfortable café,' he said. 'Did you have a good night, Jake?'

'I slept like a log.'

'I didn't sleep very well. Bill and I were out late, too.'

'Where were you?'

'Here. And after it shut we went over to that other café. The old man there speaks German and English.'

'The Café Suizo.'

'That's it. He seems like a nice old fellow. I think it's a better café than this one.'

'It's not so good in the daytime,' I said. 'Too hot. By the way, I got the bus tickets.'

'I'm not going up to-day. You and Bill go on ahead.'

'I've got your ticket.'

'Give it to me. I'll get the money back.'

'It's five pesetas.'

Robert Cohn took out a silver five-peseta piece and gave it to me.

'I ought to stay,' he said. 'You see I'm afraid there's some sort of misunderstanding.'

'Why,' I said. 'They may not come here for three or four days now if they start on parties at San Sebastian.'

'That's just it,' said Robert. 'I'm afraid they expected to meet me at San Sebastian, and that's why they stopped over.'

'What makes you think that?'

'Well, I wrote suggesting it to Brett.'

'Why in hell didn't you stay there and meet them then?' I started to say, but

The Sun Also Rises • 243

I stopped. I thought that idea would come to him by itself, but I do not believe it ever did.

He was being confidential now and it was giving him pleasure to be able to talk with the understanding that I knew there was something between him and Brett.

'Well, Bill and I will go up right after lunch,' I said.

'I wish I could go. We've been looking forward to this fishing all winter.' He was being sentimental about it. 'But I ought to stay. I really ought. As soon as they come I'll bring them right up.'

'Let's find Bill.'

'I want to go over to the barber-shop.'

'See you at lunch.'

I found Bill up in his room. He was shaving.

'Oh, yes, he told me all about it last night,' Bill said. 'He's a great little confider. He said he had a date with Brett at San Sebastian.'

'The lying bastard!'

'Oh, no,' said Bill. 'Don't get sore. Don't get sore at this stage of the trip. How did you ever happen to know this fellow, anyway?'

'Don't rub it in.'

Bill looked around, half-shaved, and then went on talking into the mirror while he lathered his face.

'Didn't you send him with a letter to me in New York last winter? Thank God, I'm a travelling man. Haven't you got some more Jewish friends you could bring along?' He rubbed his chin with his thumb, looked at it, and then started scraping again.

'You've got some fine ones yourself.'

'Oh, yes. I've got some darbs. But not alongside of this Robert Cohn. The funny thing is he's nice, too. I like him. But he's just so awful.'

'He can be damn nice.'

'I know it. That's the terrible part.'

I laughed.

'Yes. Go on and laugh,' said Bill. 'You weren't out with him last night until two o'clock.'

'Was he very bad?'

'Awful. What's all this about him and Brett, anyway? Did she ever have anything to do with him?'

He raised his chin up and pulled it from side to side.

'Sure. She went down to San Sebastian with him.'

'What a damn-fool thing to do. Why did she do that?'

'She wanted to get out of town and she can't go anywhere alone. She said she thought it would be good for him.'

'What bloody-fool things people do. Why didn't she go off with some of her own people? Or you?'—he slurred that over—'or me? Why not me?' He looked at his face carefully in the glass, put a big dab of lather on each cheek-bone. 'It's an honest face. It's a face any woman would be safe with.'

'She'd never seen it.'

'She should have. All women should see it. It's a face that ought to be thrown on every screen in the country. Every woman ought to be given a copy of this face as she leaves the altar. Mothers should tell their daughters about this face. My son'—he pointed the razor at me—'go west with this face and grow up with the country.'

He ducked down to the bowl, rinsed his face with cold water, put on some alcohol, and then looked at himself carefully in the glass, pulling down his long upper lip.

'My God!' he said, 'isn't it an awful face?'

He looked in the glass.

'And as for this Robert Cohn,' Bill said, 'he makes me sick, and he can go to hell, and I'm damn glad he's staying here so we won't have him fishing with us.'

'You're damn right.'

'We're going trout-fishing. We're going trout-fishing in the Irati River, and we're going to get tight now at lunch on the wine of the country, and then take a swell bus ride.'

'Come on. Let's go over to the Iruña and start,' I said.

11

It was baking hot in the square when we came out after lunch with our bags and the rod-case to go to Burguete. People were on top of the bus, and others were climbing up a ladder. Bill went up and Robert sat beside Bill to save a place for me, and I went back in the hotel to get a couple of bottles of wine to take with us. When I came out the bus was crowded. Men and women were sitting on all the baggage and boxes on top, and the women all had their fans going in the sun. It certainly was hot. Robert climbed down and I fitted into the place he had saved on the one wooden seat that ran across the top.

Robert Cohn stood in the shade of the arcade waiting for us start. A Basque with a big leather wine-bag in his lap lay across the top of the bus in front of our seat, leaning back against our legs. He offered the wine-skin to Bill and to me, and when I tipped it up to drink he imitated the sound of a klaxon motor-horn so well and so suddenly that I spilled some of the wine, and everybody laughed. He apologized and made me take another drink. He made the klaxon again a little later, and it fooled me the second time. He was very good at it. The Basques liked it. The man next to Bill was talking to him in Spanish and Bill was not getting it, so he offered the man one of the bottles of wine. The man waved it away. He said it was too hot and he had drunk too much at lunch. When Bill offered the bottle the second time he took a long drink, and then the bottle went all over that part of the bus. Every one took a drink very politely, and then they made us cork it up and put it away. They all wanted us to drink from their leather wine-bottles. They were peasants going up into the hills.

Finally, after a couple more false klaxons, the bus started, and Robert Cohn waved good-by to us, and all the Basques waved good-by to him. As soon as we started out on the road outside of town it was cool. It felt nice riding high up and close under the trees. The bus went quite fast and made a good breeze, and as we went out along the road with the dust powdering the trees and down the hill, we had a fine view, back through the trees, of the town rising up from the bluff above the river. The Basque lying against my knees pointed out the view with the neck of the wine-bottle, and winked at us. He nodded his head.

'Pretty nice, eh?'

'These Basques are swell people,' Bill said.

The Basque lying against my legs was tanned the color of saddle-leather. He wore a black smock like all the rest. There were wrinkles in his tanned neck. He turned around and offered his wine-bag to Bill. Bill handed him one of our bottles. The Basque wagged a forefinger at him and handed the bottle back, slapping in the cork with the palm of his hand. He shoved the wine-bag up.

'Arriba! Arriba!' he said. 'Lift it up.'

Bill raised the wine-skin and let the stream of wine spurt out and into his mouth, his head tipped back. When he stopped drinking and tipped the leather bottle down a few drops ran down his chin.

'No! No!' several Basques said. 'Not like that.' One snatched the bottle away from the owner, who was himself about to give a demonstration. He was a young fellow and he held the wine-bottle at full arms' length and raised it high up, squeezing the leather bag with his hand so the stream of wine hissed into his mouth. He held the bag out there, the wine making a flat, hard trajectory into his mouth, and he kept on swallowing smoothly and regularly.

'Hey!' the owner of the bottle shouted. 'Whose wine is that?'

The drinker waggled his little finger at him and smiled at us with his eyes. Then he bit the stream off sharp, made a quick lift with the wine-bag and lowered it down to the owner. He winked at us. The owner shook the wine-skin sadly.

We passed through a town and stopped in front of the posada, and the driver took on several packages. Then we started on again, and outside the town the road commenced to mount. We were going through farming country with rocky hills that sloped down into the fields. The grain-fields went up the hillsides. Now as we went higher there was a wind blowing the grain. The road was white and dusty, and the dust rose under the wheels and hung in the air behind us. The road climbed up into the hills and left the rich grain-fields below. Now there were only patches of grain on the bare hillsides and on each side of the water-courses. We turned sharply out to the side of the road to give room to pass to a long string of six mules, following one after the other, hauling a high-hooded wagon loaded with freight. The wagon and the mules were covered with dust. Close behind was another string of mules and another wagon. This was loaded with lumber, and the arriero driving the mules leaned back and put on the thick wooden brakes as we passed. Up here the country was quite barren and the hills were rocky and hard-baked clay furrowed by the rain.

We came around a curve into a town, and on both sides opened out a sudden green valley. A stream went through the centre of the town and fields of grapes touched the houses.

The bus stopped in front of a posada and many of the passengers got down, and a lot of the baggage was unstrapped from the roof from under the big tarpaulins and lifted down. Bill and I got down and went into the posada. There was a low, dark room with saddles and harness, and hay-forks made of white wood, and clusters of canvas rope-soled shoes and hams and slabs of bacon and white garlics and long sausages hanging from the roof. It was cool and dusky, and we stood in front of a long wooden counter with two women behind it serving drinks. Behind them were shelves stacked with supplies and goods.

We each had an aguardiente and paid forty centimes for the two drinks. I gave the woman fifty centimes to make a tip, and she gave me back the copper piece, thinking I had misunderstood the price.

Two of our Basques came in and insisted on buying a drink. So they bought a drink and then we bought a drink, and then they slapped us on the back and bought another drink. Then we bought, and then we all went out into the sunlight and the heat, and climbed back on top of the bus. There was plenty of room now for every one to sit on the seat, and the Basque who had been lying on the tin roof now sat between us. The woman who had been serving drinks came out wiping her hands on her apron and talked to somebody inside the bus. Then the driver came out swinging two flat leather mail-pouches and climbed up, and everybody waving we started off.

The road left the green valley at once, and we were up in the hills again. Bill and the wine-bottle Basque were having a conversation. A man leaned over from the other side of the seat and asked in English: 'You're Americans?'

'Sure.'

'I been there,' he said. 'Forty years ago.'

He was an old man, as brown as the others, with the stubble of a white beard.

'How was it?'

'What you say?'

'How was America?'

'Oh, I was in California. It was fine.'

'Why did you leave?'

'What you say?'

'Why did you come back here?'

'Oh! I come back to get married. I was going to go back but my wife she don't like to travel. Where you from?'

'Kansas City.'

'I been there,' he said. 'I been in Chicago, St. Louis, Kansas City, Denver,

Los Angeles, Salt Lake City.'

He named them carefully.

'How long were you over?'

'Fifteen years. Then I come back and got married.'

'Have a drink?'

'All right,' he said. 'You can't get this in America, eh?'

'There's plenty if you can pay for it.'

'What you come over here for?'

'We're going to the fiesta at Pamplona.'

'You like the bull-fights?'

'Sure. Don't you?'

'Yes,' he said. 'I guess I like them.'

Then after a little:

'Where you go now?'

'Up to Burguete to fish.'

'Well,' he said, 'I hope you catch something.'

He shook hands and turned around to the back seat again. The other Basques had been impressed. He sat back comfortably and smiled at me when I turned around to look at the country. But the effort of talking American seemed to have tired him. He did not say anything after that.

The bus climbed steadily up the road. The country was barren and rocks stuck up through the clay. There was no grass beside the road. Looking back we could see the country spread out below. Far back the fields were squares of green and brown on the hillsides. Making the horizon were the brown mountains. They were strangely shaped. As we climbed higher the horizon kept changing. As the bus ground slowly up the road we could see other mountains coming up in the south. Then the road came over the crest, flattened out, and went into a forest. It was a forest of cork oaks, and the sun came through the trees in patches, and there were cattle grazing back in the trees. We went through the forest and the road came out and turned along a rise of land, and out ahead of us was a rolling green plain, with dark mountains beyond it. These were not like the brown, heat-baked mountains we had left behind. These were wooded and there were clouds coming down from them. The green plain stretched off. It was cut by fences and the white of the road showed through the trunks of a double line of trees that crossed the plain toward the north. As we came to the edge of the rise we saw the red roofs and white houses of Burguete ahead strung out on the plain, and away off on the shoulder of the first dark mountain was the gray metal-sheathed roof of the monastery of Roncesvalles.

'There's Roncevaux,' I said.

'Where?'

'Way off there where the mountain starts.'

'It's cold up here,' Bill said.

'It's high,' I said. 'It must be twelve hundred metres.'

'It's awful cold,' Bill said.

The bus levelled down onto the straight line of road that ran to Burguete. We passed a crossroads and crossed a bridge over a stream. The houses of Burguete were along both sides of the road. There were no side-streets. We passed the church and the school-yard, and the bus stopped. We got down and the driver handed down our bags and the rod-case. A carabineer in his cocked hat and yellow leather cross-straps came up.

'What's in there?' he pointed to the rod-case.

I opened it and showed him. He asked to see our fishing permits and I got them out. He looked at the date and then waved us on.

'Is that all right?' I asked.

'Yes. Of course.'

We went up the street, past the whitewashed stone houses, families sitting in their doorways watching us, to the inn.

The fat woman who ran the inn came out from the kitchen and shook hands with us. She took off her spectacles, wiped them, and put them on again. It was cold in the inn and the wind was starting to blow outside. The woman sent a girl up-stairs with us to show the room. There were two beds, a washstand, a clothes-chest, and a big, framed steel-engraving of Nuestra Señora de Roncesvalles. The wind was blowing against the shutters. The room was on the north side of the inn. We washed, put on sweaters, and came down-stairs into the dining-room. It had a stone floor, low ceiling, and was oak-panelled. The shutters were up and it was so cold you could see your breath.

'My God!' said Bill. 'It can't be this cold to-morrow. I'm not going to wade a stream in this weather.'

There was an upright piano in the far corner of the room beyond the wooden tables and Bill went over and started to play.

'I got to keep warm,' he said.

I went out to find the woman and ask her how much the room and board was. She put her hands under her apron and looked away from me.

'Twelve pesetas.'

'Why, we only paid that in Pamplona.'

She did not say anything, just took off her glasses and wiped them on her apron.

'That's too much,' I said. 'We didn't pay more than that at a big hotel.'

'We've put in a bathroom.'

'Haven't you got anything cheaper?'

'Not in the summer. Now is the big season.'

We were the only people in the inn. Well, I thought, it's only a few days.

'Is the wine included?'

'Oh, yes.'

'Well,' I said. 'It's all right.'

I went back to Bill. He blew his breath at me to show how cold it was, and went on playing. I sat at one of the tables and looked at the pictures on the wall. There was one panel of rabbits, dead, one of pheasants, also dead, and one panel of dead ducks. The panels were all dark and smoky-looking. There was a cupboard full of liqueur bottles. I looked at them all. Bill was still playing. 'How about a hot rum punch?' he said. 'This isn't going to keep me warm permanently.'

I went out and told the woman what a rum punch was and how to make it. In a few minutes a girl brought a stone pitcher, steaming, into the room. Bill came over from the piano and we drank the hot punch and listened to the wind.

'There isn't too much rum in that.'

I went over to the cupboard and brought the rum bottle and poured a half-tumblerful into the pitcher.

'Direct action,' said Bill. 'It beats legislation.'

The girl came in and laid the table for supper.

'It blows like hell up here,' Bill said.

The girl brought in a big bowl of hot vegetable soup and the wine. We had fried trout afterward and some sort of a stew and a big bowl full of wild strawberries. We did not lose money on the wine, and the girl was shy but nice about bringing it. The old woman looked in once and counted the empty bottles.

After supper we went up-stairs and smoked and read in bed to keep warm. Once in the night I woke and heard the wind blowing. It felt good to be warm and in bed.

12

When I woke in the morning I went to the window and looked out. It had cleared and there were no clouds on the mountains. Outside under the window were some carts and an old diligence, the wood of the roof cracked and split by the weather. It must have been left from the days before the motor-buses. A goat hopped up on one of the carts and then to the roof of the diligence. He jerked his head at the other goats below and when I waved at him he bounded down.

Bill was still sleeping, so I dressed, put on my shoes outside in the hall, and went down-stairs. No one was stirring down-stairs, so I unbolted the door and went out. It was cool outside in the early morning and the sun had not yet dried the dew that had come when the wind died down. I hunted around in the shed behind the inn and found a sort of mattock, and went down toward the stream to try and dig some worms for bait. The stream was clear and shallow but it did not look trouty. On the grassy bank where it was damp I drove the mattock into the earth and loosened a chunk of sod. There were worms underneath. They slid out of sight as I lifted the sod and I dug carefully and got a good many. Digging at the edge of the damp ground I filled two empty tobacco-tins with worms and sifted dirt onto them. The goats watched me dig.

When I went back into the inn the woman was down in the kitchen, and I asked her to get coffee for us, and that we wanted a lunch. Bill was awake and sitting on the edge of the bed.

'I saw you out of the window,' he said. 'Didn't want to interrupt you. What were you doing? Burying your money?'

'You lazy bum!'

'Been working for the common good? Splendid. I want you to do that every morning.'

'Come on,' I said. 'Get up.'

'What? Get up? I never get up.'

He climbed into bed and pulled the sheet up to his chin.

'Try and argue me into getting up.'

I went on looking for the tackle and putting it all together in the tackle-bag.

'Aren't you interested?' Bill asked.

'I'm going down and eat.'

'Eat? Why didn't you say eat? I thought you just wanted me to get up for fun. Eat? Fine. Now you're reasonable. You go out and dig some more worms and I'll be right down.'

'Oh, go to hell!'

'Work for the good of all.' Bill stepped into his underclothes. 'Show irony and pity.'

I started out of the room with the tackle-bag, the nets, and the rod-case.

'Hey! come back!'

I put my head in the door.

'Aren't you going to show a little irony and pity?'

I thumbed my nose.

'That's not irony.'

As I went down-stairs I heard Bill singing, 'Irony and Pity. When you're feeling . . . Oh, Give them Irony and Give them Pity. Oh, give them Irony. When they're feeling . . . Just a little irony. Just a little pity . . .' He kept on singing until he came down-stairs. The tune was: 'The Bells are Ringing for Me and my Gal.' I was reading a week-old Spanish paper.

'What's all this irony and pity?'

'What? Don't you know about Irony and Pity?'

'No. Who got it up?'

'Everybody. They're mad about it in New York. It's just like the Fratellinis used to be.'

The girl came in with the coffee and buttered toast. Or, rather, it was bread toasted and buttered.

'Ask her if she's got any jam,' Bill said. 'Be ironical with her.'

'Have you got any jam?'

'That's not ironical. I wish I could talk Spanish.'

The coffee was good and we drank it out of big bowls. The girl brought in a glass dish of raspberry jam.

'Thank you.'

'Hey! that's not the way,' Bill said. 'Say something ironical. Make some crack about Primo de Rivera.'

'I could ask her what kind of a jam they think they've gotten into in the Riff.'

'Poor,' said Bill. 'Very poor. You can't do it. That's all. You don't understand irony. You have no pity. Say something pitiful.'

'Robert Cohn.'

'Not so bad. That's better. Now why is Cohn pitiful? Be ironic.'

He took a big gulp of coffee.

'Aw, hell!' I said. 'It's too early in the morning.'

'There you go. And you claim you want to be a writer, too. You're only a newspaper man. An expatriated newspaper man. You ought to be ironical the minute you get out of bed. You ought to wake up with your mouth full of pity.'

'Go on,' I said. 'Who did you get this stuff from?'

'Everybody. Don't you read? Don't you ever see anybody? You know what you are? You're an expatriate. Why don't you live in New York? Then you'd know these things. What do you want me to do? Come over here and tell you every year?'

'Take some more coffee,' I said.

'Good. Coffee is good for you. It's the caffeine in it. Caffeine, we are here. Caffeine puts a man on her horse and a woman in his grave. You know what's the trouble with you? You're an expatriate. One of the worst type. Haven't you heard that? Nobody that ever left their own country ever wrote anything worth printing. Not even in the newspapers.'

He drank the coffee.

'You're an expatriate. You've lost touch with the soil. You get precious. Fake European standards have ruined you. You drink yourself to death. You become obsessed by sex. You spend all your time talking, not working. You are an expatriate, see? You hang around cafés.'

'It sounds like a swell life,' I said. 'When do I work?'

'You don't work. One group claims women support you. Another group claims you're impotent.'

'No,' I said. 'I just had an accident.'

'Never mention that,' Bill said. 'That's the sort of thing that can't be spoken of. That's what you ought to work up into a mystery. Like Henry's bicycle.'

He had been going splendidly, but he stopped. I was afraid he thought he had hurt me with that crack about being impotent. I wanted to start him again.

'It wasn't a bicycle,' I said. 'He was riding horseback.'

'I heard it was a tricycle.'

'Well,' I said. 'A plane is sort of like a tricycle. The joystick works the same way.'

'But you don't pedal it.'

'No,' I said, 'I guess you don't pedal it.'

'Let's lay off that,' Bill said.

'All right. I was just standing up for the tricycle.'

'I think he's a good writer, too,' Bill said. 'And you're a hell of a good guy.

Anybody ever tell you you were a good guy?'

'I'm not a good guy.'

'Listen. You're a hell of a good guy, and I'm fonder of you than anybody on earth. I couldn't tell you that in New York. It'd mean I was a faggot. That was what the Civil War was about. Abraham Lincoln was a faggot. He was in love with General Grant. So was Jefferson Davis. Lincoln just freed the slaves on a bet. The Dred Scott case was framed by the Anti-Saloon League. Sex explains it all. The Colonel's Lady and Judy O'Grady are Lesbians under their skin.'

He stopped.

'Want to hear some more?'

'Shoot,' I said.

'I don't know any more. Tell you some more at lunch.'

'Old Bill,' I said.

'You bum!'

We packed the lunch and two bottles of wine in the rucksack, and Bill put it on. I carried the rod-case and the landing-nets slung over my back. We started up the road and then went across a meadow and found a path that crossed the fields and went toward the woods on the slope of the first hill. We walked across the fields on the sandy path. The fields were rolling and grassy and the grass was short from the sheep grazing. The cattle were up in the hills. We heard their bells in the woods.

The path crossed a stream on a foot-log. The log was surfaced off, and there was a sapling bent across for a rail. In the flat pool beside the stream tadpoles spotted the sand. We went up a steep bank and across the rolling fields. Looking back we saw Burguete, white houses and red roofs, and the white road with a truck going along it and the dust rising.

Beyond the fields we crossed another faster-flowing stream. A sandy road led down to the ford and beyond into the woods. The path crossed the stream on another foot-log below the ford, and joined the road, and we went into the woods.

It was a beech wood and the trees were very old. Their roots bulked above the ground and the branches were twisted. We walked on the road between the thick trunks of the old beeches and the sunlight came through the leaves in light patches on the grass. The trees were big, and the foliage was thick but it was not gloomy. There was no undergrowth, only the smooth grass, very green and fresh, and the big gray trees well spaced as though it were a park.

'This is country,' Bill said.

The road went up a hill and we got into thick woods, and the road kept on climbing. Sometimes it dipped down but rose again steeply. All the time we heard the cattle in the woods. Finally, the road came out on the top of the hills. We were on the top of the height of land that was the highest part of the range of wooded hills we had seen from Burguete. There were wild strawberries growing on the sunny side of the ridge in a little clearing in the trees.

Ahead the road came out of the forest and went along the shoulder of the ridge of hills. The hills ahead were not wooded, and there were great fields of yellow gorse. Way off we saw the steep bluffs, dark with trees and jutting with gray stone, that marked the course of the Irati River.

'We have to follow this road along the ridge, cross these hills, go through the woods on the far hills, and come down to the Irati valley,' I pointed out to Bill.

'That's a hell of a hike.'

'It's too far to go and fish and come back the same day, comfortably.'

'Comfortably. That's a nice word. We'll have to go like hell to get there and back and have any fishing at all.'

It was a long walk and the country was very fine, but we were tired when we came down the steep road that led out of the wooded hills into the valley of the Rio de la Fabrica.

The road came out from the shadow of the woods into the hot sun. Ahead was a river-valley. Beyond the river was a steep hill. There was a field of buckwheat on the hill. We saw a white house under some trees on the hillside. It was very hot and we stopped under some trees beside a dam that crossed the river.

Bill put the pack against one of the trees and we jointed up the rods, put on the reels, tied on leaders, and got ready to fish.

'You're sure this thing has trout in it?' Bill asked.

'It's full of them.'

'I'm going to fish a fly. You got any McGintys?'

'There's some in there.'

'You going to fish bait?'

'Yeah. I'm going to fish the dam here.'

'Well, I'll take the fly-book, then.' He tied on a fly. 'Where'd I better go? Up or down?'

'Down is the best. They're plenty up above, too.'

Bill went down the bank.

'Take a worm can.'

'No, I don't want one. If they won't take a fly I'll just flick it around.'

Bill was down below watching the stream.

'Say,' he called up against the noise of the dam. 'How about putting the wine in that spring up the road?'

'All right,' I shouted. Bill waved his hand and started down the stream. I found the two wine-bottles in the pack, and carried them up the road to where the water of a spring flowed out of an iron pipe. There was a board over the spring and I lifted it and, knocking the corks firmly into the bottles, lowered them down into the water. It was so cold my hand and wrist felt numbed. I put back the slab of wood, and hoped nobody would find the wine.

I got my rod that was leaning against the tree, took the bait-can and landing-net, and walked out onto the dam. It was built to provide a head of water for driving logs. The gate was up, and I sat on one of the squared timbers and watched the smooth apron of water before the river tumbled into the falls. In the white water at the foot of the dam it was deep. As I baited up, a trout shot up out of the white water into the falls and was carried down. Before I could finish baiting, another trout jumped at the falls, making the same lovely arc and disappearing into the water that was thundering down. I put on a good-sized sinker and dropped into the white water close to the edge of the timbers of the dam.

I did not feel the first trout strike. When I started to pull up I felt that I had one and brought him, fighting and bending the rod almost double, out of the boiling water at the foot of the falls, and swung him up and onto the dam. He was a good trout, and I banged his head against the timber so that he quivered out straight, and then slipped him into my bag.

While I had him on, several trout had jumped at the falls. As soon as I baited up and dropped in again I hooked another and brought him in the same way. In a little while I had six. They were all about the same size. I laid them out, side by side, all their heads pointing the same way, and looked at them. They were beautifully colored and firm and hard from the cold water. It was a hot day, so I slit them all and shucked out the insides, gills and all, and tossed them over across the river. I took the trout ashore, washed them in the cold, smoothly heavy water above the dam, and then picked some ferns and packed them all in the bag, three trout on a layer of ferns, then another layer of ferns, then three more trout, and then covered them with ferns. They looked nice in the ferns, and now the bag was bulky, and I put it in the shade of the tree.

It was very hot on the dam, so I put my worm-can in the shade with the bag, and got a book out of the pack and settled down under the tree to read until Bill should come up for lunch.

It was a little past noon and there was not much shade, but I sat against the trunk of two of the trees that grew together, and read. The book was something by A. E. W. Mason, and I was reading a wonderful story about a man who had been frozen in the Alps and then fallen into a glacier and disappeared, and his bride was going to wait twenty-four years exactly for his body to come out on the moraine, while her true love waited too, and they were still waiting when Bill came up.

'Get any?' he asked. He had his rod and his bag and his net all in one hand, and he was sweating. I hadn't heard him come up, because of the noise from the dam.

'Six. What did you get?'

Bill sat down, opened up his bag, laid a big trout on the grass. He took out three more, each one a little bigger than the last, and laid them side by side in the shade from the tree. His face was sweaty and happy.

'How are yours?'

'Smaller.'

'Let's see them.'

'They're packed.'

'How big are they really?'

'They're all about the size of your smallest.'

'You're not holding out on me?'

'I wish I were.'

'Get them all on worms?'

'Yes.'

'You lazy bum!'

Bill put the trout in the bag and started for the river, swinging the open bag. He was wet from the waist down and I knew he must have been wading the stream.

I walked up the road and got out the two bottles of wine. They were cold. Moisture beaded on the bottles as I walked back to the trees. I spread the lunch on a newspaper, and uncorked one of the bottles and leaned the other against a tree. Bill came up drying his hands, his bag plump with ferns.

'Let's see that bottle,' he said. He pulled the cork, and tipped up the bottle and drank. 'Whew! That makes my eyes ache.'

'Let's try it.'

The wine was icy cold and tasted faintly rusty.

'That's not such filthy wine,' Bill said.

'The cold helps it,' I said.

We unwrapped the little parcels of lunch.

'Chicken.'

'There's hard-boiled eggs.'

'Find any salt?'

'First the egg,' said Bill. 'Then the chicken. Even Bryan could see that.'

'He's dead. I read it in the paper yesterday.'

'No. Not really?'

'Yes. Bryan's dead.'

Bill laid down the egg he was peeling.

'Gentlemen,' he said, and unwrapped a drumstick from a piece of newspaper. 'I reverse the order. For Bryan's sake. As a tribute to the Great Commoner. First the chicken; then the egg.'

'Wonder what day God created the chicken?'

'Oh,' said Bill, sucking the drumstick, 'how should we know? We should not question. Our stay on earth is not for long. Let us rejoice and believe and give thanks.'

'Eat an egg.'

Bill gestured with the drumstick in one hand and the bottle of wine in the other.

'Let us rejoice in our blessings. Let us utilize the fowls of the air. Let us utilize the product of the vine. Will you utilize a little, brother?'

'After you, brother.'

Bill took a long drink.

'Utilize a little, brother,' he handed me the bottle. 'Let us not doubt, brother. Let us not pry into the holy mysteries of the hen-coop with simian fingers. Let us accept on faith and simply say—I want you to join with me in saying—What shall we say, brother?' He pointed the drumstick at me and went on. 'Let me tell you. We will say, and I for one am proud to say—and I want you to say with me, on your knees, brother. Let no man be ashamed to kneel here in the great out-of-doors. Remember the woods were God's first temples. Let us kneel and say: "Don't eat that, Lady—that's Mencken."'

'Here,' I said. 'Utilize a little of this.'
We uncorked the other bottle.
'What's the matter?' I said. 'Didn't you like Bryan?'
'I loved Bryan,' said Bill. 'We were like brothers.'
'Where did you know him?'
'He and Mencken and I all went to Holy Cross together.'
'And Frankie Fritsch.'
'It's a lie. Frankie Fritsch went to Fordham.'
'Well,' I said, 'I went to Loyola with Bishop Manning.'
'It's a lie,' Bill said. 'I went to Loyola with Bishop Manning myself.'
'You're cock-eyed,' I said.
'On wine?'
'Why not?'
'It's the humidity,' Bill said. 'They ought to take this damn humidity away.'
'Have another shot.'
'Is this all we've got?'
'Only the two bottles.'
'Do you know what you are?' Bill looked at the bottle affectionately.
'No,' I said.
'You're in the pay of the Anti-Saloon League.'
'I went to Notre Dame with Wayne B. Wheeler.'
'It's a lie,' said Bill. 'I went to Austin Business College with Wayne B. Wheeler. He was class president.'
'Well,' I said, 'the saloon must go.'
'You're right there, old classmate,' Bill said. 'The saloon must go, and I will take it with me.'
'You're cock-eyed.'
'On wine?'
'On wine.'
'Well, maybe I am.'
'Want to take a nap?'
'All right.'
We lay with our heads in the shade and looked up into the trees.
'You asleep?'
'No,' Bill said. 'I was thinking.'
I shut my eyes. It felt good lying on the ground.
'Say,' Bill said, 'what about this Brett business?'
'What about it?'

'Were you ever in love with her?'

'Sure.'

'For how long?'

'Off and on for a hell of a long time.'

'Oh, hell!' Bill said. 'I'm sorry, fella.'

'It's all right,' I said. 'I don't give a damn any more.'

'Really?'

'Really. Only I'd a hell of a lot rather not talk about it.'

'You aren't sore I asked you?'

'Why the hell should I be?'

'I'm going to sleep,' Bill said. He put a newspaper over his face.

'Listen, Jake,' he said, 'are you really a Catholic?'

'Technically.'

'What does that mean?'

'I don't know.'

'All right, I'll go to sleep now,' he said. 'Don't keep me awake by talking so much.'

I went to sleep, too. When I woke up Bill was packing the rucksack. It was late in the afternoon and the shadow from the trees was long and went out over the dam. I was stiff from sleeping on the ground.

'What did you do? Wake up?' Bill asked. 'Why didn't you spend the night?' I stretched and rubbed my eyes.

'I had a lovely dream,' Bill said. 'I don't remember what it was about, but it was a lovely dream.'

'I don't think I dreamt.'

'You ought to dream,' Bill said. 'All our biggest business men have been dreamers. Look at Ford. Look at President Coolidge. Look at Rockefeller. Look at Jo Davidson.'

I disjointed my rod and Bill's and packed them in the rod-case. I put the reels in the tackle-bag. Bill had packed the rucksack and we put one of the trout-bags in. I carried the other.

'Well,' said Bill, 'have we got everything?'

'The worms.'

'Your worms. Put them in there.'

He had the pack on his back and I put the worm-cans in one of the outside flap pockets.

'You got everything now?'

I looked around on the grass at the foot of the elm-trees.

'Yes.'

We started up the road into the woods. It was a long walk home to Burguete, and it was dark when we came down across the fields to the road, and along the road between the houses of the town, their windows lighted, to the inn.

We stayed five days at Burguete and had good fishing. The nights were cold and the days were hot, and there was always a breeze even in the heat of the day. It was hot enough so that it felt good to wade in a cold stream, and the sun dried you when you came out and sat on the bank. We found a stream with a pool deep enough to swim in. In the evenings we played three-handed bridge with an Englishman named Harris, who had walked over from Saint Jean Pied de Port and was stopping at the inn for the fishing. He was very pleasant and went with us twice to the Irati River. There was no word from Robert Cohn nor from Brett and Mike.

13

One morning I went down to breakfast and the Englishman, Harris, was already at the table. He was reading the paper through spectacles. He looked up and smiled.

'Good morning,' he said. 'Letter for you. I stopped at the post and they gave it me with mine.'

The letter was at my place at the table, leaning against a coffee-cup. Harris was reading the paper again. I opened the letter. It had been forwarded from Pamplona. It was dated San Sebastian, Sunday:

Dear Jake,

We got here Friday, Brett passed out on the train, so brought her here for 3 days rest with old friends of ours. We go to Montoya Hotel Pamplona Tuesday, arriving at I don't know what hour. Will you send a note by the bus to tell us what to do to rejoin you all on Wednesday. All our love and sorry to be late, but Brett was really done in and will be quite all right by Tues. and is practically so now. I know her so well and try to look after her but it's not so easy. Love to all the chaps,

Michael.

'What day of the week is it?' I asked Harris.

'Wednesday, I think. Yes, quite. Wednesday. Wonderful how one loses track of the days up here in the mountains.'

'Yes. We've been here nearly a week.'

'I hope you're not thinking of leaving?'

'Yes. We'll go in on the afternoon bus, I'm afraid.'

'What a rotten business. I had hoped we'd all have another go at the Irati together.'

'We have to go *into* Pamplona. We're meeting people there.'

'What rotten luck for me. We've had a jolly time here at Burguete.'

'Come on in to Pamplona. We can play some bridge there, and there's going to be a damned fine fiesta.'

'I'd like to. Awfully nice of you to ask me. I'd best stop on here, though. I've not much more time to fish.'

'You want those big ones in the Irati.'

'I say, I do, you know. They're enormous trout there.'

'I'd like to try them once more.'

'Do. Stop over another day. Be a good chap.'

'We really have to get into town,' I said.

'What a pity.'

After breakfast Bill and I were sitting warming in the sun on a bench out in front of the inn and talking it over. I saw a girl coming up the road from the centre of the town. She stopped in front of us and took a telegram out of the leather wallet that hung against her skirt.

'Por ustedes?'

I looked at it. The address was: 'Barnes, Burguete.'

'Yes. It's for us.'

She brought out a book for me to sign, and I gave her a couple of coppers. The telegram was in Spanish: 'Vengo Jueves Cohn.'

I handed it to Bill.

'What does the word Cohn mean?' he asked.

'What a lousy telegram!' I said. 'He could send ten words for the same price. "I come Thursday." That gives you a lot of dope, doesn't it?'

'It gives you all the dope that's of interest to Cohn.'

'We're going in, anyway,' I said. 'There's no use trying to move Brett and Mike out here and back before the fiesta. Should we answer it?'

'We might as well,' said Bill. 'There's no need for us to be snooty.'

We walked up to the post-office and asked for a telegraph blank.

'What will we say?' Bill asked.

'"Arriving to-night." That's enough.'

We paid for the message and walked back to the inn. Harris was there and the three of us walked up to Roncesvalles. We went through the monastery.

'It's a remarkable place,' Harris said, when we came out. 'But you know I'm not much on those sort of places.'

'Me either,' Bill said.

'It's a remarkable place, though,' Harris said. 'I wouldn't not have seen it. I'd been intending coming up each day.'

'It isn't the same as fishing, though, is it?' Bill asked. He liked Harris.

'I say not.'

We were standing in front of the old chapel of the monastery.

'Isn't that a pub across the way?' Harris asked. 'Or do my eyes deceive me?'

'It has the look of a pub,' Bill said.

'It looks to me like a pub,' I said.

'I say,' said Harris, 'let's utilize it.' He had taken up utilizing from Bill.

We had a bottle of wine apiece. Harris would not let us pay. He talked Spanish quite well, and the innkeeper would not take our money.

'I say. You don't know what it's meant to me to have you chaps up here.'

'We've had a grand time, Harris.'

Harris was a little tight.

'I say. Really you don't know how much it means. I've not had much fun since the war.'

'We'll fish together again, some time. Don't you forget it, Harris.'
'We must. We *have* had such a jolly good time.'
'How about another bottle around?'
'Jolly good idea,' said Harris.
'This is mine,' said Bill. 'Or we don't drink it.'
'I wish you'd let me pay for it. It *does* give me pleasure, you know.'
'This is going to give me pleasure,' Bill said.

The innkeeper brought in the fourth bottle. We had kept the same glasses. Harris lifted his glass.

'I say. You know this does utilize well.'

Bill slapped him on the back.

'Good old Harris.'

'I say. You know my name isn't really Harris. It's Wilson-Harris. All one name. With a hyphen, you know.'

'Good old Wilson-Harris,' Bill said. 'We call you Harris because we're so fond of you.'

'I say, Barnes. You don't know what this all means to me.'

'Come on and utilize another glass,' I said.

'Barnes. Really, Barnes, you can't know. That's all.'

'Drink up, Harris.'

We walked back down the road from Roncesvalles with Harris between us. We had lunch at the inn and Harris went with us to the bus. He gave us his card, with his address in London and his club and his business address, and as we got on the bus he handed us each an envelope. I opened mine and there were a dozen flies in it. Harris had tied them himself. He tied all his own flies.

'I say, Harris—' I began.

'No, no!' he said. He was climbing down from the bus. 'They're not first-rate flies at all. I only thought if you fished them some time it might remind you of what a good time we had.'

The bus started. Harris stood in front of the post-office. He waved. As we started along the road he turned and walked back toward the inn.

'Say, wasn't that Harris nice?' Bill said.

'I think he really did have a good time.'

'Harris? You bet he did.'

'I wish he'd come into Pamplona.'

'He wanted to fish.'

'Yes. You couldn't tell how English would mix with each other, anyway.'

'I suppose not.'

We got into Pamplona late in the afternoon and the bus stopped in front of the Hotel Montoya. Out in the plaza they were stringing electric-light wires to light the plaza for the fiesta. A few kids came up when the bus stopped, and a customs officer for the town made all the people getting down from the bus open their bundles on the sidewalk. We went into the hotel and on the stairs I met Montoya.

He shook hands with us, smiling in his embarrassed way.

'Your friends are here,' he said.

'Mr. Campbell?'

'Yes. Mr. Cohn and Mr. Campbell and Lady Ashley.'

He smiled as though there were something I would hear about.

'When did they get in?'

'Yesterday. I've saved you the rooms you had.'

'That's fine. Did you give Mr. Campbell the room on the plaza?'

'Yes. All the rooms we looked at.'

'Where are our friends now?'

'I think they went to the pelota.'

'And how about the bulls?'

Montoya smiled. 'To-night,' he said. 'To-night at seven o'clock they bring in the Villar bulls, and to-morrow come the Miuras. Do you all go down?'

'Oh, yes. They've never seen a desencajonada.'

Montoya put his hand on my shoulder.

'I'll see you there.'

He smiled again. He always smiled as though bull-fighting were a very special secret between the two of us; a rather shocking but really very deep secret that we knew about. He always smiled as though there were something lewd about the secret to outsiders, but that it was something that we understood. It would not do to expose it to people who would not understand.

'Your friend, is he aficionado, too?' Montoya smiled at Bill.

'Yes. He came all the way from New York to see the San Fermines.'

'Yes?' Montoya politely disbelieved. 'But he's not aficionado like you.'

He put his hand on my shoulder again embarrassedly.

'Yes,' I said. 'He's a real aficionado.'

'But he's not aficionado like you are.'

Aficion means passion. An aficionado is one who is passionate about the bull-fights. All the good bull-fighters stayed at Montoya's hotel; that is, those with aficion stayed there. The commercial bull-fighters stayed once, perhaps, and then did not come back. The good ones came each year. In Montoya's room were their photographs. The photographs were dedicated to Juanito Montoya or to his sister. The photographs of bull-fighters Montoya had really believed in were framed. Photographs of bull-fighters who had been without aficion Montoya kept in a drawer of his desk. They often had the most flattering inscriptions. But they did not mean anything. One day Montoya took them all out and dropped them in the waste-basket. He did not want them around.

We often talked about bulls and bull-fighters. I had stopped at the Montoya for several years. We never talked for very long at a time. It was simply the pleasure of discovering what we each felt. Men would come in from distant towns and before they left Pamplona stop and talk for a few minutes with Montoya about bulls. These men were aficionados. Those who were aficionados could always get rooms even when the hotel was full. Montoya introduced me to some of them. They were always very polite at first, and it amused them very much that I should be an American. Somehow it was taken for granted that an American could not have aficion. He might simulate it or confuse it with excitement, but he could not really have it. When they saw that I had aficion, and there was no password, no set questions that could bring it out, rather it was a sort of oral spiritual examination with the questions always a little on the defensive and never apparent, there was this same embarrassed putting the hand on the shoulder, or a 'Buen hombre.' But nearly always there was the actual touching. It seemed as though they wanted to touch you to make it certain.

Montoya could forgive anything of a bull-fighter who had aficion. He could forgive attacks of nerves, panic, bad unexplainable actions, all sorts of lapses. For one who had aficion he could forgive anything. At once he forgave me all my friends. Without his ever saying anything they were simply a little something shameful between us, like the spilling open of the horses in bull-fighting.

Bill had gone up-stairs as we came in, and I found him washing and changing in his room.

'Well,' he said, 'talk a lot of Spanish?'

'He was telling me about the bulls coming in to-night.'

'Let's find the gang and go down.'

'All right. They'll probably be at the café.'

'Have you got tickets?'

'Yes. I got them for all the unloadings.'

'What's it like?' He was pulling his cheek before the glass, looking to see if there were unshaved patches under the line of the jaw.

'It's pretty good,' I said. 'They let the bulls out of the cages one at a time, and they have steers in the corral to receive them and keep them from fighting, and the bulls tear in at the steers and the steers run around like old maids trying to quiet them down.'

'Do they ever gore the steers?'

'Sure. Sometimes they go right after them and kill them.'

'Can't the steers do anything?'

'No. They're trying to make friends.'

'What do they have them in for?'

'To quiet down the bulls and keep them from breaking horns against the stone walls, or goring each other.'

'Must be swell being a steer.'

We went down the stairs and out of the door and walked across the square toward the Café Iruña. There were two lonely looking ticket-houses standing in the square. Their windows, marked SOL, SOL Y SOMBRA, and SOMBRA, were shut. They would not open until the day before the fiesta.

Across the square the white wicker tables and chairs of the Iruña extended out beyond the Arcade to the edge of the street. I looked for Brett and Mike at the tables. There they were. Brett and Mike and Robert Cohn. Brett was wearing a Basque beret. So was Mike. Robert Cohn was bare-headed and wearing his spectacles. Brett saw us coming and waved. Her eyes crinkled up as we came up to the table.

'Hello, you chaps!' she called.

Brett was happy. Mike had a way of getting an intensity of feeling into shaking hands. Robert Cohn shook hands because we were back.

'Where the hell have you been?' I asked.

'I brought them up here,' Cohn said.

'What rot,' Brett said. 'We'd have gotten here earlier if you hadn't come.'

'You'd never have gotten here.'

'What rot! You chaps are brown. Look at Bill.'

'Did you get good fishing?' Mike asked. 'We wanted to join you.'

'It wasn't bad. We missed you.'

'I wanted to come,' Cohn said, 'but I thought I ought to bring them.'

'You bring us. What rot.'

'Was it really good?' Mike asked. 'Did you take many?'

'Some days we took a dozen apiece. There was an Englishman up there.'

'Named Harris,' Bill said. 'Ever know him, Mike? He was in the war, too.'

'Fortunate fellow,' Mike said. 'What times we had. How I wish those dear days were back.'

'Don't be an ass.'

'Were you in the war, Mike?' Cohn asked.

'Was I not.'

'He was a very distinguished soldier,' Brett said. 'Tell them about the time your horse bolted down Piccadilly.'

'I'll not. I've told that four times.'

'You never told me,' Robert Cohn said.

'I'll not tell that story. It reflects discredit on me.'

'Tell them about your medals.'

'I'll not. That story reflects great discredit on me.'

'What story's that?'

'Brett will tell you. She tells all the stories that reflect discredit on me.'

'Go on. Tell it, Brett.'

'Should I?'

'I'll tell it myself.'

'What medals have you got, Mike?'

'I haven't got any medals.'

'You must have some.'

'I suppose I've the usual medals. But I never sent in for them. One time there was this wopping big dinner and the Prince of Wales was to be there, and the cards said medals will be worn. So naturally I had no medals, and I stopped at my tailor's and he was impressed by the invitation, and I thought that's a good piece of business, and I said to him: 'You've got to fix me up with some medals.' He said: 'What medals, sir?' And I said: 'Oh, any medals. Just give me a few medals.' So he said: 'What medals *have* you, sir?' And I said: 'How should I know?' Did he think I spent all my time reading the bloody gazette? 'Just give me a good lot. Pick them out yourself.' So he got me some medals, you know, miniature medals, and handed me the box, and I put it in my pocket and forgot it. Well, I went to the dinner, and it was the night they'd shot Henry Wilson, so the Prince didn't come and the King didn't come, and no one wore any medals, and all these coves were busy taking off their medals, and I had mine in my pocket.'

He stopped for us to laugh.

'Is that all?'

'That's all. Perhaps I didn't tell it right.'

'You didn't,' said Brett. 'But no matter.'

We were all laughing.

'Ah, yes,' said Mike. 'I know now. It was a damn dull dinner, and I couldn't stick it, so I left. Later on in the evening I found the box in my pocket. What's this? I said. Medals? Bloody military medals? So I cut them all off their backing—you know, they put them on a strip—and gave them all around. Gave one to each girl. Form of souvenir. They thought I was hell's own shakes of a soldier. Give away medals in a night club. Dashing fellow.'

'Tell the rest,' Brett said.

'Don't you think that was funny?' Mike asked. We were all laughing. 'It was. I swear it was. Any rate, my tailor wrote me and wanted the medals back. Sent a man around. Kept on writing for months. Seems some chap had left them to be cleaned. Frightfully military cove. Set hell's own store by them.' Mike paused. 'Rotten luck for the tailor,' he said.

'You don't mean it,' Bill said. 'I should think it would have been grand for the tailor.'

'Frightfully good tailor. Never believe it to see me now,' Mike said. 'I used to pay him a hundred pounds a year just to keep him quiet. So he wouldn't send me any bills. Frightful blow to him when I went bankrupt. It was right after the medals. Gave his letters rather a bitter tone.'

'How did you go bankrupt?' Bill asked.

'Two ways,' Mike said. 'Gradually and then suddenly.'

'What brought it on?'

'Friends,' said Mike. 'I had a lot of friends. False friends. Then I had creditors, too. Probably had more creditors than anybody in England.'

'Tell them about in the court,' Brett said.

'I don't remember,' Mike said. 'I was just a little tight.'

'Tight!' Brett exclaimed. 'You were blind!'

'Extraordinary thing,' Mike said. 'Met my former partner the other day. Offered to buy me a drink.'

'Tell them about your learned counsel,' Brett said.

'I will not,' Mike said. 'My learned counsel was blind, too. I say this is a gloomy subject. Are we going down and see these bulls unloaded or not?'

'Let's go down.'

We called the waiter, paid, and started to walk through the town. I started off walking with Brett, but Robert Cohn came up and joined her on the other side. The three of us walked along, past the Ayuntamiento with the banners hung from the balcony, down past the market and down past the steep street that led to the bridge across the Arga. There were many people walking to go and see the bulls, and carriages drove down the hill and across the bridge, the drivers, the horses, and the whips rising above the walking people in the street. Across the bridge we turned up a road to the corrals. We passed a wine-shop with a sign in the window: Good Wine 30 Centimes A Liter.

'That's where we'll go when funds get low,' Brett said.

The woman standing in the door of the wine-shop looked at us as we passed. She called to some one in the house and three girls came to the window and stared. They were staring at Brett.

At the gate of the corrals two men took tickets from the people that went in. We went in through the gate. There were trees inside and a low, stone house. At the far end was the stone wall of the corrals, with apertures in the stone that were like loopholes running all along the face of each corral. A ladder led up to the top of the wall, and people were climbing up the ladder and spreading down to stand on the walls that separated the two corrals. As we came up the ladder, walking across the grass under the trees, we passed the big, gray painted cages with the bulls in them. There was one bull in each travelling-box. They had come by train from a bull-breeding ranch in Castile, and had been unloaded off flat-cars at the station and brought up here to be let out of their cages into the corrals. Each cage was stencilled with the name and the brand of the bull-breeder.

We climbed up and found a place on the wall looking down into the corral. The stone walls were whitewashed, and there was straw on the ground and wooden feed-boxes and water-troughs set against the wall.

'Look up there,' I said.

Beyond the river rose the plateau of the town. All along the old walls and ramparts people were standing. The three lines of fortifications made three black lines of people. Above the walls there were heads in the windows of the houses. At the far end of the plateau boys had climbed into the trees.

'They must think something is going to happen,' Brett said.

'They want to see the bulls.'

Mike and Bill were on the other wall across the pit of the corral. They waved to us. People who had come late were standing behind us, pressing against us when other people crowded them.

'Why don't they start?' Robert Cohn asked.

A single mule was hitched to one of the cages and dragged it up against the gate in the corral wall. The men shoved and lifted it with crowbars into position against the gate. Men were standing on the wall ready to pull up the gate of the corral and then the gate of the cage. At the other end of the corral a gate opened and two steers came in, swaying their heads and trotting, their lean flanks swinging. They stood together at the far end, their heads toward the gate where the bull would enter.

'They don't look happy,' Brett said.

The men on top of the wall leaned back and pulled up the door of the corral. Then they pulled up the door of the cage.

I leaned way over the wall and tried to see into the cage. It was dark. Some one rapped on the cage with an iron bar. Inside something seemed to explode. The bull, striking into the wood from side to side with his horns, made a great noise. Then I saw a dark muzzle and the shadow of horns, and then, with a clattering on the wood in the hollow box, the bull charged and came out into the corral, skidding with his forefeet in the straw as he stopped, his head up, the great hump of muscle on his neck swollen tight, his body muscles quivering as he looked up at the crowd on the stone walls. The two steers backed away against the wall, their heads sunken, their eyes watching the bull.

The bull saw them and charged. A man shouted from behind one of the boxes and slapped his hat against the planks, and the bull, before he reached the steer, turned, gathered himself and charged where the man had been, trying to reach him behind the planks with a half-dozen quick, searching drives with the right horn.

'My God, isn't he beautiful?' Brett said. We were looking right down on him.

'Look how he knows how to use his horns,' I said. 'He's got a left and a right just like a boxer.'

'Not really?'

'You watch.'

'It goes too fast.'

'Wait. There'll be another one in a minute.'

They had backed up another cage into the entrance. In the far corner a man, from behind one of the plank shelters, attracted the bull, and while the bull was facing away the gate was pulled up and a second bull came out into the corral.

He charged straight for the steers and two men ran out from behind the planks and shouted, to turn him. He did not change his direction and the men shouted: 'Hah! Hah! Toro!' and waved their arms; the two steers turned sideways to take the shock, and the bull drove into one of the steers.

'Don't look,' I said to Brett. She was watching, fascinated.

'Fine,' I said. 'If it doesn't buck you.'

'I saw it,' she said. 'I saw him shift from his left to his right horn.'

'Damn good!'

The steer was down now, his neck stretched out, his head twisted, he lay the way he had fallen. Suddenly the bull left off and made for the other steer which had been standing at the far end, his head swinging, watching it all. The steer ran awkwardly and the bull caught him, hooked him lightly in the flank, and then turned away and looked up at the crowd on the walls, his crest of muscle rising. The steer came up to him and made as though to nose at him and the bull hooked perfunctorily. The next time he nosed at the steer and then the two of them trotted over to the other bull.

When the next bull came out, all three, the two bulls and the steer, stood together, their heads side by side, their horns against the newcomer. In a few minutes the steer picked the new bull up, quieted him down, and made him one of the herd. When the last two bulls had been unloaded the herd were all together.

The steer who had been gored had gotten to his feet and stood against the stone wall. None of the bulls came near him, and he did not attempt to join the herd.

We climbed down from the wall with the crowd, and had a last look at the bulls through the loopholes in the wall of the corral. They were all quiet now, their heads down. We got a carriage outside and rode up to the café. Mike and Bill came in half an hour later. They had stopped on the way for several drinks.

We were sitting in the café.

'That's an extraordinary business,' Brett said.

'Will those last ones fight as well as the first?' Robert Cohn asked. 'They seemed to quiet down awfully fast.'

'They all know each other,' I said. 'They're only dangerous when they're alone, or only two or three of them together.'

'What do you mean, dangerous?' Bill said. 'They all looked dangerous to me.'

'They only want to kill when they're alone. Of course, if you went in there you'd probably detach one of them from the herd, and he'd be dangerous.'

'That's too complicated,' Bill said. 'Don't you ever detach me from the herd, Mike.'

'I say,' Mike said, 'they *were* fine bulls, weren't they? Did you see their horns?'

'Did I not,' said Brett. 'I had no idea what they were like.'

'Did you see the one hit that steer?' Mike asked. 'That was extraordinary.'

'It's no life being a steer,' Robert Cohn said.

'Don't you think so?' Mike said. 'I would have thought you'd loved being a steer, Robert.'

'What do you mean, Mike?'

'They lead such a quiet life. They never say anything and they're always hanging about so.'

We were embarrassed. Bill laughed. Robert Cohn was angry. Mike went on talking.

'I should think you'd love it. You'd never have to say a word. Come on, Robert. Do say something. Don't just sit there.'

'I said something, Mike. Don't you remember? About the steers.'

'Oh, say something more. Say something funny. Can't you see we're all having a good time here?'

'Come off it, Michael. You're drunk,' Brett said.

'I'm not drunk. I'm quite serious. *Is* Robert Cohn going to follow Brett around like a steer all the time?'

'Shut up, Michael. Try and show a little breeding.'

'Breeding be damned. Who has any breeding, anyway, except the bulls? Aren't the bulls lovely? Don't you like them, Bill? Why don't you say something, Robert? Don't sit there looking like a bloody funeral. What if Brett did sleep with you? She's slept with lots of better people than you.'

'Shut up,' Cohn said. He stood up. 'Shut up, Mike.'

'Oh, don't stand up and act as though you were going to hit me. That won't make any difference to me. Tell me, Robert. Why do you follow Brett around like a poor bloody steer? Don't you know you're not wanted? I know when I'm not wanted. Why don't you know when you're not wanted? You came down to San Sebastian where you weren't wanted, and followed Brett around like a bloody steer. Do you think that's right?'

'Shut up. You're drunk.'

'Perhaps I am drunk. Why aren't you drunk? Why don't you ever get drunk, Robert? You know you didn't have a good time at San Sebastian because none of our friends would invite you on any of the parties. You can't blame them hardly. Can you? I asked them to. They wouldn't do it. You can't blame them, now. Can you? Now, answer me. Can you blame them?'

'Go to hell, Mike.'

'I can't blame them. Can you blame them? Why do you follow Brett around? Haven't you any manners? How do you think it makes *me* feel?'

'You're a splendid one to talk about manners,' Brett said. 'You've such lovely manners.'

'Come on, Robert,' Bill said.

'What do you follow her around for?'

Bill stood up and took hold of Cohn.

'Don't go,' Mike said. 'Robert Cohn's going to buy a drink.'

Bill went off with Cohn. Cohn's face was sallow. Mike went on talking. I sat and listened for a while. Brett looked disgusted.

'I say, Michael, you might not be such a bloody ass,' she interrupted. 'I'm not saying he's not right, you know.' She turned to me.

The emotion left Mike's voice. We were all friends together.

'I'm not so damn drunk as I sounded,' he said.

'I know you're not,' Brett said.

'We're none of us sober,' I said.

'I didn't say anything I didn't mean.'

'But you put it so badly,' Brett laughed.

'He was an ass, though. He came down to San Sebastian where he damn well wasn't wanted. He hung around Brett and just *looked* at her. It made me damned well sick.'

'He did behave very badly,' Brett said.

'Mark you. Brett's had affairs with men before. She tells me all about everything. She gave me this chap Cohn's letters to read. I wouldn't read them.'

'Damned noble of you.'

'No, listen, Jake. Brett's gone off with men. But they weren't ever Jews, and they didn't come and hang about afterward.'

'Damned good chaps,' Brett said. 'It's all rot to talk about it. Michael and I understand each other.'

'She gave me Robert Cohn's letters. I wouldn't read them.'

'You wouldn't read any letters, darling. You wouldn't read mine.'

'I can't read letters,' Mike said. 'Funny, isn't it?'

'You can't read anything.'

'No. You're wrong there. I read quite a bit. I read when I'm at home.'

'You'll be writing next,' Brett said. 'Come on, Michael. Do buck up. You've got to go through with this thing now. He's here. Don't spoil the fiesta.'

'Well, let him behave, then.'

'He'll behave. I'll tell him.'

'You tell him, Jake. Tell him either he must behave or get out.'

'Yes,' I said, 'it would be nice for me to tell him.'

'Look, Brett. Tell Jake what Robert calls you. That is perfect, you know.'

'Oh, no. I can't.'

'Go on. We're all friends. Aren't we all friends, Jake?'

'I can't tell him. It's too ridiculous.'

'I'll tell him.'

'You won't, Michael. Don't be an ass.'

'He calls her Circe,' Mike said. 'He claims she turns men into swine. Damn good. I wish I were one of these literary chaps.'

'He'd be good, you know,' Brett said. 'He writes a good letter.'

'I know,' I said. 'He wrote me from San Sebastian.'

'That was nothing,' Brett said. 'He can write a damned amusing letter.'

'She made me write that. She was supposed to be ill.'

'I damned well was, too.'

'Come on,' I said, 'we must go in and eat.'

'How should I meet Cohn?' Mike said.

'Just act as though nothing had happened.'

'It's quite all right with me,' Mike said. 'I'm not embarrassed.'

'If he says anything, just say you were tight.'

'Quite. And the funny thing is I think I was tight.'

'Come on,' Brett said. 'Are these poisonous things paid for? I must bathe before dinner.'

We walked across the square. It was dark and all around the square were the lights from the cafés under the arcades. We walked across the gravel under the trees to the hotel.

They went up-stairs and I stopped to speak with Montoya.

'Well, how did you like the bulls?' he asked.

'Good. They were nice bulls.'

'They're all right'—Montoya shook his head—"but they're not too good.'

'What didn't you like about them?'

'I don't know. They just didn't give me the feeling that they were so good.'

'I know what you mean.'

'They're all right.'

'Yes. They're all right.'

'How did your friends like them?'

'Fine.'

'Good,' Montoya said.

I went up-stairs. Bill was in his room standing on the balcony looking out at the square. I stood beside him.

'Where's Cohn?'

'Up-stairs in his room.'

'How does he feel?'

'Like hell, naturally. Mike was awful. He's terrible when he's tight.'

'He wasn't so tight.'

'The hell he wasn't. I know what we had before we came to the café.'

'He sobered up afterward.'

'Good. He was terrible. I don't like Cohn, God knows, and I think it was a silly trick for him to go down to San Sebastian, but nobody has any business to talk like Mike.'

'How'd you like the bulls?'

'Grand. It's grand the way they bring them out.'

'To-morrow come the Miuras.'

'When does the fiesta start?'

'Day after to-morrow.'

'We've got to keep Mike from getting so tight. That kind of stuff is terrible.'

'We'd better get cleaned up for supper.'

'Yes. That will be a pleasant meal.'

'Won't it?'

As a matter of fact, supper was a pleasant meal. Brett wore a black, sleeveless evening dress. She looked quite beautiful. Mike acted as though nothing had happened. I had to go up and bring Robert Cohn down. He was reserved and formal, and his face was still taut and sallow, but he cheered up finally. He could not stop looking at Brett. It seemed to make him happy. It must have been pleasant for him to see her looking so lovely, and know he had been away with her and that every one knew it. They could not take that away from him. Bill was very funny. So was Michael. They were good together.

It was like certain dinners I remember from the war. There was much wine, an ignored tension, and a feeling of things coming that you could not prevent happening. Under the wine I lost the disgusted feeling and was happy. It seemed they were all such nice people.

14

I do not know what time I got to bed. I remember undressing, putting on a bathrobe, and standing out on the balcony. I knew I was quite drunk, and when I came in I put on the light over the head of the bed and started to read. I was reading a book by Turgenieff. Probably I read the same two pages over several times. It was one of the stories in 'A Sportsman's Sketches.' I had read it before, but it seemed quite new. The country became very clear and the feeling of pressure in my head seemed to loosen. I was very drunk and I did not want to shut my eyes because the room would go round and round. If I kept on reading that feeling would pass.

I heard Brett and Robert Cohn come up the stairs. Cohn said good night outside the door and went on up to his room. I heard Brett go into the room next door. Mike was already in bed. He had come in with me an hour before. He woke as she came in, and they talked together. I heard them laugh. I turned off the light and tried to go to sleep. It was not necessary to read any more. I could shut my eyes without getting the wheeling sensation. But I could not sleep. There is no reason why because it is dark you should look at things differently from when it is light. The hell there isn't!

I figured that all out once, and for six months I never slept with the electric light off. That was another bright idea. To hell with women, anyway. To hell with you, Brett Ashley.

Women made such swell friends. Awfully swell. In the first place, you had to be in love with a woman to have a basis of friendship. I had been having Brett for a friend. I had not been thinking about her side of it. I had been getting something for nothing. That only delayed the presentation of the bill. The bill always came. That was one of the swell things you could count on.

I thought I had paid for everything. Not like the woman pays and pays and pays. No idea of retribution or punishment. Just exchange of values. You gave up something and got something else. Or you worked for something. You paid some way for everything that was any good. I paid my way into enough things that I liked, so that I had a good time. Either you paid by learning about them, or by experience, or by taking chances, or by money. Enjoying living was learning to get your money's worth and knowing when you had it. You could get your money's worth. The world was a good place to buy in. It seemed like a fine philosophy. In five years, I thought, it will seem just as silly as all the other fine philosophies I've had.

Perhaps that wasn't true, though. Perhaps as you went along you did learn something. I did not care what it was all about. All I wanted to know was how to live in it. Maybe if you found out how to live in it you learned from that what it was all about.

I wished Mike would not behave so terribly to Cohn, though. Mike was a bad drunk. Brett was a good drunk. Bill was a good drunk. Cohn was never drunk. Mike was unpleasant after he passed a certain point. I liked to see him hurt Cohn. I wished he would not do it, though, because afterward it made me disgusted at myself. That was morality; things that made you disgusted afterward. No, that must be immorality. That was a large statement. What a lot of bilge I could think up at night. What rot, I could hear Brett say it. What rot! When you were with English you got into the habit of using English expressions in your thinking. The English spoken language—the upper classes, anyway—must have fewer words than the Eskimo. Of course I didn't know anything about the Eskimo. Maybe the Eskimo was a fine language. Say the Cherokee. I didn't know anything about the Cherokee, either. The English talked with inflected phrases. One phrase to mean everything. I liked them, though. I liked the way they talked. Take Harris. Still Harris was not the upper classes.

I turned on the light again and read. I read the Turgenieff. I knew that now, reading it in the oversensitized state of my mind after much too much brandy, I would remember it somewhere, and afterward it would seem as though it had really happened to me. I would always have it. That was another good thing you paid for and then had. Some time along toward daylight I went to sleep.

The next two days in Pamplona were quiet, and there were no more rows. The town was getting ready for the fiesta. Workmen put up the gate-posts that were to shut off the side streets when the bulls were released from the corrals and came running through the streets in the morning on their way to the ring. The workmen dug holes and fitted in the timbers, each timber numbered for its regular place. Out on the plateau beyond the town employees of the bull-ring exercised picador horses, galloping them stiff-legged on the hard, sun-baked fields behind the bull-ring. The big gate of the bull-ring was open, and inside the amphitheatre was being swept. The ring was rolled and sprinkled, and carpenters replaced weakened or cracked planks in the barrera. Standing at the edge of the smooth rolled sand you could look up in the empty stands and see old women sweeping out the boxes.

Outside, the fence that led from the last street of the town to the entrance of the bull-ring was already in place and made a long pen; the crowd would come running down with the bulls behind them on the morning of the day of the first bull-fight. Out across the plain, where the horse and cattle fair would be, some gypsies had camped under the trees. The wine and aguardiente sellers were putting up their booths. One booth advertised ANIS DEL TORO. The cloth sign hung against the planks in the hot sun. In the big square that was the centre of the town there was no change yet. We sat in the white wicker chairs on the terrasse of the café and watched the motor-buses come in and unload peasants from the country coming in to the market, and we watched the buses fill up and start out with peasants sitting with their saddle-bags full of the things they had bought in the town. The tall gray motor-buses were the only life of the square except for the pigeons and the man with a hose who sprinkled the gravelled square and watered the streets.

In the evening was the paseo. For an hour after dinner every one, all the good-looking girls, the officers from the garrison, all the fashionable people of the town, walked in the street on one side of the square while the café tables filled with the regular after-dinner crowd.

During the morning I usually sat in the café and read the Madrid papers and then walked in the town or out into the country. Sometimes Bill went along. Sometimes he wrote in his room. Robert Cohn spent the mornings studying Spanish or trying to get a shave at the barber-shop. Brett and Mike never got up until noon. We all had a vermouth at the café. It was a quiet life and no one was drunk. I went to church a couple of times, once with Brett. She said she wanted to hear me go to confession, but I told her that not only was it impossible but it was not as interesting as it sounded, and, besides, it would be in a language she did not know. We met Cohn as we came out of church, and although it was obvious he had followed us, yet he was very pleasant and nice, and we all three went for a walk out to the gypsy camp, and Brett had her fortune told.

It was a good morning, there were high white clouds above the mountains. It had rained a little in the night and it was fresh and cool on the plateau, and there was a wonderful view. We all felt good and we felt healthy, and I felt quite friendly to Cohn. You could not be upset about anything on a day like that.

That was the last day before the fiesta.

15

At noon of Sunday, the 6th of July, the fiesta exploded. There is no other way to describe it. People had been coming in all day from the country, but they were assimilated in the town and you did not notice them. The square was as quiet in the hot sun as on any other day. The peasants were in the outlying wine-shops. There they were drinking, getting ready for the fiesta. They had come in so recently from the plains and the hills that it was necessary that they make their shifting in values gradually. They could not start in paying café prices. They got their money's worth in the wine-shops. Money still had a definite value in hours worked and bushels of grain sold. Late in the fiesta it would not matter what they paid, nor where they bought.

Now on the day of the starting of the fiesta of San Fermin they had been in the wine-shops of the narrow streets of the town since early morning. Going down the streets in the morning on the way to mass in the cathedral, I heard them singing through the open doors of the shops. They were warming up. There were many people at the eleven o'clock mass. San Fermin is also a religious festival.

I walked down the hill from the cathedral and up the street to the café on the square. It was a little before noon. Robert Cohn and Bill were sitting at one of the tables. The marble-topped tables and the white wicker chairs were gone. They were replaced by cast-iron tables and severe folding chairs. The café was like a battleship stripped for action. To-day the waiters did not leave you alone all morning to read without asking if you wanted to order something. A waiter came up as soon as I sat down.

'What are you drinking?' I asked Bill and Robert.

'Sherry,' Cohn said.

'Jerez,' I said to the waiter.

Before the waiter brought the sherry the rocket that announced the fiesta went up in the square. It burst and there was a gray ball of smoke high up above the Theatre Gayarre, across on the other side of the plaza. The ball of smoke hung in the sky like a shrapnel burst, and as I watched, another rocket came up to it, trickling smoke in the bright sunlight. I saw the bright flash as it burst and another little cloud of smoke appeared. By the time the second rocket had burst there were so many people in the arcade, that had been empty a minute before, that the waiter, holding the bottle high up over his head, could hardly get through the crowd to our table. People were coming into the square from all sides, and down the street we heard the pipes and the fifes and the drums coming. They were playing the *riau-riau* music, the pipes shrill and the drums pounding, and behind them came the men and boys dancing. When the fifers stopped they all crouched down in the street, and when the reed-pipes and the fifes shrilled, and the flat, dry, hollow drums tapped it out again, they all went up in the air dancing. In the crowd you saw only the heads and shoulders of the dancers going up and down.

In the square a man, bent over, was playing on a reed-pipe, and a crowd of children were following him shouting, and pulling at his clothes. He came out of the square, the children following him, and piped them past the café and down a side street. We saw his blank pockmarked face as he went by, piping, the children close behind him shouting and pulling at him.

'He must be the village idiot,' Bill said. 'My God! look at that!'

Down the street came dancers. The street was solid with dancers, all men. They were all dancing in time behind their own fifers and drummers. They were a club of some sort, and all wore workmen's blue smocks, and red handkerchiefs around their necks, and carried a great banner on two poles. The banner danced up and down with them as they came down surrounded by the crowd.

'Hurray for Wine! Hurray for the Foreigners!' was painted on the banner.

'Where are the foreigners?' Robert Cohn asked.

'We're the foreigners,' Bill said.

All the time rockets were going up. The café tables were all full now. The square was emptying of people and the crowd was filling the cafés.

'Where's Brett and Mike?' Bill asked.

'I'll go and get them,' Cohn said.

'Bring them here.'

The fiesta was really started. It kept up day and night for seven days. The dancing kept up, the drinking kept up, the noise went on. The things that happened could only have happened during a fiesta. Everything became quite unreal finally and it seemed as though nothing could have any consequences. It seemed out of place to think of consequences during the fiesta. All during the fiesta you had the feeling, even when it was quiet, that you had to shout any remark to make it heard. It was the same feeling about any action. It was a fiesta and it went on for seven days.

That afternoon was the big religious procession. San Fermin was translated from one church to another. In the procession were all the dignitaries, civil and religious. We could not see them because the crowd was too great. Ahead of the formal procession and behind it danced the *riau-riau* dancers. There was one mass of yellow shirts dancing up and down in the crowd. All we could see of the procession through the closely pressed people that crowded all the side streets and curbs were the great giants, cigar-store Indians, thirty feet high, Moors, a King and Queen, whirling and waltzing solemnly to the *riau-riau*.

They were all standing outside the chapel where San Fermin and the dignitaries had passed in, leaving a guard of soldiers, the giants, with the men who danced in them standing beside their resting frames, and the dwarfs moving with their whacking bladders through the crowd. We started inside and there was a smell of incense and people filing back into the church, but Brett was stopped just inside the door because she had no hat, so we went out again and along the street that ran back from the chapel into town. The street was lined on both sides with people keeping their place at the curb for the return of the procession. Some dancers formed a circle around Brett and started to dance. They wore big wreaths of white garlics around their necks. They took Bill and me by the arms and put us in the circle. Bill started to dance, too. They were all chanting. Brett wanted to dance but they did not want her to. They wanted her as an image to dance around. When the song ended with the sharp *riau-riau!* they rushed us into a wine-shop.

We stood at the counter. They had Brett seated on a wine-cask. It was dark in the wine-shop and full of men singing, hard-voiced singing. Back of the counter they drew the wine from casks. I put down money for the wine, but one of the men picked it up and put it back in my pocket.

'I want a leather wine-bottle,' Bill said.

'There's a place down the street,' I said. 'I'll go get a couple.'

The dancers did not want me to go out. Three of them were sitting on the high wine-cask beside Brett, teaching her to drink out of the wine-skins. They had hung a wreath of garlics around her neck. Some one insisted on giving her a glass. Somebody was teaching Bill a song. Singing it into his ear. Beating time on Bill's back.

I explained to them that I would be back. Outside in the street I went down the street looking for the shop that made leather wine-bottles. The crowd was packed on the sidewalks and many of the shops were shuttered, and I could not find it. I walked as far as the church, looking on both sides of the street. Then I asked a man and he took me by the arm and led me to it. The shutters were up but the door was open.

Inside it smelled of fresh tanned leather and hot tar. A man was stencilling completed wine-skins. They hung from the roof in bunches. He took one down, blew it up, screwed the nozzle tight, and then jumped on it.

'See! It doesn't leak.'

'I want another one, too. A big one.'

He took down a big one that would hold a gallon or more, from the roof. He blew it up, his cheeks puffing ahead of the wine-skin, and stood on the bota holding on to a chair.

'What are you going to do? Sell them in Bayonne?'

'No. Drink out of them.'

He slapped me on the back.

'Good man. Eight pesetas for the two. The lowest price.'

The man who was stencilling the new ones and tossing them into a pile stopped.

'It's true,' he said. 'Eight pesetas is cheap.'

I paid and went out and along the street back to the wine-shop. It was darker than ever inside and very crowded. I did not see Brett and Bill, and some one said they were in the back room. At the counter the girl filled the two wine-skins for me. One held two litres. The other held five litres. Filling them both cost three pesetas sixty centimos. Some one at the counter, that I had never seen before, tried to pay for the wine, but I finally paid for it myself. The man who had wanted to pay then bought me a drink. He would not let me buy one in return, but said he would take a rinse of the mouth from the new wine-bag. He tipped the big five-litre bag up and squeezed it so the wine hissed against the back of his throat.

'All right,' he said, and handed back the bag.

In the back room Brett and Bill were sitting on barrels surrounded by the dancers. Everybody had his arms on everybody else's shoulders, and they were all singing. Mike was sitting at a table with several men in their shirt-sleeves, eating from a bowl of tuna fish, chopped onions and vinegar. They were all drinking wine and mopping up the oil and vinegar with pieces of bread.

'Hello, Jake. Hello!' Mike called. 'Come here. I want you to meet my friends. We're all having an hors-d'œuvre.'

I was introduced to the people at the table. They supplied their names to Mike and sent for a fork for me.

'Stop eating their dinner, Michael,' Brett shouted from the wine-barrels.

'I don't want to eat up your meal,' I said when some one handed me a fork.

'Eat,' he said. 'What do you think it's here for?'

I unscrewed the nozzle of the big wine-bottle and handed it around. Every one took a drink, tipping the wine-skin at arm's length.

Outside, above the singing, we could hear the music of the procession going by.

'Isn't that the procession?' Mike asked.

'Nada,' some one said. 'It's nothing. Drink up. Lift the bottle.'

'Where did they find you?' I asked Mike.

'Some one brought me here,' Mike said. 'They said you were here.'

'Where's Cohn?'

'He's passed out,' Brett called. 'They've put him away somewhere.'

'Where is he?'

'I don't know.'

'How should we know,' Bill said. 'I think he's dead.'

'He's not dead,' Mike said. 'I know he's not dead. He's just passed out on Anis del Mono.'

As he said Anis del Mono one of the men at the table looked up, brought out a bottle from inside his smock, and handed it to me.

'No,' I said. 'No, thanks!'

'Yes. Yes. Arriba! Up with the bottle!'

I took a drink. It tasted of licorice and warmed all the way. I could feel it warming in my stomach.

'Where the hell is Cohn?'

'I don't know,' Mike said. 'I'll ask. Where is the drunken comrade?' he asked in Spanish.

'You want to see him?'

'Yes,' I said.

'Not me,' said Mike. 'This gent.'

The Anis del Mono man wiped his mouth and stood up.

'Come on.'

In a back room Robert Cohn was sleeping quietly on some wine-casks. It was almost too dark to see his face. They had covered him with a coat and another coat was folded under his head. Around his neck and on his chest was a big wreath of twisted garlics.

'Let him sleep,' the man whispered. 'He's all right.'

Two hours later Cohn appeared. He came into the front room still with the wreath of garlics around his neck. The Spaniards shouted when he came in. Cohn wiped his eyes and grinned.

'I must have been sleeping,' he said.

'Oh, not at all,' Brett said.

'You were only dead,' Bill said.

'Aren't we going to go and have some supper?' Cohn asked.

'Do you want to eat?'

'Yes. Why not? I'm hungry.'

'Eat those garlics, Robert,' Mike said. 'I say. Do eat those garlics.'

Cohn stood there. His sleep had made him quite all right.

'Do let's go and eat,' Brett said. 'I must get a bath.'

'Come on,' Bill said. 'Let's translate Brett to the hotel.'

We said good-bye to many people and shook hands with many people and went out. Outside it was dark.

'What time is it do you suppose?' Cohn asked.

'It's to-morrow,' Mike said. 'You've been asleep two days.'

'No,' said Cohn, 'what time is it?'

'It's ten o'clock.'

'What a lot we've drunk.'

'You mean what a lot *we've* drunk. You went to sleep.'

Going down the dark streets to the hotel we saw the sky-rockets going up in the square. Down the side streets that led to the square we saw the square solid with people, those in the centre all dancing.

It was a big meal at the hotel. It was the first meal of the prices being doubled for the fiesta, and there were several new courses. After the dinner we were out in the town. I remember resolving that I would stay up all night to watch the bulls go through the streets at six o'clock in the morning, and being so sleepy that I went to bed around four o'clock. The others stayed up.

My own room was locked and I could not find the key, so I went up-stairs and slept on one of the beds in Cohn's room. The fiesta was going on outside in the night, but I was too sleepy for it to keep me awake. When I woke it was the sound of the rocket exploding that announced the release of the bulls from the corrals at the edge of town. They would race through the streets and out to the bull-ring. I had been sleeping heavily and I woke feeling I was too late. I put on a coat of Cohn's and went out on the balcony. Down below the narrow street was empty. All the balconies were crowded with people. Suddenly a crowd came down the street. They were all running, packed close together. They passed along and up the street toward the bull-ring and behind them came more men running faster, and then some stragglers who were really running. Behind them was a little bare space, and then the bulls galloping, tossing their heads up and down. It all went out of sight around the corner. One man fell, rolled to the gutter, and lay quiet. But the bulls went right on and did not notice him. They were all running together.

After they went out of sight a great roar came from the bull-ring. It kept on. Then finally the pop of the rocket that meant the bulls had gotten through the people in the ring and into the corrals. I went back in the room and got into bed. I had been standing on the stone balcony in bare feet. I knew our crowd must have all been out at the bull-ring. Back in bed, I went to sleep.

Cohn woke me when he came in. He started to undress and went over and closed the window because the people on the balcony of the house just across the street were looking in.

'Did you see the show?' I asked.

'Yes. We were all there.'

'Anybody get hurt?'

'One of the bulls got into the crowd in the ring and tossed six or eight people.'

'How did Brett like it?'

'It was all so sudden there wasn't any time for it to bother anybody.'
'I wish I'd been up.'
'We didn't know where you were. We went to your room but it was locked.'
'Where did you stay up?'
'We danced at some club.'
'I got sleepy,' I said.
'My gosh! I'm sleepy now,' Cohn said. 'Doesn't this thing ever stop?'
'Not for a week.'
Bill opened the door and put his head in.
'Where were you, Jake?'
'I saw them go through from the balcony. How was it?'
'Grand.'
'Where you going?'
'To sleep.'

No one was up before noon. We ate at tables set out under the arcade. The town was full of people. We had to wait for a table. After lunch we went over to the Iruña. It had filled up, and as the time for the bull-fight came it got fuller, and the tables were crowded closer. There was a close, crowded hum that came every day before the bull-fight. The café did not make this same noise at any other time, no matter how crowded it was. This hum went on, and we were in it and a part of it.

I had taken six seats for all the fights. Three of them were barreras, the first row at the ring-side, and three were sobrepuertos, seats with wooden backs, half-way up the amphitheatre. Mike thought Brett had best sit high up for her first time, and Cohn wanted to sit with them. Bill and I were going to sit in the barreras, and I gave the extra ticket to a waiter to sell. Bill said something to Cohn about what to do and how to look so he would not mind the horses. Bill had seen one season of bull-fights.

'I'm not worried about how I'll stand it. I'm only afraid I may be bored,' Cohn said.

'You think so?'

'Don't look at the horses, after the bull hits them,' I said to Brett. 'Watch the charge and see the picador try and keep the bull off, but then don't look again until the horse is dead if it's been hit.'

'I'm a little nervy about it,' Brett said. 'I'm worried whether I'll be able to go through with it all right.'

'You'll be all right. There's nothing but that horse part that will bother you, and they're only in for a few minutes with each bull. Just don't watch when it's bad.'

'She'll be all right,' Mike said. 'I'll look after her.'

'I don't think you'll be bored,' Bill said.

'I'm going over to the hotel to get the glasses and the wine-skin,' I said. 'See you back here. Don't get cock-eyed.'

'I'll come along,' Bill said. Brett smiled at us.

We walked around through the arcade to avoid the heat of the square.

'That Cohn gets me,' Bill said. 'He's got this Jewish superiority so strong that he thinks the only emotion he'll get out of the fight will be being bored.'

'We'll watch him with the glasses,' I said.

'Oh, to hell with him!'

'He spends a lot of time there.'

'I want him to stay there.'

In the hotel on the stairs we met Montoya.

'Come on,' said Montoya. 'Do you want to meet Pedro Romero?'

'Fine,' said Bill. 'Let's go see him.'

We followed Montoya up a flight and down the corridor.

'He's in room number eight,' Montoya explained. 'He's getting dressed for the bull-fight.'

Montoya knocked on the door and opened it. It was a gloomy room with a little light coming in from the window on the narrow street. There were two beds separated by a monastic partition. The electric light was on. The boy stood very straight and unsmiling in his bull-fighting clothes. His jacket hung over the back of a chair. They were just finishing winding his sash. His black hair shone under the electric light. He wore a white linen shirt and the sword-handler finished his sash and stood up and stepped back. Pedro Romero nodded, seeming very far away and dignified when we shook hands. Montoya said something about what great aficionados we were, and that we wanted to wish him luck. Romero listened very seriously. Then he turned to me. He was the best-looking boy I have ever seen.

'You go to the bull-fight,' he said in English.

'You know English,' I said, feeling like an idiot.

'No,' he answered, and smiled.

One of three men who had been sitting on the beds came up and asked us if we spoke French. 'Would you like me to interpret for you? Is there anything you would like to ask Pedro Romero?'

We thanked him. What was there that you would like to ask? The boy was nineteen years old, alone except for his sword-handler, and the three hangers-on, and the bull-fight was to commence in twenty minutes. We wished him 'Mucha suerte,' shook hands, and went out. He was standing, straight and handsome and altogether by himself, alone in the room with the hangers-on as we shut the door.

'He's a fine boy, don't you think so?' Montoya asked.

'He's a good-looking kid,' I said.

'He looks like a torero,' Montoya said. 'He has the type.'

'He's a fine boy.'

'We'll see how he is in the ring,' Montoya said.

We found the big leather wine-bottle leaning against the wall in my room, took it and the field-glasses, locked the door, and went down-stairs.

It was a good bull-fight. Bill and I were very excited about Pedro Romero.

Montoya was sitting about ten places away. After Romero had killed his first bull Montoya caught my eye and nodded his head. This was a real one. There had not been a real one for a long time. Of the other two matadors, one was very fair and the other was passable. But there was no comparison with Romero, although neither of his bulls was much.

Several times during the bull-fight I looked up at Mike and Brett and Cohn, with the glasses. They seemed to be all right. Brett did not look upset. All three were leaning forward on the concrete railing in front of them.

'Let me take the glasses,' Bill said.

'Does Cohn look bored?' I asked.

'That kike!'

Outside the ring, after the bull-fight was over, you could not move in the crowd. We could not make our way through but had to be moved with the whole thing, slowly, as a glacier, back to town. We had that disturbed emotional feeling that always comes after a bull-fight, and the feeling of elation that comes after a good bull-fight. The fiesta was going on. The drums pounded and the pipe music was shrill, and everywhere the flow of the crowd was broken by patches of dancers. The dancers were in a crowd, so you did not see the intricate play of the feet. All you saw was the heads and shoulders going up and down, up and down. Finally, we got out of the crowd and made for the café. The waiter saved chairs for the others, and we each ordered an absinthe and watched the crowd in the square and the dancers.

'What do you suppose that dance is?' Bill asked.

'It's a sort of jota.'

'They're not all the same,' Bill said. 'They dance differently to all the different tunes.'

'It's swell dancing.'

In front of us on a clear part of the street a company of boys were dancing. The steps were very intricate and their faces were intent and concentrated. They all looked down while they danced. Their rope-soled shoes tapped and spatted on the pavement. The toes touched. The heels touched. The balls of the feet touched. Then the music broke wildly and the step was finished and they were all dancing on up the street.

'Here come the gentry,' Bill said.

They were crossing the street.

'Hello, men,' I said.

'Hello, gents!' said Brett. 'You saved us seats? How nice.'

'I say,' Mike said, 'that Romero what'shisname is somebody. Am I wrong?'

'Oh, isn't he lovely,' Brett said. 'And those green trousers.'

'Brett never took her eyes off them.'

'I say, I must borrow your glasses to-morrow.'

'How did it go?'

'Wonderfully! Simply perfect. I say, it is a spectacle!'

'How about the horses?'

'I couldn't help looking at them.'

'She couldn't take her eyes off them,' Mike said. 'She's an extraordinary wench.'

'They do have some rather awful things happen to them,' Brett said. 'I couldn't look away, though.'

'Did you feel all right?'

'I didn't feel badly at all.'

'Robert Cohn did,' Mike put in. 'You were quite green, Robert.'

'The first horse did bother me,' Cohn said.

'You weren't bored, were you?' asked Bill.

Cohn laughed.

'No. I wasn't bored. I wish you'd forgive me that.'

'It's all right,' Bill said, 'so long as you weren't bored.'

'He didn't look bored,' Mike said. 'I thought he was going to be sick.'

'I never felt that bad. It was just for a minute.'

'I thought he was going to be sick. You weren't bored, were you, Robert?'

'Let up on that, Mike. I said I was sorry I said it.'

'He was, you know. He was positively green.'

'Oh, shove it along, Michael.'

'You mustn't ever get bored at your first bull-fight, Robert,' Mike said. 'It might make such a mess.'

'Oh, shove it along, Michael,' Brett said.

'He said Brett was a sadist,' Mike said. 'Brett's not a sadist. She's just a lovely, healthy wench.'

'Are you a sadist, Brett?' I asked.

'Hope not.'

'He said Brett was a sadist just because she has a good, healthy stomach.'

'Won't be healthy long.'

Bill got Mike started on something else than Cohn. The waiter brought the absinthe glasses.

'Did you really like it?' Bill asked Cohn.

'No, I can't say I liked it. I think it's a wonderful show.'

'Gad, yes! What a spectacle!' Brett said.

'I wish they didn't have the horse part,' Cohn said.

'They're not important,' Bill said. 'After a while you never notice anything disgusting.'

'It is a bit strong just at the start,' Brett said. 'There's a dreadful moment for me just when the bull starts for the horse.'

'The bulls were fine,' Cohn said.

'They were very good,' Mike said.

'I want to sit down below, next time.' Brett drank from her glass of absinthe.

'She wants to see the bull-fighters close by,' Mike said.

'They are something,' Brett said. 'That Romero lad is just a child.'

'He's a damned good-looking boy,' I said. 'When we were up in his room I never saw a better-looking kid.'

'How old do you suppose he is?'

'Nineteen or twenty.'

'Just imagine it.'

The bull-fight on the second day was much better than on the first. Brett sat between Mike and me at the barrera, and Bill and Cohn went up above. Romero was the whole show. I do not think Brett saw any other bull-fighter. No one else did either, except the hard-shelled technicians. It was all Romero. There were two other matadors, but they did not count. I sat beside Brett and explained to Brett what it was all about. I told her about watching the bull, not the horse, when the bulls charged the picadors, and got her to watching the picador place the point of his pic so that she saw what it was all about, so that it became more something that was going on with a definite end, and less of a spectacle with unexplained horrors. I had her watch how Romero took the bull away from a fallen horse with his cape, and how he held him with the cape and turned him, smoothly and suavely, never wasting the bull. She saw how Romero avoided every brusque movement and saved his bulls for the last when he wanted them, not winded and discomposed but smoothly worn down. She saw how close Romero always worked to the bull, and I pointed out to her the tricks the other bull-fighters used to make it look as though they were working closely. She saw why she liked Romero's cape-work and why she did not like the others.

Romero never made any contortions, always it was straight and pure and natural in line. The others twisted themselves like corkscrews, their elbows raised, and leaned against the flanks of the bull after his horns had passed, to give a faked look of danger. Afterward, all that was faked turned bad and gave an unpleasant feeling. Romero's bull-fighting gave real emotion, because he kept the absolute purity of line in his movements and always quietly and calmly let the horns pass him close each time. He did not have to emphasize their closeness. Brett saw how something that was beautiful done close to the bull was ridiculous if it were done a little way off. I told her how since the death of Joselito all the bull-fighters had been developing a technic that simulated this appearance of danger in order to give a fake emotional feeling, while the bull-fighter was really safe. Romero had the old thing, the holding of his purity of line through the maximum of exposure, while he dominated the bull by making him realize he was unattainable, while he prepared him for the killing.

'I've never seen him do an awkward thing,' Brett said.

'You won't until he gets frightened,' I said.

'He'll never be frightened,' Mike said. 'He knows too damned much.'

'He knew everything when he started. The others can't ever learn what he was born with.'

'And God, what looks,' Brett said.

'I believe, you know, that she's falling in love with this bull-fighter chap,'

Mike said.

'I wouldn't be surprised.'

'Be a good chap, Jake. Don't tell her anything more about him. Tell her how they beat their old mothers.'

'Tell me what drunks they are.'

'Oh, frightful,' Mike said. 'Drunk all day and spend all their time beating their poor old mothers.'

'He looks that way,' Brett said.

'Doesn't he?' I said.

They had hitched the mules to the dead bull and then the whips cracked, the men ran, and the mules, straining forward, their legs pushing, broke into a gallop, and the bull, one horn up, his head on its side, swept a swath smoothly across the sand and out the red gate.

'This next is the last one.'

'Not really,' Brett said. She leaned forward on the barrera. Romero waved his picadors to their places, then stood, his cape against his chest, looking across the ring to where the bull would come out.

After it was over we went out and were pressed tight in the crowd.

'These bull-fights are hell on one,' Brett said. 'I'm limp as a rag.'

'Oh, you'll get a drink,' Mike said.

The next day Pedro Romero did not fight. It was Miura bulls, and a very bad bull-fight. The next day there was no bull-fight scheduled. But all day and all night the fiesta kept on.

16

In the morning it was raining. A fog had come over the mountains from the sea. You could not see the tops of the mountains. The plateau was dull and gloomy, and the shapes of the trees and the houses were changed. I walked out beyond the town to look at the weather. The bad weather was coming over the mountains from the sea.

The flags in the square hung wet from the white poles and the banners were wet and hung damp against the front of the houses, and in between the steady drizzle the rain came down and drove every one under the arcades and made pools of water in the square, and the streets wet and dark and deserted; yet the fiesta kept up without any pause. It was only driven under cover.

The covered seats of the bull-ring had been crowded with people sitting out of the rain watching the concourse of Basque and Navarrais dancers and singers, and afterward the Val Carlos dancers in their costumes danced down the street in the rain, the drums sounding hollow and damp, and the chiefs of the bands riding ahead on their big, heavy-footed horses, their costumes wet, the horses' coats wet in the rain. The crowd was in the cafés and the dancers came in, too, and sat, their tight-wound white legs under the tables, shaking the water from their belled caps, and spreading their red and purple jackets over the chairs to dry. It was raining hard outside.

I left the crowd in the café and went over to the hotel to get shaved for dinner. I was shaving in my room when there was a knock on the door.

'Come in,' I called.

Montoya walked in.

'How are you?' he said.

'Fine,' I said.

'No bulls to-day.'

'No,' I said, 'nothing but rain.'

'Where are your friends?'

'Over at the Iruña.'

Montoya smiled his embarrassed smile.

'Look,' he said. 'Do you know the American ambassador?'

'Yes,' I said. 'Everybody knows the American ambassador.'

'He's here in town, now.'

'Yes,' I said. 'Everybody's seen them.'

'I've seen them, too,' Montoya said. He didn't say anything. I went on shaving.

'Sit down,' I said. 'Let me send for a drink.'

'No, I have to go.'

I finished shaving and put my face down into the bowl and washed it with cold water. Montoya was standing there looking more embarrassed.

'Look,' he said. 'I've just had a message from them at the Grand Hotel that they want Pedro Romero and Marcial Lalanda to come over for coffee to-night after dinner.'

'Well,' I said, 'it can't hurt Marcial any.'

'Marcial has been in San Sebastian all day. He drove over in a car this morning with Marquez. I don't think they'll be back to-night.'

Montoya stood embarrassed. He wanted me to say something.

'Don't give Romero the message,' I said.

'You think so?'

'Absolutely.'

Montoya was very pleased.

'I wanted to ask you because you were an American,' he said.

'That's what I'd do.'

'Look,' said Montoya. 'People take a boy like that. They don't know what he's worth. They don't know what he means. Any foreigner can flatter him. They start this Grand Hotel business, and in one year they're through.'

'Like Algabeno,' I said.

'Yes, like Algabeno.'

'They're a fine lot,' I said. 'There's one American woman down here now that collects bull-fighters.'

'I know. They only want the young ones.'

'Yes,' I said. 'The old ones get fat.'

'Or crazy like Gallo.'

'Well,' I said, 'it's easy. All you have to do is not give him the message.'

'He's such a fine boy,' said Montoya. 'He ought to stay with his own people. He shouldn't mix in that stuff.'

'Won't you have a drink?' I asked.

'No,' said Montoya, 'I have to go.' He went out.

I went down-stairs and out the door and took a walk around through the arcades around the square. It was still raining. I looked in at the Iruña for the gang and they were not there, so I walked on around the square and back to the hotel. They were eating dinner in the down-stairs dining-room.

They were well ahead of me and it was no use trying to catch them. Bill was buying shoe-shines for Mike. Bootblacks opened the street door and each one Bill called over and started to work on Mike.

'This is the eleventh time my boots have been polished,' Mike said. 'I say, Bill is an ass.'

The bootblacks had evidently spread the report. Another came in.

'Limpia botas?' he said to Bill.

'No,' said Bill. 'For this Señor.'

The bootblack knelt down beside the one at work and started on Mike's free shoe that shone already in the electric light.

'Bill's a yell of laughter,' Mike said.

I was drinking red wine, and so far behind them that I felt a little uncomfortable about all this shoe-shining. I looked around the room. At the next table was Pedro Romero. He stood up when I nodded, and asked me to come over and meet a friend. His table was beside ours, almost touching. I met the friend, a Madrid bull-fight critic, a little man with a drawn face. I told Romero how much I liked his work, and he was very pleased. We talked Spanish and the critic knew a little French. I reached to our table for my wine-bottle, but the critic took my arm. Romero laughed.

'Drink here,' he said in English.

He was very bashful about his English, but he was really very pleased with it, and as we went on talking he brought out words he was not sure of, and asked me about them. He was anxious to know the English for *Corrida de toros*, the exact translation. Bull-fight he was suspicious of. I explained that bull-fight in Spanish was the *lidia* of a *toro*. The Spanish word *corrida* means in English the running of bulls—the French translation is *Course de taureaux*. The critic put that in. There is no Spanish word for bull-fight.

Pedro Romero said he had learned a little English in Gibraltar. He was born in Ronda. That is not far above Gibraltar. He started bull-fighting in Malaga in the bull-fighting school there. He had only been at it three years. The bull-fight critic joked him about the number of *Malagueño* expressions he used. He was nineteen years old, he said. His older brother was with him as a banderillero, but he did not live in this hotel. He lived in a smaller hotel with the other people who worked for Romero. He asked me how many times I had seen him in the ring. I told him only three. It was really only two, but I did not want to explain after I had made the mistake.

'Where did you see me the other time? In Madrid?'

'Yes,' I lied. I had read the accounts of his two appearances in Madrid in the bull-fight papers, so I was all right.

'The first or the second time?'

'The first.'

'I was very bad,' he said. 'The second time I was better. You remember?' He turned to the critic.

He was not at all embarrassed. He talked of his work as something altogether apart from himself. There was nothing conceited or braggartly about him.

'I like it very much that you like my work,' he said. 'But you haven't seen it yet. To-morrow, if I get a good bull, I will try and show it to you.'

When he said this he smiled, anxious that neither the bull-fight critic nor I would think he was boasting.

'I am anxious to see it,' the critic said. 'I would like to be convinced.'

'He doesn't like my work much.' Romero turned to me. He was serious.

The critic explained that he liked it very much, but that so far it had been incomplete.

'Wait till to-morrow, if a good one comes out.'

'Have you seen the bulls for to-morrow?' the critic asked me.

'Yes. I saw them unloaded.'

Pedro Romero leaned forward.

'What did you think of them?'

'Very nice,' I said. 'About twenty-six arrobas. Very short horns. Haven't you seen them?'

'Oh, yes,' said Romero.

'They won't weigh twenty-six arrobas,' said the critic.

'No,' said Romero.

'They've got bananas for horns,' the critic said.

'You call them bananas?' asked Romero. He turned to me and smiled. '*You* wouldn't call them bananas?'

'No,' I said. 'They're horns all right.'

'They're very short,' said Pedro Romero. 'Very, very short. Still, they aren't bananas.'

'I say, Jake,' Brett called from the next table, 'you *have* deserted us.'

'Just temporarily,' I said. 'We're talking bulls.'

'You *are* superior.'

'Tell him that bulls have no balls,' Mike shouted. He was drunk.

Romero looked at me inquiringly.

'Drunk,' I said. 'Borracho! Muy borracho!'

'You might introduce your friends,' Brett said. She had not stopped looking at Pedro Romero. I asked them if they would like to have coffee with us. They both stood up. Romero's face was very brown. He had very nice manners.

I introduced them all around and they started to sit down, but there was not enough room, so we all moved over to the big table by the wall to have coffee. Mike ordered a bottle of Fundador and glasses for everybody. There was a lot of drunken talking.

'Tell him I think writing is lousy,' Bill said. 'Go on, tell him. Tell him I'm ashamed of being a writer.'

Pedro Romero was sitting beside Brett and listening to her.

'Go on. Tell him!' Bill said.

Romero looked up smiling.

'This gentleman,' I said, 'is a writer.'

Romero was impressed. 'This other one, too,' I said, pointing at Cohn.

'He looks like Villalta,' Romero said, looking at Bill. 'Rafael, doesn't he look like Villalta?'

'I can't see it,' the critic said.

'Really,' Romero said in Spanish. 'He looks a lot like Villalta. What does the drunken one do?'

'Nothing.'

'Is that why he drinks?'

'No. He's waiting to marry this lady.'

'Tell him bulls have no balls!' Mike shouted, very drunk, from the other end of the table.

'What does he say?'

'He's drunk.'

'Jake,' Mike called. 'Tell him bulls have no balls!'

'You understand?' I said.

'Yes.'

I was sure he didn't, so it was all right.

'Tell him Brett wants to see him put on those green pants.'

'Pipe down, Mike.'

'Tell him Brett is dying to know how he can get into those pants.'

'Pipe down.'

During this Romero was fingering his glass and talking with Brett. Brett was talking French and he was talking Spanish and a little English, and laughing.

Bill was filling the glasses.

'Tell him Brett wants to come into—'

'Oh, pipe down, Mike, for Christ's sake!'

Romero looked up smiling. 'Pipe down! I know that,' he said.

Just then Montoya came into the room. He started to smile at me, then he saw Pedro Romero with a big glass of cognac in his hand, sitting laughing between me and a woman with bare shoulders, at a table full of drunks. He did not even nod.

Montoya went out of the room. Mike was on his feet proposing a toast. 'Let's all drink to—' he began. 'Pedro Romero,' I said. Everybody stood up. Romero took it very seriously, and we touched glasses and drank it down, I rushing it a little because Mike was trying to make it clear that that was not at all what he was going to drink to. But it went off all right, and Pedro Romero shook hands with every one and he and the critic went out together.

'My God! he's a lovely boy,' Brett said. 'And how I would love to see him get into those clothes. He must use a shoe-horn.'

'I started to tell him,' Mike began. 'And Jake kept interrupting me. Why do you interrupt me? Do you think you talk Spanish better than I do?'

'Oh, shut up, Mike! Nobody interrupted you.'

'No, I'd like to get this settled.' He turned away from me. 'Do you think you amount to something, Cohn? Do you think you belong here among us? People who are out to have a good time? For God's sake don't be so noisy, Cohn!'

'Oh, cut it out, Mike,' Cohn said.

'Do you think Brett wants you here? Do you think you add to the party? Why don't you say something?'

'I said all I had to say the other night, Mike.'

'I'm not one of you literary chaps.' Mike stood shakily and leaned against the table. 'I'm not clever. But I do know when I'm not wanted. Why don't you see when you're not wanted, Cohn? Go away. Go away, for God's sake. Take that sad Jewish face away. Don't you think I'm right?'

He looked at us.

'Sure,' I said. 'Let's all go over to the Iruña.'

'No. Don't you think I'm right? I love that woman.'

'Oh, don't start that again. Do shove it along, Michael,' Brett said.

'Don't you think I'm right, Jake?'

Cohn still sat at the table. His face had the sallow, yellow look it got when he was insulted, but somehow he seemed to be enjoying it. The childish, drunken heroics of it. It was his affair with a lady of title.

'Jake,' Mike said. He was almost crying. 'You know I'm right. Listen, you!' He turned to Cohn: 'Go away! Go away now!'

'But I won't go, Mike,' said Cohn.

'Then I'll make you!' Mike started toward him around the table. Cohn stood up and took off his glasses. He stood waiting, his face sallow, his hands fairly low, proudly and firmly waiting for the assault, ready to do battle for his lady love.

I grabbed Mike. 'Come on to the café,' I said. 'You can't hit him here in the hotel.'

'Good!' said Mike. 'Good idea!'

We started off. I looked back as Mike stumbled up the stairs and saw Cohn putting his glasses on again. Bill was sitting at the table pouring another glass of Fundador. Brett was sitting looking straight ahead at nothing.

Outside on the square it had stopped raining and the moon was trying to get through the clouds. There was a wind blowing. The military band was playing and the crowd was massed on the far side of the square where the fireworks specialist and his son were trying to send up fire balloons. A balloon would start up jerkily, on a great bias, and be torn by the wind or blown against the houses of the square. Some fell into the crowd. The magnesium flared and the fireworks exploded and chased about in the crowd. There was no one dancing in the square. The gravel was too wet.

Brett came out with Bill and joined us. We stood in the crowd and watched Don Manuel Orquito, the fireworks king, standing on a little platform, carefully starting the balloons with sticks, standing above the heads of the crowd to launch the balloons off into the wind. The wind brought them all down, and Don Manuel Orquito's face was sweaty in the light of his complicated fireworks that fell into the crowd and charged and chased, sputtering and cracking, between the legs of the people. The people shouted as each new luminous paper bubble careened, caught fire, and fell.

'They're razzing Don Manuel,' Bill said.

'How do you know he's Don Manuel?' Brett said.

'His name's on the programme. Don Manuel Orquito, the pirotecnico of esta ciudad.'

'Globos illuminados,' Mike said. 'A collection of globos illuminados. That's what the paper said.'

The wind blew the band music away.

'I say, I wish one would go up,' Brett said. 'That Don Manuel chap is furious.'

'He's probably worked for weeks fixing them to go off, spelling out 'Hail to San Fermin,'" Bill said.

'Globos illuminados,' Mike said. 'A bunch of bloody globos illuminados.'

'Come on,' said Brett. 'We can't stand here.'

'Her ladyship wants a drink,' Mike said.

'How you know things,' Brett said.

Inside, the café was crowded and very noisy. No one noticed us come in. We could not find a table. There was a great noise going on.

'Come on, let's get out of here,' Bill said.

Outside the paseo was going in under the arcade. There were some English and Americans from Biarritz in sport clothes scattered at the tables. Some of the women stared at the people going by with lorgnons. We had acquired, at some time, a friend of Bill's from Biarritz. She was staying with another girl at the Grand Hotel. The other girl had a headache and had gone to bed.

'Here's the pub,' Mike said. It was the Bar Milano, a small, tough bar where you could get food and where they danced in the back room. We all sat down at a table and ordered a bottle of Fundador. The bar was not full. There was nothing going on.

'This is a hell of a place,' Bill said.

'It's too early.'

'Let's take the bottle and come back later,' Bill said. 'I don't want to sit here on a night like this.'

'Let's go and look at the English,' Mike said. 'I love to look at the English.'

'They're awful,' Bill said. 'Where did they all come from?'

'They come from Biarritz,' Mike said, 'They come to see the last day of the quaint little Spanish fiesta.'

'I'll festa them,' Bill said.

'You're an extraordinarily beautiful girl.' Mike turned to Bill's friend. 'When did you come here?'

'Come off it, Michael.'

'I say, she *is* a lovely girl. Where have I been? Where have I been looking all this while? You're a lovely thing. *Have* we met? Come along with me and Bill. We're going to festa the English.'

'I'll festa them,' Bill said, 'What the hell are they doing at this fiesta?'

'Come on,' Mike said. 'Just us three. We're going to festa the bloody English. I hope you're not English? I'm Scotch. I hate the English. I'm going to festa them. Come on, Bill.'

Through the window we saw them, all three arm in arm, going toward the café. Rockets were going up in the square.

'I'm going to sit here,' Brett said.

'I'll stay with you,' Cohn said.

'Oh, don't!' Brett said. 'For God's sake, go off somewhere. Can't you see Jake and I want to talk?'

'I didn't,' Cohn said. 'I thought I'd sit here because I felt a little tight.'

'What a hell of a reason for sitting with any one. If you're tight, go to bed. Go on to bed.'

'Was I rude enough to him?' Brett asked. Cohn was gone. 'My God! I'm so sick of him!'

'He doesn't add much to the gayety.'

'He depresses me so.'

'He's behaved very badly.'

'Damned badly. He had a chance to behave so well.'

'He's probably waiting just outside the door now.'

'Yes. He would. You know I do know how he feels. He can't believe it didn't mean anything.'

'I know.'

'Nobody else would behave as badly. Oh, I'm so sick of the whole thing. And Michael. Michael's been lovely, too.'

'It's been damned hard on Mike.'

'Yes. But he didn't need to be a swine.'

'Everybody behaves badly,' I said. 'Give them the proper chance.'

'You wouldn't behave badly.' Brett looked at me.

'I'd be as big an ass as Cohn,' I said.

'Darling, don't let's talk a lot of rot.'

'All right. Talk about anything you like.'

'Don't be difficult. You're the only person I've got, and I feel rather awful tonight.'

'You've got Mike.'

'Yes, Mike. Hasn't he been pretty?'

'Well,' I said, 'it's been damned hard on Mike, having Cohn around and seeing him with you.'

'Don't I know it, darling? Please don't make me feel any worse than I do.'

Brett was nervous as I had never seen her before. She kept looking away from me and looking ahead at the wall.

'Want to go for a walk?'

'Yes. Come on.'

I corked up the Fundador bottle and gave it to the bartender.

'Let's have one more drink of that,' Brett said. 'My nerves are rotten.'

We each drank a glass of the smooth amontillado brandy.

'Come on,' said Brett.

As we came out the door I saw Cohn walk out from under the arcade.

'He *was* there,' Brett said.

'He can't be away from you.'

'Poor devil!'

'I'm not sorry for him. I hate him, myself.'

'I hate him, too,' she shivered. 'I hate his damned suffering.'

We walked arm in arm down the side street away from the crowd and the lights of the square. The street was dark and wet, and we walked along it to the fortifications at the edge of town. We passed wine-shops with light coming out from their doors onto the black, wet street, and sudden bursts of music.

'Want to go in?'

'No.'

We walked out across the wet grass and onto the stone wall of the fortifications. I spread a newspaper on the stone and Brett sat down. Across the plain it was dark, and we could see the mountains. The wind was high up and took the clouds across the moon. Below us were the dark pits of the fortifications. Behind were the trees and the shadow of the cathedral, and the town silhouetted against the moon.

'Don't feel bad,' I said.

'I feel like hell,' Brett said. 'Don't let's talk.'

We looked out at the plain. The long lines of trees were dark in the moonlight. There were the lights of a car on the road climbing the mountain. Up on the top of the mountain we saw the lights of the fort. Below to the left was the river. It was high from the rain, and black and smooth. Trees were dark along the banks. We sat and looked out. Brett stared straight ahead. Suddenly she shivered.

'It's cold.'

'Want to walk back?'

'Through the park.'

We climbed down. It was clouding over again. In the park it was dark under the trees.

'Do you still love me, Jake?'

'Yes,' I said.

'Because I'm a goner,' Brett said.

'How?'

'I'm a goner. I'm mad about the Romero boy. I'm in love with him, I think.'

'I wouldn't be if I were you.'

'I can't help it. I'm a goner. It's tearing me all up inside.'

'Don't do it.'

'I can't help it. I've never been able to help anything.'

'You ought to stop it.'

'How can I stop it? I can't stop things. Feel that?'

Her hand was trembling.

'I'm like that all through.'

'You oughtn't to do it.'

'I can't help it. I'm a goner now, anyway. Don't you see the difference?'

'No.'

'I've got to do something. I've got to do something I really want to do. I've lost my self-respect.'

'You don't have to do that.'

'Oh, darling, don't be difficult. What do you think it's meant to have that damned Jew about, and Mike the way he's acted?'

'Sure.'

'I can't just stay tight all the time.'

'No.'

'Oh, darling, please stay by me. Please stay by me and see me through this.'

'Sure.'

'I don't say it's right. It is right though for me. God knows, I've never felt such a bitch.'

'What do you want me to do?'

'Come on,' Brett said. 'Let's go and find him.'

Together we walked down the gravel path in the park in the dark, under the trees and then out from under the trees and past the gate into the street that led into town.

Pedro Romero was in the café. He was at a table with other bull-fighters and bull-fight critics. They were smoking cigars. When we came in they looked up. Romero smiled and bowed. We sat down at a table half-way down the room.

'Ask him to come over and have a drink.'

'Not yet. He'll come over.'

'I can't look at him.'

'He's nice to look at,' I said.

'I've always done just what I wanted.'

'I know.'

'I do feel such a bitch.'

'Well,' I said.

'My God!' said Brett, 'the things a woman goes through.'

'Yes?'

'Oh, I do feel such a bitch.'

I looked across at the table. Pedro Romero smiled. He said something to the other people at his table, and stood up. He came over to our table. I stood up and we shook hands.

'Won't you have a drink?'

'You must have a drink with me,' he said. He seated himself, asking Brett's permission without saying anything. He had very nice manners. But he kept on smoking his cigar. It went well with his face.

'You like cigars?' I asked.

'Oh, yes. I always smoke cigars.'

It was part of his system of authority. It made him seem older. I noticed his skin. It was clear and smooth and very brown. There was a triangular scar on his cheek-bone. I saw he was watching Brett. He felt there was something between them. He must have felt it when Brett gave him her hand. He was being very careful. I think he was sure, but he did not want to make any mistake.

'You fight to-morrow?' I said.

'Yes,' he said. 'Algabeno was hurt to-day in Madrid. Did you hear?'

'No,' I said. 'Badly?'

He shook his head.

'Nothing. Here,' he showed his hand. Brett reached out and spread the fingers apart.

'Oh!' he said in English, 'you tell fortunes?'

'Sometimes. Do you mind?'

'No. I like it.' He spread his hand flat on the table. 'Tell me I live for always, and be a millionaire.'

He was still very polite, but he was surer of himself. 'Look,' he said, 'do you see any bulls in my hand?'

He laughed. His hand was very fine and the wrist was small.

'There are thousands of bulls,' Brett said. She was not at all nervous now. She looked lovely.

'Good,' Romero laughed. 'At a thousand duros apiece,' he said to me in Spanish. 'Tell me some more.'

'It's a good hand,' Brett said. 'I think he'll live a long time.'

'Say it to me. Not to your friend.'

'I said you'd live a long time.'

'I know it,' Romero said. 'I'm never going to die.'

I tapped with my finger-tips on the table. Romero saw it. He shook his head.

'No. Don't do that. The bulls are my best friends.'

I translated to Brett.

'You kill your friends?' she asked.

'Always,' he said in English, and laughed. 'So they don't kill me.' He looked at her across the table.

'You know English well.'

'Yes,' he said. 'Pretty well, sometimes. But I must not let anybody know. It would be very bad, a torero who speaks English.'

'Why?' asked Brett.

'It would be bad. The people would not like it. Not yet.'

'Why not?'

'They would not like it. Bull-fighters are not like that.'

'What are bull-fighters like?'

He laughed and tipped his hat down over his eyes and changed the angle of his cigar and the expression of his face.

'Like at the table,' he said. I glanced over. He had mimicked exactly the expression of Nacional. He smiled, his face natural again. 'No. I must forget English.'

'Don't forget it, yet,' Brett said.

'No?'

'No.'

'All right.'

He laughed again.

'I would like a hat like that,' Brett said.

'Good. I'll get you one.'

'Right. See that you do.'

'I will. I'll get you one to-night.'

I stood up. Romero rose, too.

'Sit down,' I said. 'I must go and find our friends and bring them here.'

He looked at me. It was a final look to ask if it were understood. It was understood all right.

'Sit down,' Brett said to him. 'You must teach me Spanish.'

He sat down and looked at her across the table. I went out. The hard-eyed people at the bull-fighter table watched me go. It was not pleasant. When I came back and looked in the café, twenty minutes later, Brett and Pedro Romero were gone. The coffee-glasses and our three empty cognac-glasses were on the table. A waiter came with a cloth and picked up the glasses and mopped off the table.

17

Outside the Bar Milano I found Bill and Mike and Edna. Edna was the girl's name.

'We've been thrown out,' Edna said.

'By the police,' said Mike. 'There's some people in there that don't like me.'

'I've kept them out of four fights,' Edna said. 'You've got to help me.'

Bill's face was red.

'Come back in, Edna,' he said. 'Go on in there and dance with Mike.'

'It's silly,' Edna said. 'There'll just be another row.'

'Damned Biarritz swine,' Bill said.

'Come on,' Mike said. 'After all, it's a pub. They can't occupy a whole pub.'

'Good old Mike,' Bill said. 'Damned English swine come here and insult Mike and try and spoil the fiesta.'

'They're so bloody,' Mike said. 'I hate the English.'

'They can't insult Mike,' Bill said. 'Mike is a swell fellow. They can't insult Mike. I won't stand it. Who cares if he is a damn bankrupt?' His voice broke.

'Who cares?' Mike said. 'I don't care. Jake doesn't care. Do *you* care?'

'No,' Edna said. 'Are you a bankrupt?'

'Of course I am. You don't care, do you, Bill?'

Bill put his arm around Mike's shoulder.

'I wish to hell I was a bankrupt. I'd show those bastards.'

'They're just English,' Mike said. 'It never makes any difference what the English say.'

'The dirty swine,' Bill said. 'I'm going to clean them out.'

'Bill,' Edna looked at me. 'Please don't go in again, Bill. They're so stupid.'

'That's it,' said Mike. 'They're stupid. I knew that was what it was.'

'They can't say things like that about Mike,' Bill said.

'Do you know them?' I asked Mike.

'No. I never saw them. They say they know me.'

'I won't stand it,' Bill said.

'Come on. Let's go over to the Suizo,' I said.

'They're a bunch of Edna's friends from Biarritz,' Bill said.

'They're simply stupid,' Edna said.

'One of them's Charley Blackman, from Chicago,' Bill said.

'I was never in Chicago,' Mike said.

Edna started to laugh and could not stop.

'Take me away from here,' she said, 'you bankrupts.'

'What kind of a row was it?' I asked Edna. We were walking across the square to the Suizo. Bill was gone.

'I don't know what happened, but some one had the police called to keep Mike out of the back room. There were some people that had known Mike at Cannes. What's the matter with Mike?'

'Probably he owes them money" I said. 'That's what people usually get bitter about.'

In front of the ticket-booths out in the square there were two lines of people waiting. They were sitting on chairs or crouched on the ground with blankets and newspapers around them. They were waiting for the wickets to open in the morning to buy tickets for the bull-fight. The night was clearing and the moon was out. Some of the people in the line were sleeping.

At the Café Suizo we had just sat down and ordered Fundador when Robert Cohn came up.

'Where's Brett?' he asked.

'I don't know.'

'She was with you.'

'She must have gone to bed.'

'She's not.'

'I don't know where she is.'

His face was sallow under the light. He was standing up.

'Tell me where she is.'

'Sit down,' I said. 'I don't know where she is.'

'The hell you don't!'

'You can shut your face.'

'Tell me where Brett is.'

'I'll not tell you a damn thing.'

'You know where she is.'

'If I did I wouldn't tell you.'

'Oh, go to hell, Cohn,' Mike called from the table. 'Brett's gone off with the bull-fighter chap. They're on their honeymoon.'

'You shut up.'

'Oh, go to hell!' Mike said languidly.

'Is that where she is?' Cohn turned to me.

'Go to hell!'

'She was with you. Is that where she is?'

'Go to hell!'

'I'll make you tell me'—he stepped forward—'you damned pimp.'

I swung at him and he ducked. I saw his face duck sideways in the light. He hit me and I sat down on the pavement. As I started to get on my feet he hit me twice. I went down backward under a table. I tried to get up and felt I did not have any legs. I felt I must get on my feet and try and hit him. Mike helped me up. Some one poured a carafe of water on my head. Mike had an arm around me, and I found I was sitting on a chair. Mike was pulling at my ears.

'I say, you were cold,' Mike said.

'Where the hell were you?'

'Oh, I was around.'

'You didn't want to mix in it?'

'He knocked Mike down, too,' Edna said.

'He didn't knock me out,' Mike said. 'I just lay there.'

'Does this happen every night at your fiestas?' Edna asked. 'Wasn't that Mr. Cohn?'

'I'm all right,' I said. 'My head's a little wobbly.'

There were several waiters and a crowd of people standing around.

'Vaya!' said Mike. 'Get away. Go on.'

The waiters moved the people away.

'It was quite a thing to watch,' Edna said. 'He must be a boxer.'

'He is.'

'I wish Bill had been here,' Edna said. 'I'd like to have seen Bill knocked down, too. I've always wanted to see Bill knocked down. He's so big.'

'I was hoping he would knock down a waiter,' Mike said, 'and get arrested. I'd like to see Mr. Robert Cohn in jail.'

'No,' I said.

'Oh, no,' said Edna. 'You don't mean that.'

'I do, though,' Mike said. 'I'm not one of these chaps likes being knocked about. I never play games, even.'

Mike took a drink.

'I never liked to hunt, you know. There was always the danger of having a horse fall on you. How do you feel, Jake?'

'All right.'

'You're nice,' Edna said to Mike. 'Are you really a bankrupt?'

'I'm a tremendous bankrupt,' Mike said. 'I owe money to everybody. Don't you owe any money?'

'Tons.'

'I owe everybody money,' Mike said. 'I borrowed a hundred pesetas from Montoya to-night.'

'The hell you did,' I said.

'I'll pay it back,' Mike said. 'I always pay everything back.'

'That's why you're a bankrupt, isn't it?' Edna said.

I stood up. I had heard them talking from a long way away. It all seemed like some bad play.

'I'm going over to the hotel,' I said. Then I heard them talking about me.

'Is he all right?' Edna asked.

'We'd better walk with him.'

'I'm all right,' I said. 'Don't come. I'll see you all later.'

I walked away from the café. They were sitting at the table. I looked back at them and at the empty tables. There was a waiter sitting at one of the tables with his head in his hands.

Walking across the square to the hotel everything looked new and changed. I had never seen the trees before. I had never seen the flagpoles before, nor the front of the theatre. It was all different. I felt as I felt once coming home from an out-of-town football game. I was carrying a suitcase with my football things in it, and I walked up the street from the station in the town I had lived in all my life and it was all new. They were raking the lawns and burning leaves in the road, and I stopped for a long time and watched. It was all strange. Then I went on, and my feet seemed to be a long way off, and everything seemed to come from a long way off, and I could hear my feet walking a great distance away. I had been kicked in the head early in the game. It was like that crossing the square. It was like that going up the stairs in the hotel. Going up the stairs took a long time, and I had the feeling that I was carrying my suitcase. There was a light in the room. Bill came out and met me in the hall.

'Say,' he said, 'go up and see Cohn. He's been in a jam, and he's asking for you.'

'The hell with him.'

'Go on. Go on up and see him.'

I did not want to climb another flight of stairs.

'What are you looking at me that way for?'

'I'm not looking at you. Go on up and see Cohn. He's in bad shape.'

'You were drunk a little while ago,' I said.

'I'm drunk now,' Bill said. 'But you go up and see Cohn. He wants to see you.'

'All right,' I said. It was just a matter of climbing more stairs. I went on up the stairs carrying my phantom suitcase. I walked down the hall to Cohn's room. The door was shut and I knocked.

'Who is it?'

'Barnes.'

'Come in, Jake.'

I opened the door and went in, and set down my suitcase. There was no light in the room. Cohn was lying, face down, on the bed in the dark.

'Hello, Jake.'

'Don't call me Jake.'

I stood by the door. It was just like this that I had come home. Now it was a hot bath that I needed. A deep, hot bath, to lie back in.

'Where's the bathroom?' I asked.

Cohn was crying. There he was, face down on the bed, crying. He had on a white polo shirt, the kind he'd worn at Princeton.

'I'm sorry, Jake. Please forgive me.'

'Forgive you, hell.'

'Please forgive me, Jake.'

I did not say anything. I stood there by the door.

'I was crazy. You must see how it was.'

'Oh, that's all right.'

'I couldn't stand it about Brett.'

'You called me a pimp.'

I did not care. I wanted a hot bath. I wanted a hot bath in deep water.

'I know. Please don't remember it. I was crazy.'

'That's all right.'

He was crying. His voice was funny. He lay there in his white shirt on the bed in the dark. His polo shirt.

'I'm going away in the morning.'

He was crying without making any noise.

'I just couldn't stand it about Brett. I've been through hell, Jake. It's been simply hell. When I met her down here Brett treated me as though I were a perfect stranger. I just couldn't stand it. We lived together at San Sebastian. I suppose you know it. I can't stand it any more.'

He lay there on the bed.

'Well,' I said, 'I'm going to take a bath.'

'You were the only friend I had, and I loved Brett so.'

'Well,' I said, 'so long.'

'I guess it isn't any use,' he said. 'I guess it isn't any damn use.'

'What?'

'Everything. Please say you forgive me, Jake.'

'Sure,' I said. 'It's all right.'

'I felt so terribly. I've been through such hell, Jake. Now everything's gone. Everything.'

'Well,' I said, 'so long. I've got to go.'

He rolled over, sat on the edge of the bed, and then stood up.

'So long, Jake,' he said. 'You'll shake hands, won't you?'

'Sure. Why not?'

We shook hands. In the dark I could not see his face very well.

'Well,' I said, 'see you in the morning.'

'I'm going away in the morning.'

'Oh, yes,' I said.

I went out. Cohn was standing in the door of the room.

'Are you all right, Jake?' he asked.

'Oh, yes,' I said. 'I'm all right.'

I could not find the bathroom. After a while I found it. There was a deep stone tub. I turned on the taps and the water would not run. I sat down on the edge of the bath-tub. When I got up to go I found I had taken off my shoes. I hunted for them and found them and carried them down-stairs. I found my room and went inside and undressed and got into bed.

I woke with a headache and the noise of the bands going by in the street. I remembered I had promised to take Bill's friend Edna to see the bulls go through the street and into the ring. I dressed and went down-stairs and out into the cold early morning. People were crossing the square, hurrying toward the bull-ring. Across the square were the two lines of men in front of the ticket-booths. They were still waiting for the tickets to go on sale at seven o'clock. I hurried across the street to the café. The waiter told me that my friends had been there and gone.

'How many were they?'

'Two gentlemen and a lady.'

That was all right. Bill and Mike were with Edna. She had been afraid last night they would pass out. That was why I was to be sure to take her. I drank the coffee and hurried with the other people toward the bull-ring. I was not groggy now. There was only a bad headache. Everything looked sharp and clear, and the town smelt of the early morning.

The stretch of ground from the edge of the town to the bull-ring was muddy. There was a crowd all along the fence that led to the ring, and the outside balconies and the top of the bull-ring were solid with people. I heard the rocket and I knew I could not get into the ring in time to see the bulls come in, so I shoved through the crowd to the fence. I was pushed close against the planks of the fence. Between the two fences of the runway the police were clearing the crowd along. They walked or trotted on into the bull-ring. Then people commenced to come running. A drunk slipped and fell. Two policemen grabbed him and rushed him over to the fence. The crowd were running fast now. There was a great shout from the crowd, and putting my head through between the boards I saw the bulls just coming out of the street into the long running pen. They were going fast and gaining on the crowd. Just then another drunk started out from the fence with a blouse in his hands. He wanted to do capework with the bulls. The two policemen tore out, collared him, one hit him with a club, and they dragged him against the fence and stood flattened out against the fence as the last of the crowd and the bulls went by. There were so many people running ahead of the bulls that the mass thickened and slowed up going through the gate into the ring, and as the bulls passed, galloping together, heavy, muddy-sided, horns swinging, one shot ahead, caught a man in the running crowd in the back and lifted him in the air. Both the man's arms were by his sides, his head went back as the horn went in, and the bull lifted him and then dropped him. The bull picked another man running in front, but the man disappeared into the crowd, and the crowd was through the gate and into the ring with the bulls behind them. The red door of the ring went shut, the crowd on the outside balconies of the bull-ring were pressing through to the inside, there was a shout, then another shout.

The man who had been gored lay face down in the trampled mud. People climbed over the fence, and I could not see the man because the crowd was so thick around him. From inside the ring came the shouts. Each shout meant a charge by some bull into the crowd. You could tell by the degree of intensity in the shout how bad a thing it was that was happening. Then the rocket went up that meant the steers had gotten the bulls out of the ring and into the corrals. I left the fence and started back toward the town.

Back in the town I went to the café to have a second coffee and some buttered toast. The waiters were sweeping out the café and mopping off the tables. One came over and took my order.

'Anything happen at the encierro?'

'I didn't see it all. One man was badly cogido.'

'Where?'

'Here.' I put one hand on the small of my back and the other on my chest, where it looked as though the horn must have come through. The waiter nodded his head and swept the crumbs from the table with his cloth.

'Badly cogido,' he said. 'All for sport. All for pleasure.'

He went away and came back with the long-handled coffee and milk pots. He poured the milk and coffee. It came out of the long spouts in two streams into the big cup. The waiter nodded his head.

'Badly cogido through the back,' he said. He put the pots down on the table and sat down in the chair at the table. 'A big horn wound. All for fun. Just for fun. What do you think of that?'

'I don't know.'

'That's it. All for fun. Fun, you understand.'

'You're not an aficionado?'

'Me? What are bulls? Animals. Brute animals.' He stood up and put his hand on the small of his back. 'Right through the back. A cornada right through the back. For fun—you understand.'

He shook his head and walked away, carrying the coffee-pots. Two men were going by in the street. The waiter shouted to them. They were grave-looking. One shook his head. 'Muerto!' he called.

The waiter nodded his head. The two men went on. They were on some errand. The waiter came over to my table.

'You hear? Muerto. Dead. He's dead. With a horn through him. All for morning fun. Es muy flamenco.'

'It's bad.'

'Not for me,' the waiter said. 'No fun in that for me.'

Later in the day we learned that the man who was killed was named Vicente Girones, and came from near Tafalla. The next day in the paper we read that he was twenty-eight years old, and had a farm, a wife, and two children. He had continued to come to the fiesta each year after he was married. The next day his wife came in from Tafalla to be with the body, and the day after there was a service in the chapel of San Fermin, and the coffin was carried to the railway-station by members of the dancing and drinking society of Tafalla. The drums marched ahead, and there was music on the fifes, and behind the men who carried the coffin walked the wife and two children. . . . Behind them marched all the members of the dancing and drinking societies of Pamplona, Estella, Tafalla, and Sanguesa who could stay over for the funeral. The coffin was loaded into the baggage-car of the train, and the widow and the two children rode, sitting, all three together, in an open third-class railway-carriage. The train started with a jerk, and then ran smoothly, going down grade around the edge of the plateau and out into the fields of grain that blew in the wind on the plain on the way to Tafalla.

The bull who killed Vicente Girones was named Bocanegra, was Number 118 of the bull-breeding establishment of Sanchez Tabemo, and was killed by Pedro Romero as the third bull of that same afternoon. His ear was cut by popular acclamation and given to Pedro Romero, who, in turn, gave it to Brett, who wrapped it in a handkerchief belonging to myself, and left both ear and handkerchief, along with a number of Muratti cigarette-stubs, shoved far back in the drawer of the bed-table that stood beside her bed in the Hotel Montoya, in Pamplona.

Back in the hotel, the night watchman was sitting on a bench inside the door. He had been there all night and was very sleepy. He stood up as I came in. Three of the waitresses came in at the same time. They had been to the morning show at the bull-ring. They went up-stairs laughing. I followed them up-stairs and went into my room. I took off my shoes and lay down on the bed. The window was open onto the balcony and the sunlight was bright in the room. I did not feel sleepy. It must have been half past three o'clock when I had gone to bed and the bands had waked me at six. My jaw was sore on both sides. I felt it with my thumb and fingers. That damn Cohn. He should have hit somebody the first time he was insulted, and then gone away. He was so sure that Brett loved him. He was going to stay, and true love would conquer all. Some one knocked on the door.

'Come in.'

It was Bill and Mike. They sat down on the bed.

'Some encierro,' Bill said. 'Some encierro.'

'I say, weren't you there?' Mike asked. 'Ring for some beer, Bill.'

'What a morning!' Bill said. He mopped off his face. 'My God! what a morning! And here's old Jake. Old Jake, the human punching-bag.'

'What happened inside?'

'Good God!' Bill said, 'what happened, Mike?'

'There were these bulls coming in,' Mike said. 'Just ahead of them was the crowd, and some chap tripped and brought the whole lot of them down.'

'And the bulls all came in right over them,' Bill said.

'I heard them yell.'

'That was Edna,' Bill said.

'Chaps kept coming out and waving their shirts.'

'One bull went along the barrera and hooked everybody over.'

'They took about twenty chaps to the infirmary,' Mike said.

'What a morning!' Bill said. 'The damn police kept arresting chaps that wanted to go and commit suicide with the bulls.'

'The steers took them in, in the end,' Mike said.

'It took about an hour.'

'It was really about a quarter of an hour,' Mike objected.

'Oh, go to hell,' Bill said. 'You've been in the war. It was two hours and a half for me.'

'Where's that beer?' Mike asked.

'What did you do with the lovely Edna?'

'We took her home just now. She's gone to bed.'

'How did she like it?'

'Fine. We told her it was just like that every morning.'

'She was impressed,' Mike said.

'She wanted us to go down in the ring, too,' Bill said. 'She likes action.'

'I said it wouldn't be fair to my creditors,' Mike said.

'What a morning,' Bill said. 'And what a night!'

'How's your jaw, Jake?' Mike asked.

'Sore,' I said.

Bill laughed.

'Why didn't you hit him with a chair?'

'You can talk,' Mike said. 'He'd have knocked you out, too. I never saw him hit me. I rather think I saw him just before, and then quite suddenly I was sitting down in the street, and Jake was lying under a table.'

'Where did he go afterward?' I asked.

'Here she is,' Mike said. 'Here's the beautiful lady with the beer.'

The chambermaid put the tray with the beer-bottles and glasses down on the table.

'Now bring up three more bottles,' Mike said.

'Where did Cohn go after he hit me?' I asked Bill.

'Don't you know about that?' Mike was opening a beer-bottle. He poured the beer into one of the glasses, holding the glass close to the bottle.

'Really?' Bill asked.

'Why he went in and found Brett and the bull-fighter chap in the bull-fighter's room, and then he massacred the poor, bloody bull-fighter.'

'No.'

'Yes.'

'What a night!' Bill said.

'He nearly killed the poor, bloody bull-fighter. Then Cohn wanted to take Brett away. Wanted to make an honest woman of her, I imagine. Damned touching scene.'

He took a long drink of the beer.

'He is an ass.'

'What happened?'

'Brett gave him what for. She told him off. I think she was rather good.'

'I'll bet she was,' Bill said.

'Then Cohn broke down and cried, and wanted to shake hands with the bull-fighter fellow. He wanted to shake hands with Brett, too.'

'I know. He shook hands with me.'

'Did he? Well, they weren't having any of it. The bull-fighter fellow was rather good. He didn't say much, but he kept getting up and getting knocked down again. Cohn couldn't knock him out. It must have been damned funny.'

'Where did you hear all this?'

'Brett. I saw her this morning.'

'What happened finally?'

'It seems the bull-fighter fellow was sitting on the bed. He'd been knocked down about fifteen times, and he wanted to fight some more. Brett held him and wouldn't let him get up. He was weak, but Brett couldn't hold him, and he got up. Then Cohn said he wouldn't hit him again. Said he couldn't do it. Said it would be wicked. So the bull-fighter chap sort of rather staggered over to him.

Cohn went back against the wall.

'So you won't hit me?'

'No,' said Cohn. 'I'd be ashamed to.'

'So the bull-fighter fellow hit him just as hard as he could in the face, and then sat down on the floor. He couldn't get up, Brett said. Cohn wanted to pick him up and carry him to the bed. He said if Cohn helped him he'd kill him, and he'd kill him anyway this morning if Cohn wasn't out of town. Cohn was crying, and Brett had told him off, and he wanted to shake hands. I've told you that before.'

'Tell the rest,' Bill said.

'It seems the bull-fighter chap was sitting on the floor. He was waiting to get strength enough to get up and hit Cohn again. Brett wasn't having any shaking hands, and Cohn was crying and telling her how much he loved her, and she was telling him not to be a ruddy ass. Then Cohn leaned down to shake hands with the bull-fighter fellow. No hard feelings, you know. All for forgiveness. And the bull-fighter chap hit him in the face again.'

'That's quite a kid,' Bill said.

'He ruined Cohn,' Mike said. 'You know I don't think Cohn will ever want to knock people about again.'

'When did you see Brett?'

'This morning. She came in to get some things. She's looking after this Romero lad.'

He poured out another bottle of beer.

'Brett's rather cut up. But she loves looking after people. That's how we came to go off together. She was looking after me.'

'I know,' I said.

'I'm rather drunk,' Mike said. 'I think I'll *stay* rather drunk. This is all awfully amusing, but it's not too pleasant. It's not too pleasant for me.'

He drank off the beer.

'I gave Brett what for, you know. I said if she would go about with Jews and bull-fighters and such people, she must expect trouble.' He leaned forward. 'I say, Jake, do you mind if I drink that bottle of yours? She'll bring you another one.'

'Please,' I said. 'I wasn't drinking it, anyway.'

Mike started to open the bottle. 'Would you mind opening it?' I pressed up the wire fastener and poured it for him.

'You know,' Mike went on, 'Brett was rather good. She's always rather good. I gave her a fearful hiding about Jews and bull-fighters, and all those sort of people, and do you know what she said: 'Yes. I've had such a hell of a happy life with the British aristocracy!'"

He took a drink.

'That was rather good. Ashley, chap she got the title from, was a sailor, you know. Ninth baronet. When he came home he wouldn't sleep in a bed. Always made Brett sleep on the floor. Finally, when he got really bad, he used to tell her he'd kill her. Always slept with a loaded service revolver. Brett used to take the shells out when he'd gone to sleep. She hasn't had an absolutely happy life, Brett. Damned shame, too. She enjoys things so.'

He stood up. His hand was shaky.

'I'm going in the room. Try and get a little sleep.'

He smiled.

'We go too long without sleep in these fiestas. I'm going to start now and get plenty of sleep. Damn bad thing not to get sleep. Makes you frightfully nervy.'

'We'll see you at noon at the Iruña,' Bill said.

Mike went out the door. We heard him in the next room.

He rang the bell and the chambermaid came and knocked at the door.

'Bring up half a dozen bottles of beer and a bottle of Fundador,' Mike told her.

'Si, Señorito.'

'I'm going to bed,' Bill said. 'Poor old Mike. I had a hell of a row about him last night.'

'Where? At that Milano place?'

'Yes. There was a fellow there that had helped pay Brett and Mike out of Cannes, once. He was damned nasty.'

'I know the story.'

'I didn't. Nobody ought to have a right to say things about Mike.'

'That's what makes it bad.'

'They oughtn't to have any right. I wish to hell they didn't have any right. I'm going to bed.'

'Was anybody killed in the ring?'

'I don't think so. Just badly hurt.'

'A man was killed outside in the runway.'

'Was there?' said Bill.

18

At noon we were all at the café. It was crowded. We were eating shrimps and drinking beer. The town was crowded. Every street was full. Big motor-cars from Biarritz and San Sebastian kept driving up and parking around the square. They brought people for the bull-fight. Sight-seeing cars came up, too. There was one with twenty-five Englishwomen in it. They sat in the big, white car and looked through their glasses at the fiesta. The dancers were all quite drunk. It was the last day of the fiesta.

The fiesta was solid and unbroken, but the motor-cars and tourist-cars made little islands of onlookers. When the cars emptied, the onlookers were absorbed into the crowd. You did not see them again except as sport clothes, odd-looking at a table among the closely packed peasants in black smocks. The fiesta absorbed even the Biarritz English so that you did not see them unless you passed close to a table. All the time there was music in the street. The drums kept on pounding and the pipes were going. Inside the cafés men with their hands gripping the table, or on each other's shoulders, were singing the hard-voiced singing.

'Here comes Brett,' Bill said.

I looked and saw her coming through the crowd in the square, walking, her head up, as though the fiesta were being staged in her honor, and she found it pleasant and amusing.

'Hello, you chaps!' she said. 'I say, I *have* a thirst.'

'Get another big beer,' Bill said to the waiter.

'Shrimps?'

'Is Cohn gone?' Brett asked.

'Yes,' Bill said. 'He hired a car.'

The beer came. Brett started to lift the glass mug and her hand shook. She saw it and smiled, and leaned forward and took a long sip.

'Good beer.'

'Very good,' I said. I was nervous about Mike. I did not think he had slept. He must have been drinking all the time, but he seemed to be under control.

'I heard Cohn had hurt you, Jake,' Brett said.

'No. Knocked me out. That was all.'

'I say, he did hurt Pedro Romero,' Brett said. 'He hurt him most badly.'

'How is he?'

'He'll be all right. He won't go out of the room.'

'Does he look badly?'

'Very. He was really hurt. I told him I wanted to pop out and see you chaps for a minute.'

'Is he going to fight?'

'Rather. I'm going with you, if you don't mind.'

'How's your boy friend?' Mike asked. He had not listened to anything that Brett had said.

'Brett's got a bull-fighter,' he said. 'She had a Jew named Cohn, but he turned out badly.'

Brett stood up.

'I am not going to listen to that sort of rot from you, Michael.'

'How's your boy friend?'

'Damned well,' Brett said. 'Watch him this afternoon.'

'Brett's got a bull-fighter,' Mike said. 'A beautiful, bloody bull-fighter.'

'Would you mind walking over with me? I want to talk to you, Jake.'

'Tell him all about your bull-fighter,' Mike said. 'Oh, to hell with your bull-fighter!' He tipped the table so that all the beers and the dish of shrimps went over in a crash.

'Come on,' Brett said. 'Let's get out of this.'

In the crowd crossing the square I said: 'How is it?'

'I'm not going to see him after lunch until the fight. His people come in and dress him. They're very angry about me, he says.'

Brett was radiant. She was happy. The sun was out and the day was bright.

'I feel altogether changed,' Brett said. 'You've no idea, Jake.'

'Anything you want me to do?'

'No, just go to the fight with me.'

'We'll see you at lunch?'

'No. I'm eating with him.'

We were standing under the arcade at the door of the hotel. They were carrying tables out and setting them up under the arcade.

'Want to take a turn out to the park?' Brett asked. 'I don't want to go up yet. I fancy he's sleeping.'

We walked along past the theatre and out of the square and along through the barracks of the fair, moving with the crowd between the lines of booths. We came out on a cross-street that led to the Paseo de Sarasate. We could see the crowd walking there, all the fashionably dressed people. They were making the turn at the upper end of the park.

'Don't let's go there,' Brett said. 'I don't want staring at just now.'

We stood in the sunlight. It was hot and good after the rain and the clouds from the sea.

'I hope the wind goes down,' Brett said. 'It's very bad for him.'

'So do I.'

'He says the bulls are all right.'

'They're good.'

'Is that San Fermin's?'

Brett looked at the yellow wall of the chapel.

'Yes. Where the show started on Sunday.'

'Let's go in. Do you mind? I'd rather like to pray a little for him or something.'

We went in through the heavy leather door that moved very lightly. It was dark inside. Many people were praying. You saw them as your eyes adjusted themselves to the half-light. We knelt at one of the long wooden benches. After a little I felt Brett stiffen beside me, and saw she was looking straight ahead.

'Come on,' she whispered throatily. 'Let's get out of here. Makes me damned nervous.'

Outside in the hot brightness of the street Brett looked up at the tree-tops in the wind. The praying had not been much of a success.

'Don't know why I get so nervy in church,' Brett said. 'Never does me any good.'

We walked along.

'I'm damned bad for a religious atmosphere,' Brett said. 'I've the wrong type of face.'

'You know,' Brett said, 'I'm not worried about him at all. I just feel happy about him.'

'Good.'

'I wish the wind would drop, though.'

'It's liable to go down by five o'clock.'

'Let's hope.'

'You might pray,' I laughed.

'Never does me any good. I've never gotten anything I prayed for. Have you?'

'Oh, yes.'

'Oh, rot,' said Brett. 'Maybe it works for some people, though. You don't look very religious, Jake.'

'I'm pretty religious.'

'Oh, rot,' said Brett. 'Don't start proselyting to-day. To-day's going to be bad enough as it is.'

It was the first time I had seen her in the old happy, careless way since before she went off with Cohn. We were back again in front of the hotel. All the tables were set now, and already several were filled with people eating.

'Do look after Mike,' Brett said. 'Don't let him get too bad.'

'Your frients haff gone up-stairs,' the German maître d'hôtel said in English. He was a continual eavesdropper. Brett turned to him:

'Thank you, so much. Have you anything else to say?'

'No, ma'am.'

'Good,' said Brett.

'Save us a table for three,' I said to the German. He smiled his dirty little pink-and-white smile.

'Iss madam eating here?'

'No,' Brett said.

'Den I think a tabul for two will be enuff.'

'Don't talk to him,' Brett said. 'Mike must have been in bad shape,' she said on the stairs. We passed Montoya on the stairs. He bowed and did not smile.

'I'll see you at the café,' Brett said. 'Thank you, so much, Jake.'

We had stopped at the floor our rooms were on. She went straight down the hall and into Romero's room. She did not knock. She simply opened the door, went in, and closed it behind her.

I stood in front of the door of Mike's room and knocked. There was no answer. I tried the knob and it opened. Inside the room was in great disorder. All the bags were opened and clothing was strewn around. There were empty bottles beside the bed. Mike lay on the bed looking like a death mask of himself. He opened his eyes and looked at me.

'Hello, Jake,' he said very slowly. 'I'm getting a little sleep. I've want ed a little sleep for a long time.'

'Let me cover you over.'

'No. I'm quite warm.'

'Don't go. I have n't got ten to sleep yet.'

'You'll sleep, Mike. Don't worry, boy.'

'Brett's got a bull-fighter,' Mike said. 'But her Jew has gone away.'

He turned his head and looked at me.

'Damned good thing, what?'

'Yes. Now go to sleep, Mike. You ought to get some sleep.'

'I'm just starting. I'm going to get a little sleep.'

He shut his eyes. I went out of the room and turned the door to quietly. Bill was in my room reading the paper.

'See Mike?'

'Yes.'

'Let's go and eat.'

'I won't eat down-stairs with that German head waiter. He was damned snotty when I was getting Mike up-stairs.'

'He was snotty to us, too.'

'Let's go out and eat in the town.'

We went down the stairs. On the stairs we passed a girl coming up with a covered tray.

'There goes Brett's lunch,' Bill said.

'And the kid's,' I said.

Outside on the terrace under the arcade the German head waiter came up. His red cheeks were shiny. He was being polite.

'I haff a tabul for two for you gentlemen,' he said.

'Go sit at it,' Bill said. We went on out across the street.

We ate at a restaurant in a side street off the square. They were all men eating in the restaurant. It was full of smoke and drinking and singing. The food was good and so was the wine. We did not talk much. Afterward we went to the café and watched the fiesta come to the boiling-point. Brett came over soon after lunch. She said she had looked in the room and that Mike was asleep.

When the fiesta boiled over and toward the bull-ring we went with the crowd. Brett sat at the ringside between Bill and me. Directly below us was the callejon, the passageway between the stands and the red fence of the barrera. Behind us the concrete stands filled solidly. Out in front, beyond the red fence, the sand of the ring was smooth-rolled and yellow. It looked a little heavy from the rain, but it was dry in the sun and firm and smooth. The sword-handlers and bull-ring servants came down the callejon carrying on their shoulders the wicker baskets of fighting capes and muletas. They were bloodstained and compactly folded and packed in the baskets. The sword-handlers opened the heavy leather sword-cases so the red wrapped hilts of the sheaf of swords showed as the leather case leaned against the fence. They unfolded the dark-stained red flannel of the muletas and fixed batons in them to spread the stuff and give the matador something to hold. Brett watched it all. She was absorbed in the professional details.

'He's his name stencilled on all the capes and muletas,' she said. 'Why do they call them muletas?'

'I don't know.'

'I wonder if they ever launder them.'

'I don't think so. It might spoil the color.'

'The blood must stiffen them,' Bill said.

'Funny,' Brett said. 'How one doesn't mind the blood.'

Below in the narrow passage of the callejon the sword-handlers arranged everything. All the seats were full. Above, all the boxes were full. There was not an empty seat except in the President's box. When he came in the fight would start. Across the smooth sand, in the high doorway that led into the corrals, the bull-fighters were standing, their arms furled in their capes, talking, waiting for the signal to march in across the arena. Brett was watching them with the glasses.

'Here, would you like to look?'

I looked through the glasses and saw the three matadors. Romero was in the centre, Belmonte on his left, Marcial on his right. Back of them were their people, and behind the banderilleros, back in the passageway and in the open space of the corral, I saw the picadors. Romero was wearing a black suit. His tricornered hat was low down over his eyes. I could not see his face clearly under the hat, but it looked badly marked. He was looking straight ahead. Marcial was smoking a cigarette guardedly, holding it in his hand. Belmonte looked ahead, his face wan and yellow, his long wolf jaw out. He was looking at nothing. Neither he nor Romero seemed to have anything in common with the others. They were all alone. The President came in; there was handclapping above us in the grand stand, and I handed the glasses to Brett. There was applause. The music started. Brett looked through the glasses.

'Here, take them,' she said.

Through the glasses I saw Belmonte speak to Romero. Marcial straightened up and dropped his cigarette, and, looking straight ahead, their heads back, their free arms swinging, the three matadors walked out. Behind them came all the procession, opening out, all striding in step, all the capes furled, everybody with free arms swinging, and behind rode the picadors, their pics rising like lances. Behind all came the two trains of mules and the bull-ring servants. The matadors bowed, holding their hats on, before the President's box, and then came over to the barrera below us. Pedro Romero took off his heavy gold-brocaded cape and handed it over the fence to his sword-handler. He said something to the sword-handler. Close below us we saw Romero's lips were puffed, both eyes were discolored. His face was discolored and swollen. The sword-handler took the cape, looked up at Brett, and came over to us and handed up the cape.

'Spread it out in front of you,' I said.

Brett leaned forward. The cape was heavy and smoothly stiff with gold. The sword-handler looked back, shook his head, and said something. A man beside me leaned over toward Brett.

'He doesn't want you to spread it,' he said. 'You should fold it and keep it in your lap.'

Brett folded the heavy cape.

Romero did not look up at us. He was speaking to Belmonte. Belmonte had sent his formal cape over to some friends. He looked across at them and smiled, his wolf smile that was only with the mouth. Romero leaned over the barrera and asked for the water-jug. The sword-handler brought it and Romero poured water over the percale of his fighting-cape, and then scuffed the lower folds in the sand with his slippered foot.

'What's that for?' Brett asked.

'To give it weight in the wind.'

'His face looks bad,' Bill said.

'He feels very badly,' Brett said. 'He should be in bed.'

The first bull was Belmonte's. Belmonte was very good. But because he got thirty thousand pesetas and people had stayed in line all night to buy tickets to see him, the crowd demanded that he should be more than very good. Belmonte's great attraction is working close to the bull. In bull-fighting they speak of the terrain of the bull and the terrain of the bull-fighter. As long as a bull-fighter stays in his own terrain he is comparatively safe. Each time he enters into the terrain of the bull he is in great danger. Belmonte, in his best days, worked always in the terrain of the bull. This way he gave the sensation of coming tragedy. People went to the corrida to see Belmonte, to be given tragic sensations, and perhaps to see the death of Belmonte. Fifteen years ago they said if you wanted to see Belmonte you should go quickly, while he was still alive. Since then he has killed more than a thousand bulls. When he retired the legend grew up about how his bull-fighting had been, and when he came out of retirement the public were disappointed because no real man could work as close to the bulls as Belmonte was supposed to have done, not, of course, even Belmonte.

Also Belmonte imposed conditions and insisted that his bulls should not be too large, nor too dangerously armed with horns, and so the element that was necessary to give the sensation of tragedy was not there, and the public, who wanted three times as much from Belmonte, who was sick with a fistula, as Belmonte had ever been able to give, felt defrauded and cheated, and Belmonte's jaw came further out in contempt, and his face turned yellower, and he moved with greater difficulty as his pain increased, and finally the crowd were actively against him, and he was utterly contemptuous and indifferent. He had meant to have a great afternoon, and instead it was an afternoon of sneers, shouted insults, and finally a volley of cushions and pieces of bread and vegetables, thrown down at him in the plaza where he had had his greatest triumphs. His jaw only went further out. Sometimes he turned to smile that toothed, long-jawed, lipless smile when he was called something particularly insulting, and always the pain that any movement produced grew stronger and stronger, until finally his yellow face was parchment color, and after his second bull was dead and the throwing of bread and cushions was over, after he had saluted the President with the same wolf-jawed smile and contemptuous eyes, and handed his sword over the barrera to be wiped, and put back in its case, he passed through into the callejon and leaned on the barrera below us, his head on his arms, not seeing, not hearing anything, only going through his pain. When he looked up, finally, he asked for a drink of water. He swallowed a little, rinsed his mouth, spat the water, took his cape, and went back into the ring.

Because they were against Belmonte the public were for Romero. From the moment he left the barrera and went toward the bull they applauded him. Belmonte watched Romero, too, watched him always without seeming to. He paid no attention to Marcial. Marcial was the sort of thing he knew all about. He had come out of retirement to compete with Marcial, knowing it was a competition gained in advance. He had expected to compete with Marcial and the other stars of the decadence of bull-fighting, and he knew that the sincerity of his own bull-fighting would be so set off by the false æsthetics of the bull-fighters of the decadent period that he would only have to be in the ring. His return from retirement had been spoiled by Romero. Romero did always, smoothly, calmly, and beautifully, what he, Belmonte, could only bring himself to do now sometimes. The crowd felt it, even the people from Biarritz, even the American ambassador saw it, finally. It was a competition that Belmonte would not enter because it would lead only to a bad horn wound or death. Belmonte was no longer well enough. He no longer had his greatest moments in the bull-ring. He was not sure that there were any great moments. Things were not the same and now life only came in flashes. He had flashes of the old greatness with his bulls, but they were not of value because he had discounted them in advance when he had picked the bulls out for their safety, getting out of a motor and leaning on a fence, looking over at the herd on the ranch of his friend the bull-breeder. So he had two small, manageable bulls without much horns, and when he felt the greatness again coming, just a little of it through the pain that was always with him, it had been discounted and sold in advance, and it did not give him a good feeling. It was the greatness, but it did not make bull-fighting wonderful to him any more.

Pedro Romero had the greatness. He loved bull-fighting, and I think he loved the bulls, and I think he loved Brett. Everything of which he could control the locality he did in front of her all that afternoon. Never once did he look up. He made it stronger that way, and did it for himself, too, as well as for her. Because he did not look up to ask if it pleased he did it all for himself inside, and it strengthened him, and yet he did it for her, too. But he did not do it for her at any loss to himself. He gained by it all through the afternoon.

His first 'quite' was directly below us. The three matadors take the bull in turn after each charge he makes at a picador. Belmonte was the first. Marcial was the second. Then came Romero. The three of them were standing at the left of the horse. The picador, his hat down over his eyes, the shaft of his pic angling sharply toward the bull, kicked in the spurs and held them and with the reins in his left hand walked the horse forward toward the bull. The bull was watching. Seemingly he watched the white horse, but really he watched the triangular steel point of the pic. Romero, watching, saw the bull start to turn his head. He did not want to charge. Romero flicked his cape so the color caught the bull's eye. The bull charged with the reflex, charged, and found not the flash of color but a white horse, and a man leaned far over the horse, shot the steel point of the long hickory shaft into the hump of muscle on the bull's shoulder, and pulled his horse sideways as he pivoted on the pic, making a wound, enforcing the iron into the bull's shoulder, making him bleed for Belmonte.

The bull did not insist under the iron. He did not really want to get at the horse. He turned and the group broke apart and Romero was taking him out with his cape. He took him out softly and smoothly, and then stopped and, standing squarely in front of the bull, offered him the cape. The bull's tail went up and he charged, and Romero moved his arms ahead of the bull, wheeling, his feet firmed. The dampened, mud-weighted cape swung open and full as a sail fills, and Romero pivoted with it just ahead of the bull. At the end of the pass they were facing each other again. Romero smiled. The bull wanted it again, and Romero's cape filled again, this time on the other side. Each time he let the bull pass so close that the man and the bull and the cape that filled and pivoted ahead of the bull were all one sharply etched mass. It was all so slow and so controlled. It was as though he were rocking the bull to sleep. He made four veronicas like that, and finished with a half-veronica that turned his back on the bull and came away toward the applause, his hand on his hip, his cape on his arm, and the bull watching his back going away.

In his own bulls he was perfect. His first bull did not see well. After the first two passes with the cape Romero knew exactly how bad the vision was impaired. He worked accordingly. It was not brilliant bull-fighting. It was only perfect bull-fighting. The crowd wanted the bull changed. They made a great row. Nothing very fine could happen with a bull that could not see the lures, but the President would not order him replaced.

'Why don't they change him?' Brett asked.

'They've paid for him. They don't want to lose their money.'

'It's hardly fair to Romero.'

'Watch how he handles a bull that can't see the color.'

'It's the sort of thing I don't like to see.'

It was not nice to watch if you cared anything about the person who was doing it. With the bull who could not see the colors of the capes, or the scarlet flannel of the muleta, Romero had to make the bull consent with his body. He had to get so close that the bull saw his body, and would start for it, and then shift the bull's charge to the flannel and finish out the pass in the classic manner. The Biarritz crowd did not like it They thought Romero was afraid, and that was why he gave that little sidestep each time as he transferred the bull's charge from his own body to the flannel. They preferred Belmonte's imitation of himself or Marcial's imitation of Belmonte. There were three of them in the row behind us.

'What's he afraid of the bull for? The bull's so dumb he only goes after the cloth.'

'He's just a young bull-fighter. He hasn't learned it yet.'

'But I thought he was fine with the cape before.'

'Probably he's nervous now.'

Out in the centre of the ring, all alone, Romero was going on with the same thing, getting so close that the bull could see him plainly, offering the body, offering it again a little closer, the bull watching dully, then so close that the bull thought he had him, offering again and finally drawing the charge and then, just before the horns came, giving the bull the red cloth to follow with at little, almost imperceptible, jerk that so offended the critical judgment of the Biarritz bull-fight experts.

'He's going to kill now,' I said to Brett. 'The bull's still strong. He wouldn't wear himself out.'

Out in the centre of the ring Romero profiled in front of the bull, drew the sword out from the folds of the muleta, rose on his toes, and sighted along the blade. The bull charged as Romero charged. Romero's left hand dropped the muleta over the bull's muzzle to blind him, his left shoulder went forward between the horns as the sword went in, and for just an instant he and the bull were one, Romero way out over the bull, the right arm extended high up to where the hilt of the sword had gone in between the bull's shoulders. Then the figure was broken. There was a little jolt as Romero came clear, and then he was standing, one hand up, facing the bull, his shirt ripped out from under his sleeve, the white blowing in the wind, and the bull, the red sword hilt tight between his shoulders, his head going down and his legs settling.

'There he goes,' Bill said.

Romero was close enough so the bull could see him. His hand still up, he spoke to the bull. The bull gathered himself, then his head went forward and he went over slowly, then all over, suddenly, four feet in the air.

They handed the sword to Romero, and carrying it blade down, the muleta in his other hand, he walked over to in front of the President's box, bowed, straightened, and came over to the barrera and handed over the sword and muleta.

'Bad one,' said the sword-handler.

'He made me sweat,' said Romero. He wiped off his face. The sword-handler handed him the water-jug. Romero wiped his lips. It hurt him to drink out of the jug. He did not look up at us.

Marcial had a big day. They were still applauding him when Romero's last bull came in. It was the bull that had sprinted out and killed the man in the morning running.

During Romero's first bull his hurt face had been very noticeable. Everything he did showed it. All the concentration of the awkwardly delicate working with the bull that could not see well brought it out. The fight with Cohn had not touched his spirit but his face had been smashed and his body hurt. He was wiping all that out now. Each thing that he did with this bull wiped that out a little cleaner. It was a good bull, a big bull, and with horns, and it turned and recharged easily and surely. He was what Romero wanted in bulls.

When he had finished his work with the muleta and was ready to kill, the crowd made him go on. They did not want the bull killed yet, they did not want it to be over. Romero went on. It was like a course in bull-fighting. All the passes he linked up, all completed, all slow, templed and smooth. There were no tricks and no mystifications. There was no brusqueness. And each pass as it reached the summit gave you a sudden ache inside. The crowd did not want it ever to be finished.

The bull was squared on all four feet to be killed, and Romero killed directly below us. He killed not as he had been forced to by the last bull, but as he wanted to. He profiled directly in front of the bull, drew the sword out of the folds of the muleta and sighted along the blade. The bull watched him. Romero spoke to the bull and tapped one of his feet. The bull charged and Romero waited for the charge, the muleta held low, sighting along the blade, his feet firm. Then without taking a step forward, he became one with the bull, the sword was in high between the shoulders, the bull had followed the low-swung flannel, that disappeared as Romero lurched clear to the left, and it was over. The bull tried to go forward, his legs commenced to settle, he swung from side to side, hesitated, then went down on his knees, and Romero's older brother leaned forward behind him and drove a short knife into the bull's neck at the base of the horns. The first time he missed. He drove the knife in again, and the bull went over, twitching and rigid. Romero's brother, holding the bull's horn in one hand, the knife in the other, looked up at the President's box. Handkerchiefs were waving all over the bull-ring. The President looked down from the box and waved his handkerchief. The brother cut the notched black ear from the dead bull and trotted over with it to Romero. The bull lay heavy and black on the sand, his tongue out. Boys were running toward him from all parts of the arena, making a little circle around him. They were starting to dance around the bull.

Romero took the ear from his brother and held it up toward the President. The President bowed and Romero, running to get ahead of the crowd, came toward us. He leaned up against the barrera and gave the ear to Brett. He nodded his head and smiled. The crowd were all about him. Brett held down the cape.

'You liked it?' Romero called.

Brett did not say anything. They looked at each other and smiled. Brett had the ear in her hand.

'Don't get bloody,' Romero said, and grinned. The crowd wanted him. Several boys shouted at Brett. The crowd was the boys, the dancers, and the drunks. Romero turned and tried to get through the crowd. They were all around him trying to lift him and put him on their shoulders. He fought and twisted away, and started running, in the midst of them, toward the exit. He did not want to be carried on people's shoulders. But they held him and lifted him. It was uncomfortable and his legs were spraddled and his body was very sore. They were lifting him and all running toward the gate. He had his hand on somebody's shoulder. He looked around at us apologetically. The crowd, running, went out the gate with him.

We all three went back to the hotel. Brett went up-stairs. Bill and I sat in the down-stairs dining-room and ate some hard-boiled eggs and drank several bottles of beer. Belmonte came down in his street clothes with his manager and two other men. They sat at the next table and ate. Belmonte ate very little. They were leaving on the seven o'clock train for Barcelona. Belmonte wore a blue-striped shirt and a dark suit, and ate soft-boiled eggs. The others ate a big meal. Belmonte did not talk. He only answered questions.

Bill was tired after the bull-fight. So was I. We both took a bull-fight very hard. We sat and ate the eggs and I watched Belmonte and the people at his table. The men with him were tough-looking and businesslike.

'Come on over to the café,' Bill said. 'I want an absinthe.'

It was the last day of the fiesta. Outside it was beginning to be cloudy again. The square was full of people and the fireworks experts were making up their set pieces for the night and covering them over with beech branches. Boys were watching. We passed stands of rockets with long bamboo stems. Outside the café there was a great crowd. The music and the dancing were going on. The giants and the dwarfs were passing.

'Where's Edna?' I asked Bill.

'I don't know.'

We watched the beginning of the evening of the last night of the fiesta. The absinthe made everything seem better. I drank it without sugar in the dripping glass, and it was pleasantly bitter.

'I feel sorry about Cohn,' Bill said. 'He had an awful time.'

'Oh, to hell with Cohn,' I said.

'Where do you suppose he went?'

'Up to Paris.'

'What do you suppose he'll do?'

'Oh, to hell with him.'

'What do you suppose he'll do?'

'Pick up with his old girl, probably.'

'Who was his old girl?'

'Somebody named Frances.'

We had another absinthe.

'When do you go back?' I asked.

'To-morrow.'

After a little while Bill said: 'Well, it was a swell fiesta.'

'Yes,' I said; 'something doing all the time.'

'You wouldn't believe it. It's like a wonderful nightmare.'

'Sure,' I said. 'I'd believe anything. Including nightmares.'

'What's the matter? Feel low?'

'Low as hell.'

'Have another absinthe. Here, waiter! Another absinthe for this señor.'

'I feel like hell,' I said.

'Drink that,' said Bill. 'Drink it slow.'

It was beginning to get dark. The fiesta was going on. I began to feel drunk but I did not feel any better.

'How do you feel?'

'I feel like hell.'

'Have another?'

'It won't do any good.'

'Try it. You can't tell; maybe this is the one that gets it. Hey, waiter! Another absinthe for this señor!'

I poured the water directly into it and stirred it instead of letting it drip. Bill put in a lump of ice. I stirred the ice around with a spoon in the brownish, cloudy mixture.

'How is it?'

'Fine.'

'Don't drink it fast that way. It will make you sick.'

I set down the glass. I had not meant to drink it fast.

'I feel tight.'

'You ought to.'

'That's what you wanted, wasn't it?'

'Sure. Get tight. Get over your damn depression.'

'Well, I'm tight. Is that what you want?'

'Sit down.'

'I won't sit down,' I said. 'I'm going over to the hotel.'

I was very drunk. I was drunker than I ever remembered having been. At the hotel I went up-stairs. Brett's door was open. I put my head in the room. Mike was sitting on the bed. He waved a bottle.

'Jake,' he said. 'Come in, Jake.'

I went in and sat down. The room was unstable unless I looked at some fixed point.

'Brett, you know. She's gone off with the bull-fighter chap.'

'No.'

'Yes. She looked for you to say good-bye. They went on the seven o'clock train.'

'Did they?'

'Bad thing to do,' Mike said. 'She shouldn't have done it.'

'No.'

'Have a drink? Wait while I ring for some beer.'

'I'm drunk,' I said. 'I'm going in and lie down.'

'Are you blind? I was blind myself.'

'Yes,' I said, 'I'm blind.'

'Well, bung-o,' Mike said. 'Get some sleep, old Jake.'

I went out the door and into my own room and lay on the bed. The bed went sailing off and I sat up in bed and looked at the wall to make it stop. Outside in the square the fiesta was going on. It did not mean anything. Later Bill and Mike came in to get me to go down and eat with them. I pretended to be asleep.

'He's asleep. Better let him alone.'

'He's blind as a tick,' Mike said. They went out.

I got up and went to the balcony and looked out at the dancing in the square. The world was not wheeling any more. It was just very clear and bright, and inclined to blur at the edges. I washed, brushed my hair. I looked strange to myself in the glass, and went down-stairs to the dining-room.

'Here he is!' said Bill. 'Good old Jake! I knew you wouldn't pass out.'

'Hello, you old drunk,' Mike said.

'I got hungry and woke up.'

'Eat some soup,' Bill said.

The three of us sat at the table, and it seemed as though about six people were missing.

BOOK THREE

19

In the morning it was all over. The fiesta was finished. I woke about nine o'clock, had a bath, dressed, and went down-stairs. The square was empty and there were no people on the streets. A few children were picking up rocket-sticks in the square. The cafés were just opening and the waiters were carrying out the comfortable white wicker chairs and arranging them around the marble-topped tables in the shade of the arcade. They were sweeping the streets and sprinkling them with a hose.

I sat in one of the wicker chairs and leaned back comfortably. The waiter was in no hurry to come. The white-paper announcements of the unloading of the bulls and the big schedules of special trains were still up on the pillars of the arcade. A waiter wearing a blue apron came out with a bucket of water and a cloth, and commenced to tear down the notices, pulling the paper off in strips and washing and rubbing away the paper that stuck to the stone. The fiesta was over.

I drank a coffee and after a while Bill came over. I watched him come walking across the square. He sat down at the table and ordered a coffee.

'Well,' he said, 'it's all over.'

'Yes,' I said. 'When do you go?'

'I don't know. We better get a car, I think. Aren't you going back to Paris?'

'No. I can stay away another week. I think I'll go to San Sebastian.'

'I want to get back.'

'What's Mike going to do?'

'He's going to Saint Jean de Luz.'

'Let's get a car and all go as far as Bayonne. You can get the train up from there to-night.'

'Good. Let's go after lunch.'

'All right. I'll get the car.'

We had lunch and paid the bill. Montoya did not come near us. One of the maids brought the bill. The car was outside. The chauffeur piled and strapped the bags on top of the car and put them in beside him in the front seat and we got in. The car went out of the square, along through the side streets, out under the trees and down the hill and away from Pamplona. It did not seem like a very long ride. Mike had a bottle of Fundador. I only took a couple of drinks. We came over the mountains and out of Spain and down the white roads and through the overfoliaged, wet, green, Basque country, and finally into Bayonne. We left Bill's baggage at the station, and he bought a ticket to Paris. His train left at seven-ten. We came out of the station. The car was standing out in front.

'What shall we do about the car?' Bill asked.

'Oh, bother the car,' Mike said. 'Let's just keep the car with us.'

'All right,' Bill said. 'Where shall we go?'

'Let's go to Biarritz and have a drink.'

'Old Mike the spender,' Bill said.

We drove in to Biarritz and left the car outside a very Ritz place. We went into the bar and sat on high stools and drank a whiskey and soda.

'That drink's mine,' Mike said.

'Let's roll for it.'

So we rolled poker dice out of a deep leather dice-cup. Bill was out first roll. Mike lost to me and handed the bartender a hundred-franc note. The whiskeys were twelve francs apiece. We had another round and Mike lost again. Each time he gave the bartender a good tip. In a room off the bar there was a good jazz band playing. It was a pleasant bar. We had another round. I went out on the first roll with four kings. Bill and Mike rolled. Mike won the first roll with four jacks. Bill won the second. On the final roll Mike had three kings and let them stay. He handed the dice-cup to Bill. Bill rattled them and rolled, and there were three kings, an ace, and a queen.

'It's yours, Mike,' Bill said. 'Old Mike, the gambler.'

'I'm so sorry,' Mike said. 'I can't get it.'

'What's the matter?'

'I've no money,' Mike said. 'I'm stony. I've just twenty francs. Here, take twenty francs.'

Bill's face sort of changed.

'I just had enough to pay Montoya. Damned lucky to have it, too.'

'I'll cash you a check,' Bill said.

'That's damned nice of you, but you see I can't write checks.'

'What are you going to do for money?'

'Oh, some will come through. I've two weeks allowance should be here. I can live on tick at this pub in Saint Jean.'

'What do you want to do about the car?' Bill asked me. 'Do you want to keep it on?'

'It doesn't make any difference. Seems sort of idiotic.'

'Come on, let's have another drink,' Mike said.

'Fine. This one is on me,' Bill said. 'Has Brett any money?' He turned to Mike.

'I shouldn't think so. She put up most of what I gave to old Montoya.'

'She hasn't any money with her?' I asked.

'I shouldn't think so. She never has any money. She gets five hundred quid a year and pays three hundred and fifty of it in interest to Jews.'

'I suppose they get it at the source,' said Bill.

'Quite. They're not really Jews. We just call them Jews. They're Scotsmen, I believe.'

'Hasn't she any at all with her?' I asked.

'I hardly think so. She gave it all to me when she left.'

'Well,' Bill said, 'we might as well have another drink.'

'Damned good idea,' Mike said. 'One never gets anywhere by discussing finances.'

'No,' said Bill. Bill and I rolled for the next two rounds. Bill lost and paid. We went out to the car.

'Anywhere you'd like to go, Mike?' Bill asked.

'Let's take a drive. It might do my credit good. Let's drive about a little.'

'Fine. I'd like to see the coast. Let's drive down toward Hendaye.'

'I haven't any credit along the coast.'

'You can't ever tell,' said Bill.

We drove out along the coast road. There was the green of the headlands, the white, red-roofed villas, patches of forest, and the ocean very blue with the tide out and the water curling far out along the beach. We drove through Saint Jean de Luz and passed through villages farther down the coast. Back of the rolling country we were going through we saw the mountains we had come over from Pamplona. The road went on ahead. Bill looked at his watch. It was time for us to go back. He knocked on the glass and told the driver to turn around. The driver backed the car out into the grass to turn it. In back of us were the woods, below a stretch of meadow, then the sea.

At the hotel where Mike was going to stay in Saint Jean we stopped the car and he got out. The chauffeur carried in his bags. Mike stood by the side of the car.

'Good-bye, you chaps,' Mike said. 'It was a damned fine fiesta.'

'So long, Mike,' Bill said.

'I'll see you around,' I said.

'Don't worry about money,' Mike said. 'You can pay for the car, Jake, and I'll send you my share.'

'So long, Mike.'

'So long, you chaps. You've been damned nice.'

We all shook hands. We waved from the car to Mike. He stood in the road watching. We got to Bayonne just before the train left. A porter carried Bill's bags in from the consigne. I went as far as the inner gate to the tracks.

'So long, fella,' Bill said.

'So long, kid!'

'It was swell. I've had a swell time.'

'Will you be in Paris?'

'No, I have to sail on the 17th. So long, fella!'

'So long, old kid!'

He went in through the gate to the train. The porter went ahead with the bags. I watched the train pull out. Bill was at one of the windows. The window passed, the rest of the train passed, and the tracks were empty. I went outside to the car.

'How much do we owe you?' I asked the driver. The price to Bayonne had been fixed at a hundred and fifty pesetas.

'Two hundred pesetas.'

'How much more will it be if you drive me to San Sebastian on your way back?'

'Fifty pesetas.'

'Don't kid me.'

'Thirty-five pesetas.'

'It's not worth it,' I said. 'Drive me to the Hotel Panier Fleuri.'

At the hotel I paid the driver and gave him a tip. The car was powdered with dust. I rubbed the rod-case through the dust. It seemed the last thing that connected me with Spain and the fiesta. The driver put the car in gear and went down the street. I watched it turn off to take the road to Spain. I went into the hotel and they gave me a room. It was the same room I had slept in when Bill and Cohn and I were in Bayonne. That seemed a very long time ago. I washed, changed my shirt, and went out in the town.

At a newspaper kiosque I bought a copy of the New York *Herald* and sat in a café to read it. It felt strange to be in France again. There was a safe, suburban feeling. I wished I had gone up to Paris with Bill, except that Paris would have meant more fiesta-ing. I was through with fiestas for a while. It would be quiet in San Sebastian. The season does not open there until August. I could get a good hotel room and read and swim. There was a fine beach there. There were wonderful trees along the promenade above the beach, and there were many children sent down with their nurses before the season opened. In the evening there would be band concerts under the trees across from the Café Marinas. I could sit in the Marinas and listen.

'How does one eat inside?' I asked the waiter. Inside the café was a restaurant.

'Well. Very well. One eats very well.'

'Good.'

I went in and ate dinner. It was a big meal for France but it seemed very carefully apportioned after Spain. I drank a bottle of wine for company. It was a Château Margaux. It was pleasant to be drinking slowly and to be tasting the wine and to be drinking alone. A bottle of wine was good company. Afterward I had coffee. The waiter recommended a Basque liqueur called Izzarra. He brought in the bottle and poured a liqueur-glass full. He said Izzarra was made of the flowers of the Pyrenees. The veritable flowers of the Pyrenees. It looked like hair-oil and smelled like Italian *strega*. I told him to take the flowers of the Pyrenees away and bring me a *vieux marc*. The *marc* was good. I had a second *marc* after the coffee.

The waiter seemed a little offended about the flowers of the Pyrenees, so I overtipped him. That made him happy. It felt comfortable to be in a country where it is so simple to make people happy. You can never tell whether a Spanish waiter will thank you. Everything is on such a clear financial basis in France. It is the simplest country to live in. No one makes things complicated by becoming your friend for any obscure reason. If you want people to like you you have only to spend a little money. I spent a little money and the waiter liked me. He appreciated my valuable qualities. He would be glad to see me back. I would dine there again some time and he would be glad to see me, and would want me at his table. It would be a sincere liking because it would have a sound basis. I was back in France.

Next morning I tipped every one a little too much at the hotel to make more friends, and left on the morning train for San Sebastian. At the station I did not tip the porter more than I should because I did not think I would ever see him again. I only wanted a few good French friends in Bayonne to make me welcome in case I should come back there again. I knew that if they remembered me their friendship would be loyal.

At Irun we had to change trains and show passports. I hated to leave France. Life was so simple in France. I felt I was a fool to be going back into Spain. In Spain you could not tell about anything. I felt like a fool to be going back into it, but I stood in line with my passport, opened my bags for the customs, bought a ticket, went through a gate, climbed onto the train, and after forty minutes and eight tunnels I was at San Sebastian.

Even on a hot day San Sebastian has a certain early-morning quality. The trees seem as though their leaves were never quite dry. The streets feel as though they had just been sprinkled. It is always cool and shady on certain streets on the hottest day. I went to a hotel in the town where I had stopped before, and they gave me a room with a balcony that opened out above the roofs of the town. There was a green mountainside beyond the roofs.

I unpacked my bags and stacked my books on the table beside the head of the bed, put out my shaving things, hung up some clothes in the big armoire, and made up a bundle for the laundry. Then I took a shower in the bathroom and went down to lunch. Spain had not changed to summer-time, so I was early. I set my watch again. I had recovered an hour by coming to San Sebastian.

As I went into the dining-room the concierge brought me a police bulletin to fill out. I signed it and asked him for two telegraph forms, and wrote a message to the Hotel Montoya, telling them to forward all mail and telegrams for me to this address. I calculated how many days I would be in San Sebastian and then wrote out a wire to the office asking them to hold mail, but forward all wires for me to San Sebastian for six days. Then I went in and had lunch.

After lunch I went up to my room, read a while, and went to sleep. When I woke it was half past four. I found my swimming-suit, wrapped it with a comb in a towel, and went down-stairs and walked up the street to the Concha. The tide was about half-way out. The beach was smooth and firm, and the sand yellow. I went into a bathing-cabin, undressed, put on my suit, and walked across the smooth sand to the sea. The sand was warm under bare feet. There were quite a few people in the water and on the beach. Out beyond where the headlands of the Concha almost met to form the harbor there was a white line of breakers and the open sea. Although the tide was going out, there were a few slow rollers. They came in like undulations in the water, gathered weight of water, and then broke smoothly on the warm sand. I waded out. The water was cold. As a roller came I dove, swam out under water, and came to the surface with all the chill gone. I swam out to the raft, pulled myself up, and lay on the hot planks. A boy and girl were at the other end. The girl had undone the top strap of her bathing-suit and was browning her back. The boy lay face downward on the raft and talked to her. She laughed at things he said, and turned her brown back in the sun. I lay on the raft in the sun until I was dry. Then I tried several dives. I dove deep once, swimming down to the bottom. I swam with my eyes open and it was green and dark. The raft made a dark shadow. I came out of water beside the raft, pulled up, dove once more, holding it for length, and then swam ashore. I lay on the beach until I was dry, then went into the bathing-cabin, took off my suit, sloshed myself with fresh water, and rubbed dry.

 I walked around the harbor under the trees to the casino, and then up one of the cool streets to the Café Marinas. There was an orchestra playing inside the café and I sat out on the terrace and enjoyed the fresh coolness in the hot day, and had a glass of lemon-juice and shaved ice and then a long whiskey and soda. I sat in front of the Marinas for a long time and read and watched the people, and listened to the music.

 Later when it began to get dark, I walked around the harbor and out along the promenade, and finally back to the hotel for supper. There was a bicycle-race on, the Tour du Pays Basque, and the riders were stopping that night in San Sebastian. In the dining-room, at one side, there was a long table of bicycle-riders, eating with their trainers and managers. They were all French and Belgians, and paid close attention to their meal, but they were having a good time. At the head of the table were two good-looking French girls, with much Rue du Faubourg Montmartre chic. I could not make out whom they belonged to. They all spoke in slang at the long table and there were many private jokes and some jokes at the far end that were not repeated when the girls asked to hear them. The next morning at five o'clock the race resumed with the last lap, San Sebastian-Bilbao. The bicycle-riders drank much wine, and were burned and browned by the sun. They did not take the race seriously except among themselves. They had raced among themselves so often that it did not make much difference who won. Especially in a foreign country. The money could be arranged.

 The man who had a matter of two minutes lead in the race had an attack of boils, which were very painful. He sat on the small of his back. His neck was very red and the blond hairs were sunburned. The other riders joked him about his boils. He tapped on the table with his fork.

 'Listen,' he said, 'to-morrow my nose is so tight on the handle-bars that the only thing touches those boils is a lovely breeze.'

One of the girls looked at him down the table, and he grinned and turned red. The Spaniards, they said, did not know how to pedal.

I had coffee out on the terrasse with the team manager of one of the big bicycle manufacturers. He said it had been a very pleasant race, and would have been worth watching if Bottechia had not abandoned it at Pamplona. The dust had been bad, but in Spain the roads were better than in France. Bicycle road-racing was the only sport in the world, he said. Had I ever followed the Tour de France? Only in the papers. The Tour de France was the greatest sporting event in the world. Following and organizing the road races had made him know France. Few people know France. All spring and all summer and all fall he spent on the road with bicycle road-racers. Look at the number of motor-cars now that followed the riders from town to town in a road race. It was a rich country and more *sportif* every year. It would be the most *sportif* country in the world. It was bicycle road-racing did it. That and football. He knew France. *La France Sportive*. He knew road-racing. We had a cognac. After all, though, it wasn't bad to get back to Paris. There is only one Paname. In all the world, that is. Paris is the town the most *sportif* in the world. Did I know the *Chope de Negre*? Did I not. I would see him there some time. I certainly would. We would drink another *fine* together. We certainly would. They started at six o'clock less a quarter in the morning. Would I be up for the depart? I would certainly try to. Would I like him to call me? It was very interesting. I would leave a call at the desk. He would not mind calling me. I could not let him take the trouble. I would leave a call at the desk. We said good-bye until the next morning.

In the morning when I awoke the bicycle-riders and their following cars had been on the road for three hours. I had coffee and the papers in bed and then dressed and took my bathing-suit down to the beach. Everything was fresh and cool and damp in the early morning. Nurses in uniform and in peasant costume walked under the trees with children. The Spanish children were beautiful. Some bootblacks sat together under a tree talking to a soldier. The soldier had only one arm. The tide was in and there was a good breeze and a surf on the beach.

I undressed in one of the bath-cabins, crossed the narrow line of beach and went into the water. I swam out, trying to swim through the rollers, but having to dive sometimes. Then in the quiet water I turned and floated. Floating I saw only the sky, and felt the drop and lift of the swells. I swam back to the surf and coasted in, face down, on a big roller, then turned and swam, trying to keep in the trough and not have a wave break over me. It made me tired, swimming in the trough, and I turned and swam out to the raft. The water was buoyant and cold. It felt as though you could never sink. I swam slowly, it seemed like a long swim with the high tide, and then pulled up on the raft and sat, dripping, on the boards that were becoming hot in the sun. I looked around at the bay, the old town, the casino, the line of trees along the promenade, and the big hotels with their white porches and gold-lettered names. Off on the right, almost closing the harbor, was a green hill with a castle. The raft rocked with the motion of the water. On the other side of the narrow gap that led into the open sea was another high headland. I thought I would like to swim across the bay but I was afraid of cramp.

I sat in the sun and watched the bathers on the beach. They looked very small. After a while I stood up, gripped with my toes on the edge of the raft as it tipped with my weight, and dove cleanly and deeply, to come up through the lightening water, blew the salt water out of my head, and swam slowly and steadily in to shore.

After I was dressed and had paid for the bath-cabin, I walked back to the hotel. The bicycle-racers had left several copies of *L'Auto* around, and I gathered them up in the reading-room and took them out and sat in an easy chair in the sun to read about and catch up on French sporting life. While I was sitting there the concierge came out with a blue envelope in his hand.

'A telegram for you, sir.'

I poked my finger along under the fold that was fastened down, spread it open, and read it. It had been forwarded from Paris:

> COULD YOU COME HOTEL MONTANA MADRID
> AM RATHER IN TROUBLE BRETT.

I tipped the concierge and read the message again. A postman was coming along the sidewalk. He turned in the hotel. He had a big moustache and looked very military. He came out of the hotel again. The concierge was just behind him.

'Here's another telegram for you, sir.'

'Thank you,' I said.

I opened it. It was forwarded from Pamplona.

> COULD YOU COME HOTEL MONTANA MADRID
> AM RATHER IN TROUBLE BRETT.

The concierge stood there waiting for another tip, probably.

'What time is there a train for Madrid?'

'It left at nine this morning. There is a slow train at eleven, and the Sud Express at ten to-night.'

'Get me a berth on the Sud Express. Do you want the money now?'

'Just as you wish,' he said. 'I will have it put on the bill.'

'Do that.'

Well, that meant San Sebastian all shot to hell. I suppose, vaguely, I had expected something of the sort. I saw the concierge standing in the doorway.

'Bring me a telegram form, please.'

He brought it and I took out my fountain-pen and printed:

> LADY ASHLEY HOTEL MONTANA MADRID
> ARRIVING SUD EXPRESS TOMORROW LOVE JAKE.

That seemed to handle it. That was it. Send a girl off with one man. Introduce her to another to go off with him. Now go and bring her back. And sign the wire with love. That was it all right. I went in to lunch.

I did not sleep much that night on the Sud Express. In the morning I had breakfast in the dining-car and watched the rock and pine country between Avila and Escorial. I saw the Escorial out of the window, gray and long and cold in the sun, and did not give a damn about it. I saw Madrid come up over the plain, a compact white sky-line on the top of a little cliff away off across the sun-hardened country.

The Norte station in Madrid is the end of the line. All trains finish there. They don't go on anywhere. Outside were cabs and taxis and a line of hotel runners. It was like a country town. I took a taxi and we climbed up through the gardens, by the empty palace and the unfinished church on the edge of the cliff, and on up until we were in the high, hot, modern town. The taxi coasted down a smooth street to the Puerta del Sol, and then through the traffic and out into the Carrera San Jeronimo. All the shops had their awnings down against the heat. The windows on the sunny side of the street were shuttered. The taxi stopped at the curb. I saw the sign HOTEL MONTANA on the second floor. The taxi-driver carried the bags in and left them by the elevator. I could not make the elevator work, so I walked up. On the second floor up was a cut brass sign: HOTEL MONTANA. I rang and no one came to the door. I rang again and a maid with a sullen face opened the door.

'Is Lady Ashley here?' I asked.

She looked at me dully.

'Is an Englishwoman here?'

She turned and called some one inside. A very fat woman came to the door. Her hair was gray and stiffly oiled in scallops around her face. She was short and commanding.

'Muy buenos,' I said. 'Is there an Englishwoman here? I would like to see this English lady.'

'Muy buenos. Yes, there is a female English. Certainly you can see her if she wishes to see you.'

'She wishes to see me.'

'The chica will ask her.'

'It is very hot.'

'It is very hot in the summer in Madrid.'

'And how cold in winter.'

'Yes, it is very cold in winter.'

Did I want to stay myself in person in the Hotel Montana?

Of that as yet I was undecided, but it would give me pleasure if my bags were brought up from the ground floor in order that they might not be stolen. Nothing was ever stolen in the Hotel Montana. In other fondas, yes. Not here. No. The personages of this establishment were rigidly selected. I was happy to hear it. Nevertheless I would welcome the upbringal of my bags.

The maid came in and said that the female English wanted to see the male English now, at once.

'Good,' I said. 'You see. It is as I said.'

'Clearly.'

I followed the maid's back down a long, dark corridor. At the end she knocked on a door.

'Hello,' said Brett. 'Is it you, Jake?'

'It's me.'

'Come in. Come in.'

I opened the door. The maid closed it after me. Brett was in bed. She had just been brushing her hair and held the brush in her hand. The room was in that disorder produced only by those who have always had servants.

'Darling!' Brett said.

I went over to the bed and put my arms around her. She kissed me, and while she kissed me I could feel she was thinking of something else. She was trembling in my arms. She felt very small.

'Darling! I've had such a hell of a time.'

'Tell me about it.'

'Nothing to tell. He only left yesterday. I made him go.'

'Why didn't you keep him?'

'I don't know. It isn't the sort of thing one does. I don't think I hurt him any.'

'You were probably damn good for him.'

'He shouldn't be living with any one. I realized that right away.'

'No.'

'Oh, hell!' she said, 'let's not talk about it. Let's never talk about it.'

'All right.'

'It was rather a knock his being ashamed of me. He was ashamed of me for a while, you know.'

'No.'

'Oh, yes. They ragged him about me at the café, I guess. He wanted me to grow my hair out. Me, with long hair. I'd look so like hell.'

'It's funny.'

'He said it would make me more womanly. I'd look a fright.'

'What happened?'

'Oh, he got over that. He wasn't ashamed of me long.'

'What was it about being in trouble?'

'I didn't know whether I could make him go, and I didn't have a sou to go away and leave him. He tried to give me a lot of money, you know. I told him I had scads of it. He knew that was a lie. I couldn't take his money, you know.'

'No.'

'Oh, let's not talk about it. There were some funny things, though. Do give me a cigarette.'

I lit the cigarette.

'He learned his English as a waiter in Gib.'

'Yes.'

'He wanted to marry me, finally.'

'Really?'

'Of course. I can't even marry Mike.'

'Maybe he thought that would make him Lord Ashley.'

'No. It wasn't that. He really wanted to marry me. So I couldn't go away from him, he said. He wanted to make it sure I could never go away from him. After I'd gotten more womanly, of course.'

'You ought to feel set up.'

'I do. I'm all right again. He's wiped out that damned Cohn.'

'Good.'

'You know I'd have lived with him if I hadn't seen it was bad for him. We got along damned well.'

'Outside of your personal appearance.'

'Oh, he'd have gotten used to that.'

She put out the cigarette.

'I'm thirty-four, you know. I'm not going to be one of these bitches that ruins children.'

'No.'

'I'm not going to be that way. I feel rather good, you know. I feel rather set up.'

'Good.'

She looked away. I thought she was looking for another cigarette. Then I saw she was crying. I could feel her crying. Shaking and crying. She wouldn't look up. I put my arms around her.

'Don't let's ever talk about it. Please don't let's ever talk about it.'

'Dear Brett.'

'I'm going back to Mike.' I could feel her crying as I held her close. 'He's so damned nice and he's so awful. He's my sort of thing.'

She would not look up. I stroked her hair. I could feel her shaking.

'I won't be one of those bitches,' she said. 'But, oh, Jake, please let's never talk about it.'

We left the Hotel Montana. The woman who ran the hotel would not let me pay the bill. The bill had been paid.

'Oh, well. Let it go,' Brett said. 'It doesn't matter now.'

We rode in a taxi down to the Palace Hotel, left the bags, arranged for berths on the Sud Express for the night, and went into the bar of the hotel for a cocktail. We sat on high stools at the bar while the barman shook the Martinis in a large nickelled shaker.

'It's funny what a wonderful gentility you get in the bar of a big hotel,' I said.

'Barmen and jockeys are the only people who are polite any more.'

'No matter how vulgar a hotel is, the bar is always nice.'

'It's odd.'

'Bartenders have always been fine.'

'You know,' Brett said, 'it's quite true. He is only nineteen. Isn't it amazing?'

We touched the two glasses as they stood side by side on the bar. They were coldly beaded. Outside the curtained window was the summer heat of Madrid.

'I like an olive in a Martini,' I said to the barman.

'Right you are, sir. There you are.'

'Thanks.'

'I should have asked, you know.'

The barman went far enough up the bar so that he would not hear our conversation. Brett had sipped from the Martini as it stood, on the wood. Then she picked it up. Her hand was steady enough to lift it after that first sip.

'It's good. Isn't it a nice bar?'

'They're all nice bars.'

'You know I didn't believe it at first. He was born in 1905. I was in school in Paris, then. Think of that.'

'Anything you want me to think about it?'

'Don't be an ass. *Would* you buy a lady a drink?'

'We'll have two more Martinis.'

'As they were before, sir?'

'They were very good.' Brett smiled at him.

'Thank you, ma'am.'

'Well, bung-o,' Brett said.

'Bung-o!'

'You know,' Brett said, 'he'd only been with two women before. He never cared about anything but bull-fighting.'

'He's got plenty of time.'

'I don't know. He thinks it was me. Not the show in general.'

'Well, it was you.'

'Yes. It was me.'

'I thought you weren't going to ever talk about it.'

'How can I help it?'

'You'll lose it if you talk about it.'

'I just talk around it. You know I feel rather damned good, Jake.'

'You should.'

'You know it makes one feel rather good deciding not to be a bitch.'

'Yes.'

'It's sort of what we have instead of God.'

'Some people have God,' I said. 'Quite a lot.'

'He never worked very well with me.'

'Should we have another Martini?'

The barman shook up two more Martinis and poured them out into fresh glasses.

'Where will we have lunch?' I asked Brett. The bar was cool. You could feel the heat outside through the window.

'Here?' asked Brett.

'It's rotten here in the hotel. Do you know a place called Botin's?' I asked the barman.

'Yes, sir. Would you like to have me write out the address?'

'Thank you.'

We lunched up-stairs at Botin's. It is one of the best restaurants in the world. We had roast young suckling pig and drank *rioja alta*. Brett did not eat much. She never ate much. I ate a very big meal and drank three bottles of *rioja alta*.

'How do you feel, Jake?' Brett asked. 'My God! what a meal you've eaten.'

'I feel fine. Do you want a dessert?'

'Lord, no.'

Brett was smoking.

'You like to eat, don't you?' she said.

'Yes.' I said. 'I like to do a lot of things.'

'What do you like to do?'

'Oh,' I said, 'I like to do a lot of things. Don't you want a dessert?'

'You asked me that once,' Brett said.

'Yes,' I said. 'So I did. Let's have another bottle of *rioja alta*.'

'It's very good.'

'You haven't drunk much of it,' I said.

'I have. You haven't seen.'

'Let's get two bottles,' I said. The bottles came. I poured a little in my glass, then a glass for Brett, then filled my glass. We touched glasses.

'Bung-o!' Brett said. I drank my glass and poured out another. Brett put her hand on my arm.

'Don't get drunk, Jake,' she said. 'You don't have to.'

'How do you know?'

'Don't,' she said. 'You'll be all right.'

'I'm not getting drunk,' I said. 'I'm just drinking a little wine. I like to drink wine.'

'Don't get drunk,' she said. 'Jake, don't get drunk.'

'Want to go for a ride?' I said. 'Want to ride through the town?'

'Right,' Brett said. 'I haven't seen Madrid. I should see Madrid.'

'I'll finish this,' I said.

Down-stairs we came out through the first-floor dining-room to the street. A waiter went for a taxi. It was hot and bright. Up the street was a little square with trees and grass where there were taxis parked. A taxi came up the street, the waiter hanging out at the side. I tipped him and told the driver where to drive, and got in beside Brett. The driver started up the street. I settled back. Brett moved close to me. We sat close against each other. I put my arm around her and she rested against me comfortably. It was very hot and bright, and the houses looked sharply white. We turned out onto the Gran Via.

'Oh, Jake,' Brett said, 'we could have had such a damned good time together.'

Ahead was a mounted policeman in khaki directing traffic. He raised his baton. The car slowed suddenly pressing Brett against me.

'Yes,' I said. 'Isn't it pretty to think so?'

MEN WITHOUT WOMEN

THE UNDEFEATED

Manuel Garcia climbed the stairs to Don Miguel Retana's office. He set down his suitcase and knocked on the door. There was no answer.

Manuel, standing in the hallway, felt there was someone in the room. He felt it through the door.

'Retana,' he said, listening. There was no answer.

He's there, all right, Manuel thought.

'Retana,' he said and banged the door.

'Who's there?' said someone in the office. 'Me, Manolo,' Manuel said.

'What do you want?' asked the voice. 'I want to work,' Manuel said.

Something in the door clicked several times and it swung open. Manuel went in, carrying his suitcase.

A little man sat behind a desk at the far side of the room. Over his head was a bull's head, stuffed by a Madrid taxidermist; on the walls were framed photographs and bullfight posters.

The little man sat looking at Manuel.

'I thought they'd killed you,' he said.

Manuel knocked with his knuckles on the desk. The little man sat looking at him across the desk.

'How many corridas you had this year?' Retana asked.

'One,' he answered.

'Just that one?' the little man asked. 'That's all.'

'I read about it in the papers,' Retana said. He leaned back in the chair and looked at Manuel.

Manuel looked up at the stuffed bull. He had seen it often before. He felt a certain family interest in it. It had killed his brother, the promising one, about nine years ago. Manuel remembered the day. There was a brass plate on the oak shield the bull's head was mounted on. Manuel could not read it, but he imagined it was in memory of his brother. Well, he had been a good kid.

The plate said: 'The Bull "Mariposa" of the Duke of Veragua, which accepted 9 varas for 7 caballos, and caused the death of Antonio Garcia, Novillero, April 27, 1909.'

Retana saw him looking at the stuffed bull's head.

'The lot the Duke sent me for Sunday will make a scandal,' he said. 'They're all bad in the legs. What do they say about them at the Café?'

'I don't know,' Manuel said. 'I just got in.'

'Yes,' Retana said. 'You still have your bag.'

He looked at Manuel, leaning back behind the big desk.

'Sit down,' he said. 'Take off your cap.'

Manuel sat down; his cap off, his face was changed. He looked pale, and his coleta pinned forward on his head, so that it would not show under the cap, gave him a strange look.

'You don't look well,' Retana said.

'I just got out of the hospital,' Manuel said.

'I heard they'd cut your leg off,' Retana said.

'No,' said Manuel. 'It got all right.'

Retana leaned forward across the desk and pushed a wooden box of cigarettes toward Manuel.

'Have a cigarette,' he said. 'Thanks.'

Manuel lit it.

'Smoke?' he said, offering the match to Retana.

'No,' Retana waved his hand. 'I never smoke.'

Retana watched him smoking.

'Why don't you get a job and go to work?' he said.

'I don't want to work,' Manuel said. 'I am a bullfighter.'

'There aren't any bullfighters any more,' Retana said. 'I'm a bullfighter,' Manuel said.

'Yes, while you're in there,' Retana said.

Manuel laughed.

Retana sat, saying nothing and looking at Manuel.

'I'll put you in a nocturnal if you want,' Retana offered.

'When?' Manuel asked.

'Tomorrow night.'

'I don't like to substitute for anybody,' Manuel said. That was the way they all got killed. That was the way Salvador got killed. He tapped with his knuckles on the table.

'It's all I've got,' Retana said.

'Why don't you put me on next week?' Manuel suggested.

'You wouldn't draw,' Retana said. 'All they want is Litri and Rubito and La Torre. Those kids are good.'

'They'd come to see me get it,' Manuel said, hopefully.

'No, they wouldn't. They don't know who you are any more.'

'I've got a lot of stuff,' Manuel said.

'I'm offering to put you on tomorrow night,' Retana said. 'You can work with young Hernandez and kill two novillos after the Charlots.'

'Whose novillos?' Manuel asked.

'I don't know. Whatever stuff they've got in the corrals. What the veterinaries won't pass in the daytime.'

'I don't like to substitute,' Manuel said.

'You can take it or leave it,' Retana said. He leaned forward over the papers. He was no longer interested. The appeal that Manuel had made to him for a moment when he thought of the old days was gone. He would like to get him to substitute for Larita because he could get him cheaply. He could get others cheaply too. He would like to help him though. Still, he had given him the chance. It was up to him.

'How much do I get?' Manuel asked. He was still playing with the idea of refusing. But he knew he could not refuse.

'Two hundred and fifty pesetas,' Retana said. He had thought of five hundred, but when he opened his mouth it said two hundred and fifty.

'You pay Villalta seven thousand,' Manuel said.

'You're not Villalta,' Retana said.

'I know it,' Manuel said.

'He draws it, Manolo,' Retana said in explanation.

'Sure,' said Manuel. He stood up. 'Give me three hundred, Retana.' 'All right,' Retana agreed. He reached in the drawer for a paper. 'Can I have fifty now?' Manuel asked.

'Sure,' said Retana. He took a fifty peseta note out of his pocket-book and laid it, spread out flat, on the table.

Manuel picked it up and put it in his pocket.

'What about a cuadrilla?' he asked.

'There's the boys that always work for me nights,' Retana said. 'They're all right.'

'How about picadors?' Manuel asked. 'They're not much,' Retana admitted.

'I've got to have one good pic,' Manuel said.

'Get him then,' Retana said. 'Go and get him.'

'Not out of this,' Manuel said. 'I'm not paying for any cuadrilla out of sixty duros.'

Retana said nothing but looked at Manuel across the big desk.

'You know I've got to have one good pic,' Manuel said. Retana said nothing but looked at Manuel from a long way off. 'It isn't right,' Manuel said.

Retana was still considering him, leaning back in his chair, considering him from a long way away.

'There're the regular pics,' he offered.

'I know,' Manuel said. 'I know your regular pics.'

Retana did not smile. Manuel knew it was over.

'All I want is an even break,' Manuel said reasonably. 'When I go out there I want to be able to call my shots on the bull. It only takes one good picador.'

He was talking to a man who was no longer listening.

'If you want something extra,' Retana said, 'go and get it. There will be a regular cuadrilla out there. Bring as many of your own pics as you want. The charlotada is over by ten-thirty.'

'All right,' Manuel said. 'If that's the way you feel about it.'

'That's the way,' Retana said.

'I'll see you tomorrow night,' Manuel said.

'I'll be out there,' Retana said.

Manuel picked up his suitcase and went out. 'Shut the door,' Retana called.

Manuel looked back. Retana was sitting forward looking at some papers. Manuel pulled the door tight until it clicked.

He went down the stairs and out of the door into the hot brightness of the street. It was very hot in the street and the light on the white buildings was sudden and hard on his eyes. He walked down the shady side of the steep street toward the Puerta del Sol. The shade felt solid and cool as running water. The heat came suddenly as he crossed the intersecting streets.

Manuel saw no one he knew in all the people he passed. Just before the Puerta del Sol he turned into a café.

It was quiet in the café. There were a few men sitting at tables against the wall. At one table four men played cards. Most of the men sat against the wall smoking, empty coffee-cups and liqueur-glasses before them on the tables. Manuel went through the long room to a small room in back. A man sat at a table in the corner asleep. Manuel sat down at one of the tables.

A waiter came in and stood beside Manuel's table.

'Have you seen Zurito?' Manuel asked him.

'He was in before lunch, the waiter answered. 'He won't be back before five o'clock.'

'Bring me some coffee and milk and a shot of the ordinary,' Manuel said.

The waiter came back into the room carrying a tray with a big coffee-glass and a liqueur-glass on it. In his left hand he held a bottle of brandy. He swung these down to the table and a boy who had followed him poured coffee and milk into the glass from two shiny, spouted pots with long handles.

Manuel took off his cap and the waiter noticed his pigtail pinned forward on his head. He winked at the coffee-boy as he poured out the brandy into the little glass beside Manuel's coffee. The coffee-boy looked at Manuel's pale face curiously.

'You fighting here?' asked the waiter, corking up the bottle.

'Yes,' Manuel said. 'Tomorrow.'

The waiter stood there, holding the bottle on one hip.

'You in the Charlie Chaplin's?' he asked.

The coffee-boy looked away, embarrassed. 'No. In the ordinary.'

'I thought they were going to have Chaves and Hernandez,' the waiter said. 'No. Me and another.'

'Who? Chaves or Hernandez?' 'Hernandez, I think.'

'What's the matter with Chaves?' 'He got hurt.'

'Where did you hear that?' 'Retana.'

'Hey, Looie,' the waiter called to the next room, 'Chaves got cogida.'

Manuel had taken the wrapper off the lumps of sugar and dropped them into his coffee. He stirred it and drank it down, sweet, hot, and warming in his empty stomach. He drank off the brandy.

'Give me another shot of that,' he said to the waiter.

The waiter uncorked the bottle and poured the glass full, slopping another drink into the saucer. Another waiter had come up in front of the table. The coffee-boy was gone.

'Is Chaves hurt bad?' the second waiter asked Manuel. 'I don't know,' Manuel said. 'Retana didn't say.'

'A hell of a lot he cares,' the tall waiter said. Manuel had not seen him before. He must have just come up.

'If you stand in with Retana in this town, you're a made man,' the tall waiter said. 'If you aren't in with him, you might just as well go out and shoot yourself.'

'You said it,' the other waiter who had come in said. 'You said it then.'

'You're right I said it,' said the tall waiter. 'I know what I'm talking about when I talk about that bird.'

'Look what he's done for Villalta,' the first waiter said.

'And that ain't all,' the tall waiter said. 'Look what he's done for Marcial Lalanda. Look what he's done for Nacional.'

'You said it, kid,' agreed the short waiter.

Manuel looked at them, standing talking in front of his table. He had drunk his second brandy. They had forgotten about him. They were not interested in him.

'Look at that bunch of camels,' the tall waiter went on. 'Did you ever see this Nacional II?'

'I seen him last Sunday, didn't I?' the original waiter said.

'He's a giraffe,' the short waiter said.

'What did I tell you?' the tall waiter said. 'Those are Retana's boys.'

'Say, give me another shot of that,' Manuel said. He had poured the brandy the waiter had slopped over in the saucer into his glass and drank it while they were talking.

The original waiter poured his glass full mechanically, and the three of them went out of the room talking.

In the far corner the man was still asleep, snoring slightly on the intaking breath, his head back against the wall.

Manuel drank his brandy. He felt sleepy himself. It was too hot to go out into the town. Besides there was nothing to do. He wanted to see Zurito. He would go to sleep while he waited. He kicked his suitcase under the table to be sure it was there. Perhaps it would be better to put it back under the seat, against the wall. He leaned down and shoved it under. Then he leaned forward on the table and went to sleep.

When he woke there was someone sitting across the table from him. It was a big man with a heavy brown face like an Indian. He had been sitting there some time. He had waved the waiter away and sat reading the paper and occasionally looking down at Manuel, asleep, his head on the table. He read the paper laboriously forming the words with his lips as he read. When it tired him he looked at Manuel. He sat heavily in the chair, his black Cordoba hat tipped forward.

Manuel sat up and looked at him. 'Hullo, Zurito,' he said.

'Hello, kid,' the big man said.

'I've been asleep.' Manuel rubbed his forehead with the back of his fist. 'I thought maybe you were.'

'How's everything?'

'Good. How is everything with you?'

'Not so good.'

They were both silent. Zurito, the picador, looked at Manuel's white face. Manuel looked down at the picador's enormous hands folding the paper to put away in his pocket.

'I got a favor to ask you, Manos,' Manuel said.

Manosduros was Zurito's nickname. He never heard it without thinking of his huge hands. He put them forward on the table self-consciously.

'Let's have a drink,' he said. 'Sure,' said Manuel.

The waiter came and went and came again. He went out of the room looking back at the two men at the table.

'What's the matter, Manolo?' Zurito set down his glass.

'Would you pic two bulls for me tomorrow night?' Manuel asked, looking at Zurito across the table.

'No,' said Zurito. 'I'm not pic-ing.'

Manuel looked down at his glass. He had expected that answer; now he had it. Well, he had it.

'I'm sorry, Manolo, but I'm not pic-ing.' Zurito looked at his hands.

'That's all right,' Manuel said.

'I'm too old,' Zurito said.

'I just asked you,' Manuel said. 'Is it the nocturnal tomorrow?'

'That's it. I figured if I had just one good pic, I could get away with it.' 'How much are you getting?'

'Three hundred pesetas.'

'I get more than that for pic-ing.'

'I know,' said Manuel. 'I didn't have any right to ask you.'

'What do you keep on doing it for?' Zurito asked. 'Why don't you cut off your coleta, Manolo?'

'I don't know,' Manuel said.

'You're pretty near as old as I am,' Zurito said.

'I don't know,' Manuel said. 'I got to do it. If I can fix it so that I get an even break, that's all I want. I got to stick with it Manos.'

'No you don't.'

'Yes, I do. I've tried keeping away from it.'

'I know how you feel. But it isn't right. You ought to get out and stay out.' 'I can't do it. Besides, I've been going good lately.'

Zurito looked at his face. 'You've been in the hospital.'

'But I was going great when I got hurt.'

Zurito said nothing. He tipped the cognac out of his saucer into his glass. 'The papers said they never saw a better faena,' Manuel said.

Zurito looked at him.

'You know when I get going I'm good,' Manuel said.

'You're too old,' the picador said.

'No,' said Manuel. 'You're ten years older than I am.'

'With me it's different.'

'I'm not too old,' Manuel said.

They sat silent, Manuel watching the picador's face.

'I was going great till I got hurt,' Manuel offered.

'You ought to have seen me, Manos,' Manuel said, reproachfully. 'I don't want to see you,' Zurito said. 'It makes me nervous.' 'You haven't seen me lately.'

'I've seen you plenty.'

Zurito looked at Manuel, avoiding his eyes.

'You ought to quit it, Manolo.'

'I can't,' Manuel said. 'I'm going good now, I tell you.'

Zurito leaned forward his hands on the table.

'Listen. I'll pic for you and if you don't go big tomorrow night, you'll quit. See? Will you do that?'

'Sure.'

Zurito leaned back, relieved.

'You got to quit,' he said. 'No monkey business. You got to cut the coleta.' 'I won't have to quit,' Manuel said. 'You watch me. I've got the stuff.' Zurito stood up. He felt tired from arguing.

'You got to quit,' he said. 'I'll cut your coleta myself.' 'No, you won't,' Manuel said. 'You won't have a chance.' Zurito called the waiter.

'Come on,' said Zurito. 'Come on up to the house.'

Manuel reached under the seat for his suitcase. He was happy. He knew Zurito would pic for him. He was the best picador living. It was all simple now.

'Come on up to the house and we'll eat,' Zurito said.

Manuel stood in the patio de caballos waiting for the Charlie Chaplins to be over. Zurito stood beside him. Where they stood it was dark. The high door that led into the bullring was shut. Above them they heard a shout, then another shout of laughter. Then there was silence. Manuel liked the smell of the stables about the patio de caballos. It smelt good in the dark. There was another roar from the arena and then applause, prolonged applause, going on and on.

'You ever seen these fellows?' Zurito asked, big and looming beside Manuel in the dark.

'No,' Manuel said.

'They're pretty funny,' Zurito said. He smiled to himself in the dark. The high, double, tight-fitting door into the bullring swung open and Manuel saw the ring in the hard light of the arc-lights, the plaza, dark all the way around, rising high; around the edge of the ring were running and bowing two men dressed like tramps, followed by a third in the uniform of a hotel-boy who stooped and picked up the hats and canes thrown down on to the sand and tossed them back up into the darkness.

The electric light went on in the patio.

'I'll climb onto one of those ponies while you collect the kids,' Zurito said.

Behind them came the jingle of the mules, coming out to go into the arena and be hitched onto the dead bull.

The members of the cuadrilla, who had been watching the burlesque from the runway between the barrera and the seats, came walking back and stood in a group talking, under the electric light in the patio. A good-looking lad in a silver-and-orange suit came up to Manuel and smiled.

'I'm Hernandez,' he said and put out his hand.

Manuel took it.

'They're regular elephants we've got tonight,' the boy said cheerfully.

'They're big ones with horns,' Manuel agreed.

'You drew the worst lot,' the boy said.

'That's all right,' Manuel said. 'The bigger they are, the more meat for the poor.'

'Where did you get that one?' Hernandez grinned.

'That's an old one,' Manuel said. 'You line up your cuadrilla, so I can see what I've got.'

'You've got some good kids,' Hernandez said. He was very cheerful. He had been on twice before in nocturnals and was beginning to get a following in Madrid. He was happy the fight would start in a few minutes.

'Where are the pics?' Manuel asked.

'They're back in the corrals fighting about who gets the beautiful horses,' Hernandez grinned.

The mules came through the gate in a rush, the whips snapping, bells jangling, and the young bull plowing a furrow of sand.

They formed up for the paseo as soon as the bull had gone through.

Manuel and Hernandez stood in front. The youths of the cuadrillas were behind, their heavy capes furled over their arms. In black, the four picadors, mounted, holding their steel-tipped push-poles erect in the half-dark of the corral.

'It's a wonder Retana wouldn't give us enough light to see the horses by,' one picador said.

'He knows we'll be happier if we don't get too good a look at these skins,' another pic answered.

'This thing I'm on barely keeps me off the ground,' the first picador said. 'Well, they're horses.'

'Sure, they're horses.'

They talked, sitting their gaunt horses in the dark.

Zurito said nothing. He had the only steady horse of the lot. He had tried him, wheeling him in the corrals, and he responded to the bit and the spurs. He had taken the bandage off his right eye and cut the strings where they had tied his ears tight shut at the base. He was a good, solid horse, solid on his legs. That was all he needed. He intended to ride him all through the corrida. He had already, since he had mounted, sitting in the half-dark in the big, quilted saddle, waiting for the paseo, pic-ed through the whole corrida in his mind. The other picadors went on talking on both sides of him. He did not hear them.

The two matadors stood together in front of their three peones, their capes furled over their left arms in the same fashion. Manuel was thinking about the three lads in back of him. They were all three Madrileños, like Hernandez, boys about nineteen. One of them, a gypsy, serious, aloof, and dark-faced, he liked the look of. He turned.

'What's your name, kid?' he asked the gypsy.

'Fuentes,' the gypsy said.

'That's a good name,' Manuel said.

The gypsy smiled, showing his teeth.

'You take the bull and give him a little run when he comes out,' Manuel said.

'All right,' the gypsy said. His face was serious. He began to think about just what he would do.

'Here she goes,' Manuel said to

Hernandez. 'All right. We'll go.'

Heads up, swinging with the music, their right arms swinging free, they stepped out, crossing the sanded arena under the arc-lights, the cuadrillas opening out behind, the picadors riding after, behind came the bullring servants and the jingling mules. The crowd applauded Hernandez as they marched across the arena. Arrogant, swinging, they looked straight ahead as they marched.

They bowed before the president, and the procession broke up into its component parts. The bullfighters went over to the barrera and changed their heavy mantles for the light fighting capes. The mules went out. The picadors galloped jerkily around the ring, and two rode out the gate they had come in by. The servants swept the sand smooth.

Manuel drank a glass of water poured for him by one of Retana's deputies, who was acting as his manager and sword-handler. Hernandez came over from speaking with his own manager.

'You got a good hand, kid,' Manuel complimented him.

'They like me,' Hernandez said happily.

'How did the paseo go?' Manuel asked Retana's man.

'Like a wedding,' said the handler. 'Fine. You came out like Joselito and Belmonte.'

Zurito rode by, a bulky equestrian statue. He wheeled his horse and faced him towards the toril on the far side of the ring where the bull would come out. It was strange under the arc-light. He pic-ed in the hot afternoon sun for big money. He didn't like this arc-light business. He wished they would get started.

Manuel went up to him.

'Pic him, Manos,' he said. 'Cut him down to size for me.'

'I'll pic him, kid,' Zurito spat on the sand. 'I'll make him jump out of the ring.'

'Lean on him, Manos,' Manuel said.

'I'll lean on him,' Zurito said. 'What's holding it up?'

'He's coming now,' Manuel said.

Zurito sat there, his feet in the box-stirrups, his great legs in the buckskin-covered armor gripping the horse, the reins in his left hand, the long pic held in his right hand, his broad hat well down over his eyes to shade them from the lights, watching the distant door of the toril. His horse's ears quivered. Zurito patted him with his left hand.

The red door of the toril swung back and for a moment Zurito looked into the empty passage-way far across the arena. Then the bull came out in a rush, skidding on his four legs as he came out under the lights, then charging in a gallop, moving softly in a fast gallop, silent except as he woofed through wide nostrils as he charged, glad to be free after the dark pen.

In the first row of seats, slightly bored, leaning forward to write on the cement wall in front of his knees, the substitute bullfight critic of *El Heraldo* scribbled: 'Campagnero, Negro, 42, came out at 90 miles an hour with plenty of gas—'

Manuel, leaning against the barrera, watching the bull, waved his hand and the gypsy ran out, trailing his cape. The bull, in full gallop, pivoted and charged the cape, his head down, his tail rising. The gypsy moved in a zigzag and as he passed, the bull caught sight of him and abandoned the cape to charge the man. The gyp sprinted and vaulted the red fence of the barrera as the bull struck it with his horns. He tossed into it twice with his horns, banging into the wood blindly.

The critic of *El Heraldo* lit a cigarette and tossed the match at the bull, then wrote in his notebook, 'large and with enough horns to satisfy the cash customers, Campagnero showed a tendency to cut into the terrain of the bullfighters.'

Manuel stepped out on the hard sand as the bull banged into the fence. Out of the corner of his eye he saw Zurito sitting the white horse close to the barrera, about a quarter of the way around the ring to the left. Manuel held the cape close in front of him, a fold in each hand, and shouted at the bull. 'Huh! Huh!' the bull turned, seemed to brace against the fence as he charged in a scramble, driving into the cape as Manuel side-stepped, pivoted on his heels with the charge of the bull, and swung the cape just ahead of the horns. At the end of the cape he was facing the bull again and held the cape in the same position close in front of his body, and pivoted again as the bull recharged. Each time, as he swung, the crowd shouted.

Four times he swung with the bull, lifting the cape so it billowed full, and each time bringing the bull around to charge again. Then, at the end of the fifth swing, he held the cape against his hip and pivoted, so the cape swung out like a ballet dancer's skirt and wound the bull around himself like a belt, to step clear, leaving the bull facing Zurito on the white horse, come up and planted firm, the horse facing the bull, its ears forward, its lips nervous, Zurito, his hat over his eyes, leaning forward, the long pole sticking out before and behind in a sharp angle under his right arm, held halfway down, the triangular iron point facing the bull.

El Heraldo's second-string critic, drawing on his cigarette, his eyes on the bull, wrote: 'the veteran Manolo designed a series of acceptable veronicas, ending in a very Belmontistic recorte that earned applause from the regulars, and we entered the tercio of the cavalry.'

Zurito sat his horse, measuring the distance between the bull and the end of the pic. As he looked, the bull gathered himself together and charged, his eyes on the horse's chest. As he lowered his head to hook, Zurito sunk the point of the pic in the swelling hump of muscle above the bull's shoulder, leaned all his weight on the shaft, and with his left hand pulled the white horse into the air, front hoofs pawing, and swung him to the right as he pushed the bull under and through so that the horns passed safely under the horse's belly and the horse came down, quivering, the bull's tail brushing his chest as he charged the cape Hernandez offered him.

Hernandez ran sideways, taking the bull out and away with the cape, toward the other picador. He fixed him with a swing of the cape, squarely facing the horse and rider, and stepped back. As the bull saw the horse he charged. The picador's lance slid along his back, and as the shock of the charge lifted the horse, the picador was already half-way out of the saddle, lifting his right leg clear as he missed with the lance and falling to the left side to keep the horse between him and the bull. The horse, lifted and gored, crashed over with the bull driving into him, the picador gave a shove with his boots against the horse and lay clear, waiting to be lifted and hauled away and put on his feet.

Manuel let the bull drive into the fallen horse, he was in no hurry, the picador was safe; besides, it did a picador like that good to worry. He'd stay on longer next time. Lousy pics! He looked across the sand at Zurito a little way out from the barrera, his horse rigid, waiting.

'Huh!' he called to the bull, 'Tomar!' holding the cape in both hands so it would catch his eye. The bull detached himself from the horse and charged the cape, and Manuel, running sideways and holding the cape spread wide, stopped, swung on his heels, and brought the bull sharply around facing Zurito.

'Campagnero accepted a pair of varas for the death of one rosinante, with Hernandez and Manolo at the quites,' *El Heraldo*'s critic wrote. 'He pressed on the iron and clearly showed he was no horse-lover. The veteran Zurito resurrected some of his old stuff with the pike-pole, notably the suerte—'

'Olé! Olé!' the man sitting beside him shouted. The shout was lost in the roar of the crowd, and he slapped the critic on the back. The critic looked up to see Zurito, directly below him, leaning far out over his horse, the length of the pic rising in a sharp angle under his armpit, holding the pic almost by the point, bearing down with all his weight, holding the bull off, the bull pushing and driving to get at the horse, and Zurito, far out, on top of him, holding him, holding him, and slowly pivoting the horse against the pressure, so that at last he was clear. Zurito felt the moment when the horse was clear and the bull could come past, and relaxed the absolute steel lock of his resistance, and the triangular steel point of the pic ripped in the bull's hump of shoulder muscle as he tore loose to find Hernandez's cape before his muzzle. He charged blindly into the cape and the boy took him out into the open arena.

Zurito sat patting his horse and looking at the bull charging the cape that Hernandez swung for him out under the bright light while the crowd shouted.

'You see that one?' he said to Manuel. 'It was a wonder,' Manuel said.

'I got him that time,' Zurito said. 'Look at him now.'

At the conclusion of a closely turned pass of the cape the bull slid to his knees. He was up at once, but far out across the sand Manuel and Zurito saw the shine of the pumping flow of blood, smooth against the black of the bull's shoulder.

'I got him that time,' Zurito said. 'He's a good bull,' Manuel said.

'If they gave me another shot at him, I'd kill him,' Zurito said.

'They'll change the thirds on us,' Manuel said.

'Look at him now,' Zurito said.

'I got to go over there,' Manuel said, and started on a run for the other side of the ring, where the monos were leading a horse out by the bridle toward the bull, whacking him on the legs with rods and all, in a procession, trying to get him towards the bull, who stood, dropping his head, pawing, unable to make up his mind to charge.

Zurito, sitting his horse, walking him toward the scene, not missing any detail, scowled.

Finally the bull charged, the horse leaders ran for the barrera, the picador hit too far back, and the bull got under the horse, lifted him, threw him onto his back.

Zurito watched. The monos, in their red shirts, running out to drag the picador clear. The picador, now on his feet, swearing and flopping his arms. Manuel and Hernandez standing ready with their capes. And the bull, the great, black bull, with a horse on his back, hooves dangling, the bridle caught in the horns. Black bull with a horse on his back, staggering short-legged, then arching his neck and lifting, thrusting, charging to slide the horse off, horse sliding down. Then the bull into a lunging charge at the cape Manuel spread for him.

The bull was slower now, Manuel felt. He was bleeding badly. There was a sheen of blood all down his flank.

Manuel offered him the cape again. There he came, eyes open, ugly, watching the cape. Manuel stepped to the side and raised his arms, tightening the cape ahead of the bull for the veronica.

Now he was facing the bull. Yes, his head was going down a little. He was carrying it lower. That was Zurito.

Manuel flopped the cape; there he comes; he side-stepped and swung in another veronica. He's shooting awfully accurately, he thought. He's had enough fight, so he's watching now. He's hunting now. Got his eye on me. But I always give him the cape.

He shook the cape at the bull; there he comes; he sidestepped. Awful close that time. I don't want to work that close to him.

The edge of the cape was wet with blood where it had swept along the bull's back as he went by.

All right, here's the last one.

Manuel, facing the bull, having turned with him each charge, offered the cape with his two hands. The bull looked at him. Eyes watching, horns straight forward, the bull looked at him, watching.

'Huh!' Manuel said, 'Toro!' and leaning back, swung the cape forward. Here he comes. He side-stepped, swung the cape in back of him, and pivoted, so the bull followed a swirl of cape and was then left with nothing, fixed by the pass, dominated by the cape. Manuel swung the cape under his muzzle with one hand, to show the bull was fixed, and walked away.

There was no applause.

Manuel walked across the sand towards the barrera, while Zurito rode out of the ring. The trumpet had blown to change the act to the planting of the banderillos while Manuel had been working with the bull. He had not consciously noticed it. The monos were spreading canvas over the two dead horses and sprinkling sawdust around them.

Manuel came up to the barrera for a drink of water. Retana's man handed him the heavy porous jug.

Fuentes, the tall gypsy, was standing holding a pair of banderillos, holding them together, slim, red sticks, fishhook points out. He looked at Manuel.

'Go on out there,' Manuel said.

The gypsy trotted out. Manuel set down the jug and watched. He wiped his face with his handkerchief.

The critic of *El Heraldo* reached for the bottle of warm champagne that stood between his feet, took a drink, and finished his paragraph.

'—the aged Manolo rated no applause for a vulgar series of lances with the cape and we entered the third of the palings.'

Alone in the centre of the ring the bull stood, still fixed. Fuentes, tall, flat-backed, walking towards him arrogantly, his arms spread out, the two slim, red sticks, one in each hand, held by the fingers, points straight forward.

Fuentes walked forward. Back of him and to one side was a peon with a cape. The bull looked at him and was no longer fixed.

His eyes watched Fuentes, now standing still. Now he leaned back, calling to him. Fuentes twitched the two banderillos and the light on the steel points caught the bull's eye.

His tail went up and he charged.

He came straight, his eyes on the man. Fuentes stood still, leaning back, the banderillos pointing forward. As the bull lowered his head to hook, Fuentes leaned backward, his arms came together and rose, his two hands touching, the banderillos two descending red lines, and leaning forward drove the points into the bull's shoulder, leaning far in over the bull's horns and pivoting on the two upright sticks, his legs tight together, his body curving to one side to let the bull pass.

'Olé!' from the crowd.

The bull was hooking wildly, jumping like a trout, all four feet off the ground. The red shafts of the banderillos tossed as he jumped.

Manuel, standing at the barrera, noticed that he hooked always to the right.

'Tell him to drop the next pair on the right,' he said to the kid who started to run out to Fuentes with the new banderillos.

A heavy hand fell on his shoulder. it was Zurito.

'How do you feel, kid?' he asked.

Manuel was watching the bull.

Zurito leaned forward on the barrera, leaning the weight of his body on his arms. Manuel turned to him.

'You're going good,' Zurito said.

Manuel shook his head. He had nothing to do now until the next third. The gypsy was very good with the banderillos. The bull would come to him in the next third in good shape. He was a good bull. It had all been easy up to now. The final stuff with the sword was all he worried over. He did not really worry. He did not even think about it. But standing there he had a heavy sense of apprehension. He looked out at the bull, planning his faena, his work with the red cloth that was to reduce the bull, to make him manageable.

The gypsy was walking out towards the bull again, walking heel-and-toe, insultingly, like a ballroom dancer, the red shafts of the banderillos twitching with his walk. The bull watched him, not fixed now, hunting him, but waiting to get close enough so he could be sure of getting him, getting the horns into him.

As Fuentes walked forward the bull charged. Fuentes ran across the quarter of a circle as the bull charged and, as he passed running backwards, stopped, swung forward, rose on his toes, arms straight out, and sunk the banderillos straight down into the tight of the big shoulder muscles as the bull missed him.

The crowd were wild about it.

'That kid won't stay in this night stuff long,' Retana's man said to Zurito. 'He's good,' Zurito said.

'Watch him now.' They watched.

Fuentes was standing with his back against the barrera. Two of the cuadrilla were back of him, with their capes ready to flop over the fence to distract the bull.

The bull, with his tongue out, his barrel heaving, was watching the gypsy. He thought he had him now. Back against the red planks. Only a short charge away. The bull watched him.

The gypsy bent back, drew back his arms, the banderillos pointing at the bull. He called to the bull, stamped one foot. The bull was suspicious. He wanted the man. No more barbs in the shoulder.

Fuentes walked a little closer to the bull. Bent back. Called again. Somebody in the crowd shouted a warning.

'He's too damn close,' Zurito said. 'Watch him,' Retana's man said.

Leaning back, inciting the bull with the banderillos, Fuentes jumped, both feet off the ground. As he jumped the bull's tail rose and he charged.

Fuentes came down on his toes, arms straight out, whole body arching forward, and drove the shafts straight down as he swung his body clear of the right horn.

The bull crashed into the barrera where the flopping capes had attracted his eye as he lost the man.

The gypsy came running along the barrera towards Manuel, taking the applause of the crowd. His vest was ripped where he had not quite cleared the point of the horn. He was happy about it, showing it to the spectators. He made a tour of the ring. Zurito saw him go by, smiling, pointing to his vest. He smiled.

Somebody else was planting the last pair of banderillos. Nobody was paying any attention.

Retana's man tucked a baton inside the red cloth of a muleta, folded the cloth over it, and handed it over the barrera to Manuel. He reached in the leather sword-case, took out a sword and, holding it by its leather scabbard, reached it over the fence to Manuel. Manuel pulled the blade out by the red hilt and the scabbard fell limp.

He looked at Zurito. The big man saw he was sweating. 'Now you get him, kid,' Zurito said.

Manuel nodded.

'He's in good shape,' Zurito said.

'Just like you want him,' Retana's man assured him.

Manuel nodded.

The trumpeter, up under the roof, blew for the final act, and Manuel walked across the arena towards where, up in the dark boxes, the president must be.

In the front row seats the substitute bullfight critic of *El Heraldo* took a long drink of warm champagne. He had decided it was not worthwhile to write a running story and would write up the corrida back in the office.

What the hell was it anyway? Only a nocturnal. If he missed anything he would get it out of the morning papers. He took another drink of the champagne. He had a date at Maxim's at twelve. Who were these bullfighters anyway? Kids and bums. A bunch of bums. He put his pad of paper in his pocket and looked over towards Manuel, standing very much alone in the ring, gesturing with his hat in a salute towards a box he could not see high up in the dark plaza. Out in the ring the bull stood quiet, looking at nothing.

'I dedicate this bull to you, Mr. President, and to the public of Madrid, the most intelligent and generous in the world,' was what Manuel was saying. It was a formula. He said it all. It was a little too long for nocturnal use.

He bowed at the dark, straightened, tossed his hat over his shoulder, and, carrying the muleta in his left hand and the sword in his right, walked out towards the bull.

Manuel walked toward the bull. The bull looked at him; his eyes were quick. Manuel noticed the way the banderillos hung down on his left shoulder and the steady sheen of blood from Zurito's pic-ing. He noticed the way the bull's feet were.

As he walked forward, holding the muleta in his left hand and the sword in his right, he watched the bull's feet. The bull could not charge without gathering his feet together. Now he stood square on them, dully.

Manuel walked towards him, watching his feet. This was all right. He could do this. He must work to get the bull's head down, so he could go in past the horns and kill him. He did not think about the sword, not about killing the bull. He thought about one thing at a time. The coming things oppressed him, though. Walking forward, watching the bull's feet, he saw successively his eyes, his wet muzzle, and the wide, forward-pointing spread of his horns. The bull had light circles about his eyes. His eyes watched Manuel.

He felt he was going to get this little one with the white face.

Standing still now and spreading the red cloth of the muleta with the sword, pricking the point into the cloth so that the sword, now held in his left hand, spread the red flannel like the jib of a boat, Manuel noticed the points of the bull's horns. One of them was splintered from banging against the barrera. The other was sharp as a porcupine quill. Manuel noticed while spreading the muleta that the white base of the horn was stained red. While he noticed these things he did not lose sight of the bull's feet. The bull watched Manuel steadily.

He's on the defensive now, Manuel thought. He's reserving himself. I've got to bring him out of that and get his head down. Always get his head down. Zurito had his head down once, but he's come back. He'll bleed when I" start him going and that will bring it down.

Holding the muleta, with the sword in his left hand widening it in front of him, he called to the bull.

The bull looked at him.

He leaned back insultingly and shook the widespread flannel.

The bull saw the muleta. It was a bright scarlet under the arc-light. The bull's legs tightened.

Here he comes. Whoosh! Manuel turned as the bull came and raised the muleta so that it passed over the bull's horns and swept down his broad back from head to tail. The bull had gone clean up in the air with the charge. Manuel had not moved.

At the end of the pass the bull turned like a cat coming around a corner and faced Manuel.

He was on the offensive again. His heaviness was gone. Manuel noted the fresh blood shining down the black shoulder and dripping down the bull's leg. He drew the sword out of the muleta and held it in his right hand. The muleta held low down in his left hand, leaning toward the left, he called to the bull. The bull's legs tightened, his eyes on the muleta. Here he comes, Manuel thought. Yuh!

He swung with the charge, sweeping the muleta ahead of the bull, his feet firm, the sword following the curve, a point of light under the arcs.

The bull recharged as the pase natural finished and Manuel raised the muleta for a pase de pecho. Firmly planted, the bull came by his chest under the raised muleta. Manuel leaned his head back to avoid the clattering banderillo shafts. The hot black bull body touched his chest as it passed.

Too damn close, Manuel thought. Zurito, leaning on the barrera, spoke rapidly to the gypsy who trotted out towards Manuel with a cape, Zurito pulled his hat down low and looked out across the arena at Manuel.

Manuel was facing the bull again, the muleta held low and to the left. The bull's head was down as he watched the muleta.

'If it was Belmonte doing that stuff, they'd go crazy,' Retana's man said. Zurito said nothing. He was watching Manuel out in the centre of the arena. 'Where did the boss dig this fellow up?' Retana's man asked.

'Out of the hospital,' Zurito said.

'That's where he's going damn quick,' Retana's man said.

Zurito turned on him.

'Knock on that,' he said, pointing to the barrera.

'I was just kidding, man,' Retana's man said.

'Knock on that wood.'

Retana's man leaned forward and knocked three times on the barrera.

'Watch the faena,' Zurito said.

Out in the centre of the ring, under the lights, Manuel was kneeling, facing the bull, and as he raised the muleta in both hands the bull charged, tail up.

Manuel swung his body clear and, as the bull recharged, brought around the muleta in a half-circle that pulled the bull to his knees.

'Why, that one's a great bullfighter,' Retana's man said.

'No, he's not,' said Zurito.

Manuel stood up and, the muleta in his left hand, the sword in his right, acknowledged the applause from the dark plaza.

The bull had humped himself up from his knees and stood waiting, his head hung low.

Zurito spoke to two of the other lads of the cuadrilla and they ran out to stand back of Manuel with their capes. There were four men back of him now. Hernandez had followed him since he first came out with the muleta. Fuentes stood watching, his cape held against his body, tall in repose, watching lazy-eyed. Now the two came up. Hernandez motioned them to stand one at each side. Manuel stood alone, facing the bull.

Manuel waved back the men with the capes. Stepping back cautiously, they saw his face was white and sweating.

Didn't they know enough to keep back? Did they want to catch the bull's eye with the capes after he was fixed and ready? He had enough to worry about without that kind of thing.

The bull was standing, his four feet square, looking at the muleta. Manuel furled the muleta in his left hand. The bull's eyes watched it. His body was heavy on his feet. He carried his head low, but not too low.

Manuel lifted the muleta at him. The bull did not move. Only his eyes watched.

He's all lead, Manuel thought. He's all square. He's framed right. He'll take it.

He thought in bullfight terms. Sometimes he had a thought and the particular piece of slang would not come into his mind and he could not realize the thought. His instincts and knowledge worked automatically, and his brain worked slowly and in words. He knew all about bulls. He did not have to think about them. He just did the right thing. His eyes noted things and his body performed the necessary measures without thought. If he thought about it, he would be gone.

Now, facing the bull, he was conscious of many things at the same time. There were the horns, the one splintered, the other smoothly sharp, the need to profile himself toward the left horn, lance himself short and straight, lower the muleta so the bull would follow it, and, going in over the horns, put the sword all the way into a little spot about as big as a five-peseta piece straight in back of the neck, between the sharp pitch of the bull's shoulders. He must do all this, and must then come out from between the horns. He was conscious he must do all this, but his only thought was in words: 'Corto y derecho.'

'Corto y derecho,' he thought, furling the muleta. Short and straight. Corto y derecho, he drew the sword out of the muleta, profiled on the splintered left horn, dropped the muleta across his body, so his right hand with the sword on the level with his eye made the sign of the cross, and, rising on his toes, sighted along the dipping blade of the sword at the spot high up between the bull's shoulders.

Corto y derecho he lanced himself on the bull.

There was a shock, and he felt himself go up in the air. He pushed on the sword as he went up and over, and it flew out of his hand. He hit the ground and the bull was on him. Manuel, lying on the ground, kicked at the bull's muzzle with his splippered feet. Kicking, kicking, the bull after him, missing him in his excitement, bumping him with his head, driving the horns into the sand. Kicking like a man keeping a ball in the air, Manuel kept the bull from getting a clean thrust at him.

Manuel felt the wind on his back from the capes flopping at the bull, and then the bull was gone, gone over him in a rush. Dark, as his belly went over. Not even stepped on.

Manuel stood up and picked up the muleta. Fuentes handed him the sword. It was bent where it had struck the shoulder-blade. Manuel straightened it on his knee and ran towards the bull, standing now beside one of the dead horses. As he ran, his jacket flopped where it had been ripped under the armpit.

'Get him out of there,' Manuel shouted to the gypsy. The bull had smelled the blood of the dead horse and ripped into the canvas cover with his horns. He charged Fuentes's cape, with the canvas hanging from his splintered horn, and the crowd laughed. Out in the ring, he tossed his head to rid himself of the canvas. Hernandez, running up from behind him, grabbed the end of the canvas and neatly lifted it off the horn.

The bull followed it in a half-charge and stopped still. He was on the defensive again. Manuel was walking towards him with the sword and muleta. Manuel swung the muleta before him. The bull would not charge.

Manuel profiled toward the bull, sighting along the dipping blade of the sword. The bull was motionless, seemingly dead on his feet, incapable of another charge.

Manuel rose to his toes, sighting along the steel, and charged.

Again there was the shock and he felt himself being borne back in a rush, to strike hard on the sand. There was no chance of kicking this time. The bull was on top of him. Manuel lay as though dead, his head on his arms, and the bull bumped him. Bumped his back, bumped his face in the sand. He felt the horn go into the sand between his folded arms. The bull hit him in the small of the back. His face drove into the sand. The horn drove through one of his sleeves and the bull ripped it off. Manuel was tossed clear and the bull followed the capes.

Manuel got up, found the sword and muleta, tried the point of the sword with his thumb, and then ran towards the barrera for a new sword.

Retana's man handed him the sword over the edge of the barrera.

'Wipe off your face,' he said.

Manuel, running again towards the bull, wiped his bloody face with his handkerchief. He had not seen Zurito. Where was Zurito?'

The cuadrilla had stepped away from the bull and waited with their capes. The bull stood, heavy and dull again after the action.

Manuel walked towards him with the muleta. He stopped and shook it. The bull did not respond. He passed it right and left, left and right before the bull's muzzle. The bull's eyes watched it and turned with the swing, but he would not charge. He was waiting for Manuel.

Manuel was worried. There was nothing to do but go in. Corto y derecho. He profiled close to the bull, crossed the muleta in front of his body and charged. As he pushed in the sword, he jerked his body to the left to clear the horn. The bull passed him and the sword shot up in the air, twinkling under the arc-lights, to fall red-hilted on the sand.

Manuel ran over and picked it up. It was bent and he straightened it over his knee.

As he came running towards the bull, fixed again now, he passed Hernandez standing with his cape.

'He's all bone,' the boy said encouragingly.

Manuel nodded, wiping his face. He put the bloody handkerchief in his pocket.

There was the bull. He was close to the barrera now. Damn him. Maybe he was all bone. Maybe there was not any place for the sword to go in. The hell there wasn't! He'd show them.

He tried a pass with the muleta and the bull did not move. Manuel chopped the muleta back and forth in front of the bull. Nothing doing.

He furled the muleta, drew the sword out, profiled and drove in on the bull. He felt the sword buckle as he shoved it in, leaning his weight on it, and then it shot in the air, end-over-ending into the crowd. Manuel had jerked clear as the sword jumped.

The first cushions thrown down out of the dark missed him. Then one hit him in the face, his bloody face looking towards the crowd. They were coming down fast. Spotting the sand. Somebody threw an empty champagne bottle from close range. It hit Manuel on the foot. He stood there watching the dark, where the things were coming from. Then something whished through the air and struck by him. Manuel leaned over and picked it up. It was his sword. He straightened it over his knee and gestured with it to the crowd.

'Thank you,' he said. 'Thank you.'

Oh, the dirty bastards! Dirty bastards! Oh, the lousy, dirty bastards! He kicked into a cushion as he ran.

There was the bull. The same as ever. All right, you dirty, lousy bastard! Manuel passed the muleta in front of the bull's black muzzle.

Nothing doing.

You won't. All right. He stepped close and jammed the sharp peak of the muleta into the bull's damp muzzle.

The bull was on him as he jumped back and as he tripped on a cushion he felt the horn go into him, into his side. He grabbed the horn with his two hands and rode backward, holding tight on to the place. The bull tossed him and he was clear. He lay still. It was all right. The bull was gone.

He got up coughing and feeling broken and gone. The dirty bastards!

'Give me the sword,' he shouted. 'Give me the stuff.'

Fuentes came up with the muleta and the sword. Hernandez put his arm around him.

'Go on to the infirmary, man,' he said. 'Don't be a damn fool.'

'Get away from me,' Manuel said. 'Get to hell away from me.'

He twisted free. Hernandez shrugged his shoulders. Manuel ran toward the bull.

There was the bull standing, heavy, firmly planted.

All right, you bastard! Manuel drew the sword out of the muleta, sighted with the same movement, and flung himself onto the bull. He felt the sword go in all the way. Right up to the guard. Four fingers and his thumb into the bull. The blood was hot on his knuckles, and he was on top of the bull.

The bull lurched with him as he lay on, and seemed to sink; then he was standing clear. He looked at the bull going down slowly over on his side, then suddenly four feet in the air.

Then he gestured at the crowd, his hand warm from the bull blood.

All right, you bastards! He wanted to say something, but he started to cough. It was hot and choking. He looked down for the muleta. He must go over and salute the president. President hell! He was sitting down looking at something. It was the bull. His four feet up. Thick tongue out. Things crawling around on his belly and under his legs. Crawling where the hair was thin. Dead bull. To hell with the bull! To hell with them all! He started

to get to his feet and commenced to cough. He sat down again, coughing.

Somebody came and pushed him up.

They carried him across the ring to the infirmary, running with him across the sand, standing blocked at the gate as the mules came in, then around under the dark passageway, men grunting as they took him up the stairway, and then laid him down.

The doctor and two men in white were waiting for him. They laid him out on the table. They were cutting away his shirt. Manuel felt tired. His whole chest felt scalding inside. He started to cough and they held something to his mouth. Everybody was very busy.

There was an electric light in his eyes. He shut his eyes.

He heard someone coming very heavily up the stairs. Then he did not hear it. Then he heard a noise far off. That was the crowd. Well, somebody would have to kill his other bull. They had cut away all his shirt. The doctor smiled at him. There was Retana.

'Hello, Retana!' Manuel said. He could not hear his voice.

Retana smiled at him and said something. Manuel could not hear it.

Zurito stood beside the table, bending over where the doctor was working. He was in his picador clothes, without his hat.

Zurito said something to him. Manuel could not hear it. Zurito was speaking to Retana. One of the men in white smiled and handed Retana a pair of scissors. Retana gave them to Zurito. Zurito said something to Manuel. He could not hear it.

To hell with this operating table! He'd been on plenty of operating tables before. He was not going to die. There would be a priest if he was going to die.

Zurito was saying something to him. Holding up the scissors.

That was it. They were going to cut off his coleta. They were going to cut off his pigtail.

Manuel sat up on the operating table. The doctor stepped back, angry. Someone grabbed him and held him.

'You couldn't do a thing like that, Manos,' he said. He heard suddenly, clearly, Zurito's voice.

'That's all right,' Zurito said. 'I won't do it. I was joking.'

'I was going good,' Manuel said. 'I didn't have any luck. That was all.'

Manuel lay back. They had put something over his face. It was all familiar. He inhaled deeply. He felt very tired. He was very, very tired. They took the thing away from his face.

'I was going good,' Manuel said weakly. 'I was going great.' etana looked at Zurito and started for the door.

'I'll stay here with him,' Zurito said. etana shrugged his shoulders.

Manuel opened his eyes and looked at Zurito.

'Wasn't I going good, Manos?' he asked, for confirmation. Sure,' said Zurito. 'You were going great.'

The doctor's assistant put the cone over Manuel's face and he inhaled deeply. Zurito stood awkwardly, watching.

IN ANOTHER COUNTRY

IN the fall the war was always there, but we did not go to it any more. It was cold in the fall in Milan and the dark came very early. Then the electric lights came on, and it was pleasant along the streets looking in the windows. There was much game hanging outside the shops, and the snow powdered in the fur of the foxes and the wind blew their tails. The deer hung stiff and heavy and empty, and small birds blew in the wind and the wind turned their feathers. It was a cold fall and the wind came down from the mountains.

We were all at the hospital every afternoon, and there were different ways of walking across the town through the dusk to the hospital. Two of the ways were alongside canals, but they were long. Always, though, you crossed a bridge across a canal to enter the hospital. There was a choice of three bridges. On one of them a woman sold roasted chestnuts. It was warm, standing in front of her charcoal fire, and the chestnuts were warm afterward in your pocket. The hospital was very old and very beautiful, and you entered through a gate and walked across a courtyard and out of a gate on the other side. There were usually funerals starting from the courtyard. Beyond the old hospital were the new brick pavilions, and there we met every afternoon and were all very polite and interested in what was the matter, and sat in the machines that were to make so much difference.

The doctor came up to the machine where I was sitting and said: 'What did you like best to do before the war? Did you practice a sport?'

I said: 'Yes, football.'

'Good,' he said. 'You will be able to play football again better than ever.'

My knee did not bend and the leg dropped straight from the knee to the ankle without a calf, and the machine was to bend the knee and make it move as in riding a tricycle. But it did not bend yet, and instead the machine lurched when it came to the bending part. The doctor said: 'That will all pass. You are a fortunate young man. You will play football again like a champion.'

In the next machine was a major who had a little hand like a baby's. He winked at me when the doctor examined his hand, which was between two leather straps that bounced up and down and flapped the stiff fingers, and said: 'And will I too play football, captain-doctor?' He had been a very great fencer and, before the war, the greatest fencer in Italy.

The doctor went to his office in the back room and brought a photograph which showed a hand that had been withered almost as small as the major's, before it had taken a machine course, and after was a little larger. The major held the photograph with his good hand and looked at it very carefully. 'A wound?' he asked.

'An industrial accident,' the doctor said.

'Very interesting, very interesting,' the major said, and handed it back to the doctor.

'You have confidence?' 'No,' said the major.

There were three boys who came each day who were about the same age I was. They were all three from Milan, and one of them was to be a lawyer, and one was to be a painter, and one had intended to be a soldier, and after we were finished with the machines, sometimes we walked back together to the Café Cova, which was next door to the Scala. We walked the short way through the communist quarter because we were four together. The people hated us because we were officers, and from a wine shop someone would call out, 'A basso gli ufficiali!' as we passed. Another boy who walked with us sometimes and made us five wore a black silk handkerchief across his face because he had no nose then and his face was to be rebuilt. He had gone out to the front from the military academy and been wounded within an hour after he had gone into the front line for the first time. They rebuilt his face, but he came from a very old family and they could never get the nose exactly right. He went to South America and worked in a bank. But this was a long time ago, and then we did not any of us know how it was going to be afterwards. We only knew then that there was always the war, but that we were not going to it any more.

We all had the same medals, except the boy with the black silk bandage across his face, and he had not been at the front long enough to get any medals. The tall boy with a very pale face who was to be a lawyer had been a lieutenant of Arditi and had three medals of the sort we each had only one of. He had lived a very long time with death and was a little detached. We were all a little detached, and there was nothing that held us together except that we met every afternoon at the hospital. Although, as we walked to the Cova through the tough part of the town, walking in the dark, with light and singing coming out of the wine shops, and sometimes having to walk into the street when the men and women would crowd together on the sidewalk so that we would have had to jostle them to get by, we felt held together by there being something that had happened that they, the people who disliked us, did not understand.

We ourselves all understood the Cova, where it was rich and warm and not too brightly lighted, and noisy and smoky at certain hours, and there were always girls at the tables and the illustrated papers on a rack on the wall.

The girls at the Cova were very patriotic, and I found that the most patriotic people in Italy were the café girls—and I believe they are still patriotic.

The boys at first were very polite about my medals and asked me what I had done to get them. I showed them the papers, which were written in very beautiful language and full of *fratellanza* and *abnegazione*, but which really said, with the adjectives removed, that I had been given the medals because I was an American. After that their manner changed a little toward me, although I was their friend against outsiders. I was a friend, but I was never really one of them after they had read the citations, because it had been different with them and they had done very different things to get their medals. I had been wounded, it was true; but we all knew that being wounded, after all, was really an accident. I was never ashamed of the ribbons, though, and sometimes, after the cocktail hour, I would imagine myself having done all the things they had done to get their medals; but walking home at night through the empty streets with the cold wind and all the shops closed, trying to keep near the street lights, I knew that I would never have done such things, and I was very much afraid to die, and often lay in bed at night by myself, afraid to die and wondering how I would be when I went back to the front again.

The three with the medals were like hunting-hawks; and I was not a hawk, although I might seem a hawk to those who had never hunted; they, the three, knew better and so we drifted apart. But I stayed good friends with the boy who had been wounded his first day at the front, because he would never know how he would have turned out; so he could never be accepted either, and I liked him because I thought perhaps he would not have turned out to be a hawk either.

The major, who had been the great fencer, did not believe in bravery, and spent much time while we sat in the machines correcting my grammar. He had complimented me on how I spoke Italian, and we talked together very easily. One day I had said that Italian seemed such an easy language to me that I could not take a great interest in it; everything was so easy to say. 'Ah, yes,' the major said. 'Why, then, do you not take up the use of grammar?' So we took up the use of grammar, and soon Italian was such a difficult language that I was afraid to talk to him until I had the grammar straight in my mind.

The major came very regularly to the hospital. i do not think he ever missed a day, although I am sure he did not believe in the machines. There was a time when none of us believed in the machines, and one day the major said it was all nonsense. The machines were new then and it was we who were to prove them. It was an idiotic idea, he said, 'a theory, like another". I had not learned my grammar, and he said I was a stupid impossible disgrace, and he was a fool to have bothered with me. He was a small man and he sat straight up in his chair with his right hand thrust into the machine and looked straight ahead at the wall while the straps thumped up and down with his fingers in them.

'What will you do when the war is over if it is over?' he asked me. 'Speak grammatically!'

'I will go to the States.'

'Are you married?'

'No, but I hope to be.'

'The more of a fool you are,' he said. He seemed very angry. 'A man must not marry.'

'Why, Signor Maggiore?'

'Don't call me 'Signor Maggiore".'

'Why must not a man marry?'

'He cannot marry. He cannot marry,' he said angrily. 'If he is to lose everything, he should not place himself in a position to lose that. He should not place himself in a position to lose. He should find things he cannot lose.'

He spoke very angrily and bitterly, and looked straight ahead while he talked.

'But why should he necessarily lose it?'

'He'll lose it,' the major said. He was looking at the wall. Then he looked down at the machine and jerked his little hand out from between the straps and slapped it hard against his thigh. 'He'll lose it,' he almost shouted. 'Don't argue with me!' Then he called to the attendant who ran the machines. 'Come and turn this damned thing off.'

He went back into the other room for the light treatment and the massage. Then I heard him ask the doctor if he might use his telephone and he shut the door. When he came back into the room, I was sitting in another machine. He was wearing his cape and had his cap on, and he came directly toward my machine and put his arm on my shoulder.

'I am *so* sorry,' he said, and patted me, on the shoulder with his good hand. 'I would not be rude. My wife has just died. You must forgive me.'

'Oh—' I said, feeling sick for him. 'I am so sorry.'

He stood there biting his lower lip. 'It is very difficult,' he said. 'I cannot resign myself.'

He looked straight past me and out through the window. Then he began to cry. 'I am utterly unable to resign myself,' he said and choked. And then crying, his head up, looking at nothing, carrying himself straight and soldierly, with tears on both his cheeks and biting his lips, he walked past the machines and out of the door.

The doctor told me that the major's wife, who was very young and whom he had not married until he was definitely invalided out of the war, had died of pneumonia. She had been sick only a few days. No one expected her to die. The major did not come to the hospital for three days. Then he came at the usual hour, wearing a black band on the sleeve of his uniform. When he came back, there were large framed photographs around the wall, of all sorts of wounds before and after they had been cured by the machines. In front of the machine the major used were three photographs of hands like his that were completely restored. I do not know where the doctor got them. I always understood we were the first to use the machines. The photographs did not make much difference to the major because he only looked out of the window.

HILLS LIKE WHITE ELEPHANTS

THE hills across the valley of the Ebro were long and white. On this side there was no shade and no trees and the station was between two lines of rails in the sun. Close against the side of the station there was the warm shadow of the building and a curtain, made of strings of bamboo beads, hung across the open door into the bar, to keep out flies. The American and the girl with him sat at a table in the shade, outside the building. It was very hot and the express from Barcelona would come in forty minutes. It stopped at this junction for two minutes and went on to Madrid.

'What should we drink?' the girl asked. She had taken off her hat and put it on the table.

'It's pretty hot,' the man said. 'Let's drink beer.'

'Dos cervezas,' the man said into the curtain.

'Big ones?' a woman asked from the doorway.

'Yes. Two big ones.'

The woman brought two glasses of beer and two felt pads. She put the felt pads and the beer glasses on the table and looked at the man and the girl. The girl was looking off at the line of hills. They were white in the sun and the country was brown and dry.

'They look like white elephants,' she said.

'I've never seen one.' The man drank his beer. 'No, you wouldn't have.'

'I might have,' the man said. 'Just because you say I wouldn't have doesn't prove anything.'

The girl looked at the bead curtain. 'They've painted something on it,' she said. 'What does it say?'

'Anis del Toro. It's a drink.' 'Could we try it?'

The man called 'Listen' through the curtain.

The woman came out from the bar.

'Four reales.'

'We want two Anis del Toros.' 'With water?'

'Do you want it with water?'

'I don't know,' the girl said. 'Is it good with water?'

'It's all right.'

'You want them with water?' asked the woman.

'Yes, with water.'

'It tastes like liquorice,' the girl said and put the glass down.

'That's the way with everything.'

'Yes,' said the girl. 'Everything tastes of liquorice. Especially all the things you've waited so long for, like absinthe.'

'Oh, cut it out.'

'You started it,' the girl said. 'I was being amused. I was having a fine time.'

'Well, let's try and have a fine time.'

'All right. I was trying. I said the mountains looked like white elephants. Wasn't that bright?'

'That was bright.'

'I wanted to try this new drink. That's all we do, isn't it—look at things and try new drinks?'

'I guess so.'

The girl looked across at the hills.

'They're lovely hills,' she said. 'They don't really look like white elephants. I just meant the coloring of their skin through the trees.'

'Should we have another drink?' 'All right.'

The warm wind blew the bead curtain against the table. 'The beer's nice and cool,' the man said.

'It's lovely,' the girl said.

'It's really an awfully simple operation, Jig,' the man said. 'It's not really an operation at all.'

The girl looked at the ground the table legs rested on.

'I know you wouldn't mind it, Jig. It's really not anything. It's just to let the air in.'

The girl did not say anything.

'I'll go with you and I'll stay with you all the time. They just let the air in and then it's all perfectly natural.'

'Then what will we do afterwards?'

'We'll be fine afterwards. Just like we were before.'

'What makes you think so?'

'That's the only thing that bothers us. It's the one thing that's made us unhappy.'

The girl looked at the bead curtain, put her hand out and took hold of two of the strings of beads.

'And you think then we'll be all right and be happy.'

'I know we will. You don't have to be afraid. I've known lots of people that have done it.'

'So have I,' said the girl. 'And afterward they were all so happy.'

'Well,' the man said, 'if you don't want to you don't have to. I wouldn't have you do it if you didn't want to. But I know it's perfectly simple.'

'And you really want to?'

'I think it's the best thing to do. But I don't want you to do it if you don't really want to.'

'And if I do it you'll be happy and things will be like they were and you'll love me?'

'I love you now. You know I love you.'

'I know. But if I do it, then it will be nice again if I say things are like white elephants, and you'll like it?'

'I'll love it. I love it now but I just can't think about it. You know how I get when I worry.'

'If I do it you won't ever worry?'

'I won't worry about that because it's perfectly simple.'

'Then I'll do it. Because I don't care about me.'

'What do you mean?' 'I don't care about me.'

'Well, I care about you.'

'Oh, yes. But I don't care about me. And I'll do it and then everything will be fine.'

'I don't want you to do it if you feel that way.'

The girl stood up and walked to the end of the station. Across, on the other side, were fields of grain and trees along the banks of the Ebro. Far away, beyond the river, were mountains. The shadow of a cloud moved across the field of grain and she saw the river through the trees.

'And we could have all this,' she said. 'And we could have everything and every day we make it more impossible.'

'What did you say?'

'I said we could have everything.' 'We can have everything.'

'No, we can't.'

'We can have the whole world.' 'No, we can't.'

'We can go everywhere.'

'No, we can't. It isn't ours any more.'

'It's ours.'

'No, it isn't. And once they take it away, you never get it back.'

'But they haven't taken it away.'

'We'll wait and see.'

'Come on back in the shade,' he said. 'You mustn't feel that way.' 'I don't feel any way,' the girl said. 'I just know things.'

'I don't want you to do anything that you don't want to do—'

'Nor that isn't good for me,' she said. 'I know. Could we have another beer?'

'All right. But you've got to realize—'

'I realize,' the girl said. 'Can't we maybe stop talking?'

They sat down at the table and the girl looked across at the hills on the dry side of the valley and the man looked at her and at the table.

'You've got to realize,' he said, 'that I don't want you to do it if you don't want to. I'm perfectly willing to go through with it if it means anything to you.'

'Doesn't it mean anything to you? We could get along.'

'Of course it does. But I don't want anybody but you. I don't want anyone else. And I know it's perfectly simple.'

'Yes, you know it's perfectly simple.'

'It's all right for you to say that, but I do know it.'

'Would you do something for me now?'

'I'd do anything for you.'

'Would you please please please please please please please stop talking?'

He did not say anything but looked at the bags against the wall of the station. There were labels on them from all the hotels where they had spent nights.

'But I don't want you to,' he said, 'I don't care anything about it.' 'I'll scream,' the girl said.

The woman came out through the curtains with two glasses of beer and put them down on the damp felt pads.

'The train comes in five minutes,' she said.

'What did she say?' asked the girl.

'That the train is coming in five minutes.'

The girl smiled brightly at the woman, to thank her.

'I'd better take the bags over to the other side of the station,' the man said.

She smiled at him.

'All right. Then come back and we'll finish the beer.'

He picked up the two heavy bags and carried them around the station to the other tracks. He looked up the tracks but could not see the train. Coming back, he walked through the bar-room, where people waiting for the train were drinking. He drank an Anis at the bar and looked at the people. They were all waiting reasonably for the train. He went out through the bead curtain. She was sitting at the table and smiled at him.

'Do you feel better?' he asked.

'I feel fine,' she said. 'There's nothing wrong with me. I feel fine.'

THE KILLERS

The door of Henry's lunch-room opened and two men came in. They sat down at the counter.

'What's yours?' George asked them.

'I don't know,' one of the men said. 'What do you want to eat, Al?' 'I don't know,' said Al. 'I don't know what I want to eat.'

Outside it was getting dark. The street light came on outside the window. The two men at the counter read the menu. From the other end of the counter Nick Adams watched them. He had been talking to George when they came in.

'I'll have a roast pork tenderloin with apple sauce and mashed potatoes,' the first man said.

'It isn't ready yet.'

'What the hell do you put it on the card for?'

'That's the dinner,' George explained. 'You can get that at six o'clock.'

George looked at the clock on the wall behind the counter.

'It's five o'clock.'

'The clock says twenty minutes past five,' the second man said.

'It's twenty minutes fast.'

'Oh, to hell with the clock,' the first man said. 'What have you got to eat?'

'I can give you any kind of sandwiches,' George said. 'You can have ham and eggs, bacon and eggs, liver and bacon, or a steak.'

'Give me chicken croquettes with green peas and cream sauce and mashed potatoes.'

'That's the dinner.'

'Everything we want's the dinner, eh?' That's the way you work it.' 'I can give you ham and eggs, bacon and eggs, liver—'

'I'll take ham and eggs,' the man called Al said. He wore a derby hat and a black overcoat buttoned across the chest. His face was small and white and he had tight lips. He wore a silk muffler and gloves.

'Give me bacon and eggs,' said the other man. He was about the same size as Al. Their faces were different, but they were dressed like twins. Both wore overcoats too tight for them. They sat leaning forward, their elbows on the counter.

'Got anything to drink?' Al asked.

'Silver beer, bevo, ginger-ale,' George said. 'I mean you got anything to *drink*?'

'Just those I said.'

'This is a hot town,' said the other. 'What do they call it?' 'Summit.'

'Ever hear of it?' Al asked his friend. 'No,' said the friend.

'What do you do here nights?' Al asked.

'They eat the dinner,' his friend said. 'They all come here and eat the big dinner.'

'That's right,' George said.

'So you think that's right?' Al asked George.

'Sure.'

'You're a pretty bright boy, aren't you?'

'Sure,' said George.

'Well, you're not,' said the other little man. 'Is he, Al?'

'He's dumb,' said Al. He turned to Nick. 'What's your name?'

'Adams.'

'Another bright boy,' Al said. 'Ain't he a bright boy, Max?' 'The town's full of bright boys,' Max said.

George put down two platters, one of ham and eggs, the other of bacon and eggs, on the counter. He set down two side dishes of fried potatoes and closed the wicket into the kitchen.

'Which is yours?' he asked Al. 'Don't you remember?'

'Ham and eggs.'

'Just a bright boy,' Max said. He leaned forward and took the ham and eggs. Both men ate with their gloves on. George watched them eat.

'What are *you* looking at?' Max looked at George.

'Nothing.'

'The hell you were. You were looking at me.'

'Maybe the boy meant it for a joke Max,' Al said.

George laughed.

'*You* don't have to laugh,' Max said to him. '*You* don't have to laugh at all, see?'

'All right,' said George.

'So he thinks it's all right,' Max turned to Al. 'He thinks it's all right. That's a good one.'

'Oh, he's a thinker,' Al said. They went on eating.

'What's the bright boy's name down the counter?' Al asked Max.

'Hey, bright boy,' Max said to Nick. 'You go around on the other side of the counter with your boy friend.'

'What's the idea?' Nick asked. 'There isn't any idea.'

'You better go around, bright boy,' Al said. Nick went around behind the counter.

'What's the idea?' George asked.

'None of your damn business,' Al said. 'Who's out in the kitchen?' 'The nigger.'

'What do you mean the nigger?' 'The nigger that cooks.'

'Tell him to come in.'

'What's the idea?'

'Tell him to come in.'

'Where do you think you are?'

'We know damn well where we are,, the man called Max said. 'Do we look silly?'

'You talk silly,' Al said to him. 'What the hell do you argue with this kid for? Listen,' he said to George, 'tell the nigger to come out here.'

'What are you going to do to him?'

'Nothing. Use your head, bright boy. What would we do to a nigger?'

George opened the slip that opened back into the kitchen. 'Sam,' he called. 'Come in here a minute.'

The door of the kitchen opened and the nigger came in. 'What was it?' he asked. The two men at the counter took a look at him.

'All right, nigger. You stand right there,' Al said.

Sam, the nigger, standing in his apron, looked at the two men sitting at the counter. 'Yes, sir,' he said. Al got down from his stool.

'I'm going back to the kitchen with the nigger and bright boy,' he said. 'Go back to the kitchen, nigger. You go with him, bright boy.' The little man walked after Nick and Sam, the cook, back into the kitchen. The door shut after them. The man called Max sat at the counter opposite George. He didn't look at George but looked in the mirror that ran along back of the counter. Henry's had been made over from a saloon into a lunch-counter.

'Well, bright boy,' Max said, looking into the mirror, 'why don't you say something?'

'What's it all about?'

'Hey, Al,' Max called, 'bright boy wants to know what it's all about.' 'Why don't you tell him?' Al's voice came from the kitchen.

'What do you think it's all about?' 'I don't know.'

'What do you think?'

Max looked into the mirror all the time he was talking. 'I wouldn't say.'

'Hey, Al, bright boy says he wouldn't say what he thinks it's all about.'

'I can hear you, all right,' Al said from the kitchen. He had propped open the slit that dishes passed through into the kitchen with a catsup bottle. 'Listen, bright boy,' he said from the kitchen to George. 'Stand a little further along the bar. You move a little to the left, Max.' He was like a photographer arranging for a group picture.

'Talk to me, bright boy,' Max said. 'What do you think's going to happen?'

George did not say anything.

'I'll tell you,' Max said. 'We're going to kill a Swede. Do you know a big Swede named Ole Andreson?'

'Yes.'

'He comes in here to eat every night, don't he?'

'Sometimes he comes here.'

'He comes here at six o'clock, don't he?' 'If he comes.'

'We know all that, bright boy,' Max said. 'Talk about something else. Ever go to the movies?'

'Once in a while.'

'You ought to go to the movies more. The movies are fine for a bright boy like you.'

'What are you going to kill Ole Andreson for? What did he ever do to you?'

'He never had a chance to do anything to us. He never even seen us. 'And he's only going to see us once,' Al said from the kitchen. 'What are you going to kill him for, then?' George asked.

'We're killing him for a friend. Just to oblige a friend, bright boy.' 'Shut up,' said Al from the kitchen. 'You talk too goddam much.' 'Well, I got to keep bright boy amused. Don't I, bright boy?'

'You talk too damn much,' Al said. 'The nigger and my bright boy are amused by themselves. I got them tied up like a couple of girl friends in the convent.'

'I suppose you were in a convent.' 'You never know.'

'You were in a kosher convent. That's where you were.'

George looked up at the clock.

'If anybody comes in you tell them the cook is off, and if they keep after it, you tell them you'll go back and cook yourself. Do you get that, bright boy?'

'All right,' George said. 'What you going to do with us afterwards?'

'That'll depend,' Max said. 'That's one of those things you never know at the time.'

George looked up at the clock. It was a quarter past six. The door from the street opened. A street-car motorman came in.

'Hello, George,' he said. 'Can I get supper?'

'Sam's gone out,' George said. 'He'll be back in about half an hour.'

'I'd better go up the street,' the motorman said. George looked at the clock. It was twenty minutes past six.

'That was nice, bright boy,' Max said. 'You're a regular little gentleman.' 'He knew I'd blow his head off,' Al said from the kitchen.

'No,' said Max. 'It ain't that. Bright boy is nice. He's a nice boy. I like him.'

At six-fifty-five George said: 'He's not coming.'

Two other people had been in the lunch-room. Once George had gone out to the kitchen and made a ham-and-egg sandwich 'to go' that a man wanted to take with him. Inside the kitchen he saw Al, his derby hat tilted back, sitting on a stool beside the wicket with the muzzle of a sawed-off shotgun resting on the ledge. Nick and the cook were back to back in the corner, a towel tied in each of their mouths. George had cooked the sandwich, wrapped it up in oiled paper, put it in a bag, brought it in, and the man had paid for it and gone out.

'Bright boy can do everything,' Max said. 'He can cook and everything. You'd make some girl a nice wife, bright boy.'

'Yes?' George said. 'Your friend, Ole Andreson, isn't going to come. 'We'll give him ten minutes,' Max said.

Max watched the mirror and the clock. The hands of the clock marked seven o'clock, and then five minutes past seven.

'Come on, Al,' said Max. 'We better go. He's not coming.'

'Better give him five minutes,' Al said from the kitchen.

In the five minutes a man came in, and George explained that the cook was sick.

'Why the hell don't you get another cook?' the man asked. 'Aren't you running a lunch-counter?' He went out.

'Come on, Al,' Max said.

'What about the two bright boys and the nigger?'

'They're all right.'

'You think so?'

'Sure. We're through with it.'

'I don't like it,' said Al. 'It's sloppy. You talk too much.'

'Oh, what the hell,' said Max. 'We got to keep amused, haven't we?' 'You talk too much, all the same,' Al said. He came out from the kitchen.

The cut-off barrels of the shotgun made a slight bulge under the waist of his too tight-fitting overcoat. He straightened his coat with his gloved hands.

'So long, bright boy,' he said to George. 'You got a lot of luck.' 'That's the truth,' Max said. 'You ought to play the races, bright boy.'

The two of them went out of the door. George watched them, through the window, pass under the arc-light, and cross the street. In their tight overcoats and derby hats they looked like a vaudeville team. George went back through the swinging-door into the kitchen and untied Nick and the cook.

'I don't want any more of that,' said Sam, the cook. 'I don't want any more of that.'

Nick stood up. He had never had a towel in his mouth before.

'Say,' he said. 'What the hell?' He was trying to swagger it off.

'They were going to kill Ole Andreson,' George said. 'They were going to shoot him when he came in to eat.'

'Ole
Andreson?'

'Sure.'

The cook felt the corners of his mouth with his thumbs.

'They all gone?' he asked.

'Yeah,' said George. 'They're gone now.'

'I don't like it,' said the cook. 'I don't like any of it at all.' 'Listen,' George said to Nick. 'You better go see Ole Andreson.' 'All right.'

'You better not have anything to do with it at all,' Sam, the cook, said. 'You better stay way out of it.'

'Don't go if you don't want to,' George said.

'Mixing up in this ain't going to get you anywhere,' the cook said. 'You stay out of it.'

'I'll go see him,' Nick said to George. 'Where does he live?'

The cook turned away.

'Little boys always know what they want to do,' he said.

'He lives up at Hirsch's rooming-house,' George said to Nick. 'I'll go up there.'

Outside, the arc-light shone through the bare branches of a tree. Nick walked up the street beside the car-tracks and turned at the next arc-light down a side-street. Three houses up the street was Hirsch's rooming-house. Nick walked up the two steps and pushed the bell. A woman came to the door.

'Is Ole Andreson here?'

'Do you want to see him?' 'Yes, if he's in.'

Nick followed the woman up a flight of stairs and back to the end of the corridor. She knocked on the door.

'Who is it?'

'It's somebody to see you, Mr. Andreson,' the woman said.

'It's Nick Adams.'

'Come in.'

Nick opened the door and went into the room. Ole Andreson was lying on the bed with all his clothes on. He had been a heavyweight prize-fighter and he was too long for the bed. He lay with his head on two pillows. He did not look at Nick.

'What was it?' he asked.

'I was up at Henry's,' Nick said, 'and two fellows came in and tied up me and the cook, and they said they were going to kill you.'

It sounded silly when he said it. Ole Andreson said nothing.

'They put us out in the kitchen,' Nick went on. 'They were going to shoot you when you came in to supper.'

Ole Andresen looked at the wall and did not say anything.

'George thought I'd better come and tell you about it.' 'There isn't anything I can do about it,' Ole Andreson said. 'I'll tell you what they were like.'

'I don't want to know what they were like,' Ole Andreson said. He looked at the wall. 'Thanks for coming to tell me about it.'

'That's all right.'

Nick looked at the big man lying on the bed.

'Don't you want me to go and see the police?'

'No,' Ole Andresen said. 'That wouldn't do any good.'

'Isn't there something I could do?'

'No. There ain't anything to do.' 'Maybe it was just a bluff.'

'No. It ain't just a bluff.'

Ole Andresen rolled over towards the wall.

'The only thing is,' he said, talking towards the wall, 'I just can't make up my mind to go out. I been in here all day.'

'Couldn't you get out of town?'

'No,' Ole Andresen said. 'I'm through with all that running around.' He looked at the wall.

'There ain't anything to do now.'

'Couldn't you fix it up some way?'

'No. I got in wrong.' He talked in the same flat voice. 'There ain't anything to do. After a while I'll make up my mind to go out.'

'I better go back and see George,' Nick said.

'So long,' said Ole Andreson. He did not look towards Nick. 'Thanks for coming around.'

Nick went out. As he shut the door he saw Ole Andreson with all his clothes on, lying on the bed looking at the wall.

'He's been in his room all day,' the landlady said downstairs. 'I guess he don't feel well. I said to him: 'Mr. Andreson, you ought to go out and take a walk on a nice fall day like this,' but he didn't feel like it.'

'He doesn't want to go out.'

'I'm sorry he don't feel well,' the woman said. 'He's an awfully nice man. He was in the ring, you know.'

'I know it.'

'You'd never know it except from the way his face is,' the woman said. They stood talking just inside the street door. 'He's just as gentle.'

'Well, good-night, Mrs. Hirsch,' Nick said.

'I'm not Mrs. Hirsch" the woman said. 'She owns the place. I just look after it for her, I'm Mrs. Bell.'

'Well, good-night, Mrs. Bell,' Nick said.

'Good-night,' the woman said.

Nick walked up the dark street to the corner under the arc-light, and then along the car-tracks to Henry's eating-house. George was inside, back of the counter.

'Did you see Ole?'

'Yes,' said Nick. 'He's in his room and he won't go out.'

The cook opened the door from the kitchen when he heard Nick's voice. 'I don't even listen to it,' he said and shut the door.

'Did you tell him about it?' George asked.

'Sure. I told him, but he knows what it's all about.'

'What's he going to do?'

'Nothing.'

'They'll kill him.' 'I guess they will.'

'He must have got mixed up in something in Chicago.' 'I guess so,' said Nick.

'It's a hell of a thing.'

'It's an awful thing,' Nick said.

They did not say anything. George reached down for a towel and wiped the counter.

'I wonder what he did?' Nick said.

'Double-crossed somebody. That's what they kill them for.'

'I'm going to get out of this town,' Nick said.

'Yes,' said George. 'That's a good thing to do.'

'I can't stand to think about him waiting in the room and knowing he's going to get it. It's too damned awful.'

'Well,' said George, 'you better not think about it.'

CHE TI DICE LA PATRIA?

The road of the pass was hard and smooth and not yet dusty in the early morning. Below were the hills with oak and chestnut trees, and far away below was the sea. On the other side were snowy mountains.

We came down from the pass through wooded country. There were bags of charcoal piled beside the road, and through the trees we saw charcoal-burners' huts. It was Sunday and the road, rising and falling, but always dropping away from the altitude of the pass, went through the scrub woods and through villages.

Outside the villages there were fields with vines. The fields were brown and the vines coarse and thick. The houses were white, and in the streets the men, in their Sunday clothes, were playing bowls. Against the walls of some of the houses there were pear trees, their branches candelabraed against the white walls. The pear trees had been sprayed, and the walls of the houses were stained a metallic blue-green by the spray vapor. There were small clearings around the villages where the vines grew, and then the woods.

In a village, twenty kilometers above Spezia, there was a crowd in the square, and a young man carrying a suitcase came up to the car and asked us to take him in to Spezia.

'There are only two places, and they are occupied,' I said. We had an old Ford coupé.

'I will ride on the outside.'

'You will be uncomfortable.'

'That makes nothing, I must go to Spezia.' 'Should we take him?' I asked Guy.

'He seems to be going anyway,' Guy said. The young man handed in a parcel through the window.

'Look after this,' he said. Two men tied his suitcase on the back of the car, above our suitcases. He shook hands with every one, explained that to a Fascist and a man as used to traveling as himself there was no discomfort, and climbed up on the running-board on the left-hand side of the car, holding on inside, his right arm through the open window.

'You can start,' he said. The crowd waved. He waved with his free hand. 'What did he say?' Guy asked me.

'That we could start.'

'Isn't he nice?' Guy said.

The road followed a river. Across the river were mountains. The sun was taking the frost out of the grass. It was bright and cold and the air came through the open windshield.

'How do you think he likes it out there?' Guy was looking up the road. His view out of his side of the car was blocked by our guest. The young man projected from the side of the car like the figurehead of a ship. He had turned his coat collar up and pulled his hat down and his nose looked cold in the wind.

'Maybe he'll get enough of it,' Guy said. 'That's the side our bum tire's on.'

'Oh, he'd leave us if we blew out,' I said. 'He wouldn't get his traveling clothes dirty.'

'Well, I don't mind him,' Guy said—"except the way he leans out on the turns.'

The woods were gone; the road had left the river to climb; the radiator was boiling; the young man looked annoyedly and suspiciously at the steam and rusty water; the engine was grinding, with both Guy's feet on the first-speed pedal, up and up, back and forth, and up, and, finally, out level. The grinding stopped, and in the new quiet there was a great churning bubbling in the radiator. We were at the top of the last range above Spezia and the sea. The road descended with short, barely rounded turns. Our guest hung out on the turns and nearly pulled the top-heavy car over.

'You can't tell him not to,' I said to Guy. 'It's his sense of self- preservation.'

'The great Italian sense.'

'The greatest Italian sense.'

We came down around curves, through deep dust, the dust powdering the olive trees. Spezia spread below along the sea. The road flattened outside the town. Our guest put his head in the window.

'I want to stop.'

'Stop it,' I said to Guy.

We slowed up, at the side of the road. The young man got down, went to the back of the car and untied the suitcase.

'I stop here, so you won't get into trouble carrying passengers,' he said. 'My package.'

I handed him the package. He reached in his pocket. 'How much do I owe you?'

'Nothing.' 'Why not?'

'I don't know,' I said.

'Then thanks,' the young man said, not 'thank you,' or 'thank you very much,' or 'thank you a thousand times', all of which you formerly said in

Italy to a man when he handed you a time-table or explained about a direction. The young man uttered the lowest form of the word 'thanks' and looked after us suspiciously as Guy started the car. I waved my hand at him. He was too dignified to reply. We went on into Spezia.

'That's a young man that will go a long way in Italy,' I said to Guy.

'Well,' said Guy, 'he went twenty kilometers with us.'

A MEAL IN SPEZIA

We came into Spezia looking for a place to eat. The street was wide and the houses high and yellow. We followed the tram-track into the centre of town. On the walls of the houses were stenciled eye-bugging portraits of Mussolini, with hand-painted 'vivas', the double V in black paint with drippings of paint down the wall. Side-streets went down to the harbor. It was bright and the people were all out for Sunday. The stone paving had been sprinkled and there were damp stretches in the dust. We went close to the curb to avoid a train.

'Let's eat somewhere simple,' Guy said.

We stopped opposite two restaurant signs. We were standing across the street and I was buying the papers. The two restaurants were side by side. A woman standing in the doorway of one smiled at us and we crossed the street and went in.

It was dark inside and at the back of the room three girls were sitting at a table with an old woman. Across from us, at another table, sat a sailor. He sat there neither eating nor drinking. Further back, a young man in a blue suit was writing at a table. His hair was pomaded and shining and he was very smartly dressed and clean-cut looking.

The light came through the doorway, and through the window where vegetables, fruit, steaks, and chops were arranged in a showcase. A girl came and took our order and another girl stood in the doorway. We noticed that she wore nothing under her house dress. The girl who took our order put her arm around Guy's neck while we were looking at the menu. There were three girls in all, and they all took turns going and standing in the doorway. The old woman at the table in the back of the room spoke to them and they sat down again with her.

There was no doorway leading from the room except into the kitchen. A curtain hung over it. The girl who had taken our order came in from the kitchen with spaghetti. She put it on the table and brought a bottle of red wine and sat down at the table.

'Well,' I said to Guy, 'you wanted to eat at some place simple.' 'This isn't simple. This is complicated.'

'What do you say?' asked the girl. 'Are you Germans?'

'South Germans,' I said. 'The South Germans are a gentle, lovable people.'

'Don't understand,' she said.

'What's the mechanics of this place?' Guy asked. 'Do I have to let her put her arm around my neck?'

'Certainly,' I said. 'Mussolini has abolished brothels. This is a restaurant.'

The girl wore a one-piece dress. She leaned forward against the table and put her hands on her breasts and smiled. She smiled better on one side than on the other and turned the good side towards us. The charm of the good side had been enhanced by some event which had smoothed the other side of her nose in, as warm wax can be smoothed. Her nose, however, did not look like warm wax. It was very cold and firmed, only smoothed in. 'You like me?' she asked Guy.

'He adores you,' I said. 'But he doesn't speak Italian.'

'Ich spreche Deutsch,' she said, and stroked Guy's hair.

'Speak to the lady in your native tongue, Guy.'

'Where do you come from?' asked the lady. 'Potsdam.'

'And you will stay here now for a little while?'

'In this so dear Spezia?' I asked.

'Tell him we have to go,' said Guy. 'Tell her we are very ill, and have no money.'

'My friend is a misogynist,' I said, 'an old German misogynist.' 'Tell him I love him.'

I told him.

'Will you shut your mouth and get us out of here?' Guy said. The lady had placed another arm around his neck. 'Tell him he is mine,' she said.

I told him.

'Will you get us out of here?'

'You are quarreling,' the lady said. 'You do not love one another.' 'We are Germans,' I said proudly, 'old South Germans.'

'Tell him he is a beautiful boy,' the lady said. Guy is thirty-eight and takes some pride in the fact that he is taken for a traveling salesman in France. 'You are a beautiful boy,' I said.

'Who says so?' Guy asked, 'you or her?'

'She does. I'm just your interpreter. Isn't that what you got me in on this trip for?'

'I'm glad it's her,' said Guy. 'I don't want to have to leave you here too.' 'I don't know. Spezia's a lovely place.'

'Spezia,' the lady said. 'You are talking about Spezia.'

'Lovely place,' I said.

'It is my country,' she said. 'Spezia is my home and Italy is my country.' 'She says that Italy is her country.'

'Tell her it looks like her country,' Guy said.

'What have you for dessert?' I asked.

'Fruit,' she said. 'We have bananas.'

'Bananas are all right,' Guy said. 'They've got skins on.'

'Oh, he takes bananas,' the lady said. She embraced Guy.

'What does she say?' he asked, keeping his face out of her way.

'She is pleased because you take bananas.'

'Tell her I don't take bananas.'

'The Signor does not take bananas.'

'Ah,' said the lady, crestfallen, 'he doesn't take bananas.'

'Tell her I take a cold bath every morning,' Guy said. 'The Signor takes a cold bath every morning.'

'No understand,' the lady said.

Across from us, the property sailor had not moved. No one in the place paid any attention to him.

'We want the bill,' I said. 'Oh, no. You must stay.'

'Listen,' the clean-cut young man said from the table where he was writing, 'let them go. These two are worth nothing.'

The lady took my hand. 'You won't stay? You won't ask him to stay?'

'We have to go,' I said. 'We have to get to Pisa, or if possible, Firenze, tonight. We can amuse ourselves in those cities at the end of the day. It is now the day. In the day we must cover distance.'

'To stay a little while is nice.'

'To travel is necessary during the light of day.'

'Listen,' the clean-cut young man said. 'Don't bother to talk with these two. I tell you they are worth nothing and I know.'

'Bring us the bill,' I said. She brought the bill from the old woman and went back and sat at the table. Another girl came in from the kitchen. She walked the length of the room and stood in the doorway.

'Don't bother with these two,' the clean-cut young man said in a wearied voice. 'Come and eat. They are worth nothing.'

We paid the bill and stood up. All the girls, the old woman, and the clean-cut young man sat down at the table together. The property sailor sat with his head in his hands. No one had spoken to him all the time we were at lunch. The girl brought us our change that the old woman counted out for her and went back to her place at the table. We left a tip on the table and went out. When we were seated in the car ready to start, the girl came out and stood in the door. We started and I waved to her. She did not wave, but stood there looking after us.

AFTER THE RAIN

It was raining hard when we passed through the suburbs of Genoa, and, even going very slowly behind the tramcars and the motor trucks, liquid mud splashed on to the sidewalks, so that people stepped into the doorways as they saw us coming. In San Pier d'Arena, the industrial suburb outside of Genoa, there is a wide street with two car-tracks and we drove down the centre to avoid sending the mud on to the men going home from work. On our left was the Mediterranean. There was a big sea running and waves broke and the wind blew the spray against the car. A riverbed that, when we had passed, going into Italy, had been wide, stony, and dry, was running brown, and up to the banks. The brown water discolored the sea and as the waves thinned and cleared in breaking, the light came through the yellow water and the crests, detached by the wind, blew across the road.

A big car passed us, going fast, and a sheet of muddy water rose up and over our windshield and radiator. The automatic windshield cleaner moved back and forth, spreading the film over the glass. We stopped and ate lunch at Sestri. There was no heat in the restaurant and we kept our hats and coats on. We could see the car outside, through the window. It was covered with mud and was stopped beside some boats that had been pulled up beyond the waves. In the restaurant you could see your breath.

The *pasta asciutta* was good; the wine tasted of alum, and we poured water in it. Afterwards the waiter brought beef steak and fried potatoes. A man and a woman sat at the far end of the restaurant. He was middle-aged and she was young and wore black. All during the meal she would blow out her breath in the cold damp air. The man would look at it and shake his head.

They ate without talking and the man held her hand under the table. She was good-looking and they seemed very sad. They had a traveling-bag with them.

We had the papers and I read the account of the Shanghai fighting aloud to Guy. After the meal, he left with the waiter in search for a place which did not exist in the restaurant, and I cleaned off the windshield, the lights, and the license plates with a rag. Guy came back and we backed the car out and started. The waiter had taken him across the road and into an old house. The people in the house were suspicious and the waiter had remained with Guy to see nothing was stolen.

'Although I don't know how, me not being a plumber, they expected me to steal anything,' Guy said.

As we came up on a headland beyond the town, the wind struck the car and nearly tipped it over.

'It's good, it blows us away from the sea,' Guy said.

'Well,' I said, 'they drowned Shelley somewhere along here.'

'That was down by Viareggio,' Guy said. 'Do you remember what we came to this country for?'

'Yes,' I said, 'but we didn't get it.'

'We'll be out of it tonight.'

'If we can get past Ventimiglia.'

'We'll see. I don't like to drive this coast at night.' It was early afternoon and the sun was out. Below, the sea was blue with whitecaps running towards Savona. Back beyond the cape the brown and blue waters joined. Out ahead of us, a tramp steamer was going up the coast.

'Can you still see Genoa?' Guy asked. 'Oh, yes.'

'That next big cape ought to put it out of sight.'

'We'll see it a long time yet. I can still see Portofino Cape behind it.'

Finally we could not see Genoa. I looked back as we came out and there was only the sea, and below in the bay, a line of beach and fishing-boats and above, on the side of the hill, a town and then capes far down the coast.

'It's gone now,' I said to Guy.

'Oh, it's been gone a long time now.'

'But we couldn't be sure till we got way out.'

There was a sign with a picture of an S-turn and Svolta Pericolosa. The road curved around the headland and the wind blew through the crack in the windshield. Below the cape was a flat stretch beside the sea. The wind had dried the mud and the wheels were beginning to lift dust. On the flat road we passed a Fascist riding a bicycle, a heavy revolver in a holster on his back. He held the middle of the road on his bicycle and we turned out for him. He looked up at us as we passed. Ahead there was a railway crossing, and as we came towards it the gates went down.

As we waited, the Fascist came up on his bicycle. The train went by and Guy started the engine.

'Wait,' the bicycle man shouted from behind the car. 'Your number's dirty.'

I got out with a rag. The number had been cleaned at lunch. 'You can read it,' I said.

'You think so?' 'Read it.'

'I cannot read it. It is dirty.'

I wiped it off with the rag. 'How's that?'

'Twenty-five lire.'

'What?' I said. 'You could have read it. It's only dirty from the state of the roads.'

'You don't like Italian roads?' 'They are dirty.'

'Fifty lire.' He spat in the road. 'Your car is dirty and you are dirty too.'

'Good. And give me a receipt with your name.'

He took out a receipt book, made in duplicate, and perforated, so one side could be given to the customer, and the other side filled in and kept as a stub. There was no carbon to record what the customer's ticket said.

'Give me fifty lire.'

He wrote in indelible pencil, tore out the slip, and handed it to me. I read it.

'This is for twenty-five lire.'

'A mistake,' he said, and changed the twenty-five to fifty. 'And now the other side. Make it fifty in the part you keep.'

He smiled a beautiful Italian smile and wrote something on the receipt stub, holding it so I could not see.

'Go on,' he said, 'before your number gets dirty again.'

We drove for two hours after it was dark and slept in Mentone that night. It seemed very cheerful and clean and sane and lovely. We had driven from Ventimiglia to Pisa and Florence, across the Romagna to Rimini, back through Forlì, Imola, Bologna, Parma, Piacenza, and Genoa, to Ventimiglia again. The whole trip had only taken ten days. Naturally, in such a short trip, we had no opportunity to see how things were with the country or the people.

FIFTY GRAND

'How are you going yourself Jack?' I asked him.

'You seen this Walcott?' he says.

'Just in the gym.'

'Well,' Jack says, 'I'm going to need a lot of luck with that boy.' 'He can't hit you, Jack,' Soldier said.

'I wish to hell he couldn't.'

'He couldn't hit you with a handful of bird-shot.'

'Bird-shot'd be all right,' Jack says. 'I wouldn't mind bird-shot any.' 'He looks easy to hit,' I said.

'Sure,' Jack says, 'he ain't going to last long. He ain't going to last like you and me, Jerry. But right now he's got everything.'

'You'll left-hand him to death.'

'Maybe,' Jack says. 'Sure. I got a chance to.'

'Handle him like you handled Richie Lewis'

'Richie Lewis,' Jack said. 'That kike!'

The three of us, Jack Brennan, Soldier Bartlett, and I, were in Handley's. There were a couple of broads sitting at the next table to us. They had been drinking.

'What do you mean, kike?' one of the broads says. 'What do you mean, kike, you big Irish bum?'

'Sure,' Jack says. 'That's it.'

'Kikes,' this broad goes on. 'They're always talking about kikes, these big Irishmen. What do you mean, kikes?'

'Come on. Let's get out of here.'

'Kikes,' this broad goes on. 'Whoever saw you ever buy a drink? Your wife sews your pockets up every morning. These Irishmen and their kikes? Ritchie Lewis could lick you too.'

'Sure,' Jack says. 'And you give away a lot of things free too, don't you?'

We went out. That was Jack. He could say what he wanted to when he wanted to say it.

Jack started training out at Danny Hogan's health farm over in Jersey. It was nice out there but Jack didn't like it much. He didn't like being away from his wife and the kids, and he was sore and grouchy most of the time. He liked me and we got along fine together; and he liked Hogan, but after a while Soldier Bartlett commenced to get on his nerves. A kidder gets to be an awful thing around a camp if his stuff goes sort of sour. Soldier was always kidding Jack, just sort of kidding him all the time. It wasn't very funny and it wasn't very good, and it began to get to Jack. It was sort of stuff like this. Jack would finish up with the weights and the bag and pull on the gloves.

'You want to work?' he'd say to Soldier.

'Sure. How you want me to work?' Soldier would ask. 'Want me to treat you rough like Walcott? Want me to knock you down a few times?'

'That's it,' Jack would say. He didn't like it any, though.

One morning we were all out on the road. We'd been out quite a way and now we were coming back. We'd go along fast for three minutes and then walk a minute, and then go fast for three minutes again. Jack wasn't ever what you would call a sprinter. He'd move around fast enough in the ring if he had to, but he wasn't any too fast on the road. All the time we were walking Soldier was kidding him. We came up the hill to the farmhouse.

'Well,' says Jack, 'you better go back to town, Soldier.'
'What do you mean?'
'You better go back to town and stay there.'
'What's the matter?'
'I'm sick of hearing you talk.' 'Yes?' says Soldier.
'Yes,' says Jack.
'You'll be a damn sight sicker when Walcott gets through with you.' 'Sure,' says Jack, 'maybe I will. But I know I'm sick of you.'

So Soldier went off on that train to town that same morning. I went with him to the train. He was good and sore.

'I was just kidding him,' he said. We were waiting on the platform. 'He can't pull that stuff with me, Jerry.'

'He's nervous and crabby,' I said. 'He's a good fellow, Soldier.'
'The hell he is. The hell he's ever been a good fellow.'
'Well,' I said, 'so long, Soldier.'
The train had come in. He climbed up with his bag.
'So long, Jerry,' he says. 'You be in town before the fight?' 'I don't think so.'
'See you then.'

He went in and the conductor swung up and the train went out. I rode back to the farm in the cart. Jack was on the porch writing a letter to his wife.

The mail had come and I got the papers and went over on the other side of the porch and sat down to read. Hogan came out the door and walked over to me.

'Did he have a jam with Soldier?'
'Not a jam,' I said. 'He just told him to go back to town.'
'I could see it coming,' Hogan said. 'He never liked Soldier much.' 'No. He don't like many people.'
'He's a pretty cold one,' Hogan said. 'Well, he's always been fine to me.'
'Me too,' Hogan said. 'I got no kick on him. He's a cold one though.'

Hogan went in through the screen door and I sat there on the porch and read the papers. It was just starting to get fall weather and it's nice country there in Jersey, up in the hills, and after I read the paper through I sat there and looked out at the country and the road down below against the woods with cars going along it, lifting the dust up. It was fine weather and pretty nice- looking country. Hogan came to the door and I said, 'Say, Hogan, haven't you got anything to shoot here?'

'No,' Hogan said. 'Only sparrows.'
'Seen the paper?' I said to Hogan. 'What's in it?'
'Sande booted three of them in yesterday.'
'I got that on the telephone last night.'
'You follow them pretty close, Hogan?' I asked.
'Oh, I keep in touch with them,' Hogan said.
'How about Jack?' I says. 'Does he still play them?'

'Him?' said Hogan. 'Can you see him doing it?'

Just then Jack came around the corner with the letter in his hand. He's wearing a sweater and an old pair of pants and boxing shoes.

'Got a stamp, Hogan?' he asks.

'Give me that letter,' Hogan said. 'I'll mail it for you.'

'Say, Jack,' I said, 'didn't you used to play the ponies?'

'Sure.'

'I knew you did. I knew I used to see you out at Sheepshead.'

'What did you lay off them for?' Hogan asked.

'Lost money.'

Jack sat down on the porch by me. He leaned back against a post. He shut his eyes in the sun.

'Want a chair?' Hogan asked. 'No,' said Jack.

'This is fine.'

'It's a nice day,' I said. 'It's pretty nice out in the country.' 'I'd a damn sight rather be in town with the wife.'

'Well, you only got another week.' 'Yes,' Jack says. 'That's so.'

We sat there on the porch. Hogan was inside at the office.

'What do you think about the shape I'm in?' Jack asked me.

'Well, you can't tell,' I said. 'You got a week to get around into form.' 'Don't stall me.'

'Well,' I said, 'you're not right.'

'I'm not sleeping,' Jack said.

'You'll be all right in a couple of days.'

'No,' said Jack, 'I got the insomnia.'

'What's on your mind?'

'I miss the wife.'

'Have her come out.'

'No. I'm too old for that.'

'We'll take a long walk before you turn in and get you good and tired.' 'Tired!' Jack says. 'I'm tired all the time.'

He was that way all week. He wouldn't sleep at night and he'd get up in the morning feeling that way, you know when you can't shut your hands.

'He's stale as poorhouse cake,' Hogan said. 'He's nothing.' 'I never seen Walcott,' I said.

'He'll kill him,' said Hogan. 'He'll tear him in two.'

'Well,' I said, 'everybody's got to get it sometime.'

'Not like this, though,' Hogan said. 'They'll think he never trained. It gives the farm a black eye.'

'You hear what the reporters said about him?'

'Didn't I! They said he was awful. They said they oughtn't to let him fight.'

'Well,' I said, 'they're always wrong, ain't they?'

'Yes,' said Hogan. 'But this time they're right.'

'What the hell do they know about whether a man's right or not?'

'Well,' said Hogan, 'they're not such fools.'

'All they did was pick Willard at Toledo. This Lardner, he's so wise now, ask him about when he picked Willard at Toledo.'

'Aw, he wasn't out,' Hogan said. 'He only writes the big fights.'

'I don't care who they are,' I said. 'What the hell do they know? They can write maybe, but what the hell do they know?'

'You don't think Jack's in any shape, do you?' Hogan asked.

'No. He's through. All he needs is to have Corbett pick him to win for it to be all over.'

'Well, Corbett'll pick him,' Hogan says.

'Sure. He'll pick him.'

That night Jack didn't sleep any either. The next morning was the last day before the fight. After breakfast we were out on the porch again.

'What do you think about, Jack, when you can't sleep?' I said.

'Oh, I worry,' Jack says. 'I worry about property I got up in the Bronx, I worry about property I got in Florida. I worry about the kids. I worry about the wife. Sometimes I think about fights. I think about that kike Richie

Lewis and I get sore. I got some stocks and I worry about them. What the hell don't I think about?'

'Well,' I said, 'tomorrow night it'll all be over.'

'Sure,' said Jack. 'That always helps a lot, don't it? That just fixes everything all up, I suppose. Sure.'

He was sore all day. We didn't do any work. Jack just moved around a little to loosen up. He shadow-boxed a few rounds. He didn't even look good doing that. He skipped the rope a little while. He couldn't sweat.

'He'd be better not to do any work at all,' Hogan said. We were standing watching him skip rope. 'Don't he ever sweat at all any more?'

'He can't sweat.'

'Do you suppose he's got the con? He never had any trouble making weight, did he?'

'No, he hasn't got any con. He just hasn't got anything inside any more.' 'He ought to sweat,' said Hogan.

Jack came over, skipping the rope. He was skipping up and down in front of us, forward and back, crossing his arms every third time.

'Well,' he says. 'What are you buzzards talking about?'

'I don't think you ought to work any more,' Hogan says. 'You'll be stale.'

'Wouldn't that be awful?' Jack says and skips away down the floor, slapping the rope hard.

That afternoon John Collins showed up out at the farm. Jack was up in his room. John came out in a car from town. He had a couple of friends with him. The car stopped and they all got out.

'Where's Jack?' John asked me.

'Up in his room, lying down.' 'Lying down?'

'Yes,' I said.

'How is he?'

I looked at the two fellows that were with John.

'They're friends of his,' John said.

'He's pretty bad,' I said.

'What's the matter with him?' 'He don't sleep.'

'Hell,' said John. 'That Irishman could never sleep.'

'He isn't right,' I said.

'Hell,' John said. 'He's never right. I've had him for ten years and he's never been right yet.'

The fellows who were with him laughed.

'I want you to shake hands with Mr. Morgan and Mr. Steinfelt,' John said. 'This is Mr. Doyle. He's been training Jack.'

'Glad to meet you,' I said.

'Let's go up and see the boy,' the fellow called Morgan said.

'Let's have a look at him,' Steinfelt said.

We all went upstairs.

'Where's Hogan?' John asked.

'He's out in the barn with a couple of his customers,' I said.

'He got many people out here now?' John asked.

'Just two.'

'Pretty quiet, ain't it?' Morgan said. 'Yes,' I said. 'It's pretty quiet.'

We were outside Jack's room. John knocked on the door. There wasn't an answer.

'Maybe he's asleep,' I said.

'What the hell's he sleeping in the daytime for?'

John turned the handle and we all went in. Jack was lying asleep on the bed. He was face down and his face was in the pillow. Both his arms were around the pillow.

'Hey, Jack!' John said to him.

Jack's head moved a little on the pillow. 'Jack!' John says, leaning over him. Jack just dug a little deeper in the pillow. John touched him on the shoulder. Jack sat up and looked at us. He hadn't shaved and he was wearing an old sweater.

'Christ! Why can't you let me sleep?' he says to John. 'Don't be sore,' John says. 'I didn't mean to wake you up.' 'Oh no,' Jack says. 'Of course not.'

'You know Morgan and Steinfelt,' John said.

'Glad to see you,' Jack says.

'How do you feel, Jack?' Morgan asks him.

'Fine,' Jack says. 'How the hell would I feel?'

'You look fine,' Steinfelt says.

'Yes, don't I,' says Jack. 'Say,' he says to John. 'You're my manager. You get a big enough cut. Why the hell don't you come out here when the reporters was out!

You want Jerry and me to talk to them?'

'I had Lew fighting in Philadelphia,' John said.

'What the hell's that to me?' Jack says. 'You're my manager. You get a big enough cut, don't you? You aren't making me any money in Philadelphia, are you? Why the hell aren't you out here when I ought to have you?'

'Hogan was here.'

'Hogan,' Jack says. 'Hogan's as dumb as I am.'

'Soldier Bartlett was out here wukking with you for a while, wasn't he?' Steinfelt said to change the subject.

'Yes, he was out here,' Jack says. 'He was out here all right.'

'Say, Jerry,' John said to me. 'Would you go and find Hogan and tell him we want to see him in about half an hour?'

'Sure,' I said.

'Why the hell can't he stick around?' Jack says. 'Stick around, Jerry.'

Morgan and Steinfelt looked at each other.

'Quiet down, Jack,' John said to him. 'I better go find Hogan,' I said.

'All right, if you want to go,' Jack says. 'None of these guys are going to send you away, though.'

'I'll go find Hogan,' I said.

Hogan was out in the gym in the barn. He had a couple of his health-farm patients with the gloves on. They neither one wanted to hit the other, for fear the other would come back and hit him.

'That'll do,' Hogan said when he saw me come in. 'You can stop the slaughter. You gentlemen take a shower and Bruce will rub you down.'

They climbed out through the ropes and Hogan came over to me.

'John Collins is out with a couple of friends to see Jack,' I said. 'I saw them come up in the car.'

'Who are the two fellows with John?'

'They're what you call wise boys,' Hogan said. 'Don't you know them two?'

'No,' I said.

'That's Happy Steinfelt and Lew Morgan. They got a pool-room.' 'I been away a long time,' I said.

'Sure,' said Hogan. 'That Happy Steinfelt's a big operator.'

'I've heard his name,' I said.

'He's a pretty smooth boy,' Hogan said. 'They're a couple of sharpshooters.'

'Well,' I said. 'They want to see us in half an hour.' 'You mean they don't want to see us until half an hour?' 'That's it.'

'Come into the office,' Hogan said. 'To hell with those sharpshooters.'

After about thirty minutes or so Hogan and I went upstairs. We knocked on Jack's door. They were talking inside the room.

'Wait a minute,' somebody said.

'To hell with that stuff,' Hogan said. 'When you want to see me I'm down in the office.'

We heard the door unlock. Steinfelt opened it.

'Come on in, Hogan,' he says. 'We're all going to have a drink.'

'Well,' says Hogan. 'That's something.'

We went in. Jack was sitting on the bed. John and Morgan were sitting on a couple of chairs. Steinfelt was standing up.

'You're a pretty mysterious lot of boys,' Hogan said.

'Hello, Danny,' John says.

'Hello, Danny,' Morgan says and shakes hands.

Jack doesn't say anything. He just sits there on the bed. He ain't with the others. He's all by himself. He was wearing an old blue jersey and pants and had on boxing shoes. He needed a shave. Steinfelt and Morgan were dressers. John was quite a dresser too. Jack sat there looking Irish and tough.

Steinfelt brought out a bottle and Hogan brought in some glasses and everybody had a drink. Jack and I took one and the rest of them went on and had two or three each.

'Better save some for your ride back,' Hogan said.

'Don't you worry. We got plenty,' Morgan said.

Jack hadn't drunk anything since the one drink. He was standing up and looking at them. Morgan was sitting on the bed where Jack had sat.

'Have a drink, Jack,' John said and handed him the glass and the bottle.

'No,' Jack said, 'I never liked to go to these wakes.'

They all laughed. Jack didn't laugh.

They were all feeling pretty good when they left. Jack stood on the porch when they got into the car. They waved to him.

'So long,' Jack said.

We had supper. Jack didn't say anything all during the meal except, 'Will you pass me this?' or 'Will you pass me that?' The two health-farm patients ate at the same table with us. They were pretty nice fellows. After we finished eating we went out on the porch. It was dark early.

'Like to take a walk, Jerry?' Jack said. 'Sure,' I said.

We put on our coats and started out. It was quite a way down to the main road and then we walked along the main road about a mile and a half. Cars kept going by and we would pull out to one side until they were past. Jack didn't say anything. After we had stepped out into the bushes to let a big car go by Jack said, 'To hell with this walking. Come on back to Hogan's'.

We went along a side road that cut up over the hill and cut across the fields back to Hogan's. We could see the lights of the house up on the hill. We came around to the front of the house and there standing in the doorway was Hogan.

'Have a good walk?' Hogan asked.

'Oh, fine,' Jack said. 'Listen, Hogan. Have you got any liquor?'

'Sure,' says Hogan. 'What's the idea?'

'Send it up to the room,' Jack says. 'I'm going to sleep tonight.'

'You're the doctor,' Hogan says.

'Come on up to the room, Jerry,' Jack says.

Upstairs, Jack sat on the bed with his head in his hands.

'Ain't it a life?' Jack says.

Hogan brought in a quart of liquor and two glasses.

'Want some ginger ale?'

'What do you think I want to do, get sick?'

'I just asked you,' said Hogan.

'Have a drink?' said Jack.

'No, thanks,' said Hogan. He went out. 'How about it, Jerry?'

'I'll have one with you,' I said.

Jack poured out a couple of drinks. 'Now,' he said, 'I want to take it slow and easy.'

'Put some water in it,' I said.

'Yes,' Jack said. 'I guess that's better.'

We had a couple of drinks without saying anything. Jack started to pour me another.

'No,' I said, 'that's all I want.'

'All right,' Jack said. He poured himself out another big shot and put water in it. He was lighting up a little.

'That was a fine bunch out here this afternoon,' he said.

'They don't take any chances, those two.'

Then a little later, 'Well,' he says, 'they're right. What the hell's the good in taking chances?'

'Don't you want another, Jerry?' he said. 'Come on, drink along with me.' 'I don't need it, Jack,' I said. 'I feel all right.'

'Just have one more,' Jack said. It was softening him up.

'All right,' I said.

Jack poured one for me and another big one for himself.

'You know,' he said, 'I like liquor pretty well. If I hadn't been boxing I would have drunk quite a lot.'

'Sure,' I said.

'You know,' he said, 'I missed a lot, boxing.'

'You made plenty of money.'

'Sure, that's what I'm after. You know I miss a lot, Jerry.'

'How do you mean?'

'Well,' he says, 'like about the wife. And being away from home so much. It don't do my girls any good. 'Whose your old man?' some of those society kids'll say to them. 'My old man's Jack Brennan.' That don't do them any good.'

'Hell,' I said, 'all that makes a difference is if they got dough.'

'Well,' says Jack, 'I got the dough for them all right.' He poured out another drink. The bottle was about empty.

'Put some water in it,' I said. Jack poured in some water.

'You know,' he says, 'you ain't got any idea how I miss the wife.'

'Sure.'

'You ain't got any idea. You can't have an idea what it's like.' 'It ought to be better out in the country than in town.'

'With me now,' Jack said, 'it don't make any difference where I am. You can't have an idea what it's like.'

'Have another drink.'

'Am I getting soused? Do I talk funny?'

'You're coming on all right.'

'You can't have an idea what it's like. They ain't anybody can have an idea what it's like.'

'Except the wife,' I said.

'She knows,' Jack said. 'She knows all right. She knows. You bet she knows.'

'Put some water in that,' I said.

'Jerry,' says Jack, 'you can't have an idea what it gets to be like.'

He was good and drunk. He was looking at me steady. His eyes were sort of too steady.

'You'll sleep all right,' I said.

'Listen, Jerry,' Jack says. 'You want to make some money? Get some money down on Walcott.'

'Yes?'

'Listen, Jerry.' Jack put down the glass. 'I'm not drunk now, see? You know what I'm betting on him? Fifty grand.'

'That's a lot of dough.'

'Fifty grand,' Jack says, 'at two to one. I'll get twenty-five thousand bucks. Get some money on him, Jerry.'

'It sounds good,' I said.

'How can I beat him?' Jack says. 'It ain't crooked. How can I beat him? Why not make money on it?'

'Put some water in that,' I said.

'I'm through after this fight,' Jack says. 'I'm through with it. I got to take a beating. Why shouldn't I make money on it?'

'Sure.'

'I ain't slept for a week,' Jack says. 'All night I lay awake and worry my can off. I can't sleep, Jerry. You ain't got an idea what it's like when you can't sleep.'

'Sure.'

'I can't sleep. That's all. I just can't sleep. What's the use of taking care of yourself all these years when you can't sleep?'

'It's bad.'

'You ain't got an idea what it's like, Jerry, when you can't sleep.' 'Put some water in that,' I said.

Well, about eleven o'clock Jack passes out and I put him to bed. Finally he's so he can't keep from sleeping. I helped him get his clothes off and got him into bed.

'You'll sleep all right, Jack,' I said.

'Sure,' Jack says. 'I'll sleep now.'
'Good night, Jack,' I said.
'Good night, Jerry,' Jack says. 'You're the only friend I got.'
'Oh, hell,' I said.
'You're the only friend I got,' Jack says, 'the only friend I got.' 'Go to sleep,' I said.
'I'll sleep,' Jack says.

Downstairs, Hogan was sitting at the desk in the office reading the papers. He looked up. 'Well, you get your boy friend to sleep?' he asks.

'He's off.'

'It's better for him than not sleeping,' Hogan said.

'Sure.'

'You'd have a hell of a time explaining that to these sports writers though,' Hogan said.

'Well, I'm going to bed myself,' I said.

'Good night,' said Hogan.

In the morning I came downstairs about eight o'clock and got some breakfast. Hogan had his customers out in the barn doing exercises. I went out and watched them.

'One! Two! Three! Four!' Hogan was counting for them. 'Hello, Jerry,' he said. 'Is Jack up yet?'

'No. He's still sleeping.'

I went back to my room and packed up to go to town. About nine-thirty I heard Jack getting up in the next room. When I heard him go downstairs I went down after him. Jack was sitting at the breakfast table. Hogan had come in and was standing beside the table.

'How do you feel, Jack?' I asked him. 'Not so bad.'

'Sleep well?' Hogan asked.

'I slept all right,' Jack said. 'I got a thick tongue but I ain't got a head.' 'Good,' said Hogan. 'That was good liquor.'

'Put it on the bill,' Jack says.

'What time you want to go into town?' Hogan asked.

'Before lunch,' Jack says. 'The eleven o'clock train.'

'Sit down, Jerry,' Jack said. Hogan went out.

I sat down at the table. Jack was eating a grapefruit. When he'd find a seed he'd spit it out in the spoon and dump it on the plate.

'I guess I was pretty stewed last night,' he started.

'You drank some liquor.'

'I guess I said a lot of fool things.' 'You weren't bad.'

'Where's Hogan?' he asked. He was through with the grape-fruit.

'He's out in front in the office.'

'What did I say about betting on the fight?' Jack asked. He was holding the spoon and sort of poking at the grapefruit with it.

The girl came in with some ham and eggs and took away the grape-fruit. 'Bring me another glass of milk,' Jack said to her. She went out.

'You said you had fifty grand on Walcott,' I said.

'That's right,' Jack said.

'That's a lot of money.'

'I don't feel too good about it,' Jack said.

'Something might happen.'

'No,' Jack said. 'He wants the title bad. They'll be shooting with him all right.'

'You can't ever tell.'

'No. He wants the title. It's worth a lot of money to him.'

'Fifty grand is a lot of money,' I said.

'It's business,' said Jack. 'I can't win. You know I can't win anyway.' 'As long as you're in there you got a chance.'

'No,' Jack says. 'I'm all through. It's just business.'

'How do you feel?'

'Pretty good,' Jack said. 'The sleep was what I needed.'

'You might go good.'

'I'll give them a good show,' Jack said.

After breakfast Jack called up his wife on the long-distance. He was inside the booth telephoning.

'That's the first time he's called her up since he's out here,' Hogan said. 'He writes her every day.'

'Sure,' Hogan says, 'a letter only costs two cents.'

Hogan said good-bye to us and Bruce, the nigger rubber, drove us down to the train in the cart.

'Good-bye, Mr. Brennan,' Bruce said at the train, 'I sure hope you knock his can off.'

'So long,' Jack said. He gave Bruce two dollars. Bruce had worked on him a lot. He looked kind of disappointed. Jack saw me looking at Bruce holding the two dollars.

'It's all in the bill,' he said. 'Hogan charged me for the rubbing.'

On the train going to town Jack didn't talk. He sat in the corner of the seat with his ticket in his hat-band and looked out of the window. Once he turned and spoke to me.

'I told the wife I'd take a room at the Shelby tonight,' he said. 'It's just around the corner from the Garden. I can go up to the house tomorrow morning.'

'That's a good idea,' I said. 'Your wife ever see you fight, Jack?' 'No,' Jack says. 'She never seen me fight.'

I thought he must be figuring on taking an awful beating if he doesn't want to go home afterwards. In town we took a taxi up to the Shelby. A boy came out and took our bags and we went to the desk. 'How much are the rooms?' Jack asked.

'We only have double rooms,' the clerk says. 'I can give you a nice double room for ten dollars.'

'That's too steep.'
'I can give you a double room for seven dollars.'
'With a bath?'
'Certainly.'
'You might as well bunk with me, Jerry,' Jack says.
'Oh,' I said. 'I'll sleep down at my brother-in-law's.'
'I don't mean for you to pay it,' Jack says. 'I just want to get my money's worth.'
'Will you register, please?' the clerk says. He looked at the names.
'Number 238, Mister Brennan.'

We went up in the elevator. It was a nice big room with two beds and a door opening into a bathroom.

'This is pretty good,' Jack says.

The boy who brought us up pulled up the curtains and brought in our bags. Jack didn't make any move, so I gave the boy a quarter. We washed up and Jack said we better go out and get something to eat.

We ate a lunch at Jimmy Handley's place. Quite a lot of the boys were there. When we were about half through eating, John came in and sat down with us. Jack didn't talk much.

'How are you on the weight, Jack?' John asked him. Jack was putting away a pretty good lunch.

'I could make it with my clothes on,' Jack said. He never had to worry about taking off weight. He was a natural welter-weight and he'd never gotten fat. He'd lost weight out at Hogan's.

'Well, that's one thing you never had to worry about.' John said.

'That's one thing,' Jack says.

We went around to the Garden to weigh-in after lunch. The match was made at a hundred forty-seven pounds at three o'clock. Jack stepped on the scales with a towel around him. The bar didn't move. Walcott had just weighed and was standing with a lot of people around him.

'Let's see what you weigh, Jack,' Freedman, Walcott's manager, said. 'All right, weigh *him* then,' Jack jerked his head towards Walcott. 'Drop the towel,' Freedman said.

'What do you make it?' Jack asked the fellows who were weighing.

'One hundred and forty-three pounds,' the fat man who was weighing said.

'You're down fine, Jack,' Freedman says.

'Weigh *him*,' Jack says.

Walcott came over. He was blond with wide shoulders and arms like a heavyweight. He didn't have much legs. Jack stood about half-a-head taller than he did.

'Hello, Jack,' he said. His face was plenty marked up.

'Hello,' said Jack. 'How do you feel?'

'Good,' Walcott says. He dropped the towel from around his waist and stood on the scales. He had the widest shoulders and back you ever saw.

'One hundred and forty-six pounds and twelve ounces.'

Walcott stepped off and grinned at Jack.

'Well,' John says to him, 'Jack's spotting you about four pounds.'

'More than that when I come in, kid,' Walcott says. 'I'm going to go and eat now.'

We went back and Jack got dressed. 'He's a pretty tough-looking boy,' Jack says to me.

'He looks as though he'd been hit plenty of times.'

'Oh, yes,' Jack says. 'He ain't hard to hit.'

'Where are you going?' John asked when Jack was dressed.

'Back to the hotel,' Jack says. 'You looked after everything?'

'Yes,' John says. 'It's all looked after.'

'I'm going to lie down for a while,' Jack says.

'I'll come around for you about a quarter to seven and we'll go and eat.'

'All right.'

Up at the hotel Jack took off his shoes and his coat and lay down for a while. I wrote a letter. I looked over a couple of times and Jack wasn't sleeping. He was lying perfectly still but every once in a while his eyes would open. Finally he sits up.

'Want to play some cribbage, Jerry?' he says. 'Sure,' I said.

He went over to his suitcase and got out the cards and the cribbage board. We played cribbage and he won three dollars off me. John knocked at the door and came in.

'Want to play some cribbage, John?' Jack asked him.

John put his kelly down on the table. It was all wet. His coat was wet too. 'Is it raining?' Jack asks.

'It's pouring,' John says. 'The taxi I had got tied up in the traffic and I got out and walked.'

'Come on, play some cribbage,' Jack says. 'You ought to go and eat.'

'No,' says Jack. 'I don't want to eat yet.'

So they played cribbage for about half an hour and Jack won a dollar and a half off him.

'Well, I suppose we got to go eat,' Jack says. He went to the window and looked out.

'Is it still raining?' 'Yes.'

'Let's eat in the hotel,' John says.

'All right,' Jack says, 'I'll play you once more to see who pays for the meal.'

After a little while Jack gets up and says, 'You buy the meal, John,' and we went downstairs and ate in the big dining-room.

After we ate we went upstairs and Jack played cribbage with John again and won two dollars and a half off him. Jack was feeling pretty good. John had a bag with him with all his stuff in it. Jack took off his shirt and collar and put on a jersey and a sweater, so he wouldn't catch cold when he came out, and put his ring clothes and bathrobe in a bag.

'You all ready?' John asks him. 'I'll call up and have them get a taxi. Pretty soon the telephone rang and they said the taxi was waiting.

We rode down in the elevator and went out through the lobby, and got in a taxi and rode around to the Garden. It was raining hard but there was a lot of people outside on the streets. The Garden was sold out. As we came in on our way to the dressing-room I saw how full it was. It looked like half a mile down to the ring. It was all dark. Just the lights over the ring.

'It's a good thing, with this rain, they didn't try to pull this fight in the ball park,' John said.

'They got a good crowd,' Jack says.

'This is a fight that would draw a lot more than the Garden could hold.'

'You can't tell about the weather,' Jack says.

John came to the door of the dressing-room and poked his head in. Jack was sitting there with his bathrobe on, he had his arms folded and was looking at the floor. John had a couple of handlers with him. They looked over his shoulder. Jack looked up.

'Is he in?' he asked.

'He's just gone down,' John said.

We started down. Walcott was just getting into the ring. The crowd gave him a big hand. He climbed through between the ropes and put his two fists together and smiled, and shook them at the crowd, first at one side of the ring, then at the other, and then sat down. Jack got a good hand coming down through the crowd. Jack is Irish and the Irish always get a pretty good hand. An Irishman don't draw in New York like a Jew or an Italian but they always get a good hand. Jack climbed up and bent down to go through the ropes and Walcott came over from his corner and pushed the rope down for Jack to go through. The crowd thought that was wonderful. Walcott put his hand on Jack's shoulder and they stood there just for a second.

'So you're going to be one of these popular champions,' Jack says to him. 'Take your goddam hand off my shoulder.'

'Be yourself,' Walcott says.

This is all great for the crowd. How gentlemanly the boys are before the fight! How they wish each other luck!

Solly Freedman came over to our corner while Jack is bandaging his hands and John is over in Walcott's corner. Jack put his thumb through the slit in the bandage and then wrapped his hand nice and smooth. I taped it around the wrist and twice across the knuckles.

'Hey,' Freedman says. 'Where do you get all that tape?'

'Feel of it,' Jack says. 'It's soft ain't it? Don't be a hick.'

Freedman stands there all the time while Jack bandages the other hand, and one of the boys that's going to handle him brings the gloves and I pull them on and work them around.

'Say, Freedman,' Jack asks, 'what nationality is this Walcott?' 'I don't know,' Solly says. 'He's some sort of a Dane.'

'He's a Bohemian,' the lad who brought the gloves said.

The referee called them out to the centre of the ring and Jack walks out. Walcott comes out smiling. They met and the referee put his arm on each of their shoulders.

'Hello, popularity,' Jack says to Walcott.

'Be yourself.'

'What do you call yourself 'Walcott' for?' Jack says. 'Didn't you know he was a nigger?'

'Listen—' says the referee, and he gives them the same old line. Once Walcott interrupts him. He grabs Jack's arm, and says, 'Can I hit when he's got me like this?'

'Keep your hands off me,' Jack says. 'There ain't no moving-pictures of this.'

They went back to their corners. I lifted the bathrobe off Jack and he leaned on the ropes and flexed his knees a couple of times and scuffed his shoes in the rosin. The gong rang and Jack turned quick and went out. Walcott came toward him and they touched gloves and as soon as Walcott dropped his hands Jack jumped his left into his face twice. There wasn't anybody ever boxed better than Jack. Walcott was after him, going forward all the time with his chin on his chest. He's a hooker and he carries his hands pretty low. All he knows is to get in there and sock. But every time he gets in there close, Jack has the left hand in his face. It's just as though it's automatic.

Jack just raises the left hand up and it's in Walcott's face. Three or four times Jack brings the right over but Walcott gets it on the shoulder or high up on the head. He's just like all these hookers. The only thing he's afraid of is another one of the same kind. He's covered everywhere you can hurt him. He don't care about a left hand in his face.

After about four rounds Jack has him bleeding bad and his face all cut up, but every time Walcott's got in close he's socked so hard he's got two big red patches on both sides just below Jack's ribs. Every time he gets in close, Jack ties him up, then gets one hand loose and uppercuts him, but when Walcott gets his hands loose he socks Jack in the body so they can hear it outside in the street. He's a socker.

It goes along like that for three rounds more. They don't talk any. They're working all the time. We worked over Jack plenty too, in between the rounds. He don't look good at all but he never does much work in the ring. He don't move around much and the left hand is just automatic. It's just like it was connected with Walcott's face and Jack just had to wish it in every time. Jack is always calm in close and he doesn't waste any juice. He knows everything about working in close too and he's getting away with a lot of stuff. While they were in our corner I watched him tie Walcott up, get his right hand loose, turn it, and come up with an uppercut that got Walcott's nose with the heel of the glove. Walcott was bleeding bad and leaned his nose on Jack's shoulder so as to give Jack some of it too, and Jack sort of lifted his shoulder sharp and caught him against the nose, and then brought down the right hand and did the same thing again.

Walcott was sore as hell. By the time they'd gone five rounds he hated Jack's guts. Jack wasn't sore; that is, he wasn't any sorer than he always was. He certainly did used to make the fellows he fought hate boxing. That was why he hated Richie Lewis so. He never got Richie's goat. Richie Lewis always had about three new dirty things Jack couldn't do. Jack was as safe as a church all the time he was in there, as long as he was strong. He certainly was treating Walcott rough. The funny thing was it looked as though Jack was an open classic boxer. That was because he had all that stuff too.

After the seventh round Jack says, 'My left's getting heavy.'

From then he started to take a beating. It didn't show at first. But instead of him running the fight it was Walcott was running it, instead of being safe all the time now he was in trouble. He couldn't keep him out with the left hand now. It looked as though it was the same as ever, only now instead of Walcott's punches just missing him they were just hitting him. He took an awful beating in the body.

'What's the round?' Jack asked. 'The eleventh.'

'I can't stay,' Jack says. 'My legs are going bad.'

Walcott had been hitting him for a long time. It was like a baseball catcher pulls the ball and takes some of the shock off. From now on Walcott commenced to land solid. He certainly was a socking-machine. Jack was just trying to block everything now. It didn't show what an awful beating he was taking. In between the rounds I worked on his legs. The muscles would flutter under my hands all the time I was rubbing them. He was sick as hell.

'How's it go?' he asked John, turning around, his face all swollen.

'It's his fight.'

'I think I can last,' Jack says. 'I don't want this bohunk to stop me.

It was going just the way he thought it would. He knew he couldn't beat Walcott. He wasn't strong any more. He was all right though. His money was all right and now he wanted to finish it off right to please himself. He didn't want to be knocked out.

The gong rang and we pushed him out. He went out slow. Walcott came right out after him. Jack put the left in his face and Walcott took it, came in under it and started working on Jack's body. Jack tried to tie him up and it was just like trying to hold on to a buzz-saw. Jack broke away from it and missed with the right. Walcott clipped him with a left-hook and Jack went down. He went down on his hands and knees and looked at us. The referee started counting. Jack was watching us and shaking his head. At eight John motioned to him. You couldn't hear on account of the crowd. Jack got up. The referee had been holding Walcott back with one arm while he counted.

When Jack was on his feet Walcott started toward him. 'Watch yourself, Jimmy,' I heard Solly Freedman yell to him.

Walcott came up to Jack looking at him. Jack stuck the left hand at him. Walcott just shook his head. He backed Jack up against the ropes, measured him and then hooked the left very light to the side of Jack's head and socked the right into the body as hard as he could sock, just as low as he could get it. He must have hit him five inches below the belt. I thought the eyes would come out of Jack's head. They stuck way out. His mouth came open.

The referee grabbed Walcott. Jack stepped forward. If he went down there went fifty thousand bucks. He walked as though all his insides were going to fall out.

'It wasn't low,' he said. 'It was an accident.'

The crowd were yelling so you couldn't hear anything.

'I'm all right,' Jack says. They were right in front of us. The referee looks at John and then he shakes his head.

'Come on, you polak son-of-a-bitch,' Jack says to Walcott.

John was hanging on to the ropes. He had the towel ready to chuck in. Jack was standing just a little way out from the ropes. He took a step forward. I saw the sweat come out on his face like somebody had squeezed it and a big drop went down his nose.

'Come on and fight,' Jack says to Walcott.

The referee looked at John and waved Walcott on. 'Go in there, you slob,' he says.

Walcott went in. He didn't know what to do either. He never thought Jack could have stood it. Jack put the left in his face. There was such a hell of a lot of yelling going on. They were right in front of us. Walcott hit him twice. Jack's face was the worst thing I ever saw—the look on it! He was holding himself and all his body together and it all showed on his face. All the time he was thinking and holding his body in where it was busted.

Then he started to sock. His face looked awful all the time. He started to sock with his hands low down by his side, swinging at Walcott. Walcott covered up and Jack was swinging wild at Walcott's head. Then he swung the left and it hit Walcott in the groin and the right hit Walcott right bang where he'd hit Jack. Way low below the belt. Walcott went down and grabbed himself there and rolled and twisted around.

The referee grabbed Jack and pushed him towards his corner. John jumps into the ring. There was all this yelling going on. The referee was talking with the judges and then the announcer got into the ring with the megaphone and says, 'Walcott on a foul.'

The referee is talking to John and he says, 'What could I do? Jack wouldn't take the foul. Then when he's groggy he fouls him.'

'He'd lost it anyway,' John says.

Jack's sitting on the chair. I've got his gloves off and he's holding himself in down there with both hands. When he's got something supporting it his face doesn't look so bad.

'Go over and say you're sorry,' John says into his ear. 'It'll look good.'

Jack stands up and the sweat comes out all over his face. I put the bathrobe around him and he holds himself in with one hand under the bathrobe and goes across the ring. They've picked Walcott up and they're working on him. There're a lot of people in Walcott's corner. Nobody speaks to Jack.

He leans over Walcott.

'I'm sorry,' Jack says. 'I didn't mean to foul you.' Walcott doesn't say anything. He looks too damned sick.

'Well, you're the champion now,' Jack says to him. 'I hope you get a hell of a lot of fun out of it.'

'Leave the kid alone,' Solly Freedman says.

'Hello, Solly,' Jack says. 'I'm sorry I fouled your boy.'

Freedman just looks at him.

Jack went to his corner walking that funny jerky way and we got him down through the ropes and through the reporters' tables and out down the aisle. A lot of people want to slap Jack on the back. He goes out through all that mob in his bathrobe to the dressing-room. It's a popular win for Walcott.

That's the way the money was bet in the Garden.

Once we got inside the dressing-room, Jack lay down and shut his eyes. 'We want to get to the hotel and get a doctor,' John says.

'I'm all busted inside,' Jack says.

'I'm sorry as hell, Jack,' John says. 'It's all right,' Jack says.

He lies there with his eyes shut.

'They certainly tried a nice double-cross,' John said.

'Your friends Morgan and Steinfelt,' Jack said. 'You got nice friends.'

He lies there, his eyes are open now. His face has still got that awful drawn look.

'It's funny how fast you can think when it means that much money,' Jack says.

'You're some boy, Jack,' John says. 'No,' Jack says. 'It was nothing.'

A SIMPLE ENQUIRY

Outside, the snow was higher than the window. The sunlight came in through the window and shone on a map on the pine-board wall of the hut. The sun was high and the light came in over the top of the snow. A trench had been cut along the open side of the hut, and each clear day the sun, shining on the wall, reflected heat against the snow and widened the trench. It was late March. The major sat at a table against the wall. His adjutant sat at another table.

Around the major's eyes were two white circles where his snow-glasses had protected his face from the sun on the snow. The rest of his face had been burned and then tanned and then burned through the tan. His nose was swollen and there were edges of loose skin where blisters had been. While he worked at the papers he put the forgers of his left hand into a saucer of oil and then spread the oil over his face, touching it very gently with the tips of his fingers. He was very careful to drain his fingers on the edge of the saucer so there was only a film of oil on them, and after he had stroked his forehead and his cheeks, he stroked his nose very delicately between his fingers. When he had finished he stood up, took the saucer of oil, and went into a small room of the hut where he slept. 'I'm going to take a little sleep,' he said to the adjutant. In that army an adjutant is not a commissioned officer. 'You'll finish up.'

'Yes, Signor Maggiore,' the adjutant answered. He leaned back in his chair and yawned. He took a paper-covered book out of the pocket of his coat and opened it; then laid it down on the table and lit his pipe. He leaned forward on the table to read and puffed at his pipe. Then he closed the book and put it back in his pocket. He had too much paper-work to get through. He could not enjoy reading until it was done. Outside, the sun went behind a mountain and there was no more light on the wall of the hut. A soldier came in and put some pine branches, chopped into irregular lengths, into the stove. 'Be soft, Pinin,' the adjutant said to him. 'The major is sleeping.'

Pinin was the major's orderly. He was a dark-faced boy, and he fixed the stove, putting the pine wood in carefully, shut the door, and went into the back of the but again. The adjutant went on with his papers.

'Tonani,' the major called. 'Signor Maggiore?'

'Send Pinin in to me.'

'Pinin!' the adjutant called. Pinin came into the room. 'The major wants you,' the adjutant said.

Pinin walked across the main room of the but toward the major's door. He knocked on the half-opened door. 'Signor Maggiore?'

'Come in,' the adjutant heard the major say, 'and shut the door.'

Inside the room the major lay on his bunk. Pinin stood beside the bunk. The major lay with his head on the rucksack that he had stuffed with spare clothing to make a pillow. His long, burned, oiled face looked at Pinin. His hands lay on the blankets.

'You are nineteen?' he asked. 'Yes, Signor Maggiore.' 'You have ever been in love?'

'How do you mean, Signor Maggiore?' 'In love—with a girl?'

'I have been with girls.'

'I did not ask that. I asked if you had been in love—with a girl.' 'Yes, Signor Maggiore.'

'You are in love with this girl now? You don't write her. I read all your letters.'

'I am in love with her,' Pinin said, 'but I do not write her.'

'You are sure of this?'

'I am sure.'

'Tonani,' the major said in the same tone of voice, 'can you hear me talking?'

There was no answer from the next room.

'He cannot hear,' the major said. 'And you are quite sure that you love a girl?'

'I am sure.'

'And,' the major looked at him quickly, 'that you are not corrupt?' 'I don't know what you mean, corrupt.'

'All right,' the major said. 'You needn't be superior.'

Pinin looked at the floor. The major looked at his brown face, down and up him, and at his hands. Then he went on, not smiling. 'And you really don't want—' the major paused. Pinin looked at the floor. 'That your great desire isn't really—' Pinin looked at the floor. The major leaned his head back on the rucksack and smiled. He was really relieved: life in the army was too complicated. 'You're a good boy,' he said. 'You're a good boy, Pinin. But don't be superior and be careful someone else doesn't come along and take you.'

Pinin stood still beside the bunk.

'Don't be afraid,' the major said. His hands were folded on the blankets. 'I won't touch you. You can go back to your platoon if you like. But you had better stay on as my servant. You've less chance of being killed.'

'Do you want anything of me, Signor Maggiore?'

'No,' the major said. 'Go on and get on with whatever you were doing. Leave the door open when you go out.' Pinin went out, leaving the door open. The adjutant looked up at him as he walked awkwardly across the room and out of the door. Pinin was flushed and moved differently than he had moved when he brought in the wood for the fire. The adjutant looked after him and smiled. Pinin came in with more wood for the stove. The major, lying on his bunk, looking at his cloth-covered helmet and his snow-glasses that hung from a nail on the wall, heard him walk across the floor.

The little devil, he thought, I wonder if he lied to me.

TEN INDIANS

After one Fourth of July, Nick, driving home late from town in the big wagon with Joe Garner and his family, passed nine drunken Indians along the road. He remembered there were nine because Joe Garner, driving along in the dusk, pulled up the horses, jumped down into the road, and dragged an Indian out of the wheel rut. The Indian had been asleep, face down in the sand. Joe dragged him into the bushes and got back up on the wagon-box.

'That makes nine of them,' Joe said, 'just between here and the edge of town.'

'Them Indians,' said Mrs. Garner.

Nick was on the back seat with the two Garner boys. He was looking out from the back seat to see the Indian where Joe had dragged him alongside of the road.

'Was it Billy Tableshaw?' Carl asked. 'No.'

'His pants looked mighty like Billy.'

'All Indians wear the same kind of pants.'

'I didn't see him at all,' Frank said. 'Pa was down into the road and back up again before I seen a thing. I thought he was killing a snake.'

'Plenty of Indians'll kill snakes tonight, I guess,' Joe Garner said. 'Them Indians,' said Mrs. Garner.

They drove along. The road turned off from the main highway and went up into the hills. It was hard pulling for the horses and the boys got down and walked. The road was sandy. Nick looked back from the top of the hill by the schoolhouse. He saw the lights of Petoskey and, off across Little Traverse Bay, the lights of Harbor Springs. They climbed back into the wagon again.

'They ought to put some gravel on that stretch,' Joe Garner said. The wagon went along the road through the woods. Joe and Mrs. Garner sat close together on the front seat. Nick sat between the two boys. The road came out into a clearing.

'Right here was where Pa ran over the skunk.' 'It was further on.'

'It don't make no difference where it was,' Joe said without turning his head. 'One place is just as good as another to run over a skunk.'

'I saw two skunks last night,' Nick said. 'Where?'

'Down by the lake. They were looking for dead fish along the beach.' 'They were coons probably,' Carl said.

'They were skunks. I guess I know skunks.'

'You ought to,' Carl said. 'You got an Indian girl.'

'Stop talking that way, Carl,' said Mrs. Garner.

'Well, they smell about the same.'

Joe Garner laughed.

'You stop laughing, Joe,' Mrs. Garner said. 'I won't have Carl talk that way.'

'Have you got an Indian girl, Nickie?' Joe asked.

'No.'

'He has too, Pa,' Frank said. 'Prudence Mitchell's his girl.'

'She's not.'

'He goes to see her every day.'

'I don't.' Nick, sitting between the two boys in the dark, felt hollow and happy inside himself to be teased about Prudence Mitchell. 'She ain't my girl,' he said.

'Listen to him,' said Carl. 'I see them together every day.'

'Carl can't get a girl,' his mother said, 'not even a squaw.' Carl was quiet.

'Carl ain't no good with girls,' Frank said.

'You shut up.'

'You're all right, Carl,' Joe Garner said. 'Girls never got a man anywhere. Look at your pa.'

'Yes, that's what you would say.' Mrs. Garner moved close to Joe as the wagon jolted. 'Well, you had plenty of girls in your time.'

'I'll bet pa wouldn't ever have had a squaw for a girl.'

'Don't you think it,' Joe said. 'You better watch out to keep Prudie, Nick.' His wife whispered to him and Joe laughed.

'What you laughing at?' asked Frank.

'Don't you say it, Garner,' his wife warned. Joe laughed again.

'Nickie can have Prudence,' Joe Garner said. 'I got a good girl.'

'That's the way to talk,' Mrs. Garner said.

The horses were pulling heavily in the sand. Joe reached out in the dark with the whip.

'Come on, pull into it. You'll have to pull harder than this tomorrow.'

They trotted down the long hill, the wagon jolting. At the farmhouse everybody got down. Mrs. Garner unlocked the door, went inside, and came out with a lamp in her hand. Carl and Nick unloaded the things from the back of the wagon. Frank sat on the front seat to drive to the barn and put up the horses. Nick went up the steps and opened the kitchen door. Mrs.

Garner was building a fire in the stove. She turned from pouring kerosene on the wood.

'Good-bye, Mrs. Garner,' Nick said. 'Thanks for taking me.' 'Oh shucks, Nickie.' 'I had a wonderful time.'

'We like to have you. Won't you stay and eat some supper?' 'I better go. I think Dad probably waited for me.'

'Well, get along then. Send Carl up to the house, will you?' 'All right.'

'Good night, Nickie!'

'Good night, Mrs. Garner.'

Nick went out the farmyard and down to the barn. Joe and Frank were milking.

'Good night,' Nick said. 'I had a swell time.'

'Good night, Nick,' Joe Garner called. 'Aren't you going to stay and eat?'

'No, I can't. Will you tell Carl his mother wants him?' 'All right. Good night, Nickie.'

Nick walked barefooted along the path through the meadow below the barn. The path was smooth and the dew was cool on his bare feet. He climbed a fence at the end of the meadow, went down through a ravine, his feet wet in the swamp mud, and then climbed up through the dry beech woods until he saw the lights of the cottage. He climbed over the fence and walked around to the front porch. Through the window he saw his father sitting by the table, reading in the light from the big lamp. Nick opened the door and went in.

'Well, Nickie,' his father said, 'was it a good day?'

'I had a swell time, Dad. It was a swell Fourth of July.'

'Are you hungry?'

'You bet.'

'What did you do with your shoes?'

'I left them in the wagon at Garner's.' 'Come on out to the kitchen.'

Nick's father went ahead with the lamp. He stopped and lifted the lid of the ice-box. Nick went on into the kitchen. His father brought in a piece of cold chicken on a plate and a pitcher of milk and put them on the table before Nick. He put down the lamp.

'There's some pie too,' he said. 'Will that hold you?'

'It's grand.'

His father sat down in a chair beside the oilcloth-covered table. He made a big shadow on the kitchen wall.

'Who won the ball game?' 'Petoskey. Five to three.'

His father sat watching him eat and filled his glass from the milk-pitcher. Nick drank and wiped his mouth on his napkin. His father reached over to the shelf for the pie. He cut Nick a big piece. It was huckleberry pie.

'What did you do, Dad?'
'I went out fishing in the morning.'
'What did you get?'
'Only perch.'
His father sat watching Nick eat the pie.
'What did you do this afternoon?' Nick asked.
'I went for a walk up by the Indian camp.' 'Did you see anybody?'
'The Indians were all in town getting drunk.'
'Didn't you see anybody at all?'
'I saw your friend, Prudie.' 'Where was she?'
'She was in the woods with Frank Washburn. I ran on to them. They were having quite a time.'
His father was not looking at him. 'What were they doing?'
'I didn't stay to find out.'
'Tell me what they were doing.'
'I don't know,' his father said. 'I just heard them threshing around.'
'How did you know it was them?'
'I saw them.'
'I thought you said you didn't see them.'
'Oh, yes, I saw them.'
'Who was it with her?' Nick asked. 'Frank Washburn.'
'Were they—were they—' 'Were they what?'
'Were they happy?' 'I guess so.'
His father got up from the table and went out of the kitchen screen door. When he came back Nick was looking at his plate. He had been crying.
'Have some more?' His father picked up the knife to cut the pie. 'No,' said Nick.
'You better have another piece.' 'No, I don't want any.'
His father cleared off the table.
'Where were they in the woods?' asked Nick.
'Up back of the camp.' Nick looked at his plate. His father said, 'You better go to bed, Nick.'
'All right.'
Nick went into his room, undressed, and got into bed. He heard his father moving around in the living-room. Nick lay in the bed with his face in the pillow.
'My heart's broken,' he thought. 'If I feel this way my heart must be broken.'
After a while he heard his father blow out the lamp and go into his own room. He heard a wind come up in the trees outside and felt it come in cool through the screen. He lay for a long time with his face in the pillow, and after a while he forgot to think about Prudence and finally he went to sleep. When he awoke in the night

he heard the wind in the hemlock trees outside the cottage and the waves of the lake coming in on the shore, and he went back to sleep. In the morning there was a big wind blowing and the waves were running high up on the beach and he was awake a long time before he remembered that his heart was broken.

A CANARY FOR ONE

The train passed very quickly a long, red stone house with a garden and four thick palm trees with tables under them in the shade. On the other side was the sea. Then there was a cutting through a red stone and clay, and the sea was only occasionally and far below against the rocks.

'I bought him in Palermo,' the American lady said. 'We only had an hour ashore and it was Sunday morning. The man wanted to be paid in dollars and I gave him a dollar and a half. He really sings very beautifully.'

It was very hot in the train and it was very hot in the *lit salon* compartment. There was no breeze came through the open window. The American lady pulled the window-blind down and there was no more sea, even occasionally. On the other side there was glass, then the corridor, then an open window, and outside the window were dusty trees and an oiled road and flat fields of grapes, with grey-stone hills behind them.

There was smoke from many tall chimneys coming into Marseilles, and the train slowed down and followed one track through many others into the station. The train stayed twenty-five minutes in the station at Marseilles and the American lady bought a copy of the *Daily Mail* and a half-bottle of Evian water. She walked a little way along the station platform, but she stayed near the steps of the car because at Cannes, where it stopped for twelve minutes, the train had left with no signal of departure and she had only gotten on just in time. The American lady was a little deaf and she was afraid that perhaps signals of departure were given and that she did not hear them.

The train left the station in Marseilles and there was not only the switch- yards and the factory smoke but, looking back, the town of Marseilles and the harbor with stone hills behind it and the last of the sun on the water. As it was getting dark the train passed a farmhouse burning in a field. Motor- cars were stopped along the road and bedding and things from inside the farmhouse were spread in the field. Many people were watching the house burn. After it was dark the train was in Avignon. People got on and off. At the news-stand Frenchmen, returning to Paris, bought that day's French papers. On the station platforms were Negro soldiers. They wore brown uniforms and were tall and their faces shone, close under the electric light. Their faces were very black and they were too tall to stare. The train left Avignon station with the Negroes standing there. A short white sergeant was with them.

Inside the *lit salon* compartment the porter had pulled down the three beds from inside the wall and prepared them for sleeping. In the night the American lady lay without sleeping because the train was a *rapide* and went very fast and she was afraid of the speed in the night. The American lady's bed was the one next to the window. The canary from Palermo, a cloth spread over his cage, was out of the draught in the corridor that went into the compartment washroom. There was a blue light outside the compartment, and all night the train went very fast and the American lady lay awake and waited for a wreck.

In the morning the train was near Paris, and after the American lady had come out of the washroom, looking very wholesome and middle-aged and American in spite of not having slept, and had taken the cloth off the bird-cage and hung the cage in the sun, she went back to the restaurant car for breakfast. When she came back to the *lit salon* compartment again, the beds had been pushed back into the wall and made into seats, the canary was shaking his feathers in the sunlight that came through the open window, and the train was much nearer Paris.

'He loves the sun,' the American lady said. 'He'll sing now in a little while.'

The canary shook his feathers and pecked in them. 'I've always loved birds,' the American lady said. 'I'm taking him home to my little girl. There—he's singing now.'

The canary chirped and the feathers on his throat stood out, then he dropped his bill and pecked into his feathers again. The train crossed a river and passed through a very carefully tended forest. The train passed through many outside of Paris towns. There were train-cars in the towns and big advertisements for the Belle Jardiniére and Dubonnet and Pernod on the walls toward the train. All that the train passed through looked as though it were before breakfast. For several minutes I had not listened to the American lady, who was talking to my wife.

'Is your husband American too?' asked the lady.

'Yes,' said my wife. 'We're both Americans.' 'I thought you were English.'

'Oh, no.'

'Perhaps that was because I wore braces,' I said. I had started to say suspenders and changed it to braces in the mouth, to keep my English character. The American lady did not hear. She was really quite deaf; she read lips, and I had not looked toward her. I had looked out of the window. She went on talking to my wife.

'I'm so glad you're Americans. American men make the best husbands,' the American lady was saying. 'That was why we left the Continent, you know. My daughter fell in love with a man in Vevey.' She stopped. 'They were simply madly in love.' She stopped again. 'I took her away, of course.'

'Did she get over it?' asked my wife.

'I don't think so,' said the American lady. 'She wouldn't eat anything and she wouldn't sleep at all. I've tried so very hard, but she doesn't seem to take an interest in anything. She doesn't care about things. I couldn't have her marrying a foreigner.' She paused. 'Someone, a very good friend, told me once, 'No foreigner can make an American girl a good husband.'

'No,' said my wife, 'I suppose not.'

The American lady admired my wife's traveling coat, and it turned out that the American lady had bought her own clothes for twenty years now from the same *maison de couture* in the Rue Saint Honoré. They had her measurements, and a vendeuse who knew her and her tastes picked the dresses out for her and they were sent to America. They came to the post office near where she lived uptown in New York, and the duty was never exorbitant because they opened the dresses there in the post office to appraise them and they were always very simple-looking and with no gold lace nor ornaments that would make the dresses look expensive. Before the present vendeuse, named Thérèse, there had been another vendeuse, named Amélie. Altogether there had only been these two in the twenty years. It had always been the same couturier. Prices, however, had gone up. The exchange, though, equalized that. They had her daughter's measurements now too. She was grown up and there was not much chance of their changing now. The train was now coming into Paris. The fortifications were leveled but grass had not grown. There were many cars standing on tracks—brown wooden restaurant cars and brown wooden sleeping cars that would go to Italy at five o'clock that night, if that train still left at five; the cars were marked Paris-Rome, and cars, with seats on the roofs, that went back and forth to the suburbs with, at certain hours, people in all the seats and on the roofs, if that were the way it were still done, and passing were the white walls and many windows of houses. Nothing had eaten any breakfast.

'Americans make the best husbands,' the American lady said to my wife. I was getting down the bags. 'American men are the only men in the world to marry.'

'How long ago did you leave Vevey?' asked my wife.

'Two years ago this fall. It's her, you know, that I'm taking the canary to.' 'Was the man your daughter was in love with a Swiss?'

'Yes,' said the American lady. 'He was from a very good family in Vevey. He was going to be an engineer. They met there in Vevey. They used to go on long walks together.'

'I know Vevey,' said my wife. 'We were there on our honeymoon.'

'Were you really? That must have been lovely. I had no idea, of course, that she'd fall in love with him.'

'It was a very lovely place,' said my wife.

'Yes,' said the American lady. 'Isn't it lovely? Where did you stop there?' 'We stayed at the Trois Couronnes,' said my wife.

'It's such a fine old hotel,' said the American lady.

'Yes,' said my wife. 'We had a very fine room and in the fall the country was lovely.'

'Were you there in the fall?' 'Yes,' said my wife.

We were passing three cars that had been in a wreck. They were splintered open and the roofs sagged in.

'Look,' I said. 'There's been a wreck.'

The American lady looked and saw the last car. 'I was afraid of that all night,' she said. 'I have terrific presentiments about things sometimes. I'll never travel on a *rapide* again at night. There must be other comfortable trains that don't go so fast.'

The train was in the dark of the Gare de Lyons, and then stopped and porters came up to the windows. I handed bags through the windows, and we were out on the dim longness of the platform, and the American lady put herself in charge of one of three men from Cook's who said: 'Just a moment, madame, and I'll look for your name.'

The porter brought a truck and piled on the baggage, and my wife said good-bye and I said good-bye to the American lady whose name had been found by the man from Cook's on a typewritten page in a sheaf of typewritten pages which he replaced in his pocket.

We followed the porter with the truck down the long cement platform beside the train. At the end was a gate and a man took the tickets.

We were returning to Paris to set up separate residences.

AN ALPINE IDYLL

It was hot coming down into the valley even in the early morning. The sun melted the snow from the skis we were carrying and dried the wood. It was spring in the valley but the sun was very hot. We came along the road into Galtur carrying our skis and rucksacks. As we passed the churchyard a burial was just over. I said, 'Grüss Gott,' to the priest as he walked past us coming out of the churchyard. The priest bowed.

'It's funny a priest never speaks to you,' John said.

'You'd think they'd like to say "Grüss Gott."' 'They never answer,' John said.

We stopped in the road and watched the sexton shoveling in the new earth. A peasant with a black beard and high leather boots stood beside the grave. The sexton stopped shoveling and straightened his back. The peasant in the high boots took the spade from the sexton and went on filling in the grave—spreading the earth evenly as a man spreading manure in a garden. In the bright May morning the grave-filling looked unreal. I could not imagine anyone being dead.

'Imagine being buried on a day like this,' I said to John. 'I wouldn't like it.'

'Well,' I said, 'we don't have to do it.'

We went on up the road past the houses of the town to the inn. We had been skiing in the Silvretta for a month, and it was good to be down in the valley. In the Silvretta the skiing had been all right, but it was spring skiing, the snow was only good in the early morning and again in the evening. The rest of the time it was spoiled by the sun. We were both tired of the sun. You could not get away from the sun. The only shadows were made by rocks or by the hut that was built under the protection of a rock beside a glacier, and in the shade the sweat froze in your underclothing. You could not sit outside the hut without dark glasses. It was pleasant to be burned black but the sun had been very tiring. You could not rest in it. I was glad to be down away from snow. It was too late in the spring to be up in the Silvretta. I was a little tired of skiing. We had stayed too long. I could taste the snow water we had been drinking melted off the tin roof of the hut. The taste was a part of the way I felt about skiing. I was glad there were other things beside skiing, and I was glad to be down, away from the unnatural high mountain spring, into this May morning in the valley.

The innkeeper sat on the porch of the inn his chair tipped back against the wall. Beside him sat the cook.

'Ski-heil!' said the innkeeper.

'Heil!' we said and leaned the skis against the wall and took off our packs. 'How was it up above?' asked the innkeeper.

'Schön. A little too much sun.'

'Yes. There's too much sun this time of year.'

The cook sat on in his chair. The innkeeper went in with us and unlocked his office and brought out our mail. There was a bundle of letters and some papers.

'Let's get some beer,' John said. 'Good. We'll drink it inside.'

The proprietor brought two bottles and we drank them while we read the letters.

'We better have some more beer,' John said. A girl brought it this time. She smiled as she opened the bottles.

'Many letters,' she said.

'Yes. Many.'

'Prosit,' she said and went out, taking the empty bottles.

'I'd forgotten what beer tasted like.'

'I hadn't,' John said. 'Up in the hut I used to think about it a lot.' 'Well,' I said, 'we've got it now.'

'You oughtn't to ever do anything too long.'

'No. We were up there too long.'

'Too damn long,' John said. 'It's no good doing a thing too long.'

The sun came through the open window and shone through the beer bottles on the table. The bottles were half full. There was a little froth on the beer in the bottles, not much, because it was very cold. It collared up when you poured it into the tall glasses. I looked out of the open window at the white road. The trees beside the road were dusty. Beyond was a green field and a stream. There were trees along the stream and a mill with a water wheel.

Through the open side of the mill I saw a long log and a saw in it rising and falling. No one seemed to be tending it. There were four crows walking in the green field. One crow sat in a tree watching. Outside on the porch the cook got off his chair and passed into the hall that led back into the kitchen. Inside, the sunlight shone through the empty glasses on the table. John was leaning forward with his head on his arms.

Through the window I saw two men come up the front steps. They came into the drinking room. One was the bearded peasant in the high boots. The other was the sexton. They sat down at the table under the window. The girl came in and stood by their table. The peasant did not seem to see her. He sat with his hands on the table. He wore his old army clothes. There were patches on the elbows.

'What will it be?' asked the sexton. The peasant did not pay any attention.

'What will you drink?'

'Schnapps,' the peasant said.

'And a quarter liter of red wine,' the sexton told the girl.

The girl brought the drinks and the peasant drank the schnapps. He looked out of the window. The sexton watched him. John had his head forward on the table. He was asleep.

The innkeeper came in and went over to the table. He spoke in dialect and the sexton answered him. The peasant looked out of the window. The innkeeper went out of the room. The peasant stood up. He took a folded ten-thousand kronen note out of a leather pocket-book and unfolded it. The girl came up.

'Alles?' she asked. 'Alles,' he said.

'Let me buy the wine,' the sexton said.

'Alles,' the peasant repeated to the girl. She put her hand in the pocket of her apron, brought it out full of coins and counted out the change. The peasant went out of the door. As soon as he was gone the innkeeper came into the room again and spoke to the sexton. He sat down at the table. They talked in dialect. The sexton was amused. The innkeeper was disgusted.

The sexton stood up from the table. He was a little man with a moustache. He leaned out of the window and looked up the road.

'There he goes in,' he said. 'In the Lowen?'

'Ja.'

They talked again and then the innkeeper came over to our table. The innkeeper was a tall man and old. He looked at John asleep.

'He's pretty tired.'

'Yes, we were up early.'

'Will you want to eat soon?'

'Any time,' I said. 'What is there to eat?'

'Anything you want. The girl will bring the eating-card.'

The girl brought the menu. John woke up. The menu was written in ink on a card and the card slipped into a wooden paddle.

'There's the speise-karte,' I said to John. He looked at it. He was still sleepy.

'Won't you have a drink with us?' I asked the innkeeper. He sat down. 'Those peasants are beasts,' said the innkeeper.

'We saw that one at a funeral coming in to town.'

'That was his wife.'

'Oh.'

'He's a beast. All these peasants are beasts.' 'How do you mean?'

'You wouldn't believe it. You wouldn't believe what just happened to that one.'

'Tell me.'

'You wouldn't believe it.' The innkeeper spoke to the sexton. 'Franz, come over here.' The sexton came, bringing his little bottle of wine and his glass.

'The gentlemen are just come down from the Wiesbadenerhütte,' the innkeeper said. We shook hands.

'What will you drink?' I asked.

'Nothing,' Franz shook his finger. 'Another quarter liter?'

'All right.'

'Do you understand dialect?' the innkeeper asked.

'No.'

'What's it all about?' John asked.

'He's going to tell us about the peasant we saw filling the grave, coming into town.'

'I can't understand it, anyway,' John said. 'It goes too fast for me.'

'That peasant,' the innkeeper said, 'today he brought his wife in to be buried. She died last November.'

'December,' said the sexton.

'That makes nothing. She died last December then, and he notified the commune.'

'December eighteenth,' said the sexton.

'Anyway, he couldn't bring her over to be buried until the snow was gone.'

'He lives on the other side of the Paznaun,' said the sexton. 'But he belongs to this parish.'

'He couldn't bring her out at all?' I asked.

'No. He can only come, from where he lives, on skis until the snow melts. So today he brought her in to be buried and the priest, when he looked at her face, didn't want to bury her. You go on and tell it,' he said to the sexton. 'Speak German, not dialect.'

'It was very funny with the priest,' said the sexton. 'In the report to the commune she died of heart trouble. We knew she had heart trouble here. She used to faint in church sometimes. She did not come for a long time. She wasn't strong to climb. When the priest uncovered her face he asked Olz, "Did your wife suffer much?" "No," said Olz. "When I came in the house she was dead across the bed."'

'The priest looked at her again. He didn't like it.'

'How did her face get that way?'

" 'I don't know,' Olz said.

"'You'd better find out,' the priest said, and put the blanket back. Olz didn't say anything. The priest looked at him. Olz looked back at the priest. 'You want to know?'

"'I must know,' the priest said."

'This is where it's good,' the innkeeper said. 'Listen to this. Go on Franz.'

"'Well,' said Olz, 'when she died I made the report to the commune and I put her in the shed across the top of the big wood. When I started to use the big wood she was stiff and I put her up against the wall. Her mouth was open and when I came to the shed at night to cut up the big wood, I hung the lantern from it.'

"'Why did you do that?' asked the priest.

"'I don't know,' said Olz.

"'Did you do that many times?'

"'Every time I went to work in the shed at night.'

"'It was very wrong,' said the priest. 'Did you love your wife?' "'Ja, I loved her,' Olz said. 'I loved her fine.'"

"Did you understand it all?' asked the innkeeper. 'You understand it all about his wife?'

'I heard it.'

'How about eating?' John asked.

'You order,' I said. 'Do you think it's true?' I asked the innkeeper.

'Sure it's true,' he said. 'These peasants are beasts.'

'Where did he go now?'

'He's gone to drink at my colleague's, the Lowen!'

"He didn't want to drink with me,' said the sexton.

'He didn't want to drink with him, after he knew about his wife,' said the innkeeper.

'Say,' said John. 'How about eating?' 'All right,' I said.

A PURSUIT RACE

William Campbell had been in a pursuit race with a burlesque show ever since Pittsburgh. In a pursuit race, in bicycle racing, riders start at equal intervals to ride after one another. They ride very fast because the race is usually limited to a short distance and if they slow their riding another rider who maintains his pace will make up the space that separated them equally at the start. As soon as a rider is caught and passed he is out of the race and must get down from his bicycle and leave the track. If none of the riders are caught the winner of the race is the one who has gained the most distance. In most pursuit races, if there are only two riders, one of the riders is caught inside of six miles. The burlesque show caught William Campbell at Kansas City.

William Campbell had hoped to hold a slight lead over the burlesque show until they reached the Pacific coast. As long as he preceded the burlesque show as advance man he was being paid. When the burlesque show caught up with him he was in bed. He was in bed when the manager of the burlesque troupe came into his room and after the manager had gone out he decided that he might as well stay in bed. It was very cold in Kansas City and he was in no hurry to go out. He did not like Kansas City. He reached under the bed for a bottle and drank. It made his stomach feel better. Mr.

Turner, the manager of the burlesque show, had refused a drink.

William Campbell's interview with Mr. Turner had been a little strange. Mr. Turner had knocked on the door. Campbell had said: 'Come in!' When Mr. Turner came into the room he saw clothing on a chair, an open suitcase, the bottle on a chair beside the bed, and someone lying in the bed completely covered by bedclothes.

'Mister Campbell,' Mr. Turner said.

'You can't fire me,' William Campbell said from underneath the covers. It was warm and white and close under the covers. 'You can't fire me because I've got down off my bicycle.'

'You're drunk,' Mr. Turner said.

'Oh, yes,' William Campbell said, speaking directly against the sheet and feeling the texture with his lips.

'You're a fool,' Mr. Turner said. He turned off the electric light. The electric light had been burning all night. It was now ten o'clock in the morning. 'You're a drunken fool. When did you get into this town?'

'I got into this town last night,' William Campbell said, speaking against the sheet. He found he liked to talk through a sheet. 'Did you ever talk through a sheet?'

'Don't try to be funny. You aren't funny.'

'I'm not being funny. I'm just talking through a sheet.'

'You're talking through a sheet all right.'

'You can go now, Mr. Turner,' Campbell said. 'I don't work for you any more.'

'You know that anyway.'

'I know a lot,' William Campbell said. He pulled down the sheet and looked at Mr. Turner. 'I know enough so I don't mind looking at you at all. Do you want to hear what I know?'

'No.'

'Good,' said William Campbell. 'Because really I don't know anything at all. I was just talking.' He pulled the sheet up over his face again. 'I love it under a sheet,' he said. Mr. Turner stood beside the bed. He was a middle-aged man with a large stomach and a bald head and he had many things to do. 'You ought to stop off here, Billy, and take a cure,' he said. 'I'll fix it up if you want to do it.'

'I don't want to take a cure,' William Campbell said. 'I don't want to take a cure at all. I am perfectly happy. All my life I have been perfectly happy.'

'How long have you been this way?'

'What a question!' William Campbell breathed in and out through the sheet.

'How long have you been stewed, Billy?'

'Haven't I done my work?'

'Sure. I just asked you how long you've been stewed, Billy.'

'I don't know. But I've got my wolf back.' He touched the sheet with his tongue. 'I've had him for a week.'

'The hell you have.'

'Oh, yes. My dear wolf. Every time I take a drink he goes outside the room. He can't stand alcohol. The poor little fellow.' He moved his tongue round and round on the sheet. 'He's a lovely wolf. He's just like he always was.' William Campbell shut his eyes and took a deep breath.

'You got to take a cure, Billy,' Mr. Turner said. 'You won't mind the Keeley. It isn't bad.'

'The Keeley,' William Campbell said. 'It isn't far from London.' He shut his eyes and opened them, moving the eyelashes against the sheet. 'I just love sheets,' he said. He looked at Mr. Turner.

'Listen, you think I'm drunk.' 'You *are* drunk.'

'No, I'm not.'

'You're drunk and you've had d.t.'s.'

'No.' William Campbell held the sheet around his head. 'Dear sheet,' he said. He breathed against it gently. 'Pretty sheet. You love me, don't you, sheet? It's all in the price of the room. Just like in Japan. No,' he said.

'Listen Billy, dear Sliding Billy, I have a surprise for you. I'm not drunk. I'm hopped to the eyes.'

'No,' said Mr. Turner.

'Take a look.' William Campbell pulled up the right sleeve of his pajama jacket under the sheet, then shoved the right forearm out. 'Look at that.' On the forearm, from just above the wrist to the elbow, were small blue circles around tiny dark blue punctures. The circles almost touched one another. 'That's the new development,' William Campbell said. 'I drink a little now once in a while, just to drive the wolf out of the room.'

'They got a cure for that,' 'Sliding Billy' Turner said.

'No,' William Campbell said. 'They haven't got a cure for anything.' 'You just can't quit like that, Billy,' Turner said. He sat on the bed. 'Be careful of my sheet,' William Campbell said.

'You just can't quit at your age and take to pumping yourself full of that stuff because you got into a jam.'

'There's a law against it. If that's what you mean.'

'No, I mean you got to fight it out.'

Billy Campbell caressed the sheet with his lips and his tongue. 'Dear sheet,' he said. 'I can kiss this sheet and see right through it at the same time.'

'Cut it out about the sheet. You can't just take to that stuff, Billy.'

William Campbell shut his eyes. He was beginning to feel a slight nausea. He knew that this nausea would increase steadily, without there ever being the relief of sickness, until something were done against it. It was at this point that he suggested that Mr. Turner have a drink. Mr. Turner declined. William Campbell took a drink from the bottle. It was a temporary measure. Mr. Turner watched him. Mr. Turner had been in this room much longer than he should have been, he had many things to do; although living in daily association with people who used drugs, he had a horror of drugs, and he was very fond of William Campbell; he did not wish to leave him. He was very sorry for him and he felt a cure might help. He knew there were good cures in Kansas City. But he had to go. He stood up.

'Listen, Billy,' William Campbell said, 'I want to tell you something. You're called 'Sliding Billy'. That's because you can slide. I'm called just Billy. That's because

I never could slide at all. I can't slide, Billy. I can't slide. It just catches. Every time I try it, it catches.' He shut his eyes. 'I can't slide, Billy. It's awful when you can't slide.'

'Yes,' said 'Sliding Billy' Turner.

'Yes, what?' William Campbell looked at him. 'You were saying.'

'No,' said William Campbell. 'I wasn't saying. It must have been a mistake.'

'You were saying about sliding.'

'No. It couldn't have been about sliding. But listen, Billy, and I'll tell you a secret. Stick to sheets, Billy. Keep away from women and horses and, and—' he stopped '—eagles, Billy. If you love horses you'll get horse-s—and if you love eagles you'll get eagle-s—' He stopped and put his head under the sheet.

'I got to go,' said 'Sliding Billy' Turner.

'If you love women you'll get a dose,' William Campbell said. 'If you love horses—'

'Yes, you said that.' 'Said what?'

'About horses and eagles.'

'Oh, yes. And if you love sheets.' He breathed on the sheet and stroked his nose against it. 'I don't know about sheets,' he said. 'I just started to love this sheet.'

'I have to go,' Mr. Turner said. 'I got a lot to do.'

'That's all right,' William Campbell said. 'Everybody's got to go.' 'I better go.'

'All right, you go.'

'Are you all right, Billy?'

'I was never so happy in my life.' 'And you're all right?'

'I'm fine. You go along. I'll just lie here for a little while. Around noon I'll get up.'

But when Mr. Turner came up to William Campbell's room at noon William Campbell was sleeping and as Mr. Turner was a man who knew what things in life were very valuable he did not wake him.

TODAY IS FRIDAY

Three Roman soldiers are in a drinking place at eleven o'clock at night. There are barrels around the wall. Behind the wooden counter is a Hebrew wine-seller. The three Roman soldiers are a little cock-eyed.

1st Soldier—You tried the red? *2nd Soldier*—No, I ain't tried it. *1st Soldier*—You better try it.

2nd Soldier—All right, George, we'll have a round of the red.

Hebrew Wine-seller—Here you are, gentlemen. You'll like that. [*He sets down an earthenware pitcher that he has filled from one of the casks.*] That's a nice little wine.

1st Soldier—Have a drink of it yourself. [*He turns to the third Roman soldier who is leaning on a barrel.*] What's the matter with you?'

3rd Soldier—I got a gut-ache.

2nd Soldier—You've been drinking water.

1st Soldier—Try some of the red.

3rd Soldier—I can't drink the damn stuff. It makes my gut sour.

1st Soldier—You been out here too long.

3rd Soldier—Hell, don't I know it?'

1st Soldier—Say, George, can't you give this gentleman something to fix his stomach?'

Hebrew Wine-seller—I got it right here.

[*The third Roman soldier tastes the cup that the wine-seller has mixed for him.*]

3rd Soldier—Hey, what you put in that, camel chips?

Wine-seller—You drink that right down, Lootenant. That'll fix you up right.

3rd Soldier—Well, I couldn't feel any worse.

1st Soldier—Take a chance on it. George fixed me up fine the other day.

Wine-seller—You were in bad shape, Lootenant. I know what fixes up a bad stomach.

[*The third Roman soldier drinks the cup down.*] *3rd Soldier*—Jesus Christ. [*He makes a face.*] *2nd Soldier*—That false alarm!

1st Soldier—Oh, I don't know. He was pretty good in there to-day.

2nd Soldier—Why didn't he come down off the cross?

1st Soldier—He didn't want to come down off the cross. That's not his play.

2nd Soldier—Show me a guy that doesn't want to come down off the cross.

1st Soldier—Aw, hell, you don't know anything about it. Ask George there. Did he want to come down off the cross, George?'

Wine-seller—I'll tell you, gentlemen, I wasn't out there. It's a thing I haven't taken any interest in.

2nd Soldier—Listen, I seen a lot of them—here and plenty of other places. Any time you show me one that doesn't want to get down off the cross when the time comes—when the time comes, I mean—I'll climb right up with him.

1st Soldier—I thought he was pretty good in there to-day.

3rd Soldier—He was all right.

2nd Soldier—You guys don't know what I'm talking about. I'm not saying whether he was good or not. What I mean is, when the time comes. When they first start nailing him, there isn't none of them wouldn't stop it if they could.

1st Soldier—Didn't you follow it, George?

Wine-seller—No, I didn't take any interest in it, Lootenant.

1st Soldier—I was surprised how he acted.

3rd Soldier—The part I don't like is the nailing them on. You know, that must get you pretty bad.

2nd Soldier—It isn't that that's so bad, as when they first lift 'em [*He makes a lifting gesture with his two palms together.*] When the weight starts to pull on 'em. That's when it gets 'em.

3rd Soldier—It takes some of them pretty bad.

1st Soldier—Ain't I seen 'em? I seen plenty of them. I tell you, he was pretty good in there today.

[*The second Roman soldier smiles at the Hebrew wine-seller.*] 2nd Soldier—You're a regular Christer, big boy.

1st Soldier—Sure, go on and kid him. But listen while I tell you something. He was pretty good in there today.

2nd Soldier—What about some more wine?'

[*The wine-seller looks up expectantly. The third Roman soldier is sitting with his head down. He does not look well.*]

3rd Soldier—I don't want any more.

2nd Soldier—Just for two, George.

[*The wine-seller puts out a pitcher of wine, a size smaller than the last one. He leans forward on the wooden counter.*]

1st Soldier—You see his girl?'

2nd Soldier—Wasn't I standing right by her?

1st Soldier—She's a nice looker.

2nd Soldier—I knew her before he did. [*He winks at the wine-seller.*] 1st Soldier—I used to see her around the town.

2nd Soldier—She used to have a lot of stuff. He never brought her no good luck.

1st Soldier—Oh, he ain't lucky. But he looked pretty good to me in there today.

2nd Soldier—What became of his gang?'

1st Soldier—Oh, they faded out. Just the women stuck by him.

2nd Soldier—They were a pretty yellow crowd. When they seen him go up there they didn't want any of it.

1st Soldier—The women stuck all right.

2nd Soldier—Sure, they stuck all right.

1st Soldier—You see me slip the old spear into him?

2nd Soldier—You'll get into trouble doing that some day.

1st Soldier—It was the least I could do for him. I'll tell you he looked pretty good to me in there today.

Hebrew wine-seller—Gentlemen, you know I got to close.

1st Soldier—We'll have one more round.

2nd Soldier—What's the use? This stuff don't get you anywhere. Come on, let's go.

1st Soldier—Just another round.

3rd Soldier—[*Getting up from the barrel.*] No, come on. Let's go. I feel like hell tonight.

1st Soldier—Just one more.

2nd Soldier—No, come on. We're going to go. Good night, George. Put it on the bill.

Wine-seller—Good night gentlemen. [*He looks a little worried.*] You couldn't let me have a little something on account, Lootenant?'

2nd Soldier—What the hell, George! Wednesday's payday. Wine-seller—It's all right, Lootenant. Good night, gentlemen. [*The three Roman soldiers go out the door into the street.*] [*Outside in the street.*]

    2nd Soldier—George is a kike just like all the rest of them.
    1st Soldier—Oh, George is a nice fella.
    2nd Soldier—Everybody's a nice fella to you tonight.
    3rd Soldier—Come on, let's go up to the barracks. I feel like hell tonight.
    2nd Soldier—You been out here too long.
    3rd Soldier—No, it ain't that. I feel like hell.
    2nd Soldier—You been out here too long. That's all.

CURTAIN BANAL STORY

So he ate an orange, slowly spitting out the seeds. Outside, the snow was turning to rain. Inside, the electric stove seemed to give no heat and rising from his writing-table, he sat down upon the stove. How good it felt! Here, at last, was life.

He reached for another orange. Far away in Paris, Mascart had knocked Danny Frush cuckoo in the second round. Far off in Mesopotamia, twenty- one feet of snow had fallen. Across the world in distant Australia, the English cricketers were sharpening up their wickets. *There* was Romance.

Patrons of the arts and letters have discovered The Forum, he read. It is the guide, philosopher, and friend of the thinking minority. Prize short-stories—will their authors write our best-sellers of tomorrow?'

You will enjoy these warm, homespun, American tales, bits of real life on the open ranch, in crowded tenement or comfortable home, and all with a healthy undercurrent of humor.

I must read them, he thought.

He read on. Our children's children—what of them? Who of them? New means must be discovered to find room for us under the sun. Shall this be done by war or can it be done by peaceful methods?'

Or will we all have to move to Canada?'

Our deepest convictions—will Science upset them? Our civilization—is it inferior to older orders of things—

And meanwhile, in the far-off dripping jungles of Yucatan, sounded the chopping of the axes of the gum-choppers. Do we want big men—or do we want them cultured? Take Joyce. Take President Coolidge. What star must our college students aim at? There is Jack Britton. There is Dr Henry Van Dyke. Can we reconcile the two? Take the case of Young Stribling.

And what of our daughters who must take their own Soundings? Nancy Hawthorne is obliged to make her own Soundings in the sea of life. Bravely and sensibly she faces the problems which come to every girl of eighteen.

It was a splendid booklet.

Are you a girl of eighteen? Take the case of a Joan of Arc. Take the case of Bernard Shaw. Take the case of Betsy Ross.

Think of these things in 1925—Was there a frisqué page in Puritan history?

Were there two sides to Pocahontas? Did she have a fourth dimension?'

Are modern paintings—and poetry—Art? Yes and No. Take Picasso. Have tramps codes of conduct? Send your mind adventuring.

There is Romance everywhere. *Forum* writers talk to the point, are possessed of humor and wit. But they do not try to be smart and are never long-winded.

Live the full life of the mind, exhilarated by new ideas, intoxicated by the romance of the unusual. He laid down the booklet.

And meanwhile, stretched flat on a bed in a darkened room in the house in Triana, Manuel Garcia Maera lay with a tube in each lung, drowning with the pneumonia. All the papers in Andalucia devoted special supplements to his death, which had been expected for some days. Men and boys bought full-length colored pictures of him to remember him by, and lost the picture they had of him in their memories by looking at the lithographs.

Bullfighters were very relieved he was dead, because he did always in the bullring the things they could only do sometimes. They all marched in the rain behind his coffin and there were one hundred and forty-seven bullfighters followed him out to the cemetery where they buried him in the tomb next to Joselito. After the funeral every one sat in the cafés out of the rain, and many colored pictures of Maera were sold to men who rolled them up and put them away in their pockets.

NOW I LAY ME

That night we lay on the floor in the room and I listened to the silk-worms eating. The silk-worms fed in racks of mulberry leaves and all night you could hear them eating and a dropping sound in the leaves. I myself did not want to sleep because I had been living for a long time with the knowledge that if I ever shut my eyes in the dark and let myself go, my soul would go out of my body. I had been that way for a long time, ever since I had been blown up at night and felt it go out of me and go off and then come back. I tried never to think about it, but it had started to go since, in the nights, just at the moment of going off to sleep, and I could only stop it by a very great effort. So while now I am fairly sure that it will not really have gone out, yet then, that summer, I was unwilling to make the experiment.

I had different ways of occupying myself while I lay awake. I would think of a trout stream I had fished along when I was a boy; and fish its whole length very carefully in my mind; fishing very carefully under all the logs, all the turns of the bank, the deep holes and the clear shallow stretches, sometimes catching trout and sometimes losing them. I would stop fishing at noon to eat my lunch; sometimes on a log over the stream; sometimes on a high bank under a tree, and I always ate my lunch very slowly and watched the stream below me while I ate. Often I ran out of bait because I would take only ten worms with me in a tobacco tin when I started. When I had used them all I had to find more worms, and sometimes it was very difficult digging in the bank of the stream where the cedar trees kept out the sun and there was no grass but only the bare moist earth and often I could find no worms. Always though I found some kind of bait, but one time in the swamp I could find no bait at all and had to cut up one of the trout I had caught and use him for bait.

Sometimes I found insects in the swamp meadows, in the grass or under ferns, and used them. There were beetles and insects with legs like grass stems, and grubs in old rotten logs; white grubs with brown pinching heads that would not stay on the hook and emptied into nothing in the cold water, and wood ticks under logs where sometimes I found angle-worms that slipped into the ground as soon as the log was raised. Once I used a salamander from under an old log. The salamander was very small and neat and agile and a lovely color. He had tiny feet that tried to hold on to the hook, and after that one time I never used a salamander, although I found them very often. Nor did I use crickets, because of the way they acted about the hook.

Sometimes the stream ran through an open meadow, and in the dry grass I would catch grasshoppers and use them for bait and sometimes I would catch grasshoppers and toss them into the stream and watch them float along swimming on the stream and circling on the surface as the current took them and then disappear as a trout rose. Sometimes I would fish four or five different streams in the night; starting as near as I could get to their source and fishing them down stream. When I had finished too quickly and the time did not go, I would fish the stream over again, starting where it emptied into the lake and fishing back up stream, trying for all the trout I had missed coming down. Some nights too I made up streams, and some of them were very exciting, and it was like being awake and dreaming. Some of those streams I still remember and think that I have fished in them, and they are confused with streams I really know. I gave them all names and went to them on the train and sometimes walked for miles to get to them.

But some nights I could not fish, and on those nights I was cold-awake and said my prayers over and over and tried to pray for all the people I had ever known. That took up a great amount of time, for if you try to remember all the people you have ever known, going back to the earliest thing you remember—which was, with me, the attic of the house where I was born and my mother and father's wedding-cake in a tin box hanging from one of the rafters, and, in the attic, jars of snakes and other specimens that my father had collected as a boy and preserved in alcohol sunken in the jars so the backs of some of the snakes and specimens were exposed and had turned white—if you thought back that far, you remembered a great many people. If you prayed for all of them, saying a Hail Mary and Our Father for each one, it took a long time and finally it would be light, and then you could go to sleep, if you were in a place where you could sleep in the daylight.

On those nights I tried to remember everything that had ever happened to me, starting with just before I went to the war and remembering back from one thing to another. I found I could only remember back to that attic in my grandfather's house. Then I would start there and remember this way again, until I reached the war.

I remembered, after my grandfather died we moved away from the house and to a new house designed and built by my mother. Many things that were not to be moved were burned in the backyard and I remember those jars from the attic being thrown in the fire, and how they popped in the heat and the fire flamed up from the alcohol. I remember the snakes burning in the fire in the backyard. But there were no people in that, only things. I could not remember who burned the things even, and I would go on until I came to people and then stop and pray for them.

About the new house I remember how my mother was always cleaning things out and making a good clearance. One time when my father was away on a hunting trip she made a good thorough cleaning out in the basement and burned everything that should not have been there. When my father came home and got down from his buggy and hitched the horse, the fire was still burning in the road beside the house. I went out to meet him. He handed me his shotgun and looked at the fire. 'What's this?' he asked.

'I've been cleaning out the basement, dear,' my mother said from the porch. She was standing there smiling, to meet him. My father looked at the fire and kicked at something. Then he leaned over and picked something out of the ashes. 'Get a rake, Nick,' he said to me. I went to the basement and brought a rake and my father raked very carefully in the ashes. He raked out stone axes and stone skinning knives and tools for making arrow-heads and pieces of pottery and many arrow-heads. They had all been blackened and chipped by the fire. My father raked them all out very carefully and spread them on the grass by the road. His shotgun in its leather case and his game-bags were on the grass where he had left them when he stepped down from the buggy.

'Take the gun and the bags in the house, Nick, and bring me a paper,' he said. My mother had gone inside the house. I took the shotgun, which was heavy to carry and banged against my legs, and the two game-bags and started towards the house. 'Take them one at a time,' my father said. 'Don't try and carry too much at once.' I put down the game-bags and took in the shotgun and brought out a newspaper from the pile in my father's office. My father spread all the blackened, chipped stone implements on the paper and then wrapped them up. 'The best arrow-heads went all to pieces,' he said. He walked into the house with the paper package and I stayed outside on the grass with the two game-bags. After a while, I took them in. In remembering that, there were only two people, so I would pray for them both.

Some nights, though, I could not remember my prayers even. I could only get as far as 'On earth as it is in heaven" and then have to start all over and be absolutely unable to get past that. Then I would have to recognize that I could not remember and give up saying my prayers that night and try something else. So on some nights I would try to remember all the animals in the world by name and then the birds and then fishes and then countries and cities and then kinds of food and the names of all the streets I could remember in Chicago, and when I could not remember anything at all any more I would just listen. And I do not remember a night on which you could not hear things. If I could have a light I was not afraid to sleep, because I knew my soul would only go out of me if it were dark. So, of course, many nights I was where I could have a light and then I slept because I was nearly always tired and often very sleepy. And I am sure many times too that I slept without knowing it—but I never slept knowing it, and on this night I listened to the silk-worms. You can hear silk-worms eating very clearly in the night and I lay with my eyes open and listened to them.

There was only one other person in the room and he was awake too. I listened to him being awake, for a long time. He could not lie as quietly as I could because, perhaps, he had not had so much practice being awake. We were lying on blankets spread over straw and when he moved the straw was noisy, but the silk-worms were not frightened by any noise we made and ate on steadily. There were the noises of night seven kilometers behind the lines outside but they were different from the small noises inside the room in the dark. The other man in the room tried lying quietly. Then he moved again. I moved too, so he would know I was awake. He had lived ten years in Chicago. They had taken him for a soldier in nineteen fourteen when he had come back to visit his family, and they had given him to me for an orderly because he spoke English. I heard him listening, so I moved again in the blankets.

'Can't you sleep, Signor Tenente?' he asked. 'No.'
'I can't sleep, either.' 'What's the matter?'
'I don't know. I can't sleep.' 'You feel all right?'
'Sure. I feel good. I just can't sleep.'
'You want to talk a while?' I asked.
'Sure. What can you talk about in this damn place.'
'This place is pretty good,' I said.
'Sure,' he said. 'It's all right.'
'Tell me about out in Chicago,' I said.
'Oh,' he said, 'I told you all that once.'
'Tell me about how you got married.'
'I told you that.'
'Was the letter you got Monday—from her?'
'Sure. She writes me all the time. She's making good money with the place.'
'You'll have a nice place when you go back.'
'Sure. She runs it fine. She's making a lot of money.'
'Don't you think we'll wake them up, talking?' I asked.
'No. They can't hear. Anyway, they sleep like pigs. I'm different,' he said. 'I'm nervous.'
'Talk quiet,' I said. 'Want a smoke?'
We smoked skillfully in the dark.
'You don't smoke much, Signor Tenente.'
'No. I've just about cut it out.'

'Well,' he said, 'it don't do you any good and I suppose you get so you don't miss it. Did you ever hear a blind man won't smoke because he can't see the smoke come out?'

'I don't believe it.'

'I think it's all bull, myself,' he said. 'I just heard it somewhere. You know how you hear things.'

We were both quiet and I listened to the silk-worms.

'You hear those damn silk-worms?' he asked. 'You can hear them chew.' 'It's funny,' I said.

'Say, Signor Tenente, is there something really the matter that you can't sleep? I never see you sleep. You haven't slept nights ever since I been with you.'

'I don't know, John,' I said. 'I got in pretty bad shape along early last spring and at night it bothers me.'

'Just like I am,' he said. 'I shouldn't have ever got in this war. I'm too nervous.'

'Maybe it will get better.'

'Say, Signor Tenente, what did you get in this war for anyway?' 'I don't know, John. I wanted to, then.'

'Wanted to,' he said. 'That's a hell of a reason.'

'We oughtn't to talk so loud,' I said.

'They sleep like pigs,' he said. 'They can't understand the English language, anyway. They don't know a damn thing. What are you going to do when it's over and we go back to the States?'

'I'll get a job on a paper.' 'In Chicago?'

'Maybe.'

'Do you ever read what this fellow Brisbane writes? My wife cuts it out for me and sends it to me.'

'Sure.'

'Did you ever meet him?' 'No, but I've seen him.'

'I'd like to meet that fellow. He's a fine writer. My wife don't read English but she takes the paper just like when I was home and she cuts out the editorials and the sport page and sends them to me.'

'How are your kids?'

'They're fine. One of the girls is in the fourth grade now. You know, Signor Tenente, if I didn't have the kids I wouldn't be your orderly now. They'd have made me stay in the line all the time.'

'I'm glad you've got them.'

'So am I. They're fine kids but I want a boy. Three girls and no boy. That's a hell of a note.'

'Why don't you try and go to sleep.'

'No, I can't sleep now, I'm wide awake now, Signor Tenente. Say, I'm worried about you not sleeping, though.'

'It'll be all right, John.'

'Imagine a young fellow like you not to sleep.'

'I'll get all right. It just takes a while.'

'You got to get all right. A man can't get along that don't sleep. Do you worry about anything? You got anything on your mind?'

'No, John, I don't think so.'

'You ought to get married, Signor Tenente. Then you wouldn't worry.' 'I don't know.'

'You ought to get married. Why don't you pick out some nice Italian girl with plenty of money? You could get any one you want. You're young and you got good decorations and you look nice. You been wounded a couple of times.'

'I can't talk the language well enough.'

'You talk it fine. To hell with talking the language. You don't have to talk to them. Marry them.'

'I'll think about it.'

'You know some girls, don't you?' 'Sure.'

'Well, you marry the one with the most money. Over here, the way they're brought up, they'll all make you a good wife.'

'I'll think about it.'

'Don't think about it, Signor Tenente. Do it.'

'All right.'

'A man ought to be married. You'll never regret it. Every man ought to be married.'

'All right,' I said. 'Let's try and sleep a while.'

'All right Signor Tenente. I'll try it again. But you remember what I said.' 'I'll remember it,' I said. 'Now let's sleep a while, John.'

'All right,' he said. 'I hope you sleep, Signor Tenente.'

I heard him roll in his blankets on the straw and then he was very quiet and I listened to him breathing regularly. Then he started to snore. I listened to him snore for a long time and then I stopped listening to him snore and listened to the silk-worms eating. They ate steadily, making a dropping in the leaves. I had a new thing to think about and I lay in the dark with my eyes open and thought of all the girls I had ever known and what kind of wives they would make. It was a very interesting thing to think about and for a while it killed off trout-fishing and interfered with my prayers. Finally, though, I went back to trout-fishing, because I found that I could remember all the streams and there was always something new about them, while the girls, after I had thought about them a few times, blurred and I could not call them into my mind and finally they all blurred and all became rather the same and I gave up thinking about them almost altogether. But I kept on with my prayers and I prayed very often for John in the nights and his class was removed from active service before the October offensive. I was glad he was not there, because he would have been a great worry to me. He came to the hospital in Milan to see me several months after and he was very disappointed that I had not yet married, and I know he would feel very badly if he knew that, so far, I have never married. He was going back to America and he was very certain about marriage and knew it would fix up everything.

THE OLD MAN AND THE SEA

TO CHARLIE SHRIBNER AND TO MAX PERKINS

He was an old man who fished alone in a skiff in the Gulf Stream and he had gone eighty-four days now without taking a fish. In the first forty days a boy had been with him. But after forty days without a fish the boy's parents had told him that the old man was now definitely and finally *salao*, which is the worst form of unlucky, and the boy had gone at their orders in another boat which caught three good fish the first week. It made the boy sad to see the old man come in each day with his skiff empty and he always went down to help him carry either the coiled lines or the gaff and harpoon and the sail that was furled around the mast. The sail was patched with flour sacks and, furled, it looked like the flag of permanent defeat.

The old man was thin and gaunt with deep wrinkles in the back of his neck. The brown blotches of the benevolent skin cancer the sun brings from its reflection on the tropic sea were on his cheeks. The blotches ran well down the sides of his face and his hands had the deep-creased scars from handling heavy fish on the cords. But none of these scars were fresh. They were as old as erosions in a fishless desert.

Everything about him was old except his eyes and they were the same color as the sea and were cheerful and undefeated.

'Santiago,' the boy said to him as they climbed the bank from where the skiff was hauled up. 'I could go with you again. We've made some money.'

The old man had taught the boy to fish and the boy loved him.

'No,' the old man said. 'You're with a lucky boat. Stay with them.'

'But remember how you went eighty-seven days without fish and then we caught big ones every day for three weeks.'

'I remember,' the old man said. 'I know you did not leave me because you doubted.'

'It was papa made me leave. I am a boy and I must obey him.' 'I know,' the old man said. 'It is quite normal.'

'He hasn't much faith.'

'No,' the old man said. 'But we have. Haven't we?'

'Yes,' the boy said. 'Can I offer you a beer on the Terrace and then we'll take the stuff home.'

'Why not?' the old man said. 'Between fishermen.'

They sat on the Terrace and many of the fishermen made fun of the old man and he was not angry. Others, of the older fishermen, looked at him and were sad. But they did not show it and they spoke politely about the current and the depths they had drifted their lines at and the steady good weather and of what they had seen. The successful fishermen of that day were already in and had butchered their marlin out and carried them laid full length across two planks, with two men staggering at the end of each plank, to the fish house where they waited for the ice truck to carry them to the market in Havana. Those who had caught sharks had taken them to the shark factory on the other side of the cove where they were hoisted on a block and tackle, their livers removed, their fins cut off and their hides skinned out and their flesh cut into strips for salting.

When the wind was in the east a smell came across the harbour from the shark factory; but today there was only the faint edge of the odour because the wind had backed into the north and then dropped off and it was pleasant and sunny on the Terrace.

'Santiago,' the boy said.

'Yes,' the old man said. He was holding his glass and thinking of many years ago.

'Can I go out to get sardines for you for tomorrow?'

'No. Go and play baseball. I can still row and Rogelio will throw the net.'

'I would like to go. If I cannot fish with you. I would like to serve in some way.'

'You bought me a beer,' the old man said. 'You are already a man.'

'How old was I when you first took me in a boat?'

'Five and you nearly were killed when I brought the fish in too green and he nearly tore the boat to pieces. Can you remember?'

'I can remember the tail slapping and banging and the thwart breaking and the noise of the clubbing. I can remember you throwing me into the bow where the wet coiled lines were and feeling the whole boat shiver and the noise of you clubbing him like chopping a tree down and the sweet blood smell all over me.'

'Can you really remember that or did I just tell it to you?' 'I remember everything from when we first went together.'

The old man looked at him with his sun-burned, confident loving eyes.

'If you were my boy I'd take you out and gamble,' he said. 'But you are your father's and your mother's and you are in a lucky boat.'

'May I get the sardines? I know where I can get four baits too.' 'I have mine left from today. I put them in salt in the box.'

'Let me get four fresh ones.'

'One,' the old man said. His hope and his confidence had never gone. But now they were freshening as when the breeze rises.

'Two,' the boy said.

'Two,' the old man agreed. 'You didn't steal them?' 'I would,' the boy said. 'But I bought these.'

'Thank you,' the old man said. He was too simple to wonder when he had attained humility. But he knew he had attained it and he knew it was not disgraceful and it carried no loss of true pride.

'Tomorrow is going to be a good day with this current,' he said. 'Where are you going?' the boy asked.

'Far out to come in when the wind shifts. I want to be out before it is light.'

'I'll try to get him to work far out,' the boy said. 'Then if you hook something truly big we can come to your aid.'

'He does not like to work too far out.'

'No,' the boy said. 'But I will see something that he cannot see such as a bird working and get him to come out after dolphin.'

'Are his eyes that bad?' 'He is almost blind.'

'It is strange,' the old man said. 'He never went turtle-ing. That is what kills the eyes.'

'But you went turtle-ing for years off the Mosquito Coast and your eyes are good.'

'I am a strange old man'

'But are you strong enough now for a truly big fish?' 'I think so. And there are many tricks.'

'Let us take the stuff home,' the boy said. 'So I can get the cast net and go after the sardines.'

They picked up the gear from the boat. The old man carried the mast on his shoulder and the boy carried the wooden boat with the coiled, hard-braided brown lines, the gaff and the harpoon with its shaft. The box with the baits was under the stern of the skiff along with the club that was used to subdue the big fish when they were brought alongside. No one would steal from the old man but it was better to take the sail and the heavy lines home as the dew was bad for them and, though he was quite sure no local people would steal from him, the old man thought that a gaff and a harpoon were needless temptations to leave in a boat.

They walked up the road together to the old man's shack and went in through its open door. The old man leaned the mast with its wrapped sail against the wall and the boy put the box and the other gear beside it. The mast was nearly as long as the one room of the shack. The shack was made of the tough budshields of the royal palm which are called *guano* and in it there was a bed, a table, one chair, and a place on the dirt floor to cook with charcoal. On the brown walls of the flattened, overlapping leaves of the sturdy fibered *guano* there was a picture in color of the Sacred Heart of Jesus and another of the Virgin of Cobre. These were relics of his wife. Once there had been a tinted photograph of his wife on the wall but he had taken it down because it made him too lonely to see it and it was on the shelf in the corner under his clean shirt.

'What do you have to eat?' the boy asked.

'A pot of yellow rice with fish. Do you want some?'

'No. I will eat at home. Do you want me to make the fire?' 'No. I will make it later on. Or I may eat the rice cold.' 'May I take the cast net?'

'Of course.'

There was no cast net and the boy remembered when they had sold it. But they went through this fiction every day. There was no pot of yellow rice and fish and the boy knew this too.

'Eighty-five is a lucky number,' the old man said. 'How would you like to see me bring one in that dressed out over a thousand pounds?'

'I'll get the cast net and go for sardines. Will you sit in the sun in the doorway?'

'Yes. I have yesterday's paper and I will read the baseball.'

The boy did not know whether yesterday's paper was a fiction too. But the old man brought it out from under the bed.

'Perico gave it to me at the *bodega*,' he explained.

'I'll be back when I have the sardines. I'll keep yours and mine together on ice and we can share them in the morning. When I come back you can tell me about the baseball.'

'The Yankees cannot lose.'

'But I fear the Indians of Cleveland.'

'Have faith in the Yankees my son. Think of the great DiMaggio.'

'I fear both the Tigers of Detroit and the Indians of Cleveland.'

'Be careful or you will fear even the Reds of Cincinnati and the White Sox of Chicago.'

'You study it and tell me when I come back.'

'Do you think we should buy a terminal of the lottery with an eighty-five? Tomorrow is the eighty-fifth day.'

'We can do that,' the boy said. 'But what about the eighty-seven of your great record?'

'It could not happen twice. Do you think you can find an eighty- five?'

'I can order one.

'One sheet. That's two dollars and a half. Who can we borrow that from?'

'That's easy. I can always borrow two dollars and a half.'

'I think perhaps I can too. But I try not to borrow. First you borrow. Then you beg.'

'Keep warm old man,' the boy said. 'Remember we are in September.'

'The month when the great fish come,' the old man said. 'Anyone can be a fisherman in May.'

'I go now for the sardines,' the boy said.

When the boy came back the old man was asleep in the chair and the sun was down. The boy took the old army blanket off the bed and spread it over the back of the chair and over the old man's shoulders. They were strange shoulders, still powerful although very old, and the neck was still strong too and the creases did not show so much when the old man was asleep and his head fallen forward. His shirt had been patched so many times that it was like the sail and the patches were faded to many different shades by the sun. The old man's head was very old though and with his eyes closed there was no life in his face. The newspaper lay across his knees and the weight of his arm held it there in the evening breeze. He was barefooted.

The boy left him there and when he came back the old man was still asleep.

'Wake up old man,' the boy said and put his hand on one of the old man's knees.

The old man opened his eyes and for a moment he was coming back from a long way away. Then he smiled.

'What have you got?' he asked.

'Supper,' said the boy. 'We're going to have supper.' 'I'm not very hungry.'

'Come on and eat. You can't fish and not eat.'

'I have,' the old man said getting up and taking the newspaper and folding it. Then he started to fold the blanket.

'Keep the blanket around you,' the boy said. 'You'll not fish without eating while I'm alive.'

'Then live a long time and take care of yourself,' the old man said. 'What are we eating?'

'Black beans and rice, fried bananas, and some stew.'

The boy had brought them in a two-decker metal container from the Terrace. The two sets of knives and forks and spoons were in his pocket with a paper napkin wrapped around each set.

'Who gave this to you?' 'Martin. The owner.' 'I must thank him.'

'I thanked him already,' the boy said. 'You don't need to thank him.'

'I'll give him the belly meat of a big fish,' the old man said. 'Has he done this for us more than once?'

'I think so.'

'I must give him something more than the belly meat then. He is very thoughtful for us.'

'He sent two beers.'

'I like the beer in cans best.'

'I know. But this is in bottles, Hatuey beer, and I take back the bottles.'

'That's very kind of you,' the old man said. 'Should we eat?'

'I've been asking you to,' the boy told him gently. 'I have not wished to open the container until you were ready.'

'I'm ready now,' the old man said. 'I only needed time to wash.'

Where did you wash? the boy thought. The village water supply was two streets down the road. I must have water here for him, the boy thought, and soap and a good towel. Why am I so thoughtless? I must get him another shirt and a jacket for the winter and some sort of shoes and another blanket.

'Your stew is excellent,' the old man said.

'Tell me about the baseball,' the boy asked him.

'In the American League it is the Yankees as I said,' the old man said happily.'

'They lost today,' the boy told him.

'That means nothing. The great DiMaggio is himself again.'

'They have other men on the team.'

'Naturally. But he makes the difference. In the other league, between Brooklyn and Philadelphia I must take Brooklyn. But then I think of Dick Sisler and those great drives in the old park.'

'There was nothing ever like them. He hits the longest ball I have ever seen.'

'Do you remember when he used to come to the Terrace? I wanted to take him fishing but I was too timid to ask him. Then I asked you to ask him and you were too timid.'

'I know. It was a great mistake. He might have gone with us. Then we would have that for all of our lives.'

'I would like to take the great DiMaggio fishing,' the old man said. 'They say his father was a fisherman. Maybe he was as poor as we are and would understand.'

'The great Sisler's father was never poor and he, the father, was playing in the Big Leagues when he was my age.'

'When I was your age I was before the mast on a square rigged ship that ran to Africa and I have seen lions on the beaches in the evening.'

'I know. You told me.'

'Should we talk about Africa or about baseball?'

'Baseball I think,' the boy said. 'Tell me about the great John J. McGraw.' He said *Jota* for J.

'He used to come to the Terrace sometimes too in the older days. But he was rough and harsh-spoken and difficult when he was drinking. His mind was on horses as well as baseball. At least he carried lists of horses at all times in his pocket and frequently spoke the names of horses on the telephone.'

'He was a great manager,' the boy said. 'My father thinks he was the greatest.'

'Because he came here the most times,' the old man said. 'If Durocher had continued to come here each year your father would think him the greatest manager.'

'Who is the greatest manager, really, Luque or Mike Gonzalez?' 'I think they are equal.'

'And the best fisherman is you.' 'No. I know others better.'

'*Qué va*,' the boy said. 'There are many good fishermen and some great ones. But there is only you.'

'Thank you. You make me happy. I hope no fish will come along so great that he will prove us wrong.'

'There is no such fish if you are still strong as you say.'

'I may not be as strong as I think,' the old man said. 'But I know many tricks and I have resolution.'

'You ought to go to bed now so that you will be fresh in the morning. I will take the things back to the Terrace.'

'Good night then. I will wake you in the morning.' 'You're my alarm clock,' the boy said.

'Age is my alarm clock,' the old man said. 'Why do old men wake so early? Is it to have one longer day?'

'I don't know,' the boy said. 'All I know is that young boys sleep late and hard.'

'I can remember it,' the old man said. 'I'll waken you in time.'

'I do not like for him to waken me. It is as though I were inferior.'

'I know.'

'Sleep well old man.'

The boy went out. They had eaten with no light on the table and the old man took off his trousers and went to bed in the dark. He rolled his trousers up to make a pillow, putting the newspaper inside them. He rolled himself in the blanket and slept on the other old newspapers that covered the springs of the bed.

He was asleep in a short time and he dreamed of Africa when he was a boy and the long golden beaches and the white beaches, so white they hurt your eyes, and the high capes and the great brown mountains. He lived along that coast now every night and in his dreams he heard the surf roar and saw the native boats come riding through it. He smelled the tar and oakum of the deck as he slept and he smelled the smell of Africa that the land breeze brought at morning.

Usually when he smelled the land breeze he woke up and dressed to go and wake the boy. But tonight the smell of the land breeze came very early and he knew it was too early in his dream and went on dreaming to see the white peaks of the Islands rising from the sea and then he dreamed of the different harbours and roadsteads of the Canary Islands.

He no longer dreamed of storms, nor of women, nor of great occurrences, nor of great fish, nor fights, nor contests of strength, nor of his wife. He only dreamed of places now and of the lions on the beach. They played like young cats in the dusk and he loved them as he loved the boy. He never dreamed about the boy. He simply woke, looked out the open door at the moon and unrolled his trousers and put them on. He urinated outside the shack and then went up the road to wake the boy. He was shivering with the morning cold. But he knew he would shiver himself warm and that soon he would be rowing.

The door of the house where the boy lived was unlocked and he opened it and walked in quietly with his bare feet. The boy was asleep on a cot in the first room and the old man could see him clearly with the light that came in from the dying moon. He took hold of one foot gently and held it until the boy woke and turned and looked at him. The old man nodded and the boy took his trousers from the chair by the bed and, sitting on the bed, pulled them on.

The old man went out the door and the boy came after him. He was sleepy and the old man put his arm across his shoulders and said, 'I am sorry.'

'*Qué va*,' the boy said. 'It is what a man must do.'

They walked down the road to the old man's shack and all along the road, in the dark, barefoot men were moving, carrying the masts of their boats.

When they reached the old man's shack the boy took the rolls of line in the basket and the harpoon and gaff and the old man carried the mast with the furled sail on his shoulder.

'Do you want coffee?' the boy asked.

'We'll put the gear in the boat and then get some.'

They had coffee from condensed milk cans at an early morning place that served fishermen.

'How did you sleep old man?' the boy asked. He was waking up now although it was still hard for him to leave his sleep.

'Very well, Manolin,' the old man said. 'I feel confident today.'

'So do I,' the boy said. 'Now I must get your sardines and mine and your fresh baits. He brings our gear himself. He never wants anyone to carry anything.'

'We're different,' the old man said. 'I let you carry things when you were five years old.'

'I know it,' the boy said. 'I'll be right back. Have another coffee. We have credit here.'

He walked off, bare-footed on the coral rocks, to the ice house where the baits were stored.

The old man drank his coffee slowly. It was all he would have all day and he knew that he should take it. For a long time now eating had bored him and he never carried a lunch. He had a bottle of water in the bow of the skiff and that was all he needed for the day.

The boy was back now with the sardines and the two baits wrapped in a newspaper and they went down the trail to the skiff, feeling the pebbled sand under their feet, and lifted the skiff and slid her into the water.

'Good luck old man.'

'Good luck,' the old man said. He fitted the rope lashings of the oars onto the thole pins and, leaning forward against the thrust of the blades in the water, he began to row out of the harbour in the dark. There were other boats from the other beaches going out to sea and the old man heard the dip and push of their oars even though he could not see them now the moon was below the hills.

Sometimes someone would speak in a boat. But most of the boats were silent except for the dip of the oars. They spread apart after they were out of the mouth of the harbour and each one headed for the part of the ocean where he hoped to find fish. The old man knew he was going far out and he left the smell of the land behind and rowed out into the clean early morning smell of the ocean. He saw the phosphorescence of the Gulf weed in the water as he rowed over the part of the ocean that the fishermen called the great well because there was a sudden deep of seven hundred fathoms where all sorts of fish congregated because of the swirl the current made against the steep walls of the floor of the ocean. Here there were concentrations of shrimp and bait fish and sometimes schools of squid in the deepest holes and these rose close to the surface at night where all the wandering fish fed on them.

In the dark the old man could feel the morning coming and as he rowed he heard the trembling sound as flying fish left the water and the hissing that their stiff set wings made as they soared away in the darkness. He was very fond of flying fish as they were his principal friends on the ocean. He was sorry for the birds, especially the small delicate dark terns that were always flying and looking and almost never finding, and he thought, the birds have a harder life than we do except for the robber birds and the heavy strong ones. Why did they make birds so delicate and fine as those sea swallows when the ocean can be so cruel? She is kind and very beautiful. But she can be so cruel and it comes so suddenly and such birds that fly, dipping and hunting, with their small sad voices are made too delicately for the sea.

He always thought of the sea as *la mar* which is what people call her in Spanish when they love her. Sometimes those who love her say bad things of her but they are always said as though she were a woman. Some of the younger fishermen, those who used buoys as floats for their lines and had motorboats, bought when the shark livers had brought much money, spoke of her as *el mar* which is masculine. They spoke of her as a contestant or a place or even an enemy. But the old man always thought of her as feminine and as something that gave or withheld great favours, and if she did wild or wicked things it was because she could not help them. The moon affects her as it does a woman, he thought.

He was rowing steadily and it was no effort for him since he kept well within his speed and the surface of the ocean was flat except for the occasional swirls of the current. He was letting the current do a third of the work and as it started to be light he saw he was already further out than he had hoped to be at this hour.

I worked the deep wells for a week and did nothing, he thought. Today I'll work out where the schools of bonito and albacore are and maybe there will be a big one with them.

Before it was really light he had his baits out and was drifting with the current. One bait was down forty fathoms. The second was at seventy-five and the third and fourth were down in the blue water at one hundred and one hundred and twenty-five fathoms. Each bait hung head down with the shank of the hook inside the bait fish, tied and sewed solid and all the projecting part of the hook, the curve and the point, was covered with fresh sardines. Each sardine was hooked through both eyes so that they made a half-garland on the projecting steel. There was no part of the hook that a great fish could feel which was not sweet smelling and good tasting.

The boy had given him two fresh small tunas, or albacores, which hung on the two deepest lines like plummets and, on the others, he had a big blue runner and a yellow jack that had been used before; but they were in good condition still and had the excellent sardines to give them scent and attractiveness. Each line, as thick around as a big pencil, was looped onto a green-sapped stick so that any pull or touch on the bait would make the stick dip and each line had two forty-fathom coils which could be made fast to the other spare coils so that, if it were necessary, a fish could take out over three hundred fathoms of line.

Now the man watched the dip of the three sticks over the side of the skiff and rowed gently to keep the lines straight up and down and at their proper depths. It was quite light and any moment now the sun would rise.

The sun rose thinly from the sea and the old man could see the other boats, low on the water and well in toward the shore, spread out across the current. Then the sun was brighter and the glare came on the water and then, as it rose clear, the flat sea sent it back at his eyes so that it hurt sharply and he rowed without looking into it. He looked down into the water and watched the lines that went straight down into the dark of the water. He kept them straighter than anyone did, so that at each level in the darkness of the stream there would be a bait waiting exactly where he wished it to be for any fish that swam there.

Others let them drift with the current and sometimes they were at sixty fathoms when the fishermen thought they were at a hundred.

But, he thought, I keep them with precision. Only I have no luck any more. But who knows? Maybe today. Every day is a new day. It is better to be lucky. But I would rather be exact. Then when luck comes you are ready.

The sun was two hours higher now and it did not hurt his eyes so much to look into the east. There were only three boats in sight now and they showed very low and far inshore.

All my life the early sun has hurt my eyes, he thought. Yet they are still good. In the evening I can look straight into it without getting the blackness. It has more force in the evening too. But in the morning it is painful.

Just then he saw a man-of-war bird with his long black wings circling in the sky ahead of him. He made a quick drop, slanting down on his back-swept wings, and then circled again.

'He's got something,' the old man said aloud. 'He's not just looking.'

He rowed slowly and steadily toward where the bird was circling. He did not hurry and he kept his lines straight up and down. But he crowded the current a little so that he was still fishing correctly though faster than he would have fished if he was not trying to use the bird.

The bird went higher in the air and circled again, his wings motionless. Then he dove suddenly and the old man saw flying fish spurt out of the water and sail desperately over the surface.

'Dolphin,' the old man said aloud. 'Big dolphin.'

He shipped his oars and brought a small line from under the bow. It had a wire leader and a medium-sized hook and he baited it with one of the sardines. He let it go over the side and then made it fast to a ring bolt in the stern. Then he baited another line and left it coiled in the shade of the bow. He went back to rowing and to watching the long-winged black bird who was working, now, low over the water.

As he watched the bird dipped again slanting his wings for the dive and then swinging them wildly and ineffectually as he followed the flying fish. The old man could see the slight bulge in the water that the big dolphin raised as they followed the escaping fish. The dolphin were cutting through the water below the flight of the fish and would be in the water, driving at speed, when the fish dropped. It is a big school of dolphin, he thought. They are widespread and the flying fish have little chance. The bird has no chance. The flying fish are too big for him and they go too fast.

He watched the flying fish burst out again and again and the ineffectual movements of the bird. That school has gotten away from me, he thought. They are moving out too fast and too far. But perhaps I will pick up a stray and perhaps my big fish is around them. My big fish must be somewhere.

The clouds over the land now rose like mountains and the coast was only a long green line with the gray blue hills behind it. The water was a dark blue now, so dark that it was almost purple. As he looked down into it he saw the red sifting of the plankton in the dark water and the strange light the sun made now. He watched his lines to see them go straight down out of sight into the water and he was happy to see so much plankton because it meant fish. The strange light the sun made in the water, now that the sun was higher, meant good weather and so did the shape of the clouds over the land. But the bird was almost out of sight now and nothing showed on the surface of the water but some patches of yellow, sun-bleached Sargasso weed and the purple, formalized, iridescent, gelatinous bladder of a Portuguese man-of-war floating close beside the boat. It turned on its side and then righted itself. It floated cheerfully as a bubble with its long deadly purple filaments trailing a yard behind it in the water.

'*Agua mala*,' the man said. 'You whore.'

From where he swung lightly against his oars he looked down into the water and saw the tiny fish that were coloured like the trailing filaments and swam between them and under the small shade the bubble made as it drifted. They were immune to its poison. But men were not and when some of the filaments would catch on a line and rest there slimy and purple while the old man was working a fish, he would have welts and sores on his arms and hands of the sort that poison ivy or poison oak can give. But these poisonings from the *agua mala* came quickly and struck like a whiplash.

The iridescent bubbles were beautiful. But they were the falsest thing in the sea and the old man loved to see the big sea turtles eating them. The turtles saw them, approached them from the front, then shut their eyes so they were completely carapaced and ate them filaments and all. The old man loved to see the turtles eat them and he loved to walk on them on the beach after a storm and hear them pop when he stepped on them with the horny soles of his feet.

He loved green turtles and hawk-bills with their elegance and speed and their great value and he had a friendly contempt for the huge, stupid loggerheads, yellow in their armour-plating, strange in their love-making, and happily eating the Portuguese men-of-war with their eyes shut.

He had no mysticism about turtles although he had gone in turtle boats for many years. He was sorry for them all, even the great trunk backs that were as long as the skiff and weighed a ton.

Most people are heartless about turtles because a turtle's heart will beat for hours after he has been cut up and butchered. But the old man thought, I have such a heart too and my feet and hands are like theirs. He ate the white eggs to give himself strength. He ate them all through May to be strong in September and October for the truly big fish.

He also drank a cup of shark liver oil each day from the big drum in the shack where many of the fishermen kept their gear. It was there for all fishermen who wanted it. Most fishermen hated the taste. But it was no worse than getting up at the hours that they rose and it was very good against all colds and grippes and it was good for the eyes.

Now the old man looked up and saw that the bird was circling again.

'He's found fish,' he said aloud. No flying fish broke the surface and there was no scattering of bait fish. But as the old man watched, a small tuna rose in the air, turned and dropped head first into the water. The tuna shone silver in the sun and after he had dropped back into the water another and another rose and they were jumping in all directions, churning the water and leaping in long jumps after the bait. They were circling it and driving it.

If they don't travel too fast I will get into them, the old man thought, and he watched the school working the water white and the bird now dropping and dipping into the bait fish that were forced to the surface in their panic.

'The bird is a great help,' the old man said. Just then the stern line came taut under his foot, where he had kept a loop of the line, and he dropped his oars and felt the weight of the small tuna's shivering pull as he held the line firm and commenced to haul it in. The shivering increased as he pulled in and he could see the blue back of the fish in the water and the gold of his sides before he swung him over the side and into the boat. He lay in the stern in the sun, compact and bullet shaped, his big, unintelligent eyes staring as he thumped his life out against the planking of the boat with the quick shivering strokes of his neat, fast-moving tail. The old man hit him on the head for kindness and kicked him, his body still shuddering, under the shade of the stern.

'Albacore,' he said aloud. 'He'll make a beautiful bait. He'll weigh ten pounds.'

He did not remember when he had first started to talk aloud when he was by himself. He had sung when he was by himself in the old days and he had sung at night sometimes when he was alone steering on his watch in the smacks or in the turtle boats. He had probably started to talk aloud, when alone, when the boy had left. But he did not remember. When he and the boy fished together they usually spoke only when it was necessary. They talked at night or when they were storm-bound by bad weather. It was considered a virtue not to talk unnecessarily at sea and the old man had always considered it so and respected it. But now he said his thoughts aloud many times since there was no one that they could annoy.

'If the others heard me talking out loud they would think that I am crazy,' he said aloud. 'But since I am not crazy, I do not care.

And the rich have radios to talk to them in their boats and to bring them the baseball.'

Now is no time to think of baseball, he thought. Now is the time to think of only one thing. That which I was born for. There might be a big one around that school, he thought. I picked up only a straggler from the albacore that were feeding. But they are working far out and fast. Everything that shows on the surface today travels very fast and to the north-east. Can that be the time of day? Or is it some sign of weather that I do not know?

He could not see the green of the shore now but only the tops of the blue hills that showed white as though they were snow-capped and the clouds that looked like high snow mountains above them. The sea was very dark and the light made prisms in the water. The myriad flecks of the plankton were annulled now by the high sun and it was only the great deep prisms in the blue water that the old man saw now with his lines going straight down into the water that was a mile deep.

The tuna, the fishermen called all the fish of that species tuna and only distinguished among them by their proper names when they came to sell them or to trade them for baits, were down again. The sun was hot now and the old man felt it on the back of his neck and felt the sweat trickle down his back as he rowed.

I could just drift, he thought, and sleep and put a bight of line around my toe to wake me. But today is eighty-five days and I should fish the day well.

Just then, watching his lines, he saw one of the projecting green sticks dip sharply.

'Yes,' he said. 'Yes,' and shipped his oars without bumping the boat. He reached out for the line and held it softly between the thumb and forefinger of his right hand. He felt no strain nor weight and he held the line lightly. Then it came again. This time it was a tentative pull, not solid nor heavy, and he knew exactly what it was. One hundred fathoms down a marlin was eating the sardines that covered the point and the shank of the hook where the hand-forged hook projected from the head of the small tuna.

The old man held the line delicately, and softly, with his left hand, unleashed it from the stick. Now he could let it run through his fingers without the fish feeling any tension.

This far out, he must be huge in this month, he thought. Eat them, fish. Eat them. Please eat them. How fresh they are and you down there six hundred feet in that cold water in the dark. Make another turn in the dark and come back and eat them.

He felt the light delicate pulling and then a harder pull when a sardine's head must have been more difficult to break from the hook. Then there was nothing.

'Come on,' the old man said aloud. 'Make another turn. Just smell them. Aren't they lovely? Eat them good now and then there is the tuna. Hard and cold and lovely. Don't be shy, fish. Eat them.'

He waited with the line between his thumb and his finger, watching it and the other lines at the same time for the fish might have swum up or down. Then came the same delicate pulling touch again.

'He'll take it,' the old man said aloud. 'God help him to take it.'

He did not take it though. He was gone and the old man felt nothing.

'He can't have gone,' he said. 'Christ knows he can't have gone. He's making a turn. Maybe he has been hooked before and he remembers something of it.'

Then he felt the gentle touch on the line and he was happy. 'It was only his turn,' he said. 'He'll take it.'

He was happy feeling the gentle pulling and then he felt something hard and unbelievably heavy. It was the weight of the fish and he let the line slip down, down, down, unrolling off the first of the two reserve coils. As it went down, slipping lightly through the old man's fingers, he still could feel the great weight, though the pressure of his thumb and finger were almost imperceptible.

'What a fish,' he said. 'He has it sideways in his mouth now and he is moving off with it.'

Then he will turn and swallow it, he thought. He did not say that because he knew that if you said a good thing it might not happen. He knew what a huge fish this was and he thought of him moving away in the darkness with the tuna held crosswise in his mouth. At that moment he felt him stop moving but the weight was still there. Then the weight increased and he gave more line. He tightened the pressure of his thumb and finger for a moment and the weight increased and was going straight down.

'He's taken it,' he said. 'Now I'll let him eat it well.'

He let the line slip through his fingers while he reached down with his left hand and made fast the free end of the two reserve coils to the loop of the two reserve coils of the next line. Now he was ready. He had three forty-fathom coils of line in reserve now, as well as the coil he was using.

'Eat it a little more,' he said. 'Eat it well.'

Eat it so that the point of the hook goes into your heart and kills you, he thought. Come up easy and let me put the harpoon into you. All right. Are you ready? Have you been long enough at table?

'Now!' he said aloud and struck hard with both hands, gained a yard of line and then struck again and again, swinging with each arm alternately on the cord with all the strength of his arms and the pivoted weight of his body.

Nothing happened. The fish just moved away slowly and the old man could not raise him an inch. His line was strong and made for heavy fish and he held it against his back until it was so taut that beads of water were jumping from it. Then it began to make a slow hissing sound in the water and he still held it, bracing himself against the thwart and leaning back against the pull. The boat began to move slowly off toward the north-west.

The fish moved steadily and they travelled slowly on the calm water. The other baits were still in the water but there was nothing to be done.

'I wish I had the boy" the old man said aloud. 'I'm being towed by a fish and I'm the towing bitt. I could make the line fast. But then he could break it. I must hold him all I can and give him line when he must have it. Thank God he is travelling and not going down.'

What I will do if he decides to go down, I don't know. What I'll do if he sounds and dies I don't know. But I'll do something. There are plenty of things I can do.

He held the line against his back and watched its slant in the water and the skiff moving steadily to the north-west.

This will kill him, the old man thought. He can't do this forever. But four hours later the fish was still swimming steadily out to sea, towing the skiff, and the old man was still braced solidly with the line across his back.

'It was noon when I hooked him,' he said. 'And I have never seen him.'

He had pushed his straw hat hard down on his head before he hooked the fish and it was cutting his forehead. He was thirsty too and he got down on his knees and, being careful not to jerk on the line, moved as far into the bow as he could get and reached the water bottle with one hand. He opened it and drank a little. Then he rested against the bow. He rested sitting on the un-stepped mast and sail and tried not to think but only to endure.

Then he looked behind him and saw that no land was visible. That makes no difference, he thought. I can always come in on the glow from Havana. There are two more hours before the sun sets and maybe he will come up before that. If he doesn't maybe he will come up with the moon. If he does not do that maybe he will come up with the sunrise. I have no cramps and I feel strong. It is he that has the hook in his mouth. But what a fish to pull like that. He must have his mouth shut tight on the wire. I wish I could see him. I wish I could see him only once to know what I have against me.

The fish never changed his course nor his direction all that night as far as the man could tell from watching the stars. It was cold after the sun went down and the old man's sweat dried cold on his back and his arms and his old legs. During the day he had taken the sack that covered the bait box and spread it in the sun to dry. After the sun went down he tied it around his neck so that it hung down over his back and he cautiously worked it down under the line that was across his shoulders now. The sack cushioned the line and he had found a way of leaning forward against the bow so that he was almost comfortable. The position actually was only somewhat less intolerable; but he thought of it as almost comfortable.

I can do nothing with him and he can do nothing with me, he thought. Not as long as he keeps this up.

Once he stood up and urinated over the side of the skiff and looked at the stars and checked his course. The line showed like a phosphorescent streak in the water straight out from his shoulders. They were moving more slowly now and the glow of Havana was not so strong, so that he knew the current must be carrying them to the eastward. If I lose the glare of Havana we must be going more to the eastward, he thought. For if the fish's course held true I must see it for many more hours. I wonder how the baseball came out in the grand leagues today, he thought. It would be wonderful to do this with a radio. Then he thought, think of it always. Think of what you are doing. You must do nothing stupid.

Then he said aloud, 'I wish I had the boy. To help me and to see this.'

No one should be alone in their old age, he thought. But it is unavoidable. I must remember to eat the tuna before he spoils in order to keep strong. Remember, no matter how little you want to, that you must eat him in the morning. Remember, he said to himself.

During the night two porpoises came around the boat and he could hear them rolling and blowing. He could tell the difference between the blowing noise the male made and the sighing blow of the female.

'They are good,' he said. 'They play and make jokes and love one another. They are our brothers like the flying fish.'

Then he began to pity the great fish that he had hooked. He is wonderful and strange and who knows how old he is, he thought. Never have I had such a strong fish nor one who acted so strangely. Perhaps he is too wise to jump. He could ruin me by jumping or by a wild rush. But perhaps he has been hooked many times before and he knows that this is how he should make his fight. He cannot know that it is only one man against him, nor that it is an old man. But what a great fish he is and what will he bring in the market if the flesh is good. He took the bait like a male and he pulls like a male and his fight has no panic in it. I wonder if he has any plans or if he is just as desperate as I am?

He remembered the time he had hooked one of a pair of marlin. The male fish always let the female fish feed first and the hooked fish, the female, made a wild, panic-stricken, despairing fight that soon exhausted her, and all the time the male had stayed with her, crossing the line and circling with her on the surface. He had stayed so close that the old man was afraid he would cut the line with his tail which was sharp as a scythe and almost of that size and shape. When the old man had gaffed her and clubbed her, holding the rapier bill with its sandpaper edge and clubbing her across the top of her head until her colour turned to a colour almost like the backing of mirrors, and then, with the boy's aid, hoisted her aboard, the male fish had stayed by the side of the boat. Then, while the old man was clearing the lines and preparing the harpoon, the male fish jumped high into the air beside the boat to see where the female was and then went down deep, his lavender wings, that were his pectoral fins, spread wide and all his wide lavender stripes showing. He was beautiful, the old man remembered, and he had stayed.

That was the saddest thing I ever saw with them, the old man thought. The boy was sad too and we begged her pardon and butchered her promptly.

'I wish the boy was here,' he said aloud and settled himself against the rounded planks of the bow and felt the strength of the great fish through the line he held across his shoulders moving steadily toward whatever he had chosen.

When once, through my treachery, it had been necessary to him to make a choice, the old man thought.

His choice had been to stay in the deep dark water far out beyond all snares and traps and treacheries. My choice was to go there to find him beyond all people. Beyond all people in the world. Now we are joined together and have been since noon. And no one to help either one of us.

Perhaps I should not have been a fisherman, he thought. But that was the thing that I was born for. I must surely remember to eat the tuna after it gets light.

Some time before daylight something took one of the baits that were behind him. He heard the stick break and the line begin to rush out over the gunwale of the skiff. In the darkness he loosened his sheath knife and taking all the strain of the fish on his left shoulder he leaned back and cut the line against the wood of the gunwale. Then he cut the other line closest to him and in the dark made the loose ends of the reserve coils fast. He worked skillfully with the one hand and put his foot on the coils to hold them as he drew his knots tight. Now he had six reserve coils of line. There were two from each bait he had severed and the two from the bait the fish had taken and they were all connected.

After it is light, he thought, I will work back to the forty-fathom bait and cut it away too and link up the reserve coils. I will have lost two hundred fathoms of good Catalan *cardel* and the hooks and leaders. That can be replaced. But who replaces this fish if I hook some fish and it cuts him off? I don't know what that fish was that took the bait just now. It could have been a marlin or a broadbill or a shark. I never felt him. I had to get rid of him too fast.

Aloud he said, 'I wish I had the boy.'

But you haven't got the boy, he thought. You have only yourself and you had better work back to the last line now, in the dark or not in the dark, and cut it away and hook up the two reserve coils.

So he did it. It was difficult in the dark and once the fish made a surge that pulled him down on his face and made a cut below his eye. The blood ran down his cheek a little way. But it coagulated and dried before it reached his chin and he worked his way back to the bow and rested against the wood. He adjusted the sack and carefully worked the line so that it came across a new part of his shoulders and, holding it anchored with his shoulders, he carefully felt the pull of the fish and then felt with his hand the progress of the skiff through the water.

I wonder what he made that lurch for, he thought. The wire must have slipped on the great hill of his back. Certainly his back cannot feel as badly as mine does. But he cannot pull this skiff forever, no matter how great he is. Now everything is cleared away that might make trouble and I have a big reserve of line; all that a man can ask.

'Fish,' he said softly, aloud, 'I'll stay with you until I am dead.'

He'll stay with me too, I suppose, the old man thought and he waited for it to be light. It was cold now in the time before daylight and he pushed against the wood to be warm. I can do it as long as he can, he thought. And in the first light the line extended out and down into the water. The boat moved steadily and when the first edge of the sun rose it was on the old man's right shoulder.

'He's headed north,' the old man said. The current will have set us far to the eastward, he thought. I wish he would turn with the current. That would show that he was tiring.

When the sun had risen further the old man realized that the fish was not tiring. There was only one favorable sign. The slant of the line showed he was swimming at a lesser depth. That did not necessarily mean that he would jump. But he might.

'God let him jump,' the old man said. 'I have enough line to handle him.'

Maybe if I can increase the tension just a little it will hurt him and he will jump, he thought. Now that it is daylight let him jump so that he'll fill the sacks along his backbone with air and then he cannot go deep to die.

He tried to increase the tension, but the line had been taut up to the very edge of the breaking point since he had hooked the fish and he felt the harshness as he leaned back to pull and knew he could put no more strain on it. I must not jerk it ever, he thought. Each jerk widens the cut the hook makes and then when he does jump he might throw it. Anyway I feel better with the sun and for once I do not have to look into it.

There was yellow weed on the line but the old man knew that only made an added drag and he was pleased. It was the yellow Gulf weed that had made so much phosphorescence in the night.

'Fish,' he said, 'I love you and respect you very much. But I will kill you dead before this day ends.'

Let us hope so, he thought.

A small bird came toward the skiff from the north. He was a warbler and flying very low over the water. The old man could see that he was very tired.

The bird made the stern of the boat and rested there. Then he flew around the old man's head and rested on the line where he was more comfortable.

'How old are you?' the old man asked the bird. 'Is this your first trip?'

The bird looked at him when he spoke. He was too tired even to examine the line and he teetered on it as his delicate feet gripped it fast.

'It's steady,' the old man told him. 'It's too steady. You shouldn't be that tired after a windless night. What are birds coming to?'

The hawks, he thought, that come out to sea to meet them. But he said nothing of this to the bird who could not understand him anyway and who would learn about the hawks soon enough.

'Take a good rest, small bird,' he said. 'Then go in and take your chance like any man or bird or fish.'

It encouraged him to talk because his back had stiffened in the night and it hurt truly now.

'Stay at my house if you like, bird,' he said. 'I am sorry I cannot hoist the sail and take you in with the small breeze that is rising. But I am with a friend.'

Just then the fish gave a sudden lurch that pulled the old man down onto the bow and would have pulled him overboard if he had not braced himself and given some line.

The bird had flown up when the line jerked and the old man had not even seen him go. He felt the line carefully with his right hand and noticed his hand was bleeding.

'Something hurt him then,' he said aloud and pulled back on the line to see if he could turn the fish. But when he was touching the breaking point he held steady and settled back against the strain of the line.

'You're feeling it now, fish,' he said. 'And so, God knows, am I.'

He looked around for the bird now because he would have liked him for company. The bird was gone.

You did not stay long, the man thought. But it is rougher where you are going until you make the shore. How did I let the fish cut me with that one quick pull he made? I must be getting very stupid. Or perhaps I was looking at the small bird and thinking of him. Now I will pay attention to my work and then I must eat the tuna so that I will not have a failure of strength.

'I wish the boy were here and that I had some salt,' he said aloud.

Shifting the weight of the line to his left shoulder and kneeling carefully he washed his hand in the ocean and held it there, submerged, for more than a minute watching the blood trail away and the steady movement of the water against his hand as the boat moved.

'He has slowed much,' he said.

The old man would have liked to keep his hand in the salt water longer but he was afraid of another sudden lurch by the fish and he stood up and braced himself and held his hand up against the sun. It was only a line burn that had cut his flesh. But it was in the working part of his hand. He knew he would need his hands before this was over and he did not like to be cut before it started.

'Now,' he said, when his hand had dried, 'I must eat the small tuna. I can reach him with the gaff and eat him here in comfort.'

He knelt down and found the tuna under the rn with the gaff and drew it toward him keeping it clear of the coiled lines. Holding the line with his left shoulder again, and bracing on his left hand and arm, he took the tuna off the gaff hook and put the gaff back in place. He put one knee on the fish and cut strips of dark red meat longitudinally from the back of the head to the tail. They were wedge-shaped strips and he cut them from next to the back bone down to the edge of the belly. When he had cut six strips he spread them out on the wood of the bow, wiped his knife on his trousers, and lifted the carcass of the bonito by the tail and dropped it overboard.

'I don't think I can eat an entire one,' he said and drew his knife across one of the strips. He could feel the steady hard pull of the line and his left hand was cramped. It drew up tight on the heavy cord and he looked at it in disgust.

'What kind of a hand is that,' he said. 'Cramp then if you want. Make yourself into a claw. It will do you no good.'

Come on, he thought and looked down into the dark water at the slant of the line. Eat it now and it will strengthen the hand. It is not the hand's fault and you have been many hours with the fish. But you can stay with him forever. Eat the bonito now.

He picked up a piece and put it in his mouth and chewed it slowly. It was not unpleasant.

Chew it well, he thought, and get all the juices. It would not be bad to eat with a little lime or with lemon or with salt.

'How do you feel, hand?' he asked the cramped hand that was almost as stiff as rigor mortis. 'I'll eat some more for you.'

He ate the other part of the piece that he had cut in two. He chewed it carefully and then spat out the skin.

'How does it go, hand? Or is it too early to know?' He took another full piece and chewed it.

'It is a strong full-blooded fish,' he thought. 'I was lucky to get him instead of dolphin. Dolphin is too sweet. This is hardly sweet at all and all the strength is still in it.'

There is no sense in being anything but practical though, he thought. I wish I had some salt. And I do not know whether the sun will rot or dry what is left, so I had better eat it all although I am not hungry. The fish is calm and steady. I will eat it all and then I will be ready.

'Be patient, hand,' he said. 'I do this for you.'

I wish I could feed the fish, he thought. He is my brother. But I must kill him and keep strong to do it. Slowly and conscientiously he ate all of the wedge-shaped strips of fish.

He straightened up, wiping his hand on his trousers.

'Now,' he said. 'You can let the cord go, hand, and I will handle him with the right arm alone until you stop that nonsense.' He put his left foot on the heavy line that the left hand had held and lay back against the pull against his back.

'God help me to have the cramp go,' he said. 'Because I do not know what the fish is going to do.'

But he seems calm, he thought, and following his plan. But what is his plan, he thought. And what is mine? Mine I must improvise to his because of his great size. If he will jump I can kill him. But he stays down forever. Then I will stay down with him forever.

He rubbed the cramped hand against his trousers and tried to gentle the fingers. But it would not open. Maybe it will open with the sun, he thought. Maybe it will open when the strong raw tuna is digested. If I have to have it, I will open it, cost whatever it costs. But I do not want to open it now by force. Let it open by itself and come back of its own accord. After all I abused it much in the night when it was necessary to free and untie the various lines.

He looked across the sea and knew how alone he was now. But he could see the prisms in the deep dark water and the line stretching ahead and the strange undulation of the calm. The clouds were building up now for the trade wind and he looked ahead and saw a flight of wild ducks etching themselves against the sky over the water, then blurring, then etching again and he knew no man was ever alone on the sea.

He thought of how some men feared being out of sight of land in a small boat and knew they were right in the months of sudden bad weather. But now they were in hurricane months and, when there are no hurricanes, the weather of hurricane months is the best of all the year.

If there is a hurricane you always see the signs of it in the sky for days ahead, if you are at sea. They do not see it ashore because they do not know what to look for, he thought. The land must make a difference too, in the shape of the clouds. But we have no hurricane coming now.

He looked at the sky and saw the white cumulus built like friendly piles of ice cream and high above were the thin feathers of the cirrus against the high September sky.

'Light *brisa*,' he said. 'Better weather for me than for you, fish.' His left hand was still cramped, but he was unknotting it slowly.

I hate a cramp, he thought. It is a treachery of one's own body. It is humiliating before others to have a diarrhoea from ptomaine poisoning or to vomit from it. But a cramp, he thought of it as a *calambre*, humiliates oneself especially when one is alone.

If the boy were here he could rub it for me and loosen it down from the forearm, he thought. But it will loosen up.

Then, with his right hand he felt the difference in the pull of the line before he saw the slant change in the water. Then, as he leaned against the line and slapped his left hand hard and fast against his thigh he saw the line slanting slowly upward.

'He's coming up,' he said. 'Come on hand. Please come on.'

The line rose slowly and steadily and then the surface of the ocean bulged ahead of the boat and the fish came out. He came out unendingly and water poured from his sides. He was bright in the sun and his head and back were dark purple and in the sun the stripes on his sides showed wide and a light lavender. His sword was as long as a baseball bat and tapered like a rapier and he rose his full length from the water and then re-entered it, smoothly, like a diver and the old man saw the great scythe-blade of his tail go under and the line commenced to race out.

'He is two feet longer than the skiff,' the old man said. The line was going out fast but steadily and the fish was not panicked. The old man was trying with both hands to keep the line just inside of breaking strength. He knew that if he could not slow the fish with a steady pressure the fish could take out all the line and break it.

He is a great fish and I must convince him, he thought. I must never let him learn his strength nor what he could do if he made his run. If I were him I would put in everything now and go until something broke. But, thank God, they are not as intelligent as we who kill them; although they are more noble and more able.

The old man had seen many great fish. He had seen many that weighed more than a thousand pounds and he had caught two of that size in his life, but never alone. Now alone, and out of sight of land, he was fast to the biggest fish that he had ever seen and bigger than he had ever heard of, and his left hand was still as tight as the gripped claws of an eagle.

It will uncramp though, he thought. Surely it will uncramp to help my right hand. There are three things that are brothers: the fish and my two hands. It must uncramp. It is unworthy of it to be cramped. The fish had slowed again and was going at his usual pace.

I wonder why he jumped, the old man thought. He jumped almost as though to show me how big he was. I know now, anyway, he thought. I wish I could show him what sort of man I am. But then he would see the cramped hand. Let him think I am more man than I am and I will be so. I wish I was the fish, he thought, with everything he has against only my will and my intelligence.

He settled comfortably against the wood and took his suffering as it came and the fish swam steadily and the boat moved slowly through the dark water. There was a small sea rising with the wind coming up from the east and at noon the old man's left hand was uncramped.

'Bad news for you, fish,' he said and shifted the line over the sacks that covered his shoulders.

He was comfortable but suffering, although he did not admit the suffering at all.

'I am not religious,' he said. 'But I will say ten Our Fathers and ten Hail Marys that I should catch this fish, and I promise to make a pilgrimage to the Virgin of Cobre if I catch him. That is a promise.'

He commenced to say his prayers mechanically. Sometimes he would be so tired that he could not remember the prayer and then he would say them fast so that they would come automatically. Hail Marys are easier to say than Our Fathers, he thought.

'Hail Mary full of Grace the Lord is with thee. Blessed art thou among women and blessed is the fruit of thy womb, Jesus. Holy Mary, Mother of God, pray for us sinners now and at the hour of our death. Amen.' Then he added, 'Blessed Virgin, pray for the death of this fish. Wonderful though he is.'

With his prayers said, and feeling much better, but suffering exactly as much, and perhaps a little more, he leaned against the wood of the bow and began, mechanically, to work the fingers of his left hand.

The sun was hot now although the breeze was rising gently.

'I had better re-bait that little line out over the stern,' he said. 'If the fish decides to stay another night I will need to eat again and the water is low in the bottle. I don't think I can get anything but a dolphin here. But if I eat him fresh enough he won't be bad. I wish a flying fish would come on board tonight. But I have no light to attract them. A flying fish is excellent to eat raw and I would not have to cut him up. I must save all my strength now. Christ, I did not know he was so big.'

'I'll kill him though,' he said. 'In all his greatness and his glory.'

Although it is unjust, he thought. But I will show him what a man can do and what a man endures.

'I told the boy I was a strange old man,' he said. 'Now is when I must prove it.'

The thousand times that he had proved it meant nothing. Now he was proving it again. Each time was a new time and he never thought about the past when he was doing it.

I wish he'd sleep and I could sleep and dream about the lions, he thought. Why are the lions the main thing that is left? Don't think, old man, he said to himself, Rest gently now against the wood and think of nothing. He is working. Work as little as you can.

It was getting into the afternoon and the boat still moved slowly and steadily.

But there was an added drag now from the easterly breeze and the old man rode gently with the small sea and the hurt of the cord across his back came to him easily and smoothly.

Once in the afternoon the line started to rise again. But the fish only continued to swim at a slightly higher level. The sun was on the old man's left arm and shoulder and on his back. So he knew the fish had turned east of north.

Now that he had seen him once, he could picture the fish swimming in the water with his purple pectoral fins set wide as wings and the great erect tail slicing through the dark. I wonder how much he sees at that depth, the old man thought. His eye is huge and a horse, with much less eye, can see in the dark.

Once I could see quite well in the dark. Not in the absolute dark. But almost as a cat sees.

The sun and his steady movement of his fingers had uncramped his left hand now completely and he began to shift more of the strain to it and he shrugged the muscles of his back to shift the hurt of the cord a little.

'If you're not tired, fish,' he said aloud, 'you must be very strange.'

He felt very tired now and he knew the night would come soon and he tried to think of other things. He thought of the Big Leagues, to him they were the *Gran Ligas*, and he knew that the Yankees of New York were playing the *Tigres* of Detroit.

This is the second day now that I do not know the result of the *juegos*, he thought. But I must have confidence and I must be worthy of the great DiMaggio who does all things perfectly even with the pain of the bone spur in his heel. What is a bone spur? he asked himself. *Un espuela de hueso.* We do not have them. Can it be as painful as the spur of a fighting cock in one's heel? I do not think I could endure that or the loss of the eye and of both eyes and continue to fight as the fighting cocks do. Man is not much beside the great birds and beasts. Still I would rather be that beast down there in the darkness of the sea.

'Unless sharks come,' he said aloud. 'If sharks come, God pity him and me.'

Do you believe the great DiMaggio would stay with a fish as long as I will stay with this one? he thought. I am sure he would and more since he is young and strong. Also his father was a fisherman. But would the bone spur hurt him too much?

'I do not know,' he said aloud. 'I never had a bone spur.'

As the sun set he remembered, to give himself more confidence, the time in the tavern at Casablanca when he had played the hand game with the great negro from Cienfuegos who was the strongest man on the docks. They had gone one day and one night with their elbows on a chalk line on the table and their forearms straight up and their hands gripped tight. Each one was trying to force the other's hand down onto the table. There was much betting and people went in and out of the room under the kerosene lights and he had looked at the arm and hand of the negro and at the negro's face. They changed the referees every four hours after the first eight so that the referees could sleep. Blood came out from under the fingernails of both his and the negro's hands and they looked each other in the eye and at their hands and forearms and the bettors went in and out of the room and sat on high chairs against the wall and watched. The walls were painted bright blue and were of wood and the lamps threw their shadows against them. The negro's shadow was huge and it moved on the wall as the breeze moved the lamps.

The odds would change back and forth all night and they fed the negro rum and lighted cigarettes for him. Then the negro, after the rum, would try for a tremendous effort and once he had the old man, who was not an old man then but was Santiago *El Campeón*, nearly three inches off balance. But the old man had raised his hand up to dead even again. He was sure then that he had the negro, who was a fine man and a great athlete, beaten. And at daylight when the bettors were asking that it be called a draw and the referee was shaking his head, he had unleashed his effort and forced the hand of the negro down and down until it rested on the wood. The match had started on a Sunday morning and ended on a Monday morning. Many of the bettors had asked for a draw because they had to go to work on the docks loading sacks of sugar or at the Havana Coal Company. Otherwise everyone would have wanted it to go to a finish. But he had finished it anyway and before anyone had to go to work.

For a long time after that everyone had called him The Champion and there had been a return match in the spring. But not much money was bet and he had won it quite easily since he had broken the confidence of the negro from Cienfuegos in the first match. After that he had a few matches and then no more. He decided that he could beat anyone if he wanted to badly enough and he decided that it was bad for his right hand for fishing. He had tried a few practice matches with his left hand. But his left hand had always been a traitor and would not do what he called on it to do and he did not trust it.

The sun will bake it out well now, he thought. It should not cramp on me again unless it gets too cold in the night. I wonder what this night will bring.

An airplane passed overhead on its course to Miami and he watched its shadow scaring up the schools of flying fish.

'With so much flying fish there should be dolphin,' he said, and leaned back on the line to see if it was possible to gain any on his fish. But he could not and it stayed at the hardness and water-drop shivering that preceded breaking. The boat moved ahead slowly and he watched the airplane until he could no longer see it.

It must be very strange in an airplane, he thought. I wonder what the sea looks like from that height? They should be able to see the fish well if they do not fly too high. I would like to fly very slowly at two hundred fathoms high and see the fish from above. In the turtle boats I was in the cross-trees of the mast-head and even at that height I saw much. The dolphin look greener from there and you can see their stripes and their purple spots and you can see all of the school as they swim. Why is it that all the fast-moving fish of the dark current have purple backs and usually purple stripes or spots? The dolphin looks green of course because he is really golden. But when he comes to feed, truly hungry, purple stripes show on his sides as on a marlin. Can it be anger, or the greater speed he makes that brings them out?

Just before it was dark, as they passed a great island of Sargasso weed that heaved and swung in the light sea as though the ocean were making love with something under a yellow blanket, his small line was taken by a dolphin. He saw it first when it jumped in the air, true gold in the last of the sun and bending and flapping wildly in the air. It jumped again and again in the acrobatics of its fear and he worked his way back to the stern and crouching and holding the big line with his right hand and arm, he pulled the dolphin in with his left hand, stepping on the gained line each time with his bare left foot. When the fish was at the stern, plunging and cutting from side to side in desperation, the old man leaned over the stern and lifted the burnished gold fish with its purple spots over the stern. Its jaws were working convulsively in quick bites against the hook and it pounded the bottom of the skiff with its long flat body, its tail and its head until he clubbed it across the shining golden head until it shivered and was still.

The old man unhooked the fish, re-baited the line with another sardine and tossed it over. Then he worked his way slowly back to the bow. He washed his left hand and wiped it on his trousers. Then he shifted the heavy line from his right hand to his left and washed his right hand in the sea while he watched the sun go into the ocean and the slant of the big cord.

'He hasn't changed at all,' he said. But watching the movement of the water against his hand he noted that it was perceptibly slower.

'I'll lash the two oars together across the stern and that will slow him in the night,' he said. 'He's good for the night and so am I.'

It would be better to gut the dolphin a little later to save the blood in the meat, he thought. I can do that a little later and lash the oars to make a drag at the same time. I had better keep the fish quiet now and not disturb him too much at sunset. The setting of the sun is a difficult time for all fish.

He let his hand dry in the air then grasped the line with it and eased himself as much as he could and allowed himself to be pulled forward against the wood so that the boat took the strain as much, or more, than he did.

I'm learning how to do it, he thought. This part of it anyway. Then too, remember he hasn't eaten since he took the bait and he is huge and needs much food. I have eaten the whole bonito.

Tomorrow I will eat the dolphin. He called it *dorado*. Perhaps I should eat some of it when I clean it. It will be harder to eat than the bonito. But, then, nothing is easy.

'How do you feel, fish?' he asked aloud. 'I feel good and my left hand is better and I have food for a night and a day. Pull the boat, fish.'

He did not truly feel good because the pain from the cord across his back had almost passed pain and gone into a dullness that he mistrusted. But I have had worse things than that, he thought. My hand is only cut a little and the cramp is gone from the other. My legs are all right. Also now I have gained on him in the question of sustenance.

It was dark now as it becomes dark quickly after the sun sets in September. He lay against the worn wood of the bow and rested all that he could. The first stars were out. He did not know the name of Rigel but he saw it and knew soon they would all be out and he would have all his distant friends.

'The fish is my friend too,' he said aloud. 'I have never seen or heard of such a fish. But I must kill him. I am glad we do not have to try to kill the stars.'

Imagine if each day a man must try to kill the moon, he thought. The moon runs away. But imagine if a man each day should have to try to kill the sun? We were born lucky, he thought.

Then he was sorry for the great fish that had nothing to eat and his determination to kill him never relaxed in his sorrow for him. How many people will he feed, he thought. But are they worthy to eat him? No, of course not. There is no one worthy of eating him from the manner of his behaviour and his great dignity.

I do not understand these things, he thought. But it is good that we do not have to try to kill the sun or the moon or the stars. It is enough to live on the sea and kill our true brothers.

Now, he thought, I must think about the drag. It has its perils and its merits. I may lose so much line that I will lose him, if he makes his effort and the drag made by the oars is in place and the boat loses all her lightness. Her lightness prolongs both our suffering but it is my safety since he has great speed that he has never yet employed. No matter what passes I must gut the dolphin so he does not spoil and eat some of him to be strong.

Now I will rest an hour more and feel that he is solid and steady before I move back to the stern to do the work and make the decision. In the meantime I can see how he acts and if he shows any changes. The oars are a good trick; but it has reached the time to play for safety. He is much fish still and I saw that the hook was in the corner of his mouth and he has kept his mouth tight shut. The punishment of the hook is nothing. The punishment of hunger, and that he is against something that he does not comprehend, is everything. Rest now, old man, and let him work until your next duty comes.

He rested for what he believed to be two hours. The moon did not rise now until late and he had no way of judging the time. Nor was he really resting except comparatively. He was still bearing the pull of the fish across his shoulders but he placed his left hand on the gunwale of the bow and confided more and more of the resistance to the fish to the skiff itself.

How simple it would be if I could make the line fast, he thought. But with one small lurch he could break it. I must cushion the pull of the line with my body and at all times be ready to give line with both hands.

'But you have not slept yet, old man,' he said aloud. 'It is half a day and a night and now another day and you have not slept. You must devise a way so that you sleep a little if he is quiet and steady. If you do not sleep you might become unclear in the head.'

I'm clear enough in the head, he thought. Too clear. I am as clear as the stars that are my brothers. Still I must sleep. They sleep and the moon and the sun sleep and even the ocean sleeps sometimes on certain days when there is no current and a flat calm.

But remember to sleep, he thought. Make yourself do it and devise some simple and sure way about the lines. Now go back and prepare the dolphin. It is too dangerous to rig the oars as a drag if you must sleep.

I could go without sleeping, he told himself. But it would be too dangerous.

He started to work his way back to the stern on his hands and knees, being careful not to jerk against the fish. He may be half asleep himself, he thought. But I do not want him to rest. He must pull until he dies.

Back in the stern he turned so that his left hand held the strain of the line across his shoulders and drew his knife from its sheath with his right hand. The stars were bright now and he saw the dolphin clearly and he pushed the blade of his knife into his head and drew him out from under the stern. He put one of his feet on the fish and slit him quickly from the vent up to the tip of his lower jaw. Then he put his knife down and gutted him with his right hand, scooping him clean and pulling the gills clear. He felt the maw heavy and slippery in his hands and he slit it open. There were two flying fish inside. They were fresh and hard and he laid them side by side and dropped the guts and the gills over the stern. They sank leaving a trail of phosphorescence in the water. The dolphin was cold and a leprous gray-white now in the starlight and the old man skinned one side of him while he held his right foot on the fish's head. Then he turned him over and skinned the other side and cut each side off from the head down to the tail.

He slid the carcass overboard and looked to see if there was any swirl in the water. But there was only the light of its slow descent. He turned then and placed the two flying fish inside the two fillets of fish and putting his knife back in its sheath, he worked his way slowly back to the bow. His back was bent with the weight of the line across it and he carried the fish in his right hand.

Back in the bow he laid the two fillets of fish out on the wood with the flying fish beside them. After that he settled the line across his shoulders in a new place and held it again with his left hand resting on the gunwale. Then he leaned over the side and washed the flying fish in the water, noting the speed of the water against his hand. His hand was phosphorescent from skinning the fish and he watched the flow of the water against it. The flow was less strong and as he rubbed the side of his hand against the planking of the skiff, particles of phosphorus floated off and drifted slowly astern.

'He is tiring or he is resting,' the old man said. 'Now let me get through the eating of this dolphin and get some rest and a little sleep.'

Under the stars and with the night colder all the time he ate half of one of the dolphin fillets and one of the flying fish, gutted and with its head cut off.

'What an excellent fish dolphin is to eat cooked,' he said. 'And what a miserable fish raw. I will never go in a boat again without salt or limes.'

If I had brains I would have splashed water on the bow all day and drying, it would have made salt, he thought. But then I did not hook the dolphin until almost sunset. Still it was a lack of preparation. But I have chewed it all well and I am not nauseated.

The sky was clouding over to the east and one after another the stars he knew were gone. It looked now as though he were moving into a great canyon of clouds and the wind had dropped.

'There will be bad weather in three or four days,' he said. 'But not tonight and not tomorrow. Rig now to get some sleep, old man, while the fish is calm and steady.'

He held the line tight in his right hand and then pushed his thigh against his right hand as he leaned all his weight against the wood of the bow. Then he passed the line a little lower on his shoulders and braced his left hand on it.

My right hand can hold it as long as it is braced, he thought If it relaxes in sleep my left hand will wake me as the line goes out. It is hard on the right hand. But he is used to punishment Even if I sleep twenty minutes or a half an hour it is good. He lay forward cramping himself against the line with all of his body, putting all his weight onto his right hand, and he was asleep.

He did not dream of the lions but instead of a vast school of porpoises that stretched for eight or ten miles and it was in the time of their mating and they would leap high into the air and return into the same hole they had made in the water when they leaped.

Then he dreamed that he was in the village on his bed and there was a norther and he was very cold and his right arm was asleep because his head had rested on it instead of a pillow.

After that he began to dream of the long yellow beach and he saw the first of the lions come down onto it in the early dark and then the other lions came and he rested his chin on the wood of the bows where the ship lay anchored with the evening off-shore breeze and he waited to see if there would be more lions and he was happy.

The moon had been up for a long time but he slept on and the fish pulled on steadily and the boat moved into the tunnel of clouds.

He woke with the jerk of his right fist coming up against his face and the line burning out through his right hand. He had no feeling of his left hand but he braked all he could with his right and the line rushed out. Finally his left hand found the line and he leaned back against the line and now it burned his back and his left hand, and his left hand was taking all the strain and cutting badly. He looked back at the coils of line and they were feeding smoothly. Just then the fish jumped making a great bursting of the ocean and then a heavy fall. Then he jumped again and again and the boat was going fast although line was still racing out and the old man was raising the strain to breaking point and raising it to breaking point again and again. He had been pulled down tight onto the bow and his face was in the cut slice of dolphin and he could not move.

This is what we waited for, he thought. So now let us take it. Make him pay for the line, he thought. Make him pay for it.

He could not see the fish's jumps but only heard the breaking of the ocean and the heavy splash as he fell. The speed of the line was cutting his hands badly but he had always known this would happen and he tried to keep the cutting across the calloused parts and not let the line slip into the palm nor cut the fingers.

If the boy was here he would wet the coils of line, he thought. Yes. If the boy were here. If the boy were here.

The line went out and out and out but it was slowing now and he was making the fish earn each inch of it. Now he got his head up from the wood and out of the slice of fish that his cheek had crushed. Then he was on his knees and then he rose slowly to his feet. He was ceding line but more slowly all he time. He worked back to where he could feel with his foot the coils of line that he could not see. There was plenty of line still and now the fish had to pull the friction of all that new line through the water.

Yes, he thought. And now he has jumped more than a dozen times and filled the sacks along his back with air and he cannot go down deep to die where I cannot bring him up. He will start circling soon and then I must work on him. I wonder what started him so suddenly? Could it have been hunger that made him desperate, or was he frightened by something in the night?

Maybe he suddenly felt fear. But he was such a calm, strong fish and he seemed so fearless and so confident. It is strange.

'You better be fearless and confident yourself, old man,' he said. 'You're holding him again but you cannot get line. But soon he has to circle.'

The old man held him with his left hand and his shoulders now and stooped down and scooped up water in his right hand to get the crushed dolphin flesh off of his face. He was afraid that it might nauseate him and he would vomit and lose his strength. When his face was cleaned he washed his right hand in the water over the side and then let it stay in the salt water while he watched the first light come before the sunrise. He's headed almost east, he thought. That means he is tired and going with the current. Soon he will have to circle. Then our true work begins.

After he judged that his right hand had been in the water long enough he took it out and looked at it.

'It is not bad,' he said. 'And pain does not matter to a man.'

He took hold of the line carefully so that it did not fit into any of the fresh line cuts and shifted his weight so that he could put his left hand into the sea on the other side of the skiff.

'You did not do so badly for something worthless,' he said to his left hand. 'But there was a moment when I could not find you.'

Why was I not born with two good hands? he thought. Perhaps it was my fault in not training that one properly. But God knows he has had enough chances to learn. He did not do so badly in the night, though, and he has only cramped once. If he cramps again let the line cut him off.

When he thought that he knew that he was not being clear- headed and he thought he should chew some more of the dolphin. But I can't, he told himself. It is better to be light-headed than to lose your strength from nausea. And I know I cannot keep it if I eat it since my face was in it. I will keep it for an emergency until it goes bad. But it is too late to try for strength now through nourishment. You're stupid, he told himself. Eat the other flying fish.

It was there, cleaned and ready, and he picked it up with his left hand and ate it chewing the bones carefully and eating all of it down to the tail.

It has more nourishment than almost any fish, he thought. At least the kind of strength that I need. Now I have done what I can, he thought. Let him begin to circle and let the fight come.

The sun was rising for the third time since he had put to sea when the fish started to circle.

He could not see by the slant of the line that the fish was circling. It was too early for that. He just felt a faint slackening of the pressure of the line and he commenced to pull on it gently with his right hand. It tightened, as always, but just when he reached the point where it would break, line began to come in. He slipped his shoulders and head from under the line and began to pull in line steadily and gently. He used both of his hands in a swinging motion and tried to do the pulling as much as he could with his body and his legs. His old legs and shoulders pivoted with the swinging of the pulling.

'It is a very big circle,' he said. 'But he is circling.'

Then the line would not come in any more and he held it until he saw the drops jumping from it in the sun. Then it started out and the old man knelt down and let it go grudgingly back into the dark water.

'He is making the far part of his circle now,' he said. I must hold all I can, he thought. The strain will shorten his circle each time. Perhaps in an hour I will see him. Now I must convince him and then I must kill him.

But the fish kept on circling slowly and the old man was wet with sweat and tired deep into his bones two hours later. But the circles were much shorter now and from the way the line slanted he could tell the fish had risen steadily while he swam.

For an hour the old man had been seeing black spots before his eyes and the sweat salted his eyes and salted the cut over his eye and on his forehead. He was not afraid of the black spots. They were normal at the tension that he was pulling on the line. Twice, though, he had felt faint and dizzy and that had worried him.

'I could not fail myself and die on a fish like this,' he said. 'Now that I have him coming so beautifully, God help me endure. I'll say a hundred Our Fathers and a hundred Hail Marys. But I cannot say them now.

Consider them said, he thought. I'll say them later.

Just then he felt a sudden banging and jerking on the line he held with his two hands. It was sharp and hard-feeling and heavy.

He is hitting the wire leader with his spear, he thought. That was bound to come. He had to do that. It may make him jump though and I would rather he stayed circling now. The jumps were necessary for him to take air. But after that each one can widen the opening of the hook wound and he can throw the hook.

'Don't jump, fish,' he said. 'Don't jump.'

The fish hit the wire several times more and each time he shook his head the old man gave up a little line.

I must hold his pain where it is, he thought. Mine does not matter. I can control mine. But his pain could drive him mad.

After a while the fish stopped beating at the wire and started circling slowly again. The old man was gaining line steadily now. But he felt faint again. He lifted some sea water with his left hand and put it on his head. Then he put more on and rubbed the back of his neck.

'I have no cramps,' he said. 'He'll be up soon and I can last. You have to last. Don't even speak of it.'

He kneeled against the bow and, for a moment, slipped the line over his back again. I'll rest now while he goes out on the circle and then stand up and work on him when he comes in, he decided.

It was a great temptation to rest in the bow and let the fish make one circle by himself without recovering any line. But when the strain showed the fish had turned to come toward the boat, the old man rose to his feet and started the pivoting and the weaving pulling that brought in all the line he gained.

I'm tireder than I have ever been, he thought, and now the trade wind is rising. But that will be good to take him in with. I need that badly.

'I'll rest on the next turn as he goes out,' he said. 'I feel much better. Then in two or three turns more I will have him.'

His straw hat was far on the back of his head and he sank down into the bow with the pull of the line as he felt the fish turn.

You work now, fish, he thought. I'll take you at the turn.

The sea had risen considerably. But it was a fair-weather breeze and he had to have it to get home.

'I'll just steer south and west,' he said. 'A man is never lost at sea and it is a long island.'

It was on the third turn that he saw the fish first.

He saw him first as a dark shadow that took so long to pass under the boat that he could not believe its length.

'No,' he said. 'He can't be that big.'

But he was that big and at the end of this circle he came to the surface only thirty yards away and the man saw his tail out of water. It was higher than a big scythe blade and a very pale lavender above the dark blue water. It raked back and as the fish swam just below the surface the old man could see his huge bulk and the purple stripes that banded him. His dorsal fin was down and his huge pectorals were spread wide.

On this circle the old man could see the fish's eye and the two gray sucking fish that swam around him. Sometimes they attached themselves to him.

Sometimes they darted off.

Sometimes they would swim easily in his shadow. They were each over three feet long and when they swam fast they lashed their whole bodies like eels.

The old man was sweating now but from something else besides the sun. On each calm placid turn the fish made he was gaining line and he was sure that in two turns more he would have a chance to get the harpoon in.

But I must get him close, close, close, he thought. I mustn't try for the head. I must get the heart.

'Be calm and strong, old man,' he said.

On the next circle the fish's back was out but he was a little too far from the boat. On the next circle he was still too far away but he was higher out of water and the old man was sure that by gaining some more line he could have him alongside.

He had rigged his harpoon long before and its coil of light rope was in a round basket and the end was made fast to the bitt in the bow.

The fish was coming in on his circle now calm and beautiful looking and only his great tail moving. The old man pulled on him all that he could to bring him closer. For just a moment the fish turned a little on his side. Then he straightened himself and began another circle.

'I moved him,' the old man said. 'I moved him then.'

He felt faint again now but he held on the great fish all the strain that he could. I moved him, he thought. Maybe this time I can get him over. Pull, hands, he thought. Hold up, legs. Last for me, head. Last for me. You never went. This time I'll pull him over.

But when he put all of his effort on, starting it well out before the fish came alongside and pulling with all his strength, the fish pulled part way over and then righted himself and swam away.

'Fish,' the old man said. 'Fish, you are going to have to die anyway. Do you have to kill me too?'

That way nothing is accomplished, he thought. His mouth was too dry to speak but he could not reach for the water now. I must get him alongside this time, he thought. I am not good for many more turns. Yes you are, he told himself. You're good for ever.

On the next turn, he nearly had him. But again the fish righted himself and swam slowly away.

You are killing me, fish, the old man thought. But you have a right to. Never have I seen a greater, or more beautiful, or a calmer or more noble thing than you, brother. Come on and kill me. I do not care who kills who.

Now you are getting confused in the head, he thought. You must keep your head clear. Keep your head clear and know how to suffer like a man. Or a fish, he thought.

'Clear up, head,' he said in a voice he could hardly hear. 'Clear up.'

Twice more it was the same on the turns.

I do not know, the old man thought. He had been on the point of feeling himself go each time. I do not know. But I will try it once more.

He tried it once more and he felt himself going when he turned the fish. The fish righted himself and swam off again slowly with the great tail weaving in the air.

I'll try it again, the old man promised, although his hands were mushy now and he could only see well in flashes.

He tried it again and it was the same. So he thought, and he felt himself going before he started; I will try it once again.

He took all his pain and what was left of his strength and his long gone pride and he put it against the fish's agony and the fish came over onto his side and swam gently on his side, his bill almost touching the planking of the skiff and started to pass the boat, long, deep, wide, silver and barred with purple and interminable in the water.

The old man dropped the line and put his foot on it and lifted the harpoon as high as he could and drove it down with all his strength, and more strength he had just summoned, into the fish's side just behind the great chest fin that rose high in the air to the altitude of the man's chest. He felt the iron go in and he leaned on it and drove it further and then pushed all his weight after it.

Then the fish came alive, with his death in him, and rose high out of the water showing all his great length and width and all his power and his beauty. He seemed to hang in the air above the old man in the skiff. Then he fell into the water with a crash that sent spray over the old man and over all of the skiff.

The old man felt faint and sick and he could not see well. But he cleared the harpoon line and let it run slowly through his raw hands and, when he could see, he saw the fish was on his back with his silver belly up. The shaft of the harpoon was projecting at an angle from the fish's shoulder and the sea was discolouring with the red of the blood from his heart. First it was dark as a shoal in the blue water that was more than a mile deep. Then it spread like a cloud. The fish was silvery and still and floated with the waves.

The old man looked carefully in the glimpse of vision that he had. Then he took two turns of the harpoon line around the bitt in the bow and hid his head on his hands.

'Keep my head clear,' he said against the wood of the bow. 'I am a tired old man. But I have killed this fish which is my brother and now I must do the slave work.'

Now I must prepare the nooses and the rope to lash him alongside, he thought. Even if we were two and swamped her to load him and bailed her out, this skiff would never hold him. I must prepare everything, then bring him in and lash him well and step the mast and set sail for home.

He started to pull the fish in to have him alongside so that he could pass a line through his gills and out his mouth and make his head fast alongside the bow. I want to see him, he thought, and to touch and to feel him. He is my fortune, he thought. But that is not why I wish to feel him. I think I felt his heart, he thought.

When I pushed on the harpoon shaft the second time. Bring him in now and make him fast and get the noose around his tail and another around his middle to bind him to the skiff.

'Get to work, old man,' he said. He took a very small drink of the water. 'There is very much slave work to be done now that the fight is over.'

He looked up at the sky and then out to his fish. He looked at the sun carefully. It is not much more than noon, he thought. And the trade wind is rising. The lines all mean nothing now. The boy and I will splice them when we are home.

'Come on, fish,' he said. But the fish did not come. Instead he lay there wallowing now in the seas and the old man pulled the skiff upon to him.

When he was even with him and had the fish's head against the bow he could not believe his size. But he untied the harpoon rope from the bitt, passed it through the fish's gills and out his jaws, made a turn around his sword then passed the rope through the other gill, made another turn around the bill and knotted the double rope and made it fast to the bitt in the bow. He cut the rope then and went astern to noose the tail. The fish had turned silver from his original purple and silver, and the stripes showed the same pale violet colour as his tail. They were wider than a man's hand with his fingers spread and the fish's eye looked as detached as the mirrors in a periscope or as a saint in a procession.

'It was the only way to kill him,' the old man said. He was feeling better since the water and he knew he would not go away and his head was clear. He's over fifteen hundred pounds the way he is, he thought. Maybe much more. If he dresses out two- thirds of that at thirty cents a pound?

'I need a pencil for that,' he said. 'My head is not that clear. But I think the great DiMaggio would be proud of me today. I had no bone spurs. But the hands and the back hurt truly.' I wonder what a bone spur is, he thought. Maybe we have them without knowing of it.

He made the fish fast to bow and stern and to the middle thwart. He was so big it was like lashing a much bigger skiff alongside. He cut a piece of line and tied the fish's lower jaw against his bill so his mouth would not open and they would sail as cleanly as possible. Then he stepped the mast and, with the stick that was his gaff and with his boom rigged, the patched sail drew, the boat began to move, and half lying in the stern he sailed south-west.

He did not need a compass to tell him where south-west was. He only needed the feel of the trade wind and the drawing of the sail. I better put a small line out with a spoon on it and try and get something to eat and drink for the moisture. But he could not find a spoon and his sardines were rotten. So he hooked a patch of yellow Gulf weed with the gaff as they passed and shook it so that the small shrimps that were in it fell onto the planking of the skiff. There were more than a dozen of them and they jumped and kicked like sand fleas. The old man pinched their heads off with his thumb and forefinger and ate them chewing up the shells and the tails. They were very tiny but he knew they were nourishing and they tasted good.

The old man still had two drinks of water in the bottle and he used half of one after he had eaten the shrimps. The skiff was sailing well considering the handicaps and he steered with the tiller under his arm. He could see the fish and he had only to look at his hands and feel his back against the stern to know that this had truly happened and was not a dream. At one time when he was feeling so badly toward the end, he had thought perhaps it was a dream. Then when he had seen the fish come out of the water and hang motionless in the sky before he fell, he was sure there was some great strangeness and he could not believe it. Then he could not see well, although now he saw as well as ever.

Now he knew there was the fish and his hands and back were no dream. The hands cure quickly, he thought. I bled them clean and the salt water will heal them. The dark water of the true gulf is the greatest healer that there is. All I must do is keep the head clear. The hands have done their work and we sail well. With his mouth shut and his tail straight up and down we sail like brothers. Then his head started to become a little unclear and he thought, is he bringing me in or am I bringing him in? If I were towing him behind there would be no question. Nor if the fish were in the skiff, with all dignity gone, there would be no question either. But they were sailing together lashed side by side and the old man thought, let him bring me in if it pleases him. I am only better than him through trickery and he meant me no harm.

They sailed well and the old man soaked his hands in the salt water and tried to keep his head clear. There were high cumulus clouds and enough cirrus above them so that the old man knew the breeze would last all night. The old man looked at the fish constantly to make sure it was true. It was an hour before the first shark hit him.

The shark was not an accident. He had come up from deep down in the water as the dark cloud of blood had settled and dispersed in the mile deep sea. He had come up so fast and absolutely without caution that he broke the surface of the blue water and was in the sun. Then he fell back into the sea and picked up the scent and started swimming on the course the skiff and the fish had taken.

Sometimes he lost the scent. But he would pick it up again, or have just a trace of it, and he swam fast and hard on the course.

He was a very big Mako shark built to swim as fast as the fastest fish in the sea and everything about him was beautiful except his jaws. His back was as blue as a sword fish's and his belly was silver and his hide was smooth and handsome. He was built as a sword fish except for his huge jaws which were tight shut now as he swam fast, just under the surface with his high dorsal fin knifing through the water without wavering. Inside the closed double lip of his jaws all of his eight rows of teeth were slanted inwards. They were not the ordinary pyramid-shaped teeth of most sharks. They were shaped like a man's fingers when they are crisped like claws. They were nearly as long as the fingers of the old man and they had razor-sharp cutting edges on both sides. This was a fish built to feed on all the fishes in the sea, that were so fast and strong and well armed that they had no other enemy. Now he speeded up as he smelled the fresher scent and his blue dorsal fin cut the water.

When the old man saw him coming he knew that this was a shark that had no fear at all and would do exactly what he wished. He prepared the harpoon and made the rope fast while he watched the shark come on. The rope was short as it lacked what he had cut away to lash the fish.

The old man's head was clear and good now and he was full of resolution but he had little hope. It was too good to last, he thought. He took one look at the great fish as he watched the shark close in. It might as well have been a dream, he thought. I cannot keep him from hitting me but maybe I can get him.

Dentuso, he thought. Bad luck to your mother.

The shark closed fast astern and when he hit the fish the old man saw his mouth open and his strange eyes and the clicking chop of the teeth as he drove forward in the meat just above the tail. The shark's head was out of water and his back was coming out and the old man could hear the noise of skin and flesh ripping on the big fish when he rammed the harpoon down onto the shark's head at a spot where the line between his eyes intersected with the line that ran straight back from his nose.

There were no such lines. There was only the heavy sharp blue head and the big eyes and the clicking, thrusting all-swallowing jaws. But that was the location of the brain and the old man hit it. He hit it with his blood mushed hands driving a good harpoon with all his strength. He hit it without hope but with resolution and complete malignancy.

The shark swung over and the old man saw his eye was not alive and then he swung over once again, wrapping himself in two loops of the rope. The old man knew that he was dead but the shark would not accept it. Then, on his back, with his tail lashing and his jaws clicking, the shark plowed over the water as a speedboat does. The water was white where his tail beat it and three-quarters of his body was clear above the water when the rope came taut, shivered, and then snapped. The shark lay quietly for a little while on the surface and the old man watched him. Then he went down very slowly.

'He took about forty pounds,' the old man said aloud. He took my harpoon too and all the rope, he thought, and now my fish bleeds again and there will be others.

He did not like to look at the fish anymore since he had been mutilated. When the fish had been hit it was as though he himself were hit.

But I killed the shark that hit my fish, he thought. And he was the biggest *dentuso* that I have ever seen. And God knows that I have seen big ones.

It was too good to last, he thought. I wish it had been a dream now and that I had never hooked the fish and was alone in bed on the newspapers.

'But man is not made for defeat,' he said. 'A man can be destroyed but not defeated.' I am sorry that I killed the fish though, he thought. Now the bad time is coming and I do not even have the harpoon. The *dentuso* is cruel and able and strong and intelligent. But I was more intelligent than he was. Perhaps not, he thought. Perhaps I was only better armed.

'Don't think, old man,' he said aloud. 'Sail on this course and take it when it comes.'

But I must think, he thought. Because it is all I have left. That and baseball. I wonder how the great DiMaggio would have liked the way I hit him in the brain? It was no great thing, he thought. Any man could do it. But do you think my hands were as great a handicap as the bone spurs? I cannot know. I never had anything wrong with my heel except the time the sting ray stung it when I stepped on him when swimming and paralyzed the lower leg and made the unbearable pain.

'Think about something cheerful, old man,' he said. 'Every minute now you are closer to home. You sail lighter for the loss of forty pounds.'

He knew quite well the pattern of what could happen when he reached the inner part of the current. But there was nothing to be done now.

'Yes there is,' he said aloud. 'I can lash my knife to the butt of one of the oars.'

So he did that with the tiller under his arm and the sheet of the sail under his foot.

'Now,' he said. 'I am still an old man. But I am not unarmed.'

The breeze was fresh now and he sailed on well. He watched only the forward part of the fish and some of his hope returned.

It is silly not to hope, he thought. Besides I believe it is a sin. Do not think about sin, he thought. There are enough problems now without sin. Also I have no understanding of it.

I have no understanding of it and I am not sure that I believe in it. Perhaps it was a sin to kill the fish. I suppose it was even though I did it to keep me alive and feed many people. But then everything is a sin. Do not think about sin. It is much too late for that and there are people who are paid to do it. Let them think about it. You were born to be a fisherman as the fish was born to be a fish. San Pedro was a fisherman as was the father of the great DiMaggio.

But he liked to think about all things that he was involved in and since there was nothing to read and he did not have a radio, he thought much and he kept on thinking about sin. You did not kill the fish only to keep alive and to sell for food, he thought. You killed him for pride and because you are a fisherman. You loved him when he was alive and you loved him after. If you love him, it is not a sin to kill him. Or is it more?

'You think too much, old man,' he said aloud.

But you enjoyed killing the *dentuso*, he thought. He lives on the live fish as you do. He is not a scavenger nor just a moving appetite as some sharks are. He is beautiful and noble and knows no fear of anything.

'I killed him in self-defense,' the old man said aloud. 'And I killed him well.'

Besides, he thought, everything kills everything else in some way. Fishing kills me exactly as it keeps me alive. The boy keeps me alive, he thought. I must not deceive myself too much.

He leaned over the side and pulled loose a piece of the meat of the fish where the shark had cut him. He chewed it and noted its quality and its good taste. It was firm and juicy, like meat, but it was not red. There was no stringiness in it and he knew that it would bring the highest price In the market. But there was no way to keep its scent out of the water and the old man knew that a very bad time was coming.

The breeze was steady. It had backed a little further into the north-east and he knew that meant that it would not fall off. The old man looked ahead of him but he could see no sails nor could he see the hull nor the smoke of any ship. There were only the flying fish that went up from his bow sailing away to either side and the yellow patches of Gulf weed. He could not even see a bird.

He had sailed for two hours, resting in the stern and sometimes chewing a bit of the meat from the marlin, trying to rest and to be strong, when he saw the first of the two sharks.

'*Ay*,' he said aloud. There is no translation for this word and perhaps it is just a noise such as a man might make, involuntarily, feeling the nail go through his hands and into the wood.

'*Galanos*,' he said aloud. He had seen the second fin now coming up behind the first and had identified them as shovel- nosed sharks by the brown, triangular fin and the sweeping movements of the tail. They had the scent and were excited and in the stupidity of their great hunger they were losing and finding the scent in their excitement. But they were closing all the time.

The old man made the sheet fast and jammed the tiller. Then he took up the oar with the knife lashed to it. He lifted it as lightly as he could because his hands rebelled at the pain. Then he opened and closed them on it lightly to loosen them. He closed them firmly so they would take the pain now and would not flinch and watched the sharks come. He could see their wide, flattened, shovel-pointed heads now and their white tipped wide pectoral fins. They were hateful sharks, bad smelling, scavengers as well as killers, and when they were hungry they would bite at an oar or the rudder of a boat. It was these sharks that would cut the turtles' legs and flippers off when the turtles were asleep on the surface, and they would hit a man in the water, if they were hungry, even if the man had no smell of fish blood nor of fish slime on him.

'*Ay*,' the old man said. '*Galanos*. Come on *galanos*.'

They came. But they did not come as the Mako had come. One turned and went out of sight under the skiff and the old man could feel the skiff shake as he jerked and pulled on the fish.

The other watched the old man with his slitted yellow eyes and then came in fast with his half circle of jaws wide to hit the fish where he had already been bitten. The line showed clearly on the top of his brown head and back where the brain joined the spinal cord and the old man drove the knife on the oar into the juncture, withdrew it, and drove it in again into the shark's yellow cat-like eyes. The shark let go of the fish and slid down, swallowing what he had taken as he died.

The skiff was still shaking with the destruction the other shark was doing to the fish and the old man let go the sheet so that the skiff would swing broadside and bring the shark out from under. When he saw the shark he leaned over the side and punched at him. He hit only meat and the hide was set hard and he barely got the knife in. The blow hurt not only his hands but his shoulder too. But the shark came up fast with his head out and the old man hit him squarely in the center of his flat-topped head as his nose came out of water and lay against the fish.

The old man withdrew the blade and punched the shark exactly in the same spot again. He still hung to the fish with his jaws hooked and the old man stabbed him in his left eye. The shark still hung there.

'No?' the old man said and he drove the blade between the vertebrae and the brain. It was an easy shot now and he felt the cartilage sever. The old man reversed the oar and put the blade between the shark's jaws to open them. He twisted the blade and as the shark slid loose he said, 'Go on, *galano*. Slide down a mile deep. Go see your friend, or maybe it's your mother.'

The old man wiped the blade of his knife and laid down the oar. Then he found the sheet and the sail filled and he brought the skiff onto her course.

'They must have taken a quarter of him and of the best meat,' he said aloud. 'I wish it were a dream and that I had never hooked him. I'm sorry about it, fish. It makes everything wrong.' He stopped and he did not want to look at the fish now. Drained of blood and awash he looked the colour of the silver backing of a minor and his stripes still showed.

'I shouldn't have gone out so far, fish,' he said. 'Neither for you nor for me. I'm sorry, fish.'

Now, he said to himself. Look to the lashing on the knife and see if it has been cut. Then get your hand in order because there still is more to come.

'I wish I had a stone for the knife,' the old man said after he had checked the lashing on the oar butt. 'I should have brought a stone.' You should have brought many things, he thought. But you did not bring them, old man. Now is no time to think of what you do not have. Think of what you can do with what there is.

'You give me much good counsel,' he said aloud. 'I'm tired of it.'

He held the tiller under his arm and soaked both his hands in the water as the skiff drove forward.

'God knows how much that last one took,' he said. 'But she's much lighter now.' He did not want to think of the mutilated under-side of the fish. He knew that each of the jerking bumps of the shark had been meat torn away and that the fish now made a trail for all sharks as wide as a highway through the sea.

He was a fish to keep a man all winter, he thought Don't think of that. Just rest and try to get your hands in shape to defend what is left of him. The blood smell from my hands means nothing now with all that scent in the water. Besides they do not bleed much. There is nothing cut that means anything. The bleeding may keep the left from cramping.

What can I think of now? he thought. Nothing. I must think of nothing and wait for the next ones. I wish it had really been a dream, he thought. But who knows? It might have turned out well.

The next shark that came was a single shovelnose. He came like a pig to the trough if a pig had a mouth so wide that you could put your head in it. The old man let him hit the fish and then drove the knife on the oar don into his brain. But the shark jerked backwards as he rolled and the knife blade snapped.

The old man settled himself to steer. He did not even watch the big shark sinking slowly in the water, showing first life-size, then small, then tiny. That always fascinated the old man. But he did not even watch it now.

'I have the gaff now,' he said. 'But it will do no good. I have the two oars and the tiller and the short club.'

Now they have beaten me, he thought. I am too old to club sharks to death. But I will try it as long as I have the oars and the short club and the tiller.

He put his hands in the water again to soak them. It was getting late in the afternoon and he saw nothing but the sea and the sky. There was more wind in the sky than there had been, and soon he hoped that he would see land.

'You're tired, old man,' he said. 'You're tired inside.' The sharks did not hit him again until just before sunset.

The old man saw the brown fins coming along the wide trail the fish must make in the water. They were not even quartering on the scent. They were headed straight for the skiff swimming side by side.

He jammed the tiller, made the sheet fast and reached under the stern for the club. It was an oar handle from a broken oar sawed off to about two and a half feet in length. He could only use it effectively with one hand because of the grip of the handle and he took good hold of it with his right hand, flexing his hand on it, as he watched the sharks come. They were both *galanos*.

I must let the first one get a good hold and hit him on the point of the nose or straight across the top of the head, he thought.

The two sharks closed together and as he saw the one nearest him open his jaws and sink them into the silver side of the fish, he raised the club high and brought it down heavy and slamming onto the top of the shark's broad head. He felt the rubbery solidity as the club came down. But he felt the rigidity of bone too and he struck the shark once more hard across the point of the nose as he slid down from the fish.

The other shark had been in and out and now came in again with his jaws wide. The old man could see pieces of the meat of the fish spilling white from the corner of his jaws as he bumped the fish and closed his jaws. He swung at him and hit only the head and the shark looked at him and wrenched the meat loose. The old man swung the club down on him again as he slipped away to swallow and hit only the heavy solid rubberiness.

'Come on, *galano*,' the old man said. 'Come in again.'

The shark came in a rush and the old man hit him as he shut his jaws. He hit him solidly and from as high up as he could raise the club. This time he felt the bone at the base of the brain and he hit him again in the same place while the shark tore the meat loose sluggishly and slid down from the fish.

The old man watched for him to come again but neither shark showed. Then he saw one on the surface swimming in circles. He did not see the fin of the other.

I could not expect to kill them, he thought. I could have in my time. But I have hurt them both badly and neither one can feel very good. If I could have used a bat with two hands I could have killed the first one surely. Even now, he thought.

He did not want to look at the fish. He knew that half of him had been destroyed. The sun had gone down while he had been in the fight with the sharks.

'It will be dark soon,' he said. 'Then I should see the glow of Havana.. If I am too far to the eastward I will see the lights of one of the new beaches.'

I cannot be too far out now, he thought. I hope no one has been too worried. There is only the boy to worry, of course. But I am sure he would have confidence. Many of the older fishermen will worry. Many others too, he thought. I live in a good town.

He could not talk to the fish anymore because the fish had been ruined too badly. Then something came into his head.

'Half fish,' he said. 'Fish that you were. I am sorry that I went too far out. I ruined us both. But we have killed many sharks, you and I, and ruined many others. How many did you ever kill, old fish? You do not have that spear on your head for nothing.'

He liked to think of the fish and what he could do to a shark if he were swimming free. I should have chopped the bill off to fight them with, he thought. But there was no hatchet and then there was no knife.

But if I had, and could have lashed it to an oar butt, what a weapon. Then we might have fought them together. What will you do now if they come in the night? What can you do?

'Fight them,' he said. 'I'll fight them until I die.'

But in the dark now and no glow showing and no lights and only the wind and the steady pull of the sail he felt that perhaps he was already dead. He put his two hands together and felt the palms. They were not dead and he could bring the pain of life by simply opening and closing them. He leaned his back against the stern and knew he was not dead. His shoulders told him.

I have all those prayers I promised if I caught the fish, he thought. But I am too tired to say them now. I better get the sack and put it over my shoulders.

He lay in the stern and steered and watched for the glow to come in the sky. I have half of him, he thought. Maybe I'll have the luck to bring the forward half in. I should have some luck. No, he said. You violated your luck when you went too far outside.

'Don't be silly,' he said aloud. 'And keep awake and steer. You may have much luck yet.'

'I'd like to buy some if there's any place they sell it,' he said.

What could I buy it with? he asked himself. Could I buy it with a lost harpoon and a broken knife and two bad hands?

'You might,' he said. 'You tried to buy it with eighty-four days at sea. They nearly sold it to you too.'

I must not think nonsense, he thought. Luck is a thing that comes in many forms and who can recognize her? I would take some though in any form and pay what they asked. I wish I could see the glow from the lights, he thought. I wish too many things. But that is the thing I wish for now. He tried to settle more comfortably to steer and from his pain he knew he was not dead.

He saw the reflected glare of the lights of the city at what must have been around ten o'clock at night. They were only perceptible at first as the light is in the sky before the moon rises. Then they were steady to see across the ocean which was rough now with the increasing breeze. He steered inside of the glow and he thought that now, soon, he must hit the edge of the stream.

Now it is over, he thought. They will probably hit me again. But what can a man do against them in the dark without a weapon?

He was stiff and sore now and his wounds and all of the strained parts of his body hurt with the cold of the night. I hope I do not have to fight again, he thought. I hope so much I do not have to fight again.

But by midnight he fought and this time he knew the fight was useless. They came in a pack and he could only see the lines in the water that their fins made and their phosphorescence as they threw themselves on the fish. He clubbed at heads and heard the jaws chop and the shaking of the skiff as they took hold below. He clubbed desperately at what he could only feel and hear and he felt something seize the club and it was gone.

He jerked the tiller free from the rudder and beat and chopped with it, holding it in both hands and driving it down again and again. But they were up to the bow now and driving in one after the other and together, tearing off the pieces of meat that showed glowing below the sea as they turned to come once more.

One came, finally, against the head itself and he knew that it was over. He swung the tiller across the shark's head where the jaws were caught in the heaviness of the fish's head which would not tear. He swung it once and twice and again. He heard the tiller break and he lunged at the shark with the splintered butt. He felt it go in and knowing it was sharp he drove it in again. The shark let go and rolled away. That was the last shark of the pack that came. There was nothing more for them to eat.

The old man could hardly breathe now and he felt a strange taste in his mouth. It was coppery and sweet and he was afraid of it for a moment. But there was not much of it.

He spat into the ocean and said, 'Eat that, *galanos*. And make a dream you've killed a man.'

He knew he was beaten now finally and without remedy and he went back to the stern and found the jagged end of the tiller would fit in the slot of the rudder well enough for him to steer. He settled the sack around his shoulders and put the skiff on her course. He sailed lightly now and he had no thoughts nor any feelings of any kind. He was past everything now and he sailed the skiff to make his home port as well and as intelligently as he could. In the night sharks hit the carcass as someone might pick up crumbs from the table. The old man paid no attention to them and did not pay any attention to anything except steering. He only noticed how lightly and how well the skiff sailed now there was no great weight beside her.

She's good, he thought. She is sound and not harmed in any way except for the tiller. That is easily replaced.

He could feel he was inside the current now and he could see the lights of the beach colonies along the shore. He knew where he was now and it was nothing to get home.

The wind is our friend, anyway, he thought. Then he added, sometimes. And the great sea with our friends and our enemies. And bed, he thought. Bed is my friend. Just bed, he thought. Bed will be a great thing. It is easy when you are beaten, he thought. I never knew how easy it was. And what beat you, he thought.

'Nothing,' he said aloud. 'I went out too far.'

When he sailed into the little harbour the lights of the Terrace were out and he knew everyone was in bed. The breeze had risen steadily and was blowing strongly now. It was quiet in the harbour though and he sailed up onto the little patch of shingle below the rocks. There was no one to help him so he pulled the boat up as far as he could. Then he stepped out and made her fast to a rock.

He unstepped the mast and furled the sail and tied it. Then he shouldered the mast and started to climb. It was then he knew the depth of his tiredness. He stopped for a moment and looked back and saw in the reflection from the street light the great tail of the fish standing up well behind the skiff's stern. He saw the white naked line of his backbone and the dark mass of the head with the projecting bill and all the nakedness between.

He started to climb again and at the top he fell and lay for some time with the mast across his shoulder. He tried to get up. But it was too difficult and he sat there with the mast on his shoulder and looked at the road. A cat passed on the far side going about its business and the old man watched it. Then he just watched the road.

Finally he put the mast down and stood up. He picked the mast up and put it on his shoulder and started up the road. He had to sit down five times before he reached his shack.

Inside the shack he leaned the mast against the wall. In the dark he found a water bottle and took a drink. Then he lay down on the bed. He pulled the blanket over his shoulders and then over his back and legs and he slept face down on the newspapers with his arms out straight and the palms of his hands up.

He was asleep when the boy looked in the door in the morning. It was blowing so hard that the drifting-boats would not be going out and the boy had slept late and then come to the old man's shack as he had come each morning. The boy saw that the old man was breathing and then he saw the old man's hands and he started to cry. He went out very quietly to go to bring some coffee and all the way down the road he was crying.

Many fishermen were around the skiff looking at what was lashed beside it and one was in the water, his trousers rolled up, measuring the skeleton with a length of line.

The boy did not go down. He had been there before and one of the fishermen was looking after the skiff for him.

'How is he?' one of the fishermen shouted.

'Sleeping,' the boy called. He did not care that they saw him crying. 'Let no one disturb him.'

'He was eighteen feet from nose to tail,' the fisherman who was measuring him called.

'I believe it,' the boy said.

He went into the Terrace and asked for a can of coffee. 'Hot and with plenty of milk and sugar in it.'

'Anything more?'

'No. Afterwards I will see what he can eat.'

'What a fish it was,' the proprietor said. 'There has never been such a fish. Those were two fine fish you took yesterday too.'

'Damn my fish,' the boy said and he started to cry again. 'Do you want a drink of any kind?' the proprietor asked.

'No,' the boy said. 'Tell them not to bother Santiago. I'll be back.'

'Tell him how sorry I am.' 'Thanks,' the boy said.

The boy carried the hot can of coffee up to the old man's shack and sat by him until he woke. Once it looked as though he were waking. But he had gone back into heavy sleep and the boy had gone across the road to borrow some wood to heat the coffee.

Finally the old man woke.

'Don't sit up,' the boy said. 'Drink this.' He poured some of the coffee in a glass.

The old man took it and drank it.

'They beat me, Manolin,' he said. 'They truly beat me.' '*He* didn't beat you. Not the fish.'

'No. Truly. It was afterwards.'

'Pedrico is looking after the skiff and the gear. What do you want done with the head?'

'Let Pedrico chop it up to use in fish traps.' 'And the spear?'

'You keep it if you want it.'

'I want it,' the boy said. 'Now we must make our plans about the other things.'

'Did they search for me?'

'Of course. With coast guard and with planes.'

'The ocean is very big and a skiff is small and hard to see,' the old man said. He noticed how pleasant it was to have someone to talk to instead of speaking only to himself and to the sea. 'I missed you,' he said. 'What did you catch?'

'One the first day. One the second and two the third.' 'Very good.'

'Now we fish together again.'

'No. I am not lucky. I am not lucky anymore.'

'The hell with luck,' the boy said. 'I'll bring the luck with me.' 'What will your family say?'

'I do not care. I caught two yesterday. But we will fish together now for I still have much to learn.'

'We must get a good killing lance and always have it on board. You can make the blade from a spring leaf from an old Ford. We can grind it in Guanabacoa. It should be sharp and not tempered so it will break. My knife broke.'

'I'll get another knife and have the spring ground.' How many days of heavy *brisa* have we?'

'Maybe three. Maybe more.'

'I will have everything in order,' the boy said. 'You get your hands well old man.'

'I know how to care for them. In the night I spat something strange and felt something in my chest was broken.'

'Get that well too,' the boy said. 'Lie down, old man, and I will bring you your clean shirt. And something to eat.'

'Bring any of the papers of the time that I was gone,' the old man said.

'You must get well fast for there is much that I can learn and you can teach me everything. How much did you suffer?' 'Plenty,' the old man said.

'I'll bring the food and the papers,' the boy said. 'Rest well, old man. I will bring stuff from the drugstore for your hands.'

'Don't forget to tell Pedrico the head is his.' 'No. I will remember.'

As the boy went out the door and down the worn coral rock road he was crying again.

That afternoon there was a party of tourists at the Terrace and looking down in the water among the empty beer cans and dead barracudas a woman saw a great long white spine with a huge tail at the end that lifted and swung with the tide while the east wind blew a heavy steady sea outside the entrance to the harbour.

'What's that?' she asked a waiter and pointed to the long backbone of the great fish that was now just garbage waiting to go out with the tide.

'Tiburon,' the waiter said. 'Shark.' He was meaning to explain what had happened.

'I didn't know sharks had such handsome, beautifully formed tails.'

'I didn't either,' her male companion said.

Up the road, in his shack, the old man was sleeping again. He was still sleeping on his face and the boy was sitting by him watching him. The old man was dreaming about the lions.

FOR WHOM THE BELL TOLLS

No man is an *Iland*, intire of it selfe; every man is a peece of the *Continent*, a part of the *maine*; if a *Clod* bee washed away by the *Sea*, *Europe* is the lesse, as well as if a *Promontorie* were, as well as if a *Mannor* of thy *friends* or of thine owne were; any man's *death* diminishes *me*, because I am involved in *Mankinde*; And therefore never send to know for whom the *bell* tolls; It tolls for *thee*.

—John Donne

1

He Lay flat on the brown, pine-needled floor of the forest, his chin on his folded arms, and high overhead the wind blew in the tops of the pine trees. The mountainside sloped gently where he lay; but below it was steep and he could see the dark of the oiled road winding through the pass. There was a stream alongside the road and far down the pass he saw a mill beside the stream and the falling water of the dam, white in the summer sunlight.

'Is that the mill?' he asked.

'Yes.'

'I do not remember it.'

'It was built since you were here. The old mill is farther down; much below the pass.'

He spread the photostated military map out on the forest floor and looked at it carefully. The old man looked over his shoulder. He was a short and solid old man in a black peasant's smock and gray iron stiff trousers and he wore rope-soled shoes. He was breathing heavily from the climb and his hand rested on one of the two heavy packs they had been carrying.

'Then you cannot see the bridge from here.'

'No,' the old man said. 'This is the easy country of the pass where the stream flows gently. Below, where the road turns out of sight in the trees, it drops suddenly and there is a steep gorge—'

'I remember.'

'Across this gorge is the bridge.'

'And where are their posts?'

'There is a post at the mill that you see there.'

The young man, who was studying the country, took his glasses from the pocket of his faded, khaki flannel shirt, wiped the lenses with a handkerchief, screwed the eyepieces around until the boards of the mill showed suddenly clearly and he saw the wooden bench beside the door; the huge pile of sawdust that rose behind the open shed where the circular saw was, and a stretch of the flume that brought the logs down from the mountainside on the other bank of the stream.

The stream showed clear and smooth-looking in the glasses and, below the curl of the falling water, the spray from the dam was blowing in the wind.

'There is no sentry.'

'There is smoke coming from the millhouse,' the old man said. 'There are also clothes hanging on a line.'

'I see them but I do not see any sentry.'

'Perhaps he is in the shade,' the old man explained. 'It is hot there now. He would be in the shadow at the end we do not see.'

'Probably. Where is the next post?'

'Below the bridge. It is at the roadmender's hut at kilometer five from the top of the pass.'

'How many men are here?' He pointed at the mill.

'Perhaps four and a corporal.'

'And below?'

'More. I will find out.'

'And at the bridge?'

'Always two. One at each end.'

'We will need a certain number of men,' he said. 'How many men can you get?'

'I can bring as many men as you wish,' the old man said. 'There are many men now here in the hills.'

'How many?'

'There are more than a hundred. But they are in small bands. How many men will you need?'

'I will let you know when we have studied the bridge.'

'Do you wish to study it now?'

'No. Now I wish to go to where we will hide this explosive until it is time. I would like to have it hidden in utmost security at a distance no greater than half an hour from the bridge, if that is possible.'

'That is simple,' the old man said. 'From where we are going, it will all be downhill to the bridge. But now we must climb a little in seriousness to get there. Are you hungry?'

'Yes,' the young man said. 'But we will eat later. How are you called? I have forgotten.' It was a bad sign to him that he had forgotten.

'Anselmo,' the old man said. 'I am called Anselmo and I come from Barcode Avila. Let me help you with that pack.'

The young man, who was tall and thin, with sun-streaked fair hair, and a wind and sun-burned face, who wore the sun-faded flannel shirt, a pair of peasant's trousers and rope-soled shoes, leaned over, put his arm through one of the leather pack straps and swung the heavy pack up onto his shoulders. He worked his arm through the other strap and settled the weight of the pack against his back. His shirt was still wet from where the pack had rested.

'I have it up now,' he said. 'How do we go?'

'We climb,' Anselmo said.

Bending under the weight of the packs, sweating, they climbed steadily in the pine forest that covered the mountainside. There was no trail that the young man could see, but they were working up and around the face of the mountain and now they crossed a small stream and the old man went steadily on ahead up the edge of the rocky stream bed. The climbing now was steeper and more difficult, until finally the stream seemed to drop down over the edge of a smooth granite ledge that rose above them and the old man waited at the foot of the ledge for the young man to come up to him.

'How are you making it?'

'All right,' the young man said. He was sweating heavily and his thigh muscles were twitchy from the steepness of the climb.

'Wait here now for me. I go ahead to warn them. You do not want to be shot at carrying that stuff.'

'Not even in a joke,' the young man said. 'Is it far?'

'It is very close. How do they call thee?'

'Roberto,' the young man answered. He had slipped the pack off and lowered it gently down between two boulders by the stream bed.

'Wait here, then, Roberto, and I will return for you.'

'Good,' the young man said. 'But do you plan to go down this way to the bridge?'

'No. When we go to the bridge it will be by another way. Shorter and easier.'

'I do not want this material to be stored too far from the bridge.'

'You will see. If you are not satisfied, we will take another place.'

'We will see,' the young man said.

He sat by the packs and watched the old man climb the ledge. It was not hard to climb and from the way he found hand-holds without searching for them the young man could see that he had climbed it many times before. Yet whoever was above had been very careful not to leave any trail.

The young man, whose name was Robert Jordan, was extremely hungry and he was worried. He was often hungry but he was not usually worried because he did not give any importance to what happened to himself and he knew from experience how simple it was to move behind the enemy lines in all this country. It was as simple to move behind them as it was to cross through them, if you had a good guide. It was only giving importance to what happened to you if you were caught that made it difficult; that and deciding whom to trust. You had to trust the people you worked with completely or not at all, and you had to make decisions about the trusting. He was not worried about any of that. But there were other things.

This Anselmo had been a good guide and he could travel wonderfully in the mountains. Robert Jordan could walk well enough himself and he knew from following him since before daylight that the old man could walk him to death. Robert Jordan trusted the man, Anselmo, so far, in everything except judgment. He had not yet had an opportunity to test his judgment, and, anyway, the judgment was his own responsibility. No, he did not worry about Anselmo and the problem of the bridge was no more difficult than many other problems. He knew how to blow any sort of bridge that you could name and he had blown them of all sizes and constructions. There was enough explosive and all equipment in the two packs to blow this bridge properly even if it were twice as big as Anselmo reported it, as he remembered it when he had walked over it on his way to La Granja on a walking trip in 1933, and as Golz had read him the description of its night before last in that upstairs room in the house outside of the Escorial.

'To blow the bridge is nothing,' Golz had said, the lamplight on his scarred, shaved head, pointing with a pencil on the big map. 'You understand?'

'Yes, I understand.'

'Absolutely nothing. Merely to blow the bridge is a failure.'

'Yes, Comrade General.'

'To blow the bridge at a stated hour based on the time set for the attack is how it should be done. You see that naturally. That is your right and how it should be done.'

Golz looked at the pencil, then tapped his teeth with it.

Robert Jordan had said nothing.

'You understand that is your right and how it should be done,' Golz went on, looking at him and nodding his head. He tapped on the map now with the pencil. 'That is how I should do it. That is what we cannot have.'

'Why, Comrade General?'

'Why?' Golz said, angrily. 'How many attacks have you seen and you ask me why? What is to guarantee that my orders are not changed? What is to guarantee that the attack is not annulled? What is to guarantee that the attack is not postponed? What is to guarantee that it starts within six hours of when it should start? Has any attack ever been as it should?'

'It will start on time if it is your attack,' Robert Jordan said.

'They are never my attacks,' Golz said. 'I make them. But they are not mine. The artillery is not mine. I must put in for it. I have never been given what I ask for even when they have it to give. That is the least of it. There are other things. You know how those people are. It is not necessary to go into all of it. Always there is something. Always some one will interfere. So now be sure you understand.'

'So, when is the bridge to be blown?' Robert Jordan had asked. 'After the attack starts. As soon as the attack has started and not before. So that no reinforcements will come up over that road.' He pointed with his pencil. 'I must know that nothing will come up over that road.'

'And when is the attack?'

'I will tell you. But you are to use the date and hour only as an indication of a probability. You must be ready for that time. You will blow the bridge after the attack has started. You, see?' he indicated with the pencil. 'That is the only road on which they can bring up reinforcements. That is the only road on which they can get up tanks, or artillery, or even move a truck toward the pass which I attack.

I must know that bridge is gone. Not before, so it can be repaired if the attack is postponed. No. It must go when the attack starts and I must know it is gone. There are only two sentries. The man who will go with you has just come from there. He is a very reliable man, they say. You will see. He has people in the mountains. Get as many men as you need. Use as few as possible, but use enough. I do not have to tell you these things.'

'And how do I determine that the attack has started?'

'It is to be made with a full division. There will be an aerial bombardment as preparation. You are not deaf, are you?'

'Then I may take it that when the planes unload, the attack has started?'

'You could not always take it like that,' Golz said and shook his head. 'But in this case, you may. It is my attack.'

'I understand it,' Robert Jordan had said. 'I do not say I like it very much.'

'Neither do I like it very much. If you do not want to undertake it, say so now. If you think you cannot do it, say so now.'

'I will do it,' Robert Jordan had said. 'I will do it all right.'

'That is all I have to know,' Golz said. 'That nothing comes up over that bridge. That is absolute.'

'I understand.'

'I do not like to ask people to do such things and in such a way,' Golz went on. 'I could not order you to do it. I understand what you may be forced to do through my putting such conditions. 1 explain very carefully so that you understand and that you understand all of the possible difficulties and the importance.'

'And how will you advance on La Granja if that bridge is blown?'

'We go forward prepared to repair it after we have stormed the pass. It is a very complicated and beautiful operation. As complicated and as beautiful as always. The plan has been manufactured in Madrid. It is another of Vicente Rojo, the unsuccessful professor's, masterpieces. I make the attack and I make it, as always, not in sufficient force. It is a very possible operation, in spite of that. I am much happier about it than usual. It can be successful with that bridge eliminated. We can take Segovia. Look, I show you how it goes. You, see? It is not the top of the pass where we attack. We hold that. It is much beyond. Look—Here—Like this—'

'I would rather not know,' Robert Jordan said.

'Good,' said Golz. 'It is less of baggage to carry with you on the other side, yes?'

'I would always rather not know. Then, no matter what can happen, it was not me that talked.'

'It is better not to know,' Golz stroked his forehead with the pencil. 'Many times, I wish I did not know myself. But you do know the one thing you must know about the bridge?'

'Yes. I know that.'

'I believe you do,' Golz said. 'I will not make you any little speech. Let us now have a drink. So much talking makes me very thirsty, Comrade Hordan. You have a funny name in Spanish, Comrade Hordown.'

'How do you say Golz in Spanish, Comrade General?'

'Hotze,' said Golz grinning, making the sound deep in his throat as though hawking with a bad cold. 'Hotze,' he croaked. 'Comrade Heneral Khotze. If I had known how they pronounced Golz in Spanish I would pick me out a better name before I come to war here. When I think I come to command a division and I can pick out any name I want and I pick out Hotze. General Hotze. Now it is too late to change. How do you like partisan work?' It was the Russian term for guerilla work behind the lines.

'Very much,' Robert Jordan said. He grinned. 'It is very healthy in the open air.'

'I like it very much when I was your age, too,' Golz said. 'They tell me you blow bridges very well. Very scientific. It is only hearsay. I have never seen you do anything myself. Maybe nothing ever happens really. You really blow them?' He was teasing now. 'Drink this,' he handed the glass of Spanish brandy to Robert Jordan. 'You *really* blow them?'

'Sometimes.'

'You better not have any sometimes on this bridge. No, let us not talk any more about this bridge. You understand enough now about that bridge. We are very serious so we can make very strong jokes. Look, do you have many girls on the other side of the lines?'

'No, there is no time for girls.'

'I do not agree. The more irregular the service, the more irregular the life. You have very irregular service. Also, you need a haircut.'

'I have my hair cut as it needs it,' Robert Jordan said. He would be damned if he would have his head shaved like Golz. 'I have enough to think about without girls,' he said sullenly.

'What sort of uniform am I supposed to wear?' Robert Jordan asked.

'None,' Golz said. 'Your haircut is all right. I tease you. You are very different from me,' Golz had said and filled up the glasses again.

'You never think about only girls. I never think at all. Why should I? I am *General Sovietique*. I never think. Do not try to trap me into thinking.'

Someone on his staff, sitting on a chair working over a map on a drawing board, growled at him in the language Robert Jordan did not understand.

'Shut up,' Golz had said, in English. 'I joke if I want. I am so serious is why I can joke. Now drink this and then go. You understand, huh?'

'Yes,' Robert Jordan had said. 'I understand.'

They had shaken hands and he had saluted and gone out to the staff car where the old man was waiting asleep and, in that car, they had ridden over the road past Guadarrama, the old man still asleep, and up the Navacerrada road to the Alpine Club hut where he, Rebert Jordan, slept for three hours before they started.

That was the last he had seen of Golz with his strange white face that never tanned, his hawk eyes, the big nose and thin lips and the shaven head crossed with wrinkles and with scars. Tomorrow night they would be outside the Escorial in the dark along the road; the long lines of trucks loading the infantry in the darkness; the men, heavy loaded, climbing up into the trucks; the machinegun sections lifting their guns into the trucks; the tanks being run up on the skids onto the long-bodied tank trucks; pulling the Division out to move them in the night for the attack on the pass. He would not think about that. That was not his business. That was Golz's business. He had only one thing to do and that was what he should think about and he must think it out clearly and take everything as it came along, and not worry. To worry was as bad as to be afraid. It simply made things more difficult.

He sat no by the stream watching the clear water flowing between the rocks and, across the stream, he noticed there was a thick bed of watercress. He crossed the stream, picked a double handful, washed the muddy roots clean in the current and then sat down again beside his pack and ate the clean, cool green leaves and the crisp, peppery-tasting stalks. He knelt by the stream and, pushing his automatic pistol around on his belt to the small of his back so that it would not be wet, he lowered himself with a hand on each of two boulders and drank from the stream. The water was achingly cold.

Pushing himself up on his hands he turned his head and saw the old man coming down the ledge. With him was another man, also in a black peasant's smock and the dark gray trousers that were almost a uniform in that province, wearing rope-soled shoes and with a carbine slung over his back. This man was bareheaded. The two of them came scrambling down the rock like goats.

They came up to him and Robert Jordan got to his feet.

'*Salud, Camarada,*' he said to the man with the carbine and smiled.

'*Salud,*' *the* other said, grudgingly. Robert Jordan looked at the man's heavy, beard-stubbled face. It was almost round and his head was round and set close on his shoulders. His eyes were small and set too wide apart and his ears were small and set close to his head. He was a heavy man about five feet ten inches tall and his hands and feet were large. His nose had been broken and his mouth was cut at one corner and the line of the scar across the upper lip and lower jaw showed through the growth of beard over his face.

The old man nodded his head at this man and smiled.

'He is the boss here,' he grinned, then flexed his arms as though to make the muscles stand out and looked at the man with the carbine in a half-mocking admiration. 'A very strong man.'

'I can see it,' Robert Jordan said and smiled again. He did not like the look of this man and inside himself he was not smiling at all.

'What have you to justify your identity?' Asked the man with the carbine.

Robert Jordan unpinned a safety pin that ran through his pocket flap and took a folded paper out of the left breast pocket of his flannel shirt and handed it to the man, who opened it, looked at it doubtfully and turned it in his hands.

So, he cannot read, Robert Jordan noted.

'Look at the seal,' he said.

The old man pointed to the seal and the man with the carbine studied it, turning it in his fingers.

'What seal is that?'

'Have you never seen it?'

'No.'

'There are two,' said Robert Jordan. 'One is S.I.M., the service of the military intelligence. The other is the General Staff.'

'Yes, I have seen that seal before. But here no one commands but me,' the other said sullenly. 'What have you in the packs?'

'Dynamite,' the old man said proudly. 'Last night we crossed the lines in the dark and all day we have carried this dynamite over the mountain.'

'I can use dynamite,' said the man with the carbine. He handed back the paper to Robert Jordan and looked him over. 'Yes. I have use for dynamite. How much have you brought me?'

'I have brought you no dynamite,' Robert Jordan said to him evenly. 'The dynamite is for another purpose. What is your name?'

'What is that to you?'

'He is Pablo,' said the old man. The man with the carbine looked at them both sullenly.

'Good. I have heard much good of you,' said Robert Jordan.

'What have you heard of me?' asked Pablo.

'I have heard that you are an excellent guerilla leader, that you are loyal to the republic and prove your loyalty through your acts, and that you are a man both serious and valiant. I bring you greetings from the General Staff.'

'Where did you hear all this?' asked Pablo. Robert Jordan registered that he was not taking any of the flattery.

'I heard it from Buitrago to the Escorial,' he said, naming all the stretch of country on the other side of the lines.

'I know no one in Buitrago nor in Escorial,' Pablo told him.

'There are many people on the other side of the mountains who were not there before. Where are you from?'

'Avila. What are you going to do with the dynamite?'

'Blow up a bridge.'

'What bridge?'

'That is my business.'

'If it is in this territory, it is my business. You cannot blow bridges close to where you live. You must live in one place and operate in another. I know my business One who is alive, now, after a year, knows his business.'

'This is my business,' Robert Jordan said. 'We can discuss it together. Do you wish to help us with the sacks?'

'No,' said Pablo and shook his head.

The old man turned toward him suddenly and spoke rapidly and furiously in a dialect that Robert Jordan could just follow. It was like reading Quevedo.

Anselmo was speaking old Castilian and it went something like this, 'Art thou a brute? Yes. Art thou a beast? Yes, many times. Hast thou a brain? Nay. None. Now we come for something of consummate importance and thee, with thy dwelling place to be undisturbed, puts thy fox-hole before the interests of humanity. Before the interests of thy people. I this and that in the this and that of thy father. I this and that and that in thy this. *Pick up that bag.*'

Pablo looked down.

'Everyone has to do what he can do according to how it can be truly done,' he said. 'I live here and I operate beyond Segovia. If you make a disturbance here, we will be hunted out of these mountains. It is only by doing nothing here that we are able to live in these mountains. It is the principle of the fox.'

'Yes,' said Anselmo bitterly. 'It is the principle of the fox when we need the wolf.'

'I am more wolf than thee,' Pablo said and Robert Jordan knew that he would pick up the sack.

'Hi. Ho...,' Anselmo looked at him. 'Thou art more wolf than me and I am sixty-eight years old.'

He spat on the ground and shook his head.

'You have that many years?' Robert Jordan asked, seeing that now, for the moment, it would be all right and trying to make it go easier.

'Sixty-eight in the month of July.'

'If we should ever see that month,' said Pablo. 'Let me help you with the pack,' he said to Robert Jordan.

'Leave the other to the old man.' He spoke, not sullenly, but almost sadly now. 'He is an old man of great strength.'

'I will carry the pack,' Robert Jordan said.

'Nay,' said the old man. 'Leave it to this other strong man.'

'I will take it,' Pablo told him, and in his sullenness, there was a sadness that was disturbing to Robert Jordan. He knew that sadness and to see it here worried him.

'Give me the carbine then,' he said and when Pablo handed it to him, he slung it over his back and, with the two men climbing ahead of him, they went heavily, pulling and climbing up the granite shelf and over its upper edge to where there was a green clearing in the forest.

They skirted the edge of the little meadow and Robert Jordan, striding easily now without the pack, the carbine pleasantly rigid over his shoulder after the heavy, sweating pack weight, noticed that the grass was cropped down in several places and signs that picket pins had been driven into the earth. He could see a trail through the grass where horses had been led to the stream to drink and there was the fresh manure of several horses. They picket them here to feed at night and keep them out of sight in the timber in the daytime, he thought. I wonder how many horses this Pablo has?

He remembered now noticing, without realizing it, that Pablo's trousers were worn soapy shiny in the knees and thighs. I wonder if he has a pair of boots or if he rides in those apparatus, *he* thought. He must have quite an outfit. But I don't like that sadness, he thought. That sadness is bad. That's the sadness they get before they quit or before they betray. That is the sadness that comes before the sell-out.

Ahead of them a horse whinnied in the timber and then, through the brown trunks of the pine trees, only a little sunlight coming down through their thick, almost-touching tops, he saw the corral made by roping around the tree trunks. The horses had their heads pointed toward the men as they approached, and at the foot of a tree, outside the corral, the saddles were piled together and covered with a tarpaulin.

As they came up, the two men with the packs stopped, and Robert Jordan knew it was for him to admire the horses.

'Yes,' he said. 'They are beautiful.' He turned to Pablo. 'You have your cavalry and all.'

There were five horses in the rope corral, three bays, a sorrel, and a buckskin. Sorting them out carefully with his eyes after he had seen them first together, Robert Jordan looked them over individually. Pablo and Anselmo knew how good they were and while Pablo stood now proud and less sad-looking, watching them lovingly, the old man acted as though they were some great surprises that he had produced, suddenly, himself.

'How do they look to you?' he asked.

'All these I have taken,' Pablo said and Robert Jordan was pleased to hear him speak proudly.

'That,' said Robert Jordan, pointing to one of the bays, a big stall lion with a white blaze on his forehead and a single white foot, the near front, 'is much horse.'

He was a beautiful horse that looked as though he had come out of a painting by Velasquez.

'They are all good,' said Pablo. 'You know horses?'

'Yes.'

'Less bad,' said Pablo. 'Do you see a defect in one of these?'

Robert Jordan knew that now his papers were being examined by the man who could not read.

The horses all still had their heads up looking at the man. Robert Jordan slipped through between the double rope of the corral and slapped the buckskin on the haunch. He leaned back against the ropes of the enclosure and watched the horses circle the corral, stood watching them a minute more, as they stood still, then leaned down and came out through the ropes.

'The sorrel is lame in the off-hind foot,' he said to Pablo, not looking at him. 'The hoof is split and although it might not get worse soon if shod properly, she could break down if she travels over much hard ground.'

'The hoof was like that when we took her,' Pablo said.

'The best horse that you have, the white-faced bay stallion, has a swelling on the upper part of the cannon bone that I do not like.'

'It is nothing,' said Pablo. 'He knocked it three days ago. If it were to be anything it would have become so already.'

He pulled back the tarpaulin and showed the saddles. There were two ordinary vaquero's or herdsman's saddles, like American stock saddles, one very ornate vaquero's saddle, with hand-tooled leather and heavy, hooded stirrups, and two military saddles in black leather.

'We killed a pair of *guardians civil*,' he said, explaining the military saddles.

'That is big game.'

'They had dismounted on the road between Segovia and Santa Maria del Real. They had dismounted to ask papers of the driver of a cart. We were able to kill them without injuring the horses.'

'Have you killed many civil guards?' Robert Jordan asked. 'Several,' Pablo said. 'But only these two without injury to the horses.'

'It was Pablo who blew up the train at Arevalo,' Anselmo said. 'That was Pablo.'

'There was a foreigner with us who made the explosion,' Pablo said. 'Do you know him?'

'What is he called?'

'I do not remember. It was a very rare name.'

'What did he look like?'

'He was fair, as you are, but not as tall and with large hands and a broken nose.'

'Kashkin,' Robert Jordan said. 'That would be Kashkin.'

'Yes,' said Pablo. 'It was a very rare name. Something like that. What has become of him?'

'He is dead since April.'

'That is what happens to everybody,' Pablo said, gloomily. 'That is the way we will all finish.'

'That is the way all men end,' Anselmo said. 'That is the way men have always ended. What is the matter with you, man? What hast thou in the stomach? '

'*They are* very strong,' Pablo said. It was as though he were talking to himself. He looked at the horses gloomily. 'You do not realize how strong they are. I seem them always stronger, always better armed. Always with more material. Here am I with horses like these. And what can I look forward to? To be hunted and to die. Nothing more.'

'You hunt as much as you are hunted,' Anselmo said.

'No,' said Pablo. 'Not any more. And if we leave these mountains now, where can we go? Answer me that? Where now?'

'In Spain there are many mountains. There are the Sierra de Grew dos if one leaves here.'

'Not for me,' Pablo said. 'I am tired of being hunted. Here we are all right. Now if you blow a bridge here, we will be hunted. If they know we are here and hunt for us with planes, they will find us. If they send Moors to hunt us out, they will find us and we must go. I am tired of all this. You hear?' He turned to Robert Jordan. 'What right have you, a foreigner, to come to me and tell me what I must do?'

'I have not told you anything you must do,' Robert Jordan said to him.

'You will though,' Pablo said. 'There. There is the badness.'

He pointed at the two heavy packs that they had lowered to the ground while they had watched the horses. Seeing the horses had seemed to bring this all to a head in him and seeing that Robert Jordan knew horses had seemed to loosen his tongue. The three of them stood now by the rope corral and the patchy sunlight shone on the coat of the bay stallion. Pablo looked at him and then pushed with his foot against the heavy pack. 'There is the badness.'

'I come only for my duty,' Robert Jordan told him. 'I come under orders from those who are conducting the war. If I ask you to help me, you can refuse and I will find others who will help me. I have not even asked you for help yet. I have to do what I am ordered to do and I can promise you of its importance. That I am a foreigner is not my fault. I would rather have been born here.'

'To me, now, the most important is that we be not disturbed here,' Pablo said. 'To me, now, my duty is to those who are with me and to myself.'

'Thyself. Yes,' Anselmo said. 'Thyself now since a long time. Thyself and thy horses. Until thou hadst horses thou wert with us. Now thou art another capitalist more.'

'That is unjust,' said Pablo. 'I expose the horses all the time for the cause.'

'Very little,' said Anselmo scornfully. 'Very little in my judgment. To steal, yes. To eat well, yes. To murder, yes. To fight, no.'

'You are an old man who will make himself trouble with his mouth.'

'I am an old man who is afraid of no one,' Anselmo told him. 'Also, I am an old man without horses.'

'You are an old man who may not live long.'

'I am an old man who will live until I die,' Anselmo said. 'And I am not afraid of foxes.'

Pablo said nothing but picked up the pack.

'Nor of wolves either,' Anselmo said, picking up the other pack. 'If thou art a wolf.'

'Shut thy mouth,' Pablo said to him. 'Thou art an old man who always talks too much.'

'And would do whatever he said he would do,' Anselmo said, bent under the pack. 'And who now is hungry. And thirsty. Go on, guerilla leader with the sad face. Lead us to something to eat.'

It is starting badly enough, Robert Jordan thought. But Anselmo's a man. They are wonderful when they are good, he thought. There are no people like them when they are good and when they go bad there is no people that is worse. Anselmo must have known what he was doing when he brought us here. But I don't like it. I don't like any of it.

The only good sign was that Pablo was carrying the pack and that he had given him the carbine. Perhaps he is always like that, Robert Jordan thought. Maybe he is just one of the gloomy ones.

No, he said to himself, don't fool yourself You do not know how he was before; but you do know that he is going bad fast and without hiding it. When he starts to hide it, he will have made a decision. Remember that, he told himself the first friendly thing he does, he will have made a decision. They are awfully good horses, though, he thought, beautiful horses. I wonder what could make me feel the way those horses make Pablo feel. The old man was right. The horses made him rich and as soon as he was rich, he wanted to enjoy life. Pretty soon he'll feel bad because he can't join the Jockey Club, I guess, he thought. Pauvre Pablo. Il a manqué son Jockey.

That idea made him feel better. He grinned, looking at the two bent backs and the big packs ahead of him moving through the trees. He had not made any jokes with himself all day and now that he had made one, he felt much better. You're getting to be as all the rest of them, he told himself. You're getting gloomy, too. He'd certainly been solemn and gloomy with Golz. The job had overwhelmed him a little. Slightly overwhelmed, he thought. Plenty overwhelmed. Golz was gay and he had wanted him to be gay too before he left, but he hadn't been.

All the best ones, when you thought it over, were gay. It was much better to be gay and it was a sign of something too. It was like having immortality while you were still alive. That was a complicated one. There were not many of them left though. No, there were not many of the gay ones left. There were very damned few of them left. And if you keep on thinking like that, my boy, you won't be left either. Turn off the thinking now, old timer, old comrade. You're a bridge blower now. Not a thinker. Man, I'm hungry, he thought. I hope Pablo eats well.

2

They had come through the heavy timber to the cup-shaped upper end of the little valley and he saw where the camp must be under the rim-rock that rose ahead of them through the trees.

That was the camp all right and it was a good camp. You did not see it at all until you were up to it and Robert Jordan knew it could not be spotted from the air. Nothing would show from above. It was as well-hidden as a bear's den. But it seemed to be little better guarded. He looked at it carefully as they came up.

There was a large cave in the rim-rock formation and beside the opening a man sat with his back against the rock, his legs stretched out on the ground and his carbine leaning against the rock. He was cutting away on a stick with a knife and he stared at them as they came up, then went on whittling.

'Hola,' said the seated man. 'What is this that comes?'

'The old man and a dynamiter,' Pablo told him and lowered the pack inside the entrance to the cave. Anselmo lowered his pack, too, and Robert Jordan unslung the rifle and leaned it against the rock.

'Don't leave it so close to the cave,' the whittling man, who had blue eyes in a dark, good-looking lazy gypsy face, the color of smoked leather, said. 'There's a fire in there.'

'Get up and put it away thyself,' Pablo said. 'Put it by that tree.' The gypsy did not move but said something unprintable, then, 'Leave it there. Blow thyself up,' he said lazily. ''Twill cure thy diseases.'

'What do you make?' Robert Jordan sat down by the gypsy. The gypsy showed him. It was a figure four trap and he was whittling the crossbar for it.

'For faxes,' he said. 'With a log for a dead-fall. It breaks their backs.' He grinned at Jordan. 'Like this, see?' He made a motion of the framework of the trap collapsing, the log falling, then shook his head, drew in his hand, and spread his arms to show the fox with a broken back. 'Very practical,' he explained.

'He catches rabbits,' Anselmo said. 'He is a gypsy. So, if he catches rabbits, he says it is faxes. If he catches a fox, he would say it was an elephant.'

'And if I catch an elephant?' the gypsy asked and showed his white teeth again and winked at Robert Jordan.

'You'd say it was a tank,' Anselmo told him.

'I'll get a tank,' the gypsy told him. 'I will get a tank. And you can say it is what you please.'

'Gypsies talk much and kill little,' Anselmo told him.

The gypsy winked at Robert Jordan and went on whittling.

Pablo had gone in out of sight in the cave. Robert Jordan hoped he had gone for food. He sat on the ground by the gypsy and the afternoon sunlight came down through the tree tops and was warm on his outstretched legs. He could smell food now in the cave, the smell of oil and of onions and of meat frying and his stomach moved with hunger inside of him.

'We can get a tank,' he said to the gypsy. 'It is not to differ cult.'

'With this?' the gypsy pointed toward the two sacks.

'Yes,' Robert Jordan told him. 'I will teach you. You make a trap. It is not too difficult.'

'You and me?'

'Sure,' said Robert Jordan. 'Why not?'

'Hey,' the gypsy said to Anselmo. 'Move those two sacks to where they will be safe, will you? They're valuable.'

Anselmo grunted. 'I am going for wine,' he told Robert Jordan. Robert Jordan got up and lifted the sacks away from the cave entrance and leaned them, one on each side of a tree trunk. He knew what was in them and he never liked to see them close to gather.

'Bring a cup for me,' the gypsy told him.

'Is there wine?' Robert Jordan asked, sitting down again by the gypsy.

'Wine? Why not? A whole skinful. Half a skinful, anyway.' 'And what to eat?'

'Everything, man,' the gypsy said. 'We eat like generals.' 'And what do gypsies do in the war?' Robert Jordan asked him. 'They keep on being gypsies.'

'That's a good job.'

'The best,' the gypsy said. 'How do they call thee?'

'Roberto. And there?'

'Rafael. And this of the tank is serious?'

'Surely. Why not?'

Anselmo came out of the mouth of the cave with a deep stone basin full of red wine and with his fingers through the handles of three cups. 'Look,' he said. 'They have cups and all.' Pablo came out behind them.

'There is food soon,' he said. 'Do you have tobacco?'

Robert Jordan went over to the packs and opening one, felt in side an inner pocket and brought out one of the flat boxes of Russian cigarettes he had gotten at Golz's headquarters. He ran his thumbnail around the edge of the box and, opening the lid, handed them to Pablo who took half a dozen. Pablo, holding them in one of his huge hands, picked one up and looked at it against the light. They were long narrow cigarettes with paste board cylinders for mouthpieces.

'Much air and little tobacco,' he said. 'I know these. The other with the rare name had them.'

'Kashkin,' Robert Jordan said and offered the cigarettes to the gypsy and Anselmo, who each took one.

'Take more,' he said and they each took another. He gave them each four more, they making a double nod with the hand holding the cigarettes so that the cigarette dipped its end as a man salutes with a sword, to thank him.

'Yes,' Pablo said. 'It was a rare name.'

'Here is the wine.' Anselmo dipped a cup out of the bowl and handed it to Robert Jordan, then dipped for himself and the gypsy.

'Is there no wine for me?' Pablo asked. They were all sitting together by the cave entrance.

Anselmo handed him his cup and went into the cave for another. Coming out he leaned over the bowl and dipped the cup full and they all touched cup edges.

The wine was good, tasting faintly resinous from the wineskin, but excellent, light and clean on his tongue. Robert Jordan drank it slowly, feeling it spread warmly through his tiredness.

'The food comes shortly,' Pablo said. 'And this foreigner with the rare name, how did he die?'

'He was captured and he killed himself.'

'How did that happen?'

'He was wounded and he did not wish to be a prisoner.'

'What were the details?'

'I don't know,' he lied. He knew the details very well and he knew they would not make good talking now.

'He made us promise to shoot him in case he was wounded at the business of the train and should be unable to get away,' Pablo said. 'He spoke in a very rare manner.'

He must have been jumpy even then, Robert Jordan thought. Poor old Kashkin.

'He had a prejudice against killing himself,' Pablo said. 'He told me that. Also, he had a great fear of being tortured.'

'Did he tell you that, too?' Robert Jordan asked him.

'Yes,' the gypsy said. 'He spoke like that to all of us.'

'Were you at the train, too?'

'Yes. All of us were at the train.'

'He spoke in a very rare manner,' Pablo said. 'But he was very brave.'

Poor old Kashkin, Robert Jordan thought. He must have been doing more harm than good around here. I wish I would have known he was that jumpy as far back as then. They should have pulled him out. You can't have people around doing this sort of work and talking like that. That is no way to talk. Even if they accomplish their mission, they are doing more harm than good, talking that sort of stuff.

'He was a little strange,' Robert Jordan said. 'I think he was a little crazy.'

'But very dexterous at producing explosions,' the gypsy said. 'And very brave.'

'But crazy,' Robert Jordan said. 'In this you have to have very much head and be very cold in the head. That was no way to talk.'

'And you,' Pablo said. 'If you are wounded in such a thing as this bridge, you would be willing to be left behind?'

'Listen,' Robert Jordan said and, leaning forward, he dipped himself another cup of the wine. 'Listen to me clearly. If ever I should have any little favors to ask of any man, I will ask him at the time.'

'Good,' said the gypsy approvingly. 'In this way speak the good ones. Ah! Here it comes.'

'You have eaten,' said Pablo.

'And I can eat twice more,' the gypsy told him. 'Look now who brings it.'

The girl stooped as she came out of the cave mouth carrying the big iron cooking platter and Robert Jordan saw her face turned at an angle and at the same time saw the strange thing about her. She smiled and said, *Hola, Comrade,*' and Robert Jordan said, '*Salud*,' and was careful not to stare and not to look away. She set down the flat iron platter in front of him and he noticed her handsome brown hands. Now she looked him full in the face and smiled. Her teeth were white in her brown face and her skin and her eyes were the same golden tawny brown. She had high cheek bones, merry eyes and a straight mouth with full lips. Her hair was the golden brown of a grain field that has been burned dark in the sun but it was cut short all over her head so that it was but little longer than the fur on a beaver pelt. She smiled in Robert Jordan's face and put her brown hand up and ran it over her head, flattening the hair which rose again as her hand passed. She has a beautiful face Robert Jordan thought. She'd be beautiful if they hadn't cropped her hair.

'That is the way I comb it,' she said to Robert Jordan and laughed. 'Go ahead and eat. Don't stare at me. They gave me this haircut in Valladolid. It's almost grown out now.'

She sat down opposite him and looked at him. He looked back at her and she smiled and folded her hands together over her knees. Her legs slanted long and clean from the open cuffs of the trousers as she sat with her hands across her knees and he could see the shape of her small up-tilted breasts under the gray shirt. Every time Robert Jordan looked at her, he could feel a thickness in his throat.

'There are no plates,' Anselmo said. 'Use your own knife.' The girl had leaned four forks, tines down, against the sides of the iron dish.

They were all eating out of the platter, not speaking, as is the Spanish custom. It was rabbit cooked with onions and green peppers and there were chick peas in the red wine sauce. It was well cooked, the rabbit meat flaked off the bones, and the sauce was delicious. Robert Jordan drank another cup of wine while he ate. The girl watched him all through the meal. Everyone else was watching his food and eating. Robert Jordan wiped up the last of the sauce in front of him with a piece of bread, piled the rabbit bones to one side, wiped the spot where they had been for sauce, then wiped his fork clean with the bread, wiped his knife and put it away and ate the bread. He leaned over and dipped his cup full of wine and the girl still watched him.

Robert Jordan drank half the cup of wine but the thickness still came in his throat when he spoke to the girl.

'How art thou called?' he asked. Pablo looked at him quickly when he heard the tone of his voice. Then he got up and walked away.

'Maria. And there?'

'Roberto. Have you been long in the mountains?'

'Three months.'

'Three months?' He looked at her Hair, that was as thick and short and rippling when she passed her hand over it, now in embarrassment, as a grain field in the wind on a hillside. 'It was shaved,' she said. 'They shaved it regularly in the prison at Val ladled. It has taken three months to grow to this. I was on the train. They were taking me to the south. Many of the prisoners were caught after the train was blown up but I was not. I came with these.'

'I found her hidden in the rocks,' the gypsy said. 'It was when we were leaving. Man, but this one was ugly. We took her along but many times I thought we would have to leave her.'

'And the other one who was with them at the train?' asked Maria. 'The other blond one. The foreigner. Where is he?'

'Dead,' Robert Jordan said. 'In April.'

'In April? The train was in April.'

'Yes,' Robert Jordan said. 'He died ten days after the train.'

'Poor man,' she said. 'He was very brave. And you do that same business?'

'Yes.'

'You have done trains, too?'

'Yes. Three trains.'

'Here?'

'In Estremadura,' he said. 'I was in Estremadura before I came here. We do very much in Estremadura. There are many of us working in Estremadura.'

'And why do you come to these mountains now?'

'I take the place of the other blond one. Also, I know this country from before the movement.'

'You know it well?'

'No, not really well. But I learn fast. I have a good map and I have a good guide.'

'The old man,' she nodded. 'The old man is very good.' 'Thank you,' Anselmo said to her and Robert Jordan realized suddenly that he and the girl were not alone and he realized too that it was hard for him to look at her because it made his voice change so. He was violating the second rule of the two rules for getting on well with people that speak Spanish; give the men tobacco and leave the women alone; and he realized, very suddenly, that he did not care. There were so many things that he had not to care about, why should he care about that?

'You have a very beautiful face,' he said to Maria. 'I wish I would have had the luck to see you before your hair was cut.'

'It will grow out,' she said. 'In six months, it will be long enough.'

'You should have seen her when we brought her from the train. She was so ugly it would make you sick.'

'Whose woman, are you?' Robert Jordan asked, trying not to pull out of it. 'Are you Pablo's?'

She looked at him and laughed, then slapped him on the knee.

'Of Pablo? You have seen Pablo?'

'Well, then, of Rafael. I have seen Rafael.'

'Of Rafael neither.'

'Of no one,' the gypsy said. 'This is a very strange woman. Is of no one. But she cooks well.'

'Really of no one?' Robert Jordan asked her.

'Of no one. No one. Neither in joke nor in seriousness. Nor of thee either.'

'No?' Robert Jordan said and he could feel the thickness coming in his throat again. 'Good. I have no time for any woman. That is true.'

'Not fifteen minutes?' the gypsy asked teasingly. 'Not a quarter of an hour?' Robert Jordan did not answer. He looked at the girl, Maria, and his throat felt too thick for him to trust himself to speak.

Maria looked at him and laughed, then blushed suddenly but kept on looking at him.

'You are blushing,' Robert Jordan said to her. 'Do you blush much?'

'Never.'

'You are blushing now.'

'Then I will go into the cave.'

'Stay here, Maria.'

'No,' she said and did not smile at him. 'I will go into the cave now.' She picked up the iron plate they had eaten from and the four forks. She moved awkwardly as a colt moves, but with that same grace as of a young animal.

'Do you want the cups?' she asked.

Robert Jordan was still looking at her and she blushed again. 'Don't make me do that,' she said. 'I do not like to do that.'

'Leave them,' they gypsy said to her. 'Here,' he dipped into the stone bowl and handed the full cup to Robert Jordan who watched the girl duck her head and go into the cave carrying the heavy iron dish.

'Thank you,' Robert Jordan said. His voice was all right again, now that she was gone. 'This is the last one. We've had enough of this.'

'We will finish the bowl,' the gypsy said. 'There is over half a skin. We packed it in on one of the horses.'

'That was the last raid of Pablo,' Anselmo said. 'Since then, he has done nothing.'

'How many are you?' Robert Jordan asked.

'We are seven and there are two women.'

'Two?'

'Yes. The *muter* of Pablo.'

'And she?'

'In the cave. The girl can cook a little. I said she cooks well to please her. But mostly she helps the *muter* of Pablo.'

'And how is she, the *muter* of Pablo?'

'Something barbarous,' the gypsy grinned. 'Something *very* barbarous. If you think Pablo is ugly you should see his woman. But brave. A hundred times braver than Pablo. But something barbarous.'

'Pablo was brave in the beginning,' Anselmo said. 'Pablo was something serious in the beginning.'

'He killed more people than the cholera,' the gypsy said. 'At the start of the movement, Pablo killed more people than the typhoid fever.'

'But since a long time, he is *muy flojo,* Anselmo said. 'He is very flaccid. He is very much afraid to die.'

'It is possible that it is because he has killed so many at the beginning,' the gypsy said philosophically. 'Pablo killed more than the bubonic plague.'

'That and the riches,' Anselmo said. 'Also, he drinks very much. Now he would like to retire like a *matador de taros*. Like a bullfighter. But he cannot retire.'

'If he crosses to the other side of the lines, they will take his horses and make him go in the army,' the gypsy said. 'In me there is no love for being in the army either.' 'Nor is there in any other gypsy,' Anselmo said.

'Why should there be?' the gypsy asked. 'Who wants to be in an army? Do we make the revolution to be in an army? I am willing to fight but not to be in an army.'

'Where are the others?' asked Robert Jordan. He felt comfort able and sleepy now from the wine and lying back on the floor of the forest he saw through the tree tops the small afternoon clouds of the mountains moving slowly in the high Spanish sky.

'There are two asleep in the cave,' the gypsy said. 'Two are on guard above where we have the gun. One is on guard below. They are probably all asleep.'

Robert Jordan rolled over on his side.

'What kind of a gun is it?'

'A very rare name,' the gypsy said. 'It has gone away from me for the moment. It is a machine gun.'

It must be an automatic rifle, Robert Jordan thought.

'How much does it weigh?' he asked.

'One man can carry it but it is heavy. It has three legs that fold. We got it in the last serious raid. The one before the wine.'

'How many rounds have you for it?'

'An infinity,' the gypsy said. 'One whole case of an unbelievable heaviness.'

Sounds like about five hundred rounds, Robert Jordan thought. 'Does it feed from a pan or a belt?'

'From round iron cans on the top of the gun.'

Hell, it's a Lewis gun, Robert Jordan thought.

'Do you know anything about a machine gun?' he asked the old man.

'*Nada*,' said Anselmo. 'Nothing.'

'And thou?' to the gypsy.

'That they fire with much rapidity and become so hot the barrel burns the hand that touches it,' the gypsy said proudly.

'Everyone knows that,' Anselmo said with contempt.

'Perhaps,' the gypsy said. 'But he asked me to tell what I know about a *maquila* and I told him.' Then he added, 'Also, unlike an ordinary rifle, they continue to fire as long as you exert pressure on the trigger.'

'Unless they jam, run out of ammunition or get so hot they melt,' Robert Jordan said in English.

'What do you say?' Anselmo asked him.

'Nothing,' Robert Jordan said. 'I was only looking into the future in English.'

'That is something truly rare,' the gypsy said. 'Looking into the future in *Inglés*. Can you read in the palm of the hand?'

'No,' Robert Jordan said and he dipped another cup of wine. 'But if thou canst I wish thee would read in the palm of my hand and tell me what is going to pass in the next three days.'

'The *mujer* of Pablo reads in the hands,' the gypsy said. 'But she is so irritable and of such a barbarousness that I do not know if she will do it.'

Robert Jordan sat up now and took a swallow of the wine.

'Let us see the *mujer* of Pablo now,' he said. 'If it is that bad let us get it over with.'

'I would not disturb her,' Rafael said. 'She has a strong hatred for me.'

'Why?'

'She treats me as a time waster.'

'What injustice,' Anselmo taunted.

'She is against gypsies.'

'What an error,' Anselmo said.

'She has gypsy blood,' Rafael said. 'She knows of what she speaks.' He grinned. 'But she has a tongue that scalds and that bites like a bull whip. With this tongue she takes the hide from anyone. In strips. She is of an unbelievable barbarousness.'

'How does she get along with the girl, Maria?' Robert Jordan asked.

'Good. She likes the girl. But let anyone come near her seriously—' He shook his head and clucked with his tongue.

'She is very good with the girl,' Anselmo said. 'She takes good care of her.'

'When we picked the girl up at the time of the train, she was very strange,' Rafael said. 'She would not speak and she cried all the time and if any one touched her, she would shiver like a wet dog. Only lately has she been better. Lately she has been much better. Today she was fine. Just now, talking to you, she was very good. We would have left her after the train. Certainly, it was not worth being delayed by something so sad and ugly and apparently worthless. But the old woman tied a rope to her and when the girl thought she could not go further, the old woman beat her with the end of the rope to make her go. Then when she could not really go further, the old woman carried her over her shoulder. When the old woman could not carry her, I carried her. We were going up that hill breast high in the gorse and heather. And when I could no longer carry her, Pablo carried her. But what the old woman had to say to us to make us do it!' He shook his head at the memory. 'It is true that the girl is long in the legs but is not heavy. The bones are light and she weighs little. But she weighs enough when we had to carry her and stop to fire and then carry her again with the old woman lashing at Pablo with the rope and carrying his rifle, putting it in his hand when he would drop the girl, making him pick her up again and loading the gun for him while she cursed him; taking the shells from his pouches and shoving them down into the magazine and cursing him. The dusk was coming well on then and when the night came it was all right. But it was lucky that they had no cavalry.'

'It must have been very hard at the train,' Anselmo said. 'I was not there,' he explained to Robert Jordan. 'There was the band of Pablo, of El Sardo, whom we will see tonight, and two other bands of these mountains. I had gone to the other side of the lines.'

'In addition to the blond one with the rare name—' the gypsy said.

'Kashkin.'

'Yes. It is a name I can never dominate. We had two with a machine gun. They were sent also by the army. They could not get the gun away and lost it. Certainly, it weighed no more than that girl and if the old woman had been over them, they would have gotten it away.' He shook his head remembering, then went on. 'Never in my life have I seen such a thing as when the explosion was produced. The train was coming steadily. We saw it far away. And I had an excitement so great that I cannot tell it. We saw steam from it and then later came the noise of the whistle. Then it came chu-chu-chu-chu-chu-chu steadily larger and larger and then, at the moment of the explosion, the front wheels of the engine rose up and all of the earth seemed to rise in a great cloud of blackness and a roar and the engine rose high in the cloud of dirt and of the wooden ties rising in the air as in a dream and then it fell onto its side like a great wounded animal and there was an explosion of white steam before the clods of the other explosion had ceased to fall on us and the *maquila* commenced to speak tat-tat-tat-tat!' went the gypsy shaking his two clenched fists up and down in front of him, thumbs up, on an imaginary machine gun. 'Ta! Ta! Tat! Tat! Tat! Ta!' he exulted. 'Never in my life have I seen such a thing, with the troops running from the train and the *máquina speaking* into them and the men falling. It was then that I put my hand on the máquina *in* my excitement and discovered that the barrel burned and at that moment the old woman slapped me on the side of the face and said, 'Shoot, you fool! Shoot or I will kick your brains in!' Then I commenced to shoot but it was very hard to hold my gun steady and the troops were running up the far hill. Later, after we had been down at the train to see what there was to take, an officer forced some troops back toward us at the point of a pistol. He kept waving the pistol and shouting at them and we were all shooting at him but no one hit him. Then some troops lay down and commenced firing and the officer walked up and down behind them with his pistol and still we could not hit him and the *máquina could* not fire on him because of the position of the train. This officer shot two men as they lay and still, they would not get up and he was cursing them and finally they got up, one two and three at a time and came running toward us and the train. Then they lay flat again and fired. Then we left, with the *máquina* still speaking over us as we left. It was then I found the girl where she had run from the train to the rocks and she ran with us. It was those troops who hunted us until that night.'

'It must have been something very hard,' Anselmo said. 'Of much emotion.'

'It was the only good thing we have done,' said a deep voice. 'What are you doing now, your lazy drunken obscene unsayable son of an unnamable unmarried gypsy obscenity? What are you doing?'

Robert Jordan saw a woman of about fifty almost as big as Pablo, almost as wide as she was tall, in black peasant skirt and waist, with heavy wool socks on heavy legs, black rope-soled shoes and a brown face like a model for a granite monument. She had big but nice-looking hands and her thick curly black hair was twisted into a knot on her neck.

'Answer me,' she said to the gypsy, ignoring the others.

'I was talking to these comrades. This one comes as a dynamiter.' 'I know all that,' the *mujer* of Pablo said. 'Get out of here now and relieve Andres who is on guard at the top.'

'*Me Voy*,' the gypsy said. 'I go.' He turned to Robert Jordan. 'I will see thee at the hour of eating.'

'Not even in a joke,' said the woman to him. 'Three times you have eaten today according to my count. Go now and send me Andres.

'*Hola*,' she said to Robert Jordan and put out her hand and smiled. 'How are you and how is everything in the Republic?' 'Good,' he said and returned her strong hand grip. 'Both with me and with the Republic.'

'I am happy,' she told him. She was looking into his face and smiling and he noticed she had fine gray eyes. 'Do you come for us to do another train?'

'No,' said Robert Jordan, trusting her instantly. 'For a bridge.'

'*No es nada,*' she said. 'A bridge is nothing. When do we do another train now that we have horses?'

'Later. This bridge is of great importance.'

'The girl told me your comrade who was with us at the train is dead.'

'Yes.'

'What a pity. Never have I seen such an explosion. He was a man of talent. He pleased me very much. It is not possible to do another train now? There are many men here now in the hills. Too many. It is already hard to get food. It would be better to get out. And we have horses.'

'We have to do this bridge.'

'Where is it?'

'Quite close.'

'All the better,' the *mujer* of Pablo said. 'Let us blow all the bridges there are here and get out. I am sick of this place. Here is too much concentration of people. No good can come of it. Here is a stagnation that is repugnant.'

She sighted Pablo through the trees.

'*Borracho*' she called to him. 'Drunkard. Rotten drunkard!' She turned back to Robert Jordan cheerfully. 'He's taken a leather wine bottle to drink alone in the woods,' she said. 'He's drinking all the time. This life is running him. Young man, I am very con tent that you have come.' She clapped him on the back. 'Ah,' she said. 'You're bigger than you look,' and ran her hand over his shoulder, feeling the muscle under the flannel shirt. 'Good. I am very content that you have come.'

'And I equally.'

'We will understand each other,' she said. 'Have a cup of wine'

'We have already had some,' Robert Jordan said. 'But, will you?'

'Not until dinner,' she said. 'It gives me heartburn.' Then she sighted Pablo again. '*Borracho!*' she shouted. 'Drunkard!' She turned to Robert Jordan and shook her head. 'He was a very good man,' she told him. 'But now he is terminated. And listen to me about another thing. Be very good and careful about the girl. The Maria. She has had a bad time. Understandest thou?'

'Yes. Why do you say this?'

'I saw how she was from seeing thee when she came into the cave. I saw her watching thee before she came out.'

'I joked with her a little.'

'She was in a very bad state,' the woman of Pablo said. 'Now she is better, she ought to get out of here.'

'Clearly, she can be sent through the lines with Anselmo.' 'You and the Anselmo can take her when this terminates.'

Robert Jordan felt the ache in his throat and his voice thickening. 'That might be done,' he said.

The *mujer* of Pablo looked at him and shook her head. 'Ayee. Ayee,' she said. 'Are all men like that?'

'I said nothing. She is beautiful, you know that.'

'No, she is not beautiful. But she begins to be beautiful, you mean,' the woman of Pablo said. 'Men. It is a shame to us women that we make them. No. In seriousness. Are there not homes to care for such as her under the Republic?'

'Yes,' said Robert Jordan. 'Good places. On the coast near Valencia. In other places too. There they will treat her well and she can work with children. There are the children from evacuated villages. They will teach her the work.'

'That is what I want,' the *mujer* of Pablo said. 'Pablo has a sickness for her already. It is another thing which destroys him. It lies on him like a sickness when he sees her. It is best that she goes now.'

'We can take her after this is over.'

'And you will be careful of her now if I trust you? I speak to you as though I knew you for a long time.'

'It is like that,' Robert Jordan said, 'when people understand one another.'

'Why if I would not take her?'

'Because I do not want her crazy here after you will go. I have had her crazy before and I have enough without that.'

'We will take her after the bridge,' Robert Jordan said. 'If we are alive after the bridge, we will take her.'

'I do not like to hear you speak in that manner. That manner of speaking never brings luck.'

'I spoke in that manner only to make a promise,' Robert Jordan said. 'I am not if those who speak gloomily.'

'Let me see thy hand,' the woman said. Robert Jordan put his hand out and the woman opened it, held it in her own big hand, rubbed her thumb over it and looked at it, carefully, then dropped it. She stood up. He got up too and she looked at him without smiling.

'What did you see in it?' Robert Jordan asked her. 'I don't believe in it. You won't scare me.'

'Nothing,' she told him. 'I saw nothing in it.'

'Yes, you did. I am only curious. I do not believe in such things.'

'In what do you believe?'

'In many things but not in that.'

'In what?'

'In my work.'

'Yes, I saw that.'

'Tell me what else you saw.'

'I saw nothing else,' she said bitterly. 'The bridge is very difficult you said?'

'No. I said it is very important.'

'But it can be difficult?'

'Yes. And now I go down to look at it. How many men have you here?'

'Five that are any good. The gypsy is worthless although his intentions are good. He has a good heart. Pablo I no longer trust.'

'How many men has El Sordo that are good?'

'Perhaps eight. We will see tonight. He is coming here. He is a very practical man. He also has some dynamite. Not very much, though. You will speak with him.'

'Have you sent for him?'

'He comes every night. He is a neighbor. Also, a friend as well as a comrade.'

'What do you think of him?'

'He is a very good man. Also, very practical. In the business of the train, he was enormous.'

'And in the other bands?'

'Advising them in time, it should be possible to unite fifty rifles of a certain dependability.'

'How dependable?'

'Dependable within the gravity of the situation.'

'And how many cartridges per rifle?'

'Perhaps twenty. Depending how many they would bring for this bush. If they would come for this business. Remember thee that in this of a bridge there is no money and no loot and in thy reservations of talking, much danger, and that afterwards there must be a moving from these mountains. Many will oppose this of the bridge.'

'Clearly.'

'In this way it is better not to speak of it unnecessarily.'

'I am in accord.'

'Then after thou hast studied thy bridge we will talk tonight with El Sordo.'

'I go down now with Anselmo.'

'Wake him then,' she said. 'Do you want a carbine?'

'Thank you,' he told her. 'It is good to have but I will not use it. I go to look, not to make disturbances. Thank you for what you have told me. I like very much your way of speaking.'

'I try to speak frankly.'

'Then tell me what you saw in the hand.'

'No,' she said and shook her head. 'I saw nothing. Go now to thy bridge. I will look after thy equipment.'

'Cover it and that no one should touch it. It is better there than in the cave.'

'It shall be covered and no one shall touch it,' the woman of Pablo said. 'Go now to thy bridge.'

'Anselmo,' Robert Jordan said, putting his hand on the shoulder of the old man who lay sleeping, his head on his arms.

The old man looked up. 'Yes,' he said. 'Of course. Let us go.'

3

They came down the last two hundred yards, moving carefully from tree to tree in the shadows and now, through the last pines of the steep hillside, the bridge was only fifty yards away. The late afternoon sun that still came over the brown shoulder of the mountain showed the bridge dark against the steep emptiness of the gorge. It was a steel bridge of a single span and there was a sentry box at each end. It was wide enough for two motor cars to pass and it spanned, in solid- flung metal grace, a deep gorge at the bottom of which, far below, a brook leaped in white water through rocks and boulders down to the main stream of the pass.

The sun was in Robert Jordan's eyes and the bridge showed only in outline. Then the sun lessened and was gone and looking up through the trees at the brown, rounded height that it had gone behind, he saw, now, that he no longer looked into the glare, that the mountain slope was a delicate new green and that there were patches of old snow under the crest.

Then he was watching the bridge again in the sudden short trueness of the little light that would be left, and studying its construction. The problem of its demolition was not difficult. As he watched he took out a notebook from his breast pocket and made several quick line sketches. As he made the drawings, he did not figure the charges. He would do that later. Now he was noting the points where the explosive should be placed in order to cut the support of the span and drop a section of it into the gorge. It could be done unhurriedly, scientifically and correctly with a half dozen charges laid and braced to explode simultaneously; or it could be done roughly with two big ones. They would need to be very big ones, on opposite sides and should go at the same time. He sketched quickly and happily; glad at last to have the problem under his hand; glad at last actually to be engaged upon it. Then he shut his notebook, pushed the pencil into its leather holder in the edge of the flap, put the notebook in his pocket and buttoned the pocket.

While he had sketched, Anselmo had been watching the road, the bridge and the sentry boxes. He thought they had come too close to the bridge for safety and when the sketching was finished, he was relieved.

As Robert Jordan buttoned the flap of his pocket and then lay flat behind the pine trunk, looking out from behind it, Anselmo put his hand on his elbow and pointed with one finger.

In the sentry box that faced toward them up the road, the sentry was sitting holding his rifle, the bayonet fixed, between his knees. He was smoking a cigarette and he wore a knitted cap and blanket style cape. At fifty yards, you could not see anything about his face. Robert Jordan put up his field glasses, shading the lenses carefully with his cupped hands even though there was now no sun to make a glint, and there was the rail of the bridge as clear as though you could reach out and touch it and there was the face of the sentry so clear he could see the sunken cheeks, the ash on the cigarette and the greasy shine of the bayonet. It was a peasant's face, the cheeks hollow under the high cheekbones, the beard stubbled, the eyes shaded by the heavy brows, big hands holding the rifle, heavy boots showing beneath the folds of the blanket cape. There was a worn, blackened leather wine bottle on the wall of the sentry box, there were some newspapers and there was no telephone. There could, of course, be a telephone on the side he could not see; but there were no wires running from the box that were visible. A telephone line ran along the road and its wires were carried over the bridge. There was a charcoal brazier outside the sentry box, made from an old petrol tin with the top cut off and holes punched in it, which rested on two stones; but he held no fire. There were some fire-blackened empty tins in the ashes under it.

Robert Jordan handed the glasses to Anselmo who lay flat be side him. The old man grinned and shook his head. He tapped his skull beside his eye with one finger.

'*Ya lo Veo*, 'he said in Spanish. 'I have seen him,' speaking frvom the front of his mouth with almost no movement of his lips in the way that is quieter than any whisper. He looked at the sentry as Robert Jordan smiled at him and, pointing with one finger, drew the other across his throat. Robert Jordan nodded but he did not smile.

The sentry box at the far end of the bridge faced away from them and down the road and they could not see into it. The road, which was broad and oiled and well-constructed, made a turn to the left at the far end of the bridge and then swung out of sight around a curve to the right. At this point it was enlarged from the old road to its present width by cutting into the solid bastion of the rock on the far side of the gorge; and its left or western edge, looking down from the pass and the bridge, was marked and protested by a line of upright cut blocks of stone where its edge fell sheer away to the gorge. The gorge was almost a canyon here, where the brook, that the bridge was flung over, merged with the main stream of the pass.

'And the other post?' Robert Jordan asked Anselmo.

'Five hundred meters below that turn. In the roadmender's hut that is built into the side of the rock.'

'How many men?' Robert Jordan asked.

He was watching the sentry again with his glasses. The sentry rubbed his cigarette out on the plank wall of the box, then took a leather tobacco pouch from his pocket, opened the paper of the dead cigarette and emptied the remnant of used tobacco into the pouch. The sentry stood up, leaned his rifle against the wall of the box and stretched, then picked up his rifle, slung it over his shoulder and walked out onto the bridge. Anselmo flattened on the ground and Robert Jordan slipped his glasses into his shirt pocket and put his head well behind the pine tree.

'There are seven men and a corporal,' Anselmo said close to his ear. 'I informed myself from the gypsy.'

'We will go now as soon as he is quiet,' Robert Jordan said. 'We are too close.'

'Hast, thou seen what thou needest?'

'Yes. All that I need.'

It was getting cold quickly now with the sun down and the light was failing as the afterglow from the last sunlight on the mountains behind them faded.

'How does it look to thee?' Anselmo said softly as they watched the sentry walk across the bridge toward the other box, his bayonet bright in the last of the afterglow, his figure unshapely in the blanket coat.

'Very good,' Robert Jordan said. 'Very, very good.'

'I am glad,' Anselmo said. 'Should we go? Now there is no chance that he sees us.'

The sentry was standing, his back toward them, at the far end of the bridge. From the gorge came the noise of the stream in the boulders. Then through this noise came another noise, a steady, racketing drone and they saw the sentry looking up, his knitted cap slanted back, and turning their heads and looking up they saw, high in the evening sky, three monoplanes in V formation, showing minute and silvery at that height where there still was sun, passing unbelievably quickly across the sky, their motors now throbbing steadily.

'Ours?' Anselmo asked.

'They seem so,' Robert Jordan said but knew that at that height you never could be sure. They could be an evening patrol of either side. But you always said pursuit planes were ours because it made people feel better. Bombers were another matter.

Anselmo evidently felt the same. 'They are ours,' he said. 'I recognize them. They are *Moscas*.'

'Good,' said Robert Jordan. 'They seem to me to be Moscas, too.'

'They are *Moscas*,' Anselmo said.

Robert Jordan could have put the glasses on them and been sure instantly but he preferred not to. It made no difference to him who they were tonight and if it pleased the old man to have them be ours, he did not want to take them away. Now, as they moved out of sight toward Segovia, they did not look to be the green, red wing-tipped, low-wing Russian conversion of the Boeing P32 that the Spaniards called Moscas. You could not see the colors but the cut was wrong. No. It was a Fascist Patrol coming home.

The sentry was still standing at the far box with his back turned.

'Let us go,' Robert Jordan said. He started up the hill, moving carefully and taking advantage of the cover until they were out of sight. Anselmo followed him at a hundred yards distance. When they were well out of sight of the bridge, he stopped and the old man came up and went into the lead and climbed steadily through the pass, up the steep slope in the dark.

'We have a formidable aviation,' the old man said happily.

'Yes.'

'And we will win.'

'We have to win.'

'Yes. And after we have won, you must come to hunt.'

'To hunt what?'

'The boar, the bear, the wolf, the ibex—'

'You like to hunt?'

'Yes, man. More than anything. We all hunt in my village. You do not like to hunt?'

'No,' said Robert Jordan. 'I do not like to kill animals.'

'With me it is the opposite,' the old man said. 'I do not like to kill men.'

'Nobody does except those who are disturbed in the head,' Robert Jordan said. 'But I feel nothing against it when it is necessary. When it is for the cause.'

'It is a different thing, though,' Anselmo said. 'In my house, when I had a house, and now I have no house, there were the tusks of boar I had shot in the lower forest. There were the hides of wolves I had shot. In the winter, hunting them in the snow. One very big one, I killed at dusk in the outskirts of the village on my way home one night in November. There were four wolf hides on the floor of my house. They were worn by stepping on them but they were wolf hides. There were the horns of ibex that I had killed in the high Sierra, and there was an eagle stuffed by an embalmer of birds of Avila, with his wings spread, and eyes as yellow and real as the eyes of an eagle alive. It was a very beautiful thing and all of those things gave me great pleasure to contemplate.'

'Yes,' said Robert Jordan.

'On the door of the church of my village was nailed the paw of a bear that I killed in the spring, finding him on a hillside in the snow, overturning a log with this same paw.'

'When was this?'

'Six years ago. And every time I saw that paw, like the hand of a man, but with those long claws, dried and nailed through the palm to the door of the church, I received a pleasure.'

'Of pride?'

'Of pride of remembrance of the encounter with the bear on that hillside in the early spring. But of the killing of a man, who is a man as we are, there is nothing good that remains.'

'You can't nail his paw to the church,' Robert Jordan said.

'No. Such a barbarity is unthinkable. Yet the hand of a man is like the paw of a bear.'

'So is the chest of a man like the chest of a bear,' Robert Jordan said. 'With the hide removed from the bear, there are many similarities in the muscles.'

'Yes,' Anselmo said. 'The gypsies believe the bear to be a brother of man.'

'So do the Indians in America,' Robert Jordan said. 'And when they kill a bear, they apologize to him and ask his pardon. They put his skull in a tree and they ask him to forgive them be fore they leave it.'

'The gypsies believe the bear to be a brother to man because he has the same body beneath his hide, because he drinks beer, be because he enjoys music and because he likes to dance.'

'So also believe the Indians?

'Are the Indians then gypsies?'

'No. But they believe alike about the bear.'

'Clearly. The gypsies also believe he is a brother because he steals for pleasure.'

'Have you gypsy blood?'

'No. But I have seen much of them and clearly, since the movement, more. There are many in the hills. To them it is not a sin to kill outside the tribe. They deny this but it is true.'

'Like the Moors.'

'Yes. But the gypsies have many laws they do not admit to having. In the war many gypsies have become bad again as they were in olden times.'

'They do not understand why the war is made. They do not know for what we fight.'

'No,' Anselmo said. 'They only know now there is a war and people may kill again as in the olden times without a surety of punishment.'

'You have killed?' Robert Jordan asked in the intimacy of the dark and of their day together.

'Yes. Several times. But not with pleasure. To me it is a sin to kill a man. Even Fascists, whom we must kill. To me there is a great difference between the bear and the man and I do not believe the wizardry of the gypsies about the brotherhood with animals. No. I am against all killing of men.'

'Yet you have killed.'

'Yes. And will again. But if I live later, I will try to live in such a way, doing no harm to any one, that it will be forgiven.'

'By whom?'

'Who knows? Since we do not have God here anymore, neither His Son nor the Holy Ghost, who forgives? 1 do not know.'

'You have not God anymore?'

'No. Man. Certainly not. If there were God, never would He have permitted what 1 have seen with my eyes. Let *them have* God.'

'They claim Him.'

'Clearly I miss Him, having been brought up in religion. But now a man must be responsible to himself.'

'Then it is thyself who will forgive thee for killing.'

'I believe so,' Anselmo said. 'Since you put it clearly m that way 1 believe that must be it. But with or without God, I think it is a sin to kill. To take the life of another is to me very grave. I will do it whenever necessary but I am not of the race of Pablo.'

'To win a war we must kill our enemies. That has always been true.'

'Clearly. In war we must kill. But I have very rare ideas,' Anselmo said.

They were walking now close together in the dark and he spoke softly, sometimes turning his head as he climbed. 'I would not kill even a Bishop. I would not kill a proprietor of any kind. I would make them work each day as we have worked in the fields and as we work in the mountains with the timber, all of the rest of their lives. So, they would see what man is born to. That they should sleep where we sleep. That they should eat as we eat. But above all that they should work.

Thus, they would learn.'

'And they would survive to enslave thee again.'

'To kill them teaches nothing,' Anselmo said. 'You cannot exterminate them because from their seed comes more with greater hatred. Prison is nothing Prison only makes hatred. That all our enemies should learn.'

'But still thou hast killed.'

'Yes,' Anselmo said. 'Many times, and will again. But not with pleasure and regarding it as a sin.'

'And the sentry. You joked of killing the sentry.'

'That was in joke. I would kill the sentry. Yes. Certainly, and with a clear heart considering our task. But not with pleasure.'

'We will leave them to those who enjoy it,' Robert Jordan said. 'There are eight and five. That is thirteen for those who enjoy it.'

'There are many of those who enjoy it,' Anselmo said in the dark. 'We have many of those. More of those than of men who would serve for a battle.'

'Hast thou ever been in a battle r'

'Nay,' the old man said. 'We fought in Segovia at the start of the movement but we were beaten and we ran. I ran with the others. We did not truly understand what we were doing, nor how it should be done. Also, I had only a shotgun with cartridges of large buckshot and the *guardia civil* had Mausers. I could not hit them with buckshot at a hundred yards, and at three hundred yards they shot us as they wished as though we were rabbits. They shot much and well and we were like sheep before them.' He was silent. Then asked, 'Thinkest thou there will be a battle at the bridge?'

'There is a chance.'

'I have never seen a battle without running,' Anselmo said. 'I do not know how I would comport myself. I am an old man and I have wondered.'

'I will respond for thee,' Robert Jordan told him.

'And hast thou been in many battles?'

'Several.'

'And what thinkest thou of this of the bridge r'

'First I think of the bridge. That my businesses. It is not difficult to destroy the bridge. Then we will make the dispositions for the rest. For the preliminaries. It will all be written.'

'Very few of these people read,' Anselmo said.

'It will be written for every one's knowledge so that all know, but also it will be clearly explained.'

'I will do that to which I am assigned,' Anselmo said. 'But remembering the shooting in Segovia, if there is to be a battle or even much exchanging of shots, I would wish to have it very clear what I must do under all circumstances to avoid running. I remember that I had a great tendency to run at Segovia.'

'We will be together,' Robert Jordan told him. 'I will tell you what there is to do at all times.'

'Then there is no problem,' Anselmo said. 'I can do anything that I am ordered.'

'For us will be the bridge and the battle, should there be one,' Robert Jordan said and saying it in the dark, he felt a little theatrical but it sounded well in Spanish.

'It should be of the highest interest,' Anselmo said and hearing him say it honestly and clearly and with no pose, neither the English pose of understatement nor any Latin bravado, Robert Jordan thought he was very lucky to have this old man and having seen the bridge and worked out and simplified the problem it would have been to surprise the posts and blow it in a normal way, he resented Golz's orders, and the necessity for them. He resented them for what they could do to him and for what they could do to this old man. They were bad orders all right for those who would have to carry them out.

And that is not the way to think, he told himself, and there is not you, and there are no people that things must not happen to. Neither you nor this old man is anything. You are instruments to do your duty. There are necessary orders that are no fault of yours and there is a bridge and that bridge can be the point on which the future of the human race can turn. As it can turn on every thing that happens in this war. You have only one thing to do and you must do it. Only one thing, hell, he thought. If it were one thing it was easy. Stop worrying, you windy bastard, he said to himself. Think about something else.

So, he thought about the girl Maria, with her skin, the hair and the eyes all the same golden tawny brown, the hair a little darker than the rest but it would be lighter as her skin tanned deeper, the smooth skin, pale gold on the surface with a darkness underneath. Smooth it would be, all of her body smooth, and she moved awkwardly as though there were something of her and about her that embarrassed her as though it were visible, though it was not, but only in her mind. And she blushed with he looked at her, and she sitting, her hands clasped around her knees and the shirt open at the throat, the cup of her breasts uptilted against the shirt, and as he thought of her, his throat was choky and there was a difficulty in walking and he and Anselmo spoke no more until the old man said, 'Now we go down through these rocks and to the camp.'

As they came through the rocks in the dark, a man spoke to them, 'Halt. Who goes?' They heard a rifle bolt snick as it was drawn back and then the knock against the wood as it was pushed forward and down on the stock.

'Comrades,' Anselmo said.

'What comrades?'

'Comrades of Pablo,' the old man told him. 'Dost thou not know us?'

'Yes,' the voice said. 'But it is an order. Have you the password? '

'No. We come from below.'

'I know,' the man said in the dark. 'You come from the bridge. I know all of that. The order is not mine. You must know the second half of a password.'

'What is the first half then?' Robert Jordan said.

'I have forgotten it,' the man said in the dark and laughed. 'Go then unprintably to the campfire with thy obscene dynamite.'

'That is called guerilla discipline,' Anselmo said. 'Uncock thy piece.'

'It is uncocked,' the man said in the dark. 'I let it down with my thumb and forefinger.'

'Thou wilt do that with a Mauser sometime which has no knurl on the bolt and it will fire.'

'This is a Mauser,' the man said. 'But I have a grip of thumb and forefinger beyond description. Always I let it down that way.'

'Where is the rifle pointed?' asked Anselmo into the dark.

'At thee,' the man said, 'all the time that I descended the bolt. And when thou comest to the camp, order that someone should relieve me because I have indescribable and unprintable hunger and I have forgotten the password.'

'How art thou called?' Robert Jordan asked.

'Agustin,' the man said. 'I am called Agustin and I am dying with boredom in this spot.'

'We will take the message,' Robert Jordan said and he thought how the word *abutment* which means boredom in Spanish was a word no peasant would use in any other language. Yet it is one of the most common words in the mouth of a Spaniard of any class.

'Listen to me,' Agustin said, and coming close he put his hand on Robert Jordan's shoulder. Then striking a flint and steel together he held it up and blowing on the end of the cork, looked at the young man's face in its glow.

'You look like the other one,' he said. 'But something different. Listen,' he put the lighter down and stood holding his rifle. 'Tell me this. Is it true about the bridge?'

'What about the bridge?'

'That we blow up an obscene bridge and then have to obscenely well obscenity ourselves off out of these mountains?'

'I know not.'

'*You* know not,' Agustin said. 'What a barbarity! Whose then is the dynamite?'

'Mine.'

'And knowest thou not what it is for? Don't tell me tales.'

'I know what it is for and so will you in time,' Robert Jordan said. 'But now we go to the camp.'

'Go to the unprintable,' Agustin said. 'And unprint thyself. But do you want me to tell you something of service to you?'

'Yes,' said Robert Jordan. 'If it is not unprintable,' naming the principal obscenity that had larded the conversation. The man, Agustin, spoke so obscenely, coupling an obscenity to every noun as an adjective, using the same obscenity as a verb, that Robert Jordan wondered if he could speak a straight sentence. Agustin laughed in the dark when he heard the word. 'It is a way of speaking I have. Maybe it is ugly. Who knows? Each one speaks according to his manner. Listen to me. The bridge is nothing to me. As well the bridge as another thing. Also, I have a boredom in these mountains. That we should go if it is needed. These mountains say nothing to me. That we should leave them. But I would say one thing. Guard well thy explosive.'

'Thank you,' Robert Jordan said. 'From thee?'

'No,' Agustin said. 'From people less unprintably equipped than I.'

'So?' asked Robert Jordan.

'You understand Spanish,' Agustin said seriously now. 'Care well for thy unprintable explosive.'

'Thank you.'

'No. Don't thank me. Look after thy stuff.'

'Has anything happened to it? '

'No, or I would not waste thy time talking in this fashion.'

'Thank you all the same. We go now to camp.'

'Good,' said Agustin, 'and that they send some one here who knows the password.'

'Will we see you at the camp?'

'Yes, man. And shortly.'

'Come on,' Robert Jordan said to Anselmo.

They were walking down the edge of the meadow now and there was a gray mist. The grass was lush underfoot after the pine-needle floor of the forest and the dew on the grass wet through their canvas rope-soled shoes. Ahead, through the trees, Robert Jordan could see a light where he knew the mouth of the cave must be.

'Agustin is a very good man,' Anselmo said. 'He speaks very filthily and always in jokes but he is a very serious man.'

'You know him well?'

'Yes. For a long time. I have much confidence in him.'

'And what he says?'

'Yes, man. This Pablo is bad now, as you could see.'

'And the best thing to do?'

'One shall guard it at all times.'

'Who?'

'You. Me. The woman and Agustin. Since he sees the danger.'

'Did you think things were as bad as they are here?'

'No,' Anselmo said. 'They have gone bad very fast. But it was necessary to come here. This is the country of Pablo and of El Sordo. In their country we must deal with them unless it is something that can be done alone.'

'And El Sordo?'

'Good,' Anselmo said. 'As good as the other is bad.'

'You believe now that he is truly bad?'

'All afternoon I have thought of it and since we have heard what we have heard, I think now, yes. Truly.'

'It would not be better to leave, speaking of another bridge, and obtain men from other bands?'

'No,' Anselmo said. 'This is his country. You could not move that he would not know it. But one must move with much precautions.'

4

They came down to the mouth of the cave, where a light shone out from the edge of a blanket that hung over the opening. The two packs were at the foot of the tree covered with a canvas and Robert Jordan knelt down and felt the canvas wet and stiff over them. In the dark he felt under the canvas in the outside pocket of one of the packs and took out a leather-covered flask and slipped it in his pocket. Unlocking the long barred padlocks that passed through the grommet that closed the opening of the mouth of the packs, and untying the drawstring at the top of each pack, he felt inside them and verified their contents with his hands. Deep in one pack he felt the bundled blocks in the sacks, the sacks wrapped in the sleeping robe, and tying the strings of that and pushing the lock shut again, he put his hands into the other and felt the sharp wood outline of the box of the old exploder, the cigar box with the caps, each little cylinder wrapped round and round with its two wires (the lot of them packed as carefully as he had packed his collection of wild bird eggs when he was a boy), the stock of the submachine gun, disconnected from the barrel and wrapped in his leather jacket, the two pans and five clips in one of the inner pockets of the big pack-sack and the small coils of copper wire and the big coil of light insulated wire in the other. In the pocket with the wire he felt his pliers and the two wooden awls for making holes in the end of the blocks and then, from the last inside pocket, he took a big box of the Russian cigarettes of the lot he had from Golz's headquarters and tying the mouth of the pack shut, he pushed the lock in, buckled the flaps down and again covered both packs with the canvas. Anselmo had gone on into the cave.

Robert Jordan stood up to follow him, then reconsidered and, lifting the canvas off the two packs, picked them up, one in each hand, and started with them, just able to carry them, for the mouth of the cave. He laid one pack down and lifted the blanket aside, then with his head stooped and with a pack in each hand, carrying by the leather shoulder straps, he went into the cave.

It was warm and smoky in the cave. There was a table along one wall with a tallow candle stuck in a bottle on it and at the table were seated Pablo, three men he did not know, and the gypsy, Rafael. The candle made shadows on the wall behind the men and Anselmo stood where he had come in to the right of the table. The wife of Pablo was standing over the charcoal fire on the open fire hearth in the corner of the cave. The girl knelt by her stirring in an iron pot. She lifted the wooden spoon out and looked at Robert Jordan as he stood there in the doorway and he saw, in the glow from the fire the woman was blowing with a bellows, the girl's face, her arm and the drops running down from the spoon and dropping into the iron pot.

'What do you carry?' Pablo said.

'My things,' Robert Jordan said and set the two packs down a little way apart where the cave opened out on the side away from the table.

'Are they not well outside?' Pablo asked.

'Someone might trip over them in the dark,' Robert Jordan said and walked over to the table and laid the box of cigarettes on it.

'I do not like to have dynamite here in the cave,' Pablo said.

'It is far from the fire,' Robert Jordan said. 'Take some cigarettes.' He ran his thumbnail along the side of the paper box with the big colored figure of a warship on the cover and pushed the box toward Pablo.

Anselmo brought him a rawhide-covered stool and he sat down at the table. Pablo looked at him as though he were going to speak again, then reached for the cigarettes.

Robert Jordan pushed them toward the others. He was not looking at them yet. But he noted one man took cigarettes and two did not. All of his concentration was on Pablo.

'How goes it, gypsy?' he said to Rafael.

'Good,' the gypsy said. Robert Jordan could tell they had been talking about him when he came in. Even the gypsy was not at ease.

'She is going to let you eat again?' Robert Jordan asked the gypsy.

'Yes. Why not?' the gypsy said. It was a long way from the friendly joking they had together in the afternoon.

The woman of Pablo said nothing and went on blowing up the coals of the fire.

'One called Agustin says he dies of boredom above,' Robert Jordan said.

'That doesn't kill,' Pablo said. 'Let him die a little.'

'Is there wine?' Robert Jordan asked the table at large, leaning forward, his hands on the table.

'There is little left,' Pablo said sullenly. Robert Jordan decided he had better look at the other three and try to see where he stood.

'In that case, let me have a cup of water. Thou,' he called to the girl. 'Bring me a cup of water.'

The girl looked at the woman, who said nothing, and gave no sign of having heard, then she went to a kettle containing water and dipped a cup full. She brought it to the table and put it down before him. Robert Jordan smiled at her. At the same time he sucked in on his stomach muscles and swung a little to the left on his stool so that his pistol slipped around on his belt closer to where he wanted it. He reached his hand down toward his hip pocket and Pablo watched him. He knew they all were watching him, too, but he watched only Pablo. His hand came up from the hip pocket with the leather-covered flask and he unscrewed the top and then, lifting the cup, drank half the water and poured very slowly from the flask into the cup.

'It is too strong for thee or I would give thee some,' he said to the girl and smiled at her again. 'There is little left or I would offer some to thee,' he said to Pablo.

'I do not like anis,' Pablo said.

The acrid smell had carried across the table and he had picked out the one familiar component.

'Good,' said Robert Jordan. 'Because there is very little left.'

'What drink is that?' the gypsy asked.

'A medicine,' Robert Jordan said. 'Do you want to taste it?'

'What is it for?'

'For everything,' Robert Jordan said. 'It cures everything. If you have anything wrong this will cure it.'

'Let me taste it,' the gypsy said.

Robert Jordan pushed the cup toward him. It was a milky yellow now with the water and he hoped the gypsy would not take more than a swallow. There was very little of it left and one cup of it took the place of the evening papers, of all the old evenings in cafes, of all chestnut trees that would be in bloom now in this month, of the great slow horses of the outer boulevards, of book shops, of kiosques, and of galleries, of the Parc Montsouris, of the Stade Buffalo, and of the Butte Chaumont, of the Guaranty Trust Company and the Ile de la Cite, of Foyot's old hotel, and of being able to read and relax in the evening; of all the things he had enjoyed and forgotten and that came back to him when he tasted that opaque, bitter, tongue-numbing, brain-warming, stomachwarming, idea-changing liquid alchemy.

The gypsy made a face and handed the cup back. 'It smells of anis but it is bitter as gall,' he said. 'It is better to be sick than have that medicine.'

'That's the wormwood,' Robert Jordan told him. 'In this, the real absinthe, there is wormwood. It's supposed to rot your brain out but I don't believe it. It only changes the ideas. You should pour water into it very slowly, a few drops at a time. But I poured it into the water.'

'What are you saying?' Pablo said angrily, feeling the mockery. 'Explaining the medicine,' Robert Jordan told him and grinned. 'I bought it in Madrid. It was the last bottle and it's lasted me three weeks.' He took a big swallow of it and felt it coasting over his tongue in delicate anesthesia. He looked at Pablo and grinned again.

'How's business?' he asked.

Pablo did not answer and Robert Jordan looked carefully at the other three men at the table. One had a large flat face, flat and brown as a Serrano ham with a nose flattened and broken, and the long thin Russian cigarette, projecting at an angle, made the face look even flatter. This man had short gray hair and a gray stubble of beard and wore the usual black smock buttoned at the neck. He looked down at the table when Robert Jordan looked at him but his eyes were steady and they did not blink. The other two were evidently brothers. They looked much alike and were both short, heavily built, dark haired, their hair growing low on their foreheads, dark-eyed and brown. One had a scar across his forehead above his left eye and as he looked at them, they looked back at him steadily. One looked to be about twenty-six or eight, the other perhaps two years older.

'What are you looking at?' one brother, the one with the scar, asked.

'Thee,' Robert Jordan said.

'Do you see anything rare?'

'No,' said Robert Jordan. 'Have a cigarette?'

'Why not?' the brother said. He had not taken any before.

'These are like the other had. He of the train.'

'Were you at the train?'

'We were all at the train,' the brother said quietly. 'All except the old man.'

'That is what we should do now,' Pablo said. 'Another train.'

'We can do that,' Robert Jordan said. 'After the bridge.'

He could see that the wife of Pablo had turned now from the fire and was listening. When he said the word bridge every one was quiet.

'After the bridge,' he said again deliberately and took a sip of the absinthe. I might as well bring it on, he thought. It's coming anyway.

'I do not go for the bridge,' Pablo said, looking down at the table. 'Neither me nor my people.'

Robert Jordan said nothing. He looked at Anselmo and raised the cup. 'Then we shall do it alone, old one,' he said and smiled.

'Without this coward,' Anselmo said.

'What did you say?' Pablo spoke to the old man.

'Nothing for thee. I did not speak to thee,' Anselmo told him.

Robert Jordan now looked past the table to where the wife of Pablo was standing by the fire. She had said nothing yet, nor given any sign. But now she said something he could not hear to the girl and the girl rose from the cooking fire, slipped along the wall, opened the blanket that hung over the mouth of the cave and went out. I think it is going to come now, Robert Jordan thought. I believe this is it. I did not want it to be this way but this seems to be the way it is.

'Then we will do the bridge without thy aid,' Robert Jordan said to Pablo.

'No,' Pablo said, and Robert Jordan watched his face sweat. 'Thou wilt blow no bridge here.'

'No?'

'Thou wilt blow no bridge,' Pablo said heavily.

'And thou?' Robert Jordan spoke to the wife of Pablo who was standing, still and huge, by the fire. She turned toward them and said, 'I am for the bridge.' Her face was lit by the fire and it was flushed and it shone warm and dark and handsome now in the firelight as it was meant to be.

'What do you say?' Pablo said to her and Robert Jordan saw the betrayed look on his face and the sweat on his forehead as he turned his head.

'I am for the bridge and against thee,' the wife of Pablo said. 'Nothing more.'

'I am also for the bridge,' the man with the flat face and the broken nose said, crushing the end of the cigarette on the table.

'To me the bridge means nothing,' one of the brothers said. 'I am for the *mujer* of Pablo.'

'Equally,' said the other brother.

'Equally,' the gypsy said.

Robert Jordan watched Pablo and as he watched, letting his right hand hang lower and lower, ready if it should be necessary, half hoping it would be (feeling perhaps that were the simplest and easiest yet not wishing to spoil what had gone so well, knowing how quickly all of a family, all of a clan, all of a band, can turn against a stranger in a quarrel, yet thinking what could be done with the hand were the simplest and best and surgically the most sound now that this had happened), saw also the wife of Pablo standing there and watched her blush proudly and soundly and healthily as the allegiances were given.

'I am for the Republic,' the woman of Pablo said happily. 'And the Republic is the bridge. Afterwards we will have time for other projects.'

'And thou,' Pablo said bitterly. 'With your head of a seed bull and your heart of a whore. Thou thinkest there will be an afterwards from this bridge? Thou hast an idea of that which will pass?'

'That which must pass,' the woman of Pablo said. 'That which must pass, will pass.'

'And it means nothing to thee to be hunted then like a beast after this thing from which we derive no profit? Nor to die in it?' 'Nothing,' the woman of Pablo said. 'And do not try to frighten me, coward.'

'Coward,' Pablo said bitterly. 'You treat a man as coward because he has a tactical sense. Because he can see the results of an idiocy in advance. It is not cowardly to know what is foolish.'

'Neither is it foolish to know what is cowardly,' said Anselmo, unable to resist making the phrase.

'Do you want to die?' Pablo said to him seriously and Robert Jordan saw how unrhetorical was the question.

'No.'

'Then watch thy mouth. You talk too much about things you do not understand. Don't you see that this is serious?' he said almost pitifully. 'Am I the only one who sees the seriousness of this?'

I believe so, Robert Jordan thought. Old Pablo, old boy, I believe so. Except me. You can see it and I see it and the woman read it in my hand but she doesn't see it, yet. Not yet she doesn't see it.

'Am I a leader for nothing?' Pablo asked. 'I know what I speak of. You others do not know. This old man talks nonsense. He is an old man who is nothing but a messenger and a guide for foreigners. This foreigner comes here to do a thing for the good of the foreigners. For his good we must be sacrificed. I am for the good and the safety of all.'

'Safety,' the wife of Pablo said. 'There is no such thing as safety. There are so many seeking safety here now that they make a great danger. In seeking safety now you lose all.'

She stood now by the table with the big spoon in her hand.

'There is safety,' Pablo said. 'Within the danger there is the safety of knowing what chances to take. It is like the bullfighter who knowing what he is doing, takes no chances and is safe.'

'Until he is gored,' the woman said bitterly. 'How many times have I heard matadors talk like that before they took a goring. How often have I heard Finito say that it is all knowledge and that the bull never gored the man; rather the man gored himself on the horn of the bull. Always do they talk that way in their arrogance before a goring. Afterwards we visit them in the clinic.' Now she was mimicking a visit to a bedside, 'Hello, old timer. Hello,' she boomed. Then, '*Buenas, Compadre*. How goes it, Pilar?' imitating the weak voice of the wounded bullfighter. 'How did this happen, Finito, *Chico*, how did this dirty accident occur to thee?' booming it out in her own voice. Then talking weak and small,' 'It is nothing, woman. Pilar, it is nothing. It shouldn't have happened. I killed him very well, you understand. Nobody could have killed him better. Then having killed him exactly as I should and him absolutely dead, swaying on his legs, and ready to fall of his own weight, I walked away from him with a certain amount of arrogance and much style and from the back he throws me this horn between the cheeks of my buttocks and it comes out of my liver.' She commenced to laugh, dropping the imitation of the almost effeminate bullfighter's voice and booming again now. 'You and your safety! Did I live nine years with three of the worst paid matadors in the world not to learn about fear and about safety? Speak to me of anything but safety. And thee. What illusions I put in thee and how they have turned out! From one year of war thou has become lazy, a drunkard and a coward.'

'In that way thou hast no right to speak,' Pablo said. 'And less even before the people and a stranger.'

'In that way will I speak,' the wife of Pablo went on. 'Have you not heard? Do you still believe that you command here?'

'Yes,' Pablo said. 'Here I command.'

'Not in joke,' the woman said. 'Here I command! Haven't you heard *la gente*? Here no one commands but me. You can stay if you wish and eat of the food and drink of the wine, but not too bloody much, and share in the work if thee wishes. But here I command.'

'I should shoot thee and the foreigner both,' Pablo said sullenly.

'Try it,' the woman said. 'And see what happens.'

'A cup of water for me,' Robert Jordan said, not taking his eyes from the man with his sullen heavy head and the woman standing proudly and confidently holding the big spoon as authoritatively as though it were a baton.

'Maria,' called the woman of Pablo and when the girl came in the door she said, 'Water for this comrade.'

Robert Jordan reached for his flask and, bringing the flask out, as he brought it he loosened the pistol in the holster and swung it on top of his thigh. He poured a second absinthe into his cup and took the cup of water the girl brought him and commenced to drip it into the cup, a little at a time. The girl stood at his elbow, watching him.

'Outside,' the woman of Pablo said to her, gesturing with the spoon.

'It is cold outside,' the girl said, her cheek close to Robert Jordan's, watching what was happening in the cup where the liquor was clouding.

'Maybe,' the woman of Pablo said. 'But in here it is too hot.' Then she said, kindly, 'It is not for long.'

The girl shook her head and went out.

I don't think he is going to take this much more, Robert Jordan thought to himself. He held the cup in one hand and his other hand rested, frankly now, on the pistol. He had slipped the safety catch and he felt the worn comfort of the checked grip chafed almost smooth and touched the round, cool companionship of the trigger guard. Pablo no longer looked at him but only at the woman. She went on, 'Listen to me, drunkard. You understand who commands here?'

'I command.'

'No. Listen. Take the wax from thy hairy ears. Listen well. I command.'

Pablo looked at her and you could tell nothing of what he was thinking by his face. He looked at her quite deliberately and then he looked across the table at Robert Jordan. He looked at him a long time contemplatively and then he looked back at the woman, again.

'All right. You command,' he said. 'And if you want he can command too. And the two of you can go to hell.' He was looking the woman straight in the face and he was neither dominated by her nor seemed to be much affected by her. 'It is possible that I am lazy and that I drink too much. You may consider me a coward but there you are mistaken. But I am not stupid.' He paused. 'That you should command and that you should like it. Now if you are a woman as well as a commander, that we should have something to eat.'

'Maria,' the woman of Pablo called.

The girl put her head inside the blanket across the cave mouth. 'Enter now and serve the supper.'

The girl came in and walked across to the low table by the hearth and picked up the enameled-ware bowls and brought them to the table.

'There is wine enough for all,' the woman of Pablo said to Robert Jordan. 'Pay no attention to what that drunkard says. When this is finished we will get more. Finish that rare thing thou art drinking and take a cup of wine.'

Robert Jordan swallowed down the last of the absinthe, feeling it, gulped that way, making a warm, small, fume-rising, wet, chemical-change-producing heat in him and passed the cup for wine. The girl dipped it full for him and smiled.

'Well, did you see the bridge?' the gypsy asked. The others, who had not opened their mouths after the change of allegiance, were all leaning forward to listen now.

'Yes,' Robert Jordan said. 'It is something easy to do. Would you like me to show you?'

'Yes, man. With much interest.'

Robert Jordan took out the notebook from his shirt pocket and showed them the sketches.

'Look how it seems,' the flat-faced man, who was named Primitivo, said. 'It is the bridge itself.'

Robert Jordan with the point of the pencil explained how the bridge should be blown and the reason for the placing of the charges.

'What simplicity,' the scarred-faced brother, who was called Andres, said. 'And how do you explode them?'

Robert Jordan explained that too and, as he showed them, he felt the girl's arm resting on his shoulder as she looked. The woman of Pablo was watching too. Only Pablo took no interest, sitting by himself with a cup of wine that he replenished by dipping into the big bowl Maria had filled from the wineskin that hung to the left of the entrance to the cave.

'Hast thou done much of this?' the girl asked Robert Jordan softly.

'Yes.'

'And can we see the doing of it?'

'Yes. Why not?'

'You will see it,' Pablo said from his end of the table. 'I believe that you will see it.'

'Shut up,' the woman of Pablo said to him and suddenly remembering what she had seen in the hand in the afternoon she was wildly, unreasonably angry. 'Shut up, coward. Shut up, bad luck bird. Shut up, murderer.'

'Good,' Pablo said. 'I shut up. It is thou who commands now and you should continue to look at the pretty pictures. But remember that 1 am not stupid.'

The woman of Pablo could feel her rage changing to sorrow and to a feeling of the thwarting of all hope and promise. She knew this feeling from when she was a girl and she knew the things that caused it all through her life. It came now suddenly and she put it away from her and would not let it touch her, neither her nor the Republic, and she said, 'Now we will eat. Serve the bowls from the pot, Maria.'

5

Robert Jordan pushed aside the saddle blanket that hung over the mouth of the cave and, stepping out, took a deep breath of the cold night air. The mist had cleared away and the stars were out. There was no wind, and, outside now of the warm air of the cave, heavy with smoke of both tobacco and charcoal, with the odor of cooked rice and meat, saffron, pimentos, and oil, the tarry, wine-spilled smell of the big skin hung beside the door, hung by the neck and the four legs extended, wine drawn from a plug fitted in one leg, wine that spilled a little onto the earth of the floor, settling the dust smell; out now from the odors of different herbs whose names he did not know that hung in bunches from the ceiling, with long ropes of garlic, away now from the copper-penny, red wine and garlic, horse sweat and man sweat dried in the clothing (acrid and gray the man sweat, sweet and sickly the dried brushed-off lather of horse sweat), of the men at the table,

Robert Jordan breathed deeply of the clear night air of the mountains that smelled of the pines and of the dew on the grass in the meadow by the stream. Dew had fallen heavily since the wind had dropped, but, as he stood there, he thought there would be frost by morning.

As he stood breathing deep and then listening to the night, he heard first, firing far away, and then he heard an owl cry in the timber below, where the horse corral was slung. Then inside the cave he could hear the gypsy starting to sing and the soft chording of a guitar.

'*I had an inheritance from my father*,' the artificially hardened voice rose harshly and hung there. Then went on:

'*It was the moon and the sun*

'*And though I roam all over the world 'The spending of it's never done.*'

The guitar thudded with chorded applause for the singer. 'Good,' Robert Jordan heard some one say. 'Give us the Catalan, gypsy.'

'No.'

'Yes. Yes. The Catalan.'

'All right,' the gypsy said and sang mournfully,

'*My nose is flat. 'My face is black.*

'*But still I am a man.*'

'Ole!' some one said. 'Go on, gypsy!'

The gypsy's voice rose tragically and mockingly.

'*Thank God I am a Negro.*

'*And not a Catalan!*'

'There is much noise,' Pablo's voice said. 'Shut up, gypsy.' 'Yes,' he heard the woman's voice. 'There is too much noise. You could call the *guardia civil* with that voice and still it has no quality.' 'I know another verse,' the gypsy said and the guitar commenced.

'Save it,' the woman told him.

The guitar stopped.

'I am not good in voice tonight. So there is no loss,' the gypsy said and pushing the blanket aside he came out into the dark.

Robert Jordan watched him walk over to a tree and then come toward him.

'Roberto,' the gypsy said softly.

'Yes, Rafael,' he said. He knew the gypsy had been affected by the wine from his voice. He himself had drunk the two absinthes and some wine but his head was clear and cold from the strain of the difficulty with Pablo.

'Why didst thou not kill Pablo?' the gypsy said very softly. 'Why kill him?'

'You have to kill him sooner or later. Why did you not approve of the moment?'

'Do you speak seriously?'

'What do you think they all waited for? What do you think the woman sent the girl away for? Do you believe that it is possible to continue after what has been said?'

'That you all should kill him.'

'*Que va*,' the gypsy said quietly. 'That is your business. Three or four times we waited for you to kill him. Pablo has no friends.'

'I had the idea,' Robert Jordan said. 'But I left it.'

'Surely all could see that. Every one noted your preparations. Why didn't you do it?'

'I thought it might molest you others or the woman.'

'*Que va*. And the woman waiting as a whore waits for the flight of the big bird. Thou art younger than thou appearest.'

'It is possible.'

'Kill him now,' the gypsy urged. 'That is to assassinate.'

'Even better,' the gypsy said very softly. 'Less danger. Go on. Kill him now.'

'I cannot in that way. It is repugnant to me and it is not how one should act for the cause.'

'Provoke him then,' the gypsy said. 'But you have to kill him. There is no remedy.'

As they spoke, the owl flew between the trees with the softness of all silence, dropping past them, then rising, the wings beating quickly, but with no noise of feathers moving as the bird hunted.

'Look at him,' the gypsy said in the dark. 'Thus should men move.'

'And in the day, blind in a tree with crows around him,' Robert Jordan said.

'Rarely,' said the gypsy. 'And then by hazard. Kill him,' he went on. 'Do not let it become difficult.'

'Now the moment is passed.'

'Provoke it,' the gypsy said. 'Or take advantage of the quiet.'

The blanket that closed the cave door opened and light came out. Some one came toward where they stood.

'It is a beautiful night,' the man said in a heavy, dull voice. 'We will have good weather.'

It was Pablo.

He was smoking one of the Russian cigarettes and in the glow, as he drew on the cigarette, his round face showed. They could see his heavy, long-armed body in the starlight.

'Do not pay any attention to the woman,' he said to Robert Jordan. In the dark the cigarette glowed bright, then showed in his hand as he lowered it. 'She is difficult sometimes. She is a good woman. Very loyal to the Republic.' The light of the cigarette jerked slightly now as he spoke. He must be talking with it in the corner of his mouth, Robert Jordan thought. 'We should have no difficulties. We are of accord. I am glad you have come.' The cigarette glowed brightly. 'Pay no attention to arguments,' he said. 'You are very welcome here.

'Excuse me now,' he said. 'I go to see how they have picketed the horses.'

He went off through the trees to the edge of the meadow and they heard a horse nicker from below.

'You see?' the gypsy said. 'Now you see? In this way has the moment escaped.'

Robert Jordan said nothing.

'I go down there,' the gypsy said angrily.

'To do what?'

'Que va, to do what. At least to prevent him leaving.'

'Can he leave with a horse from below?'

'No.'

'Then go to the spot where you can prevent him.'

'Agustin is there.'

'Go then and speak with Agustin. Tell him that which has happened.'

'Agustin will kill him with pleasure.'

'Less bad,' Robert Jordan said. 'Go then above and tell him all as it happened.'

'And then?'

'I go to look below in the meadow.'

'Good. Man. Good,' he could not see Rafael's face in the dark but he could feel him smiling. 'Now you have tightened your garters,' the gypsy said approvingly.

'Go to Agustin.' Robert Jordan said to him.'

Yes, Roberto, yes,' said the gypsy.

Robert Jordan walked through the pines, feeling his way from tree to tree to the edge of the meadow. Looking across it in the darkness, lighter here in the open from the starlight, he saw the dark bulks of the picketed horses. He counted them where they were scattered between him and the stream. There were five. Robert Jordan sat down at the foot of a pine tree and looked out across the meadow.

I am tired, he thought, and perhaps my judgment is not good. But my obligation is the bridge and to fulfill that, I must take no useless risk of myself until I complete that duty. Of course it is sometimes more of a risk not to accept chances which are necessary to take but I have done this so far, trying to let the situation take its own course. If it is true, as the gypsy says, that they expected me to kill Pablo then I should have done that. But it was never clear to me that they did expect that. For a stranger to kill where he must work with the people afterwards is very bad. It may be done in action, and it may be done if backed by sufficient discipline, but in this case I think it would be very bad, although it was a temptation and seemed a short and simple way. But I do not believe anything is that short nor that simple in this country and, while I trust the woman absolutely, I could not tell how she would react to such a drastic thing. One dying in such a place can be very ugly, dirty and repugnant. You could not tell how she would react. Without the woman there is no organization nor any discipline here and with the woman it can be very good. It would be ideal if she would kill him, or if the gypsy would (but he will not) or if the sentry, Agustin, would. Anselmo will if I ask it, though he says he is against all killing. He hates him, I believe, and he already trusts me and believes in me as a representative of what he believes in. Only he and the woman really believe in the Republic as far as I can see; nut it is too early to know that yet.

As his eyes became used to the starlight he could see that Pablo was standing by one of the horses. The horse lifted his head from grazing; then dropped it impatiently. Pablo was standing by the horse, leaning against him, moving with him as he swung with the length of the picket rope and patting him on the neck. The horse was impatient at the tenderness while he was feeding. Robert Jordan could not see what Pablo was doing, nor hear what he was saying to the horse, but he could see that he was neither unpicketing nor saddling. He sat watching him, trying to think his problem out clearly.

'Thou my big good little pony,' Pablo was saying to the horse in the dark; it was the big bay stallion he was speaking to. 'Thou lovely white-faced big beauty. Thou with the big neck arching like the viaduct of my pueblo,' he stopped. 'But arching more and much finer.' The horse was snatching grass, swinging his head sideways as he pulled, annoyed by the man and his talking. 'Thou art no woman nor a fool,' Pablo told the bay horse. 'Thou, oh, thou, thee, thee, my big little pony. Thou art no woman like a rock that is burning. Thou art no colt of a girl with cropped head and the movement of a foal still wet from its mother. Thou dost not insult nor lie nor not understand. Thou, oh, thee, oh my good big little pony.'

It would have been very interesting for Robert Jordan to have heard Pablo speaking to the bay horse but he did not hear him because now, convinced that Pablo was only down checking on his horses, and having decided that it was not a practical move to kill him at this time, he stood up and walked back to the cave. Pablo stayed in the meadow talking to the horse for a long time. The horse understood nothing that he said; only, from the tone of the voice, that they were endearments and he had been in the corral all day and was hungry now, grazing impatiently at the limits of his picket rope, and the man annoyed him. Pablo shifted the picket pin finally and stood by the horse, not talking now. The horse went on grazing and was relieved now that the man did not bother him.

6

Inside the cave, Robert Jordan sat on one of the rawhide stools in a corner by the fire listening to the woman. She was washing the dishes and the girl, Maria, was drying them and putting them away, kneeling to place them in the hollow dug in the wall that was used as a shelf.

'It is strange,' she said. 'That El Sordo has not come. He should have been here an hour ago.'

'Did you advise him to come?'

'No. He comes each night.'

'Perhaps he is doing something. Some work.'

'It is possible,' she said. 'If he does not come we must go to see him tomorrow.'

'Yes. Is it far from here?'

'No. It will be a good trip. I lack exercise.' 'Can I go?' Maria asked. 'May I go too, Pilar?'

'Yes, beautiful,' the woman said, then turning her big face, 'Isn't she pretty?' she asked Robert Jordan. 'How does she seem to thee? A little thin?'

'To me she seems very well,' Robert Jordan said. Maria filled his cup with wine. 'Drink that,' she said. 'It will make me seem even better. It is necessary to drink much of that for me to seem beautiful.'

'Then I had better stop,' Robert Jordan said. 'Already thou seemest beautiful and more.'

'That's the way to talk,' the woman said. 'You talk like the good ones. What more does she seem?'

'Intelligent,' Robert Jordan said lamely. Maria giggled and the woman shook her head sadly. 'How well you begin and how it ends, Don Roberto.'

'Don't call me Don Roberto.'

'It is a joke. Here we say Don Pablo for a joke. As we say the Senorita Maria for a joke.'

'I don't joke that way,' Robert Jordan said. 'Camarada to me is what all should be called with seriousness in this war. In the joking commences a rottenness.'

'Thou art very religious about thy politics,' the woman teased him. 'Thou makest no jokes?'

'Yes. I care much for jokes but not in the form of address. It is like a flag.'

'I could make jokes about a flag. Any flag,' the woman laughed. 'To me no one can joke of anything. The old flag of yellow and gold we called pus and blood. The flag of the Republic with the purple added we call blood, pus and permanganate. It is a joke.'

'He is a Communist,' Maria said. 'They are very serious *gente*.'

'Are you a Communist?'

'No I am an anti-fascist.'

'For a long time?'

'Since I have understood fascism.'

'How long is that?'

'For nearly ten years.'

'That is not much time,' the woman said. 'I have been a Republican for twenty years.'

'My father was a Republican all his life,' Maria said. 'It was for that they shot him.'

'My father was also a Republican all his life. Also my grandfather,' Robert Jordan said.

'In what country?'

'The United States.'

'Did they shoot them?' the woman asked.

'*Que va*,' Maria said. 'The United States is a country of Republicans. They don't shoot you for being a Republican there.'

'All the same it is a good thing to have a grandfather who was a Republican,' the woman said. 'It shows a good blood.'

'My grandfather was on the Republican national committee,' Robert Jordan said. That impressed even Maria.

'And is thy father still active in the Republic?' Pilar asked.

'No. He is dead.'

'Can one ask how he died?'

'He shot himself.'

'To avoid being tortured?' the woman asked.

'Yes,' Robert Jordan said. 'To avoid being tortured.'

Maria looked at him with tears in her eyes. 'My father,' she said, 'could not obtain a weapon. Oh, I am very glad that your father had the good fortune to obtain a weapon.'

'Yes. It was pretty lucky,' Robert Jordan said. 'Should we talk about something else?'

'Then you and me we are the same,' Maria said. She put her hand on his arm and looked in his face. He looked at her brown face and at the eyes that, since he had seen them, had never been as young as the rest of her face but that now were suddenly hungry and young and wanting.

'You could be brother and sister by the look,' the woman said. 'But I believe it is fortunate that you are not.'

'Now I know why I have felt as I have,' Maria said. 'Now it is clear.'

'*Que va*,' Robert Jordan said and reaching over, he ran his handover the top of her head. He had been wanting to do that all day and now he did it, he could feel his throat swelling. She moved her head under his hand and smiled up at him and he felt the thick but silky roughness of the cropped head rippling between his fingers. Then his hand was on her neck and then he dropped it.

'Do it again,' she said. 'I wanted you to do that all day.'

'Later,' Robert Jordan said and his voice was thick.

'And me,' the woman of Pablo said in her booming voice. 'I am expected to watch all this? I am expected not to be moved? One cannot. For fault of anything better; that Pablo should come back.'

Maria took no notice of her now, nor of the others playing cards at the table by the candlelight.

'Do you want another cup of wine, Roberto?' she asked.'

Yes,' he said. 'Why not?'

'You're going to have a drunkard like I have,' the woman of Pablo said. 'With that rare thing he drank in the cup and all. Listen to me, *Inglés*.'

'Not *Inglés*. American.'

'Listen, then, American. Where do you plan to sleep?'

'Outside. I have a sleeping robe.'

'Good,' she said. 'The night is clear?'

'And will be cold.'

'Outside then,' she said. 'Sleep thee outside. And thy materials can sleep with me.'

'Good,' said Robert Jordan.

'Leave us for a moment,' Robert Jordan said to the girl and put his hand on her shoulder.

'Why?'

'I wish to speak to Pilar.'

'Must I go?'

'Yes.'

'What is it?' the woman of Pablo said when the girl had gone over to the mouth of the cave where she stood by the big wineskin, watching the card players.

'The gypsy said I should have-' he began.

'No,' the woman interrupted. 'He is mistaken.'

'If it is necessary that I—' Robert Jordan said quietly but with difficulty.

'Thee would have done it, I believe,' the woman said. 'Nay, it is not necessary. I was watching thee. But thy judgment was good.'

'But if it is needful—'

'No,' the woman said. 'I tell you it is not needful. The mind of the gypsy is corrupt.'

'But in weakness a man can be a great danger.'

'No. Thou dost not understand. Out of this one has passed all capacity for danger.'

'I do not understand.'

'Thou art very young still,' she said. 'You will understand.' Then, to the girl, 'Come, Maria. We are not talking more.'

The girl came over and Robert Jordan reached his hand out and patted her head. She stroked under his hand like a kitten. Then he thought that she was going to cry. But her lips drew up again and she looked at him and smiled.

'Thee would do well to go to bed now,' the woman said to Robert Jordan. 'Thou hast had a long journey.'

'Good,' said Robert Jordan. 'I will get my things.'

7

He was asleep in the robe and he had been asleep, he thought, for a long time. The robe was spread on the forest floor in the lee of the rocks beyond the cave mouth and as he slept, he turned, and turning rolled on his pistol which was fastened by a lanyard to one wrist and had been by his side under the cover when he went to sleep, shoulder and back weary, leg-tired, his muscles pulled with tiredness so that the ground was soft, and simply stretching in the robe against the flannel lining was voluptuous with fatigue. Waking, he wondered where he was, knew, and then shifted the pistol from under his side and settled happily to stretch back into sleep, his hand on the pillow of his clothing that was bundled neatly around his rope-soled shoes. He had one arm around the pillow.

Then he felt her hand on his shoulder and turned quickly, his right hand holding the pistol under the robe.

'Oh, it is thee,' he said and dropping the pistol he reached both arms up and pulled her down. With his arms around her he could feel her shivering.

'Get in,' he said softly. 'It is cold out there.'

'No. I must not.'

'Get in,' he said. 'And we can talk about it later.'

She was trembling and he held her wrist now with one hand and held her lightly with the other arm. She had turned her head away.

'Get in, little rabbit,' he said and kissed her on the back of the neck.

'I am afraid.'

'No. Do not be afraid. Get in.'

'How?'

'Just slip in. There is much room. Do you want me to help you?'

'No,' she said and then she was in the robe and he was holding her tight to him and trying to kiss her lips and she was pressing her face against the pillow of clothing but holding her arms close around his neck. Then he felt her arms relax and she was shivering again as he held her.

'No,' he said and laughed. 'Do not be afraid. That is the pistol.' He lifted it and slipped it behind him.

'I am ashamed,' she said, her face away from him.

'No. You must not be. Here. Now.'

'No, I must not. I am ashamed and frightened.'

'No. My rabbit. Please.'

'I must not. If thou dost not love me.'

'I love thee.'

'I love thee. Oh, I love thee. Put thy hand on my head,' she said away from him, her face still in the pillow. He put his hand on her head and stroked it and then suddenly her face was away from the pillow and she was in his arms, pressed close against him, and her face was against his and she was crying.

He held her still and close, feeling the long length of the young body, and he stroked her head and kissed the wet saltiness of her eyes, and as she cried he could feel the rounded, firm-pointed breasts touching through the shirt she wore.

'I cannot kiss,' she said. 'I do not know how.'

'There is no need to kiss.'

'Yes. I must kiss. I must do everything.'

'There is no need to do anything. We are all right. But thou many hast clothes.'

'What should I do?'

'I will help you.'

'Is that better?'

'Yes. Much. It is not better to thee?'

'Yes. Much better. And I can go with thee as Pilar said?'

'Yes.'

'But not to a home. With thee.'

'No, to a home.'

'No. No. No. With thee and I will be thy woman.'

Now as they lay all that before had been shielded was unshielded. Where there had been roughness of fabric all was smooth with a smoothness and firm rounded pressing and a long warm coolness, cool outside and warm within, long and light and closely holding, closely held, lonely, hollow-making with contours, happy-making, young and loving and now all warmly smooth with a hollowing, chest-aching, tight-held loneliness that was such that Robert Jordan felt he could not stand it and he said, 'Hast thou loved others?'

'Never.'

Then suddenly, going dead in his arms, 'But things were done to me.'

'By whom?'

'By various.'

Now she lay perfectly quietly and as though her body were dead and turned her head away from him.

'Now you will not love me.'

'I love you,' he said.

But something had happened to him and she knew it.

'No,' she said and her voice had gone dead and flat. 'Thou wilt not love me. But perhaps thou wilt take me to the home. And I will go to the home and I will never be thy woman nor anything.'

'I love thee, Maria.'

'No. It is not true,' she said. Then as a last thing pitifully and hopefully.

'But I have never kissed any man.'

'Then kiss me now.'

'I wanted to,' she said. 'But I know not how. Where things were done to me I fought until I could not see. I fought until-until-until one sat upon my head-and I bit him-and then they tied my mouth and held my arms behind my head-and others did things to me.'

'I love thee, Maria,' he said. 'And no one has done anything to thee. Thee, they cannot touch. No one has touched thee, little rabbit.'

'You believe that?'

'I know it.'

'And you can love me?' warm again against him now.

'I can love thee more.'

'I will try to kiss thee very well.'

'Kiss me a little.'

'I do not know how.'

'Just kiss me.'

She kissed him on the cheek.

'No.'

'Where do the noses go? I always wondered where the noses would go.'

'Look, turn thy head,' and then their mouths were tight together and she lay close pressed against him and her mouth opened a little gradually and then, suddenly, holding her against him, he was happier than he had ever been, lightly, lovingly, exultingly, innerly happy and unthinking and untired and unworried and only feeling a great delight and he said, 'My little rabbit. My darling. My sweet. My long lovely.'

'What do you say?' she said as though from a great distance away.

'My lovely one,' he said.

They lay there and he felt her heart beating against his and with the side of his foot he stroked very lightly against the side of hers.

'Thee came barefooted,' he said.

'Yes.'

'Then thee knew thou wert coming to the bed.'

'Yes.'

'And you had no fear.'

'Yes. Much. But more fear of how it would be to take my shoes off.'

'And what time is it now? *lo sabes?*'

'No. Thou hast no watch?'

'Yes. But it is behind thy back.'

'Take it from there.'

'No.'

'Then look over my shoulder.'

It was one o'clock. The dial showed bright in the darkness that the robe made.

'Thy chin scratches my shoulder.'

'Pardon it. I have no tools to shave.'

'I like it. Is thy beard blond?'

'Yes.'

'And will it be long?'

'Not before the bridge. Maria, listen. Dost thou—?' 'Do I what?'

'Dost thou wish?'

'Yes. Everything. Please. And if we do everything together, the other maybe never will have been.'

'Did you think of that?'

'No. I think it in myself but Pilar told me.' 'She is very wise.'

'And another thing,' Maria said softly. 'She said for me to tell you that I am not sick. She knows about such things and she said to tell you that.'

'She told you to tell me?'

'Yes. I spoke to her and told her that I love you. I loved you when I saw you today and I loved you always but I never saw you before and I told Pilar and she said if I ever told you anything about anything, to tell you that I was not sick. The other thing she told me long ago. Soon after the train.'

'What did she say?'

'She said that nothing is done to oneself that one does not accept and that if I loved some one it would take it all away. I wished to die, you see.'

'What she said is true.'

'And now I am happy that I did not die. I am so happy that I did not die. And you can love me?'

'Yes. I love you now.'

'And I can be thy woman?'

'I cannot have a woman doing what I do. But thou art my woman now.'

'If once I am, then I will keep on. Am I thy woman now?' 'Yes, Maria. Yes, my little rabbit.'

She held herself tight to him and her lips looked for his and then found them and were against them and he felt her, fresh, new and smooth and young and lovely with the warm, scalding coolness and unbelievable to be there in the robe that was as familiar as his clothes, or his shoes, or his duty and then she said, frightenedly, 'And now let us do quickly what it is we do so that the other is all gone.'

'You want?'

'Yes,' she said almost fiercely. 'Yes. Yes. Yes.'

8

It was cold in the night and Robert Jordan slept heavily. Once he woke and, stretching, realized that the girl was there, curled far down in the robe, breathing lightly and regularly, and in the dark, bringing his head in from the cold, the sky hard and sharp with stars, the air cold in his nostrils, he put his head under the warmth of the robe and kissed her smooth shoulder. She did not wake and he rolled onto his side away from her and with his head out of the robe in the cold again, lay awake a moment feeling the long, seeping luxury of his fatigue and then the smooth tactile happiness of their two bodies touching and then, as he pushed his legs out deep as they would go in the robe, he slipped down steeply into sleep.

He woke at first daylight and the girl was gone. He knew it as he woke and, putting out his arm, he felt the robe warm where she had been. He looked at the mouth of the cave where the blanket showed frost-rimmed and saw the thin gray smoke from the crack in the rocks that meant the kitchen fire was lighted.

A man came out of the timber, a blanket worn over his head like a poncho. Robert Jordan saw it was Pablo and that he was smoking a cigarette. He's been down corralling the horses, he thought.

Pablo pulled open the blanket and went into the cave without looking toward Robert Jordan.

Robert Jordan felt with his hand the light frost that lay on the worn, spotted green balloon silk outer covering of the five-year-old down robe, then settled into it again. *Bueno*, he said to himself, feeling the familiar caress of the flannel lining as he spread his legs wide, then drew them together and then turned on his side so that his head would be away from the direction where he knew the sun would come. *Qué más da,* I might as well sleep some more.

He slept until the sound of airplane motors woke him.

Lying on his back, he saw them, a fascist patrol of three Fiats, tiny, bright, fast-moving across the mountain sky, headed in the direction from which Anselmo and he had come yesterday. The three passed and then came nine more, flying much higher in the minute, pointed formations of threes, threes and threes.

Pablo and the gypsy were standing at the cave mouth, in the shadow, watching the sky and as Robert Jordan lay still, the sky now full of the high hammering roar of motors, there was a new droning roar and three more planes came over at less than a thousand feet above the clearing. These three were Heinkel one elevens, twin-motor bombers.

Robert Jordan, his head in the shadow of the rocks, knew they would not see him, and that it did not matter if they did. He knew they could possibly see the horses in the corral if they were looking for anything in these mountains. If they were not looking for anything they might still see them but would naturally take them for some of their own cavalry mounts. Then came a new and louder droning roar and three more Heinkel one-elevens showed coming steeply, stiffly, lower yet, crossing in rigid formation, their pounding roar approaching in crescendo to an absolute of noise and then receding as they passed the clearing.

Robert Jordan unrolled the bundle of clothing that made his pillow and pulled on his shirt. It was over his head and he was pulling it down when he heard the next planes coming and he pulled his trousers on under the robe and lay still as three more of the Heinkel bi-motor bombers came over. Before they were gone over the shoulder of the mountain, he had buckled on his pistol, rolled the robe and placed it against the rocks and sat now, close against the rocks, tying his rope-soled shoes when the approaching droning turned to a greater clattering roar than ever before and nine more Heinkel light bombers came in echelons; hammering the sky apart as they went over.

Robert Jordan slipped along the rocks to the mouth of the cave where one of the brothers, Pablo, the gypsy, Anselmo, Agustin and the woman stood in the mouth looking out.

'Have there been planes like this before?' he asked.

'Never,' said Pablo. 'Get in. They will see thee.'

The sun had not yet hit the mouth of the cave. It was just now shining on the meadow by the stream and Robert Jordan knew they could not be seen in the dark, early morning shadow of the trees and the solid shade the rocks made, but he went in the cave in order not to make them nervous.

'They are many,' the woman said.

'And there will be more,' Robert Jordan said.

'How do you know?' Pablo asked suspiciously.

'Those, just now, will have pursuit planes with them.'

Just then they heard them, the higher, whining drone, and as they passed at about five thousand feet, Robert Jordan counted fifteen Fiats in echelon of echelons like a wild-goose flight of the V-shaped threes.

In the cave entrance their faces all looked very sober and Robert Jordan said, 'You have not seen this many planes?'

'Never,' said Pablo.

'There are not many at Segovia?'

'Never has there been, we have seen three usually. Sometimes six of the chasers. Perhaps three Junkers, the big ones with the three motors, with the chasers with them. Never have we seen planes like this.'

It is bad, Robert Jordan thought. This is really bad. Here is a concentration of planes which means something very bad. I must listen for them to unload. But no, they cannot have brought up the troops yet for the attack. Certainly not before tonight or tomorrow night, certainly not yet. Certainly they will not be moving anything at this hour.

He could still hear the receding drone. He looked at his watch. By now they should be over the lines, the first ones anyway. He pushed the knob that set the second hand to clicking and watched it move around. No, perhaps not yet. By now. Yes. Well over by now. Two hundred and fifty miles an hour for those one-elevens anyway Five minutes would carry them there. By now they're well beyond the pass with Castile all yellow and tawny beneath them now in the morning, the yellow crossed by white roads and spotted with the small villages and the shadows of the Heinkels moving over the land as the shadows of sharks pass over a sandy floor of the ocean.

There was no bump, bump, bumping thud of bombs. His watch ticked on.

They're going on to Colmenar, to Escorial, or to the flying field at Manzanares el Real, he thought, with the old castle above the lake with the ducks in the reeds and the fake airfield just behind the real field with the dummy planes, not quite hidden, their props turning in the wind. That's where they must be headed. They can't know about the attack, he told himself and something in him said, why can't they? They've known about all the others.

'Do you think they saw the horses?' Pablo asked.

'Those weren't looking for horses,' Robert Jordan said. 'But did they see them?'

'Not unless they were asked to look for them.'

'Could they see them?'

'Probably not,' Robert Jordan said. 'Unless the sun were on the trees.'

'It is on them very early,' Pablo said miserably.

'I think they have other things to think of besides thy horses,' Robert Jordan said.

It was eight minutes since he had pushed the lever on the stop watch and there was still no sound of bombing.

'What do you do with the watch?' the woman asked. 'I listen where they have gone.'

'Oh,' she said. At ten minutes he stopped looking at the watch knowing it would be too far away to hear, now, even allowing a minute for the sound to travel, and said to Anselmo, 'I would speak to thee.'

Anselmo came out of the cave mouth and they walked a little way from the entrance and stood beside a pine tree.

'*Qué tal?*' Robert Jordan asked him. 'How goes it?'

'All right.'

'Hast thou eaten?'

'No. No one has eaten.'

'Eat then and take something to eat at mid-day. I want you to go to watch the road. Make a note of everything that passes both up and down the road.'

'I do not write.'

'There is no need to,' Robert Jordan took out two leaves from his notebook and with his knife cut an inch from the end of his pencil. 'Take this and make a mark for tanks thus,' he drew a slanted tank, 'and then a mark for each one and when there are four, cross the four strokes for the fifth.'

'In this way we count also.'

'Good. Make another mark, two wheels and a box, for trucks. If they are empty make a circle. If they are full of troops make a straight mark. Mark for guns. Big ones, thus. Small ones, thus. Mark for cars. Mark for ambulances. Thus, two wheels and a box with a cross on it. Mark for troops on foot by companies, like this, see? A little square and then mark beside it. Mark for cavalry, like this, you see? Like a horse. A box with four legs. That is a troop of twenty horse. You understand? Each troop a mark.'

'Yes. It is ingenious.'

'Now,' he drew two large wheels with circles around them and a short line for a gun barrel. 'These are anti-tanks. They have rubber tires. Mark for them. These are anti-aircraft,' two wheels with the gun barrel slanted up. 'Mark for them also. Do you understand? Have you seen such guns?'

'Yes,' Anselmo said. 'Of course. It is clear.'

'Take the gypsy with you that he will know from what point you will be watching so you may be relieved. Pick a place that is safe, not too close and from where you can see well and comfortably. Stay until you are relieved.'

'I understand.'

'Good. And that when you come back, I should know everything that moved upon the road. One paper is for movement up. One is for movement down the road.'

They walked over toward the cave.

'Send Rafael to me,' Robert Jordan said and waited by the tree. He watched Anselmo go into the cave, the blanket falling behind him. The gypsy sauntered out, wiping his mouth with his hand.

'Que *tal?*' the gypsy said. 'Did you divert yourself last night?'

'I slept.'

'Less bad,' the gypsy said and grinned. 'Have you a cigarette? '

'Listen,' Robert Jordan said and felt in his pocket for the cigarettes. 'I wish you to go with Anselmo to a place from which he will observe the road. There you will leave him, noting the place in order that you may guide me to it or guide whoever will relieve him later. You will then go to where you can observe the saw mill and note if there are any changes in the post there.'

'What changes?'

'How many men are there now?'

'Eight. The last I knew.'

'See how many are there now. See at what intervals the guard is relieved at that bridge.'

'Intervals?'

'How many hours the guard stays on and at what time a change is made.'

'I have no watch.'

'Take mine.' He unstrapped it.

'What a watch,' Rafael said admiringly. 'Look at what complications. Such a watch should be able to read and write. Look at what complications of numbers. It's a watch to end watches.'

'Don't fool with it,' Robert Jordan said. 'Can you tell time?' 'Why not? Twelve o'clock mid-day. Hunger. Twelve o'clock midnight. Sleep. Six o'clock in the morning, hunger. Six o'clock at night, drunk. With luck. Ten o'clock at night—'

'Shut up,' Robert Jordan said. 'You don't need to be a clown. I want you to check on the guard at the big bridge and the post on the road below in the same manner as the post and the guard at the saw mill and the small bridge.'

'It is much work,' the gypsy smiled. 'You are sure there is no one you would rather send than me?'

'No, Rafael. It is very important. That you should do it very carefully and keeping out of sight with care.'

'I believe I will keep out of sight,' the gypsy said. 'Why do you tell me to keep out of sight? You think I want to be shot?'

'Take things a little seriously,' Robert Jordan said. 'This is serious.'

'Thou askest me to take things seriously? After what thou didst last night? When thou needest to kill a man and instead did what you did? You were supposed to kill one, not make one! When we have just seen the sky full of airplanes of a quantity to kill us back to our grandfathers and forward to all unborn grandsons including all cats, goats and bedbugs. Airplanes making a noise to curdle the milk in your mother's breasts as they pass over darkening the sky and roaring like lions and you ask me to take things seriously. I take them too seriously already.'

'All right,' said Robert Jordan and laughed and put his hand on the gypsy's shoulder. '*Don 't* take them too seriously then. Now finish your breakfast and go.'

'And thou?' the gypsy asked. 'What do you do?'

'I go to see El Sordo.'

'After those airplanes it is very possible that thou wilt find nobody in the whole mountains,' the gypsy said. 'There must have been many people sweating the big drop this morning when those passed.'

'Those have other work than hunting guerillas.'

'Yes,' the gypsy said. Then shook his head. 'But when they care to undertake that work.'

'*Qué va*,' Robert Jordan said. 'Those are the best of the German light bombers. They do not send those after gypsies.'

'They give me a horror,' Rafael said. 'Of such things, yes, I am frightened.'

'They go to bomb an airfield,' Robert Jordan told him as they went into the cave. 'I am almost sure they go for that.'

'What do you say?' the woman of Pablo asked. She poured him a bowl of coffee and handed him a can of condensed milk.

'There is milk? What luxury! '

'There is everything,' she said. 'And since the planes there IS Much fear. Where did you say they went?'

Robert Jordan dripped some of the thick milk into his coffee from the slit cut in the can, wiped the can on the rim of the cup, and stirred the coffee until it was light brown.

'They go to bomb an airfield I believe. They might go to Escorial and Colmenar. Perhaps all three.'

'That they should go a long way and keep away from here,' Pablo said.

'And why are they here now?' the woman asked. 'What brings them now? Never have we seen such planes. Nor in such quantity. Do they prepare an attack?'

'What movement was there on the road last night?' Robert Jordan asked. The girl Maria was close to him but he did not look at her.

'You,' the woman said. 'Fernando. You were in La Granja last night. What movement was there?'

'Nothing,' a short, open-faced man of about thirty-five with a cast in one eye, whom Robert Jordan had not seen before, answered. 'A few camions as usual. Some cars. No movement of troops while I was there.'

'You go into La Granja every night?' Robert Jordan asked him. 'I or another,' Fernando said. 'Someone goes.'

'They go for the news. For tobacco. For small things,' the woman said.

'We have people there?'

'Yes. Why not? Those who work the power plant. Some others.'

'What was the news?'

'*Pues nada.* There was nothing. It still goes badly in the north. That is not news. In the north it has gone badly now since the beginning.'

'Did you hear anything from Segovia?'

'No, *hombre*. I did not ask.'

'Do you go into Segovia?'

'Sometimes,' Fernando said. 'But there IS danger. There are controls where they ask for your papers.'

'Do you know the airfield?'

'No, *hombre*. I know where it is but I was never close to it. There, there is much asking for papers.'

'No one spoke about these planes last night?'

'In La Granja? Nobody. But they will talk about them tonight certainly. They talked about the broadcast of Quiepo de Llano. Nothing more. Oh, yes. It seems that the Republic is preparing an offensive.'

'That what?'

'That the Republic is preparing an offensive.'

'Where?'

'It is not certain. Perhaps here. Perhaps for another part of the Sierra. Hast thou heard of it?'

'They say this in La Granja?'

'Yes, *hombre*. I had forgotten it. But there is always much talk of offensives.'

'Where does this talk come from?'

'Where? Why from different people. The officers speak in the cafes in Segovia and Avila and the waiters note it. The rumors come running. Since some time they speak of an offensive by the Republic in these parts.'

'By the Republic or by the Fascists?'

'By the Republic. If it were by the Fascists all would know of it. No, this is an offensive of quite some size. Some say there are two. One here and the other over the Alto del Le6n near the Escorial. Have you heard aught of this?'

'What else did you hear?'

'*Nada, hombre*. Nothing. Oh, yes. There was some talk that the Republicans would try to blow up the bridges, if there was to be an offensive. But the bridges are guarded.'

'Art thou joking?' Robert Jordan said, sipping his coffee.

'No, *hombre*,' said Fernando.

'This one doesn't joke,' the woman said. 'Bad luck that he doesn't.'

'Then,' said Robert Jordan. 'Thank you for all the news. Did you hear nothing more?'

'No. They talk, as always, of troops to be sent to clear out these mountains. There is some talk that they are on the way. That they have been sent already from Valladolid. But they always talk in that way. It is not to give any importance to.'

'And thou,' the woman of Pablo said to Pablo almost viciously. 'With thy talk of safety.'

Pablo looked at her reflectively and scratched his chin. 'Thou,' he said. 'And thy bridges.'

'What bridges?' asked Fernando cheerfully.

'Stupid,' the woman said to him. 'Thick head. *Tonto*. Take another cup of coffee and try to remember more news.'

'Don't be angry, Pilar,' Fernando said calmly and cheerfully. 'Neither should one become alarmed at rumors. I have told thee and this comrade all that I remember.'

'You don't remember anything more?' Robert Jordan asked. 'No,' Fernando said with dignity. 'And I am fortunate to remember this because, since it was but rumors, I paid no attention to any of it.'

'Then there may have been more?'

'Yes. It is possible. But I paid no attention. For a year I have heard nothing but rumors.'

Robert Jordan heard a quick, control-breaking sniff of laughter from the girl, Maria, who was standing behind him.

'Tell us one more rumor, Fernandito,' she said and then her shoulders shook again.

'If I could remember, I would not,' Fernando said. 'It is beneath a man's dignity to listen and give importance to rumors.' 'And with this we will save the Republic,' the woman said. 'No. *You* will save it by blowing bridges,' Pablo told her.

'Go,' said Robert Jordan to Anselmo and Rafael. 'If you have eaten.'

'We go now,' the old man said and the two of them stood up. Robert Jordan felt a hand on his shoulder. It was Maria. 'Thou shouldst eat,' she said and let her hand rest there. 'Eat well so that thy stomach can support more rumors.'

'The rumors have taken the place of the appetite.'

'No. It should not be so. Eat this now before more rumors come.' She put the bowl before him.

'Do not make a joke of me,' Fernando said to her. 'I am thy good friend, Maria.'

'I do not joke at thee, Fernando. I only joke with him and he should eat or he will be hungry.'

'We should all eat,' Fernando said. 'Pilar, what passes that we are not served?'

'Nothing, man,' the woman of Pablo said and filled his bowl with the meat stew. 'Eat. Yes, that's what you *can* do. Eat now.'

'It is very good, Pilar,' Fernando said, all dignity intact.

'Thank you,' said the woman. 'Thank you and thank you again.'

'Are you angry at me?' Fernando asked.

'No. Eat. Go ahead and eat.'

'I will,' said Fernando. 'Thank you.'

Robert Jordan looked at Maria and her shoulders started shaking again and she looked away. Fernando ate steadily, a proud and dignified expression on his face, the dignity of which could not be affected even by the huge spoon that he was using or the slight dripping of juice from the stew which ran from the corners of his mouth.

'Do you like the food?' the woman of Pablo asked him.

'Yes, Pilar,' he said with his mouth full. 'It is the same as usual.'

Robert Jordan felt Maria's hand on his arm and felt her fingers tighten with delight.

'It is for *that* that you like it?' the woman asked Fernando.

'Yes,' she said. 'I see. The stew; as usual. *Como siempre*. Things are bad in the north; as usual. An offensive here; as usual. That troops come to hunt us out; as usual. You could serve as a monument to as usual.'

'But the last two are only rumors, Pilar.'

'Spain,' the woman of Pablo said bitterly. Then turned to Robert Jordan. 'Do they have people such as this in other countries?'

'There are no other countries like Spain,' Robert Jordan said politely.

'You are right,' Fernando said. 'There is no other country in the world like Spain.'

'Hast thou ever seen any other country?' the woman asked him.

'Nay,' said Fernando. 'Nor do I wish to.'

'You see?' the woman of Pablo said to Robert Jordan.

'Fernandito,' Maria said to him. 'Tell us of the time thee went to Valencia.'

'I did not like Valencia.'

'Why?' Maria asked and pressed Robert Jordan's arm again. 'Why did thee not like it?'

'The people had no manners and I could not understand them. All they did was shout *che* at one another.'

'Could they understand thee?' Maria asked.

'They pretended not to,' Fernando said.

'And what did thee there?'

'I left without even seeing the sea,' Fernando said. 'I did not like the people.'

'Oh, get out of here, you old maid,' the woman of Pablo said. 'Get out of here before you make me sick. In Valencia I had the best time of my life. *Vamos!* Valencia. Don't talk to me of Valencia.'

'What did thee there?' Maria asked. The woman of Pablo sat down at the table with a bowl of coffee, a piece of bread and a bowl of the stew.

'*Que?* what did we there. I was there when Finito had a contract for three fights at the Feria. Never have I seen so many people. Never have I seen cafes so crowded. For hours it would be impossible to get a seat and it was impossible to board the tram cars. In Valencia there was movement all day and all night.'

'But what did you do?' Maria asked.

'All things,' the woman said. 'We went to the beach and lay in the water and boats with sails were hauled up out of the sea by oxen.

The oxen driven to the water until they must swim; then harnessed to the boats, and, when they found their feet, staggering up the sand. Ten yokes of oxen dragging a boat with sails out of the sea in the morning with the line of the small waves breaking on the beach. That is Valencia.'

'But what did thee besides watch oxen?'

'We ate in pavilions on the sand. Pastries made of cooked and shredded fish and red and green peppers and small nuts like grains of rice. Pastries delicate and flaky and the fish of a richness that was incredible. Prawns fresh from the sea sprinkled with lime juice. They were pink and sweet and there were four bites to a prawn. Of those we ate many. Then we ate *paella* with fresh sea food, clams in their shells, mussels, crayfish, and small eels. Then we ate even smaller eels alone cooked in oil and as tiny as bean sprouts and curled in all directions and so tender they disappeared in the mouth without chewing. All the time drinking a white wine, cold, light and good at thirty centimos the bottle. And for an end, melon. That is the home of the melon.'

'The melon of Castile is better,' Fernando said.

'*Que va,* 'said the woman of Pablo. 'The melon of Castile is for self abuse. The melon of Valencia for eating. When I think of those melons long as one's arm, green like the sea and crisp and juicy to cut and sweeter than the early morning in summer. Aye, when I think of those smallest eels, tiny, delicate and in mounds on the plate. Also the beer in pitchers all through the afternoon, the beer sweating in its coldness in pitchers the size of water jugs.'

'And what did thee when not eating nor drinking?'

'We made love in the room with the strip wood blinds hanging over the balcony and a breeze through the opening of the top of the door which turned on hinges. We made love there, the room dark in the day time from the hanging blinds, and from the streets there was the scent of the flower market and the smell of burned powder from the firecrackers of the *traca* that ran though the streets exploding each noon during the Feria. It was a line of fireworks that ran through all the city, the firecrackers linked together and the explosions running along on poles and wires of the tramways, exploding with great noise and a jumping from pole to pole with a sharpness and a cracking of explosion you could not believe.

'We made love and then sent for another pitcher of beer with the drops of its coldness on the glass and when the girl brought it, I took it from the door and I placed the coldness of the pitcher against the back of Finito as he lay, now, asleep, not having wakened when the beer was brought, and he said, 'No, Pilar. No, woman, let me sleep.' And I said, 'No, wake up and drink this to see how cold,' and he drank without opening his eyes and went to sleep again and I lay with my back against a pillow at the foot of the bed and watched him sleep, brown and dark-haired and young and quiet in his sleep, and drank the whole pitcher, listening now to the music of a band that was passing. You,' she said to Pablo. 'Do you know aught of such things?'

'We have done things together,' Pablo said.

'Yes,' the woman said. 'Why not? And thou wert more man than Finito in your time. But never did we go to Valencia. Never did we lie in bed together and hear a band pass in Valencia.'

'It was impossible,' Pablo told her. 'We have had no opportunity to go to Valencia. Thou knowest that if thou wilt be reasonable. But, with Finito, neither did thee blow up any train.'

'No,' said the woman. 'That is what is left to us. The train. Yes. Always the train. No one can speak against that. That remains of all the laziness, sloth and failure. That remains of the cowardice of this moment. There were many other things before too. I do not want to be unjust. But no one can speak against Valencia either. You hear me?'

'I did not like it,' Fernando said quietly. 'I did not like Valencia.'

'Yet they speak of the mule as stubborn,' the woman said.

'Clean up, Maria, that we may go.'

As she said this they heard the first sound of the planes returning.

9

They stood in the mouth of the cave and watched them. The bombers were high now in fast, ugly arrow-heads beating the sky apart with the noise of their motors. They are shaped like sharks, Robert Jordan thought, the wide-finned, sharp-nosed sharks of the Gulf Stream. But these, wide-finned in silver, roaring, the light mist of their propellers in the sun, these do not move like sharks. They move like no thing there has ever been. They move like mechanized doom.

You ought to write, he told himself. Maybe you will again some time. He felt Maria holding to his arm. She was looking up and he said to her, 'What do they look like to you, *guapa?*'

'I don't know,' she said. 'Death, I think.'

'They look like planes to me,' the woman of Pablo said. 'Where are the little ones?'

'They may be crossing at another part,' Robert Jordan said. 'Those bombers are too fast to have to wait for them and have come back alone. We never follow them across the lines to fight. There aren't enough planes to risk it.'

Just then three Heinkel fighters in V formation came low over the clearing coming toward them, just over the tree tops, like clattering, wing-tilting, pinch-nosed ugly toys, to enlarge suddenly, fearfully to their actual size; pouring past in a whining roar. They were so low that from the cave mouth all of them could see the pilots, helmeted, goggled, a scarf blowing back from behind the patrol leader's head.

'*Those* can see the horses,' Pablo said.

'Those can see thy cigarette butts,' the woman said. 'Let fall the blanket.'

No more planes came over. The others must have crossed farther up the range and when the droning was gone they went out of the cave into the open.

The sky was empty now and high and blue and clear.

'It seems as though they were a dream that you wake from,' Maria said to Robert Jordan. There was not even the last almost unheard hum that comes like a finger faintly touching and leaving and touching again after the sound is gone almost past hearing.

'They are no dream and you go in and clean up,' Pilar said to her. 'What about it?' she turned to Robert Jordan. 'Should we ride or walk?'

Pablo looked at her and grunted.

'As you will,' Robert Jordan said.

'Then let us walk,' she said. 'I would like it for the liver.'

'Riding is good for the liver.'

'Yes, but hard on the buttocks. We will walk and thou' She turned to Pablo. 'Go down and count thy beasts and see they have not flown away with any.'

'Do you want a horse to ride?' Pablo asked Robert Jordan.

'No. Many thanks. What about the girl?'

'Better for her to walk,' Pilar said. 'She'll get stiff in too many places and serve for nothing.'

Robert Jordan felt his face reddening.

'Did you sleep well?' Pilar asked. Then said, 'It is true that there is no sickness. There could have been. I know not why there wasn't. There probably still is God after all, although we have abolished Him. Go on,' she said to Pablo. 'This does not concern thee. This is of people younger than thee. Made of other material. Get on.' Then to Robert Jordan, 'Agustin is looking after thy things. We go when he comes.'

It was a clear, bright day and warm now in the sun. Robert Jordan looked at the big, brown-faced woman with her kind, widely set eyes and her square, heavy face, lined and pleasantly ugly, the eyes merry, but the face sad until the lips moved. He looked at her and then at the man, heavy and stolid, moving off through the trees toward the corral. The woman, too, was looking after him.

'Did you make love?' the woman said.

'What did she say?'

'She would not tell me.'

'I neither.'

'Then you made love,' the woman said. 'Be as careful with her as you can.'

'What if she has a baby?'

'That will do no harm,' the woman said. 'That will do less harm.'

'This is no place for that.'

'She will not stay here. She will go with you.'

'And where will I go? I can't take a woman where I go.'

'Who knows? You may take two where you go.'

'That is no way to talk.'

'Listen,' the woman said. 'I am no coward, but I see things very clearly in the early morning and I think there are many that we know that are alive now who will never see another Sunday.'

'In what day are we?'

'Sunday.'

'*Que va*,' said Robert Jordan. 'Another Sunday is very far. If we see Wednesday we are all right. But I do not like to hear thee talk like this.'

'Every one needs to talk to some one,' the woman said. 'Before we had religion and other nonsense. Now for every one there should be some one to whom one can speak frankly, for all the valor that one could have one becomes very alone.'

'We are not alone. We are all together.'

'The sight of those machines does things to one,' the woman said. 'We are nothing against such machines.'

'Yet we can beat them.'

'Look,' the woman said. 'I confess a sadness to you, but do not think I lack resolution. Nothing has happened to my resolution.'

'The sadness will dissipate as the sun rises. It is like a mist.'

'Clearly,' the woman said. 'If you want it that way. Perhaps it came from talking that foolishness about Valencia. And that failure of a man who has gone to look at his horses. I wounded him much with the story. Kill him, yes. Curse him, yes. But wound him, no.'

'How came you to be with him?'

'How is one with any one? In the first days of the movement and before too, he was something. Something serious. But now he is finished. The plug has been drawn and the wine has all run out of the skin.'

'I do not like him.'

'Nor does he like you, and with reason. Last night I slept with him.' She smiled now and shook her head. *'Vamos a ver,'* she said.

'I said to him, "Pablo, why did you not kill the foreigner?"

'"He's a good boy, Pilar," he said. "He's a good boy."

'So I said, "You understand now that I command?"

'"Yes, Pilar. Yes," he said. Later in the night I hear him awake and he is crying. He is crying in a short and ugly manner as a man cries when it is as though there is an animal inside that is shaking him.

'"What passes with thee, Pablo?" I said to him and I took hold of him and held him.

'"Nothing, Pilar. Nothing."

'"Yes. Something passes with thee."

'"The people," he said. "The way they left me. The *gente*."

'"Yes, but they are with me," I said, "and I am thy woman."

'"Pilar," he said, "remember the train." Then he said, "May God aid thee, Pilar."

'"What are you talking of God for?" I said to him. "What way is that to speak?"

'"Yes," he said. "God and the *Virgen*."

'"*Que va*, God and the *Virgen*," I said to him. "Is that any way to talk?"

'"I am afraid to die, Pilar," he said. *"Tengo miedo de morir.* Dost thou understand?"

'"Then get out of bed," I said to him. "There is not room in one bed for me and thee and thy fear all together."

'Then he was ashamed and was quiet and I went to sleep but, man, he's a ruin.'

Robert Jordan said nothing.

'All my life I have had this sadness at intervals,' the woman said. 'But it is not like the sadness of Pablo. It does not affect my resolution.'

'I believe that.'

'It may be it is like the times of a woman,' she said. 'It may be it is nothing,' she paused, then went on. 'I put great illusion in the Republic. I believe firmly in the Republic and I have faith. I believe in it with fervor as those who have religious faith believe in the mysteries.'

'I believe you.'

'And you have this same faith?'

'In the Republic?'

'Yes.'

'Yes,' he said, hoping it was true.

'I am happy,' the woman said. 'And you have no fear?'

'Not to die,' he said truly.

'But other fears?'
'Only of not doing my duty as I should.'
'Not of capture, as the other had?'
'No,' he said truly. 'Fearing that, one would be so preoccupied as to be useless.'
'You are a very cold boy.'
'No,' he said. 'I do not think so.'
'No. In the head you are very cold.'
'It is that I am very preoccupied with my work.'
'But you do not like the things of life?'
'Yes. Very much. But not to interfere with my work.'
'You like to drink, I know. I have seen.'
'Yes. Very much. But not to interfere with my work.'
'And women?'
'I like them very much, but I have not given them much importance.'
'You do not care for them?'
'Yes. But I have not found one that moved me as they say they should move you.'
'I think you lie.'
'Maybe a little.'
'But you care for Maria.'
'Yes. Suddenly and very much.'
'I, too. I care for her very much. Yes. Much.'
'I, too,' said Robert Jordan, and could feel his voice thickening. 'I, too. Yes.' It gave him pleasure to say it and he said it quite formally in Spanish. 'I care for her very much.'
'I will leave you alone with her after we have seen El Sordo.'
Robert Jordan said nothing. Then he said, 'That is not necessary.'
'Yes, man. It is necessary. There is not much time.'
'Did you see that in the hand?' he asked.
'No. Do not remember that nonsense of the hand.'
She had put that away with all the other things that might do ill to the Republic.
Robert Jordan said nothing. He was looking at Maria putting away the dishes inside the cave. She wiped her hands and turned and smiled at him. She could not hear what Pilar was saying, but as she smiled at Robert Jordan she blushed dark under the tawny skin and then smiled at him again.
'There is the day also,' the woman said. 'You have the night, but there is the day, too. Clearly, there is no such luxury as in Valencia in my time. But you could pick a few wild strawberries or something.' She laughed.
Robert Jordan put his arm on her big shoulder. 'I care for thee, too,' he said. 'I care for thee very much.'
'Thou art a regular Don Juan Tenorio,' the woman said, embarrassed now with affection. 'There is a commencement of caring for every one. Here comes Agustin.'
Robert Jordan went into the cave and up to where Maria was standing. She

watched him come toward her, her eyes bright, the blush again on her cheeks and throat.

'Hello, little rabbit,' he said and kissed her on the mouth. She held him tight to her and looked in his face and said, 'Hello. Oh, hello. Hello.'

Fernando, still sitting at the table smoking a cigarette, stood up, shook his head and walked out, picking up his carbine from where it leaned against the wall.

'It is very unformal,' he said to Pilar. 'And I do not like it. You should take care of the girl.'

'I am,' said Pilar. 'That comrade is her *novio*.'

'Oh,' said Fernando. 'In that case, since they are engaged, I counter it to be perfectly normal.'

'I am pleased,' the woman said.

'Equally,' Fernando agreed gravely. '*Sa Iud*, Pilar.'

'Where are you going?'

'To the upper post to relieve Primitivo.'

'Where the hell are you going?' Agustin asked the grave little man as he came up.

'To my duty,' Fernando said with dignity.

'Thy duty,' said Agustin mockingly. 'I besmirch the milk of thy duty.' Then turning to the woman, 'Where the un-nameable is this vileness that I am to guard?'

'In the cave,' Pilar said. 'In two sacks. And I am tired of thy obscenity.'

'I obscenity in the milk of thy tiredness,' Agustin said.

'Then go and befoul thyself,' Pilar said to him without heat.

'Thy mother,' Agustin replied.

'Thou never had one,' Pilar told him, the insults having reached the ultimate formalism in Spanish in which the acts are never stated but only implied.

'What are they doing in there?' Agustin now asked confidentially.

'Nothing,' Pilar told him. '*Nada*. We are, after all, in the spring, animal.'

'Animal,' said Agustin, relishing the word. 'Animal. And thou. Daughter of the great whore of whores. I befoul myself in the milk of the sprin6time.'

Pilar slapped him on the shoulder.

'You,' she said, and laughed that booming laugh. 'You lack variety in your cursing. But you have force. Did you see the planes?' 'I un-name in the milk of their motors,' Agustin said, nodding his head and biting his lower lip.

'That's something,' Pilar said. 'That is really something. But really difficult of execution.'

'At that altitude, yes,' Agustin grinned. '*Desde luego*. But it is better to joke.'

'Yes,' the woman of Pablo said. 'It is much better to joke, and you are a good man and you joke with force.'

'Listen, Pilar,' Agustin said seriously. 'Something is preparing. It is not true?'

'How does it seem to you?'

'Of a foulness that cannot be worse. Those were many planes, woman. Many planes.'

'And thou hast caught fear from them like all the others?'

'Que va,' said Agustin. 'What do you think they are preparing?'

'Look,' Pilar said. 'From this boy coming for the bridges obviously the Republic is preparing an offensive. From these planes obviously the Fascists are preparing to meet it. But why show the planes?'

'In this war are many foolish things,' Agustin said. 'In this war there is an idiocy without bounds.'

'Clearly,' said Pilar. 'Otherwise we could not be here.'

'Yes,' said Agustfn. 'We swim within the idiocy for a year now. But Pablo is a man of much understanding. Pablo is very wily.'

'Why do you say this?'

'I say it.'

'But you must understand,' Pilar explained. 'It is now too late to be saved by wiliness and he has lost the other.'

'I understand,' said Agustin. 'I know we must go. And since we must win to survive ultimately, it is necessary that the bridges must be blown. But Pablo, for the coward that he now is, is very smart.'

'I, too, am smart.'

'No, Pilar,' Agustin said. 'You are not smart. You are brave. You are loyal. You have decision. You have intuition. Much decision and much heart. But you are not smart.'

'You believe that?' the woman asked thoughtfully.

'Yes, Pilar.'

'The boy is smart,' the woman said. 'Smart and cold. Very cold in the head.'

'Yes,' Agustin said. 'He must know his business or they would not have him doing this. But I do not know that he is smart. Pablo I *know* is smart.'

'But rendered useless by his fear and his disinclination to action.' 'But still smart.'

'And what do you say?'

'Nothing. I try to consider it intelligently. In this moment we need to act with intelligence. After the bridge we must leave at once. All must be prepared. We must know for where we are leaving and how.'

'Naturally.'

'For this Pablo. It must be done smartly.'

'I have no confidence in Pablo.'

'In this, yes.'

'No. You do not know how far he is ruined.'

'*Pero es muy vivo*. He is very smart. And if we do not do this smartly we are obscenitied.'

'I will think about it,' Pilar said. 'I have the day to think about it.'

'For the bridges; the boy,' Agustin said. 'This he must know. Look at the fine manner in which the other organized the train.'

'Yes,' Pilar said. 'It was really he who planned all.'

'You for energy and resolution,' Agustín said. 'But Pablo for the moving. Pablo for the retreat. Force him now to study it.'

'You are a man of intelligence.'

'Intelligent, yes,' Agustín said. 'But *sin picardia*. Pablo for that.'

'With his fear and all?'

'With his fear and all.'

'And what do you think of the bridges?'

'It is necessary. That I know. Two things we must do. We must leave here and we must win. The bridges are necessary if we are to win.'

'If Pablo is so smart, why does he not see that?'

'He wants things as they are for his own weakness. He wants to stay in the eddy of his own weakness. But the river is rising. Forced to a change, he will be smart in the change. *Es muy vivo.*'

'It is good that the boy did not kill him.'

'*Que va.* The gypsy wanted me to kill him last night. The gypsy is an animal.'

'You're an animal, too,' she said. 'But intelligent.'

'We are both intelligent,' Agustín said. 'But the talent is Pablo!' 'But difficult to put up with. You do not know how ruined.'

'Yes. But a talent. Look, Pilar. To make war all you need is intelligence. But to win you need talent and material.'

'I will think it over,' she said. 'We must start now. We are late.' Then, raising her voice, 'English!' she called. '*Inglés!* Come on! Let us go.'

10

'Let us rest,' Pilar said to Robert Jordan. 'Sit down here, Maria, and let us rest.'

'We should continue,' Robert Jordan said. 'Rest when we get there. I must see this man.'

'You will see him,' the woman told him. 'There is no hurry. Sit down here, Maria.'

'Come on,' Robert Jordan said. 'Rest at the top.'

'I rest now,' the woman said, and sat down by the stream. The girl sat by her in the heather, the sun shining on her hair. Only Robert Jordan stood looking across the high mountain meadow with the trout brook running through it. There was heather growing where he stood. There were gray boulders rising from the yellow bracken that replaced the heather in the lower part of the meadow and below was the dark line of the pines.

'How fa r is it to El Sordo's?' he asked.

'Not far,' the woman said. 'It is across this open country, down into the next valley and above the timber at the head of the stream. Sit thee down and forget thy seriousness.'

'I want to see him and get it over with.'

'I want to bathe my feet,' the woman said and, taking off her rope-soled shoes and pulling off a heavy wool stocking, she put her right foot into the stream. 'My God, it's cold.'

'We should have taken horses,' Robert Jordan told her.

'This is good for me,' the woman said. 'This is what I have been missing. What's the matter with you?'

'Nothing, except that I am in a hurry.'

'Then calm yourself. There is much time. What a day it is and how I am contented not to be in pine trees. You cannot imagine how one can tire of pine trees. Aren't you tired of the pines, *guapa*?'

'I like them,' the girl said. 'What can you like about them?'

'I like the odor and the feel of the needles under foot. I like the wind in the high trees and the creaking they make against each other.'

'You like anything,' Pilar said. 'You are a gift to any man if you could cook a little better. But the pine tree makes a forest of boredom. Thou hast never known a forest of beech, nor of oak, nor of chestnut. Those are forests. In such forests each tree differs and there is character and beauty. A forest of pine trees is boredom. What do you say, *Inglés*?'

'I like the pines, too.'

'*Pero, venga*,' Pilar said. 'Two of you. So do I like the pines, but we have been too long in these pines. Also I am tired of the mountains. In mountains there are only two directions. Down and up and down leads only to the road and the towns of the Fascists.'

'Do you ever go to Segovia?'

'*Que va*. With this face? This is a face that is known. How would you like to be ugly, beautiful one?' she said to Maria.

'Thou art not ugly.'

'*Vamos*, I'm not ugly. I was born ugly. All my life I have been ugly. You, *Inglés*, who know nothing about women. Do you know how an ugly woman feels? Do you know what it is to be ugly all your life and inside to feel that you are beautiful? It is very rare,' she put the other foot in the stream, then removed it. 'God, it's cold. Look at the water wagtail,' she said and pointed to the gray ball of a bird that was bobbing up and down on a stone up the stream. 'Those are no good for anything. Neither to sing nor to eat. Only to jerk their tails up and down. Give me a cigarette, *Inglés*,' she said and taking it, lit it from a flint and steel lighter in the pocket of her skirt. She puffed on the cigarette and looked at Maria and Robert Jordan.

'Life is very curious,' she said, and blew smoke from her nostrils. 'I would have made a good man, but I am all woman and all ugly. Yet many men have loved me and I have loved many men. It is curious. Listen, *Inglés*, this is interesting. Look at me, as ugly as I am. Look closely, *Inglés*.'

'Thou art not ugly.'

'*Que no*? Don't lie to me. Or,' she laughed the deep laugh. 'Has it begun to work with thee? No. That is a joke. No. Look at the ugliness. Yet one has a feeling within one that blinds a man while he loves you. You, with that feeling, blind him, and blind yourself. Then one day, for no reason, he sees you ugly as you really are and he is not blind any more and then you see yourself as ugly as he sees you and you lose your man and your feeling. Do you understand, guapa?' She patted the girl on the shoulder.

'No,' said Maria. 'Because thou art not ugly.'

'Try to use thy head and not thy heart, and listen,' Pilar said. 'I am telling you things of much interest. Does it not interest you, Inglés?'

'Yes. But we should go.'

'Que va, go. I am very well here. Then,' she went on, addressing herself to Robert Jordan now as though she were speaking to a classroom; almost as though she were lecturing. 'After a while, when you are as ugly as I am, as ugly as women can be, then, as I say, after a while the feeling, the idiotic feeling that you are beautiful, grows slowly in one again. It grows like a cabbage. And then, when the feeling is grown, another man sees you and thinks you are beautiful and it is all to do over. Now I think I am past it, but it still might come. You are lucky, guapa, that you are not ugly.'

'But I *am* ugly,' Maria insisted.

'Ask *him*,' said Pilar. 'And don't put thy feet in the stream because it will freeze them.'

'If Roberto says we should go, I think we should go,' Maria said.

'Listen to you,' Pilar said. 'I have as much at stake in this as thy Roberto and I say that we are well off resting here by the stream and that there is much time. Furthermore, I like to talk. It is the only civilized thing we have. How otherwise can we divert ourselves? Does what I say not hold interest for you, Inglés?'

'You speak very well. But there are other things that interest me more than talk of beauty or lack of beauty.'

'Then let us talk of what interests thee.' 'Where were you at the start of the movement?' 'In my town.'

'Avila?'

'Que va, Avila.'

'Pablo said he was from Avila.'

'He lies. He wanted to take a big city for his town. It was this town,' and she named a town.

'And what happened?'

'Much,' the woman said. 'Much. And all of it ugly. Even that which was glorious.'

'Tell me about it,' Robert Jordan said.

'It is brutal,' the woman said. 'I do not like to tell it before the girl.'

'Tell it,' said Robert Jordan. 'And if it is not for her, that she should not listen.'

'I can hear it,' Maria said. She put her hand on Robert Jordan's. 'There is nothing that I cannot hear.'

'It isn't whether you can hear it,' Pilar said. 'It is whether I should tell it to thee and make thee bad dreams.'

'I will not get bad dreams from a story,' Maria told her. 'You think after all that has happened with us I should get bad dreams from a story?'

'Maybe it will give the *Inglés* bad dreams.'

'Try it and see.'

'No, *Inglés*, I am not joking. Didst thou see the start of the movement in any small town?'

'No,' Robert Jordan said.

'Then thou hast seen nothing. Thou hast seen the ruin that now is Pablo, but you should have seen Pablo on that day.'

'Tell it.'

'Nay. I do not want to.'

'Tell it.'

'All right, then. I will tell it truly as it was. But thee, *guapa,* if it reaches a point that it molests thee, tell me.'

'I will not listen to it if it molests me,' Maria told her. 'It cannot be worse than many things.'

'I believe it can,' the woman said. 'Give me another cigarette, Inglés, and vamonos.'

The girl leaned back against the heather on the bank of the stream and Robert Jordan stretched himself out, his shoulders against the ground and his head against a clump of the heather. He reached out and found Maria's hand and held it in his, rubbing their two hands against the heather until she opened her hand and laid it flat on top of his as they listened.

'It was early in the morning when the *civiles* surrendered at the barracks,' Pilar began.' You had assaulted the barracks?' Robert Jordan asked.

'Pablo had surrounded it in the dark, cut the telephone wires, placed dynamite under one wall and called on the *guardia civil* to surrender. They would not. And at daylight he blew the wall open. There was fighting. Two *civiles* were killed. Four were wounded and four surrendered.

'We all lay on roofs and on the ground and at the edge of walls and of buildings in the early morning light and the dust cloud of the explosion had not yet settled, for it rose high in the air and there was no wind to carry it, and all of us were firing into the broken side of the building, loading and firing into the smoke, and from within there was still the flashing of rifles and then there was a shout from in the smoke not to fire more, and out came the four *civiles* with their hands up. A big part of the roof had fallen in and the wall was gone and they came out to surrender.

'Are there more inside?' Pablo shouted.' 'There are wounded.'

'Guard these,' Pablo said to four who had come up from where we were firing. 'Stand there. Against the wall,' he told the *civiles*. The four *civiles* stood against the wall, dirty, dusty, smoke-grimed, with the four who were guarding them pointing their guns at them and Pablo and the others went in to finish the wounded.

'After they had done this and there was no longer any noise of the wounded, neither groaning, nor crying out, nor the noise of shooting in the barracks, Pablo and the others came out and Pablo had his shotgun over his back and was carrying in his hand a Mauser pistol.

'Look, Pilar,' he said. 'This was in the hand of the officer who killed himself. Never have I fired a pistol. You,' he said to one of the guards, 'show me how it works. No. Don't show me. Tell me.' 'The four *civiles* had stood against the wall, sweating and saying nothing while the shooting had gone on inside the barracks. They were all tall men with the faces of *guardias civiles,* which is the same model of face as mine is. Except that their faces were covered with the small stubble of this their last morning of not yet being shaved and they stood there against the wall and said nothing.

'You,' said Pablo to the one who stood nearest him. 'Tell me how it works.'

'Pull the small lever down,' the man said in a very dry voice. 'Pull the receiver back and let it snap forward.'

'What is the receiver?' asked Pablo, and he looked at the four *civiles*. 'What is the receiver?'

'The block on top of the action.'

'Pablo pulled it back, but it stuck. 'What now?' he said. 'It is jammed. You have lied to me.'

'Pull it farther back and let it snap lightly forward,' the *civil* said, and I have never heard such a tone of voice. It was grayer than a morning without sunrise.

'Pablo pulled and let go as the man had told him and the block snapped forward into place and the pistol was cocked with the hammer back. It is an ugly pistol, small in the round handle, large and flat in the barrel, and unwieldy. All this time the *civiles* had been watching him and they had said nothing.

'What are you going to do with us?' one asked him.

'Shoot thee,' Pablo said.

'When?' the man asked in the same gray voice.

'Now,' said Pablo.

'Where?' asked the man.

'Here,' said Pablo. 'Here. Now. Here and now. Have you anything to say?'

'*Nada,*' said the *civil*. 'Nothing. But it is an ugly thing.'

'And you are an ugly thing,' Pablo said. 'You murderer of peasants. You who would shoot your own mother.'

'I have never killed any one,' the *civil* said. 'And do not speak of my mother.'

'Show us how to die. You, who have always done the killing.'

'There is no necessity to insult us,' another *civil* said. 'And we know how to die.'

'Kneel down against the wall with your heads against the wall,' Pablo told them. The *civiles* looked at one another.

'Kneel, I say,' Pablo said. 'Get down and kneel.'

'How does it seem to you, Paco?' one *civil* said to the tallest, who had spoken with Pablo about the pistol. He wore a corporal's stripes on his sleeves and was sweating very much although the early morning was still cool.

'It is as well to kneel,' he answered. 'It is of no importance.'

'It is closer to the earth,' the first one who had spoken said, trying to make a joke, but they were all too grave for a joke and no one smiled.

'Then let us kneel,' the first *civil* said, and the four knelt, looking very awkward with their heads against the wall and their hands by their sides, and Pablo passed behind them and shot each in turn in the back of the head with the pistol, going from one to another and putting the barrel of the pistol against the back of their heads, each man slipping down as he fired. I can hear the pistol still, sharp and yet muffled, and see the barrel jerk and the head of the man drop forward. One held his head still when the pistol touched it. One pushed his head forward and pressed his forehead against the stone. One shivered in his whole body and his head was shaking. Only one put his hands in front of his eyes, and he was the last one, and the four bodies were slumped against the wall when Pablo turned away from them and came toward us with the pistol still in his hand.

'Hold this for me, Pilar,' he said. 'I do not know how to put down the hammer,' and he handed me the pistol and stood there looking at the four guards as they lay against the wall of the barracks. All those who were with us stood there too, looking at them, and no one said anything.

'We had won the town and it was still early in the morning and no one had eaten nor had any one drunk coffee and we looked at each other and we were all powdered with dust from the blowing up of the barracks, as powdered as men are at a threshing, and I stood holding the pistol and it was heavy in my hand and I felt weak in the stomach when I looked at the guards dead there against the wall; they all as gray and as dusty as we were, but each one was now moistening with his blood the dry dirt by the wall where they lay. And as we stood there the sun rose over the far hills and shone now on the road where we stood and on the white wall of the barracks and the dust in the air was golden in that first sun and the peasant who was beside me looked at the wall of the barracks and what lay there and then looked at us and then at the sun and said, *Vaya*. a day that commences.'

'Now let us go and get coffee,' I said.

'Good, Pilar, good,' he said. And we went up into the town to the Plaza, and those were the last people who were shot in the village.'

'What happened to the others?' Robert Jordan asked. 'Were there no other fascists in the village?'

'Que *va*, were there no other fascists? There were more than twenty. But none was shot.' 'What was done?'

'Pablo had them beaten to death with flails and thrown from the top of the cliff into the river.'

'All twenty?'

'I will tell you. It is not so simple. And in my life never do I wish to see such a scene as the flailing to death in the plaza on the top of the cliff above the river.

'The town is built on the high bank above the river and there is a square there with a fountain and there are benches and there are big trees that give a shade for the benches. The balconies of the houses look out on the plaza. Six streets enter on the plaza and there is an arcade from the houses that goes around the plaza so that one can walk in the shade of the arcade when the sun is hot. On three sides of the plaza is the arcade and on the fourth side is the walk shaded by the trees beside the edge of the cliff with, far below, the river. It is three hundred feet down to the river.

'Pablo organized it all as he did the attack on the barracks. First he had the entrances to the streets blocked off with carts as though to organize the plaze for a *capea*. For an amateur bullfight. The fascists were all held in the *Ayuntamiento*, the city hall, which was the largest building on one side of the plaza. It was there the clock was set in the wall and it was in the buildings under the arcade that the club of the fascists was. And under the arcade on the sidewalk in front of their club was where they had their chairs and tables for their club. It was there, before the movement, that they were accustomed to take the aperitifs. The chairs and the tables were of wicker. It looked like a cafe but was more elegant.'

'But was there no fighting to take them?'

'Pablo had them seized in the night before he assaulted the barracks. But he had already surrounded the barracks. They were all seized in their homes at the same hour the attack started. That was intelligent. Pablo is an organizer. Otherwise he would have had people attacking him at his flanks and at his rear while he was assaulting the barracks of the *guardia civil*.

'Pablo is very intelligent but very brutal. He had this of the village well planned and well ordered. Listen. After the assault was successful, and the last four guards had surrendered, and he had shot them against the wall, and we had drunk coffee at the cafe that always opened earliest in the morning by the corner from which the early bus left, he proceeded to the organization of the plaza. Carts were piled exactly as for a *capea* except that the side toward the river was not enclosed. That was left open. Then Pablo ordered the priest to confess the fascists and give them the necessary sacraments.'

'Where was this done?'

'In the *Ayuntamiento*, as I said. There was a great crowd outside and while this was going on inside with the priest, there was some levity outside and shouting of obscenities, but most of the people were very serious and respectful. Those who made jokes were those who were already drunk from the celebration of the taking of the barracks and there were useless characters who would have been drunk at any time.

'While the priest was engaged in these duties, Pablo organized those in the plaza into two lines.

'He placed them in two lines as you would place men for a rope pulling contest, or as they stand in a city to watch the ending of a bicycle road race with just room for the cyclists to pass between, or as men stood to allow the passage of a holy image in a procession. Two meters was left between the lines and they extended from the door of the *Ayuntamiento* clear across the plaza to the edge of the cliff. So that, from the doorway of the *Ayuntamiento*, looking across the plaza, one coming out would see two solid lines of people waiting.

'They were armed with flails such as are used to beat out the grain and they were a good flail's length apart. All did not have flails, as enough flails could not be obtained. But most had flails obtained from the store of Don Guillermo Martin, who was a fascist and sold all sorts of agricultural implements. And those who did not have flails had heavy herdsman's clubs, or ox-goads, and some had wooden pitchforks; those with wooden tines that are used to fork the chaff and straw into the air after the flailing. Some had sickles and reaping hooks but these Pablo placed at the far end where the lines reached the edge of the cliff.

'These lines were quiet and it was a clear day, as today is clear, and there were clouds high in the sky, as there are now, and the plaza was not yet dusty for there had been a heavy dew in the night, and the trees cast a shade over the men in the lines and you could hear the water running from the brass pipe in the mouth of the lion and falling into the bowl of the fountain where the women bring the water jars to fill them.

'Only near the *Ayuntamiento*, where the priest was complying with his duties with the fascists, was there any ribaldry, and that came from those worthless ones who, as I said, were already drunk and were crowded around the windows shouting obscenities and jokes in bad taste in through the iron bars of the windows. Most of the men in the lines were waiting quietly and I heard one say to another, 'Will there be women?'

'And another said, 'I hope to Christ, no.'

'Then one said, 'Here is the woman of Pablo. Listen, Pilar. Will there be women?'

'I looked at him and he was a peasant dressed in his Sunday jacket and sweating heavily and I said, 'No, Joaquin. There are no women. We are not killing the women. Why should we kill their women?'

'And he said, 'Thanks be to Christ, there are no women and when does it start?'

'And I said, 'As soon as the priest finishes.'

'And the priest?'

'I don't know,' I told him and I saw his face working and the sweat coming down on his forehead. 'I have never killed a man,' he said.

'Then you will learn,' the peasant next to him said. 'But I do not think one blow with this will kill a man,' and he held his flail in both hands and looked at it with doubt.

'That is the beauty of it,' another peasant said. 'There must be many blows.'

'*They* have taken Valladolid. *They* have Avila,' some one said. 'I heard that before we came into town.'

'*They* will never take this town. *This* town is ours. We have struck ahead of them,' I said, 'Pablo is not one to wait for them to strike.'

'Pablo is able,' another said. 'But in this finishing off of the *civiles* he was egoistic. Don't you think so, Pilar?'

'Yes,' I said. 'But now all are participating in this.'

'Yes,' he said. 'It is well organized. But why do we not hear more news of the movement? '

'Pablo cut the telephone wires before the assault on the barracks. They are not yet repaired.'

'Ah,' he said. 'It is for this we hear nothing. I had my news from the road mender's station early this morning.' 'Why is this done thus, Pilar?' he said to me.

'To save bullets,' I said. 'And that each man should have his share in the responsibility.'

'That it should start then. That it should start.' And I looked at him and saw that he was crying.

'Why are you crying, Joaquin?' I asked him. 'This is not to cry about.'

'I cannot help it, Pilar,' he said. 'I have never killed any one.'

If you have not seen the day of revolution in a small town where all know all in the town and always have known all, you have seen nothing. And on this day most of the men in the double line across the plaza wore the clothes in which they worked in the fields, having come into town hurriedly, but some, not knowing how one should dress for the first day of a movement, wore their clothes for Sundays or holidays, and these, seeing that the others, including those who had attacked the barracks, wore their oldest clothes, were ashamed of being wrongly dressed. But they did not like to take off their jackets for fear of losing them, or that they might be stolen by the worthless ones, and so they stood, sweating in the sun and waiting for it to commence.

Then the wind rose and the dust was now dry in the plaza for the men walking and standing and shuffling had loosened it and it commenced to blow and a man in a dark blue Sunday jacket shouted 'Agua! Agua!' and the caretaker of the plaza, whose duty it was to sprinkle the plaza each morning with a hose, came and turned the hose on and commenced to lay the dust at the edge of the plaza, and then toward the center. Then the two lines fell back and let him lay the dust over the center of the plaza; the hose sweeping in wide arcs and the water glistening in the sun and the men leaning on their flails or the clubs or the white wood pitchforks and watching the sweep of the stream of water. And then, when the plaza was nicely moistened and the dust settled, the lines formed up again and a peasant shouted, 'When do we get the first fascist? When does the first one come out of the box?' 'Soon,' Pablo shouted from the door of the *Ayuntamiento*. 'Soon the first one comes out.' His voice was hoarse from shouting in the assault and from the smoke of the barracks. 'What's the delay?' some one asked.

'They're still occupied with their sins,' Pablo shouted.

'Clearly, there are twenty of them,' a man said.

'More,' said another.

'Among twenty there are many sins to recount.'

'Yes, but I think it's a trick to gain time. Surely facing such an emergency one could not remember one's sins except for the biggest.'

'Then have patience. For with more than twenty of them there are enough of the biggest sins to take some time.'

'I have patience,' said the other. 'But it is better to get it over with. Both for them and for us. It is July and there is much work. We have harvested but we have not threshed. We are not yet in the time of fairs and festivals.'

'But this will be a fair and festival today,' another said. 'The Fair of Liberty and from this day, when these are extinguished, the town and the land are ours.'

'We thresh fascists today,' said one, 'and out of the chaff comes the freedom of this pueblo.'

'We must administer it well to deserve it,' said another. 'Pillar,' he said tome, 'when do we have a meeting for the organization?'

'Immediately after this is completed,' I told him. 'In the same building of the *Ayuntamiento*.'

'I was wearing one of the three-cornered patent leather hats of the *guardia civil* as a joke and I had put the hammer down on the pistol, holding it with my thumb to lower it as I pulled on the trigger as seemed natural, and the pistol was held in a rope I had around my waist, the long barrel stuck under the rope. And when I put it on the joke seemed very good to me, although afterwards I wished I had taken the holster of the pistol instead of the hat. But one of the men in the line said to me, 'Pilar, daughter. It seems to me bad taste for thee to wear that hat. Now we have finished with such things as the *guardia civil*.'

'Then,' I said, 'I will take it off.' And I did.

'Give it to me,' he said. 'It should be destroyed.'

'And as we were at the far end of the line where the walk runs along the cliff by the river, he took the hat in his hand and sailed it off over the cliff with the motion a herdsman makes throwing a stone underhand at the bulls to herd them. The hat sailed far out into space and we could see it smaller and smaller, the patent leather shining in the clear air, sailing down to the river. I looked back over the square and at all the windows and all the balconies there were people crowded and there was the double line of men across the square to the doorway of the *Ayuntamiento* and the crowd swarmed outside against the windows of that building and there was the noise of many people talking, and then I heard a shout and some one said 'Here comes the first one,' and it was Don Benito Garcia, the Mayor, and he came out bareheaded walking slowly from the door and down the porch and nothing happened; and he walked between the line of men with the flails and nothing happened. He passed two men, four men, eight men, ten men and nothing happened and he was walking between that line of men, his head up, his fat face gray, his eyes looking ahead and then flickering from side to side and walking steadily. And nothing happened.

'From a balcony some one cried out, '*Que pasa, cobardes?* What is the matter, cowards?' and still Don Benito walked along between the men and nothing happened. Then I saw a man three men down from where I was standing and his face was working and he was biting his lips and his hands were white on his flail. I saw him looking toward Don Benito, watching him come on. And still nothing happened. Then, just before Don Benito came abreast of this man, the man raised his flail high so that it struck the man beside him and smashed a blow at Don Benito that hit him on the side of the head and Don Benito looked at him and the man struck again and shouted, 'That for you, *Cabron*,' and the blow hit Don Benito in the face and he raised his hands to his face and they beat him until he fell and the man who had struck him first called to others to help him and he pulled on the collar of Don Benito's shirt and others took hold of his arms and with his face in the dust of the plaza, they dragged him over the walk to the edge of the cliff and threw him over and into the river. And the man who hit him first was kneeling by the edge of the cliff looking over after him and saying, 'The Cabron! The Cabron! Oh, the Cabron!' He was a tenant of Don Benito and they had never gotten along together. There had been a dispute about a piece of land by the river that Don Benito had taken from this man and let to another and this man had long hated him. This man did not join the line again but sat by the cliff looking down where Don Benito had fallen.

'After Don Benito no one would come out. There was no noise now in the plaza as all were waiting to see who it was that would come out. Then a drunkard shouted in a great voice, 'Que *Jalga el toro!* Let the bull out!'

'Then some one from by the windows of the *Ayuntamiento* yelled, 'They won't move! They are all praying!'

'Another drunkard shouted, 'Pull them out. Come on, pull them out. The time for praying is finished.'

'But none came out and then I saw a man coming out of the door. 'It was Don Federico Gonzalez, who owned the mill and feed store and was a fascist of the first order. He was tall and thin and his hair was brushed over the top of his head from one side to the other to cover a baldness and he wore a nightshirt that was tucked into his trousers. He was barefooted as when he had been taken from his home and he walked ahead of Pablo holding his hands above his head, and Pablo walked behind him with the barrels of his shotgun pressing against the back of Don Federico Gonzalez until Don Federico entered the double line. But when Pablo left him and returned to the door of the *Ayuntamiento,* Don Federico could not walk forward, and stood there, his eyes turned up to heaven and his hands reaching up as though they would grasp the sky.

'He has no legs to walk,' some one said.

'What's the matter, Don Federico? Can't you walk?' some one shouted to him. But Don Federico stood there with his hands up and only his lips were moving.

'Get on,' Pablo shouted to him from the steps. 'Walk.'

'Don Federico stood there and could not move. One of the drunkards poked him in the backside with a flail handle and Don Federico gave a quick jump as a balky horse might, but still stood in the same place, his hands up, and his eyes up toward the sky.

'Then the peasant who stood beside me said, 'This is shameful. I have nothing against him but such a spectacle must terminate.' So he walked down the line and pushed through to where Don Federico was standing and said, 'With your permission,' and hit him a great blow alongside of the head with a club.

'Then Don Federico dropped his hands and put them over the top of his head where the bald place was and with his head bent and covered by his hands, the thin long hairs that covered the bald place escaping through his fingers, he ran fast through the double line with flails falling on his back and shoulders until he fell and those at the end of the line picked him up and swung him over the cliff. Never did he open his mouth from the moment he came out pushed by the shotgun of Pablo. His only difficulty was to move forward. It was as though he had no command of his legs.

'After Don Federico, I saw there was a concentration of the hardest men at the end of the lines by the edge of the cliff and I left there and I went to the Arcade of the *Ayuntamiento* and pushed aside two drunkards and looked in the window. In the big room of the *Ayuntamiento* they were all kneeling in a half circle praying and the priest was kneeling and praying with them. Pablo and one named *Cuatro Dedos*, Four Fingers, a cobbler, who was much with Pablo then, and two others were standing with shotguns and Pablo said to the priest, 'Who goes now?' and the priest went on praying and did not answer him.

'Listen, you,' Pablo said to the priest in his hoarse voice, 'who goes now? Who is ready now?'

'The priest would not speak to Pablo and acted as though he were not there and I could see Pablo was becoming very angry.

'Let us all go together,' Don Ricardo Montalvo, who was a land owner, said to Pablo, raising his head and stopping praying to speak.

'*Que va,*' said Pablo. 'One at a time as you are ready.'

'Then I go now,' Don Ricardo said. 'I'll never be any more ready.' The priest blessed him as he spoke and blessed him again as he stood up, without interrupting his praying, and held up a crucifix for Don Ricardo to kiss and Don Ricardo kissed it and then turned and said to Pablo, 'Nor ever again as ready. You *Cabron* of the bad milk. Let us go.'

'Don Ricardo was a short man with gray hair and a thick neck and he had a shirt on with no collar. He was bow-legged from much horseback riding. 'Goodby,' he said to all those who were kneeling. 'Don't be sad. To die is nothing. The only bad thing is to die at the hands of this *canalla*. Don't touch me,' he said to Pablo. 'Don't touch me with your shotgun.'

'He walked out of the front of the *Ayuntamiento* with his gray hair and his small gray eyes and his thick neck looking very short and angry. He looked at the double line of peasants and he spat on the ground. He could spit actual saliva which, in such a circumstance, as you should know, *Inglés*, is very rare and he said, '*Arriba Espana!* Down with the miscalled Republic and I obscenity in the milk of your fathers.'

'So they clubbed him to death very quickly because of the insult, beating him as soon as he reached the first of the men, beating him as he tried to walk with his head up, beating him until he fell and chopping at him with reaping hooks and the sickles, and many men bore him to the edge of the cliff to throw him over and there was blood now on their hands and on their clothing, and now began to be the feeling that these who came out were truly enemies and should be killed.

'Until Don Ricardo came out with that fierceness and calling those insults, many in the line would have given much, I am sure, never to have been in the line. And if any one had shouted from the line, 'Come, let us pardon the rest of them. Now they have had their lesson,' I am sure most would have agreed.

'But Don Ricardo with all his bravery did a great disservice to the others. For he aroused the men in the line and where, before, they were performing a duty and with no great taste for it, now they were angry, and the difference was apparent.

'Let the priest out and the thing will go faster,' some one shouted. 'Let out the priest.'

'We've had three thieves, let us have the priest. 'Two thieves,' a short peasant said to the man who had shouted. 'It was two thieves with Our Lord.'

'Whose Lord?' the man said, his face angry and red. 'In the manner of speaking it is said Our Lord.'

'He isn't my Lord; not in joke,' said the other. 'And thee hadst best watch thy mouth if thou dost not want to walk between the lines.'

'I am as good a Libertarian Republican as thou,' the short peasant said. 'I struck Don Ricardo across the mouth. I struck Don Federico across the back. I missed Don Benito. But I say Our Lord is the formal way of speaking of the man in question and that it was two thieves.'

'I obscenity in the milk of thy Republicanism. You speak of Don this and Don that.'

'Here are they so called.'

'Not by me, the *cabrones*. And thy Lord-Hi! Here comes a new one!'

'It was then that we saw a disgraceful sight, for the man who walked out of the doorway of the *Ayuntamiento* was Don Faustino Rivero, the oldest son of his father, Don Celestino Rivero, a land owner. He was tall and his hair was yellow and it was freshly combed back from his forehead for he always carried a comb in his pocket and he had combed his hair now before coming out. He was a great annoyer of girls, and he was a coward, and he had always wished to be an amateur bullfighter. He went much with gypsies and with bullfighters and with bull raisers and delighted to wear the Andalucian costume, but he had no courage and was considered a joke. One time he was announced to appear in an amateur benefit fight for the old people's home in Avila and to kill a bull from on horseback in the Andalucian style, which he had spent much time practising, and when he had seen the size of the bull that had been substituted for him in place of the little one, weak in the legs, he had picked out himself, he had said he was sick and, some said, put three fingers down his throat to make himself vomit.

'When the lines saw him, they commenced to shout, '*Hola,* Don Faustino. Take care not to vomit.'

'Listen to me, Don Faustino. There are beautiful girls over the cliff.'

'Don Faustino. Wait a minute and we will bring out a bull bigger than the other.'

'And another shouted, 'Listen to me, Don Faustino. Hast thou ever heard speak of death?'

'Don Faustino stood there, still acting brave. He was still under the impulse that had made him announce to the others that he was going out. It was the same impulse that had made him announce himself for the bullfight. That had made him believe and hope that he could be an amateur matador. Now he was inspired by the example of Don Ricardo and he stood there looking both handsome and brave and he made his face scornful. But he could not speak.

'Come, Don Faustino,' some one called from the line. 'Come, Don Faustino. Here is the biggest bull of all.'

'Don Faustino stood looking out and I think as he looked, that there was no pity for him on either side of the line. Still he looked both handsome and superb; but time was shortening and there was only one direction to go.

'Don Faustino,' some one called. 'What are you waiting for, Don Faustino?'

'He is preparing to vomit,' some one said and the lines laughed.

'Don Faustino,' a peasant called. 'Vomit if it will give thee pleasure. To me it is all the same.'

'Then, as we watched, Don Faustino looked along the lines and across the square to the cliff and then when he saw the cliff and the emptyness beyond, he turned quickly and ducked back toward the entrance of the *Ayuntamiento*.

'All the lines roared and some one shouted in a high voice, 'Where do you go, Don Faustino? Where do you go?'

'He goes to throw up,' shouted another and they all laughed again.

'Then we saw Don Faustino coming out again with Pablo behind him with the shotgun. All of his style was gone now. The sight of the lines had taken away his type and his style and he came out now with Pablo behind him as though Pablo were cleaning a street and Don Faustino was what he was pushing ahead of him. Don Faustino came out now and he was crossing himself and praying and then he put his hands in front of his eyes and walked down the steps toward the lines.

'Leave him alone,' some one shouted. 'Don't touch him.'

'The lines understood and no one made a move to touch Don Faustino and, with his hands shaking and held in front of his eyes, and with his mouth moving, he walked along between the lines.

'No one said anything and no one touched him and, when he was halfway through the lines, he could go no farther and fell to his knees.

'No one struck him. I was walking along parallel to the line to see what happened to him and a peasant leaned down and lifted him to his feet and said, 'Get up, Don Faustino, and keep walking. The bull has not yet come out.'

'Don Faustino could not walk alone and the peasant in a black smock helped him on one side and another peasant in a black smock and herdsman's boots helped him on the other, supporting him by the arms and Don Faustino walking along between the lines with his hands over his eyes, his lips never quiet, and his yellow hair slicked on his head and shining in the sun, and as he passed the peasants would say, 'Don Faustino, *buen provecho*. Don Faustino, that you should have a good appetite,' and others said, 'Don Faustino, *a sus ordenes*. Don Faustino at your orders,' and one, who had failed at bullfighting himself, said, 'Don Faustino. *Matador, a sus ordenes,*' and another said, 'Don Faustino, there are beautiful girls in heaven, Don Faustino.' And they walked Don Faustino through the lines, holding him close on either side, holding him up as he walked, with him with his hands over his eyes. But he must have looked through his fingers, because when they came to the edge of the cliff with him, he knelt again, throwing himself down and clutching the ground and holding to the grass, saying, 'No. No. No. Please. NO. Please. Please. No. No.'

'Then the peasants who were with him and the others, the hard ones of the end of the line, squatted quickly behind him as he knelt, and gave him a rushing push and he was over the edge without ever having been beaten and you heard him crying loud and high as he fell.

'It was then I knew that the lines had become cruel and it was first the insults of Don Ricardo and second the cowardice of Don Faustino that had made them so.

'Let us have another,' a peasant called out and another peasant slapped him on the back and said, 'Don Faustino! What a thing! Don Faustino!'

'He's seen the big bull now,' another said. 'Throwing up will never help him, now.'

'In my life,' another peasant said, 'in my life I've never seen a thing like Don Faustino.'

'There are others,' another peasant said. 'Have patience. Who knows what we may yet see?'

'There may be giants and dwarfs,' the first peasant said. 'There may be Negroes and rare beasts from Africa. But for me never, never will there be anything like Don Faustino. But let's have another one! Come on. Let's have another one!'

'The drunkards were handing around bottles of anis and cognac that they had looted from the bar of the club of the fascists, drinking them down like wine, and many of the men in the lines were beginning to be a little drunk, too, from drinking after the strong emotion of Don Benito, Don Federico, Don Ricardo and especially Don Faustino. Those who did not drink from the bottles of liquor were drinking from leather wineskins that were passed about and one handed a wineskin to me and I took a long drink, letting the wine run cool down my throat from the leather *bota* for I was very thirsty, too.

'To kill gives much thirst,' the man with the wineskin said to me.

'*Que va*,' I said. 'Hast thou killed?'

'We have killed four,' he said, proudly. 'Not counting the *civiles*. Is it true that thee killed one of the *civiles*, Pilar?'

'Not one,' I said. 'I shot into the smoke when the wall fell, as did the others. That is all.'

'Where got thee the pistol, Pilar?'

'From Pablo. Pablo gave it to me after he killed the *civiles*.'

'Killed he them with this pistol?'

'With no other,' I said. 'And then he armed me with it.' 'Can I see it, Pilar? Can I hold it?'

'Why not, man?' I said, and I took it out from under the rope and handed it to him. But I was wondering why no one else had come out and just then who should come out but Don Guillermo Martin from whose store the flails, the herdsman's clubs, and the wooden pitchforks had been taken. Don Guillermo was a fascist but otherwise there was nothing against him.

'It is true he paid little to those who made the flails but he charged little for them too and if one did not wish to buy flails from Don Guillermo, it was possible to make them for nothing more than the cost of the wood and the leather. He had a rude way of speaking and he was undoubtedly a fascist and a member of their club and he sat at noon and at evening in the cane chairs of their club to read *El Debate,* to have his shoes shined, and to drink vermouth and seltzer and eat roasted almonds, dried shrimps, and anchovies. But one does not kill for that, and I am sure if it had not been for the insults of Don Ricardo Montalvo and the lamentable spectacle of Don Faustino, and the drinking consequent on the emotion of them and the others, some one would have shouted, "That Don Guillermo should go in peace. We have his flails. Let him go."

'Because the people of this town are as kind as they can be cruel and they have a natural sense of justice and a desire to do that which is right. But cruelty had entered into the lines and also drunkenness or the beginning of drunkenness and the lines were not as they were when Don Benito had come out. I do not know how it is in other countries, and no one cares more for the pleasure of drinking than I do, but in Spain drunkenness, when produced by other elements than wine, is a thing of great ugliness and the people do things that they would not have done. Is it not so in your country, *Inglés?*'

'It is so,' Robert Jordan said. 'When I was seven years old and going with my mother to attend a wedding in the state of Ohio at which I was to be the boy of a pair of boy and girl who carried flowers–'

'Did you do that?' asked Maria. 'How nice!'

'In this town a Negro was hanged to a lamp post and later burned. It was an arc light. A light which lowered from the post to the pavement. And he was hoisted, first by the mechanism which was used to hoist the arc light but this broke—'

'A Negro,' Maria said. 'How barbarous!'

'Were the people drunk?' asked Pilar. 'Were they drunk thus to burn a Negro?'

'I do not know,' Robert Jordan said. 'Because I saw it only looking out from under the blinds of a window in the house which stood on the corner where the arc light was. The street was full of people and when they lifted the Negro up for the second time—'

'If you had only seven years and were in a house, you could not tell if they were drunk or not,' Pilar said.

'As I said, when they lifted the Negro up for the second time, my mother pulled me away from the window, so I saw no more,' Robert Jordan said. 'But since I have had experiences which demonstrate that drunkenness is the same in my country. It is ugly and brutal.'

'You were too young at seven,' Maria said. 'You were too young for such things. I have never seen a Negro except in a circus. Unless the Moors are Negroes.'

'Some are Negroes and some are not,' Pilar said. 'I can talk to you of the Moors.'

'Not as I can,' Maria said. 'Nay, not as I can.'

'Don't speak of such things,' Pilar said. 'It is unhealthy. Where were we?'

'Speaking of the drunkenness of the lines,' Robert Jordan said. 'Go on.'

'It is not fair to say drunkenness,' Pilar said. 'For, yet, they were a long way from drunkenness. But already there was a change in them, and when Don Guillermo came out, standing straight, near-sighted, gray-headed, of medium height, with a shirt with a collar button but no collar, standing there and crossing himself once and looking ahead, but seeing little without his glasses, but walking forward well and calmly, he was an appearance to excite pity. But some one shouted from the line, 'Here, Don Guillermo. Up here, Don Guillermo. In this direction. Here we all have your products.'

'They had had such success joking at Don Faustino that they could not see, now, that Don Guillermo was a different thing, and if Don Guillermo was to be killed, he should be killed quickly and with dignity.

'Don Guillermo,' another shouted. 'Should we send to the house for thy spectacles?'

'Don Guillermo's house was no house, since he had not much money and was only a fascist to be a snob and to console himself that he must work for little, running a wooden-implement shop. He was a fascist, too, from the religiousness of his wife which he accepted as his own due to his love for her. He lived in an apartment in the building three houses down the square and when Don Guillermo stood there, looking near-sightedly at the lines, the double lines he knew he must enter, a woman started to scream from the balcony of the apartment where he lived. She could see him from the balcony and she was his wife.

'Guillermo,' she cried. 'Guillermo. Wait and I will be with thee.' Don Guillermo turned his head toward where the shouting came from. He could not see her. He tried to say something but he could not. Then he waved his hand in the direction the woman had called from and started to walk between the lines.

'Guillermo!' she cried. 'Guillermo! Oh, Guillermo!' She was holding her hands on the rail of the balcony and shaking back and forth. 'Guillermo!'

'Don Guillermo waved his hand again toward the noise and walked into the lines with his head up and you would not have known what he was feeling except for the color of his face.

'Then some drunkard yelled, 'Guillermo!' from the lines, imitating the high cracked voice of his wife and Don Guillermo rushed toward the man, blindly, with tears now running down his cheeks and the man hit him hard across the face with his flail and Don Guillermo sat down from the force of the blow and sat there crying, but not from fear, while the drunkards beat him and one drunkard jumped on top of him, astride his shoulders, and beat him with a bottle. After this many of the men left the lines and their places were taken by the drunkards who had been jeering and saying things in bad taste through the windows of the *Ayuntamiento.*

'I myself had felt much emotion at the shooting of the *guardia civil* by Pablo,' Pilar said. 'It was a thing of great ugliness, but I had thought if this is how it must be, this is how it must be, and at least there was no cruelty, only the depriving of life which, as we all have learned in these years, is a thing of ugliness but also a necessity to do if we are to win, and to preserve the Republic.

'When the square had been closed off and the lines formed, I had admired and understood it as a conception of Pablo, although it seemed to me to be somewhat fantastic and that it would be necessary for all that was to be done to be done in good taste if it were not to be repugnant. Certainly if the fascists were to be executed by the people, it was better for all the people to have a part in it, and I wished to share the guilt as much as any, just as I hoped to share in the benefits when the town should be ours. But after Don Guillermo I felt a feeling of shame and distaste, and with the coming of the drunkards and the worthless ones into the lines, and the abstention of those who left the lines as a protest after Don Guillermo, I wished that I might disassociate myself altogether from the lines, and I walked away, across the square, and sat down on a bench under one of the big trees that gave shade there.

'Two peasants from the lines walked over, talking together, and one of them called to me, 'What passes with thee, Pilar?'

'Nothing, man,' I told him.

'Yes,' he said. 'Speak. What passes.'

'I think that I have a belly-full,' I told him.

'Us, too,' he said and they both sat down on the bench. One of them had a leather wineskin and he handed it to me.

'Rinse out thy mouth,' he said and the other said, going on with the talking they had been engaged in, 'The worst is that it will bring bad luck. Nobody can tell me that such things as the killing of Don Guillermo in that fashion will not bring bad luck.'

'Then the other said, 'If it is necessary to kill them all, and I am not convinced of that necessity, let them be killed decently and without mockery.'

'Mockery is justified in the case of Don Faustino,' the other said. 'Since he was always a farcer and was never a serious man. But to mock such a serious man as Don Guillermo is beyond all right.'

'I have a belly-full,' I told him, and it was literally true because I felt an actual sickness in all of me inside and a sweating and a nausea as though I had swallowed bad sea food.

'Then, nothing,' the one peasant said. 'We will take no further part in it. But I wonder what happens in the other towns.'

'They have not repaired the telephone wires yet,' I said. 'It is a lack that should be remedied.'

'Clearly,' he said. 'Who knows but what we might be better employed putting the town into a state of defense than massacring people with this slowness and brutality.'

'I will go to speak with Pablo, I told them and I stood up from the bench and started toward the arcade that led to the door of the *Ayuntamiento* from where the lines spread across the square. The lines now were neither straight nor orderly and there was much and very grave drunkenness. Two men had fallen down and lay on their backs in the middle of the square and were passing a bottle back and forth between them. One would take a drink and then shout, *Viva la Anarquial'* lying on his back and shouting as though he were a madman. He had a red-and-black handkerchief around his neck. The other shouted, *Viva la Libertad!*' and kicked his feet in the air and then bellowed, *Viva la Libertadl*' again. He had a red-and-black handkerchief too and he waved it in one hand and waved the bottle with the other.

'A peasant who had left the lines and now stood in the shade of the arcade looked at them in disgust and said, 'They should shout, 'Long live drunkenness.' That's all they believe in.'

'They don't believe even in that,' another peasant said. 'Those neither understand nor believe in anything.'

'Just then, one of the drunkards got to his feet and raised both arms with his fists clenched over his head and shouted, 'Long live Anarchy and Liberty and I obscenity in the milk of the Republic!' 'The other drunkard who was still lying on his back, took hold of the ankle of the drunkard who was shouting and rolled over, so that the shouting drunkard fell with him, and they rolled over together and then sat up and the one who had pulled the other down put his arm around the shouter's neck and then handed the shouter a bottle and kissed the red-and-black handkerchief he wore and they both drank together.

'Just then, a yelling went up from the lines and, looking up the arcade, I could not see who it was that was coming out because the man's head did not show above the heads of those crowded about the door of the *Ayuntamiento*. All I could see was that some one was being pushed out by Pablo and Cuatro Dedos with their shotguns but I could not see who it was and I moved on close toward the lines where they were packed against the door to try to see.

'There was much pushing now and the chairs and the tables of the fascists' cafe had been overturned except for one table on which a drunkard was lying with his head hanging down and his mouth open and I picked up a chair and set it against one of the pillars and mounted on it so that I could see over the heads of the crowd.

'The man who was being pushed out by Pablo and Cuatro Dedos was Don Anastasio Rivas, who was an undoubted fascist and the fattest man in the town. He was a grain buyer and the agent for several insurance companies and he also loaned money at high rates of interest. Standing on the chair, I saw him walk down the steps and toward the lines, his fat neck bulging over the back of the collar band of his shirt, and his bald head shining in the sun, but he never entered them because there was a shout, not as of different men shouting, but of all of them. It was an ugly noise and was the cry of the drunken lines all yelling together and the lines broke with the rush of men toward him and I saw Don Anastasio throw himself down with his hands over his head and then you could not see him for the men piled on top of him. And when the men got up from him, Don Anastasio was dead from his head being beaten against the stone flags of the paving of the arcade and there were no more lines but only a mob.

'We're going in,' they commenced to shout. 'We're going in after them.'

'He's too heavy to carry,' a man kicked at the body of Don Anastasio, who was lying there on his face. 'Let him stay there.'

'Why should we lug that tub of tripe to the cliff? Let him lie there.'

'We are going to enter and finish with them inside,' a man shouted. 'We're going in.'

'Why wait all day in the sun?' another yelled. 'Come on. Let us go.'

'The mob was now pressing into the arcade. They were shouting and pushing and they made a noise now like an animal and they were all shouting 'Open up! Open up!' for the guards had shut the doors of the *Ayuntamiento* when the lines broke.

'Standing on the chair, I could see in through the barred window into the hall of the *Ayuntamiento* and in there it was as it had been before. The priest was standing, and those who were left were kneeling in a half circle around him and they were all praying Pablo was sitting on the big table in front of the Mayor's chair with his shotgun slung over his back. His legs were hanging down from the table and he was rolling a cigarette. Cuatro Dedos was sitting in the Mayor's chair with his feet on the table and he was smoking a cigarette. All the guards were sitting in different chairs of the administration holding their guns. The key to the big door was on the table beside Pablo.

'The mob was shouting, 'Open up! Open up! Open up!' as though it were a chant and Pablo was sitting there as though he did not hear them. He said something to the priest but I could not hear what he said for the noise of the mob.

'The priest, as before, did not answer him but kept on praying. With many people pushing me, I moved the chair close against the wall, shoving it ahead of me as they shoved me from behind. I stood on the chair with my face close against the bars of the window and held on by the bars. A man climbed on the chair too and stood with his arms around mine, holding the wider bars.

'The chair will break,' I said to him.

'What does it matter?' he said. 'Look at them. Look at them pray.'

'His breath on my neck smelled like the smell of the mob, sour, like vomit on paving stones and the smell of drunkenness, and then he put his mouth against the opening in the bars with his head over my shoulder, and shouted, 'Open up! Open!' and it was as though the mob were on my back as a devil is on your back in a dream.

'Now the mob was pressed tight against the door so that those in front were being crushed by all the others who were pressing and from the square a big drunkard in a black smock with a redand-black handkerchief around his neck, ran and threw himself against the press of the mob and fell forward onto the pressing men and then stood up and backed away and then ran forward again and threw himself against the backs of those men who were pushing, shouting, 'Long live me and long live Anarchy.'

'As I watched, this man turned away from the crowd and went and sat down and drank from a bottle and then, while he was sitting down, he saw Don Anastasio, who was still lying face down on the stones, but much trampled now, and the drunkard got up and went over to Don Anastasio and leaned over and poured out of the bottle onto the head of Don Anastasio and onto his clothes, and then he took a matchbox out of his pocket and lit several matches, trying to make a fire with Don Anastasio. But the wind was blowing hard now and it blew the matches out and after a little the big drunkard sat there by Don Anastasio, shaking his head and drinking out of the bottle and every once in a while, leaning over and patting Don Anastasio on the shoulders of his dead body.

'All this time the mob was shouting to open up and the man on the chair with me was holding tight to the bars of the window and shouting to open up until it deafened me with his voice roaring past my ear and his breath foul on me and I looked away from *watching* the drunkard who had been trying to set fire to Don Anastasio and into the hall of the *Ayuntamiento* again; and it was just as it had been. They were still praying as they had been, the men all kneeling, with their shirts open, some with their heads down, others with their heads up, looking toward the priest and toward the crucifix that he held, and the priest praying fast and hard and looking out over their heads, and in back of them Pablo, with his cigarette now lighted, was sitting there on the table swinging his legs, his shotgun slung over his back, and he was playing with the key.

'I saw Pablo speak to the priest again, leaning forward from the table and I could not hear what he said for the shouting. But the priest did not answer him but went on praying. Then a man stood up from among the half circle of those who were praying and I saw he wanted to go out. It was Don Jose Castro, whom every one called Don Pepe, a confirmed fascist, and a dealer in horses, and he stood up now small, neat-looking even unshaven and wearing a pajama top tucked into a pair of gray-striped trousers. He kissed the crucifix and the priest blessed him and he stood up and looked at Pablo and jerked his head toward the door.

'Pablo shook his head and went on smoking. I could see Don Pepe say something to Pablo but could not hear it. Pablo did not answer; he simply shook his head again and nodded toward the door.

'Then I saw Don Pepe look full at the door and realized that he had not known it was locked. Pablo showed him the key and he stood looking at it an instant and then he turned and went and knelt down again. I saw the priest look around at Pablo and Pablo grinned at him and showed him the key and the priest seemed to realize for the first time that the door was locked and he seemed as though he started to shake his head, but he only inclined it and went back to praying.'

'I do not know how they could not have understood the door was locked unless it was that they were so concentrated on their praying and their own thoughts; but now they certainly understood and they understood the shouting and they must have known now that all was changed. But they remained the same as before.

'By now the shouting was so that you could hear nothing and the drunkard who stood on the chair with me shook with his hands at the bars and yelled, 'Open up! Open up!' until he was hoarse.

'I watched Pablo speak to the priest again and the priest did not answer. Then I saw Pablo unsling his shotgun and he reached over and tapped the priest on the shoulder with it. The priest paid no attention to him and I saw Pablo shake his head. Then he spoke over his shoulder to Cuatro Dedas and Cuatro Dedas spoke to the other guards and they all stood up and walked back to the far end of the room and stood there with their shotguns.

'I saw Pablo say something to Cuatro Dedas and he moved over two tables and some benches and the guards stood behind them with their shotguns. It made a barricade in that corner of the room. Pablo leaned over and tapped the priest on the shoulder again with the shotgun and the priest did not pay attention to him but I saw Don Pepe watching him while the others paid no attention but went on praying. Pablo shook his head and, seeing Don Pepe looking at him, he shook his head at Don Pepe and showed him the key, holding it up in his hand. Don Pepe understood and he dropped his head and commenced to pray very fast.

'Pablo swung his legs down from the table and walked around it to the big chair of the Mayor on the raised platform behind the long council table. He sat down in it and rolled himself a cigarette, all the time watching the fascists who were praying with the priest. You could not see any expression on his face at all. The key was on the table in front of him. It was a big key of iron, over a foot long. Then Pablo called to the guards something I could not hear and one guard went down to the door. I could see them all praying faster than ever and I knew that they all knew now.

'Pablo said something to the priest but the priest did not answer. Then Pablo leaned forward, picked up the key and tossed it underhand to the guard at the door. The guard caught it and Pablo smiled at him. Then the guard put the key in the door, turned it, and pulled the door toward him, ducking behind it as the mob rushed in.

'I saw them come in and just then the drunkard on the chair with me commenced to shout 'Ayee! Ayee! Ayee!' and pushed his head forward so 1 could not see and then he shouted 'Kill them! Kill them! Club them! Kill them!' and he pushed me aside with his two arms and 1 could see nothing.

'I hit my elbow into his belly and 1 said, 'Drunkard, whose chair is this? Let me see.'

'But he just kept shaking his hands and arms against the bars and shouting, 'Kill them! Club them! Club them! that's it. Club them! Kill them! *Cabrones! Cabrones! Cabronesf'*

'I hit him hard with my elbow and said, '*Cabron!* Drunkard! Let me see.'

'Then he put both his hands on my head to push me down and so he might see better and leaned all his weight on my head and went on shouting, 'Club them! that's it. Club them!'

'Club yourself,' I said and I hit him hard where it would hurt him and it hurt him and he dropped his hands from my head and grabbed himself and said. '*No hay derecho, mujer.* This, woman, you have no right to do.' And in that moment, looking through the bars, I saw the hall full of men flailing away with clubs and striking with flails, and poking and striking and pushing and heaving against people with the white wooden pitchforks that now were red and with their tines broken, and this was going on all over the room while Pablo sat in the big chair with his shotgun on his knees, watching, and they were shouting and clubbing and stabbing and men were screaming as horses scream in a fire. And 1 saw the priest with his skirts tucked up scrambling over a bench and those after him were chopping at him with the sickles and the reaping hooks and then some one had hold of his robe and there was another scream and another scream and 1 saw two men chopping into his back with sickles while a third man held the skirt of his robe and the priest's arms were up and he was clinging to the back of a chair and then the chair 1 was standing on broke and the drunkard and I were on the pavement that smelled of spilled wine and vomit and the drunkard was shaking his finger at me and saying, '*No hay derecho, mujer, no hay derecho.* You could have done me an injury,' and the people were trampling over us to get into the hall of the *Ayuntamiento* and all I could see was legs of people going in the doorway and the drunkard sitting there facing me and holding himself where I had hit him.

'That was the end of the killing of the fascists in our town and I was glad I did not see more of it and, but for that drunkard, I would have seen it all. So he served some good because in the *Ayuntamiento* it was a thing one is sorry to have seen.

'But the other drunkard was something rarer still. As we got up after the breaking of the chair, and the people were still crowding into the *Ayuntamiento*, I saw this drunkard of the square with his red-and-black scarf, again pouring something over Don Anastasio. He was shaking his head from side to side and it was very hard for him to sit up, but he was pouring and lighting matches and then pouring and lighting matches and I walked over to him and said, 'What are you doing, shameless?'

'*Nada, mujer, nada,*' he said. 'Let me alone.'

'And perhaps because I was standing there so that my legs made a shelter from the wind, the match caught and a blue flame began to run up the shoulder of the coat of Don Anastasio and onto the back of his neck and the drunkard put his head up and shouted in a huge voice, 'They're burning the dead! They're burning the dead'

'Who?' somebody said.

'Where?' shouted some one else.

'Here,' bellowed the drunkard. 'Exactly here!'

'Then some one hit the drunkard a great blow alongside the head with a flail and he fell back, and lying on the ground, he looked up at the man who had hit him and then shut his eyes and crossed his hands on his chest, and lay there beside Don Anastasio as though he were asleep. The man did not hit him again and he lay there and he was still there when they picked up Don Anastasio and put him with the others in the cart that hauled them all over to the cliff where they were thrown over that evening with the others after there had been a cleaning up in the *Ayuntamiento*. It would have been better for the town if they had thrown over twenty or thirty of the drunkards, especially those of the red-andblack scarves, and if we ever have another revolution I believe they should be destroyed at the start. But then we did not know this. But in the next days we were to learn.

'But that night we did not know what was to come. After the slaying in the *Ayuntamiento* there was no more killing but we could not have a meeting that night because there were too many drunkards. It was impossible to obtain order and so the meeting was postponed until the next day.

'That night I slept with Pablo. I should not say this to you, *guapa*, but on the other hand, it is good for you to know everything and at least what I tell you is true. Listen to this, *Inglés*. It is very curious.

'As I say, that night we ate and it was very curious. It was as after a storm or a flood or a battle and every one was tired and no one spoke much. I, myself, felt hollow and not well and I was full of shame and a sense of wrongdoing and I had a great feeling of oppression and of bad to come, as this morning after the planes. And certainly, bad came within three days.

'Pablo, when we ate, spoke little.

'Did you like it, Pilar?' he asked finally with his mouth full of roast young goat. We were eating at the inn from where the busses leave and the room was crowded and people were singing and there was difficulty serving.

'No,' I said. 'Except for Don Faustino, I did not like it.'

'I liked it,' he said.

'All of it?' I asked him.

'All of it,' he said and cut himself a big piece of bread with his knife and commenced to mop up gravy with it. 'All of it, except the priest.'

'You didn't like it about the priest?' because I knew he hated priests even worse than he hated fascists.

'He was a disillusionment to me,' Pablo said sadly.

'So many people were singing that we had to almost shout to hear one another.

'Why?'

'He died very badly,' Pablo said. 'He had very little dignity.'

'How did you want him to have dignity when he was being chased by the mob?' I said. 'I thought he had much dignity all the time before. All the dignity that one could have.'

'Yes,' Pablo said. 'But in the last minute he was frightened.'

'Who wouldn't be?' I said. 'Did you see what they were chasing him with?'

'Why would I not see?' Pablo said. 'But I find he died badly.'

'In such circumstances any one dies badly,' I told him. 'What do you want for your money? Everything that happened in the *Ayuntamiento* was scabrous.'

'Yes,' said Pablo. 'There was little organization. But a priest. He has an example to set. '

'I thought you hated priests.'

'Yes,' said Pablo and cut some more bread. 'But a *Spanish* priest. A *Spanish* priest should die very well.'

'I think he died well enough,' I said. 'Being deprived of all formality.'

'No,' Pablo said. 'To me he was a great disillusion. All day I had waited for the death of the priest. I had thought he would be the last to enter the lines. I awaited it with great anticipation. I expected something of a culmination. I had never seen a priest die.'

'There is time,' I said to him sarcastically. 'Only today did the movement start.'

'No,' he said. 'I am disillusioned.'

'Now,' I said. 'I suppose you will lose your faith.'

'You do not understand, Pilar,' he said. 'He was a *Spanish* priest.' 'What people the Spaniards are,' I said to him. And what a people they are for pride, eh, *Inglis*? What a people.'

'We must get on,' Robert Jordan said. He looked at the sun. 'It's nearly noon.'

'Yes,' Pilar said. 'We will go now. But let me tell you about Pablo. That night he said to me, 'Pilar, tonight we will do nothing.'

'Good,' I told him. 'That pleases me.'

'I think it would be bad taste after the killing of so many people.'

'*Que va*', I told him. 'What a saint you are. You think I lived years with bullfighters not to know how they are after the Corrida?'

'Is it true, Pilar?' he asked me.

'When did I lie to you?' I told him.

'It is true, Pilar, I am a finished man this night. You do not reproach me?'

'No, *hombre*,' I said to him. 'But don't kill people every day, Pablo.'

'And he slept that night like a baby and I woke him in the morning at daylight but I could not sleep that night and I got up and sat in a chair and looked out of the window and I could see the square in the moonlight where the lines had been and across the square the trees shining in the moonlight, and the darkness of their shadows, and the benches bright too in the moonlight, and the scattered bottles shining, and beyond the edge of the cliff where they had all been thrown. And there was no sound but the splashing of the water in the fountain and I sat there and I thought we have begun badly.

'The window was open and up the square from the Fonda I could hear a woman crying. I went out on the balcony standing there in my bare feet on the iron and the moon shone on the faces of all the buildings of the square and the crying was coming from the balcony of the house of Don Guillermo. It was his wife and she was on the balcony kneeling and crying.

'Then I went back inside the room and I sat there and I did not wish to think for that was the worst day of my life until one other day.'

'What was the other?' Maria asked.

'Three days later when the fascists took the town.'

'Do not tell me about it,' said Maria. 'I do not want to hear it. This is enough. This was too much.'

'I told you that you should not have listened,' Pilar said. 'See. I did not want you to hear it. Now you will have bad dreams.'

'No,' said Maria. 'But I do not want to hear more.'

'I wish you would tell me of it sometime,' Robert Jordan said. 'I will,' Pilar said. 'But it is bad for Maria.'

'I don't want to hear it,' Maria said pitifully. 'Please, Pilar. And do not tell it if I am there, for I might listen in spite of myself.'

Her lips were working and Robert Jordan thought she would cry. 'Please, Pilar, do not tell it.'

'Do not worry, little cropped head,' Pilar said. 'Do not worry. But I will tell the *Inglis* sometime.'

'But I want to be there when he is there,' Maria said. 'Oh, Pilar, do not tell it at all.'

'I will tell it when thou art working.'

'No. No. Please. Let us not tell it at all,' Maria said.

'It is only fair to tell it since I have told what we did,' Pilar said. 'But you shall never hear it.'

'Are there no pleasant things to speak of?' Maria said. 'Do we have to talk always of horrors?'

'This afternoon,' Pilar said, 'thou and *Inglis*. The two of you can speak of what you wish.'

'Then that the afternoon should come,' Maria said. 'That it should come flying.'

'It will come,' Pilar told her. 'It will come flying and go the same way and tomorrow will fly, too.'

'This afternoon,' Maria said. 'This afternoon. That this afternoon should come.'

11

As they came up, still deep in the shadow of the pines, after dropping down from the high meadow into the wooden valley and climbing up it on a trail that paralleled the stream and then left it to gain, steeply, the top of a rim-rock formation, a man with a carbine stepped out from behind a tree.

'Halt,' he said. Then, '*Hola*, Pilar. Who is this with thee?'

'An *Inglés*,' Pilar said. 'But with a Christian name-Roberto. And what an obscenity of steepness it is to arrive here.'

'*Salud, Camarada*,' the guard said to Robert Jordan and put out his hand. 'Are you well?'

'Yes,' said Robert Jordan. 'And thee?'

'Equally,' the guard said. He was very young, with a light build, thin, rather hawk-nosed face, high cheekbones and gray eyes. He wore no hat, his hair was black and shaggy and his handclasp was strong and friendly. His eyes were friendly too.

'Hello, Maria,' he said to the girl. 'You did not tire yourself?'

'*Que va,* Joaquin,' the girl said. 'We have sat and talked more than we have walked.'

'Are you the dynamiter?' Joaquin asked. 'We have heard you were here.'

'We passed the night at Pablo's,' Robert Jordan said. 'Yes, I am the dynamiter.'

'We are glad to see you,' Joaquin said. 'Is it for a train?' 'Were you at the last train?' Robert Jordan asked and smiled.

'Was I not,' Joaquin said. 'That's where we got this,' he grinned at Maria. 'You are pretty now,' he said to Maria. 'Have they told thee how pretty?'

'Shut up, Joaquin, and thank you very much,' Maria said. 'You'd be pretty with a haircut.'

'I carried thee,' Joaquin told the girl. 'I carried thee over my shoulder.'

'As did many others,' Pilar said in the deep voice. 'Who didn't carry her? Where is the old man?'

'At the camp.'

'Where was he last night?'

'In Segovia.'

'Did he bring news?'

'Yes,' Joaquin said, 'there is news.'

'Good or bad?'

'I believe bad.'

'Did you see the planes?'

'Ay,' said Joaquin and shook his head. 'Don't talk to me of that. Comrade Dynamiter, what planes were those?'

'Heinkel one eleven bombers. Heinkel and Fiat pursuit,' Robert Jordan told him.

'What were the big ones with the low wings?' 'Heinkel one elevens.'

'By any names they are as bad,' Joaquin said. 'But I am delaying you. I will take you to the commander.'

'The commander?' Pilar asked.

Joaquin nodded seriously. 'I like it better than "chief",' he said. 'It is more military.'

'You are militarizing heavily,' Pilar said and laughed at him. 'No,' Joaquin said. 'But I like military terms because it makes orders clearer and for better discipline.'

'Here is one according to thy taste, *Inglés,*' Pilar said. 'A very serious boy.'

'Should I carry thee?' Joaquin asked the girl and put his arm on her shoulder and smiled in her face.

'Once was enough,' Maria told him. 'Thank you just the same.' 'Can you remember it?' Joaquin asked her.

'I can remember being carried,' Maria said. 'By you, no. I remember the gypsy because he dropped me so many times. But I thank thee, Joaquin, and I'll carry thee sometime.'

'I can remember it well enough,' Joaquin said. 'I can remember holding thy two legs and thy belly was on my shoulder and thy head over my back and thy arms hanging down against my back.'

'Thou hast much memory,' Maria said and smiled at him. 'I remember nothing of that. Neither thy arms nor thy shoulders nor thy back.'

'Do you want to know something? Joaquin asked her. 'What is it?'

'I was glad thou wert hanging over my back when the shots were coming from behind us.'

'What a swine,' Maria said. 'And was it for this the gypsy too carried me so much?'

'For that and to hold onto thy legs.' 'My heroes,' Maria said. 'My saviors.'

'Listen, *guapa*,' Pilar told her. 'This boy carried thee much, and in that moment thy legs said nothing to any one. In that moment only the bullets talked clearly. And if he would have dropped thee he could soon have been out of range of the bullets.' 'I have thanked him,' Maria said. 'And I will carry him sometime. Allow us to joke. I do not have to cry, do I, because he carried me?'

'I'd have dropped thee,' Joaquin went on teasing her. 'But I was afraid Pilar would shoot me.'

'I shoot no one,' Pilar said.

'*No hace faIta*,' Joaquin told her. 'You don't need to. You scare them to death with your mouth.'

'What a way to speak,' Pilar told him. 'And you used to be such a polite little boy. What did you do before the movement, little boy?'

'Very little,' Joaquin said. 'I was sixteen.' 'But what, exactly?'

'A few pairs of shoes from time to time.' 'Make them?'

'No. Shine them.'

'*Que va*,' said Pilar. 'There is more to it than that.' She looked at his brown face, his lithe build, his shock of hair, and the quick heel-and-toe way that he walked. 'Why did you fail at it?'

'Fail at what?'

'What? You know what. You're growing the pigtail now.'

'I guess it was fear,' the boy said.

'You've a nice figure,' Pilar told him. 'But the face isn't much. So it was fear, was it? You were all right at the train.'

'I have no fear of them now,' the boy said. 'None. And we have seen much worse things and more dangerous than the bulls. It is clear no bull is as dangerous as a machine gun. But if I were in the ring with one now I do not know if I could dominate my legs.'

'He wanted to be a bullfighter,' Pilar explained to Robert Jordan. 'But he was afraid.'

'Do you like the bulls, Comrade Dynamiter?' Joaquin grinned, showing white teeth.

'Very much,' Robert Jordan said. 'Very, very much.' 'Have you seen them in Valladolid?' asked Joaquin. 'Yes. In September at the feria.'

'That's my town,' Joaquin said. 'What a fine town but how the *buena gente,* the good people of that town, have suffered in this war.' Then, his face grave, 'There they shot my father. My mother. My brother-in-law and now my sister.'

'What barbarians,' Robert Jordan said.

How many times had he heard this? How many times had he watched people say it with difficulty? How many times had he seen their eyes fill and their throats harden with the difficulty of saying my father, or my brother, or my mother, or my sister? He could not remember how many times he had heard them mention their dead in this way. Nearly always they spoke as this boy did now; suddenly and apropos of the mention of the town and always you said, 'What barbarians.'

You only heard the statement of the loss. You did not see the father fall as Pilar made him see the fascists die in that story she had told by the stream. You knew the father died in some courtyard, or against some wall, or in some field or orchard, or at night, in the lights of a truck, beside some road. You had seen the lights of the car from the hills and heard the shooting and afterwards you had come down to the road and found the bodies. You did not see the mother shot, nor the sister, nor the brother. You heard about it; you heard the shots; and you saw the bodies.

Pilar had made him see it in that town.

If that woman could only write. He would try to write it and if he had luck and could remember it perhaps he could get it down as she told it. God, how she could tell a story. She's better than Quevedo, he thought. He never wrote the death of any Don Faustino as well as she told it. I wish I could write well enough to write that story, he thought. What we did. Not what the others did to us. He knew enough about that. He knew plenty about that behind the lines. But you had to have known the people before. You had to know what they had been in the village.

Because of our mobility and because we did not have to stay afterwards to take the punishment we never knew how anything really ended, he thought. You stayed with a peasant and his family. You came at night and ate with them. In the day you were hidden and the next night you were gone. You did your job and cleared out. The next time you came that way you heard that they had been shot. It was as simple as that.

But you were always gone when it happened. The *partizans* did their damage and pulled out. The peasants stayed and took the punishment. I've always known about the other, he thought. What we did to them at the start. I've always known it and hated it and I have heard it mentioned shamelessly and shamefully, bragged of, boasted of, defended, explained and denied. But that damned woman made me see it as though I had been there.

Well, he thought, it is part of one's education. It will be quite an education when it's finished. You learn in this war if you listen. You most certainly did. He was lucky that he had lived parts of ten years in Spain before the war. They trusted you on the language, principally. They trusted you on understanding the language completely and speaking it idiomatically and having a knowledge of the different places. A Spaniard was only really loyal to his village in the end. First Spain of course, then his own tribe, then his province, then his village, his family and finally his trade. If you knew Spanish he was prejudiced in your favor, if you knew his province it was that much better, but if you knew his village and his trade you were in as far as any foreigner ever could be. He never felt like a foreigner in Spanish and they did not really treat him like a foreigner most of the time; only when they turned on you.

Of course they turned on you. They turned on you often but they always turned on every one. They turned on themselves, too. If you had three together, two would unite against one, and then the two would start to betray each other. Not always, but often enough for you to take enough cases and start to draw it as a conclusion.

This was no way to think; but who censored his thinking? Nobody but himself. He would not think himself into any defeatism. The first thing was to win the war. If we did not win the war everything was lost. But he noticed, and listened to, and remembered everything. He was serving in a war and he gave absolute loyalty and as complete a performance as he could give while he was serving. But nobody owned his mind, nor his faculties for seeing and hearing, and if he were going to form judgments he would form them afterwards. And there would be plenty of material to draw them from. There was plenty already. There was a little too much sometimes.

Look at the Pilar woman, he thought. No matter what comes, if there is time, I must make her tell me the rest of that story. Look at her walking along with those two kids. You could not get three better-looking products of Spain than those. She is like a mountain and the boy and the girl are like young trees. The old trees are all cut down and the young trees are growing clean like that. In spite of what has happened to the two of them they look as fresh and clean and new and untouched as though they had never heard of misfortune. But according to Pilar, Maria has just gotten sound again. She must have been in an awful shape.

He remembered a Belgian boy in the Eleventh Brigade who had enlisted with five other boys from his village. It was a village of about two hundred people and the boy had never been away from the village before. When he first saw the boy, out at Hans' Brigade Staff, the other five from the village had all been killed and the boy was in very bad shape and they were using him as an orderly to wait on table at the staff. He had a big, blond, ruddy Flemish face and huge awkward peasant hands and he moved, with the dishes, as powerfully and awkwardly as a draft horse. But he cried all the time. All during the meal he cried with no noise at all.

You looked up and there he was, crying. If you asked for the wine, he cried and if you passed your plate for stew, he cried; turning away his head. Then he would stop; but if you looked up at him, tears would start coming again. Between courses he cried in the kitchen. Every one was very gentle with him. But it did no good. He would have to find out what became of him and whether he ever cleared up and was fit for soldiering again.

Maria was sound enough now. She seemed so anyway. But he was no psychiatrist. Pilar was the psychiatrist. It probably had been good for them to have been together last night. Yes, unless it stopped. It certainly had been good for him. He felt fine today; sound and good and unworried and happy. The show looked bad enough but he was awfully lucky, too. He had been in others that announced themselves badly. Announced themselves; that was thinking in Spanish. Maria was lovely.

Look at her, he said to himself. Look at her.

He looked at her striding happily in the sun; her khaki shirt open at the neck. She walks like a colt moves, he thought. You do not run onto something like that. Such things don't happen. Maybe it never did happen, he thought. Maybe you dreamed it or made it up and it never did happen. Maybe it is like the dreams you have when some one you have seen in the cinema comes to your bed at night and is so kind and lovely. He'd slept with them all that way when he was asleep in bed. He could remember Garbo still, and Harlow. Yes, Harlow many times. Maybe it was like those dreams.

But he could still remember the time Garbo came to his bed the night before the attack at Pozoblanco and she was wearing a soft silky wool sweater when he put his arm around her and when she leaned forward her hair swept forward and over his face and she said why had he never told her that he loved her when she had loved him all this time? She was not shy, nor cold, nor distant. She was just lovely to hold and kind and lovely and like the old days with Jack Gilbert and it was as true as though it happened and he loved her much more than Harlow though Garbo was only there once while Harlow-maybe this was like those dreams.

Maybe it isn't too, he said to himself. Maybe I could reach over and touch that Maria now, he said to himself. Maybe you are afraid to he said to himself. Maybe you would find out that it never happened and it was not true and it was something you made up like those dreams about the people of the cinema or how all your old girls come back and sleep in that robe at night on all the bare floors, in the straw of the haybarns, the stables, the *corrales* and the *cortjjos,* the woods, the garages, the trucks and all the hills of Spain. They all came to that robe when he was asleep and they were all much nicer than they ever had been in life. Maybe it was like that. Maybe you would be afraid to touch her to see if it was true. Maybe you would, probably it is something that you made up or that you dreamed.

He took a step across the trail and put his hand on the girl's arm. Under his fingers he felt the smoothness of her arm in the worn khaki. She looked at him and smiled.

'Hello, Maria,' he said.

'Hello, *Inglés,*' she answered and he saw her tawny brown face and the yellow-gray eyes and the full lips smiling and the cropped sun-burned hair and she lifted her face at him and smiled in his eyes. It was true all right.

Now they were in sight of El Sordo's camp in the last of the pines, where there was a rounded gulch-head shaped like an upturned basin. All these limestone upper basins must be full of caves, he thought. There are two caves there ahead. The scrub pines growing in the rock hide them well. This is as good or a better place than Pablo's.

'How was this shooting of thy family?' Pilar was saying to Joaquin.

'Nothing, woman,' Joaquin said. 'They were of the left as many others in Valladolid. When the fascists purified the town they shot first the father. He had voted Socialist. Then they shot the mother. She had voted the same. It was the first time she had ever voted. After that they shot the husband of one of the sisters. He was a member of the syndicate of tramway drivers. Clearly he could not drive a tram without belonging to the syndicate. But he was without politics. I knew him well. He was even a little bit shameless. I do not think he was even a good comrade. Then the husband of the other girl, the other sister, who was also in the trams, had gone to the hills as I had. They thought she knew where he was. But she did not. So they shot her because she would not tell them where he was.'

'What barbarians,' said Pilar. 'Where is El Sordo? I do not see him.'

'He is here. He is probably inside,' answered Joaquin and stopping now, and resting the rifle butt on the ground, said, 'Pilar, listen to me. And thou, Maria. Forgive me if I have molested you speaking of things of the family. I know that all have the same troubles and it is more valuable not to speak of them.'

'That you should speak,' Pilar said. 'For what are we born if not to aid one another? And to listen and say nothing is a cold enough aid.'

'But it can molest the Maria. She has too many things of her own.'

'*Que va*,' Maria said. 'Mine are such a big bucket that yours falling in will never fill it. I am sorry, Joaquin, and I hope thy sister is well.'

'So far she's all right,' Joaquin said. 'They have her in prison and it seems they do not mistreat her much.'

'Are there others in the family?' Robert Jordan asked.

'No,' the boy said. 'Me. Nothing more. Except the brother-in-law who went to the hills and I think he is dead.'

'Maybe he is all right,' Maria said. 'Maybe he is with a band in other mountains.'

'For me he is dead,' Joaquin said. 'He was never too good at getting about and he was conductor of a tram and that is not the best preparation for the hills. I doubt if he could last a year. He was somewhat weak in the chest too.'

'But he may be all right,' Maria put her arm on his shoulder. 'Certainly, girl. Why not?' said Joaquin.

As the boy stood there, Maria reached up, put her arms around his neck and kissed him. Joaquin turned his head away because he was crying.

'That is as a brother,' Maria said to him. 'I kiss thee as a brother.'

The boy shook his head, crying without making any noise.

'I am thy sister,' Maria said. 'And I love thee and thou hast a family. We are all thy family.'

'Including the *Inglés*,' boomed Pilar. 'Isn't it true, *Inglés*?'

'Yes,' Robert Jordan said to the boy, 'we are all thy family, Joaquin.'

'He's your brother,' Pilar said. 'Hey *Inglés*?'

Robert Jordan put his arm around the boy's shoulder. 'We are all brothers,' he said. The boy shook his head.

'I am ashamed to have spoken,' he said. 'To speak of such things makes it more difficult for all. I am ashamed of molesting you.'

'I obscenity in the milk of my shame,' Pilar said in her deep lovely voice. 'And if the Maria kisses thee again I will commence kissing thee myself. It's years since I've kissed a bullfighter, even an unsuccessful one like thee, I would like to kiss an unsuccessful bullfighter turned Communist. Hold him, *Inglés*, till I get a good kiss at him.'

'*Deja*,' the boy said and turned away sharply. 'Leave me alone. I am all right and I am ashamed.'

He stood there, getting his face under control. Maria put her hand in Robert Jordan's. Pilar stood with her hands on her hips looking at the boy mockingly now.

'When I kiss thee,' she said to him, 'it will not be as any sister. This trick of kissing as a sister.'

'It is not necessary to joke,' the boy said. 'I told you I am all right, I am sorry that I spoke.'

'Well then let us go and see the old man,' Pilar said. 'I tire myself with such emotion.'

The boy looked at her. From his eyes you could see he was suddenly very hurt.

'Not thy emotion,' Pilar said to him. 'Mine. What a tender thing thou art for a bullfighter.'

'I was a failure,' Joaquin said. 'You don't have to keep insisting on it.'

'But you are growing the pigtail another time.'

'Yes, and why not? Fighting stock serves best for that purpose economically. It gives employment to many and the State will control it. And perhaps now I would not be afraid.'

'Perhaps not,' Pilar said. 'Perhaps not.'

'Why do you speak in such a brutal manner, Pilar?' Maria said to her. 'I love thee very much but thou art acting very barbarous.' 'It is possible that I am barbarous,' Pilar said. 'Listen, *Inglés*.

Do you know what you are going to say to El Sordo?'

'Yes.'

'Because he is a man of few words unlike me and thee and this sentimental menagerie.'

'Why do you talk thus?' Maria asked again, angrily.

'I don't know,' said Pilar as she strode along. 'Why do you think?' 'I do not know.'

'At times many things tire me,' Pilar said angrily. 'You understand? And one of them is to have forty-eight years. You hear me? Forty-eight years and an ugly face. And another is to see panic in the face of a failed bullfighter of Communist tendencies when I say, as a joke, I might kiss him.'

'It's not true, Pilar,' the boy said. 'You did not see that.'

'*Que va*, it's not true. And I obscenity in the milk of all of you. Ah, there he is. *Hola*, Santiago! *Que tal?*'

The man to whom Pilar spoke was short and heavy, brown-faced, with broad cheekbones; gray haired, with wide-set yellow-brown eyes, a thin-bridged, hooked nose like an Indian's, a long upper lip and a wide, thin mouth. He was clean shaven and he walked toward them from the mouth of the cave, moving with the bow-legged walk that went with his cattle herdsman's breeches and boots. The day was warm but he had on a sheep's-wool-lined short leather jacket buttoned up to the neck. He put out a big brown hand to Pilar. '*Hola*, woman,' he said. '*Hola*,' he said to Robert Jordan and shook his hand and looked him keenly in the face. Robert Jordan saw his eyes were yellow as a cat's and flat as reptile's eyes are. '*Guapa*,' he said to Maria and patted her shoulder.

'Eaten?' he asked Pilar. She shook her head.

'Eat,' he said and looked at Robert Jordan. 'Drink?' he asked, making a motion with his hand decanting his thumb downward.

'Yes, thanks.'

'Good,' El Sordo said. 'Whiskey?'

'You have whiskey?'

El Sordo nodded. '*Inglés?*' he asked. 'Not *Ruso?*'

'*Americana.*'

'Few Americans here,' he said.

'Now more.'

'Less bad. North or South?'

'North.'

'Same as *Inglés*. When blow bridge?'

'You know about the bridge?'

El Sordo nodded.

'Day after tomorrow morning.'

'Good,' said El Sordo.

'Pablo?' he asked Pilar.

She shook her head. El Sordo grinned.

'Go away,' he said to Maria and grinned again. 'Come back,' he looked at a large watch he pulled out on a leather thong from inside his coat. 'Half an hour.'

He motioned to them to sit down on a flattened log that served as a bench and looking at Joaquin, jerked his thumb down the trail in the direction they had come from.

'I'll walk down with Joaquin and come back,' Maria said.

El Sordo went into the cave and came out with a pinch bottle of Scotch whiskey and three glasses. The bottle was under one arm, and three glasses were in the hand of that arm, a finger in each glass, and his other hand was around the neck of an earthenware jar of water. He put the glasses and the bottle down on the log and set the jug on the ground.

'No ice,' he said to Robert Jordan and handed him the bottle. 'I don't want any,' Pilar said and covered her glass with her hand.

'Ice last night on ground,' El Sordo said and grinned. 'All melt. Ice up there,' El Sordo said and pointed to the snow that showed on the bare crest of the mountains. 'Too far.'

Robert Jordan started to pour into El Sordo's glass but the deaf man shook his head and made a motion for the other to pour for himself.

Robert Jordan poured a big drink of Scotch into the glass and El Sordo watched him eagerly and when he had finished, handed him the water jug and Robert Jordan filled the glass with the cold water that ran in a stream from the earthenware spout as he tipped up the jug.

El Sordo poured himself half a glassful of whiskey and filled the glass with water.

'Wine?' he asked Pilar.

'No. Water.'

'Take it,' he said. 'No good,' he said to Robert Jordan and grinned. 'Knew many English. Always much whiskey.'

'Where?'

'Ranch,' El Sordo said. 'Friends of boss.'

'Where do you get the whiskey?'

'What?' he could not hear.

'You have to shout,' Pilar said. 'Into the other ear.' El Sordo pointed to his better ear and grinned.

'Where do you get the whiskey?' Robert Jordan shouted. 'Make it,' El Sordo said and watched Robert Jordan's hand check on its way to his mouth with the glass.

'No,' El Sordo said and patted his shoulder. 'Joke. Comes from La Granja. Heard last night comes English dynamiter. Good. Very happy. Get whiskey. For you. You like?'

'Very much,' said Robert Jordan. 'It's very good whiskey.' 'Am contented,' Sordo grinned. 'Was bringing tonight with information.'

'What information?'

'Much troop movement.'

'Where?'

'Segovia. Planes you saw.'

'Yes.'

'Bad, eh?'

'Bad.'

'Troop movement?'

'Much between Villacastin and Segovia. On Valladolid road. Much between Villacastin and San Rafael. Much. Much.'

'What do you think?'

'We prepare something?'

'Possibly.'

'They know. Prepare too.'

'It is possible.'

'Why not blow bridge tonight?'

'Orders.'

'Whose orders?'

'General Staff.'

'So,'

'Is the time of the blowing important?' Pilar asked.

'Of all importance.'

'But if they are moving up troops?'

'I will send Anselmo with a report of all movement and concentrations. He is checking the road.'

'You have some one at road?' Sordo asked.

Robert Jordan did not know how much he had heard. You never know with a deaf man.

'Yes,' he said.

'Me, too. Why not blow bridge now?'

'I have my orders.'

'I don't like it,' El Sardo said. 'This I do not like.'

'Nor I,' said Robert Jordan.

El Sardo shook his head and took a sip of the whiskey. 'You want of me?'

'How many men have you?'

'Eight.'

'To cut the telephone, attack the post at the house of the road- menders, take it, and fall back on the bridge.'

'It is easy.'

'It will all be written out.'

'Don't trouble. And Pablo?'

'Will cut the telephone below, attack the post at the sawmill, take it and fall back on the bridge.'

'And afterwards for the retreat?' Pilar asked. 'We are seven men, two women and five horses. You are,' she shouted into Sardo's ear.

'Eight men and four horses. *Faltan caballos,*' he said. 'Lacks horses.'

'Seventeen people and nine horses,' Pilar said. 'Without accounting for transport.'

Sordo said nothing.

'There is no way of getting horses?' Robert Jordan said into Sardo's best ear.

'In war a year,' Sordo said. 'Have four.' He showed four fingers. 'Now you want eight for tomorrow.'

'Yes,' said Robert Jordan. 'Knowing you are leaving. Having no need to be careful as you have been in this neighborhood. Not having to be cautious here now. You could not cut out and steal eight head of horses?'

'Maybe,' Sordo said. 'Maybe none. Maybe more.'

'You have an automatic rifle?' Robert Jordan asked.

Sordo nodded.

'Where?'

'Up the hill.'

'What kind?'

'Don't know name. With pans.'

'How many rounds?'

'Five pans.'

'Does any one know how to use it?'

'Me. A little. Not shoot too much. Not want make noise here. Not want use cartridges.'

'I will look at it afterwards,' Robert Jordan said. 'Have you hand grenades?'

'Plenty.'

'How many rounds per rifle?'

'Plenty.'

'How many?'

'One hundred fifty. More maybe.'

'What about other people?'

'For what?'

'To have sufficient force to take the posts and cover the bridge while I am blowing it. We should have double what we have.'

'Take posts don't worry. What time day?'

'Daylight.'

'Don't worry.'

'I could use twenty more men, to be sure,' Robert Jordan said. 'Good ones do not exist. You want undependables?'

'No. How many good ones?'

'Maybe four.'

'Why so few?'

'No trust.'

'For horseholders?'

'Must trust much to be horseholders.'

'I'd like ten more good men if I could get them.'

'Four.'

'Anselmo told me there were over a hundred here in these hills.'

'No good.'

'You said thirty,' Robert Jordan said to Pilar. 'Thirty of a certain degree of dependability.'

'What about the people of Elias?' Pilar shouted to Sordo. He shook his head.

'No good.'

'You can't get ten?' Robert Jordan asked. Sardo looked at him with his flat, yellow eyes and shook his head.

'Four,' he said and held up four fingers.

'Yours are good?' Robert Jordan asked, regretting it as he said it.

Sardo nodded.

'*Dentro de fa gra vedad,*' he said in Spanish. 'Within the limits of the danger.' He grinned. 'Will be bad, eh?'

'Possibly.'

'Is the same to me,' Sordo said simply and not boasting. 'Better four good than much bad. In this war always much bad, very little good. Every day fewer good. And Pablo?' he looked at Pilar.

'As you know,' Pilar said. 'Worse every day.'

Sordo sh rugged his shoulders.

'Take drink,' Sardo said to Robert Jordan. 'I bring mine and four more. Makes twelve. Tonight we discuss all. I have sixty sticks dynamite. You want?'

'What per cent?'

'Don't know. Common dynamite. I bring.'

'We'll blow the small bridge above with that,' Robert Jordan said. 'That is fine. You'll come down tonight? Bring that, will you? I've no orders for that but it should be blown.'

'I come tonight. Then hunt horses.'

'What chance for horses?'

'Maybe. Now eat.'

Does he talk that way to every one? Robert Jordan thought. Or is that his idea of how to make foreigners understand?

'And where are we going to go when this is done?' Pilar shouted into Sordo's ear.

He shrugged his shoulders.

'All that must be arranged,' the woman said.

'Of course,' said Sardo. 'Why not?'

'It is bad enough,' Pilar said. 'It must be planned very well.'

'Yes, woman,' Sardo said. 'What has thee worried?'

'Everything,' Pilar shouted.

Sardo grinned at her.

'You've been going about with Pablo,' he said.

So he does only speak that pidgin Spanish for foreigners, Robert Jordan thought. Good. I'm glad to hear him talking straight.

'Where do you think we should go?' Pilar asked.

'Where?'

'Yes, where?'

'There are many places,' Sordo said. 'Many places. You know Gredos?'

'There are many people there. All these places will be cleaned up as soon as they have time.'

'Yes. But it is a big country and very wild.'

'It would be very difficult to get there,' Pilar said.

'Everything is difficult, difficult,' El Sordo said. 'We can get to Gredos as well as to anywhere else. Travelling at night. Here it is very dangerous now. It is a miracle we have been here this long. Gredos is safer country than this.'

'Do you know where I want to go?' Pilar asked him.

'Where? The Paramera? That's no good.'

'No,' Pilar said. 'Not the Sierra de Paramera. I want to go to the Republic.'

'That is possible.'

'Would your people go?'

'Yes. If I say to.'

'Of mine, I do not know,' Pilar said. 'Pablo would not want to although, truly, he might feel safer there. He is too old to have to go for a soldier unless they call more classes. The gypsy will not wish to go. I do not know about the others.'

'Because nothing passes her for so long they do not realize the danger,' El Sordo said.

'Since the planes today they will see it more,' Robert Jordan said. 'But I should think you could operate very well from the Gredos.'

'What?' El Sordo said and looked at him with his eyes very flat. There was no friendliness in the way he asked the question.

'You could raid more effectively from there,' Robert Jordan said. 'So,' El Sardo said. 'You know Gredos?'

Yes. You could operate against the main line of the railway from there. You could keep cutting it as we are doing farther south In Estremadura. To operate from there would be better than returning to the Republic,' Robert Jordan said. 'You are more useful there.'

They had both gotten sullen as he talked.

Sordo looked at Pilar and she looked back at him.

'You know Gredos?'

Sordo asked. 'Truly?'

'Sure,' said Robert Jordan.

'Where would you go?'

'Above Barco de Avila. Better places than here. Raid against the main road and the railroad between Bejar and Plasencia.'

'Very difficult,' Sordo said.

'We have worked against that same railroad in much more dangerous country in Estremadura,' Robert Jordan said.

'Who is we?'

'The *guerrilleros* group of Estremadura.' 'You are many?'

'About forty.'

'Was the one with the bad nerves and the strange name from there?' asked Pilar.

'Yes.'

'Where is he now?'

'Dead, as I told you.'

'You are from there, too?'

'Yes.'

'You see what I mean?' Pilar said to him.

And I have made a mistake, Robert Jordan thought to himself. I have told Spaniards we can do something better than they can when the rule is never to speak of your own exploits or abilities. When I should have flattered them I have told them what I think they should do and now they are furious. Well, they will either get over it or they will not. They are certainly much more useful in the Credos than here. The proof is that here they have done nothing since the train that Kashkin organized. It was not much of a show. It cost the fascists one engine and killed a few troops but they all talk as though it were the high point of the war. Maybe they will shame into going to the Gredos. Yes and maybe I will get thrown out of here too. Well, it is not a very rosy-looking dish anyway that you look into it.

'Listen *Inglés*,' Pilar said to him. 'How are your nerves?'

'All right,' said Robert Jordan. 'O.K.'

'Because the last dynamiter they sent to work with us, although a formidable technician, was very nervous.'

'We have nervous ones,' Robert Jordan said.

'I do not say that he was a coward because he comported himself very well,' Pilar went on. 'But he spoke in a very rare and windy way.' She raised her voice. 'Isn't it true, Santiago, that the last dynamiter, he of the train, was a little rare?'

'*Alga raro*,' the deaf man nodded and his eyes went over Robert Jordan's face in a way that reminded him of the round opening at the end of the wand of a vacuum cleaner. '*Si, alga raro, pero buena.*'

'*Murio*,' Robert Jordan said into the deaf man's ear. 'He is dead.'

'How was that?' the deaf man asked, dropping his eyes down from Robert Jordan's eyes to his lips.

'I shot him,' Robert Jordan said. 'He was too badly wounded to travel and I shot him.'

'He was always talking of such a necessity,' Pilar said. 'It was his obsession.'

'Yes,' said Robert Jordan. 'He was always talking of such a necessity and it was his obsession.'

'*Como fue?*' the deaf man asked. 'Was it a train?'

'It was returning from a train,' Robert Jordan said. 'The train was successful. Returning in the dark we encountered a fascist patrol and as we ran he was shot high in the back but without hitting any bone except the shoulder blade. He travelled quite a long way, but with the wound was unable to travel more. He was unwilling to be left behind and I shot him.'

'*Menos mal*,' said El Sordo. 'Less bad.'

'Are you sure your nerves are all right?' Pilar said to Robert Jordan.

'Yes,' he told her. 'I am sure that my nerves are all right and I think that when we terminate this of the bridge you would do well to go to the Gredos.'

As he said that, the woman started to curse in a flood of obscene invective that rolled over and around him like the hot white water splashing down from the sudden eruption of a geyser.

The deaf man shook his head at Robert Jordan and grinned in delight. He continued to shake his head happily as Pilar went on vilifying and Robert Jordan knew that it was all right again now. Finally she stopped cursing, reached for the water jug, tipped it up and took a drink and said, calmly, 'Then just shut up about what we are to do afterwards, will you, *Inglés*? You go back to the Republic and you take your piece with you and leave us others alone here to decide what part of these hills we'll die in.'

'Live in,' El Sordo said. 'Calm thyself, Pilar.'

'Live in and die in,' Pilar said. 'I can see the end of it well enough. I like thee, *Inglés*, but keep thy mouth off of what we must do when thy business is finished.'

'It is thy business,' Robert Jordan said. 'I do not put my hand in it.'

'But you did,' Pilar said. 'Take thy little cropped-headed whore and go back to the Republic but do not shut the door on others who are not foreigners and who loved the Republic when thou wert wiping thy mother's milk off thy chin.'

Maria had come up the trail while they were talking and she heard this last sentence which Pilar, raising her voice again, shouted at Robert Jordan. Maria shook her head at Robert Jordan violently and shook her finger warningly. Pilar saw Robert Jordan looking at the girl and saw him smile and she turned and said, 'Yes. I said whore and I mean it. And I suppose that you'll go to Valencia together and we can eat goat crut in Gredos.'

'I'm a whore if thee wishes, Pilar,' Maria said. 'I suppose I am in all case if you say so. But calm thyself. What passes with thee?'

'Nothing,' Pilar said and sat down on the bench, her voice calm now and all the metallic rage gone out of it. 'I do not call thee that. But I have such a desire to go to the Republic.'

'We can all go,' Maria said.

'Why not?' Robert Jordan said. 'Since thou seemest not to love the Gredos.'

Sordo grinned at him.

'We'll see,' Pilar said, her rage gone now. 'Give me a glass of that rare drink. I have worn my throat out with anger. We'll see. We'll see what happens.'

'You see, Comrade,' El Sardo explained. 'It is the morning that is difficult.' He was not talking the pidgin Spanish now and he was looking into Robert Jordan's eyes calmly and explainingly; not searchingly nor suspiciously, nor with the flat superiority of the old campaigner that had been in them before. 'I understand your needs and I know the posts must be exterminated and the bridge covered while you do your work. This I understand perfectly. This is easy to do before daylight or at daylight.'

'Yes,' Robert Jordan said. 'Run along a minute, will you?' he said to Maria without looking at her.

The girl walked away out of hearing and sat down, her hands clasped over her ankles.

'You see,' Sordo said. 'In that there is no problem. But to leave afterward and get out of this country in daylight presents a grave problem.'

'Clearly,' said Robert Jordan. 'I have thought of it. It is daylight for me also.'

'But you are one,' El Sardo said. 'We are various.'

'There is the possibility of returning to the camps and leaving from there at dark,' Pilar said, putting the glass to her lips and then lowering it.

'That is very dangerous, too,' El Sordo explained. 'That is perhaps even more dangerous.'

'I can see how it would be,' Robert Jordan said.

'To do the bridge in the night would be easy,' El Sordo said. 'Since you make the condition that it must be done at daylight, it brings grave consequences.'

'I know it.'

'You could not do it at night?' 'I would be shot for it.'

'It is very possible we will all be shot for it if you do it in the daytime.'

'For me myself that is less important once the bridge is blown,' Robert Jordan said. 'But I see your viewpoint. You cannot work out a retreat for daylight?'

'Certainly,' El Sardo said. 'We will work out such a retreat. But I explain to you why one is preoccupied and why one is irritated. You speak of going to Gredos as though it were a military manoeuvre to be accomplished. To arrive at Gredos would be a miracle.'

Robert Jordan said nothing.

'Listen to me,' the deaf man said. 'I am speaking much. But it is so we may understand one another. We exist here by a miracle. By a miracle of laziness and stupidity of the fascists which they will remedy in time. Of course, we are very careful and we make no disturbance in these hills.'

'I know.'

'But now, with this, we must go. We must think much about the manner of our going.'

'Clearly.'

'Then,' said El Sordo. 'Let us eat now. I have talked much.'

'Never have I heard thee talk s o much,' Pilar said. 'Is it this?' she held up the glass.

'No,' El Sordo shook his head. 'It isn't whiskey. I t is that never have I had so much to talk of.'

'I appreciate your aid and your loyalty,' Robert Jordan said. 'I appreciate the difficulty caused by the timing of the blowing of the bridge.'

'Don't talk of that,' El Sordo said. 'We are here to do what we can do. But this is complicated.'

'And on paper very simple,' Robert Jordan grinned. 'On paper the bridge is blown at the moment the attack starts in order that nothing shall come up the road. It is very simple.'

'That they should let us do something on paper,' El Sordo said. 'That we should conceive and execute something on paper.'

'Paper bleeds little,' Robert Jordan quoted the proverb.

'But it is very useful,' Pilar said. 'Es muy uti!. What I would like to do is use thy orders for that purpose.'

'Me too,' said Robert Jordan. 'But you could never win a war like that.'

'No,' the big woman said. 'I suppose not. But do you know what I would like?'

'To go to the Republic,' E l Sordo said. He had put his good ear close to her as she spoke. 'Ya irds, mujet: Let us win this and it will all be Republic.'

'All right,' Pilar said. 'And now, for God's sake let us eat.'

12

They left El Sordo's after eating and started down the trail. El Sardo had walked with them as far as the lower post.

'*Sa iud,*' he said. 'Until tonight.'

'*Salud, Camarada,*' Robert Jordan had said to him and the three of them had gone on down the trail, the deaf man standing looking after them. Maria had turned and waved her hand at him and El Sordo waved disparagingly with the abrupt, Spanish upward flick of the forearm as though something were being tossed away which seems the negation of all salutation which has not to do with business. Through the meal he had never unbuttoned his sheepskin coat and he had been carefully polite, careful to turn his head to hear and had returned to speaking his broken Spanish, asking Robert Jordan about conditions in the Republic politely; but it was obvious he wanted to be rid of them.

As they had left him, Pilar had said to him, 'Well, Santiago?' 'Well, nothing, woman,' the deaf man said. 'It is all right. But I am thinking.'

'Me, too,' Pilar had said and now as they walked down the trail, the walking easy and pleasant down the steep trail through the pines that they had toiled up, Pilar said nothing. Neither Robert Jordan nor Maria spoke and the three of them travelled along fast until the trail rose steeply out of the wooded valley to come up through the timber, leave it, and come out into the high meadow.

It was hot in the late May afternoon and halfway up this last steep grade the woman stopped. Robert Jordan, stopping and looking back, saw the sweat beading on her forehead. He thought her brown face looked pallid and the skin sallow and that there were dark areas under her eyes.

'Let us rest a minute,' he said. 'We go to fast.'

'No,' she said. 'Let us go on.'

'Rest, Pilar,' Maria said. 'You look badly.'

'Shut up,' the woman said. 'Nobody asked for thy advice.'

She started on up the trail but at the top she was breathing heavily and her face was wet with perspiration and there was no doubt about her pallor now.

'Sit down, Pilar,' Maria said. 'Please, please sit down.'

'All right,' said Pilar and the three of them sat down under a pine tree and looked across the mountain meadow to where the tops of the peaks seemed to jut out from the roll of the high country with snow shining bright on them now in the early afternoon sun.

'What rotten stuff is the snow and how beautiful it looks,' Pilar said. 'What an illusion is the snow.' She turned to Maria. 'I am sorry I was rude to thee, *guapa*. I don't know what has held me today. I have an evil temper.'

'I never mind what you say when you are angry,' Maria told her. 'And you are angry often.'

'Nay, it is worse than anger,' Pilar said, looking across at the peaks.

'Thou art not well,' Maria said.

'Neither is it that,' the woman said. 'Come here, *guapa,* and put thy head in my lap.'

Maria moved close to her, put her arms out and folded them as one does who goes to sleep without a pillow and lay with her head on her arms. She turned her face up at Pilar and smiled at her but the big woman looked on across the meadow at the mountains. She stroked the girl's head without looking down at her and ran a blunt finger across the girl's forehead and then around the line of her ear and down the line where the hair grew on her neck.

'You can have her in a little while, *Inglés,*' she said. Robert Jordan was sitting behind her.

'Do not talk like that,' Maria said.

'Yes, he can have thee,' Pilar said and looked at neither of them. 'I have never wanted thee. But I am jealous.'

'Pilar,' Maria said. 'Do not talk thus.'

'He can have thee,' Pilar said and ran her finger around the lobe of the girl's ear. 'But I am very jealous.'

'But Pilar,' Maria said. 'It was thee explained to me there was nothing like that between us.'

'There is always something like that,' the woman said. 'There is always something like something that there should not be. But with me there is not. Truly there is not. I want thy happiness and nothing more.'

Maria said nothing but lay there, trying to make her head rest lightly.

'Listen, *guapa,*' said Pilar and ran her finger now absently but tracingly over the contours of her cheeks. 'Listen, *guapa,* I love thee and he can have thee, I am no *tortillera* but a woman made for men. That is true. But now it gives me pleasure to say thus, in the daytime, that I care for thee.'

'I love thee, too.'

'*Qué va.* Do not talk nonsense. Thou dost not know even of what I speak.'

'I know.'

'*Qué va,* that you know. You are for the *Inglés.* That is seen and as it should be. That I would have. Anything else I would not have. I do not make perversions. I only tell you something true. Few people will ever talk to thee truly and no women. I am jealous and say it and it is there. And I say it.'

'Do not say it,' Maria said. 'Do not say it, Pilar.'

'*Par qué*, do not say it,' the woman said, still not looking at either of them. 'I will say it until it no longer pleases me to say it. And,' she looked down at the girl now, 'that time has come already. I do not say it more, you understand?'

'Pilar,' Maria said. 'Do not talk thus.'

'Thou art a very pleasant little rabbit,' Pilar said. 'And lift thy 'head now because this silliness is over.'

'It was not silly,' said Maria. 'And my head is well where it is.' 'Nay. Lift it,' Pilar told her and put her big hands under the girl's head and raised it. 'And thou, *Inglés?*' she said, still holding the girl's head as she looked across at the mountains. 'What cat has eaten thy tongue?'

'No cat,' Robert Jordan said.

'What animal then?' She laid the girl's head down on the ground.

'No animal,' Robert Jordan told her. 'You swallowed it yourself, eh?'

'I guess so,' Robert Jordan said.

'And did you like the taste?' Pilar turned now and grinned at him.

'Not much.'

'I thought not,' Pilar said. 'I *thought* not. But I give you back our rabbit. Nor ever did I try to take your rabbit. That's a good name for her. I heard you call her that this morning.'

Robert Jordan felt his face redden.

'You are a very hard woman,' he told her.

'No,' Pilar said. 'But so simple I am very complicated. Are you very complicated, *Inglés?*'

'No. Nor not so simple.'

'You please me, *Inglés*,' Pilar said. Then she smiled and leaned forward and smiled and shook her head. 'Now if I could take the rabbit from thee and take thee from the rabbit.'

'You could not.'

'I know it,' Pilar said and smiled again. 'Nor would I wish to. But when I was young I could have.'

'I believe it.'

'You believe it?'

'Surely,' Robert Jordan said. 'But such talk is nonsense.' 'It is not like thee,' Maria said.

'I am not much like myself today,' Pilar said. 'Very little like myself. Thy bridge has given me a headache, *Inglés*.'

'We can tell it the Headache Bridge,' Robert Jordan said. 'But I will drop it in that gorge like a broken bird cage.'

'Good,' said Pilar. 'Keep on talking like that.'

'I'll drop it as you break a banana from which you have removed the skin.'

'I could eat a banana now,' said Pilar. 'Go on, *Inglés*. Keep on talking largely.'

'There is no need,' Robert Jordan said. 'Let us get to camp.' 'Thy duty,' Pilar said. 'It will come quickly enough. I said that I would leave the two of you.' 'No. I have much to do.'

'That is much too and does not take long.'

'Shut thy mouth, Pilar,' Maria said. 'You speak grossly.'

'I am gross,' Pilar said. 'But I am also very delicate. *Soy muy delicada.* I will leave the two of you. And the talk of jealousness is nonsense. I was angry at Joaquin because I saw from his look how ugly I am. I am only jealous that you are nineteen. It is not a jealousy which lasts. You will not be always. Now I go.'

She stood up and with a hand on one hip looked at Robert Jordan, who was also standing. Maria sat on the ground under the tree, her head dropped forward.

'Let us all go to camp together,' Robert Jordan said. 'It is better and there is much to do.'

Pilar nodded with her head toward Maria, who sat there, her head turned away from them, saying nothing.

Pilar smiled and shrugged her shoulders almost imperceptibly and said, 'You know the way?'

'I know it,' Maria said, not raising her head.

'*Pues me voy,*' Pilar said. 'Then I am going. We'll have something hearty for you to eat, *Inglés.*'

She started to walk off into the heather of the meadow toward the stream that led down through it toward the camp.

'Wait,' Robert Jordan called to her. 'It is better that we should all go together.'

Maria sat there and said nothing. Pilar did not turn.

'*Que va,* go together,' she said. 'I will see thee at the camp.'

Robert Jordan stood there.

'Is she all right?' he asked Maria. 'She looked ill before.' 'Let her go,' Maria said, her head still down.

'I think I should go with her.'

'Let her go,' said Maria. 'Let her go!'

13

They were walking through the heather of the mountain meadow and Robert Jordan felt the brushing of the heather against his legs, felt the weight of his pistol in its holster against his thigh, felt the sun on his head, felt the breeze from the snow of the mountain peaks cool on his back and, in his hand, he felt the girl's hand firm and strong, the fingers locked in his. From it, from the palm of her hand against the palm of his, from their fingers locked together, and from her wrist across his wrist something came from her hand, her fingers and her wrist to his that was as fresh as the first light air that moving toward you over the sea barely wrinkles the glassy surface of a calm, as light as a feather moved across one's lip, or a leaf falling when there is no breeze; so light that it could be felt with the touch of their fingers alone, but that was so strengthened, so intensified, and made so urgent, so aching and so strong by the hard pressure of their fingers and the close pressed palm and wrist, that it was as though a current moved up his arm and filled his whole body with an aching hollowness of wanting. With the sun shining on her hair, tawny as wheat, and on her gold-brown smooth-lovely face and on the curve of her throat he bent her head back and held her to him and kissed her. He felt her trembling as he kissed her and he held the length of her body tight to him and felt her breasts against his chest through the two khaki shirts, he felt them small and firm and he reached and undid the buttons on her shirt and bent and kissed her and she stood shivering, holding her head back, his arm behind her. Then she dropped her chin to his head and then he felt her hands holding his head and rocking it against her. He straightened and with his two arms around her held her so tightly that she was lifted off the ground, tight against him, and he felt her trembling and then her lips were on his throat, and then he put her down and said, 'Maria, oh, my, Maria.'

Then he said, 'Where should we go?'

She did not say anything but slipped her hand inside of his shirt and he felt her undoing the shirt buttons and she said, 'You, too. I want to kiss, too.'

'No, little rabbit.'

'Yes. Yes. Everything as you.'

'Nay. That is an impossibility.'

'Well, then. Oh, then. Oh, then. Oh.'

Then there was the smell of heather crushed and the roughness of the bent stalks under her head and the sun bright on her closed eyes and all his life he would remember the curve of her throat with her head pushed back into the heather roots and her lips that moved smally and by themselves and the fluttering of the lashes on the eyes tight closed against the sun and against everything, and for her everything was red, orange, gold-red from the sun on the closed eyes, and it all was that color, all of it, the filling, the possessing, the having, all of that color, all in a blindness of that color. For him it was a dark passage which led to nowhere, then to nowhere, then again to nowhere, once again to nowhere, always and forever to nowhere, heavy on the elbows in the earth to nowhere, dark, never any end to nowhere, hung on all time always to unknowing nowhere, this time and again for always to nowhere, now not to be borne once again always and to nowhere, now beyond all bearing up, up, up and into nowhere, suddenly, scaldingly, holdingly all nowhere gone and time absolutely still and they were both there, time having stopped and he felt the earth move out and away from under them.

Then he was lying on his side, his head deep in the heather, smelling it and the smell of the roots and the earth and the sun came through it and it was scratchy on his bare shoulders and along his flanks and the girl was lying opposite him with her eyes still shut and then she opened them and smiled at him and he said very tiredly and from a great but friendly distance, 'Hello, rabbit.' And she smiled and from no distance said, 'Hello, my *Inglés*.'

'I'm not an *Inglés*,' he said very lazily.

'Oh yes, you are,' she said. 'You're my *Inglés*,' and reached and took hold of both his ears and kissed him on the forehead.

'There,' she said. 'How is that? Do I kiss thee better?'

Then they were walking along the stream together and he said, 'Maria, I love thee and thou art so lovely and so wonderful and so beautiful and it does such things to me to be with thee that I feels though J wanted to die when I am loving thee.'

'Oh,' she said. 'I die each time. Do you not die?'

'No. Almost. But did thee feel the earth move?'

'Yes. As I died. Put thy arm around me, please.'

'No. I have thy hand. Thy hand is enough.'

He looked at her and across the meadow where a hawk was hunting and the big afternoon clouds were coming now over the mountains.

'And it is not thus for thee with others?' Maria asked him, they now walking hand in hand.

'No. Truly.'

'Thou hast loved many others.'

'Some. But not as thee.'

'And it was not thus? Truly?'

'It was a pleasure but it was not thus.'

'And then the earth moved. The earth never moved before? '

'Nay. Truly never.'

'Ay,' she said. 'And this we have for one day.'

He said nothing.

'But we have had it now at least,' Maria said. 'And do you like me too? Do I please thee? I will look better later.'

'Thou art very beautiful now.'

'Nay,' she said. 'But stroke thy hand across my head.'

He did that feeling her cropped hair soft and flattening and then rising between his fingers and he put both hands on her head and turned her face up to his and kissed her.

'I like to kiss very much,' she said. 'But I do not do it well.'

'Thou hast no need to kiss.'

'Yes, I have. If I am to be thy woman I should please thee in all ways.'

'You please me enough. I would not be more pleased. There is nothing I could do if I were more pleased.'

'But you will see,' she said very happily. 'My hair amuses thee now because it is odd. But every day it is growing. It will be long and then I will not look ugly and perhaps you will love me very much.'

'Thou hast a lovely body,' he said. 'The loveliest in the world.' 'It is only young and thin.'

'No. In a fine body there is magic. I do not know what makes it in one and not in another. But thou hast it.'

'For thee,' she said. 'Nay.'

'Yes. For thee and for thee always and only for thee. But it is little to bring thee. I would learn to take good care of thee. But tell me truly. Did the earth never move for thee before?'

'Never,' he said truly.

'Now am I happy,' she said. 'Now am I truly happy.'

'You are thinking of something else now?' she asked him. 'Yes. My work.'

'I wish we had horses to ride,' Maria said. 'In my happiness I would like to be on a good horse and ride fast with thee riding fast beside me and we would ride faster and faster, galloping, and never pass my happiness.'

'We could take thy happiness in a plane,' he said absently.

'And go over and over in the sky like the little pursuit planes shining in the sun,' she said. 'Rolling it in loops and in dives. *Que buena!*' she laughed. 'My happiness would not even notice it.'

'Thy happiness has a good stomach,' he said half hearing what she said.

Because now he was not there. He was walking beside her but his mind was thinking of the problem of the bridge now and it was all clear and hard and sharp as when a camera lens is brought into focus. He saw the two posts and Anselmo and the gypsy watching. He saw the road empty and he saw movement on it. He saw where he would place the two automatic rifles to get the most level field of fire, and who will serve them, he thought, me at the end, but who at the start? He placed the charges, wedged and lashed them, sunk his caps and crimped them, ran his wires, hooked them up and got back to where he had placed the old box of the exploder and then he started to think of all the things that could have happened and that might go wrong. Stop it, he told himself. You have made love to this girl and now your head is clear, properly clear, and you start to worry. It is one thing to think you must do and it is another thing to worry. Don't worry. You mustn't worry. You know the things that you may have to do and you know what may happen. Certainly it may happen.

You went into it knowing what you were fighting for. You were fighting against exactly what you were doing and being forced into doing to have any chance of winning. So now he was compelled to use these people whom he liked as you should use troops toward whom you have no feeling at all if you were to be successful. Pablo was evidently the smartest. He knew how bad it was instantly. The woman was all for it, and still was; but the realization of what it really consisted in had overcome her steadily and it had done plenty to her already. Sordo recognized it instantly and would do it but he did not like it any more than he, Robert Jordan, liked it.

So you say that it is not that which will happen to yourself but that which may happen to the woman and the girl and to the others that you think of. All right. What would have happened to them if you had not come? What happened to them and what passed with them before you were ever here? You must not think in that way. You have no responsibility for them except in action. The orders do not come from you. They come from Golz. And who is Golz? A good general. The best you've ever served under. But should a man carry out impossible orders knowing what they lead to? Even though they come from Golz, who is the party as well as the army? Yes. He should carry them out because it is only in the performing of them that they can prove to be impossible. How do you know they are impossible until you have tried them? If every one said orders were impossible to carry out when they were received where would you be? Where would we all be if you just said, 'Impossible,' when orders came?

He had seen enough of commanders to whom all orders were impossible. That swine Gomez in Estremadura. He had seen enough attacks when the flanks did not advance because it was impossible. No, he would carry out the orders and it was bad luck that you liked the people you must do it with.

In all the work that they, the *partizans,* did, they brought added danger and bad luck to the people that sheltered them and worked with them. For what? So that, eventually, there should be no more danger and so that the country should be a good place to live in. That was true no matter how trite it sounded.

If the Republic lost it would be impossible for those who believed in it to live in Spain. But would it? Yes, he knew that it would be, from the things that happened in the parts the fascists had already taken.

Pablo was a swine but the others were fine people and was it not a betrayal of them all to get them to do this? Perhaps it was. But if they did not do it two squadrons of cavalry would come and hunt them out of these hills in a week.

No. There was nothing to be gained by leaving them alone. Except that all people should be left alone and you should interfere with no one. So he believed that, did he? Yes, he believed that. And what about a planned society and the rest of it? That was for the others to do. He had something else to do after this war. He fought now in this war because it had started in a country that he loved and he believed in the Republic and that if it were destroyed life would be unbearable for all those people who believed in it. He was under Communist discipline for the duration of the war. Here in Spain the Communists offered the best discipline and the soundest and sanest for the prosecution of the war. He accepted their discipline for the duration of the war because, in the conduct of the war, they were the only party whose program and whose discipline he could respect.

What were his politics then? He had none now, he told himself. But do not tell any one else that, he thought. Don't ever admit that. And what are you going to do afterwards? I am going back and earn my living teaching Spanish as before, and I am going to write a true book. I'll bet, he said. I'll bet that will be easy.

He would have to talk with Pablo about politics. It would certainly be interesting to see what his political development had been. The classical move from left to right, probably; like old Lerroux. Pablo was quite a lot like Lerroux. Prieto was as bad. Pablo and Prieto had about an equal faith in the ultimate victory. They all had the politics of horse thieves. He believed in the Republic as a form of government but the Republic would have to get rid of all of that bunch of horse thieves that brought it to the pass it was in when the rebellion started. Was there ever a people whose leaders were as truly their enemies as this one?

Enemies of the people. That was a phrase he might omit. That was a catch phrase he would skip. That was one thing that sleeping with Maria had done. He had gotten to be as bigoted and hide-bound about his politics as a hard-shelled Baptist and phrases like enemies of the people came into his mind without his much criticizing them in any way. Any sort of *cliches* both revolutionary and patriotic. His mind employed them without criticism. Of course they were true but it was too easy to be nimble about using them. But since last night and this afternoon his mind was much clearer and cleaner on that business. Bigotry is an odd thing. To be bigoted you have to be absolutely sure that you are right and nothing makes that surety and righteousness like continence. Continence is the foe of heresy.

How would that premise stand up if he examined it? That was probably why the Communists were always cracking down on Bohemianism. When you were drunk or when you committed either fornication or adultery you recognized your own personal fallibility of that so mutable substitute for the apostles' creed, the party line. Down with Bohemianism, the sin of Mayakovsky.

But Mayakovsky was a saint again. That was because he was safely dead. You'll be safely dead yourself, he told himself. Now stop thinking that sort of thing. Think about Maria.

Maria was very hard on his bigotry. So far she had not affected his resolution but he would much prefer not to die. He would abandon a hero's or a martyr's end gladly. He did not want to make a Thermopyla:, nor be Horatius at any bridge, nor be the Dutch boy with his finger in that dyke. No. He would like to spend some time with Maria. That was the simplest expression of it. He would like to spend a long, long time with her.

He did not believe there was ever going to be any such thing as a long time any more but if there ever was such a thing he would like to spend it with her. We could go into the hotel and register as Doctor and Mrs. Livingstone I presume, he thought.

Why not marry her? Sure, he thought. I will marry her. Then we will be Mr. and Mrs. Robert Jordan of Sun Valley, Idaho. Or Corpus Christi, Texas, or Butte, Montana.

Spanish girls make wonderful wives. I've never had one so I know. And when I get my job back at the university she can be an instructor's wife and when undergraduates who take Spanish IV come in to smoke pipes in the evening and have those so valuable informal discussions about Quevedo, Lope de Vega, Gald6s and the other always admirable dead, Maria can tell them about how some of the blue-shirted crusaders for the true faith sat on her head while others twisted her arms and pulled her skirts up and stuffed them in her mouth.

I wonder how they will like Maria in Missoula, Montana? That is if I can get a job back in Missoula. I suppose that I am ticketed as a Red there now for good and will be on the general blacklist. Though you never know. You never can tell.

They've no proof of what you do, and as a matter of fact they would never believe it if you told them, and my passport was valid for Spain before they issued the restrictions.

The time for getting back will not be until the fall of thirty-seven. I left in the summer of thirty-six and though the leave is for a year you do not need to be back until the fall term opens in the following year. There is a lot of time between now and the fall term. There is a lot of time between now and day after tomorrow if you want to put it that way. No. I think there is no need to worry about the university. Just you turn up there in the fall and it will be all right. Just try and turn up there.

But it has been a strange life for a long time now. Damned if it hasn't. Spain was your work and your job, so being in Spain was natural and sound. You had worked summers on engineering projects and in the forest service building roads and in the park and learned to handle powder, so the demolition was a sound and normal job too. Always a little hasty, but once you accept the idea of demolition as a problem it is only a problem. But there was plenty that was not so good that went with it although God knows you took it easily enough. There was the constant attempt to approximate the conditions of successful assassination that accompanied the demolition. Did big words make it more defensible? Did they make killing any more palatable? You took to it a little too readily if you ask me, he told himself. And what you will be like or just exactly what you will be suited for when you leave the service of the Republic is, to me, he thought, extremely doubtful. But my guess is you will get rid of all that by writing about it, he said. Once you write it down it is all gone. It will be a good book if you can write it. Much better than the other.

But in the meantime all the life you have or ever will have is today, tonight, tomorrow, today, tonight, tomorrow, over and over again (I hope), he thought and so you had better take what time there is and be very thankful for it. If the bridge goes bad. It does not look too good just now.

But Maria has been good. Has she not? Oh, has she not, he thought. Maybe that is what I am to get now from life. Maybe that is my life and instead of it being threescore years and ten it is forty-eight hours or just threescore hours and ten or twelve rather. Twenty-four hours in a day would be threescore and twelve for the three full days.

I suppose it is possible to live as full a life in seventy hours as in seventy years; grantedthat your life has been full up to the time that the hours start and that you have reached a certain age.

What nonsense, he thought. What rot you get to thinking by yourself. That is *really* nonsense. And maybe it isn't nonsense too. Well, we will see. The last time I slept with a girl was in Madrid. No it wasn't. It was in the Escorial and, except that I woke in the night and thought it was someone else and was excited until I realized who it really was, it was just dragging ashes; except that it was pleasant enough. And the time before that was in Madrid and except for some lying and pretending I did to myself as to identity while things were going on, it was the same or something less. So I am no romantic glorifier of the Spanish Woman nor did I ever think of a casual piece as anything much other than a casual piece in any country. But when I am with Maria I love her so that I feel, literally, as though I would die and I never believed in that nor thought that it could happen.

So if your life trades its seventy years for seventy hours I have that value now and I am lucky enough to know it. And if there is not any such thing as a long time, nor the rest of your lives, nor from now on, but there is only now, why then now is the thing to praise and T am very happy with it. Now, *ahora, maintenant, heute.* Now, it has a funny sound to be a whole world and your life. *Esta noche,* tonight, *ce soir, heute abend.* Life and wife, *Vie* and *Mari.* No it didn't work out. The French turned it into a husband. There was now and *frau*; but that did not prove anything either. Take dead, *mort, muerto,* and *todt. Todt* was the deadest of them all. War, *guerre, guerra,* and *krieg. Krieg* was the most like war, or was it? Or was it only that he knew German the least well? Sweetheart, *cherie, prenda,* and *schatz.* He would trade them all for Maria. There was a name.

Well, they would all be doing it together and it would not be long now. It certainly looked worse all the time. It was just something that you could not bring off in the morning. In an impossible situation you hang on until night to get away. You try to last out until night to get back in. You are all right, maybe, if you can stick it out until dark and then get in. So what if you start this sticking it out at daylight? How about that? And that poor bloody Sordo abandoning his pidgin Spanish to explain it to him so carefully. As though he had not thought about that whenever he had done any particularly bad thinking ever since Golz had first mentioned it. As though he hadn't been living with that like a lump of undigested dough in the pit of his stomach ever since the night before the night before last.

What a business. You go along your whole life and they seem as though they mean something and they always end up not meaning anything There was never any of what this is. You think that is one thing that you will never have. And then, on a lousy show like this, coordinating two chicken-crut guerilla bands to help you blow a bridge under impossible conditions, to abort a counteroffensive that will probably already be started, you run into a girl like this Maria. Sure. That is what you would do. You ran into her rather late, that was all.

So a woman like that Pilar practically pushed this girl into your sleeping bag and what happens? Yes, what happens? What happens? You tell me what happens, please. Yes. That is just what happens. That is exactly what happens.

Don't lie to yourself about Pilar pushing her into your sleeping robe and try to make it nothing or to make it lousy. You gone were when you first saw her. When she first opened her mouth and spoke to you it was there already and you know it. Since you have it and you never thought you would have it, there is no sense throwing dirt at it, when you know what it is and you know it came the first time you looked at her as she came out bent over carrying that iron cooking platter.

It hit you then and you know it and so why lie about it?

You went all strange inside every time you looked at her and every time she looked at you. So why don't you admit it? All right, I'll admit it. And as for Pilar pushing her onto you, all Pilar did was be an intelligent woman. She had taken good care of the girl and she saw what was coming the minute the girl came back into the cave with the cooking dish.

So she made things easier. She made things easier so that there was last night and this afternoon. She is a damned sight more civilized than you are and she knows what time is all about. Yes, he said to himself, I think we can admit that she has certain notions about the value of time. She took a beating and all because she did not want other people losing what she'd lost and then the idea of admitting it was lost was too big a thing to swallow. So she took a beating back there on the hill and I guess we did not make it any easier for her.

Well, so that is what happens and what has happened and you might as well admit it and now you will never have two whole nights with her. Not a lifetime, not to live together, not to have what people were always supposed to have, not at all. One night that is past, once one afternoon, one night to come; maybe. No, sir.

Not time, not happiness, not fun, not children, not a house, not a bathroom, not a clean pair of pajamas, not the morning paper, not to wake up together, not to wake and know she's there and that you're not alone. No. None of that. But why, when this is all you are going to get in life of what you want; when you have found it; why not just one night in a bed with sheets?

You ask for the impossible. You ask for the ruddy impossible. So if you love this girl as much as you say you do, you had better love her very hard and make up in intensity what the relation will lack in duration and in continuity. Do you hear that? In the old days people devoted a lifetime to it. And now when you have found it if you get two nights you wonder where all the luck came from. Two nights. Two nights to love, honor and cherish. For better and for worse. In sickness and in death. No that wasn't it. In sickness and in health. Till death do us part. In two nights. Much more than likely. Much more than likely and now lay off that sort of thinking. You can stop that now. That's not good for you. Do nothing that is not good for you. Sure that's it.

This was what Golz had talked about. The longer he was around, the smarter Golz seemed. So this was what he was asking about; the compensation of irregular service. Had Golz had this and was it the urgency and the lack of time and the circumstances that made it? Was this something that happened to every one given comparable circumstances? And did he only think it was something special because it was happening to him? Had Golz slept around in a hurry when he was commanding irregular cavalry in the Red Army and had the combination of the circumstances and the rest of it made the girls seem the way Maria was?

Probably Golz knew all about this too and wanted to make the point that you must make your whole life in the two nights that are given to you; that living as we do now you must concentrate all of that which you should always have into the short time that you can have it.

It was a good system of belief. But he did not believe that Maria had only been made by the circumstances. Unless, of course, she is a reaction from her own circumstance as well as his. Her one circumstance is not so good, he thought. No, not so good.

If this was how it was then this was how it was. But there was no law that made him say he liked it. I did not know that I could ever feel what I have felt, he thought. Nor that this could happen to me. I would like to have it for my whole life. You will, the other part of him said. You will. You have it now and that is all your whole life is; now. There is nothing else than now. There is neither yesterday, certainly, nor is there any tomorrow. How old must you be before you know that? There is only now, and if now is only two days, then two days is your life and everything in it will be in proportion. This is how you live a life in two days. And if you stop complaining and asking for what you never will get, you will have a good life. A good life is not measured by any biblical span.

So now do not worry, take what you have, and do your work and you will have a long life and a very merry one. Hasn't it been merry lately? What are you complaining about? That's the thing about this sort of work, he told himself, and was very pleased with the thought, it isn't so much what you learn as it is the people you meet. He was pleased then because he was joking and he came back to the girl.

'I love you, rabbit,' he said to the girl. 'What was it you were saying?'

'I was saying,' she told him, 'that you must not worry about your work because I will not bother you nor interfere. If there is anything I can do you will tell me.'

'There's nothing,' he said. 'It is really very simple.'

'I will learn from Pilar what I should do to take care of a man well and those things I will do,' Maria said. 'Then, as I learn, I will discover things for myself and other things you can tell me.'

'There is nothing to do.'

'*Qué va,* man, there is nothing! Thy sleeping robe, this morning, should have been shaken and aired and hung somewhere in the sun. Then, before the dew comes, it should be taken into shelter.'

'Go on, rabbit.'

'Thy socks should be washed and dried. I would see thee had two pair.'

'What else?'

'If thou would show me I would clean and oil thy pistol.' 'Kiss me,' Robert Jordan said.

'Nay, this is serious. Wilt thou show me about the pistol? Pilar has rags and oil. There is a cleaning rod inside the cave that should fit it.'

'Sure. I'll show you.'

'Then,' Maria said. 'If you will teach me to shoot it either one of us could shoot the other and himself, or herself, if one were wounded and it were necessary to avoid capture.'

'Very interesting,' Robert Jordan said. 'Do you have many ideas like that?'

'Not many,' Maria said. 'But it is a good one. Pilar gave me this and showed me how to use it,' she opened the breast pocket of her shirt and took out a cut-down leather holder such as pocket combs are carried in and, removing a wide rubber band that closed both ends, took out a Gem type, single-edged razor blade. 'I keep this always,' she explained. 'Pilar says you must make the cut here just below the ear and draw it toward here.' She showed him with her finger. 'She says there is a big artery there and that drawing the blade from there you cannot miss it. Also, she says there is no pain and you must simply press firmly below the ear and draw it downward. She says it is nothing and that they cannot stop it if it is done.'

'That's right,' said Robert Jordan. 'That's the carotid artery.' So she goes around with that all the time, he thought, as a definitely accepted and properly organized possibility.

'But I would rather have thee shoot me,' Maria said. 'Promise if there is ever any need that thou wilt shoot me.'

'Sure,' Robert Jordan said. 'I promise.'

'Thank thee very much,' Maria told him. 'I know it is not easy to do.'

'That's all right,' Robert Jordan said.

You forget all this, he thought. You forget about the beauties of a civil war when you keep your mind too much on your work. You have forgotten this. Well, you are supposed to. Kashkin couldn't forget it and it spoiled his work. Or do you think the old boy had a hunch? It was very strange because he had experienced absolutely no emotion about the shooting of Kashkin. He expected that at some time he might have it. But so far there had been absolutely none.

'But there are other things I can do for thee,' Maria told him, walking close beside him, now, very serious and womanly.

'Besides shoot me?'

'Yes. I can roll cigarettes for thee when thou hast no more of those with tubes. Pilar has taught me to roll them very well, tight and neat and not spilling.'

'Excellent,' said Robert Jordan. 'Do you lick them yourself?' 'Yes,' the girl said, 'and when thou art wounded I will care for thee and dress thy wound and wash thee and feed thee—' 'Maybe I won't be wounded,' Robert Jordan said.

'Then when you are sick I will care for thee and make thee soups and clean thee and do all for thee. And I will read to thee.'

'Maybe I won't get sick.'

'Then I will bring thee coffee in the morning when thou wakest—'

'Maybe I don't like coffee,' Robert Jordan told her.

'Nay, but you do,' the girl said happily. 'This morning you took two cups.'

'Suppose I get tired of coffee and there's no need to shoot me and I'm neither wounded nor sick and I give up smoking and have only one pair of socks and hang up my robe myself. What then, rabbit?' he patted her on the back. 'What then?'

'Then,' said Maria, 'I will borrow the scissors of Pilar and cut thy hair.'

'I don't like to have my hair cut.'

'Neither do I,' said Maria. 'And I like thy hair as it is. So. If there is nothing to do for thee, I will sit by thee and watch thee and in the nights we will make love.'

'Good,' Robert Jordan said. 'The last project is very sensible.'

'To me it seems the same,' Maria smiled.

'Oh, *Inglés*,' she said.

'My name is Roberto.'

'Nay. But I call thee *Inglés* as Pilar does.' 'Still it is Roberto.'

'No,' she told him. 'Now for a whole day it is *Inglés*. And *Inglés*, can I help thee with thy work?'

'No. What I do now I do alone and very coldly in my head.' 'Good,' she said. 'And when will it be finished?'

'Tonight, with luck.' 'Good,' she said.

Below them was the last woods that led to the camp. 'Who is that?' Robert Jordan asked and pointed.

'Pilar,' the girl said, looking along his arm. 'Surely it is Pilar.'

At the lower edge of the meadow where the first trees grew the woman was sitting, her head on her arms. She looked like a dark bundle from where they stood; black against the brown of the tree trunk.

'Come on,' Robert Jordan said and started to run toward her through the knee-high heather. It was heavy and hard to run in and when he had run a little way, he slowed and walked. He could see the woman's head was on her folded arms and she looked broad and black against the tree trunk. He came up to her and said, 'Pilar!' sharply.

The woman raised her head and looked up at him. 'Oh,' she said. 'You have terminated already?' 'Art thou ill?' he asked and bent down by her. '*Que va*,' she said. 'I was asleep.'

'Pilar,' Maria, who had come up, said and kneeled down by her. 'How are you? Are you all right?'

'I'm magnificent,' Pilar said but she did not get up. She looked at the two of them. 'Well, *Inglés*,' she said. 'You have been doing manly tricks again?'

'You are all right?' Robert Jordan asked, ignoring the words. 'Why not? I slept. Did you?'

'No.'

'Well,' Pilar said to the girl. 'It seems to agree with you.' Maria blushed and said nothing.

'Leave her alone,' Robert Jordan said.

'No one spoke to thee,' Pilar told him. 'Maria,' she said and her voice was hard. The girl did not look up.

'Maria,' the woman said again. 'I said it seems to agree with thee.'

'Oh, leave her alone,' Robert Jordan said again.

'Shut up, you,' Pilar said without looking at him. 'Listen, Maria, tell me one thing.'

'No,' Maria said and shook her head.

'Maria,' Pilar said, and her voice was as hard as her face and there was nothing friendly in her face. 'Tell me one thing of thy own volition.'

The girl shook her head.

Robert Jordan was thinking, if I did not have to work with this woman and her drunken man and her chicken-crut outfit, I would slap her so hard across the face that—

'Go ahead and tell me,' Pilar said to the girl. 'No,' Maria said. 'No.'

'Leave her alone,' Robert Jordan said and his voice did not sound like his own voice. I'll slap her anyway and the hell with it, he thought.

Pilar did not even speak to him. It was not like a snake charming a bird, nor a cat with a bird. There was nothing predatory. Nor was there anything perverted about it. There was a spreading, though, as a cobra's hood spreads. He could feel this. He could feel the menace of the spreading. But the spreading was a domination, not of evil, but of searching. I wish I did not see this, Robert Jordan thought. But it is not a business for slapping.

'Maria,' Pilar said. 'I will not touch thee. Tell me now of thy own volition.'

'De tu propia voluntad,' the words were in Spanish.

The girl shook her head.

'Maria,' Pilar said. 'Now and of thy own volition. You hear me? Anything at all.'

'No,' the girl said softly. 'No and no.'

'Now you will tell me,' Pilar told her. 'Anything at all. You will see. Now you will tell me.'

'The earth moved,' Maria said, not looking at the woman. 'Truly. It was a thing I cannot tell thee.'

'So,' Pilar said and her voice was warm and friendly and there was no compulsion in it. But Robert Jordan noticed there were small drops of perspiration on her forehead and her lips. 'So there was that. So that was it.'

'It is true,' Maria said and bit her lip.

'Of course it is true,' Pilar said kindly. 'But do not tell it to your own people for they never will believe you. You have no *Cali* blood, *Inglés?*'

She got to her feet, Robert Jordan helping her up. 'No,' he said. 'Not that I know of.'

'Nor has the Maria that she knows of,' Pilar said, *'Pues es muy raro.* It is very strange.'

'But it happened, Pilar,' Maria said.

'Cómo que no, hija?' Pilar said. 'Why not, daughter? When I was young the earth moved so that you could feel it all shift in space and were afraid it would go out from under you. It happened every night.'

'You lie,' Maria said.

'Yes,' Pilar said. 'I lie. It never moves more than three times in a lifetime. Did it *really* move?'

'Yes,' the girl said. 'Truly.'

'For you, *Inglés?*' Pilar looked at Robert Jordan. 'Don't lie.' 'Yes,' he said. 'Truly.'

'Good,' said Pilar. 'Good. That is something.'

'What do you mean about the three times?' Maria asked. 'Why do you say that?'

'Three times,' said Pilar. 'Now you've had one.'

'Only three times?'

'For most people, never,' Pilar told her. 'You are sure it moved?'

'One could have fallen off,' Maria said.

'I guess it moved, then,' Pilar said. 'Come, then, and let us get to camp.'

'What's this nonsense about three times?' Robert Jordan said to the big woman as they walked through the pines together.

'Nonsense?' she looked at him wryly. 'Don't talk to me of nonsense, little English.'

'Is it a wizardry like the palms of the hands?'

'Nay, it is common and proven knowledge with *Gitanos*.'

'But we are not *Gitanos*.'

'Nay. But you have had a little luck. Non-gypsies have a little luck sometimes.'

'You mean it truly about the three times?'

She looked at him again, oddly. 'Leave me, *Inglés*,' she said. 'Don't molest me. You are too young for me to speak to.'

'But, Pilar,' Maria said.

'Shut up,' Pilar told her. 'You have had one and there are two more in the world for thee.'

'And you?' Robert Jordan asked her.

'Two,' said Pilar and put up two fingers. 'Two. And there will never be a third.'

'Why not?' Maria asked.

'Oh, shut up,' Pilar said. 'Shut up. *Busnes* of thy age bore me.' 'Why not a third?' Robert Jordan asked.

'Oh, shut up, will you?' Pilar said. 'Shut up!'

All right, Robert Jordan said to himself. Only I am not having any. I've known a lot of gypsies and they are strange enough. But so are we. The difference is we have to make an honest living. Nobody knows what tribes we came from nor what our tribal inheritance is nor what the mysteries were in the woods where the people lived that we came from. All we know is that we do not know. We know nothing about what happens to us in the nights. When it happens in the day though, it *is* something. Whatever happened, happened and now this woman not only has to make the girl say it when she did not want to; but she has to take it over and make it her own. She has to make it into a gypsy thing. I thought she took a beating up the hill but she was certainly dominating just now back there. If it had been evil she should have been shot. But it wasn't evil. It was only wanting to keep her hold on life. To keep it through Maria.

When you get through with this war you might take up the study of women, he said to himself. You could start with Pilar. She has put in a pretty complicated day, if you ask me. She never brought in the gypsy stuff before. Except the hand, he thought. Yes, of course the hand. And I don't think she was faking about the hand. She wouldn't tell me what she saw, of course. Whatever she saw she believed in herself. But that proves nothing.

'Listen, Pilar,' he said to the woman. Pilar looked at him and smiled. 'What is it?' she asked.

'Don't be so mysterious,' Robert Jordan said. 'These mysteries tire me very much.'

'So?' Pilar said.

'I do not believe in ogres, soothsayers, fortune tellers, or chicken-crut gypsy witchcraft.'

'Oh,' said Pilar.

'No. And you can leave the girl alone.' 'I will leave the girl alone.'

'And leave the mysteries,' Robert Jordan said. 'We have enough work and enough things that will be done without complicating it with chicken-crut. Fewer mysteries and more work.'

'I see,' said Pilar and nodded her head in agreement. 'And listen, *Inglés*,' she said and smiled at him. 'Did the earth move?'

'Yes, God damn you. It moved.'

Pilar laughed and laughed and stood looking at Robert Jordan laughing.

'Oh, *Inglés. Inglés*,' she said laughing. 'You are very comical. You must do much work now to regain thy dignity.'

The Hell with you, Robert Jordan thought. But he kept his mouth shut. While they had spoken the sun had clouded over and as he looked back up toward the mountains the sky was now heavy and gray.

'Sure,' Pilar said to him, looking at the sky. 'It will snow.'

'Now? almost in June?'

'Why not? These mountains do not know the names of the months. We are in the moon of May.'

'It can't be snow,' he said. 'It *can't* snow.'

'Just the same, *Inglés*,' she said to him, 'it will snow.'

Robert Jordan looked up at the thick gray of the sky with the sun gone faintly yellow, and now as he watched gone completely and the gray becoming uniform so that it was soft and heavy; the gray now cutting off the tops of the mountains.

'Yes,' he said. 'I guess you are right.'

14

By the time they reached the camp it was snowing and the flakes were dropping diagonally through the pines. They slanted through the trees, sparse at first and circling as they fell, and then, as the cold wind came driving down the mountain, they came whirling and thick and Robert Jordan stood in front of the cave in a rage and watched them.

'We will have much snow,' Pablo said. His voice was thick and his eyes were red and bleary.

'Has the gypsy come in?' Robert Jordan asked him. 'No,' Pablo said. 'Neither him nor the old man.'

'Will you come with me to the upper post on the road?' 'No,' Pablo said. 'I will take no part in this.'

'I will find it myself.'

'In this storm you might miss it,' Pablo said. 'I would not go now.' 'It's just downhill to the road and then follow it up.'

'You could find it. But thy two sentries will be coming up now with the snow and you would miss them on the way.'

'The old man is waiting for me.'

'Nay. He will come in now with the snow.'

Pablo looked at the snow that was blowing fast now past the mouth of the cave and said, 'You do not like the snow, *Inglés?*'

Robert Jordan swore and Pablo looked at him through his bleary eyes and laughed.

'With this thy offensive goes, *Inglés,*' he said. 'Come into the cave and thy people will be in directly.'

Inside the cave Maria was busy at the fire and Pilar at the kitchen table. The fire was smoking but, as the girl worked with it, poking in a stick of wood and then fanning it with a folded paper, there was a puff and then a flare and the wood was burning, drawing brightly as the wind sucked a draft out of the hole in the roof.

'And this snow,' Robert Jordan said. 'You think there will be much?'

'Much,' Pablo said contentedly. Then called to Pilar, 'You don't like it, woman, either? Now that you command you do not like this snow?'

'*A mi qué?*' Pilar said, over her shoulder. 'If it snows it snows.'

'Drink some wine, *Inglés,* 'Pablo said. 'I have been drinking all day waiting for the snow.'

'Give me a cup,' Robert Jordan said.

'To the snow,' Pablo said and touched cups with him. Robert Jordan looked him in the eyes and clinked his cup. You blearyeyed murderous sod, he thought. I'd like to clink this cup against your teeth. *Take it easy,* he told himself, *take it easy.*

'It is very beautiful the snow,' Pablo said. 'You won't want to sleep outside with the snow falling.'

So *that's* on your mind too is it? Robert Jordan thought. You've a lot of troubles, haven't you, Pablo?

'No?' he said, politely.

'No. Very cold,' Pablo said. 'Very wet.'

You don't know why those old eiderdowns cost sixty-five dollars, Robert Jordan thought. I'd like to have a dollar for every time I've slept in that thing in the snow.

'Then I should sleep in here?' he asked politely. 'Yes.'

'Thanks,' Robert Jordan said. 'I'll be sleeping outside.' 'In the snow?'

'Yes' (damn your bloody, red pig-eyes and your swine-bristly swines-end of a face). 'In the snow.' (In the utterly-damned, ruinous, unexpected, slutting, defeat-conniving, bastard-cessary of the snow.)

He went over to where Maria had just put another piece of pine on the fire.

'Very beautiful, the snow,' he said to the girl.

'But it is bad for the work, isn't it?' she asked him. 'Aren't you worried?'

'*Que va*,' he said. 'Worrying is no good. When will supper be ready?'

'I thought you would have an appetite,' Pilar said. 'Do you want a cut of cheese now?'

'Thanks,' he said and she cut him a slice, reaching up to unhook the big cheese that hung in a net from the ceiling, drawing a knife across the open end and handing him the heavy slice. He stood, eating it. It was just a little too goaty to be enjoyable.

'Maria,' Pablo said from the table where he was sitting. 'What?' the girl asked.

'Wipe the table clean, Maria,' Pablo said and grinned at Robert Jordan.

'Wipe thine own spillings,' Pilar said to him. 'Wipe first thy chin and thy shirt and then the table.'

'Maria,' Pablo called.

'Pay no heed to him. He is drunk,' Pilar said.

'Maria,' Pablo called. 'It is still snowing and the snow is beautiful.'

He doesn't know about that robe, Robert Jordan thought. Good old pig-eyes doesn't know why I paid the Woods boys sixty-five dollars for that robe. I wish the gypsy would come in though. As soon as the gypsy comes I'll go after the old man. I should go now but it is very possible that I would miss them. I don't know where he is posted.

'Want to make snowballs?' he said to Pablo. 'Want to have a snowball fight?'

'What?' Pablo asked. 'What do you propose?'

'Nothing,' Robert Jordan said. 'Got your saddles covered up good?'

'Yes.'

Then in English Robert Jordan said, 'Going to gram those horses or peg them out and let them dig for it?'

'What?'

'Nothing. It's your problem, old pal. I'm going out of here on my feet.'

'Why do you speak in English?' Pablo asked.

'I don't know,' Robert Jordan said. 'When I get very tired sometimes I speak English. Or when I get very disgusted. Or baffled, say. When I get highly baffled I just talk English to hear the sound of it. It's a reassuring noise. You ought to try it sometime.'

'What do you say, *Inglés?*' Pilar said. 'It sounds very interesting but I do not understand.'

'Nothing,' Robert Jordan said. 'I said, 'nothing' in English.'

'Well then, talk Spanish,' Pilar said. 'It's shorter and simpler in Spanish.'

'Surely,' Robert Jordan said. But oh boy, he thought, oh Pablo, oh Pilar, oh Maria, oh you two brothers in the corner whose names I've forgotten and must remember, but I get tired of it sometimes. Of it and of you and of me and of the war and why in all why did it have to snow now? That's too bloody much. No, it's not.

Nothing is too bloody much. You just have to take it and fight out of it and now stop prima-donnaing and accept the fact that it is snowing as you did a moment ago and the next thing is to check with your gypsy and pick up your old man. But to snow! Now in this month. Cut it out, he said to himself. Cut it out and take it. It's that cup, you know. How did it go about that cup? He'd either have to improve his memory or else never think of quotations because when you missed one it hung in your mind like a name you had forgotten and you could not get rid of it. How did it go about that cup?

'Let me have a cup of wine, please,' he said in Spanish. Then, 'Lots of snow? Eh?' he said to Pablo. '*Mucha nieve.*'

The drunken man looked up at him and grinned. He nodded his head and grinned again.

'No offensive. No *aviones*. No bridge. Just snow,' Pablo said.

'You expect it to last a long time?' Robert Jordan sat down by him. 'You think we're going to be snowed in all summer, Pablo, old boy?'

'All summer, no,' Pablo said. 'Tonight and tomorrow, yes.' 'What makes you think so?'

'There are two kinds of storms,' Pablo said, heavily and judiciously. 'One comes from the Pyrenees. With this one there is great cold. It is too late for this one.'

'Good,' Robert Jordan said. 'That's something.'

'This storm comes from the Cantabrico,' Pablo said. 'It comes from the sea. With the wind in this direction there will be a great storm and much snow.'

'Where did you learn all this, old timer?' Robert Jordan asked.

Now that his rage was gone he was excited by this storm as he was always by all storms. In a blizzard, a gale, a sudden line squall, a tropical storm, or a summer thunder shower in the mountains there was an excitement that came to him from no other thing. It was like the excitement of battle except that it was clean. There is a wind that blows through battle but that was a hot wind; hot and dry as your mouth; and it blew heavily; hot and dirtily; and it rose and died away with the fortunes of the day. He knew that wind well.

But a snowstorm was the opposite of all of that. In the snowstorm you came close to wild animals and they were not afraid. They travelled across country not knowing where they were and the deer stood sometimes in the lee of the cabin. In a snowstorm you rode up to a moose and he mistook your horse for another moose and trotted forward to meet you. In a snowstorm it always seemed, for a time, as though there were no enemies. In a snowstorm the wind could blow a gale; but it blew a white cleanness and the air was full of a driving whiteness and all things were changed and when the wind stopped there would be the stillness. This was a big storm and he might as well enjoy it. It was ruining everything, but you might as well enjoy it.

'I was an arroyero for many years,' Pablo said. 'We trucked freight across the mountains with the big carts before the camions came into use. In that business we learned the weather.'

'And how did you get into the movement?'

'I was always of the left,' Pablo said. 'We had many contacts with the people of Asturias where they are much developed politically. I have always been for the Republic.'

'But what were you doing before the movement?'

'I worked then for a horse contractor of Zaragoza. He furnished horses for the bull rings as well as remounts for the army. It was then that I met Pilar who was, as she told you, with the matador Finito de Palencia.'

He said this with considerable pride.

'He wasn't much of a matador,' one of the brothers at the table said looking at Pilar's back where she stood in front of the stove.

'No?' Pilar said, turning around and looking at the man. 'He wasn't much of a matador?'

Standing there now in the cave by the cooking fire she could see him, short and brown and sober-faced, with the sad eyes, the cheeks sunken and the black hair curled wet on his forehead where the tight-fitting matador's hat had made a red line that no one else noticed. She saw him stand, now, facing the five-year-old bull, facing the horns that had lifted the horses high, the great neck thrusting the horse up, up, as that rider poked into that neck with the spiked pole, thrusting up and up until the horse went over with a crash and the rider fell against the wooden fence and, with the bull's legs thrusting him forward, the big neck swung the horns that searched the horse for the life that was in him. She saw him, Finito, the not-so-good matador, now standing in front of the bull and turning sideways toward him. She saw him now clearly as he furled the heavy flannel cloth around the stick; the flannel hanging blood-heavy from the passes where it had swept over the bull's head and shoulders and the wet streaming shine of his withers and on down and over his back as the bull raised into the air and the banderillas clattered. She saw Finito stand five paces from the bull's head, profiled, the bull standing still and heavy, and draw the sword slowly up until it was level with his shoulder and then sight along the dipping blade at a point he could not yet see because the bull's head was higher than his eyes. He would bring that head down with the sweep his left arm would make with the wet, heavy cloth; but now he rocked back a little on his heels and sighted along the blade, profiled in front of the splintered horn; the bull's chest heaving and his eyes watching the cloth.

She saw him very clearly now and she heard his thin, clear voice as he turned his head and looked toward the people in the first row of the ring above the red fence and said, 'Let's see if we can kill him like this!'

She could hear the voice and then see the first bend of the knee as he started forward and watch his voyage in onto the horn that lowered now magically as the bull's muzzle followed the low swept cloth, the thin, brown wrist controlled, sweeping the horns down and past, as the sword entered the dusty height of the withers.

She saw its brightness going in slowly and steadily as though the bull's rush plucked it into himself and out from the man's hand and she watched it move in until the brown knuckles rested against the taut hide and the short, brown man whose eyes had never left the entry place of the sword now swung his sucked-in belly clear of the horn and rocked clear from the animal, to stand holding the cloth on the stick in his left hand, raising his right hand to watch the bull die.

She saw him standing, his eyes watching the bull trying to hold the ground, watching the bull sway like a tree before it falls, watching the bull fight to hold his feet to the earth, the short man's hand raised in a formal gesture of triumph. She saw him standing there in the sweated, hollow relief of it being over, feeling the relief that the bull was dying, feeling the relief that there had been no shock, no blow of the horn as he came clear from it and then, as he stood, the bull could hold to the earth no longer and crashed over, rolling dead with all four feet in the air, and she could see the short, brown man walking tired and unsmiling to the fence.

She knew he could not run across the ring if his life depended on it and she watched him walk slowly to the fence and wipe his mouth on a towel and look up at her and shake his head and then wipe his face on the towel and start his triumphant circling of the ring.

She saw him moving slowly, dragging around the ring, smiling, bowing, smiling, his assistants walking behind him, stooping, picking up cigars, tossing back hats; he circling the ring sad-eyed and smiling, to end the circle before her. Then she looked over and saw him sitting now on the step of the wooden fence, his mouth in a towel.

Pilar saw all this as she stood there over the fire and she said, 'So he wasn't a good matador? With what class of people is my life passed now!'

'He was a good matador,' Pablo said. 'He was handicapped by his short stature.'

'And clearly he was tubercular,' Primitivo said.

'Tubercular?' Pilar said. 'Who wouldn't be tubercular from the punishment he received? In this country where no poor man can ever hope to make money unless he is a criminal like Juan March, or a bullfighter, or a tenor in the opera? Why wouldn't he be tubercular? In a country where the bourgeoisie over-eat so that their stomachs are all ruined and they cannot live without bicarbonate of soda and the poor are hungry from their birth till the day they die, why wouldn't he be tubercular? If you travelled under the seats in third-class carriages to ride free when you were following the fairs learning to fight as a boy, down there in the dust and dirt with the fresh spit and the dry spit, wouldn't you be tubercular if your chest was beaten out by horns?'Clearly,' Primitivo said. 'I only said he was tubercular.'

'Of course he was tubercular,' Pilar said, standing there with the big wooden stirring spoon in her hand. 'He was short of stature and he had a thin voice and much fear of bulls. Never have I seen a man with more fear before the bullfight and never have I seen a man with less fear in the ring. 'You,' she said to Pablo. 'You are afraid to die now. You think that is something of importance. But Finito was afraid all the time and in the ring he was like a lion.'

'He had the fame of being very valiant,' the second brother said.

'Never have I known a man with so much fear,' Pilar said. 'He would not even have a bull's head in the house. One time at the feria of Valladolid he killed a bull of Pablo Romero very well—'

'I remember,' the first brother said. 'I was at the ring. It was a soap-colored one with a curly forehead and with very high horns. It was a bull of over thirty arrobas. It was the last bull he killed in Valladolid.'

'Exactly,' Pilar said. 'And afterwards the club of enthusiasts who met in the Cafe Colon and had taken his name for their club had the head of the bull mounted and presented it to him at a small banquet at the Cafe Colon. During the meal they had the head on the the wall, but it was covered with a cloth. I was at the table and others were there, Pastora, who is uglier than I am, and the Nina de los Peines, and other gypsies and whores of great category. It was a banquet, small but of great intensity and almost of a violence due to a dispute between Pastora and one of the most significant whores over a question of propriety. I, myself, was feeling more than happy and I was sitting by Finito and I noticed he would not look up at the bull's head, which was shrouded in a purple cloth as the images of the saints are covered in church during the week of the passion of our former Lord.

'Finito did not eat much because he had received a *palotaxo*, a blow from the flat of the horn when he had gone in to kill in his last corrida of the year at Zaragoza, and it had rendered him unconscious for some time and even now he could not hold food on his stomach and he would put his handkerchief to his mouth and deposit a quantity of blood in it at intervals throughout the banquet. What was I going to tell you?'

'The bull's head,' Primitivo said. 'The stuffed head of the bull.' 'Yes,' Pilar said. 'Yes. But I must tell certain details so that you will see it. Finito was never very merry, you know. He was essentially solemn and I had never known him when we were alone to laugh at anything. Not even at things which were very comic. He took everything with great seriousness. He was almost as serious as Fernando. But this was a banquet given him by a club of *aficionados* banded together into the *Club Finito* and it was necessary for him to give an appearance of gaiety and friendliness and merriment. So all during the meal he smiled and made friendly remarks and it was only I who noticed what he was doing with the handkerchief. He had three handkerchiefs with him and he filled the three of them and then he said to me in a very low voice, 'Pilar, I can support this no further. I think I must leave.'

'Let us leave then,' I said. For I saw he was suffering much. There was great hilarity by this time at the banquet and the noise was tremendous.

'No. I cannot leave,' Finito said to me. 'After all it is a club named for me and I have an obligation.'

'If thou art ill let us go,' I said.

'Nay,' he said. 'I will stay. Give me some of that manzanilla.'

'I did not think it was wise of him to drink, since he had eaten nothing, and since he had such a condition of the stomach; but he was evidently unable to support the merriment and the hilarity and the noise longer without taking something. So I watched him drink, very rapidly, almost a bottle of the manzanilla. Having exhausted his handkerchiefs he was now employing his napkin for the use he had previously made of his handkerchiefs.

'Now indeed the banquet had reached a stage of great enthusiasm and some of the least heavy of the whores were being paraded around the table on the shoulders of various of the club members. Pastora was prevailed upon to sing and El Nino Ricardo played the guitar and it was very moving and an occasion of true joy and drunken friendship of the highest order. Never have I seen a banquet at which a higher pitch of *realjlamenco* enthusiasm was reached and yet we had not arrived at the unveiling of the bull's head which was, after all, the reason for the celebration of the banquet.

'I was enjoying myself to such an extent and I was so busy clapping my hands to the playing of Ricardo and aiding to make up a team to clap for the singing of the Nina de los Peines that I did not notice that Finito had filled his own napkin by now, and that he had taken mine. He was drinking more manzanilla now and his eyes were very bright, and he was nodding very happily to every one. He could not speak much because at any time, while speaking, he might have to resort to his napkin; but he was giving an appearance of great gayety and enjoyment which, after all, was what he was there for.

'So the banquet proceeded and the man who sat next to me had been the former manager of Rafael eI Gallo and he was telling me a story, and the end of it was, 'So Rafael came to me and said,' You are the best friend I have in the world and the noblest. I love you like a brother and I wish to make you a present.' So then he gave me a beautiful diamond stick pin and kissed me on both cheeks and we were both very moved. Then Rafael el Gallo, having given me the diamond stick pin, walked out of the cafe and I said to Retana who was sitting at the table, 'That dirty gypsy had just signed a contract with another manager.' '

'What do you mean?' Retana asked.'

'I've managed him for ten years and he has never given me a present before,' the manager of El Gallo had said. 'That's the only thing it can mean.' And sure enough it was true and that was how El Gallo left him.

'But at this point, Pastora intervened in the conversation, not perhaps as much to defend the good name of Rafael, since no one had ever spoken harder against him than she had herself, but because the manager had spoken against the gypsies by employing the phrase, 'Dirty gypsy.' She intervened so forcibly and in such terms that the manager was reduced to silence. I intervened to quiet Pastora and another *Gitana* intervened to quiet me and the din was such that no one could distinguish any words which passed except the one great word 'whore' which roared out above all other words until quiet was restored and the three of us who had intervened sat looking down into our glasses and then I noticed that Finito was staring at the bull's head, still draped in the purple cloth, with a look of horror on his face. 'At this moment the president of the Club commenced the speech which was to precede the unveiling of the head and all through the speech which was applauded with shouts of *'Ole!'* and poundings on the table I was watching Finito who was making use of his, no, my, napkin and sinking further back in his chair and staring with horror and fascination at the shrouded bull's head on the wall opposite him.

'Toward the end of the speech, Finito began to shake his head and he got further back in the chair all the time.

'How are you, little one?' I said to him but when he looked at me he did not recognize me and he only shook his head and said, 'No. No. No.'

'So the president of the Club reached the end of the speech and then, with everybody cheering him, he stood on a chair and reached up and untied the cord that bound the purple shroud over the head and slowly pulled it clear of the head and it stuck on one of the horns and he lifted it clear and pulled it off the sharp polished horns and there was that great yellow bull with black horns that swung way out and pointed forward, their white tips sharp as porcupine quills, and the head of the bull was as though he were alive; his forehead was curly as in life and his nostrils were open and his eyes were bright and he was there looking straight at Finito.

'Every one shouted and applauded and Finito sunk further back in the chair and then every one was quiet and looking at him and he said, 'No. No,' and looked at the bull and pulled further back and then he said, 'No!' very loudly and a big blob of blood came out and he didn't even put up the napkin and it slid down his chin and he was still looking at the bull and he said, 'All season, yes. To make money, yes. To eat, yes. But I can't eat. Hear me? My stomach's bad. But now with the season finished! No! No! No!' He looked around at the table and then he looked at the bull's head and said, 'No,' once more and then he put his head down and he put his napkin up to his mouth and then he just sat there like that and said nothing and the banquet, which had started so well, and promised to mark an epoch in hilarity and good fellowship was not a success.'

'Then how long after that did he die?' Primitivo asked.

'That winter,' Pilar said. 'He never recovered from that last blow with the flat of the horn in Zaragoza. They are worse than a goring, for the injury is internal and it does not heal. He received one almost every time he went in to kill and it was for this reason he was not more successful. It was difficult for him to get out from over the horn because of his short stature. Nearly always the side of the horn struck him. But of course many were only glancing blows.'

'If he was so short he should not have tried to be a matador,' Primitivo said.

Pilar looked at Robert Jordan and shook her head. Then she bent over the big iron pot, still shaking her head.

What a people they are, she thought. What a people are the Spaniards, 'and if he was so short he should not have tried to be a matador.' And I hear it and say nothing. I have no rage for that and having made an explanation I am silent. How simple it is when one knows nothing. *Quesencillo!* Knowing nothing one says, 'He was not much of a matador.' Knowing nothing another says, 'He was tubercular.'

And another says, after one, knowing, has explained, 'If he was so short he should not have tried to be a matador.'

Now, bending over the fire, she saw on the bed again the naked brown body with the gnarled scars in both thighs, the deep, seared whorl below the ribs on the right side of the chest and the long white welt along the side that ended in the armpit. She saw the eyes closed and the solemn brown face and the curly black hair pushed back now from the forehead and she was sitting by him on the bed rubbing the legs, chafing the taut muscles of the calves, kneading them, loosening them, and then tapping them lightly with her folded hands, loosening the cramped muscles.

'How is it?' she said to him. 'How are the legs, little one?' 'Very well, Pilar,' he would say without opening his eyes. 'Do you want me to rub the chest?'

'Nay, Pilar. Please do not touch it.' 'And the upper legs?'

'No. They hurt too badly.'

'But if I rub them and put liniment on, it will warm them and they will be better.'

'Nay, Pilar. Thank thee. I would rather they were not touched.' 'I will wash thee with alcohol.'

'Yes. Do it very lightly.'

'You were enormous in the last bull,' she would say to him and he would say, 'Yes, I killed him very well.'

Then, having washed him and covered him with a sheet, she would lie by him in the bed and he would put a brown hand out and touch her and say, 'Thou art much woman, Pilar.' It was the nearest to a joke he ever made and then, usually, after the fight, he would go to sleep and she would lie there, holding his hand in her two hands and listening to him breathe.

He was often frightened in his sleep and she would feel his hand grip tightly and see the sweat bead on his forehead and if he woke, she said, 'It's nothing,' and he slept again. She was with him thus five years and never was unfaithful to him, that is almost never, and then after the funeral, she took up with Pablo who led picador horses in the ring and was like all the bulls that Finito had spent his life killing. But neither bull force nor bull courage lasted, she knew now, and what did last? I last, she thought. Yes, I have lasted. But for what?

'Maria,' she said. 'Pay some attention to what you are doing. That is a fire to cook with. Not to burn down a city.'

Just then the gypsy came in the door. He was covered with snow and he stood there holding his carbine and stamping the snow from his feet.

Robert Jordan stood up and went over to the door, 'Well?' he said to the gypsy.

'Six-hour watches, two men at a time on the big bridge,' the gypsy said. 'There are eight men and a corporal at the road mender's hut. Here is thy chronometer.'

'What about the sawmill post?'

'The old man is there. He can watch that and the road both.' 'And the road?' Robert Jordan asked.

'The same movement as always,' the gypsy said. 'Nothing out of the usual. Several motor cars.'

The gypsy looked cold, his dark face was drawn with the cold and his hands were red. Standing in the mouth of the cave he took off his jacket and shook it.

'I stayed until they changed the watch,' he said. 'It was changed at noon and at six. That is a long watch. I am glad I am not in their army.'

'Let us go for the old man,' Robert Jordan said, putting on his leather coat.

'Not me,' the gypsy said. 'I go now for the fire and the hot soup. I will tell one of these where he is and he can guide you. Hey, loafers,' he called to the men who sat at the table. 'Who wants to guide the *Inglés* to where the old man is watching the road?'

'I will go,' Fernando rose. 'Tell me where it is.'

'Listen,' the gypsy said. 'It is here-' and he told him where the old man, Anselmo, was posted.

15

Anselmo was crouched in the lee of the trunk of a big tree and the snow blew past on either side. He was pressed close against the tree and his hands were inside of the sleeves of his jacket, each hand shoved up into the opposite sleeve, and his head was pulled as far down into the jacket as it would go. If I stay here much longer I will freeze, he thought, and that will be of no value. The *Inglés* told me to stay until I was relieved but he did not know then about this storm. There has been no abnormal movement on the road and I know the dispositions and the habits of this post at the sawmill across the road. I should go now to the camp. Anybody with sense would be expecting me to return to the camp. I will stay a little longer, he thought, and then go to the camp. It is the fault of the orders, which are too rigid. There is no allowance for a change in circumstance. He rubbed his feet together and then took his hands out of the jacket sleeves and bent over and rubbed his legs with them and patted his feet together to keep the circulation going. It was less cold there, out of the wind in the shelter of the tree, but he would have to start walking shortly.

As he crouched, rubbing his feet, he heard a motorcar on the road. It had on chains and one link of chain was slapping and, as he watched, it came up the snow-covered road, green and brown painted, in broken patches of daubed color, the windows blued over so that you could not see in, with only a half circle left clear in the blue for the occupants to look out through. It was a two-year-old RollsRoyce town car camouflaged for the use of the General Staff but Anselmo did not know that. He could not see into the car where three officers sat wrapped in their capes. Two were on the back seat and one sat on the folding chair. The officer on the folding chair was looking out of the slit in the blue of the window as the car passed but Anselmo did not know this. Neither of them saw the other.

The car passed in the snow directly below him. Anselmo saw the chauffeur, red-faced and steel-helmeted, his face and helmet projecting out of the blanket cape he wore and he saw the forward jut of the automatic rifle the orderly who sat beside the chauffeur carried. Then the car was gone up the road and Anselmo reached into the inside of his jacket and took out from his shirt pocket the two sheets torn from Robert Jordan's notebook and made a mark after the drawing of a motorcar. It was the tenth car up for the day. Six had come down. Four were still up. It was not an unusual amount of cars to move upon that road but Anselmo did not distinguish between the Fords, Fiats, Opels, Renaults, and Citroens of the staff of the Division that held the passes and the line of the mountain and the Rolls-Royces, Lancias, Mercedes, and Isottas of the General Staff. This was the sort of distinction that Robert Jordan should have made and, if he had been there instead of the old man, he would have appreciated the significance of these cars which had gone up. But he was not there and the old man simply made a mark for a motorcar going up the road, on the sheet of note paper.

Anselmo was now so cold that he decided he had best go to camp before it was dark. He had no fear of missing the way, but he thought it was useless to stay longer and the wind was blowing colder all the time and there was no lessening of the snow. But when he stood up and stamped his feet and looked through the driving snow at the road he did not start off up the hillside but stayed leaning against the sheltered side of the pine tree.

The *Inglés* told me to stay, he thought. Even now he may be on the way here and, if I leave this place, he may lose himself in the snow searching for me. All through this war we have suffered from a lack of discipline and from the disobeying of orders and I will wait a while still for the *Inglés*. But if he does not come soon I must go in spite of all orders for I have a report to make now, and I have much to do in these days, and to freeze here is an exaggeration and without utility.

Across the road at the sawmill smoke was coming out of the chimney and Anselmo could smell it blown toward him through the snow. The fascists are warm, he thought, and they are comfortable, and tomorrow night we will kill them. It is a strange thing and I do not like to think of it. I have watched them all day and they are the same men that we are. I believe that I could walk up to the mill and knock on the door and I would be welcome except that they have orders to challenge all travellers and ask to see their papers. It is only orders that come between us. Those men are not fascists. I call them so, but they are not. They are poor men as we are. They should never be fighting against us and I do not like to think of the killing.

These at this post are Gallegos. I know that from hearing them talk this afternoon. They cannot desert because if they do their families will be shot. Gallegos are either very intelligent or very dumb and brutal. I have known both kinds. Lister is a Gallego from the same town as Franco. I wonder what these Gallegos think of this snow now at this time of year. They have no high mountains such as these and in their country it always rains and it is always green.

A light showed in the window of the sawmill and Anselmo shivered and thought, damn that *Inglés!* There are the Gallegos warm and in a house here in our country, and I am freezing behind a tree and we live in a hole in the rocks like beasts in the mountain. But tomorrow, he thought, the beasts will come out of their hole and these that are now so comfortable will die warm in their blankets. As those died in the night when we raided Otero, he thought. He did not like to remember Otero.

In Otero, that night, was when he first killed and he hoped he would not have to kill in this of the suppressing of these posts. It was in Otero that Pablo knifed the sentry when Anselmo pulled the blanket over his head and the sentry caught Anselmo's foot and held it, smothered as he was in the blanket, and made a crying noise in the blanket and Anselmo had to feel in the blanket and knife him until he let go of the foot and was still. He had his knee across the man's throat to keep him silent and he was knifing into the bundle when Pablo tossed the bomb through the window into the room where the men of the post were all sleeping. And when the flash came it was as though the whole world burst red and yellow before your eyes and two more bombs were in already. Pablo had pulled the pins and tossed them quickly through the window, and those who were not killed in their beds were killed as they rose from bed when the second bomb exploded. That was in the great days of Pablo when he scourged the country like a tartar and no fascist post was safe at night.

And now, he is as finished and as ended as a boar that has been altered, Anselmo thought, and, when the altering has been accomplished and the squealing is over you cast the two stones away and the boar, that is a boar no longer, goes snouting and rooting up to them and eats them. No, he is not that bad, Anselmo grinned, one can think too badly even of Pablo. But he is ugly enough and changed enough.

It is too cold, he thought. That the *Inglés* should come and that I should not have to kill in this of the posts. These four Gallegos and their corporal are for those who like the killing. The *Inglés* said that. I will do it if it is my duty but the *Inglés* said that I would be with him at the bridge and that this would be left to others. At the bridge there will be a battle and, if I am able to endure the battle, then I will have done all that an old man may do in this war. But let the *Inglés* come now, for I am cold and to see the light in the mill where I know that the Gallegos are warm makes me colder still. I wish that I were in my own house again and that this war were over. But you have no house now, he thought. We must win this war before you can ever return to your house.

Inside the sawmill one of the soldiers was sitting on his bunk and greasing his boots. Another lay in his bunk sleeping. The third was cooking and the corporal was reading a paper. Their helmets hung on nails driven into the wall and their rifles leaned against the plank wall.

'What kind of country is this where it snows when it is almost June?' the soldier who was sitting on the bunk said.

'It is a phenomenon,' the corporal said.

'We are in the moon of May,' the soldier who was cooking said. 'The moon of May has not yet terminated.'

'What kind of a country is it where it snows in May?' the soldier on the bunk insisted.

'In May snow is no rarity in these mountains,' the corporal said. 'I have been colder in Madrid in the month of May than in any other month.'

'And hotter, too,' the soldier who was cooking said.

'May is a month of great contrasts in temperature,' the corporal said. 'Here, in Castile, May is a month of great heat but it can have much cold.'

'Or rain,' the soldier on the bunk said. 'In this past May it rained almost every day.'

'It did not,' the soldier who was cooking said. 'And anyway this past May was the moon of April.'

'One could go crazy listening to thee and thy moons,' the corporal said. 'Leave this of the moons alone.'

'Any one who lives either by the sea or by the land knows that it is the moon and not the month which counts,' the soldier who was cooking said. 'Now for example, we have just started the moon of May. Yet it is coming on June.'

'Why then do we not get definitely behind in the seasons?' the corporal said. 'The whole proposition gives me a headache.'

'You are from a town,' the soldier who was cooking said. 'You are from Lugo. What would you know of the sea or of the land?' 'One learns more in a town than you *anal Jabetos* learn in thy sea or thy land.'

'In this moon the first of the big schools of sardines come,' the soldier who was cooking said. 'In this moon the sardine boats will be outfitting and the mackerel will have gone north.'

'Why are you not in the navy if you come from Noya?' the corporal asked.

'Because I am not inscribed from Noya but from Negreira, where I was born. And from Negreira, which is up the river Tambre, they take you for the army.'

'Worse luck,' said the corporal.

'Do not think the navy is without peril,' the soldier who was sitting on the bunk said. 'Even without the possibility of combat that is a dangerous coast in the winter.'

'Nothing can be worse than the army,' the corporal said.

'And you a corporal,' the soldier who was cooking said. 'What a way of speaking is that?'

'Nay,' the corporal said. 'I mean for dangers. I mean the endurance of bombardments, the necessity to attack, the life of the parapet.'

'Here we have little of that,' the soldier on the bunk said.

'By the Grace of God,' the corporal said. 'But who knows when we will be subject to it again? Certainly we will not have something as easy as this forever!'

'How much longer do you think we will have this detail?'

'I don't know,' the corporal said. 'But I wish we could have it for all of the war.'

'Six hours is too long to be on guard,' the soldier who was cooking said.

'We will have three-hour watches as long as this storm holds,' the corporal said. 'That is only normal.'

'What about all those staff cars?' the soldier on the bunk asked. 'I did not like the look of all those staff cars.'

'Nor I,' the corporal said. 'All such things are of evil omen.' 'And aviation,' the soldier who was cooking said. 'Aviation IS another bad sign.'

'But we have formidable aviation,' the corporal said. 'The Reds have no aviation such as we have. Those planes this morning were something to make any man happy.'

'I have seen the Red planes when they were something serious,' the soldier on the bunk said. 'I have seen those two motor bombers when they were a horror to endure.'

'Yes. But they are not as formidable as our aviation,' the corporal said. 'We have an aviation that is insuperable.'

This was how they were talking in the sawmill while Anselmo waited in the snow watching the road and the light in the sawmill window.

I hope I am not for the killing, Anselmo was thinking. I think that after the war there will have to be some great penance done for the killing. If we no longer have religion after the war then I think there must be some form of civic penance organized that all may be cleansed from the killing or else we will never have a true and human basis for living. The killing is necessary, I know, but still the doing of it is very bad for a man and I think that, after all this is over and we have won the war, there must be a penance of some kind for the cleansing of us all.

Anselmo was a very good man and whenever he was alone for long, and he was alone much of the time, this problem of the killing returned to him.

I wonder about the *Inglés*, he thought. He told me that he did not mind it. Yet he seems to be both sensitive and kind. It may be that in the younger people it does not have an importance. It may be that in foreigners, or in those who have not had our religion, there is not the same attitude. But I think any one doing it will be brutalized in time and I think that even though necessary, it is a great sin and that afterwards we must do something very strong to atone for it.

It was dark now and he looked at the light across the road and shook his arms against his chest to warm them. Now, he thought, he would certainly leave for the camp; but something kept him there beside the tree above the road. It was snowing harder and Anselmo thought: if only we could blow the bridge tonight. On a night like this it would be nothing to take the posts and blow the bridge and it would all be over and done with. On a night like this you could do anything.

Then he stood there against the tree stamping his feet softly and he did not think any more about the bridge. The coming of the dark always made him feel lonely and tonight he felt so lonely that there was a hollowness in him as of hunger. In the old days he could help this loneliness by the saying of prayers and often coming home from hunting he would repeat a great number of the same prayer and it made him feel better. But he had not prayed once since the movement. He missed the prayers but he thought it would be unfair and hypocritical to say them and he did not wish to ask any favors or for any different treatment than all the men were receiving.

No, he thought, I am lonely. But so are all the soldiers and the wives of all the soldiers and all those who have lost families or parents. I have no wife, but I am glad that she died before the movement. She would not have understood it. I have no children and I never will have any children. I am lonely in the day when I am not working but when the dark comes it is a time of great loneliness. But one thing I have that no man nor any God can take from me and that is that I have worked well for the Republic. I have worked hard for the good that we will all share later. I have worked my best from the first of the movement and I have done nothing that I am ashamed of.

All that I am sorry for is the killing. But surely there will be an opportunity to atone for that because for a sin of that sort that so many bear, certainly some just relief will be devised. I would like to talk with the *Inglés* about it but, being young, it is possible that he might not understand. He mentioned the killing before. Or was it I that mentioned it? He must have killed much, but he shows no signs of liking it. In those who like it there is always a rottenness.

It must really be a great sin, he thought. Because certainly it is the one thing we have no right to do even though, as I know, it is necessary. But in Spain it is done too lightly and often without true necessity and there is much quick injustice which, afterward, can never be repaired. I wish I did not think about it so much, he thought. I wish there were a penance for it that one could commence now because it is the only thing that I have done in all my life that makes me feel badly when I am alone. All the other things are forgiven or one had a chance to atone for them by kindness or in some decent way. But I think this of the killing must be a very great sin and I would like to fix it up. Later on there may be certain days that one can work for the state or something that one can do that will remove it. It will probably be something that one pays as in the days of the Church, he thought, and smiled. The Church was well organized for sin. That pleased him and he was smiling in the dark when Robert Jordan came up to him. He came silently and the old man did not see him until he was there.

'Hola, *viejo*,' Robert Jordan whispered and clapped him on the back. 'How's the old one?'

'Very cold,' Anselmo said. Fernando was standing a little apart, his back turned against the driving snow.

'Come on,' Robert Jordan whispered. 'Get on up to camp and get warm. It was a crime to leave you here so long.'

'That is their light,' Anselmo pointed. 'Where's the sentry?'

'You do not see him from here. He is around the bend.'

'The hell with them,' Robert Jordan said. 'You tell me at camp. Come on, let's go.'

'Let me show you,' Anselmo said.

'I'm going to look at it in the morning,' Robert Jordan said. 'Here, take a swallow of this.'

He handed the old man his flask. Anselmo tipped it up and swallowed.

'*Ayee*,' he said and rubbed his mouth. 'It is fire.'

'Come on,' Robert Jordan said in the dark. 'Let us go.'

It was so dark now you could only see the flakes blowing past and the rigid dark of the pine trunks. Fernando was standing a little way up the hill. Look at that cigar store Indian, Robert Jordan thought. I suppose I have to offer him a drink.

'Hey, Fernando,' he said as he came up to him. 'A swallow?'

'No,' said Fernando. 'Thank you.'

Thank *you*, I mean, Robert Jordan thought. I'm glad cigar store Indians don't drink. There isn't too much of that left. Boy, I'm glad to see this old man, Robert Jordan thought. He looked at Anselmo and then clapped him on the back again as they started up the hill.

'I'm glad to see you, *viejo*,' he said to Anselmo. 'If I ever get gloomy, when I see you it cheers me up. Come on, let's get up there.'

They were going up the hill in the snow.

'Back to the palace of Pablo,' Robert Jordan said to Anselmo. It sounded wonderful in Spanish.

'*El Palacio del Miedo*,' Anselmo said. 'The Palace of Fear.'

'*La cueva de los huevos perdidos*,' Robert Jordan capped the other happily. 'The cave of the lost eggs.'

'What eggs?' Fernando asked.

'A joke,' Robert Jordan said. 'Just a joke. Not eggs, you know. The others.'

'But why are they lost?' Fernando asked.

'I don't know,' said Robert Jordan. 'Take a book to tell you. Ask Pilar,' then he put his arm around Anselmo's shoulder and held him tight as they walked and shook him. 'Listen,' he said. 'I'm glad to see you, hear? You don't know what it means to find somebody in this country in the same place they were left.'

It showed what confidence and intimacy he had that he could say anything against the country.

'I am glad to see thee,' Anselmo said. 'But I was just about to leave.'

'Like hell you would have,' Robert Jordan said happily. 'You'd have frozen first.'

'How was it up above?' Anselmo asked. 'Fine,' said Robert Jordan. 'Everything is fine.'

He was very happy with that sudden, rare happiness that can come to any one with a command in a revolutionary arm; the happiness of finding that even one of your flanks holds. If both flanks ever held I suppose it would be too much to take, he thought. I don't know who is prepared to stand that. And if you extend along a flank, any flank, it eventually becomes one man. Yes, one man. This was not the axiom he wanted. But this was a good man. One good man. You are going to be the left flank when we have the battle, he thought. I better not tell you that yet. It's going to be an awfully small battle, he thought. But it's going to be an awfully good one. Well, I always wanted to fight one on my own. I always had an opinion on what was wrong with everybody else's, from Agin court down. I will have to make this a good one. It is going to be small but very select. If I have to do what I think I will have to do it will be very select indeed.

'Listen,' he said to Anselmo. 'I'm awfully glad to see you.'

'And me to see thee,' the old man said.

As they went up the hill in the dark, the wind at their backs, the storm blowing past them as they climbed, Anselmo did not feel lonely. He had not been lonely since the *Inglés* had clapped him on the shoulder. The *Inglés* was pleased and happy and they joked together. The *Inglés* said it all went well and he was not worried. The drink in his stomach warmed him and his feet were warming now climbing.

'Not much on the road,' he said to the *Inglés*.

'Good,' the *Inglés* told him. 'You will show me when we get there.'

Anselmo was happy now and he was very pleased that he had stayed there at the post of observation.

If he had come in to camp it would have been all right. It would have been the intelligent and correct thing to have done under the circumstances, Robert Jordan was thinking. But he stayed as he was told, Robert Jordan thought. That's the rarest thing that can happen in Spain. To stay in a storm, in a way, corresponds to a lot of things. It's not for nothing that the Germans call an attack a storm. I could certainly use a couple more who would stay. I most certainly could. I Wonder if that Fernando would stay. It's just possible. After all, he is the one who suggested coming out just now. Do you suppose he would stay? Wouldn't that be good? He's just about stubborn enough. I'll have to make some inquiries. Wonder what the old cigar store Indian is thinking about now.

'What are you thinking about, Fernando?' Robert Jordan asked. 'Why do you ask?'

'Curiosity,' Robert Jordan said. 'I am a man of great curiosity.'

'I was thinking of supper,' Fernando said. 'Do you like to eat?'

'Yes. Very much.'

'How's Pilar's cooking?'

'Average,' Fernando answered.

He's a second Coolidge, Robert Jordan thought. But, you know, I have just a hunch that he would stay.

The three of them plodded up the hill in the snow.

16

'El Sordo was here,' Pilar said to Robert Jordan. They had come in out of the storm to the smoky warmth of the cave and the woman had motioned Robert Jordan over to her with a nod of her head. 'He's gone to look for horses.'

'Good. Did he leave any word for me?' 'Only that he had gone for horses.'

'And we?'

'*No sé*,' she said. 'Look at him.'

Robert Jordan had seen Pablo when he came in and Pablo had grinned at him. Now he looked over at him sitting at the board table and grinned and waved his hand.

'Inglés,' Pablo called. 'It's still falling, Inglés.'

Robert Jordan nodded at him.

'Let me take thy shoes and dry them,' Maria said. 'I will hang them here in the smoke of the fire.'

'Watch out you don't burn them,' Robert Jordan told her. 'I don't want to go around here barefoot. What's the matter?' he turned to Pilar. 'Is this a meeting? Haven't you any sentries out?'

'In this storm? Qué va.'

There were six men sitting at the table and leaning back against the wall. Anselmo and Fernando were still shaking the snow from their jackets, beating their trousers and rapping their feet against the wall by the entrance.

'Let me take thy jacket,' Maria said. 'Do not let the snow melt on it.'

Robert Jordan slipped out of his jacket, beat the snow from his trousers, and untied his shoes.

'You will get everything wet here,' Pilar said. 'It was thee who called me.'

'Still there IS no impediment to returning to the door for thy brushing.'

'Excuse me,' Robert Jordan said, standing in his bare feet on the dirt floor. 'Hunt me a pair of socks, Maria.' 'The Lord and Master,' Pilar said and poked a piece of wood into the fire.

'Hay que aprovechar el tiempo,' Robert Jordan told her.

'You have to take advantage of what time there is.'

'It is locked,' Maria said.

'Here is the key,' and he tossed it over.

'It does not fit this sack.'

'It is the other sack. They are on top and at the side.'

The girl found the pair of socks, closed the sack, locked it and brought them over with the key.

'Sit down and put them on and rub thy feet well,' she said. Robert Jordan grinned at her.

'Thou canst not dry them with thy hair?' he said for Pilar to hear.

'What a swine,' she said. 'First he is the Lord of the Manor. Now he is our ex-Lord Himself. Hit him with a chunk of wood, Maria.'

'Nay,' Robert Jordan said to her. 'I am joking because I am happy.'

'You are happy?'

'Yes,' he said. 'I think everything goes very well.'

'Roberto,' Maria said. 'Go sit down and dry thy feet and let me bring thee something to drink to warm thee.'

'You would think that man had never dampened foot before,' Pilar said. 'Nor that a flake of snow had ever fallen.'

Maria brought him a sheepskin and put it on the dirt floor of the cave.

'There,' she said. 'Keep that under thee until thy shoes are dry.'

The sheepskin was fresh dried and not tanned and as Robert Jordan rested his stocking feet on it he could feel it crackle like parchment.

The fire was smoking and Pilar called to Maria, 'Blow up the fire, worthless one. This is no smokehouse.'

'Blow it thyself,' Maria said. 'I am searching for the bottle that El Sordo left.'

'It is behind his packs,' Pilar told her. 'Must you care for him as a sucking child?'

'No,' Maria said. 'As a man who is cold and wet. And a man who has just come to his house. Here it is.' She brought the bottle to where Robert Jordan sat. 'It is the bottle of this noon. With this bottle one could make a beautiful lamp. When we have electricity again, what a lamp we can make of this bottle.' She looked at the pinch-hattie admiringly. 'How do you take this, Roberto?'

'I thought I was *Inglés*,' Robert Jordan said to her.

'I call thee Roberto before the others,' she said in a low voice and blushed. 'How do you want it, Roberto?'

'Roberto,' Pablo said thickly and nodded his head at Robert Jordan. 'How do you want it, Don Roberto?'

'Do you want some?' Robert Jordan asked him.

Pablo shook his head. 'I am making myself drunk with wine,' he said with dignity.

'Go with Bacchus,' Robert Jordan said in Spanish. 'Who is Bacchus?' Pablo asked.

'A comrade of thine,' Robert Jordan said.

'Never have I heard of him,' Pablo said heavily. 'Never in these mountains.'

'Give a cup to Anselmo,' Robert Jordan said to Maria. 'It is he who is cold.' He was putting on the dry pair of socks and the whiskey and water in the cup tasted clean and thinly warming. But it does not curl around inside of you the way the absinthe does, he thought. There is nothing like absinthe.

Who would imagine they would have whiskey up here, he thought. But La Granja was the most likely place in Spain to find it when you thought it over. Imagine Sordo getting a bottle for the visiting dynamiter and then remembering to bring it down and leave it. It wasn't just manners that they had. Manners would have been producing the bottle and having a formal drink. That was what the French would have done and then they would have saved what was left for another occasion. No, the true thoughtfulness of thinking the visitor would like it and then bringing it down for him to enjoy when you yourself were engaged in something where there was every reason to think of no one else but yourself and of nothing but the matter in hand-that was Spanish. One kind of Spanish, he thought. Remembering to bring the whiskey was one of the reasons you loved these people. Don't go romanticizing them, he thought.

There are as many sorts of Spanish as there are Americans. But still, bringing the whiskey was very handsome.

'How do you like it?' he asked Anselmo.

The old man was sitting by the fire with a smile on his face, his big hands holding the cup. He shook his head.

'No?' Robert Jordan asked him.

'The child put water in it,' Anselmo said.

'Exactly as Roberto takes it,' Maria said. 'Art thou something special?'

'No,' Anselmo told her. 'Nothing special at all. But I like to feel it burn as it goes down.'

'Give me that,' Robert Jordan told the girl, 'and pour him some of that which burns.'

He tipped the contents of the cup into his own and handed it back empty to the girl, who poured carefully into it from the bottle.

'Ah,' Anselmo took the cup, put his head back and let it run down his throat. He looked at Maria standing holding the bottle and winked at her, tears coming from both eyes. 'That,' he said. 'That.' Then he licked his lips. '*That* is what kills the worm that haunts us.'

'Roberto,' Maria said and came over to him, still holding the bottle. 'Are you ready to eat?'

'Is it ready?'

'It is ready when you wish it.'

'Have the others eaten?'

'All except you, Anselmo and Fernando.'

'Let us eat then,' he told her. 'And thou?' 'Afterwards with Pilar.'

'Eat now with us.'

'No. It would not be well.'

'Come on and eat. In my country a man does not eat before his woman.'

'That is thy country. Here it is better to eat after.'

'Eat with him,' Pablo said, looking up from the table. 'Eat with him. Drink with him. Sleep with him. Die with him. Follow the customs of his country.'

'Are you drunk?' Robert Jordan said, standing in front of Pablo. The dirty, stubble-faced man looked at him happily.

'Yes,' Pablo said. 'Where is thy country, *Inglés*, where the women eat with the men?'

'In *Estados Unidos* in the state of Montana.'

'Is it there that the men wear skirts as do the women?' 'No. That is in Scotland.'

'But listen,' Pablo said. 'When you wear skirts like that, *Inglés*—'

'I don't wear them,' Robert Jordan said.

'When you are wearing those skirts,' Pablo went on, 'what do you wear under them?'

'I don't know what the Scotch wear,' Robert Jordan said. 'I've wondered myself.'

'Not the *Escoceses*,' Pablo said. 'Who cares about the *Escoceses*? Who cares about anything with a name as rare as that? Not me. I don't care. You, I say, *Inglés*. You. What do you wear under your ski rts in your country?'

'Twice I have told you that we do not wear skirts,' Robert Jordan said. 'Neither drunk nor in joke.'

'But under your skirts,' Pablo insisted. 'Since it is well known that you wear skirts. Even the soldiers. I have seen photographs and also I have seen them in the Circus of Price. What do you wear under your skirts, *Inglés?*'

'*Los cojones,*' Robert Jordan said.

Anselmo laughed and so did the others who were listening; all except Fernando. The sound of the word, of the gross word spoken before the women, was offensive to him.

'Well, that is normal,' Pablo said. 'But it seems to me that with enough *cojones* you would not wear skirts.'

'Don't let him get started again, *Inglés,*' the flat-faced man with the broken nose who was called Primitivo said. 'He is drunk. Tell me, what do they raise in your country?'

'Cattle and sheep,' Robert Jordan said. 'Much grain also and beans. And also much beets for sugar.'

The three were at the table now and the others sat close by except Pablo, who sat by himself in front of a bowl of the wine. It was the same stew as the night before and Robert Jordan ate it hungrily.

'In your country there are mountains? With that name surely there are mountains,' Primitivo asked politely to make conversation. He was embarrassed at the drunkenness of Pablo.

'Many mountains and very high.' 'And are there good pastures?'

'Excellent; high pasture in the summer in forests controlled by the government. Then in the fall the cattle are brought down to the lower ranges.'

'Is the land there owned by the peasants?'

'Most land is owned by those who farm it. Originally the land was owned by the state and by living on it and declaring the intention of improving it, a man could obtain a title to a hundred and fifty hectares.'

'Tell me how this is done,' Agustin asked. 'That is an agrarian reform which means something.'

Robert Jordan explained the process of homesteading. He had never thought of it before as an agrarian reform.

'That is magnificent,' Primitivo said. 'Then you have a communism in your country?'

'No. That is done under the Republic.'

'For me,' Agustin said, 'everything can be done under the Re- public. I see no need for other form of government.'

'Do you have no big proprietors?' Andres asked. 'Many.'

'Then there must be abuses.'

'Certainly. There are many abuses.' 'But you will do away with them?'

'We try to more and more. But there are many abuses still.'

'But there are not great estates that must be broken up?'

'Yes. But there are those who believe that taxes will break them up.'

'How?'

Robert Jordan, wiping out the stew bowl with bread, explained how the income tax and inheritance tax worked. 'But the big estates remain. Also there are taxes on the land,' he said.

'But surely the big proprietors and the rich will make a revolution against such taxes. Such taxes appear to me to be revolutionary. They will revolt against the government when they see that they are threatened, exactly as the fascists have done here,' Primitivo said.

'It is possible.'

'Then you will have to fight in your country as we fight here.'

'Yes, we will have to fight.'

'But are there not many fascists in your country?'

'There are many who do not know they are fascists but will find it out when the time comes.'

'But you cannot destroy them until they rebel?'

'No,' Robert Jordan said. 'We cannot destroy them. But we can educate the people so that they will fear fascism and recognize it as it appears and combat it.'

'Do you know where there are no fascists?' Andres asked.

'Where?'

'In the town of Pablo,' Andres said and grinned.

'You know what was done in that village?' Primitivo asked Robert Jordan.

'Yes. I have heard the story.'

'From Pilar?'

'Yes.'

'You could not hear all of it from the woman,' Pablo said heavily. 'Because she did not see the end of it because she fell from a chair outside of the window.'

'You tell him what happened then,' Pilar said. 'Since I know not the story, let you tell it.'

'Nay,' Pablo said. 'I have never told it.'

'No,' Pilar said. 'And you will not tell it. And now you wish it had not happened.'

'No,' Pablo said. 'That is not true. And if all had killed the fascists as I did we would not have this war. But I would not have had it happen as it happened.'

'Why do you say that?' Primitivo asked him. 'Are you changing your politics?'

'No. But it was barbarous,' Pablo said. 'In those days I was very barbarous.'

'And now you are drunk,' Pilar said.

'Yes,' Pablo said. 'With your permission.'

'I liked you better when you were barbarous,' the woman said. 'Of all men the drunkard is the foulest. The thief when he is not stealing is like another. The extortioner does not practise in the home. The murderer when he is at home can wash his hands. But the drunkard stinks and vomits in his own bed and dissolves his organs in alcohol.

'You are a woman and you do not understand,' Pablo said equably. 'I am drunk on wine and I would be happy except for those people I have killed. All of them fill me with sorrow.' He shook his head lugubriously.

'Give him some of that which Sordo brought,' Pilar said. 'Give him something to animate him. He is becoming too sad to bear.'

'If I could restore them to life, I would,' Pablo said.

'Go and obscenity thyself,' Agustin said to him. 'What sort of place is this?'

'I would bring them all back to life,' Pablo said sadly. 'Everyone.'

'Thy mother,' Agustin shouted at him. 'Stop talking like this or get out. Those were fascists you killed.'

'You heard me,' Pablo said. 'I would restore them all to life.'

'And then you would walk on the water,' Pilar said. 'In my in life I have never seen such a man. Up until yesterday you preserved some remnants of manhood. And today there is not enough of you left to make a sick kitten. Yet you are happy your soddenness.'

'We should have killed all or none,' Pablo nodded his head. 'All or none.'

'Listen, *Inglés*,' Agustin said. 'How did you happen to come to Spain? Pay no attention to Pablo. He is drunk.'

'I came first twelve years ago to study the country and the language,' Robert Jordan said. 'I teach Spanish in a university.'

'You look very little like a professor,' Primitivo said.

'He has no beard,' Pablo said. 'Look at him. He has no beard.'

'Are you truly a professor?'

'An instructor.' 'But you teach?'

'Yes.'

'But why Spanish?' Andres asked. 'Would it not be easier to teach English since you are English?'

'He speaks Spanish as we do,' Anselmo said. 'Why should he not teach Spanish?'

'Yes. But it is, in a way, presumptuous for a foreigner to teach Spanish,' Fernando said. 'I mean nothing against you, Don Roberto.'

'He's a false professor,' Pablo said, very pleased with himself. 'He hasn't got a beard.'

'Surely you know English better,' Fernando said. 'Would it not be better and easier and clearer to teach English?'

'He doesn't teach it to Spaniards-' Pilar started to intervene. 'I should hope not,' Fernando said.

'Let me finish, you mule,' Pilar said to him. 'He teaches Spanish to Americans. North Americans.'

'Can they not speak Spanish?' Fernando asked. 'South Americans can.'

'Mule,' Pilar said. 'He teaches Spanish to North Americans who speak English.'

'Still and all I think it would be easier for him to teach English if that is what he speaks,' Fernando said.

'Can't you hear he speaks Spanish?' Pilar shook her head hopelessly at Robert Jordan.

'Yes. But with an accent.'

'Of where?' Robert Jordan asked.

'Of Estremadura,' Fernando said primly.

'Oh my mother,' Pilar said. 'What a people!'

'It is possible,' Robert Jordan said. 'I have come here from there.' 'As he well knows,' Pilar said.' You old maid,' she turned to Fernando. 'Have you had enough to eat?'

'I could eat more if there is a sufficient quantity,' Fernando told her. 'And do not think that I wish to say anything against you, Don Roberto—'

'Milk,' Agustin said simply. 'And milk again. Do we make the revolution in order to say Don Roberto to a comrade?'

'For me the revolution is so that all will say Don to all,' Fernando said. 'Thus should it be under the Republic.'

'Milk,' Agustin said. 'Black milk.'

'And I still think it would be easier and clearer for Don Roberto to teach English.'

'Don Roberto has no beard,' Pablo said. 'He is a false professor.'

'What do you mean, I have no beard?' Robert Jordan said. 'What's this?' He stroked his chin and his cheeks where the three-day growth made a blond stubble.

'Not a beard,' Pablo said. He shook his head. 'That's not a beard.' He was almost jovial now. 'He's a false professor.'

'I obscenity in the milk of all,' Agustin said, 'if it does not seem like a lunatic asylum here.'

'You should drink,' Pablo said to him.' To me everything appears normal. Except the lack of beard of Don Roberto.'

Maria ran her hand over Robert Jordan's cheek. 'He has a beard,' she said to Pablo.

'You should know,' Pablo said and Robert Jordan looked at him.

I don't think he is so drunk, Robert Jordan thought. No, not so drunk. And I think I had better watch myself.

'Thou,' he said to Pablo. 'Do you think this snow will last?' 'What do you think?'

'I asked you.'

'Ask another,' Pablo told him. 'I am not thy service of information. You have a paper from thy service of information. Ask the woman. She commands.'

'I asked thee.'

'Go and obscenity thyself,' Pablo told him. 'Thee and the woman and the girl.'

'He is drunk,' Primitivo said. 'Pay him no heed, *Inglés*.'

'I do not think he is so drunk,' Robert Jordan said.

Maria was standing behind him and Robert Jordan saw Pablo watching her over his shoulder. The small eyes, like a boar's, were watching her out of the round, stubble-covered head and Robert Jordan thought: I have known many killers in this war and some before and they were all different; there is no common trait nor feature; nor any such thing as the criminal type; but Pablo is certainly not handsome.

'I don't believe you can drink,' he said to Pablo. 'Nor that you're drunk.'

'I am drunk,' Pablo said with dignity. 'To drink is nothing. It is to be drunk that is important. *Estoy muy borracho.*'

'I doubt it,' Robert Jordan told him. 'Cowardly, yes.'

It was so quiet in the cave, suddenly, that he could hear the hissing noise the wood made burning on the hearth where Pilar cooked. He heard the sheepskin crackle as he rested his weight on his feet. He thought he could almost hear the snow falling outside. He could not, but he could hear the silence where it fell.

I'd like to kill him and have it over with, Robert Jordan was thinking. I don't know what he is going to do, but it is nothing good. Day after tomorrow is the bridge and this man is bad and he constitutes a danger to the success of the whole enterprise. Come on. Let us get it over with.

Pablo grinned at him and put one finger up and wiped it across his throat. He shook his head that turned only a little each way on his thick, short neck.

'Nay, *Inglés*,' he said. 'Do not provoke me.' He looked at Pilar and said to her, 'It is not thus that you get rid of me.'

'*Sinverguenza*,' Robert Jordan said to him, committed now in his own mind to the action. '*Cobarde.*'

'It is very possible,' Pablo said. 'But I am not to be provoked. Take something to drink, *Inglés*, and signal to the woman it was not successful.'

'Shut thy mouth,' Robert Jordan said. 'I provoke thee for myself.'

'It is not worth the trouble,' Pablo told him. 'I do not provoke.' 'Thou art a *bicho raro*,' Robert Jordan said, not wanting to let it go; not wanting to have it fail for the second time; knowing as he spoke that this had all been gone through before; having that feeling that he was playing a part from memory of something that he had read or had dreamed, feeling it all moving in a circle.

'Very rare, yes,' Pablo said. 'Very rare and very drunk. To your health, *Inglés*.' He dipped a cup in the wine bowl and held it up. '*Saiud y cojones.*'

He's rare, all right, Robert Jordan thought, and smart, and very complicated. He could no longer hear the fire for the sound of his own breathing.

'Here's to you,' Robert Jordan said, and dipped a cup into the wine. Betrayal wouldn't amount to anything without all these pledges, he thought. Pledge up. '*Saiud*,' he said. '*Salud* and *Salud* again,' you *salud*, he thought. *Salud*, you *salud*.

'Don Roberto,' Pablo said heavily. 'Don Pablo,' Robert Jordan said.

'You're no professor,' Pablo said, 'because you haven't got a beard.

And also to do away with me you have to assassinate me and, for this, you have not *cojones*.'

He was looking at Robert Jordan with his mouth closed so that his lips made a tight line, like the mouth of a fish, Robert Jordan thought. With that head it is like one of those porcupine fish that swallow air and swell up after they are caught.

'*Salud*, Pablo,' Robert Jordan said and raised the cup up and drank from it. 'I am learning much from thee.'

'I am teaching the professor,' Pablo nodded his head. 'Come on, Don Roberto, we will be friends.'

'We are friends already,' Robert Jordan said.

'But now we will be good friends.'

'We are good friends already.'

'I'm going to get out of here,' Agustin said. 'Truly, it is said that we must eat a ton of it in this life but I have twenty-five pounds of it stuck in each of my ears this minute.'

'What is the matter, *negro?*' Pablo said to him. 'Do you not like to see friendship between Don Roberto and me?'

'Watch your mouth about calling me *negro.*' Agustin went over to him and stood in front of Pablo holding his hands low.

'So you are called,' Pablo said.

'Not by thee.'

'Well, then, *blanco—*'

'Nor that, either.'

'What are you then, Red?'

'Yes. Red. *Roja*. With the Red star of the army and in favor of the Republic. And my name is Agustin.'

'What a patriotic man,' Pablo said. 'Look, *Inglés,* what an exemplary patriot.'

Agustin hit him hard across the mouth with his left hand, bringing it forward in a slapping, backhand sweep. Pablo sat there. The corners of his mouth were wine-stained and his expression did not change, but Robert Jordan watched his eyes narrow, as a cat's pupils close to vertical slits in a strong light.

'Nor this,' Pablo said. 'Do not count on this, woman.' He turned his head toward Pilar. 'I am not provoked.'

Agustin hit him again. This time he hit him on the mouth with his closed fist. Robert Jordan was holding his pistol in his hand under the table. He had shoved the safety catch off and he pushed Maria away with his left hand. She moved a little way and he pushed her hard in the ribs with his left hand again to make her get really away. She was gone now and he saw her from the corner of his eye, slipping along the side of the cave toward the fire and now Robert Jordan watched Pablo's face.

The round-headed man sat staring at Agustin from his flat little eyes. The pupils were even smaller now. He licked his lips then, put up an arm and wiped his mouth with the back of his hand, looked down and saw the blood on his hand. He ran his tongue over his lips, then spat.

'Nor that,' he said. 'I am not a fool. I do not provoke.'

'*Cabrón,*' Agustin said.

'You should know,' Pablo said. 'You know the woman.'

Agustin hit him again hard in the mouth and Pablo laughed at him, showing the yellow, bad, broken teeth in the reddened line of his mouth.

'Leave it alone,' Pablo said and reached with a cup to scoop some wine from the bowl. 'Nobody here has *cojones* to kill me and this of the hands is silly.'

'*Cobarde,*' Agustin said.

'Nor words either,' Pablo said and made a swishing noise rinsing the wine in his mouth. He spat on the floor. 'I am far past words.'

Agustin stood there looking down at him and cursed him, speaking slowly, clearly, bitterly and contemptuously and cursing as steadily as though he were dumping manure on a field, lifting it with a dung fork out of a wagon.

'Nor of those,' Pablo said. 'Leave it, Agustin. And do not hit me more. Thou wilt injure thy hands.'

Agustin turned from him and went to the door.

'Do not go out,' Pablo said. 'It is snowing outside. Make thyself comfortable in here.'

'And thou! Thou!' Agustin turned from the door and spoke to him, putting all his contempt in the single, '*Yu*.'

'Yes, me,' said Pablo. 'I will be alive when you are dead.'

He dipped up another cup of wine and raised it to Robert Jordan. 'To the professor,' he said. Then turned to Pilar. 'To the Senora Commander.' Then toasted them all, 'To all the illusioned ones.'

Agustin walked over to him and, striking quickly with the side of his hand, knocked the cup out of his hand.

'That is a waste,' Pablo said. 'That is silly.' Agustin said something vile to him.

'No,' Pablo said, dipping up another cup. 'I am drunk, seest thou? When I am not drunk I do not talk. You have never heard me talk much. But an intelligent man is sometimes forced to be drunk to spend his time with fools.'

'Go and obscenity in the milk of thy cowardice,' Pillar said to him. 'I know too much about thee and thy cowardice.'

'How the woman talks,' Pablo said. 'I will be going out to sec the horses.'

'Go and befoul them,' Agustin said. 'Is not that one of thy customs?'

'No,' Pablo said and shook his head. He was taking down his big blanket cape from the wall and he looked at Agustin. 'Thou,' he said, 'and thy violence.'

'What do you go to do with the horses?' Agustin said.

'Look to them,' Pablo said.

'Befoul them,' Agustin said. 'Horse lover.'

'I care for them very much,' Pablo said. 'Even from behind they are handsomer and have more sense than these people. Divert yourselves,' he said and grinned. 'Speak to them of the bridge, *Inglés*. Explain their duties in the attack. Tell them how to conduct the retreat. Where will you take them, *Inglés*, after the bridge? Where will you take your patriots? I have thought of it all day while I have been drinking.'

'What have you thought?' Agustin asked.

'What have I thought?' Pablo said and moved his tongue around exploringly inside his lips. '*Que te importa*, what have I thought.'

'Say it,' Agustin said to him.

'Much,' Pablo said. He pulled the blanket coat over his head, the roundness of his head protruding now from the dirty yellow folds of the blanket. 'I have thought much.'

'What?' Agustin said. 'What?'

'I have thought you are a group of illusioned people,' Pablo said. 'Led by a woman with her brains between her thighs and a foreigner who comes to destroy you.'

'Get out,' Pilar shouted at him. 'Get out and fist yourself into the snow. Take your bad milk out of here, you horse exhausted maricon.'

'Thus one talks,' Agustin said admiringly, but absent-mindedly. He was worried.

'I go,' said Pablo. 'But I will be back shortly.' He lifted the blanket over the door of the cave and stepped out. Then from the door he called, 'It's still falling, *Inglés*.'

17

The Only noise in the cave now was the hissing from the hearth where snow was falling through the hole in the roof onto the coals of the fire.

'Pilar,' Fernando said. 'Is there more of the stew?'

'Oh, shut up,' the woman said. But Maria took Fernando's bowl over to the big pot set back from the edge of the fire and ladled into it. She brought it over to the table and set it down and then patted Fernando on the shoulder as he bent to eat. She stood for a moment beside him, her hand on his shoulder. But Fernando did not look up. He was devoting himself to the stew.

Agustin stood beside the fire. The others were seated. Pilar sat at the table opposite Robert Jordan.

'Now, *Inglés*,' she said, 'you have seen how he is.' 'What will he do?' Robert Jordan asked.

'Anything,' the woman looked down at the table. 'Anything. He is capable of doing anything.'

'Where is the automatic rifle?' Robert Jordan asked.

'There in the corner wrapped in the blanket,' Primitivo said. 'Do you want it?'

'Later,' Robert Jordan said. 'I wished to know where it is.'

'It is there,' Primitivo said. 'I brought it in and I have wrapped it in my blanket to keep the action dry. The pans are in that sack.'

'He would not do that,' Pilar said. 'He would not do anything with the *máquina*.'

'I thought you said he would do anything.'

'He might,' she said. 'But he has no practice with the *máquina*. He could toss in a bomb. That is more his style.'

'It is an idiocy and a weakness not to have killed him,' the gypsy said. He had taken no part in any of the talk all evening. 'Last night Roberto should have killed him.'

'Kill him,' Pilar said. Her big face was dark and tired looking. 'I am for it now.'

'I was against it,' Agustin said. He stood in front of the fire, his long arms hanging by his sides, his cheeks, stubble-shadowed below the cheekbones, hollow in the firelight. 'Now I am for it,' he said. 'He is poisonous now and he would like to see us all destroyed.'

'Let all speak,' Pilar said and her voice was tired. 'Thou, Andres? '

'*Matarlo*,' 'the brother with the dark hair growing far down in the point on his forehead said and nodded his head. 'Eladio?'

'Equally,' the other brother said. 'To me he seems to constitute a great danger. And he serves for nothing.'

'Primitivo?'

'Equally.'

'Fernando?'

'Could we not hold him as a prisoner?' Fernando asked.

'Who would look after a prisoner?' Primitivo said. 'It would take two men to look after a prisoner and what would we do with him in the end?'

'We could sell him to the fascists,' the gypsy said. 'None of that,' Agustin said. 'None of that filthiness.'

'It was only an idea,' Rafael, the gypsy, said. 'It seems to me that *the facciosos* would be happy to have him.'

'Leave it alone,' Agustin said. 'That is filthy.'

'No filthier than Pablo,' the gypsy justified himself.

'One filthiness does not justify another,' Agustin said. 'Well, that is all. Except for the old man and the *Inglés*.'

'They are not in it,' Pilar said. 'He has not been their leader.'

'One moment,' Fernando said. 'I have not finished.'

'Go ahead,' Pilar said. 'Talk until he comes back. Talk until he rolls a hand grenade under that blanket and blows this all up. Dynamite and all.'

'I think that you exaggerate, Pilar,' Fernando said. 'I do not think that he has any such conception.'

'I do not think so either,' Agustin said. 'Because that would blow the wine up too and he will be back in a little while to the wine.'

'Why not turn him over to El Sordo and let El Sordo sell him to the fascists?' Rafael suggested. 'You could blind him and he would be easy to handle.'

'Shut up,' Pilar said. 'I feel something very justified against thee too when thou talkest.'

'The fascists would pay nothing for him anyway,' Primitivo said. 'Such things have been tried by others and they pay nothing. They will shoot thee too.'

'I believe that blinded he could be sold for something,' Rafael said.

'Shut up,' Pilar said. 'Speak of blinding again and you can go with the other.'

'But, he, Pablo, blinded the *guardia civil* who was wounded,' the gypsy insisted. 'You have forgotten that?'

'Close thy mouth,' Pilar said to him. She was embarrassed be- fore Robert Jordan by this talk of blinding.

'I have not been allowed to finish,' Fernando interrupted. 'Finish,' Pilar told him. 'Go on. Finish.'

'Since it is impractical to hold Pablo as a prisoner,' Fernando commenced, 'and since it is repugnant to offer him—'

'Finish,' Pilar said. 'For the love of God, finish.'

'—in any class of negotiation,' Fernando proceeded calmly, 'I am agreed that it is perhaps best that he should be eliminated in order that the operations projected should be insured of the maximum possibility of success.'

Pilar looked at the little man, shook her head, bit her lips and said nothing.

'That is my opinion,' Fernando said. 'I believe we are justified in believing that he constitutes a danger to the Republic—'

'Mother of God,' Pilar said. 'Even here one man can make a bureaucracy with his mouth.'

'Both from his own words and his recent actions,' Fernando continued. 'And while he is deserving of gratitude for his actions in the early part of the movement and up until the most recent time—'

Pilar had walked over to the fire. Now she came up to the table. 'Fernando,' Pilar said quietly and handed a bowl to him. 'Take this stew please in all formality and fill thy mouth with it and talk no more. We are in possession of thy opinion.'

'But, how then—' Primitivo asked and paused without completing the sentence.

'*Estoy listo*,' Robert Jordan said. 'I am ready to do it. Since you are all decided that it should be done it is a service that I can do.'

What's the matter? he thought. From listening to him I am beginning to talk like Fernando. That language must be infectious. French, the language of diplomacy. Spanish, the language of bureaucracy.

'No,' Maria said. 'No.'

'This is none of thy business,' Pilar said to the girl. 'Keep thy mouth shut.'

'I will do it tonight,' Robert Jordan said.

He saw Pilar looking at him, her fingers on her lips. She was looking toward the door.

The blanket fastened across the opening of the cave was lifted and Pablo put his head in. He grinned at them all, pushed under the blanket and then turned and fastened it again. He turned around and stood there, then pulled the blanket cape over his head and shook the snow from it.

'You were speaking of me?' he addressed them all. 'I am interrupting?'

No one answered him and he hung the cape on a peg in the wall and walked over to the table.

'Que *tal?*' he asked and picked up his cup which had stood empty on the table and dipped it into the wine bowl. 'There is no wine,' he said to Maria. 'Go draw some from the skin.'

Maria picked up the bowl and went over to the dusty, heavily distended, black-tarred wineskin that hung neck down from the wall and unscrewed the plug from one of the legs enough so that the wine squirted from the edge of the plug into the bowl. Pablo watched her kneeling, holding the bowl up and watched the light red wine flooding into the bowl so fast that it made a whirling motion as it filled it.

'Be careful,' he said to her. 'The wine's below the chest now.' No one said anything.

'I drank from the belly-button to the chest today,' Pablo said. 'It's a day's work. What's the matter with you all? Have you lost your tongues?'

'No one said anything at all.

'Screw it up, Maria,' Pablo said. 'Don't let it spill.'

'There'll be plenty of wine,' Agustin said. 'You'll be able to be drunk.'

'One has encountered his tongue,' Pablo said and nodded to Agustin. 'Felicitations. I thought you'd been struck dumb.'

'By what?' Agustin asked. 'By my entry.'

'Thinkest thou that thy entry carries importance–'

He's working himself up to it, maybe, Robert Jordan thought. Maybe Agustin is going to do it. He certainly hates him enough. I don't hate him, he thought. No, I don't hate him. He is disgusting but I do not hate him. Though that blinding business puts him in a special class. Still this is their war. But he is certainly nothing to have around for the next two days. I am going to keep away out of it, he thought. I made a fool of myself with him once tonight and am perfectly willing to liquidate him. But I am not going to fool with him beforehand. And there are not going to be any shooting matches or monkey business in here with that dynamite around either. Pablo thought of that, of course. And did you think of it, he said to himself? No, you did not and neither did Agustin. You deserve whatever happens to you, he thought.

'Agustin,' he said.

'What?' Agustin looked up sullenly and turned his head away from Pablo.

'I wish to speak to thee,' Robert Jordan said. 'Later.'

'Now,' Robert Jordan said. *'Par favor.'*

Robert Jordan had walked to the opening of the cave and Pablo followed him with his eyes. Agustin, tall and sunken cheeked, stood up and came over to him. He moved reluctantly and contemptuously.

'Thou hast forgotten what is in the sacks?' Robert Jordan said to him, speaking so low that it could not be heard.

'Milk!' Agustin said. 'One becomes accustomed and one forgets.'

'I, too, forgot.'

'Milk!' Agustin said. *'Leche!* What fools we are.' He swungback loose-jointedly to the table and sat down. 'Have a drink, Pablo, old boy,' he said. 'How were the horses?'

'Very good,' Pablo said. 'And it is snowing less.' 'Do you think it will stop?'

'Yes,' Pablo said. 'It is thinning now and there are small, hard pellets. The wind will blow but the snow is going. The wind has changed.'

'Do you think it will clear tomorrow?' Robert Jordan asked him.

'Yes,' Pablo said. 'I believe it will be cold and clear. This wind is shifting.'

Look at him, Robert Jordan thought. Now he is friendly. He has shifted like the wind. He has the face and the body of a pig and I know he is many times a murderer and yet he has the sensitivity of a good aneroid. Yes, he thought, and the pig is a very intelligent animal, too. Pablo has hatred for us, or perhaps it is only for our projects, and pushes his hatred with insults to the point where you are ready to do away with him and when he sees that this point has been reached he drops it and starts all new and clean again.

'We will have good weather for it, *Inglés,*' Pablo said to Robert Jordan.

'*We,*' Pilar said. '*We?*'

'Yes, we,' Pablo grinned at her and drank some of the wine. 'Why not? I thought it over while I was outside. Why should we not agree?'

'In what?' the woman asked. 'In what now?'

'In all,' Pablo said to her. 'In this of the bridge. I am with thee now.'

'You are with us now?' Agustín said to him. 'After what you have said?'

'Yes,' Pablo told him. 'With the change of the weather I am with thee.'

Agustín shook his head. 'The weather,' he said and shook his head again. 'And after me hitting thee in the face?'

'Yes,' Pablo grinned at him and ran his fingers over his lips. 'After that too.'

Robert Jordan was watching Pilar. She was looking at Pablo as at some strange animal. On her face there was still a shadow of the expression the mention of the blinding had put there. She shook her head as though to be rid of that, then tossed it back. 'Listen,' she said to Pablo.

'Yes, woman.'

'What passes with thee?'

'Nothing,' Pablo said. 'I have changed my opinion. Nothing more.'

'You were listening at the door,' she told him.

'Yes,' he said. 'But I could hear nothing.'

'You fear that we will kill thee.'

'No,' he told her and looked at her over the wine cup. 'I do not fear that. You know that.'

'Well, what passes with thee?' Agustín said. 'One moment you are drunk and putting your mouth on all of us and disassociating yourself from the work in hand and speaking of our death in a dirty manner and insulting the women and opposing that which should be done—'

'I was drunk,' Pablo told him.

'And now—'

'I am not drunk,' Pablo said. 'And I have changed my mind.'

'Let the others trust thee. I do not,' Agustín said.

'Trust me or not,' Pablo said. 'But there is no one who can take thee to Credos as I can.'

'Credos?'

'It is the only place to go after this of the bridge.'

Robert Jordan, looking at Pilar, raised his hand on the side away from Pablo and tapped his right ear questioningly.

The woman nodded. Then nodded again. She said something to Maria and the girl came over to Robert Jordan's side.

'She says, "Of course he heard,"' Maria said in Robert Jordan's ear.

'Then Pablo,' Fernando said judicially. 'Thou art with us now and in favor of this of the bridge?'

'Yes, man,' Pablo said. He looked Fernando squarely in the eye and nodded.

'In truth?' Primitivo asked.

'*De veras,*' Pablo told him.

'And you think it can be successful?' Fernando asked. 'You now have confidence?'

'Why not?' Pablo said. 'Haven't you confidence?'

'Yes,' Fernando said. 'But I always have confidence.'

'I'm going to get out of here,' Agustin said.

'It is cold outside,' Pablo told him in a friendly tone.

'Maybe,' Agustin said. 'But I can't stay any longer in this *manicomio*.'

'Do not call this cave an insane asylum,' Fernando said.

'A *manicomio* for criminal lunatics,' Agustin said. 'And I'm getting out before I'm crazy, too.'

18

IT IS LIKE a merry-go-round, Robert Jordan thought. Not a merry-go-round that travels fast, and with a calliope for music, and the children ride on cows with gilded horns, and there are rings to catch with sticks, and there is the blue, gas-Rare-lit early dark of the Avenue du Maine, with fried fish sold from the next stall, and a wheel of fortune turning with the leather Raps slapping against the posts of the numbered compartments, and the packages of lump sugar piled in pyramids for prizes. No, it is not that kind of a merry-go-round; although the people are waiting, like the men in caps and the women in knitted sweaters, their heads bare in the gaslight and their hair shining, who stand in front of the wheel of fortune as it spins. Yes, those are the people. But this is another wheel. This is like a wheel that goes up and around.

It has been around twice now. It is a vast wheel, set at an angle, and each time it goes around and then is back to where it starts. One side is higher than the other and the sweep it makes lifts you back and down to where you started. There are no prizes either, he thought, and no one would choose to ride this wheel. You ride it each time and make the turn with no intention ever to have mounted. There is only one turn; one large, elliptical, rising and falling turn and you are back where you have started. We are back again now, he thought, and nothing is settled.

It was warm in the cave and the wind had dropped outside. Now he was sitting at the table with his notebook in front of him figuring all the technical part of the bridge-blowing. He drew three sketches, figured his formulas, marked the method of blowing with two drawings as clearly as a kindergarten project so that Anselmo could complete it in case anything should happen to himself during the process of the demolition. He finished these sketches and studied them.

Maria sat beside him and looked over his shoulder while he worked. He was conscious of Pablo across the table and of the others talking and playing cards and he smelled the odors of the cave which had changed now from those of the meal and the cooking to the fire smoke and man smell, the tobacco, red-wine and brassy, stale body smell, and when Maria, watching him finishing a drawing, put her hand on the table he picked it up with his left hand and lifted it to his face and smelled the coarse soap and water freshness from her washing of the dishes. He laid her hand down without looking at her and went on working and he could not see her blush. She let her hand lie there, close to his, but he did not lift it again.

Now he had finished the demolition project and he took a new page of the notebook and commenced to write out the operation orders. He was thinking clearly and well on these and what he wrote pleased him. He wrote two pages in the notebook and read them over carefully.

I think that is all, he said to himself. It is perfectly clear and I do not think there are any holes in it. The two posts will be destroyed and the bridge will be blown according to Golz's orders and that is all of my responsibility. All of this business of Pablo is something with which I should never have been saddled and it will be solved one way or another. There will be Pablo or there will be nu Pablo. I care nothing about it either way. But I am not going to get on that wheel again. Twice I have been on that wheel and twice it has gone around and come back to where it started and I am taking no more rides on it.

He shut the notebook and looked up at Maria. 'Hola, guapa,' he said to her. 'Did you make anything out of all that?'

'No, Roberto,' the girl said and put her hand on his hand that still held the pencil. 'Have you finished?'

'Yes. Now it is all written out and ordered.'

'What have you been doing, *Inglés?*' Pablo asked from across the table. His eyes were bleary again.

Robert Jordan looked at him closely. Stay off that wheel, he said to himself. Don't step on that wheel. I think it is going to start to swing again.

'Working on the problem of the bridge,' he said civilly.

'How is it?' asked Pablo.

'Very good,' Robert Jordan said. 'All very good.'

'I have been working on the problem of the retreat,' Pablo said and Robert Jordan looked at his drunken pig eyes and at the wine bow!. The wine bowl was nearly empty.

Keep off the wheel, he told himself. He is drinking again. Sure. But don't you get on that wheel now. Wasn't Grant supposed to be drunk a good part of the time during the Civil War? Certainly he was. I'll bet Grant would be furious at the comparison if he could see Pablo. Grant was a cigar smoker, too. Well, he would have to see about getting Pablo a cigar. That was what that face really needed to complete it; a half chewed cigar. Where could he get Pablo a cigar?

'How does it go?' Robert Jordan asked politely.

'Very well,' Pablo said and nodded his head heavily and judiciously. '*Muy bien.*'

'You've thought up something?' Agustin asked from where they were playing cards.

'Yes,' Pablo said. 'Various things.'

'Where did you find them? In that bowl?' Agustin demanded.

'Perhaps,' Pablo said. 'Who knows? Maria, fill the bowl, will you, please?'

'In the wineskin itself there should be some fine ideas,' Agustin turned back to the card game. 'Why don't you crawl in and look for them inside the skin?'

'Nay,' said Pablo equably. 'I search for them in the bowl.'

He is not getting on the wheel either, Robert Jordan thought. It must be revolving by itself. I suppose you cannot ride that wheel too long. That is probably quite a deadly wheel. I'm glad we are off of it. It was making me dizzy there a couple of times. Hut it is the thing that drunkards and those who are truly mean or cruel ride until they die. It goes around and up and the swing is never quite the same and then it comes around down. Let it swing, he thought. They will not get me onto it again. No sir, General Grant, I am off that wheel.

Pilar was sitting by the fire, her chair turned so that she could see over the shoulders of the two card players who had their backs to her. She was watching the game.

Here it is the shift from deadliness to normal family life that is the strangest, Robert Jordan thought. It is when the damned wheel comes down that it gets you. But I am off that wheel, he thought. And nobody is going to get me onto it again.

Two days ago I never knew that Pilar, Pablo nor the rest existed, he thought. There was no such thing as Maria in the world. It was certainly a much simpler world. I had instructions from Golz that were perfectly clear and seemed perfectly possible to carry out although they presented certain difficulties and involved certain consequences. After we blew the bridge I expected either to get back to the lines or not get back and if we got back I was going to ask for some time in Madrid. No one has any leave in this war but I am sure I could get two or three days in Madrid.

In Madrid I wanted to buy some books, to go to the Florida Hotel and get a room and to have a hot bath, he thought. I was going to send Luis the porter out for a bottle of absinthe if he could locate one at the Mantequerfas Leonesas or at any of the places off the Gran Via and I was going to lie in bed and read after the bath and drink a couple of absinthes and then I was going to call up Gaylord's and see if I could come up there and eat.

He did not want to eat at the Gran Via because the food was no good really and you had to get there on time or whatever there was of it would be gone. Also there were too many newspaper men there he knew and he did not want to have to keep his mouth shut. He wanted to drink the absinthes and to feel like talking and then go up to Gaylord's and eat with Karkov, where they had good food and real beer, and find out what was going on in the war.

He had not liked Gaylord's, the hotel in Madrid the Russians had taken over, when he first went there because it seemed too luxurious and the food was too good for a besieged city and the talk too cynical for a war. But I corrupted very easily, he thought. Why should you not have as good food as could be organized when you came back from something like this? And the talk that he had thought of as cynicism when he had first heard it had turned out to be much too true. This will be something to tell at Gaylord's, he thought, when this is over. Yes, when this is over.

Could you take Maria to Gaylord's? No. You couldn't. But you could leave her in the hotel and she could take a hot bath and be there when you came back from Gaylord's. Yes, you could do that and after you had told Karkov about her, you could bring her later because they would be curious about her and want to see her.

Maybe you wouldn't go to Gaylord's at all. You could eat early at the Gran Via and hurry back to the Florida. But you knew you would go to Gaylord's because you wanted to see all that again; you wanted to eat that food again and you wanted to see all the comfort of it and the luxury of it after this. Then you would come back to the Florida and there Maria would be. Sure, she would be there after this was over. After this was over. Yes, after this was over. If he did this well he would rate a meal at Gaylord's.

Gaylord's was the place where you met famous peasant and worker Spanish commanders who had sprung to arms from the people at the start of the war without any previous military training and found that many of them spoke Russian. That had been the first big disillusion to him a few months back and he had started to be cynical to himself about it. But when he realized how it happened it was all right. They were peasants and workers. They had been active in the 1 934 revolution and had to flee the country when it failed and in Russia they had sent them to the military academy and to the Lenin Institute the Comintern maintained so they would be ready to fight the next time and have the necessary military education to command.

The Comintern had educated them there. In a revolution you could not admit to outsiders who helped you nor that any one knew more than he was supposed to know. He had learned that. If a thing was right fundamentally the lying was not supposed to matter. There was a lot of lying though. He did not care for the lying at first. He hated it. Then later he had come to like it. It was part of being an insider but it was a very corrupting business.

It was at Gaylord's that you learned that Valentin Gonzalez, called El Campesino or The Peasant, had never been a peasant but was an ex-sergeant in the Spanish Foreign Legion who had deserted and fought with Abd el Krim. That was all right, too. Why shouldn't he be? You had to have these peasant leaders quickly in this sort of war and a real peasant leader might be a little too much like Pablo. You couldn't wait for the real Peasant Leader to arrive and he might have too many peasant characteristics when he did. So you had to manufacture one. At that, from what he had seen of Campesino, with his black beard, his thick negroid lips, and his feverish, staring eyes, he thought he might give almost as much trouble as a real peasant leader. The last time he had seen him he seemed to have gotten to believe his own publicity and think he was a peasant. He was a brave, tough man; no braver in the world. But God, how he talked too much. And when he was excited he would say anything no matter what the consequences of his indiscretion. And those consequences had been many already. He was a wonderful Brigade Commander though in a situation where it looked as though everything was lost. He never knew when everything was lost and if it was, he would fight out of it.

At Gaylord's, too, you met the simple stonemason, Enrique Lister from Galicia, who now commanded a division and who talked Russian, too. And you met the cabinet worker, Juan Modesto from Andaluda who had just been given an Army Corps. He never learned his Russian in Puerto de Santa Maria although he might have if they had a Berlitz School there that the cabinet makers went to. He was the most trusted of the young soldiers by the Russians because he was a true party man, 'a hundred per cent' they said, proud to use the Americanism. He was much more intelligent than Lister or El Campesino.

Sure, Gaylord's was the place you needed to complete your education. It was there you learned how it was all really done instead of how it was supposed to be done. He had only started his education, he thought. He wondered whether he would continue with it long. Gaylord's was good and sound and what he needed. At the start when he had still believe all the nonsense it had come as a shock to him. But now he knew enough to accept the necessity for all the deception and what he learned at Gaylord's only strengthened him in his belief in the things that he did hold to be true. He liked to know how it really was; not how it was supposed to be. There was always lying in a war. But the truth of Lister, Modesto, and El Campesino was much better than the lies and legends. Well, some day they would tell the truth to everyone and meantime he was glad there was a Gaylord's for his own learning of it.

Yes, that was where he would go in Madrid after he had bought the books and after he had lain in the hot bath and had a couple of drinks and had read awhile. But that was before Maria had come into all this that he had that plan. All right. They would have two rooms and she could do what she liked while he went up there and he'd come back from Gaylord's to her. She had waited up in the hills all this time. She could wait a little while at the Hotel Florida. They would have three days in Madrid. Three days could be a long time. He'd take her to see the Marx Brothers at the Opera. That had been running for three months now and would certainly be good for three months more. She'd like the Marx Brothers at the Opera, he thought.

She'd like that very much.

It was a long way from Gaylord's to this cave though. No, that was not the long way. The long way was going to be from this cave to Gaylord's. Kashkin had taken him there first and he had not liked it. Kashkin had said he should meet Karkov because Karkov wanted to know Americans and because he was the greatest lover of Lope de Vega in the world and thought 'Fuente Ovejuna' was the greatest play ever written. Maybe it was at that, but he, Robert Jordan, did not think so.

He had liked Karkov but not the place. Karkov was the most intelligent man he had ever met. Wearing black riding boots, gray breeches, and a gray tunic, with tiny hands and feet, puffily fragile of face and body, with a spitting way of talking through his bad teeth, he looked comic when Robert Jordan first saw him. But he had more brains and more inner dignity and outer insolence and humor than any man that he had ever known.

Gaylord's itself had seemed indecently luxurious and corrupt. But why shouldn't the representatives of a power that governed a sixth of the world have a few comforts? Well, they had them and Robert Jordan had at first been repelled by the whole business and then had accepted it and enjoyed it. Kashkin had made him out to be a hell of a fellow and Karkov had at first been insultingly polite and then, when Robert Jordan had not played at being a hero but had told a story that was really funny and obscenely discreditable to himself, Karkov had shifted from the politeness to a relieved rudeness and then to insolence and they had become friends.

Kashkin had only been tolerated there. There was something wrong with Kashkin evidently and he was working it out In Spain. They would not tell him what it was but maybe they would now that he was dead. Anyway, he and Karkov had become friends and he had become friends too with the incredibly thin, drawn, dark, loving, nervous, deprived and unbitter woman with a lean, neglected body and dark, gray-streaked hair cut short who was Karkov's wife and who served as an interpreter with the tank corps. He was a friend too of Karkov's mistress, who had cat-eyes, reddish gold hair (sometimes more red; sometimes more gold, depending on the coiffeurs), a lazy sensual body (made to fit well against other bodies), a mouth made to fit other mouths, and a stupid, ambitious and utterly loyal mind. This mistress loved gossip and enjoyed a periodically controlled promiscuity which seemed only to amuse Karkov. Karkov was supposed to have another wife somewhere besides the tank-corps one, maybe two more, but nobody was very sure about that. Robert Jordan liked both the wife he knew and the mistress. He thought he would probably like the other wife, too, if he knew her, if there was one. Karkov had good taste in women.

There were sentries with bayonets downstairs outside the portecochere at Gaylord's and tonight it would be the pleasantest and most comfortable place in all of besieged Madrid. He would like to be there tonight instead of here. Though it was all right here, now they had stopped that wheel. And the snow was stopping too.

He would like to show his Maria to Karkov but he could not take her there unless he asked first and he would have to see how he was received after this trip. Golz would be there after this attack was over and if he had done well they would all know it from Golz. Golz would make fun of him, too, about Maria. After what he'd said to him about no girls.

He reached over to the bowl in front of Pablo and dipped up a cup of wine. 'With your permission,' he said.

Pablo nodded. He is engaged in his military studies, I imagine, Robert Jordan thought. Not seeking the bubble reputation in the cannon's mouth but seeking the solution to the problem in yonder bowl. But you know the bastard must be fairly able to have run this band successfully for as long as he did. Looking at Pablo he wondered what sort of guerilla leader he would have been in the American Civil War. There were lots of them, he thought. But we know very little about them. Not the Quantrills, nor the Mosbys, nor his own grandfather, but the little ones, the bushwhackers. And about the drinking. Do you suppose Grant really was a drunk? His grandfather always claimed he was. That he was always a little drunk by four o'clock in the afternoon and that before Vicksburg sometimes during the siege he was very drunk for a couple of days. But grandfather claimed that he functioned perfectly normally no matter how much he drank except that sometimes it was very hard to wake him. But if you *could* wake him he was normal.

There wasn't any Grant, nor any Sherman nor any Stonewall Jackson on either side so far in this war. No. Nor any Jeb Stuart either. Nor any Sheridan. It was overrun with McClellans though. The fascists had plenty of McClellans and we had at least three of them.

He had certainly not seen any military geniuses in this war. Not a one. Nor anything resembling one. Kleber, Lucasz, and Hans had done a fine job of their share in the defense of Madrid with the International Brigades and then the old bald, spectacled, conceited, stupid-as-an-owl, unintelligent-in-conversation, braveand-as-dumb-as-a-bull, propaganda-build-up defender of Madrid, Miaja, had been so jealous of the publicity Kleber received that he had forced the Russians to relieve Kleber of his command and send him to Valencia. Kleber was a good soldier; but limited and he *did* talk too much for the job he had. Golz was a good general and a fine soldier but they always kept him in a subordinate position and never gave him a free hand. This attack was going to be his biggest show so far and Robert Jordan did not like too much what he had heard about the attack. Then there was Gall, the Hungarian, who ought to be shot if you could believe half you heard at Gaylord's. Make it if you can believe ten per cent of what you hear at Gaylord's, Robert Jordan thought.

He wished that he had seen the fighting on the plateau beyond Guadalajara when they beat the Italians. But he had been down in Estremadura then. Hans had told him about it one night in Gaylord's two weeks ago and made him see it all. There was one moment when it was really lost when the Italians had broken the line near Trijueque and the Twelfth Brigade would have been cut off if the Torija-Brihuega road had been cut. 'But knowing they were Italians,' Hans had said, 'we attempted to maneuver which would have been unjustifiable against other troops. And it was successful.'

Hans had shown it all to him on his maps of the battle. Hans carried them around with him in his map case all the time and still seemed marvelled and happy at the miracle of it. Hans was a fine soldier and a good companion. Lister's and Modesto's and Campesino's Spanish troops had all fought well in that battle, Hans had told him, and that was to be credited to their leaders and to the discipline they enforced. But Lister and Campesino and Modesto had been told many of the moves they should make by their Russian military advisers. They were like students flying a machine with dual controls which the pilot could take over whenever they made a mistake. Well, this year would show how much and how well they learned. After a while there would not be dual controls and then we would see how well they handled divisions and army corps alone.

They were Communists and they were disciplinarians. The discipline that they would enforce would make good troops. Lister was murderous in discipline. He was a true fanatic and he had the complete Spanish lack of respect for life. In a few armies since the Tartar's first invasion of the West were men executed summarily for as little reason as they were under his command. But he knew how to forge a division into a fighting unit. It is one thing to hold positions. It is another to attack positions and take them and it is something very different to maneuver an army in the field, Robert Jordan thought as he sat there at the table. From what I have seen of him, I wonder how Lister will be at that once the dual controls are gone? But maybe they won't go, he thought. I wonder if they will go? Or whether they will strengthen? I wonder what the Russian stand is on the whole business? Gaylord's is the place, he thought. There is much that I need to know now that I can learn only at Gaylord's.

At one time he had thought Gaylord's had been bad for him. It was the opposite of the puritanical, religious communism of Velazquez 63, the Madrid palace that had been turned into the

International Brigade headquarters in the capital. At Velazquez 63 it was like being a member of a religious order-and Gaylord's was a long way away from the feeling you had at the headquarters of the Fifth Regiment before it had been broken up into the brigades of the new army.

At either of those places you felt that you were taking part in a crusade. That was the only word for it although it was a word that had been so worn and abused that it no longer gave its true meaning. You felt, in spite of all bureaucracy and inefficiency and party strife, something that was like the feeling you expected to have and did not have when you made your first communion. It was a feeling of consecration to a duty toward all of the oppressed of the world which would be as difficult and embarrassing to speak about as religious experience and yet it was authentic as the feeling you had when you heard Bach, or stood in Chartres Cathedral or the Cathedral at León and saw the light coming through the great windows; or when you saw Mantegna and Greco and Brueghel in the Prado. It gave you a part in something that you could believe in wholly and completely and in which you felt an absolute brotherhood with the others who were engaged in it. It was something that you had never known before but that you had experienced now and you gave such importance to it and the reasons for it that your own death seemed of complete unimportance; only a thing to be avoided because it would interfere with the performance of your duty. But the best thing was that there was something you could do about this feeling and this necessity too. You could fight.

So you fought, he thought. And in the fighting soon there was no purity of feeling for those who survived the fighting and were good at it. Not after the first six months.

The defense of a position or of a city is a part of war in which you can feel that first sort of feeling. The fighting in the Sierras had been that way. They had fought there with the true comradeship of the revolution. Up there when there had been the first necessity for the enforcement of discipline he had approved and understood it. Under the shelling men had been cowards and had run. *He* had seen them shot and left to swell beside the road, nobody bothering to do more than strip them of their cartridges and their valuables. Taking their cartridges, their boots and their leather coats was right. Taking the valuables was only realistic. It only kept the anarchists from getting them.

It had seemed just and right and necessary that the men who ran were shot. There was nothing wrong about it. Their running was a selfishness The fascists had attacked and we had stopped them on that slope in the gray rocks, the scrub pines and the gorse of the Guadarrama hillsides. We had held along the road under the bombing from the planes and the shelling when they brought their artillery up and those who were left at the end of that day had counterattacked and driven them back. Later, when they had tried to come down on the left, sifting down between the rocks and through the trees, we had held out in the Sanitarium firing from the windows and the roof although they had passed it on both sides, and we lived through knowing what it was to be surrounded until the counterattack had cleared them back behind the road again.

In all that, in the fear that dries your mouth and your throat, in the smashed plaster dust and the sudden panic of a wall falling, collapsing in the flash and roar of a shell burst, clearing the gun, dragging those away who had been serving it, lying face downward and covered with rubble, your head behind the shield working on a stoppage, getting the broken case out, straightening the belt again, you now lying straight behind the shield, the gun searching the roadside again; you did the thing there was to do and knew that you were right. You learned the dry-mouthed, fear-purged, purging ecstasy of battle and you fought that summer and that fall for all the poor in the world, against all tyranny, for all the things that you believed and for the new world you had been educated into. You learned that fall, he thought, how to endure and how to ignore suffering in the long time of cold and wetness, of mud and of digging and fortifying. And the feeling of the summer and the fall was buried deep under tiredness, sleepiness, and nervousness and discomfort. But it was still there and all that you went through only served to validate it. It was in those days, he thought, that you had a deep and sound and selfless pride-that would have made you a bloody bore at Gaylord's, he thought suddenly.

No, you would not have been so good at Gaylord's then, he thought. You were too naive. You were in a sort of state of grace. But Gaylord's might not have been the way it was now at that time, either. No, as a matter of fact, it was not that way, he told himself. It was not that way at all. There was not any Gaylord's then.

Karkov had told him about those days. At that time what Russians there were had lived at the Palace Hotel. Robert Jordan had known none of them then. That was before the first *partizan* groups had been formed; before he had met Kashkin or any of the others. Kashkin had been in the north at Irun, at San Sebastian and in the abortive fighting toward Vitoria. He had not arrived in Madrid until January and while Robert Jordan had fought at Carabanchel and at Usera in those three days when they stopped the right wing of the fascist attack on Madrid and drove the Moors and the *Tercia* back from house to house to clear that battered suburb on the edge of the gray, sun-baked plateau and establish a line of defense along the heights that would protect that corner of the city, Karkov had been in Madrid.

Karkov was not cynical about those times either when he talked. Those were the days they all shared when everything looked lost and each man retained now, better than any citation or decoration, the knowledge of just how he would act when everything looked lost. The government had abandoned the city, taking all the motor cars from the ministry of war in their flight and old Miaja had to ride down to inspect his defensive positions on a bicycle. Robert Jordan did not believe that one. He could not see Miaja on a bicycle even in his most patriotic imagination, but Karkov said it was true. But then he had written it for Russian papers so he probably wanted to believe it was true after writing it.

But there was another story that Karkov had not written. He had three wounded Russians in the Palace Hotel for whom he was responsible. They were two tank drivers and a flyer who were too bad to be moved, and since, at that time, it was of the greatest importance that there should be no evidence of any Russian intervention to justify an open intervention by the fascists, it was Karkov's responsibility that these wounded should not fall into the hands of the fascists in case the city should be abandoned.

In the event the city should be abandoned, Karkov was to poison them to destroy all evidence of their identity before leaving the Palace Hotel. No one could prove from the bodies of three wounded men, one with three bullet wounds in his abdomen, one with his jaw shot away and his vocal cords exposed, one with his femur smashed to bits by a bullet and his hands and face so badly burned that his face was just an eyelashless, eyebrowless, hairless blister that they were Russians. No one could tell from the bodies of these wounded men he would leave in beds at the Palace, that they were Russians. Nothing proved a naked dead man was a Russian. Your nationality and your politics did not show when you were dead.

Robert Jordan had asked Karkov how he felt about the necessity of performing this act and Karkov had said that he had not looked forward to it. 'How were you going to do it?' Robert Jordan had asked him and had added, 'You know it isn't so simple just suddenly to poison people.' And Karkov had said, 'Oh, yes, it is when you carry it always for your own use.' Then he had opened his cigarette case and showed Robert Jordan what he carried in one side of it.

'But the first thing anybody would do if they took you prisoner would be to take your cigarette case,' Robert Jordan had objected. 'They would have your hands up.'

'But I have a little more here,' Karkov had grinned and showed the lapel of his jacket. 'You simply put the lapel in your mouth like this and bite it and swallow.'

'That's much better,' Robert Jordan had said. 'Tell me, does it smell like bitter almonds the way it always does in detective stories?'

'I don't know,' Karkov said delightedly. 'I have never smelled it. Should we break a little tube and smell it?'

'Better keep it.'

'Yes,' Karkov said and put the cigarette case away. 'I am not a defeatist, you understand, but it is always possible that such serious times might come again and you cannot get this anywhere. Have you seen the communique from the Cordoba front? It is very beautiful. It is now my favorite among all the communiques.'

'What did it say?' Robert Jordan had come to Madrid from the Córdoban Front and he had the sudden stiffening that comes when some one jokes about a thing which you yourself may joke about but which they may not. 'Tell me?'

'*Nuestra gloriosa tropa siga avanzando sin perder ni una sola palma de terreno*,' Karkov said in his strange Spanish.

'It didn't really say that,' Robert Jordan doubted.

'Our glorious troops continue to advance without losing a foot of ground,' Karkov repeated in English. 'It is in the communique. I will find it for you.'

You could remember the men you knew who died in the fighting around Pozoblanco; but it was a joke at Gaylord's.

So that was the way it was at Gaylord's now. Still there had not always been Gaylord's and if the situation was now one which produced such a thing as Gaylord's out of the survivors of the early days, he was glad to see Gaylord's and to know about it. You are a long way from how you felt in the Sierra and at Carabanchel and at Usera, he thought. You corrupt very easily, he thought. But was it corruption or was it merely that you lost the naivete that you started with? Would it not be the same in anything? Who else kept that first chastity of mind about their work that young doctors, young priests, and young soldiers usually started with? The priests certainly kept it, or they got out. I suppose the Nazis keep it, he thought, and the Communists who have a severe enough self-discipline. But look at Karkov.

He never tired of considering the case of Karkov. The last time he had been at Gaylord's Karkov had been wonderful about a certain British economist who had spent much time in Spain. Robert Jordan had read this man's writing for years and he had always respected him without knowing anything about him. He had not cared very much for what this man had written about Spain. It was too clear and simple and too open and shut and many of the statistics he knew were faked by wishful thinking. But he thought you rarely cared for journalism written about a country you really knew about and he respected the man for his intentions.

Then he had seen the man, finally, on the afternoon when they had attacked at Carabanchel. They were sitting in the lee of the bull ring and there was shooting down the two streets and every one was nervous waiting for the attack. A tank had been promised and it had not come up and Montero was sitting with his head in his hand saying, 'The tank has not come. The tank has not come.'

It was a cold day and the yellow dust was blowing down the street and Montero had been hit in the left arm and the arm was stiffening. 'We have to have a tank,' he said.' We must wait for the tank, but we cannot wait.' His wound was making him sound petulant.

Robert Jordan had gone back to look for the tank which Montero said he thought might have stopped behind the apartment building on the corner of the tram-line. It was there all right. But it was not a tank. Spaniards called anything a tank in those days. It was an old armored car. The driver did not want to leave the angle of the apartment house and bring it up to the bull ring. He was standing behind it with his arms folded against the metal of the car and his head in the leather-padded helmet on his arms. He shook his head when Robert Jordan spoke to him and kept it pressed against his arms. Then he turned his head without looking at Robert Jordan.

'I have no orders to go there,' he said sullenly.

Robert Jordan had taken his pistol out of the holster and pushed the muzzle of the pistol against the leather coat of the armored car driver.

'Here are your orders,' he had told him. The man shook his head with the big padded-leather helmet like a football player's on it and said, 'There is no ammunition for the machine gun.'

'We have ammunition at the bull ring,' Robert Jordan had told him. 'Come on, let's go. We will fill the belts there. Come on.'

'There is no one to work the gun,' the driver said. 'Where is he?

Where is your mate?'

'Dead,' the driver had said. 'Inside there.'

'Get him out,' Robert Jordan had said. 'Get him out of there.'

'I do not like to touch him,' the driver had said. 'And he is bent over between the gun and the wheel and I cannot get past him.'

'Come on,' Robert Jordan had said. 'We will get him out together.'

He had banged his head as he climbed into the armored car and it had made a small cut over his eyebrow that bled down onto his face. The dead man was heavy and so stiff you could not bend him and he had to hammer at his head to get it out from where it had wedged, face down, between his seat and the wheel. Finally he got it up by pushing with his knee up under the dead man's head and then, pulling back on the man's waist now that the head was loose, he pulled the dead man out himself toward the door.

'Give me a hand with him,' he had said to the driver.

'I do not want to touch him,' the driver had said and Robert Jordan had seen that he was crying. The tears ran straight down on each side of his nose on the powder-grimed slope of his face and his nose was running, too.

Standing beside the door he had swung the dead man out and the dead man fell onto the sidewalk beside the tram-line still in that hunched-over, doubled-up position. He lay there, his face waxy gray against the cement sidewalk, his hands bent under him as they had been in the car.

'Get in, God damn it,' Robert Jordan had said, motioning now with his pistol to the driver. 'Get in there now.'

Just then he had seen this man who had come out from the lee of the apartment house building. He had on a long overcoat and he was bareheaded and his hair was gray, his cheekbones broad and his eyes were deep and set close together. He had a package of Chesterfields in his hand and he took one out and handed it toward Robert Jordan who was pushing the driver into the armored car with his pistol.

'Just a minute, Comrade,' he had said to Robert Jordan in Spanish. 'Can you explain to me something about the fighting?'

Robert Jordan took the cigarette and put it in the breast pocket of his blue mechanic jumper. He had recognized this comrade from his pictures. It was the British economist.

'Go muck yourself,' he said in English and then, in Spanish, to the armored car driver. 'Down there. The bull ring. See?' And he had pulled the heavy side door to with a slam and locked it and they had started down that long slope in the car and the bullets had commenced to hit against the car, sounding like pebbles tossed against an iron boiler. Then when the machine gun opened on them, they were like sharp hammer tappings. They had pulled up behind the shelter of the bull ring with the last October posters still pasted up beside the ticket window and the ammunition boxes knocked open and the comrades with the rifles, the grenades on their belts and in their pockets, waiting there in the lee and Montero had said, 'Good. Here is the tank. Now we can attack.'

Later that night when they had the last houses on the hill, he lay comfortable behind a brick wall with a hole knocked in the bricks for a loophole and looked across the beautiful level field of fire they had between them and the ridge the fascists had retired to and thought, with a comfort that was almost voluptuous, of the rise of the hill with the smashed villa that protected the left flank. He had lain in a pile of straw in his sweat-soaked clothes and wound a blanket around him while he dried. Lying there he thought of the economist and laughed, and then felt sorry he had been rude. But at the moment, when the man had handed him the cigarette, pushing it out almost like offering a tip for information, the combatant's hatred for the noncombatant had been too much for him.

Now he remembered Gaylord's and Karkov speaking of this same man. 'So it was there you met him,' Karkov had said. 'I did not get farther than the Puente de Toledo myself on that day. He was very far toward the front. That was the last day of his bravery I believe. He left Madrid the next day. Toledo was where he was the bravest, I believe. At Toledo he was enormous. He was one of the architects of our capture of the Alcazar. You should have seen him at Toledo. I believe it was largely through his efforts and his advice that our siege was successful. That was the silliest part of the war. It reached an ultimate in silliness but tell me, what is thought of him in America?'

'In America,' Robert Jordan said, 'he is supposed to be very close to Moscow.'

'He is not,' said Karkov. 'But he has a wonderful face and his face and his manners are very successful. Now with my face I could do nothing. What little I have accomplished was all done in spite of my face which does not either inspire people nor move them to love me and to trust me. But this man Mitchell has a face he makes his fortune with. It is the face of a conspirator. All who have read of conspirators in books trust him instantly. Also he has the true manner of the conspirator. Any one seeing him enter a room knows that he is instantly in the presence of a conspirator of the first mark. All of your rich compatriots who wish sentimentally to aid the Soviet Union as they believe or to insure themselves a little against any eventual success of the party see instantly in the face of this man, and in his manner that he can be none other than a trusted agent of the Comintern.'

'Has he no connections in Moscow?'

'None. Listen, Comrade Jordan. Do you know about the two kinds of fools?'

'Plain and damn?'

'No. The two kinds of fools we have in Russia,' Karkov grinned and began. 'First there is the winter fool. The winter fool comes to the door of your house and he knocks loudly. You go to the door and you see him there and you have never seen him before. He is an impressive sight. He is a very big man and he has on high boots and a fur coat and a fur hat and he is all covered with snow. First he stamps his boots and snow falls from them. Then he takes off his fur coat and shakes it and more snow falls. Then he takes off his fur hat and knocks it against the door. More snow falls from his fur hat. Then he stamps his boots again and advances into the room. Then you look at him and you see he is a fool. That is the winter fool.

'Now in the summer you see a fool going down the street and he is waving his arms and jerking his head from side to side and everybody from two hundred yards away can tell he is a fool. That is a summer fool. This economist is a winter fool.'

'But why do people trust him here?' Robert Jordan asked.

'His face,' Karkov said. 'His beautiful *gueule de conspirateur*. And his invaluable trick of just having come from somewhere else where he is very trusted and important. Of course,' he smiled, 'he must travel very much to keep the trick working. You know the Spanish are very strange,' Karkov went on. 'This government has had much money. Much gold. They will give nothing to their friends. You are a friend. All right. You will do it for nothing and should not be rewarded. But to people representing an important firm or a country which is not friendly but must be influenced—to such people they give much. It is very interesting when you follow it closely.'

'I do not like it. Also that money belongs to the Spanish workers.'

'You are not supposed to like things. Only to understand,' Karkov had told him. 'I teach you a little each time I see you and eventually you will acquire an education. It would be very interesting for a professor to be educated.'

'I don't know whether I'll be able to be a professor when I get back. They will probably run me out as a Red.'

'Well, perhaps you will be able to come to the Soviet Union and continue your studies there. That might be the best thing for you to do.'

'But Spanish is my field.'

'There are many countries where Spanish is spoken,' Karkov had said. 'They cannot all be as difficult to do anything with as Spain is. Then you must remember that you have not been a professor now for almost nine months. In nine months you may have learned a new trade. How much dialectics have you read?'

'I have read the Handbook of Marxism that Emil Burns edited. That is all.'

'If you have read it all that is quite a little. There are fifteen hundred pages and you could spend some time on each page. But there are some other things you should read.'

'There is no time to read now.'

'I know,' Karkov had said. 'I mean eventually. There are many things to read which will make you understand some of these things that happen. But out of this will come a book which is very necessary; which will explain many things which it is necessary to know. Perhaps I will write it. I hope that it will be me who will write it.'

'I don't know who could write it better.'

'Do not flatter,' Karkov had said. 'I am a journalist. But like all journalists I wish to write literature. Just now, I am very busy on a study of Calvo Sotelo. He was a very good fascist; a true Spanish fascist. Franco and these other people are not. I have been studying all of Sotelo's writing and speeches. He was very intelligent and it was very intelligent that he was killed.'

'I thought that you did not believe in political assassination.'

'It is practised very extensively,' Karkov said. 'Very, very extensively.'

'But—'

'We do not believe in acts of terrorism by individuals,' Karkov had smiled. 'Not of course by criminal terrorist and counterrevolutionary organizations. We detest with horror the duplicity and villainy of the murderous hyenas of Bukharinite wreckers and such dregs of humanity as Zinoviev, Kamenev, Rykov and their henchmen. We hate and loathe these veritable fiends,' he smiled again. 'But I still believe that political assassination can be said to be practised very extensively.'

'You mean—'

'I mean nothing. But certainly we execute and destroy such veritable fiends and dregs of humanity and the treacherous dogs of generals and the revolting spectacle of admirals unfaithful to their trust. These are destroyed. They are not assassinated. You see the difference?'

'I see,' Robert Jordan had said.

'And because I make jokes sometime: and you know how dangerous it is to make jokes even in joke? Good. Because I make jokes, do not think that the Spanish people will not live to regret that they have not shot certain generals that even now hold commands. I do not like the shootings, you understand.'

'I don't mind them,' Robert Jordan said. 'I do not like them but I do not mind them any more.'

'I know that,' Karkov had said. 'I have been told that.'

'Is it important?' Robert Jordan said. 'I was only trying to be truthful about it.'

'It is regrettable,' Karkov had said. 'But it is one of the things that makes people be treated as reliable who would ordinarily have to spend much more time before attaining that category.'

'Am I supposed to be reliable?'

'In your work you are supposed to be very reliable. I must talk to you sometime to see how you are in your mind. It is regrettable that we never speak seriously.'

'My mind is in suspension until we win the war,' Robert Jordan had said.

'Then perhaps you will not need it for a long time. But you should be careful to exercise it a little.'

'I read *Mundo Obrero*,' Robert Jordan had told him and Karkov had said, 'All right. Good. I can take a joke too. But there are very intelligent things in *Mundo Obrero*. The only intelligent things written on this war.'

'Yes,' Robert Jordan had said. 'I agree with you. But to get a full picture of what is happening you cannot read only the party organ.'

'No,' Karkov had said. 'But you will not find any such picture if you read twenty papers and then, if you had it, I do not know what you would do with it. I have such a picture almost constantly and what I do is try to forget it.'

'You think it is that bad?'

'It is better now than it was. We are getting rid of some of the worst. But it is very rotten. We are building a huge army now and some of the elements, those of Modesto, of El Campesino, of Lister and of Duran, are reliable. They are more than reliable. They arc magnificent. You will see that. Also we still have the Brigades although their role is changing. But an army that is made up of good and bad elements cannot win a war. All must be brought to a certain level of political development; all must know why they are fighting, and its importance. All must believe in the fight they are to make and all must accept discipline. We are making a huge conscript army without the time to implant the discipline that a conscript army must have, to behave properly under fire. We call it a people's army but it will not have the assets of a true people's army and it will not have the iron discipline that a conscript army needs. You will see. It is a very dangerous procedure.'

'You are not very cheerful today.'

'No,' Karkov had said. 'I have just come back from Valencia where I have seen many people. No one comes back very cheerful from Valencia. In Madrid you feel good and clean and with no possibility of anything but winning. Valencia is something else. The cowards who fled from Madrid still govern there. They have settled happily into the sloth and bureaucracy of governing. They have only contempt for those of Madrid. Their obsession now is the weakening of the commissariat for war. And Barcelona. You should see Barcelona.'

'How is it?'

'It is all still comic opera. First it was the paradise of the crackpots and the romantic revolutionists. Now it is the paradise of the fake soldier. The soldiers who like to wear uniforms, who like to strut and swagger and wear red-and-black scarves. Who like everything about war except to fight. Valencia makes you sick and Barcelona makes you laugh.'

'What about the P.O.U.M. putsch?'

'The P.O.U.M. was never serious. It was a heresy of crackpots and wild men and it was really just an infantilism. There were some honest misguided people. There was one fairly good brain and there was a little fascist money. Not much. The poor P.O.U.M. They were very silly people.' 'But were many killed in the putsch?'

'Not so many as were shot afterwards or will be shot. The P.O.U.M. It is like the name. Not serious. They should have called it the M.U.M.P.S. or the M.E.A.S.L.E.S. But no. The Measles is much more dangerous. It can affect both sight and hearing. But they made one plot you know to kill me, to kill Walter, to kill Modesto and to kill Prieto. You see how badly mixed up they were? We are not at all alike. Poor P. O. U. M. They never did kill anybody. Not at the front nor anywhere else. A few in Barcelona, yes.'

'Were you there?'

'Yes. I have sent a cable describing the wickedness of that infamous organization of Trotskyite murderers and their fascist machinations all beneath contempt but, between us, it is not very serious, the P.O.U.M. Nin was their only man. We had him but he escaped from our hands.'

'Where is he now?'

'In Paris. We say he is in Paris. He was a very pleasant fellow but with bad political aberrations.'

'But they were in communication with the fascists, weren't they?'

'Who is not?' 'We are not.'

'Who knows? I hope we are not. You go often behind their lines,' he grinned. 'But the brother of one of the secretaries of the Republican Embassy at Paris made a trip to St. Jean de Luz last week to meet people from Burgos.'

'I like it better at the front,' Robert Jordan had said. 'The closer to the front the better the people.'

'How do you like it behind the fascist lines?' 'Very much. We have fine people there.'

'Well, you see they must have their fine people behind our lines the same way. We find them and shoot them and they find ours and shoot them. When you are in their country you must always think of how many people they must send over to us.'

'I have thought about them.'

'Well,' Karkov had said. 'You have probably enough to think about for today, so drink that beer that is left in the pitcher and run along now because I have to go upstairs to see people. Upstairs people. Come again to see me soon.'

Yes, Robert Jordan thought. You learned a lot at Gaylord's. Karkov had read the one and only book he had published. The book had not been a success. It was only two hundred pages long and he doubted if two thousand people had ever read it. He had put in it what he had discovered about Spain in ten years of travelling in it, on foot, in third-class carriages, by bus, on horse- and mule-back and in trucks. He knew the Basque country, Navarre, Aragon, Galicia, the two Castiles and Estremadura well. There had been such good books written by Borrow and Ford and the rest that he had been able to add very little. But Karkov said it was a good book.

'It is why I bother with you,' he said. 'I think you write absolutely truly and that is very rare. So I would like you to know some things.'

All right. He would write a book when he got through with this. But only about the things he knew, truly, and about what he knew. But I will have to be a much better writer than I am now to handle them, he thought. The things he had come to know in this war were not so simple.

19

'WHAT do you do sitting there?' Maria asked him. She was standing close beside him and he turned his head and smiled at her.

'Nothing,' he said. 'I have been thinking.' 'What of? The bridge?'

'No. The bridge is terminated. Of thee and of a hotel in Madrid where I know some Russians, and of a book I will write some time.'

'Are there many Russians in Madrid?'

'No. Very few.'

'But in the fascist periodicals it says there are hundreds of thousands.'

'Those are lies. There are very few.'

'Do you like the Russians? The one who was here was a Russian.'

'Did you like him?'

'Yes. I was sick then but I thought he was very beautiful and very brave.'

'What nonsense, beautiful,' Pilar said. 'His nose was flat as my hand and he had cheekbones as wide as a sheep's buttocks.'

'He was a good friend and comrade of mine,' Robert Jordan said to Maria. 'I cared for him very much.'

'Sure,' Pilar said. 'But you shot him.'

When she said this the card players looked up from the table and Pablo stared at Robert Jordan. Nobody said anything and then the gypsy, Rafael, asked, 'Is it true, Roberto?'

'Yes,' Robert Jordan said. He wished Pilar had not brought this up and he wished he had not told it at El Sardo's. 'At his request. He was badly wounded.'

'Que *cosa mas rara*,' the gypsy said. 'All the time he was with us he talked of such a possibility. I don't know how many times I have promised him to perform such an act. What a rare thing,' he said again and shook his head.

'He was a very rare man,' Primitivo said. 'Very singular.'

'Look,' Andres, one of the brothers, said. 'You who are Professor and all. Do you believe in the possibility of a man seeing ahead what is to happen to him?'

'I believe he cannot see it,' Robert Jordan said. Pablo was staring at him curiously and Pilar was watching him with no expression on her face. 'In the case of this Russian comrade he was very nervous from being too much time at the front. He had fought at Irun which, you know, was bad. Very bad. He had fought later in the north. And since the first groups who did this work behind the lines were formed he had worked here, in Estremadura and in Andaluda. I think he was very tired and nervous and he imagined ugly things.'

'He would undoubtedly have seen many evil things,' Fernando said.

'Like all the world,' Andres said. 'But listen to me, *Inglés*. Do you think there is such a thing as a man knowing in advance what will befall him?'

'No,' Robert Jordan said. 'That is ignorance and superstition.' 'Go on,' Pilar said. 'Let us hear the viewpoint of the professor.' She spoke as though she were talking to a precocious child.

'I believe that fear produces evil visions,' Robert Jordan said. 'Seeing bad signs—'

'Such as the airplanes today,' Primitivo said.

'Such as thy arrival,' Pablo said softly and Robert Jordan looked across the table at him, saw it was not a provocation but only an expressed thought, then went on. 'Seeing bad signs, one, with fear, imagines an end for himself and one thinks that imagining comes by divination,' Robert Jordan concluded.

'I believe there is nothing more to it than that. I do not believe in ogres, nor soothsayers, nor in the supernatural things.'

'But this one with the rare name saw his fate clearly,' the gypsy said. 'And that was how it happened.'

'He did not see it,' Robert Jordan said. 'He had a fear of such a possibility and it became an obsession. No one can tell me that he saw anything.'

'Not I?' Pilar asked him and picked some dust up from the fire and blew it off the palm of her hand. 'I cannot tell thee either?'

'No. With all wizardry, gypsy and all, thou canst not tell me either.'

'Because thou art a miracle of deafness,' Pilar said, her big face harsh and broad in the candlelight. 'It is not that thou art stupid. Thou art simply deaf. One who is deaf cannot hear music. Neither can he hear the radio. So he might say, never having heard them, that such things do not exist. *Que va, Inglés.* I saw the death of that one with the rare name in his face as though it were burned there with a branding iron.'

'You did not,' Robert Jordan insisted. 'You saw fear and apprehension. The fear was made by what he had been through. The apprehension was for the possibility of evil he imagined.'

'*Que va,*' Pilar said. 'I saw death there as plainly as though it were sitting on his shoulder. And what is more he smelt of death.' 'He smelt of death,' Robert Jordan jeered. 'Of fear maybe. There is a smell to fear.'

'*De la muerte,*' Pilar said. 'Listen. When Blanquet, who was the greatest *peon de brega* who ever lived, worked under the orders of Granero he told me that on the day of Manolo Granero's death, when they stopped in the chapel on the way to the ring, the odor of death was so strong on Manolo that it almost made Blanquet sick. And he had been with Manolo when he had bathed and dressed at the hotel before setting out for the ring. The odor was not present in the motorcar when they had sat packed tight together riding to the bull ring. Nor was it distinguishable to any one else but Juan Luis de la Rosa in the chapel. Neither Marcial nor Chicuelo smelled it neither then nor when the four of them lined up for the paseo. But Juan Luis was dead white, Blanquet told me, and he, Blanquet, spoke to him saying, 'Thou also?'

'So that I cannot breathe,' Juan Luis said to him. 'And from thy matador.'

'*Pues nada,*' Blanquet said. 'There is nothing to do. Let us hope we are mistaken.'

'And the others?' Juan Luis asked Blanquet.

'*Nada:* Blanquet said. 'Nothing. But this one stinks worse than Jose at Talavera.'

'And it was on that afternoon that the bull *Pocapena* of the ranch of Veragua destroyed Manolo Granero against the planks of the barrier in front of *tendido* two in the Plaza de Toros of Madrid. I was there with Finito and I saw it. The horn entirely destroyed the cranium, the head of Manolo being wedged under the *estribo* at the base of the *barrem* where the bull had tossed him.'

'But did you smell anything?' Fernando asked.

'Nay,' Pilar said. 'I was too far away. We were in the seventh row of the *tendido* three. It was thus, being at an angle, that I could see all that happened. But that same night Blanquet who had been under the orders of Joselito when he too was killed told Finito about it at Fornos, and Finito asked Juan Luis de la Rosa and he would say nothing. But he nodded his head that it was true. I was present when this happened. So, *Inglés,* it may be that thou art deaf to things as Chicuelo and Marcial Lalanda and all of their *banderillems* and picadors and all of the *gente* of Juan and Manolo Granero were deaf to this thing on this day. But Juan Luis and Blanquet were not deaf. Nor am I deaf to such things.'

'Why do you say deaf when it is a thing of the nose?' Fernando asked.

'*Leche!*' Pilar said. 'Thou shouldst be the professor in place of the *Inglés.* But I could tell thee of other things, *Inglés,* and do not doubt what thou simply cannot see nor cannot hear. Thou canst not hear what a dog hears. Nor canst thou smell what a dog smells. But already thou hast experienced a little of what can happen to man.'

Maria put her hand on Robert Jordan's shoulder and let it rest there and he thought suddenly, let us finish all this nonsense and take advantage of what time we have. But it is too early yet. We have to kill this part of the evening. So he said to Pablo, 'Thou, believest thou in this wizardry?'

'I do not know,' Pablo said. 'I am more of thy opinion. No supernatural thing has ever happened to me. But fear, yes certainly. Plenty. But I believe that the Pilar can divine events from the hand. If she does not lie perhaps it is true that she has smelt such a thing.' '*Que va* that I should lie,' Pilar said. 'This is not a thing of my invention. This man Blanquet was a man of extreme seriousness and furthermore very devout. He was no gypsy but a bourgeois from Valencia. Hast thou never seen him?'

'Yes,' Robert Jordan said. 'I have seen him many times. He was small, gray-faced and no one handled a cape better. He was quick on his feet as a rabbit.'

'Exactly,' Pilar said. 'He had a gray face from heart trouble and gypsies said that he carried death with him but that he could flick it away with a cape as you might dust a table. Yet he, was who no gypsy, smelled death on Joselito when he fought at Talavera. Although I do not see how he could smell it above the smell of manzanilla. Blanquet spoke of this afterwards with much diffidence but those to whom he spoke said that it was a fantasy and that what he had smelled was the life that Jose led at that time coming out in sweat from his armpits. But then, later, came this of Manolo Granero in which Juan Luis de la Rosa also participated. Clearly Juan Luis was a man of very little honor, but of much sensitiveness in his work and he was also a great layer of women. But Blanquet was serious and very quiet and completely incapable of telling an untruth. And I tell you that I smelled death on your colleague who was here.'

'I do not believe it,' Robert Jordan said. 'Also you said that Blanquet smelled this just before the paseo. Just before the bullfight started. Now this was a successful action here of you and Kashkin and the train. He was not killed in that. How could you smell it then?'

'That has nothing to do with it,' Pilar explained. 'In the last season of Ignacio Sanchez Mejias he smelled so strongly of death that many refused to sit with him in the cafe. All gypsies knew of this.'

'After the death such things are invented,' Robert Jordan argued. 'Every one knew that Sanchez Mejias was on the road to a *cornada* because he had been too long out of training, because his style was heavy and dangerous, and because his strength and the agility in his legs were gone and his reflexes no longer as they had been.'

'Certainly,' Pilar told him. 'All of that is true. But all the gypsies knew also that he smelled of death and when he would come into the Villa Rosa you would see such people as Ricardo and Felipe Gonzalez leaving by the small door behind the bar.'

'They probably owed him money,' Robert Jordan said.

'It is possible,' Pilar said. 'Very possible. But they also smelled the thing and all knew of it.'

'What she says is true, *Inglés*,' the gypsy, Rafael, said. 'It is a well-known thing among us.'

'I believe nothing of it,' Robert Jordan said.

'Listen, *Inglés*,' Anselmo began. 'I am against all such wizardry. But this Pilar has the fame of being very advanced in such things.'

'But what does it smell like?' Fernando asked. 'What odor has it? If there be an odor it must be a definite odor.'

'You want to know, Fernandito?' Pilar smiled at him. 'You think that you could smell it?'

'If it actually exists why should I not smell it as well as another?' 'Why not?' Pilar was making fun of him, her big hands folded across her knees. 'Hast thou ever been aboard a ship, Fernando?'

'Nay. And I would not wish to.'

'Then thou might not recognize it. For part of it is the smell that comes when, on a ship, there is a storm and the portholes are closed up. Put your nose against the brass handle of a screwedtight porthole on a rolling ship that is swaying under you so that you are faint and hollow in the stomach and you have a part of that smell.'

'It would be impossible for me to recognize because I will go on no ship,' Fernando said.

'I have been on ships several times,' Pilar said. 'Both to go to Mexico and to Venezuela.'

'What's the rest of it?' Robert Jordan asked. Pilar looked at him mockingly, remembering now, proudly, her voyages.

'All right, *Inglés*. Learn. That's the thing. Learn. All right. After that of the ship you must go down the hill in Madrid to the Puente de Toledo early in the morning to the *matadero* and stand there on the wet paving when there is a fog from the Manzanares and wait for the old women who go before daylight to drink the blood of the beasts that are slaughtered. When such an old woman comes out of the *matadero*, holding her shawl around her, with her face gray and her eyes hollow, and the whiskers of age on her chin, and on her cheeks, set in the waxen white of her face as the sprouts grow from the seed of the bean, not bristles, but pale sprouts in the death of her face; put your arms tight around her, *Inglés*, and hold her to you and kiss her on the mouth and you will know the second part that odor is made of.'

'That one has taken my appetite,' the gypsy said. 'That of the sprouts was too much.'

'Do you want to hear some more?' Pilar asked Robert Jordan.

'Surely,' he said. 'If it is necessary for one to learn let us learn.'

'That of the sprouts in the face of the old women sickens me,' the gypsy said. 'Why should that occur in old women, Pilar? With us it is not so.'

'Nay,' Pilar mocked at him. 'With us the old woman, who was so slender in her youth, except of course for the perpetual bulge that is the mark of her husband's favor, that every gypsy pushes always before her—'

'Do not speak thus,' Rafael said. 'It is ignoble.'

'So thou art hurt,' Pilar said. 'Hast thou ever seen a *gitana* who was not about to have, or just to have had, a child?'

'Thou.'

'Leave it,' Pilar said. 'There is no one who cannot be hurt. What I was saying is that age brings its own form of ugliness to all. There is no need to detail it. But if the *Inglés* must learn that odor that he covets to recognize he must go to the *matadero* early in the morning.'

'I will go,' Robert Jordan said. 'But I will get the odor as they pass without kissing one. I fear the sprouts, too, as Rafael does.'

'Kiss one,' Pilar said. 'Kiss one, *Inglés,* for thy knowledge's sake and then, with this in thy nostrils, walk back up into the city and when thou seest a refuse pail with dead flowers in it plunge thy nose deep into it and inhale so that scent mixes with those thou hast already in thy nasal passages.'

'Now have I done it,' Robert Jordan said. 'What flowers were they?'

'Chrysanthemums.'

'Continue,' Robert Jordan said. 'I smell them.'

'Then,' Pilar went on, 'it is important that the day be in autumn with rain, or at least some fog, or early winter even and now thou shouldst continue to walk through the city and down the Calle de Salud smelling what thou wilt smell where they are sweeping out the *casas de putas* and emptying the slop jars into the drains and, with this odor of love's labor lost mixed sweetly with soapy water and cigarette butts only faintly reaching thy nostrils, thou shouldst go on to the Jardin Botanico where at night those girls who can no longer work in the houses do their work against the iron gates of the park and the iron picketed fences and upon the sidewalks. It is there in the shadow of the trees against the iron railings that they will perform all that a man wishes; from the simplest requests at a remuneration of ten centimos up to a peseta for that great act that we are born to and there, on a dead flower bed that has not yet been plucked out and replanted, and so serves to soften the earth that is so much softer than the sidewalk, thou wilt find an abandoned gunny sack with the odor of the wet earth, the dead flowers, and the doings of that night. In this sack will be contained the essence of it all, both the dead earth and the dead stalks of the flowers and their rotted blooms and the smell that is both the death and birth of man. Thou wilt wrap this sack around thy head and try to breathe through it.'

'No.'

'Yes,' Pilar said. 'Thou wilt wrap this sack around thy head and try to breathe and then, if thou hast not lost any of the previous odors, when thou inhalest deeply, thou wilt smell the odor of death-to-come as we know it.'

'All right,' Robert Jordan said. 'And you say Kashkin smelt like that when he was here?'

'Yes.'

'Well,' said Robert Jordan gravely. 'If that is true it is a good thing that I shot him.'

'*Ole,*' the gypsy said. The others laughed.

'Very good,' Primitivo approved. 'That should hold her for a while.'

'But Pilar,' Fernando said. 'Surely you could not expect one of Don Roberto's education to do such vile things.'

'No,' Pilar agreed.

'All of that is of the utmost repugnance.' 'Yes,' Pilar agreed.

'You would not expect him actually to perform those degrading acts?'

'No,' Pilar said. 'Go to bed, will you?' 'But, Pilar—' Fernando went on.

'Shut up, will you?' Pilar said to him suddenly and viciously. 'Do not make a fool of thyself and I will try not to make a fool of myself talking with people who cannot understand what one speaks of.'

'I confess I do not understand,' Fernando began.

'Don't confess and don't try to understand,' Pilar said. 'Is it still snowing outside?'

Robert Jordan went to the mouth of the cave, lifted the blanket and looked out. It was clear and cold in the night outside and no snow was falling. He looked through the tree trunks where the whiteness lay and up through the trees to where the sky was now clear. The air came into his lungs sharp and cold as he breathed.

'El Sordo will leave plenty of tracks if he has stolen horses tonight,' he thought.

He dropped the blanket and came back into the smoky cave. 'It is clear,' he said. 'The storm is over.'

20

Now in the night he lay and waited for the girl to come to him. There was no wind now and the pines were still in the night. The trunks of the pines projected from the snow that covered all the ground, and he lay in the robe feeling the suppleness of the bed under him that he had made, his legs stretched long against the warmth of the robe, the air sharp and cold on his head and in his nostrils as he breathed. Under his head, as he lay on his side, was the bulge of the trousers and the coat that he had wrapped around his shoes to make a pillow and against his side was the cold metal of the big automatic pistol he had taken from the holster when he undressed and fastened by its lanyard to his right wrist. He pushed the pistol away and settled deeper into the robe as he watched, across the snow, the dark break in the rocks that was the entrance to the cave. The sky was clear and there was enough light reflected from the snow to see the trunks of the trees and the bulk of the rocks where the cave was.

Earlier in the evening he had taken the ax and gone outside of the cave and walked through the new snow to the edge of the clearing and cut down a small spruce tree. In the dark he had dragged it, butt first, to the lee of the rock wall. There close to the rock, he had held the tree upright, holding the trunk firm with one hand, and, holding the ax-haft close to the head had lopped off all the boughs until he had a pile of them. Then, leaving the pile of boughs, he had laid the bare pole of the trunk down in the snow and gone into the cave to get a slap of wood he had seen against the wall. With this slab he scraped the ground clear of the snow along the rock wall and then picked up his boughs and shaking them clean of snow laid them in rows, like over-lapping plumes, until he had a bed. He put the pole across the foot of the bough bed to hold the branches in place and pegged it firm with two pointed pieces of wood he split from the edge of the slab.

Then he carried the slab and the ax back into the cave, ducking under the blanket as he came in, and leaned them both against the wall.

'What do you do outside?' Pilar had asked. 'I made a bed.'

'Don't cut pieces from my new shelf for thy bed.' 'I am sorry.'

'It has no importance,' she said. 'There are more slabs at the sawmill. What sort of bed hast thou made?'

'As in my country.'

'Then sleep well on it,' she had said and Robert Jordan had opened one of the packs and pulled the robe out and replaced those things wrapped in it back in the pack and carried the robe out, ducking under the blanket again, and spread it over the boughs so that the closed end of the robe was against the pole that was pegged cross-wise at the foot of the bed. The open head of the robe was protected by the rock wall of the cliff. Then he went back into the cave for his packs but Pilar said, 'They can sleep with me as last night.'

'Will you not have sentries?' he asked. 'The night is clear and the storm is over.'

'Fernando goes,' Pilar said.

Maria was in the back of the cave and Robert Jordan could not see her.

'Good night to every one,' he had said. 'I am going to sleep.'

Of the others, who were laying out blankets and bedrolls on the floor in front of the cooking fire, pushing back the slab tables and the rawhide-covered stools to make sleeping space, Primitivo and Andres looked up and said, *'Buenas naches.'*

Anselmo was already asleep in a corner, rolled in his blanket and his cape, not even his nose showing. Pablo was asleep in his chair.

'Do you want a sheep hide for thy bed?' Pilar asked Robert Jordan softly.

'Nay,' he said. 'Thank thee. I do not need it.'

'Sleep well,' she said. 'I will respond for thy material.'

Fernando had gone out with him and stood a moment where Robert Jordan had spread the sleeping robe.

'You have a curious idea to sleep in the open, Don Roberto,' he said standing there in the dark, muffled in his blanket cape, his carbine slung over his shoulder.

'I am accustomed to it. Good night.'

'Since you are accustomed to it.'

'When are you relieved?'

'At four.'

'There is much cold between now and then.'

'I am accustomed to it,' Fernando said.

'Since, then, you are accustomed to it–' Robert Jordan said politely.

'Yes,' Fernando agreed. 'Now I must get up there. Good night, Don Roberto.'

'Good night, Fernando.'

Then he had made a pillow of the things he took off and gotten into the robe and then lain and waited, feeling the spring of the boughs under the flannelly, feathered lightness of the robe warmth, watching the mouth of the cave across the snow; feeling his heart beat as he waited.

The night was clear and his head felt as clear and cold as the air. He smelled the odor of the pine boughs under him, the piney smell of the crushed needles and the sharper odor of the resinous sap from the cut limbs. Pilar, he thought. Pilar and the smell of death. This is the smell I love. This and fresh-cut clover, the crushed sage as you ride after cattle, wood-smoke and the burning leaves of autumn. That must be the odor of nostalgia, the smell of the smoke from the piles of raked leaves burning in the streets in the fall in Missoula. Which would you rather smell? Sweet grass the Indians used in their baskets? Smoked leather? The odor of the ground in the spring after rain? The smell of the sea as you walk through the gorse on a headland in Galicia? Or the wind from the land as you come in toward Cuba in the dark? That was the odor of the cactus flowers, mimosa and the seagrape shrubs. Or would you rather smell frying bacon in the morning when you are hungry? Or coffee in the morning? Or a Jonathan apple as you bit into it? Or a cider mill in the grinding, or bread fresh from the oven? You must be hungry, he thought, and he lay on his side and watched the entrance of the cave in the light that the stars reflected from the snow.

Someone came out from under the blanket and he could see whoever it was standing by the break in the rock that made the entrance. Then he heard a slithering sound in the snow and then whoever it was ducked down and went back in.

I suppose she won't come until they are all asleep, he thought. It is a waste of time. The night is half gone. Oh, Maria. Come now quickly, Maria, for there is little time. He heard the soft sound of snow falling from a branch onto the snow on the ground. A little wind was rising. He felt it on his face. Suddenly he felt a panic that she might not come. The wind rising now reminded him how soon it would be morning. More snow fell from the branches as he heard the wind now moving the pine tops.

Come now, Maria. Please come here now quickly, he thought. Oh, come here now. Do not wait. There is no importance any more to your waiting until they are asleep.

Then he saw her coming out from under the blanket that covered the cave mouth. She stood there a moment and he knew it was she but he could not see what she was doing. He whistled a low whistle and she was still at the cave mouth doing something in the darkness of the rock shadow. Then she came running, carrying something in her hands and he saw her running longlegged through the snow. Then she was kneeling by the robe, her head pushed hard against him, slapping snow from her feet. She kissed him and handed him her bundle.

'Put it with thy pillow,' she said. 'I took these off there to save time.'

'You came barefoot through the snow?'

'Yes,' she said, 'and wearing only my wedding shirt.'

He held her close and tight in his arms and she rubbed her head against his chin.

'Avoid the feet,' she said. 'They are very cold, Roberto.'

'Put them here and warm them.'

'Nay,' she said. 'They will warm quickly. But say quickly now that you love me.'
'I love thee.'
'Good. Good. Good.'
'I love thee, little rabbit.'
'Do you love my wedding shirt?'
'It is the same one as always.'
'Yes. As last night. It is my wedding shirt.'
'Put thy feet here.'
'Nay, that would be abusive. They will warm of themselves. They are warm to me. It is only that the snow has made them cold toward thee. Say it again.'
'I love thee, my little rabbit.'
'I love thee, too, and I am thy wife.'
'Were they asleep?'
'No,' she said. 'But I could support it no longer. And what importance has it?'
'None,' he said, and felt her against him, slim and long and warmly lovely. 'No other thing has importance.'
'Put thy hand on my head,' she said, 'and then let me see if I can kiss thee.'
'Was it well?' she asked.
'Yes,' he said. 'Take off thy wedding shirt.'
'You think I should?'
'Yes, if thou wilt not be cold.'
'*Qué va*, cold. I am on fire.'
'I, too. But afterwards thou wilt not be cold?'
'No. Afterwards we will be as one animal of the forest and be so close that neither one can tell that one of us is one and not the other. Can you not feel my heart be your heart?'
'Yes. There is no difference.'
'Now, feel. I am thee and thou art me and all of one is the other. And I love thee, oh, I love thee so. Are you not truly one? Canst thou not feel it?'
'Yes,' he said. 'It is true.'
'And feel now. Thou hast no heart but mine.'
'Nor any other legs, nor feet, nor of the body.'
'But we are different,' she said. 'I would have us exactly the same.'
'You do not mean that.'
'Yes I do. I do. That is a thing I had to tell thee.' 'You do not mean that.'
'Perhaps I do not,' she said speaking softly with her lips against his shoulder. 'But I wished to say it. Since we are different I am glad that thou art Roberto and I Maria. But if thou should ever wish to change I would be glad to change. I would be thee because I love thee so.'
'I do not wish to change. It is better to be one and each one to be the one he is.'
'But we will be one now and there will never be a separate one.' Then she said, 'I will be thee when thou are not there. Oh, I love thee so and I must care well for thee.'

'Maria.'
'Yes.'
'Maria.'
'Yes.'
'Maria.'
'Oh, yes. Please.'
'Art thou not cold?'
'Oh, no. Pull the robe over thy shoulders.'
'Maria.'
'I cannot speak.'
'Oh, Maria. Maria. Maria.'

Then afterwards, close, with the night cold outside, in the long warmth of the robe, her head touching his cheek, she lay quiet and happy against him and then said softly, 'And thou?'

'*Como tu*,' he said.

'Yes,' she said. 'But it was not as this afternoon.'

'No.'

'But I loved it more. One does not need to die.'

'*Ojala no*,' he said. 'I hope not.' 'I did not mean that.'

'I know. I know what thou meanest. We mean the same.'

'Then why did you say that instead of what I meant?'

'With a man there is a difference.'

'Then I am glad that we are different.'

'And so am I,' he said. 'But I understood about the dying. I only spoke thus, as a man, from habit. I feel the same as thee.'

'However thou art and however thou speakest is how I would have thee be.'

'And I love thee and I love thy name, Maria.'

'It is a common name.'

'No,' he said.

'It is not common.'

'Now should we sleep?' she said. 'I could sleep easily.'

'Let us sleep,' he said, and he felt the long light body, warm against him, comforting against him, abolishing loneliness against him, magically, by a simple touching of flanks, of shoulders and of feet, making an alliance against death with him, and he said, 'Sleep well, little long rabbit.'

She said, 'I am asleep already.'

'I am going to sleep,' he said. 'Sleep well, beloved.' Then he was asleep and happy as he slept.

But in the night he woke and held her tight as though she were all of life and it was being taken from him. He held her feeling she was all of life there was and it was true. But she was sleeping well and soundly and she did not wake. So he rolled away onto his side and pulled the robe over her head and kissed her once on her neck under the robe and then pulled the pistol lanyard up and put the pistol by his side where he could reach it handily and then he lay there in the night thinking.

21

A Warm wind came with daylight and he could hear the snow melting in the trees and the heavy sound of its falling. It was a late spring morning. He knew with the first breath he drew that the snow had been only a freak storm in the mountains and it would be gone by noon. Then he heard a horse coming, the hoofs balled with the wet snow thumping dully as the horseman trotted. He heard the noise of a carbine scabbard slapping loosely and the creak of leather.

'Maria,' he said, and shook the girl's shoulder to waken her. 'Keep thyself under the robe,' and he buttoned his shirt with one hand and held the automatic pistol in the other, loosening the safety catch with his thumb. He saw the girl's cropped head disappear with a jerk under the robe and then he saw the horseman coming through the trees. He crouched now in the robe and holding the pistol in both hands aimed it at the man as he rode toward him. He had never seen this man before.

The horseman was almost opposite him now. He was riding a big gray gelding and he wore a khaki beret, a blanket cape like a poncho, and heavy black boots. From the scabbard on the right of his saddle projected the stock and the long oblong clip of a short automatic rifle. He had a young, hard face and at this moment he saw Robert Jordan.

He reached his hand down toward the scabbard and as he swung low, turning and jerking at the scabbard, Robert Jordan saw the scarlet of the formalized device he wore on the left breast of his khaki blanket cape.

Aiming at the center of his chest, a little lower than the device, Robert Jordan fired.

The pistol roared in the snowy woods.

The horse plunged as though he had been spurred and the young man, still tugging at the scabbard, slid over toward the ground, his right foot caught in the stirrup. The horse broke off through the trees dragging him, bumping, face downward, and Robert Jordan stood up holding the pistol now in one hand.

The big gray horse was galloping through the pines. There was a broad swath in the snow where the man dragged with a scarlet streak along one side of it. People were coming out of the mouth of the cave. Robert Jordan reached down and unrolled his trousers from the pillow and began to put them on.

'Get thee dressed,' he said to Maria.

Overhead he heard the noise of a plane flying very high. Through the trees he saw where the gray horse had stopped and was standing, his rider still hanging face down from the stirrup.

'Go catch that horse,' he called to Primitivo who had started over toward him. Then, 'Who was on guard at the top?'

'Rafael,' Pilar said from the cave. She stood there, her hair still down her back in two braids.

'There's cavalry out,' Robert Jordan said. 'Get your damned gun up there.'

He heard Pilar call, 'Agustin,' into the cave. Then she went into the cave and then two men came running out, one with the automatic rifle with its tripod swung on his shoulder; the other with a sackful of the pans.

'Get up there with them,' Robert Jordan said to Anselmo. 'You lie beside the gun and hold the legs still,' he said.

The three of them went up the trail through the woods at a run.

The sun had not yet come up over the tops of the mountains and Robert Jordan stood straight buttoning his trousers and tightening his belt, the big pistol hanging from the lanyard on his wrist. He put the pistol in its holster on his belt and slipped the knot down on the lanyard and passed the loop over his head.

Somebody will choke you with that sometime, he thought. Well, this has done it. He took the pistol out of the holster, removed the clip, inserted one of the cartridges from the row alongside of the holster and shoved the clip back into the butt of the pistol.

He looked through the trees to where Primitivo, holding the reins of the horse, was twisting the rider's foot out of the stirrup. The body lay face down in the snow and as he watched Primitivo was going through the pockets.

'Come on,' he called. 'Bring the horse. 'As he knelt to put on his rope-soled shoes, Robert Jordan could feel Maria against his knees, dressing herself under the robe. She had no place in his life now.

That cavalryman did not expect anything, he was thinking. He was not following horse tracks and he was not even properly alert, let alone alarmed. He was not even following the tracks up to the post. He must have been one of a patrol scattered out in these hills. But when the patrol misses him they will follow his tracks here. Unless the snow melts first, he thought. Unless something happens to the patrol.

'You better get down below,' he said to Pablo.

They were all out of the cave now, standing there with the carbines and with grenades on their belts. Pilar held a leather bag of grenades toward Robert Jordan and he took three and put them in his pocket. He ducked into the cave, found his two packs, opened the one with the submachine gun in it and took out the barrel and stock, slipped the stock onto the forward assembly and put one clip into the gun and three in his pockets. He locked the pack and started for the door. I've got two pockets full of hardware, he thought. I hope the seams hold. He came out of the cave and said to Pablo, 'I'm going up above. Can Agustin shoot that gun?'

'Yes,' Pablo said. He was watching Primitivo leading up the horse.

'*Mira que caballo*,' he said. 'Look, what a horse.'

The big gray was sweating and shivering a little and Robert Jordan patted him on the withers.

'I will put him with the others,' Pablo said.

'No,' Robert Jordan said. 'He has made tracks into here. He must make them out.'

'True,' agreed Pablo. 'I will ride him out and will hide him and bring him in when the snow is melted. Thou hast much head today, *Inglés*.'

'Send some one below,' Robert Jordan said. 'We've got to get up there.'

'It is not necessary,' Pablo said. 'Horsemen cannot come that way. But we can get out, by there and by two other places. It is better not to make tracks if there are planes coming. Give me the *bota* with wine, Pilar.'

'To go off and get drunk,' Pilar said. 'Here, take these instead.' He reached over and put two of the grenades in his pockets.

'*Que va*, to get drunk,' Pablo said. 'There is gravity in the situation. But give me the *bota*. I do not like to do all this on water.'

He reached his arms up, took the reins and swung up into the saddle. He grinned and patted the nervous horse. Robert Jordan saw him rub his leg along the horse's flank affectionately.

'Que *caballo más bonito*,' he said and patted the big gray again.

'*Que caballo más hermoso*. Come on. The faster this gets out of here the better.'

He reached down and pulled the light automatic rifle with its ventilated barrel, really a submachine gun built to take the 9 mm. pistol cartridge, from the scabbard, and looked at it. 'Look how they are armed,' he said. 'Look at modern cavalry.'

'There's modern cavalry over there on his face,' Robert Jordan said. '*Vamonos*.'

'Do you, Andres, saddle and hold the horses in readiness. If you hear firing bring them up to the woods behind the gap. Come with thy arms and leave the women to hold the horses. Fernando, see that my sacks are brought also. Above all, that my sacks are brought carefully. Thou to look after my sacks, too,' he said to Pilar. 'Thou to verify that they come with the horses. *Vamonos*,' he said. 'Let us go.'

'The Maria and I will prepare all for leaving,' Pilar said. Then to Robert Jordan, 'Look at him,' nodding at Pablo on the gray horse, sitting him in the heavy-thighed herdsman manner, the horse's nostrils widening as Pablo replaced the clip in the automatic rifle. 'See what a horse has done for him.'

'That I should have two horses,' Robert Jordan said fervently.

'Danger is thy horse.'

'Then give me a mule,' Robert Jordan grinned.

'Strip me that,' he said to Pilar and jerked his head toward where the man lay face down in the snow. 'And bring everything, all the letters and papers, and put them in the outside pocket of my sack. Everything, understand?'

'Yes.'

'*Vamonos*,' he said.

Pablo rode ahead and the two men followed in a single file in order not to track up the snow. Robert Jordan carried the submachine gun muzzle down, carrying it by its forward hand grip. I wish it took the same ammunition that saddle gun takes, he thought. But it doesn't. This is a German gun. This was old Kashkin's gun.

The sun was coming over the mountains now. A warm wind was blowing and the snow was melting. It was a lovely late spring morning.

Robert Jordan looked back and saw Maria now standing with Pilar. Then she came running up the trail. He dropped behind Primitivo to speak to her.

'Thou,' she said. 'Can I go with thee?'

'No. Help Pilar.'

She was walking behind him and put her hand on his arm.

'I'm coming.'

'Nay.'

She kept on walking close behind him.

'I could hold the legs of the gun in the way thou told Anselmo.'

'Thou wilt hold no legs. Neither of guns nor of nothing.'

Walking beside him she reached forward and put her hand in his pocket.

'No,' he said. 'But take good care of thy wedding shirt.'

'Kiss me,' she said, 'if thou goest.'

'Thou art shameless,' he said.

'Yes,' she said. 'Totally.'

'Get thee back now. There is much work to do. We may fight here if they follow these horse tracks.'

'Thou,' she said. 'Didst thee see what he wore on his chest?'

'Yes. Why not?'

'It was the Sacred Heart.'

'Yes. All the people of Navarre wear it.'

'And thou shot for that?'

'No. Below it. Get thee back now.'

'Thou,' she said. 'I saw all.'

'Thou saw nothing. One man. One man from a horse. *Vete*. Get thee back.'

'Say that you love me.'

'No. Not now.'

'Not love me now?'

'*Dejamos*. Get thee back. One does not do that and love all at the same moment.'

'I want to go to hold the legs of the gun and while it speaks love thee all in the same moment.'

'Thou art crazy. Get thee back now.' 'I am crazy,' she said. 'I love thee.' 'Then get thee back.'

'Good. I go. And if thou dost not love me, I love thee enough for both.'

He looked at her and smiled through his thinking.

'When you hear firing,' he said, 'come with the horses. Aid the Pilar with my sacks. It is possible there will be nothing. I hope so.'

'I go,' she said. 'Look what a horse Pablo rides.' The big gray was moving ahead up the trail.

'Yes. But go.'

'I go.'

Her fist, clenched tight in his pocket, beat hard against his thigh. He looked at her and saw there were tears in her eyes. She pulled her fist out of his pocket and put both arms tight around his and kissed him.

'I go,' she said. '*Me voy.* I go.'

He looked back and saw her standing there, the first morning sunlight on her brown face and the cropped, tawny, burned-gold hair. She lifted her fist at him and turned and walked back down the trail, her head down.

Primitivo turned around and looked after her.

'If she did not have her hair cut so short she would be a pretty girl,' he said.

'Yes,' Robert Jordan said. He was thinking of something else. 'How is she in the bed?' Primitivo asked.

'What?' 'In the bed.'

'Watch thy mouth.'

'One should not be offended when—'

'Leave it,' Robert Jordan said. He was looking at the position.

22

'Cut Me pine branches,' Robert Jordan said to Primitivo, 'and bring them quickly.'

'I do not like the gun there,' he said to Agustin.

'Why?'

'Place it over there,' Robert Jordan pointed, 'and later I will tell thee.'

'Here, thus. Let me help thee. Here,' he said, then squatted down.

He looked out across the narrow oblong, noting the height of the rocks on either side.

'It must be farther,' he said, 'farther out. Good. Here. That will do until it can be done properly. There. Put the stones there. Here is one. Put another there at the side. Leave room for the muzzle to swing. The stone must be farther to this side. Anselmo. Get thee down to the cave and bring me an ax. Quickly.'

'Have you never had a proper emplacement for the gun?' he said to Agustin.

'We always placed it here.

'Kashkin never said to put it there?'

'No. The gun was brought after he left.'

'Did no one bring it who knew how to use it?'

'No. It was brought by porters.'

'What a way to do things,' Robert Jordan said. 'It was just given to you without instruction?'

'Yes, as a gift might be given. One for us and one for El Sardo. Four men brought them. Anselmo guided them.'

'It was a wonder they did not lose them with four men to cross the lines.'

'I thought so, too,' Agustin said. 'I thought those who sent them meant for them to be lost. But Anselmo brought them well.'

'You know how to handle it?'

'Yes. I have experimented. I know. Pablo knows. Primitivo knows. So does Fernando. We have made a study of taking it apart and putting it together on the table in the cave. Once we had it apart and could not get it together for two days.

Since then we have not had it apart.'

'Does it shoot now?'

'Yes. But we do not let the gypsy nor others frig with it.'

'You see? From there it was useless,' he said. 'Look. Those rocks which should protect your flanks give cover to those who will attack you. With such a gun you must seek a flatness over which to fire. Also you must take them sideways. See? Look now. All that is dominated.'

'I see,' said Agustin. 'But we have never fought in defense except when our town was taken. At the train there were soldiers with the *máquina*.'

'Then we will all learn together,' Robert Jordan said. 'There are a few things to observe. Where is the gypsy who should be here?'

'I do not know.'

'Where is it possible for him to be?'

'I do not know.'

Pablo had ridden out through the pass and turned once and ridden in a circle across the level space at the top that was the field of fire for the automatic rifle. Now Robert Jordan watched him riding down the slope alongside the tracks the horse had left when he was ridden in. He disappeared in the trees turning to the left.

'I hope he doesn't run right into cavalry,' Robert Jordan thought. 'I'm afraid we'd have him right here in our laps.'

Primitivo brought the pine branches and Robert Jordan stuck them through the snow into the unfrozen earth, arching them over the gun from either side.

'Bring more,' he said. 'There must be cover for the two men who serve it. This is not good but it will serve until the ax comes. Listen,' he said, 'if you hear a plane lie flat wherever thou art in the shadows of the rocks. I am here with the gun.'

Now with the sun up and the warm wind blowing it was pleasant on the side of the rocks where the sun shone. Four horses, Robert Jordan thought. The two women and me, Anselmo, Primitivo, Fernando, Agustin, what the hell is the name of the other brother? That's eight. Not counting the gypsy. Makes nine. Plus Pablo gone with one horse makes ten. Andres is his name. The other brother.

Plus the other, Eladio. Makes ten. That's not one-half a horse apiece. Three men can hold this and four can get away. Five with Pablo. That's two left over. Three with Eladio. Where the hell is he?

God knows what will happen to Sordo today if they picked up the trail of those horses in the snow. That was tough; the snow stopping that way. But it melting today will even things up. But not for Sardo. I'm afraid it's too late to even it up for Sordo.

If we can last through today and not have to fight we can swing the whole show tomorrow with what we have. I know we can. Not well, maybe. Not as it should be, to be foolproof, not as we would have done; but using everybody we can swing it. *If we don't have to fight today.* God help us if we have to fight today.

I don't know any place better to lay up in the meantime than this. If we move now we only leave tracks. This is as good a place as any and if the worst gets to be the worst there are three ways out of this place. There is the dark then to come and from wherever we are in these hills, I can reach and do the bridge at daylight. I don't know why I worried about it before. It seems easy enough now. I hope they get the planes up on time for once. I certainly hope that. Tomorrow is going to be a day with dust on the road.

Well, today will be very interesting or very dull. Thank God we've got that cavalry mount out and away from here. I don't think even if they ride right up here they will go in the way those tracks are now. They'll think he stopped and circled and they'll pick up Pablo's tracks. I wonder where the old swine will go. He'll probably leave tracks like an old bull elk spooking out of the country and work way up and then when the snow melts circle back below. That horse certainly did things for him. Of course he may have just mucked off with him too. Well, he should be able to take care of himself. He's been doing this a long time. I wouldn't trust him farther than you can throw Mount Everest, though.

I suppose it's smarter to use these rocks and build a good blind for this gun than to make a proper emplacement for it. You'd be digging and get caught with your pants down if they come or if the planes come. She will hold this, the way she is, as long as it is any use to hold it, and anyway I can't stay to fight. I have to get out of here with that stuff and I'm going to take Anselmo with me. Who would stay to cover us while we got away if we have to fight here r

Just then, while he was watching all of the country that was visible, he saw the gypsy coming through the rocks to the left. He was walking with a loose, high-hipped, sloppy swing, his carbine was slung on his back, his brown face was grinning and he carried two big hares, one in each hand. He carried them by the legs, heads swinging.

'*Hola*, Roberto,' he called cheerfully.

Robert Jordan put his hand to his mouth, and the gypsy looked startled. He slid over behind the rocks to where Robert Jordan was crouched beside the brush-shielded automatic rifle. He crouched down and laid the hares in the snow. Robert Jordan looked up at him.

'You *hijo de la gran puta!*' he said softly. 'Where the obscenity have you been r'

'I tracked them,' the gypsy said. 'I got them both. They had made love in the snow.'

'And thy post?'

'It was not for long,' the gypsy whispered. 'What passes r Is there an alarm r'

'There is cavalry out.'

'*Rediós!*' the gypsy said. 'Hast thou seen them?'

'There is one at the camp now,' Robert Jordan said. 'He came for breakfast.'

'I thought I heard a shot or something like one,' the gypsy said.

'I obscenity in the milk! Did he come through here?'

'Here. *Thy* post.'

'*Ay, mi madre!*' the gypsy said. 'I am a poor, unlucky man.'

'If thou wert not a gypsy, I would shoot thee.'

'No, Roberto. Don't say that. I am sorry. It was the hares. Before daylight I heard the male thumping in the snow. You cannot imagine what a debauch they were engaged in. I went toward the noise but they were gone. I followed the tracks in the snow and high up I found them together and slew them both. Feel the fatness of the two for this time of year. Think what the Pilar will do with those two. I am sorry, Roberto, as sorry as thee. Was the cavalryman killed?'

'Yes.'

'By thee?'

'Yes.'

'*Que tio!*' the gypsy said in open flattery. 'Thou art a veritable phenomenon.'

'Thy mother!' Robert Jordan said. He could not help grinning at the gypsy. 'Take thy hares to camp and bring us up some breakfast.'

He put a hand out and felt of the hares that lay limp, long, heavy, thick-furred, big-footed and long-eared in the snow, their round dark eyes open.

'They *are* fat,' he said.

'Fat!' the gypsy said. 'There's a tub of lard on the ribs of each one. In my life have I never dreamed of such hares.'

'Go then,' Robert Jordan said, 'and come quickly with the breakfast and bring to me the documentation of that *requete*. Ask Pilar for it.'

'You are not angry with me, Roberto?'

'Not angry. Disgusted that you should leave your post. Suppose it had been a troop of cavalry?'

'*Rediós*,' the gypsy said. 'How reasonable you are.'

'Listen to me. You cannot leave a post again like that. Never. I do not speak of shooting lightly.'

'Of course not. And another thing. Never would such an opportunity as the two hares present itself again. Not in the life of one man.'

'*Anda!*' Robert Jordan said. 'And hurry back.'

The gypsy picked up the two hares and slipped back through the rocks and Robert Jordan looked out across the flat opening and the slopes of the hill below. Two crows circled overhead and then lit in a pine tree below. Another crow joined them and Robert Jordan, watching them, thought: those are my sentinels. As long as those are quiet there is no one coming through the trees.

The gypsy, he thought. He is truly worthless. He has no political development, nor any discipline, and you could not rely on him for anything. But I need him for tomorrow. I have a use for him tomorrow. It's odd to see a gypsy in a war. They should be exempted like conscientious objectors. Or as the physically and mentally unfit. They are worthless. But conscientious objectors weren't exempted in this war. No one was exempted. It came to one and all alike. Well, it had come here now to this lazy outfit. They had it now.

Agustin and Primitivo came up with the brush and Robert Jordan built a good blind for the automatic rifle, a blind that would conceal the gun from the air and that would look natural from the forest. He showed them where to place a man high in the rocks to the right where he could see all the country below and to the right, and another where he could command the only stretch where the left wall might be climbed.

'Do not fire if you see any one from there,' Robert Jordan said. 'Roll a rock down as a warning, a small rock, and signal to us with thy rifle, thus,' he lifted the rifle and held it over his head as though guarding it. 'Thus for numbers,' he lifted the rifle up and down. 'If they are dismounted point thy rifle muzzle at the ground. Thus. Do not fire from there until thou hearest the máquina fire. Shoot at a man's knees when you shoot from that height. If you hear me whistle twice on this whistle get down, keeping behind cover, and come to these rocks where the *máquina* is.'

Primitivo raised the rifle.

'I understand,' he said. 'It is very simple.'

'Send first the small rock as a warning and indicate the direction and the number. See that you are not seen.'

'Yes,' Primitivo said. 'If I can throw a grenade?'

'Not until the *máquina* has spoken. It may be that cavalry will come searching for their comrade and still not try to enter. They may follow the tracks of Pablo. We do not want combat if it can be avoided. Above all that we should avoid it. Now get up there.'

'*Me voy*,' Primitivo said, and climbed up into the high rocks with his carbine.

'Thou, Agustin,' Robert Jordan said. 'What do you know of the gun?'

Agustin squatted there, tall, black, stubbly-jeweled, with his sunken eyes and thin mouth and his big work-worn hands.

'*Pues*, to load it. To aim it. To shoot it. Nothing more.'

'You must not fire until they are within fifty meters and only when you are sure they will be coming into the pass which leads to the cave,' Robert Jordan said.

'Yes. How far is that?'

'That rock.'

'If there is an officer shoot him first. Then move the gun onto the others. Move very slowly. It takes little movement. I will teach Fernando to tap it. Hold it tight so that it does not jump and sight carefully and do not fire more than six shots at a time if you can help it. For the fire of the gun jumps upward. But each time fire at one man and then move from him to another. At a man on a horse, shoot at his belly.'

'Yes.'

'One man should hold the tripod still so that the gun does not jump. Thus. He will load the gun for thee.'

'And where will you be?'

'I will be here on the left. Above, where I can see all and I will cover thy left with this small *máquina*. Here. If they should come it would be possible to make a massacre. But you must not fire until they are that close.'

'I believe that we could make a massacre. *Menuda matanza!*'

'But I hope they do not come.'

'If it were not for thy bridge we could make a massacre here and get out.'

'It would avail nothing. That would serve no purpose. The bridge is a part of a plan to win the war. This would be nothing. This would be an incident. A nothing.'

'*Que va,* nothing. Every fascist dead is a fascist less.'

'Yes. But with this of the bridge we can take Segovia. The Capital of a Province. Think of that. It will be the first one we will take.'

'Thou believest in this seriously? That we can take Segovia?'

'Yes. It is possible with the bridge blown correctly.'

'I would like to have the massacre here and the bridge, too.'

'Thou hast much appetite,' Robert Jordan told him.

All this time he had been watching the crows. Now he saw one was watching something. The bird cawed and flew up. But the other crow still stayed in the tree. Robert Jordan looked up toward Primitivo's place high in the rocks. He saw him watching out over the country below but he made no signal. Robert Jordan leaned forward and worked the lock on the automatic rifle, saw the round in the chamber and let the lock down. The crow was still there in the tree. The other circled wide over the snow and then settled again. In the sun and the warm wind the snow was falling from the laden branches of the pines.

'I have a massacre for thee for tomorrow morning,' Robert Jordan said. 'It is necessary to exterminate the post at the sawmill.'

'I am ready,' Agustin said, '*Estoy listo*.'

'Also the post at the road mender's hut below the bridge.'

'For the one or for the other,' Agustin said. 'Or for both.'

'Not for both. They will be done at the same time,' Robert Jordan said.

'Then for either one,' Agustin said. 'Now for a long time have I wished for action in this war. Pablo has rotted us here with inaction.'

Anselmo came up with the ax.

'Do you wish more branches?' he asked. 'To me it seems well hidden.'

'Not branches,' Robert Jordan said. 'Two small trees that we can plant here and there to make it look more natural. There are not enough trees here for it to be truly natural.'

'I will bring them.'

'Cut them well back, so the stumps cannot be seen.'

Robert Jordan heard the ax sounding in the woods behind him. He looked up at Primitivo above in the rocks and he looked down at the pines across the clearing. The one crow was still there. Then he heard the first high, throbbing murmur of a plane coming. He looked up and saw it high and tiny and silver in the sun, seeming hardly to move in the high sky.

'They cannot see us,' he said to Agustin. 'But it is well to keep down. That is the second observation plane today.'

'And those of yesterday?' Agustin asked.

'They are like a bad dream now,' Robert Jordan said.

'They must be at Segovia. The bad dream waits there to become a reality.'

The plane was out of sight now over the mountains but the sound of its motors still persisted.

As Robert Jordan looked, he saw the crow fly up. He flew straight away through the trees without cawing.

23

'Get thee down,' Robert Jordan whispered to Agustin, and he turned his head and flicked his hand *Down, Down,* to Anselmo who was coming through the gap with a pine tree, carrying it over his shoulder like a Christmas tree. He saw the old man drop his pine tree behind a rock and then he was out of sight in the rocks and Robert Jordan was looking ahead across the open space toward the timber. He saw nothing and heard nothing but he could feel his heart pounding and then he heard the clack of stone on stone and the leaping, dropping clicks of a small rock falling. He turned his head to the right and looking up saw Primitivo's rifle raised and lowered four times horizontally. Then there was nothing more to see but the white stretch in front of him with the circle of horse tracks and the timber beyond.

'Cavalry,' he said softly to Agustin.

Agustin looked at him and his dark, sunken cheeks widened at their base as he grinned. Robert Jordan noticed he was sweating. He reached over and put his hand on his shoulder. His hand was still there as they saw the four horsemen ride out of the timber and he felt the muscles in Agustin's back twitch under his hand.

One horseman was ahead and three rode behind. The one ahead was following the horse tracks. He looked down as he rode. The other three came behind him, fanned out through the timber. They were all watching carefully. Robert Jordan felt his heart beating against the snowy ground as he lay, his elbows spread wide and watched them over the sights of the automatic rifle.

The man who was leading rode along the trail to where Pablo had circled and stopped. The others rode up to him and they all stopped.

Robert Jordan saw them clearly over the blued steel barrel of the automatic rifle. He saw the faces of the men, the sabers hanging, the sweat-darkened flanks of the horses, and the cone like slope of the khaki capes, and the Navarrese slant of the khaki berets. The leader turned his horse directly toward the opening in the rocks where the gun was placed and Robert Jordan saw his young, sun- and wind-darkened face, his close-set eyes, hawk nose and the over-long wedge-shaped chin.

Sitting his horse there, the horse's chest toward Robert Jordan, the horse's head high, the butt of the light automatic rifle projecting forward from the scabbard at the right of the saddle, the leader pointed toward the opening where the gun was.

Robert Jordan sunk his elbows into the ground and looked along the barrel at the four riders stopped there in the snow. Three of them had their automatic rifles out. Two carried them across the pommels of their saddles. The other sat his' horse with the rifle swung out to the right, the butt resting against his hip.

You hardly ever see them at such range, he thought. Not along the barrel of one of these do you see them like this. Usually the rear sight is raised and they seem miniatures of men and you have hell to make it carry up there; or they come running, flopping, running, and you beat a slope with fire or bar a certain street, or keep it on the windows; or far away you see them marching on a road. Only at the trains do you see them like this. Only then are they like now, and with four of these you can make them scatter. Over the gun sights, at this range, it makes them twice the size of men.

Thou, he thought, looking at the wedge of the front sight placed now firm in the slot of the rear sight, the top of the wedge against the center of the leader's chest, a little to the right of the scarlet device that showed bright in the morning sun against the khaki cape. Though, he thought, thinking in Spanish now and pressing his fingers forward against the trigger guard to keep it away from where it would bring the quick, shocking, hurtling rush from the automatic rifle. Thou, he thought again, thou art dead now in thy youth. And thou, he thought, and thou, and thou. But let it not happen. Do not let it happen.

He felt Agustin beside him start to cough, felt him hold it, choke and swallow. Then as he looked along the oiled blue of the barrel out through the opening between the branches, his finger still pressed forward against the trigger guard, he saw the leader turn his horse and point into the timber where Pablo's trail led. The four of them trotted into the timber and Agustin said softly, '*Cabrones!*'

Robert Jordan looked behind him at the rocks where Anselmo had dropped the tree.

The gypsy, Rafael, was coming toward them through the rocks, carrying a pair of cloth saddlebags, his rifle slung on his back. Robert Jordan waved him down and the gypsy ducked out of sight.

'We could have killed all four,' Agustin said quietly. He was still wet with sweat.

'Yes,' Robert Jordan whispered. 'But with the firing who knows what might have come?'

Just then he heard the noise of another rock falling and he looked around quickly. But both the gypsy and Anselmo were out of sight. He looked at his wrist watch and then up to where Primitivo was raising and lowering his rifle in what seemed an infinity of short jerks. Pablo has forty-five minutes' start, Robert Jordan thought, and then he heard the noise of a body of cavalry coming.

'*No te apures,*' he whispered to Agustin. 'Do not worry. They will pass as the others.'

They came into sight trotting along the edge of the timber in column of twos, twenty mounted men, armed and uniformed as the others had been, their sabers swinging, their carbines in their holsters; and then they went down into the timber as the others had.

'*Tu ves?*' Robert Jordan said to Agustin. 'Thou seest?'

'There were many,' Agustin said.

'These would we have had to deal with if we had destroyed the others,' Robert

Jordan said very softly. His heart had quieted now and his shirt felt wet on his chest from the melting snow. There was a hollow feeling in his chest.

The sun was bright on the snow and it was melting fast. He could see it hollowing away from the tree trunks and just ahead of the gun, before his eyes, the snow surface was damp and lacily fragile as the heat of the sun melted the top and the warmth of the earth breathed warmly up at the snow that lay upon it.

Robert Jordan looked up at Primitivo's post and saw him signal, 'Nothing,' crossing his two hands, palms down.

Anselmo's head showed above a rock and Robert Jordan motioned him up. The old man slipped from rock to rock until he crept up and lay down flat beside the gun.

'Many,' he said. 'Many!'

'I do not need the trees,' Robert Jordan said to him. 'There is no need for further forestal improvement.'

Both Anselmo and Agustin grinned.

'This has stood scrutiny well and it would be dangerous to plant trees now because those people will return and perhaps they are not stupid.'

He felt the need to talk that, with him, was the sign that there had just been much danger. He could always tell how bad it had been by the strength of the desire to talk that came after.

'It was a good blind, eh?' he said.

'Good,' said Agustin. 'To obscenity with all fascism good. We could have killed the four of them. Didst thou see?' he said to Anselmo.

'I saw.'

'Thou,' Robert Jordan said to Anselmo. 'Thou must go to the post of yesterday or another good post of thy selection to watch the road and report on all movement as of yesterday. Already we are late in that. Stay until dark. Then come in and we will send another.'

'But the tracks that I will make?'

'Go from below as soon as the snow is gone. The road will be muddied by the snow. Note if there has been much traffic of trucks or if there are tank tracks in the softness on the road. That is all we can tell until you are there to observe.'

'With your permission?' the old man asked. 'Surely.'

'With your permission, would it not be better for me to go into La Granja and inquire there what passed last night and arrange for one to observe today thus in the manner you have taught me? Such a one could report tonight or, better, I could go again to La Granja for the report.'

'Have you no fear of encountering cavalry?'

'Not when the snow is gone.'

'Is there some one in La Crania capable of this?'

'Yes. Of this, yes. It would be a woman. There are vanous women of trust in La Crania.'

'I believe it,' Agustin said. 'More, I know it, and several who serve for other purposes. You do not wish me to go?'

'Let the old man go. You understand this gun and the day is not over.'

'I will go when the snow melts,' Anselmo said. 'And the snow is melting fast.'

'What think you of their chance of catching Pablo?' Robert Jordan asked Agustin.

'Pablo is smart,' Agustin said. 'Do men catch a wise stag without hounds?'

'Sometimes,' Robert Jordan said.

'Not Pablo,' Agustin said. 'Clearly, he is only a garbage of what he once was. But it is not for nothing that he is alive and comfortable in these hills and able to drink himself to death while there are so many others that have died against a wall.'

'Is he as smart as they say?'

'He is much smarter.'

'He has not seemed of great ability here.'

'*Como que no?* If he were not of great ability he would have died last night. It seems to me you do not understand politics, *Inglés,* nor guerilla warfare. In politics and this other the first thing is to continue to exist. Look how he continued to exist last night. And the quantity of dung he ate both from me and from thee.'

Now that Pablo was back in the movements of the unit, Robert Jordan did not wish to talk against him and as soon as he had uttered it he regretted saying the thing about his ability. He knew himself how smart Pablo was. It was Pablo who had seen instantly all that was wrong with the orders for the destruction of the bridge. He had made the remark only from dislike and he knew as he made it that it was wrong. It was part of the talking too much after a strain. So now he dropped the matter and said to Anselmo, 'And to go into La Crania in daylight?'

'It is not bad,' the old man said. 'I will not go with a military band.'

'Nor with a bell around his neck,' Agustin said. 'Nor carrying a banner.'

'How will you go?'

'Above and down through the forest.'

'But if they pick you up.'

'I have papers.'

'So have we all but thou must eat the wrong ones quickly.'

Anselmo shook his head and tapped the breast pocket of his smock.

'How many times have I contemplated that,' he said. 'And never did I like to swallow paper.'

'I have thought we should carry a little mustard on them all,' Robert Jordan said. 'In my left breast pocket I carry our papers. In my right the fascist papers. Thus one does not make a mistake in an emergency.'

It must have been bad enough when the leader of the first patrol of cavalry had pointed toward the entry because they were all talking very much. Too much, Robert Jordan thought.

'But look, Roberto,' Agustin said. 'They say the government moves further to the right each day. That in the Republic they no longer say Comrade but Senor and Senora. Canst shift thy pockets?' 'When it moves far enough to the right I will carry them in my hip pocket,' Robert Jordan said, 'and sew it in the center.'

'That they should stay in thy shirt,' Agustin said. 'Are we to win this war and lose the revolution?'

'Nay,' Robert Jordan said. 'But if we do not win this war there will be no revolution nor any Republic nor any thou nor any me nor anything but the most grand *carajo*.'

'So say I,' Anselmo said. 'That we should win the war.'

'And afterwards shoot the anarchists and the Communists and all this *canalla* except the good Republicans,' Agustin said.

'That we should win this war and shoot nobody,' Anselmo said. 'That we should govern justly and that all should participate in the benefits according as they have striven for them. And that those who have fought against us should be educated to see their error.'

'We will have to shoot many,' Agustin said. 'Many, many, many.'

He thumped his closed right fist against the palm of his left hand.

'That we should shoot none. Not even the leaders. That they should be reformed by work.'

'I know the work I'd put them at,' Agustin said, and he picked up some snow and put it in his mouth.

'What, bad one?' Robert Jordan asked.

'Two trades of the utmost brilliance.'

'They are?'

Agustin put some more snow in his mouth and looked across the clearing where the cavalry had ridden. Then he spat the melted snow out. '*Vaya*. What a breakfast,' he said. 'Where is the filthy gypsy?'

'What trades?' Robert Jordan asked him. 'Speak, bad mouth.'

'Jumping—from planes without parachutes,' Agustin said, and his eyes shone. 'That for those that we care for. And being nailed to the tops of fence posts to be pushed over backwards for the others.'

'That way of speaking is ignoble,' Anselmo said. 'Thus we will never have a Republic.'

'I would like to swim ten leagues in a strong soup made from the *cojones* of all of them,' Agustin said. 'And when I saw those four there and thought that we might kill them I was like a mare in the corral waiting for the stallion.'

'You know why we did not kill them, though?' Robert Jordan said quietly.

'Yes,' Agustin said. 'Yes. But the necessity was on me as it is on a mare in heat. You cannot know what it is if you have not felt it.'

'You sweated enough,' Robert Jordan said. 'I thought it was fear.'

'Fear, yes,' Agustin said. 'Fear and the other. And in this life there is no stronger thing than the other.'

Yes, Robert Jordan thought. We do it coldly but they do not, nor ever have. It is their extra sacrament. Their old one that they had before the new religion came from the far end of the Mediterranean, the one they have never abandoned but only suppressed and hidden to bring it out again in wars and inquisitions. They are the people of the Auto de Fe; the act of faith. Killing is something one must do, but ours are different from theirs. And you, he thought, you have never been corrupted by it? You never had it in the Sierra? Nor at Usera? Nor through all the time in Estremadura? Nor at any time? *Qué va*, he told himself At every train.

Stop making dubious literature about the Berbers and the old Iberians and admit that you have liked to kill as all who are soldiers by choice have enjoyed it at some time whether they lie about it or not. Anselmo does not like to because he is a hunter, not a soldier. Don't idealize him, either. Hunters kill animals and soldiers kill men. Don't lie to yourself, he thought. Nor make up literature about it. You have been tainted with it for a long time now. And do not think against Anselmo either. He is a Christian. Something very rare in Catholic countries.

But with Agustin I had thought it was fear, he thought. That natural fear before action. So it was the other, too. Of course, he may be bragging now. There was plenty of fear. I felt the fear under my hand. Well, it was time to stop talking.

'See if the gypsy brought food,' he said to Anselmo. 'Do not let him come up. He is a fool. Bring it yourself. And however much he brought, send back for more. I am hungry.'

24

Now the morning was late May, the sky was high and clear and the wind blew warm on Robert Jordan's shoulders. The snow was going fast and they were eating breakfast. There were two big sandwiches of meat and the goaty cheese apiece, and Robert Jordan had cut thick slices of onion with his clasp knife and put them on each side of the meat and cheese between the chunks of bread.

'You will have a breath that will carry through the forest to the fascists,' Agustin said, his own mouth full.

'Give me the wineskin and I will rinse the mouth,' Robert Jordan said, his mouth full of meat, cheese, onion and chewed bread.

He had never been hungrier and he filled his mouth with wine, faintly tarry-tasting from the leather bag, and swallowed. Then he took another big mouthful of wine, lifting the bag up to let the jet of wine spurt into the back of his mouth, the wineskin touching the needles of the blind of pine branches that covered the automatic rifle as he lifted his hand, his head leaning against the pine branches as he bent it back to let the wine run down.

'Dost thou want this other sandwich?' Agustin asked him, handing it toward him across the gun.

'No. Thank you. Eat it.'

'I cannot. I am not accustomed to eat in the morning.' 'You do not want it, truly?'

'Nay. Take it.'

Robert Jordan took it and laid it on his lap while he got the onion out of his side jacket pocket where the grenades were and opened his knife to slice it. He cut off a thin sliver of the surface that had dirtied in his pocket, then cut a thick slice. An outer segment fell and he picked it up and bent the circle together and put it into the sandwich.

'Eatest thou always onions for breakfast?' Agustin asked.'

'When there are any.'

'Do all in thy country do this?'

'Nay,' Robert Jordan said. 'It is looked on badly there.'

'I am glad,' Agustin said. 'I had always considered America a civilized country.'

'What hast thou against the onion?'

'The odor. Nothing more. Otherwise it is like the rose.' Robert Jordan grinned at him with his mouth full.

'Like the rose,' he said. 'Mighty like the rose. A rose is a rose is an onion.'

'Thy onions are affecting thy brain,' Agustin said. 'Take care.' 'An onion is an onion is an onion,' Robert Jordan said cheerily and, he thought, a stone is a stein is a rock is a boulder is a pebble.

'Rinse thy mouth with wine,' Agustin said. 'Thou art very rare, *Inglés*. There is great difference between thee and the last dynamiter who worked with us.'

'There is one great difference.'

'Tell it to me.'

'I am alive and he is dead,' Robert Jordan said. Then: what's the matter with you? he thought. Is that the way to talk? Does food make you that slap happy? What are you, drunk on onions? Is that all it means to you, now? It never meant much, he told himself truly. You tried to make it mean something, but it never did. There is no need to lie in the time that is left.

'No,' he said, seriously now. 'That one was a man who had suffered greatly.'

'And thou? Hast thou not suffered?'

'No,' said Robert Jordan. 'I am of those who suffer little.'

'Me also,' Agustin told him. 'There are those who suffer and those who do not. I suffer very little.'

'Less bad,' Robert Jordan tipped up the wineskin again. 'And with this, less.'

'I suffer for others.'

'As all good men should.'

'But for myself very little.'

'Hast thou a wife?'

'No.'

'Me neither.'

'But now you have the Maria.'

'Yes.'

'There is a rare thing,' Agustin said. 'Since she came to us at the train the Pilar has kept her away from all as fiercely as though she were in a convent of Carmelites. You cannot imagine with what fierceness she guarded her. You come, and she gives her to thee as a present. How does that seem to thee?'

'It was not thus.'

'How was it, then?'

'She has put her in my care.'

'And thy care is to *joder* with her all night?'

'With luck.'

'What a manner to care for one.'

'You do not understand that one can take good care of one thus?'

'Yes, but such care could have been furnished by any one of us.'

'Let us not talk of it any more,' Robert Jordan said. 'I care for her seriously.'

'Seriously?'

'As there can be nothing more serious in this world.'

'And afterwards? After this of the bridge?'

'She goes with me.'

'Then,' Agustín said. 'That no one speaks of it further and that the two of you go with all luck.'

He lifted the leather wine bag and took a long pull, then handed it to Robert Jordan.

'One thing more, *Inglés*,' he said.

'Of course.'

'I have cared much for her, too.'

Robert Jordan put his hand on his shoulder.

'Much,' Agustín said. 'Much. More than one is able to imagine.'

'I can imagine.'

'She has made an impression on me that does not dissipate.'

'I can imagine.'

'Look. I say this to thee in all seriousness.'

'Say it.'

'I have never touched her nor had anything to do with her but I care for her greatly. *Inglés*, do not treat her lightly. Because she sleeps with thee she is no whore.'

'I will care for her.'

'I believe thee. But more. You do not understand how such a girl would be if there had been no revolution. You have much responsibility. This one, truly, has suffered much. She is not as we are.'

'I will marry her.'

'Nay. Not that. There is no need for that under the revolution. But—' he nodded his head—'it would be better.'

'I will marry her,' Robert Jordan said and could feel his throat swelling as he said it. 'I care for her greatly.'

'Later,' Agustín said. 'When it is convenient. The important thing is to have the intention.'

'I have it.'

'Listen,' Agustín said. 'I am speaking too much of a matter in which I have no right to intervene, but hast thou known many girls of this country?'

'A few.'
'Whores?'
'Some who were not.'
'How many?'
'Several.'
'And did you sleep with them?'
'No.'
'You see?'
'Yes.'
'What I mean is that this Maria does not do this lightly.'
'Nor I.'
'If I thought you did I would have shot you last night as you lay with her. For this we kill much here.'

'Listen, old one,' Robert Jordan said. 'It is because of the lack of time that there has been informality. What we do not have is time. Tomorrow we must fight. To me that is nothing. But for the Maria and me it means that we must live all of our life in this time.'

'And a day and a night is little time,' Agustin said.

'Yes. But there has been yesterday and the night before and last night.'

'Look,' Agustin said. 'If I can aid thee.' 'No. We are all right.'

'If I could do anything for thee or for the cropped head'

'No.'

'Truly, there is little one man can do for another.'

'No. There is much.'

'What?'

'No matter what passes today and tomorrow in respect to combat, give me thy confidence and obey even though the orders may appear wrong.'

'You have my confidence. Since this of the cavalry and the sending away of the horse.'

'That was nothing. You see that we are working for one thing. To win the war. Unless we win, all other things are futile. Tomorrow we have a thing of great importance. Of true importance. Also we will have combat. In combat there must be discipline. For many things are not as they appear. Discipline must come from trust and confidence.'

Agustin spat on the ground.

'The Maria and all such things are apart,' he said. 'That you and the Maria should make use of what time there is as two human beings. If I can aid thee I am at thy orders. But for the thing of tomorrow I will obey thee blindly. If it is necessary that one should die for the thing of tomorrow one goes gladly and with the heart light.'

'Thus do I feel,' Robert Jordan said. 'But to hear it from thee brings pleasure.'

'And more,' Agustin said. 'That one above,' he pointed toward Primitivo, 'is a dependable value. The Pilar is much, much more than thou canst imagine. The old man Anselmo, also. Andres also. Eladio also. Very quiet, but a dependable element. And Fernando. I do not know how thou hast appreciated him. It is true he is heavier than mercury. He is fuller of boredom than a steer drawing a cart on the highroad. But to fight and to do as he is told. *Esmuy hombre!* Thou wilt see.'

'We are lucky.'

'No. We have two weak elements. The gypsy and Pablo. But the band of Sordo are as much better than we are as we are better than goat manure.'

'All is well then.'

'Yes,' AgustIn said. 'But I wish it was for today.'

'Me, too. To finish with it. But it is not.'

'Do you think it will be bad?'

'It can be.'

'But thou are very cheerful now, *Inglés*.'

'Yes.'

'Me also. In spite of this of the Maria and all.'

'Do you know why?'

'No.'

'Me neither. Perhaps it is the day. The day is good.'

'Who knows? Perhaps it is that we will have action.'

'I think it is that,' Robert Jordan said. 'But not today. Of all things; of all importance we must avoid it today.'

As he spoke he heard something. It was a noise far off that came above the sound of the warm wind in the trees. He could not be sure and he held his mouth open and listened, glancing up at Primitivo as he did so. He thought he heard it but then it was gone. The wind was blowing in the pines and now Robert Jordan strained all of himself to listen. Then he heard it faintly coming down the wind.

'It is nothing tragic with me,' he heard Agustin say. 'That I should never have the Maria is nothing. I will go with the whores as always.'

'Shut up,' he said, not listening, and lying beside him, his head having been turned away. Agustin looked over at him suddenly.

'Que pasa?' he asked.

Robert Jordan put his hand over his own mouth and went on listening. There it came again. It came faint, muted, dry and far away. But there was no mistaking it now. It was the precise, crackling, curling roll of automatic rifle fire. It sounded as though pack after pack of miniature firecrackers were going off at a distance that was almost out of hearing.

Robert Jordan looked up at Primitivo who had his head up now, his face looking toward them, his hand cupped to his ear. As he looked Primitivo pointed up the mountain toward the highest country.

'They are fighting at El Sordo's,' Robert Jordan said.

'Then let us go to aid them,' Agustin said. 'Collect the people. Vamonos.'

'No,' Robert Jordan said. 'We stay here.'

25

ROBERT JORDAN looked up at where Primitivo stood now in his lookout post, holding his rifle and pointing. He nodded his head but the man kept pointing, putting his hand to his ear and then pointing insistently and as though he could not possibly have been understood.

'Do you stay with this gun and unless it is sure, sure, sure that they are coming in do not fire. And then not until they reach that shrub,' Robert Jordan pointed. 'Do you understand?'

'Yes. But—'

'No but. I will explain to thee later. I go to Primitivo.'

Anselmo was by him and he said to the old man:

'*Viejo*, stay there with Agustin with the gun.' He spoke slowly and unhurriedly. 'He must not fire unless cavalry is actually entering. If they merely present themselves he must let them alone as we did before. If he must fire, hold the legs of the tripod firm for him and hand him the pans when they are empty.'

'Good,' the old man said. 'And La Granja?' 'Later.'

Robert Jordan climbed up, over and around the gray boulders that were wet now under his hands as he pulled himself up. The sun was melting the snow on them fast. The tops of the boulders were drying and as he climbed he looked across the country and saw the pine woods and the long open glade and the dip of the country before the high mountains beyond. Then he stood beside Primitivo in a hollow behind two boulders and the short, brownfaced man said to him, 'They are attacking Sordo. What is it that we do?'

'Nothing,' Robert Jordan said.

He heard the firing clearly here and as he looked across the country, he saw, far off, across the distant valley where the country rose steeply again, a troop of cavalry ride out of the timber and cross the snowy slope riding uphill in the direction of the firing. He saw the oblong double line of men and horses dark against the snow as they forced at an angle up the hill. He watched the double line top the ridge and go into the farther timber.

'We have to aid them,' Primitivo said. His voice was dry and flat.

'It is impossible,' Robert Jordan told him. 'I have expected this all morning.'

'How?'

'They went to steal horses last night. The snow stopped and they tracked them up there.'

'But we have to aid them,' Primitivo said. 'We cannot leave them alone to this. Those are our comrades.'

Robert Jordan put his hand on the other man's shoulder. 'We can do nothing,' he said. 'If we could I would do it.'

'There is a way to reach there from above. We can take that way with the horses and the two guns. This one below and thine. We can aid them thus.'

'Listen-' Robert Jordan said.

'*That* is what I listen to,' Primitivo said.

The firing was rolling in overlapping waves. Then they heard the noise of hand grenades heavy and sodden in the dry rolling of the automatic rifle fire.

'They are lost,' Robert Jordan said. 'They were lost when the snow stopped. If we go there we are lost, too. It is impossible to divide what force we have.'

There was a gray stubble of beard stippled over Primitivo's jaws, his lip and his neck. The rest of his face was flat brown with a broken, flattened nose and deep-set gray eyes, and watching him Robert Jordan saw the stubble twitching at the corners of his mouth and over the cord of his throat.

'Listen to it,' he said. 'It is a massacre.'

'If they have surrounded the hollow it is that,' Robert Jordan said. 'Some may have gotten out.'

'Coming on them now we could take them from behind,' Primitivo said. 'Let four of us go with the horses.'

'And then what? What happens after you take them from be hind?'

'We join with Sordo.'

'To die there? Look at the sun. The day is long.' The sky was high and cloudless and the sun was hot on their backs. There were big bare patches now on the southern slope of the open glade below them and the snow was all dropped from the pine trees. The boulders below them that had been wet as the snow melted were steaming faintly now in the hot sun.

'You have to stand it,' Robert Jordan said. *'Hay que aguantarse.* There are things like this in a war.'

'But there is nothing we can do? Truly?' Primitivo looked at him and Robert Jordan knew he trusted him. 'Thou couldst not send me and another with the small machine gun?'

'It would be useless,' Robert Jordan said.

He thought he saw something that he was looking for but it was a hawk that slid down into the wind and then rose above the line of the farthest pine woods. 'It would be useless if we all went,' he said.

Just then the firing doubled in intensity and in it was the heavy bumping of the hand grenades.

'Oh, obscenity them,' Primitivo said with an absolute devoutness of blasphemy, tears in his eyes and his cheeks twitching. 'Oh, God and the Virgin, obscenity them in the milk of their filth.'

'Calm thyself,' Robert Jordan said. 'You will be fighting them soon enough. Here comes the woman.'

Pilar was climbing up to them, making heavy going of it in the boulders.

Primitivo kept saying. 'Obscenity them. Oh, God and the Virgin, befoul them,' each time for firing rolled down the wind, and Robert Jordan climbed down to help Pilar up.

'Que tal, woman,' he said, taking hold of both her wrists and hoisting as she climbed heavily over the last boulder.

'Thy binoculars,' she said and lifted their strap over her head. 'So it has come to Sordo?'

'Yes.'

'*Pabre*,' she said in commiseration. 'Poor Sordo.'

She was breathing heavily from the climb and she took hold of Robert Jordan's hand and gripped it tight in hers as she looked out over the country.

'How does the combat seem?' 'Bad. Very bad.'

'He's *jadida?*' 'I believe so.'

'*Pobre*,' she said. 'Doubtless because of the horses?' 'Probably.'

'*Pabre*,' Pilar said. Then, 'Rafael recounted me all of an entire novel of dung about cavalry. What came?' 'A patrol and part of a squadron.'

'Up to what point?'

Robert Jordan pointed out where the patrol had stopped and showed her where the gun was hidden. From where they stood they could just sec one of Agustin's boots protruding from the rear of the blind.

'The gypsy said they rode to where the gun muzzle pressed against the chest of the horse of the leader,' Pilar said. 'What a race! Thy glasses were in the cave.'

'Have you packed?'

'All that can be taken. Is there news of Pablo?'

'He was forty minutes ahead of the cavalry. They took his trail.'

Pilar grinned at him. She still held his hand. Now she dropped it. 'They'll never see him,' she said. 'Now for Sordo. Can we do anything?'

'Nothing.'

'*Pabre*,' she said. 'I was fond of Sordo. Thou art sure, *sure* that he is *jodido?*'

'Yes. I have seen much cavalry.'

'More than were here?'

'Another full troop on their way up there.'

'Listen to it,' Pilar said. '*Pobre, pobre Sardo.*' They listened to the firing.

'Primitivo wanted to go up there,' Robert Jordan said.

'Art thou crazy?' Pilar said to the flat-faced man. 'What kind of *locos* are we producing here?'

'I wish to aid them.'

'Que *va*,' Pilar said. 'Another romantic. Dost thou not believe thou wilt die quick enough here without useless voyages?'

Robert Jordan looked at her, at the heavy brown face with the high Indian cheekbones, the wide-set dark eyes and the laughing mouth with the heavy, bitter upper lip.

'Thou must act like a man,' she said to Primitivo. 'A grown man. You with your gray hairs and all.'

'Don't joke at me,' Primitivo said sullenly. 'If a man has a little heart and a little imagination—'

'He should learn to control them,' Pilar said. 'Thou wilt die soon enough with us. There is no need to seek that with strangers. As for thy imagination. The gypsy has enough for all. What a novel he told me.'

'If thou hadst seen it thou wouldst not call it a novel,' Primitivo said. 'There was a moment of great gravity.'

'*Que va*,' Pilar said. 'Some cavalry rode here and they rode away. And you all make yourselves a heroism. It is to this we have come with so much inaction.'

'And this of Sordo is not grave?' Primitivo said contemptuously now. He suffered visibly each time the firing came down the wind and he wanted either to go to the combat or have Pilar go and leave him alone.

'*Total, que?*' Pilar said. 'It has come so it has come. Don't lose thy *cojones* for the misfortune of another.'

'Go defile thyself,' Primitivo said. 'There are women of a stupidity and brutality that is insupportable.'

'In order to support and aid those men poorly equipped for procreation,' Pilar said, 'if there is nothing to see I am going.'

Just then Robert Jordan heard the plane high overhead. He looked up and in the high sky it looked to be the same observation plane that he had seen earlier in the morning. Now it was returning from the direction of the lines and it was moving in the direction of the high country where El Sordo was being attacked.

'There is the bad luck bird,' Pilar said. 'Will it see what goes on there?'

'Surely,' Robert Jordan said. 'If they are not blind.'

They watched the plane moving high and silvery and steady in the sunlight. It was coming from the left and they could see the round disks of light the two propellers made.

'Keep down,' Robert Jordan said.

Then the plane was overhead, its shadows passing over the open glade, the throbbing reaching its maximum of portent. Then it was past and headed toward the top of the valley. They watched it go steadily on its course until it was just out of sight and then they saw it coming back in a wide dipping circle, to circle twice over the high country and then disappear in the direction of Segovia.

Robert Jordan looked at Pilar. There was perspiration on her forehead and she shook her head. She had been holding her lower lip between her teeth.

'For each one there is something,' she said. 'For me it is those.' 'Thou hast not caught my fear?' Primitivo said sarcastically. 'Nay,' she put her hand on his shoulder. 'Thou hast no fear to catch. I know that. I am sorry I joked too roughly with thee. We are all in the same caldron.' Then she spoke to Robert Jordan. 'I will send up food and wine. Dost need anything more?'

'Not in this moment. Where are the others?'

'Thy reserve is intact below with the horses,' she grinned. 'Everything is out of sight. Everything to go is ready. Maria is with thy material.'

'If by any chance we *should* have aviation keep her in the cave.' 'Yes, my Lord *Inglés*,' Pilar said. '*Thy* gypsy (I give him to thee) I have sent to gather mushrooms to cook with the hares. There are many mushrooms now and it seemed to me we might as well eat the hares although they would be better tomorrow or the day after.'

'I think it is best to eat them,' Robert Jordan said, and Pilar put her big hand on his shoulder where the strap of the submachine gun crossed his chest, then reached up and mussed his hair with her fingers. 'What an *Inglés*,' Pilar said. 'I will send the Maria with the *puchero* when they are cooked.'

The firing from far away and above had almost died out and now there was only an occasional shot.

'You think it is over?' Pilar asked.

'No,' Robert Jordan said. 'From the sound that we have heard they have attacked and been beaten off. Now I would say the attackers have them surrounded. They have taken cover and they wait for the planes.'

Pilar spoke to Primitivo, 'Thou. Dost understand there was no intent to insult thee?'

'*Ya lo sé*,' said Primitivo. 'I have put up with worse than that from thee. Thou hast a vile tongue. But watch thy mouth, woman. Sordo was a good comrade of mine.'

'And not of mine?' Pilar asked him. 'Listen, flat face. In war one cannot say what one feels. We have enough of our own without taking Sordo's.'

Primitivo was still sullen.

'You should take a physic,' Pilar told him. 'Now I go to prepare the meal.'

'Did you bring the documentation of the *requeté*?' Robert Jordan asked her.

'How stupid I am,' she said. 'I forgot it. I will send the Maria.'

26

It was three o'clock in the afternoon before the planes came. The snow had all been gone by noon and the rocks were hot now in the sun. There were no clouds in the sky and Robert Jordan sat in the rocks with his shirt off browning his back in the sun and reading the letters that had been in the pockets of the dead cavalryman. From time to time he would stop reading to look across the open slope to the line of the timber, look over the high country above and then return to the letters. No more cavalry had appeared. At intervals there would be the sound of a shot from the direction of El Sordo's camp. But the firing was desultory.

From examining his military papers he knew the boy was from Tafalla in Navarra, twenty-one years old, unmarried, and the son of a blacksmith. His regiment was the Nth cavalry, which surprised Robert Jordan, for he had believed that regiment to be in the North. He was a Carlist, and he had been wounded at the fighting for Irun at the start of the war.

I've probably seen him run through the streets ahead of the bulls at the Feria in Pamplona, Robert Jordan thought. You never kill any one that you want to kill in a war, he said to himself. Well, hardly ever, he amended and went on reading the letters.

The first letters he read were very formal, very carefully written and dealt almost entirely with local happenings. They were from his sister and Robert Jordan learned that everything was all right in Tafalla, that father was well, that mother was the same as always but with certain complaints about her back, that she hoped he was well and not in too great danger and she was happy he was doing away with the Reds to liberate Spain from the domination of the Marxist hordes. Then there was a list of those boys from Tafalla who had been killed or badly wounded since she wrote last. She mentioned ten who were killed. That is a great many for a town the size of Tafalla, Robert Jordan thought.

There was quite a lot of religion in the letter and she prayed to Saint Anthony, to the Blessed Virgin of Pilar, and to other Virgins to protect him and she wanted him never to forget that he was also protected by the Sacred Heart of Jesus that he wore still, she trusted, at all times over his own heart where it had been proven innumerable-this was underlined-times to have the power of stopping bullets. She was as always his loving sister Concha.

This letter was a little stained around the edges and Robert Jordan put it carefully back with the military papers and opened a letter with a less severe handwriting. It was from the boy's *novia*, his fiancée, and it was quietly, formally, and completely hysterical with concern for his safety. Robert Jordan read it through and then put all the letters together with the papers into his hip pocket. He did not want to read the other letters.

I guess I've done my good deed for today, he said to himself. I guess you have all right, he repeated.

'What are those you were reading?' Primitivo asked him.

'The documentation and the letters of that *requete* we shot this morning. Do you want to see it?'

'I can't read,' Primitivo said. 'Was there anything interesting?' 'No,' Robert Jordan told him. 'They are personal letters.'

'How are things going where he came from? Can you tell from the letters?'

'They seem to be going all right,' Robert Jordan said. 'There are many losses in his town.' He looked down to where the blind for the automatic rifle had been changed a little and improved after the snow melted. It looked convincing enough. He looked off across the country.

'From what town is he?' Primitivo asked. 'Tafalla,' Robert Jordan told him.

All right, he said to himself. I'm sorry, if that does any good. It doesn't, he said to himself.

All right then, drop it, he said to himself. All right, it's dropped.

But it would not drop that easily. How many is that you have killed? he asked himself. I don't know. Do you think you have a right to kill any one? No. But I have to. How many of those you have killed have been real fascists? Very few. But they are all the enemy to whose force we are opposing force. But you like the people of Navarra better than those of any other part of Spain. Yes. And you kill them. Yes. If you don't believe it go down there to the camp. Don't you know it is wrong to kill? Yes. But you do it? Yes. And you still believe absolutely that your cause is right? Yes.

It is right, he told himself, not reassuringly, but proudly. I believe in the people and their right to govern themselves as they wish. But you mustn't believe in killing, he told himself. You must do it as a necessity but you must not believe in it. If you believe in it the whole thing is wrong.

But how many do you suppose you have killed? I don't know because I won't keep track. But do you know? Yes. How many? You can't be sure how many. Blowing the trains you kill many. Very many. But you can't be sure. But of those you are sure of? More than twenty. And of those how many were real fascists? Two that I am sure of. Because I had to shoot them when we took them prisoners at Usera. And you did not mind that? No. Nor did you like it? No. I decided never to do it again. I have avoided it. I have avoided killing those who are unarmed.

Listen, he told himself. You better cut this out. This is very bad for you and for your work. Then himself said back to him, You listen, see? Because you are doing something very serious and I have to see you understand it all the time. I have to keep you straight in your head. Because if you are not absolutely straight in your head you have no right to do the things you do for all of them are crimes and no man has a right to take another man's life unless it is to prevent something worse happening to other people. So get it straight and do not lie to yourself.

But I won't keep a count of people I have killed as though it were a trophy record or a disgusting business like notches in a gun, he told himself. I have a right to not keep count and I have a right to forget them.

No, himself said. You have no right to forget anything. You have no right to shut your eyes to any of it nor any right to forget any of it nor to soften it nor to change it.

Shut up, he told himself. You're getting awfully pompous. Nor ever to deceive yourself about it, himself went on.

All right, he told himself. Thanks for all the good advice and is it all right for me to love Maria?

Yes, himself said.

Even if there isn't supposed to be any such thing as love in a purely materialistic conception of society?

Since when did you ever have any such conception? himself asked. Never. And you never could have. You're not a real Marxist and you know it. You believe in Liberty, Equality and Fraternity. You believe in Life, Liberty and the Pursuit of Happiness. Don't ever kid yourself with too much dialectics. They are for some but not for you. You have to know them in order not to be a sucker. You have put many things in abeyance to win a war. If this war is lost all of those things are lost.

But afterwards you can discard what you do not believe in. There is plenty you do not believe in and plenty that you do believe in.

And another thing. Don't ever kid yourself about loving some one. It is just that most people are not lucky enough ever to have it. You never had it before and now you have it. What you have with Maria, whether it lasts just through today and a part of tomorrow, or whether it lasts for a long life is the most important thing that can happen to a human being. There will always be people who say it does not exist because they cannot have it. Rut I tell you it is true and that you have it and that you are lucky even if you die tomorrow.

Cut out the dying stuff, he said to himself. That's not the way we talk. That's the way our friends the anarchists talk. Whenever things get really bad they want to

For Whom the Bell Tolls • 677

set fire to something and to die. It's a very odd kind of mind they have. Very odd. Well, we're getting through today, old timer, he told himself. It's nearly three o'clock now and there is going to be some food sooner or later. They are still shooting up at Sordo's, which means that they have him surrounded and are waiting to bring up more people, probably. Though they have to make it before dark.

I wonder what it is like up at Sordo's. That's what we all have to expect, given enough time. I imagine it is not too jovial up at Sordo's. We certainly got Sordo into a fine jam with that horse business. How does it go in Spanish? *Un callejón sin salida.* A passageway with no exit. I suppose I could go through with it all right. You only have to do it once and it is soon over with. But wouldn't it be luxury to fight in a war some time where, when you were surrounded, you could surrender? *Estamos copados.* We are surrounded. That was the great panic cry of this war. Then the next thing was that you were shot; with nothing bad before if you were lucky. Sordo wouldn't be lucky that way. Neither would they when the time ever came.

It was three o'clock. Then he heard the far-off, distant th robbing and, looking up, he saw the planes.

27

El Sardo was making his fight on a hilltop. He did not like this hill and when he saw it he thought it had the shape of a chancre. But he had had no choice except this hill and he had picked it as far away as he could see it and galloped for it, the automatic rifle heavy on his back, the horse laboring, barrel heaving between his thighs, the sack of grenades swinging against one side, the sack of automatic rifle pans banging against the other, and Joaquin and Ignacio halting and firing, halting and firing to give him time to get the gun in place.

There had still been snow then, the snow that had ruined them, and when his horse was hit so that he wheezed in a slow, jerking, climbing stagger up the last part of the crest, splattering the snow with a bright, pulsing jet, Sordo had hauled him along by the bridle, the reins over his shoulder as he climbed. He climbed as hard as he could with the bullets spatting on the rocks, with the two sacks heavy on his shoulders, and then, holding the horse by the mane, had shot him quickly, expertly, and tenderly just where he had needed him, so that the horse pitched, head forward down to plug a gap between two rocks. He had gotten the gun to firing over the horse's back and he fired two pans, the gun clattering, the empty shells pitching into the snow, the smell of burnt hair from the burnt hide where the hot muzzle rested, him firing at what came up to the hill, forcing them to scatter for cover, while all the time there was a chill in his back from not knowing what was behind him. Once the last of the five men had reached the hilltop the chill went out of his back and he had saved the pans he had left until he would need them.

There were two more horses dead along the slope and three more were dead here on the hilltop. He had only succeeded in stealing three horses last night and one had bolted when they tried to mount him bareback in the corral at the camp when the first shooting had started. Of the five men who had reached the hilltop three were wounded. Sordo was wounded in the calf of his leg and in two places in his left arm. He was very thirsty, his wounds had stiffened, and one of the wounds in his left arm was very painful. He also had a bad headache and as he lay waiting for the planes to come he thought of a joke in Spanish. It was, *'Hay que tomar la muerte como si fuera aspirina,'* which means, 'You will have to take death as an aspirin.' But he did not make the joke aloud. He grinned somewhere inside the pain in his head and inside the nausea that came whenever he moved his arm and looked around at what there was left of his band.

The five men were spread out like the points of a five-pointed star. They had dug with their knees and hands and made mounds in front of their heads and shoulders with the dirt and piles of stones. Using this cover, they were linking the individual mounds up with stones and dirt. Joaquin, who was eighteen years old, had a steel helmet that he dug with and he passed dirt in it.

He had gotten this helmet at the blowing up of the train. It had a bullet hole through it and every one had always joked at him for keeping it. Hut he had hammered the jagged edges of the bullet hole smooth and driven a wooden plug into it and then cut the plug off and smoothed it even with the metal inside the helmet.

When the shooting started he had clapped this helmet on his head so hard it banged his head as though he had been hit with a casserole and, in the last lung-aching, leg-dead, mouth-dry, bulletspatting, bullet-cracking, bullet-singing run up the final slope of the hill after his horse was killed, the helmet had seemed to weigh a great amount and to ring his bursting forehead with an iron band. But he had kept it. Now he dug with it in a steady, almost machinelike desperation. He had not yet been hit.

'It serves for something finally,' Sordo said to him in his deep, throaty voice.

'Resistiry fortifiear es vencer,' Joaquin said, his mouth stiff with the dryness of fear which surpassed the normal thirst of battle. It was one of the slogans of the Communist party and it meant, 'Hold out and fortify, and you will win.'

Sordo looked away and down the slope at where a cavalryman was sniping from behind a boulder. He was very fond of this boy and he was in no mood for slogans.

'What did you say?'

One of the men turned from the building that he was doing. This man was lying flat on his face, reaching carefully up with his hands to put a rock in place while keeping his chin flat against the ground.

Joaquin repeated the slogan in his dried-up boy's voice without checking his digging for a moment.

'What was the last word?' the man with his chin on the ground asked.

'Veneer,' the boy said. 'Win.'

'Mierda,' the man with his chin on the ground said.

For Whom the Bell Tolls • 679

'There is another that applies to here,' Joaquin said, bringing them out as though they were talismans, 'Pasionaria says it is better to die on your feet than to live on your knees.'

'*Mierda* again,' the man said and another man said, over his shoulder, 'We're on our bellies, not our knees.'

'Thou. Communist. Do you know your Pasionaria has a son thy age in Russia since the start of the movement?'

'It's a lie,' Joaquin said.

'*Que va*, it's a lie,' the other said. 'The dynamiter with the rare name told me. He was of thy party, too. Why should he lie?'

'It's a lie,' Joaquin said. 'She would not do such a thing as keep a son hidden in Russia out of the war.'

'I wish I were in Russia,' another of Sordo's men said. 'Will not thy Pasionaria send me now from here to Russia, Communist?'

'If thou believest so much in thy Pasionaria, get her to get us off this hill,' one of the men who had a bandaged thigh said.

'The fascists will do that,' the man with his chin in the dirt said. 'Do not speak thus,' Joaquin said to him.

'Wipe the pap of your mother's breasts off thy lips and give me a hatful of that dirt,' the man with his chin on the ground said. 'No one of us will see the sun go down this night.'

El Sordo was thinking: It is shaped like a chancre. Or the breast of a young girl with no nipple. Or the top cone of a volcano. You have never seen a volcano, he thought. Nor will you ever see one. And this hill is like a chancre. Let the volcanos alone. It's late now for the volcanos.

He looked very carefully around the withers of the dead horse and there was a quick hammering of firing from behind a boulder well down the slope and he heard the bullets from the submachine gun thud into the horse. He crawled along behind the horse and looked out of the angle between the horse's hindquarters and the rock. There were three bodies on the slope just below him where they had fallen when the fascists had rushed the crest under cover of the automatic rifle and submachine gunfire and he and the others had broken down the attack by throwing and rolling down hand grenades. There were other bodies that he could not see on the other sides of the hill crest. There was no dead ground by which attackers could approach the summit and Sordo knew that as long as his ammunition and grenades held out and he had as many as four men they could not get him out of there unless they brought up a trench mortar. He did not know whether they had sent to La Granja for a trench mortar. Perhaps they had not, because surely, soon, the planes would come. It had been four hours since the observation plane had flown over them.

This hill is truly like a chancre, Sordo thought, and we are the very pus of it. But we killed many when they made that stupidness. How could they think that they would take us thus? They have such modern armament that they lose all their sense with overconfidence. He had killed the young officer who had led the assault with a grenade that had gone bouncing and rolling down the slope as they came up it, running, bent half over. In the yellow flash and gray roar of smoke he had seen the officer dive forward to where he lay now like a heavy, broken bundle of old clothing marking the farthest point that the assault had reached. Sordo looked at this body and then, down the hill, at the others.

They are brave but stupid people, he thought. But they have sense enough now not to attack us again until the planes come. Unless, of course, they have a mortar coming. It would be easy with a mortar. The mortar was the normal thing and he knew that they would die as soon as a mortar came up, but when he thought of the planes coming up he felt as naked on that hilltop as though all of his clothing and even his skin had been removed. There is no nakeder thing than I feel, he thought. A flayed rabbit is as well covered as a bear in comparison. But why should they bring planes? They could get us out of here with a trench mortar easily. They are proud of their planes, though, and they will probably bring them. Just as they were so proud of their automatic weapons that they made that stupidness. But undoubtedly they must have sent for a mortar, too. One of the men fired. Then jerked the bolt and fired again, quickly.

'Save thy cartridges,' Sordo said.

'One of the sons of the great whore tried to reach that boulder,' the man pointed.

'Did you hit him?' Sordo asked, turning his head with difficulty. 'Nay,' the man said. 'The fornicator ducked back.'

'Who is a whore of whores is Pilar,' the man with his chin in the dirt said. 'That whore knows we are dying here.'

'She could do no good,' Sordo said. The man had spoken on the side of his good ear and he had heard him without turning his head. 'What could she do?'

'Take these sluts from the rear.'

'*Que va*,' Sordo said. 'They are spread around a hillside. How would she come on them? There are a hundred and fifty of them. Maybe more now.'

'But if we hold out until dark,' Joaquin said.

'And if Christmas comes on Easter,' the man with his chin on the ground said.

'And if thy aunt had *cojones* she would be thy uncle,' another said to him. 'Send for thy Pasionaria. She alone can help us.'

'I do not believe that about the son,' Joaquin said. 'Or if he is there he is training to be an aviator or something of that sort.'

'He is hidden there for safety,' the man told him.

'He is studying dialectics. Thy Pasionaria has been there. So have Lister and Modesto and others. The one with the rare name told me.'

'That they should go to study and return to aid us,' Joaquin said.

'That they should aid us now,' another man said. 'That all the cruts of Russian sucking swindlers should aid us now.' He fired and said, '*Me cago en tal*; I missed him again.'

'Save thy cartridges and do not talk so much or thou wilt be very thirsty,' Sordo said. 'There is no water on this hill.'

'Take this,' the man said and rolling on his side he pulled a wineskin that he wore slung from his shoulder over his head and handed it to Sordo. 'Wash thy mouth out, old one. Thou must have much thirst with thy wounds.'

'Let all take it,' Sordo said. 'Then I will have some first,' the owner said and squirted a long stream into his mouth before he handed the leather bottle around.

'Sordo, when thinkest thou the planes will come?' the man with his chin in the dirt asked.

'Any time,' said Sordo. 'They should have come before.'

'Do you think these sons of the great whore will attack again?' 'Only if the planes do not come.'

He did not think there was any need to speak about the mortar. They would know it soon enough when the mortar came.

'God knows they've enough planes with what we saw yesterday.' 'Too many,' Sordo said.

His head hurt very much and his arm was stiffening so that the pain of moving it was almost unbearable. He looked up at the bright, high, blue early summer sky as he raised the leather wine bottle with his good arm. He was fifty-two years old and he was sure this was the last time he would see that sky.

He was not at all afraid of dying but he was angry at being trapped on this hill which was only utilizable as a place to die. If we could have gotten clear, he thought. If we could have made them come up the long valley or if we could have broken loose across the road it would have been all right. But this chancre of a hill. We must use it as well as we can and we have used it very well so far.

If he had known how many men in history have had to use a hill to die on it would not have cheered him any for, in the moment he was passing through, men are not impressed by what has happened to other men in similar circumstances any more than a widow of one day is helped by the knowledge that other loved husbands have died. Whether one has fear of it or not, one's death is difficult to accept. Sordo had accepted it but there was no sweetness in its acceptance even at fifty-two, with three wounds and him surrounded on a hill.

He joked about it to himself but he looked at the sky and at the far mountains and he swallowed the wine and he did not want it. If one must die, he thought, and clearly one must, I can die. But I hate it.

Dying was nothing and he had no picture of it nor fear of it in his mind. But living was a field of grain blowing in the wind on the side of a hill. Living was a hawk in the sky. Living was an earthen jar of water in the dust of the threshing with the grain flailed out and the chaff blowing. Living was a horse between your legs and a carbine under one leg and a hill and a valley and a stream with trees along it and the far side of the valley and the hills beyond. Sordo passed the wine bottle back and nodded his head in thanks. He leaned forward and patted the dead horse on the shoulder where the muzzle of the automatic rifle had burned the hide.

He could still smell the burnt hair. He thought how he had held the horse there, trembling, with the fire around them, whispering and cracking, over and around them like a curtain, and had carefully shot him just at the intersection of the crosslines between the two eyes and the ears. Then as the horse pitched he had dropped down behind his warm, wet back to get the gun to going as they came up the hill.

'Eras mucho caballo,' he said, meaning. 'Thou wert plenty of horse.'

El Sordo lay now on his good side and looked up at the sky. He was lying on a heap of empty cartridge hulls but his head was protected by the rock and his body lay in the lee of the horse. His wounds had stiffened badly and he had much pain and he felt too tired to move.

'What passes with thee, old one?' the man next to him asked. 'Nothing. I am taking a little rest.'

'Sleep,' the other said. '*They* will wake us when they come.'

Just then some one shouted from down the slope.

'Listen, bandits!' the voice came from behind the rocks where the closest automatic rifle was placed. 'Surrender now before the planes blow you to pieces.'

'What is it he says?' Sordo asked.

Joaquin told him. Sordo rolled to one side and pulled himself up so that he was crouched behind the gun again.

'Maybe the planes aren't coming,' he said. 'Don't answer them and do not fire. Maybe we can get them to attack again.'

'If we should insult them a little?' the man who had spoken to Joaquin about La Pasionaria's son in Russia asked.

'No,' Sordo said. 'Give me thy big pistol. Who has a big pistol?'

'Here.'

'Give it to me.' Crouched on his knees he took the big 9 mm. Star and fired one shot into the ground beside the dead horse, waited, then fired again four times at irregular intervals. Then he waited while he counted sixty and then fired a final shot directly into the body of the dead horse. He grinned and handed back the pistol.

'Reload it,' he whispered, 'and that every one should keep his mouth shut and no one shoot.'

'*Bandidos!*' the voice shouted from behind the rocks.

No one spoke on the hill.

'*Bandidos!* Surrender now before we blow thee to little pieces.' 'They're biting,' Sordo whispered happily.

As he watched, a man showed his head over the top of the rocks. There was no shot from the hilltop and the head went down again. El Sordo waited, watching, but nothing more happened. He turned his head and looked at the others who were all watching down their sectors of the slope. As he looked at them the others shook their heads.

'Let no one move,' he whispered.

'Sons of the great whore,' the voice came now from behind the rocks again.

'Red swine. Mother rapers. Eaters of the milk of thy fathers.'

Sordo grinned. He could just hear the bellowed insults by turning his good ear. This is better than the aspirin, he thought. How many will we get? Can they be that foolish?

The voice had stopped again and for three minutes they heard nothing and saw no movement. Then the sniper behind the boulder a hundred yards down the slope exposed himself and fired. The bullet hit a rock and ricocheted with a sharp whine. Then Sardo saw a man, bent double, run from the shelter of the rocks where the automatic rifle was across the open ground to the big boulder behind which the sniper was hidden. He almost dove behind the boulder.

Sordo looked around. They signalled to him that there was no movement on the other slopes. El Sordo grinned happily and shook his head. This is ten times better than the aspirin, he thought, and he waited, as happy as only a hunter can be happy.

Below on the slope the man who had run from the pile of stones to the shelter of the boulder was speaking to the sniper.

'Do you believe it?'

'I don't know,' the sniper said.

'It would be logical,' the man, who was the officer in command, said. 'They are surrounded. They have nothing to expect but to die.'

The sniper said nothing.

'What do you think?' the officer asked. 'Nothing,' the sniper said.

'Have you seen any movement since the shots?' 'None at all.'

The officer looked at his wrist watch. It was ten minutes to three o'clock.

'The planes should have come an hour ago,' he said. Just then another officer flopped in behind the boulder. The sniper moved over to make room for him.

'Thou, Paco,' the first officer said. 'How does it seem to thee?'

The second officer was breathing heavily from his sprint up and across the hillside from the automatic rifle position.

'For me it is a trick,' he said.

'But if it is not? What a ridicule we make waiting here and laying siege to dead men.'

'We have done something worse than ridiculous already,' the second officer said. 'Look at that slope.'

He looked up the slope to where the dead were scattered close to the top. From where he looked the line of the hilltop showed the scattered rocks, the belly, projecting legs, shod hooves jutting out, of Sordo's horse, and the fresh dirt thrown up by the digging.

'What about the mortars?' asked the second officer. 'They should be here in an hour. If not before.'

'Then wait for them. There has been enough stupidity already.' *'Bandidos!'* the first officer shouted suddenly, getting to his feet and putting his head well up above the boulder so that the crest of the hill looked much closer as he stood upright.

'Red swine! Cowards!'

The second officer looked at the sniper and shook his head. The sniper looked away but his lips tightened.

The first officer stood there, his head all clear of the rock and with his hand on his pistol butt. He cursed and vilified the hilltop. Nothing happened. Then he stepped clear of the boulder and stood there looking up the hill.

'Fire, cowards, if you are alive,' he shouted. 'Fire on one who has no fear of any Red that ever came out of the belly of the great whore.'

This last was quite a long sentence to shout and the officer's face was red and congested as he finished.

The second officer, who was a thin sunburned man with quiet eyes, a thin, long-lipped mouth and a stubble of beard over his hollow cheeks, shook his head again. It was this officer who was shouting who had ordered the first assault. The young lieutenant who was dead up the slope had been the best friend of this other lieutenant who was named Paco Berrendo and who was listening to the shouting of the captain, who was obviously in a state of exaltation.

'Those are the swine who shot my sister and my mother,' the captain said. He had a red face and a blond, British-looking moustache and there was something wrong about his eyes. They were a light blue and the lashes were light, too. As you looked at them they seemed to focus slowly. Then 'Reds,' he shouted. 'Cowards!' and commenced cursing again.

He stood absolutely clear now and, sighting carefully, fired his pistol at the only target that the hiltop presented: the dead horse that had belonged to Sardo. The bullet threw up a puff of dirt fifteen yards below the horse. The captain fired again. The bullet hit a rock and sung off.

The captain stood there looking at the hilltop. The Lieutenant Berrendo was looking at the body of the other lieutenant just below the summit. The sniper was looking at the ground under his eyes. Then he looked up at the captain.

'There is no one alive up there,' the captain said. 'Thou,' he said to the sniper, 'go up there and see.'

The sniper looked down. He said nothing.

'Don't you hear me?' the captain shouted at him.

'Yes, my captain,' the sniper said, not looking at him.

'Then get up and go.' The captain still had his pistol out. 'Do you hear me?'

'Yes, my captain.'

'Why don't you go, then?' 'I don't want to, my captain.'

'You don't *want* to?' The captain pushed the pistol against the small of the man's back. 'You don't *want* to?'

'I am afraid, my captain,' the soldier said with dignity.

Lieutenant Berrendo, watching the captain's face and his odd eyes, thought he was going to shoot the man then.

'Captain Mora,' he said. 'Lieutenant Berrendo?'

'It is possible the soldier is right.'

For Whom the Bell Tolls • 685

'That he is right to say he is afraid? That he is right to say he does not *want* to obey an order?'

'No. That he is right that it is a trick.'

'They are all dead,' the captain said. 'Don't you hear me say they are all dead?'

'You mean our comrades on the slope?' Berrendo asked him. 'I agree with you.'

'Paco,' the captain said, 'don't be a fool. Do you think you are the only one who cared for Julian? I tell you the Reds are dead. Look I'

He stood up, then put both hands on top of the boulder and pulled himself up, kneeing-up awkwardly, then getting on his feet.

'Shoot,' he shouted, standing on the gray granite boulder and waved both his arms. 'Shoot me! Kill me!'

On the hilltop El Sordo lay behind the dead horse and grinned.

What a people, he thought. He laughed, trying to hold it in because the shaking hurt his arm.

'Reds,' came the shout from below. 'Red canaille. Shoot me! Kill me!'

Sordo, his chest shaking, barely peeped past the horse's crupper and saw the captain on top of the boulder waving his arms. Another officer stood by the boulder. The sniper was standing at the other side. Sordo kept his eye where it was and shook his head happily.

'Shoot me,' he said softly to himself. 'Kill me!' Then his shoulders shook again. The laughing hurt his arm and each time he laughed his head felt as though it would burst. But the laughter shook him again like a spasm.

Captain Mora got down from the boulder.

'Now do you believe me, Paco?' he questioned Lieutenant Berrendo.

'No,' said Lieutenant Berrendo.

'*Cojones!*' the captain said. 'Here there is nothing but idiots and cowards.'

The sniper had gotten carefully behind the boulder again and Lieutenant Berrendo was squatting beside him.

The captain, standing in the open beside the boulder, commenced to shout filth at the hilltop. There is no language so filthy as Spanish. There are words for all the vile words in English and there are other words and expressions that are used only in countries where blasphemy keeps pace with the austerity of religion. Lieutenant Berrendo was a very devout Catholic. So was the sniper. They were Carlists from Navarra and while both of them cursed and blasphemed when they were angry they regarded it as a sin which they regularly confessed.

As they crouched now behind the boulder watching the captain and listening to what he was shouting, they both disassociated themselves from him and what he was saying. They did not want to have that sort of talk on their consciences on a day in which they might die. Talking thus will not bring luck, the sniper thought. Speaking thus of the *Virgen* is bad luck. This one speaks worse than the Reds.

Julian is dead, Lt. Berrendo was thinking. Dead there on the slope on such a day as this is. And this foul mouth stands there bringing more ill fortune with his blasphemies.

Now the captain stopped shouting and turned to Lieutenant His eyes looked stranger than ever.

'Paco,' he said, happily, 'you and I will go up there.'

'Not me.'

'What?' The captain had his pistol out again.

I hate these pistol brandishers, Berrendo was thinking. They cannot give an order without jerking a gun out. They probably pull out their pistols when they go to the toilet and order the move they will make.

'I will go if you order me to. But under protest,' Lieutenant Berrendo told the captain.

'Then I will go alone,' the captain said. 'The smell of cowardice is too strong here.'

Holding his pistol in his right hand, he strode steadily up the slope. Rerrendo and the sniper watched him. He was making no attempt to take any cover and he was looking straight ahead of him at the rocks, the dead horse, and the fresh-dug dirt of the hilltop.

El Sordo lay behind the horse at the corner of the rock, watching the captain come striding up the hill.

Only one, he thought. We get only one. But from his manner of speaking he is *caza mayor*. Look at him walking. Look what an animal. Look at him stride forward. This one is for me. This one I take with me on the trip. This one coming now makes the same voyage I do. Come on, Comrade Voyager. Come striding. Come right along. Come along to meet it. Come on. Keep on walking. Don't slow up. Come right along. Come as thou art coming. Don't stop and look at those. That's right. Don't even look down. Keep on coming with your eyes forward. Look, he has a moustache. What do you think of that? He runs to a moustache, the Comrade Voyager. He is a captain. Look at his sleeves. I said he was *caza mayor*. He has the face of an *Inglés*. Look. With a red face and blond hair and blue eyes. With no cap on and his moustache is yellow. With blue eyes. With pale blue eyes. With pale blue eyes with something wrong with them. With pale blue eyes that don't focus. Close enough. Too close. Yes, Comrade Voyager. Take it, Comrade Voyager.

He squeezed the trigger of the automatic rifle gently and it pounded back three times against his shoulder with the slippery jolt the recoil of a tripoded automatic weapon gives.

The captain lay on his face on the hillside. His left arm was under him. His right arm that had held the pistol was stretched forward of his head. From all down the slope they were firing on the hill crest again.

Crouched behind the boulder, thinking that now he would have to sprint across that open space under fire, Lieutenant Berrendo heard the deep hoarse voice of Sordo from the hilltop.

'*Bandidos!*' the voice came. '*Bandidos!* Shoot me! Kill me!'

On the top of the hill El Sordo lay behind the automatic rifle laughing so that his chest ached, so that he thought the top of his head would burst.

'*Bandidos*,' he shouted again happily. 'Kill me, *bandidos!*' Then he shook his head happily. We have lots of company for the Voyage, he thought.

He was going to try for the other officer with the automatic rifle when he would leave the shelter of the boulder. Sooner or later he would have to leave it. Sardo knew that he could never command from there and he thought he had a very good chance to get him.

Just then the others on the hill heard the first sound of the coming of the planes.

El Sardo did not hear them. He was covering the down-slope edge of the boulder with his automatic rifle and he was thinking: when I see him he will be running already and I will miss him if I am not careful. I could shoot behind him all across that stretch. I should swing the gun with him and ahead of him. Or let him start and then get on him and ahead of him. I will try to pick him up there at the edge of the rock and swing just ahead of him. Then he felt a touch on his shoulder and he turned and saw the gray, fear-drained face of Joaquin and he looked where the boy was pointing and saw the three planes coming.

At this moment Lieutenant Berrendo broke from behind the boulder and, with his head bent and his legs plunging, ran down and across the slope to the shelter of the rocks where the automatic rifle was placed.

Watching the planes, Sardo never saw him go.

'Help me to pull this out,' he said to Joaquin and the boy dragged the automatic rifle clear from between the horse and the rock.

The planes were coming on steadily. They were in echelon and each second they grew larger and their noise was greater.

'Lie on your backs to fire at them,' Sordo said. 'Fire ahead of them as they come.'

He was watching them all the time. '*Cabrones! Hijos de puta!*' he said rapidly.

'Ignacio!' he said. 'Put the gun on the shoulder of the boy. Thou!' to Joaquin, 'Sit there and do not move. Crouch over. More. No. More.'

He lay back and sighted with the automatic rifle as the planes came on steadily.

'Thou, Ignacio, hold me the three legs of that tripod.' They were dangling down the boy's back and the muzzle of the gun was shaking from the jerking of his body that Joaquin could not control as he crouched with bent head hearing the droning roar of their coming.

Lying flat on his belly and looking up into the sky watching them come, Ignacio gathered the legs of the tripod into his two hands and steadied the gun.

'Keep thy head down,' he said to Joaquin. 'Keep thy head forward.'

'Pasionaria says "Better to die on thy-"' Joaquin was saying to himself as the drone came nearer them. Then he shifted suddenly into 'Hail Mary, full of grace, the Lord is with thee; Blessed art thou among women and Blessed is the fruit of thy womb, Jesus. Holy Mary, Mother of God, pray for us sinners now and at the hour of our death. Amen. Holy Mary, Mother of God,' he started, then he remembered quickly as the roar came now unbearably and started an act of contrition racing in it, 'Oh my God, I am heartily sorry for having offended thee who art worthy of all my love-'

Then there were the hammering explosions past his ears and the gun barrel hot against his shoulder. It was hammering now again and his ears were deafened by the muzzle blast. Ignacio was pulling down hard on the tripod and the barrel was burning his back. It was hammering now in the roar and he could not remember the act of contrition.

All he could remember was at the hour of our death. Amen. At the hour of our death. Amen. At the hour. At the hour. Amen. The others all were firing. Now and at the hour of our death. Amen.

Then, through the hammering of the gun, there was the whistle of the air splitting apart and then in the red black roar the earth rolled under his knees and then waved up to hit him in the face and then dirt and bits of rock were falling all over and Ignacio was lying on him and the gun was lying on him. But he was not dead because the whistle came again and the earth rolled under him with the roar. Then it came again and the earth lurched under his belly and one side of the hilltop rose into the air and then fell slowly over them where they lay.

The planes came back three times and bombed the hilltop but no one on the hilltop knew it. Then the planes machine-gunned the hilltop and went away. As they dove on the hill for the last time with their machine guns hammering, the first plane pulled up and winged over and then each plane did the same and they moved from echelon to V-formation and went away into the sky in the direction of Segovia.

Keeping a heavy fire on the hilltop, Lieutenant Berrendo pushed a patrol up to one of the bomb craters from where they could throw grenades onto the crest. He was taking no chances of any one being alive and waiting for them in the mess that was up there and he threw four grenades into the confusion of dead horses, broken and split rocks, and torn yellow-stained explosivestinking earth before he climbed out of the bomb crater and walked over to have a look.

No one was alive on the hilltop except the boy Joaquin, who was unconscious under the dead body of Ignacio. Joaquin was bleeding from the nose and from the ears. He had known nothing and had no feeling since he had suddenly been in the very heart of the thunder and the breath had been wrenched from his body when the one bomb struck so close and Lieutenant Berrendo made the sign of the cross and then shot him in the back of the head, as quickly and as gently, if such an abrupt movement can be gentle, as Sordo had shot the wounded horse.

Lieutenant Berrendo stood on the hilltop and looked down the slope at his own dead and then across the country seeing where they had galloped before Sordo had turned at bay here. He noticed all the dispositions that had been made of the troops and then he ordered the dead men's horses to be brought up and the bodies tied across the saddles so that they might be packed in to La Granja.

'Take that one, too,' he said. 'The one with his hands on the automatic rifle. That should be Sordo. He is the oldest and it was he with the gun. No. Cut the head off and wrap it in a poncho.' He considered a minute. 'You might as well take all the heads. And of the others below on the slope and where we first found them. Collect the rifles and pistols and pack that gun on a horse.'

Then he walked down to where the lieutenant lay who had been killed in the first assault. He looked down at him but did not touch him.

'*Que cosa mas mala es la guerra,*' he said to himself, which meant, 'What a bad thing war is.'

Then he made the sign of the cross again and as he walked down the hill he said five Our Fathers and five Hail Marys for the repose of the soul of his dead comrade. He did not wish to stay to see his orders being carried out.

28

After the planes went away Robert Jordan and Primitivo heard the firing start and his heart seemed to start again with it. A cloud of smoke drifted over the last ridge that he could see in the high country and the planes were three steadily receding specks in the sky.

'They've probably bombed hell out of their own cavalry and never touched Sordo and Company,' Robert Jordan said to himself. 'The damned planes scare you to death but they don't kill you.'

'The combat goes on,' Primitivo said, listening to the heavy firing. He had winced at each bomb thud and now he licked his dry lips.

'Why not?' Robert Jordan said. 'Those things never kill anybody.'

Then the firing stopped absolutely and he did not hear another shot. Lieutenant Berrendo's pistol shot did not carry that far.

When the firing first stopped it did not affect him. Then as the quiet kept on a hollow feeling came in his chest. Then he heard the grenades burst and for a moment his heart rose. Then everything was quiet again and the quiet kept on and he knew that it was over.

Maria came up from the camp with a tin bucket of stewed hare with mushrooms sunken in the rich gravy and a sack with bread, a leather wine bottle, four tin plates, two cups and four spoons. She stopped at the gun and ladled out two plates for Agustin and Eladio, who had replaced Anselmo at the gun, and gave them bread and unscrewed the horn tip of the wine bottle and poured two cups of wine.

Robert Jordan watched her climbing lithely up to his lookout post, the sack over her shoulder, the bucket in one hand, her cropped head bright in the sun. He climbed down and took the bucket and helped her up the last boulder.

'What did the aviation do?' she asked, her eyes frightened.

'Bombed Sordo.'

He had the bucket open and was ladling out stew onto a plate.

'Are they still fighting?'

'No. It is over.'

'Oh,' she said and bit her lip and looked out across the country.

'I have no appetite,' Primitivo said.

'Eat anyway,' Robert Jordan told him.

'I could not swallow food.'

'Take a drink of this, man,' Robert Jordan said and handed him the wine bottle. 'Then eat.'

'This of Sordo has taken away desire,' Primitivo said. 'Eat, thou. I have no desire.'

Maria went over to him and put her arms around his neck and kissed him.

'Eat, old one,' she said. 'Each one should take care of his strength.'

Primitivo turned away from her. He took the wine bottle and tipping his head back swallowed steadily while he squirted a jet of wine into the back of his mouth. Then he filled his plate from the bucket and commenced to eat.

Robert Jordan looked at Maria and shook his head. She sat down by him and put her arm around his shoulder. Each knew how the other felt and they sat there and Robert Jordan ate the stew, taking time to appreciate the mushrooms completely, and he drank the wine and they said nothing.

'You may stay here, *guapa*, if you want,' he said after a while when the food was all eaten.

'Nay,' she said. 'I must go to Pilar.'

'It is all right to stay here. I do not think that anything will happen now.'

'Nay. I must go to Pilar. She is giving me instruction.'

'What does she give thee?'

'Instruction.' She smiled at him and then kissed him. 'Did you never hear of religious instruction?' She blushed. 'It is something like that.' She blushed again. 'But different.'

'Go to thy instruction,' he said and patted her on the head. She smiled at him again, then said to Primitivo, 'Do you want any thing from below—'

'No, daughter,' he said. They both saw that he was still not yet recovered.

'*Salud*, old one,' she said to him.

'Listen,' Primitivo said. 'I have no fear to die but to leave them alone thus—' his voice broke.

'There was no choice,' Robert Jordan told him.

'I know. But all the same.'

'There was no choice,' Robert Jordan repeated. 'And now it is better not to speak of it.'

'Yes. But there alone with no aid from us—'

'Much better not to speak of it,' Robert Jordan said. 'And thou, *guapa*, get thee to thy instruction.'

He watched her climb down through the rocks. Then he sat there for a long time thinking and watching the high country.

Primitivo spoke to him but he did not answer. It was hot in the sun but he did not notice the heat while he sat watching the hill slopes and the long patches of pine trees that stretched up the highest slope. An hour passed and the sun was far to his left now when he saw them coming over the crest of the slope and he picked up his glasses.

The horses showed small and minute as the first two riders came into sight on the long green slope of the high hill. Then there were four more horsemen coming down, spread out across the wide hill and then through his glasses he saw the double column of men and horses ride into the sharp clarity of his vision. As he watched them he felt sweat come from his armpits and run down his flanks. One man rode at the head of the column. Then came more horsemen. Then came the riderless horses with their burdens tied across the saddles. Then there were two riders. Then came the wounded with men walking by them as they rode. Then came more cavalry to close the column.

Robert Jordan watched them ride down the slope and out of sight into the timber. He could not see at that distance the load one saddle bore of a long rolled poncho tied at each end and at intervals so that it bulged between each lashing as a pod bulges with peas. This was tied across the saddle and at each end it was lashed to the stirrup leathers. Alongside this on the top of the saddle the automatic rifle Sordo had served was lashed arrogantly.

Lieutenant Berrendo, who was riding at the head of the column, his flankers out, his point pushed well forward, felt no arrogance. He felt only the hollowness that comes after action. He was thinking: taking the heads is barbarous. But proof and identifica tion is necessary. I will have trouble enough about this as it is and who knows? This of the heads may appeal to them. There are those of them who like such things. It is possible they will send them all to Burgos. It is a barbarous business. The planes were *muchos*. Much. Much. But we could have done it all, and almost without losses, with a Stokes mortar. Two mules to carry the shells and a mule with a mortar on each side of the pack saddle. What an army we would be then! With the fire power of all these automatic weapons. And another mule. No, two mules to carry ammunition. Leave it alone, he told himself. It is no longer cavalry. Leave it alone. You're building yourself an army. Next you will want a mountain gun.

Then he thought of Julian, dead on the hill, dead now, tied across a horse there in the first troop, and as he rode down into the dark pine forest, leaving the sunlight behind him on the hill, riding now in the quiet dark of the forest, he started to say a prayer for him again.

'Hail, holy queen mother of mercy,' he started. 'Our life, our sweetness and our hope. To thee do we send up our sighs, mournings and weepings in this valley of tears—'

He went on with the prayer, the horses' hooves soft on the fallen pine needles, the light coming through the tree trunks in patches as it comes through the columns of a cathedral, and as he prayed he looked ahead to see his flankers riding through the trees.

He rode out of the forest onto the yellow road that led into La Granja and the horses' hooves raised a dust that hung over them as they rode. It powdered the dead who were tied face down across the saddles and the wounded, and those who walked beside them, were in thick dust.

It was here that Anselmo saw them ride past in their dust.

He counted the dead and the wounded and he recognized Sordo's automatic rifle. He did not know what the poncho-wrapped bundle was which flapped against the led horse's flanks as the stirrup leathers swung but when, on his way home, he came in the dark onto the hill where Sordo had fought, he knew at once what the long poncho roll contained. In the dark he could not tell who had been up on the hill. But he counted those that lay there and then made off across the hills for Pablo's camp.

Walking alone in the dark, with a fear like a freezing of his heart from the feeling the holes of the bomb craters had given him, from them and from what he had found on the hill, he put all thought of the next day out of his mind. He simply walked as fast as he could to bring the news. And as he walked he prayed for the souls of Sordo and of all his band. It was the first time he had prayed since the start of the movement.

'Most kind, most sweet, most clement Virgin,' he prayed.

But he could not keep from thinking of the next day finally. So he thought: I will do exactly as the *Inglés* says and as he says to do it. But let me be close to him, 0 Lord, and may his instructiosn be exact for I do not think that I could control myself under the bombardment of the planes. Help me, 0 Lord, tomorrow to comport myself as a man should in his last hours. Help me, 0 Lord, to understand clearly the needs of the day. Help me, 0 Lord, to dominate the movement of my legs that I should not run when the bad moment comes. Help me, 0 Lord, to comport myself as a man tomorrow in the day of battle. Since I have asked this aid of thee, please grant it, knowing I would not ask it if it were not serious, and I will ask nothing more of thee again.

Walking in the dark alone he felt much better from having prayed and he was sure, now, that he would comport himself well. Walking now down from the high country, he went back to praying for the people of Sordo and in a short time he had reached the upper post where Fernando challenged him.

'It is I,' he answered, 'Anselmo.'

'Good,' Fernando said.

'You know of this of Sordo, old one?' Anselmo asked Fernando, the two of them standing at the entrance of the big rocks in the dark.

'Why not?' Fernando said. 'Pablo has told us.'

'He was up there?'

'Why not?' Fernando said stolidly. 'He visited the hill as soon as the cavalry left.'

'He told you—'

'He told us as,' Fernando said. 'What barbarians these fascists are! We must do away with all such barbarians in Spain.' He stopped, then said bitterly, 'In them is lacking all conception of dignity.'

Anselmo grinned in the dark. An hour ago he could not have imagined that he would ever smile again. What a marvel, that Fernando, he thought.

'Yes,' he said to Fernando. 'We must teach them. We must take away their planes, their automatic weapons, their tanks, their artillery and teach them dignity.'

'Exactly,' Fernando said. 'I am glad that you agree.'

Anselmo left him standing there alone with his dignity and went on down to the cave.

29

Anselmo found Robert Jordan sitting at the plank table inside the cave with Pablo opposite him. They had a bowl poured full of wine between them and each had a cup of wine on the table. Robert Jordan had his notebook out and he was holding a pencil. Pilar and Maria were in the back of the cave out of sight. There was no way for Anselmo to know that the woman was keeping the girl back there to keep her from hearing the conversation and he thought that it was odd that Pilar was not at the table.

Robert Jordan looked up as Anselmo came in under the blanket that hung over the opening. Pablo stared straight at the table. His eyes were focused on the wine bowl but he was not seeing it.

'I come from above,' Anselmo said to Robert Jordan. 'Pablo has told us,' Robert Jordan said.

'There were six dead on the hill and they had taken the heads,' Anselmo said. 'I was there in the dark.'

Robert Jordan nodded. Pablo sat there looking at the wine bowl and saying nothing. There was no expression on his face and his small pig-eyes were looking at the wine bowl as though he had never seen one before.

'Sit down,' Robert Jordan said to Anselmo.

The old man sat down at the table on one of the hide-covered stools and Robert Jordan reached under the table and brought up the pinch-bottle of whiskey that had been the gift of Sardo. It was about half-full. Robert Jordan reached down the table for a cup and poured a drink of whiskey into it and shoved it along the table to Anselmo.

'Drink that, old one,' he said.

Pablo looked from the wine bowl to Anselmo's face as he drank and then he looked back at the wine bowl.

As Anselmo swallowed the whiskey he felt a burning in his nose, his eyes and his mouth, and then a happy, comforting warmth in his stomach. He wiped his mouth with the back of his hand.

Then he looked at Robert Jordan and said, 'Can I have another?'

'Why not?' Robert Jordan said and poured another drink from the bottle and handed it this time instead of pushing it.

This time there was not the burning when he swallowed but the warm comfort doubled. It was as good a thing for his spirit as a saline injection is for a man who has suffered a great hemorrhage.

The old man looked toward the bottle again.

'The rest is for tomorrow,' Robert Jordan said. 'What passed on the road, old one?'

'There was much movement,' Anselmo said. 'I have it all noted down as you showed me. I have one watching for me and noting now. Later I will go for her report.'

'Did you see anti-tank guns? Those on rubber tires with the long barrels?'

'Yes,' Anselmo said. 'There were four camions which passed on the road. In each of them there was such a gun with pine branches spread across the barrels. In the trucks rode six men with each gun.'

'Four guns, you say?' Robert Jordan asked him.

'Four,' Anselmo said. He did not look at his papers.

'Tell me what else went up the road.'

While Robert Jordan noted Anselmo told him everything he had seen move past him on the road. He told it from the beginning and in order with the wonderful memory of those who cannot read or write, and twice, while he was talking, Pablo reached out for more wine from the bowl.

'There was also the cavalry which entered La Granja from the high country where El Sardo fought,' Anselmo went on.

Then he told the number of the wounded he had seen and the number of the dead across the saddles.

'There was a bundle packed across one saddle that I did not understand,' he said. 'But now I know it was the heads.' He went on without pausing. 'It was a squad ron of cavalry. They had only one officer left. He was not the one who was here in the early morning when you were by the gun. He must have been one of the dead. Two of the dead were officers by their sleeves. They were lashed face down over the saddles, their arms hanging. Also they had the *máquina* of El Sordo tied to the saddle that bore the heads. The barrel was bent. That is all,' he finished.

'It is enough,' Robert Jordan said and dipped his cup into the wine bowl. 'Who beside you has been through the lines to the side of the Republic?'

'Andres and Eladio.'

'Which is the better of those two?'

'Andres.'

'How long would it take him to get to Navacerrada from here?'

'Carrying no pack and taking his precautions, in three hours with luck. We came by a longer, safer route because of the material.' 'He can surely make it?'

'*No se,* there is no such thing as surely.'

'Not for thee either?'

'Nay.'

That decides that, Robert Jordan thought to himself. If he had said that he could make it surely, surely I would have sent him.

'Andres can get there as well as thee?' 'As well or better. He is younger.' 'But this must absolutely get there.'

'If nothing happens he will get there. If anything happens it could happen to any one.'

'I will write a dispatch and send it by him,' Robert Jordan said. 'I will explain to him where he can find the General. He will be at the Estado Mayor of the Division.'

'He will not understand all this of divisions and all,' Anselmo said. 'Always has it confused me. He should have the name of the General and where he can be found.'

'But it is at the Estado Mayor of the Division that he will be found.'

'But is that not a place?'

'Certainly it is a place, old one,' Robert Jordan explained patiently. 'But it is a place the General will have selected. It is where he will make his headquarters for the battle.'

'Where is it then?' Anselmo was tired and the tiredness was making him stupid. Also words like Brigades, Divisions, Army Corps confused him. First there had been columns, then there were regiments, then there were brigades. Now there were brigades and divisions, both. He did not understand. A place was a place.

'Take it slowly, old one,' Robert Jordan said. He knew that if he could not make Anselmo understand he could never explain it clearly to Andres either. 'The Estado Mayor of the Division is a place the General will have picked to set up his organization to command. He commands a division, which is two brigades. I do not know where it is because I was not there when it was picked. It will probably be a cave or dugout, a refuge, and wires will run to it. Andres must ask for the General and for the Estado Mayor of the Division. He must give this to the General or to the Chief of his Estado Mayor or to another whose name I will write. One of them will surely be there even if the others are out inspecting the preparations for the attack. Do you understand now?'

'Yes.'

'Then get Andres and I will write it now and seal it with this seal.' He showed him the small, round, wooden-backed rubber stamp with the seal of the S.I.M. and the round, tin-covered inking pad no bigger than a fifty-cent piece he carried in his pocket. 'That seal they will honor. Get Andres now and I will explain to him. He must go quickly but first he must understand.'

'He will understand if I do. But you must make it very clear. This of staffs and divisions is a mystery to me. Always have I gone to such things as definite places such as a house. In Navacerrada it is in the old hotel where the place of command is. In Guadarrama it is in a house with a garden.'

'With this General,' Robert Jordan said, 'it will be some place very close to the lines. It will be underground to protect from the planes. Andrés will find it easily by asking, if he knows what to ask for. He will only need to show what I have written. But fetch him now for this should get there quickly.'

Anselmo went out, ducking under the hanging blanket. Robert Jordan commenced writing in his notebook.

'Listen, *Inglés*,' Pablo said, still looking at the wine bowl.

'I am writing,' Robert Jordan said without looking up.

'Listen, *Inglés*,' Pablo spoke directly to the wine bowl. 'There is no need to be disheartened in this. Without Sordo we have plenty of people to take the posts and blow thy bridge.'

'Good,' Robert Jordan said without stopping writing.

'Plenty,' Pablo said. 'I have admired thy judgment much today, *Inglés*,' Pablo told the wine bowl. 'I think thou hast much *picardia*. That thou art smarter than I am. I have confidence in thee.'

Concentrating on his report to Golz, trying to put it in the fewest words and still make it absolutely convincing, trying to put it so the attack would be cancelled, absolutely, yet convince them he wasn't trying to have it called off because of any fears he might have about the danger of his own mission, but wished only to put them in possession of all the facts, Robert Jordan was hardly half listening.

'*Inglés*,' Pablo said.

'I am writing,' Robert Jordan told him without looking up.

I probably should send two copies, he thought. But if I do we will not have enough people to blow it if I have to blow it. What do I know about why this attack is made? Maybe it is only a holding attack. Maybe they want to draw those troops from somewhere else. Perhaps they make it to draw those planes from the North. Maybe that is what it is about. Perhaps it is not expected to succeed. What do I know about it? This is my report to Golz. I do not blow the bridge until the attack starts. My orders are clear and if the attack is called off I blow nothing. But I've got to keep enough people here for the bare minimum necessary to carry the orders out.

'What did you say?' he asked Pablo.

'That I have confidence, *Inglés*.' Pablo was still addressing the wine bowl.

Man, I wish I had, Robert Jordan thought. He went on writing.

30

So now everything had been done that there was to do that night. All orders had been given. Every one knew exactly what he was to do in the morning. Andres had been gone three hours. Either it would come now with the coming of the daylight or it would not come. I believe that it will come, Robert Jordan told himself, walking back down from the upper post where he had gone to speak to Primitivo.

Golz makes the attack but he has not the power to cancel it. Permission to cancel it will have to come from Madrid. The chances are they won't be able to wake anybody up there and if they do wake up they will be too sleepy to think. I should have gotten word to Golz sooner of the preparations they have made to meet the attack, but how could I send word about something until it happened? They did not move up that stuff until just at dark. They did not want to have any movement on the road spotted by planes. But what about all their planes? What about those fascist planes?

Surely our people must have been warned by them. But perhaps the fascists were faking for another offensive down through Guadalajara with them. There were supposed to be Italian troops concentrated in Soria, and at Siguenza again besides those operating in the North. They haven't enough troops or material to run two major offensives at the same time though. That is impossible; so it must be just a bluff.

But we know how many troops the Italians have landed all last month and the month before at Cadiz. It is always possible they will try again at Guadalajara, not stupidly as before, but with three main fingers coming down to broaden it out and carry it along the railway to the west of the plateau. There was a way that they could do it all right. Hans had shown him. They made many mistakes the first time. The whole conception was unsound. They had not used any of the same troops in the Arganda offensive against the Madrid Valencia road that they used at Guadalajara. Why had they not made those same drives simultaneously? Why? Why? When would we know why?

Yet we had stopped them both times with the very same troops. We never could have stopped them if they had pulled both drives at once. Don't worry, he told himself. Look at the miracles that have happened before this. Either you will have to blow that bridge in the morning or you will not have to. But do not start deceiving yourself into thinking you won't have to blow it. You will blow it one day or you will blow it another. Or if it is not this bridge it will be some other bridge. It is not you who decides what shall be done. You follow orders. Follow them and do not try to think beyond them.

The orders on this are very clear. Too very clear. But you must not worry nor must you be frightened. For if you allow yourself the luxury of normal fear that fear will infect those who must work with you.

But that heads business was quite a thing all the same, he told himself. And the old man running onto them on the hilltop alone. How would you have liked to run onto them like that? That impressed you, didn't it? Yes, that impressed you, Jordan. You have been quite impressed more than once today. But you have behaved O.K. So far you have behaved all right.

You do very well for an instructor in Spanish at the University of Montana, he joked at himself. You do all right for that. But do not start to thinking that you are anything very special. You haven't gotten very far in this business. Just remember Duran, who never had any military training and who was a composer and lad about town before the movement and is now a damned good general commanding a brigade. It was all as simple and easy to learn and understand to Duran as chess to a child chess prodigy. You had read on and studied the art of war ever since you were a boy and your grandfather had started you on the American Civil War. Except that Grandfather always called it the War of the Rebellion. But compared with Duran you were like a good sound chess player against a boy prodigy. Old

Duran. It would be good to see Duran again. He would see him at Gaylord's after this was over. Yes. After this was over. See how well he was behaving?

I'll see him at Gaylord's, he said to himself again, after this is over. Don't kid yourself, he said. You do it all perfectly O.K. Cold. Without kidding yourself. You aren't going to see Duran any more and it is of no importance. Don't be that way either, he told himself. Don't go in for any of those luxuries.

Nor for heroic resignation either. We do not want any citizens full of heroic resignation in these hills. Your grandfather fought four years in our Civil War and you are just finishing your first year in this war. You have a long time to go yet and you are very well fitted for the work. And now you have Maria, too. Why, you've got everything. You shouldn't worry. What is a little brush between a guerilla band and a squadron of cavalry? That isn't anything. What if they took the heads? Does that make any difference? None at all.

The Indians always took the scalps when Grandfather was at Fort Kearny after the war. Do you remember the cabinet in your father's office with the arrowheads spread out on a shelf, and the eagle feathers of the war bonnets that hung on the wall, their plumes slanting, the smoked buckskin smell of the leggings and the shirts and the feel of the beaded moccasins? Do you remember the great stave of the buffalo bow that leaned in a corner of the cabinet and the two quivers of hunting and war arrows, and how the bundle of shafts felt when you closed your hand around them?

Remember something like that. Remember something concrete and practical. Remember Grandfather's saber, bright and well oiled in its dented scabbard and Grandfather showed you how the blade had been thinned from the many times it had been to the grinder's. Remember Grandfather's Smith and Wesson. It was a single action, officer's model .32 caliber and there was no trigger guard. It had the softest, sweetest trigger pull you had ever felt and it was always well oiled and the bore was clean although the finish was all worn off and the brown metal of the barrel and the cylinder was worn smooth from the leather of the holster. It was kept in the holster with a U.S. on the flap in a drawer in the cabinet with its cleaning equipment and two hundred round of cartridges. Their cardboard boxes were wrapped and tied neatly with waxed twine.

You could take the pistol out of the drawer and hold it. 'Handle it freely,' was Grandfather's expression. But you could not play with it because it was 'a serious weapon.'

You asked Grandfather once if he had ever killed any one with it and he said, 'Yes.' Then you said, 'When, Grandfather?' and he said, 'In the War of the Rebellion and afterwards.'

You said, 'Will you tell me about it, Grandfather?' And he said, 'I do not care to speak about it, Robert.'

Then after your father had shot himself with this pistol, and you had come home from school and they'd had the funeral, the coroner had returned it after the inquest saying, 'Bob, I guess you might want to keep the gun. I'm supposed to hold it, but I know your dad set a lot of store by it because his dad packed it all through the War, besides out here when he first came out with the Cavalry, and it's still a hell of a good gun. I had her out trying her this afternoon. She don't throw much of a slug but you can hit things with her.'

He had put the gun back in the drawer in the cabinet where it belonged, but the next day he took it out and he had ridden up to the top of the high country above Red Lodge, with Chub, where they had built the road to Cooke City now over the pass and across the Bear Tooth plateau, and up there where the wind was thin and there was snow all summer on the hills they had stopped by the lake which was supposed to be eight hundred feet deep and was a deep green color, and Chub held the two horses and he climbed out on a rock and leaned over and saw his face in the still water, and saw himself holding the gun, and then he dropped it, holding it by the muzzle, and saw it go down making bubbles until it was just as big as a watch charm in that clear water, and then it was out of sight. Then he came back off the rock and when he swung up into the saddle he gave old Bess such a clout with the spurs she started to buck like an old rocking horse. He bucked her out along the shore of the lake and as soon as she was reasonable they went on back along the trail.

'I know why you did that with the old gun, Bob,' Chub said.

'Well, then we don't have to talk about it,' he had said.

They never talked about it and that was the end of Grandfather's side arms except for the saber. He still had the saber in his trunk with the rest of his things at Missoula.

I wonder what Grandfather would think of this situation, he thought. Grandfather was a hell of a good soldier, everybody said. They said if he had been with Custer that day he never would have let him be sucked in that way. How could he ever not have seen the smoke nor the dust of all those lodges down there in the draw along the Little Big Horn unless there must have been a heavy morning mist? But there wasn't any mist.

I wish Grandfather were here instead of me. Well, maybe we will all be together by tomorrow night. If there should be any such damn fool business as a hereafter, and I'm sure there isn't, he thought, I would certainly like to talk to him. Because there are a lot of things I would like to know. I have a right to ask him now because I have had to do the same sort of things myself. I don't think he'd mind my asking now. I had no right to ask before. I understand him not telling me because he didn't know me. But now I think that we would get along all right. I'd like to be able to talk to him now and get his advice. Hell, if I didn't get advice I'd just like to talk to him. It's a shame there is such a jump in time between ones like us.

Then, as he thought, he realized that if there was any such thing as ever meeting, both he and his grandfather would be acutely embarrassed by the presence of his father. Any one has a right to do it, he thought. But it isn't a good thing to do. I understand it, but I do not approve of it. *Lache* was the word. But you *do* understand it? Sure, I understand it but. Yes, but. You have to be awfully occupied with yourself to do a thing like that.

Aw hell, I wish Grandfather was here, he thought. For about an hour anyway. Maybe he sent me what little I have through that other one that misused the gun. Maybe that is the only communication that we have. But, damn it. Truly damn it, but I wish the time-lag wasn't so long so that I could have learned from him what the other one never had to teach me. But suppose the fear he had to go through and dominate and just get rid of finally in four years of that and then in the Indian fighting, although in that, mostly, there couldn't have been so much fear, had made a *cobarde* out of the other one the way second generation bullfighters almost always are? Suppose that? And maybe the good juice only came through straight again after passing through that one?

I'll never forget how sick it made me the first time I knew he was a *cobarde*. Go on, say it in English. Coward. It's easier when you have it said and there is never any point in referring to a son of a bitch by some foreign term. He wasn't any son of a bitch, though. He was just a coward and that was the worst luck any man could have. Because if he wasn't a coward he would have stood up to that woman and not let her bully him. I wonder what I would have been like if he had married a different woman? That's something you'll never know, he thought, and grinned. Maybe the bully in her helped to supply what was missing in the other. And you. Take it a little easy. Don't get to referring to the good juice and such other things until you are through tomorrow. Don't be snotty too soon. And then don't be snotty at all. We'll see what sort of juice you have tomorrow.

But he started thinking about Grandfather again.

'George Custer was not an intelligent leader of cavalry, Robert,' his grandfather had said. 'He was not even an intelligent man.'

He remembered that when his grandfather said that he felt resentment that any one should speak against that figure in the buckskin shirt, the yellow curls blowing, that stood on that hill holding a service revolver as the Sioux closed in around him in the old Anheuser-Busch lithograph that hung on the poolroom wall in Red Lodge.

'He just had great ability to get himself in and out of trouble,' his grandfather went on, 'and on the Little Big Horn he got into it but he couldn't get out.'

'Now Phil Sheridan was an intelligent man and so was Jeb Stuart. But John Mosby was the finest cavalry leader that ever lived.'

He had a letter in his things in the trunk at Missoula from General Phil Sheridan to old Killy-the-Horse Kilpatrick that said his grandfather was a finer leader of irregular cavalry than John Mosby.

I ought to tell Golz about my grandfather, he thought. He wouldn't ever have heard of him though. He probably never even heard of John Mosby. The British all had heard of them though because they had to study our Civil War much more than people did on the Continent. Karkov said after this was over I could go to the Lenin Institute in Moscow if I wanted to. He said I could go to the military academy of the Red Army if I wanted to do that. I wonder what Grandfather would think of that? Grandfather, who never knowingly sat at table with a Democrat in his life.

Well, I don't want to be a soldier, he thought. I know that. So that's out. I just want us to win this war. I guess really good soldiers are really good at very little else, he thought. That's obviously un-true. Look at Napoleon and Wellington. You're very stupid this evening, he thought.

Usually his mind was very good company and tonight it had been when he thought about his grandfather. Then thinking of his father had thrown him off. He understood his father and he forgave him everything and he pitied him but he was ashamed of him.

You better not think at all, he told himself. Soon you will be with Maria and you won't have to think. That's the best way now that everything is worked out. When you have been concentrating so hard on something you can't stop and your brain gets to racing like a flywheel with the weight gone. You better just not think.

But just suppose, he thought. Just suppose that when the planes unload they smash those anti-tank guns and just blow hell out of the positions and the old tanks roll good up whatever hill it is for once and old Golz boots that bunch of drunks, *clochards,* bums, fanatics and heroes that make up the Quatorzieme Brigade ahead of him, and I *know* how good Duran's people are in Golz's other brigade, and we are in Segovia tomorrow night.

Yes. Just suppose, he said to himself. I'll settle for La Granja, he told himself. But you are going to have to blow that bridge, he suddenly knew absolutely. There won't be any calling off. Because the way you have just been supposing there for a minute is how the possibilities of that attack look to those who have ordered it. Yes, you will have to blow the bridge, he knew truly. Whatever happens to Andres doesn't matter.

Coming down the trail there in the dark, alone with the good feeling that everything that had to be done was over for the next four hours, and with the confidence that had come from thinking back to concrete things, the knowledge that he would surely have to blow the bridge came to him almost with comfort.

The uncertainty, the enlargement of the feeling of being uncertain, as when, through a misunderstanding of possible dates, one does not know whether the guests are really coming to a party, that had been with him ever since he had dispatched Andres with the report to Golz, had all dropped from him now. He was sure now that the festival would not be cancelled. It's much better to be sure, he thought. It's always much better to be sure.

31

So now they were in the robe again together and it was late in the last night. Maria lay close against him and he felt the long smoothness of her thighs against his and her breasts like two small hills that rise out of the long plain where there is a well, and the far country beyond the hills was the valley of her throat where his lips were. He lay very quiet and did not think and she stroked his head with her hand.

'Roberto,' Maria said very softly and kissed him. 'I am ashamed. I do not wish to disappoint thee but there is a great soreness and much pain. I do not think I would be any good to thee.'

'There is always a great soreness and much pain,' he said. 'Nay, rabbit. That is nothing. We will do nothing that makes pain.'

'It is not that. It is that I am not good to receive thee as I wish to.'

'That is of no importance. That is a passing thing. We are together when we lie together.'

'Yes, but I am ashamed. I think it was from when things were done to me that it comes. Not from thee and me.'

'Let us not talk of that.'

'Nor do I wish to. I meant I could not bear to fail thee now on this night and so I sought to excuse myself.'

'Listen, rabbit,' he said. 'All such things pass and then there is no problem.' But he thought; it was not good luck for the last night.

Then he was ashamed and said, 'Lie close against me, rabbit. I love thee as much feeling thee against me in here in the dark as I love thee making love.'

'I am deeply ashamed because I thought it might be again tonight as it was in the high country when we came down from El Sordo's.'

'Qué va,' he said to her. 'That is not for every day. I like it thus as well as the other.' He lied, putting aside disappointment. 'We will be here together quietly and we will sleep. Let us talk together. I know thee very little from talking.'

'Should we speak of tomorrow and of thy work? I would like to be intelligent about thy work.'

'No,' he said and relaxed completely into the length of the robe and lay now quietly with his cheek against her shoulder, his left arm under her head. 'The most intelligent is not to talk about tomorrow nor what happened today. In this we do not discuss the losses and what we must do tomorrow we will do. Thou art not afraid?'

'Que va,' she said. 'I am always afraid. But now I am afraid for thee so much I do not think of me.'

'Thou must not, rabbit. I have been in many things. And worse than this,' he lied.

Then suddenly surrendering to something, to the luxury of going into unreality, he said, 'Let us talk of Madrid and of us in Madrid.'

'Good,' she said. Then, 'Oh, Roberto, I am sorry I have failed thee. Is there not some other thing that I can do for thee?'

He stroked her head and kissed her and then lay close and relaxed beside her, listening to the quiet of the night.

'Thou canst talk with me of Madrid,' he said and thought: I'll keep any oversupply of that for tomorrow. I'll need all of that there is tomorrow. There are no pine needles that need that now as I will need it tomorrow. Who was it cast his seed upon the ground in the Bible? Onan. How did Onan turn out? he thought. I don't remember ever hearing any more about Onan. He smiled in the dark.

Then he surrendered again and let himself slip into it, feeling a voluptuousness of surrender into unreality that was like a sexual acceptance of something that could come in the night when there was no understanding, only the delight of acceptance.

'My beloved,' he said, and kissed her. 'Listen. The other night I was thinking about Madrid and I thought how I would get there and leave thee at the hotel while I went up to see people at the hotel of the Russians. But that was false. I would not leave thee at any hotel.'

'Why not?'

'Because I will take care of thee. I will not ever leave thee. I will go with thee to the Seguridad to get papers. Then I will go with thee to buy those clothes that are needed.'

'They are few, and I can buy them.'

'Nay, they are many and we will go together and buy good ones and thou wilt be beautiful in them.'

'I would rather we stayed in the room in the hotel and sent out for the clothes. Where is the hotel?'

'It is on the Plaza del Callao. We will be much in that room in that hotel. There is a wide bed with clean sheets and there is hot running water in the bathtub and there are two closets and I will keep my things in one and thou wilt take the other. And there are tall, wide windows that open, and outside, in the streets, there is the spring. Also I know good places to eat that are illegal but with good food, and I know shops where there is still wine and whiskey. And we will keep things to eat in the room for when we are hungry and also whiskey for when I wish a drink and I will buy thee manzanilla.'

'I would like to try the whiskey.'

'But since it is difficult to obtain and if thou likest manzanilla.' 'Keep thy whiskey, Roberto,' she said 'Oh, I love thee very much.

Thou and thy whiskey that I could not have. What a pig thou art.' 'Nay, you shall try it. But it is not good for a woman.'

'And I have only had things that were good for a woman,' Maria said. 'Then there in bed I will still wear my wedding shirt?'

'Nay. I will buy thee various nightgowns and pajamas too if you should prefer them.'

'I will buy seven wedding shirts,' she said. 'One for each day of the week. And I will buy a clean wedding shirt for thee. Dost ever wash thy shirt?'

'Sometimes.'

'I will keep everything clean and I will pour thy whiskey and put the water in it as it was done at Sardo's. I will obtain olives and salted codfish and hazel nuts for thee to eat while thou drinkest and we will stay in the room for a month and never leave it. If I am fit to receive thee,' she said, suddenly unhappy.

'That is nothing,' Robert Jordan told her. 'Truly it is nothing. It is possible thou wert hurt there once and now there is a scar that makes a further hurting. Such a thing is possible. All such things pass. And also there are good doctors in Madrid if there is truly anything.'

'But all was good before,' she said pleadingly. 'That is the promise that all will be good again.'

'Then let us talk again about Madrid.' She curled her legs between his and rubbed the top of her head against his shoulder. 'But will I not be so ugly there with this cropped head that thou wilt be ashamed of me?'

'Nay. Thou art lovely. Thou hast a lovely face and a beautiful body, long and light, and thy skin is smooth and the color of burnt gold and every one will try to take thee from me.'

'*Qué va*, take me from thee,' she said. 'No other man will ever touch me till I die. Take me from thee! *Qué va*.'

'But many will try. Thou wilt see.'

'They will see I love thee so that they will know it would be as unsafe as putting their hands into a caldron of melted lead to touch me. But thou? When thou seest beautiful women of the same culture as thee? Thou wilt not be ashamed of me?'

'Never. And I will marry thee.'

'If you wish,' she said. 'But since we no longer have the Church I do not think it carries importance.'

'I would like us to be married.'

'If you wish. But listen. If we were ever in another country where there still was the Church perhaps we could be married in it there?'

'In my country they still have the Church,' he told her. 'There we can be married in it if it means aught to thee. I have never been married. There is no problem.'

'I am glad thou hast never been married,' she said. 'But I am glad thou knowest about such things as you have told me for that means thou hast been with many women and the Pilar told me that it is only such men who are possible for husbands. But thou wilt not run with other women now? Because it would kill me.'

'I have never run with many women,' he said, truly. 'Until thee I did not think that I could love one deeply.'

She stroked his cheeks and then held her hands clasped behind his head. 'Thou must have known very many.'

'Not to love them.'

'Listen. The Pilar told me something–'

'Say it.'

'No. It is better not to. Let us talk again about Madrid.'

'What was it you were going to say?'

'I do not wish to say it.'

'Perhaps it would be better to say it if it could be important.'

'You think it is important?'

'Yes.'

'But how can you know when you do not know what it is?'

'From thy manner.'

'I will not keep it from you then. The Pilar told me that we would all die tomorrow and that you know it as well as she does and that you give it no importance. She said this not in criticism but in admiration.'

'She said that?' he said. The crazy bitch, he thought, and he said, 'That is more of her gypsy manure. That is the way old market women and cafe cowards talk. That is manuring obscenity.' He felt the sweat that came from under his armpits and slid down between his arm and his side and he said to himself, 'So you are scared, eh?' and aloud he said, 'She is a manure-mouthed superstitious bitch. Let us talk again of Madrid.'

'Then you know no such thing?'

'Of course not. Do not talk such manure,' he said, using a stronger, ugly word.

But this time when he talked about Madrid there was no slipping into make-believe again. Now he was just lying to his girl and to himself to pass the night before battle and he knew it. He liked to do it, but all the luxury of the acceptance was gone. But he started again.

'I have thought about thy hair,' he said. 'And what we can do about it. You see it grows now all over thy head the same length like the fur of an animal and it is lovely to feel and 1 love it very much and it is beautiful and it flattens and rises like a wheatfield in the wind when 1 pass my hand over it.'

'Pass thy hand over it.'

He did and left his hand there and went on talking to her throat, as he felt his own throat swell. 'But in Madrid I thought we could go together to the coiffeur's and they could cut it neatly on the sides and in the back as they cut mine and that way it would look better in the town while it is growing out.'

'I would look like thee,' she said and held him close to her. 'And then 1 never would want to change it.' Nay. It will grow all the time and that will only be to keep it neat at the start while it is growing long. How long will it take it to grow long?'

'Really long?

'No. I mean to thy shoulders. It is thus I would have thee wear it.'

'As Garbo in the cinema?' 'Yes,' he said thickly.

Now the making believe was coming back in a great rush and he would take it all to him. It had him now, and again he surrendered and went on. 'So it will hang straight to thy shoulders and curl at the ends as a wave of the sea curls, and it will be the color of ripe wheat and thy face the color of burnt gold and thine eyes the only color they could be with thy hair and thy skin, gold with the dark flecks in them, and I will push thy head back and look in thy eyes and hold thee tight against me—'

'Where?'

'Anywhere. Wherever it is that we are. How long will it take for thy hair to grow?'

'I do not know because it never had been cut before. But I think in six months it should be long enough to hang well below my ears and in a year as long as thou couldst ever wish. But do you know what will happen first?'

'Tell me.'

'We will be in the big clean bed in thy famous room in our famous hotel and we will sit in the famous bed together and look into the mirror of the *armoire* and there will be thee and there will be me in the glass and then I will turn to thee thus, and put my arms around thee thus, and then I will kiss thee thus.'

Then they lay quiet and close together in the night, hot-aching, rigid, close together and holding her, Robert Jordan held closely too all those things that he knew could never happen, and he went on with it deliberately and said, 'Rabbit, we will not always live in that hotel.'

'Why not?'

'We can get an apartment in Madrid on that street that runs along the Parque of the Buen Retiro. I know an American woman who furnished apartments and rented them before the movement and I know how to get such an apartment for only the rent that was paid before the movement. There are apartments there that face on the park and you can see all of the park from the windows; the iron fence, the gardens, and the gravel walks and the green of the lawns where they touch the gravel, and the trees deep with shadows and the many fountains, and now the chestnut trees will be in bloom. In Madrid we can walk in the park and row on the lake if the water is back in it now.'

'Why would the water be out?'

'They drained it in November because it made a mark to sight from when the planes came over for bombing. But I think that the water is back in it now. I am not sure. But even if there is no water in it we can walk through all the park away from the lake and there is a part that is like a forest with trees from all parts of the world with their names on them, with placards that tell what trees they are and where they came from.'

'I would almost as soon go the cinema,' Maria said. 'But the trees sound very interesting and I will learn them all with thee if I can remember them.'

'They are not as in a museum,' Robert Jordan said. 'They grow naturally and there are hills in the park and part of the park is like a jungle. Then below it there is the book fair where along the sidewalks there are hundreds of booths with second-hand books in them and now, since the movement, there are many books, stolen in the looting of the houses which have been bombed and from the houses of the fascists, and brought to the book fair by those who stole them. I could spend all day every day at the stalls of the book fair as I once did in the days before the movement, if I ever could have any time in Madrid.'

'While thou art visiting the book fair I will occupy myself with the apartment,' Maria said. 'Will we have enough money for a servant?'

'Surely. I can get Petra who is at the hotel if she pleases thee. She cooks well and is clean. I have eaten there with newspapermen that she cooks for. They have electric stoves in their rooms.'

'If you wish her,' Maria said. 'Or I can find some one. But wilt thou not be away much with thy work? They would not let me go with thee on such work as this.'

'Perhaps I can get work in Madrid. I have done this work now for a long time and I have fought since the start of the movement. It is possible that they would give me work now in Madrid. I have never asked for it. I have always been at the front or in such work as this.

'Do you know that until I met thee I have never asked for anything? Nor wanted anything? Nor thought of anything except the movement and the winning of this war? Truly I have been very pure in my ambitions. I have worked much and now I love thee and,' he said it now in a complete embracing of all that would not be, 'I love thee as I love all that we have fought for. I love thee as I love liberty and dignity and the rights of all men to work not be hungry. I love thee as I love Madrid that we have defended and as I love all my comrades that have died. And many have died. Many. Many. Thou canst not think how many. But I love thee as I love what I love most in the world and I love thee more. I love thee very much, rabbit. More than I can tell thee. But I say this now to tell thee a little. I have never had a wife and now I have thee for a wife and I am happy.'

'I will make thee as good a wife as I can,' Maria said. 'Clearly I am not well trained but I will try to make up for that. If we live in Madrid; good. If we must live in any other place; good. If we live nowhere and I can go with thee; better. If we go to thy country I will learn to talk *Inglés* like the most *Inglés* that there is. I will study all their manners and as they do so will I do.'

'Thou wilt be very comic.'

'Surely. I will make mistakes but you will tell me and I will never make them twice, or maybe only twice. Then in thy country if thou art lonesome for our food I can cook for thee. And I will go to a school to learn to be a wife, if there is such a school, and study at it.'

'There are such schools but thou dost not need that schooling.'

'Pilar told me that she thought they existed in your country. She had read of them in a periodical. And she told me also that I must learn to speak *Inglés* and to speak it well so thou wouldst never be ashamed of me.'

'When did she tell you this?'

'Today while we were packing. Constantly she talked to me about what I should do to be thy wife.'

I guess she was going to Madrid too, Robert Jordan thought, and said, 'What else did she say?'

'She said I must take care of my body and guard the line of my figure as though I were a bullfighter. She said this was of great importance.'

'It is,' Robert Jordan said. 'But thou hast not to worry about that for many years.'

'No. She said those of our race must watch that always as it can come suddenly. She told me she was once as slender as I but that in those days women did not take exercise. She told me what exercises I should take and that I must not eat too much. She told me which things not to eat. But I have forgotten and must ask her again.'

'Potatoes,' he said.

'Yes,' she went on. 'It was potatoes and things that are fried. Also when I told her about this of the soreness she said I must not tell thee but must support the pain and not let thee know. But I told thee because I do not wish to lie to thee ever and also I feared that thou might think we did not have the joy in common any longer and that other, as it was in the high country, had not truly happened.'

'It was right to tell me.'

'Truly? For I am ashamed and I will do anything for thee that thou should wish. Pilar has told me of things one can do for a husband.'

'There is no need to do anything. What we have we have together and we will keep it and guard it. I love thee thus lying beside thee and touching thee and knowing thou art truly there and when t 'Nay. We will have our necessities together. I have no necessities apart from hou art ready again we will have all.'

'But hast thou not necessities that I can care for? She explained that to me.'thee.'

'That seems much better to me. But understand always that I will do what you wish. But thou must tell me for I have great ignorance and much of what she told me I did not understand clearly. For I was ashamed to ask and she is of such great and varied wisdom.'

'Rabbit,' he said. 'Thou art very wonderful.'

'*Qué va*,' she said. 'But to try to learn all of that which goes into wifehood in a day while we are breaking camp and packing for a battle with another battle passing in the country above is a rare thing and if I make serious mistakes thou must tell me for I love thee. It could be possible for me to remember things incorrectly and much that she told me was very complicated.'

'What else did she tell thee?'

'*Pues* so many things I cannot remember them. She said I could tell thee of what was done to me if I ever began to think of it again because thou art a good man and already have understood it all. But that it were better never to speak of it unless it came on me as a black thing as it had been before and then that telling it to thee might rid me of it.'

'Does it weigh on thee now?'

'No. It is as though it had never happened since we were first together. There is the sorrow for my parents always. But that there will be always. But I would have thee know that which you should know for thy own pride if I am to be thy wife. Never did I submit to any one. Always I fought and always it took two of them or more to do me the harm. One would sit on my head and hold me. I tell thee this for thy pride.'

'My pride is in thee. Do not tell it.'

'Nay, I speak of thy own pride which it is necessary to have in thy wife. And another thing. My father was the mayor of the village and an honorable man. My mother was an honorable woman and a good Catholic and they shot her with my father because of the politics of my father who was a Republican. I saw both of them shut and my father said, '*Viva la Republica*,' when they shot him standing against the wall of the slaughterhouse of our village.

'My mother standing against the same wall said, 'Viva my husband who was the Mayor of this village,' and I hoped they would shoot me too and I was going to say *'Viva la Republica y vivan mis padres,'* but instead there was no shooting but instead the doing of the things.

'Listen. I will tell thee of one thing since it affects us. After the shooting at the *matadero* they took us, those relatives who had seen it but were not shot, back from the *matadero* up the steep hill into the main square of the town. Nearly all were weeping but some were numb with what they had seen and the tears had dried in them. I myself could not cry. I did not notice anything that passed for I could only see my father and my mother at the moment of the shooting and my mother saying, 'Long live my husband who was Mayor of this village,' and this was in my head like a scream that would not die but kept on and on. For my mother was not a Republican and she would not say, *'Viva la Republica,'* but only *Viva* my father who lay there, on his face, by her feet.

'But what she had said, she had said very loud, like a shriek and then they shot and she fell and I tried to leave the line to go to her but we were all tied. The shooting was done by the *guardia civil* and they were still there waiting to shoot more when the Falangists herded us away and up the hill leaving the *guardias civiles* leaning on their rifles and leaving all the bodies there against the wall. We were tied by the wrists in a long line of girls and women and they herded us up by the hill and through the streets to the square and in the square they stopped in front of the barbershop which was across the square from the city hall.

'Then the two men looked at us and one said, 'That is the daughter of the Mayor,' and the other said, 'Commence with her.'

'Then they cut the rope that was on each of my wrists, one saying to others of them, 'Tie up the line,' and these two took me by the arms and into the barbershop and lifted me up and put me in the barber's chair and held me there.

'I saw my face in the mirror of the barbershop and the faces of those who were holding me and the faces of three others who were leaning over me and I knew none of their faces but in the glass I saw myself and them, but they saw only me. And it was as though one were in the dentist's chair and there were many dentists and they were all insane. My own face I could hardly recognize because my grief had changed it but I looked at it and knew that it was me. But my grief was so great that I had no fear nor any feeling but my grief.

'At that time I wore my hair in two braids and as I watched in the mirror one of them lifted one of the braids and pulled on it so it hurt me suddenly through my grief and then cut it off close to my head with a razor. And I saw myself with one braid and a slash where the other had been. Then he cut off the other braid but without pulling on it and the razor made a small cut on my ear and I saw blood come from it. thou feel the scar with thy finger?'

'Yes. But would it be better not to talk of this?'

'This is nothing. I will not talk of that which is bad. So he had cut both braids close to my head with a razor and the others laughed and I did not even feel the cut on my ear and then he stood in front of me and struck me across the face with the braids while the other two held me and he said, 'This is how we make Red nuns. This will show thee how to unite with thy proletarian brothers. Bride of the Red Christ!'

'And he struck me again and again across the face with the braids which had been mine and then he put the two of them in my mouth and tied them tight around my neck, knotting them in the back to make a gag and the two holding me laughed.

'And all of them who saw it laughed and when I saw them laugh in the mirror I commenced to cry because until then I had been too frozen in myself from the shooting to be able to cry.

'Then the one who had gagged me ran a clippers all over my head; first from the forehead all the way to the back of the neck and then across the top and then all over my head and close behind my ears and they held me so I could see into the glass of the barber's mirror all the time that they did this and I could not believe it as I saw it done and I cried and I cried but I could not look away from the horror that my face made with the mouth open and the braids tied in it and my head coming naked under the clippers.

'And when the one with the clippers was finsihed he took a bottle of iodine from the shelf of the barber (they had shot the barber too for he belonged to a syndicate, and he lay in the doorway of the shop and they had lifted me over him as they brought me in) and with the glass wand that is in the iodine bottle he touched me on the ear where it had been cut and the small pain of that came through my grief and through my horror.

'Then he stood in front of me and wrote U. H. P. on my forehead with the iodine, lettering it slowly and carefully as though he were an artist and I saw all of this as it happened in the mirror and I no longer cried for my heart was frozen in me for my father and my mother and what happened to me now was nothing and I knew it.

'Then when he had finished the lettering, the Falangist stepped back and looked at me to examine his work and then he put down the iodine bottle and picked up the clippers and said, 'Next,' and they took me out of the barbershop holding me tight by each arm and I stumbled over the barber lying there still in the doorway on his back with his gray face up, and we nearly collided with Concepcion Grada, my best friend, that two of them were bringing in and when she saw me she did not recognize me, and then she recognized me, and she screamed, and I could hear her screaming all the time they were shoving me across the square, and into the doorway, and up the stairs of the city hall and into the office of my father where they laid me onto the couch. And it was there that the bad things were done.'

'My rabbit,' Robert Jordan said and held her as close and as gently as he could. But he was as full of hate as any man could be. 'Do not talk more about it. Do not tell me any more for I cannot bear my hatred now.'

She was stiff and cold in his arms and she said, 'Nay. I will never talk more of it. But they are bad people and I would like to kill some of them with thee if I could. But I have told thee this only for thy pride if! am to be thy wife. So thou wouldst understand.'

'I am glad you told me,' he said. 'For tomorrow, with luck, we will kill plenty.'

'But will we kill Falangists? It was they who did it.'

'They do not fight,' he said gloomily. 'They kill at the rear. It is not them we fight in battle.'

'But can we not kill them in some way? I would like to kill some very much.'

'I have killed them,' he said. 'And we will kill them again. At the trains we have killed them.'

'I would like to go for a train with thee,' Maria said. 'The time of the train that Pilar brought me back from I was somewhat crazy. Did she tell thee how I was?'

'Yes. Do not talk of it.'

'I was dead in my head with a numbness and all I could do was cry. But there is another thing that I must tell thee. This I must. Then perhaps thou wilt not marry me. But, Roberto, if thou should not wish to marry me, can we not, then, just be always together?'

'I will marry thee.'

'Nay. I had forgotten this. Perhaps you should not. It is possible that I can never bear thee either a son or a daughter for the Pilar says that if I could it would have happened to me with the things which were done. I must tell thee that. Oh, I do not know why I had forgotten that.'

'It is of no importance, rabbit,' he said. 'First it may not be true. That is for a doctor to say. Then I would not wish to bring either a son or a daughter into this world as this world is. And also you take all the love I have to give.'

'I would like to bear thy son and thy daughter,' she told him. 'And how can the world be made better if there are no children of us who fight against the fascists?'

'Thou,' he said. 'I love thee. Hearest thou? And now we must sleep, rabbit. For I must be up long before daylight and the dawn comes early in this month.'

'Then it is all right about the last thing I said? We can still be married?'

'We are married, now. I marry thee now. Thou art my wife. But go to sleep, my rabbit, for there is little time now.'

'And we will truly be married? Not just a talking?'

'Truly.'

'Then I will sleep and think of that if I wake.'

'I, too.'

'Good night, my husband.'

'Good night,' he said. 'Good night, wife.'

He heard her breathing steadily and regularly now and he knew she was asleep and he lay awake and very still not wanting to waken her by moving. He thought of all the part she had not told him and he lay there hating and he was pleased there would be killing in the morning. But I must not take any of it personally, he thought.

Though how can I keep from it? I know that we did dreadful things to them too. But it was because we were uneducated and knew no better. But they did that on purpose and deliberately. Those who did that are the last flowering of what their education has produced. Those are the flowers of Spanish chivalry. What a people they have been. What sons of bitches from Cortez, Pizarro, Menendez de Avila all down through Enrique Lister to Pablo. And what wonderful people. There is no finer and no worse people in the world. No kinder people and no crueler. And who understands them? Not me, because if I did I would forgive it all. To understand is to forgive. That's not true. Forgiveness has been exaggerated. Forgiveness is a Christian idea and Spain has never been a Christian country. It has always had its own special idol worship within the Church. *Otra Virgen más.* I suppose that was why they had to destroy the virgins of their enemies. Surely it was deeper with them, with the Spanish religion fanatics, than it was with the people. The people had grown away from the Church because the Church was in the government and the government had always been rotten. This was the only country that the reformation never reached. They were paying for the Inquisition now, all right.

Well, it was something to think about. Something to keep your mind from worrying about your work. It was sounder than pretending. God, he had done a lot of pretending tonight. And Pilar had been pretending all day. Sure. What if they were killed tomorrow? What did it matter as long as they did the bridge properly? That was all they had to do tomorrow.

It didn't. You couldn't do these things indefinitely. But you weren't supposed to live forever. Maybe I have had all my life in three days, he thought. If that's true I wish we would have spent the last night differently. But last nights are never any good. Last nothings are any good. Yes, last words were good sometimes.

'*Viva* my husband who was Mayor of this town' was good.

He knew it was good because it made a tingle run all over him when he said it to himself. He leaned over and kissed Maria who did not wake. In English he whispered very quietly, 'I'd like to marry you, rabbit. I'm very proud of your family.'

32

On that same night in Madrid there were many people at the Hotel Gaylord. A car pulled up under the porte-cochere of the hotel, its headlights painted over with blue calcimine and a little man in black riding boots, gray riding breeches and a short, gray high-buttoned jacket stepped out and returned the salute of the two sentries as he opened the door, nodded to the secret policeman who sat at the concierge's desk and stepped into the elevator. There were two sentries seated on chairs inside the door, one on each side of the marble entrance hall, and these only looked up as the little man passed them at the door of the elevator. It was their business to feel every one they did not know along the flanks, under the armpits, and over the hip pockets to see if the person entering carried a pistol and, if he did, have him check it with the concierge. Rut they knew the short man in riding boots very well and they hardly looked up as he passed.

The apartment where he lived in Gaylord's was crowded as he entered. People were sitting and standing about and talking together as in any drawing room and the men and the women were drinking vodka, whiskey and soda, and beer from small glasses filled from great pitchers. Four of the men were in uniform. The others wore windbreakers or leather jackets and three of the four women were dressed in ordinary street dresses while the fourth, who was haggardly thin and dark, wore a sort of severely cut militiawoman's uniform with a skirt with high boots under it.

When he came into the room, Karkov went at once to the woman in the uniform and bowed to her and shook hands. She was his wife and he said something to her in Russian that no one could hear and for a moment the insolence that had been in his eyes as he entered the room was gone. Then it lighted again as he saw the mahogany-colored head and the love-lazy face of the well-constructed girl who was his mistress and he strode with short, precise steps over to her and bowed and shook her hand in such a way that no one could tell it was not a mimicry of his greeting to his wife. His wife had not looked after him as he walked across the room. She was standing with a tall, good-looking Spanish officer and they were talking Russian now.

'Your great love is getting a little fat,' Karkov was saying to the girl. 'All of our heroes are fattening now as we approach the second year.' He did not look at the man he was speaking of.

'You are so ugly you would be jealous of a toad,' the girl told him cheerfully. She spoke in German. 'Can I go with thee to the offensive tomorrow?'

'No. Nor is there one.'

'Every one knows about it,' the girl said. 'Don't be so mysterious. Dolores is going. I will go with her or Carmen. Many people are going.'

'Go with whoever will take you,' Karkov said. 'I will not.'

Then he turned to the girl and asked seriously, 'Who told thee of it? Be exact.'

'Richard,' she said as seriously.

Karkov shrugged his shoulders and left her standing.

'Karkov,' a man of middle height with a gray, heavy, sagging face, puffed eye pouches and a pendulous under-lip called to him in a dyspeptic voice. 'Have you heard the good news?'

Karkov went over to him and the man said, 'I only have it now. Not ten minutes ago. It is wonderful. All day the fascists have been fighting among themselves near Segovia. They have been forced to quell the mutinies with automatic rifle and machine gun fire. In the afternoon they were bombing their own troops with planes.'

'Yes?' asked Karkov.

'That is true,' the puffy-eyed man said. 'Dolores brought the news herself. She was here with the news and was in such a state of radiant exultation as I have never seen. The truth of the news shone from her face. That great face-' he said happily.

'That great face,' Karkov said with no tone in his voice at all.

'If you could have heard her,' the puffy-eyed man said. 'The news itself shone from her with a light that was not of this world. In her voice you could tell the truth of what she said. I am putting it in an article for *Izvestia*. It was one of the greatest moments of the war to me when I heard the report in that great voice where pity, compassion and truth are blended. Goodness and truth shine from her as from a true saint of the people. Not for nothing IS she called La Pasionaria.'

'Not for nothing,' Karkov said in a dull voice. 'You better write it for *Izvestia* now, before you forget that last beautiful lead.'

'That is a woman that is not to joke about. Not even by a cynic like you,' the puffy-eyed man said. 'If you could have been here to hear her and to see her face.'

'That great voice,' Karkov said. 'That great face. Write it,' he said. 'Don't tell it to me. Don't waste whole paragraphs on me. Go and write it now.'

'Not just now.'

'I think you'd better,' Karkov said and looked at him, and then looked away. The puffy-eyed man stood there a couple of minutes more holding his glass of vodka, his eyes, puffy as they were, absorbed in the beauty of what he had seen and heard and then he left the room to write it.

Karkov went over to another man of about forty-eight, who was short, chunky, jovial-looking with pale blue eyes, thinning blond hair and a gay mouth under a bristly yellow moustache. This man was in uniform. He was a divisional commander and he was a Hungarian.

'Were you here when the Dolores was here?' Karkov asked the man.

'Yes.'

'What was the stuff?'

'Something about the fascists fighting among themselves. Beautiful if true.'

'You hear much talk of tomorrow.'

'Scandalous. All the journalists should be shot as well as most of the people in this room and certainly the intriguing German unmentionable of a Richard. Whoever gave that Sunday *Juggler* command of a brigade should be shot. Perhaps you and me should be shot too. It is possible,' the General laughed. 'Don't suggest it though.'

'That is a thing I never like to talk about,' Karkov said. 'That American who comes here sometimes is over there. You know the one, Jordan, who is with the *partizan* group. He is there where this business they spoke of is supposed to happen.'

'Well, he should have a report through on it tonight then,' the General said. 'They don't like me down there or I'd go down and find out for you. He works with Golz on this, doesn't he? You'll see Golz tomorrow.'

'Early tomorrow.'

'Keep out of his way until it's going well,' the General said. 'He hates you bastards as much as I do. Though he has a much better temper.'

'But about this—'

'It was probably the fascists having maneuvers,' the General grinned. 'Well, we'll see if Golz can maneuvers them a little. Let Golz try his hand at it. We maneuvers them at Guadalajara.'

'I hear you are travelling too,' Karkov said, showing his bad teeth as he smiled. The General was suddenly angry.

'And me too. Now is the mouth on me. And on all of us always. This filthy sewing circle of gossip. One man who could keep his mouth shut could save the country if he believed he could.'

'Your friend Prieto can keep his mouth shut.'

'But he doesn't believe he can win. How can you win without belief in the people?'

'You decide that,' Karkov said. 'I am going to get a little sleep.'

He left the smoky, gossip-filled room and went into the back bedroom and sat down on the bed and pulled his boots off. He could still hear them talking so he shut the door and opened the window. He did not bother to undress because at two o'clock he would be starting for the drive by Colmenar, Cerceda, and Navacerrada up to the front where Golz would be attacking in the morning.

33

It was two o'clock in the morning when Pilar waked him. As her hand touched him he thought, at first, it was Maria and he rolled toward her and said, 'Rabbit.' Then the woman's big hand shook his shoulder and he was suddenly, completely and absolutely awake and his hand was around the butt of the pistol that lay alongside of his bare right leg and all of him was as cocked as the pistol with its safety catch slipped off.

In the dark he saw it was Pilar and he looked at the dial of his wrist watch with the two hands shining in the short angle close to the top and seeing it was only two, he said, 'What passes with thee, woman?'

'Pablo is gone,' the big woman said to him.

Robert Jordan put on his trousers and shoes. Maria had not waked. 'When?' he asked.

'It must be an hour.'

'And?'

'He has taken something of thine,' the woman said miserably. 'So. What?'

'I do not know,' she told him. 'Come and see.'

In the dark they walked over to the entrance of the cave, ducked under the blanket and went in. Robert Jordan followed her in the dead-ashes, bad-air and sleeping-men smell of the cave, shining his electric torch so that he would not step on any of those who were sleeping on the floor. Anselmo woke and said, 'Is it time?'

'No,' Robert Jordan whispered. 'Sleep, old one.'

The two sacks were at the head of Pilar's bed which was screened off with a hanging blanket from the rest of the cave. The bed smelt stale and sweat-dried and sickly-sweet the way an Indian's bed does as Robert Jordan knelt on it and shone the torch on the two sacks. There was a long slit from top to bottom in each one. Holding the torch in his left hand, Robert Jordan felt in the first sack with his right hand. This was the one that he carried his robe in and it should not be very full. It was not very full. There was some wire in it still but the square wooden box of the exploder was gone. So was the cigar box with the carefully wrapped and packed detonators. So was the screw-top tin with the fuse and the caps.

Robert Jordan felt in the other sack. It was still full of explosive. There might be one packet missing.

He stood up and turned to the woman. There is a hollow empty feeling that a man can have when he is waked too early in the morning that is almost like the feeling of disaster and he had this multiplied a thousand times.

'And this is what you call guarding one's materials,' he said.

'I slept with my head against them and one arm touching them,' Pilar told him.

'You slept well.'

'Listen,' the woman said. 'He got up in the night and I said, 'Where do you go, Pablo?' 'To urinate, woman,' he told me and I slept again. When I woke again I did not know what time had passed but I thought, when he was not there, that he had gone down to look at the horses as was his custom. Then,' she finished miserably, 'when he did not come I worried and when I worried I felt of the sacks to be sure all was well and there were the slit places and I came to thee.'

'Come on,' Robert Jordan said.

They were outside now and it was still so near the middle of the night that you could not feel the morning coming.

'Can he get out with the horses other ways than by the sentry?'

'Two ways.'

'Who's at the top?'

'Eladio.'

Robert Jordan said nothing more until they reached the meadow where the horses were staked out to feed. There were three horses feeding in the meadow. The big bay and the gray were gone.

'How long ago do you think it was he left you?'

'It must have been an hour.'

'Then that is that,' Robert Jordan said. 'I go to get what is left of my sacks and go back to bed.'

'I will guard them.'

'Que va, you will guard them. You've guarded them once already.' 'Inglés,' the woman said, 'I feel in regard to this as you do. There is nothing I would not do to bring back thy property. You have no need to hurt me. We have both been betrayed by Pablo.'

As she said this Robert Jordan realized that he could not afford the luxury of being bitter, that he could not quarrel with this woman. He had to work with this woman on that day that was already two hours and more gone.

He put his hand on her shoulder. 'It is nothing, Pilar,' he told her. 'What is gone is of small importance. We shall improvise something that will do as well.'

'But what did he take?'

'Nothing, woman. Some luxuries that one permits oneself.'

'Was it part of thy mechanism for the exploding?'

'Yes. But there are other ways to do the exploding. Tell me, did Pablo not have caps and fuse? Surely they would have equipped him with those?'

'He has taken them,' she said miserably. 'I looked at once for them. They are gone, too.'

They walked back through the woods to the entrance of the cave.

'Get some sleep,' he said. 'We are better off with Pablo gone.' 'I go to see Eladio.'

'He will have gone another way.'

'I go anyway. I have betrayed thee with my lack of smartness.' 'Nay,' he said. 'Get some sleep, woman. We must be under way at four.'

He went into the cave with her and brought out the two sacks, carrying them held together in both arms so that nothing could spill from the slits.

'Let me sew them up.'

'Before we start,' he said softly. 'I take them not against you but so that J can sleep.'

'I must have them early to sew them.'

'You shall have them early,' he told her. 'Get some sleep, woman.'

'Nay,' she said. 'I have failed thee and I have failed the Republic.'

'Get thee some sleep, woman,' he told her gently. 'Get thee some sleep.'

34

The fascists held the crests of the hills here. Then there was a valley that no one held except for a fascist post in a farmhouse with its outbuildings and its barn that they had fortified. Andres, on his way to Golz with the message from Robert Jordan, made a wide circle around this post in the dark. He knew where there was a trip wire laid that fired a set-gun and he located it in the dark, stepped over it, and started along the small stream bordered with poplars whose leaves were moving with the night wind. A cock crowed at the farmhouse that was the fascist post and as he walked along the stream he looked back and saw, through the trunks of the poplars, a light showing at the lower edge of one of the windows of the farmhouse. The night was quiet and clear and Andres left the stream and struck across the meadow.

There were four haycocks in the meadow that had stood there ever since the fighting in July of the year before. No one had ever carried the hay away and the four seasons that had passed had flattened the cocks and made the hay worthless.

Andres thought what a waste it was as he stepped over a trip wire that ran between two of the haycocks. But the Republicans would have had to carry the hay up the steep Guadarrama slope that rose beyond the meadow and the fascists did not need it, I suppose, he thought.

They have all the hay they need and all the grain. They have much, he thought. But we will give them a blow tomorrow morning. Tomorrow morning we will give them something for Sardo. What barbarians they are! But in the morning there will be dust on the road.

He wanted to get this message-taking over and be back for the attack on the posts in the morning. Did he really want to get back though or did he only pretend he wanted to be back? He knew the reprieved feeling he had felt when the *Inglés* had told him he was to go with the message. He had faced the prospect of the morning calmly. It was what was to be done. He had voted for it and would do it. The wiping out of Sardo had impressed him deeply. But, after all, that was Sardo. That was not them. What they had to do they would do.

But when the *Inglés* had spoken to him of the message he had felt the way he used to feel when he was a boy and he had wakened in the morning of the festival of his village and heard it raining hard so that he knew that it would be too wet and that the bullbaiting in the square would be cancelled.

He loved the bullbaiting when he was a boy and he looked forward to it and to the moment when he would be in the square in the hot sun and the dust with the carts ranged all around to close the exits and to make a closed place into which the bull would come, sliding down out of his box, braking with all four feet, when they pulled the end-gate up. He looked forward with excitement, delight and sweating fear to the moment when, in the square, he would hear the clatter of the bull's horns knocking against the wood of his travelling box, and then the sight of him as he came, sliding, braking out into the square, his head up, his nostrils wide, his ears twitching, dust in the sheen of his black hide, dried crut splashed on his flanks, watching his eyes set wide apart, unblinking eyes under the widespread horns as smooth and solid as driftwood polished by the sand, the sharp tips uptilted so that to see them did something to your heart.

He looked forward all the year to that moment when the bull would come out into the square on that day when you watched his eyes while he made his choice of whom in the square he would attack in that sudden head-lowering, horn-reaching, quick cat-gallop that stopped your heart dead when it started. He had looked forward to that moment all the year when he was a boy; but the feeling when the *Inglés* gave the order about the message was the same as when you woke to hear the reprieve of the rain falling on the slate roof, against the stone wall and into the puddles on the dirt street of the village.

He had always been very brave with the bull in those village *capeas,* as brave as any in the village or of the other near-by villages, and not for anything would he have missed it any year although he did not go to the *capeas* of other villages. He was able to wait still when the bull charged and only jumped aside at the last moment. He waved a sack under his muzzle to draw him off when the bull had some one down and many times he had held and pulled on the horns when the bull had some one on the ground and pulled sideways on the horn, had slapped and kicked him in the face until he left the man to charge some one else.

He had held the bull's tail to pull him away from a fallen man, bracing hard and pulling and twisting. Once he had pulled the tail around with one hand until he could reach a horn with the other and when the bull had lifted his head to charge him he had run backwards, circling with the bull, holding the tail in one hand and the horn in the other until the crowd had swarmed onto the bull with their knives and stabbed him. In the dust and the heat, the shouting, the bull and man and wine smell, he had been in the first of the crowd that threw themselves onto the bull and he knew the feeling when the bull rocked and bucked under him and he lay across the withers with one arm locked around the base of the horn and his hand holding the other horn tight, his fingers locked as his body tossed and wrenched and his left arm felt as though it would tear from the socket while he lay on the hot, dusty, bristly, tossing slope of muscle, the ear clenched tight in his teeth, and drove his knife again and again and again into the swelling, tossing bulge of the neck that was now spouting hot on his fist as he let his weight hang on the high slope of the withers and banged and banged into the neck.

The first time he had bit the ear like that and held onto it, his neck and jaws stiffened against the tossing, they had all made fun of him afterwards. But though they joked him about it they had great respect for him. And every year after that he had to repeat it. They called him the bulldog of Villaconejos and joked about him eating cattle raw. But every one in the village looked forward to seeing him do it and every year he knew that first the bull would come out, then there would be the charges and the tossing, and then when they yelled for the rush for the killing he would place himself to rush through the other attackers and leap for his hold. Then, when it was over, and the bull settled and sunk dead finally under the weight of the killers, he would stand up and walk away ashamed of the ear part, but also as proud as a man could be. And he would go through the carts to wash his hands at the stone fountain and men would clap him on the back and hand him wineskins and say, 'Hurray for you, Bulldog. Long life to your mother.'

Or they would say, 'That's what it is to have a pair of *cojones!* Year after year!'

Andres would be ashamed, empty-feeling, proud and happy, and he would shake them all off and wash his hands and his right arm and wash his knife well and then take one of the wineskins and rinse the ear-taste out of his mouth for that year; spitting the wine on the stone flags of the plaza before he lifted the wineskin high and let the wine spurt into the back of his mouth.

Surely. He was the Bulldog of Villaconejos and not for anything would he have missed doing it each year in his village. But he knew there was no better feeling than that one the sound of the rain gave when he knew he would not have to do it.

But I must go back, he told himself. There is no question but that I must go back for the affair of the posts and the bridge. My brother Eladio is there, who is of my own bone and flesh. Anselmo, Primitivo, Fernando, Agustin, Rafael, though clearly he is not serious, the two women, Pablo and the *Inglés*, though the *Inglés* does not count since he is a foreigner and under orders. They are all in for it. It is impossible that r should escape this proving through the accident of a message. I must deliver this message now quickly and well and then make all haste to return in time for the assault on the posts. It would be ignoble of me not to participate in this action because of the accident of this message. That could not be clearer. And besides, he told himself, as one who suddenly remembers that there will be pleasure too in an engagement only the onerous aspects of which he has been considering, and besides I will enjoy the killing of some fascists. It has been too long since we have destroyed any. Tomorrow can be a day of much valid action. Tomorrow can be a day of concrete acts. Tomorrow can be a day which is worth something. That tomorrow should come and that I should be there.

Just then, as knee deep in the gorse he climbed the steep slope that led to the Republican lines, a partridge flew up from under his feet, exploding in a whirr of wingbeats in the dark and he felt a sudden breath-stopping fright. It is the suddenness, he thought. How can they move their wings that fast? She must be nesting now. I probably trod close to the eggs. If there were not this war I would tie a handkerchief to the bush and come back in the daytime and search out the nest and I could take the eggs and put them under a setting hen and when they hatched we would have little partridges in the poultry yard and I would watch them grow and, when they were grown, I'd use them for callers. I wouldn't blind them because they would be tame. Or do you suppose they would fly off? Probably. Then I would have to blind them.

But I don't like to do that after I have raised them. I could clip the wings or tether them by one leg when I used them for calling. If there was no war I would go with Eladio to get crayfish from that stream back there by the fascist post. One time we got four dozen from that stream in a day. If we go to the Sierra de Gredos after this of the bridge there are fine streams there for trout and for crayfish also. I hope we go to Gredos, he thought. We could make a good life in Gredos in the summer time and in the fall but it would be terribly cold in winter. But by winter maybe we will have won the war.

If our father had not been a Republican both Eladio and I would be soldiers now with the fascists and if one were a soldier with them then there would be no problem. One would obey orders and one would live or die and in the end it would be however it would be. It was easier to live under a regime than to fight it.

But this irregular fighting was a thing of much responsibility. There was much worry if you were one to worry. Eladio thinks more than I do. Also he worries. I believe truly in the cause and I do not worry. But it is a life of much responsibility.

I think that we are born into a time of great difficulty, he thought. I think any other time was probably easier. One suffers little because all of us have been formed to resist suffering. They who suffer are unsuited to this climate. But it is a time of difficult decisions. The fascists attacked and made our decision for us. We fight to live. But I would like to have it so that I could tie a handkerchief to that bush back there and come in the daylight and take the eggs and put them under a hen and be able to see the chicks of the partridge in my own courtyard. I would like such small and regular things.

But you have no house and no courtyard in your no-house, he thought. You have no family but a brother who goes to battle tomorrow and you own nothing but the wind and the sun and an empty belly. The wind is small, he thought, and there is no sun. You have four grenades in your pocket but they are only good to throw away. You have a carbine on your back but it is only good to give away bullets. You have a message to give away. And you' re full of crap that you can give to the earth, he grinned in the dark. You can anoint it also with urine. Everything you have is to give. Thou art a phenomenon of philosophy and an unfortunate man, he told himself and grinned again.

But for all his noble thinking a little while before there was in him that reprieved feeling that had always come with the sound of rain in the village on the morning of the fiesta. Ahead of him now at the top of the ridge was the government position where he knew he would be challenged.

35

Robert Jordan lay in the robe beside the girl Maria who was still sleeping. He lay on his side turned away from the girl and he felt her long body against his back and the touch of it now was just an irony. You, you, he raged at himself. Yes, you. You told yourself the first time you saw him that when he would be friendly would be when the treachery would come. You damned fool. You utter blasted damned fool. Chuck all that. That's not what you have to do now.

What are the chances that he hid them or threw them away? Not so good. Besides you'd never find them in the dark. He would have kept them. He took some dynamite, too. Oh, the dirty, vile, treacherous sod. The dirty rotten crut. Why couldn't he have just mucked off and not have taken the exploder and the detonators? Why was I such an utter god damned fool as to leave them with that bloody woman? The smart, treacherous ugly bastard. The dirty *cabron*.

Cut it out and take it easy, he told himself. You had to take chances and that was the best there was. You're just mucked, he told himself. You're mucked for good and higher than a kite. Keep your damned head and get the anger out and stop this cheap lamenting like a damned wailing wall. It's gone. God damn you, it's gone. Oh damn the dirty swine to hell. You can muck your way out of it. You've got to, you know you've got to blow it if you have to stand there and-cut out that stuff, too. Why don't you ask your grandfather?

Oh, muck my grandfather and muck this whole treacherous muckfaced mucking country and every mucking Spaniard in it on either side and to hell forever. Muck them to hell together, Largo, Prieto, Asensio, Miaja, Raja, all of them. Muck every one of them to death to hell. Much the whole treachery-ridden country. Muck their egotism and their selfishness and their selfishness and their egotism and their conceit and their treachery. Muck them to hell and always. Muck them before we die for them. Muck them after we die for them. Muck them to death and hell. God muck Pablo. Pablo is all of them. God pity the Spanish people. Any leader they have will muck them. One good man, Pablo Iglesias, in two thousand years and everybody else mucking them. How do we know how he would have stood up in this war? I remember when I thought Largo was O.K. Durruti was good and his own people shot him there at the Puente de los Franceses. Shot him because he wanted them to attack. Shot him in the glorious discipline of indiscipline. The cowardly swine. Oh muck them all to hell and be damned. And that Pablo that just mucked off with my exploder and my box of detonators. Oh muck him to deepest hell. But no. He's mucked us instead. They always muck you instead, from Cortez and Menendez de Avila down to Miaja. Look at what Miaja did to Kleber. The bald egotistical swine. The stupid egg-headed bastard. Muck all the insane, egotistical, treacherous swine that have always governed Spain and ruled her armies. Muck everybody but the people and then be damned careful what they turn into when they have power.

His rage began to thin as he exaggerated more and more and spread his scorn and contempt so widely and unjustly that he could no longer believe in it himself. If that were true what are you here for? It's not true and you know it. Look at all the good ones. Look at all the fine ones. He could not bear to be unjust. He hated injustice as he hated cruelty and he lay in his rage that blinded his mind until gradually the anger died down and the red, black, blinding, killing anger was all gone and his mind now as quiet, empty-calm and sharp, cold-seeing as a man is after he has had sexual intercourse with a woman that he does not love.

'And you, you poor rabbit,' he leaned over and said to Maria, who smiled in her sleep and moved close against him. 'I would have struck thee there awhile back if thou had spoken. What an animal a man is in a rage.'

He lay close to the girl now with his arms around her and his chin on her shoulder and lying there he figured out exactly what he would have to do and how he would have to do it.

And it isn't so bad, he thought. It really isn't so bad at all. I don't know whether any one has ever done it before. But there will always be people who will do it from now on, given a similar jam. If we do it and if they hear about it. If they hear about it, yes. If they do not just wonder how it was we did it. We are too short of people but there is no sense to worry about that. I will do the bridge with what we have. God, I'm glad I got over being angry. It was like not being able to breathe in a storm. That being angry is another damned luxury you can't afford.

'It's all figured out, *guapa*,' he said softly against Maria's shoulder. 'You haven't been bothered by any of it. You have not known about it. We'll be killed but we'll blow the bridge. You have not had to worry about it. That isn't much of a wedding present But is not a good night's sleep supposed to be priceless? You had a good night's sleep. See if you can wear that like a ring on your finger. Sleep, *guapa*. Sleep well, my beloved. I do not wake thee. That is all I can do for thee now.'

He lay there holding her very lightly, feeling her breathe and feeling her heart beat, and keeping track of the time on his wrist watch.

36

Andres had challenged at the government position. That is, he had lain down where the ground fell sharply away below the triple belt of wire and shouted up at the rock and earth parapet. There was no continual defensive line and he could easily have passed this position in the dark and made his way farther into the government territory before running into some one who would challenge him. But it seemed safer and simpler to get it over here.

'*Saludf*' he had shouted. '*SaIud, milicianosf*'

He heard a bolt snick as it was pulled back. Then, from farther down the parapet, a rifle fired. There was a crashing crack and a downward stab of yellow in the dark. Andres had flattened at the click, the top of his head hard against the ground.

'Don't shoot, Comrades,' Andres shouted. 'Don't shoot! I want to come in.'

'How many are you?' some one called from behind the parapet. 'One. Me. Alone.'

'Who are you?'

'Andres Lopez of Villaconejos. From the band of Pablo. With a message.'

'Have you your rifle and equipment?' 'Yes, man.'

'We can take in none without rifle and equipment,' the voice said. 'Nor in larger groups than three.'

'I am alone,' Andres shouted. 'It is important. Let me come in.'

He could hear them talking behind the parapet but not what they were saying. Then the voice shouted again, 'How many are you?'

'One. Me. Alone. For the love of God.'

They were talking behind the parapet again. Then the voice came, 'Listen, fascist.'

'I am not a fascist,' Andres shouted. 'I am a *guerrillero* from the band of Pablo. I come with a message for the General Staff.'

'He's crazy,' he heard some one say. 'Toss a bomb at him.' 'Listen,' Andres said. 'I am alone. I am completely by myself. I obscenity in the midst of the holy mysteries that I am alone. Let me come in.'

'He speaks like a Christian,' he heard some one say and laugh.

Then some one else said, 'The best thing is to toss a bomb down on him.'

'No,' Andres shouted. 'That would be a great mistake. This is important. Let me come in.'

It was for this reason that he had never enjoyed trips back and forth between the lines. Sometimes it was better than others. But it was never good.

'You are alone?' the voice called down again.

'*Me cago en la leche,*' Andres shouted. 'How many times must I tell thee? I AM ALONE.'

'Then if you should be alone stand up and hold thy rifle over thy head.'

Andres stood up and put the carbine above his head, holding it in both hands.

'Now come through the wire. We have thee covered with the *máquina,*' the voice called.

Andres was in the first zigzag belt of wire. 'I need my hands to get through the wire,' he shouted.

'Keep them up,' the voice commanded.

'I am held fast by the wire,' Andres called.

'It would have been simpler to have thrown a bomb at him,' a voice said.

'Let him sling his rifle,' another voice said. 'He cannot come through there with his hands above his head. Use a little reason.'

'All these fascists are the same,' the other voice said. 'They demand one condition after another.'

'Listen,' Andres shouted. 'I am no fascist but a *guerrillem* from the band of Pablo. We've killed more fascists than the typhus.'

'I have never heard of the band of Pablo,' the man who was evidently in command of the post said. 'Neither of Peter nor of Paul nor of any of the other saints nor apostles. Nor of their bands. Sling thy rifle over thy shoulder and use thy hands to come through the wire.'

'Before we loose the *máquina* on thee,' another shouted. '*Quepoco amables sois!*' Andres said. 'You're not very amiable.' He was working his way through the wire.

'*Amables,*' some one shouted at him. 'We are in a war, man.'

'It begins to appear so,' Andres said.

'What's he say?' Andres heard a bolt click again.

'Nothing,' he shouted. 'I say nothing. Do not shoot until I get through this fornicating wire.'

'Don't speak badly of our wire,' some one shouted. 'Or we'll toss a bomb on you.'

'*Quiero decir, que buena alambrada,*' Andres shouted. 'What beautiful wire. God in a latrine. What lovely wire. Soon I will be with thee, brothers.'

'Throw a bomb at him,' he heard the one voice say. 'I tell you that's the soundest way to deal with the whole thing.'

'Brothers,' Andres said. He was wet through with sweat and he knew the bomb advocate was perfectly capable of tossing a grenade at any moment. 'I have no importance.'

'I believe it,' the bomb man said.

'You are right,' Andres said. He was working carefully through the third belt of wire and he was very close to the parapet. 'I have no importance of any kind. But the affair is serious. *Muy, muy serio.*'

'There is no more serious thing than liberty,' the bomb man shouted. 'Thou thinkest there is anything more serious than liberty?' he asked challengingly.

'No, man,' Andres said, relieved. He knew now he was up against the crazies; the ones with the black-and-red scarves.

'*Viva la Libertad!*'

'*Viva la F. A. I. Vviala C. N. T.,*' they shouted back at him from the parapet.

'*Viva el anarco-sindicalismo* and liberty.'

'*Viva nosotros*,' Andres shouted. 'Long life to us.'

'He is a coreligionary of ours,' the bomb man said. 'And I might have killed him with this.'

He looked at the grenade in his hand and was deeply moved as Andres climbed over the parapet. Putting his arms around him, the grenade still in one hand, so that it rested against Andres's shoulder blade as he embraced him, the bomb man kissed him on both cheeks.

'I am content that nothing happened to thee, brother,' he said. 'I am very content.'

'Where is thy officer?' Andres asked.

'I command here,' a man said. 'Let me see thy papers.'

He took them into a dugout and looked at them with the light of a candle. There was the little square of folded silk with the colors of the Republic and the seal of the S. I. M. in the center. There was the *Salvoconducto* or safe-conduct pass giving his name, age, height, birthplace and mission that Robert Jordan had written out on a sheet from his notebook and sealed with the S. I. M. rubber stamp and there were the four folded sheets of the dispatch to Golz which were tied around with a cord and sealed with wax and the impression of the metal S. I. M. seal that was set in the top end of the wooden handle of the rubber stamp.

'This 1 have seen,' the man in command of the post said and handed back the piece of silk. 'This you all have, 1 know. But its possession proves nothing without this.' He lifted the *Salvoconducto* and read it through again. 'Where were you born?'

'Villaconejos,' Andres said.

'And what do they raise there?'

'Melons,' Andres said. 'As all the world knows.'

'Who do you know there?'

'Why? Are you from there?'

'Nay. But I have been there. 1 am from Aranjuez.'

'Ask me about any one.'

'Describe Jose Rincon.'

'Who keeps the bodega?'

'Naturally.'

'With a shaved head and a big belly and a cast in one eye.'

'Then this is valid,' the man said and handed him back the paper. 'But what do you do on their side?'

'Our father had installed himself at Villacastin before the movement,' Andres said. 'Down there beyond the mountains on the plain. It was there we were surprised by the movement. Since the movement I have fought with the band of Pablo. But I am in a great hurry, man, to take that dispatch.'

'How goes it in the country of the fascists?' the man commanding asked. He was in no hurry.

'Today we had much *tomate*,' Andres said proudly. 'Today there was plenty of dust on the road all day. Today they wiped out the band of Sordo.'

'And who is Sordo?' the other asked deprecatingly. 'The leader of one of the best bands in the mountains.'

'All of you should come in to the Republic and join the army,' the officer said. 'There is too much of this silly guerilla nonsense going on All of you should come in and submit to our Libertarian discipline. Then when we wished to send out guerillas we would send them out as they are needed.'

Andres was a man endowed with almost supreme patience. He had taken the coming in through the wire calmly. None of this examination had flustered him. He found it perfectly normal that this man should have no understanding of them nor of what they were doing and that he should talk idiocy was to be expected. That it should all go slowly should be expected too; but now he wished to go.

'Listen, *Compadre*,' he said. 'It is very possible that you are right. But I have orders to deliver that dispatch to the General commanding the thirty-fifth Division, which makes an attack at daylight in these hills and it is already late at night and I must go.'

'What attack? What do you know of an attack?'

'Nay. I know nothing. But I must go now to Navacerrada and go on from there. Wilt thou send me to thy commander who will give me transport to go on from there? Send one with me now to respond to him that there be no delay.'

'I distrust all of this greatly,' he said. 'It might have been better to have shot thee as thou approached the wire.'

'You have seen my papers, Comrade, and I have explained my mission,' Andres told him patiently.

'Papers can be forged,' the officer said. 'Any fascist could invent such a mission. I will go with thee myself to the Commander.'

'Good,' Andres said. 'That you should come. But that we should go quickly.'

'Thou, Sanchez. Thou commandest in my place,' the officer said. 'Thou knowest thy duties as well as I do. I take this socalled Comrade to the Commander.'

They started down the shallow trench behind the crest of the hill and in the dark Andres smelt the foulness the defenders of the hill crest had made all through the bracken on that slope. He did not like these people who were like dangerous children; dirty, foul, undisciplined, kind, loving, silly and ignorant but always dangerous because they were armed. He, Andres, was without politics except that he was for the Republic. He had heard these people talk many times and he thought what they said was often beautiful and fine to hear but he did not like them. It is not liberty not to bury the mess one makes, he thought. No animal has more liberty than the cat; but it buries the mess it makes. The cat is the best anarchist. Until they learn that from the cat I cannot respect them.

Ahead of him the officer stopped suddenly. 'You have your *carabine* still,' he said.

'Yes,' Andres said. 'Why not?'

'Give it to me,' the officer said. 'You could shoot me in the back with it.'

'Why?' Andres asked him. 'Why would I shoot thee in the back?'

For Whom the Bell Tolls • 727

'One never knows,' the officer said. 'I trust no one. Give me the carbine.'

Andres unslung it and handed it to him.

'If it pleases thee to carry it,' he said.

'It is better,' the officer said. 'We are safer that way.'

They went on down the hill in the dark.

37

Now Robert Jordan lay with the girl and he watched time passing on his wrist. It went slowly, almost imperceptibly, for it was a small watch and he could not see the second hand. But as he watched the minute hand he found he could almost check its motion with his concentration. The girl's head was under his chin and when he moved his head to look at the watch he felt the cropped head against his cheek, and it was as soft but as alive and silkily rolling as when a marten's fur rises under the caress of your hand when you spread the trap jaws open and lift the marten clear and, holding it, stroke the fur smooth. His throat swelled when his cheek moved against Maria's hair and there was a hollow aching from his throat all through him as he held his arms around her; his head dropped, his eyes close to the watch where the lance-pointed, luminous splinter moved slowly up the left face of the dial. He could see its movement clearly and steadily now and he held Maria close now to slow it. He did not want to wake her but he could not leave her alone now in this last time and he put his lips behind her ear and moved them up along her neck, feeling the smooth skin and the soft touch of her hair on them. He could see the hand moving on the watch and he held her tighter and ran the tip of his tongue along her cheek and onto the lobe of her ear and along the lovely convolutions to the sweet, firm rim at the top, and his tongue was trembling. He felt the trembling run through all of the hollow aching and he saw the hand of the watch now mounting in sharp angle toward the top where the hour was. Now while she still slept he turned her head and put his lips to hers. They lay there, just touching lightly against the sleep-firm mouth and he swung them softly across it, feeling them brush lightly. He turned himself toward her and he felt her shiver along the long, light lovely body and then she sighed, sleeping, and then she, still sleeping, held him too and then, unsleeping, her lips were against his firm and hard and pressing and he said, 'But the pain.'

And she said, 'Nay, there is no pain.'

'Rabbit.'

'Nay, speak not.'

'My rabbit.'

'Speak not. Speak not.'

Then they were together so that as the hand on the watch moved, unseen now, they knew that nothing could ever happen to the one that did not happen to the other, that no other thing could happen more than this; that this was all and always; this was what had been and now and whatever was to come. This, that they were not to have, they were having. They were having now and before and always and now and now and now. Oh, now, now, now, the only now, and above all now, and there is no other now but thou now and now is thy prophet. Now and forever now. Come now, now, for there is no now but now. Yes, now. Now, please now, only now, not anything else only this now, and where are you and where am I and where is the other one, and not why, not ever why, only this now; and on and always please then always now, always now, for now always one now; one only one, there is no other one but one now, one, going now, rising now, sailing now, leaving now, wheeling now, soaring now, away now, all the way now, all of all the way now; one and one is one, is one, is one, is one, is still one, is still one, is one descendingly, is one softly, is one longingly, is one kindly, is one happily, is one in goodness, is one to cherish, is one now on earth with elbows against the cut and slept-on branches of the pine tree with the smell of the pine boughs and the night; to earth conclusively now, and with the morning of the day to come. Then he said, for the other was only in his head and he had said nothing, 'Oh, Maria, I love thee and I thank thee for this.'

Maria said, 'Do not speak. It is better if we do not speak.'

'I must tell thee for it is a great thing.'

'Nay.'

'Rabbit—'

But she held him tight and turned her head away and he asked softly, 'Is it pain, rabbit?'

'Nay,' she said. 'It is that I am thankful too to have been another time in *la gloria*.'

Then afterwards they lay quiet, side by side, all length of ankle, thigh, hip and shoulder touching, Robert Jordan now with the watch where he could see it again and Maria said, 'We have had much good fortune.'

'Yes,' he said, 'we are people of much luck.'

'There is not time to sleep?'

'No,' he said, 'it starts soon now.'

'Then if we must rise let us go to get something to eat.'

'All right.'

'Thou. Thou art not worried about anything?'

'No.'

'Truly?'

'No. Not now.'

'But thou hast worried before?'

'For a while.'

'Is it aught I can help?'

'Nay,' he said. 'You have helped enough.'

'That? That was for me.'

'That was for us both,' he said. 'No one is there alone. Come, rabbit, let us dress.'

But his mind, that was his best companion, was thinking La Gloria. She said La Gloria. It has nothing to do with glory nor La Gloire that the French write and speak about. It is the thing that is in the Cante Hondo and in the Saetas. It is in Greco and in San Juan de la Cruz, of course, and in the others. I am no mystic, but to deny it is as ignorant as though you denied the telephone or that the earth revolves around the sun or that there are other planets than this.

How little we know of what there is to know. I wish that I were going to live a long time instead of going to die today because I have learned much about life in these four days; more, I think, than in all the other time. I'd like to be an old man and to really know. I wonder if you keep on learning or if there is only a certain amount each man can understand. I thought I knew about so many things that I know nothing of. I wish there was more time.

'You taught me a lot, *guapa*,' he said in English.

'What did you say?'

'I have learned much from thee.'

'*Que va*,' she said, 'it is thou who art educated.'

'Educated, he thought. I have the very smallest beginnings of an education. The very small beginnings. If I die on this day it is a waste because I know a few things now. I wonder if you only learn them now because you are over sensitized because of the shortness of the time? There is no such thing as a shortness of time, though. You should have sense enough to know that too. I have been all my life in these hills since I have been here. Anselmo is my oldest friend. I know him better than I know Charles, than I know Chub, than I know Guy, than I know Mike, and I know them well. Agustin, with his vile mouth, is my brother, and I never had a brother. Maria is my true love and my wife. I never had a true love. I never had a wife. She is also my sister, and I never had a sister, and my daughter, and I never will have a daughter. I hate to leave a thing that is so good. He finished tying his rope-soled shoes.

'I find life very interesting,' he said to Maria. She was sitting beside him on the robe, her hands clasped around her ankles. Some one moved the blanket aside from the entrance to the cave and they both saw the light. It was night still and here was no promise of morning except that as he looked up through the pines he saw how low the stars had swung. The morning would be coming fast now in this month.

'Roberto,' Maria said.

'Yes, *guapa*.'

'In this of today we will be together, will we not?'

'After the start, yes.'

'Not at the start?'

'No. Thou wilt be with the horses.'

'I cannot be with thee?'

'No. I have work that only I can do and I would worry about thee.'

'But you will come fast when it is done?'

'Very fast,' he said and grinned in the dark. 'Come, *guapa*, let us go and eat.'

'And thy robe?'

'Roll it up, if it pleases thee.'

'It pleases me,' she said.

'I will help thee.'

'Nay. Let me do it alone.'

She knelt to spread and roll the robe, then changed her mind and stood up and shook it so it flapped. Then she knelt down again to straighten it and roll it. Robert Jordan picked up the two packs, holding them carefully so that nothing would spill from the slits in them, and walked over through the pines to the cavemouth where the smoky blanket hung. It was ten minutes to three by his watch when he pushed the blanket aside with his elbow and went into the cave.

38

They were in the cave and the men were standing before the fire Maria was fanning. Pilar had coffee ready in a pot. She had not gone back to bed at all since she had roused Robert Jordan and now she was sitting on a stool in the smoky cave sewing the rip in one of Jordan's packs. The other pack was already sewed. The firelight lit up her face.

'Take more of the stew,' she said to Fernando. 'What does it matter if thy belly should be full? There is no doctor to operate if you take a goring.'

'Don't speak that way, woman,' Agustin said. 'Thou hast the tongue of the great whore.'

He was leaning on the automatic rifle, its legs folded close against the fretted barrel, his pockets were full of grenades, a sack of pans hung from one shoulder, and a full bandolier of ammunition hung over the other shoulder. He was smoking a cigarette and he held a bowl of coffee in one hand and blew smoke onto its surface as he raised it to his lips.

'Thou art a walking hardware store,' Pilar said to him. 'Thou canst not walk a hundred yards with all that.'

'Que va, woman,' Agustin said. 'It is all downhill.'

'There is a climb to the post,' Fernando said. 'Before the downward slope commences.'

'I will climb it like a goat,' Agustin said.

'And thy brother?' he asked Eladio. 'Thy famous brother has mucked off? '

Eladio was standing against the wall.

'Shut up,' he said.

He was nervous and he knew they all knew it. He was always nervous and irritable before action. He moved from the wall to the table and began filling his pockets with grenades from one of the raw-hide-covered panniers that leaned, open, against the table leg. Robert Jordan squatted by the pannier beside him. He reached into the pannier and picked out four grenades. Three were the oval Mill bomb type, serrated, heavy iron with a spring level held down in position by a cotter pin with pulling rig attached.

'Where did these come from?' he asked Eladio.

'Those? Those are from the Republic. The old man brought them.'

How are they?'

'*Valen mas que pesan*,' Eladio said. 'They are worth a fortune apiece.'

'I brought those,' Anselmo said. 'Sixty in one pack. Ninety pounds, *Inglés*.'

'Have you used those?' Robert Jordan asked Pilar.

'*Que va* have we used them?' the woman said. 'It was with those Pablo slew the post at Otero.'

When she mentioned Pablo, Agustin started cursing. Robert Jordan saw the look on Pilar's face in the firelight.

'Leave it,' she said to Agustin sharply. 'It does no good to talk.' 'Have they always exploded?' Robert Jordan held the gray painted grenade in his hand, trying the bend of the cotter pin with his thumbnail.

'Always,' Eladio said. 'There was not a dud in any of that lot we used.'

'And how quickly?'

'In the distance one can throw it. Quickly. Quickly enough.' 'And these?'

He held up a soup-tin-shaped bomb, with a tape wrapping around a wire loop.

'They are a garbage,' Eladio told him. 'They blow. Yes. But it is all flash and no fragments.'

'But do they always blow?'

'*Que* va, always,' Pilar said. 'There is no always either with our munitions or theirs.'

'But you said the other always blew.'

'Not me,' Pilar told him. 'You asked another, not me. I have seen no *always* in any of that stuff.'

'They all blew,' Eladio insisted. 'Speak the truth, woman.'

'How do you know they all blew?' Pilar asked him. 'It was Pablo who threw them. You killed no one at Otero.' 'That son of the great whore,' Agustin began.

'Leave it alone,' Pilar said sharply. Then she went on. 'They are all much the same, *Inglés*. But the corrugated ones are more simple.'

I'd better use one of each on each set, Robert Jordan thought. But the serrated type will lash easier and more securely.

'Are you going to be throwing bombs, *Inglés*?' Agustín asked. 'Why not?' Robert Jordan said.

But crouched there, sorting out the grenades, what he was thinking was: it is impossible. How I could have deceived myself about it I do not know. We were as sunk when they attacked Sordo as Sordo was sunk when the snow stopped. It is that you can't accept it. You have to go on and make a plan that you know is impossible to carry out. You made it and now you know it is no good. It's no good, now, in the morning. You can take either of the posts absolutely O.K. with what you've got here. But you can't take them both. You can't be sure of it, I mean. Don't deceive yourself. Not when the daylight comes.

Trying to take them both will never work. Pablo knew that all the time. I suppose he always intended to muck off but he knew we were cooked when Sordo was attacked. You can't base an operation on the presumption that miracles are going to happen. You will kill them all off and not even get your bridge blown if you have nothing better than what you have now. You will kill off Pilar, Anselmo, AgustIn, Primitivo, this jumpy Eladio, the worthless gypsy and old Fernando, and you won't get your bridge blown. Do you suppose there will be a miracle and Golz will get the message from Andres and stop it? If there isn't, you are going to kill them all off with those orders. Maria too. You'll kill her too with those orders. Can't you even get her out of it? God damn Pablo to hell, he thought.

No. Don't get angry. Getting angry is as bad as getting scared. But instead of sleeping with your girl you should have ridden all night through these hills with the woman to try to dig up enough people to make it work. Yes, he thought. And if anything happened to me so I was not here to blow it. Yes. That. That's why you weren't out. And you couldn't send anybody out because you couldn't run a chance of losing them and being short one more. You had to keep what you had and make a plan to do it with them.

But your plan stinks. It stinks, I tell you. It was a night plan and it's morning now. Night plans aren't any good in the morning. The way you think at night is no good in the morning. So now you know it is no good.

What if John Mosby did get away with things as impossible as this? Sure he did. Much more difficult. And remember, do not undervaluate the element of surprise. Remember that. Remember it isn't goofy if you can make it stick. But that is not the way you are supposed to make it. You should make it not only possible but sure. But look at how it all has gone. Well, it was wrong in the first place and such things accentuate disaster as a snowball rolls up wet snow.

He looked up from where he was squatted by the table and saw Maria and she smiled at him. He grinned back with the front of his face and selected four more grenades and put them in his pockets. I could unscrew the detonators and just use them, he thought. But I don't think the fragmentation will have any bad effect. It will come instantaneously with the explosion of the charge and it won't disperse it. At least, I don't think it will. I'm sure it won't. Have a little confidence, he told himself. And you, last night, thinking about how you and your grandfather were so terrific and your father was a coward. Show yourself a little confidence now.

He grinned at Maria again but the grin was still no deeper than the skin that felt tight over his cheekbones and his mouth.

She thinks you're wonderful, he thought. I think you stink. And the *gloria* and all that nonsense that you had. You had wonderful ideas, didn't you? You had this world all taped, didn't you? The hell with all of that.

Take it easy, he told himself. Don't get into a rage. That's just a way out too. There are always ways out. You've got to bite on the nail now. There isn't any need to deny everything there's been just because you are going to lose it. Don't be like some damned snake with a broken back biting at itself; and your back isn't broken either, you hound. Wait until you're hurt before you start to cry. Wait until the fight before you get angry. There's lots of time for it in a fight. It will be some use to you in a fight.

Pilar came over to him with the bag.

'It is strong now,' she said. 'Those grenades are very good, *Inglés*. You can have confidence in them.'

'How do you feel, woman?'

She looked at him and shook her head and smiled. He wondered how far into her face the smile went. It looked deep enough.

'Good,' she said. *'Dentro de la gravedad.'*

Then she said, squatting by him, 'How does it seem to thee now that it is really starting?'

'That we are few,' Robert Jordan said to her quickly.

'To me, too,' she said. 'Very few.'

Then she said still to him alone, 'The Maria can hold the horses by herself. I am not needed for that. We will hobble them. They are cavalry horses and the firing will not panic them. I will go to the lower post and do that which was the duty of Pablo. In this way we are one more.'

'Good,' he said. 'I thought you might wish to.'

'Nay, *Inglis*,' Pilar said looking at him closely. 'Do not be worried. All will be well. Remember they expect no such thing to come to them.'

'Yes,' Robert Jordan said.

'One other thing, *Inglés*,' Pilar said as softly as her harsh whisper could be soft. 'In that thing of the hand—'

'What thing of the hand?' he said angrily.

'Nay, listen. Do not be angry, little boy. In regard to that thing of the hand. That is all gypsy nonsense that I make to give myself an importance. There is no such thing.'

'Leave it alone,' he said coldly.

'Nay,' she said harshly and lovingly. 'It is just a lying nonsense that I make. I would not have thee worry in the day of battle.'

'I am not worried,' Robert Jordan said.

'Yes, *Inglis*,' she said. 'Thou art very worried, for good cause. But all will be well, *Inglés*. It is for this that we are born.'

'I don't need a political commissar,' Robert Jordan told her.

She smiled at him again, smiling fairly and truly with the harsh lips and the wide mouth, and said, 'I care for thee very much, *Inglés*.'

'I don't want that now,' he said. *'Ni tu, ni Dios.'*

'Yes,' Pilar said in that husky whisper. 'I know. I only wished to tell thee. And do not worry. We will do all very well.'

'Why not?' Robert Jordan said and the very thinnest edge of the skin in front of his face smiled. 'Of course we will. All will be well.'

'When do we go?' Pilar asked.

Robert Jordan looked at his watch.

'Any time,' he said.

He handed one of the packs to Anselmo.

'How are you doing, old one?' he asked.

The old man was finishing whittling the last of a pile of wedges he had copied from a model Robert Jordan had given him. These were extra wedges in case they should be needed.

'Well,' the old man said and nodded. 'So far, very well.' He held his hand out. 'Look,' he said and smiled. His hands were perfectly steady.

'*Bueno, y que?*' Robert Jordan said to him. 'I can always keep the whole hand steady. Point with one finger.'

Anselmo pointed. The finger was trembling. He looked at Robert Jordan and shook his head.

'Mine too,' Robert Jordan showed him. 'Always. That is normal.'

'Not for me,' Fernando said. He put his right forefinger out to show them. Then the left forefinger.

'Canst thou spit?' Agustin asked him and winked at Robert Jordan.

Fernando hawked and spat proudly onto the floor of the cave, then rubbed it in the dirt with his foot.

'You filthy mule,' Pilar said to him. 'Spit in the fire if thou must vaunt thy courage.'

'I would not have spat on the floor, Pilar, if we were not leaving this place,' Fernando said primly.

'Be careful where you spit today,' Pilar told him. 'It may be some place you will not be leaving.'

'That one speaks like a black cat,' Agustin said. He had the nervous necessity to joke that is another form of what they all felt.

'I joke,' said Pilar.

'Me too,' said Agustin. 'But *me cago en fa feche*, but I will be content when it starts.'

'Where is the gypsy?' Robert Jordan asked Eladio.

'With the horses,' Eladio said. 'You can see him from the cave mouth.'

'How is he?'

Eladio grinned. 'With much fear,' he said. It reassured him to speak of the fear of another.

'Listen, *Inglés*—' Pilar began. Robert Jordan looked toward her and as he did he saw her mouth open and the unbelieving look come on her face and he swung toward the cave mouth reaching for his pistol. There, holding the blanket aside with one hand, the short automatic rifle muzzle with its flash-cone jutting above his shoulder, was Pablo standing short, wide, bristly-faced, his small red-rimmed eyes looking toward no one in particular.

'Thou—' Pilar said to him unbelieving. 'Thou.'

'Me,' said Pablo evenly. He came into the cave.

'*Hola, Inglés,*' he said. 'I have five from the bands of Elias and Alejandro above with their horses.'

'And the exploder and the detonators?' Robert Jordan said. 'And the other material?'

'I threw them down the gorge into the river,' Pablo said still looking at no one. 'But I have thought of a way to detonate using a grenade.'

'So have I,' Robert Jordan said.

'Have you a drink of anything?' Pablo asked wearily.

Robert Jordan handed him the flask and he swallowed fast, then wiped his mouth on the back of his hand.

'What passes with you?' Pilar asked.

'*Nada,*' Pablo said, wiping his mouth again. 'Nothing. I have come back.'

'But what?'

'Nothing. I had a moment of weakness. I went away but I am come back.'

He turned to Robert Jordan. '*En el fondo no soy cobarde,*' he said. 'At bottom I am not a coward.'

But you are very many other things, Robert Jordan thought. Damned if you're not. But I'm glad to see you, you son of a bitch.

'Five was all I could get from Elias and Alejandro,' Pablo said. 'I have ridden since I left here. Nine of you could never have done it. Never. I knew that last night when the *Inglés* explained it. Never. There are seven men and a corporal at the lower post. Suppose there is an alarm or that they fight?'

He looked at Robert Jordan now. 'When I left I thought you would know that it was impossible and would give it up. Then after I had thrown away thy material I saw it in another manner.' 'I am glad to see thee,' Robert Jordan said. He walked over to him. 'We are all right with the grenades. That will work. The other does not matter now.'

'Nay,' Pablo said. 'I do nothing for thee. Thou art a thing of bad omen. All of this comes from thee. Sardo also. But after I had thrown away thy material I found myself too lonely.'

'Thy mother—' Pilar said.

'So I rode for the others to make it possible for it to be successful. I have brought the best that I could get. I have left them at the top so I could speak to you, first. They think I am the leader.'

'Thou art,' Pilar said. 'If thee wishes.' Pablo looked at her and said nothing. Then he said simply and quietly, 'I have thought much since the thing of Sardo. I believe if we must finish we must finish together. But thou, *Inglés*. I hate thee for bringing this to us.'

'But Pablo—' Fernando, his pockets full of grenades, a bandolier of cartridges over his shoulder, he still wiping in his pan of stew with a piece of bread, began. 'Do you not believe the operation can be successful? Night before last you said you were convinced it would be.'

'Give him some more stew,' Pilar said viciously to Maria. Then to Pablo, her eyes softening, 'So you have come back, eh?'

'Yes, woman,' Pablo said.

'Well, thou art welcome,' Pilar said to him. 'I did not think thou couldst be the ruin thou appeared to be.'

'Having done such a thing there is a loneliness that cannot be borne,' Pablo said to her quietly.

'That cannot be borne,' she mocked him. 'That cannot be borne by thee for fifteen minutes.'

'Do not mock me, woman. I have come back.'

'And thou art welcome,' she said. 'Didst not hear me the first time? Drink thy coffee and let us go. So much theatre tires me.'

'Is that coffee?' Pablo asked. 'Certainly,' Fernando said.

'Give me some, Maria,' Pablo said. 'How art thou?' He did not look at her.

'Well,' Maria told him and brought him a bowl of coffee. 'Do you want stew?' Pablo shook his head.

'No me gusta estar solo,' Pablo went on explaining to Pilar as though the others were not there. 'I do not like to be alone. *Sabes?* Yesterday all day alone working for the good of all I was not lonely. But last night. *Hombre! Que mal 10 pase!'*

'Thy predecessor the famous Judas Iscariot hanged himself,' Pilar said.

'Don't talk to me that way, woman,' Pablo said. 'Have you not seen? I am back. Don't talk of Judas nor nothing of that. I am back.'

'How are these people thee brought?' Pilar asked him. 'Hast brought anything worth bringing?'

'Son buenos,' Pablo said. He took a chance and looked at Pilar squarely, then looked away.

'Buenos y *bobos.* Good ones and stupids. Ready to die and all. *A tu gusto.* According to thy taste. The way you like them.'

Pablo looked Pilar in the eyes again and this time he did not look away. He kept on looking at her squarely with his small, red-rimmed pig eyes.

'Thou,' she said and her husky voice was fond again. 'Thou. I suppose if a man has something once, always something of it remains.'

'Listo,' Pablo said, looking at her squarely and flatly now. 'I am ready for what the day brings.'

'I believe thou art back,' Pilar said to him. 'I believe it. But, *hombre,* thou wert a long way gone.'

'Lend me another swallow from thy bottle,' Pablo said to Robert Jordan. 'And then let us be going.'

39

In the dark they came up the hill through the timber to the narrow pass at the top. They were all loaded heavily and they climbed slowly. The horses had loads too, packed over the saddles.

'We can cut them loose if it is necessary,' Pilar had said. 'But with that, if we can keep it, we can make another camp.'

'And the rest of the ammunition?' Robert Jordan had asked as they lashed the packs.

'In those saddle bags.'

Robert Jordan felt the weight of his heavy pack, the dragging on his neck from the pull of his jacket with its pockets full of grenades, the weight of his pistol against his thigh, and the bulging of his trouser pockets where the clips for the submachine gun were. In his mouth was the taste of the coffee, in his right hand he carried the submachine gun and with his left hand he reached and pulled up the collar of his jacket to ease the pull of the pack straps.

'*Inglés*' Pablo said to him, walking close beside him in the dark. 'What, man?'

'These I have brought think this is to be successful because I have brought them,' Pablo said. 'Do not say anything to disillusion them.'

'Good,' Robert Jordan said. 'But let us make it successful.' 'They have five horses, *sabes?*' Pablo said cautiously.

'Good,' said Robert Jordan. 'We will keep all the horses together.'

'Good,' said Pablo, and nothing more.

I didn't think you had experienced any complete conversion on the road to Tarsus, old Pablo, Robert Jordan thought. No. Your coming back was miracle enough. I don't think there will ever be any problem about canonizing you.

'With those five I will deal with the lower post as well as Sordo would have,' Pablo said. 'I will cut the wire and fall back upon the bridge as we convened.'

We went over this all ten minutes ago, Robert Jordan thought. I wonder why this now.

'There is a possibility of making it to Gredos,' Pablo said. 'Truly, I have thought much of it.'

I believe you've had another flash in the last few minutes, Robert Jordan said to himself. You have had another revelation. But you're not going to convince me that I am invited. No, Pablo. Do not ask me to believe too much.

Ever since Pablo had come into the cave and said he had five men Robert Jordan felt increasingly better. Seeing Pablo again had broken the pattern of tragedy into which the whole operation had seemed grooved ever since the snow, and since Pablo had been back he felt not that his luck had turned, since he did not believe in luck, but that the whole thing had turned for the better and that now it was possible. Instead of the surety of failure he felt confidence rising in him as a tire begins to fill with air from a slow pump. There was little difference at first, although there was a definite beginning, as when the pump starts and the rubber of the tube crawls a little, but it came now as steadily as a tide rising or the sap rising in a tree until he began to feel the first edge of that negation of apprehension that often turned into actual happiness before action.

This was the greatest gift that he had, the talent that fitted him for war; that ability not to ignore but to despise whatever bad ending there could be. This quality was destroyed by too much responsibility for others or the necessity of undertaking something ill planned or badly conceived. For in such things the bad ending, failure, could not be ignored. It was not simply a possibility of harm to one's self, which *could* be ignored. He knew he himself was nothing, and he knew death was nothing. He knew that truly, as truly as he knew anything. In the last few days he had learned that he himself, with another person, could be everything. But inside himself he knew that this was the exception. That we have had, he thought. In that I have been most fortunate. That was given to me, perhaps, because I never asked for it. That cannot be taken away nor lost. But that is over and done with now on this morning and what there is to do now is our work.

And you, he said to himself, I am glad to see you getting a little something back that was badly missing for a time. But you were pretty bad back there. I was ashamed enough of you, there for a while. Only I was you. There wasn't any me to judge you. We were all in bad shape. You and me and both of us. Come on now. Quit thinking like a schizophrenic. One at a time, now. You're all right again now. But listen, you must not think of the girl all day ever. You can do nothing now to protect her except to keep her out of it, and that you are doing. There are evidently going to be plenty of horses if you can believe the signs. The best thing you can do for her is to do the job well and fast and get out, and thinking of her will only handicap you in this. So do not think of her ever.

Having thought this out he waited until Maria came up walking with Pilar and Rafael and the horses.

'Hi, *guapa*,' he said to her in the dark, 'how are you?'

'I am well, Roberto,' she said.

'Don't worry about anything,' he said to her and shifting the gun to his left hand he put a hand on her shoulder.

'I do not,' she said.

'It is all very well organized,' he told her. 'Rafael will be with thee with the horses.'

'I would rather be with thee.'

'Nay. The horses is where thou art most useful.'

'Good,' she said. 'There 1 will be.'

Just then one of the horses whinnied and from the open place below the opening through the rocks a horse answered, the neigh rising into a shrill sharply broken quaver.

Robert Jordan saw the bulk of the new horses ahead in the dark. He pressed forward and came up to them with Pablo. The men were standing by their mounts.

'*Salud*,' Robert Jordan said.

'*Salud*,' they answered in the dark. He could not see their faces. 'This is the *Inglés* who comes with us,' Pablo said. 'The dynamiter.'

No one said anything to that. Perhaps they nodded in the dark. 'Let us get going, Pablo,' one man said. 'Soon we will have the daylight on us.'

'Did you bring any more grenades?' another asked.

'Plenty,' said Pablo. 'Supply yourselves when we leave the animals.'

'Then let us go,' another said. 'We've been waiting here half the night.'

'*Hola*, Pilar,' another said as the woman came up.

'*Que me maten,* if it is not Pepe,' Pilar said huskily. 'How are you, shepherd?'

'Good,' said the man. '*Dentro de la gravedad.*'

'What are you riding?' Pilar asked him.

'The gray of Pablo,' the man said. 'It is much horse.'

'Come on,' another man said. 'Let us go. There is no good in gossiping here.'

'How art thou, Elicio?' Pilar said to him as he mounted.

'How would I be?' he said rudely. 'Come on, woman, we have work to do.'

Pablo mounted the big bay horse.

'Keep thy mouths shut and follow me,' he said. 'I will lead you to the place where we will leave the horses.'

40

During the time that Robert Jordan had slept through, the time he had spent planning the destruction of the bridge and the time that he had been with Maria, Andres had made slow progress. Until he had reached the Republican lines he had travelled across country and through the fascist lines as fast as a countryman in good physical condition who knew the country well could travel in the dark. But once inside the Republican lines it went very slowly.

In theory he should only have had to show the safe-conduct given him by Robert Jordan stamped with the seal of the S. I. M. and the dispatch which bore the same seal and be passed along toward his destination with the greatest speed. But first he had encountered the company commander in the front line who had regarded the whole mission with owlishly grave suspicion.

He had followed this company commander to battalion headquarters where the battalion commander, who had been a barber before the movement, was filled with enthusiasm on hearing the account of his mission. This commander, who was named Gomez, cursed the company commander for his stupidity, patted Andres on the back, gave him a drink of bad brandy and told him that he himself, the ex-barber, had always wanted to be a *guerrillero*. He had then roused his adjutant, turned over the battalion to him, and sent his orderly to wake up and bring his motorcyclist. Instead of sending Andres back to brigade headquarters with the motorcyclist, Gomez had decided to take him there himself in order to expedite things and, with Andres holding tight onto the seat ahead of him, they roared, bumping down the shell-pocked mountain road between the double row of big trees, the headlight of the motorcycle showing their whitewashed bases and the places on the trunks where the whitewash and the bark had been chipped and torn by shell fragments and bullets during the fighting along this road in the first summer of the movement. They turned into the little smashed-roofed mountain-resort town where brigade headquarters was and Gomez had braked the motorcycle like a dirt-track racer and leaned it against the wall of the house where a sleepy sentry came to attention as Gomez pushed by him into the big room where the walls were covered with maps and a very sleepy officer with a green eyeshade sat at a desk with a reading lamp, two telephones and a copy of *Mundo Obrero*.

This officer looked up at Gomez and said, 'What doest thou here? Have you never heard of the telephone?'

'I must see the Lieutenant-Colonel,' Gomez said.

'He is asleep,' the officer said. 'I could see the lights of that bicycle of thine for a mile coming down the road. Dost wish to bring on a shelling?'

'Call the Lieutenant-Colonel,' Gomez said. 'This is a matter of the utmost gravity.'

'He is asleep, I tell thee,' the officer said. 'What sort of a bandit is that with thee?' he nodded toward Andres.

'He is *a guerrillero* from the other side of the lines with a dispatch of the utmost importance for the General Golz who commands the attack that is to be made at dawn beyond Navacerrada,' Gomez said excitedly and earnestly. 'Rouse the *Teniente-Coronel* for the love of God.'

The officer looked at him with his droopy eyes shaded by the green celluloid.

'All of you are crazy,' he said. 'I know of no General Golz nor of no attack. Take this sportsman and get back to your battalion.'

'Rouse the *Teniente-Coronel*, I say,' Gomez said and Andres saw his mouth tightening.

'Go obscenity yourself,' the officer said to him lazily and turned away.

Gomez took his heavy 9 mm. Star pistol out of its holster and shoved it against the officer's shoulder.

'Rouse him, you fascist bastard,' he said. 'Rouse him or I'll kill you.'

'Calm yourself,' the officer said. 'All you barbers are emotional.' Andres saw Gomez's face draw with hate in the light of the reading lamp. But all he said was, 'Rouse him.'

'Orderly,' the officer called in a contemptuous voice. A soldier came to the door and saluted and went out.

'His fiancée is with him,' the officer said and went back to reading the paper. 'It is certain he will be delighted to see you.' 'It is those like thee who obstruct all effort to win this war,' Gomez said to the staff officer.

The officer paid no attention to him. Then, as he read on, he remarked, as though to himself, 'What a curious periodical this is!'

'Why don't you real *El Debate* then? That is your paper,' Gomez said to him naming the leading Catholic-Conservative organ published in Madrid before the movement.

'Don't forget I am thy superior officer and that a report by me on thee carries weight,' the officer said without looking up. 'I never read *El Debate*. Do not make false accusations.'

'No. You read A. B. C.,' Gomez said. 'The army is still rotten with such as thee. With professionals such as thee. But it will not always be. We are caught between the ignorant and the cynical. But we will educate the one and eliminate the other.'

'Purge' is the word you want,' the officer said, still not looking up. 'Here it reports the purging of more of thy famous Russians. They are purging more than the epsom salts in this epoch.'

'By any name,' Gomez said passionately. 'By any name so that such as thee are liquidated.'

'Liquidated,' the officer said insolently as though speaking to himself. 'Another new word that has little of Castilian in it.'

'Shot, then,' Gomez said. 'That is Castilian. Canst understand it?'

'Yes, man, but do not talk so loudly. There are others beside the *Teniente-Coronel* asleep in this Brigade Staff and thy emotion bores me. It was for that reason that I always shaved myself. I never liked the conversation.'

Gomez looked at Andres and shook his head. His eyes were shining with the moistness that rage and hatred can bring. But he shook his head and said nothing as he stored it all away for some time in the future. He had stored much in the year and a half in which he had risen to the command of a battalion in the Sierra and now, as the Lieutenant-Colonel came into the room in his pajamas he drew himself stiff and saluted.

The Lieutenant-Colonel Miranda, who was a short, gray-faced man, who had been in the army all his life, who had lost the love of his wife in Madrid while he was losing his digestion in Morocco, and become a Republican when he found he could not divorce his wife (there was never any question of recovering his digestion), had entered the civil war as a Lieutenant-Colonel. He had only one ambition, to finish the war with the same rank. He had defended the Sierra well and he wanted to be left alone there to defend it whenever it was attacked. He felt much healthier in the war, probably due to the forced curtailment of the number of meat courses, he had an enormous stock of sodium-bicarbonate, he had his whiskey in the evening, his twenty-three-year-old mistress was having a baby, as were nearly all the other girls who had started out as *milicianas* in the July of the year before, and now he came into the room, nodded in answer to Gomez's salute and put out his hand.

'What brings thee, Gomez?' he asked and then, to the officer at the desk who was his chief of operation, 'Give me a cigarette, please, Pepe.'

Gomez showed him Andres's papers and the dispatch. The Lieutenant-Colonel looked at the *Salvoconducto* quickly, looked at Andres, nodded and smiled, and then looked at the dispatch hungrily. He felt of the seal, tested it with his forefinger, then handed both the safe-conduct and dispatch back to Andres.

'Is the life very hard there in the hills?' he asked. 'No, my Lieutenant-Colonel,' Andres said.

'Did they tell thee where would be the closest point to find General Golz's headquarters?'

'Navacerrada, my Lieutenant-Colonel,' Andres said. 'The *Inglés* said it would be somewhere close to Navacerrada behind the lines to the right of there.'

'What *Inglés*?' the Lieutenant-Colonel asked quietly.

'The *Inglés* who is with us as a dynamiter.'

The Lieutenant-Colonel nodded. It was just another sudden unexplained rarity of this war. 'The *Inglés* who is with us as a dynamiter.'

'You had better take him, Gomez, on the motor,' the LieutenantColonel said.

'Write them a very strong *Salvoconducto* to the *Estado Mayor* of General Golz for me to sign,' he said to the officer in the green celluloid eyeshade. 'Write it on the machine, Pepe. Here are the details,' he motioned for Andres to hand over his safeconduct, 'and put on two seals.' He turned to Gomez. 'You will need something strong tonight. It is rightly so. People should be careful when an offensive is projected. I will give you something as strong as I can make it.' Then to Andres, very kindly, he said, 'Dost wish anything? To eat or to drink?'

'No, my Lieutenant-Colonel,' Andres said. 'I am not hungry. They gave me cognac at the last place of command and more would make me seasick.'

'Did you see any movement or activity opposite my front as you came through?' the Lieutenant-Colonel asked Andres politely.

'It was as usual, my Lieutenant-Colonel. Quiet. Quiet.'

'Did I not meet thee in Cercedilla about three months back?' the Lieutenant-Colonel asked.

'Yes, my Lieutenant-Colonel.'

'I thought so,' the Lieutenant-Colonel patted him on the shoulder. 'You were with the old man Anselmo. How is he?'

'He is well, my Lieutenant-Colonel,' Andres told him.

'Good. It makes me happy,' the Lieutenant-Colonel said. The officer showed him what he had typed and he read it over and signed it. 'You must go now quickly,' he said to Gomez and Andres. 'Be careful with the motor,' he said to Gomez. 'Use your lights. Nothing will happen from a sillgle motor and you must be careful. My compliments to Comrade General Golz. We met after Peguerinos.' He shook hands with them both. 'Button the papers inside thy shirt,' he said. 'There is much wind on a motor.'

After they went out he went to a cabinet, took out a glass and a bottle, and poured himself some whiskey and poured plain water into it from an earthenware crock that stood on the floor against the wall. Then holding the glass and sipping the whiskey very slowly he stood in front of the big map on the wall and studied the offensive possibilities in the country above Navacerrada.

'I am glad it is Golz and not me,' he said finally to the officer who sat at the table. The officer did not answer and looking away from the map and at the officer the Lieutenant-Colonel saw he was asleep with his head on his arms. The Lieutenant-Colonel went over to the desk and pushed the two phones close together so that one touched the officer's head on either side. Then he walked to the cupboard, poured himself another whiskey, put water in it, and went back to the map again.

Andres, holding tight onto the seat where Gomez was forking the motor, bent his head against the wind as the motorcycle moved, noisily exploding, into the light-split darkness of the country road that opened ahead sharp with the high black of the poplars beside it, dimmed and yellow-soft now as the road dipped into the fog along a steam bed, sharpening hard again as the road rose and, ahead of them at the crossroads, the headlight showed the gray bulk of the empty trucks coming down from the mountains.

41

Parlo stopped and dismounted in the dark. Robert Jordan heard the creaking and the heavy breathing as they all dismounted and the clinking of a bridle as a horse tossed his head. He smelled the horses and the unwashed and sour slept-in-clothing smell of the new men and the wood-smoky sleep-stale smell of the others who had been in the cave. Pablo was standing close to him and he smelled the brassy, dead-wine smell that came from him like the taste of a copper coin in your mouth. He lit a cigarette, cupping his hand to hide the light, pulled deep on it, and heard Pablo say very softly, 'Get the grenade sack, Pilar, while we hobble these.'

'Agustin,' Robert Jordan said in a whisper, 'you and Anselmo come now with me to the bridge. Have you the sack of pans for the *máquina?*'

'Yes,' Agustin said. 'Why not?'

Robert Jordan went over to where Pilar was unpacking one of the horses with the help of Primitivo.

'Listen, woman,' he said softly.

'What now?' she whispered huskily, swinging a cinch hook clear from under the horse's belly.

'Thou understandest that there is to be no attack on the post until thou hearest the falling of the bombs?'

'How many times dost thou have to tell me?' Pilar said. 'You are getting like an old woman, *Inglés.*'

'Only to check,' Robert Jordan said. 'And after the destruction of the post you fall back onto the bridge and cover the road from above and my left flank.'

'The first time thou outlined it I understood it as well as I will ever understand it,' Pilar whispered to him. 'Get thee about thy business.'

'That no one should make a move nor fire a shot nor throw a bomb until the noise of the bombardment comes,' Robert Jordan said softly.

'Do not molest me more,' Pilar whispered angrily. 'I have understood this since we were at Sordo's.'

Robert Jordan went to where Pablo was tying the horses. 'I have only hobbled those which are liable to panic,' Pablo said. 'These are tied so a pull of the rope will release them, see?'

'Good.'

'I will tell the girl and the gypsy how to handle them,' Pablo said. His new men were standing in a group by themselves leaning on their carbines.

'Dost understand all?' Robert Jordan asked.

'Why not?' Pablo said. 'Destroy the post. Cut the wire. Fall back on the bridge. Cover the bridge until thou blowest.'

'And nothing to start until the commencement of the bombardment.'

'Thus it is.'

'Well then, much luck.'

Pablo grunted. Then he said, 'Thou wilt cover us well with the *máquina* and with thy small *máquina* when we come back, eh, *Inglés?*'

'*De la primera*,' Robert Jordan said. 'Off the top of the basket.' 'Then,' Pablo said. 'Nothing more. But in that moment thou must be very careful, *Inglés*. It will not be simple to do that unless thou art very careful.'

'I will handle the *máquina* myself,' Robert Jordan said to him. 'Hast thou much experience? For I am of no mind to be shot by Agustin with his belly full of good intentions.'

'I have much experience. Truly. And if Agustin uses either *méquina* I will see that he keeps it way above thee. Above, above and above.'

'Then nothing more,' Pablo said. Then he said softly and confidentially, 'There is still a lack of horses.'

The son of a bitch, Robert Jordan thought. Or does he think I did not understand him the first time.

'I go on foot,' he said. 'The horses are thy affair.'

'Nay, there will be a horse for thee, *Inglés*,' Pablo said softly. 'There will be horses for all of us.'

'That is thy problem,' Robert Jordan said. 'Thou dost not have to count me. Hast enough rounds for thy new *mdquina?*'

'Yes,' Pablo said. 'All that the cavalryman carried. I have fired only four to try it. I tried it yesterday in the high hills.'

'We go now,' Robert Jordan said. 'We must be there early and well hidden.'

'We all go now,' Pablo said. '*Suerte, Inglés.*'

I wonder what the bastard is planning now, Robert Jordan said. But I am pretty sure I know. Well, that is his, not mine. Thank God I do not know these new men.

He put his hand out and said, '*Suerte, Pablo,*' and their two hands gripped in the dark.

Robert Jordan, when he put his hand out, expected that it would be like grasping something reptilian or touching a leper. He did not know what Pablo's hand would feel like. But in the dark Pablo's hand gripped his hard and pressed it frankly and he returned the grip. Pablo had a good hand in the dark and feeling it gave Robert Jordan the strangest feeling he had felt that morning. We must be allies now, he thought. There was always much handshaking with allies. Not to mention decorations and kissing on both cheeks, he thought. I'm glad we do not have to do that. I suppose all allies are like this. They always hate each other *au fond*. But this Pablo is a strange man.

'*Suerte,* Pablo,' he said and gripped the strange, firm, purposeful hand hard. 'I will cover thee well. Do not worry.'

'I am sorry for having taken thy material,' Pablo said. 'It was an equivocation.'

'But thou has brought what we needed.'

'I do not hold this of the bridge against thee, *Inglés*,' Pablo said. 'I see a successful termination for it.'

'What are you two doing? Becoming *maricones?*' Pilar said suddenly beside them in the dark. 'That is all thou hast lacked,' she said to Pablo. 'Get along, *Inglés*, and cut thy good-bys short before this one steals the rest of thy explosive.'

'Thou dost not understand me, woman,' Pablo said. 'The *Inglés* and I understand one another.'

'Nobody understands thee. Neither God nor thy mother,' Pilar said. 'Nor I either. Get along, *Inglés*. Make thy good-bys with thy cropped head and go. *Me cago en tu padre*, but I begin to think thou art afraid to see the bull come out.'

'Thy mother,' Robert Jordan said.

'Thou never hadst one,' Pilar whispered cheerful ly. 'Now go, because I have a great desire to start this and get it over with. Go with thy people,' she said to Pablo. 'Who knows how long their stern resolution is good for? Thou hast a couple that I would not trade thee for. Take them and go.'

Robert Jordan slung his pack on his back and walked over to the horses to find Maria.

'Good-by, *guapa*,' he said. 'I will see thee soon.'

He had an unreal feeling about all of this now as though he had said it all before or as though it were a train that were going, especially as though it were a train and he was standing on the platform of a railway station.

'Good-by, Roberto,' she said. 'Take much care.'

'Of course,' he said. He bent his head to kiss her and his pack rolled forward against the back of his head so that his forehead bumped hers hard. As this happened he knew this had happened before too.

'Don't cry,' he said, awkward not only from the load. 'I do not,' she said. 'But come back quickly.'

'Do not worry when you hear the firing. There is bound to be much firing.'

'Nay. Only come back quickly.'

'Good-by, *guapa*,' he said awkwardly.

'*Salud*, Roberto.'

Robert Jordan had not felt this young since he had taken the train at Red Lodge to go down to Billings to get the train there to go away to school for the first time. He had been afraid to go and he did not want any one to know it and, at the station, just before the conductor picked up the box he would step up on to reach the steps of the day coach, his father had kissed him good-by and said, 'May the Lord watch between thee and me while we are absent the one from the other.' His father had been a very religious man and he had said it simply and sincerely. But his moustache had been moist and his eyes were damp with emotion and Robert Jordan had been so embarrassed by all of it, the damp religious sound of the prayer, and by his father kissing him good-by, that he had felt suddenly so much older than his father and sorry for him that he could hardly bear it.

After the train started he had stood on the rear platform and watched the station and the water tower grow smaller and smaller and the rails crossed by the ties narrowed toward a point where the station and the water tower stood now minute and tiny in the steady clicking that was taking him away.

The brakeman said, 'Dad seemed to take your going sort of hard, Bob.'

'Yes,' he had said watching the sagebrush that ran from the edge of the road bed between the passing telegraph poles across to the streaming-by dusty stretching of the road. He was looking for sage hens.

'You don't mind going away to school?' 'No,' he had said and it was true.

It would not have been true before but it was true that minute and it was only now, at this parting, that he ever felt as young again as he had felt before that train left. He felt very young now and very awkward and he was saying good-by as awkwardly as one can be when saying good-by to ;:l young girl when you are a boy in school, saying good-by at the front porch, not knowing whether to kiss the girl or not. Then he knew it was not the good-by he was being awkward about. It was the meeting he was going to. The good-by was only a part of the awkwardness he felt about the meeting.

You're getting them again, he told himself. But I suppose there is no one that does not feel that he is too young to do it. He would not put a name to it. Come on, he said to himself. Come on. It is too early for your second childhood.

'Good-by, *guapa*,' he said. 'Good-by, rabbit.'

'Good-by, my Roberto,' she said and he went over to where Anselmo and Agustin were standing and said, '*Vámonos.*'

Anselmo swung his heavy pack up. Agustin, fully loaded since the cave, was leaning against a tree, the automatic rifle jutting over the top of his load.

'Good,' he said, '*Vcimonos.*'

The three of them started down the hill.

'*Buena suerte*, Don Roberto,' Fernando said as the three of them passed him as they moved in single file between the trees. Fernando was crouched on his haunches a little way from where they passed but he spoke with great dignity.

'*Buena suerte* thyself, Fernando,' Robert Jordan said.

'In everything thou doest,' Agustin said.

'Thank you, Don Roberto,' Fernando said, undisturbed by Agustin.

'That one is a phenomenon, *Inglés*,' Agustin whispered.

'I believe thee,' Robert Jordan said. 'Can I help thee? Thou art loaded like a horse.'

'I am all right,' Agustin said. 'Man, but I am content we are started.'

'Speak softly,' Anselmo said. 'From now on speak little and softly.'

Walking carefully, downhill, Anselmo in the lead, Agustin next, Robert Jordan placing his feet carefully so that he would not slip, feeling the dead pine needles under his rope-soled shoes, bumping a tree root with one foot and putting a hand forward and feeling the cold metal jut of the automatic rifle barrel and the folded legs of the tripod, then working sideways down the hill, his shoes sliding and grooving the forest floor, putting his left hand out again and touching the rough bark of a tree trunk, then as he braced himself his hand feeling a smooth place, the base of the palm of his hand coming away sticky from the resinous sap where a blaze had been cut, they dropped down the steep wooded hillside to the point above the bridge where Robert Jordan and Anselmo had watched the first day.

Now Anselmo was halted by a pine tree in the dark and he took Robert

Jordan's wrist and whispered, so low Jordan could hardly hear him, 'Look. There is the fire in his brazier.'

It was a point of light below where Robert Jordan knew the bridge joined the road.

'Here is where we watched,' Anselmo said. He took Robert Jordan's hand and bent it down to touch a small fresh blaze low on a tree trunk. 'This I marked while thou watched. To the right is where thou wished to put the *máquina*.'

'We will place it there.'

'Good.'

They put the packs down behind the base of the pine trunks and the two of them followed Anselmo over to the level place where there was a clump of seedling pines.

'It is here,' Anselmo said. 'Just here.'

'From here, with daylight,' Robert Jordan crouched behind the small trees whispered to Agustin, 'thou wilt see a small stretch of road and the entrance to the bridge. Thou wilt see the length of the bridge and a small stretch of road at the other end before it rounds the curve of the rocks.'

Agustin said nothing.

'Here thou wilt lie while we prepare the exploding and fire on anything that comes from above or below.'

'Where is that light?' Agustin asked.

'In the sentry box at this end,' Robert Jordan whispered.

'Who deals with the sentries?'

'The old man and I, as I told thee. But if we do not deal with them, thou must fire into the sentry boxes and at them if thou seest them.'

'Yes. You told me that.'

'After the explosion when the people of Pablo come around that corner, thou must fire over their heads if others come after them. Thou must fire high above them when they appear in any event that others must not come. Understandest thou?'

'Why not? It is as thou saidst last night.' 'Hast any questions?'

'Nay. I have two sacks. I can load them from above where it will not be seen and bring them here.'

'But do no digging here. Thou must be as well hid as we were at the top.'

'Nay. I will bring the dirt in them in the dark. You will see. They will not show as I will fix them.'

'Thou are very close. *Sabes?* In the daylight this clump shows clearly from below.'

'Do not worry, *Inglés*. Where goest thou?'

'I go close below with the small *mciquina* of mine. The old man will cross the gorge now to be ready for the box of the other end. It faces in that direction.'

'Then nothing more,' said Agustin. '*Sa lud, Inglés*. Hast thou tobacco?'

'Thou canst not smoke. It is too close.'

'Nay. Just to hold in the mouth. To smoke later.'

Robert Jordan gave him his cigarette case and Agustin took three cigarettes and put them inside the front flap of his herdsman's flat cap. He spread the legs of his tripod with the gun muzzle in the low pines and commenced unpacking his load by touch and laying the things where he wanted them.

'*Nada mas*,' he said. 'Well, nothing more.'

Anselmo and Robert Jordan left him there and went back to where the packs were.

'Where had we best leave them?' Robert Jordan whispered.

'I think here. But canst thou be sure of the sentry with thy small *máquina* from here?'

'Is this exactly where we were on that day?'

'The same tree,' Anselmo said so low Jordan could barely hear him and he knew he was speaking without moving his lips as he had spoken that first day. 'I marked it with my knife.'

Robert Jordan had the feeling again of it all having happened before, but this time it came from his own repetition of a query and Anselmo's answer. It had been the same with Agustin, who had asked a question about the sentries although he knew the answer.

'It is close enough. Even too close,' he whispered. 'But the light is behind us. We are all right here.'

'Then I will go now to cross the gorge and be in position at the other end,' Anselmo said. Then he said, 'Pardon me, *Inglés*. So that there is no mistake. In case I am stupid.'

'What?' breathed very softly.

'Only to repeat it so that I will do it exactly.'

'When I fire, thou wilt fire. When thy man is eliminated, cross the bridge to me. I will have the packs down there and thou wilt do as I tell thee in the placing of the charges. Everything I will tell thee. If aught happens to me do it thyself as I showed thee. Take thy time and do it well, wedging all securely with the wooden wedges and lashing the grenades firmly.'

'It is all clear to me,' Anselmo said. 'I remember it all. Now I go. Keep thee well covered, *Inglés*, when daylight comes.' 'When thou firest,' Robert Jordan said, 'take a rest and make very sure. Do not think of it as a man but as a target, *de acuerdo?* Do not shoot at the whole man but at a point. Shoot for the exact center of the belly-if he faces thee. At the middle of the back, if he is looking away. Listen, old one. When I fire if the man is sitting down he will stand up before he runs or crouches. Shoot then. If he is still sitting down shoot. Do not wait. But make sure. Get to within fifty yards. Thou art a hunter. Thou hast no problem.'

'I will do as thou orderest,' Anselmo said.

'Yes. I order it thus,' Robert Jordan said.

I'm glad I remembered to make it an order, he thought. That helps him out. That takes some of the curse off. I hope it does, anyway. Some of it. I had forgotten about what he told me that first day about the killing.

'It is thus I have ordered,' he said. 'Now go.'

'*Me voy,*' said Anselmo. 'Until soon, *Inglés.*'

'Until soon, old one,' Robert Jordan said.

He remembered his father in the railway station and the wetness of that farewell and he did not say *Salud* nor good-by nor good luck nor anything like that.

'Hast wiped the oil from the bore of thy gun, old one?' he whispered. 'So it will not throw wild?'

'In the cave,' Anselmo said. 'I cleaned them all with the pull-through.'

'Then until soon,' Robert Jordan said and the old man went off, noiseless on his rope-soled shoes, swinging wide through the trees.

Robert Jordan lay on the pine-needle floor of the forest and listened to the first stirring in the branches of the pines of the wind that would come with daylight. He took the clip out of the submachine gun and worked the lock back and forth. Then he turned the gun, with the lock open and in the dark he put the muzzle to his lips and blew through the barrel, the metal tasting greasy and oily as his tongue touched the edge of the bore. He laid the gun across his forearm, the action up so that no pine needles or rubbish could get in it, and shucked all the cartridges out of the clip with his thumb and onto a handkerchief he had spread in front of him. Then, feeling each cartridge in the dark and turning it in his fingers, he pressed and slid them one at a time back into the clip. Now the clip was heavy again in his hand and he slid it back into the submachine gun and felt it click home. He lay on his belly behind the pine trunk, the gun across his left forearm and watched the point of light below him. Sometimes he could not see it and then he knew that the man in the sentry box had moved in front of the brazier. Robert Jordan lay there and waited for daylight.

42

During the time that Pablo had ridden back from the hills to the cave and the time the band had dropped down to where they had left the horses Andres had made rapid progress toward Golz's headquarters. Where they came onto the main highroad to Navacerrada on which the trucks were rolling back from the mountain there was a control. But when Gomez showed the sentry at the control his safe-conduct from the Lieutenant-Colonel Miranda the sentry put the light from a flashlight on it, showed it to the other sentry with him, then handed it back and saluted.

'*Siga,*' he said. 'Continue. But without lights.'

The motorcycle roared again and Andres was holding tight onto the forward seat and they were moving along the highway, Gomez riding carefully in the traffic. None of the trucks had lights and they were moving down the road in a long convoy. There were loaded trucks moving up the road too, and all of them raised a dust that Andres could not see in that dark but could only feel as a cloud that blew in his face and that he could bite between his teeth.

They were close behind the tailboard of a truck now, the motorcycle chugging, then Gomez speeded up and passed it and another, and another, and another with the other trucks roaring and rolling down past them on the left. There was a motorcar behind them now and it blasted into the truck noise and the dust with its klaxon again and again; then flashed on lights that showed the dust like a solid yellow cloud and surged past them in a whining rise of gears and a demanding, threatening, bludgeoning of klaxoning.

Then ahead all the trucks were stopped and riding on, working his way ahead past ambulances, staff cars, an armored car, another, and a third, all halted, like heavy, metal, gun-jutting turtles in the hot yet settled dust, they found another control where there had been a smash-up. A truck, halting, had not been seen by the truck which followed it and the following truck had run into it smashing the rear of the first truck in and scattering cases of small-arms ammunition over the road. One case had burst open on landing and as Gomez and Andres stopped and wheeled the motorcycle forward through the stalled vehicles to show their safe-conduct at the control Andres walked over the brass hulls of the thousand of cartridges scattered across the road in the dust. The second truck had its radiator completely smashed in. The truck behind it was touching its tail gate. A hundred more were piling up behind and an overbooted officer was running back along the road shouting to the drivers to back so that the smashed truck could be gotten off the road.

There were too many trucks for them to be able to back unless the officer reached the end of the ever mounting line and stopped it from increasing and Andres saw him running, stumbling, with his flashlight, shouting and cursing and, in the dark, the trucks kept coming up.

The man at the control would not give the safe-conduct back. There were two of them, with rifles slung on their backs and flashlights in their hands and they were shouting too. The one carrying the safe-conduct in his hand crossed the road to a truck going in the downhill direction to tell it to proceed to the next control and tell them there to hold all trucks until his jam was straightened out. The truck driver listened and went on. Then, still holding the safe-conduct, the control patrol came over, shouting, to the truck driver whose load was spilled.

'Leave it and get ahead for the love of God so we can clear this!' he shouted at the driver.

'My transmission is smashed,' the driver, who was bent over by the rear of his truck, said.

'Obscene your transmission. Go ahead, I say.'

'They do not go ahead when the differential is smashed,' the driver told him and bent down again.

'Get thyself pulled then, get ahead so that we can get this other obscenity off the road.'

The driver looked at him sullenly as the control man shone the electric torch on the smashed rear of the truck.

'Get ahead. Get ahead,' the man shouted, still holding the safe conduct pass in his hand.

'And my paper,' Gomez spoke to him. 'My safe-conduct. We are in a hurry.'

'Take thy safe-conduct to hell,' the man said and handing it to him ran across the road to halt a down-coming truck.

'Turn thyself at the crossroads and put thyself in position to pull this wreck forward,' he said to the driver.

'My orders are–'

'Obscenity thy orders. Do as I say.'

The driver let his truck into gear and rolled straight ahead down the road and was gone in the dust.

As Gomez started the motorcycle ahead onto the now clear right-hand side of the road past the wrecked truck, Andres, holding tight again, saw the control guard halting another truck and the driver leaning from the cab and listening to him.

Now they went fast, swooping along the road that mounted steadily toward the mountain. All forward traffic had been stalled at the control and there were only the descending trucks passing, passing and passing on their left as the motorcycle climbed fast and steadily now until it began to overtake the mounting traffic which had gone on ahead before the disaster at the control.

Still without lights they passed four more armored cars, then a long line of trucks loaded with troops. The troops were silent in the dark and at first Andres only felt their presence rising above him, bulking above the truck bodies through the dust as they passed. Then another staff came behind them blasting with its klaxon and flicking its lights off and on, and each time the lights shone Andres saw the troops, steel-helmeted, their rifles vertical, their machine guns pointed up against the dark sky, etched sharp against the night that they dropped into when the light flicked off. Once as he passed close to a troop truck and the lights flashed he saw their faces fixed and sad in the sudden light. In their steel helmets, riding in the trucks in the dark toward something that they only knew was an attack, their faces were drawn with each man's own problem in the dark and the light revealed them as they would not have looked in day, from shame to show it to each other, until the bombardment and the attack would commence, and no man would think about his face.

Andres now passing them truck after truck, Gomez still keeping successfully ahead of the following staff car, did not think any of this about their faces. He only thought, 'What an army. What equipment. What a mechanization. *Vaya gente!* Look at such people. Here we have the army of the Republic. Look at them. Camion after camion. All uniformed alike. All with casques of steel on their heads. Look at the *máquinas* rising from the trucks against the coming of planes. Look at the army that has been builded!'

And as the motorcycle passed the high gray trucks full of troops, gray trucks with high square cabs and square ugly radiators, steadily mounting the road in the dust and the flicking lights of the pursuing staff car, the red star of the army showing in the light when it passed over the tail gates, showing when the light came onto the sides of the dusty truck bodies, as they passed, climbing steadily now, the air colder and the road starting to turn in bends and switchbacks now, the trucks laboring and grinding, some steaming in the light flashes, the motorcycle laboring now too, and Andres clinging tight to the front seat as they climbed, Andres thought this ride on a motorcycle was *mucha, mucha*. He had never been on a motorcycle before and now they were climbing a mountain in the midst of all the movement that was going to an attack and, as they climbed, he knew now there was no problem of ever being back in time for the assault on the posts. In this movement and confusion he would be lucky to get back by the next night. He had never seen an offensive or any of the preparations for one before and as they rode up the road he marvelled at the size and power of this army that the Republic had built.

Now they rode on a long slanting, rising stretch of road that ran across the face of the mountain and the grade was so steep as they neared the top that Gomez told him to get down and together they pushed the motorcycle up the last steep grade of the pass. At the left, just past the top, there was a loop of road where cars could turn and there were lights winking in front of a big stone building that bulked long and dark against the night sky.

'Let us go to ask there where the headquarters is,' Gomez said to Andres and they wheeled the motorcycle over to where two sentries stood in front of the closed door of the great stone building. Gomez leaned the motorcycle against the wall as a motorcyclist in a leather suit, showing against the light from inside the building as the door opened, came out of the door with a dispatch case hung over his shoulder, a wooden-holstered Mauser pistol swung against his hip. As the light went off, he found his motorcycle in the dark by the door, pushed it until it sputtered and caught, then roared off up the road.

At the door Gomez spoke to one of the sentries. 'Captain Gomez of the Sixty-Fifth Brigade,' he said. 'Can you tell me where to find the headquarters of General Golz commanding the Thirty-Fifth Division?'

'It isn't here,' the sentry said.

'What is here?'

'The Comandancia.'

'What comandancia?'

'Well, the Comandancia.'

'The comandancia of what?'

'Who art thou to ask so many questions?' the sentry said to Gomez in the dark. Here on the top of the pass the sky was very clear with the stars out and Andres, out of the dust now, could see quite clearly in the dark. Below them, where the road turned to the right, he could see clearly the outline of the trucks and cars that passed against the sky line.

'I am Captain Rogelio Gomez of the first battalion of the Sixty Fifth Brigade and I ask where is the headquarters of General Gulz,' Gomez said.

The sentry opened the door a little way. 'Call the corporal of the guard,' he shouted inside.

Just then a big staff car came up over the turn of the road and circled toward the big stone building where Andres and Gomez were standing waiting for the corporal of the guard. It came toward them and stopped outside the door.

A large man, old and heavy, in an oversized khaki beret, such as *chasseurs a pied* wear in the French Army, wearing an overcoat, carrying a map case and wearing a pistol strapped around his greatcoat, got out of the back of the car with two other men in the uniform of the International Brigades.

He spoke in French, which Andres did not understand and of which Gomez, who had been a barber, knew only a few words, to his chauffeur telling him to get the car away from the door and into shelter.

As he came into the door with the other two officers, Gomez saw his face clearly in the light and recognized him. He had seen him at political meetings and he had often read articles by him in *Mundo Obrero* translated from the French. He recognized his bushy eyebrows, his watery gray eyes, his chin and the double chin under it, and he knew him for one of France's great modern revolutionary figures who had led the mutiny of the French Navy in the Black Sea. Gomez knew this man's high political place in the International Brigades and he knew this man would know where Golz's headquarters were and be able to direct him there. He did not know what this man had become with time, disappointment, bitterness both domestic and political, and thwarted ambition and that to question him was one of the most dangerous things that any man could do. Knowing nothing of this he stepped forward into the path of this man, saluted with his clenched fist and said, 'Comrade Marty, we are the bearers of a dispatch for General Golz. Can you direct us to his headquarters? It is urgent.'

The tall, heavy old man looked at Gomez with his outthrust head and considered him carefully with his watery eyes. Even here at the front in the light of a bare electric bulb, he having just come in from driving in an open car on a brisk night, his gray face had a look of decay. His face looked as though it were modelled from the waste material you find under the claws of a very old lion.

'You have what, Comrade?' he asked Gomez, speaking Spanish with a strong Catalan accent. His eyes glanced sideways at Andres, slid over him, and went back to Gomez.

'A dispatch for General Golz to be delivered at his headquarters, Comrade Marty.'

'Where is it from, Comrade?'

'From behind the fascist lines,' Gomez said.

Andre Marty extended his hand for the dispatch and the other papers. He glanced at them and put them in his pocket.

'Arrest them both,' he said to the corporal of the guard. 'Have them searched and bring them to me when I send for them.'

With the dispatch in his pocket he strode on into the interior of the big stone house.

Outside in the guard room Gomez and Andres were being searched by the guard.

'What passes with that man?' Gomez said to one of the guards.

'*Esta loco*,' the guard said. 'He is crazy.'

'No. He is a political figure of great importance,' Gomez said. 'He is the chief commissar of the International Brigades.'

'*Apesar de eso, esta loco*,' the corporal of the guard said. 'All the same he's crazy. What do you behind the fascist lines?'

'This comrade is a guerilla from there,' Gomez told him while the man searched him. 'He brings a dispatch to General Golz. Guard well my papers. Be careful with that money and that bullet on the string. It is from my first wound at Guadarama.'

'Don't worry,' the corporal said. 'Everything will be in this drawer. Why didn't you ask me where Golz was?'

'We tried to. I asked the sentry and he called you.'

'But then came the crazy and you asked him. No one should ask him anything. He is crazy. Thy Golz is up the road three kilometers from here and to the right in the rocks of the forest.'

'Can you not let us go to him now?'

'Nay. It would be my head. I must take thee to the crazy. Besides, he has thy dispatch.'

'Can you not tell some one?'

'Yes,' the corporal said. 'I will tell the first responsible one I see. All know that he is crazy.'

'I had always taken him for a great figure,' Gomez said. 'For one of the glories of France.'

'He may be a glory and all,' the corporal said and put his hand on Andres's shoulder. 'But he is crazy as a bedbug. He has a mania for shooting people.'

'Truly shooting them?'

'*Como 10 ayes*,' the corporal said. 'That old one kills more than the bubonic plague. *Mata mas que la peste bubonica*. But he doesn't kill fascists like we do. *Que va*. Not in joke. *Mata bichos raros*. He kills rare things. Trotzkyites. Divagationers. Any type of rare beasts.'

Andrés did not understand any of this.

'When we were at Escorial we shot I don't know how many for him,' the corporal said. 'We always furnish the firing party. The men of the Brigades would not shoot their own men. Especially the French. To avoid difficulties it is always us who do it. We shot French. We have shot Belgians. We have shot others of divers nationality. Of all types. *Tiene mania de fusilar gente*. Always for political things. He's crazy. *Purifica mas que el Salvarsan*. He purifies more than Salvarsan.'

'But you will tell some one of this dispatch?'

'Yes, man. Surely. I know every one of these two Brigades. Every one comes through here. I know even up to and through the Russians, although only a few speak Spanish. We will keep this crazy from shooting Spaniards.'

'But the dispatch.'

'The dispatch, too. Do not worry, Comrade. We know how to deal with this crazy. He is only dangerous with his own people. We understand him now.'

'Bring in the two prisoners,' came the voice of Andre Marty.

'*Quereis echar un trago?*' the corporal asked. 'Do you want a drink?'

'Why not?'

The corporal took a bottle of Anis from a cupboard and both Gomez and Andres drank. So did the corporal. He wiped his mouth on his hand.

'*Vámonos,*' he said.

They went out of the guard room with the swallowed burn of the Anis warming their mouths, their bellies and their hearts and walked down the hall and entered the room where Marty sat behind a long table, his map spread in front of him, his red-and-blue pencil, with which he played at being a general officer, in his hand. To Andres it was only one more thing. There had been many tonight. There were always many. If your papers were in order and your heart was good you were in no danger. Eventually they turned you loose and you were on your way. But the *Inglés* had said to hurry. He knew now he could never get back for the bridge but they had a dispatch to deliver and this old man there at the table had put it in his pocket.

'Stand there,' Marty said without looking up.

'Listen, Comrade Marty,' Gomez broke out, the Anis fortifying his anger. 'Once tonight we have been impeded by the ignorance of the anarchists. Then by the sloth of a bureaucratic fascist. Now by the over suspicion of a Communist.'

'Close your mouth,' Marty said without looking up.

'This not a meeting.'

'Comrade Marty, this is a matter of utmost urgency,' Gomez said. 'Of the greatest importance.'

The corporal and the soldier with them were taking a lively interest in this as though they were at a play they had seen many times but whose excellent moments they could always savor.

'Everything is of urgency,' Marty said. 'All things are of importance.' Now he looked up at them, holding the pencil. 'How did you know Golz was here? Do you understand how serious it is to come asking for an individual general before an attack? How could you know such a general would be here?'

'Tell him, *tu,*' Gomez said to Andres.

'Comrade General,' Andres started-Andre Marty did not correct him in the mistake in rank-' I was given that packet on the other side of the lines—'

'On the other side of the Lines?' Marty said. 'Yes, I heard him say you came from the fascist lines.'

'It was given to me, Comrade General, by an *Inglés* named Roberto who had come to us as a dynamiter for this of the bridge. Understandeth?'

'Continue thy story,' Marty said to Andres; using the term story as you would say lie, falsehood, or fabrication.

'Well, Comrade General, the *Inglés* told me to bring it to the General Golz with all speed. He makes an attack in these hills now on this day and all we ask is to take it to him now promptly if it pleases the Comrade General.'

Marty shook his head again. He was looking at Andres but he was not seeing him.

Golz, he thought in a mixture of horror and exultation as a man might feel hearing that a business enemy had been killed in a particularly nasty motor accident or that some one you hated but whose probity you had never doubted had been guilty of defalcation. That Golz should be one of them, too. That Golz should be in such obvious communication with the fascists. Golz that he had known for nearly twenty years. Golz who had captured the gold train that winter with Lucacz in Siberia. Golz who had fought against Kolchak, and in Poland. In the Caucasus. In China, and here since the first October. But he *had* been close to Tukachevsky. To Voroshilov, yes, too. But to Tukachevsky. And to who else? Here to Karkov, of course. And to Lucacz. But all the Hungarians had been intriguers. He hated Gall. Golz hated Gall. Remember that. Make a note of that. Golz has always hated Gall. But he favors Putz. Remember that. And Duval is his chief of staff. See what stems from that. You've heard him say Copic's a fool. That is definitive. That exists. And now this dispatch from the fascist lines. Only by pruning out of these rotten branches can the tree remain healthy and grow. The rot must become apparent for it is to be destroyed. But Golz of all men. That Golz should be one of the traitors. He knew that you could trust no one. No one. Ever. Not your wife. Not your brother. Not your oldest comrade. No one. Ever.

'Take them away,' he said to the guards. 'Guard them carefully.' The corporal looked at the soldier. This had been very quiet for one of Marty's performances.

'Comrade Marty,' Gomez said. 'Do not be insane. Listen to me, a loyal officer and comrade. That is a dispatch that must be delivered. This comrade has brought it through the fascist lines to give to Comrade General Golz.'

'Take them away,' Marty said, now kindly, to the guard. He was sorry for them as human beings if it should be necessary to liquidate them. But it was the tragedy of Gol z that oppressed him. That it should be Golz, he thought. He would take the fascist communication at once to Varloff. No, better he would take it to Golz himself and watch him as he received it. That was what he would do. How could he be sure of Varloff if Golz was one of them? No. This was a thing to be very careful about.

Andres turned to Gomez, 'You mean he is not going to send the dispatch?' he asked, unbelieving.

'Don't you see?' Gomez said.

'Me cago en su puta madre!' Andres said. *'Estd loco.'*

'Yes,' Gomez said. 'He is crazy. You are crazy! Hear! Crazy!' he shouted at Marty who was back now bending over the map with his red-and-blue pencil. 'Hear me, you crazy murderer?'

'Take them away,' Marty said to the guard. 'Their minds are unhinged by their great guilt.'

There was a phrase the corporal recognized. He had heard that before.

'You crazy murderer!' Gomez shouted.

'Hijo de fa gran puta,' Andres said to him. 'Loco.'

The stupidity of this man angered him. If he was a crazy let him be removed as a crazy. Let the dispatch be taken from his pocket. God damn this crazy to hell. His heavy Spanish anger was rising out of his usual calm and good temper. In a little while it would blind him.

Marty, looking at his map, shook his head sadly as the guards took Gomez and Andres out. The guards had enjoyed hearing him cursed but on the whole they had been disappointed in the performance. They had seen much better ones. Andre Marty did not mind the men cursing him. So many men had cursed him at the end. He was always genuinely sorry for them as human beings. He always told himself that and it was one of the last true ideas that was left to him that had ever been his own.

He sat there, his moustache and his eyes focused on the map, on the map that he never truly understood, on the brown tracing of the contours that were traced fine and concentric as a spider's web. He could see the heights and the valleys from the contours but he never really understood why it should be this height and why this valley was the one. Rut at the General Staff where, because of the system of Political Commissars, he could intervene as the political head of the Brigades, he would put his finger on such and such a numbered, brown-thin-lined encircled spot among the greens of woods cut by the lines of roads that parallel the never casual winding of a river and say, 'There. That is the point of weakness.'

Gall and Copic, who were men of politics and of ambition, would agree and later, men who never saw the map, but heard the number of the hill before they left their starting place and had the earth of diggings on it pointed out, would climb its side to find their death along its slope or, being halted by machine guns placed in olive groves would never get up it at all. Or on other fronts they might scale it easily and be no better off than they had been before. But when Marty put his finger on the map in Golz's staff the scarheaded, white-faced General's jaw muscles would tighten and he would think, 'I should shoot you, Andre Marty, before I let you put that gray rotten finger on a contour map of mine. Damn you to hell for all the men you've killed by interfering in matters you know nothing of. Damn the day they named tractor factories and villages and co-operatives for you so that you are a symbol that I cannot touch. Go and suspect and exhort and intervene and denounce and butcher some other place and leave my staff alone.'

But instead of saying that Golz would only lean back away from the leaning bulk, the pushing finger, the watery gray eyes, the gray-white moustache and the bad breath and say, 'Yes, Comrade Marty. I see your point. It is not well taken, however, and I do not agree. You can try to go over my head if you like. Yes. You can make it a Party matter as you say. But I do not agree.'

So now Andre Marty sat working over his map at the bare table with the raw light on the unshaded electric light bulb over his head, the overwide beret pulled forward to shade his eyes, referring to the mimeographed copy of the orders for the attack and slowly and laboriously working them out on the map as a young officer might work a problem at a staff college. He was engaged in war. In his mind he was commanding troops; he had the right to interfere and this he believed to constitute command. So he sat there with Robert Jordan's dispatch to Golz in his pocket and Gomez and Andres waited in the guard room and Robert Jordan lay in the woods above the bridge.

It is doubtful if the outcome of Andres's mission would have been any different if he and Gomez had been allowed to proceed without Andre Marty's hindrance. There was no one at the front with sufficient authority to cancel the attack. The machinery had been in motion much too long for it to be stopped suddenly now. There is a great inertia about all military operations of any size. But once this inertia has been overcome and movement is under way they are almost as hard to arrest as to initiate.

But on this night the old man, his beret pulled forward, was still sitting at the table with his map when the door opened and Karkov the Russian journalist came in with two other Russians in civilian clothes, leather coats and caps. The corporal of the guard closed the door reluctantly behind them. Karkov had been the first responsible man he had been able to communicate with.

'Tovarich Marty,' said Karkov in his politely disdainful lisping voice and smiled, showing his bad teeth.

Marty stood up. He did not like Karkov, but Karkov, coming from *Pravda* and in direct communication with Stalin, was at this moment one of the three most important men in Spain.

'Tovarich Karkov,' he said.

'You are preparing the attack?' Karkov said insolently, nod- ding toward the map.

'I am studying it,' Marty answered.

'Are you attacking? Or is it Golz?' Karkov asked smoothly. 'I am only a commissar, as you know,' Marty told him.

'No,' Karkov said. 'You are modest. You are really a general. You have your map and your field glasses. But were you not an admiral once, Comrade Marty?'

'I was a gunner's mate,' said Marty. It was a lie. He had really been a chief yeoman at the time of the mutiny. But he thought now, always, that he had been a gunner's mate.

'Ah. I thought you were a first-class yeoman,' Karkov said. 'I always get my facts wrong. It is the mark of the journalist.'

The other Russians had taken no part in the conversation. They were both looking over Marty's shoulder at the map and occasionally making a remark to each other in their own language. Marty and Karkov spoke French after the first greeting.

'It is better not to get facts wrong in *Pravda*,' Marty said. He said it brusquely to build himself up again. Karkov always punctured him. The French word is *degonfler* and Marty was worried and made wary by him. It was hard, when Karkov spoke, to remember with what importance he, Andre Marty, came from the Central Committee of the French Communist Party. It was hard to remember, too, that he was untouchable. Karkov seemed always to touch him so lightly and whenever he wished. Now Karkov said, 'I usually correct them before I send them to *Pravda*, I am quite accurate in *Pravda*. Tell me, Comrade Marty, have you heard anything of any message coming through for Golz from one of our *partizan* group operating toward Segovia? There is an American comrade there named Jordan that we should have heard from. There have been reports of fighting there behind the fascist lines. He would have sent a message through to Golz.'

'An American?' Marty asked. Andres had said an *Inglés*. So that is what it was. So he had been mistaken. Why had those fools spoken to him anyway?'

'Yes,' Karkov looked at him contemptuously, 'a young American of slight political development but a great way with the Spaniards and a fine *partizan* record. Just give me the dispatch, Comrade Marty. It has been delayed enough.'

'What dispatch?' Marty asked. It was a very stupid thing to say and he knew it. But he was not able to admit he was wrong that quickly and he said it anyway to delay the moment of humiliation, not accepting any humiliation. 'And the safe-conduct pass,' Karkov said through his bad teeth.

Andre Marty put his hand in his pocket and laid the dispatch on the table. He looked Karkov squarely in the eye. All right. He was wrong and there was nothing he could do about it now but he was not accepting any humiliation. 'And the safe-conduct pass,' Karkov said softly.

Marty laid it beside the dispatch.

'Comrade Corporal,' Karkov called in Spanish.

The corporal opened the door and came in. He looked quickly at Andre Marty, who stared back at him like an old boar which has been brought to bay by hounds. There was no fear on Marty's face and no humiliation. He was only angry, and he was only temporarily at bay. He knew these dogs could never hold him.

'Take these to the two comrades in the guard room and direct them to General Golz's headquarters,' Karkov said. 'There has been too much delay.'

The corporal went out and Marty looked after him, then looked at Karkov.

'Tovarich Marty,' Karkov said, 'I am going to find out just how untouchable you are.'

Marty looked straight at him and said nothing.

'Don't start to have any plans about the corporal, either,' Karkov went on. 'It was not the corporal. I saw the two men in the guard room and they spoke to me' (this was a lie). 'I hope all men always will speak to me' (this was the truth although it was the corporal who had spoken). But Karkov had this belief in the good which could come from his own accessibility and the humanizing possibility of benevolent intervention. It was the one thing he was never cynical about.

'You know when I am in the U.S.S.R. people write to me in *Pravda* when there is an injustice in a town in Azerbaijan. Did you know that? They say 'Karkov will help us.''

Andre Marty looked at him with no expression on his face except anger and dislike. There was nothing in his mind now but that Karkov had done something against him. All right, Karkov, power and all, could watch out.

'This is something else,' Karkov went on, 'but it is the same principle. I am going to find out just how untouchable you are, Comrade Marty. I would like to know if it could not be possible to change the name of that tractor factory.'

Andre Marty looked away from him and back to the map. 'What did young Jordan say?' Karkov asked him.

'I did not read it,' Andre Marty said. *'Et maintenant fiche moi fa paix,* Comrade Karkov.'

'Good,' said Karkov. 'I leave you to your military labors.'

He stepped out of the room and walked to the guard room. Andres and Gomez were already gone and he stood there a moment looking up the road and at the mountain tops beyond that showed now in the first gray of daylight. We must get on up there, he thought. It will be soon, now.

Andres and Gomez were on the motorcycle on the road again and it was getting light. Now Andres, holding again to the back of the seat ahead of him as the motorcycle climbed turn after switchback turn in a faint gray mist that lay over the top of the pass, felt the motorcycle speed under him, then skid and stop and they were standing by the motorcycle on a long, down-slope of road and in the woods, on their left, were tanks covered with pine branches. There were troops here all through the woods. Andres saw men carrying the long poles of stretchers over their shoulders. Three staff cars were off the road to the right, in under the trees, with branches laid against their sides and other pine branches over their tops.

Gomez wheeled the motorcycle up to one of them. He leaned it against a pine tree and spoke to the chauffeur who was sitting by the car, his back against a tree.

'I'll take you to him,' the chauffeur said. 'Put thy *moto* out of sight and cover it with these.' He pointed to a pile of cut branches.

With the sun just starting to come through the high branches of the pine trees, Gomez and Andres followed the chauffeur, whose name was Vicente, through the pines across the road and up the slope to the entrance of a dugout from the roof of which signal wires ran on up over the wooded slope. They stood outside while the chauffeur went in and Andres admired the construction of the dugout which showed only as a hole in the hillside, with no dirt scattered about, but which he could see, from the entrance, was both deep and profound with men moving around in it freely with no need to duck their heads under the heavy timbered roof.

Vicente, the chauffeur, came out.

'He is up above where they are deploying for the attack,' he said. 'I gave it to his Chief of Staff. He signed for it. Here.'

He handed Gomez the receipted envelope. Gomez gave it to Andres, who looked at it and put it inside his shirt.

'What is the name of him who signed?' he asked.

'Duval,' Vicente said.

'Good,' said Andres. 'He was one of the three to whom I might give it.'

'Should we wait for an answer?' G'Jmez asked Andres.

'It might be best. Though where I will find the *Inglés* and the others after that of the bridge neither God knows.'

'Come wait with me,' Vicente said, 'until the General returns. And I will get thee coffee. Thou must be hungry.'

'And these tanks,' Gomez said to him.

They were passing the branch-covered, mud-colored tanks, each with two deep-ridged tracks over the pine needles showing where they had swung and backed from the road. Their 45-mm. guns jutted horizontally under the branches and the drivers and gunners in their leather coats and ridged helmets sat with their backs against the trees or lay sleeping on the ground.

'These are the reserve,' Vicente said. 'Also these troops are in reserve. Those who commence the attack are above.'

'They are many,' Andres said.

'Yes,' Vicente said. 'It is a full division.'

Inside the dugout Duval, holding the opened dispatch from Robert Jordan in his left hand, glancing at his wrist watch on the same hand, reading the dispatch for the fourth time, each time feeling the sweat come out from under his armpit and run down his flank, said into the telephone, 'Get me position Segovia, then. He's left? Get me position Avila.'

He kept on with the phone. It wasn't any good. He had talked to both brigades. Golz had been up to inspect the dispositions for the attack and was on his way to an observation post. He called the observation post and he was not there.

'Get me planes one,' Duval said, suddenly taking all responsibility. He would take responsibility for holding it up. It was better to hold it up. You could not send them to a surprise attack against an enemy that was waiting for it. You couldn't do it. It was just murder. You couldn't. You mustn't. No matter what. They could shoot him if they wanted. He would call the airfield directly and get the bombardment cancelled. But suppose it's just a holding attack? Suppose we were supposed to draw off all that material and those forces? Suppose that is what it is for? They never tell you it is a holding attack when you make it.

'Cancel the call to planes one,' he told the signaller. 'Get me the 69th Brigade observation post.'

He was still calling there when he heard the first sound of the planes.

It was just then he got through to the observation post. 'Yes,' Golz said quietly.

He was sitting leaning back against the sandbag, his feet against a rock, a cigarette hung from his lower lip and he was looking up and over his shoulder while he was talking. He was seeing the expanding wedges of threes, silver and thundering in the sky that were coming over the far shoulder of the mountain where the first sun was striking. He watched them come shining and beautiful in the sun. He saw the twin circles of light where the sun shone on the propellers as they came.

'Yes,' he said into the telephone, speaking in French because it was Duval on the wire. *'Nous sommes foutus. Qui. Comme toujours. Qui. C'est dommage. Qui.* It's a shame it came too late.'

His eyes, watching the planes coming, were very proud. He saw the red wing markings now and he watched their steady, stately roaring advance. This was how it could be. These were our planes. They had come, crated on ships, from the Black Sea through the Straits of Marmora, through the Dardanelles, through the Mediterranean and to here, unloaded lovingly at Alicante, assembled ably, tested and found perfect and now flown in lovely hammering precision, the V's tight and pure as they came now high and silver in the morning sun to blast those ridges across there and blow them roaring high so that we can go through.

Golz knew that once they had passed overhead and on, the bombs would fall, looking like porpoises in the air as they tumbled. And then the ridge tops would spout and roar in jumping clouds and disappear in one great blowing cloud. Then the tanks would grind clanking up those two slopes and after them would go his two brigades. And if it had been a surprise they could go on and down and over and through, pausing, cleaning up, dealing with, much to do, much to be done intelligently with the tanks helping with the tanks wheeling and returning, giving covering fire and others bringing the attackers up then slipping on and over and through and pushing down beyond. This was how it would be if there was no treason and if all did what they should.

There were the two ridges, and there were the tanks ahead and there were his two good brigades ready to leave the woods and here came the planes now. Everything he had to do had been done as it should be.

But as he watched the planes, almost up to him now, he felt sick at his stomach for he knew from having heard Jordan's dispatch over the phone that there would be no one on those two ridges. They'd be withdrawn a little way below in narrow trenches to escape the fragments, or hiding in the timber and when the bombers passed they'd get back up there with their machine guns and their automatic weapons and the anti-tank guns Jordan had said went up the road, and it would be one famous balls up more. But the planes, now coming deafeningly, were how it could have been and Golz watching them, looking up, said into the telephone, 'No. *Rien a faire. Rien. Faut pas penser. Faut accepter.*'

Golz watched the planes with his hard proud eyes that knew how things could be and how they would be instead and said, proud of how they could be, believing in how they could be, even if they never were, '*Bon. Nous ferons notre petit possible,*' and hung up.

But Duval did not hear him. Sitting at the table holding the receiver, all he heard was the roar of the planes and he thought, now, maybe this time, listen to them come, maybe the bombers will blow them all off, maybe we will get a breakthrough, maybe he will get the reserves he asked for, maybe this is it, maybe this is the time. Go on. Come on. Go on. The roar was such that he could not hear what he was thinking.

43

Robert Jordan lay behind the trunk of a pine tree on the slope of the hill above the road and the bridge and watched it become daylight. He loved this hour of the day always and now he watched it; feeling it gray within him, as though he were a part of the slow lightening that comes before the rising of the sun; when solid things darken and space lightens and the lights that have shone in the night go yellow and then fade as the day comes. The pine trunks below him were hard and clear now, their trunks solid and brown and the road was shiny with a wisp of mist over it. The dew had wet him and the forest floor was soft and he felt the give of the brown, dropped pine needles under his elbows. Below he saw, through the light mist that rose from the stream bed, the steel of the bridge, straight and rigid across the gap, with the wooden sentry boxes at each end. But as he looked the structure of the bridge was still spidery and fine in the mist that hung over the stream.

He saw the sentry now in his box as he stood, his back with the hanging blanket coat topped by the steel casque on his head showing as he leaned forward over the hole-punched petrol tin of the brazier, warming his hands. Robert Jordan heard the stream, far down in the rocks, and he saw a faint, thin smoke that rose from the sentry box.

He looked at his watch and thought, I wonder if Andres got through to Golz? If we are going to blow it I would like to breathe very slowly and slow up the time again and feel it. Do you think he made it? Andres? And if he did would they call it off? If they had time to call it off? Que va. Do not worry. They will or they won't. There are no more decisions and in a little while you will know. Suppose the attack is successful. Golz said it could be. That there was a possibility. With our tanks coming down that road, the people coming through from the right and down and past La Grania and the whole left of the mountains turned. Why don't you ever think of how it is to win? You've been on the defensive for so long that you can't think of that. Sure. But that was before all that stuff went up this road. That was before all the planes came. Don't be so naive. But remember this that as long as we can hold them here we keep the fascists tied up. They can't attack any other country until they finish with us and they can never finish with us. If the French help at all, if only they leave the frontier open and if we get planes from America they can never finish with us. Never, if we get anything at all. These people will fight forever if they're well armed.

No you must not expect victory here, not for several years maybe. This is just a holding attack. You must not get illusions about it now. Suppose we got a breakthrough today? This is our first big attack. Keep your sense of proportion. But what if we should have it? Don't get excited, he told himself. Remember what went up the road. You've done what you could about that. We should have portable shortwave sets, though. We will, in time. But we haven't yet. You just watch now and do what you should.

Today is only one day in all the days that will ever be. But what will happen in all the other days that ever come can depend on what you do today. It's been that way all this year. It's been that way so many times. All of this war is that way. You are getting very pompous in the early morning, he told himself. Look there what's coming now.

He saw the two men in blanket capes and steel helmets come around the corner of the road walking toward the bridge, their rifles slung over their shoulders. One stopped at the far end of the bridge and was out of sight in the sentry box. The other came on across the bridge, walking slowly and heavily. He stopped on the bridge and spat into the gorge, then came on slowly to the near end of the bridge where the other sentry spoke to him and then started off back over the bridge. The sentry who was relieved walked faster than the other had done (because he's going to coffee, Robert Jordan thought) but he too spat down into the gorge.

I wonder if that is superstition? Robert Jordan thought. I'll have to take me a spit in that gorge too. If I can spit by then. No. It can't be very powerful medicine. It can't work. I'll have to prove it doesn't work before I am out there.

The new sentry had gone inside the box and sat down. His rifle with the bayonet fixed was leaning against the wall. Robert Jordan took his glasses from his shirt pocket and turned the eyepieces until the end of the bridge showed sharp and gray-painted-metal clear. Then he moved them onto the sentry box.

The sentry sat leaning against the wall. His helmet hung on a peg and his face showed clearly. Robert Jordan saw he was the same man who had been there on guard two days before in the afternoon watch. He was wearing the same knitted stocking-cap. And he had not shaved. His cheeks were sunken and his cheekbones prominent. He had bushy eyebrows that grew together in the center. He looked sleepy and as Robert Jordan watched him he yawned. Then he took out a tobacco pouch and a packet of papers and rolled himself a cigarette. He tried to make a lighter work and finally put it in his pocket and went over to the brazier, leaned over, reached inside, brought up a piece of charcoal, juggled it in one hand while he blew on it, then lit the cigarette and tossed the lump of charcoal back into the brazier.

Robert Jordan, looking through the Zeiss 8-power glasses, watched his face as he leaned against the wall of the sentry box drawing on the cigarette. Then he took the glasses down, folded them together and put them in his pocket.

I won't look at him again, he told himself.

He lay there and watched the road and tried not to think at all. A squirrel chittered from a pine tree below him and Robert Jordan watched the squirrel come down the tree trunk, stopping on his way down to turn his head and look toward where the man was watching. He saw the squirrel's eyes, small and bright, and watched his tail jerk in excitement. Then the squirrel crossed to another tree, moving on the ground in long, small-pawed, tail-exaggerated bounds. On the tree trunk he looked back at Robert Jordan, then pulled himself around the trunk and out of sight. Then Robert Jordan heard the squirrel chitter from a high branch of the pine tree and he watched him there, spread flat along the branch, his tail jerking.

Robert Jordan looked down through the pines to the sentry box again. He would like to have had the squirrel with him in his pocket. He would like to have had anything that he could touch. He rubbed his elbows against the pine needles but it was not the same. Nobody knows how lonely you can be when you do this. Me, though, I know. I hope that Rabbit will get out of this all right. Stop that now. Yes, sure. But I can hope that and I do. That I blow it well and that she gets out all right. Good. Sure. Just that. That is all I want now.

He lay there now and looked away from the road and the sentry box and across to the far mountain. Just do not think at all, he told himself. He lay there quietly and watched the morning come. It was a fine early summer morning and it came very fast now in the end of May. Once a motorcyclist in a leather coat and allleather helmet with an automatic rifle in a holster by his left leg came across the bridge and went on up the road. Once an ambulance crossed the bridge, passed below him, and went up the road. But that was all. He smelled the pines and he heard the stream and the bridge showed clear now and beautiful in the morning light. He lay there behind the pine tree, with the submachine gun across his left forearm, and he never looked at the sentry box again until, long after it seemed that it was never coming, that nothing could happen on such a lovely late May morning, he heard the sudden, clustered, thudding of the bombs.

As he heard the bombs, the first thumping noise of them, before the echo of them came back in thunder from the mountain, Robert Jordan drew in a long breath and lifted the submachine gun from where it lay. His arm felt stiff from its weight and his fingers were heavy with reluctance.

The man in the sentry box stood up when he heard the bombs. Robert Jordan saw him reach for his rifle and step forward out of the box listening. He stood in the road with the sun shining on him. The knitted cap was on the side of his head and the sun was on his unshaved face as he looked up into the sky toward where the planes were bombing.

There was no mist on the road now and Robert Jordan saw the man, clearly and sharply, standing there on the road looking up at the sky. The sun shone bright on him through the trees.

Robert Jordan felt his own breath tight now as though a strand of wire bound his chest and, steadying his elbows, feeling the corrugations of the forward grip against his fingers, he put the oblong of the foresight, settled now in the notch of the rear, onto the center of the man's chest and squeezed the trigger gently.

He felt the quick, liquid, spastic lurching of the gun against his shoulder and on the road the man, looking surprised and hurt, slid forward on his knees and his forehead doubled to the road. His rifle fell by him and lay there with one of the man's fingers twisted through the trigger guard, his wrist bent forward. The rifle lay, bayonet forward on the road. Robert Jordan looked away from the man lying with his head doubled under on the road to the bridge, and the sentry box at the other end. He could not see the other sentry and he looked down the slope to the right where he knew Agustin was hidden. Then he heard Anselmo shoot, the shot smashing an echo back from the gorge. Then he heard him shoot again.

With that second shot came the cracking boom of grenades from around the corner below the bridge. Then there was the noise of grenades from well up the road to the left. Then he heard rifle-firing up the road and from below came the noise of Pablo's cavalry automatic rifle spat-spat-spat-spatting into the noise of grenades. He saw Anselmo scrambling down the steep cut to the far end of the bridge and he slung the submachine gun over his shoulder and picked up the two heavy packs from behind the pine trunks and with one in each hand, the packs pulling his arms so that he felt the tendons would pull out of his shoulders, he ran lurching down the steep slope to the road.

As he ran he heard Agustin shouting, '*Buena, caza, Inglts.*

Buena cazaf' and he thought, 'Nice hunting, like hell, nice hunting,' and just then he heard Anselmo shoot at the far end of the bridge, the noise of the shot clanging in the steel girders. He passed the sentry where he lay and ran onto the bridge, the packs swinging.

The old man came running toward him, holding his carbine in one hand. '*Sin novedad,*' he shouted. 'There's nothing wrong. *Tuve que rematarlo.* I had to finish him.'

Robert Jordan, kneeling, opening the packs in the center of the bridge taking out his material, saw that tears were running down Anselmo's cheeks through the gray beard stubble.

'*Yo mate uno tambien,*' he said to Anselmo. 'I killed one too,' and jerked his head toward where the sentry lay hunched over in the road at the end of the bridge.

'Yes, man, yes,' Anselmo said. 'We have to kill them and we kill them.'

Robert Jordan was climbing down into the framework of the bridge. The girders were cold and wet with dew under his hands and he climbed carefully, feeling the sun on his back, bracing himself in a bridge truss, hearing the noise of the tumbling water below him, hearing firing, too much firing, up the road at the upper post. He was sweating heavily now and it was cool under the bridge. He had a coil of wire around one arm and a pair of pliers hung by a thong from his wrist.

'Hand me that down a package at a time, *viejo,*' he called up to Anselmo. The old man leaned far over the edge handing down the oblong blocks of explosive and Robert Jordan reached up for them, shoved them in where he wanted them, packed them close, braced them, 'Wedges, *viejo!* Give me wedges!' smelling the fresh shingle smell of the new whittled wedges as he tapped them in tight to hold the charge between the girders.

Now as he worked, placing, bracing, wedging, lashing tight with wire, thinking only of demolition, working fast and skillfully as a surgeon works, he heard a rattle of firing from below on the road. Then there was the noise of a grenade. Then another, booming through the rushing noise the water made. Then it was quiet from that direction.

'Damn,' he thought. 'I wonder what hit them then?'

There was still firing up the road at the upper post. Too damned much firing, and he was lashing two grenades side by side on top of the braced blocks of explosive, winding wire over their corrugations so they would hold tight and firm and lashing it tight; twisting it with the pliers. He felt of the whole thing and then, to make it more solid, tapped in a wedge above the grenades that blocked the whole charge firmly in against the steel.

'The other side now, *viejo*,' he shouted up to Anselmo and climbed across through the trestling, like a bloody Tarzan in a rolled steel forest, he thought, and then coming out from under the dark, the stream tumbling below him, he looked up and saw Anselmo's face as he reached the packages of explosive down to him. Goddamn good face, he thought. Not crying now. That's all to the good. And one side done. This side now and we're done.

This will drop it like what all. Come on. Don't get excited. Do it. Clean and fast as the last one. Don't fumble with it. Take your time. Don't try to do it faster than you can. You can't lose now. Nobody can keep you from blowing one side now. You're doing it just the way you should. This is a cool place. Christ, it feels cool as a wine cellar and there's no crap. Usually working under a stone bridge it's full of crap. This is a dream bridge. A bloody dream bridge. It's the old man on top who's in a bad spot. Don't try to do it faster than you can. I wish that shooting would be over up above. 'Give me some wedges, *viejo*.' I don't like that shooting still. Pilar has got in trouble there. Some of the post must have been out. Out back; or behind the mill. They're still shooting. That means there's somebody still at the mill. And all that damned sawdust. Those big piles of sawdust. Sawdust, when it's old and packed, is good stuff to fight behind. There must be several of them still. It's quiet below with Pablo. I wonder what that second flare-up was. It must have been a car or a motorcyclist. I hope to God they don't have any armored cars come up or any tanks. Go on. Put it in just as fast as you can and wedge it tight and lash it fast. You're shaking, like a Goddamn woman. What the hell is the matter with you? You're trying to do it too fast. I'll bet that Goddamn woman up above isn't shaking. That Pilar. Maybe she is too. She sounds as though she were in plenty trouble. She'll shake if she gets in enough. Like everybody bloody else.

He leaned out and up into the sunlight and as he reached his hand up to take what Anselmo handed him, his head now above the noise of the falling water, the firing increased sharply up the road and then the noise of grenades again. Then more grenades.

'They rushed the sawmill then.'

It's lucky I've got this stuff in blocks, he thought. Instead of sticks. What the hell. It's just neater. Although a lousy canvas sack full of jelly would be quicker. Two sacks. No. One of that would do. And if we just had detonators and the old exploder. That son of a bitch threw my exploder in the river. That old box and the places that it's been. In this river he threw it. That bastard Pablo. He gave them hell there below just now. 'Give me some more of that, *viejo*.'

The old man's doing very well. He's in quite a place up there. He hated to shoot that sentry. So did I but I didn't think about it. Nor do I think about it now. You have to do that. But then Anselmo got a cripple. I know about cripples. I think that killing a man with an automatic weapon makes it easier. I mean on the one doing it. It is different. After the first touch it is it that does it. Not you. Save that to go into some other time. You and your head. You have a nice thinking head old Jordan. Roll Jordan, Roll! They used to yell that at football when you lugged the ball. Do you know the damned Jordan is really not much bigger than that creek down there below. At the source, you mean. So is anything else at the source. This is a place here under this bridge. A home away from home. Come on Jordan, pull yourself together. This is serious Jordan. Don't you understand? Serious. It's less so all the time. Look at that other side. *Para que?* I'm all right now however she goes. As Maine goes so goes the nation. As Jordan goes so go the bloody Israelites. The bridge, I mean. As Jordan goes, so goes the bloody bridge, other way around, really.

'Give me some more of that, Anselmo old boy,' he said. The old man nodded. 'Almost through,' Robert Jordan said. The old man nodded again.

Finishing wiring the grenades down he no longer heard the firing from up the road. Suddenly he was working only with the noise of the stream. He looked down and saw it boiling up white below him through the boulders and then dropping down to a clear pebbled pool where one of the wedges he had dropped swung around in the current. As he looked a trout rose for some insect and made a circle on the surface close to where the chip was turning. As he twisted the wire tight with the pliers that held these two grenades in place, he saw, through the metal of the bridge, the sunlight on the green slope of the mountain. It was brown three days ago, he thought.

Out from the cool dark under the bridge he leaned into the bright sun and shouted to Anselmo's bending face, 'Give me the big coil of wire.'

The old man handed it down.

For God's sake don't loosen them any yet. This will pull them. I wish you could string them through. But with the length of wire you are using it's O.K., Robert Jordan thought as he felt the cotter pins that held the rings that would release the levers on the hand grenades. He checked that the grenades, lashed on their sides, had room for the levers to spring when the pins were pulled (the wire that lashed them ran through under the levers), then he attached a length of wire to one ring, wired it onto the main wire that ran to the ring of the outside grenade, paid off some slack from the coil and passed it around a steel brace and then handed the coil up to Anselmo. 'Hold it carefully,' he said.

He climbed up onto the bridge, took the coil from the old man and walked back as fast as he could pay out wire toward where the sentry was slumped in the road, leaning over the side of the bridge and paying out wire from the coil as he walked.

'Bring the sacks,' he shouted to Anselmo as he walked backwards. As he passed he stooped down and picked up the submachine gun and slung it over his shoulder again.

It was then, looking up from paying out wire, that he saw, well up the road, those who were coming back from the upper post.

There were four of them, he saw, and then he had to watch his wire so it would be clear and not foul against any of the outer work of the bridge. Eladio was not with them.

Robert Jordan carried the wire clear past the end of the bridge, took a loop around the last stanchion and then ran along the road until he stopped beside a stone marker. He cut the wire and handed it to Anselmo.

'Hold this, *viejo*,' he said. 'Now walk back with me to the bridge. Take up on it as you walk. No. I will.'

At the bridge he pulled the wire back out through the hitch so it now ran clear and unfouled to the grenade rings and handed it, stretching alongside the bridge but running quite clear, to Anselmo.

'Take this back to that high stone,' he said. 'Hold it easily but firmly. Do not put any force on it. When thou pullest hard, hard, the bridge will blow. *Comprendes?*'

'Yes.'

'Treat it softly but do not let it sag so it will foul. Keep it lightly firm but not pulling until thou pullest. *Comprendes?*'

'Yes.'

'When thou pullest really pull. Do not jerk.'

Robert Jordan while he spoke was looking up the road at the remainder of Pilar's band. They were close now and he saw Primitivo and Rafael were supporting Fernando. He looked to be shot through the groin for he was holding himself there with both hands while the man and the boy held him on either side. His right leg was dragging, the side of the shoe scraping on the road as they walked him. Pilar was climbing the bank into the timber carrying three rifles. Robert Jordan could not see her face but her head was up and she was climbing as fast as she could.

'How does it go?' Primitivo called.

'Good. We're almost finished,' Robert Jordan shouted back.

There was no need to ask how it went with them. As he looked away the three were on the edge of the road and Fernando was shaking his head as they tried to get him up the bank.

'Give me a rifle here,' Robert Jordan heard him say in a choky voice.

'No, *hombre*. We will get thee to the horses.'

'What would I do with a horse?' Fernando said. 'I am very well here.'

Robert Jordan did not hear the rest for he was speaking to Anselmo.

'Blow it if tanks come,' he said. 'But only if they come onto it. Blow it if armored cars come. If they come onto it. Anything else Pablo will stop.'

'I will not blow it with thee beneath it.'

'Take no account of me. Blow it if thou needest to. I fix the other wire and come back. Then we will blow it together.'

He started running for the center of the bridge.

Anselmo saw Robert Jordan run up the bridge, coil of wire over his arm, pliers hanging from one wrist and the submachine gun slung over his back. He saw him climb down under the rail of the bridge and out of sight. Anselmo held the wire in his hand, his right hand, and he crouched behind the stone marker and looked down the road and across the bridge. Halfway between him and the bridge was the sentry, who had settled now closer to the road, sinking closer onto the smooth road surface as the sun weighed on his back. His rifle, lying on the road, the bayonet fixed, pointed straight toward Anselmo. The old man looked past him along the surface of the bridge crossed by the shadows of the bridge rail to where the road swung to the left along the gorge and then turned out of sight behind the rocky wall. He looked at the far sentry box with the sun shining on it and then, conscious of the wire in his hand, he turned his head to where Fernando was speaking to Primitivo and the gypsy.

'Leave me here,' Fernando said. 'It hurts much and there is much hemorrhage inside. I feel it in the inside when I move.'

'Let us get thee up the slope,' Primitivo said. 'Put thy arms around our shoulders and we will take thy legs.'

'It is inutile,' Fernando said. 'Put me here behind a stone. I am as useful here as above.'

'But when we go,' Primitivo said.

'Leave me here,' Fernando said. 'There is no question of my travelling with this. Thus it gives one horse more. I am very well here. Certainly they will come soon.'

'We can take thee up the hill,' the gypsy said. 'Easily.'

He was, naturally, in a deadly hurry to be gone, as was Primitivo. But they had brought him this far.

'Nay,' Fernando said. 'I am very well here. What passes with Eladio?'

The gypsy put his finger on his head to show where the wound had been.

'Here,' he said. 'After thee. When we made the rush.'

'Leave me,' Fernando said. Anselmo could see he was suffering much. He held both hands against his groin now and put his head back against the bank, his legs straight out before him. His face was gray and sweating.

'Leave me now please, for a favor,' he said. His eyes were shut with pain, the edges of the lips twitching. 'I find myself very well here.'

'Here is a rifle and cartridges,' Primitivo said. 'Is it mine?' Fernando asked, his eyes shut.

'Nay, the Pilar has thine,' Primitivo said. 'This is mine.'

'I would prefer my own,' Fernando said. 'I am more accustomed to it.'

'I will bring it to thee,' the gypsy lied to him. 'Keep this until it comes.'

'I am in a very good position here,' Fernando said. 'Both for up the road and for the bridge.' He opened his eyes, turned his head and looked across the bridge, then shut them as the pain came. The gypsy tapped his head and motioned with his thumb to Primitivo for them to be off.

'Then we will be down for thee,' Primitivo said and started up the slope after the gypsy, who was climbing fast.

Fernando lay back against the bank. In front of him was one of the whitewashed stones that marked the edge of the road. His head was in the shadow but the sun shone on his plugged and bandaged wound and on his hands that were cupped over it. His legs and his feet also were in the sun. The rifle lay beside him and there were three clips of cartridges shining in the sun beside the rifle. A fly crawled on his hands but the small tickling did not come through the pain.

'Fernando!' Anselmo called to him from where he crouched, holding the wire. He had made a loop in the end of the wire and twisted it close so he could hold it in his fist.

'Fernando!' he called again.

Fernando opened his eyes and looked at him.

'How does it go?' Fernando asked.

'Very good,' Anselmo said. 'Now in a minute we will be blowing it.'

'I am pleased. Anything you need me for advise me,' Fernando said and shut his eyes again and the pain lurched in him.

Anselmo looked away from him and out onto the bridge.

He was watching for the first sight of the coil of wire being handed up onto the bridge and for the *Inglés's* sunburnt head and face to follow it as he would pull himself up the side. At the same time he was watching beyond the bridge for anything to come around the far corner of the road. He did not feel afraid now at all and he had not been afraid all the day. It goes so fast and it is so normal, he thought. I hated the shooting of the guard and it made me an emotion but that is passed now. How could the *Inglés* say that the shooting of a man is like the shooting of an animal? In all hunting I have had an elation and no feeling of wrong. But to shoot a man gives a feeling as though one had struck one's own brother when you are grown men. And to shoot him various times to kill him. Nay, do not think of that. That gave thee too much emotion and thee ran blubbering down the bridge like a woman.

That is over, he told himself, and thou canst try to atone for it as for the others. But now thou has what thou asked for last night coming home across the hills. Thou art in battle and thou hast no problem. If I die on this morning now it is all right.

Then he looked at Fernando lying there against the bank with his hands cupped over the groove of his hip, his lips blue, his eyes tight shut, breathing heavily and slowly, and he thought, If I die may it be quickly. Nay I said I would ask nothing more if I were granted what I needed for today. So I will not ask. Understand? I ask nothing. Nothing in any way. Give me what I asked for and I leave all the rest according to discretion.

He listened to the noise that came, far away, of the battle at the pass and he said to himself, Truly this is a great day. I should realize and know what a day this is.

But there was no lift or any excitement in his heart. That was all gone and there was nothing but a calmness. And now, as he crouched behind the marker stone with the looped wire in his hand and another loop of it around his wrist and the gravel beside the road under his knees he was not lonely nor did he feel in any way alone. He was one with the wire in his hand and one with the bridge, and one with the charges the *Inglés* had placed. He was one with the *Inglés* still working under the bridge and he was one with all of the battle and with the Republic.

But there was no excitement. It was all calm now and the sun beat down on his neck and on his shoulders as he crouched and as he looked up he saw the high, cloudless sky and the slope of the mountain rising beyond the river and he was not happy but he was neither lonely nor afraid.

Up the hill slope Pilar lay behind a tree watching the road that came down from the pass. She had three loaded rifles by her and she handed one to Primitivo as he dropped down beside her.

'Get down there,' she said. 'Behind that tree. Thou, gypsy, over there,' she pointed to another tree below. 'Is he dead?'

'Nay. Not yet,' Primitivo said.

'It was bad luck,' Pilar said. 'If we had had two more it need not have happened. He should have crawled around the sawdust pile. Is he all right there where he is?'

Primitivo shook his head.

'When the *Inglés* blows the bridge will fragments come this far?' the gypsy asked from behind his tree.

'I don't know,' Pilar said. 'But Agustin with the *máquina* is closer than thee. The *Inglés* would not have placed him there if it were too close.'

'But I remember with the blowing of the train the lamp of the engine blew by over my head and pieces of steel flew by like swallows.'

'Thou hast poetic memories,' Pilar said. 'Like swallows. *joder!* They were like wash boilers. Listen, gypsy, thou hast comported thyself well today. Now do not let thy fear catch up with thee.'

'Well, I only asked if it would blow this far so I might keep well behind the tree trunk,' the gypsy said.

'Keep it thus,' Pilar told him. 'How many have we killed?'

'*Pues* five for us. Two here. Canst thou not see the other at the far end - Look there toward the bridge. See the box? Look! Dost see?' He pointed. 'Then there were eight below for Pablo. I watched that post for the *Inglés*.'

Pilar grunted. Then she said violently and raging, 'What passes with that *Inglés*? What is he obscenitying off under that bridge. *Vaya mandanga!* Is he building a bridge or blowing one?'

She raised her head and looked down at Anselmo crouched behind the stone marker.

'Hey, *viejo!*' she shouted. 'What passes with thy obscenity of an Inglés?'

'Patience, woman,' Anselmo called up, holding the wire lightly but firmly. 'He is terminating his work.'

'But what in the name of the great whore does he take so much time about?'

'*Es muy condenzudo!*' Anselmo shouted. 'It is a scientific labor.' 'I obscenity in the milk of science,' Pilar raged to the gypsy.

'Let the filth-faced obscenity blow it and be done. Maria!' she shouted in her deep voice up the hill. 'Thy *Inglés*—' and she shouted a flood of obscenity about Jordan's imaginary actions under the bridge.

'Calm yourself, woman,' Anselmo called from the road. 'He is doing an enormous work. He is finishing it now.'

'The hell with it,' Pilar raged. 'It is speed that counts.'

Just then they all heard firing start down the road where Pablo was holding the post he had taken. Pilar stopped cursing and listened. 'Ay,' she said. 'Ayee. Ayee. That's it.'

Robert Jordan heard it as he swung the coil of wire up onto the bridge with one hand and then pulled himself up after it. As his knees rested on the edge of the iron of the bridge and his hands were on the surface he heard the machine gun firing around the bend below. It was a different sound from Pablo's automatic rifle. He got to his feet, leaned over, passed his coil of wire clear and commenced to pay out wire as he walked backwards and sideways along the bridge.

He heard the firing and as he walked he felt it in the pit of his stomach as though it echoed on his own diaphragm. It was closer now as he walked and he looked back at the bend of the road. But it was still clear of any car, or tank or men. It was still clear when he was halfway to the end of the bridge. It was still clear when he was three quarters of the way, his wire running clear and unfouled, and it was still clear as he climbed around behind the sentry box, holding his wire out to keep it from catching on the iron work. Then he was on the road and it was still clear below on the road and then he was moving fast backwards up the little washed-out gully by the lower side of the road as an outfielder goes backwards for a long fly ball, keeping the wire taut, and now he was almost opposite Anselmo's stone and it was still clear below the bridge.

Then he heard the truck coming down the road and he saw it over his shoulder just coming onto the long slope and he swung his wrist once around the wire and yelled to Anselmo, 'Blow her!' and he dug his heels in and leaned back hard onto the tension of the wire with a turn of it around his wrist and the noise of the truck was coming behind and ahead there was the road with the dead sentry and the long bridge and the stretch of road below, still clear and then there was a cracking roar and the middle of the bridge rose up in the air like a wave breaking and he felt the blast from the explosion roll back against him as he dove on his face in the pebbly gully with his hands holding tight over his head. His face was down against the pebbles as the bridge settled where it had risen and the familiar yellow smell of it rolled over him in acrid smoke and then it commenced to rain pieces of steel.

After the steel stopped falling he was still alive and he raised his head and looked across the bridge. The center section of it was gone. There were jagged pieces of steel on the bridge with their bright, new torn edges and ends and these were all over the road. The truck had stopped up the road about a hundred yards. The driver and the two men who had been with him were running toward a culvert.

Fernando was still lying against the bank and he was still breathing. His arms straight by his sides, his hands relaxed.

Anselmo lay face down behind the white marking stone. His left arm was doubled under his head and his right arm was stretched straight out. The loop of wire was still around his right fist. Robert Jordan got to his feet, crossed the road, knelt by him and made sure that he was dead. He did not turn him over to see what the piece of steel had done. He was dead and that was all.

He looked very small, dead, Robert Jordan thought. He looked small and gray-headed and Robert Jordan thought, I wonder how he ever carried such big loads if that is the size he really was. Then he saw the shape of the calves and the thighs in the tight, gray herdsman's breeches and the worn soles of the rope-soled shoes and he picked up Anselmo's carbine and the two sacks, practically empty now and went over and picked up the rifle that lay beside Fernando. He kicked a jagged piece of steel off the surface of the road. Then he swung the two rifles over his shoulder, holding them by the muzzles, and started up the slope into the timber. He did not look back nor did he even look across the bridge at the road. They were still firing around the bend below but he cared nothing about that now.

He was coughing from the TNT fumes and he felt numb all through himself.

He put one of the rifles down by Pilar where she lay behind the tree. She looked and saw that made three rifles that she bad again.

'You are too high up here,' he said. 'There's a truck up the road where you can't see it. They thought it was planes. You better get further down. I'm going down with Agustin to cover Pablo.'

'The old one?' she asked him, looking at his face. 'Dead.'

He coughed again, wrackingly, and spat on the ground.

'Thy bridge is blown, *Inglés*,' Pilar looked at him. 'Don't forget that.'

'I don't forget anything,' he said.' You have a big voice,' he said to Pilar. 'I have heard thee bellow. Shout up to the Maria and tell her that I am all right.'

'We lost two at the sawmill,' Pilar said, trying to make him understand.

'So I saw,' Robert Jordan said. 'Did you do something stupid?'

'Go and obscenity thyself, *Inglés*,' Pilar said.

'Fernando and Eladio were men, too.'

'Why don't you go up with the horses?' Robert Jordan said. 'I can cover here better than thee.'

'Thou art to cover Pablo.'

'The hell with Pablo. Let him cover himself with *mierda*.'

'Nay, *Inglés*. He came back. He has fought much below there. Thou hast not listened? He is fighting now. Against something bad. Do you not hear?'

'I'll cover him. But obscenity all of you. Thou and Pablo both.'

'*Inglés*,' Pilar said. 'Calm thyself. I have been with thee in this as no one could be. Pablo did thee a wrong but he returned.'

'If I had had the exploder the old man would not have been killed. I could have blown it from here.'

'If, if, if-' Pilar said.

The anger and the emptiness and the hate that had come with the let-down after the bridge, when he had looked up from where he had lain and crouching, seen Anselmo dead, were still all through him. In him, too, was despair from the sorrow that soldiers turn to hatred in order that they may continue to be soldiers. Now it was over he was lonely, detached and unelated and he hated every one he saw.

'If there had been no snow—' Pilar said. And then, not suddenly, as a physical release could have been (if the woman would have put her arm around him, say) but slowly and from his head he began to accept it and let the hate go out. Sure, the snow. That had done it. The snow. Done it to others. Once you saw it again as it was to others, once you got rid of your own self, the always ridding of self that you had to do in war. Where there could be no self. Where yourself is only to be lost. Then, from his losing of it, he heard Pilar say, 'Sordo—'

'What?' he said.

'Sordo—'

'Yes,' Robert Jordan said. He grinned at her, a cracked, stiff, tootightened-facial-tendoned grin. 'Forget it. I was wrong. I am sorry, woman. Let us do this well and all together. And the bridge *is* blown, as thou sayest.'

'Yes. Thou must think of things in their place.'

'Then I go now to Agustin. Put thy gypsy much farther down so that he can see well up the road. Give those guns to Primitivo and take this *máquina*. Let me show thee.'

'Keep the *máquina*,' Pilar said. 'We will not be here any time.

Pablo should come now and we will be going.'

'Rafael,' Robert Jordan said, 'come down here with me. Here. Good. See those coming out of the culvert. There, above the truck? Coming toward the truck? Hit me one of those. Sit. Take it easy.'

The gypsy aimed carefully and fired and as he jerked the bolt back and ejected the shell Robert Jordan said, 'Over. You threw against the rock above. See the rock dust? Lower, by two feet. Now, careful. They're running. Good. *Sigue tirando*.'

'I got one,' the gypsy said. The man was down in the road halfway between the culvert and the truck. The other two did not stop to drag him. They ran for the culvert and ducked in.

'Don't shoot at him,' Robert Jordan said. 'Shoot for the top part of a front tire on the truck. So if you miss you'll hit the engine. Good.' He watched with the glasses. 'A little lower. Good. You shoot like hell. *Mucha! Mucho!* Shoot me the top of the radiator. Anywhere on the radiator. Thou art a champion. Look. Don't let anything come past that point there. See?'

'Watch me break the windshield in the truck,' the gypsy said happily.

'Nay. The truck is already sick,' Robert Jordan said. 'Hold thy fire until anything comes down the road. Start firing when it is opposite the culvert. Try to hit the driver. That you all should fire, then,' he spoke to Pilar who had come farther down the slope with Primitivo. 'You are wonderfully placed here. See how that steepness guards thy flank?'

'That you should get about thy business with Agustín,' Pilar said. 'Desist from thy lecture. I have seen terrain in my time.'

'Put Primitivo farther up there,' Robert Jordan said. 'There. See, man? This side of where the bank steepens.'

'Leave me,' said Pilar. 'Get along, *Inglés*. Thou and thy perfection. Here there is no problem.' Just then they heard the planes.

Maria had been with the horses for a long time, but they were no comfort to her. Nor was she any to them. From where she was in the forest she could not see the road nor could she see the bridge and when the firing started she put her arm around the neck of the big white-faced bay stallion that she had gentled and brought gifts to many times when the horses had been in the corral in the trees below the camp. But her nervousness made the big stallion nervous, too, and he jerked his head, his nostrils widening at the firing and the noise of the bombs. Maria could not keep still and she walked around patting and gentling the horses and making them all more nervous and agitated.

She tried to think of the firing not as just a terrible thing that was happening, but to realize that it was Pablo below with the new men, and Pilar with the others above, and that she must not worry nor get into a panic but must have confidence in Roberto. But she could not do this and all the firing above and below the bridge and the distant sound of the battle that rolled down from the pass like the noise of a far-off storm with a dried, rolling rattle in it and the irregular beat of the bombs was simply a horrible thing that almost kept her from breathing.

Then later she heard Pilar's big voice from away below on the hillside shouting up some obscenity to her that she could not understand and she thought, Oh, God no, no. Don't talk like that with him in peril. Don't offend any one and make useless risks. Don't give any provocation.

Then she commenced to pray for Roberto quickly and automatically as she had done at school, saying the prayers as fast as she could and counting them on the fingers of her left hand, praying by tens of each of the two prayers she was repeating. Then the bridge blew and one horse snapped his halter when he rose and jerked his head at the cracking roar and he went off through the trees. Maria caught him finally and brought him back, shivering, trembling, his chest dark with sweat, the saddle down, and coming back through the trees she heard shooting below and she thought I cannot stand this longer. I cannot live not knowing any longer. I cannot breathe and my mouth is so dry. And I am afraid and I am no good and I frighten the horses and only caught this horse by hazard because he knocked the saddle down against a tree and caught himself kicking into the stirrups and now as I get the saddle up, Oh, God, I do not know. I cannot bear it. Oh please have him be all right for all my heart and all of me is at the bridge. The Republic is one thing and we must win is another thing. But, Oh, Sweet Blessed Virgin, bring him back to me from the bridge and I will do anything thou sayest ever. Because I am not here. There isn't any me. I am only with him. Take care of him for me and that will be me and then I will do the things for thee and he will not mind. Nor will it be against the Republic. Oh, please forgive me for I am very confused. I am too confused now. But if thou takest care of him I will do whatever is right. I will do what he says and what you say. With the two of me I will do it. But this now not knowing I cannot endure.

Then, the horse tied again, she with the saddle up now, the blanket smoothed, hauling tight on the cinch she heard the big, deep voice from the timber below, 'Maria! Maria! Thy *Inglés* is all right. Hear me? All right. *Sin Novedadl* '

Maria held the saddle with both hands and pressed her cropped head hard against it and cried. She heard the deep voice shouting again and she turned from the saddle and shouted, choking,' Yes! Thank you!' Then, choking again, 'Thank you! Thank you very much!'

When they heard the planes they all looked up and the planes were coming from Segovia very high in the sky, silvery in the high sky, their drumming rising over all the other sounds.

'Those!' Pilar said. 'There has only lacked those!'

Robert Jordan put his arm on her shoulders as he watched them. 'Nay, woman,' he said. 'Those do not come for us. Those have no time for us. Calm thyself.'

'I hate them.'

'Me too. But now I must go to Agustin.'

He circled the hillside through the pines and all the time there was the throbbing, drumming of the planes and across the shattered bridge on the road below, around the bend of the road there was the intermittent hammering fire of a heavy machine gun.

Robert Jordan dropped down to where Agustin lay in the clump of scrub pines behind the automatic rifle and more planes were coming all the time.

'What passes below?' Agustin said. 'What is Pablo doing? Doesn't he know the bridge is gone?'

'Maybe he can't leave.'

'Then let us leave. The hell with him.'

'He will come now if he is able,' Robert Jordan said. 'We should see him now.'

'I have not heard him,' Agustin said. 'Not for five minutes. No. There! Listen! There he is. That's him.'

There was a burst of the spot-spot-spotting fire of the cavalry submachine gun, then another, then another.

'That's the bastard,' Robert Jordan said.

He watched still more planes coming over in the high cloudless blue sky and he watched Agustin's face as he looked up at them. Then he looked down at the shattered bridge and across to the stretch of road which still was clear. He coughed and spat and listened to the heavy machine gun hammer again below the bend. It sounded to be in the same place that it was before.

'And what's that?' Agustin asked. 'What the unnameable is that?' 'It has been going since before I blew the bridge,' Robert Jordan said. He looked down at the bridge now and he could see the stream through the torn gap where the center had fallen, hanging like a bent steel apron. He heard the first of the planes that had gone over now bombing up above at the pass and more were still coming. The noise of their motors filled all the high sky and looking up he saw their pursuit, minute and tiny, circling and wheeling high above them.

'I don't think they ever crossed the lines the other morning,' Primitivo said. 'They must have swung off to the west and then come back. They could not be making an attack if they had seen these.'

'Most of these are new,' Robert Jordan said.

He had the feeling of something that had started normally and had then brought great, outsized, giant repercussions. It was as though you had thrown a stone and the stone made a ripple and the ripple returned roaring and toppling as a tidal wave. Or as though you shouted and the echo came back in rolls and peals of thunder, and the thunder was deadly. Or as though you struck one man and he fell and as far as you could see other men rose up all armed and armored. He was glad he was not with Golz up at the pass.

Lying there, by Agustin, watching the planes going over, listening for firing behind him, watching the road below where he knew he would see something but not what it would be, he still felt numb with the surprise that he had not been killed at the bridge. He had accepted being killed so completely that all of this now seemed unreal. Shake out of that, he said to himself. Get rid of that. There is much, much, much to be done today. But it would not leave him and he felt, consciously, all of this becoming like a dream.

'You swallowed too much of that smoke,' he told himself. But he knew it was not that. He could feel, solidly, how unreal it all was through the absolute reality and he looked down at the bridge and then back to the sentry lying on the road, to where Anselmo lay, to Fernando against the bank and back up the smooth, brown road to the stalled truck and still it was unreal.

'You better sell out your part of you quickly,' he told himself. 'You're like one of those cocks in the pit where nobody has seen the wound given and it doesn't show and he is already going cold with it.'

'Nuts,' he said to himself. 'You are a little groggy is all, and you have a let-down after responsibility, is all. Take it easy.'

Then Agustin grabbed his arm and pointed and he looked across the gorge and saw Pablo.

They saw Pablo come running around the corner of the bend in the road. At the sheer rock where the road went out of sight they saw him stop and lean against the rock and fire back up the road. Robert Jordan saw Pablo, short, heavy and stocky, his cap gone, leaning against the rock wall and firing the short cavalry automatic rifle and he could see the bright flicker of the cascading brass hulls as the sun caught them. They saw Pablo crouch and fire another burst. Then, without looking back, he came running, short, bowlegged, fast, his head bent down straight toward the bridge.

Robert Jordan had pushed Agustin over and he had the stock of the big automatic rifle against his shoulder and was sighting on the bend of the road. His own submachine gun lay by his left hand. It was not accurate enough for that range.

As Pablo came toward them Robert Jordan sighted on the bend but nothing came. Pablo had reached the bridge, looked over his shoulder once, glanced at the bridge, and then turned to his left and gone down into the gorge and out of sight. Robert Jordan was still watching the bend and nothing had come in sight. Agustin got up on one knee. He could see Pablo climbing down into the gorge like a goat. There had been no noise of firing below since they had first seen Pablo.

'You see anything up above? On the rocks above?' Robert Jordan asked.

'Nothing.'

Robert Jordan watched the bend of the road. He knew the wall just below that was too steep for any one to climb but below it eased and some one might have circled up above.

If things had been unreal before, they were suddenly real enough now. It was as though a reflex lens camera had been suddenly brought into focus. It was then he saw the low-bodied, angled snout and squat green, gray and brown-splashed turret with the projecting machine gun come around the bend into the bright sun. He fired on it and he could hear the spang against the steel. The little whippet tank scuttled back behind the rock wall. Watching the corner, Robert Jordan saw the nose just reappear, then the edge of the turret showed and the turret swung so that the gun was pointing down the road.

'It seems like a mouse coming out of his hole,' Agustin said. 'Look, *Inglés*.'

'He has little confidence,' Robert Jordan said.

'This is the big insect Pablo has been fighting,' Agustin said. 'Hit him again, *Inglés*.'

'Nay. I cannot hurt him. I don't want him to see where we are.'

The tank commenced to fire down the road. The bullets hit the road surface and sung off and now they were pinging and clanging in the iron of the bridge. It was the same machine gun they had heard below.

'*Cabron!*' Agustin said. 'Is that the famous tanks, *Inglés?*'

'That's a baby one.'

Cabron. If I had a baby bottle full of gasoline I would climb up there and set fire to him. What will he do, *Inglés?*'

'After a while he will have another look.'

'And these are what men fear,' Agustin said. 'Look, *Inglés!* He's rekilling the sentries.'

'Since he has no other target,' Robert Jordan said. 'Do not reproach him.'

But he was thinking, Sure, make fun of him. But suppose it was you, way back here in your own country and they held you up with firing on the main road. Then a bridge was blown. Wouldn't you think it was mined ahead or that there was a trap? Sure you would. He's done all right. He's waiting for something else to come up. He's engaging the enemy. It's only us. But he can't tell that. Look at the little bastard.

The little tank had nosed a little farther around the corner.

Just then Agustin saw Pablo coming over the edge of the gorge, pulling himself over on hands and knees, his bristly face running with sweat.

'Here comes the son of a bitch,' he said.

'Who?'

'Pablo.'

Robert Jordan looked, saw Pablo, and then he commenced firing at the part of the camouflaged turret of the tank where he knew the slit above the machine gun would be. The little tank whirred backwards, scuttling out of sight and Robert Jordan picked up the automatic rifle, clamped the tripod against the barrel and swung the gun with its still hot muzzle over his shoulder. The muzzle was so hot it burned his shoulder and he shoved it far behind him turning the stock flat in his hand.

'Bring the sack of pans and my little *máquina*,' he shouted, 'and come running.'

Robert Jordan ran up the hill through the pines. Agustin was close behind him and behind him Pablo was coming.

'Pilar!' Jordan shouted across the hill. 'Come on, woman!'

The three of them were going as fast as they could up the steep slope. They could not run any more because the grade was too severe and Pablo, who had no load but the light cavalry submachine gun, had closed up with the other two.

'And thy people?' Agustin said to Pablo out of his dry mouth.

'All dead,' Pablo said. He was almost unable to breathe. Agustin turned his head and looked at him.

'We have plenty of horses now, *Inglés*,' Pablo panted.

'Good,' Robert Jordan said. The murderous bastard, he thought. 'What did you encounter?'

'Everything,' Pablo said. He was breathing in lunges. 'What passed with Pilar?'

'She lost Fernando and the brother—' 'Eladio,' Agustin said.

'And thou?' Pablo asked.

'I lost Anselmo.'

'There are lots of horses,' Pablo said. 'Even for the baggage.' Agustin bit his lip, looked at Robert Jordan and shook his head.

Below them, out of sight through the trees, they heard the tank firing on the road and bridge again.

Robert Jordan jerked his head. 'What passed with that?' he said to Pablo. He did not like to look at Pablo, nor to smell him, but he wanted to hear him.

'I could not leave with that there,' Pablo said. 'We were barricaded at the lower bend of the post. Finally it went back to look for something and I came.'

'What were you shooting at, at the bend?' Agustin asked bluntly.

Pablo looked at him, started to grin, thought better of it, and said nothing.

'Did you shoot them all?' Agustin asked. Robert Jordan was thinking, keep your mouth shut. It is none of your business now. They have done all that you could expect and more. This is an inter-tribal matter. Don't make moral judgments.

What do you expect from a murderer? You're working with a murderer. Keep your mouth shut. You knew enough about him before. This is nothing new. But you dirty bastard, he thought. You dirty, rotten bastard.

His chest was aching with climbing as though it would split after the running and ahead now through the trees he saw the horses.

'Go ahead,' Agustin was saying. 'Why do you not say you shot them?'

'Shut up,' Pablo said. 'I have fought much today and well. Ask the *Inglés*.'

'And now get us through today,' Robert Jordan said. 'For it is thee who has the plan for this.'

'I have a good plan,' Pablo said. 'With a little luck we will be all right.'

He was beginning to breathe better.

'You're not going to kill any of us, are you?' Agustin said. 'For I will kill thee now.'

'Shut up,' Pablo said. 'I have to look after thy interest and that of the band. This is war. One cannot do what one would wish.'

'*Cabron*,' said Agustin. 'You take all the prizes.'

'Tell me what thou encountered below,' Robert Jordan said to Pablo.

'Everything,' Pablo repeated. He was still breathing as though it were tearing his chest but he could talk steadily now and his face and head were running with sweat and his shoulders and chest were soaked with it. He looked at Robert Jordan cautiously to see if he were really friendly and then he grinned. 'Everything,' he said again. 'First we took the post. Then came a motorcyclist. Then another. Then an ambulance. Then a camion. Then the tank. Just before thou didst the bridge.'

'Then—'

'The tank could not hurt us but we could not leave for it commanded the road. Then it went away and I came.'

'And thy people?' Agustin put in, still looking for trouble.

'Shut up,' Pablo looked at him squarely, and his face was the face of a man who had fought well before any other thing had happened. 'They were not of our band.'

Now they could see the horses tied to the trees, the sun coming down on them through the pine branches and them tossing their heads and kicking against the botflies and Robert Jordan saw Maria and the next thing he was holding her tight, tight, with the automatic rifle leaning against his side, the flash-cone pressing against his ribs and Maria saying, 'Thou, Roberto. Oh, thou.'

'Yes, rabbit. My good, good rabbit. Now we go.'

'Art thou here truly?'

'Yes. Yes. Truly. Oh, thou!'

He had never thought that you could know that there was a woman if there was battle; nor that any part of you could know it, or respond to it; nor that if there was a woman that she should have breasts small, round and tight against you through a shirt; nor that they, the breasts, could know about the two of them in battle. But it was true and he thought, good. That's good. I would not have believed that and he held her to him once hard, hard, but he did not look at her, and then he slapped her where he never had slapped her and said, 'Mount. Mount. Get on that saddle, *guapa*.'

Then they were untying the halters and Robert Jordan had given the automatic rifle back to Agustin and slung his own submachine gun over his back, and he was putting bombs out of his pockets into the saddlebags, and he stuffed one empty pack inside the other and tied that one behind his saddle. Then Pilar came up, so breathless from the climb she could not talk, but only motioned.

Then Pablo stuffed three hobbles he had in his hand into a saddlebag, stood up and said, '*Que tal*, woman?' and she only nodded, and then they were all mounting.

Robert Jordan was on the big gray he had first seen in the snow of the morning of the day before and he felt that it was much horse between his legs and under his hands. He was wearing rope-soled shoes and the stirrups were a little too short; his submachine gun was slung over his shoulder, his pockets were full of clips and he was sitting reloading the one used clip, the reins under one arm, tight, watching Pilar mount into a strange sort of seat on top of the duffle lashed onto the saddle of the buckskin.

'Cut that stuff loose for God's sake,' Primitivo said. 'Thou wilt fall and the horse cannot carry it.'

'Shut up,' said Pilar. 'We go to make a life with this.'

'Canst ride like that, woman?' Pablo asked her from the *guardia-civil* saddle on the great bay horse.

'Like any milk peddler,' Pilar told him. 'How do you go, old one?'

'Straight down. Across the road. Up the far slope and into the timber where it narrows.'

'Across the road?' Agustin wheeled beside him, kicking his soft-heeled, canvas shoes against the stiff, unresponsive belly of one of the horses Pablo had recruited in the night.

'Yes, man. It is the only way,' Pablo said. He handed him one of the lead ropes. Primitivo and the gypsy had the others.

'Thou canst come at the end if thou will, *Inglés*,' Pablo said.

'We cross high enough to be out of range of that *máquina*. But we will go separately and riding much and then be together where it narrows above.'

'Good,' said Robert Jordan.

They rode down through the timber toward the edge of the road. Robert Jordan rode just behind Maria. He could not ride beside her for the timber. He caressed the gray once with his thigh muscles, and then held him steady as they dropped down fast and sliding through the pines, telling the gray with his thighs as they dropped down what the spurs would have told him if they had been on level ground.

'Thou,' he said to Maria, 'go second as they cross the road. First is not so bad though it seems bad. Second is good. It is later that they are always watching for.'

'But thou—'

'I will go suddenly. There will be no problem. It is the places in line that are bad.'

He was watching the round, bristly head of Pablo, sunk in his shoulders as he rode, his automatic rifle slung over his shoulder. He was watching Pilar, her head bare, her shoulders broad, her knees higher than her thighs as her heels hooked into the bundles. She looked back at him once and shook her head.

'Pass the Pilar before you cross the road,' Robert Jordan said to Maria.

Then he was looking through the thinning trees and he saw the oiled dark of the road below and beyond it the green slope of the hillside. We are above the culvert, he saw, and just below the height where the road drops down straight toward the bridge in that long sweep. We are around eight hundred yards above the bridge. That is not out of range for the Fiat in that little tank if they have come up to the bridge.

'Maria,' he said. 'Pass the Pilar before we reach the road and ride wide up that slope.'

She looked back at him but did not say anything. He did not look at her except to see that she had understood.

'*Comprendes?*' he asked her.

She nodded.

'Move up,' he said. She shook her head. 'Move up!'

'Nay,' she told him, turning around and shaking her head. 'I go in the order that I am to go.'

Just them Pablo dug both his spurs into the big bay and he plunged down the last pine-needled slope and cross the road in a pounding, sparking of shod hooves. The othersbehind him and Robert Jordan saw them crossing the road and slamming on up the green slope and heard the machine gun hammer at the bridge. Then he heard a noise come sweeeish-crack-boom! The boom was a sharp crack that widened in the cracking and on the hillside he saw a small fountain of earth rise with a plume of gray smoke. Sweeish-crack-boom! It came again, the swishing like the noise of a rocket and there was another up-pulsing of dirt and smoke farther up the hillside.

Ahead of him the gypsy was stopped beside the road in the shelter of the last trees. He looked ahead at the slope and then he looked back toward Robert Jordan.

'Go ahead, Rafael,' Robert Jordan said. 'Gallop, man!'

The gypsy was holding the lead rope with the pack-horse pulling his head taut behind him.

'Drop the pack-horse and gallop!' Robert Jordan said.

He saw the gypsy's hand extended behind him, rising higher and higher, seeming to take forever as his heels kicked into the horse he was riding and the rope came taut, then dropped, and he was across the road and Robert Jordan was kneeing against a frightened pack-horse that bumped back into him as the gypsy crossed the hard, dark road and he heard his horse's hooves clumping as he galloped up the slope.

Wheeeeeeish-ca-raek! The flat trajectory of the shell came and he saw the gypsy jink like a running boar as the earth spouted the little black and gray geyser ahead of him. He watched him galloping, slow and reaching now, up the long green slope and the gun threw behind him and ahead of him and he was under the fold of the hill with the others.

I can't take the damned pack-horse, Robert Jordan thought. Though I wish I could keep the son of a bitch on my off side. I'd like to have him between me and that 47 mm. they're throwing with. By God, I'll try to get him up there anyway.

He rode up to the pack-horse, caught hold of the hackamore, and then, holding the rope, the horse trotting behind him, rode fifty yards up through the trees. At the edge of the trees he looked down the road past the truck to the bridge. He could see men out on the bridge and behind it looked like a traffic jam on the road. Robert Jordan looked around, saw what he wanted finally and reached up and broke a dead limb from a pine tree. He dropped the hackamore, edged the pack-horse up to the slope that slanted down to the road and then hit him hard across the rump with the tree branch. 'Go on, you son of a bitch,' he said, and threw the dead branch after him as the pack-horse crossed the road and started across the slope. The branch hit him and the horse broke from a run into a gallop.

Robert Jordan rode thirty yards farther up the road; beyond that the bank was too steep. The gun was firing now with the rocket whish and the cracking, dirt-spouting boom. 'Come on, you big gray fascist bastard,' Robert Jordan said to the horse and put him down the slope in a sliding plunge. Then he was out in the open, over the road that was so hard under the hooves he felt the pound of it come up all the way to his shoulders, his neck and his teeth, onto the smooth of the slope, the hooves finding it, cutting it, pounding it, reaching, throwing, going, and he looked down across the slope to where the bridge showed now at a new angle he had never seen. It crossed in profile now without foreshortening and in the center was the broken place and behind it on the road was the little tank and behind the little tank was a big tank with a gun that flashed now yellow-bright as a mirror and the screech as the air ripped apart seemed almost over the gray neck that stretched ahead of him, and he turned his head as the dirt fountained up the hillside. The pack-horse was ahead of him swinging too far to the right and slowing down and Robert Jordan, galloping, his head turned a little toward the bridge, saw the line of trucks halted behind the turn that showed now clearly as he was gaining height, and he saw the bright yellow flash that signalled the instant whish and boom, and the shell fell short, but he heard the metal sailing from where the dirt rose.

He saw them all ahead in the edge of the timber watching him and he said, 'Arre caballo! Go on, horse!' and felt his big horse's chest surging with the steepening of the slope and saw the gray neck stretching and the gray ears ahead and he reached and patted the wet gray neck, and he looked back at the bridge and saw the bright flash from the heavy, squat, mud-colored tank there on the road and then he did not hear any whish but only a banging acrid smelling clang like a boiler being ripped apart and he was under the gray horse and the gray horse was kicking and he was trying to pull out from under the weight.

He could move all right. He could move toward the right. But his left leg stayed perfectly flat under the horse as he moved to the right. It was as though there was a new joint in it; not the hip joint but another one that went sideways like a hinge. Then he knew what it was all right and just then the gray horse knee-ed himself up and Robert Jordan's right leg, that had kicked the stirrup loose just as it should, slipped clear over the saddle and came down beside him and he felt with his two hands of his thigh bone where the left leg lay flat against the ground and his hands both felt the sharp bone and where it pressed against the skin.

The gray horse was standing almost over him and he could see his ribs heaving. The grass was green where he sat and there were meadow flowers in it and he looked down the slope across to the road and the bridge and the gorge and the road and saw the tank and waited for the next flash. It came almost at once with again no whish and in the burst of it, with the smell of the high explosive, the dirt clods scattering and the steel whirring off, he saw the big gray horse sit quietly down beside him as though it were a horse in a circus. And then, looking at the horse sitting there, he heard the sound the horse was making.

Then Primitivo and Agustin had him under the armpits and were dragging him up the last slope and the new joint in his leg let it swing any way the ground swung it. Once a shell whished close over them and they dropped him and fell flat, but the dirt scattered over them and the metal sung off and they picked him up again. And then they had him up to the shelter of the long draw in the timber where the horses were, and Maria, Pilar and Pablo were standing over him.

Maria was kneeling by him and saying, 'Roberto, what hast thou?' He said, sweating heavily, 'The left leg is broken, *guapa*.'

'We will bind it up,' Pilar said. 'Thou canst ride that.' She pointed to one of the horses that was packed. 'Cut off the load.'

Robert Jordan saw Pablo shake his head and he nodded at him. 'Get along,' he said. Then he said, 'Listen, Pablo. Come here.'

The sweat-streaked, bristly face bent down by him and Robert Jordan smelt the full smell of Pablo. 'Let us speak,' he said to Pilar and Maria. 'I have to speak to Pablo.'

'Does it hurt much?' Pablo asked. He was bending close over Robert Jordan.

'No. I think the nerve is crushed. Listen. Get along. I am mucked, see? I will talk to the girl for a moment. When I say to take her, take her. She will want to stay. I will only speak to her for a moment.'

'Clearly, there is not much time,' Pablo said. 'Clearly.'

'I think you would do better in the Republic,' Robert Jordan said.

'Nay. I am for Gredos.' 'Use thy head.'

'Talk to her now,' Pablo said. 'There is little time. I am sorry thou hast this, *Inglés*.'

'Since I have it-' Robert Jordan said. 'Let us not speak of it. But use thy head. Thou hast much head. Use it.'

'Why would I not?' said Pablo. 'Talk now fast, *Inglés*. There is no time.'

Pablo went over to the nearest tree and watched down the slope, across the slope and up the road across the gorge. Pablo was looking at the gray horse on the slope with true regret on his face and Pilar and Maria were with Robert Jordan where he sat against the tree trunk.

'Slit the trouser, will thee?' he said to Pilar. Maria crouched by him and did not speak. The sun was on her hair and her face was twisted as a child's contorts before it cries. But she was not crying.

Pilar took her knife and slit his trouser leg down below the left-hand pocket. Robert Jordan spread the cloth with his hands and looked at the stretch of his thigh. Ten inches below the hip joint there was a pointed, purple swelling like a sharp-peaked little tent and as he touched it with his fingers he could feel the snapped-off thigh bone tight against the skin. His leg was lying at an odd angle. He looked looked up at Pilar. Her face had the same expression as Maria's.

'*Anda*,' he said to her. 'Go.'

She went away with her head down without saying anything nor looking back and Robert Jordan could see her shoulders shaking.

'*Guapa*,' he said to Maria and took hold of her two hands. 'Listen. We will not be going to Madrid—'

Then she started to cry.

'No, *guapa*, don't,' he said. 'Listen. We will not go to Madrid now but I go always with thee wherever thou goest. Understand?'

She said nothing and pushed her head against his cheek with her arms around him.

'Listen to this well, rabbit,' he said. He knew there was a great hurry and he was sweating very much, but this had to be said and understood. 'Thou wilt go now, rabbit. But I go with thee. As long as there is one of us there is both of us. Do you understand?'

'Nay, I stay with thee.'

'Nay, rabbit. What I do now I do alone. I could not do it well with thee. If thou goest then I go, too. Do you not see how it is? Whichever one there is, is both.'

'I will stay with thee.'

'Nay, rabbit. Listen. That people cannot do together. Each one must do it alone. But if thou goest then I go with thee. It is in that way that I go too. Thou wilt go now, I know. For thou art good and kind. Thou wilt go now for us both.'

'But it is easier if I stay with thee,' she said. 'It is better for me.' 'Yes. Therefore go for a favor. Do it for me since it is what thou canst do.'

'But you don't understand, Roberto. What about *me*? It is worse for me to go.'

'Surely,' he said. 'It is harder for thee. But I am thee also now.' She said nothing.

He looked at her and he was sweating heavily and he spoke now, trying harder to do something than he had ever tried in all his life.

'Now you will go for us both,' he said.' You must not be selfish, rabbit. You must do your duty now.'

She shook her head.

'You are me now,' he said. 'Surely thou must feel it, rabbit.'

'Rabbit, listen,' he said. 'Truly thus I go too. I swear it to thee.'

She said nothing.

'Now you see it,' he said. 'Now I see it is clear. Now thou wilt go. Good. Now you are going. Now you have said you will go.' She had said nothing.

'Now I thank thee for it. Now you are going well and fast and far and we both go in thee. Now put thy hand here. Now put thy head down. Nay, put it down. That is right. Now I put my hand there. Good. Thou art so good. Now do not think more. Now art thou doing what thou should. Now thou art obeying. Not me but us both. The me in thee. Now you go for us both. Truly. We both go in thee now. This I have promised thee. Thou art very good to go and very kind.'

He jerked his head at Pablo, who was half-looking at him from the tree and Pablo started over. He motioned with his thumb to Pilar.

'We will go to Madrid another time, rabbit,' he said.' Truly. Now stand up and go and we both go. Stand up. See?'

'No,' she said and held him tight around the neck.

He spoke now still calmly and reasonably but with great authority.

'Stand up,' he said. 'Thou art me too now. Thou art all there will be of me. Stand up.'

She stood up slowly, crying, and with her head down. Then she dropped quickly beside him and then stood up again, slowly and tiredly, as he said, 'Stand up, *guapa*.'

Pilar was holding her by the arm and she was standing there.

'*Vamonos*,' Pilar said. 'Dost lack anything, *Inglés?*' She looked at him and shook her head.

'No,' he said and went on talking to Maria.

'There is no good-by, *guapa*, because we are not apart. That it should be good in the Gredos. Go now. Go good. Nay,' he spoke now still calmly and reasonably as Pilar walked the girl along. 'Do not turn around. Put thy foot in. Yes. Thy foot in. Help her up,' he said to Pilar. 'Get her in the saddle. Swing up now.'

He turned his head, sweating, and looked down the slope, then back toward where the girl was in the saddle with Pilar by her and Pablo just behind. 'Now go,' he said. 'Go.'

She started to look around. 'Don't look around,' Robert Jordan said. 'Go.' And Pablo hit the horse across the crupper with a hobbling strap and it looked as though Maria tried to slip from the saddle but Pilar and Pablo were riding close up against her and Pilar was holding her and the three horses were going up the draw. 'Roberto,' Maria turned and shouted. 'Let me stay! Let me stay!'

'I am with thee,' Robert Jordan shouted. 'I am with thee now. We are both there. Go!' Then they were out of sight around the corner of the draw and he was soaking wet with sweat and looking at nothing.

Agustin was standing by him.

'Do you want me to shoot thee, *Inglés?*' he asked, leaning down close. '*Quieres?* It is nothing.'

'*No hace falta,*' Robert Jordan said. 'Get along. I am very well here.'

'*Me cago en la leche que me han dado!*' Agustin said. He was crying so he could not see Robert Jordan clearly. '*Sa Iud, Inglés.*'

'*Salud,* old one,' Robert Jordan said. He was looking down the slope now. 'Look well after the cropped head, wilt thou?'

'There is no problem,' Agustin said. 'Thou has what thou needest?'

'There are very few shells for this *máquina,* so I will keep it,' Robert Jordan said. 'Thou canst now get more. For that other and the one of Pablo, yes.'

'I cleaned out the barrel,' Agustin said. 'Where thou plugged it in the dirt with the fall.'

'What became of the pack-horse?'

'The gypsy caught it.'

Agustin was on the horse now but he did not want to go. He leaned far over toward the tree where Robert Jordan lay.

'Go on, *viejo,*' Robert Jordan said to him. 'In war there are many things like this.'

'*Que puta es la guerra,*' Agustin said. 'War is a bitchery.'

'Yes, man, yes. But get on with thee.'

'*Sa Iud, Inglés,*' Agustin said, clenching his right fist.

'*Sa Iud,*' Robert Jordan said. 'But get along, man.'

Agustin wheeled his horse and brought his right fist down as though he cursed again with the motion of it and rode up the draw. All the others had been out of sight long before. He looked back where the draw turned in the timber and waved his fist. Robert Jordan waved and then Agustin, too, was out of sight Robert Jordan looked down the green slope of the hillside to the road and the bridge. I'm as well this way as any, he thought. It wouldn't be worth risking getting over on my belly yet, not as close as that thing was to the surface, and I can see better this way.

He felt empty and drained and exhausted from all of it and from them going and his mouth tasted of bile. Now, finally and at last, there was no problem. However all of it had been and however all of it would ever be now, for him, no longer was there any problem.

They were all gone now and he was alone with his back against a tree. He looked down across the green slope, seeing the gray horse where Agustin had shot him, and on down the slope to the road with the timber-covered country behind it. Then he looked at the bridge and across the bridge and watched the activity on the bridge and the road. He could see the trucks now, all down the lower road. The gray of the trucks showed through the trees. Then he looked back up the road to where it came down over the hill. They will be coming soon now, he thought.

Pilar will take care of her as well as any one can. You know that. Pablo must have a sound plan or he would not have tried it. You do not have to worry about

Pablo. It does no good to think about Maria. Try to believe what you told her. That is the best. And who says it is not true? Not you. You don't say it, any more than you would say the things did not happen that happened. Stay with what you believe now. Don't get cynical. The time is too short and you have just sent her away. Each one does what he can. You can do nothing for yourself but perhaps you can do something for another. Well, we had all our luck in four days. Not four days. It was afternoon when I first got there and it will not be noon today. That makes not quite three days and three nights. Keep it accurate, he said. Quite accurate.

I think you better get down now, he thought. You better get fixed around some way where you will be useful instead of leaning against this tree like a tramp. You have had much luck. There are many worse things than this. Every one has to do this, one day or another. You are not afraid of it once you know you have to do it, are you? No, he said, truly. It was lucky the nerve was crushed, though. I cannot even feel that there is anything below the break. He touched the lower part of his leg and it was as though it were not part of his body.

He looked down the hill slope again and he thought, I hate to leave it, is all. I hate to leave it very much and I hope I have done some good in it. I have tried to with what talent I had. *Have,* you *mean. All right, have.*

I have fought for what I believed in for a year now. If we win here we will win everywhere. The world is a fine place and worth the fighting for and I hate very much to leave it. And you had a lot of luck, he told himself, to have had such a good life. You've had just as good a life as grandfather's though not as long. You've had as good a life as any one because of these last days. You do not want to complain when you have been so lucky. I wish there was some way to pass on what I've learned, though. Christ, I was learning fast there at the end. I'd like to talk to Karkov. That is in Madrid. Just over the hills there, and down across the plain. Down out of the gray rocks and the pines, the heather and the gorse, across the yellow high plateau you see it rising white and beautiful. That part is just as true as Pilar's old women drinking the blood down at the slaughterhouse. There's no *one* thing that's true. It's all true. The way the planes are beautiful whether they are ours or theirs. The hell they are, he thought.

You take it easy, now, he said. Get turned over now while you still have time. Listen, one thing. Do you remember? Pilar and the hand? Do you believe that crap? No, he said. Not with everything that's happened? No, I don't believe it. She was nice about it early this morning before the show started. She was afraid maybe I believed it. I don't, though. But she does. They see something. Or they feel something. Like a bird dog. What about extra-sensory per ception? What about obscenity? he said. She wouldn't say good-by, he thought, because she knew if she did Maria would never go. That Pilar. Get yourself turned over, Jordan. But he was reluctant to try it. Then he remembered that he had the small flask in his hip pocket and he thought, I'll take a good spot of the giant killer and then I'll try it. But the flask was not there when he felt for it. Then he felt that much more alone because he knew there was not going to be even that. I guess I'd counted on that, he said.

Do you suppose Pablo took it? Don't be silly. You must have lost it at the bridge. 'Come on now, Jordan,' he said. 'Over you go.' Then he took hold of his left leg with both hands and pulled on it hard, pulling toward the foot while he lay down beside the tree he had been resting his back against. Then lying flat and pulling hard on the leg, so the broken end of the bone would not come up and cut through the thigh, he turned slowly around on his rump until the back of his head was facing downhill. Then with his broken leg, held by both hands, uphill, he put the sale of his right foot against the instep of his left foot and pressed hard while he rolled, sweating, over onto his face and chest. He got onto his elbows, stretched the left leg well behind him with both hands and a far, sweating, push with the right foot and there he was. He felt with his fingers on the left thigh and it was all right. The bone end had not punctured the skin and the broken end was well into the muscle now.

The big nerve must have been truly smashed when that damned horse rolled on it, he thought. It truly doesn't hurt at all. Except now in certain changes of positions. That's when the bone pinches something else. You see? he said. You see what luck is? You didn't need the giant killer at all.

He reached over for the submachine gun, took the clip out that was in the magazine, felt in his pocket for clips, opened the action and looked through the barrel, put the clip back into the groove of the magazine until it clicked, and then looked down the hill slope. Maybe half an hour, he thought. Now take it easy.

Then he looked at the hillside and he looked at the pines and he tried not to think at all.

Then he looked at the stream and he remembered how it had been under the bridge in the cool of the shadow. I wish they would come, he thought. I do not want to get in any sort of mixed-up state before they come.

Who do you suppose has it easier? Ones with religion or just taking it straight? It comforts them very much but we know there is no thing to fear. It is only missing it that's bad. Dying is only bad when it takes a long time and hurts so much that it humiliates you. That is where you have all the luck, see? You don't have any of that.

It's wonderful they've got away. I don't mind this at all now they are away. It *is* sort of the way I said. It is really very much that way. Look how different it would be if they were all scattered out across that hill where that gray horse is. Or if we were all cooped up here waiting for it. No. They're gone. They're away. Now if the attack were only a success. What do you want? Everything. I want everything and I will take whatever I get. If this attack is no good another one will be. I never noticed when the planes came back. *God, that was lucky I could make her go.*

I'd like to tell grandfather about this one. I'll bet he never had to go over and find his people and do a show like this. How do you know? He may have done fifty. No, he said. Be accurate. Nobody did any fifty like this one. Nobody did five. Nobody did one maybe not just like this. Sure. They must have.

I wish they would come now, he said. I wish they would come right now because the leg is starting to hurt now. It must be the swelling.

We were going awfully good when that thing hit us, he thought. But it was only luck it didn't come while I was under the bridge. When a thing is wrong something's bound to happen. You were bitched when they gave Golz those orders. That was what you knew and it was probably that which Pilar felt. But later on we will have these things much better organized. We ought to have portable short wave transmitters. *Yes, there's a lot of things we ought to have.* I ought to carry a spare leg, too.

He grinned at that sweatily because the leg, where the big nerve had been bruised by the fall, was hurting badly now. Oh, let them come, he said. I don't want to do that business that my father did. I will do it all right but I'd much prefer not to have to. I'm against that. Don't think about that. Don't think at all. I wish the bastards would come, he said. I wish so very much they'd come.

His leg was hurting very badly now. The pain had started suddenly with the swelling after he had moved and he said, Maybe I'll just do it now. I guess I'm not awfully good at pain. Listen, if I do that now you wouldn't misunderstand, would you? *Who are you talking to?* Nobody, he said. Grandfather, I guess. No. Nobody. Oh bloody it, I wish that they would come.

Listen, I may have to do that because if I pass out or anything like that I am no good at all and if they bring me to they will ask me a lot of questions and do things and all and that is no good. It's much best not to have them do those things. So why wouldn't it be all right to just do it now and then the whole thing would be over with? Because oh, listen, yes, listen, *let them come now.*

You're not good at this, Jordan, he said. Not so good at this.

And who is so good at this? I don't know and I don't really care right now. But you are not. That's right. You're not at all. Oh not at all, at all. I think it would be all right to do it now? Don't you?

No, it isn't. Because there is something you can do yet. As long as you know what it is you have to do it. As long as you remember what it is you have to wait for that. *Come on. Let them come. Let them come. Let them come!*

Think about them being away, he said. Think about them going through the timber. Think about them crossing a creek. Think about them riding through the heather. Think about them going up the slope. Think about them O. K. tonight. Think about them travelling, all night. Think about them hiding up tomorrow. Think about them. God damn it, think about them. *That's just as for as I can think about them,* he said.

Think about Montana. *I can't.* Think about Madrid. *I can't.*

Think about a cool drink of water. *All right.* That's what it will be like. Like a cool drink of water. *You're a liar.* It will just be nothing. That's all it will be. Just nothing. Then do it. *Do it.* Do it now. It's all right to do it now. Go on and do it now. *No, you have to wait.* What for? You know all right. *Then wait.*

I can't wait any longer now, he said. If I wait any longer I'll pass out. I know because I've felt it starting to go three times now and I've held it. I held it all right. But I don't know about any more. What I think is you've got an internal hemorrhage there from where that thigh bone's cut around inside. Especially on that turning business. That makes the swelling and that's what weakens you and makes you start to pass. It would be all right to do it now. Really, I'm telling you that it would be all right.

And if you wait and hold them up even a little while or just get the officer that may make all the difference. One thing well done can make—

All right, he said. And he lay very quietly and tried to hold on to himself that he felt slipping away from himself as you feel snow starting to slip sometimes on a mountain slope, and he said, now quietly, then let me last until they come.

Robert Jordan's luck held very good because he saw, just then, the cavalry ride out of the timber and cross the road. He watched them coming riding up the slope. He saw the trooper who stopped by the gray horse and shouted to the officer who rode over to him. He watched them both looking down at the gray horse. They recognized him of course. He and his rider had been missing since the early morning of the day before.

Robert Jordan saw them there on the slope, close to him now, and below he saw the road and the bridge and the long lines of vehicles below it. He was completely integrated now and he took a good long look at everything. Then he looked up at the sky. There were big white clouds in it. He touched the palm of his hand against the pine needles where he lay and he touched the bark of the pine trunk that he lay behind.

Then he rested easily as he could with his two elbows in the pine needles and the muzzle of the submachine gun resting against the trunk of the pine tree.

As the officer came trotting now on the trail of the horses of the band he would pass twenty yards below where Robert Jordan lay. At that distance there would be no problem. The officer was Lieutenant Berrendo. He had come up from La Granja when they had been ordered up after the first report of the attack on the lower post. They had ridden hard and had then had to swing back, because the bridge had been blown, to cross the gorge high above and come around through the timber. Their horses were wet and blown and they had to be urged into the trot.

Lieutenant Berrendo, watching the trail, came riding up, his thin face serious and grave. His submachine gun lay across his saddle in the crook of his left arm. Robert Jordan lay behind the tree, holding onto himself very carefully and delicately to keep his hands steady. He was waiting until the officer reached the sunlit place where the first trees of the pine forest joined the green slope of the meadow. He could feel his heart beating against the pine needle floor of the forest.